CHARLES DICKENS

CHARLES DICKENS

David Copperfield
The Old Curiosity Shop
Hard Times

BARNES
&NOBLE
BOOKS
NEW YORK

This edition published by Barnes & Noble, Inc.

1993 Barnes & Noble Books

Book design by Jennifer Roberts

ISBN 1-56619-100-9

Printed and bound in the United States of America

M 9 8 7 6 5 4 3 2

Contents

Contents

Introduction

THERE are few novelists whose reputation for greatness in their own lives has remained so unchanged for over a century. Fewer still are so solidly associated with exposing society's ills. Charles Dickens is one of those few. But beyond the greatness of his literature or his passion for social reform, beyond his tremendous contemporary and posthumous popularity, there was perhaps no other novelist who so captured the world in which he lived. His effect was so profound that no examination of Victorian England would be complete without an examination of his life.

The second of eight children of John and Elizabeth Dickens, Charles Dickens was born near Portsmouth, England on February 7, 1812. His family was, as he would later describe, "of the liquid, rather than solid, middle class," meaning that their fortunes rose and fell without any stability. This social ambiguity in such a strictly class-conscious society led Dickens to think of himself as an outsider at an early age and for the rest of his life, despite the success and acceptance he would achieve.

While both parents were of middle-class origin, his father, a clerk in the Navy Pay Office, was continually frustrated in his aspiration to be a gentleman. A loving father and an easygoing, if restless, man, he was unfortunately hugely irresponsible with money. The consequences of this certainly contributed to his son's fierce ambition for commercial success as well as his deep sense of social injustice. Dickens would twice sketch his father in fiction: in a lighter spirit as Mr. Micawber in *David Copperfield*, and in a darker, more realistic light as Dorrit.

John Dickens moved his family to London in 1814, to Chatham in 1817, and back to London in 1822. It was in Chatham that young Charles spent the happiest years of his childhood. The town was a shipbuilding center and was by all accounts a wonderful place for a boy to grow up in and explore. His parents had many books and encouraged him to read such eighteenth-century writers as Henry Fielding, Oliver Goldsmith, and Daniel Defoe. But the rapid growth of the family and his father's inability to live within his means brought about an abrupt downturn in the family fortunes and ended this youthful idyll.

They were forced to return to London where his father found himself in severe financial trouble. When Charles, who had been left in Chatham to finish the school term, joined them in the city, he was shocked to find the family living in poverty. Just two days past his twelfth birthday he was taken out of school and sent to work in a warehouse full of child laborers, pasting labels on shoe-blacking pots to supplement the family income. At the same time his father was arrested for debt and taken to Marshalsea debtor's prison.

While both father and son were released from these humiliations only about four months later, this experience was to have a profound and obvious effect on Dickens, both as a man and as an artist. This episode of his life was so wounding that his own wife and children never knew of it while he was alive. It colored his artistic and social vision so deeply that the experience now would be described as "Dickensian." It was a shattering loss of innocence from which he would never fully recover.

It might be argued, however, that something positive—or at least formative—did come from this experience. It instilled in the boy a relentless drive for success, and at the same time an uncompromising social conscience. It brought him a deepening under-standing of the society around him and the need for reform. Scenes of children in workhouses abound in his literature, perhaps none so powerfully as in *Oliver Twist.*

A fortuitously timed legacy left to the elder Dickens relieved the family of its immediate poverty, and Charles returned to school. It was at this time, between the ages of twelve and fifteen, that he began writing. He submitted what he called "penny-a-line stuff" to his father's new employer, the *British Press:* information about fires, accidents, or police reports that were missed by regular reporters. Finally, in 1828, at the age of sixteen, he learned shorthand and became a full-time reporter in the London law courts. At twenty he began reporting on Parliament.

As a sideline to earn extra money he started writing small fictional sketches of London life for magazines. These pieces gained almost immediate attention by critics and popularity with readers for both their realism and humor. When they were published in 1836 in a two-volume collection called *Sketches by Boz,* his literary career had begun.

The success of *Sketches by Boz* brought Dickens to the attention of Edward Chap-man and William Hall, two booksellers who had begun to make forays into publishing. They asked Dickens to write a series of fictional sketches to accompany the illustrations of Robert Seymour, a popular comic artist. He agreed to write twenty installments that would sell for one shilling apiece.

On April 2, 1836, with twenty-nine pounds advance money, he married Catherine Hogarth, daughter of the editor of the *Evening Chronicle.* A quiet, dreamy woman, she would bear him ten children in fifteen years. For many years the marriage appeared to be a happy one, but the couple would separate permanently in 1858, due primarily to Dickens' restlessness, to his need to put his writing first, and to "that wayward and unsettled feeling which is part (I suppose) of the tenure on which one holds an imagina-tive life."

The week they married, the first installment of the new project, known as *The Pickwick Papers,* was published. It sold 400 copies. The final installment, in October, 1837, sold 40,000 copies, and overnight Dickens was a literary superstar, a position he would hold until his death. The success of the novel had tremendous influence on both the literature of the time and the method of publishing novels. Up to that time, serializa-tion was very rare; most books were published in two or three volumes. *The Pickwick Papers* found a new way to connect with an audience, particularly those who could not afford to buy a novel. By combining the inexpensive, shilling-a-month appeal of journal-ism with the emotional engagement of fiction, Dickens opened up contemporary litera-ture to a new audience. All of his subsequent novels were published in installments, and many other writers followed suit.

Following the initial success of *The Pickwick Papers,* Dickens worked hard to establish himself as both a major writer and a man of considerable means; he was determined that his children would never experience the insecurity he had known. His ambition drove him to consolidate and extend his fame and financial security, and in the next several years, as his family grew, he worked feverishly on his literature and his business and social contacts, becoming the center of the London literary circle. Over a period of eight years he produced five novels, dozens of stories, essays, and plays.

Oliver Twist (1837–39) established Dickens not only as the preeminent storyteller of his day, but as a social reformer as well. If not quite his best work, it may still be seen as the quintessential Dickens novel: the combination of pathos and humor, melodrama and adventure, sharp plot twists and social commentary set a pattern, became a kind of paradigm for other novels that followed. The opening scenes set in the children's workhouse were obviously based on his own experiences; they were also a reaction to the New Poor Law, which he had heard debated while he was a Parliamentary reporter and which he viewed as institutionalized repression. Public reaction was again tremendous, and it encouraged Dickens to use his fiction to expose the social ills he perceived around him.

This was followed by *Nicholas Nickelby* (1838–39) which expanded on the use of melodrama so popular in *Oliver Twist;* and *The Old Curiosity Shop,* which perfected it. Perhaps because fiction has a different place in our world, it is difficult today to understand the effect *The Old Curiosity Shop* had on English society: the entire nation wept for the death of little Nell. It was a scene, however, a bit too close to the author's life. The character was based on Mary Hogarth, his sister-in-law, to whom he was very close. She came to live with his family shortly after he married, but was suddenly taken ill at the age of seventeen and actually died in his arms. Her memory haunted him for years.

Feeling financially secure for the first time in his life, Dickens embarked, in 1842, on a six-month tour of America, a country that had captured his imagination since childhood. The trip was not completely for pleasure; an unjust copyright law allowed American publishers to pirate his popular works, and he went with the intent of negotiating some kind of settlement. He was lionized by the literary community in New York and Boston, but the rest of the trip seems to have been a disappointment. American newspapers criticized his liberal social ideas, the *New York Herald* saying he had a "coarse, vulgar, imprudent, and superficial mind." Also he was, understandably, horrified by what he saw of the slave society in the south. America, at that time, was not the utopia he had hoped it would be.

In addition to his fiction, Dickens at this time was also writing journalism, contributing essays to a variety of newspapers and magazines. Nearly all of these pieces address some social injustice: attacking the use of female labor in coal mines, capital punishment, children's workhouses. He briefly became editor of the *Daily News,* by far the most left-wing publication in England, but resigned to return to fiction.

He also at this time became involved in theater, forming his own amateur company that toured London and the provinces, performing once for Queen Victoria herself.

In the late 1840s he tried writing his autobiography, but after struggling with the episode in the blackening factory, he abandoned it as too painful. Instead, he began his "favourite child," *David Copperfield* (1849–50), which was to be his most autobiographical novel. It was life in Victorian society as he saw it, and he was determined to hold nothing back. In his own words his most "human document," it is one of his least sentimental yet most passionate works, and certainly the one closest to his heart.

This novel and the ones that followed showed a more somber and less exuberant world view than his early works. *Bleak House* (1852–53) and particularly *Hard Times* (1854) can be seen as attacks not just on the capitalism of the time, but of the dehumanization and soulessness of the industrial revolution.

The last decade of his life was not a very happy one. The separation from his wife and his association with a young actress named Ellen Ternan made scandalous headlines in the newspapers. His true relationship with Miss Ternan is still not completely understood, but the publicity surrounding them did cause him pain. The breakup of his family was also disturbing, particularly the activities of his sons, who, like their grandfather, were wastrels with money. His last great work—and perhaps his greatest—was *Great Expectations* (1860–61), but he seemed to get little pleasure from its success.

In failing health, but to ensure his family's fortunes, he embarked on a grand reading tour from 1867–1868, through England and then back to America. The tour was a tremendous success, but left him exhausted and ill.

His final work was left unfinished. *The Mystery of Edwin Drood* was to be a detective story in the style of his friend Wilkie Collins, but the mystery remains unsolved. A sudden stroke killed him on June 9, 1870. He was buried in Westminster Abbey five days later, and as with the death of little Nell, all of England wept.

The question of whether Dickens was England's finest novelist has been debated for over a century. It is certainly not an unreasonable supposition. But more important, there may be no novelist of any nationality who so succinctly captured the society in which he lived. Indeed, the adjective "Dickensian" is firmly entrenched in our language. His wonderful powers of storytelling and his passion for social reform have made him a giant not just in the history of literature, but in the history of humankind.

Steven J. Kasdin
1993

David Copperfield

Affectionately Inscribed To

THE HON. MR. AND MRS. RICHARD WATSON,

OF ROCKINGHAM, NORTHAMPTONSHIRE.

Contents

Preface To 1850 Edition

I DO not find it easy to get sufficiently far away from this Book, in the first sensations of having finished it, to refer to it with the composure which this formal heading would seem to require. My interest in it, is so recent and strong; and my mind is so divided between pleasure and regret—pleasure in the achievement of a long design, regret in the separation from many companions—that I am in danger of wearying the reader whom I love, with personal confidences, and private emotions.

Besides which, all that I could say of the Story, to any purpose, I have endeavoured to say in it.

It would concern the reader little, perhaps, to know, how sorrowfully the pen is laid down at the close of a two-years' imaginative task; or how an Author feels as if he were dismissing some portion of himself into the shadowy world, when a crowd of the creatures of his brain are going from him for ever. Yet, I have nothing else to tell; unless, indeed, I were to confess (which might be of less moment still) that no one can ever believe this Narrative, in the reading, more than I have believed it in the writing.

Instead of looking back, therefore, I will look forward. I cannot close this Volume more agreeably to myself, than with a hopeful glance towards the time when I shall again put forth my two green leaves once a month, and with a faithful remembrance of the genial sun and showers that have fallen on these leaves of David Copperfield, and made me happy.

London,
October, 1850.

Preface To
The Charles Dickens Edition

I REMARKED in the original Preface to this Book, that I did not find it easy to get sufficiently far away from it, in the first sensations of having finished it, to refer to it with the composure which this formal heading would seem to require. My interest in it was so recent and strong, and my mind was so divided between pleasure and regret— pleasure in the achievement of a long design, regret in the separation from many companions—that I was in danger of wearying the reader with personal confidences and private emotions.

Besides which, all that I could have said of the Story to any purpose, I had endeavoured to say in it.

It would concern the reader little, perhaps, to know how sorrowfully the pen is laid down at the close of a two-years' imaginative task; or how an Author feels as if he were dismissing some portion of himself into the shadowy world, when a crowd of the creatures of his brain are going from him for ever. Yet, I had nothing else to tell; unless, indeed, I were to confess (which might be of less moment still), that no one can ever believe this Narrative, in the reading, more than I believed it in the writing.

So true are these avowals at the present day, that I can now only take the reader into one confidence more. Of all my books, I like this the best. It will be easily believed that I am a fond parent to every child of my fancy, and that no one can ever love that family as dearly as I love them. But, like many fond parents, I have in my heart of hearts a favourite child. And his name is DAVID COPPERFIELD.

1869

Chapter I

I AM BORN

WHETHER I shall turn out to be the hero of my own life, or whether that station will be held by anybody else, these pages must show. To begin my life with the beginning of my life, I record that I was born (as I have been informed and believe) on a Friday, at twelve o'clock at night. It was remarked that the clock began to strike, and I began to cry, simultaneously.

In consideration of the day and hour of my birth, it was declared by the nurse, and by some sage women in the neighbourhood who had taken a lively interest in me several months before there was any possibility of our becoming personally acquainted, first, that I was destined to be unlucky in life; and secondly, that I was privileged to see ghosts and spirits; both these gifts inevitably attaching, as they believed, to all unlucky infants of either gender, born towards the small hours on a Friday night.

I need say nothing here, on the first head, because nothing can show better than my history whether that prediction was verified or falsified by the result. On the second branch of the question, I will only remark, that unless I ran through that part of my inheritance while I was still a baby, I have not come into it yet. But I do not at all complain of having been kept out of this property; and if anybody else should be in the present enjoyment of it, he is heartily welcome to keep it.

I was born with a caul, which was advertised for sale, in the newspapers, at the low price of fifteen guineas. Whether sea-going people were short of money about that time, or were short of faith and preferred cork jackets, I don't know; all I know is, that there was but one solitary bidding, and that was from an attorney connected with the bill-broking business, who offered two pounds in cash, and the balance in sherry, but declined to be guaranteed from drowning on any higher bargain. Consequently the advertisement was withdrawn at a dead loss—for as to sherry, my poor dear mother's own sherry was in the market then—and ten years afterwards, the caul was put up in a raffle down in our part of the country, to fifty members at half-a-crown a head, the winner to spend five shillings. I was present myself, and I remember to have felt quite uncomfortable and confused, at a part of myself being disposed of in that way. The caul was won, I recollect, by an old lady with a hand-basket, who, very reluctantly, produced from it the stipulated five shillings, all in halfpence, and twopence halfpenny short—as it took an immense time and a great waste of arithmetic, to endeavour without any effect to prove to her. It is a fact which will be long remembered as remarkable down there, that she was never drowned, but died triumphantly in bed, at ninety-two. I have understood that it was, to the last, her proudest boast, that she never had been on the water in her life, except upon a bridge; and that over her tea (to which she was extremely partial) she, to the last, expressed her indignation at the impiety of mariners and others, who had the presumption to go "meandering" about the world. It was in vain to represent to her that some conveniences, tea perhaps included, resulted from this objectionable practice. She always returned, with greater emphasis and with an instinctive knowledge of the strength of her objection, "Let us have no meandering."

Not to meander myself, at present, I will go back to my birth.

I was born at Blunderstone, in Suffolk, or "thereby," as they say in Scotland. I was a posthumous child. My father's eyes had closed upon the light of this world six months, when mine opened on it. There is something strange to me, even now, in the reflection that he never saw me; and something stranger yet in the shadowy remembrance that I have of my first childish associations with his white grave-stone in the churchyard, and of the indefinable compassion I used to feel for it lying out alone there in the dark night, when our little parlour was warm and bright with fire and candle, and the doors of our house were—almost cruelly, it seemed to me sometimes—bolted and locked against it.

An aunt of my father's, and consequently a great-aunt of mine, of whom I shall have more to relate by and by, was the principal magnate of our family. Miss Trotwood, or Miss Betsey, as my poor mother always called her, when she sufficiently overcame her dread of this formidable personage to mention her at all (which was seldom), had been married to a husband younger than herself, who was very handsome, except in the sense of the homely adage, "handsome is, that handsome does"—for he was strongly suspected of having beaten Miss Betsey, and even of having once, on a disputed question of supplies, made some hasty but determined arrangements to throw her out of a two pair of stairs' window. These evidences of an incompatibility of temper induced Miss Betsey to pay him off, and effect a separation by mutual consent. He went to India with his capital, and there, according to a wild legend in our family, he was once seen riding on an elephant, in company with a Baboon; but I think it must have been a Baboo—or a Begum. Anyhow, from India tidings of his death reached home, within ten years. How they affected my aunt, nobody knew; for immediately upon the separation, she took her maiden name again, bought a cottage in a hamlet on the sea-coast a long way off, established herself there as a single woman with one servant, and was understood to live secluded, ever afterwards, in an inflexible retirement.

My father had once been a favourite of hers, I believe; but she was mortally affronted by his marriage, on the ground that my mother was "a wax doll." She had never seen my mother, but she knew her to be not yet twenty. My father and Miss Betsey never met again. He was double my mother's age when he married, and of but a delicate constitution. He died a year afterwards, and, as I have said, six months before I came into the world.

This was the state of matters, on the afternoon of, what I may be excused for calling, that eventful and important Friday. I can make no claim therefore to have known, at that time, how matters stood; or to have any remembrance, founded on the evidence of my own senses, of what follows.

My mother was sitting by the fire, but poorly in health, and very low in spirits, looking at it through her tears, and desponding heavily about herself and the fatherless little stranger, who was already welcomed by some grosses of prophetic pins, in a drawer upstairs, to a world not at all excited on the subject of his arrival; my mother, I say, was sitting by the fire, that bright, windy March afternoon, very timid and sad, and very doubtful of ever coming alive out of the trial that was before her, when, lifting her eyes as she dried them, to the window opposite, she saw a strange lady coming up the garden.

My mother had a sure foreboding at the second glance, that it was Miss Betsey. The setting sun was glowing on the strange lady, over the garden-fence, and she came walking up to the door with a fell rigidity of figure and composure of countenance that could have belonged to nobody else.

When she reached the house, she gave another proof of her identity. My father had often hinted that she seldom conducted herself like any ordinary Christian; and now, instead of ringing the bell, she came and looked in at that identical window, pressing the end of her nose against the glass to that extent, that my poor dear mother used to say it became perfectly flat and white in a moment.

She gave my mother such a turn, that I have always been convinced I am indebted to Miss Betsey for having been born on a Friday.

My mother had left her chair in her agitation, and gone behind it in the corner. Miss Betsey, looking round the room, slowly and inquiringly, began on the other side, and carried her eyes on, like a Saracen's Head in a Dutch clock, until they reached my mother. Then she made a frown and a gesture to my mother, like one who was accustomed to be obeyed, to come and open the door. My mother went.

"Mrs David Copperfield, I *think,*" said Miss Betsey; the emphasis referring, perhaps, to my mother's mourning weeds, and her condition.

"Yes," said my mother, faintly.

"Miss Trotwood," said the visitor. "You have heard of her, I dare say?"

My mother answered she had had that pleasure. And she had a disagreeable consciousness of not appearing to imply that it had been an overpowering pleasure.

"Now you see her," said Miss Betsey. My mother bent her head, and begged her to walk in.

They went into the parlour my mother had come from, the fire in the best room on the other side of the passage not being lighted—not having been lighted, indeed, since my father's funeral; and when they were both seated, and Miss Betsey said nothing, my mother, after vainly trying to restrain herself, began to cry.

"Oh tut, tut, tut!" said Miss Betsey, in a hurry. "Don't do that! Come, come!"

My mother couldn't help it notwithstanding, so she cried until she had had her cry out.

"Take off your cap, child," said Miss Betsey, "and let me see you."

My mother was too much afraid of her to refuse compliance with this odd request, if she had any disposition to do so. Therefore she did as she was told, and did it with such nervous hands that her hair (which was luxuriant and beautiful) fell all about her face.

"Why, bless my heart!" exclaimed Miss Betsey. "You are a very Baby!"

My mother was, no doubt, unusually youthful in appearance even for her years; she hung her head, as if it were her fault, poor thing, and said, sobbing, that indeed she was afraid she was but a childish widow, and would be but a childish mother if she lived. In a short pause which ensued, she had a fancy that she felt Miss Betsey touch her hair, and that with no ungentle hand; but, looking at her, in her timid hope, she found that lady sitting with the skirt of her dress tucked up, her hands folded on one knee, and her feet upon the fender, frowning at the fire.

"In the name of Heaven," said Miss Betsey, suddenly, "why Rookery?"

"Do you mean the house, ma'am?" asked my mother.

"Why Rookery?" said Miss Betsey. "Cookery would have been more to the purpose, if you had had any practical ideas of life, either of you."

"The name was Mr Copperfield's choice," returned my mother. "When he bought the house, he liked to think that there were rooks about it."

The evening wind made such a disturbance just now, among some tall old elm-trees at the bottom of the garden, that neither my mother nor Miss Betsey could forbear glancing that way. As the elms bent to one another, like giants who were whispering secrets, and after a few seconds of such repose, fell into a violent flurry, tossing their wild arms about, as if their late confidences were really too wicked for their peace of mind, some weatherbeaten ragged old rooks'-nests, burdening their higher branches, swung like wrecks upon a stormy sea.

"Where are the birds?" asked Miss Betsey.

"The——?" My mother had been thinking of something else.

"The rooks—what has become of them?" asked Miss Betsey.

"There have not been any since we have lived here," said my mother. "We thought—Mr Copperfield thought—it was quite a large rookery; but the nests were very old ones, and the birds have deserted them a long while."

"David Copperfield all over!" cried Miss Betsey. "David Copperfield from head to foot! Calls a house a rookery when there's not a rook near it, and takes the birds on trust, because he sees the nests!"

"Mr Copperfield," returned my mother, "is dead, and if you dare to speak unkindly of him to me——"

My poor dear mother, I suppose, had some momentary intention of committing an assault and battery upon my aunt, who could easily have settled her with one hand, even if my mother had been in far better training for such an encounter than she was that evening. But it passed with the action of rising from her chair; and she sat down again very meekly, and fainted.

When she came to herself, or when Miss Betsey had restored her, whichever it was, she found the latter standing at the window. The twilight was by this time shading down into darkness; and dimly as they saw each other, they could not have done that without the aid of the fire.

"Well?" said Miss Betsey, coming back to her chair as if she had only been taking a casual look at the prospect; "and when do you expect——"

"I am all in a tremble," faltered my mother. "I don't know what's the matter. I shall die, I am sure!"

"No, no, no," said Miss Betsey. "Have some tea."

"Oh dear me, dear me, do you think it will do me any good?" cried my mother in a helpless manner.

"Of course it will," said Miss Betsey. "It's nothing but fancy. What do you call your girl?"

"I don't know that it will be a girl, yet, ma'am," said my mother innocently.

"Bless the Baby!" exclaimed Miss Betsey, unconsciously quoting the second sentiment of the pincushion in the drawer upstairs, but applying it to my mother instead of me, "I don't mean that. I mean your servant-girl."

"Peggotty," said my mother.

"Peggotty!" repeated Miss Betsey, with some indignation. "Do you mean to say, child, that any human being has gone into a Christian church, and got herself named Peggotty?"

"It's her surname," said my mother, faintly. "Mr Copperfield called her by it, because her Christian name was the same as mine."

"Here! Peggotty!" cried Miss Betsey, opening the parlour door. "Tea. Your mistress is a little unwell. Don't dawdle."

Having issued this mandate with as much potentiality as if she had been a recognized authority in the house ever since it had been a house, and having looked out to confront the amazed Peggotty coming along the passage with a candle at the sound of a strange voice, Miss Betsey shut the door again, and sat down as before: with her feet on the fender, the skirt of her dress tucked up, and her hands folded on one knee.

"You were speaking about its being a girl," said Miss Betsey. 'I have no doubt it will be a girl. I have a presentiment that it must be a girl. Now child, from the moment of the birth of this girl—"

"Perhaps boy," my mother took the liberty of putting in.

"I tell you I have a presentiment that it must be a girl," returned Miss Betsey. "Don't contradict. From the moment of this girl's birth, child, I intend to be her friend. I intend to be her godmother, and I beg you'll call her Betsey Trotwood Copperfield. There must be no mistakes in life with *this* Betsey Trotwood. There must be no trifling with *her* affections, poor dear. She must be well brought up, and well guarded from reposing any foolish confidences where they are not deserved. I must make that *my* care."

There was a twitch of Miss Betsey's head, after each of these sentences, as if her own old wrongs were working within her, and she repressed any plainer reference to them by strong constraint. So my mother suspected, at least, as she observed her by the low glimmer of the fire: too much scared by Miss Betsey, too uneasy in herself, and too subdued and bewildered altogether, to observe anything very clearly, or to know what to say.

"And was David good to you, child?" asked Miss Betsey, when she had been silent for a little while, and these motions of her head had gradually ceased. "Were you comfortable together?"

"We were very happy," said my mother. "Mr Copperfield was only too good to me."

"What, he spoilt you, I suppose?" returned Miss Betsey.

"For being quite alone and dependent on myself in this rough world again, yes, I fear he did indeed," sobbed my mother.

"Well! Don't cry!" said Miss Betsey. "You were not equally matched, child—if any two people *can* be equally matched—and so I asked the question. You were an orphan, weren't you?"

"Yes."

"And a governess?"

"I was nursery-governess in a family where Mr Copperfield came to visit. Mr Copperfield was very kind to me, and took a great deal of notice of me, and paid me a good deal of attention, and at last proposed to me. And I accepted him. And so we were married," said my mother simply.

"Ha! Poor Baby!" mused Miss Betsey, with her frown still bent upon the fire. "Do you know anything?"

"I beg your pardon, ma'am," faltered my mother.

"About keeping house, for instance," said Miss Betsey.

"Not much, I fear," returned my mother. "Not so much as I could wish. But Mr Copperfield was teaching me—"

("Much he knew about it himself!") said Miss Betsey in a parenthesis.

—"And I hope I should have improved, being very anxious to learn, and he very patient to teach me, if the great misfortune of his death"—my mother broke down again here, and could get no farther.

"Well, well!" said Miss Betsey.

—"I kept my housekeeping-book regularly, and balanced it with Mr Copperfield every night," cried my mother in another burst of distress, and breaking down again.

"Well, well!" said Miss Betsey. "Don't cry any more."

—"And I am sure we never had a word of difference respecting it, except when Mr Copperfield objected to my threes and fives being too much like each other, or to my putting curly tails to my sevens and nines," resumed my mother in another burst, and breaking down again.

"You'll make yourself ill," said Miss Betsey, "and you know that will not be good either for you or for my god-daughter. Come! You mustn't do it!"

This argument had some share in quieting my mother, though her increasing indisposition had a larger one. There was an interval of silence, only broken by Miss Betsey's occasionally ejaculating "Ha!" as she sat with her feet upon the fender.

"David had bought an annuity for himself with his money, I know," said she, by and by. "What did he do for you?"

"Mr Copperfield," said my mother, answering with some difficulty, "was so considerate and good as to secure the reversion of a part of it to me."

"How much?" asked Miss Betsey.

"A hundred and five pounds a year," said my mother.

"He might have done worse," said my aunt.

The word was appropriate to the moment. My mother was so much worse that Peggotty, coming in with the teaboard and candles, and seeing at a glance how ill she was,—as Miss Betsey might have done sooner if there had been light enough,—conveyed her upstairs to her own room with all speed; and immediately dispatched Ham Peggotty, her nephew, who had been for some days past secreted in the house, unknown to my mother, as a special messenger in case of emergency, to fetch the nurse and doctor.

Those allied powers were considerably astonished, when they arrived within a few minutes of each other, to find an unknown lady of portentous appearance, sitting before the fire, with her bonnet tied over her left arm, stopping her ears with jewellers' cotton. Peggotty knowing nothing about her, and my mother saying nothing about her, she was quite a mystery in the parlour; and the fact of her having a magazine of jewellers' cotton in her pocket, and sticking the article in her ears in that way, did not detract from the solemnity of her presence.

The doctor having been upstairs and come down again, and having satisfied himself, I suppose, that there was a probability of this unknown lady and himself having to sit there, face to face, for some hours, laid himself out to be polite and social. He was the meekest of his sex, the mildest of little men. He sidled in and out of a room, to take up the less space. He walked as softly as the Ghost in Hamlet, and more slowly. He carried his head on one side, partly in modest depreciation of himself, partly in modest propitiation of everybody else. It is nothing to say that he hadn't a word to throw at a dog. He couldn't have *thrown* a word at a mad dog. He might have offered him one gently, or half a one, or a fragment of one; for he spoke as slowly as he walked; but he wouldn't have been rude to him, and he couldn't have been quick with him, for any earthly consideration.

Mr Chillip, looking mildly at my aunt with his head on one side, and making her a little bow, said, in allusion to the jewellers' cotton, as he softly touched his left ear:

"Some local irritation, ma'am?"

"What!" replied my aunt, pulling the cotton out of one ear like a cork.

Mr Chillip was so alarmed by her abruptness—as he told my mother afterwards—that it was a mercy he didn't lose his presence of mind. But he repeated sweetly:

"Some local irritation, ma'am?"

"Nonsense!" replied my aunt, and corked herself again, at one blow.

Mr Chillip could do nothing after this, but sit and look at her feebly, as she sat and looked at the fire, until he was called upstairs again. After some quarter of an hour's absence, he returned.

"Well?" said my aunt, taking the cotton out of the ear nearest to him.

"Well, ma'am," returned Mr Chillip, "we are—we are progressing slowly, ma'am."

"Ba—a—ah!" said my aunt, with a perfect shake on the contemptuous interjection. And corked herself as before.

Really—really—as Mr Chillip told my mother, he was almost shocked; speaking in a professional point of view alone, he was almost shocked. But he sat and looked at her, notwithstanding, for nearly two hours, as she sat looking at the fire, until he was again called out. After another absence, he again returned.

"Well?" said my aunt, taking out the cotton on that side again.

"Well, ma'am," returned Mr Chillip, "we are—we are progressing slowly, ma'am."

"Ya—a—ah!" said my aunt. With such a snarl at him, that Mr Chillip absolutely could not bear it. It was really calculated to break his spirit, he said afterwards. He preferred to go and sit upon the stairs, in the dark and a strong draught, until he was again sent for.

Ham Peggotty, who went to the national school, and was a very dragon at his catechism, and who may therefore be regarded as a credible witness, reported next day, that happening to peep in at the parlour-door an hour after this, he was instantly descried by Miss Betsey, then walking to and fro in a state of agitation, and pounced upon before he could make his escape. That there were now occasional sounds of feet and voices overhead which he inferred the cotton did not exclude, from the circumstance of his evidently being clutched by the lady as a victim on whom to expend her superabundant agitation when the sounds were loudest. That, marching him constantly up and down by the collar (as if he had been taking too much laudanum), she, at those times, shook him, rumpled his hair, made light of his linen, stopped *his* ears as if she confounded them with her own, and otherwise tousled and maltreated him. This was in part confirmed by his aunt, who saw him at half past twelve o'clock, soon after his release, and affirmed that he was then as red as I was.

The mild Mr Chillip could not possibly bear malice at such a time, if at any time. He sidled into the parlour as soon as he was at liberty, and said to my aunt in his meekest manner:

"Well, ma'am, I am happy to congratulate you."

"What upon?" said my aunt, sharply.

Mr Chillip was fluttered again, by the extreme severity of my aunt's manner; so he made her a little bow and gave her a little smile, to mollify her.

"Mercy on the man, what's he doing!" cried my aunt, impatiently. "Can't he speak?"

"Be calm, my dear ma'am," said Mr Chillip, in his softest accents. "There is no longer any occasion for uneasiness, ma'am. Be calm."

It has since been considered almost a miracle that my aunt didn't shake him, and shake what he had to say, out of him. She only shook her own head at him, but in a way that made him quail.

"Well, ma'am," resumed Mr Chillip, as soon as he had courage, "I am happy to congratulate you. All is now over, ma'am, and well over."

During the five minutes or so that Mr Chillip devoted to the delivery of this oration, my aunt eyed him narrowly.

"How is she?" said my aunt, folding her arms with her bonnet still tied on one of them.

"Well, ma'am, she will soon be quite comfortable, I hope," returned Mr Chillip. "Quite as comfortable as we can expect a young mother to be, under these melancholy domestic circumstances. There cannot be any objection to your seeing her presently, ma'am. It may do her good."

"And *she*. How is *she?*" said my aunt, sharply.

Mr Chillip laid his head a little more on one side, and looked at my aunt like an amiable bird.

"The baby," said my aunt. "How is she?"

"Ma'am," returned Mr Chillip, "I apprehended you had known. It's a boy."

My aunt said never a word, but took her bonnet by the strings, in the manner of a sling, aimed a blow at Mr Chillip's head with it, put it on bent, walked out, and never came back. She vanished like a discontented fairy; or like one of those supernatural beings, whom it was popularly supposed I was entitled to see; and never came back any more.

No. I lay in my basket, and my mother lay in her bed; but Betsey Trotwood Copperfield was for ever in the land of dreams and shadows, the tremendous region whence I had so lately travelled; and the light upon the window of our room shone out upon the earthly bourne of all such travellers, and the mound above the ashes and the dust that once was he, without whom I had never been.

Chapter II

I OBSERVE

THE first objects that assume a distinct presence before me, as I look far back, into the blank of my infancy, are my mother with her pretty hair and youthful shape, and Peggotty with no shape at all, and eyes so dark that they seemed to darken their whole neighbourhood in her face, and cheeks and arms so hard and red that I wondered the birds didn't peck her in preference to apples.

I believe I can remember these two at a little distance apart, dwarfed to my sight by stooping down or kneeling on the floor, and I going unsteadily from the one to the other. I have an impression on my mind which I cannot distinguish from actual remembrance, of the touch of Peggotty's forefinger as she used to hold it out to me, and of its being roughened by needlework, like a pocket nutmeg-grater.

This may be fancy, though I think the memory of most of us can go farther back into such times than many of us suppose; just as I believe the power of observation in numbers of very young children to be quite wonderful for its closeness and accuracy. Indeed, I think that most grown men who are remarkable in this respect, may with greater propriety be said not to have lost the faculty, than to have acquired it; the rather, as I generally observe such men to retain a certain freshness, and gentleness, and capacity of being pleased, which are also an inheritance they have preserved from their childhood.

I might have a misgiving that I am "meandering" in stopping to say this, but that it brings me to remark that I build these conclusions, in part upon my own experience of myself; and if it should appear from anything I may set down in this narrative that I was a child of close observation, or that as a man I have a strong memory of my childhood, I undoubtedly lay claim to both of these characteristics.

Looking back, as I was saying, into the blank of my infancy, the first objects I can remember as standing out by themselves from a confusion of things, are my mother and Peggotty. What else do I remember? Let me see.

There comes out of the cloud, our house—not new to me, but quite familiar, in its earliest remembrance. On the ground-floor is Peggotty's kitchen, opening into a back yard; with a pigeon-house on a pole, in the centre, without any pigeons in it; a great dog-kennel in a corner, without any dog; and a quantity of fowls that look terribly tall to me, walking about, in a menacing and ferocious manner. There is one cock who gets upon a post to crow, and seems to take particular notice of me as I look at him through the kitchen window, who makes me shiver, he is so fierce. Of the geese outside the side-gate who come waddling after me with their long necks stretched out when I go that way, I dream at night: as a man environed by wild beasts might dream of lions.

Here is a long passage—what an enormous perspective I make of it!—leading from Peggotty's kitchen to the front door. A dark store-room opens out of it, and that is a place to be run past at night; for I don't know what may be among those tubs and jars and old tea-chests, when there is nobody in there with a dimly-burning light, letting a mouldy air come out of the door, in which there is the smell of soap, pickles, pepper, candles, and coffee, all at one whiff. Then there are the two parlours: the parlour in which we sit of an evening, my mother and I and Peggotty—for Peggotty is quite our companion, when her work is done and we are alone—and the best parlour where we sit on a Sunday; grandly, but not so comfortably. There is something of a doleful air about that room to me, for Peggotty has told me—I don't know when, but apparently ages ago—about my father's funeral, and the company having their black cloaks put on. One Sunday night my mother reads to Peggotty and me in there, how Lazarus was raised up from the dead. And I am so frightened that they are afterwards obliged to take me out of bed, and shew me the quiet churchyard out of the bedroom window, with the dead all lying in their graves at rest, below the solemn moon.

There is nothing half so green that I know anywhere, as the grass of that churchyard; nothing half so shady as its trees; nothing half so quiet as its tombstones. The sheep are feeding there, when I kneel up, early in the morning, in my little bed in a closet within my mother's room, to look out at it; and I see the red light shining on the sun-dial, and think within myself, "Is the sun-dial glad, I wonder, that it can tell the time again?"

Here is our pew in the church. What a high-backed pew! With a window near it, out of which our house can be seen, and *is* seen many times during the morning's service, by Peggotty, who likes to make herself as sure as she can that it's not being robbed, or is not in flames. But though Peggotty's eye wanders, she is much offended if mine does, and frowns to me, as I stand upon the seat, that I am to look at the clergyman. But I can't always look at him—I know him without that white thing on, and I am afraid of his wondering why I stare so, and perhaps stopping the service to inquire—and what am I to do? It's a dreadful thing to gape, but I must do something. I look at my mother, but *she* pretends not to see me. I look at a boy in the aisle, and *he* makes faces at me. I look at the sunlight coming in at the open door through the porch, and there I see a stray sheep—I don't mean a sinner, but mutton—half making up his mind to come into the church. I feel that if I looked at him any longer, I might be tempted to say something out loud; and what would become of me then! I look up at the monumental tablets on the wall, and try to think of Mr Bodgers late of this parish, and what the feelings of Mrs Bodgers must have been, when affliction sore, long time Mr Bodgers bore, and physicians were in vain. I wonder whether they called in Mr Chillip, and he was in vain; and if so, how he likes to be reminded of it once a week. I look from Mr Chillip, in his Sunday neckcloth, to the pulpit; and think what a good place it would be to play in, and what a castle it would make, with another boy coming up the stairs to attack it, and having the velvet cushion with the tassels thrown down on his head. In time my eyes gradually shut up; and, from seeming to hear the clergyman singing a drowsy song in the heat, I hear nothing, until I fall off the seat with a crash, and am taken out, more dead than alive, by Peggotty.

And now I see the outside of our house, with the latticed bedroom-windows standing open to let in the sweet-smelling air, and the ragged old rooks'-nests still dangling in the elm-trees at the bottom of the front garden. Now I am in the garden at the back, beyond the yard where the empty pigeon-house and dog-kennel are—a very preserve of butterflies, as I remember it, with a high fence, and a gate and padlock; where the fruit clusters on the trees, riper and richer than fruit has ever been since, in any other garden, and where my mother gathers some in a basket, while I stand by, bolting furtive gooseberries, and trying to look unmoved. A great wind rises, and the summer is gone in a moment. We are playing in the winter twilight, dancing about the parlour. When my mother is out of breath and rests herself in an elbow-chair, I watch her winding her bright curls round her fingers, and straitening her waist, and nobody knows better than I do that she likes to look so well, and is proud of being so pretty.

That is among my very earliest impressions. That, and a sense that we were both a little afraid of Peggotty, and submitted ourselves in most things to her direction, were among the first opinions—if they may be so called—that I ever derived from what I saw.

Peggotty and I were sitting one night by the parlour fire, alone. I had been reading to Peggotty about crocodiles. I must have read very perspicuously, or the poor soul must have been deeply interested, for I remember she had a cloudy impression, after I had done, that they were a sort of vegetable. I was tired of reading, and dead sleepy; but having leave, as a high treat, to sit up until my mother came home from spending the evening at a neighbour's, I would rather have died upon my post (of course) than have gone to bed. I had reached that stage of sleepiness when Peggotty seemed to swell and grow immensely large. I propped my eyelids open with my two forefingers, and looked perseveringly at her as she sat at work; at the little bit of wax-candle she kept for her thread—how old it looked, being so wrinkled in all directions!—at the little house with a thatched roof, where the yard-measure lived; at her work-box with a sliding lid, with a view of St Paul's Cathedral (with a pink dome) painted on the top; at the brass thimble on her finger; at herself, whom I thought lovely. I felt so sleepy, that I knew if I lost sight of anything for a moment, I was gone.

"Peggotty," says I, suddenly, "were you ever married?"

"Lord, Master Davy," replied Peggotty. "What's put marriage in your head?"

She answered with such a start, that it quite awoke me. And then she stopped in her work, and looked at me, with her needle drawn out to its thread's length.

"But *were* you ever married, Peggotty?" says I. "You are a very handsome woman, an't you?"

I thought her in a different style from my mother, certainly; but of another school of beauty, I considered her a perfect example. There was a red velvet footstool in the best parlour, on which my mother had painted a nosegay. The ground-work of that stool, and

Peggotty's complexion appeared to me to be one and the same thing. The stool was smooth, and Peggotty was rough, but that made no difference.

"Me handsome, Davy!" said Peggotty. "Lawk, no, my dear! But what put marriage in your head?"

"I don't know!—You mustn't marry more than one person at a time, may you, Peggotty?"

"Certainly not," says Peggotty, with the promptest decision.

"But if you marry a person, and the person dies, why then you may marry another person, mayn't you, Peggotty?"

"You MAY," says Peggotty, "if you choose, my dear. That's a matter of opinion."

"But what is your opinion, Peggotty?" said I.

I asked her, and looked curiously at her, because she looked so curiously at me.

"My opinion is," said Peggotty, taking her eyes from me, after a little indecision and going on with her work, "that I never was married myself, Master Davy, and that I don't expect to be. That's all I know about the subject."

"You an't cross, I suppose, Peggotty, are you?" said I, after sitting quiet for a minute.

I really thought she was, she had been so short with me; but I was quite mistaken: for she laid aside her work (which was a stocking of her own), and opening her arms wide, took my curly head within them, and gave it a good squeeze. I know it was a good squeeze, because, being very plump, whenever she made any little exertion after she was dressed, some of the buttons on the back of her gown flew off. And I recollect two bursting to the opposite side of the parlour, while she was hugging me.

"Now let me hear some more about the Crorkindills," said Peggotty, who was not quite right in the name yet, "for I an't heard half enough."

I couldn't quite understand why Peggotty looked so queer, or why she was so ready to go back to the crocodiles. However, we returned to those monsters, with fresh wakefulness on my part, and we left their eggs in the sand for the sun to hatch; and we ran away from them, and baffled them by constantly turning, which they were unable to do quickly, on account of their unwieldy make; and we went into the water after them, as natives, and put sharp pieces of timber down their throats; and in short we ran the whole crocodile gauntlet. I did, at least; but I had my doubts of Peggotty, who was thoughtfully sticking her needle into various parts of her face and arms, all the time.

We had exhausted the crocodiles, and begun with the alligators, when the garden-bell rang. We went out to the door; and there was my mother, looking unusually pretty, I thought, and with her a gentleman with beautiful black hair and whiskers, who had walked home with us from church last Sunday.

As my mother stooped down on the threshold to take me in her arms and kiss me, the gentleman said I was a more highly privileged little fellow than a monarch—or something like that; for my later understanding comes, I am sensible, to my aid here.

"What does that mean?" I asked him, over her shoulder.

He patted me on the head; but somehow, I didn't like him or his deep voice, and I was jealous that his hand should touch my mother's in touching me—which it did. I put it away, as well as I could.

"Oh, Davy!" remonstrated my mother.

"Dear boy!" said the gentleman. "I cannot wonder at his devotion!"

I never saw such a beautiful colour on my mother's face before. She gently chid me for being rude; and, keeping me close to her shawl, turned to thank the gentleman for taking so much trouble as to bring her home. She put her hand to him as she spoke, and, as he met it with his own, she glanced, I thought, at me.

"Let us say 'good night,' my fine boy," said the gentleman, when he had bent his head—*I* saw him!—over my mother's little glove.

"Good night!" said I.

"Come! Let us be the best friends in the world!" said the gentleman, laughing. "Shake hands!"

My right hand was in my mother's left, so I gave him the other.

"Why, that's the wrong hand, Davy!" laughed the gentleman.

My mother drew my right hand forward, but I was resolved, for my former reason, not to give it him, and I did not. I gave him the other, and he shook it heartily, and said I was a brave fellow, and went away.

At this minute I see him turn round in the garden, and give us a last look with his ill-omened black eyes, before the door was shut.

Peggotty, who had not said a word or moved a finger, secured the fastenings instantly, and we all went into the parlour. My mother, contrary to her usual habit, instead of coming to the elbow-chair by the fire, remained at the other end of the room, and sat singing to herself.

"—Hope you have had a pleasant evening, ma'am," said Peggotty, standing as stiff as a barrel in the centre of the room, with a candlestick in her hand.

"Much obliged to you, Peggotty," returned my mother, in a cheerful voice, "I have had a *very* pleasant evening."

"A stranger or so makes an agreeable change," suggested Peggotty.

"A very agreeable change, indeed," returned my mother.

Peggotty continuing to stand motionless in the middle of the room, and my mother resuming her singing, I fell asleep, though I was not so sound asleep but that I could hear voices, without hearing what they said. When I half awoke from this uncomfortable doze, I found Peggotty and my mother both in tears, and both talking.

"Not such a one as this, Mr Copperfield wouldn't have liked," said Peggotty. "That I say, and that I swear!"

"Good Heavens!" cried my mother, "you'll drive me mad! Was ever any poor girl so ill-used by her servants as I am! Why do I do myself the injustice of calling myself a girl? Have I never been married, Peggotty?"

"God knows you have, ma'am," returned Peggotty.

"Then, how can you dare," said my mother—"you know I don't mean how can you dare, Peggotty, but how can you have the heart—to make me so uncomfortable and say such bitter things to me, when you are well aware that I haven't, out of this place, a single friend to turn to?"

"The more's the reason," returned Peggotty, "for saying that it won't do. No! That it won't do. No! No price could make it do. No!"—I thought Peggotty would have thrown the candlestick away, she was so emphatic with it.

"How can you be so aggravating," said my mother, shedding more tears than before, "as to talk in such an unjust manner! How can you go on as if it was all settled and arranged, Peggotty, when I tell you over and over again, you cruel thing, that beyond the commonest civilities nothing has passed! You talk of admiration. What am I to do? If people are so silly as to indulge the sentiment, is it my fault? What am I to do, I ask you? Would you wish me to shave my head and black my face, or disfigure myself with a burn, or a scald, or something of that sort? I dare say you would, Peggotty. I dare say you'd quite enjoy it."

Peggotty seemed to take this aspersion very much to heart, I thought.

"And my dear boy," cried my mother, coming to the elbow-chair in which I was, and caressing me, "my own little Davy! Is it to be hinted to me that I am wanting in affection for my precious treasure, the dearest little fellow that ever was!"

"Nobody never went and hinted no such a thing," said Peggotty.

"You did, Peggotty!" returned my mother. "You know you did. What else was it possible to infer from what you said, you unkind creature, when you know as well as I do, that on his account only last quarter I wouldn't buy myself a new parasol, though that old green one is frayed the whole way up, and the fringe is perfectly mangy? You know it is, Peggotty. You can't deny it." Then, turning affectionately to me, with her cheek against mine, "Am I a naughty mama to you, Davy? Am I a nasty, cruel, selfish, bad mama? Say I am, my child; say 'yes,' dear boy, and Peggotty will love you; and Peggotty's love is a great deal better than mine, Davy. I don't love you at all, do I?"

At this, we all fell a-crying together. I think I was the loudest of the party, but I am sure we were all sincere about it. I was quite heart-broken myself, and am afraid that in the first transports of wounded tenderness I called Peggotty a "Beast." That honest creature was in deep affliction, I remember, and must have become quite buttonless on the occasion; for a little volley of those explosives went off, when, after having made it up with my mother, she kneeled down by the elbow-chair, and made it up with me.

We went to bed greatly dejected. My sobs kept waking me, for a long time; and when one very strong sob quite hoisted me up in bed, I found my mother sitting on the coverlet, and leaning over me. I fell asleep in her arms, after that, and slept soundly.

Whether it was the following Sunday when I saw the gentleman again, or whether there was any greater lapse of time before he reappeared, I cannot recall. I don't profess to be clear about dates. But there he was, in church, and he walked home with us afterwards. He came in, too, to look at a famous geranium we had, in the parlour-window. It did not appear to me that he took much notice of it, but before he went he asked my mother to give him a bit of the blossom. She begged him to choose it for himself, but he refused to do that—I could not understand why—so she plucked it for him, and gave it into his hand. He said he would never, never, part with it any more; and I thought he must be quite a fool not to know that it would fall to pieces in a day or two.

Peggotty began to be less with us, of an evening, than she had always been. My mother deferred to her very much—more than usual, it occurred to me—and we were all three excellent friends; still we were different from what we used to be, and were not so comfortable among ourselves. Sometimes I fancied that Peggotty perhaps objected to my mother's wearing all the pretty dresses she had in her drawers, or to her going so often to visit at that neighbour's; but I couldn't, to my satisfaction, make out how it was.

Gradually, I became used to seeing the gentleman with the black whiskers. I liked him no better than at first, and had the same uneasy jealousy of him; but if I had any reason for it beyond a child's instinctive dislike, and a general idea that Peggotty and I could make much of my mother without any help, it certainly was not *the* reason that I might have found if I had been older. No such thing came into my mind, or near it. I could observe, in little pieces, as it were; but as to making a net of a number of these pieces, and catching anybody in it, that was, as yet, beyond me.

One autumn morning I was with my mother in the front garden, when Mr Murdstone—I knew him by that name now—came by, on horseback. He reined up his horse to salute my mother, and said he was going to Lowestoft to see some friends who were there with a yacht, and merrily proposed to take me on the saddle before him if I would like the ride.

The air was so clear and pleasant, and the horse seemed to like the idea of the ride so much himself, as he stood snorting and pawing at the garden-gate, that I had a great desire to go. So I was sent upstairs to Peggotty to be made spruce; and in the meantime Mr Murdstone dismounted, and, with his horse's bridle drawn over his arm, walked slowly up and down on the outer side of the sweetbriar fence, while my mother walked slowly up and down on the inner to keep him company. I recollect Peggotty and I peeping out at them from my little window; I recollect how closely they seemed to be examining the sweetbriar between them, as they strolled along; and how, from being in a perfectly angelic temper, Peggotty turned cross in a moment, and brushed my hair the wrong way, excessively hard.

Mr Murdstone and I were soon off, and trotting along on the green turf by the side of the road. He held me quite easily with one arm, and I don't think I was restless usually; but I could not make up my mind to sit in front of him without turning my head sometimes, and looking up in his face. He had that kind of shallow black eye—I want a better word to express an eye that has no depth in it to be looked into—which, when it is abstracted, seems from some peculiarity of light to be disfigured, for a moment at a time, by a cast. Several times when I glanced at him, I observed that appearance with a sort of awe, and wondered what he was thinking about so closely. His hair and whiskers were blacker and thicker, looked at so near, than even I had given them credit for being. A squareness about the lower part of his face, and the dotted indication of the strong black beard he shaved close every day, reminded me of the wax-work that had travelled into our neighbourhood some half-a-year before. This, his regular eyebrows, and the rich white, and black, and brown, of his complexion—confound his complexion, and his memory!—made me think him, in spite of my misgivings, a very handsome man. I have no doubt that my poor dear mother thought him so too.

We went to an hotel by the sea, where two gentlemen were smoking cigars in a room by themselves. Each of them was lying on at least four chairs, and had a large rough jacket on. In a corner was a heap of coats and boat-cloaks, and a flag, all bundled up together.

They both rolled on to their feet in an untidy sort of manner, when we came in, and said, "Halloa, Murdstone! We thought you were dead!"

"Not yet," said Mr Murdstone.

"And who's this shaver?" said one of the gentlemen, taking hold of me.

"That's Davy," returned Mr Murdstone.

"Davy who?" said the gentleman. "Jones?"

"Copperfield," said Mr Murdstone.

"What! Bewitching Mrs Copperfield's encumbrance?" cried the gentleman. "The pretty little widow?"

"Quinion," said Mr Murdstone, "take care, if you please. Somebody's sharp."

"Who is?" asked the gentleman, laughing.

I looked up, quickly; being curious to know.

"Only Brooks of Sheffield," said Mr Murdstone.

I was quite relieved to find that it was only Brooks of Sheffield; for, at first, I really thought it was I.

There seemed to be something very comical in the reputation of Mr Brooks of Sheffield, for both the gentlemen laughed heartily when he was mentioned, and Mr Murdstone was a good deal amused also. After some laughing, the gentleman whom he had called Quinion, said:

"And what is the opinion of Brooks of Sheffield, in reference to the projected business?"

"Why, I don't know that Brooks understands much about it at present," replied Mr

Murdstone; "but he is not generally favourable, I believe."

There was more laughter at this, and Mr Quinion said he would ring the bell for some sherry in which to drink to Brooks. This he did; and when the wine came, he made me have a little, with a biscuit, and, before I drank it, stand up and say, "Confusion to Brooks of Sheffield!" The toast was received with great applause, and such hearty laughter that it made me laugh too; at which they laughed the more. In short, we quite enjoyed ourselves.

We walked about on the cliff after that, and sat on the grass, and looked at things through a telescope—I could make out nothing myself when it was put to my eye, but I pretended I could—and then we came back to the hotel to an early dinner. All the time we were out, the two gentlemen smoked incessantly—which, I thought, if I might judge from the smell of their rough coats, they must have been doing, ever since the coats had first come home from the tailor's. I must not forget that we went on board the yacht, where they all three descended into the cabin, and were busy with some papers. I saw them quite hard at work, when I looked down through the open skylight. They left me, during this time, with a very nice man with a very large head of red hair and a very small shiny hat upon it, who had got a cross-barred shirt or waist-coat on, with "Skylark" in capital letters across the chest. I thought it was his name; and that as he lived on board ship and hadn't a street door to put his name on, he put it there instead; but when I called him Mr Skylark, he said it meant the vessel.

I observed all day that Mr Murdstone was graver and steadier than the two gentlemen. They were very gay and careless. They joked freely with one another, but seldom with him. It appeared to me that he was more clever and cold than they were, and that they regarded him with something of my own feeling. I remarked that, once or twice when Mr Quinion was talking, he looked at Mr Murdstone sideways, as if to make sure of his not being displeased; and that once when Mr Passnidge (the other gentleman) was in high spirits, he trod upon his foot, and gave him a secret caution with his eyes, to observe Mr Murdstone, who was sitting stern and silent. Nor do I recollect that Mr Murdstone laughed at all that day, except at the Sheffield joke—and that, by the by, was his own.

We went home early in the evening. It was a very fine evening, and my mother and he had another stroll by the sweetbriar, while I was sent in to get my tea. When he was gone, my mother asked me all about the day I had had, and what they had said and done. I mentioned what they had said about her, and she laughed, and told me they were impudent fellows who talked nonsense—but I knew it pleased her. I knew it quite as well as I know it now. I took the opportunity of asking if she was at all acquainted with Mr Brooks of Sheffield, but she answered No, only she supposed he must be a manufacturer in the knife and fork way.

Can I say of her face—altered as I have reason to remember it, perished as I know it is—that it is gone, when here it comes before me at this instant, as distinct as any face that I may choose to look on in a crowded street? Can I say of her innocent and girlish beauty, that it faded, and was no more, when its breath falls on my cheek now, as it fell that night? Can I say she ever changed, when my remembrance brings her back to life, thus only; and, truer to its loving youth than I have been, or man ever is, still holds fast what it cherished then?

I write of her just as she was when I had gone to bed after this talk, and she came to bid me good night. She kneeled down playfully by the side of the bed, and laying her chin upon her hands, and laughing, said:

"What was it they said, Davy? Tell me again. I can't believe it."

" 'Bewitching——' " I began.

My mother put her hands upon my lips to stop me.

"It was never bewitching," she said, laughing. "It never could have been bewitching, Davy. Now I know it wasn't!"

"Yes, it was. 'Bewitching Mrs Copperfield,' " I repeated stoutly. "And, 'pretty.' "

"No, no, it was never pretty. Not pretty," interposed my mother, laying her fingers on my lips again.

"Yes it was. 'Pretty little widow.' "

"What foolish, impudent creatures!" cried my mother, laughing and covering her face. "What ridiculous men! An't they? Davy dear——"

"Well, Ma."

"Don't tell Peggotty; she might be angry with them. I am dreadfully angry with them myself; but I would rather Peggotty didn't know."

I promised, of course; and we kissed one another over and over again, and I soon fell fast asleep.

It seems to me, at this distance of time, as if it were the next day when Peggotty broached the striking and adventurous proposition I am about to mention; but it was probably about two months afterwards.

We were sitting as before, one evening (when my mother was out as before), in company with the stocking and the yard-measure, and the bit of wax, and the box with St Paul's on the lid, and the crocodile book, when Peggotty, after looking at me several times, and opening her mouth as if she were going to speak, without doing it—which I thought was merely gaping, or I should have been rather alarmed—said coaxingly:

"Master Davy, how should you like to go along with me and spend a fortnight at my brother's at Yarmouth? Wouldn't *that* be a treat?"

"Is your brother an agreeable man, Peggotty?" I inquired, provisionally.

"Oh, what an agreeable man he is!" cried Peggotty, holding up her hands. "Then there's the sea; and the boats and ships; and the fishermen; and the beach; and Am to play with——"

Peggotty meant her nephew Ham, mentioned in my first chapter; but she spoke of him as a morsel of English Grammar.

I was flushed by her summary of delights, and replied that it would indeed be a treat, but what would my mother say?

"Why then I'll as good as bet a guinea," said Peggotty, intent upon my face, "that she'll let us go. I'll ask her, if you like, as soon as ever she comes home. There now!"

"But what's she to do while we're away?" said I, putting my small elbows on the table to argue the point. "She can't live by herself."

If Peggotty were looking for a hole, all of a sudden, in the heel of that stocking, it must have been a very little one indeed, and not worth darning.

"I say! Peggotty! She can't live by herself, you know."

"Oh, bless you!" said Peggotty, looking at me again at last. "Don't you know? She's going to stay for a fortnight with Mrs Grayper. Mrs Grayper's going to have a lot of company."

Oh! If that was it, I was quite ready to go. I waited, in the utmost impatience, until my mother came home from Mrs Grayper's (for it was that identical neighbour), to ascertain if we could get leave to carry out this great idea. Without being nearly so much surprised as I had expected, my mother entered into it readily; and it was all arranged that night, and my board and lodging during the visit were to be paid for.

The day soon came for our going. It was such an early day that it came soon, even to me, who was in a fever of expectation, and half afraid that an earthquake or a fiery mountain, or some other great convulsion of nature, might interpose to stop the expedition. We were to go in a carrier's cart, which departed in the morning after breakfast. I would have given any money to have been allowed to wrap myself up over-night, and sleep in my hat and boots.

It touches me nearly now, although I tell it lightly, to recollect how eager I was to leave my happy home; to think how little I suspected what I did leave for ever.

I am glad to recollect that when the carrier's cart was at the gate, and my mother stood there kissing me, a grateful fondness for her and for the old place I had never turned my back upon before, made me cry. I am glad to know that my mother cried too, and that I felt her heart beat against mine.

I am glad to recollect that when the carrier began to move, my mother ran out at the gate, and called to him to stop, that she might kiss me once more. I am glad to dwell upon the earnestness and love with which she lifted up her face to mine, and did so.

As we left her standing in the road, Mr Murdstone came up to where she was, and seemed to expostulate with her for being so moved. I was looking back round the awning of the cart, and wondered what business it was of his. Peggotty, who was also looking back on the other side, seemed anything but satisfied; as the face she brought back in the cart denoted.

I sat looking at Peggotty for some time, in a reverie on this supposititious case: whether, if she were employed to lose me like the boy in the fairy tale, I should be able to track my way home again by the buttons she would shed.

Chapter III

I HAVE A CHANGE

THE carrier's horse was the laziest horse in the world, I should hope, and shuffled along, with his head down, as if he liked to keep people waiting to whom the packages were directed. I fancied, indeed, that he sometimes chuckled audibly over this reflection, but the carrier said he was only troubled with a cough.

The carrier had a way of keeping his head down, like his horse, and of drooping sleepily forward as he drove, with one of his arms on each of his knees. I say "drove," but it struck me that the cart would have gone to Yarmouth quite as well without him, for the horse did all that; and as to conversation, he had no idea of it but whistling.

Peggotty had a basket of refreshments on her knee, which would have lasted us out handsomely, if we had been going to London by the same conveyance. We ate a good deal, and slept a good deal. Peggotty always went to sleep with her chin upon the handle of the basket, her hold of which never relaxed; and I could not have believed unless I had heard her do it, that one defenceless woman could have snored so much.

We made so many deviations up and down lanes, and were such a long time delivering a bedstead at a public-house, and calling at other places, that I was quite tired, and very glad, when we saw Yarmouth. It looked rather spongy and soppy, I thought, as I carried my eye over the great dull waste that lay across the river; and I could not help wondering, if the world were really as round as my geography book said, how any part of it came to be so flat. But I reflected that Yarmouth might be situated at one of the poles; which would account for it.

As we drew a little nearer, and saw the whole adjacent prospect lying a straight low line under the sky, I hinted to Peggotty that a mound or so might have improved it; and also that if the land had been a little more separated from the sea, and the town and the tide had not been quite so much mixed up, like toast and water, it would have been nicer. But Peggotty said, with greater emphasis than usual, that we must take things as we found them, and that, for her part, she was proud to call herself a Yarmouth Bloater.

When we got into the street (which was strange enough to me) and smelt the fish, and pitch, and oakum, and tar, and saw the sailors walking about, and the carts jingling up and down over the stones, I felt that I had done so busy a place an injustice; and said as much to Peggotty, who heard my expressions of delight with great complacency, and told me it was well known (I suppose to those who had the good fortune to be born Bloaters) that Yarmouth was, upon the whole, the finest place in the universe.

"Here's my Am!" screamed Peggotty, "growed out of knowledge!"

He was waiting for us, in fact, at the public-house; and asked me how I found myself, like an old acquaintance. I did not feel, at first, that I knew him as well as he knew me, because he had never come to our house since the night I was born, and naturally he had the advantage of me. But our intimacy was much advanced by his taking me on his back to carry me home. He was, now, a huge, strong fellow of six feet high, broad in proportion, and round-shouldered; but with a simpering boy's face and curly light hair that gave him quite a sheepish look. He was dressed in a canvas jacket, and a pair of such very stiff trousers that they would have stood quite as well alone, without any legs in them. And you couldn't so properly have said he wore a hat, as that he was covered in a-top, like an old building, with something pitchy.

Ham carrying me on his back and a small box of ours under his arm, and Peggotty carrying another small box of ours, we turned down lanes bestrewn with bits of chips and little hillocks of sand, and went past gas-works, rope-walks, boat-builders' yards, shipwrights' yards, ship-breakers' yards, caulkers' yards, riggers' lofts, smiths' forges, and a great litter of such places, until we came out upon the dull waste I had already seen at a distance; when Ham said,

"Yon's our house, Mas'r Davy!"

I looked in all directions, as far as I could stare over the wilderness, and away at the sea, and away at the river, but no house could *I* make out. There was a black barge, or some other kind of superannuated boat, not far off, high and dry on the ground, with an iron funnel sticking out of it for a chimney and smoking very cosily; but nothing else in the way of a habitation that was visible to *me*.

"That's not it?" said I. "That ship-looking thing?"

"That's it, Mas'r Davy," returned Ham.

If it had been Aladdin's palace, roc's egg and all, I suppose I could not have been more charmed with the romantic idea of living in it. There was a delightful door cut in the side, and it was roofed in, and there were little windows in it; but the wonderful charm of it was, that it was a real boat which had no doubt been upon the water hundreds of times, and which had never been intended to be lived in, on dry land. That was the captivation of it to me. If it had ever been meant to be lived in, I might have thought it small, or inconvenient, or lonely; but never having been designed for any such use, it became a perfect abode.

It was beautifully clean inside, and as tidy as possible. There was a table, and a Dutch clock, and a chest of drawers, and on the chest of drawers there was a tea-tray with a painting on it of a lady with a parasol, taking a walk with a military-looking child who was trundling a hoop. The tray was kept from tumbling down, by a bible; and the tray, if it had tumbled down, would have smashed a quantity of cups and saucers and a teapot that were grouped around the book. On the walls there were some common coloured pictures, framed and glazed, of scripture subjects; such as I have never seen since in the hands of pedlars, without seeing the whole interior of Peggotty's brother's house again, at one view. Abraham in red going to sacrifice Isaac in blue, and Daniel in yellow cast into a den of green lions, were the most prominent of these. Over the little mantelshelf, was a picture of the "Sarah Jane" lugger, built at Sunderland, with a real little wooden stern stuck on to it; a work of art, combining composition with carpentry, which I considered to be one of the most enviable possessions that the world could afford. There were some hooks in the beams of the ceiling, the use of which I did not divine then; and some lockers and boxes and conveniences of that sort, which served for seats and eked out the chairs.

All this I saw in the first glance after I crossed the threshold—child-like, according to my theory—and then Peggotty opened a little door and showed me my bedroom. It was the completest and most desirable bedroom ever seen—in the stern of the vessel; with a little window, where the rudder used to go through; a little looking-glass, just the right height for me, nailed against the wall, and framed with oyster-shells; a little bed, which there was just room enough to get into; and a nosegay of seaweed in a blue mug on the table. The walls were whitewashed as white as milk, and the patchwork counterpane made my eyes quite ache with its brightness. One thing I particularly noticed in this delightful house, was the smell of fish; which was so searching, that when I took out my pocket-handkerchief to wipe my nose, I found it smelt exactly as if it had wrapped up a lobster. On my imparting this discovery in confidence to Peggotty, she informed me that her brother dealt in lobsters, crabs, and crawfish; and I afterwards found that a heap of these creatures, in a state of wonderful conglomeration with one another, and never leaving off pinching whatever they laid hold of, were usually to be found in a little wooden outhouse where the pots and kettles were kept.

We were welcomed by a very civil woman in a white apron, whom I had seen curtseying at the door when I was on Ham's back, about a quarter of a mile off. Likewise by a most beautiful little girl (or I thought her so) with a necklace of blue beads on, who wouldn't let me kiss her when I offered to, but ran away and hid herself. By and by, when we had dined in a sumptuous manner off boiled dabs, melted butter, and potatoes, with a chop for me, a hairy man with a very good-natured face came home. As he called Peggotty "Lass," and gave her a hearty smack on the cheek, I had no doubt, from the general propriety of her conduct, that he was her brother; and so he turned out—being presently introduced to me as Mr Peggotty, the master of the house.

"Glad to see you, sir," said Mr Peggotty. "You'll find us rough, sir, but you'll find us ready."

I thanked him, and replied that I was sure I should be happy in such a delightful place.

"How's your Ma, sir?" said Mr Peggotty. "Did you leave her pretty jolly?"

I gave Mr Peggotty to understand that she was as jolly as I could wish, and that she desired her compliments—which was a polite fiction on my part.

"I'm much obleeged to her, I'm sure," said Mr Peggotty. "Well, sir, if you can make out here, fur a fortnut, 'long wi' her," nodding at his sister, "and Ham, and little Em'ly, we shall be proud of your company."

Having done the honours of his house in this hospitable manner, Mr Peggotty went out to wash himself in a kettleful of hot water, remarking that "cold would never get *his* muck off." He soon returned, greatly improved in appearance; but so rubicund, that I couldn't help thinking his face had this in common with the lobsters, crabs, and crawfish,—that it went into the hot water very black, and came out very red.

After tea, when the door was shut and all was made snug (the nights being cold and misty now), it seemed to me the most delicious retreat that the imagination of man could conceive. To hear the wind getting up out at sea, to know that the fog was creeping over the desolate flat outside, and to look at the fire, and think that there was no house near but this one, and this one a boat, was like enchantment. Little Em'ly had overcome her shyness, and was sitting by my side upon the lowest and least of the lockers, which was just large enough for us two, and just fitted into the chimney corner. Mrs Peggotty with the white apron, was knitting on the opposite side of the fire. Peggotty at her needlework was as much at home with St Paul's and the bit of wax-candle, as if they had never known any other roof. Ham, who had been giving me my first lesson in all-fours, was trying to recollect a scheme of telling fortunes with the dirty cards, and was printing off fishy impressions of his thumb on all the cards he turned. Mr Peggotty was smoking his pipe. I felt it was a time for conversation and confidence.

"Mr Peggotty!" says I.

"Sir," says he.

"Did you give your son the name of Ham, because you lived in a sort of ark?"

Mr Peggotty seemed to think it a deep idea, but answered:

"No, sir. I never giv him no name."

"Who gave him that name, then?" said I, putting question number two of the catechism to Mr Peggotty.

"Why, sir, his father giv it him," said Mr Peggotty.

"I thought you were his father!"

"My brother Joe was *his* father," said Mr Peggotty.

"Dead, Mr Peggotty?" I hinted, after a respectful pause.

"Drowndead," said Mr Peggotty.

I was very much surprised that Mr Peggotty was not Ham's father, and began to wonder whether I was mistaken about his relationship to anybody else there. I was so curious to know, that I made up my mind to have it out with Mr Peggotty.

"Little Em'ly," I said, glancing at her. "She is your daughter, isn't she, Mr Peggotty?"

"No, sir. My brother-in-law, Tom, was *her* father."

I couldn't help it. "—Dead, Mr Peggotty?" I hinted, after another respectful silence.

"Drowndead," said Mr Peggotty.

I felt the difficulty of resuming the subject, but had not got to the bottom of it yet, and must get to the bottom somehow. So I said:

"Haven't you *any* children, Mr Peggotty?"

"No, master," he answered with a short laugh. "I'm a bacheldore."

"A bachelor!" I said, astonished. "Why, who's that, Mr Peggotty?" pointing to the person in the apron who was knitting.

"That's Missis Gummidge," said Mr Peggotty.

"Gummidge, Mr Peggotty?"

But at this point Peggotty—I mean my own peculiar Peggotty—made such impressive motions to me not to ask any more questions, that I could only sit and look at all the silent company, until it was time to go to bed. Then, in the privacy of my own little cabin, she informed me that Ham and Em'ly were an orphan nephew and niece, whom my host had at different times adopted in their childhood, when they were left destitute: and that Mrs Gummidge was the widow of his partner in a boat, who had died very poor. He was but a poor man himself, said Peggotty, but as good as gold and as true as steel—those were her similes. The only subject, she informed me, on which he ever showed a violent temper or swore an oath, was this generosity of his; and if it were ever referred to, by any one of them, he struck the table a heavy blow with his right hand (had split it on one such occasion), and swore a dreadful oath that he would be "Gormed" if he didn't cut and run for good, if it was ever mentioned again. It appeared, in answer to my inquiries, that nobody had the least idea of the etymology of this terrible verb passive to be gormed; but that they all regarded it as constituting a most solemn imprecation.

I was very sensible of my entertainer's goodness, and listened to the women's going to bed in another little crib like mine at the opposite end of the boat, and to him and Ham hanging up two hammocks for themselves on the hooks I had noticed in the roof, in a very luxurious state of mind, enhanced by my being sleepy. As slumber gradually stole upon me, I heard the wind howling out at sea and coming on across the flat so fiercely, that I had a lazy apprehension of the great deep rising in the night. But I bethought myself that I was in a boat, after all; and that a man like Mr Peggotty was not a bad person to have on board if anything did happen.

Nothing happened, however, worse than morning. Almost as soon as it shone upon the oyster-shell frame of my mirror I was out of bed, and out with little Em'ly, picking up stones upon the beach.

"You're quite a sailor, I suppose?" I said to Em'ly. I don't know that I supposed anything of the kind, but I felt it an act of gallantry to say something; and a shining sail close to us made such a pretty little image of itself, at the moment, in her bright eye, that it came into my head to say this.

"No," replied Em'ly, shaking her head, "I'm afraid of the sea."

"Afraid!" I said, with a becoming air of boldness, and looking very big at the mighty ocean. "*I* an't!"

"Ah! but it's cruel," said Em'ly. "I have seen it very cruel to some of our men. I have seen it tear a boat as big as our house, all to pieces."

"I hope it wasn't the boat that—"

"That father was drownded in?" said Em'ly. "No. Not that one, I never see that boat."

"Nor him?" I asked her.

Little Em'ly shook her head. "Not to remember!"

Here was a coincidence! I immediately went into an explanation how I had never seen my own father; and how my mother and I had always lived by ourselves in the happiest state imaginable, and lived so then, and always meant to live so; and how my father's grave was in the churchyard near our house, and shaded by a tree, beneath the boughs of which I had walked and heard the birds sing many a pleasant morning. But there were some differences between Em'ly's orphanhood and mine, it appeared. She had lost her mother before her father; and where her father's grave was no one knew, except that it was somewhere in the depths of the sea.

"Besides," said Em'ly, as she looked about for shells and pebbles, "your father was a gentleman and your mother is a lady; and my father was a fisherman and my mother was a fisherman's daughter, and my uncle Dan is a fisherman."

"Dan is Mr Peggotty, is he?" said I.

"Uncle Dan—yonder," answered Em'ly, nodding at the boat-house.

"Yes. I mean him. He must be very good, I should think?"

"Good?" said Em'ly. "If I was ever to be a lady, I'd give him a sky-blue coat with diamond buttons, nankeen trousers, a red velvet waistcoat, a cocked hat, a large gold watch, a silver pipe, and a box of money."

I said I had no doubt that Mr Peggotty well deserved these treasures. I must acknowledge that I felt it difficult to picture him quite at his ease in the raiment proposed for him by his grateful little niece, and that I was particularly doubtful of the policy of the cocked hat; but I kept these sentiments to myself.

Little Em'ly had stopped and looked up at the sky in her enumeration of these articles, as if they were a glorious vision. We went on again, picking up shells and pebbles.

"You would like to be a lady?" I said.

Emily looked at me, and laughed and nodded "yes."

"I should like it very much. We would all be gentlefolks together, then. Me, and uncle, and Ham, and Mrs Gummidge. We wouldn't mind then, when there comes stormy weather.—Not for our own sakes, I mean. We would for the poor fishermen's, to be sure, and we'd help 'em with money when they come to any hurt."

This seemed to me to be a very satisfactory and therefore not at all improbable picture. I expressed my pleasure in the contemplation of it, and little Em'ly was emboldened to say, shyly,

"Don't you think you are afraid of the sea, now?"

It was quiet enough to reassure me, but I have no doubt if I had seen a moderately large wave come tumbling in, I should have taken to my heels, with an awful recollection of her drowned relations. However, I said "No," and I added, "You don't seem to be either, though you say you are,"—for she was walking much too near the brink of a sort of old jetty or wooden causeway we had strolled upon, and I was afraid of her falling over.

"I'm not afraid in this way," said little Em'ly. "But I wake when it blows, and tremble to think of Uncle Dan and Ham and believe I hear 'em crying out for help. That's why I should like so much to be a lady. But I'm not afraid in this way. Not a bit. Look here!"

She started from my side, and ran along a jagged timber which protruded from the place we stood upon, and overhung the deep water at some height, without the least defence. The incident so impressed on my remembrance, that if I were a draughtsman I could draw its form here, I dare say, accurately as it was that day, and little Em'ly springing forward to her destruction (as it appeared to me), with a look that I have never forgotten, directed far out to sea.

The light, bold, fluttering little figure turned and came back safe to me, and I soon laughed at my fears, and at the cry I had uttered; fruitlessly in any case, for there was no one near. But there have been times since, in my manhood, many times there have been, when I have thought, Is it possible, among the possibilities of hidden things, that in the sudden rashness of the child and her wild look so far off, there was any merciful attraction of her into danger, any tempting her towards him permitted on the part of her dead father, that her life might have a chance of ending that day? There has been a time since when I have wondered whether, if the life before her could have been revealed to me at a glance, and so revealed as that a child could fully comprehend it, and if her preservation could have depended on a motion of my hand, I ought to have held it up to save her. There has been a time since—I do not say it lasted long, but it has been—when I have asked myself the question, would it have been better for little Em'ly to have had the waters close above her head that morning in my sight; and when I have answered Yes, it would have been.

This may be premature. I have set it down too soon, perhaps. But let it stand.

We strolled a long way, and loaded ourselves with things that we thought curious, and put some stranded star-fish carefully back into the water—I hardly know enough of the race at this moment to be quite certain whether they had reason to feel obliged to us for doing so, or the reverse—and then made our way home to Mr Peggotty's dwelling. We stopped under the lee of the lobster-outhouse to exchange an innocent kiss, and went in to breakfast glowing with health and pleasure.

"Like two young mavishes," Mr Peggotty said. I knew this meant, in our local dialect, like two young thrushes, and received it as a compliment.

Of course I was in love with little Em'ly. I am sure I loved that baby quite as truly, quite as tenderly, with greater purity and more disinterestedness, than can enter into the best love of a later time of life, high and ennobling as it is. I am sure my fancy raised up something round that blue-eyed mite of a child, which etherealized, and made a very angel of her. If, any sunny forenoon, she had spread a little pair of wings and flown away before my eyes, I don't think I should have regarded it as much more than I had had reason to expect.

We used to walk about that dim old flat at Yarmouth in a loving manner, hours and hours. The days sported by us, as if Time had not grown up himself yet, but were a child too, and always at play. I told Em'ly I adored her, and that unless she confessed she adored me I should be reduced to the necessity of killing myself with a sword. She said she did, and I have no doubt she did.

As to any sense of inequality, or youthfulness, or other difficulty in our way, little Em'ly and I had no such trouble, because we had no future. We made no more provision for growing older, than we did for growing younger. We were the admiration of Mrs Gummidge and Peggotty, who used to whisper of an evening when we sat, lovingly, on our little locker side by side, "Lor! wasn't it beautiful!" Mr Peggotty smiled at us from behind his pipe, and Ham grinned all the evening and did nothing else. They had something of the sort of pleasure in us, I suppose, that they might have had in a pretty toy, or a pocket model of the Colosseum.

I soon found out that Mrs Gummidge did not always make herself so agreeable as she might have been expected to do, under the circumstances of her residence with Mr Peggotty. Mrs Gummidge's was rather a fretful disposition, and she whimpered more sometimes than was comfortable for other parties in so small an establishment. I was very sorry for her; but there were moments when it would have been more agreeable, I thought, if Mrs Gummidge had had a convenient apartment of her own to retire to, and had stopped there until her spirits revived.

Mr Peggotty went occasionally to a public-house called The Willing Mind. I discovered this, by his being out on the second or third evening of our visit, and by Mrs Gummidge's looking up at the Dutch clock, between eight and nine, and saying he was there, and that, what was more, she had known in the morning he would go there.

Mrs Gummidge had been in a low state all day, and had burst into tears in the forenoon, when the fire smoked. "I am a lone lorn creetur'," were Mrs Gummidge's words, when that unpleasant occurrence took place, "and everythink goes contrairy with me."

"Oh, it'll soon leave off," said Peggotty—I again mean our Peggotty—"and besides, you know, it's not more disagreeable to you than to us."

"I feel it more," said Mrs Gummidge.

It was a very cold day, with cutting blasts of wind. Mrs Gummidge's peculiar corner of the fireside seemed to me to be the warmest and snuggest in the place, as her chair was certainly the easiest, but it didn't suit her that day at all. She was constantly complaining of the cold, and of its occasioning a visitation in her back which she called "the creeps." At last she shed tears on that subject, and said again that she was "a lone lorn creetur' and everythink went contrairy with her."

"It is certainly very cold," said Peggotty. "Everybody must feel it so."

"I feel it more than other people," said Mrs Gummidge.

So at dinner; when Mrs Gummidge was always helped immediately after me, to whom the preference was given as a visitor of distinction. The fish were small and bony, and the potatoes were a little burnt. We all acknowledged that we felt this something of a disappointment; but Mrs Gummidge said she felt it more than we did, and shed tears again, and made that former declaration with great bitterness.

Accordingly, when Mr Peggotty came home about nine o'clock, this unfortunate Mrs Gummidge was knitting in her corner, in a very wretched and miserable condition. Peggotty had been working cheerfully. Ham had been patching up a great pair of waterboots; and I, with little Em'ly by my side, had been reading to them. Mrs Gummidge had never made any other remark than a forlorn sigh, and had never raised her eyes since tea.

"Well, mates," said Mr Peggotty, taking his seat, "and how are you?"

We all said something, or looked something, to welcome him, except Mrs Gummidge, who only shook her head over her knitting.

"What's amiss?" said Mr Peggotty, with a clap of his hands. "Cheer up, old Mawther!" (Mr Peggotty meant old girl.)

Mrs Gummidge did not appear to be able to cheer up. She took out an old black silk handkerchief and wiped her eyes; but instead of putting it in her pocket, kept it out, and wiped them again, and still kept it out, ready for use.

"What's amiss, dame?" said Mr Peggotty.

"Nothing," returned Mrs Gummidge. "You've come from The Willing Mind, Dan'l?"

"Why yes, I've took a short spell at The Willing Mind tonight," said Mr Peggotty.

"I'm sorry I should drive you there," said Mrs Gummidge.

"Drive! I don't want no driving," returned Mr Peggotty with an honest laugh. "I only go too ready."

"Very ready," said Mrs Gummidge, shaking her head, and wiping her eyes. "Yes, yes, very ready. I am sorry it should be along of me that you're so ready."

"Along o' you! It an't along o' you!" said Mr Peggotty. "Don't ye believe a bit on it."

"Yes, yes, it is," cried Mrs Gummidge. "I know what I am. I know that I am a lone lorn creetur', and not only that everythink goes contrairy with me, but that I go contrairy with everybody. Yes, yes. I feel more than other people do, and I show it more. It's my misfortun'."

I really couldn't help thinking, as I sat taking in all this, that the misfortune extended to some other members of that family besides Mrs Gummidge. But Mr Peggotty made no such retort, only answering with another entreaty to Mrs Gummidge to cheer up.

"I an't what I could wish myself to be," said Mrs Gummidge. "I am far from it. I know what I am. My troubles has made me contrairy. I feel my troubles, and they make me contrairy. I wish I didn't feel 'em, but I do. I wish I could be hardened to 'em, but I an't.

I make the house uncomfortable. I don't wonder at it. I've made your sister so all day, and Master Davy."

Here I was suddenly melted, and roared out, "No, you haven't, Mrs Gummidge," in great mental distress.

"It's far from right that I should do it," said Mrs Gummidge. "It an't a fit return. I had better go into the house and die. I am a lone lorn creetur', and had much better not make myself contrairy here. If things must go contrairy with me, and I must go contrairy myself, let me go contrairy in my parish. Dan'l, I'd better go into the house, and die and be a riddance!"

Mrs Gummidge retired with these words, and betook herself to bed. When she was gone, Mr Peggotty, who had not exhibited a trace of any feeling but the profoundest sympathy, looked round upon us, and nodding his head with a lively expression of that sentiment still animating his face, said in a whisper:

"She's been thinking of the old 'un!"

I did not quite understand what old one Mrs Gummidge was supposed to have fixed her mind upon, until Peggotty, on seeing me to bed, explained that it was the late Mr Gummidge; and that her brother always took that for a received truth on such occasions, and that it always had a moving effect upon him. Some time after he was in his hammock that night, I heard him myself repeat to Ham, "Poor thing! She's been thinking of the old 'un!" And whenever Mrs Gummidge was overcome in a similar manner during the remainder of our stay (which happened some few times), he always said the same thing in extenuation of the circumstance, and always with the tenderest commiseration.

So the fortnight slipped away, varied by nothing but the variation of the tide, which altered Mr Peggotty's times of going out and coming in, and altered Ham's engagements also. When the latter was unemployed, he sometimes walked with us to show us the boats and ships, and once or twice he took us for a row. I don't know why one slight set of impressions should be more particularly associated with a place than another, though I believe this obtains with most people, in reference especially to the associations of their childhood. I never hear the name, or read the name, of Yarmouth, but I am reminded of a certain Sunday morning on the beach, the bells ringing for church, little Em'ly leaning on my shoulder, Ham lazily dropping stones into the water, and the sun, away at sea, just breaking through the heavy mist, and showing us the ships, like their own shadows.

At last the day came for going home. I bore up against the separation from Mr Peggotty and Mrs Gummidge, but my agony of mind at leaving little Em'ly was piercing. We went arm-in-arm to the public-house where the carrier put up, and I promised, on the road, to write to her. (I redeemed that promise afterwards, in characters larger than those in which apartments are usually announced in manuscript, as being to let.) We were greatly overcome at parting; and if ever, in my life, I have had a void made in my heart, I had one made that day.

Now, all the time I had been on my visit, I had been ungrateful to my home again, and had thought little or nothing about it. But I was no sooner turned towards it, than my reproachful young conscience seemed to point that way with a ready finger; and I felt, all the more for the sinking of my spirits, that it was my nest, and that my mother was my comforter and friend.

This gained upon me as we went along; so that the nearer we drew, the more familiar the objects became that we passed, the more excited I was to get there, and to run into her arms. But Peggotty, instead of sharing in those transports, tried to check them (though very kindly), and looked confused and out of sorts.

Blunderstone Rookery would come, however, in spite of her, when the carrier's horse pleased—and did. How well I recollect it, on a cold grey afternoon, with a dull sky, threatening rain!

The door opened, and I looked, half laughing and half crying in my pleasant agitation, for my mother. It was not she, but a strange servant.

"Why, Peggotty!" I said, ruefully, "isn't she come home?"

"Yes, yes, Master Davy," said Peggotty. "She's come home. Wait a bit, Master Davy, and I'll—I'll tell you something."

Between her agitation, and her natural awkwardness in getting out of the cart, Peggotty was making a most extraordinary festoon of herself, but I felt too blank and strange to tell her so. When she had got down, she took me by the hand; led me, wondering, into the kitchen; and shut the door.

"Peggotty!" said I, quite frightened. "What's the matter?"

"Nothing's the matter, bless you, Master Davy dear!" she answered, assuming an air of sprightliness.

"Something's the matter, I'm sure. Where's mama?"

"Where's mama, Master Davy?" repeated Peggotty.

"Yes. Why hasn't she come out to the gate, and what have we come in here for? Oh, Peggotty!" My eyes were full, and I felt as if I were going to tumble down.

"Bless the precious boy!" cried Peggotty, taking hold of me. "What is it? Speak, my pet!"

"Not dead, too! Oh, she's not dead, Peggotty?"

Peggotty cried out No! with an astonishing volume of voice; and then sat down, and began to pant, and said I had given her a turn.

I gave her a hug to take away the turn, or to give her another turn in the right direction, and then stood before her, looking at her in anxious inquiry.

"You see, dear, I should have told you before now," said Peggotty, "but I hadn't an opportunity. I ought to have made it, perhaps, but I couldn't azackly"—that was always the substitute for exactly, in Peggotty's militia of words—"bring my mind to it."

"Go on, Peggotty," said I, more frightened than before.

"Master Davy," said Peggotty, untying her bonnet with a shaking hand, and speaking in a breathless sort of way. "What do you think? You have got a Pa!"

I trembled, and turned white. Something—I don't know what, or how—connected with the grave in the churchyard, and the raising of the dead, seemed to strike me like an unwholesome wind.

"A new one," said Peggotty.

"A new one?" I repeated.

Peggotty gave a gasp, as if she were swallowing something that was very hard, and, putting out her hand, said:

"Come and see him."

"I don't want to see him."

—"And your mama," said Peggotty.

I ceased to draw back, and we went straight to the best parlour, where she left me. On one side of the fire, sat my mother; on the other, Mr Murdstone. My mother dropped her work, and arose hurriedly, but timidly I thought.

"Now, Clara my dear," said Mr Murdstone. "Recollect! control yourself, always control yourself! Davy boy, how do you do?"

I gave him my hand. After a moment of suspense, I went and kissed my mother: she kissed me, patted me gently on the shoulder, and sat down again to her work. I could not look at her, I could not look at him, I knew quite well that he was looking at us both; and I turned to the window and looked out there, at some shrubs that were drooping their heads in the cold.

As soon as I could creep away, I crept upstairs. My old dear bedroom was changed, and I was to lie a long way off. I rambled downstairs to find anything that was like itself, so altered it all seemed; and roamed into the yard. I very soon started back there, for the empty dog-kennel was filled up with a great dog—deep mouthed and black-haired like Him—and he was very angry at the sight of me, and sprang out to get at me.

Chapter IV

I FALL INTO DISGRACE

IF the room to which my bed was removed were a sentient thing that could give evidence, I might appeal to it at this day—who sleeps there now, I wonder!—to bear witness for me what a heavy heart I carried to it. I went up there, hearing the dog in the yard bark after me all the way while I climbed the stairs; and, looking as blank and strange upon the room as the room looked upon me, sat down with my small hands crossed, and thought.

I thought of the oddest things. Of the shape of the room, of the cracks in the ceiling, of the paper on the walls, of the flaws in the window-glass making ripples and dimples on the prospect, of the washing-stand being rickety on its three legs, and having a discontented something about it, which reminded me of Mrs Gummidge under the influence of the old one. I was crying all the time, but, except that I was conscious of being cold and dejected, I am sure I never thought why I cried. At last in my desolation I began to consider that I was dreadfully in love with little Em'ly, and had been torn away from her to come here where no one seemed to want me, or to care about me, half as much as she did. This made such a very miserable piece of business of it, that I rolled myself up in a corner of the counterpane, and cried myself to sleep.

I was awoke by somebody saying "Here he is!" and uncovering my hot head. My mother and Peggotty had come to look for me, and it was one of them who had done it.

"Davy," said my mother. "What's the matter?"

I thought it was very strange that she should ask me, and answered, "Nothing." I turned over on my face, I recollect, to hide my trembling lip, which answered her with greater truth.

"Davy," said my mother. "Davy, my child!"

I dare say no words she could have uttered would have affected me so much, then, as her calling me her child. I hid my tears in the bedclothes, and pressed her from me with my hand, when she would have raised me up.

"This is your doing, Peggotty, you cruel thing!" said my mother. "I have no doubt at all about it. How can you reconcile it to your conscience, I wonder, to prejudice my own boy against me, or against anybody who is dear to me? What do you mean by it, Peggotty?"

Poor Peggotty lifted up her hands and eyes, and only answered, in a sort of paraphrase of the grace I usually repeated after dinner, "Lord forgive you, Mrs Copperfield, and for what you have said this minute, may you never be truly sorry!"

"It's enough to distract me," cried my mother. "In my honeymoon, too, when my most inveterate enemy might relent, one would think, and not envy me a little peace of mind and happiness. Davy, you naughty boy! Peggotty, you savage creature! Oh, dear me!" cried my mother, turning from one of us to the other, in her pettish wilful manner, "what a troublesome world this is, when one has the most right to expect it to be as agreeable as possible!"

I felt the touch of a hand that I knew was neither hers nor Peggotty's, and slipped to my feet at the bed-side. It was Mr Murdstone's hand, and he kept it on my arm as he said:

"What's this? Clara, my love, have you forgotten?—Firmness, my dear!"

"I am very sorry, Edward," said my mother. "I meant to be very good, but I am so uncomfortable."

"Indeed!" he answered. "That's a bad hearing, so soon, Clara."

"I say it's very hard I should be made so now," returned my mother, pouting; "and it is—very hard—isn't it?"

He drew her to him, whispered in her ear, and kissed her. I knew as well, when I saw my mother's head lean down upon his shoulder, and her arm touch his neck—I knew as well that he could mould her pliant nature into any form he chose, as I know, now, that he did it.

"Go you below, my love," said Mr Murdstone. "David and I will come down, together. My friend," turning a darkening face on Peggotty, when he had watched my mother out, and dismissed her with a nod and a smile; "do you know your mistress's name?"

"She has been my mistress a long time, sir," answered Peggotty, "I ought to know it."

"That's true," he answered. "But I thought I heard you, as I came upstairs, address her by a name that is not hers. She has taken mine, you know. Will you remember that?"

Peggotty, with some uneasy glances at me, curtseyed herself out of the room without replying; seeing, I suppose, that she was expected to go, and had no excuse for remaining. When we two were left alone, he shut the door, and sitting on a chair, and holding me standing before him, looked steadily into my eyes. I felt my own attracted, no less steadily, to his. As I recall our being opposed thus, face to face, I seem again to hear my heart beat fast and high.

"David," he said, making his lips thin, by pressing them together, "if I have an obstinate horse or dog to deal with, what do you think I do?"

"I don't know."

"I beat him."

I had answered in a kind of breathless whisper, but I felt, in my silence, that my breath was shorter now.

"I make him wince, and smart. I say to myself, 'I'll conquer that fellow'; and if it were to cost him all the blood he had, I should do it. What is that upon your face?"

"Dirt," I said.

He knew it was the mark of tears as well as I. But if he had asked the question twenty times, each time with twenty blows, I believe my baby heart would have burst before I would have told him so.

"You have a good deal of intelligence for a little fellow," he said, with a grave smile that belonged to him, "and you understood me very well, I see. Wash that face, sir, and come down with me."

He pointed to the washing-stand, which I had made out to be like Mrs Gummidge, and motioned me with his head to obey him directly. I had little doubt then, and I have less doubt now, that he would have knocked me down without the least compunction, if I had hesitated.

"Clara, my dear," he said, when I had done his bidding, and he walked me into the parlour, with his hand still on my arm; "you will not be made uncomfortable any more, I hope. We shall soon improve our youthful humours."

God help me, I might have been improved for my whole life, I might have been made another creature perhaps, for life, by a kind word at that season. A word of encouragement and explanation, of pity for my childish ignorance, of welcome home, of reassurance to me that it *was* home, might have made me dutiful to him in my heart henceforth, instead of in my hypocritical outside, and might have made me respect instead of hate him. I thought my mother was sorry to see me standing in the room so scared and strange, and that, presently, when I stole to a chair, she followed me with her eyes more sorrowfully still—missing, perhaps, some freedom in my childish tread—but the word was not spoken, and the time for it was gone.

We dined alone, we three together. He seemed to be very fond of my mother—I am afraid I liked him none the better for that—and she was very fond of him. I gathered from what they said, that an elder sister of his was coming to stay with them, and that she was expected that evening. I am not certain whether I found out then, or afterwards, that, without being actively concerned in any business, he had some share in, or some annual charge upon the profits of, a wine-merchant's house in London, with which his family had been connected from his great-grandfather's time, and in which his sister had a similar interest; but I may mention it in this place, whether or no.

After dinner, when we were sitting by the fire, and I was meditating an escape to Peggotty without having the hardihood to slip away, lest it should offend the master of the house, a coach drove up to the garden-gate and he went out to receive the visitor. My mother followed him. I was timidly following her, when she turned round at the parlour door, in the dusk, and taking me in her embrace as she had been used to do, whispered me to love my new father and be obedient to him. She did this hurriedly and secretly, as if it were wrong, but tenderly; and, putting out her hand behind her, held mine in it, until we came near to where he was standing in the garden, where she let mine go, and drew hers through his arm.

It was Miss Murdstone who was arrived, and a gloomy-looking lady she was; dark, like her brother, whom she greatly resembled in face and voice; and with very heavy eyebrows, nearly meeting over her large nose, as if, being disabled by the wrongs of her sex from wearing whiskers, she had carried them to that account. She brought with her, two uncompromising hard black boxes, with her initials on the lids in hard brass nails. When she paid the coachman she took her money out of a hard steel purse, and she kept the purse in a very jail of a bag which hung upon her arm by a heavy chain, and shut up like a bite. I had never, at that time, seen such a metallic lady altogether as Miss Murdstone was.

She was brought into the parlour with many tokens of welcome, and there formally recognized my mother as a new and near relation. Then she looked at me, and said:

"Is that your boy, sister-in-law?"

My mother acknowledged me.

"Generally speaking," said Miss Murdstone, "I don't like boys. How d'ye do, boy?"

Under these encouraging circumstances, I replied that I was very well, and that I hoped she was the same; with such an indifferent grace, that Miss Murdstone disposed of me in two words:

"Wants manner!"

Having uttered which, with great distinctness, she begged the favour of being shewn to her room, which became to me from that time forth a place of awe and dread, wherein the two black boxes were never seen open or known to be left unlocked, and where (for I peeped in once or twice when she was out) numerous little steel fetters and rivets, with which Miss Murdstone embellished herself when she was dressed, generally hung upon the looking-glass in formidable array.

As well as I could make out, she had come for good, and had no intention of ever going again. She began to "help" my mother next morning, and was in and out of the store-closet all day, putting things to rights, and making havoc in the old arrangements. Almost the first remarkable thing I observed in Miss Murdstone was, her being constantly haunted by a suspicion that the servants had a man secreted somewhere on the premises. Under the influence of this delusion, she dived into the coal-cellar at the most untimely hours, and scarcely ever opened the door of a dark cupboard without clapping it to again, in the belief that she had got him.

Though there was nothing very airy about Miss Murdstone, she was a perfect Lark in point of getting up. She was up (and, as I believe to this hour, looking for that man) before anybody in the house was stirring. Peggotty gave it as her opinion that she even slept with one eye open; but I could not concur in this idea; for I tried it myself after hearing the suggestion thrown out, and found it couldn't be done.

On the very first morning after her arrival she was up and ringing her bell at cock-crow. When my mother came down to breakfast and was going to make the tea, Miss Murdstone gave her a kind of peck on the cheek, which was her nearest approach to a kiss, and said:

"Now, Clara, my dear, I am come here, you know, to relieve you of all the trouble I can. You're much too pretty and thoughtless"—my mother blushed but laughed, and seemed not to dislike this character—"to have any duties imposed upon you that can be undertaken by me. If you'll be so good as give me your keys, my dear, I'll attend to all this sort of thing in future."

From that time, Miss Murdstone kept the keys in her own little jail all day, and under her pillow all night, and my mother had no more to do with them than I had.

My mother did not suffer her authority to pass from her without a shadow of protest. One night when Miss Murdstone had been developing certain household plans to her brother, of which he signified his approbation, my mother suddenly began to cry, and said she thought she might have been consulted.

"Clara!" said Mr Murdstone sternly. "Clara! I wonder at you."

"Oh, it's very well to say you wonder, Edward!" cried my mother, "and it's very well for you to talk about firmness, but you wouldn't like it yourself."

Firmness, I may observe, was the grand quality on which both Mr and Miss Murdstone took their stand. However I might have expressed my comprehension of it at that time, if I had been called upon, I nevertheless did clearly comprehend in my own way, that it was another name for tyranny; and for a certain gloomy, arrogant, devil's humour, that was in them both. The creed, as I should state it now, was this. Mr Murdstone was firm; nobody in his world was to be so firm as Mr Murdstone; nobody else in his world was to be firm at all, for everybody was to be bent to his firmness. Miss Murdstone was an exception. She might be firm, but only by relationship, and in an inferior and tributary degree. My mother was another exception. She might be firm, and must be; but only in bearing their firmness, and firmly believing there was no other firmness upon earth.

"It's very hard," said my mother, "that in my own house—"

"*My* own house?" repeated Mr Murdstone. "Clara!"

"*Our* own house, I mean," faltered my mother, evidently frightened—"I hope you must know what I mean, Edward—it's very hard that in *your* own house I may not have a word to say about domestic matters. I am sure I managed very well before we were married. There's evidence," said my mother, sobbing; "ask Peggotty if I didn't do very well when I wasn't interfered with!"

"Edward," said Miss Murdstone, "let there be an end of this. I go tomorrow."

"Jane Murdstone," said her brother, "be silent! How dare you to insinuate that you don't know my character better than your words imply?"

"I am sure," my poor mother went on, at a grievous disadvantage, and with many tears, "I don't want anybody to go. I should be very miserable and unhappy if anybody was to go. I don't ask much. I am not unreasonable. I only want to be consulted sometimes. I am very much obliged to anybody who assists me, and I only want to be consulted as a mere form, sometimes. I thought you were pleased, once, with my being a little inexperienced and girlish, Edward—I am sure you said so—but you seem to hate me for it now, you are so severe."

"Edward," said Miss Murdstone, again, "let there be an end of this. I go tomorrow."

"Jane Murdstone," thundered Mr Murdstone. "Will you be silent? How dare you?"

Miss Murdstone made a jail-delivery of her pocket-handkerchief, and held it before her eyes.

"Clara," he continued, looking at my mother, "you surprise me! You astound me! Yes, I had a satisfaction in the thought of marrying an inexperienced and artless person, and forming her character, and infusing into it some amount of that firmness and decision of which it stood in need. But when Jane Murdstone is kind enough to come to my assistance in this endeavour, and to assume, for my sake, a condition something like a housekeeper's, and when she meets with a base return—"

"Oh, pray, pray, Edward," cried my mother, "don't accuse me of being ungrateful. I am sure I am not ungrateful. No one ever said I was before. I have many faults, but not that. Oh, don't, my dear!"

"When Jane Murdstone meets, I say," he went on, after waiting until my mother was silent, "with a base return, that feeling of mine is chilled and altered."

"Don't, my love, say that!" implored my mother very piteously. "Oh, don't, Edward! I can't bear to hear it. Whatever I am, I am affectionate. I know I am affectionate. I wouldn't say it, if I wasn't sure that I am. Ask Peggotty. I am sure she'll tell you I'm affectionate."

"There is no extent of mere weakness, Clara," said Mr Murdstone in reply, "that can have the least weight with me. You lose breath."

"Pray let us be friends," said my mother, "I couldn't live under coldness or unkindness. I am so sorry. I have a great many defects, I know, and it's very good of you, Edward, with your strength of mind, to endeavour to correct them for me. Jane, I don't object to anything. I should be quite broken-hearted if you thought of leaving—" My mother was too much overcome to go on.

"Jane Murdstone," said Mr Murdstone to his sister, "any harsh words between us are,

I hope, uncommon. It is not my fault that so unusual an occurrence has taken place tonight. I was betrayed into it by another. Nor is it your fault. You were betrayed into it by another. Let us both try to forget it. And as this," he added, after these magnanimous words, "is not a fit scene for the boy—David, go to bed!"

I could hardly find the door, through the tears that stood in my eyes. I was so sorry for my mother's distress; but I groped my way out, and groped my way up to my room in the dark, without even having the heart to say good night to Peggotty, or to get a candle from her. When her coming up to look for me, an hour or so afterwards, awoke me, she said that my mother had gone to bed poorly, and that Mr and Miss Murdstone were sitting alone.

Going down next morning rather earlier than usual, I paused outside the parlour door, on hearing my mother's voice. She was very earnestly and humbly entreating Miss Murdstone's pardon, which that lady granted, and a perfect reconciliation took place. I never knew my mother afterwards to give an opinion on any matter, without first appealing to Miss Murdstone, or without having first ascertained by some sure means, what Miss Murdstone's opinion was; and I never saw Miss Murdstone, when out of temper (she was infirm that way), move her hand towards her bag as if she were going to take out the keys and offer to resign them to my mother, without seeing that my mother was in a terrible fright.

The gloomy taint that was in the Murdstone blood, darkened the Murdstone religion, which was austere and wrathful. I have thought, since, that its assuming that character was a necessary consequence of Mr Murdstone's firmness, which wouldn't allow him to let anybody off from the utmost weight of the severest penalties he could find any excuse for. Be this as it may, I well remember the tremendous visages with which we used to go to church, and the changed air of the place. Again, the dreaded Sunday comes round, and I file into the old pew first, like a guarded captive brought to a condemned service. Again, Miss Murdstone, in a black velvet gown, that looks as if it had been made out of a pall, follows close upon me; then my mother; then her husband. There is no Peggotty now, as in the old time. Again, I listen to Miss Murdstone mumbling the responses, and emphasizing all the dread words with a cruel relish. Again, I see her dark eyes roll round the church when she says "miserable sinners," as if she were calling all the congregation names. Again, I catch rare glimpses of my mother, moving her lips timidly between the two, with one of them muttering at each ear like low thunder. Again, I wonder with a sudden fear whether it is likely that our good old clergyman can be wrong, and Mr and Miss Murdstone right, and that all the angels in Heaven can be destroying angels. Again, if I move a finger or relax a muscle of my face, Miss Murdstone pokes me with her prayer-book, and makes my side ache.

Yes, and again, as we walk home, I note some neighbours looking at my mother and at me, and whispering. Again, as the three go on arm-in-arm, and I linger behind alone, I follow some of those looks, and wonder if my mother's step be really not so light as I have seen it, and if the gaiety of her beauty be really almost worried away. Again, I wonder whether any of the neighbours call to mind, as I do, how we used to walk home together, she and I; and I wonder stupidly about that, all the dreary dismal day.

There had been some talk on occasions of my going to boarding-school. Mr and Miss Murdstone had originated it, and my mother had of course agreed with them. Nothing, however, was concluded on the subject yet. In the meantime, I learnt lessons at home.

Shall I ever forget those lessons! They were presided over nominally by my mother, but really by Mr Murdstone and his sister, who were always present, and found them a favourable occasion for giving my mother lessons in that miscalled firmness, which was the bane of both our lives. I believe I was kept at home for that purpose. I had been apt enough to learn, and willing enough, when my mother and I had lived alone together. I can faintly remember learning the alphabet at her knee. To this day, when I look upon the fat black letters in the primer, the puzzling novelty of their shapes, and the easy good-nature of O and Q and S, seem to present themselves again before me as they used to do. But they recall no feeling of disgust or reluctance. On the contrary, I seem to have walked along a path of flowers as far as the crocodile-book, and to have been cheered by the gentleness of my mother's voice and manner all the way. But these solemn lessons which succeeded those, I remember as the death-blow of my peace, and a grievous daily drudgery and misery. They were very long, very numerous, very hard—perfectly unintelligible, some of them, to me—and I was generally as much bewildered by them as I believe my poor mother was herself.

Let me remember how it used to be, and bring one morning back again.

I come into the second-best parlour after breakfast, with my books, and an exercise-book, and a slate. My mother is ready for me at her writing-desk, but not half so ready as Mr Murdstone in his easy-chair by the window (though he pretends to be reading a book), or as Miss Murdstone, sitting near my mother stringing steel beads. The very sight of these two has such an influence over me, that I begin to feel the words I have been at infinite pains to get into my head, all sliding away, and going I don't know where. I wonder where they *do* go, by the by?

I hand the first book to my mother. Perhaps it is a grammar, perhaps a history, or geography. I take a last drowning look at the page as I give it into her hand, and start off aloud at a racing pace while I have got it fresh. I trip over a word. Mr Murdstone looks up. I trip over another word. Miss Murdstone looks up. I redden, tumble over half-a-dozen words, and stop. I think my mother would show me the book if she dared, but she does not dare, and she says softly:

"Oh, Davy, Davy!"

"Now, Clara," says Mr Murdstone, "be firm with the boy. Don't say, 'Oh, Davy, Davy!' That's childish. He knows his lesson, or he does not know it."

"He does *not* know it," Miss Murdstone interposes awfully.

"I am really afraid he does not," says my mother.

"Then, you see, Clara," returns Miss Murdstone, "you should just give him the book back, and make him know it."

"Yes, certainly," says my mother; "that is what I intend to do, my dear Jane. Now, Davy, try once more, and don't be stupid."

I obey the first clause of the injunction by trying once more, but am not so successful with the second, for I am very stupid. I tumble down before I get to the old place, at a point where I was all right before, and stop to think. But I can't think about the lesson. I think of the number of yards of net in Miss Murdstone's cap, or of the price of Mr Murdstone's dressing-gown, or any such ridiculous problem that I have no business with, and don't want to have anything at all to do with. Mr Murdstone makes a movement of impatience which I have been expecting for a long time. Miss Murdstone does the same. My mother glances submissively at them, shuts the book, and lays it by as an arrear to be worked out when my other tasks are done.

There is a pile of these arrears very soon, and it swells like a rolling snowball. The bigger it gets, the more stupid *I* get. The case is so hopeless, and I feel that I am wallowing in such a bog of nonsense, that I give up all idea of getting out, and abandon myself to my fate. The despairing way in which my mother and I look at each other, as

I blunder on, is truly melancholy. But the greatest effect in these miserable lessons is when my mother (thinking nobody is observing her) tries to give me the cue by the motion of her lips. At that instant, Miss Murdstone, who has been lying in wait for nothing else all along, says in a deep warning voice:

"Clara!"

My mother starts, colours, and smiles faintly. Mr Murdstone comes out of his chair, takes the book, throws it at me or boxes my ears with it, and turns me out of the room by the shoulders.

Even when the lessons are done, the worst is yet to happen, in the shape of an appalling sum. This is invented for me, and delivered to me orally by Mr Murdstone, and begins, "If I go into a cheesemonger's shop, and buy five thousand double-Gloucester cheeses at fourpence-halfpenny each, present payment"—at which I see Miss Murdstone secretly overjoyed. I pore over these cheeses without any result or enlightenment until dinner-time, when, having made a Mulatto of myself by getting the dirt of the slate into the pores of my skin, I have a slice of bread to help me out with the cheeses, and am considered in disgrace for the rest of the evening.

It seems to me, at this distance of time, as if my unfortunate studies generally took this course. I could have done very well if I had been without the Murdstones; but the influence of the Murdstones upon me was like the fascination of two snakes on a wretched young bird. Even when I did get through the morning with tolerable credit, there was not much gained but dinner; for Miss Murdstone never could endure to see me untasked, and if I rashly made any show of being unemployed, called her brother's attention to me by saying, "Clara, my dear, there's nothing like work—give your boy an exercise"; which caused me to be clapped down to some new labour, there and then. As to any recreation with other children of my age, I had very little of that; for the gloomy theology of the Murdstones made all children out to be a swarm of little vipers (though there *was* a child once set in the midst of the Disciples), and held that they contaminated one another.

The natural result of this treatment, continued, I suppose, for some six months or more, was to make me sullen, dull, and dogged. I was not made the less so by my sense of being daily more and more shut out and alienated from my mother. I believe I should have been almost stupefied but for one circumstance.

It was this. My father had left a small collection of books in a little room upstairs, to which I had access (for it adjoined my own) and which nobody else in our house ever troubled. From that blessed little room, Roderick Random, Peregrine Pickle, Humphrey Clinker, Tom Jones, the Vicar of Wakefield, Don Quixote, Gil Blas, and Robinson Crusoe, came out, a glorious host, to keep me company. They kept alive my fancy, and my hope of something beyond that place and time,—they, and the *Arabian Nights,* and the *Tales of the Genii,*—and did me no harm; for whatever harm was in some of them was not there for me; *I* knew nothing of it. It is astonishing to me now, how I found time, in the midst of my porings and blunderings over heavier themes, to read those books as I did. It is curious to me how I could ever have consoled myself under my small troubles (which were great troubles to me), by impersonating my favourite characters in them— as I did—and by putting Mr and Miss Murdstone into all the bad ones—which I did too. I have been Tom Jones (a child's Tom Jones, a harmless creature) for a week together. I have sustained my own idea of Roderick Random for a month at a stretch, I verily believe. I had a greedy relish for a few volumes of Voyages and Travels—I forget what, now—that were on those shelves; and for days and days I can remember to have gone about my region of our house, armed with the centre-piece out of an old set of boot-trees—the perfect realization of Captain Somebody, of the Royal British Navy, in danger of being beset by savages, and resolved to sell his life at a great price. The Captain never lost dignity, from having his ears boxed with the Latin Grammar. I did; but the Captain was a Captain and a hero, in despite of all the grammars of all the languages in the world, dead or alive.

This was my only and my constant comfort. When I think of it, the picture always rises in my mind, of a summer evening, the boys at play in the churchyard, and I sitting on my bed, reading as if for life. Every barn in the neighbourhood, every stone in the church, and every foot of the churchyard, had some association of its own, in my mind, connected with these books, and stood for some locality made famous in them. I have seen Tom Pipes go climbing up the church-steeple; I have watched Strap, with the knapsack on his back, stopping to rest himself upon the wicket-gate; and I *know* that Commodore Trunnion held that club with Mr Pickle, in the parlour of our little village alehouse.

The reader now understands, as well as I do, what I was when I came to that point of my youthful history to which I am now coming again.

One morning when I went into the parlour with my books, I found my mother looking anxious, Miss Murdstone looking firm, and Mr Murdstone binding something round the bottom of a cane—a lithe and limber cane, which he left off binding when I came in, and poised and switched in the air.

"I tell you, Clara," said Mr Murdstone, "I have been often flogged myself."

"To be sure; of course," said Miss Murdstone.

"Certainly, my dear Jane," faltered my mother, meekly. "But—but do you think it did Edward good?"

"Do you think it did Edward harm, Clara?" asked Mr Murdstone, gravely.

"That's the point," said his sister.

To this my mother returned, "Certainly, my dear Jane," and said no more.

I felt apprehensive that I was personally interested in this dialogue, and sought Mr Murdstone's eye as it lighted on mine.

"Now, David," he said—and I saw that cast again as he said it—"you must be far more careful today than usual." He gave the cane another poise, and another switch; and having finished his preparation of it, laid it down beside him, with an impressive look, and took up his book.

This was a good freshener to my presence of mind, as a beginning. I felt the words of my lessons slipping off, not one by one, or line by line, but by the entire page; I tried to lay hold of them; but they seemed, if I may so express it, to have put skates on, and to skim away from me with a smoothness there was no checking.

We began badly, and went on worse. I had come in with an idea of distinguishing myself rather, conceiving that I was very well prepared; but it turned out to be quite a mistake. Book after book was added to the heap of failures, Miss Murdstone being firmly watchful of us all the time. And when we came at last to the five thousand cheeses (canes he made it that day, I remember), my mother burst out crying.

"Clara!" said Miss Murdstone, in her warning voice.

"I am not quite well, my dear Jane, I think," said my mother.

I saw him wink, solemnly, at his sister, as he rose and said, taking up the cane:

"Why, Jane, we can hardly expect Clara to bear, with perfect firmness, the worry and torment that David has occasioned her today. That would be stoical. Clara is greatly strengthened and improved, but we can hardly expect so much from her. David, you and I will go upstairs, boy."

As he took me out at the door, my mother ran towards us. Miss Murdstone said, "Clara! are you a perfect fool?" and interfered. I saw my mother stop her ears then, and I heard her crying.

He walked me up to my room slowly and gravely—I am certain he had a delight in that formal parade of executing justice—and when we got there, suddenly twisted my head under his arm.

"Mr Murdstone! Sir!" I cried to him. "Don't! Pray don't beat me! I have tried to learn, sir, but I can't learn while you and Miss Murdstone are by. I can't indeed!"

"Can't you, indeed, David?" he said. "We'll try that."

He had my head as in a vice, but I twined round him somehow, and stopped him for a moment, entreating him not to beat me. It was only a moment that I stopped him, for he cut me heavily an instant afterwards, and in the same instant I caught the hand with which he held me in my mouth, between my teeth, and bit it through. It sets my teeth on edge to think of it.

He beat me then, as if he would have beaten me to death. Above all the noise we made, I heard them running up the stairs, and crying out—I heard my mother crying out—and Peggotty. Then he was gone; and the door was locked outside; and I was lying, fevered and hot, and torn, and sore, and raging in my puny way, upon the floor.

How well I recollect, when I became quiet, what an unnatural stillness seemed to reign through the whole house! How well I remember, when my smart and passion began to cool, how wicked I began to feel!

I sat listening for a long while, but there was not a sound. I crawled up from the floor, and saw my face in the glass, so swollen, red, and ugly that it almost frightened me. My stripes were sore and stiff, and made me cry afresh, when I moved; but they were nothing to the guilt I felt. It lay heavier on my breast than if I had been a most atrocious criminal, I dare say.

It had begun to grow dark, and I had shut the window (I had been lying, for the most part, with my head upon the sill, by turns crying, dozing, and looking listlessly out), when the key was turned, and Miss Murdstone came in with some bread and meat, and milk. These she put down upon the table without a word, glaring at me the while with exemplary firmness, and then retired, locking the door after her.

Long after it was dark I sat there, wondering whether anybody else would come. When this appeared improbable for that night, I undressed, and went to bed; and, there, I began to wonder fearfully what would be done to me. Whether it was a criminal act that I had committed? Whether I should be taken into custody, and sent to prison? Whether I was at all in danger of being hanged?

I never shall forget the waking, next morning; the being cheerful and fresh for the first moment, and then the being weighed down by the stale and dismal oppression of remembrance. Miss Murdstone reappeared before I was out of bed; told me, in so many words, that I was free to walk in the garden for half an hour and no longer; and retired, leaving the door open, that I might avail myself of that permission.

I did so, and did so every morning of my imprisonment, which lasted five days. If I could have seen my mother alone, I should have gone down on my knees to her and besought her forgiveness; but I saw no one, Miss Murdstone excepted, during the whole time—except at evening prayers in the parlour; to which I was escorted by Miss Murdstone after everybody else was placed; where I was stationed, a young outlaw, all alone by myself near the door; and whence I was solemnly conducted by my jailer, before any one arose from the devotional posture. I only observed that my mother was as far off from me as she could be, and kept her face another way so that I never saw it; and that

Mr Murdstone's hand was bound up in a large linen wrapper.

The length of those five days I can convey no idea of to any one. They occupy the place of years in my remembrance. The way in which I listened to all the incidents of the house that made themselves audible to me; the ringing of bells, the opening and shutting of doors, the murmuring of voices, the footsteps on the stairs; to any laughing, whistling, or singing, outside, which seemed more dismal than anything else to me in my solitude and disgrace—the uncertain pace of the hours, especially at night, when I would wake thinking it was morning, and find that the family were not yet gone to bed, and that all the length of night had yet to come—the depressed dreams and nightmares I had—the return of day, noon, afternoon, evening, when the boys played in the churchyard, and I watched them from a distance within the room, being ashamed to show myself at the window lest they should know I was a prisoner—the strange sensation of never hearing myself speak—the fleeting intervals of something like cheerfulness, which came with eating and drinking, and went away with it—the setting in of rain one evening, with a fresh smell, and its coming down faster and faster between me and the church, until it and gathering night seemed to quench me in gloom, and fear, and remorse—all this appears to have gone round and round for years instead of days, it is so vividly and strongly stamped on my remembrance.

On the last night of my restraint, I was awakened by hearing my own name spoken in a whisper. I started up in bed, and putting out my arms in the dark, said:

"Is that you, Peggotty?"

There was no immediate answer, but presently I heard my name again, in a tone so very mysterious and awful, that I think I should have gone into a fit, if it had not occurred to me that it must have come through the keyhole.

I groped my way to the door, and putting my own lips to the keyhole, whispered: "Is that you, Peggotty dear?"

"Yes, my own precious Davy," she replied. "Be as soft as a mouse, or the Cat'll hear us."

I understood this to mean Miss Murdstone, and was sensible of the urgency of the case; her room being close by.

"How's mama, dear Peggotty? Is she very angry with me?"

I could hear Peggotty crying softly on her side of the keyhole, as I was doing on mine, before she answered. "No. Not very."

"What is going to be done with me, Peggotty dear? Do you know?"

"School. Near London," was Peggotty's answer. I was obliged to get her to repeat it, for she spoke it the first time quite down my throat, in consequence of my having forgotten to take my mouth away from the keyhole and put my ear there; and though her words tickled me a good deal, I didn't hear them.

"When, Peggotty?"

"Tomorrow."

"Is that the reason why Miss Murdstone took the clothes out of my drawers?" which she had done, though I have forgotten to mention it.

"Yes," said Peggotty. "Box."

"Shan't I see mama?"

"Yes," said Peggotty. "Morning."

Then Peggotty fitted her mouth close to the keyhole, and delivered these words through it with as much feeling and earnestness as a keyhole has ever been the medium of communicating, I will venture to assert: shooting in each broken little sentence in a convulsive little burst of its own.

"Davy, dear. If I ain't been azackly as intimate with you. Lately, as I used to be. It ain't because I don't love you. Just as well and more, my pretty poppet. It's because I thought it better for you. And for someone else besides. Davy, my darling, are you listening? Can you hear?"

"Ye-ye-ye-yes, Peggotty!" I sobbed.

"My own!" said Peggotty, with infinite compassion. "What I want to say, is. That you must never forget me. For I'll never forget you. And I'll take as much care of your mama, Davy. As ever I took of you. And I won't leave her. The day may come when she'll be glad to lay her poor head. On her stupid, cross old Peggotty's arm again. And I'll write to you, my dear. Though I ain't no scholar. And I'll—I'll—" Peggotty fell to kissing the keyhole, as she couldn't kiss me.

"Thank you, dear Peggotty!" said I. "Oh, thank you! Thank you! Will you promise me one thing, Peggotty? Will you write and tell Mr Peggotty and little Em'ly, and Mrs Gummidge and Ham, that I am not so bad as they might suppose, and that I sent 'em all my love—especially to little Em'ly? Will you, if you please, Peggotty?"

The kind soul promised, and we both of us kissed the keyhole with the greatest affection—I patted it with my hand, I recollect, as if it had been her honest face—and parted. From that night there grew up in my breast a feeling for Peggotty which I cannot very well define. She did not replace my mother; no one could do that; but she came into a vacancy in my heart, which closed upon her, and I felt towards her something I have never felt for any other human being. It was a sort of comical affection, too; and yet if she had died, I cannot think what I should have done, or how I should have acted out the tragedy it would have been to me.

In the morning Miss Murdstone appeared as usual, and told me I was going to school; which was not altogether such news to me as she supposed. She also informed me that when I was dressed, I was to come downstairs into the parlour, and have my breakfast. There, I found my mother, very pale and with red eyes: into whose arms I ran, and begged her pardon from my suffering soul.

"Oh, Davy!" she said. "That you could hurt anyone I love! Try to be better, pray to be better! I forgive you; but I am so grieved, Davy, that you should have such bad passions in your heart."

They had persuaded her that I was a wicked fellow, and she was more sorry for that than for my going away. I felt it sorely. I tried to eat my parting breakfast, but my tears dropped upon my bread-and-butter, and trickled into my tea. I saw my mother look at me sometimes, and then glance at the watchful Miss Murdstone, and then look down, or look away.

"Master Copperfield's box there!" said Miss Murdstone, when wheels were heard at the gate.

I looked for Peggotty, but it was not she; neither she nor Mr Murdstone appeared. My former acquaintance, the carrier, was at the door; the box was taken out to his cart, and lifted in.

"Clara!" said Miss Murdstone, in her warning note.

"Ready, my dear Jane," returned my mother. "Good-bye, Davy. You are going for your own good. Good-bye, my child. You will come home in the holidays, and be a better boy."

"Clara!" Miss Murdstone repeated.

"Certainly, my dear Jane," replied my mother, who was holding me. "I forgive you, my dear boy. God bless you!"

"Clara!" Miss Murdstone repeated.

Miss Murdstone was good enough to take me out to the cart, and to say on the way that she hoped I would repent, before I came to a bad end; and then I got into the cart, and the lazy horse walked off with it.

Chapter V

I AM SENT AWAY FROM HOME

W E might have gone about half a mile, and my pocket-handkerchief was quite wet through, when the carrier stopped short.

Looking out to ascertain for what, I saw, to my amazement, Peggotty burst from a hedge and climb into the cart. She took me in both her arms, and squeezed me to her stays until the pressure on my nose was extremely painful, though I never thought of that till afterwards when I found it very tender. Not a single word did Peggotty speak. Releasing one of her arms, she put it down in her pocket to the elbow, and brought out some paper bags of cakes which she crammed into my pockets, and a purse which she put into my hand, but not one word did she say. After another and a final squeeze with both arms, she got down from the cart and ran away; and, my belief is, and has always been, without a solitary button on her gown. I picked up one, of several that were rolling about, and treasured it as a keepsake for a long time.

The carrier looked at me, as if to inquire if she were coming back. I shook my head, and said I thought not. "Then, come up," said the carrier to the lazy horse; who came up accordingly.

Having by this time cried as much as I possibly could, I began to think it was of no use crying any more, especially as neither Roderick Random, nor that Captain in the Royal British Navy, had ever cried, that I could remember, in trying situations. The carrier, seeing me in this resolution, proposed that my pocket-handkerchief should be spread upon the horse's back to dry. I thanked him, and assented; and particularly small it looked, under those circumstances.

I had now leisure to examine the purse. It was a stiff leather purse, with a snap, and had three bright shillings in it, which Peggotty had evidently polished up with whitening, for my greater delight. But its most precious contents were two half-crowns folded together in a bit of paper, on which was written, in my mother's hand, "For Davy. With my love." I was so overcome by this, that I asked the carrier to be so good as to reach me my pocket-handkerchief again; but he said he thought I had better do without it, and I thought I really had, so I wiped my eyes on my sleeve and stopped myself.

For good, too; though, in consequence of my previous emotions, I was still occasionally seized with a stormy sob. After we had jogged on for some little time, I asked the carrier if he was going all the way.

"All the way where?" inquired the carrier.

"There," I said.

"Where's there?" inquired the carrier.

"Near London," I said.

"Why that horse," said the carrier, jerking the rein to point him out, "would be deader than pork afore he got over half the ground."

"Are you only going to Yarmouth then?" I asked.

"That's about it," said the carrier. "And there I shall take you to the stage-cutch, and the stage-cutch that'll take you to—wherever it is."

As this was a great deal for the carrier (whose name was Mr Barkis) to say—he being, as I observed in a former chapter, of a phlegmatic temperament, and not at all conversational—I offered him a cake as a mark of attention, which he ate at one gulp, exactly like an elephant, and which made no more impression on his big face than it would have done on an elephant's.

"Did *she* make 'em, now?" said Mr Barkis, always leaning forward, in his slouching way, on the footboard of the cart with an arm on each knee.

"Peggotty, do you mean, sir?"

"Ah!" said Mr Barkis. "Her."

"Yes. She makes all our pastry, and does all our cooking."

"Do she though?" said Mr Barkis.

He made up his mouth as if to whistle, but he didn't whistle. He sat looking at the horse's ears, as if he saw something new there; and sat so, for a considerable time. By and by, he said:

"No sweethearts, I b'lieve?"

"Sweetmeats did you say, Mr Barkis?" For I thought he wanted something else to eat, and had pointedly alluded to that description of refreshment.

"Hearts," said Mr Barkis. "Sweet hearts; no person walks with her!"

"With Peggotty?"

"Ah!" he said. "Her."

"Oh, no. She never had a sweetheart."

"Didn't she, though!" said Mr Barkis.

Again he made up his mouth to whistle, and again he didn't whistle, but sat looking at the horse's ears.

"So she makes," said Mr Barkis, after a long interval of reflection, "all the apple parsties, and doos all the cooking, do she?".

I replied that such was the fact.

"Well. I'll tell you what," said Mr Barkis. "P'raps you might be writin' to her?"

"I shall certainly write to her," I rejoined.

"Ah!" he said, slowly turning his eyes towards me. "Well! If you was writin' to her, p'raps you'd recollect to say that Barkis was willin'; would you?"

"That Barkis is willing," I repeated, innocently. "Is that all the message?"

"Ye-es," he said, considering. "Ye-es. Barkis is willin'."

"But you will be at Blunderstone again tomorrow, Mr Barkis," I said, faltering a little at the idea of my being far away from it then, "and could give your own message so much better."

As he repudiated this suggestion, however, with a jerk of his head, and once more confirmed his previous request by saying, with profound gravity, "Barkis is willin'. That's the message," I readily undertook its transmission. While I was waiting for the coach in the hotel at Yarmouth that very afternoon, I procured a sheet of paper and an inkstand, and wrote a note to Peggotty, which ran thus: "My dear Peggotty. I have come here safe. Barkis is willing. My love to mama. Yours affectionately. P.S. He says he particularly wants you to know—*Barkis is willing.*"

When I had taken this commission on myself prospectively, Mr Barkis relapsed into perfect silence; and I, feeling quite worn out by all that had happened lately, lay down on a sack in the cart and fell asleep. I slept soundly until we got to Yarmouth; which was so entirely new and strange to me in the inn-yard to which we drove, that I at once abandoned a latent hope I had had of meeting with some of Mr Peggotty's family there, perhaps even with little Em'ly herself.

The coach was in the yard, shining very much all over, but without any horses to it as yet; and it looked in that state as if nothing was more unlikely than its ever going to London. I was thinking this, and wondering what would ultimately become of my box, which Mr Barkis had put down on the yard-pavement by the pole (he having driven up the yard to turn his cart), and also what would ultimately become of me, when a lady looked out of a bow-window where some fowls and joints of meat were hanging up, and said:

"Is that the little gentleman from Blunderstone?"

"Yes, ma'am," I said.

"What name?" inquired the lady.

"Copperfield, ma'am," I said.

"That won't do," returned the lady. "Nobody's dinner is paid for here, in that name."

"Is it Murdstone, ma'am?" I said.

"If you're Master Murdstone," said the lady, "why do you go and give another name, first?"

I explained to the lady how it was, who then rang a bell, and called out, "William! show the coffee-room!" upon which a waiter came running out of a kitchen on the opposite side of the yard to show it, and seemed a good deal surprised when he was only to show it to me.

It was a large long room with some large maps in it. I doubt if I could have felt much stranger if the maps had been real foreign countries, and I cast away in the middle of them. I felt it was taking a liberty to sit down, with my cap in my hand, on the corner of the chair nearest the door; and when the waiter laid a cloth on purpose for me, and put a set of castors on it, I think I must have turned red all over with modesty.

He brought me some chops, and vegetables, and took the covers off in such a bouncing manner that I was afraid I must have given him some offence. But he greatly relieved my mind by putting a chair for me at the table, and saying, very affably, "Now, six-foot! come on!"

I thanked him, and took my seat at the board; but found it extremely difficult to handle my knife and fork with anything like dexterity, or to avoid splashing myself with the gravy, while he was standing opposite, staring so hard, and making me blush in the most dreadful manner every time I caught his eye. After watching me into the second chop, he said:

"There's half a pint of ale for you. Will you have it now?"

I thanked him and said, "Yes." Upon which he poured it out of a jug into a large tumbler, and held it up against the light, and made it look beautiful.

"My eye!" he said. "It seems a good deal, don't it?"

"It does seem a good deal," I answered with a smile. For it was quite delightful to me, to find him so pleasant. He was a twinkling-eyed, pimple-faced man, with his hair standing upright all over his head; and as he stood with one arm a-kimbo, holding up the glass to the light with the other hand, he looked quite friendly.

"There was a gentleman here, yesterday," he said—"a stout gentleman, by the name of Topsawyer—perhaps you know him?"

"No," I said, "I don't think—"

"In breeches and gaiters, broad-brimmed hat, grey coat, speckled choker," said the waiter.

"No," I said bashfully, "I haven't the pleasure—"

"He came in here," said the waiter, looking at the light through the tumbler, "ordered a glass of this ale—*would* order it—I told him not—drank it, and fell dead. It was too old for him. It oughtn't to be drawn; that's the fact."

I was very much shocked to hear of this melancholy accident, and said I thought I had better have some water.

"Why you see," said the waiter, still looking at the light through the tumbler, with one of his eyes shut up, "our people don't like things being ordered and left. It offends 'em. But *I*'ll drink it, if you like. I'm used to it, and use is everything. I don't think it'll hurt me, if I throw my head back, and take it off quick. Shall I?"

I replied that he would much oblige me by drinking it, if he thought he could do it safely, but by no means otherwise. When he did throw his head back, and take it off quick, I had a horrible fear, I confess, of seeing him meet the fate of the lamented Mr Topsawyer, and fall lifeless on the carpet. But it didn't hurt him. On the contrary, I thought he seemed the fresher for it.

"What have we got here?" he said, putting a fork into my dish. "Not chops?"

"Chops," I said.

"Lord bless my soul!" he exclaimed, "I didn't know they were chops. Why, a chop's the very thing to take off the bad effects of that beer! Ain't it lucky?"

So he took a chop by the bone in one hand, and a potato in the other, and ate away with a very good appetite, to my extreme satisfaction. He afterwards took another chop, and another potato; and after that, another chop and another potato. When we had done, he brought me a pudding, and having set it before me, seemed to ruminate, and to become absent in his mind for some moments.

"How's the pie?" he said, rousing himself.

"It's a pudding," I made answer.

"Pudding!" he exclaimed. "Why, bless me, so it is! What!" looking at it nearer. "You don't mean to say it's a batter-pudding!"

"Yes, it is indeed."

"Why, a batter-pudding," he said, taking up a table-spoon, "is my favourite pudding! Ain't that lucky? Come on, little 'un, and let's see who'll get most."

The waiter certainly got most. He entreated me more than once to come in and win, but what with his table-spoon to my tea-spoon, his dispatch to my dispatch, and his appetite to my appetite, I was left far behind at the first mouthful, and had no chance with him. I never saw anyone enjoy a pudding so much, I think; and he laughed, when it was all gone, as if his enjoyment of it lasted still.

Finding him so very friendly and companionable, it was then that I asked for the pen and ink and paper, to write to Peggotty. He not only brought it immediately, but was good enough to look over me while I wrote the letter. When I had finished it, he asked me where I was going to school.

I said, "Near London," which was all I knew.

"Oh! my eye!" he said, looking very low-spirited, "I am sorry for that."

"Why?" I asked him.

"Oh, Lord!" he said, shaking his head, "that's the school where they broke the boy's ribs—two ribs—a little boy he was. I should say he was—let me see—how old are you, about?"

I told him between eight and nine.

"That's just his age," he said. "He was eight years and six months old when they broke his first rib; eight years and eight months old when they broke his second, and did for him."

I could not disguise from myself or from the waiter, that this was an uncomfortable coincidence, and inquired how it was done. His answer was not cheering to my spirits, for it consisted of two dismal words, "With whopping."

The blowing of the coach-horn in the yard was a seasonable diversion, which made me get up and hesitatingly inquire, in the mingled pride and diffidence of having a purse (which I took out of my pocket), if there were anything to pay.

"There's a sheet of letter-paper," he returned. "Did you ever buy a sheet of letter-paper?"

I could not remember that I ever had.

"It's dear," he said, "on account of the duty. Threepence. That's the way we're taxed in this country. There's nothing else, except the waiter. Never mind the ink. *I* lose by that."

"What should you—what should I—how much ought I to—what would it be right to pay the waiter, if you please?" I stammered, blushing.

"If I hadn't a family, and that family hadn't the cowpock," said the waiter, "I wouldn't take a sixpence. If I didn't support a aged pairint, and a lovely sister,"—here the waiter was greatly agitated—"I wouldn't take a farthing. If I had a good place, and was treated well here, I should beg acceptance of a trifle, instead of taking of it. But I live on broken wittles—and I sleep on the coals"—here the waiter burst into tears.

I was very much concerned for his misfortunes, and felt that any recognition short of ninepence would be mere brutality and hardness of heart. Therefore I gave him one of my three bright shillings, which he received with much humility and veneration, and spun up with his thumb, directly afterwards, to try the goodness of.

It was a little disconcerting to me, to find, when I was being helped up behind the coach, that I was supposed to have eaten all the dinner without any assistance. I discovered this, from overhearing the lady in the bow-window say to the guard, "Take care of that child, George, or he'll burst!" and from observing that the women-servants who were about the place came out to look and giggle at me as a young phenomenon. My unfortunate friend the waiter, who had quite recovered his spirits, did not appear to be disturbed by this, but joined in the general admiration without being at all confused. If I had any doubt of him, I suppose this half awakened it; but I am inclined to believe that with the simple confidence of a child, and the natural reliance of a child upon superior years (qualities I am very sorry any children should prematurely change for worldly wisdom), I had no serious mistrust of him on the whole, even then.

I felt it rather hard, I must own, to be made, without deserving it, the subject of jokes between the coachman and guard as to the coach drawing heavy behind, on account of my sitting there, and as to the greater expediency of my travelling by waggon. The story of my supposed appetite getting wind among the outside passengers, they were merry upon it likewise; and asked me whether I was going to be paid for, at school, as two brothers or three, and whether I was contracted for, or went upon the regular terms; with other pleasant questions. But the worst of it was, that I knew I should be ashamed to eat anything, when an opportunity offered, and that, after a rather light dinner, I should remain hungry all night—for I had left my cakes behind, at the hotel, in my hurry. My apprehensions were realized. When we stopped for supper I couldn't muster courage to take any, though I should have liked it very much, but sat by the fire and said I didn't want anything. This did not save me from more jokes, either; for a husky-voiced gentleman with a rough face, who had been eating out of a sandwich-box nearly all the way, except when he had been drinking out of a bottle, said I was like a boa-constrictor who took enough at one meal to last him a long time; after which, he actually brought a rash out upon himself with boiled beef.

We had started from Yarmouth at three o'clock in the afternoon, and we were due in London about eight next morning. It was Midsummer weather, and the evening was very pleasant. When we passed through a village, I pictured to myself what the insides of the houses were like, and what the inhabitants were about; and when boys came running after us, and got up behind and swung there for a little way, I wondered whether their fathers were alive, and whether they were happy at home. I had plenty to think of, therefore, besides my mind running continually on the kind of place I was going to—which was an awful speculation. Sometimes, I remember, I resigned myself to thoughts of home and Peggotty; and to endeavouring, in a confused blind way, to recall how I had felt, and what sort of boy I used to be, before I bit Mr Murdstone: which I couldn't satisfy myself about by any means, I seemed to have bitten him in such a remote antiquity.

The night was not so pleasant as the evening, for it got chilly; and being put between two gentlemen (the rough-faced one and another) to prevent my tumbling off the coach, I was nearly smothered by their falling asleep, and completely blocking me up. They squeezed me so hard sometimes, that I could not help crying out, "Oh! If you please!"— which they didn't like at all, because it woke them. Opposite me was an elderly lady in a great fur cloak, who looked in the dark more like a haystack than a lady, she was wrapped up to such a degree. This lady had a basket with her, and she hadn't known what to do with it, for a long time, until she found that on account of my legs being short, it could go underneath me. It cramped and hurt me so, that it made me perfectly miserable; but if I moved in the least, and made a glass that was in the basket rattle against something else (as it was sure to do), she gave me the cruellest poke with her foot, and said, "Come, don't *you* fidget. *Your* bones are young enough, *I'm* sure!"

At last the sun rose, and then my companions seemed to sleep easier. The difficulties under which they had laboured all night, and which had found utterance in the most terrific gasps and snorts, are not to be conceived. As the sun got higher, their sleep became lighter, and so they gradually one by one awoke. I recollect being very much surprised by the feint everybody made, then, of not having been to sleep at all, and by the uncommon indignation with which everyone repelled the charge. I labour under the same kind of astonishment to this day, having invariably observed that of all human weaknesses, the one to which our common nature is the least disposed to confess (I cannot imagine why) is the weakness of having gone to sleep in a coach.

What an amazing place London was to me when I saw it in the distance, and how I believed all the adventures of all my favourite heroes to be constantly enacting and re-enacting there, and how I vaguely made it out in my own mind to be fuller of wonders and wickedness than all the cities of the earth, I need not stop here to relate. We approached it by degrees, and got, in due time, to the inn in the Whitechapel district, for which we were bound. I forget whether it was the Blue Bull, or the Blue Boar; but I know it was the Blue Something, and that its likeness was painted up on the back of the coach.

The guard's eye lighted on me as he was getting down, and he said at the booking-office door:

"Is there anybody here for a youngster booked in the name of Murdstone, from Bloonderstone, Sooffolk, to be left till called for?"

Nobody answered.

"Try Copperfield, if you please, sir," said I, looking helplessly down.

"Is there anybody here for a yoongster, booked in the name of Murdstone, from Bloonderstone, Sooffolk, but owning to the name of Copperfield, to be left till called for?" said the guard. "Come! *Is* there anybody?"

No. There was nobody. I looked anxiously around; but the inquiry made no impression on any of the bystanders, if I except a man in gaiters, with one eye, who suggested that they had better put a brass collar round my neck, and tie me up in the stable.

A ladder was brought, and I got down after the lady, who was like a haystack: not daring to stir, until her basket was removed. The coach was clear of passengers by that time, the luggage was very soon cleared out, the horses had been taken out before the luggage, and now the coach itself was wheeled and backed off by some hostlers, out of the way. Still, nobody appeared, to claim the dusty youngster from Blunderstone, Suffolk.

More solitary than Robinson Crusoe, who had nobody to look at him and see that he was solitary, I went into the booking-office, and, by invitation of the clerk on duty, passed behind the counter, and sat down on the scale at which they weighed the luggage. Here, as I sat looking at the parcels, packages, and books, and inhaling the smell of stables (ever since associated with that morning), a procession of most tremendous considerations began to march through my mind. Supposing nobody should ever fetch me, how long would they consent to keep me there? Would they keep me long enough to spend seven shillings? Should I sleep at night in one of those wooden bins, with the other luggage, and wash myself at the pump in the yard in the morning; or should I be turned out every night, and expected to come again to be left till called for, when the office opened next day? Supposing there was no mistake in the case, and Mr Murdstone had devised this plan to get rid of me, what should I do? If they allowed me to remain there until my seven shillings were spent, I couldn't hope to remain there when I began to starve. That would obviously be inconvenient and unpleasant to the customers, besides entailing on the Blue Whatever-it-was, the risk of funeral expenses. If I started off at once, and tried to walk back home, how could I ever find my way, how could I ever hope to walk so far, how could I make sure of anyone but Peggotty, even if I got back? If I found out the nearest proper authorities, and offered myself to go for a soldier, or a sailor, I was such a little fellow that it was most likely they wouldn't take me in. These thoughts, and a hundred other such thoughts, turned me burning hot, and made me giddy with apprehension and dismay. I was in the height of my fever when a man entered and whispered to the clerk, who presently slanted me off the scale, and pushed me over to him, as if I were weighed, bought, delivered, and paid for.

As I went out of the office, hand in hand with this new acquaintance, I stole a look at him. He was a gaunt, sallow young man, with hollow cheeks, and a chin almost as black as Mr Murdstone's; but there the likeness ended, for his whiskers were shaved off, and his hair, instead of being glossy, was rusty and dry. He was dressed in a suit of black clothes which were rather rusty and dry too, and rather short in the sleeves and legs; and he had a white neck-kerchief on, that was not over-clean. I did not, and do not, suppose that this neck-kerchief was all the linen he wore, but it was all he showed or gave any hint of.

"You're the new boy?" he said.

"Yes, sir," I said.

I supposed I was. I didn't know.

"I'm one of the masters at Salem House," *he* said.

I made him a bow and felt very much overawed. I was so ashamed to allude to a commonplace thing like my box, to a scholar and a master at Salem House, that we had gone some little distance from the yard before I had the hardihood to mention it. We turned back, on my humbly insinuating that it might be useful to me hereafter; and he told the clerk that the carrier had instructions to call for it at noon.

"If you please, sir," I said, when we had accomplished about the same distance as before, "is it far?"

"It's down by Blackheath," he said.

"Is *that* far, sir?" I diffidently asked.

"It's a good step," he said. "We shall go by the stage-coach. It's about six miles."

I was so faint and tired, that the idea of holding out for six miles more, was too much for me. I took heart to tell him that I had had nothing all night, and that if he would allow me to buy something to eat, I should be very much obliged to him. He appeared surprised at this—I see him stop and look at me now—and after considering for a few moments, said he wanted to call on an old person who lived not far off, and that the best way would be for me to buy some bread, or whatever I liked best that was wholesome, and make my breakfast at her house, where we could get some milk.

Accordingly we looked in at a baker's window, and after I had made a series of proposals to buy everything that was bilious in the shop, and he had rejected them one by one, we decided in favour of a nice little loaf of brown bread, which cost me threepence. Then, at a grocer's shop, we bought an egg and a slice of streaky bacon; which still left what I thought a good deal of change, out of the second of the bright shillings, and made me consider London a very cheap place. These provisions laid in, we went on through a great noise and uproar that confused my weary head beyond description, and over a bridge which, no doubt, was London Bridge (indeed I think he told me so, but I was half asleep), until we came to the poor person's house, which was a part of some alms-houses, as I knew by their look, and by an inscription on a stone over the gate, which said they were established for twenty-five poor women.

The Master at Salem House lifted the latch of one of a number of little black doors that were all alike, and had each a little diamond-paned window on one side, and another little diamond-paned window above; and we went into the little house of one of these poor old women, who was blowing a fire to make a little saucepan boil. On seeing the master enter, the old woman stopped with the bellows on her knee, and said something that I thought sounded like "My Charley!" but on seeing me come in too, she got up, and rubbing her hands made a confused sort of half curtsey.

"Can you cook this young gentleman's breakfast for him, if you please?" said the Master at Salem House.

"Can I?" said the old woman. "Yes can I, sure!"

"How's Mrs Fibbitson today?" said the Master, looking at another old woman in a large chair by the fire, who was such a bundle of clothes that I feel grateful to this hour for not having sat upon her by mistake.

"Ah, she's poorly," said the first old woman. "It's one of her bad days. If the fire was to go out, through any accident, I verily believe she'd go out too, and never come to life again."

As they looked at her, I looked at her also. Although it was a warm day, she seemed to think of nothing but the fire. I fancied she was jealous even of the saucepan on it; and I have reason to know that she took its impressment into the service of boiling my egg and broiling my bacon, in dudgeon; for I saw her, with my own discomfited eyes, shake her fist at me once, when those culinary operations were going on, and no one else was looking. The sun streamed in at the little window, but she sat with her own back and the back of the large chair towards it, screening the fire as if she were sedulously keeping *it* warm, instead of it keeping her warm, and watching it in a most distrustful manner. The completion of the preparations for my breakfast, by relieving the fire, gave her such extreme joy that she laughed aloud—and a very unmelodious laugh she had, I must say.

I sat down to my brown loaf, my egg, and my rasher of bacon, with a basin of milk besides, and made a most delicious meal. While I was yet in the full enjoyment of it, the old woman of the house said to the Master:

"Have you got your flute with you?"

"Yes," he returned.

"Have a blow at it," said the old woman, coaxingly. "Do!"

The Master, upon this, put his hand underneath the skirts of his coat, and brought out his flute in three pieces, which he screwed together, and began immediately to play. My impression is, after many years of consideration, that there never can have been anybody in the world who played worse. He made the most dismal sounds I have ever heard produced by any means, natural or artificial. I don't know what the tunes were—if there were such things in the performance at all, which I doubt—but the influence of the strain upon me was, first, to make me think of all my sorrows until I could hardly keep my tears back; then to take away my appetite; and lastly, to make me so sleepy that I couldn't keep my eyes open. They begin to close again, and I begin to nod, as the recollection rises fresh upon me. Once more the little room, with its open corner cupboard, and its square-backed chairs, and its angular little staircase leading to the room above, and its three peacock's feathers displayed over the mantelpiece—I remember wondering when I first went in, what that peacock would have thought if he had known what his finery was doomed to come to—fades from before me, and I nod, and sleep. The flute becomes inaudible, the wheels of the coach are heard instead, and I am on my journey. The coach jolts, I wake with a start, and the flute has come back again, and the Master at Salem House is sitting with his legs crossed, playing it dolefully, while the old woman of the house looks on delighted. She fades in her turn, and he fades, and all fades, and there is no flute, no Master, no Salem House, no David Copperfield, no anything but heavy sleep.

I dreamed, I thought, that once while he was blowing into this dismal flute, the old woman of the house, who had gone nearer and nearer to him in her ecstatic admiration, leaned over the back of his chair and gave him an affectionate squeeze round the neck, which stopped his playing for a moment. I was in the middle state between sleeping and waking, either then or immediately afterwards; for, as he resumed—it was a real fact that he had stopped playing—I saw and heard the same old woman ask Mrs Fibbitson if it wasn't delicious (meaning the flute), to which Mrs Fibbitson replied, "Ay, ay! yes!" and nodded at the fire: to which, I am persuaded, she gave the credit of the whole performance.

When I seemed to have been dozing a long while, the Master at Salem House unscrewed his flute into the three pieces, put them up as before, and took me away. We found the coach very near at hand, and got upon the roof; but I was so dead sleepy, that when we stopped on the road to take up somebody else, they put me inside where there were no passengers, and where I slept profoundly, until I found the coach going at a footpace up a steep hill among green leaves. Presently, it stopped, and had come to its destination.

A short walk brought us—I mean the Master and me—to Salem House, which was enclosed with a high brick wall, and looked very dull. Over a door in this wall was a

board with SALEM HOUSE upon it; and through a grating in this door we were surveyed
when we rang the bell by a surly face, which I found, on the door being opened,
belonged to a stout man with a bull-neck, a wooden leg, overhanging temples, and his
hair cut close all round his head.

"The new boy," said the Master.

The man with the wooden leg eyed me all over—it didn't take long, for there was
not much of me—and locked the gate behind us, and took out the key. We were going
up to the house, among some dark heavy trees, when he called after my conductor.

"Hallo!"

We looked back, and he was standing at the door of a little lodge, where he lived,
with a pair of boots in his hand.

"Here! The cobbler's been," he said, "since you've been out, Mr Mell, and he says
he can't mend 'em any more. He says there ain't a bit of the original boot left, and he
wonders you expect it."

With these words he threw the boots towards Mr Mell, who went back a few paces
to pick them up, and looked at them (very disconsolately, I was afraid), as we went on
together. I observed then, for the first time, that the boots he had on were a good deal
the worse for wear, and that his stocking was just breaking out in one place, like a bud.

Salem House was a square brick building with wings; of a bare and unfurnished
appearance. All about it was so very quiet, that I said to Mr Mell I supposed the boys were
out; but he seemed surprised at my not knowing that it was holiday-time. That all the
boys were at their several homes. That Mr Creakle, the proprietor, was down by the
sea-side with Mrs and Miss Creakle; and that I was sent in holiday-time as a punishment
for my misdoing, all of which he explained to me as we went along.

I gazed upon the schoolroom into which he took me, as the most forlorn and
desolate place I had ever seen. I see it now. A long room with three long rows of desks,
and six of forms, and bristling all round with pegs for hats and slates. Scraps of old
copy-books and exercises litter the dirty floor. Some silkworms' houses, made of the
same materials, are scattered over the desks. Two miserable little white mice, left behind
by their owner, are running up and down in a fusty castle made of pasteboard and wire,
looking in all the corners with their red eyes for anything to eat. A bird, in a cage very
little bigger than himself, makes a mournful rattle now and then in hopping on his perch,
two inches high, or dropping from it; but neither sings nor chirps. There is a strange
unwholesome smell upon the room, like mildewed corduroys, sweet apples wanting air,
and rotten books. There could not well be more ink splashed about it, if it had been
roofless from its first construction, and the skies had rained, snowed, hailed, and blown
ink through the varying seasons of the year.

Mr Mell having left me while he took his irreparable boots upstairs, I went softly to
the upper end of the room, observing all this as I crept along. Suddenly I came upon a
pasteboard placard, beautifully written, which was lying on the desk, and bore these
words: *"Take care of him. He bites."*

I got upon the desk immediately, apprehensive of at least a great dog underneath.
But, though I looked all round with anxious eyes, I could see nothing of him. I was still
engaged in peering about, when Mr Mell came back, and asked me what I did up there?

"I beg your pardon, sir," says I, "if you please, I'm looking for the dog."

"Dog?" he says. "What dog?"

"Isn't it a dog, sir?"

"Isn't what a dog?"

"That's to be taken care of, sir; that bites."

"No, Copperfield," says he, gravely, "that's not a dog. That's a boy. My instructions are, Copperfield, to put this placard on your back. I am sorry to make such a beginning with you, but I must do it."

With that he took me down, and tied the placard, which was neatly constructed for the purpose, on my shoulders like a knapsack; and wherever I went, afterwards, I had the consolation of carrying it.

What I suffered from that placard, nobody can imagine. Whether it was possible for people to see me or not, I always fancied that somebody was reading it. It was no relief to turn round and find nobody; for wherever my back was, there I imagined somebody always to be. That cruel man with the wooden leg aggravated my sufferings. He was in authority; and if he ever saw me leaning against a tree, or a wall, or the house, he roared out from his lodge door in a stupendous voice, "Hallo, you sir! You Copperfield! Show that badge conspicuous, or I'll report you!" The playground was a bare gravelled yard, open to all the back of the house and the offices; and I knew that the servants read it, and the butcher read it, and the baker read it; that everybody, in a word, who came backwards and forwards to the house, of a morning when I was ordered to walk there, read that I was to be taken care of, for I bit. I recollect that I positively began to have a dread of myself, as a kind of wild boy who did bite.

There was an old door in this playground, on which the boys had a custom of carving their names. It was completely covered with such inscriptions. In my dread of the end of the vacation and their coming back, I could not read a boy's name, without inquiring in what tone and with what emphasis *he* would read, "Take care of him. He bites." There was one boy—a certain J. Steerforth—who cut his name very deep and very often, who, I conceived, would read it in a rather strong voice, and afterwards pull my hair. There was another boy, one Tommy Traddles, who I dreaded would make game of it, and pretend to be dreadfully frightened of me. There was a third, George Demple, who I fancied would sing it. I have looked, a little shrinking creature, at that door, until the owners of all the names—there were five-and-forty of them in the school then, Mr Mell said—seemed to send me to Coventry by general acclamation, and to cry out, each in his own way, "Take care of him. He bites!"

It was the same with the places at the desks and forms. It was the same with the groves of deserted bedsteads I peeped at, on my way to, and when I was in, my own bed. I remember dreaming night after night, of being with my mother as she used to be, or of going to a party at Mr Peggotty's, or of travelling outside the stage-coach, or of dining again with my unfortunate friend the waiter, and in all these circumstances making people scream and stare, by the unhappy disclosure that I had nothing on but my little night-shirt, and that placard.

In the monotony of my life, and in my constant apprehension of the re-opening of the school, it was such an insupportable affliction! I had long tasks every day to do with Mr Mell; but I did them, there being no Mr and Miss Murdstone here, and got through them without disgrace. Before, and after them, I walked about—supervised, as I have mentioned, by the man with the wooden leg. How vividly I call to mind the damp about the house, the green cracked flagstones in the court, an old leaky water-butt, and the discoloured trunks of some of the grim trees, which seemed to have dripped more in the rain than other trees, and to have blown less in the sun! At one we dined, Mr Mell and I, at the upper end of a long bare dining-room, full of deal tables, and smelling of fat. Then, we had more tasks until tea, which Mr Mell drank out of a blue teacup, and I out of a tin pot. All day long, and until seven or eight in the evening, Mr Mell, at his own detached desk in the schoolroom, worked hard with pen, ink, ruler, books, and writing-paper, making out the bills (as I found) for last half-year. When he had put up his things for the night he took out his flute, and blew at it, until I almost thought he would gradually blow his whole being into the large hole at the top, and ooze away at the keys.

I picture my small self in the dimly-lighted rooms, sitting with my head upon my hand, listening to the doleful performance of Mr Mell, and conning tomorrow's lessons. I picture myself with my books shut up, still listening to the doleful performance of Mr Mell, and listening through it to what used to be at home, and to the blowing of the wind on Yarmouth flats, and feeling very sad and solitary. I picture myself going up to bed, among the unused rooms, and sitting on my bed-side crying for a comfortable word from Peggotty. I picture myself coming downstairs in the morning, and looking through a long ghastly gash of a staircase window at the school-bell hanging on the top of an out-house with a weathercock above it; and dreading the time when it shall ring J. Steerforth and the rest to work: which is only second, in my foreboding apprehensions, to the time when the man with the wooden leg shall unlock the rusty gate to give admission to the awful Mr Creakle. I cannot think I was a very dangerous character in any of these aspects, but in all of them I carried the same warning on my back.

Mr Mell never said much to me, but he was never harsh to me. I suppose we were company to each other, without talking. I forgot to mention that he would talk to himself sometimes, and grin, and clench his fist, and grind his teeth, and pull his hair in an unaccountable manner. But he had these peculiarities: and at first they frightened me, though I soon got used to them.

Chapter VI

I ENLARGE MY CIRCLE OF ACQUAINTANCE

I HAD led this life about a month, when the man with the wooden leg began to stump about with a mop and a bucket of water, from which I inferred that preparations were making to receive Mr Creakle and the boys. I was not mistaken; for the mop came into the schoolroom before long, and turned out Mr Mell and me, who lived where we could, and got on how we could, for some days, during which we were always in the way of two or three young women, who had rarely shown themselves before, and were so continually in the midst of dust that I sneezed almost as much as if Salem House had been a great snuff-box.

One day I was informed by Mr Mell that Mr Creakle would be home that evening. In the evening, after tea, I heard that he was come. Before bedtime, I was fetched by the man with the wooden leg to appear before him.

Mr Creakle's part of the house was a good deal more comfortable than ours, and he had a snug bit of garden that looked pleasant after the dusty playground, which was such a desert in miniature, that I thought no one but a camel, or a dromedary, could have felt at home in it. It seemed to me a bold thing even to take notice that the passage looked comfortable, as I went on my way, trembling, to Mr Creakle's presence: which so abashed me, when I was ushered into it, that I hardly saw Mrs Creakle or Miss Creakle (who were both there, in the parlour), or anything but Mr Creakle, a stout gentleman with a bunch of watch-chain and seals, in an arm-chair, with a tumbler and bottle beside him.

"So!" said Mr Creakle. "This is the young gentleman whose teeth are to be filed! Turn him round."

The wooden-legged man turned me about so as to exhibit the placard; and having afforded time for a full survey of it, turned me about again, with my face to Mr Creakle, and posted himself at Mr Creakle's side. Mr Creakle's face was fiery, and his eyes were small, and deep in his head; he had thick veins in his forehead, a little nose, and a large chin. He was bald on the top of his head; and had some thin wet-looking hair that was just turning grey, brushed across each temple, so that the two sides interlaced on his forehead. But the circumstance about him which impressed me most, was, that he had no voice, but spoke in a whisper. The exertion this cost him, or the consciousness of talking in that feeble way, made his angry face so much more angry, and his thick veins so much thicker, when he spoke, that I am not surprised, on looking back, at this peculiarity striking me as his chief one.

"Now," said Mr Creakle. "What's the report of this boy?"

"There's nothing against him yet," returned the man with the wooden leg. "There has been no opportunity."

I thought Mr Creakle was disappointed. I thought Mrs and Miss Creakle (at whom I now glanced for the first time, and who were, both, thin and quiet) were not disappointed.

"Come here, sir!" said Mr Creakle, beckoning to me.

"Come here!" said the man with the wooden leg, repeating the gesture.

"I have the happiness of knowing your father-in-law," whispered Mr Creakle, taking me by the ear; "and a worthy man he is, and a man of a strong character. He knows me, and I know him. Do *you* know me? Hey?" said Mr Creakle, pinching my ear with ferocious playfulness.

"Not yet, sir," I said, flinching with the pain.

"Not yet? Hey?" repeated Mr Creakle. "But you will soon. Hey?"

"You will soon. Hey?" repeated the man with the wooden leg. I afterwards found that he generally acted, with his strong voice, as Mr Creakle's interpreter to the boys.

I was very much frightened, and said, I hoped so, if he pleased. I felt, all this while, as if my ear were blazing; he pinched it so hard.

"I'll tell you what I am," whispered Mr Creakle, letting it go at last, with a screw at parting that brought the water into my eyes. "I'm a Tartar."

"A Tartar," said the man with the wooden leg.

"When I say I'll do a thing, I do it," said Mr Creakle; "and when I say I will have a thing done, I will have it done."

"—Will have a thing done, I will have it done," repeated the man with the wooden leg.

"I am a determined character," said Mr Creakle. "That's what I am. I do my duty. That's what *I* do. My flesh and blood"—he looked at Mrs Creakle as he said this—"when it rises against me, is not my flesh and blood. I discard it. Has that fellow"—to the man with the wooden leg—"been here again?"

"No," was the answer.

"No," said Mr Creakle. "He knows better. He knows me. Let him keep away. I say let him keep away," said Mr Creakle, striking his hand upon the table, and looking at Mrs

Creakle, "for he knows me. Now you have begun to know me too, my young friend, and you may go. Take him away."

I was very glad to be ordered away, for Mrs and Miss Creakle were both wiping their eyes, and I felt as uncomfortable for them as I did for myself. But I had a petition on my mind which concerned me so nearly, that I couldn't help saying, though I wondered at my own courage:

"If you please, sir—"

Mr Creakle whispered, "Hah! What's this?" and bent his eyes upon me, as if he would have burnt me up with them.

"If you please, sir," I faltered, "if I might be allowed (I am very sorry indeed, sir, for what I did) to take this writing off, before the boys come back—"

Whether Mr Creakle was in earnest, or whether he only did it to frighten me, I don't know, but he made a burst out of his chair, before which I precipitately retreated, without waiting for the escort of the man with the wooden leg, and never once stopped until I reached my own bedroom, where, finding I was not pursued, I went to bed, as it was time, and lay quaking, for a couple of hours.

Next morning Mr Sharp came back. Mr Sharp was the first master, and superior to Mr Mell. Mr Mell took his meals with the boys, but Mr Sharp dined and supped at Mr Creakle's table. He was a limp, delicate-looking gentleman, I thought, with a good deal of nose, and a way of carrying his head on one side, as if it were a little too heavy for him. His hair was very smooth and wavy; but I was informed by the very first boy who came back that it was a wig (a second-hand one *he* said), and that Mr Sharp went out every Saturday afternoon to get it curled.

It was no other than Tommy Traddles who gave me this piece of intelligence. He was the first boy who returned. He introduced himself by informing me that I should find his name on the right-hand corner of the gate, over the top-bolt; upon that I said, "Traddles?" to which he replied, "The same," and then he asked me for a full account of myself and family.

It was a happy circumstance for me that Traddles came back first. He enjoyed my placard so much, that he saved me from the embarrassment of either disclosure or concealment, by presenting me to every other boy who came back, great or small, immediately on his arrival, in this form of introduction, "Look here! Here's a game!" Happily, too, the greater part of the boys came back low-spirited, and were not so boisterous at my expense as I had expected. Some of them certainly did dance about me like wild Indians, and the greater part could not resist the temptation of pretending that I was a dog, and patting and soothing me, lest I should bite, and saying, "Lie down, sir!" and calling me Towzer. This was naturally confusing, among so many strangers, and cost me some tears, but on the whole it was much better than I had anticipated.

I was not considered as being formally received into the school, however, until J. Steerforth arrived. Before this boy, who was reputed to be a great scholar, and was very good-looking, and at least half-a-dozen years my senior, I was carried as before a magistrate. He inquired, under a shed in the playground, into the particulars of my punishment, and was pleased to express his opinion that it was "a jolly shame"; for which I became bound to him ever afterwards.

"What money have you got, Copperfield?" he said, walking aside with me when he had disposed of my affair in these terms.

I told him seven shillings.

"You had better give it to me to take care of," he said. "At least, you can if you like. You needn't if you don't like."

I hastened to comply with his friendly suggestion, and opening Peggotty's purse, turned it upside down into his hand.

"Do you want to spend anything now?" he asked me.

"No thank you," I replied.

"You can, if you like, you know," said Steerforth. "Say the word."

"No, thank you, sir," I repeated.

"Perhaps you'd like to spend a couple of shillings or so, in a bottle of currant wine by and by, up in the bedroom?" said Steerforth. "You belong to my bedroom, I find."

It certainly had not occurred to me before, but I said, Yes, I should like that.

"Very good," said Steerforth. "You'll be glad to spend another shilling or so, in almond cakes, I dare say?"

I said, Yes, I should like that, too.

"And another shilling or so in biscuits, and another in fruit, eh?" said Steerforth. "I say, young Copperfield, you're going it!"

I smiled because he smiled, but I was a little troubled in my mind, too.

"Well!" said Steerforth. "We must make it stretch as far as we can; that's all. I'll do the best in my power for you. I can go out when I like, and I'll smuggle the prog in." With these words he put the money in his pocket, and kindly told me not to make myself uneasy; he would take care it should be all right.

He was as good as his word, if that were all right which I had a secret misgiving was nearly all wrong—for I feared it was a waste of my mother's two half-crowns—though I had preserved the piece of paper they were wrapped in: which was a precious saving. When we went upstairs to bed, he produced the whole seven shillings' worth, and laid it out on my bed in the moonlight, saying:

"There you are, young Copperfield, and a royal spread you've got."

I couldn't think of doing the honours of the feast, at my time of life, while he was by; my hand shook at the very thought of it. I begged him to do me the favour of presiding; and my request being seconded by the other boys who were in that room, he acceded to it, and sat upon my pillow, handing round the viands—with perfect fairness, I must say—and dispensing the currant wine in a little glass without a foot, which was his own property. As to me, I sat on his left hand, and the rest were grouped about us, on the nearest beds and on the floor.

How well I recollect our sitting there, talking in whispers; or their talking, and my respectfully listening, I ought rather to say; the moonlight falling a little way into the room, through the window, painting a pale window on the floor, and the greater part of us in shadow, except when Steerforth dipped a match into a phosphorus-box, when he wanted to look for anything on the board, and shed a blue glare over us that was gone directly! A certain mysterious feeling, consequent on the darkness, the secrecy of the revel, and the whisper in which everything was said, steals over me again, and I listen to all they tell me with a vague feeling of solemnity and awe, which makes me glad that they are all so near, and frightens me (though I feign to laugh) when Traddles pretends to see a ghost in the corner.

I heard all kinds of things about the school and all belonging to it. I heard that Mr Creakle had not preferred his claim to being a Tartar without reason; that he was the sternest and most severe of masters; that he laid about him, right and left, every day of his life, charging in among the boys like a trooper, and slashing away, unmercifully. That he knew nothing himself, but the art of slashing, being more ignorant (J. Steerforth said) than the lowest boy in the school; that he had been, a good many years ago, a small hop-dealer in the Borough, and had taken to the schooling business after being bankrupt in hops, and making away with Mrs Creakle's money. With a good deal more of that sort, which I wondered how they knew.

I heard that the man with the wooden leg, whose name was Tungay, was an obstinate barbarian who had formerly assisted in the hop business, but had come into the scholastic line with Mr Creakle, in consequence, as was supposed among the boys, of his having broken his leg in Mr Creakle's service, and having done a deal of dishonest work for him, and knowing his secrets. I heard that with the single exception of Mr Creakle, Tungay considered the whole establishment, masters and boys, as his natural enemies, and that the only delight of his life was to be sour and malicious. I heard that Mr Creakle had a son, who had not been Tungay's friend, and who, assisting in the school, had once held some remonstrance with his father on an occasion when its discipline was very cruelly exercised, and was supposed, besides, to have protested against his father's usage of his mother. I heard that Mr Creakle had turned him out of doors, in consequence; and that Mrs and Miss Creakle had been in a sad way, ever since.

But the greatest wonder that I heard of Mr Creakle was, there being one boy in the school on whom he never ventured to lay a hand, and that boy being J. Steerforth. Steerforth himself confirmed this when it was stated, and said that he should like to begin to see him do it. On being asked by a mild boy (not me) how he would proceed if he did begin to see him do it, he dipped a match into his phosphorus-box on purpose to shed a glare over his reply, and said he would commence by knocking him down with a blow on the forehead from the seven-and-sixpenny ink-bottle that was always on the mantelpiece. We sat in the dark for some time, breathless.

I heard that Mr Sharp and Mr Mell were both supposed to be wretchedly paid; and that when there was hot and cold meat for dinner at Mr Creakle's table, Mr Sharp was always expected to say he preferred cold; which was again corroborated by J. Steerforth, the only parlour-boarder. I heard that Mr Sharp's wig didn't fit him; and that he needn't be so "bounceable"—somebody else said "bumptious"—about it, because his own red hair was very plainly to be seen behind.

I heard that one boy, who was a coal-merchant's son, came as a set-off against the coal-bill, and was called, on that account, "Exchange or Barter"—a name selected from the arithmetic book as expressing this arrangement. I heard that the table beer was a robbery of parents, and the pudding an imposition. I heard that Miss Creakle was regarded by the school in general as being in love with Steerforth; and I am sure, as I sat in the dark, thinking of his nice voice, and his fine face, and his easy manner, and his curling hair, I thought it very likely. I heard that Mr Mell was not a bad sort of fellow, but hadn't a sixpence to bless himself with; and that there was no doubt that old Mrs Mell, his mother, was as poor as Job. I thought of my breakfast then, and what had sounded like "My Charley!" but I was, I am glad to remember, as mute as a mouse about it.

The hearing of all this, and a good deal more, outlasted the banquet some time. The greater part of the guests had gone to bed as soon as the eating and drinking were over; and we, who had remained whispering and listening half-undressed, at last betook ourselves to bed, too.

"Good night, young Copperfield," said Steerforth. "I'll take care of you."

"You're very kind," I gratefully returned. "I am very much obliged to you."

"You haven't got a sister, have you?" said Steerforth, yawning.

"No," I answered.

"That's a pity," said Steerforth. "If you had had one, I should think she would have been a pretty, timid, little, bright-eyed sort of girl. I should have liked to know her. Good night, young Copperfield."

"Good night, sir," I replied.

I thought of him very much after I went to bed, and raised myself, I recollect, to look at him where he lay in the moonlight, with his handsome face turned up, and his head reclining easily on his arm. He was a person of great power in my eyes; that was, of course, the reason of my mind running on him. No veiled future dimly glanced upon him in the moonbeams. There was no shadowy picture of his footsteps, in the garden that I dreamed of walking in all night.

Chapter VII

MY "FIRST HALF" AT SALEM HOUSE

SCHOOL began in earnest next day. A profound impression was made upon me, I remember, by the roar of voices in the schoolroom suddenly becoming hushed as death when Mr Creakle entered after breakfast, and stood in the doorway looking round upon us like a giant in a story-book surveying his captives.

Tungay stood at Mr Creakle's elbow. He had no occasion, I thought, to cry out "Silence!" so ferociously, for the boys were all struck speechless and motionless.

Mr Creakle was seen to speak, and Tungay was heard, to this effect.

"Now, boys, this is a new half. Take care what you're about, in this new half. Come fresh up to the lessons, I advise you, for I come fresh up to the punishment. I won't flinch. It will be of no use your rubbing yourselves; you won't rub the marks out that I shall give you. Now get to work, every boy!"

When this dreadful exordium was over, and Tungay had stumped out again, Mr Creakle came to where I sat, and told me that if I were famous for biting, he was famous for biting, too. He then showed me the cane, and asked me what I thought of *that,* for a tooth? Was it a sharp tooth, hey? Was it a double tooth, hey? Had it a deep prong, hey? Did it bite, hey? Did it bite? At every question he gave me a fleshy cut with it that made me writhe; so I was very soon made free of Salem House (as Steerforth said), and was very soon in tears also.

Not that I mean to say these were special marks of distinction, which only I received. On the contrary, a large majority of the boys (especially the smaller ones) were visited with similar instances of notice, as Mr Creakle made the round of the schoolroom. Half the establishment was writhing and crying, before the day's work began; and how much of it had writhed and cried before the day's work was over, I am really afraid to recollect, lest I should seem to exaggerate.

I should think there never can have been a man who enjoyed his profession more than Mr Creakle did. He had a delight in cutting at the boys, which was like the satisfaction of a craving appetite. I am confident that he couldn't resist a chubby boy, especially; that there was a fascination in such a subject, which made him restless in his mind, until he had scored and marked him for the day. I was chubby myself, and ought to know. I am sure when I think of the fellow now, my blood rises against him with the disinterested indignation I should feel if I could have known all about him without having ever been in his power; but it rises hotly, because I know him to have been an incapable brute, who had no more right to be possessed of the great truth he held, than to be Lord High Admiral, or Commander-in-Chief: in either of which capacities it is probable that he would have done infinitely less mischief.

Miserable little propitiators of a remorseless Idol, how abject we were to him! what a launch in life I think it now, on looking back, to be so mean and servile to a man of such parts and pretensions!

Here I sit at the desk again, watching his eye—humbly watching his eye, as he rules a ciphering-book for another victim whose hands have just been flattened by that identical ruler, and who is trying to wipe the sting out with a pocket-handkerchief. I have plenty to do. I don't watch his eye in idleness, but because I am morbidly attracted to it, in a dread desire to know what he will do next, and whether it will be my turn to suffer, or somebody else's. A lane of small boys beyond me, with the same interest in his eye, watch it too. I think he knows it, though he pretends he don't. He makes dreadful mouths as he rules the ciphering-book; and now he throws his eye sideways down our lane, and we all droop over our books and tremble. A moment afterwards we are again eyeing him. An unhappy culprit, found guilty of imperfect exercise, approaches at his command. The culprit falters excuses, and professes a determination to do better tomorrow. Mr Creakle cuts a joke before he beats him, and we laugh at it,—miserable little dogs, we laugh, with our visages as white as ashes, and our hearts sinking into our boots.

Here I sit at the desk again, on a drowsy summer afternoon. A buzz and hum go up around me, as if the boys were so many bluebottles. A cloggy sensation of the lukewarm fat of meat is upon me (we dined an hour or two ago), and my head is as heavy as so much lead. I would give the world to go to sleep. I sit with my eye on Mr Creakle, blinking at him like a young owl; when sleep overpowers me for a minute, he still looms through my slumber, ruling those ciphering-books, until he softly comes behind me and wakes me to plainer perception of him, with a red ridge across my back.

Here I am in the playground, with my eye still fascinated by him, though I can't see him. The window at a little distance from which I know he is having his dinner, stands for him, and I eye that instead. If he shows his face near it, mine assumes an imploring and submissive expression. If he looks out through the glass, the boldest boy (Steerforth excepted) stops in the middle of a shout or yell, and becomes contemplative. One day, Traddles (the most unfortunate boy in the world) breaks that window accidentally, with a ball. I shudder at this moment with the tremendous sensation of seeing it done, and feeling that the ball has bounded on to Mr Creakle's sacred head.

Poor Traddles! In a tight sky-blue suit that made his arms and legs like German sausages, or roly-poly puddings, he was the merriest and most miserable of all the boys. He was always being caned—I think he was caned every day that half-year, except one holiday Monday when he was only ruler'd on both hands—and was always going to write to his uncle about it, and never did. After laying his head on the desk for a little while, he would cheer up, somehow, begin to laugh again, and draw skeletons all over his slate, before his eyes were dry. I used at first to wonder what comfort Traddles found in drawing skeletons; and for some time looked upon him as a sort of hermit, who reminded himself by those symbols of mortality that caning couldn't last for ever. But I believe he only did it because they were easy, and didn't want any features.

He was very honourable, Traddles was, and held it as a solemn duty in the boys to stand by one another. He suffered for this on several occasions; and particularly once, when Steerforth laughed in church, and the Beadle thought it was Traddles, and took him out. I see him now, going away in custody, despised by the congregation. He never said who was the real offender, though he smarted for it next day, and was imprisoned so many hours that he came forth with a whole churchyard-full of skeletons swarming all over his Latin Dictionary. But he had his reward. Steerforth said there was nothing of the sneak in Traddles, and we all felt that to be the highest praise. For my part, I could have gone through a good deal (though I was much less brave than Traddles, and nothing like so old) to have won such a recompense.

To see Steerforth walk to church before us, arm-in-arm with Miss Creakle, was one of the great sights of my life. I didn't think Miss Creakle equal to little Em'ly in point of beauty, and I didn't love her (I didn't dare); but I thought her a young lady of extraordinary attractions, and in point of gentility not to be surpassed. When Steerforth, in white trousers, carried her parasol for her, I felt proud to know him; and believed that she could not choose but adore him with all her heart. Mr Sharp and Mr Mell were both notable personages in my eyes; but Steerforth was to them what the sun was to two stars.

Steerforth continued his protection of me, and proved a very useful friend; since nobody dared to annoy one whom he honoured with his countenance. He couldn't—or at all events he didn't—defend me from Mr Creakle, who was very severe with me; but whenever I had been treated worse than usual, he always told me that I wanted a little of his pluck, and that he wouldn't have stood it himself; which I felt he intended for encouragement, and considered to be very kind of him. There was one advantage, and only one that I know of, in Mr Creakle's severity. He found my placard in his way when he came up or down behind the form on which I sat, and wanted to make a cut at me in passing; for this reason it was soon taken off, and I saw it no more.

An accidental circumstance cemented the intimacy between Steerforth and me, in a manner that inspired me with great pride and satisfaction, though it sometimes led to inconvenience. It happened on one occasion, when he was doing me the honour of talking to me in the playground, that I hazarded the observation that something or somebody—I forget what now—was like something or somebody in *Peregrine Pickle*. He said nothing at the time; but when I was going to bed at night, asked me if I had got that book?

I told him no, and explained how it was that I had read it, and all those other books of which I have made mention.

"And do you recollect them?" Steerforth said.

"Oh yes," I replied; I had a good memory, and I believed I recollected them very well.

"Then I tell you what, young Copperfield," said Steerforth, "you shall tell 'em to me. I can't get to sleep very early at night, and I generally wake rather early in the morning. We'll go over 'em one after another. We'll make some regular Arabian Nights of it."

I felt extremely flattered by this arrangement, and we commenced carrying it into execution that very evening. What ravages I committed on my favourite authors in the course of my interpretation of them, I am not in a condition to say, and should be very unwilling to know; but I had a profound faith in them, and I had, to the best of my belief, a simple, earnest manner of narrating what I did narrate; and these qualities went a long way.

The drawback was, that I was often sleepy at night, or out of spirits and indisposed to resume the story; and then it was rather hard work, and it must be done; for to disappoint or to displease Steerforth was of course out of the question. In the morning, too, when I felt weary, and should have enjoyed another hour's repose very much, it was a tiresome thing to be roused, like the Sultana Scheherazade, and forced into a long story before the getting-up bell rang; but Steerforth was resolute; and as he explained to me, in return, my sums and exercises, and anything in my tasks that was too hard for me, I was no loser by the transaction. Let me do myself justice, however. I was moved by no interested or selfish motive, nor was I moved by fear of him. I admired and loved him, and his approval was return enough. It was so precious to me that I look back on these trifles, now, with an aching heart.

Steerforth was considerate, too; and showed his consideration, in one particular instance, in an unflinching manner that was a little tantalizing, I suspect, to poor Traddles and the rest. Peggotty's promised letter—what a comfortable letter it was!—arrived before "the half" was many weeks old; and with it a cake in a perfect nest of oranges, and two bottles of cowslip wine. This treasure, as in duty bound, I laid at the feet of Steerforth, and begged him to dispense.

"Now, I'll tell you what, young Copperfield," said he: "the wine shall be kept to wet your whistle when you are story-telling."

I blushed at the idea, and begged him, in my modesty, not to think of it. But he said he had observed I was sometimes hoarse—a little roopy was his exact expression—and it should be, every drop, devoted to the purpose he had mentioned. Accordingly, it was locked up in his box, and drawn off by himself in a phial, and administered to me through a piece of quill in the cork, when I was supposed to be in want of a restorative. Sometimes, to make it a more sovereign specific, he was so kind as to squeeze orange juice into it, or to stir it up with ginger, or dissolve a peppermint drop in it; and although I cannot assert that the flavour was improved by these experiments, or that it was exactly the compound one would have chosen for a stomachic, the last thing at night and the first thing in the morning, I drank it gratefully and was very sensible of his attention.

We seem, to me, to have been months over Peregrine, and months more over the other stories. The institution never flagged for want of a story, I am certain; and the wine lasted out almost as well as the matter. Poor Traddles—I never think of that boy but with a strange disposition to laugh, and with tears in my eyes—was a sort of chorus, in general; and affected to be convulsed with mirth at the comic parts, and to be overcome with fear when there was any passage of an alarming character in the narrative. This rather put me out, very often. It was a great jest of his, I recollect, to pretend that he couldn't keep his teeth from chattering, whenever mention was made of an Alguazil in connexion with the adventures of Gil Blas; and I remember that when Gil Blas met the captain of the robbers in Madrid, this unlucky joker counterfeited such an ague of terror, that he was overheard by Mr Creakle, who was prowling about the passage, and handsomely flogged for disorderly conduct in the bedroom.

Whatever I had within me that was romantic and dreamy, was encouraged by so much story-telling in the dark; and in that respect the pursuit may not have been very profitable to me. But the being cherished as a kind of plaything in my room, and the consciousness that this accomplishment of mine was bruited about among the boys, and attracted a good deal of notice to me though I was the youngest there, stimulated me to exertion. In a school carried on by sheer cruelty, whether it is presided over by a dunce or not, there is not likely to be much learnt. I believe our boys were, generally, as ignorant a set as any schoolboys in existence; they were too much troubled and knocked about to learn; they could no more do that to advantage, than any one can do anything to advantage in a life of constant misfortune, torment, and worry. But my little vanity, and

Steerforth's help, urged me on somehow; and without saving me from much, if anything, in the way of punishment, made me, for the time I was there, an exception to the general body, insomuch that I did steadily pick up some crumbs of knowledge.

In this I was much assisted by Mr Mell, who had a liking for me that I am grateful to remember. It always gave me pain to observe that Steerforth treated him with systematic disparagement, and seldom lost an occasion of wounding his feelings, or inducing others to do so. This troubled me the more for a long time, because I had soon told Steerforth, from whom I could no more keep such a secret, than I could keep a cake or any other tangible possession, about the two old women Mr Mell had taken me to see; and I was always afraid that Steerforth would let it out, and twit him with it.

We little thought, any one of us, I dare say, when I ate my breakfast that first morning, and went to sleep under the shadow of the peacock's feathers to the sound of the flute, what consequences would come of the introduction into those alms-houses of my insignificant person. But the visit had its unforeseen consequences; and of a serious sort, too, in their way.

One day when Mr Creakle kept the house from indisposition, which naturally diffused a lively joy through the school, there was a good deal of noise in the course of the morning's work. The great relief and satisfaction experienced by the boys made them difficult to manage; and though the dreaded Tungay brought his wooden leg in twice or thrice, and took notes of the principal offenders' names, no great impression was made by it, as they were pretty sure of getting into trouble tomorrow, do what they would, and thought it wise, no doubt, to enjoy themselves today.

It was, properly, a half-holiday; being Saturday. But as the noise in the playground would have disturbed Mr Creakle, and the weather was not favourable for going out walking, we were ordered into school in the afternoon, and set some lighter tasks than usual, which were made for the occasion. It was the day of the week on which Mr Sharp went out to get his wig curled; so Mr Mell, who always did the drudgery, whatever it was, kept school by himself.

If I could associate the idea of a bull or a bear with anyone so mild as Mr Mell, I should think of him, in connexion with that afternoon when the uproar was at its height, as of one of those animals, baited by a thousand dogs. I recall him bending his aching head, supported on his bony hand, over the book on his desk, and wretchedly endeavouring to get on with his tiresome work, amidst an uproar that might have made the Speaker of the House of Commons giddy. Boys started in and out of their places, playing at puss in the corner with other boys; there were laughing boys, singing boys, talking boys, dancing boys, howling boys; boys shuffled with their feet, boys whirled about him, grinning, making faces, mimicking him behind his back and before his eyes; mimicking his poverty, his boots, his coat, his mother, everything belonging to him that they should have had consideration for.

"Silence!" cried Mr Mell, suddenly rising up, and striking his desk with the book. "What does this mean! It's impossible to bear it. It's maddening. How can you do it to me, boys?"

It was my book that he struck his desk with; and as I stood beside him, following his eye as it glanced round the room, I saw the boys all stop, some suddenly surprised, some half afraid, and some sorry perhaps.

Steerforth's place was at the bottom of the school, at the opposite end of the long room. He was lounging with his back against the wall, and his hands in his pockets, and looked at Mr Mell with his mouth shut up as if he were whistling, when Mr Mell looked at him.

"Silence, Mr Steerforth!" said Mr Mell.

"Silence yourself," said Steerforth, turning red. "Whom are you talking to?"

"Sit down," said Mr Mell.

"Sit down yourself," said Steerforth, "and mind your business."

There was a titter, and some applause; but Mr Mell was so white, that silence immediately succeeded; and one boy, who had darted out behind him to imitate his mother again, changed his mind, and pretended to want a pen mended.

"If you think, Steerforth," said Mr Mell, "that I am not acquainted with the power you can establish over any mind here"——he laid his hand, without considering what he did (as I supposed), upon my head——"or that I have not observed you, within a few minutes, urging your juniors on to every sort of outrage against me, you are mistaken."

"I don't give myself the trouble of thinking at all about you," said Steerforth, coolly; "so I'm not mistaken, as it happens."

"And when you make use of your position of favouritism here, sir," pursued Mr Mell, with his lip trembling very much, "to insult a gentleman——"

"A what?——where is he?" said Steerforth.

Here somebody cried out, "Shame, J. Steerforth! Too bad!" It was Traddles; whom Mr Mell instantly discomfited by bidding him hold his tongue.

——"To insult one who is not fortunate in life, sir, and who never gave you the least offence, and the many reasons for not insulting whom you are old enough and wise enough to understand," said Mr Mell, with his lips trembling more and more, "you commit a mean and base action. You can sit down or stand up as you please, sir. Copperfield, go on."

"Young Copperfield," said Steerforth, coming forward up the room, "stop a bit. I tell you what, Mr Mell, once for all. When you take the liberty of calling me mean or base, or anything of that sort, you are an impudent beggar. You are always a beggar, you know; but when you do that, you are an impudent beggar."

I am not clear whether he was going to strike Mr Mell, or Mr Mell was going to strike him, or there was any such intention on either side. I saw a rigidity come upon the whole school as if they had been turned into stone, and found Mr Creakle in the midst of us, with Tungay at his side, and Mrs and Miss Creakle looking in at the door as if they were frightened. Mr Mell, with his elbows on his desk and his face in his hands, sat, for some moments, quite still.

"Mr Mell," said Mr Creakle, shaking him by the arm; and his whisper was so audible now, that Tungay felt it unnecessary to repeat his words; "you have not forgotten yourself, I hope?"

"No, sir, no," returned the Master, showing his face, and shaking his head, and rubbing his hands in great agitation. "No, sir. No. I have remembered myself, I——no, Mr Creakle, I have not forgotten myself, I——I have remembered myself, sir. I——I——could wish you had remembered me a little sooner, Mr Creakle. It——it——would have been more kind, sir, more just, sir. It would have saved me something, sir."

Mr Creakle, looking hard at Mr Mell, put his hand on Tungay's shoulder, and got his feet upon the form close by, and sat upon the desk. After still looking hard at Mr Mell from his throne, as he shook his head, and rubbed his hands, and remained in the same state of agitation, Mr Creakle turned to Steerforth, and said:

"Now, sir, as he don't condescend to tell me, what *is* this?"

Steerforth evaded the question for a little while; looking in scorn and anger on his opponent, and remaining silent. I could not help thinking even in that interval, I remember, what a noble fellow he was in appearance, and how homely and plain Mr Mell looked opposed to him.

"What did he mean by talking about favourites, then?" said Steerforth at length.

"Favourites?" repeated Mr Creakle, with the veins in his forehead swelling quickly. "Who talked about favourites?"

"He did," said Steerforth.

"And pray, what did you mean by that, sir?" demanded Mr Creakle, turning angrily on his assistant.

"I meant, Mr Creakle," he returned in a low voice, "as I said; that no pupil had a right to avail himself of his position of favouritism to degrade me."

"To degrade *you?*" said Mr Creakle. "My stars! But give me leave to ask you, Mr What's-your-name"; and here Mr Creakle folded his arms, cane and all, upon his chest, and made such a knot of his brows that his little eyes were hardly visible below them; "whether, when you talk about favourites, you showed proper respect to me? To me, sir," said Mr Creakle, darting his head at him suddenly, and drawing it back again, "the principal of this establishment, and your employer."

"It was not judicious, sir, I am willing to admit," said Mr Mell. "I should not have done so, if I had been cool."

Here Steerforth struck in.

"Then he said I was mean, and then he said I was base, and then I called him a beggar. If *I* had been cool, perhaps I shouldn't have called him a beggar. But I did, and I am ready to take the consequences of it."

Without considering, perhaps, whether there were any consequences to be taken, I felt quite in a glow at this gallant speech. It made an impression on the boys too, for there was a low stir among them, though no one spoke a word.

"I am surprised, Steerforth—although your candour does you honour," said Mr Creakle, "does you honour, certainly—I am surprised, Steerforth, I must say, that you should attach such an epithet to any person employed and paid in Salem House, sir."

Steerforth gave a short laugh.

"That's not an answer, sir," said Mr Creakle, "to my remark. I expect more than that from you, Steerforth."

If Mr Mell looked homely, in my eyes, before the handsome boy, it would be quite impossible to say how homely Mr Creakle looked.

"Let him deny it," said Steerforth.

"Deny that he is a beggar, Steerforth?" cried Mr Creakle. "Why, where does he go a begging?"

"If he is not a beggar himself, his near relation's one," said Steerforth. "It's all the same."

He glanced at me, and Mr Mell's hand gently patted me upon the shoulder. I looked up with a flush upon my face and remorse in my heart, but Mr Mell's eyes were fixed on Steerforth. He continued to pat me kindly on the shoulder, but he looked at him.

"Since you expect me, Mr Creakle, to justify myself," said Steerforth, "and to say what I mean,—what I have to say is, that his mother lives on charity in an alms-house."

Mr Mell still looked at him, and still patted me kindly on the shoulder, and said to himself, in a whisper, if I heard right: "Yes, I thought so."

Mr Creakle turned to his assistant, with a severe frown and laboured politeness:

"Now, you hear what this gentleman says, Mr Mell. Have the goodness, if you please, to set him right before the assembled school."

"He is right, sir, without correction," returned Mr Mell, in the midst of a dead silence; "what he has said, is true."

"Be so good then as declare publicly, will you," said Mr Creakle, putting his head on one side, and rolling his eyes round the school, "whether it ever came to my knowledge until this moment?"

"I believe not directly," he returned.

"Why, you know not," said Mr Creakle. "Don't you, man?"

"I apprehend you never supposed my worldly circumstances to be very good," replied the assistant. "You know what my position is, and always has been, here."

"I apprehend, if you come to that," said Mr Creakle, with his veins swelling again bigger than ever, "that you've been in a wrong position altogether, and mistook this for a charity school. Mr Mell, we'll part, if you please. The sooner the better."

"There is no time," answered Mr Mell, rising, "like the present."

"Sir, to you!" said Mr Creakle.

"I take my leave of you, Mr Creakle, and all of you," said Mr Mell, glancing round the room, and again patting me gently on the shoulders. "James Steerforth, the best wish I can leave you is that you may come to be ashamed of what you have done today. At present I would prefer to see you anything rather than a friend, to me, or to anyone in whom I feel an interest."

Once more he laid his hand upon my shoulder; and then taking his flute and a few books from his desk, and leaving the key in it for his successor, he went out of the school, with his property under his arm. Mr Creakle then made a speech, through Tungay, in which he thanked Steerforth for asserting (though perhaps too warmly) the independence and respectability of Salem House; and which he wound up by shaking hands with Steerforth, while we gave three cheers—I did not quite know what for, but I supposed for Steerforth, and so joined in them ardently, though I felt miserable. Mr Creakle then caned Tommy Traddles for being discovered in tears, instead of cheers, on account of Mr Mell's departure; and went back to his sofa, or his bed, or wherever he had come from.

We were left to ourselves now, and looked very blank, I recollect, on one another. For myself, I felt so much self-reproach and contrition for my part in what had happened, that nothing would have enabled me to keep back my tears but the fear that Steerforth, who often looked at me, I saw, might think it unfriendly—or, I should rather say, considering our relative ages, and the feeling with which I regarded him, undutiful—if I showed the emotion which distressed me. He was very angry with Traddles, and said he was glad he had caught it.

Poor Traddles, who had passed the stage of lying with his head upon the desk, and was relieving himself as usual with a burst of skeletons, said he didn't care. Mr Mell was ill-used.

"Who has ill-used him, you girl?" said Steerforth.

"Why, you have," returned Traddles.

"What have I done?" said Steerforth.

"What have you done?" retorted Traddles. "Hurt his feelings, and lost him his situation."

"His feelings?" repeated Steerforth disdainfully. "His feelings will soon get the better of it, I'll be bound. His feelings are not like yours, Miss Traddles. As to his situation—which was a precious one, wasn't it?—do you suppose I am not going to write home, and take care that he gets some money? Polly?"

We thought this intention very noble in Steerforth, whose mother was a widow, and rich, and would do almost anything, it was said, that he asked her. We were all extremely glad to see Traddles so put down, and exalted Steerforth to the skies: especially when he told us, as he condescended to do, that what he had done had been done expressly for us, and for our cause; and that he had conferred a great boon upon us by unselfishly doing it.

But I must say that when I was going on with a story in the dark that night, Mr Mell's old flute seemed more than once to sound mournfully in my ears; and that when at last Steerforth was tired, and I lay down in my bed, I fancied it playing so sorrowfully somewhere, that I was quite wretched.

I soon forgot him in the contemplation of Steerforth, who, in an easy amateur way, and without any book (he seemed to me to know everything by heart), took some of his classes until a new master was found. The new master came from a grammar school; and before he entered on his duties, dined in the parlour one day, to be introduced to Steerforth. Steerforth approved of him highly, and told us he was a Brick. Without exactly understanding what learned distinction was meant by this, I respected him greatly for it, and had no doubt whatever of his superior knowledge: though he never took the pains with me—not that *I* was anybody—that Mr Mell had taken.

There was only one other event in this half-year, out of the daily school-life, that made an impression upon me which still survives. It survives for many reasons.

One afternoon, when we were all harassed into a state of dire confusion, and Mr Creakle was laying about him dreadfully, Tungay came in, and called out in his usual strong way: "Visitors for Copperfield!"

A few words were interchanged between him and Mr Creakle, as, who the visitors were, and what room they were to be shown into; and then I, who had, according to custom, stood up on the announcement being made, and felt quite faint with astonishment, was told to go by the back stairs and get a clean frill on, before I repaired to the dining-room. These orders I obeyed, in such a flutter and hurry of my young spirits as I had never known before; and when I got to the parlour door, and the thought came into my head that it might be my mother—I had only thought of Mr or Miss Murdstone until then—I drew back my hand from the lock, and stopped to have a sob before I went in.

At first I saw nobody; but feeling a pressure against the door, I looked round it, and there, to my amazement, were Mr Peggotty and Ham, ducking at me with their hats, and squeezing one another against the wall. I could not help laughing; but it was much more in the pleasure of seeing them, than at the appearance they made. We shook hands in a very cordial way; and I laughed and laughed, until I pulled out my pocket-handkerchief and wiped my eyes.

Mr Peggotty (who never shut his mouth once, I remember, during the visit) showed great concern when he saw me do this, and nudged Ham to say something.

"Cheer up, Mas'r Davy bor'!" said Ham, in his simpering way. "Why, how you have growed!"

"Am I grown?" I said, drying my eyes. I was not crying at anything in particular that I know of; but somehow it made me cry, to see old friends.

"Growed, Mas'r Davy bor'? Ain't he growed!" said Ham.

"Ain't he growed!" said Mr Peggotty.

They made me laugh again by laughing at each other, and then we all three laughed until I was in danger of crying again.

"Do you know how mama is, Mr Peggotty?" I said. "And how my dear, dear, old Peggotty is?"

"Oncommon," said Mr Peggotty.

"And little Em'ly, and Mrs Gummidge?"

"On—common," said Mr Peggotty.

There was a silence. Mr Peggotty, to relieve it, took two prodigious lobsters, and an enormous crab, and a large canvas bag of shrimps, out of his pockets, and piled them up in Ham's arms.

"You see," said Mr Peggotty, "knowing as you was partial to a little relish with your wittles when you was along with us, we took the liberty. The old Mawther biled 'em, she did. Mrs Gummidge biled 'em. Yes," said Mr Peggotty, slowly, who I thought appeared to stick to the subject on account of having no other subject ready, "Mrs Gummidge, I do assure you, she biled 'em."

I expressed my thanks; and Mr Peggotty, after looking at Ham, who stood smiling sheepishly over the shellfish, without making any attempt to help him, said:

"We come, you see, the wind and tide making in our favour, in one of our Yarmouth lugs to Gravesen'. My sister she wrote to me the name of this here place, and wrote to me as if ever I chanced to come to Gravesen', I was to come over and inquire for Mas'r Davy and give her dooty, humbly wishing him well and reporting of the fam'ly as they was oncommon toe-be-sure. Little Em'ly, you see, she'll write to my sister when I go back, as I see you and as you was similarly oncommon, and so we make it quite a merry-go-rounder."

I was obliged to consider a little before I understood what Mr Peggotty meant by this figure, expressive of a complete circle of intelligence. I then thanked him heartily; and said, with a consciousness of reddening, that I supposed little Em'ly was altered too, since we used to pick up shells and pebbles on the beach?

"She's getting to be a woman, that's wot she's getting to be," said Mr Peggotty. "Ask him."

He meant Ham, who beamed with delight and assent over the bag of shrimps.

"Her pretty face!" said Mr Peggotty, with his own shining like a light.

"Her learning!" said Ham.

"Her writing!" said Mr Peggotty. "Why it's as black as jet! And so large it is, you might see it anywheres."

It was perfectly delightful to behold with what enthusiasm Mr Peggotty became inspired when he thought of his little favourite. He stands before me again, his bluff hairy face irradiating with a joyful love and pride, for which I can find no description. His honest eyes fire up, and sparkle, as if their depths were stirred by something bright. His broad chest heaves with pleasure. His strong loose hands clench themselves, in his earnestness; and he emphasizes what he says with a right arm that shows, in my pigmy view, like a sledge-hammer.

Ham was quite as earnest as he. I dare say they would have said much more about her, if they had not been abashed by the unexpected coming in of Steerforth, who, seeing me in a corner speaking with two strangers, stopped in a song he was singing, and said: "I didn't know you were here, young Copperfield!" (for it was not the usual visiting room) and crossed by us on his way out.

I am not sure whether it was in the pride of having such a friend as Steerforth, or in the desire to explain to him how I came to have such a friend as Mr Peggotty, that I called to him as he was going away. But I said, modestly—Good Heaven, how it all comes back to me this long time afterwards!—

"Don't go, Steerforth, if you please. These are two Yarmouth boatmen—very kind, good people——who are relations of my nurse, and have come from Gravesend to see me."

"Aye, aye?" said Steerforth, returning. "I am glad to see them. How are you both?"

There was an ease in his manner——a gay and light manner it was, but not swaggering——which I still believe to have borne a kind of enchantment with it. I still believe him, in virtue of this carriage, his animal spirits, his delightful voice, his handsome face and figure, and, for aught I know, of some inborn power of attraction besides (which I think a few people possess), to have carried a spell with him to which it was a natural weakness to yield, and which not many persons could withstand. I could not but see how pleased they were with him, and how they seemed to open their hearts to him in a moment.

"You must let them know at home, if you please, Mr Peggotty," I said, "when that letter is sent, that Mr Steerforth is very kind to me, and that I don't know what I should ever do here without him."

"Nonsense!" said Steerforth, laughing. "You mustn't tell them anything of the sort."

"And if Mr Steerforth ever comes into Norfolk or Suffolk, Mr Peggotty," I said, "while I am there, you may depend upon it I shall bring him to Yarmouth, if he will let me, to see your house. You never saw such a good house, Steerforth. It's made out of a boat!"

"Made out of a boat, is it?" said Steerforth. "It's the right sort of a house for such a thorough-built boatman."

"So 'tis, sir, so 'tis, sir," said Ham, grinning. "You're right, young gen'l'm'n! Mas'r Davy bor', gen'l'm'n's right. A thorough-built boatman! Hor, hor! That's what he is, too!"

Mr Peggotty was no less pleased than his nephew, though his modesty forbade him to claim a personal compliment so vociferously.

"Well, sir," he said, bowing and chuckling, and tucking in the ends of his neckerchief at his breast: "I thankee, sir, I thankee! I do my endeavours in my line of life, sir."

"The best of men can do no more, Mr Peggotty," said Steerforth. He had got his name already.

"I'll pound it, it's wot you do yourself, sir," said Mr Peggotty, shaking his head, "and wot you do well——right well! I thankee, sir. I'm obleeged to you, sir, for your welcoming manner of me. I'm rough, sir, but I'm ready——least ways, I *hope* I'm ready, you unnerstand. My house ain't much for to see, sir, but it's hearty at your service if ever you should come along with Mas'r Davy to see it. I'm a reg'lar Dodman, I am," said Mr Peggotty, by which he meant snail, and this was in allusion to his being slow to go, for he had attempted to go after every sentence, and had somehow or other come back again; "but I wish you both well, and I wish you happy!"

Ham echoed this sentiment, and we parted with them in the heartiest manner. I was almost tempted that evening to tell Steerforth about pretty little Em'ly, but I was too timid of mentioning her name, and too much afraid of his laughing at me. I remember that I thought a good deal, and in an uneasy sort of way, about Mr Peggotty having said that she was getting on to be a woman; but I decided that was nonsense.

We transported the shellfish, or the "relish" as Mr Peggotty had modestly called it, up into our room unobserved, and made a great supper that evening. But Traddles couldn't get happily out of it. He was too unfortunate even to come through a supper like anybody else. He was taken ill in the night——quite prostrate he was——in consequence of Crab; and after being drugged with black draughts and blue pills, to an extent which Demple (whose father was a doctor) said was enough to undermine a horse's constitution, received a caning and six chapters of Greek Testament for refusing to confess.

The rest of the half-year is a jumble in my recollection of the daily strife and struggle of our lives; of the waning summer and the changing season; of the frosty mornings when we were rung out of bed, and the cold, cold smell of the dark nights when we were rung into bed again; of the evening schoolroom dimly lighted and indifferently warmed, and the morning schoolroom which was nothing but a great shivering-machine; of the alternation of boiled beef with roast beef, and boiled mutton with roast mutton; of clods of bread-and-butter, dog's-eared lesson-books, cracked slates, tear-blotted copy-books, canings, rulerings, hair-cuttings, rainy Sundays, suet-puddings, and a dirty atmosphere of ink, surrounding all.

I well remember though, how the distant idea of the holidays, after seeming for an immense time to be a stationary speck, began to come towards us, and to grow and grow. How from counting months, we came to weeks, and then to days; and how I then began to be afraid that I should not be sent for and when I learnt from Steerforth that I *had* been sent for, and was certainly to go home, had dim forebodings that I might break my leg first. How the breaking-up day changed its place fast, at last, from the week after next to next week, this week, the day after tomorrow, tomorrow, today, tonight— when I was inside the Yarmouth mail, and going home.

I had many a broken sleep inside the Yarmouth mail, and many an incoherent dream of all these things. But when I awoke at intervals, the ground outside the window was not the playground of Salem House, and the sound in my ears was not the sound of Mr Creakle giving it to Traddles, but the sound of the coachman touching up the horses.

Chapter VIII

MY HOLIDAYS. ESPECIALLY ONE HAPPY AFTERNOON

WHEN we arrived before day at the inn where the mail stopped, which was not the inn where my friend the waiter lived, I was shown up to a nice little bedroom, with DOLPHIN painted on the door. Very cold I was I know, notwithstanding the hot tea they had given me before a large fire downstairs; and very glad I was to turn into the Dolphin's bed, pull the Dolphin's blankets round my head, and go to sleep.

Mr Barkis the carrier was to call for me in the morning at nine o'clock. I got up at eight, a little giddy from the shortness of my night's rest, and was ready for him before the appointed time. He received me exactly as if not five minutes had elapsed since we were last together, and I had only been into the hotel to get change for sixpence, or something of that sort.

As soon as I and my box were in the cart, and the carrier seated, the lazy horse walked away with us all at his accustomed pace.

"You look very well, Mr Barkis," I said, thinking he would like to know it.

Mr Barkis rubbed his cheek with his cuff, and then looked at his cuff as if he expected to find some of the bloom upon it; but made no other acknowledgement of the compliment.

"I gave your message, Mr Barkis," I said: "I wrote to Peggotty."

"Ah!" said Mr Barkis.

Mr Barkis seemed gruff, and answered drily.

"Wasn't it right, Mr Barkis?" I asked, after a little hesitation.

"Why, no," said Mr Barkis.

"Not the message?"

"The message was right enough, perhaps," said Mr Barkis; "but it come to an end there."

Not understanding what he meant, I repeated inquisitively: "Came to an end, Mr Barkis?"

"Nothing come of it," he explained, looking at me sideways. "No answer."

"There was an answer expected, was there, Mr Barkis?" said I, opening my eyes. For this was a new light to me.

"When a man says he's willin'," said Mr Barkis, turning his glance slowly on me again, "it's as much as to say, that man's a-waitin' for a answer."

"Well, Mr Barkis?"

"Well," said Mr Barkis, carrying his eyes back to his horse's ears; "that man's been a-waitin' for a answer ever since."

"Have you told her so, Mr Barkis?"

"No—no," growled Mr Barkis, reflecting about it. "I ain't got no call to go and tell her so. I never said six words to her myself, I ain't a-goin' to tell her so."

"Would you like me to do it, Mr Barkis?" said I, doubtfully.

"You might tell her, if you would," said Mr Barkis, with another slow look at me, "that Barkis was a-waitin' for a answer. Says you—what name is it?"

"Her name?"

"Ah!" said Mr Barkis, with a nod of his head.

"Peggotty."

"Chrisen name? Or nat'ral name?" said Mr Barkis.

"Oh, it's not her Christian name. Her Christian name is Clara."

"Is it though?" said Mr Barkis.

He seemed to find an immense fund of reflection in this circumstance, and sat pondering and inwardly whistling for some time.

"Well!" he resumed at length. "Says you, 'Peggotty! Barkis is waitin' for a answer.' Says she, perhaps, 'Answer to what?' Says you, 'To what I told you.' 'What is that?' says she. 'Barkis is willin',' says you."

This extremely artful suggestion, Mr Barkis accompanied with a nudge of his elbow that gave me quite a stitch in my side. After that, he slouched over his horse in his usual manner; and made no other reference to the subject except, half an hour afterwards, taking a piece of chalk from his pocket, and writing up, inside the tilt of the cart, "Clara Peggotty"—apparently as a private memorandum.

Ah, what a strange feeling it was to be going home when it was not home, and to find that every object I looked at, reminded me of the happy old home, which was like a dream I could never dream again! The days when my mother and I and Peggotty were all in all to one another, and there was no one to come between us, rose up before me so sorrowfully on the road, that I am not sure I was glad to be there—not sure but that I would rather have remained away, and forgotten it in Steerforth's company. But there

I was; and soon I was at our house, where the bare old elm-trees wrung their many hands in the bleak wintry air, and shreds of the old rooks'-nests drifted away upon the wind.

The carrier put my box down at the garden-gate, and left me. I walked along the path towards the house, glancing at the windows, and fearing at every step to see Mr Murdstone or Miss Murdstone lowering out of one of them. No face appeared, however; and being come to the house, and knowing how to open the door, before dark, without knocking, I went in with a quiet, timid step.

God knows how infantine the memory may have been, that was awakened within me by the sound of my mother's voice in the old parlour, when I set foot in the hall. She was singing in a low tone. I think I must have lain in her arms, and heard her singing so to me when I was but a baby. The strain was new to me, and yet it was so old that it filled my heart brim-full; like a friend come back from a long absence.

I believed, from the solitary and thoughtful way in which my mother murmured her song, that she was alone. And I went softly into the room. She was sitting by the fire, suckling an infant, whose tiny hand she held against her neck. Her eyes were looking down upon its face, and she sat singing to it. I was so far right, that she had no other companion.

I spoke to her, and she started, and cried out. But seeing me, she called me her dear Davy, her own boy! and coming half across the room to meet me, kneeled down upon the ground and kissed me, and laid my head down on her bosom near the little creature that was nestling there, and put its hand to my lips.

I wish I had died. I wish I had died then, with that feeling in my heart! I should have been more fit for Heaven than I ever have been since.

"He is your brother," said my mother, fondling me. "Davy, my pretty boy! My poor child!" Then she kissed me more and more, and clasped me round the neck. This she was doing when Peggotty came running in, and bounced down on the ground beside us, and went mad about us both for a quarter of an hour.

It seemed that I had not been expected so soon, the carrier being much before his usual time. It seemed, too, that Mr and Miss Murdstone had gone out upon a visit in the neighbourhood, and would not return before night. I had never hoped for this. I had never thought it possible that we three could be together undisturbed, once more; and I felt, for the time, as if the old days were come back.

We dined together by the fireside. Peggotty was in attendance to wait upon us, but my mother wouldn't let her do it, and made her dine with us. I had my own old plate, with a brown view of a man-of-war in full sail upon it, which Peggotty had hoarded somewhere all the time I had been away, and would not have had broken, she said, for a hundred pounds. I had my own old mug with David on it, and my own old little knife and fork that wouldn't cut.

While we were at table, I thought it a favourable occasion to tell Peggotty about Mr Barkis, who, before I had finished what I had to tell her, began to laugh, and throw her apron over her face.

"Peggotty," said my mother. "What's the matter?"

Peggotty only laughed the more, and held her apron tight over her face when my mother tried to pull it away, and sat as if her head were in a bag.

"What are you doing, you stupid creature?" said my mother, laughing.

"Oh, drat the man!" cried Peggotty. "He wants to marry me."

"It would be a very good match for you; wouldn't it?" said my mother.

"Oh! I don't know," said Peggotty. "Don't ask me. I wouldn't have him if he was made of gold. Nor I wouldn't have anybody."

"Then, why don't you tell him so, you ridiculous thing?" said my mother.

"Tell him so," retorted Peggotty, looking out of her apron. "He has never said a word to me about it. He knows better. If he was to make so bold as say a word to me, I should slap his face."

Her own was as red as ever I saw it, or any other face, I think; but she only covered it again, for a few moments at a time, when she was taken with a violent fit of laughter; and after two or three of those attacks, went on with her dinner.

I remarked that my mother, though she smiled when Peggotty looked at her, became more serious and thoughtful. I had seen at first that she was changed. Her face was very pretty still, but it looked careworn, and too delicate; and her hand was so thin and white that it seemed to me to be almost transparent. But the change to which I now refer was superadded to this: it was in her manner, which became anxious and fluttered. At last she said, putting out her hand, and lying it affectionately on the hand of her old servant,

"Peggotty, dear, you are not going to be married?"

"Me, ma'am?" returned Peggotty, staring. "Lord bless you, no!"

"Not just yet?" said my mother, tenderly.

"Never!" cried Peggotty.

My mother took her hand, and said:

"Don't leave me, Peggotty. Stay with me. It will not be for long, perhaps. What should I ever do without you!"

"Me leave you, my precious!" cried Peggotty. "Not for all the world and his wife. Why, what's put that in your silly little head?"—For Peggotty had been used of old to talk to my mother sometimes like a child.

But my mother made no answer, except to thank her, and Peggotty went running on in her own fashion.

"Me leave you? I think I see myself. Peggotty go away from you? I should like to catch her at it! No, no, no," said Peggotty, shaking her head, and folding her arms; "not she, my dear. It isn't that there ain't some Cats that would be well enough pleased if she did, but they sha'n't be pleased. They shall be aggravated. I'll stay with you till I am a cross cranky old woman. And when I'm too deaf, and too lame, and too blind, and too mumbly for want of teeth, to be of any use at all, even to be found fault with, than I shall go to my Davy, and ask him to take me in."

"And, Peggotty," says I, "I shall be glad to see you, and I'll make you as welcome as a queen."

"Bless your dear heart!" cried Peggotty. "I know you will!" And she kissed me beforehand, in grateful acknowledgement of my hospitality. After that, she covered her head up with her apron again and had another laugh about Mr Barkis. After that, she took the baby out of its little cradle, and nursed it. After that, she cleared the dinner table; after that, came in with another cap on, and her work-box, and the yard-measure, and the bit of wax-candle, all just the same as ever.

We sat round the fire, and talked delightfully. I told them what a hard master Mr Creakle was, and they pitied me very much. I told them what a fine fellow Steerforth was, and what a patron of mine, and Peggotty said she would walk a score of miles to see him. I took the little baby in my arms when it was awake, and nursed it lovingly. When it was asleep again, I crept close to my mother's side according to my old custom, broken now a long time, and sat with my arms embracing her waist, and my little red cheek on her shoulder, and once more felt her beautiful hair drooping over me—like an angel's wing as I used to think, I recollect—and was very happy indeed.

While I sat thus, looking at the fire, and seeing pictures in the red-hot coals, I almost believed that I had never been away; that Mr and Miss Murdstone were such pictures, and would vanish when the fire got low; and that there was nothing real in all that I remembered, save my mother, Peggotty, and I.

Peggotty darned away at a stocking as long as she could see, and then sat with it drawn on her left hand like a glove, and her needle in her right, ready to take another stitch whenever there was a blaze. I cannot conceive whose stockings they can have been that Peggotty was always darning, or where such an unfailing supply of stockings in want of darning can have come from. From my earliest infancy she seems to have been always employed in that class of needlework, and never by any chance in any other.

"I wonder," said Peggotty, who was sometimes seized with a fit of wondering on some most unexpected topic, "what's become of Davy's great-aunt?"

"Lor, Peggotty!" observed my mother, rousing herself from a reverie, "what nonsense you talk!"

"Well, but I really do wonder, ma'am," said Peggotty.

"What can have put such a person in your head?" inquired my mother. "Is there nobody else in the world to come there?"

"I don't know how it is," said Peggotty, "unless it's on account of being stupid, but my head never can pick and choose its people. They come and they go, and they don't come and they don't go, just as they like. I wonder what's become of her?"

"How absurd you are, Peggotty!" returned my mother. "One would suppose you wanted a second visit from her."

"Lord forbid!" cried Peggotty.

"Well then, don't talk about such uncomfortable things, there's a good soul," said my mother. "Miss Betsey is shut up in her cottage by the sea, no doubt, and will remain there. At all events, she is not likely ever to trouble us again."

"No!" mused Peggotty. "No, that ain't likely at all.—I wonder, if she was to die, whether she'd leave Davy anything?"

"Good gracious me, Peggotty," returned my mother, "what a nonsensical woman you are! when you know that she took offence at the poor dear boy's ever being born at all."

"I suppose she wouldn't be inclined to forgive him now," hinted Peggotty.

"Why should she be inclined to forgive him now?" said my mother, rather sharply.

"Now that he's got a brother, I mean," said Peggotty.

My mother immediately began to cry, and wondered how Peggotty dared to say such a thing.

"As if this poor little innocent in its cradle had ever done any harm to you or anybody else, you jealous thing!" said she. "You had much better go and marry Mr Barkis, the carrier. Why don't you?"

"I should make Miss Murdstone happy, if I was to," said Peggotty.

"What a bad disposition you have, Peggotty!" returned my mother. "You are as jealous of Miss Murdstone as it is possible for a ridiculous creature to be. You want to keep the keys yourself, and give out all the things, I suppose? I shouldn't be surprised if you did. When you know that she only does it out of kindness and the best intentions! You know she does, Peggotty—you know it well."

Peggotty muttered something to the effect of "Bother the best intentions!" and something else to the effect that there was a little too much of the best intentions going on.

"I know what you mean, you cross thing," said my mother. "I understand you,

Peggotty, perfectly. You know I do, and I wonder you don't colour up like fire. But one point at a time. Miss Murdstone is the point now, Peggotty, and you sha'n't escape from it. Haven't you heard her say, over and over again, that she thinks I am too thoughtless and too—a—a—"

"Pretty," suggested Peggotty.

"Well," returned my mother, half laughing, "and if she is so silly as to say so, can I be blamed for it?"

"No one says you can," said Peggotty.

"No, I should hope not, indeed!" returned my mother. "Haven't you heard her say, over and over again, that on this account she wished to spare me a great deal of trouble, which she thinks I am not suited for. and which I really don't know myself that I *am* suited for; and isn't she up early and late, and going to and fro continually—and doesn't she do all sorts of things, and grope into all sorts of places, coal-holes and pantries and I don't know where, that can't be very agreeable—and do you mean to insinuate that there is not a sort of devotion in that?"

"I don't insinuate at all," said Peggotty.

"You do, Peggotty," returned my mother. "You never do anything else, except your work. You are always insinuating. You revel in it. And when you talk of Mr Murdstone's good intentions—"

"I never talked of 'em," said Peggotty.

"No, Peggotty," returned my mother, "but you insinuated. That's what I told you just now. That's the worst of you. You *will* insinuate. I said, at the moment, that I understood you, and you see I did. When you talk of Mr Murdstone's good intentions, and pretend to slight them (for I don't believe you really do, in your heart, Peggotty), you must be as well convinced as I am how good they are, and how they actuate him in everything. If he seems to have been at all stern with a certain person, Peggotty—you understand, and so I am sure does Davy, that I am not alluding to anybody present—it is solely because he is satisfied that it is for a certain person's benefit. He naturally loves a certain person, on my account; and acts solely for a certain person's good. He is better able to judge of it than I am; for I very well know that I am a weak, light, girlish creature, and that he is a firm, grave, serious man. And he takes," said my mother, with the tears which were engendered in her affectionate nature, stealing down her face, "he takes great pains with me; and I ought to be very thankful to him, and very submissive to him even in my thoughts; and when I am not, Peggotty, I worry and condemn myself, and feel doubtful of my own heart, and don't know what to do."

Peggotty sat with her chin on the foot of the stocking, looking silently at the fire.

"There, Peggotty," said my mother, changing her tone, "don't let us fall out with one another, for I couldn't bear it. You are my true friend, I know, if I have any in the world. When I call you a ridiculous creature, or a vexatious thing, or anything of that sort, Peggotty, I only mean that you are my true friend, and always have been, ever since the night when Mr Copperfield first brought me home here, and you came out to the gate to meet me."

Peggotty was not slow to respond, and ratify the treaty of friendship by giving me one of her best hugs. I think I had some glimpses of the real character of this conversation at the time; but I am sure, now, that the good creature originated it, and took her part in it, merely that my mother might comfort herself with the little contradictory summary in which she had indulged. The design was efficacious; for I remember that my mother seemed more at ease during the rest of the evening, and that Peggotty observed her less.

When we had had our tea, and the ashes were thrown up, and the candles snuffed,

I read Peggotty a chapter out of the Crocodile Book, in remembrance of old times—she took it out of her pocket: I don't know whether she had kept it there ever since—and then we talked about Salem House, which brought me round again to Steerforth, who was my great subject. We were very happy; and that evening, as the last of its race, and destined evermore to close that volume of my life, will never pass out of my memory.

It was almost ten o'clock before we heard the sound of wheels. We all got up then; and my mother said hurriedly that, as it was so late, and Mr and Miss Murdstone approved of early hours for young people, perhaps I had better go to bed. I kissed her, and went upstairs with my candle directly, before they came in. It appeared to my childish fancy, as I ascended to the bedroom where I had been imprisoned, that they brought a cold blast of air into the house which blew away the old familiar feeling like a feather.

I felt uncomfortable about going down to breakfast in the morning, as I had never set eyes on Mr Murdstone since the day when I committed my memorable offence. However, as it must be done, I went down, after two or three false starts half-way, and as many runs back on tiptoe to my own room, and presented myself in the parlour.

He was standing before the fire with his back to it, while Miss Murdstone made the tea. He looked at me steadily as I entered, but made no sign of recognition whatever.

I went up to him, after a moment of confusion, and said: "I beg your pardon, sir. I am very sorry for what I did, and I hope you will forgive me."

"I am glad to hear you are sorry, David," he replied.

The hand he gave me was the hand I had bitten. I could not restrain my eye from resting for an instant on a red spot upon it; but it was not so red as I turned, when I met that sinister expression in his face.

"How do you do, ma'am?" I said to Miss Murdstone.

"Ah, dear me!" sighed Miss Murdstone, giving me the tea-caddy scoop instead of her fingers. "How long are the holidays?"

"A month, ma'am."

"Counting from when?"

"From today, ma'am."

"Oh!" said Miss Murdstone. "Then here's *one* day off."

She kept a calendar of the holidays in this way, and every morning checked a day off in exactly the same manner. She did it gloomily until she came to ten, but when she got into two figures she became more hopeful, and, as the time advanced, even jocular.

It was on this very first day that I had the misfortune to throw her, though she was not subject to such weakness in general, into a state of violent consternation. I came into the room where she and my mother were sitting; and the baby (who was only a few weeks old) being on my mother's lap, I took it very carefully in my arms. Suddenly Miss Murdstone gave such a scream that I all but dropped it.

"My dear Jane!" cried my mother.

"Good heavens, Clara, do you see?" exclaimed Miss Murdstone.

"See what, my dear Jane?" said my mother; "where?"

"He's got it!" cried Miss Murdstone. "The boy has got the baby!"

She was limp with horror; but stiffened herself to make a dart at me, and take it out of my arms. Then, she turned faint; and was so very ill that they were obliged to give her cherry brandy. I was solemnly interdicted by her, on her recovery, from touching my brother any more on any pretence whatever; and my poor mother, who, I could see, wished otherwise, meekly confirmed the interdict, by saying: "No doubt you are right, my dear Jane."

On another occasion, when we three were together, this same dear baby—it was truly dear to me, for our mother's sake—was the innocent occasion of Miss Murdstone's going into a passion. My mother, who had been looking at its eyes as it lay upon her lap, said:

"Davy! come here!" and looked at mine.

I saw Miss Murdstone lay her beads down.

"I declare," said my mother, gently, "they are exactly alike. I suppose they are mine. I think they are the colour of mine. But they are wonderfully alike."

"What are you talking about, Clara?" said Miss Murdstone.

"My dear Jane," faltered my mother, a little abashed by the harsh tone of this inquiry, "I find that the baby's eyes and Davy's are exactly alike."

"Clara!" said Miss Murdstone, rising angrily, "you are a positive fool sometimes."

"My dear Jane," remonstrated my mother.

"A positive fool," said Miss Murdstone. "Who else could compare my brother's baby with your boy? They are not at all alike. They are exactly unlike. They are utterly dissimilar in all respects. I hope they will ever remain so. I will not sit here, and hear such comparisons made." With that she stalked out, and made the door bang after her.

In short, I was not a favourite with Miss Murdstone. In short, I was not a favourite there with anybody, not even with myself; for those who did like me could not show it, and those who did not, showed it so plainly that I had a sensitive consciousness of always appearing constrained, boorish, and dull.

I felt that I made them as uncomfortable as they made me. If I came into the room where they were, and they were talking together and my mother seemed cheerful, an anxious cloud would steal over her face from the moment of my entrance. If Mr Murdstone were in his best humour, I checked him. If Miss Murdstone were in her worst, I intensified it. I had perception enough to know that my mother was the victim always; that she was afraid to speak to me or to be kind to me, lest she should give them some offence by her manner of doing so, and receive a lecture afterwards; that she was not only ceaselessly afraid of her own offending, but of my offending, and uneasily watched their looks if I only moved. Therefore I resolved to keep myself as much out of their way as I could; and many a wintry hour did I hear the church clock strike, when I was sitting in my cheerless bedroom, wrapped in my little great-coat, poring over a book.

In the evening, sometimes, I went and sat with Peggotty in the kitchen. There I was comfortable, and not afraid of being myself. But neither of these resources was approved of in the parlour. The tormenting humour which was dominant there stopped them both. I was still held to be necessary to my poor mother's training, and, as one of her trials, could not be suffered to absent myself.

"David," said Mr Murdstone, one day after dinner when I was going to leave the room as usual; "I am sorry to observe that you are of a sullen disposition."

"As sulky as a bear!" said Miss Murdstone.

I stood still, and hung my head.

"Now, David," said Mr Murdstone, "a sullen obdurate disposition is, of all tempers, the worst."

"And the boy's is, of all such dispositions that ever I have seen," remarked his sister, "the most confirmed and stubborn. I think, my dear Clara, even you must observe it?"

"I beg your pardon, my dear Jane," said my mother, "but are you quite sure—I am certain you'll excuse me, my dear Jane—that you understand Davy?"

"I should be somewhat ashamed of myself, Clara," returned Miss Murdstone, "if I could not understand the boy, or any boy. I don't profess to be profound; but I do lay claim to common sense."

"No doubt, my dear Jane," returned my mother, "your understanding is very vigorous——"

"Oh dear, no! Pray don't say that, Clara," interposed Miss Murdstone, angrily.

"But I am sure it is," resumed my mother; "and everybody knows it is. I profit so much by it myself, in many ways—at least I ought to—that no one can be more convinced of it than myself; and therefore I speak with great diffidence, my dear Jane, I assure you."

"We'll say I don't understand the boy, Clara," returned Miss Murdstone, arranging the little fetters on her wrists. "We'll agree, if you please, that I don't understand him at all. He is much too deep for me. But perhaps my brother's penetration may enable him to have some insight into his character. And I believe my brother was speaking on the subject when we—not very decently—interrupted him."

"I think, Clara," said Mr Murdstone, in a low grave voice, "that there may be better and more dispassionate judges of such a question than you."

"Edward," replied my mother, timidly, "you are a far better judge of all questions than I pretend to be. Both you and Jane are. I only said——"

"You only said something weak and inconsiderate," he replied. "Try not to do it again, my dear Clara, and keep a watch upon yourself."

My mother's lips moved, as if she answered "Yes, my dear Edward," but she said nothing aloud.

"I was sorry, David, I remarked," said Mr Murdstone, turning his head and his eyes stiffly towards me, "to observe that you are of a sullen disposition. This is not a character that I can suffer to develop itself beneath my eyes without an effort at improvement. You must endeavour, sir, to change it. We must endeavour to change it for you."

"I beg your pardon, sir," I faltered. "I have never meant to be sullen since I came back."

"Don't take refuge in a lie, sir!" he returned so fiercely, that I saw my mother involuntarily put out her trembling hand as if to interpose between us. "You have withdrawn yourself in your sullenness to your own room. You have kept your own room when you ought to have been here. You know now, once for all, that I require you to be here, and not there. Further, that I require you to bring obedience here. You know me, David. I will have it done."

Miss Murdstone gave a hoarse chuckle.

"I will have a respectful, prompt, and ready bearing towards myself," he continued, "and towards Jane Murdstone, and towards your mother. I will not have this room shunned as if it were infected, at the pleasure of a child. Sit down."

He ordered me like a dog, and I obeyed like a dog.

"One thing more," he said. "I observe that you have an attachment to low and common company. You are not to associate with servants. The kitchen will not improve you, in the many respects in which you need improvement. Of the woman who abets you, I say nothing—since you, Clara," addressing my mother in a lower voice, "from old associations and long-established fancies, have a weakness respecting her which is not yet overcome."

"A most unaccountable delusion it is!" cried Miss Murdstone.

"I only say," he resumed, addressing me, "that I disapprove of your preferring such company as Mistress Peggotty, and that it is to be abandoned. Now, David, you understand me, and you know what will be the consequence if you fail to obey me to the letter."

I knew well—better perhaps than he thought, as far as my poor mother was concerned—and I obeyed him to the letter. I retreated to my own room no more; I took refuge with Peggotty no more; but sat wearily in the parlour day after day, looking forward to night, and bedtime.

What irksome constraint I underwent, sitting in the same attitude hours upon hours, afraid to move an arm or a leg lest Miss Murdstone should complain (as she did on the least pretence) of my restlessness, and afraid to move an eye lest she should light on some look of dislike or scrutiny that would find new cause for complaint in mine! What intolerable dulness to sit listening to the ticking of the clock; and watching Miss Murdstone's little shiny steel beads as she strung them; and wondering whether she would ever be married, and if so, to what sort of unhappy man; and counting the divisions in the moulding of the chimney-piece; and wandering away, with my eyes, to the ceiling, among the curls and corkscrews in the paper on the wall!

What walks I took alone, down muddy lanes, in the bad winter weather, carrying that parlour, and Mr and Miss Murdstone in it, everywhere: a monstrous load that I was obliged to bear, a daymare that there was no possibility of breaking in, a weight that brooded on my wits, and blunted them!

What meals I had in silence and embarrassment, always feeling that there were a knife and fork too many, and that mine; an appetite too many, and that mine; a plate and chair too many, and those mine; a somebody too many, and that I!

What evenings, when the candles came, and I was expected to employ myself, but, not daring to read an entertaining book, pored over some hard-headed, harder-hearted treatise on arithmetic; when the tables of weights and measures set themselves to tunes, as "Rule Britannia," or "Away with Melancholy"; when they wouldn't stand still to be learnt, but would go threading my grandmother's needle through my unfortunate head, in at one ear and out at the other!

What yawns and dozes I lapsed into, in spite of all my care; what starts I came out of concealed sleeps with; what answers I never got, to little observations that I rarely made; what a blank space I seemed, which everybody overlooked, and yet was in everybody's way; what a heavy relief it was to hear Miss Murdstone hail the first stroke of nine at night, and order me to bed!

Thus the holidays lagged away, until the morning came when Miss Murdstone said: "Here's the last day off!" and gave me the closing cup of tea of the vacation.

I was not sorry to go. I had lapsed into a stupid state; but I was recovering a little and looking forward to Steerforth, albeit Mr Creakle loomed behind him. Again Mr Barkis appeared at the gate, and again Miss Murdstone in her warning voice, said: "Clara!" when my mother bent over me, to bid me farewell.

I kissed her, and my baby brother, and was very sorry then; but not sorry to go away, for the gulf between us was there, and the parting was there, every day. And it is not so much the embrace she gave me, that lives in my mind, though it was as fervent as could be, as what followed the embrace.

I was in the carrier's cart when I heard her calling to me. I looked out, and she stood at the garden-gate alone, holding her baby up in her arms for me to see. It was cold still weather; and not a hair of her head, nor a fold of her dress, was stirred, as she looked intently at me, holding up her child.

So I lost her. So I saw her afterwards, in my sleep at school—a silent presence near my bed—looking at me with the same intent face—holding up her baby in her arms.

Chapter IX

I HAVE A MEMORABLE BIRTHDAY

I PASS over all that happened at school, until the anniversary of my birthday came round in March. Except that Steerforth was more to be admired than ever, I remember nothing. He was going away at the end of the half-year, if not sooner, and was more spirited and independent than before in my eyes, and therefore more engaging than before; but beyond this I remember nothing. The great remembrance by which that time is marked in my mind, seems to have swallowed up all lesser recollections, and to exist alone.

It is even difficult for me to believe that there was a gap of full two months between my return to Salem House and the arrival of that birthday. I can only understand that the fact was so, because I know it must have been so; otherwise I should feel convinced that there was no interval, and that the one occasion trod upon the other's heels.

How well I recollect the kind of day it was! I smell the fog that hung about the place; I see the hoar frost, ghostly, through it; I feel my rimy hair fall clammy on my cheek; I look along the dim perspective of the schoolroom, with a sputtering candle here and there to light up the foggy morning, and the breath of the boys wreathing and smoking in the raw cold as they blow upon their fingers, and tap their feet upon the floor.

It was after breakfast, and we had been summoned in from the playground, when Mr Sharp entered and said:

"David Copperfield is to go into the parlour."

I expected a hamper from Peggotty, and brightened at the order. Some of the boys about me put in their claim not to be forgotten in the distribution of the good things, as I got out of my seat with great alacrity.

"Don't hurry, David," said Mr Sharp. "There's time enough, my boy, don't hurry."

I might have been surprised by the feeling tone in which he spoke, if I had given it a thought; but I gave it none until afterwards. I hurried away to the parlour; and there I found Mr Creakle, sitting at his breakfast with the cane and a newspaper before him, and Mrs Creakle with an opened letter in her hand. But no hamper.

"David Copperfield," said Mrs Creakle, leading me to a sofa, and sitting down beside me. "I want to speak to you very particularly. I have something to tell you, my child."

Mr Creakle, at whom of course I looked, shook his head without looking at me, and stopped up a sigh with a very large piece of buttered toast.

"You are too young to know how the world changes every day," said Mrs Creakle, "and how the people in it pass away. But we all have to learn it, David; some of us when we are young, some of us when we are old, some of us at all times of our lives."

I looked at her earnestly.

"When you came away from home at the end of the vacation," said Mrs Creakle, after a pause, "were they all well?" After another pause, "Was your mama well?"

I trembled without distinctly knowing why, and still looked at her earnestly, making no attempt to answer.

"Because," said she, "I grieve to tell you that I hear this morning your mama is very ill."

A mist rose between Mrs Creakle and me, and her figure seemed to move in it for an instant. Then I felt the burning tears run down my face, and it was steady again.

"She is very dangerously ill," she added.

I knew all now.

"She is dead."

There was no need to tell me so. I had already broken out into a desolate cry, and felt an orphan in the wide world.

She was very kind to me. She kept me there all day, and left me alone sometimes; and I cried, and wore myself to sleep, and awoke and cried again. When I could cry no more, I began to think; and then the oppression on my breast was heaviest, and my grief a dull pain that there was no ease for.

And yet my thoughts were idle; not intent on the calamity that weighed upon my heart, but idly loitering near it. I thought of our house shut up and hushed. I thought of the little baby, who, Mrs Creakle said, had been pining away for some time, and who, they believed, would die too. I thought of my father's grave in the churchyard, by our house, and of my mother lying there beneath the tree I knew so well. I stood upon a chair when I was left alone, and looked into the glass to see how red my eyes were, and how sorrowful my face. I considered, after some hours were gone, if my tears were really hard to flow now, as they seemed to be, what, in connexion with my loss, it would affect me most to think of when I drew near home—for I was going home to the funeral. I am sensible of having felt that a dignity attached to me among the rest of the boys, and that I was important in my affliction.

If ever child were stricken with sincere grief, I was. But I remember that this importance was a kind of satisfaction to me, when I walked in the playground that afternoon while the boys were in school. When I saw them glancing at me out of the windows, as they went up to their classes, I felt distinguished, and looked more melancholy, and walked slower. When school was over, and they came out and spoke to me, I felt it rather good in myself not to be proud to any of them, and to take exactly the same notice of them all, as before.

I was to go home next night; not by the mail, but by the heavy night-coach, which was called the Farmer, and was principally used by country-people travelling short intermediate distances upon the road. We had no story-telling that evening, and Traddles insisted on lending me his pillow. I don't know what good he thought it would do me, for I had one of my own: but it was all he had to lend, poor fellow, except a sheet of letter-paper full of skeletons; and that he gave me at parting, as a soother of my sorrows and a contribution to my peace of mind.

I left Salem House upon the morrow afternoon. I little thought then that I left it, never to return. We travelled very slowly all night, and did not get into Yarmouth before nine or ten o'clock in the morning. I looked out for Mr Barkis, but he was not there; and instead of him a fat, short-winded, merry-looking, little old man in black, with rusty little bunches of ribbons at the knees of his breeches, black stockings, and a broad-brimmed hat, came puffing up to the coach window, and said:

"Master Copperfield?"

"Yes, sir."

"Will you come with me, young sir, if you please," he said, opening the door, "and I shall have the pleasure of taking you home."

I put my hand in his, wondering who he was, and we walked away to a shop in a narrow street, on which was written OMER, DRAPER, TAILOR, HABERDASHER, FUNERAL FURNISHER, &c. It was a close and stifling little shop; full of all sorts of clothing, made and unmade, including one window full of beaver-hats and bonnets. We went into a little back-parlour behind the shop, where we found three young women at work on a quantity of black materials, which were heaped upon the table, and little bits and cuttings of which were littered all over the floor. There was a good fire in the room, and a breathless smell of warm black crape—I did not know what the smell was then, but I know now.

The three young women, who appeared to be very industrious and comfortable, raised their heads to look at me, and then went on with their work. Stitch, stitch, stitch. At the same time there came from a workshop across a little yard outside the window, a regular sound of hammering that kept a kind of tune: RAT—tat-tat, RAT—tat-tat, RAT—tat-tat, without any variation.

"Well," said my conductor to one of the three young women. "How do you get on, Minnie?"

"We shall be ready by the trying-on time," she replied gaily, without looking up. "Don't you be afraid, father."

Mr Omer took off his broad-brimmed hat, and sat down and panted. He was so fat that he was obliged to pant some time before he could say:

"That's right."

"Father!" said Minnie, playfully. "What a porpoise you do grow!"

"Well, I don't know how it is, my dear," he replied, considering about it. "I *am* rather so."

"You are such a comfortable man, you see," said Minnie. "You take things so easy."

"No use taking 'em otherwise, my dear," said Mr Omer.

"No, indeed," returned his daughter. "We are all pretty gay here, thank Heaven! Ain't we, father?"

"I hope so, my dear," said Mr Omer. "As I have got my breath now, I think I'll measure this young scholar. Would you walk into the shop, Master Copperfield?"

I preceded Mr Omer, in compliance with his request; and after showing me a roll of cloth which he said was extra super, and too good mourning for anything short of parents, he took my various dimensions, and put them down in a book. While he was recording them he called my attention to his stock in trade, and to certain fashions which he said had "just come up," and to certain other fashions which he said had "just gone out."

"And by that sort of thing we very often lose a little mint of money," said Mr Omer. "But fashions are like human beings. They come in, nobody knows when, why, or how; and they go out, nobody knows when, why, or how. Everything is like life, in my opinion, if you look at it in that point of view."

I was too sorrowful to discuss the question, which would possibly have been beyond me under any circumstances; and Mr Omer took me back into the parlour, breathing with some difficulty on the way.

He then called down a little break-neck range of steps behind a door: "Bring up that tea and bread-and-butter!" which, after some time, during which I sat looking about me and thinking, and listening to the stitching in the room and the tune that was being hammered across the yard, appeared on a tray, and turned out to be for me.

"I have been acquainted with you," said Mr Omer, after watching me for some minutes, during which I had not made much impression on the breakfast, for the black things destroyed my appetite, "I have been acquainted with you a long time, my young friend."

"Have you, sir?"

"All your life," said Mr Omer. "I may say before it. I knew your father before you. He was five foot nine and a half, and he lays in five-and-twen-ty foot of ground."

"Rᴀᴛ—tat-tat, ʀᴀᴛ—tat-tat, ʀᴀᴛ—tat-tat," across the yard.

"He lays in five and twen-ty foot of ground, if he lays in a fraction," said Mr Omer, pleasantly. "It was either his request or her direction, I forget which."

"Do you know how my little brother is, sir?" I inquired.

Mr Omer shook his head.

"Rᴀᴛ—tat-tat, ʀᴀᴛ—tat-tat, ʀᴀᴛ—tat-tat."

"He is in his mother's arms," said he.

"Oh. poor little fellow! Is he dead?"

"Don't mind it more than you can help," said Mr Omer. "Yes. The baby's dead."

My wounds broke out afresh at this intelligence. I left the scarcely-tasted breakfast, and went and rested my head on another table, in a corner of the little room, which Minnie hastily cleared, lest I should spot the mourning that was lying there with my tears. She was a pretty good-natured girl, and put my hair away from my eyes with a soft kind touch; but she was very cheerful at having nearly finished her work and being in good time, and was so different from me!

Presently the tune left off, and a good-looking young fellow came across the yard into the room. He had a hammer in his hand, and his mouth was full of little nails, which he was obliged to take out before he could speak.

"Well, Joram!" said Mr Omer. "How do *you* get on?"

"All right," said Joram. "Done, sir."

Minnie coloured a little, and the other two girls smiled at one another.

"What! you were at it by candle-light last night, when I was at the club, then? Were you?" said Mr Omer, shutting up one eye.

"Yes," said Joram. "As you said we could make a little trip of it, and go over together, if it was done, Minnie and me—and you."

"Oh! I thought you were going to leave me out altogether," said Mr Omer, laughing till he coughed.

"—As you was so good as to say that," resumed the young man, "why I turned to with a will, you see. Will you give me your opinion of it?"

"I will," said Mr Omer, rising. "My dear"; and he stopped and turned to me: "would you like to see your—"

"No, father," Minnie interposed.

"I thought it might be agreeable, my dear," said Mr Omer. "But perhaps you're right."

I can't say how I knew it was my dear, dear mother's coffin that they went to look at. I had never heard one making; I had never seen one that I know of: but it came into my mind what the noise was, while it was going on; and when the young man entered, I am sure I knew what he had been doing.

The work being now finished, the two girls, whose names I had not heard, brushed the shreds and threads from their dresses, and went into the shop to put that to rights, and wait for customers. Minnie stayed behind to fold up what they had made, and pack it in two baskets. This she did upon her knees, humming a lively little tune the while. Joram, who I had no doubt was her lover, came in and stole a kiss from her while she was busy (he didn't appear to mind me, at all), and said her father was gone for the chaise, and he must make haste and get himself ready. Then he went out again; and then she put her thimble and scissors in her pocket, and stuck a needle threaded with black thread neatly in the bosom of her gown, and put on her outer clothing smartly, at a little glass behind the door, in which I saw the reflection of her pleased face.

All this I observed, sitting at the table in the corner with my head leaning on my hand, and my thoughts running on very different things. The chaise soon came round to the front of the shop, and the baskets being put in first, I was put in next, and those three followed. I remember it as a kind of half chaise-cart, half pianoforte-van, painted of a sombre colour, and drawn by a black horse with a long tail. There was plenty of room for us all.

I do not think I have ever experienced so strange a feeling in my life (I am wiser now, perhaps) as that of being with them, remembering how they had been employed, and seeing them enjoy the ride. I was not angry with them; I was more afraid of them, as if I were cast away among creatures with whom I had no community of nature. They were very cheerful. The old man sat in front to drive, and the two young people sat behind him, and whenever he spoke to them leaned forward, the one on one side of his chubby face and the other on the other, and made a great deal of him. They would have talked to me too, but I held back, and moped in my corner; scared by their love-making and hilarity, though it was far from boisterous, and almost wondering that no judgment came upon them for their hardness of heart.

So, when they stopped to bait the horse, and ate and drank and enjoyed themselves, I could touch nothing that they touched, but kept my fast unbroken. So, when we reached home, I dropped out of the chaise behind, as quickly as possible, that I might not be in their company before those solemn windows, looking blindly on me like closed eyes once bright. And oh, how little need I had had to think what would move me to tears when I came back—seeing the window of my mother's room, and next it that which, in the better time, was mine!

I was in Peggotty's arms before I got to the door, and she took me into the house. Her grief burst out when she first saw me; but she controlled it soon, and spoke in whispers, and walked softly, as if the dead could be disturbed. She had not been in bed, I found, for a long time. She sat up at night still, and watched. As long as her poor dear pretty was above the ground, she said, she would never desert her.

Mr Murdstone took no heed of me when I went into the parlour where he was, but sat by the fireside, weeping silently, and pondering in his elbow-chair. Miss Murdstone, who was busy at her writing-desk, which was covered with letters and papers, gave me her cold finger-nails, and asked me, in an iron whisper, if I had been measured for my mourning.

I said: "Yes."

"And your shirts," said Miss Murdstone; "have you brought 'em home?"

"Yes, ma'am. I have brought home all my clothes."

This was all the consolation that her firmness administered to me. I do not doubt that she had a choice pleasure in exhibiting what she called her self-command, and her firmness, and her strength of mind, and her common sense, and the whole diabolical catalogue of her unamiable qualities, on such an occasion. She was particularly proud of her turn for business; and she showed it now in reducing everything to pen and ink, and being moved by nothing. All the rest of that day, and from morning to night afterwards, she sat at that desk, scratching composedly with a hard pen, speaking in the same imperturbable whisper to everybody; never relaxing a muscle of her face, or softening a tone of her voice, or appearing with an atom of her dress astray.

Her brother took a book sometimes, but never read it that I saw. He would open it and look at it as if he were reading, but would remain for a whole hour without turning the leaf, and then put it down and walk to and fro in the room. I used to sit with folded hands watching him, and counting his footsteps, hour after hour. He very seldom spoke to her, and never to me. He seemed to be the only restless thing, except the clocks, in the whole motionless house.

In these days before the funeral, I saw but little of Peggotty, except that, in passing up or down stairs, I always found her close to the room where my mother and her baby lay, and except that she came to me every night, and sat by my bed's head while I went to sleep. A day or two before the burial—I think it was a day or two before, but I am conscious of confusion in my mind about that heavy time, with nothing to mark its progress—she took me into the room. I only recollect that underneath some white covering on the bed, with a beautiful cleanliness and freshness all around it, there seemed to me to lie embodied the solemn stillness that was in the house; and that when she would have turned the cover gently back, I cried: "Oh no! oh no!" and held her hand.

If the funeral had been yesterday, I could not recollect it better. The very air of the best parlour, when I went in at the door, the bright condition of the fire, the shining of the wine in the decanters, the patterns of the glasses and plates, the faint sweet smell of cake, the odour of Miss Murdstone's dress, and our black clothes. Mr Chillip is in the room, and comes to speak to me.

"And how is Master David?" he says, kindly.

I cannot tell him very well. I give him my hand, which he holds in his.

"Dear me!" says Mr Chillip, meekly smiling, with something shining in his eye. "Our little friends grow up around us. They grow out of our knowledge, ma'am?"

This is to Miss Murdstone, who makes no reply.

"There is a great improvement here, ma'am?" says Mr Chillip.

Miss Murdstone merely answers with a frown and a formal bend: Mr Chillip, discomfited, goes into a corner, keeping me with him, and opens his mouth no more.

I remark this, because I remark everything that happens, not because I care about myself, or have done since I came home. And now the bell begins to sound, and Mr Omer and another come to make us ready. As Peggotty was wont to tell me, long ago, the followers of my father to the same grave were made ready in the same room.

There are Mr Murdstone, our neighbour Mr Grayper, Mr Chillip, and I. When we go out to the door, the Bearers and their load are in the garden; and they move before us down the path, and past the elms, and through the gate, and into the churchyard, where I have so often heard the birds sing on a summer morning.

We stand around the grave. The day seems different to me from every other day, and the light not of the same colour—of a sadder colour. Now there is a solemn hush, which we have brought from home with what is resting in the mould; and while we stand bareheaded, I hear the voice of the clergyman, sounding remote in the open air, and yet distinct and plain, saying: "I am the Resurrection and the Life, saith the Lord!" Then I hear sobs; and, standing apart among the lookers-on, I see that good and faithful servant, whom of all the people upon earth I love the best, and unto whom my childish heart is certain that the Lord will one day say: "Well done."

There are many faces that I know, among the little crowd; faces that I knew in church, when mine was always wandering there; faces that first saw my mother, when she came to the village in her youthful bloom. I do not mind them—I mind nothing but my grief—and yet I see and know them all; and even in the background, far away, see Minnie looking on, and her eye glancing on her sweetheart, who is near me.

It is over, and the earth is filled in, and we turn to come away. Before us stands our house, so pretty and unchanged, so linked in my mind with the young idea of what is gone, that all my sorrow has been nothing to the sorrow it calls forth. But they take me on; and Mr Chillip talks to me; and when we get home, puts some water to my lips; and when I ask his leave to go up to my room, dismisses me with the gentleness of a woman.

All this, I say, is yesterday's event. Events of later date have floated from me to the shore where all forgotten things will reappear, but this stands like a high rock in the ocean.

I knew that Peggotty would come to me in my room. The Sabbath stillness of the time (the day was so like Sunday! I have forgotten that) was suited to us both. She sat down by my side upon my little bed; and holding my hand, and sometimes putting it to her lips, and sometimes smoothing it with hers, as she might have comforted my little brother, told me, in her way, all that she had to tell concerning what had happened.

"She was never well," said Peggotty, "for a long time. She was uncertain in her mind, and not happy. When her baby was born, I thought at first she would get better, but she was more delicate, and sunk a little every day. She used to like to sit alone before her baby came, and then she cried; but afterwards she used to sing to it—so soft, that I once thought, when I heard her, it was like a voice up in the air, that was rising away.

"I think she got to be more timid, and more frightened-like, of late; and that a hard word was like a blow to her. But she was always the same to me. She never changed to her foolish Peggotty, didn't my sweet girl."

Here Peggotty stopped, and softly beat upon my hand a little while.

"The last time that I saw her like her own old self, was the night when you came home, my dear. The day you went away, she said to me, 'I never shall see my pretty darling again. Something tells me so, that tells the truth, I know.' "

"She tried to hold up after that; and many a time, when they told her she was thoughtless and light-hearted, made believe to be so; but it was all a bygone then. She never told her husband what she had told me—she was afraid of saying it to anybody else—till one night, a little more than a week before it happened, when she said to him: 'My dear, I think I am dying.' "

" 'It's off my mind now, Peggotty,' she told me, when I laid her in her bed that night. 'He will believe it more and more, poor fellow, every day for a few days to come; and then it will be past. I am very tired. If this is sleep, sit by me while I sleep: don't leave me. God bless both my children! God protect and keep my fatherless boy!' "

"I never left her afterwards," said Peggotty. "She often talked to them two down-stairs—for she loved them; she couldn't bear not to love anyone who was about her—but when they went away from her bed-side, she always turned to me, as if there was rest where Peggotty was, and never fell asleep in any other way.

"On the last night, in the evening, she kissed me, and said: 'If my baby should die too, Peggotty, please let them lay him in my arms, and bury us together.' (It was done; for the poor lamb lived but a day beyond her.) 'Let my dearest boy go with us to our resting-place,' she said, 'and tell him that his mother, when she lay here, blessed him not once, but a thousand times.' "

Another silence followed this, and another gentle beating on my hand.

"It was pretty far in the night," said Peggotty, "when she asked me for some drink; and when she had taken it, gave me such a patient smile, the dear!—so beautiful!

"Daybreak had come, and the sun was rising, when she said to me, how kind and considerate Mr Copperfield had always been to her, and how he had borne with her, and told her, when she doubted herself, that a loving heart was better and stronger than wisdom, and that he was a happy man in hers. 'Peggotty, my dear,' she said then, 'put me nearer to you,' for she was very weak. 'Lay your good arm underneath my neck,' she said, 'and turn me to you, for your face is going far off, and I want it to be near.' I put it as she asked; and oh Davy! the time had come when my first parting words to you were true—when she was glad to lay her poor head on her stupid cross old Peggotty's arm—and she died like a child that had gone to sleep!"

Thus ended Peggotty's narration. From the moment of my knowing of the death of my mother, the idea of her as she had been of late had vanished from me. I remembered her, from that instant, only as the young mother of my earliest impressions, who had been used to wind her bright curls round and round her finger, and to dance with me at twilight in the parlour. What Peggotty had told me now, was so far from bringing me back to the later period, that it rooted the earlier image in my mind. It may be curious, but it is true. In her death she winged her way back to her calm untroubled youth, and cancelled all the rest.

The mother who lay in the grave, was the mother of my infancy; the little creature in her arms, was myself, as I had once been, hushed for ever on her bosom.

Chapter X

I BECOME NEGLECTED, AND AM PROVIDED FOR

THE first act of business Miss Murdstone performed when the day of the solemnity was over, and light was freely admitted into the house, was to give Peggotty a month's warning. Much as Peggotty would have disliked such a service, I believe she would have retained it, for my sake, in preference to the best upon earth. She told me we must part, and told me why; and we condoled with one another, in all sincerity.

As to me or my future, not a word was said, or a step taken. Happy they would have been, I dare say, if they could have dismissed me at a month's warning too. I mustered courage once, to ask Miss Murdstone when I was going back to school; and she answered dryly, she believed I was not going back at all. I was told nothing more. I was very anxious to know what was going to be done with me, and so was Peggotty; but neither she nor I could pick up any information on the subject.

There was one change in my condition, which, while it relieved me of a great deal of present uneasiness, might have made me, if I had been capable of considering it closely, yet more uncomfortable about the future. It was this. The constraint that had been put upon me, was quite abandoned. I was so far from being required to keep my dull post in the parlour, that on several occasions, when I took my seat there, Miss Murdstone frowned to me to go away. I was so far from being warned off from Peggotty's society, that, provided I was not in Mr Murdstone's, I was never sought out or inquired for. At first I was in daily dread of his taking my education in hand again, or of Miss Murdstone's devoting herself to it; but I soon began to think that such fears were groundless, and that all I had to anticipate was neglect.

I do not conceive that this discovery gave me much pain then. I was still giddy with the shock of my mother's death, and in a kind of stunned state as to all tributary things.

I can recollect, indeed, to have speculated, at odd times, on the possibility of my not being taught any more, or cared for any more; and growing up to be a shabby moody man, lounging an idle life away, about the village; as well as on the feasibility of my getting rid of this picture by going away somewhere, like the hero in a story, to seek my fortune: but these were transient visions, daydreams I sat looking at sometimes, as if they were faintly painted or written on the wall of my room, and which, as they melted away, left the wall blank again.

"Peggotty," I said in a thoughtful whisper, one evening, when I was warming my hands at the kitchen fire, "Mr Murdstone likes me less than he used to. He never liked me much, Peggotty; but he would rather not even see me now, if he can help it."

"Perhaps it's his sorrow," said Peggotty, stroking my hair.

"I am sure, Peggotty, I am sorry too. If I believed it was his sorrow, I should not think of it at all. But it's not that; oh, no, it's not that."

"How do you know it's not that?" said Peggotty, after a silence.

"Oh, his sorrow is another and quite a different thing. He is sorry at this moment, sitting by the fireside with Miss Murdstone; but if I was to go in, Peggotty, he would be something besides."

"What would he be?" said Peggotty.

"Angry," I answered, with an involuntary imitation of his dark frown. "If he was only sorry, he wouldn't look at me as he does. I am only sorry, and it makes me feel kinder."

Peggotty said nothing for a little while; and I warmed my hands, as silent as she.

"Davy," she said at length.

"Yes, Peggotty?"

"I have tried, my dear, all ways I could think of—all the ways there are, and all the ways there ain't, in short—to get a suitable service here, in Blunderstone; but there's no such a thing, my love."

"And what do you mean to do, Peggotty," says I, wistfully. "Do you mean to go and seek your fortune?"

"I expect I shall be forced to go to Yarmouth," replied Peggotty, "and live there."

"You might have gone farther off," I said, brightening a little, "and been as bad as lost. I shall see you sometimes, my dear old Peggotty, there. You won't be quite at the other end of the world, will you?"

"Contrary ways, please God!" cried Peggotty, with great animation. "As long as you are here, my pet, I shall come over every week of my life to see you. One day, every week of my life!"

I felt a great weight taken off my mind by this promise: but even this was not all, for Peggotty went on to say:

"I'm a-going, Davy, you see, to my brother's, first, for another fortnight's visit—just till I have had time to look about me, and get to be something like myself again. Now, I have been thinking that perhaps, as they don't want you here at present, you might be let to go along with me."

If anything, short of being in a different relation to every one about me, Peggotty excepted, could have given me a sense of pleasure at that time, it would have been this project of all others. The idea of being again surrounded by those honest faces, shining welcome on me; of renewing the peacefulness of the sweet Sunday morning, when the bells were ringing, the stones dropping in the water, and the shadowy ships breaking through the mist; of roaming up and down with little Em'ly, telling her my troubles, and finding charms against them in the shells and pebbles on the beach; made a calm in my heart. It was ruffled next moment, to be sure, by a doubt of Miss Murdstone's giving her consent; but even that was set at rest soon, for she came out to take an evening grope in the store-closet while we were yet in conversation, and Peggotty, with a boldness that amazed me, broached the topic on the spot.

"The boy will be idle there," said Miss Murdstone, looking into a pickle-jar, "and idleness is the root of all evil. But, to be sure, he would be idle here—or anywhere, in my opinion."

Peggotty had an angry answer ready, I could see; but she swallowed it for my sake, and remained silent.

"Humph!" said Miss Murdstone, still keeping her eye on the pickles; "it is of more importance than anything else—it is of paramount importance—that my brother should not be disturbed or made uncomfortable. I suppose I had better say yes."

I thanked her, without making any demonstration of joy, lest it should induce her to withdraw her assent. Nor could I help thinking this a prudent course, since she looked at me out of the pickle-jar, with as great an access of sourness as if her black eyes had absorbed its contents. However, the permission was given, and was never retracted; for when the month was out, Peggotty and I were ready to depart.

Mr Barkis came into the house for Peggotty's boxes. I had never known him to pass the garden-gate before, but on this occasion he came into the house. And he gave me a look as he shouldered the largest box and went out, which I thought had meaning in it, if meaning could ever be said to find its way into Mr Barkis's visage.

Peggotty was naturally in low spirits at leaving what had been her home so many years, and where the two strong attachments of her life—for my mother and myself—had been formed. She had been walking in the churchyard, too, very early; and she got into the cart, and sat in it with her handkerchief at her eyes.

So long as she remained in this condition, Mr Barkis gave no sign of life whatever. He sat in his usual place and attitude like a great stuffed figure. But when she began to look about her, and to speak to me, he nodded his head and grinned several times. I have not the least notion at whom, or what he meant by it.

"It's a beautiful day, Mr Barkis!" I said, as an act of politeness.

"It ain't bad," said Mr Barkis, who generally qualified his speech, and rarely committed himself.

"Peggotty is quite comfortable now, Mr Barkis," I remarked, for his satisfaction.

"Is she, though?" said Mr Barkis.

After reflecting about it, with a sagacious air, Mr Barkis eyed her, and said:

"*Are* you pretty comfortable?"

Peggotty laughed, and answered in the affirmative.

"But really and truly, you know. Are you?" growled Mr Barkis, sliding nearer to her on the seat, and nudging her with his elbow. "Are you? Really and truly pretty comfortable? Are you? Eh?" At each of these inquiries Mr Barkis shuffled nearer to her, and gave her another nudge; so that at last we were all crowded together in the left-hand corner of the cart, and I was so squeezed that I could hardly bear it.

Peggotty calling his attention to my sufferings, Mr Barkis gave me a little more room at once, and got away by degrees. But I could not help observing that he seemed to think he had hit upon a wonderful expedient for expressing himself in a neat, agreeable, and pointed manner, without the inconvenience of inventing conversation. He manifestly chuckled over it for some time. By and by he turned to Peggotty again, and repeating, "Are you pretty comfortable though?" bore down upon us as before, until the breath was nearly edged out of my body. By and by he made another descent upon us with the same inquiry, and the same result. At length, I got up whenever I saw him coming, and standing on the foot-board, pretended to look at the prospect; after which I did very well.

He was so polite as to stop at a public-house, expressly on our account, and entertain us with broiled mutton and beer. Even when Peggotty was in the act of drinking, he was seized with one of those approaches, and almost choked her. But as we drew nearer to the end of our journey, he had more to do and less time for gallantry; and when we got on Yarmouth pavement, we were all too much shaken and jolted, I apprehend, to have any leisure for anything else.

Mr Peggotty and Ham waited for us at the old place. They received me and Peggotty in an affectionate manner, and shook hands with Mr Barkis, who, with his hat on the very back of his head, and a shame-faced leer upon his countenance, and pervading his very legs, presented but a vacant appearance, I thought. They each took one of Peggotty's trunks, and we were going away, when Mr Barkis solemnly made a sign to me with his forefinger to come under an archway.

"I say," growled Mr Barkis, "it was all right."

I looked up into his face, and answered, with an attempt to be very profound: "Oh!"

"It didn't come to a end there," said Mr Barkis, nodding confidentially. "It was all right."

Again I answered, "Oh!"

"You know who was willin'," said my friend. "It was Barkis, and Barkis only."

I nodded assent.

"It's all right," said Mr Barkis, shaking hands; "I'm a friend of your'n. You made it all right, first. It's all right."

In his attempts to be particularly lucid, Mr Barkis was so extremely mysterious, that I might have stood looking in his face for an hour, and most assuredly should have got as much information out of it as out of the face of a clock that had stopped, but for Peggotty's calling me away. As we were going along, she asked me what he had said; and I told her he had said it was all right.

"Like his impudence," said Peggotty, "but I don't mind that! Davy dear, what should you think if I was to think of being married?"

"Why—I suppose you would like me as much then, Peggotty, as you do now?" I returned, after a little consideration.

Greatly to the astonishment of the passengers in the street, as well as of her relations going on before, the good soul was obliged to stop and embrace me on the spot, with many protestations of her unalterable love.

"Tell me what should you say, darling?" she asked again, when this was over, and we were walking on.

"If you were thinking of being married—to Mr Barkis, Peggotty?"

"Yes," said Peggotty.

"I should think it would be a very good thing. For then you know, Peggotty, you would always have the horse and cart to bring you over to see me, and could come for nothing, and be sure of coming."

"The sense of the dear!" cried Peggotty. "What I have been thinking of, this month back! Yes, my precious; and I think I should be more independent altogether, you see; let alone my working with a better heart in my own house, than I could in anybody else's now. I don't know what I might be fit for, now, as a servant to a stranger. And I shall be always near my pretty's resting-place," said Peggotty, musing, "and be able to see it when I like; and when *I* lie down to rest, I may be laid not far off from my darling girl!"

We neither of us said anything for a little while.

"But I wouldn't so much as give it another thought," said Peggotty, cheerily "if my

Davy was anyways against it—not if I had been asked in church thirty ti nes three times over, and was wearing out the ring in my pocket."

"Look at me, Peggotty," I replied; "and see if I am not really glad, and don't truly wish it!" As indeed I did, with all my heart.

"Well, my life," said Peggotty, giving me a squeeze, "I have thought of it night and day, every way I can, and I hope the right way; but I'll think of it again, and speak to my brother about it, and in the meantime we'll keep it to ourselves, Davy, you and me. Barkis is a good plain creatur'," said Peggotty, "and if I tried to do my duty by him, I think it would be my fault if I wasn't—if I wasn't pretty comfortable," said Peggotty, laughing heartily.

This quotation from Mr Barkis was so appropriate, and tickled us bot 1 so much, that we laughed again and again, and were quite in a pleasant humour when ve came within view of Mr Peggotty's cottage.

It looked just the same, except that it may, perhaps, have shrunk a little in my eyes; and Mrs Gummidge was waiting at the door as if she had stood there ever since. All within was the same, down to the seaweed in the blue mug in my bedroom. I went into the out-house to look about me; and the very same lobsters, crabs, and crawfish possessed by the same desire to pinch the world in general, appeared to be in the same state of conglomeration in the same old corner.

But there was no little Em'ly to be seen, so I asked Mr Peggotty where she was.

"She's at school, sir," said Mr Peggotty, wiping the heat consequent on the porterage of Peggotty's box from his forehead; "she'll be home," looking at the Dutch clock, "in from twenty minutes to half-an-hour's time. We all on us feel the loss of her, bless ye!"

Mrs Gummidge moaned.

"Cheer up, Mawther!" cried Mr Peggotty.

"I feel it more than anybody else," said Mrs Gummidge; "I'm a lone lorn creetur', and she used to be a'most the only thing that didn't go contrairy with me."

Mrs Gummidge, whimpering and shaking her head, applied herself to blowing the fire. Mr Peggotty, looking round upon us while she was so engaged, said in a low voice, which he shaded with his hand: "The old 'un!" From this I rightly conjectured that no improvement had taken place since my last visit in the state of Mrs Gummidge's spirits.

Now, the whole place was, or it should have been, quite as delightful a place as ever; and yet it did not impress me in the same way. I felt rather disappointed with it. Perhaps it was because little Em'ly was not at home. I knew the way by which she would come, and presently found myself strolling along the path to meet her.

A figure appeared in the distance before long, and I soon knew it to be Em'ly, who was a little creature still in stature, though she was grown. But when she drew nearer, and I saw her blue eyes looking bluer, and her dimpled face looking brighter, and her whole self prettier and gayer, a curious feeling came over me that made me pretend not to know her, and pass by as if I were looking at something a long way off. I have done such a thing since in later life, or I am mistaken.

Little Em'ly didn't care a bit. She saw me well enough; but instead of turning round and calling after me, ran away laughing. This obliged me to run after her, and she ran so fast that we were very near the cottage before I caught her.

"Oh, it's you, is it?" said little Em'ly.

"Why, you knew who it was, Em'ly," said I.

"And didn't *you* know who it was?" said Em'ly. I was going to kiss her, but she covered her cherry lips with her hands, and said she wasn't a baby now, and ran away, laughing more than ever, into the house.

She seemed to delight in teasing me, which was a change in her I wondered at very much. The tea table was ready, and our little locker was put out in its old place, but instead of coming to sit by me, she went and bestowed her company upon that grumbling Mrs Gummidge: and on Mr Peggotty's inquiring why, rumpled her hair all over her face to hide it, and could do nothing but laugh.

"A little puss, it is!" said Mr Peggotty, patting her with his great hand.

"So sh'is! so sh'is!" cried Ham. "Mas'r Davy bor', so sh'is!" and he sat and chuckled at her for some time, in a state of mingled admiration and delight, that made his face a burning red.

Little Em'ly was spoiled by them all, in fact; and by no one more than Mr Peggotty himself, whom she could have coaxed into anything, by only going and laying her cheek against his rough whisker. That was my opinion, at least, when I saw her do it; and I held Mr Peggotty to be thoroughly in the right. But she was so affectionate and sweet-natured, and had such a pleasant manner of being both sly and shy at once, that she captivated me more than ever.

She was tender-hearted, too; for when, as we sat round the fire after tea, an allusion was made by Mr Peggotty over his pipe to the loss I had sustained, the tears stood in her eyes, and she looked at me so kindly across the table, that I felt quite thankful to her.

"Ah!" said Mr Peggotty, taking up her curls, and running them over his hand like water, "here's another orphan, you see, sir. And here," said Mr Peggotty, giving Ham a backhanded knock in the chest, "is another of 'em, though he don't look much like it."

"If I had you for my guardian, Mr Peggotty," said I, shaking my head, "I don't think I should *feel* much like it."

"Well said, Mas'r Davy bor'!" cried Ham, in an ecstasy. "Hoorah! Well said! Nor more you wouldn't! Hor! Hor!"—Here he returned Mr Peggotty's back-hander, and little Em'ly got up and kissed Mr Peggotty.

"And how's your friend, sir?" said Mr Peggotty to me.

"Steerforth?" said I.

"That's the name!" cried Mr Peggotty, turning to Ham. "I knowed it was something in our way."

"You said it was Rudderford," observed Ham, laughing.

"Well!" retorted Mr Peggotty. "And ye steer with a rudder, don't ye? It ain't fur off. How is he, sir?"

"He was very well indeed when I came away, Mr Peggotty."

"There's a friend!" said Mr Peggotty, stretching out his pipe. "There's a friend, if you talk of friends! Why, Lord love my heart alive, if it ain't a treat to look at him!"

"He is very handsome, is he not?" said I, my heart warming with this praise.

"Handsome!" cried Mr Peggotty. "He stands up to you like—like a—why I don't know what he *don't* stand up to you like. He's so bold!"

"Yes! That's just his character," said I. "He's as brave as a lion, and you can't think how frank he is, Mr Peggotty."

"And I do suppose, now," said Mr Peggotty, looking at me through the smoke of his pipe, "that in the way of book-larning he'd take the wind out of a'most anything."

"Yes," said I, delighted; "he knows everything. He is astonishingly clever."

"There's a friend!" murmured Mr Peggotty, with a grave toss of his head.

"Nothing seems to cost him any trouble," said I. "He knows a task if he only looks at it. He is the best cricketer you ever saw. He will give you almost as many men as you like at draughts, and beat you easily."

Mr Peggotty gave his head another toss, as much as to say: "Of course he will."

"He is such a speaker," I pursued, "that he can win anybody over; and I don't know what you'd say if you were to hear him sing, Mr Peggotty."

Mr Peggotty gave his head another toss, as much as to say: "I have no doubt of it."

"Then, he's such a generous, fine, noble fellow," said I, quite carried away by my favourite theme, "that it's hardly possible to give him as much praise as he deserves. I am sure I can never feel thankful enough for the generosity with which he has protected me, so much younger and lower in the school than himself."

I was running on, very fast indeed, when my eyes rested on little Em'ly's face, which was bent forward over the table, listening with the deepest attention, her breath held, her blue eyes sparkling like jewels, and the colour mantling in her cheeks. She looked so extraordinarily earnest and pretty, that I stopped in a sort of wonder; and they all observed her at the same time, for as I stopped, they laughed and looked at her.

"Em'ly is like me," said Peggotty, "and would like to see him."

Em'ly was confused by our all observing her, and hung down her head, and her face was covered with blushes. Glancing up presently through her stray curls, and seeing that we were all looking at her still (I am sure I, for one, could have looked at her for hours), she ran away, and kept away till it was nearly bedtime.

I lay down in the old little bed in the stern of the boat, and the wind came moaning on across the flat as it had done before. But I could not help fancying, now, that it moaned of those who were gone; and instead of thinking that the sea might rise in the night and float the boat away, I thought of the sea that had risen, since I last heard those sounds, and drowned my happy home. I recollect, as the wind and water began to sound fainter in my ears, putting a short clause into my prayers, petitioning that I might grow up to marry little Em'ly, and so dropping lovingly asleep.

The days passed pretty much as they had passed before, except—it was a great exception—that little Em'ly and I seldom wandered on the beach now. She had tasks to learn, and needle-work to do; and was absent during a great part of each day. But I felt that we should not have had those old wanderings, even if it had been otherwise. Wild and full of childish whims as Em'ly was, she was more of a little woman than I had supposed. She seemed to have got a great distance away from me, in little more than a year. She liked me, but she laughed at me, and tormented me; and when I went to meet her, stole home another way, and was laughing at the door when I came back, disappointed. The best times were when she sat quietly at work in the doorway, and I sat on the wooden step at her feet, reading to her. It seems to me, at this hour, that I have never seen such sunlight as on those bright April afternoons; that I have never seen such a sunny little figure as I used to see, sitting in the doorway of the old boat; that I have never beheld such sky, such water, such glorified ships sailing away into golden air.

On the very first evening after our arrival, Mr Barkis appeared in an exceedingly vacant and awkward condition, and with a bundle of oranges tied up in a handkerchief. As he made no allusion of any kind to this property, he was supposed to have left it behind him by accident when he went away; until Ham, running after him to restore it, came back with the information that it was intended for Peggotty. After that occasion he appeared every evening at exactly the same hour, and always with a little bundle, to which he never alluded, and which he regularly put behind the door and left there. These offerings of affection were of a most various and eccentric description. Among them I remember a double set of pigs' trotters, a huge pin-cushion, half a bushel or so of apples, a pair of jet earrings, some Spanish onions, a box of dominoes, a canary bird and cage, and a leg of pickled pork.

Mr Barkis's wooing, as I remember it, was altogether of a peculiar kind. He very seldom said anything; but would sit by the fire in much the same attitude as he sat in his cart, and stare heavily at Peggotty, who was opposite. One night, being, as I suppose, inspired by love, he made a dart at the bit of wax-candle she kept for her thread, and put it in his waistcoat-pocket and carried it off. After that, his great delight was to produce it when it was wanted, sticking to the lining of his pocket, in a partially melted state, and pocket it again when it was done with. He seemed to enjoy himself very much, and not to feel at all called upon to talk. Even when he took Peggotty out for a walk on the flats, he had no uneasiness on that head, I believe; contenting himself with now and then asking her if she was pretty comfortable; and I remember that sometimes, after he was gone, Peggotty would throw her apron over her face, and laugh for half-an-hour. Indeed, we were all more or less amused, except that miserable Mrs Gummidge, whose courtship would appear to have been of an exactly parallel nature, she was so continu- ally reminded by these transactions of the old one.

At length, when the term of my visit was nearly expired, it was given out that Peggotty and Mr Barkis were going to make a day's holiday together, and that little Em'ly and I were to accompany them. I had but a broken sleep the night before, in anticipation of the pleasure of a whole day with Em'ly. We were all astir betimes in the morning; and while we were yet at breakfast, Mr Barkis appeared in the distance, driving a chaise-cart towards the object of his affections.

Peggotty was dressed as usual, in her neat and quiet mourning; but Mr Barkis bloomed in a new blue coat, of which the tailor had given him such good measure, that the cuffs would have rendered gloves unnecessary in the coldest weather, while the collar was so high that it pushed his hair up on end on the top of his head. His bright buttons, too, were of the largest size. Rendered complete by drab pantaloons and a buff waistcoat, I thought Mr Barkis a phenomenon of respectability.

When we were all in a bustle outside the door, I found that Mr Peggotty was prepared with an old shoe, which was to be thrown after us for luck, and which he offered to Mrs Gummidge for that purpose.

"No. It had better be done by somebody else, Dan'l," said Mrs Gummidge. "I'm a lone lorn creetur' myself, and everythink that reminds me of creetur's that ain't lone and lorn, goes contrairy with me."

"Come, old gal!" cried Mr Peggotty. "Take and heave it."

"No, Dan'l," returned Mrs Gummidge, whimpering and shaking her head. "If I felt less, I could do more. You don't feel like me, Dan'l; thinks don't go contrairy with you, nor you with them; you had better do it yourself."

But here Peggotty, who had been going about from one to another in a hurried way, kissing everybody, called out from the cart, in which we all were by this time (Em'ly and I on two little chairs, side by side), that Mrs Gummidge must do it. So Mrs Gummidge did it; and, I am sorry to relate, cast a damp upon the festive character of our departure, by immediately bursting into tears, and sinking subdued into the arms of Ham, with the declaration that she knowed she was a burden, and had better be carried to the House at once. Which I really thought was a sensible idea, that Ham might have acted on.

Away we went, however, on our holiday excursion; and the first thing we did was to stop at a church, where Mr Barkis tied the horse to some rails, and went in with Peggotty, leaving little Em'ly and me alone in the chaise. I took that occasion to put my arm round Em'ly's waist, and propose that as I was going away so very soon now, we should determine to be very affectionate to one another, and very happy, all day. Little Em'ly consenting, and allowing me to kiss her, I became desperate; informing her, I recollect, that I never could love another, and that I was prepared to shed the blood of anybody who should aspire to her affections.

How merry little Em'ly made herself about it! With what a demure assumption of being immensely older and wiser than I, the fairy little woman said I was "a silly boy"; and then laughed so charmingly that I forgot the pain of being called by that disparaging name, in the pleasure of looking at her.

Mr Barkis and Peggotty were a good while in the church, but came out at last, and then we drove away into the country. As we were going along, Mr Barkis turned to me, and said, with a wink,—by the by, I should hardly have thought, before, that he *could* wink:

"What name was it as I wrote up in the cart?"

"Clara Peggotty," I answered.

"What name would it be as I should write up now, if there was a tilt here?"

"Clara Peggotty, again?" I suggested.

"Clara Peggotty Barkis!" he returned, and burst into a roar of laughter that shook the chaise.

In a word, they were married, and had gone into the church for no other purpose. Peggotty was resolved that it should be quietly done; and the clerk had given her away, and there had been no witnesses of the ceremony. She was a little confused when Mr Barkis made this abrupt announcement of their union, and could not hug me enough in token of her unimpaired affection; but she soon became herself again, and said she was very glad it was over.

We drove to a little inn in a by-road, where we were expected, and where we had a very comfortable dinner, and passed the day with great satisfaction. If Peggotty had been married every day for the last ten years, she could hardly have been more at her ease about it; it made no sort of difference in her: she was just the same as ever, and went out for a stroll with little Em'ly and me before tea, while Mr Barkis philosophically smoked his pipe, and enjoyed himself, I suppose, with the contemplation of his happiness. If so, it sharpened his appetite; for I distinctly call to mind that, although he had eaten a good deal of pork and greens at dinner, and had finished off with a fowl or two, he was obliged to have cold boiled bacon for tea, and disposed of a large quantity without any emotion.

I have often thought, since, what an odd, innocent, out-of-the-way kind of wedding it must have been! We got into the chaise again soon after dark, and drove cosily back, looking up at the stars, and talking about them. I was their chief exponent, and opened Mr Barkis's mind to an amazing extent. I told him all I knew, but he would have believed anything I might have taken it into my head to impart to him; for he had a profound veneration for my abilities, and informed his wife in my hearing, on that very occasion, that I was "a young Roeshus"—by which I think he meant prodigy.

When we had exhausted the subject of the stars, or rather when I had exhausted the mental faculties of Mr Barkis, little Em'ly and I made a cloak of an old wrapper, and sat under it for the rest of the journey. Ah, how I loved her! What happiness (I thought) if we were married, and were going away anywhere to live among the trees and in the fields, never growing older, never growing wiser, children ever, rambling hand in hand through sunshine and among flowery meadows, laying down our heads on moss at night, in a sweet sleep of purity and peace, and buried by the birds when we were dead! Some such picture, with no real world in it, bright with the light of our innocence, and vague as the stars afar off, was in my mind all the way. I am glad to think there were two such guileless hearts at Peggotty's marriage as little Em'ly's and mine. I am glad to think the Loves and Graces took such airy forms in its homely procession.

Well, we came to the old boat again in good time at night; and there Mr and Mrs Barkis bade us good-bye, and drove away snugly to their own home. I felt then, for the first time, that I had lost Peggotty. I should have gone to bed with a sore heart indeed under any other roof but that which sheltered little Em'ly's head.

Mr Peggotty and Ham knew what was in my thoughts as well as I did, and were ready with some supper and their hospitable faces to drive it away. Little Em'ly came and sat beside me on the locker for the only time in all that visit; and it was altogether a wonderful close to a wonderful day.

It was a night tide; and soon after we went to bed, Mr Peggotty and Ham went out to fish. I felt very brave at being left alone in the solitary house, the protector of Em'ly and Mrs Gummidge, and only wished that a lion or a serpent, or any ill-disposed monster, would make an attack upon us, that I might destroy him, and cover myself with glory. But as nothing of the sort happened to be walking about on Yarmouth flats that night, I provided the best substitute I could by dreaming of dragons until morning.

With morning came Peggotty; who called to me, as usual, under my window as if Mr Barkis the carrier had been from first to last a dream too. After breakfast she took me to her own home, and a beautiful little home it was. Of all the moveables in it, I must have been impressed by a certain old bureau of some dark wood in the parlour (the tile-floored kitchen was the general sitting-room), with a retreating top which opened, let down, and became a desk, within which was a large quarto edition of Foxe's *Book of Martyrs.* This precious volume, of which I do not recollect one word, I immediately discovered and immediately applied myself to; and I never visited the house afterwards, but I kneeled on a chair, opened the casket where this gem was enshrined, spread my arms over the desk, and fell to devouring the book afresh. I was chiefly edified, I am afraid, by the pictures, which were numerous, and represented all kinds of dismal horrors; but the Martyrs and Peggotty's house have been inseparable in my mind ever since, and are now.

I took leave of Mr Peggotty, and Ham, and Mrs Gummidge, and little Em'ly, that day; and passed the night at Peggotty's, in a little room in the roof (with the Crocodile Book on a shelf by the bed's head) which was to be always mine, Peggotty said, and should always be kept for me in exactly the same state.

"Young or old, Davy dear, as long as I am alive and have this house over my head," said Peggotty, "you shall find it as if I expected you here directly minute. I shall keep it every day, as I used to keep your old little room, my darling; and if you was to go to China, you might think of it as being kept just the same, all the time you were away."

I felt the truth and constancy of my dear old nurse, with all my heart, and thanked her as well as I could. That was not very well, for she spoke to me thus, with her arms round my neck, in the morning, and I was going home in the morning, and I went home in the morning, with herself and Mr Barkis in the cart. They left me at the gate, not easily or lightly; and it was a strange sight to me to see the cart go on, taking Peggotty away, and leaving me under the old elm-trees looking at the house, in which there was no face to look on mine with love or liking any more.

And now I fell into a state of neglect, which I cannot look back upon without compassion. I fell at once into a solitary condition,—apart from all friendly notice, apart from the society of all other boys of my own age, apart from all companionship but my own spiritless thoughts,—which seems to cast its gloom upon this paper as I write.

What would I have given, to have been sent to the hardest school that ever was kept!——to have been taught something, anyhow, anywhere! No such hope dawned upon me. They disliked me; and they sullenly, sternly, steadily, overlooked me. I think Mr Murdstone's means were straitened at about this time; but it is little to the purpose. He could not bear me; and in putting me from him he tried, as I believe, to put away the notion that I had any claim upon him——and succeeded.

I was not actively ill-used. I was not beaten, or starved; but the wrong that was done to me had no intervals of relenting, and was done in a systematic, passionless manner. Day after day, week after week, month after month, I was coldly neglected. I wonder sometimes, when I think of it, what they would have done if I had been taken with an illness; whether I should have lain down in my lonely room, and languished through it in my usual solitary way, or whether anybody would have helped me out.

When Mr and Miss Murdstone were at home, I took my meals with them; in their absence, I ate and drank by myself. At all times I lounged about the house and neighbourhood quite disregarded, except that they were jealous of my making any friends: thinking, perhaps, that if I did, I might complain to someone. For this reason, though Mr Chillip often asked me to go and see him (he was a widower, having, some years before that, lost a little small light-haired wife, whom I can just remember connecting in my own thoughts with a pale tortoise-shell cat), it was but seldom that I enjoyed the happiness of passing an afternoon in his closet of a surgery; reading some book that was new to me, with the smell of the whole pharmacopoeia coming up my nose, or pounding something in a mortar under his mild directions.

For the same reason, added no doubt to the old dislike of her, I was seldom allowed to visit Peggotty. Faithful to her promise, she either came to see me, or met me somewhere near, once every week, and never empty-handed; but many and bitter were the disappointments I had, in being refused permission to pay a visit to her at her house. Some few times, however, at long intervals, I was allowed to go there; and then I found out that Mr Barkis was something of a miser, or as Peggotty dutifully expressed it, was "a little near," and kept a heap of money in a box under his bed, which he pretended was only full of coats and trousers. In this coffer, his riches hid themselves with such a tenacious modesty, that the smallest instalments could only be tempted out by artifice; so that Peggotty had to prepare a long and elaborate scheme, a very Gunpowder Plot, for every Saturday's expenses.

All this time I was so conscious of the waste of any promise I had given, and of my being utterly neglected, that I should have been perfectly miserable, I have no doubt, but for the old books. They were my only comfort; and I was as true to them as they were to me, and read them over and over I don't know how many times more.

I now approach a period of my life, which I can never lose the remembrance of, while I remember anything: and the recollection of which has often, without my invocation, come before me like a ghost, and haunted happier times.

I had been out, one day, loitering somewhere, in the listless, meditative manner that my way of life engendered, when, turning the corner of a lane near our house, I came upon Mr Murdstone walking with a gentleman. I was confused, and was going by them, when the gentleman cried:

"What! Brooks!"

"No, sir, David Copperfield," I said.

"Don't tell me. You are Brooks," said the gentleman. "You are Brooks of Sheffield. That's your name."

At these words, I observed the gentleman more attentively. His laugh coming to my remembrance too, I knew him to be Mr Quinion, whom I had gone over to Lowestoft with Mr Murdstone to see, before—it is no matter—I need not recall when.

"And how do you get on, and where are you being educated, Brooks?" said Mr Quinion.

He had put his hand upon my shoulder, and turned me about, to walk with them. I did not know what to reply, and glanced dubiously at Mr Murdstone.

"He is at home at present," said the latter. "He is not being educated anywhere. I don't know what to do with him. He is a difficult subject."

That old, double look was on me for a moment; and then his eyes darkened with a frown, as it turned, in its aversion, elsewhere.

"Humph!" said Mr Quinion, looking at us both, I thought. "Fine weather!"

Silence ensued, and I was considering how I could best disengage my shoulder from his hand, and go away, when he said:

"I suppose you are a pretty sharp fellow still? Eh, Brooks?"

"Aye! He is sharp enough," said Mr Murdstone, impatiently. "You had better let him go. He will not thank you for troubling him."

On this hint, Mr Quinion released me, and I made the best of my way home. Looking back as I turned into the front garden, I saw Mr Murdstone leaning against the wicket of the churchyard, and Mr Quinion talking to him. They were both looking after me, and I felt that they were speaking of me.

Mr Quinion lay at our house that night. After breakfast, the next morning, I had put my chair away, and was going out of the room, when Mr Murdstone called me back. He then gravely repaired to another table, where his sister sat herself at her desk. Mr Quinion, with his hands in his pockets, stood looking out of window; and I stood looking at them all.

"David," said Mr Murdstone, "to the young this is a world for action; not for moping and droning in."

—"As you do," added his sister.

"Jane Murdstone, leave it to me, if you please. I say, David, to the young this is a world for action, and not for moping and droning in. It is especially so for a young boy of your disposition, which requires a great deal of correcting; and to which no greater service can be done than to force it to conform to the ways of the working world, and to bend it and break it."

"For stubbornness won't do here," said his sister "What it wants is, to be crushed. And crushed it must be. Shall be, too!"

He gave her a look, half in remonstrance, half in approval, and went on:

"I suppose you know, David, that I am not rich. At any rate, you know it now. You have received some considerable education already. Education is costly; and even if it were not, and I could afford it, I am of opinion that it would not be at all advantageous to you to be kept at school. What is before you, is a fight with the world; and the sooner you begin it, the better."

I think it occurred to me that I had already begun it, in my poor way: but it occurs to me now, whether or no.

"You have heard the 'counting-house' mentioned sometimes," said Mr Murdstone.

"The counting-house, sir?" I repeated.

"Of Murdstone and Grinby, in the wine trade," he replied.

I suppose I looked uncertain, for he went on hastily:

"You have heard the 'counting-house' mentioned, or the business, or the cellars, or the wharf, or something about it."

"I think I have heard the business mentioned, sir," I said, remembering what I vaguely knew of his and his sister's resources. "But I don't know when."

"It does not matter when," he returned. "Mr Quinion manages that business."

I glanced at the latter deferentially as he stood looking out of window.

"Mr Quinion suggests that it gives employment to some other boys, and that he sees no reason why it shouldn't, on the same terms, give employment to you."

"He having," Mr Quinion observed in a low voice, and half turning round, "no other prospect, Murdstone."

Mr Murdstone, with an impatient, even an angry gesture, resumed, without noticing what he had said:

"Those terms are, that you will earn enough for yourself to provide for your eating and drinking, and pocket-money. Your lodging (which I have arranged for) will be paid by me. So will your washing—"

"—Which will be kept down to my estimate," said his sister.

"Your clothes will be looked after for you, too," said Mr Murdstone; "as you will not be able, yet awhile, to get them for yourself. So you are now going to London, David, with Mr Quinion, to begin the world on your own account."

"In short, you are provided for," observed his sister; "and will please to do your duty."

Though I quite understood that the purpose of this announcement was to get rid of me, I have no distinct remembrance whether it pleased or frightened me. My impression is, that I was in a state of confusion about it, and, oscillating between the two points, touched neither. Nor had I much time for the clearing of my thoughts, as Mr Quinion was to go upon the morrow.

Behold me, on the morrow, in a much-worn little white hat, with a black crape round it for my mother, a black jacket, and a pair of hard stiff corduroy trousers—which Miss Murdstone considered the best armour for the legs in that fight with the world which was now to come off: behold me so attired, and with my little worldly all before me in a small trunk, sitting, a lone lorn child (as Mrs Gummidge might have said), in the post-chaise that was carrying Mr Quinion to the London coach at Yarmouth! See, how our house and church are lessening in the distance; how the grave beneath the tree is blotted out by intervening objects; how the spire points upwards from my old play-ground no more, and the sky is empty!

Chapter XI

I BEGIN LIFE ON MY OWN ACCOUNT,
AND DON'T LIKE IT

I KNOW enough of the world now, to have almost lost the capacity of being much surprised by anything; but it is matter of some surprise to me, even now, that I can have been so easily thrown away at such an age. A child of excellent abilities, and with strong powers of observation, quick, eager, delicate, and soon hurt bodily or mentally, it seems wonderful to me that nobody should have made any sign in my behalf. But none was made; and I became, at ten years old, a little labouring hind in the service of Murdstone and Grinby.

Murdstone and Grinby's warehouse was at the waterside. It was down in Blackfriars. Modern improvements have altered the place; but it was the last house at the bottom of a narrow street, curving down hill to the river, with some stairs at the end, where people took boat. It was a crazy old house with a wharf of its own, abutting on the water when the tide was in, and on the mud when the tide was out, and literally overrun with rats. Its panelled rooms, discoloured with the dirt and smoke of a hundred years, I dare say; its decaying floors and staircase; the squeaking and scuffling of the old grey rats down in the cellars; and the dirt and rottenness of the place; are things, not of many years ago, in my mind, but of the present instant. They are all before me, just as they were in the evil hour when I went among them for the first time, with my trembling hand in Mr Quinion's.

Murdstone and Grinby's trade was among a good many kinds of people, but an important branch of it was the supply of wines and spirits to certain packet ships. I forget now where they chiefly went, but I think there were some among them that made voyages both to the East and West Indies. I know that a great many empty bottles were one of the consequences of this traffic, and that certain men and boys were employed to examine them against the light, and reject those that were flawed, and to rinse and wash them. When the empty bottles ran short, there were labels to be pasted on full ones, or corks to be fitted to them, or seals to be put upon the corks, or finished bottles to be packed in casks. All this work was my work, and of the boys employed upon it I was one.

There were three or four of us, counting me. My working place was established in a corner of the warehouse, where Mr Quinion could see me, when he chose to stand up on the bottom rail of his stool in the counting-house, and look at me through a window above the desk. Hither, on the first morning of my so auspiciously beginning life on my own account, the oldest of the regular boys was summoned to show me my business. His name was Mick Walker, and he wore a ragged apron and a paper cap. He informed me that his father was a bargeman, and walked, in a black velvet head-dress, in the Lord Mayor's Show. He also informed me that our principal associate would be another boy whom he introduced by the—to me—extraordinary name of Mealy Potatoes. I discovered, however, that this youth had not been christened by that name, but that it had been bestowed upon him in the warehouse, on account of his complexion, which was pale or mealy. Mealy's father was a waterman, who had the additional distinction of being a fireman, and was engaged as such at one of the large theatres; where some young relation of Mealy's—I think his little sister—did Imps in the Pantomimes.

No words can express the secret agony of my soul as I sunk into this companionship; compared these henceforth everyday associates with those of my happier childhood—not to say with Steerforth, Traddles, and the rest of those boys; and felt my hopes of growing up to be a learned and distinguished man, crushed in my bosom. The deep remembrance of the sense I had, of being utterly without hope now; of the shame I felt in my position; of the misery it was to my young heart to believe that day by day what I had learned, and thought, and delighted in, and raised my fancy and my emulation up by, would pass away from me, little by little, never to be brought back any more; cannot be written. As often as Mick Walker went away in the course of that forenoon, I mingled my tears with the water in which I was washing the bottles; and sobbed as if there were a flaw in my own breast, and it were in danger of bursting.

The counting-house clock was at half past twelve, and there was general preparation for going to dinner, when Mr Quinion tapped at the counting-house window, and beckoned to me to go in. I went in, and found there a stoutish, middle-aged person, in a brown surtout and black tights and shoes, with no more hair upon his head (which was a large one, and very shining) than there is upon an egg, and with a very extensive face, which he turned full upon me. His clothes were shabby, but he had an imposing shirt-collar on. He carried a jaunty sort of a stick, with a large pair of rusty tassels to it; and a quizzing-glass hung outside his coat,—for ornament, I afterwards found, as he very seldom looked through it, and couldn't see anything when he did.

"This," said Mr Quinion, in allusion to myself, "is he."

"This," said the stranger, with a certain condescending roll in his voice, and a certain indescribable air of doing something genteel, which impressed me very much, "is Master Copperfield. I hope I see you well, sir?"

I said I was very well, and hoped he was. I was sufficiently ill at ease, Heaven knows; but it was not in my nature to complain much at that time of my life, so I said I was very well, and hoped he was.

"I am," said the stranger, "thank Heaven, quite well. I have received a letter from Mr Murdstone, in which he mentions that he would desire me to receive into an apartment in the rear of my house, which is at present unoccupied—and is, in short, to be let as a—in short," said the stranger, with a smile and in a burst of confidence, "as a bedroom—the young beginner whom I have now the pleasure to—" and the stranger waved his hand, and settled his chin in his shirt-collar.

"This is Mr Micawber," said Mr Quinion to me.

"Ahem!" said the stranger, "that is my name."

"Mr Micawber," said Mr Quinion, "is known to Mr Murdstone. He takes orders for us on commission, when he can get any. He has been written to by Mr Murdstone, on the subject of your lodgings, and he will receive you as a lodger."

"My address," said Mr Micawber, "is Windsor Terrace, City Road. I—in short," said Mr Micawber, with the same genteel air, and in another burst of confidence—"I live there."

I made him a bow.

"Under the impression," said Mr Micawber, "that your peregrinations in this metropolis have not as yet been extensive, and that you might have some difficulty in penetrating the arcana of the Modern Babylon in the direction of the City Road,—in short," said Mr Micawber, in another burst of confidence, "that you might lose yourself—I shall be happy to call this evening, and install you in the knowledge of the nearest way."

I thanked him with all my heart, for it was friendly in him to offer to take that trouble.

"At what hour," said Mr Micawber, "shall I—"

"At about eight," said Mr Quinion.

"At about eight," said Mr Micawber. "I beg to wish you good day, Mr Quinion. I will intrude no longer."

So he put on his hat, and went out with his cane under his arm: very upright, and humming a tune when he was clear of the counting-house.

Mr Quinion then formally engaged me to be as useful as I could in the warehouse of Murdstone and Grinby, at a salary, I think, of six shillings a week. I am not clear whether it was six or seven. I am inclined to believe, from my uncertainty on this head, that it was six at first and seven afterwards. He paid me a week down (from his own pocket, I believe), and I gave Mealy sixpence out of it to get my trunk carried to Windsor

Terrace that night: it being too heavy for my strength, small as it was. I paid sixpence more for my dinner, which was a meat pie and a turn at a neighbouring pump; and passed the hour which was allowed for that meal, in walking about the streets.

At the appointed time in the evening, Mr Micawber reappeared. I washed my hands and face, to do the greater honour to his gentility, and we walked to our house, as I suppose I must now call it, together; Mr Micawber impressing the name of streets, and the shapes of corner houses upon me, as we went along, that I might find my way back, easily, in the morning.

Arrived at this house in Windsor Terrace (which I noticed was shabby like himself, but also, like himself, made all the show it could), he presented me to Mrs Micawber, a thin and faded lady, not at all young, who was sitting in the parlour (the first floor was altogether unfurnished, and the blinds were kept down to delude the neighbours), with a baby at her breast. This baby was one of twins; and I may remark here that I hardly ever, in all my experience of the family, saw both the twins detached from Mrs Micawber at the same time. One of them was always taking refreshment.

There were two other children; Master Micawber, aged about four, and Miss Micawber, aged about three. These, and a dark-complexioned young woman, with a habit of snorting, who was servant to the family, and informed me, before half an hour had expired, that she was "a Orfling," and came from St Luke's workhouse, in the neighbourhood, completed the establishment. My room was at the top of the house, at the back: a close chamber; stencilled all over with an ornament which my young imagination represented as a blue muffin; and very scantily furnished.

"I never thought," said Mrs Micawber, when she came up, twin and all, to show me the apartment, and sat down to take breath, "before I was married, when I lived with papa and mama, that I should ever find it necessary to take a lodger. But Mr Micawber being in difficulties, all considerations of private feeling must give way."

I said: "Yes, ma'am."

"Mr Micawber's difficulties are almost overwhelming just at present," said Mrs Micawber; "and whether it is possible to bring him through them, I don't know. When I lived at home with papa and mama, I really should have hardly understood what the word meant, in the sense in which I now employ it, but experientia does it—as papa used to say."

I cannot satisfy myself whether she told me that Mr Micawber had been an officer in the Marines, or whether I have imagined it. I only know that I believe to this hour that he *was* in the Marines once upon a time, without knowing why. He was a sort of town traveller for a number of miscellaneous houses, now; but made little or nothing of it, I am afraid.

"If Mr Micawber's creditors *will not* give him time," said Mrs Micawber, "they must take the consequences; and the sooner they bring it to an issue the better. Blood cannot be obtained from a stone, neither can anything on account be obtained at present (not to mention law expenses) from Mr Micawber."

I never can quite understand whether my precocious self-dependence confused Mrs Micawber in reference to my age, or whether she was so full of the subject that she would have talked about it to the very twins if there had been nobody else to communicate with, but this was the strain in which she began, and she went on accordingly all the time I knew her.

Poor Mrs Micawber! She said she had tried to exert herself; and so, I have no doubt, she had. The centre of the street door was perfectly covered with a great brass-plate, on which was engraved "Mrs Micawber's Boarding Establishment for Young Ladies": but I never found that any young lady had ever been to school there; or that any young lady ever came, or proposed to come; or that the least preparation was ever made to receive any young lady. The only visitors I ever saw, or heard of, were creditors. *They* used to come at all hours, and some of them were quite ferocious. One dirty-faced man, I think he was a boot-maker, used to edge himself into the passage as early as seven o'clock in the morning, and call up the stairs to Mr Micawber—"Come! You ain't out yet, you know. Pay us, will you? Don't hide, you know; that's mean. I wouldn't be mean if I was you. Pay us, will you? You just pay us, d'ye hear? Come!" Receiving no answer to these taunts, he would mount in his wrath to the words "swindlers" and "robbers"; and these being ineffectual too, would sometimes go to the extremity of crossing the street, and roaring up at the windows of the second floor, where he knew Mr Micawber was. At these times, Mr Micawber would be transported with grief and mortification, even to the length (as I was once made aware by a scream from his wife) of making motions at himself with a razor; but within half-an-hour afterwards, he would polish up his shoes with extraordinary pains, and go out, humming a tune with a greater air of gentility than ever. Mrs Micawber was quite as elastic. I have known her to be thrown into fainting fits by the king's taxes at three o'clock, and to eat lamb chops, breaded, and drink warm ale (paid for with two tea-spoons that had gone to the pawnbroker's) at four. On one occasion, when an execution had just been put in, coming home through some chance as early as six o'clock, I saw her lying (of course with a twin) under the grate in a swoon, with her hair all torn about her face; but I never knew her more cheerful than she was, that very same night, over a veal cutlet before the kitchen fire, telling me stories about her papa and mama, and the company they used to keep.

In this house, and with this family, I passed my leisure time. My own exclusive breakfast of a penny loaf and a pennyworth of milk, I provided myself. I kept another small loaf, and a modicum of cheese, on a particular shelf of a particular cupboard, to make my supper on when I came back at night. This made a hole in the six or seven shillings, I know well; and I was out at the warehouse all day, and had to support myself on that money all the week. From Monday morning until Saturday night, I had no advice, no counsel, no encouragement, no consolation, no assistance, no support, of any kind, from anyone, that I can call to mind, as I hope to go to heaven!

I was so young and childish, and so little qualified—how could I be otherwise?—to undertake the whole charge of my own existence, that often, in going to Murdstone and Grinby's, of a morning, I could not resist the stale pastry put out for sale at half-price at the pastrycooks' doors, and spent in that the money I should have kept for my dinner. Then, I went without my dinner, or bought a roll or a slice of pudding. I remember two pudding shops, between which I was divided, according to my finances. One was in a court close to St Martin's Church— at the back of the church,—which is now removed altogether. The pudding at that shop was made of currants, and was rather a special pudding, but was dear, twopennyworth not being larger than a pennyworth of more ordinary pudding. A good shop for the latter was in the Strand—somewhere in that part which has been rebuilt since. It was a stout pale pudding, heavy and flabby, and with great flat raisins in it, stuck in whole at wide distances apart. It came up hot at about my time every day, and many a day did I dine off it. When I dined regularly and handsomely, I had a saveloy and a penny loaf, or a fourpenny plate of red beef from a cook's shop; or a plate of bread and cheese and a glass of beer, from a miserable old public-house opposite our place of business, called the Lion, or the Lion and something else that I have forgotten. Once, I remember carrying my own bread (which I had brought from home in the morning) under my arm, wrapped in a piece of paper, like a book, and going to a famous alamode beef-house near Drury Lane, and ordering a "small plate" of that delicacy to eat with it. What the waiter thought of such a strange little apparition coming in all alone, I don't know; but I can see him now, staring at me as I ate my dinner, and bringing up the other waiter to look. I gave him a halfpenny for himself, and I wish he hadn't taken it.

We had half-an-hour, I think, for tea. When I had money enough, I used to get half-a-pint of ready-made coffee and a slice of bread and butter. When I had none, I used to look at a venison shop in Fleet Street; or I have strolled, at such a time, as far as Covent Garden Market, and stared at the pineapples. I was fond of wandering about the Adelphi, because it was a mysterious place, with those dark arches. I see myself emerging one evening from some of these arches, on a little public-house close to the river, with an open space before it, where some coal-heavers were dancing; to look at whom I sat down upon a bench. I wonder what they thought of me!

I was such a child, and so little, that frequently when I went into the bar of a strange public-house for a glass of ale or porter, to moisten what I had had for dinner, they were afraid to give it me. I remember one hot evening I went into the bar of a public-house, and said to the landlord:

"What is your best—your *very best*—ale a glass?" For it was a special occasion. I don't know what. It may have been my birthday.

"Twopence-halfpenny," says the landlord, "is the price of the Genuine Stunning ale."

"Then," says I, producing the money, "just draw me a glass of the Genuine Stunning, if you please, with a good head to it."

The landlord looked at me in return over the bar, from head to foot, with a strange smile on his face; and instead of drawing the beer, looked round the screen and said something to his wife. She came out from behind it, with her work in her hand, and joined him in surveying me. Here we stand, all three, before me now. The landlord in his shirt-sleeves, leaning against the bar window-frame; his wife looking over the little half-door; and I, in some confusion, looking up at them from outside the partition. They asked me a good many questions; as, what my name was, how old I was, where I lived, how I was employed, and how I came there. To all of which, that I might commit nobody, I invented, I am afraid, appropriate answers. They served me with the ale, though I suspect it was not the Genuine Stunning; and the landlord's wife, opening the little half-door of the bar, and bending down, gave me my money back, and gave me a kiss that was half admiring and half compassionate, but all womanly and good, I am sure.

I know I do not exaggerate, unconsciously and unintentionally, the scantiness of my resources or the difficulties of my life. I know that if a shilling were given me by Mr Quinion at any time, I spent it in a dinner or a tea. I know that I worked, from morning until night, with common men and boys, a shabby child. I know that I lounged about the streets, insufficiently and unsatisfactorily fed. I know that, but for the mercy of God, I might easily have been, for any care that was taken of me, a little robber or a little vagabond.

Yet I held some station at Murdstone and Grinby's too. Besides that Mr Quinion did what a careless man so occupied, and dealing with a thing so anomalous, could, to treat me as one upon a different footing from the rest, I never said, to man or boy, how it was that I came to be there, or gave the least indication of being sorry that I was there. That I suffered in secret, and that I suffered exquisitely, no one ever knew but I. How much I suffered, it is, as I have said already, utterly beyond my power to tell. But I kept my own counsel, and I did my work. I knew from the first, that, if I could not do my work as well as any of the rest, I could not hold myself above slight and contempt. I soon became at least as expeditious and as skilful as either of the other boys. Though perfectly familiar with them, my conduct and manner were different enough from theirs to place a space between us. They and the men generally spoke of me as "the little gent," or "the young Suffolker." A certain man named Gregory, who was foreman of the packers, and another named Tripp, who was the carman, and wore a red jacket, used to address me sometimes as "David" but I think it was mostly when we were very confidential, and when I had made some efforts to entertain them, over our work, with some results of the old readings; which were fast perishing out of my remembrance. Mealy Potatoes uprose once, and rebelled against my being so distinguished; but Mick Walker settled him in no time.

My rescue from this kind of existence I considered quite hopeless, and abandoned, as such, altogether. I am solemnly convinced that I never for one hour was reconciled to it, or was otherwise than miserably unhappy; but I bore it; and even to Peggotty, partly for the love of her and partly for shame, never in any letter (though many passed between us) revealed the truth.

Mr Micawber's difficulties were an addition to the distressed state of my mind. In my forlorn state I became quite attached to the family, and used to walk about, busy with Mrs Micawber's calculations of ways and means, and heavy with the weight of Mr Micawber's debts. On a Saturday night, which was my grand treat,—partly because it was a great thing to walk home with six or seven shillings in my pocket, looking into the shops and thinking what such a sum would buy, and partly because I went home early,—Mrs Micawber would make the most heart-rending confidences to me; also on a Sunday morning, when I mixed the portion of tea or coffee I had bought over-night, in a little shaving-pot, and sat late at my breakfast. It was nothing at all unusual for Mr Micawber to sob violently at the beginning of one of these Saturday night conversations, and sing about Jack's delight being his lovely Nan, towards the end of it. I have known him come home to supper with a flood of tears, and a declaration that nothing was now left but a jail; and go to bed making a calculation of the expense of putting bow-windows to the house, "in case anything turned up," which was his favourite expression. And Mrs Micawber was just the same.

A curious equality of friendship, originating, I suppose, in our respective circumstances, sprung up between me and these people, notwithstanding the ludicrous disparity in our years. But I never allowed myself to be prevailed upon to accept any invitation to eat and drink with them out of their stock (knowing that they got on badly with the butcher and baker, and had often not too much for themselves), until Mrs Micawber took me into her entire confidence. This she did one evening as follows:

"Master Copperfield," said Mrs Micawber, "I make no stranger of you, and therefore do not hesitate to say that Mr Micawber's difficulties are coming to a crisis."

It made me very miserable to hear it, and I looked at Mrs Micawber's red eyes with the utmost sympathy.

"With the exception of the heel of a Dutch cheese—which is not adapted to the wants of a young family"—said Mrs Micawber, "there is really not a scrap of anything in the larder. I was accustomed to speak of the larder when I lived with papa and mama, and I use the word almost unconsciously. What I mean to express is, that there is nothing to eat in the house."

"Dear me!" I said, in great concern.

I had two or three shillings of my week's money in my pocket—from which I presume that it must have been on a Wednesday night when we held this conversation—

and I hastily produced them, and with heartfelt emotion begged Mrs Micawber to accept of them as a loan. But that lady, kissing me, and making me put them back in my pocket, replied that she couldn't think of it.

"No, my dear Master Copperfield," said she, "far be it from my thoughts! But you have a discretion beyond your years, and can render me another kind of service, if you will; and a service I will thankfully accept of."

I begged Mrs Micawber to name it.

"I have parted with the plate myself," said Mrs Micawber. "Six tea, two salt, and a pair of sugars, I have at different times borrowed money on, in secret, with my own hands. But the twins are a great tie; and to me, with my recollections, of papa and mama, these transactions are very painful. There are still a few trifles that we could part with. Mr Micawber's feelings would never allow *him* to dispose of them; and Clickett"—this was the girl from the workhouse—"being of a vulgar mind, would take painful liberties if so much confidence was reposed in her. Master Copperfield, if I might ask you—"

I understood Mrs Micawber now, and begged her to make use of me to any extent. I began to dispose of the more portable articles of property that very evening; and went out on a similar expedition almost every morning, before I went to Murdstone and Grinby's.

Mr Micawber had a few books on a little chiffonier, which he called the library; and those went first. I carried them, one after another, to a bookstall in the City Road—one part of which, near our house, was almost all bookstalls and bird shops then—and sold them for whatever they would bring. The keeper of this bookstall, who lived in a little house behind it, used to get tipsy every night, and to be violently scolded by his wife every morning. More than once, when I went there early, I had audience of him in a turn-up bedstead, with a cut in his forehead or a black eye, bearing witness to his excesses over-night (I am afraid he was quarrelsome in his drink), and he, with a shaking hand, endeavouring to find the needful shillings in one or other of the pockets of his clothes, which lay upon the floor, while his wife, with a baby in her arms and her shoes down at heel, never left off rating him. Sometimes he had lost his money, and then he would ask me to call again; but his wife had always got some—had taken his, I dare say, while he was drunk—and secretly completed the bargain on the stairs, as we went down together.

At the pawnbroker's shop, too, I began to be very well known. The principal gentleman who officiated behind the counter, took a good deal of notice of me; and often got me, I recollect, to decline a Latin noun or adjective, or to conjugate a Latin verb, in his ear, while he transacted my business. After all these occasions Mrs Micawber made a little treat, which was generally a supper; and there was a peculiar relish in these meals which I well remember.

At last Mr Micawber's difficulties came to a crisis, and he was arrested early one morning, and carried over to the King's Bench Prison in the Borough. He told me, as he went out of the house, that the God of day had now gone down upon him—and I really thought his heart was broken and mine too. But I heard, afterwards, that he was seen to play a lively game at skittles, before noon.

On the first Sunday after he was taken there, I was to go and see him, and have dinner with him. I was to ask my way to such a place, and just short of that place I should see such another place, and just short of that I should see a yard, which I was to cross, and keep straight on until I saw a turnkey. All this I did; and when at last I did see a turnkey (poor little fellow that I was!), and thought how, when Roderick Random was in a debtors' prison, there was a man there with nothing on him but an old rug, the turnkey swam before my dimmed eyes and my beating heart.

Mr Micawber was waiting for me within the gate, and we went up to his room (top story but one), and cried very much. He solemnly conjured me, I remember, to take warning by his fate; and to observe that if a man had twenty pounds a-year for his income, and spent nineteen pounds nineteen shillings and sixpence, he would be happy, but that if he spent twenty pounds one he would be miserable. After which he borrowed a shilling of me for porter, gave me a written order on Mrs Micawber for the amount, and put away his pocket-handkerchief, and cheered up.

We sat before a little fire, with two bricks put within the rusted grate, one on each side, to prevent its burning too many coals; until another debtor, who shared the room with Mr Micawber, came in from the bakehouse with the loin of mutton which was our joint-stock repast. Then I was sent up to "Captain Hopkins" in the room overhead, with Mr Micawber's compliments, and I was his young friend, and would Captain Hopkins lend me a knife and fork.

Captain Hopkins lent me the knife and fork, with his compliments to Mr Micawber. There was a very dirty lady in his little room, and two wan girls, his daughters, with shock heads of hair. I thought it was better to borrow Captain Hopkins's knife and fork, than Captain Hopkins's comb. The Captain himself was in the last extremity of shabbiness, with large whiskers, and an old, old brown great-coat with no other coat below it. I saw his bed rolled up in a corner; and what plates and dishes and pots he had, on a shelf; and I divined (God knows how) that though the two girls with the shock heads of hair were Captain Hopkins's children, the dirty lady was not married to Captain Hopkins. My timid station on his threshold was not occupied more than a couple of minutes at most; but I came down again with all this in my knowledge, as surely as the knife and fork were in my hand.

There was something gipsy-like and agreeable in the dinner, after all. I took back Captain Hopkins's knife and fork early in the afternoon, and went home to comfort Mrs Micawber with an account of my visit. She fainted when she saw me return, and made a little jug of egg-hot afterwards to console us while we talked it over.

I don't know how the household furniture came to be sold for the family benefit, or who sold it, except that *I* did not. Sold it was, however, and carried away in a van; except the bed, a few chairs, and the kitchen table. With these possessions we en-camped, as it were, in the two parlours of the emptied house in Windsor Terrace; Mrs Micawber, the children, the Orfling, and myself; and lived in those rooms night and day. I have no idea for how long, though it seems to me for a long time. At last Mrs Micawber resolved to move into the prison, where Mr Micawber had now secured a room to himself. So I took the key of the house to the landlord, who was very glad to get it; and the beds were sent over to the King's Bench, except mine, for which a little room was hired outside the walls in the neighbourhood of that Institution, very much to my satisfaction, since the Micawbers and I had become too used to one another, in our troubles, to part. The Orfling was likewise accommodated with an inexpensive lodging in the same neighbourhood. Mine was a quiet back-garret with a sloping roof, com-manding a pleasant prospect of a timberyard; and when I took possession of it, with the reflection that Mr Micawber's troubles had come to a crisis at last, I thought it quite a paradise.

All this time I was working at Murdstone and Grinby's in the same common way, and with the same common companions, and with the same sense of unmerited degra-dation as at first. But I never, happily for me no doubt, made a single acquaintance, or spoke to any of the many boys whom I saw daily in going to the warehouse, in coming from it, and in prowling about the streets at meal-times. I led the same secretly unhappy life; but I led it in the same lonely, self-reliant manner. The only changes I am conscious of are, firstly, that I had grown more shabby, and secondly, that I was now relieved of much of the weight of Mr and Mrs Micawber's cares; for some relatives or friends had engaged to help them at their present pass, and they lived more comfortably in the prison than they had lived for a long while out of it. I used to breakfast with them now, in virtue of some arrangement, of which I have forgotten the details. I forget, too, at what hour the gates were opened in the morning, admitting of my going in; but I know that I was often up at six o'clock, and that my favourite lounging-place in the interval was old London Bridge, where I was wont to sit in one of the stone recesses, watching the people going by, or to look over the balustrades at the sun shining in the water, and lighting up the golden flame on the top of the Monument. The Orfling met me here sometimes, to be told some astonishing fictions respecting the wharves and the Tower; of which I can say no more than that I hope I believed them myself. In the evening I used to go back to the prison, and walk up and down the parade with Mr Micawber; or play casino with Mrs Micawber, and hear reminiscences of her papa and mama. Whether Mr Murdstone knew where I was, I am unable to say. I never told them at Murdstone and Grinby's.

Mr Micawber's affairs, although past their crisis, were very much involved by reason of a certain "Deed," of which I used to hear a great deal, and which I suppose, now, to have been some former composition with his creditors, though I was so far from being clear about it then, that I am conscious of having confounded it with those demoniacal parchments which are held to have, once upon a time, obtained to a great extent in Germany. At last this document appeared to be got out of the way, somehow; at all events it ceased to be the rock-ahead it had been; and Mrs Micawber informed me that "her family" had decided that Mr Micawber should apply for his release under the Insolvent Debtors Act, which would set him free, she expected, in about six weeks.

"And then," said Mr Micawber, who was present, "I have no doubt I shall, please Heaven, begin to be beforehand with the world, and to live in a perfectly new manner, if—in short, if anything turns up."

By way of going in for anything that might be on the cards, I call to mind that Mr Micawber, about this time, composed a petition to the House of Commons, praying for an alteration in the law of imprisonment for debt. I set down this remembrance here, because it is an instance to myself of the manner in which I fitted my old books to my altered life, and made stories for myself, out of the streets, and out of men and women; and how some main points in the character I shall unconsciously develop, I suppose, in writing my life, were gradually forming all this while.

There was a club in the prison, in which Mr Micawber, as a gentleman, was a great authority. Mr Micawber had stated his idea of this petition to the club, and the club had strongly approved of the same. Wherefore Mr Micawber (who was a thoroughly good-natured man, and as active a creature about everything but his own affairs as ever existed, and never so happy as when he was busy about something that could never be of any profit to him) set to work at the petition, invented it, engrossed it on an immense sheet of paper, spread it out on a table, and appointed a time for all the club, and all within the walls if they chose, to come up to his room and sign it.

When I heard of this approaching ceremony, I was so anxious to see them all come in, one after another, though I knew the greater part of them already, and they me, that I got an hour's leave of absence from Murdstone and Grinby's, and established myself in a corner for that purpose. As many of the principal members of the club as could be got into the small room without filling it, supported Mr Micawber in front of the petition, while my old friend Captain Hopkins (who had washed himself, to do honour to so solemn an occasion) stationed himself close to it, to read it to all who were unacquainted with its contents. The door was then thrown open, and the general population began to come in, in a long file: several waiting outside, while one entered, affixed his signature, and went out. To everybody in succession, Captain Hopkins said: "Have you read it?"—"No."—"Would you like to hear it read?" If he weakly showed the least disposition to hear it, Captain Hopkins, in a loud sonorous voice, gave him every word of it. The Captain would have read it twenty thousand times, if twenty thousand people would have heard him, one by one. I remember a certain luscious roll he gave to such phrases as "The people's representatives in Parliament assembled," "Your petitioners therefore humbly approach your honourable house," "His gracious Majesty's unfortunate sub-jects," as if the words were something real in his mouth, and delicious to taste; Mr Micawber, meanwhile, listening with a little of an author's vanity, and contemplating (not severely) the spikes on the opposite wall.

As I walked to and fro daily between Southwark and Blackfriars, and lounged about at meal-times in obscure streets, the stones of which may, for anything I know, be worn at this moment by my childish feet, I wonder how many of these people were wanting in the crowd that used to come filing before me in review again, to the echo of Captain Hopkins's voice! When my thoughts go back, now, to that slow agony of my youth, I wonder how much of the histories I invented for such people hangs like a mist of fancy over well-remembered facts! When I tread the old ground, I do not wonder that I seem to see and pity, going on before me, an innocent romantic boy, making his imaginative world out of such strange experiences and sordid things!

Chapter XII

LIKING LIFE ON MY OWN ACCOUNT NO BETTER, I FORM A GREAT RESOLUTION

IN due time, Mr Micawber's petition was ripe for hearing; and that gentleman was ordered to be discharged under the Act, to my great joy. His creditors were not implacable; and Mrs Micawber informed me that even the revengeful boot-maker had declared in open court that he bore him no malice, but that when money was owing to him he liked to be paid. He said he thought it was human nature.

Mr Micawber returned to the King's Bench when his case was over, as some fees were to be settled, and some formalities observed, before he could be actually released. The club received him with transport, and held an harmonic meeting that evening in his honour; while Mrs Micawber and I had a lamb's fry in private, surrounded by the sleeping family.

"On such an occasion I will give you, Master Copperfield," said Mrs Micawber, "in a little more flip," for we had been having some already, "the memory of my papa and mama."

"Are they dead, ma'am?" I inquired, after drinking the toast in a wine-glass.

"My mama departed this life," said Mrs Micawber, "before Mr Micawber's difficulties commenced, or at least before they became pressing. My papa lived to bail Mr Micawber several times, and then expired, regretted by a numerous circle."

Mrs Micawber shook her head, and dropped a pious tear upon the twin who happened to be in hand.

As I could hardly hope for a more favourable opportunity of putting a question in which I had a near interest, I said to Mrs Micawber:

"May I ask, ma'am, what you and Mr Micawber intend to do, now that Mr Micawber is out of his difficulties, and at liberty? Have you settled yet?"

"My family," said Mrs Micawber, who always said those two words with an air, though I never could discover who came under the denomination, "my family are of opinion that Mr Micawber should quit London, and exert his talents in the country. Mr Micawber is a man of great talent, Master Copperfield."

I said I was sure of that.

"Of great talent," repeated Mrs Micawber. "My family are of opinion, that, with a little interest, something might be done for a man of his ability in the Custom House. The influence of my family being local, it is their wish that Mr Micawber should go down to Plymouth. They think it indispensable that he should be upon the spot."

"That he may be ready?" I suggested.

"Exactly," returned Mrs Micawber. "That he may be ready—in case of anything turning up."

"And do you go too, ma'am?"

The events of the day, in combination with the twins, if not with the flip, had made Mrs Micawber hysterical, and she shed tears as she replied:

"I never will desert Mr Micawber. Mr Micawber may have concealed his difficulties from me in the first instance, but his sanguine temper may have led him to expect that he would overcome them. The pearl necklace and bracelets which I inherited from mama, have been disposed of for less than half their value; and the set of coral, which was the wedding gift of my papa, has been actually thrown away for nothing. But I never will desert Mr Micawber. No!" cried Mrs Micawber, more affected than before, "I never will do it! It's of no use asking me!"

I felt quite uncomfortable—as if Mrs Micawber supposed I had asked her to do anything of the sort!—and sat looking at her in alarm.

"Mr Micawber has his faults. I do not deny that he is improvident. I do not deny that he has kept me in the dark as to his resources and his liabilities both," she went on, looking at the wall; "but I never will desert Mr Micawber!"

Mrs Micawber having now raised her voice into a perfect scream, I was so frightened that I ran off to the club-room, and disturbed Mr Micawber in the act of presiding at a long table, and leading the chorus of

> Gee up, Dobbin,
> Gee ho, Dobbin,
> Gee up, Dobbin,
> Gee up, and gee ho-o-o!

—with the tidings that Mrs Micawber was in an alarming state, upon which he immediately burst into tears, and came away with me with his waistcoat full of the heads and tails of shrimps, of which he had been partaking.

"Emma, my angel!" cried Mr Micawber, running into the room; "what is the matter?"

"I never will desert you, Micawber!" she exclaimed.

"My life!" said Mr Micawber, taking her in his arms. "I am perfectly aware of it."

"He is the parent of my children! He is the father of my twins! He is the husband of my affections," cried Mrs Micawber, struggling; "and I ne—ver—will—desert Mr Micawber!"

Mr Micawber was so deeply affected by this proof of her devotion (as to me, I was dissolved in tears), that he hung over her in a passionate manner, imploring her to look up, and to be calm. But the more he asked Mrs Micawber to look up, the more she fixed her eyes on nothing; and the more he asked her to compose herself, the more she wouldn't. Consequently Mr Micawber was soon so overcome, that he mingled his tears with hers and mine; until he begged me to do him the favour of taking a chair on the staircase, while he got her into bed. I would have taken my leave for the night, but he would not hear of my doing that until the strangers' bell should ring. So I sat at the staircase window, until he came out with another chair and joined me.

"How is Mrs Micawber now, sir?" I said.

"Very low," said Mr Micawber, shaking his head; "reaction. Ah, this has been a dreadful day! We stand alone now—everything is gone from us!"

Mr Micawber pressed my hand, and groaned, and afterwards shed tears. I was greatly touched, and disappointed too, for I had expected that we should be quite gay on this happy and long-looked-for occasion. But Mr and Mrs Micawber were so used to their old difficulties, I think, that they felt quite shipwrecked when they came to consider that they were released from them. All their elasticity was departed, and I never saw them half so wretched as on this night; insomuch that when the bell rang, and Mr Micawber walked with me to the lodge, and parted from me there with a blessing, I felt quite afraid to leave him by himself, he was so profoundly miserable.

But through all the confusion and lowness of spirits in which we had been, so unexpectedly to me, involved, I plainly discerned that Mr and Mrs Micawber and their family were going away from London, and that a parting between us was near at hand. It was in my walk home that night, and in the sleepless hours which followed when I lay in bed, that the thought first occurred to me—though I don't know how it came into my head—which afterwards shaped itself into a settled resolution.

I had grown to be so accustomed to the Micawbers, and had been so intimate with them in their distresses, and was so utterly friendless without them, that the prospect of being thrown upon some new shift for a lodging, and going once more among unknown people, was like being that moment turned adrift into my present life, with such a knowledge of it ready made as experience had given me. All the sensitive feelings it wounded so cruelly, all the shame and misery it kept alive within my breast, became more poignant as I thought of this; and I determined that the life was unendurable.

That there was no hope of escape from it, unless the escape was my own act, I knew quite well. I rarely heard from Miss Murdstone, and never from Mr Murdstone: but two or three parcels of made or mended clothes had come up for me, consigned to Mr Quinion, and in each there was a scrap of paper to the effect that J. M. trusted D. C. was applying himself to business, and devoting himself wholly to his duties—not the least hint of my ever being anything else than the common drudge into which I was fast settling down.

The very next day showed me, while my mind was in the first agitation of what it had conceived, that Mrs Micawber had not spoken of their going away without warrant. They took a lodging in the house where I lived, for a week; at the expiration of which time they were to start for Plymouth. Mr Micawber himself came down to the counting-house, in the afternoon, to tell Mr Quinion that he must relinquish me on the day of his departure, and to give me a high character, which I am sure I deserved. And Mr Quinion, calling in Tipp the carman, who was a married man, and had a room to let, quartered me prospectively on him—by our mutual consent, as he had every reason to think; for I said nothing, though my resolution was now taken.

I passed my evenings with Mr and Mrs Micawber, during the remaining term of our residence under the same roof; and I think we became fonder of one another as the time went on. On the last Sunday, they invited me to dinner; and we had a loin of pork and apple sauce, and a pudding. I had bought a spotted wooden horse over-night as a parting gift to little Wilkins Micawber—that was the boy—and a doll for little Emma. I had also bestowed a shilling on the Orfling, who was about to be disbanded.

We had a very pleasant day, though we were all in a tender state about our approaching separation.

"I shall never, Master Copperfield," said Mrs Micawber, "revert to the period when Mr Micawber was in difficulties, without thinking of you. Your conduct has always been of the most delicate and obliging description. You have never been a lodger. You have been a friend."

"My dear," said Mr Micawber; "Copperfield," for so he had been accustomed to call me, of late, "has a heart to feel for the distresses of his fellow-creatures when they are behind a cloud, and a head to plan, and a hand to—in short, a general ability to dispose of such available property as could be made away with."

I expressed my sense of this commendation, and said I was very sorry we were going to lose one another.

"My dear young friend," said Mr Micawber, "I am older than you; a man of some experience in life, and—and of some experience, in short, in difficulties, generally speaking. At present, and until something turns up (which I am, I may say, hourly expecting), I have nothing to bestow but advice. Still my advice is so far worth taking, that—in short, that I have never taken it myself, and am the"—here Mr Micawber, who had been beaming and smiling, all over his head and face, up to the present moment, checked himself and frowned—"the miserable wretch you behold."

"My dear Micawber!" urged his wife.

"I say," returned Mr Micawber, quite forgetting himself, and smiling again, "the miserable wretch you behold. My advice is, never do tomorrow what you can do today. Procrastination is the thief of time. Collar him!"

"My poor papa's maxim," Mrs Micawber observed.

"My dear," said Mr Micawber, "your papa was very well in his way, and Heaven forbid that I should disparage him. Take him for all in all, we ne'er shall—in short, make the acquaintance, probably, of anybody else possessing, at his time of life, the same legs for gaiters, and able to read the same description of print, without spectacles. But he applied that maxim to our marriage, my dear; and that was so far prematurely entered into, in consequence, that I never recovered the expense."

Mr Micawber looked aside at Mrs Micawber, and added: "Not that I am sorry for it. Quite the contrary, my love." After which, he was grave for a minute or so.

"My other piece of advice, Copperfield," said Mr Micawber, "you know. Annual income twenty pounds, annual expenditure nineteen nineteen and six, result happiness. Annual income twenty pounds, annual expenditure twenty pounds ought and six, result misery. The blossom is blighted, the leaf is withered, the god of day goes down upon the dreary scene, and—and in short you are for ever floored. As I am!"

To make his example the more impressive, Mr Micawber drank a glass of punch with an air of great enjoyment and satisfaction, and whistled the College Hornpipe.

I did not fail to assure him that I would store these precepts in my mind, though indeed I had no need to do so, for, at the time, they affected me visibly. Next morning I met the whole family at the coach office, and saw them, with a desolate heart, take their places outside, at the back.

"Master Copperfield," said Mrs Micawber, "God bless you! I never can forget all that, you know, and I never would if I could."

"Copperfield," said Mr Micawber, "farewell! Every happiness and prosperity! If, in the progress of revolving years, I could persuade myself that my blighted destiny had been a warning to you, I should feel that I had not occupied another man's place in existence altogether in vain. In case of anything turning up (of which I am rather confident), I shall be extremely happy if it should be in my power to improve your prospects."

I think, as Mrs Micawber sat at the back of the coach, with the children, and I stood in the road looking wistfully at them, a mist cleared from her eyes, and she saw what a little creature I really was. I think so, because she beckoned to me to climb up, with quite a new and motherly expression in her face, and put her arm round my neck, and gave me just such a kiss as she might have given to her own boy. I had barely time to get down again before the coach started, and I could hardly see the family for the handkerchiefs they waved. It was gone in a minute. The Orfling and I stood looking vacantly at each other in the middle of the road, and then shook hands and said good-bye; she going back, I suppose, to St Luke's workhouse, as I went to begin my weary day at Murdstone and Grinby's.

But with no intention of passing many more weary days there. No. I had resolved to run away.—To go, by some means or other, down into the country, to the only relation I had in the world, and tell my story to my aunt, Miss Betsey.

I have already observed that I don't know how this desperate idea came into my brain. But, once there, it remained there; and hardened into a purpose than which I have never entertained a more determined purpose in my life. I am far from sure that I believed there was anything hopeful in it, but my mind was thoroughly made up that it must be carried into execution.

Again, and again, and a hundred times again, since the night when the thought had first occurred to me and banished sleep, I had gone over that old story of my poor mother's about my birth, which it had been one of my great delights in the old time to hear her tell, and which I knew by heart. My aunt walked into that story, and walked out of it, a dread and awful personage; but there was one little trait in her behaviour which I liked to dwell on, and which gave me some faint shadow of encouragement. I could not forget how my mother had thought that she felt her touch her pretty hair with no ungentle hand; and though it might have been altogether my mother's fancy, and might have had no foundation whatever in fact, I made a little picture, out of it, of my terrible aunt relenting towards the girlish beauty that I recollected so well and loved so much, which softened the whole narrative. It is very possible that it had been in my mind a long time, and had gradually engendered my determination.

As I did not even know where Miss Betsey lived, I wrote a long letter to Peggotty, and asked her, incidentally, if she remembered; pretending that I had heard of such a lady living at a certain place I named at random, and had a curiosity to know if it were the same. In the course of that letter, I told Peggotty that I had a particular occasion for half a guinea; and that if she could lend me that sum until I could repay it, I should be very much obliged to her, and would tell her afterwards what I had wanted it for.

Peggotty's answer soon arrived, and was, as usual, full of affectionate devotion. She enclosed the half guinea (I was afraid she must have had a world of trouble to get it out of Mr Barkis's box), and told me that Miss Betsey lived near Dover, but whether at Dover itself, at Hythe, Sandgate, or Folkestone, she could not say. One of our men, however, informing me on my asking him about these places, that they were all close together, I deemed this enough for my object, and resolved to set out at the end of that week.

Being a very honest little creature, and unwilling to disgrace the memory I was going to leave behind me at Murdstone and Grinby's, I considered myself bound to remain until Saturday night; and, as I had been paid a week's wages in advance when I first came there, not to present myself in the counting-house at the usual hour, to receive my stipend. For this express reason, I had borrowed the half-guinea, that I might not be without a fund for my travelling-expenses. Accordingly, when the Saturday night came, and we were all waiting in the warehouse to be paid, and Tipp the carman, who always took precedence, went in first to draw his money, I shook Mick Walker by the hand; asked him, when it came to his turn to be paid, to say to Mr Quinion that I had gone to move my box to Tipp's; and, bidding a last good night to Mealy Potatoes, ran away.

My box was at my old lodging, over the water, and I had written a direction for it on the back of one of our address cards that we nailed on the casks: "Master David, to be left till called for, at the Coach Office, Dover." This I had in my pocket ready to put on the box, after I should have got it out of the house; and as I went towards my lodging, I looked about me for someone who would help me to carry it to the booking-office.

There was a long-legged young man with a very little empty donkey-cart, standing near the Obelisk, in the Blackfriars Road, whose eye I caught as I was going by, and who, addressing me as "Sixpenn'orth of bad ha'pence," hoped "I should know him agin to swear to"—in allusion, I have no doubt, to my staring at him. I stopped to assure him that I had not done so in bad manners, but uncertain whether he might or might not like a job.

"Wot job?" said the long-legged young man.

"To move a box," I answered.

"Wot box?" said the long-legged young man.

I told him mine, which was down that street there, and which I wanted him to take to the Dover coach office for sixpence.

"Done with you for a tanner!" said the long-legged young man, and directly got upon his cart, which was nothing but a large wooden-tray on wheels, and rattled away at such a rate, that it was as much as I could do to keep pace with the donkey.

There was a defiant manner about this young man, and particularly about the way in which he chewed straw as he spoke to me, that I did not much like; as the bargain was made, however, I took him upstairs to the room I was leaving, and we brought the box down, and put it on his cart. Now, I was unwilling to put the direction-card on there, lest any of my landlord's family should fathom what I was doing, and detain me; so I said to the young man that I would be glad if he would stop for a minute, when he came to the dead-wall of the King's Bench prison. The words were no sooner out of my mouth, than he rattled away as if he, my box, the cart, and the donkey, were all equally mad; and I was quite out of breath with running and calling after him, when I caught him at the place appointed.

Being much flushed and excited, I tumbled my half-guinea out of my pocket in pulling the card out. I put it in my mouth for safety, and though my hands trembled a good deal, had just tied the card on very much to my satisfaction, when I felt myself violently, chucked under the chin by the long-legged young man, and saw my half-guinea fly out of my mouth into his hand.

"Wot!" said the young man, seizing me by my jacket collar, with a frightful grin. "This is a pollis case, is it? You're a-going to bolt, are you? Come to the pollis, you young warmin, come to the pollis!"

"You give me my money back, if you please," said I, very much frightened; "and leave me alone."

"Come to the pollis!" said the young man. "You shall prove it yourn to the pollis."

"Give me my box and money, will you," I cried, bursting into tears.

The young man still replied: "Come to the pollis!" and was dragging me against the donkey in a violent manner, as if there were any affinity between that animal and a magistrate, when he changed his mind, jumped into the cart, sat upon my box, and, exclaiming that he would drive to the pollis straight, rattled away harder than ever.

I ran after him as fast as I could, but I had no breath to call out with, and should not have dared to call out, now, if I had. I narrowly escaped being run over, twenty times at least, in half a mile. Now I lost him, now I saw him, now I lost him, now I was cut at with a whip, now shouted at, now down in the mud, now up again, now running into somebody's arms, now running headlong at a post. At length, confused by fright and heat, and doubting whether half London might not by this time be turning out for my apprehension, I left the young man to go where he would with my box and money; and, panting and crying, but never stopping, faced about for Greenwich, which I had understood was on the Dover Road: taking very little more out of the world, towards the retreat of my aunt, Miss Betsey, than I had brought into it, on the night when my arrival gave her so much umbrage.

Chapter XIII

THE SEQUEL OF MY RESOLUTION

FOR anything I know, I may have had some wild idea of running all the way to Dover, when I gave up the pursuit of the young man with the donkey-cart, and started for Greenwich. My scattered senses were soon collected as to that point, if I had; for I came to a stop in the Kent Road, at a terrace with a piece of water before it, and a great foolish image in the middle, blowing a dry shell. Here I sat down on a doorstep, quite spent and exhausted with the efforts I had already made, and with hardly breath enough to cry for the loss of my box and half-guinea.

It was by this time dark; I heard the clocks strike ten, as I sat resting. But it was a summer night, fortunately, and fine weather. When I had recovered my breath, and had got rid of a stifling sensation in my throat, I rose up and went on. In the midst of my distress, I had no notion of going back. I doubt if I should have had any, though there had been a Swiss snow-drift in the Kent Road.

But my standing possessed of only three-halfpence in the world (and I am sure I wonder how *they* came to be left in my pocket on a Saturday night!) troubled me none the less because I went on. I began to picture to myself, as a scrap of newspaper intelligence, my being found dead in a day or two, under some hedge; and I trudged on miserably, though as fast as I could, until I happened to pass a little shop, where it was written up that ladies' and gentlemen's wardrobes were bought, and that the best price was given for rags, bones, and kitchen-stuff. The master of this shop was sitting at the door in his shirt-sleeves, smoking; and as there were a great many coats and pairs of trousers dangling from the low ceiling, and only two feeble candles burning inside to show what they were, I fancied that he looked like a man of a revengeful disposition, who had hung all his enemies, and was enjoying himself.

My late experiences with Mr and Mrs Micawber suggested to me that here might be a means of keeping off the wolf for a little while. I went up the next by-street, took off my waistcoat, rolled it neatly under my arm, and came back to the shop door. "If you please, sir," I said, "I am to sell this for a fair price."

Mr Dolloby—Dolloby was the name over the shop door, at least—took the waist-coat, stood his pipe on its head against the door-post, went into the shop, followed by me, snuffed the two candles with his fingers, spread the waistcoat on the counter, and looked at it there, held it up against the light, and looked at it there, and ultimately said:

"What do you call a price, now, for this here little weskit?"

"Oh! you know best, sir," I returned modestly.

"I can't be buyer and seller too," said Mr Dolloby. "Put a price on this here little weskit."

"Would eighteenpence be?"—I hinted, after some hesitation.

Mr Dolloby rolled it up again, and gave it me back. "I should rob my family," he said, "if I was to offer ninepence for it."

This was a disagreeable way of putting the business; because it imposed upon me, a perfect stranger, the unpleasantness of asking Mr Dolloby to rob his family on my account. My circumstances being so very pressing, however, I said I would take nine-pence for it, if he pleased. Mr Dolloby, not without some grumbling, gave ninepence. I wished him good night, and walked out of the shop, the richer by that sum, and the poorer by a waistcoat. But when I buttoned my jacket, that was not much.

Indeed, I foresaw pretty clearly that my jacket would go next, and that I should have to make the best of my way to Dover in a shirt and a pair of trousers, and might deem myself lucky if I got there even in that trim. But my mind did not run so much on this as might be supposed. Beyond a general impression of the distance before me, and of the young man with the donkey-cart having used me cruelly, I think I had no very urgent sense of my difficulties when I once again set off with my ninepence in my pocket.

A plan had occurred to me for passing the night, which I was going to carry into execution. This was, to lie behind the wall at the back of my old school, in a corner where there used to be a haystack. I imagined it would be a kind of company to have the boys, and the bedroom where I used to tell the stories, so near me: although the boys would know nothing of my being there, and the bedroom would yield me no shelter.

I had had a hard day's work, and was pretty well jaded when I came climbing out, at last, upon the level of Blackheath. It cost me some trouble to find out Salem House; but I found it, and I found a haystack in the corner, and I lay down by it; having first walked round the wall, and looked up at the windows, and seen that all was dark and silent within. Never shall I forget the lonely sensation of first lying down, without a roof above my head!

Sleep came upon me as it came on many other outcasts, against whom house-doors were locked, and house-dogs barked, that night—and I dreamed of lying on my old school-bed, talking to the boys in my room; and found myself sitting upright, with Steerforth's name upon my lips, looking wildly at the stars that were glistening and glimmering above me. When I remembered where I was at that untimely hour, a feeling stole upon me that made me get up, afraid of I don't know what, and walk about. But the fainter glimmering of the stars, and the pale light in the sky where the day was coming, reassured me: and my eyes being very heavy, I lay down again, and slept—though with a knowledge in my sleep that it was cold—until the warm beams of the sun, and the ringing of the getting-up bell at Salem House, awoke me. If I could have hoped that Steerforth was there, I would have lurked about until he came out alone; but I knew he must have left long since. Traddles still remained, perhaps, but it was very doubtful; and I had not sufficient confidence in his discretion or good luck, however strong my reliance was on his good nature, to wish to trust him with my situation. So I crept away from the wall as Mr Creakle's boys were getting up, and struck into the long dusty track which I had first known to be the Dover Road when I was one of them, and when I little expected that any eyes would ever see me the wayfarer I was now, upon it.

What a different Sunday morning from the old Sunday morning at Yarmouth! In due time I heard the church-bells ringing, as I plodded on; and I met people who were going to church; and I passed a church or two where the congregation were inside, and the sound of singing came out into the sunshine, while the beadle sat and cooled himself in the shade of the porch, or stood beneath the yew-tree, with his hand to his forehead, glowering at me going by. But the peace and rest of the old Sunday morning were on everything, except me. That was the difference. I felt quite wicked in my dirt and dust, with my tangled hair. But for the quiet picture I had conjured up, of my mother in her youth and beauty, weeping by the fire, and my aunt relenting to her, I hardly think I should have had the courage to go on until next day. But it always went before me, and I followed.

I got, that Sunday, through three-and-twenty miles on the straight road, though not very easily, for I was new to that kind of toil. I see myself, as evening closes in, coming over the bridge at Rochester, footsore and tired, and eating bread that I had bought for supper. One or two little houses, with the notice, "Lodgings for Travellers," hanging out, had tempted me; but I was afraid of spending the few pence I had, and was even more afraid of the vicious looks of the trampers I had met or overtaken. I sought no shelter, therefore, but the sky; and toiling into Chatham,—which, in that night's aspect, is a mere dream of chalk, and drawbridges, and mastless ships in a muddy river, roofed like Noah's arks,—crept, at last, upon a sort of grass-grown battery overhanging a lane, where a sentry was walking to and fro. Here I lay down, near a cannon; and, happy in the society of the sentry's footsteps, though he knew no more of my being above him than the boys at Salem House had known of my lying by the wall, slept soundly until morning.

Very stiff and sore of foot I was in the morning, and quite dazed by the beating of drums and marching of troops, which seemed to hem me in on every side when I went down towards the long narrow street. Feeling that I could go but a very little way that day, if I were to reserve any strength for getting to my journey's end, I resolved to make the sale of my jacket its principal business. Accordingly, I took the jacket off, that I might learn to do without it; and carrying it under my arm, began a tour of inspection of the various slop-shops.

It was a likely place to sell a jacket in; for the dealers in second-hand clothes were numerous, and were, generally speaking, on the look-out for customers at their shop doors. But as most of them had, hanging up among their stock, an officer's coat or two, epaulettes and all, I was rendered timid by the costly nature of their dealings, and walked about for a long time without offering my merchandise to anyone.

This modesty of mine directed my attention to the marine-store shops, and such shops as Mr Dolloby's, in preference to the regular dealers. At last I found one that I thought looked promising, at the corner of a dirty lane, ending in an enclosure full of stinging-nettles, against the palings of which some second-hand sailors' clothes, that seemed to have overflowed the shop, were fluttering among some cots, and rusty guns, and oilskin hats, and certain trays full of so many old rusty keys of so many sizes that they seemed various enough to open all the doors in the world.

Into this shop, which was low and small, and which was darkened rather than lighted by a little window, overhung with clothes, and was descended into by some steps, I went with a palpitating heart; which was not relieved when an ugly old man, with the lower part of his face all covered with a stubbly grey beard, rushed out of a dirty den behind it, and seized me by the hair of my head. He was a dreadful old man to look at, in a filthy flannel waistcoat, and smelling terribly of rum. His bedstead, covered with a tumbled and ragged piece of patchwork, was in the den he had come from, where another little window showed a prospect of more stinging-nettles, and a lame donkey.

"Oh, what do you want?" grinned this old man, in a fierce, monotonous whine. "Oh, my eyes and limbs, what do you want? Oh, my lungs and liver, what do you want? Oh, goroo, goroo!"

I was so much dismayed by these words, and particularly by the repetition of the last unknown one, which was a kind of rattle in his throat, that I could make no answer; hereupon the old man, still holding me by the hair, repeated:

"Oh, what do you want? Oh, my eyes and limbs, what do you want? Oh, my lungs and liver, what do you want? Oh, goroo!"—which he screwed out of himself, with an energy that made his eyes start in his head.

"I wanted to know," I said, trembling, "if you would buy a jacket."

"Oh, let's see the jacket!" cried the old man. "Oh, my heart on fire, show the jacket to us! Oh, my eyes and limbs, bring the jacket out!"

With that he took his trembling hands, which were like the claws of a great bird, out of my hair; and put on a pair of spectacles, not at all ornamental to his inflamed eyes.

"Oh, how much for the jacket?" cried the old man, after examining it. "Oh—goroo!—how much for the jacket?"

"Half-a-crown," I answered, recovering myself.

"Oh, my lungs and liver," cried the old man, "no! Oh, my eyes, no! Oh, my limbs, no! Eighteenpence. Goroo!"

Every time he uttered this ejaculation, his eyes seemed to be in danger of starting out; and every sentence he spoke, he delivered in a sort of tune, always exactly the same, and more like a gust of wind, which begins low, mounts up high, and falls again, than any other comparison I can find for it.

"Well," said I, glad to have closed the bargain, "I'll take eighteenpence."

"Oh, my liver!" cried the old man, throwing the jacket on a shelf. "Get out of the shop! Oh, my lungs, get out of the shop! Oh, my eyes and limbs—goroo!—don't ask for money; make it an exchange.

I never was so frightened in my life, before or since; but I told him humbly that I wanted money, and that nothing else was of any use to me, but that I would wait for it, as he desired, outside, and had no wish to hurry him. So I went outside, and sat down in the shade in a corner. And I sat there so many hours, that the shade became sunlight, and the sunlight became shade again, and still I sat there waiting for the money.

There never was such another drunken madman in that line of business, I hope. That he was well known in the neighbourhood, and enjoyed the reputation of having sold himself to the devil, I soon understood from the visits he received from the boys, who continually came skirmishing about the shop, shouting that legend, and calling to him to bring out his gold. "You ain't poor, you know, Charley, as you pretend. Bring out your gold. Bring out some of the gold you sold yourself to the devil for. Come! It's in the lining of the mattress, Charley. Rip it open and let's have some!" This, and many offers to lend him a knife for the purpose, exasperated him to such a degree, that the whole day was a succession of rushes on his part, and flights on the part of the boys. Sometimes in his rage he would take me for one of them, and come at me, mouthing as if he were going to tear me in pieces; then, remembering me, just in time, would dive into the shop, and lie upon his bed, as I thought from the sound of his voice, yelling in a frantic way, to his own windy tune, the "Death of Nelson"; with an Oh! before every line, and innumerable Goroos interspersed. As if this were not bad enough for me, the boys, connecting me with the establishment, on account of the patience and perseverance with which I sat outside, half-dressed, pelted me, and used me very ill all day.

He made many attempts to induce me to consent to an exchange; at one time coming out with a fishing-rod, at another with a fiddle, at another with a cocked hat, at another with a flute. But I resisted all these overtures, and sat there in desperation; each time asking him, with tears in my eyes, for my money or my jacket. At last he began to pay me in halfpence at a time; and was full two hours getting by easy stages to a shilling.

"Oh, my eyes and limbs!" he then cried, peeping hideously out of the shop, after a long pause, "will you go for twopence more?"

"I can't," I said; "I shall be starved."

"Oh, my lungs and liver, will you go for threepence?"

"I would go for nothing, if I could," I said, "but I want the money badly."

"Oh, go——roo!" (it is really impossible to express how he twisted this ejaculation out of himself, as he peeped round the door-post at me, showing nothing but his crafty old head); "will you go for fourpence?"

I was so faint and weary that I closed with this offer; and taking the money out of his claw, not without trembling, went away more hungry and thirsty than I had ever been, a little before sunset. But at an expense of threepence I soon refreshed myself completely; and, being in better spirits then, limped seven miles upon my road.

My bed at night was under another haystack, where I rested comfortably, after having washed my blistered feet in a stream, and dressed them as well as I was able, with some cool leaves. When I took the road again next morning, I found that it lay through a succession of hop-grounds and orchards. It was sufficiently late in the year for the orchards to be ruddy with ripe apples; and in a few places the hop-pickers were already at work. I thought it all extremely beautiful, and made up my mind to sleep among the hops that night: imagining some cheerful companionship in the long perspectives of poles, with the graceful leaves twining round them.

The trampers were worse than ever that day, and inspired me with a dread that is yet quite fresh in my mind. Some of them were most ferocious-looking ruffians, who stared at me as I went by; and stopped, perhaps, and called after me to come back and speak to them, and when I took to my heels, stoned me. I recollect one young fellow——a tinker, I suppose, from his wallet and brazier——who had a woman with him, and who faced about and stared at me thus; and then roared to me in such a tremendous voice to come back, that I halted and looked round.

"Come here, when you're called," said the tinker, "or I'll rip your young body open."

I thought it best to go back. As I drew nearer to them, trying to propitiate the tinker by my looks, I observed that the woman had a black eye.

"Where are you going?" said the tinker, gripping the bosom of my shirt with his blackened hand.

"I am going to Dover," I said.

"Where do you come from?" asked the tinker, giving his hand another turn in my shirt, to hold me more securely.

"I come from London," I said.

"What lay are you upon?" asked the tinker. "Are you a prig?"

"N—no," I said.

"Ain't you, by G——? If you make a brag of your honesty to me," said the tinker, "I'll knock your brains out."

With his disengaged hand he made a menace of striking me, and then looked at me from head to foot.

"Have you got the price of a pint of beer about you?" said the tinker. "If you have, out with it, afore I take it away!"

I should certainly have produced it, but that I met the woman's look, and saw her very slightly shake her head, and form "No!" with her lips.

"I am very poor," I said, attempting to smile, "and have got no money."

"Why, what do you mean?" said the tinker, looking so sternly at me, that I almost feared he saw the money in my pocket.

"Sir!" I stammered.

"What do you mean," said the tinker, "by wearing my brother's silk handkerchief! Give it over here!" And he had mine off my neck in a moment, and tossed it to the woman.

The woman burst into a fit of laughter, as if she thought this a joke, and tossed it back to me, nodded once, as slightly as before, and made the word "Go!" with her lips. Before I could obey, however, the tinker seized the handkerchief out of my hand with a roughness that threw me away like a feather, and putting it loosely round his own neck, turned upon the woman with an oath, and knocked her down. I never shall forget seeing her fall backward on the hard road, and lie there with her bonnet tumbled off, and her hair all whitened in the dust; nor, when I looked back from a distance, seeing her sitting on the pathway, which was a bank by the roadside, wiping the blood from her face with a corner of her shawl, while he went on ahead.

This adventure frightened me so, that, afterwards, when I saw any of these people coming, I turned back until I could find a hiding-place, where I remained until they had gone out of sight; which happened so often, that I was very seriously delayed. But under this difficulty, as under all the other difficulties of my journey, I seemed to be sustained and led on by my fanciful picture of my mother in her youth, before I came into the world. It always kept me company. It was there, among the hops, when I lay down to sleep; it was with me on my waking in the morning; it went before me all day. I have associated it, ever since, with the sunny street of Canterbury, dozing as it were in the hot light; and with the sight of its old houses and gateways, and the stately, grey Cathedral, with the rooks sailing round the towers. When I came, at last, upon the bare, wide downs near Dover, it relieved the solitary aspect of the scene with hope; and not until I reached that first great aim of my journey, and actually set foot in the town itself, on the sixth day of my flight, did it desert me. But then, strange to say, when I stood with my ragged shoes, and my dusty, sunburnt, half-clothed figure, in the place so long desired, it seemed to vanish like a dream, and to leave me helpless and dispirited.

I inquired about my aunt among the boatmen first, and received various answers. One said she lived in the South Foreland Light, and had singed her whiskers by doing so; another, that she was made fast to the great buoy outside the harbour, and could only be visited at half-tide; a third, that she was locked up in Maidstone Jail for child-stealing; a fourth, that she was seen to mount a broom in the last high wind, and make direct for Calais. The fly-drivers, among whom I inquired next, were equally jocose and equally disrespectful; and the shopkeepers, not liking my appearance, generally replied, without hearing what I had to say, that they had got nothing for me. I felt more miserable and destitute than I had done at any period of my running away. My money was all gone, I had nothing left to dispose of; I was hungry, thirsty, and worn out; and seemed as distant from my end as if I had remained in London.

The morning had worn away in these inquiries, and I was sitting on the step of an empty shop at a street corner, near the market-place, deliberating upon wandering towards those other places which had been mentioned, when a fly-driver, coming by with his carriage, dropped a horsecloth. Something good-natured in the man's face, as I handed it up, encouraged me to ask him if he could tell me where Miss Trotwood lived; though I had asked the question so often, that it almost died upon my lips.

"Trotwood," said he. "Let me see. I know the name, too. Old lady?"

"Yes," I said, "rather."

"Pretty stiff in the back?" said he, making himself upright.

"Yes," I said. "I should think it very likely."

"Carries a bag?" said he—"bag with a good deal of room in it—is gruffish, and comes down upon you, sharp?"

My heart sank within me as I acknowledged the undoubted accuracy of this description.

"Why then, I tell you what," said he. "If you go up there," pointing with his whip towards the heights, "and keep right on till you come to some houses facing the sea, I think you'll hear of her. My opinion is she won't stand anything, so here's a penny for you."

I accepted the gift thankfully, and bought a loaf with it. Dispatching this refreshment by the way, I went in the direction my friend had indicated, and walked on a good distance without coming to the houses he had mentioned. At length I saw some before me; and approaching them, went into a little shop (it was what we used to call a general shop, at home), and inquired if they could have the goodness to tell me where Miss Trotwood lived. I addressed myself to a man behind the counter, who was weighing some rice for a young woman; but the latter, taking the inquiry to herself, turned round quickly.

"My mistress?" she said. "What do you want with her, boy?"

"I want," I replied, "to speak to her, if you please."

"To beg of her, you mean," retorted the damsel.

"No," I said, "indeed." But suddenly remembering that in truth I came for no other purpose, I held my peace in confusion, and felt my face burn.

My aunt's handmaid, as I supposed she was from what she had said, put her rice in a little basket and walked out of the shop; telling me that I could follow her, if I wanted to know where Miss Trotwood lived. I needed no second permission; though I was by this time in such a state of consternation and agitation, that my legs shook under me. I followed the young woman, and we soon came to a very neat little cottage with cheerful bow-windows: in front of it, a small square gravelled court or garden full of flowers, carefully tended, and smelling deliciously.

"This is Miss Trotwood's," said the young woman. "Now you know; and that's all I have got to say." With which words she hurried into the house, as if to shake off the responsibility of my appearance; and left me standing at the garden-gate, looking disconsolately over the top of it towards the parlour window, where a muslin curtain partly undrawn in the middle, a large round green screen or fan fastened on to the windowsill, a small table, and a great chair, suggested to me that my aunt might be at that moment seated in awful state.

My shoes were by this time in a woeful condition. The soles had shed themselves bit by bit, and the upper leathers had broken and burst until the very shape and form of shoes had departed from them. My hat (which had served me for a night-cap, too) was so crushed and bent, that no old battered handleless saucepan on a dunghill need have been ashamed to vie with it. My shirt and trousers, stained with heat, dew, grass, and the Kentish soil on which I had slept—and torn besides—might have frightened the birds from my aunt's garden, as I stood at the gate. My hair had known no comb or brush since I left London. My face, neck, and hands, from unaccustomed exposure to the air and sun, were burnt to a berry-brown. From head to foot I was powdered almost as white with chalk and dust, as if I had come out of a lime-kiln. In this plight, and with a strong consciousness of it, I waited to introduce myself to, and make my first impression on, my formidable aunt.

The unbroken stillness of the parlour window leading me to infer, after a while, that she was not there, I lifted up my eyes to the window above it, where I saw a florid, pleasant-looking gentleman, with a grey head, who shut up one eye in a grotesque manner, nodded his head at me several times, shook it at me as often, laughed, and went away.

I had been discomposed enough before; but I was so much the more discomposed by this unexpected behaviour, that I was on the point of slinking off, to think how I had best proceed, when there came out of the house a lady with her handkerchief tied over her cap, and a pair of gardening gloves on her hands, wearing a gardening pocket like a toll-man's apron, and carrying a great knife. I knew her immediately to be Miss Betsey, for she came stalking out of the house exactly as my poor mother had so often described her stalking up our garden at Blunderstone Rookery.

"Go away!" said Miss Betsey, shaking her head, and making a distant chop in the air with her knife. "Go along! No boys here!"

I watched her, with my heart at my lips, as she marched to a corner of her garden, and stooped to dig up some little root there. Then, without a scrap of courage, but with a great deal of desperation, I went softly in and stood beside her, touching her with my finger.

"If you please, ma'am," I began.

She started and looked up.

"If you please, aunt."

"Eh?" exclaimed Miss Betsey, in a tone of amazement I have never heard approached.

"If you please, aunt, I am your nephew."

"Oh, Lord!" said my aunt. And sat flat down in the garden-path.

"I am David Copperfield, of Blunderstone, in Suffolk—where you came, on the night when I was born, and saw my dear mamma. I have been very unhappy since she died. I have been slighted, and taught nothing, and thrown upon myself, and put to work not fit for me. It made me run away to you. I was robbed at first setting out, and have walked all the way, and have never slept in a bed since I began the journey." Here my self-support gave way all at once; and with a movement of my hands, intended to show her my ragged state, and call it to witness that I had suffered something, I broke into a passion of crying, which I suppose had been pent up within me all the week.

My aunt, with every sort of expression but wonder discharged from her countenance, sat on the gravel, staring at me, until I began to cry; when she got up in a great hurry, collared me, and took me into the parlour. Her first proceeding there was to unlock a tall press, bring out several bottles, and pour some of the contents of each into my mouth. I think they must have been taken out at random, for I am sure I tasted aniseed water, anchovy sauce, and salad dressing. When she had administered these restoratives, as I was still quite hysterical, and unable to control my sobs, she put me on the sofa, with a shawl under my head, and the handkerchief from her own head under my feet, lest I should sully the cover; and then, sitting herself down behind the green fan or screen I have already mentioned, so that I could not see her face, ejaculated at intervals, "Mercy on us!" letting those exclamations off like minute guns.

After a time she rang the bell. "Janet," said my aunt, when her servant came in. "Go upstairs, give my compliments to Mr Dick, and say I wish to speak to him."

Janet looked a little surprised to see me lying stiffly on the sofa (I was afraid to move lest it should be displeasing to my aunt), but went on her errand. My aunt, with her hands behind her, walked up and down the room, until the gentleman who had squinted at me from the upper window came in laughing.

"Mr Dick," said my aunt, "don't be a fool, because nobody can be more discreet than you can, when you choose. We all know that. So don't be a fool, whatever you are."

The gentleman was serious immediately, and looked at me, I thought, as if he would entreat me to say nothing about the window.

"Mr Dick," said my aunt, "you have heard me mention David Copperfield? Now don't pretend not to have a memory, because you and I know better."

"David Copperfield?" said Mr Dick, who did not appear to me to remember much about it. *"David* Copperfield? Oh yes, to be sure. David, certainly."

"Well," said my aunt, "this is his boy—his son. He would be as like his father as it's possible to be, if he was not so like his mother, too."

"His son?" said Mr Dick. "David's son? Indeed!"

"Yes," pursued my aunt, "and he has done a pretty piece of business. He has run away. Ah! His sister, Betsey Trotwood, never would have run away." My aunt shook her head firmly, confident in the character and behaviour of the girl who never was born.

"Oh! you think she wouldn't have run away?" said Mr Dick.

"Bless and save the man," exclaimed my aunt, sharply, "how he talks! Don't I know she wouldn't? She would have lived with her god-mother, and we should have been devoted to one another. Where, in the name of wonder, should his sister, Betsey Trotwood, have run from, or to?"

"Nowhere," said Mr Dick.

"Well then," returned my aunt, softened by the reply, "how can you pretend to be wool-gathering, Dick, when you are as sharp as a surgeon's lancet? Now, here you see young David Copperfield, and the question I put to you is, what shall I do with him?"

"What shall you do with him?" said Mr Dick, feebly, scratching his head. "Oh! do with him?"

"Yes," said my aunt, with a grave look, and her forefinger held up. "Come! I want some very sound advice."

"Why, if I was you," said Mr Dick, considering, and looking vacantly at me, "I should—" The contemplation of me seemed to inspire him with a sudden idea, and he added, briskly, "I should wash him!"

"Janet," said my aunt, turning round with a quiet triumph, which I did not then understand, "Mr Dick sets us all right. Heat the bath!"

Although I was deeply interested in this dialogue, I could not help observing my aunt, Mr Dick, and Janet, while it was in progress, and completing a survey I had already been engaged in making of the room.

My aunt was a tall, hard-featured lady, but by no means ill-looking. There was an inflexibility in her face, in her voice, in her gait and carriage, amply sufficient to account for the effect she had made upon a gentle creature like my mother; but her features were rather handsome than otherwise, though unbending and austere. I particularly noticed that she had a very quick, bright eye. Her hair, which was grey, was arranged in two plain divisions, under what I believe would be called a mob-cap; I mean a cap, much more common then than now, with side-pieces fastening under the chin. Her dress was of a lavender colour, and perfectly neat; but scantily made, as if she desired to be as little encumbered as possible. I remember that I thought it, in form, more like a riding-habit with the superfluous skirt cut off, than anything else. She wore at her side a gentleman's gold watch, if I might judge from its size and make, with an appropriate chain and seals; she had some linen at her throat not unlike a shirt-collar, and things at her wrists like little shirt-wristbands.

Mr Dick, as I have already said, was grey-headed, and florid: I should have said all about him, in saying so, had not his head been curiously bowed—not by age; it reminded me of one of Mr Creakle's boys' heads after a beating—and his grey eyes prominent and large, with a strange kind of watery brightness in them that made me, in combination with his vacant manner, his submission to my aunt, and his childish delight when she praised him, suspect him of being a little mad; though, if he were mad, how he came to be there puzzled me extremely. He was dressed like any other ordinary gentleman, in a loose grey morning coat and waistcoat, and white trousers; and had his watch in his fob, and his money in his pockets: which he rattled as if he were very proud of it.

Janet was a pretty blooming girl, of about nineteen or twenty, and a perfect picture of neatness. Though I made no further observation of her at the moment, I may mention here what I did not discover until afterwards, namely, that she was one of a series of protégées whom my aunt had taken into her service expressly to educate in a renounce-ment of mankind, and who had generally completed their abjuration by marrying the baker.

The room was as neat as Janet or my aunt. As I laid down my pen, a moment since, to think of it, the air from the sea came blowing in again, mixed with the perfume of the flowers; and I saw the old-fashioned furniture brightly rubbed and polished, my aunt's inviolable chair and table by the round green fan in the bow-window, the drugget-covered carpet, the cat, the kettle-holder, the two canaries, the old china, the punchbowl full of dried roseleaves, the tall press guarding all sorts of bottles and pots, and, wonder-fully out of keeping with the rest, my dusty self upon the sofa, taking note of everything.

Janet had gone away to get the bath ready, when my aunt, to my great alarm, became in one moment rigid with indignation, and had hardly voice to cry out, "Janet! Donkeys!"

Upon which, Janet came running up the stairs as if the house were in flames, darted out on a little piece of green in front, and warned off two saddle-donkeys, lady-ridden, that had presumed to set hoof upon it: while my aunt, rushing out of the house, seized the bridle of a third animal laden with a bestriding child, turned him, led him forth from those sacred precincts, and boxed the ears of the unlucky urchin in attendance who had dared to profane that hallowed ground.

To this hour I don't know whether my aunt had any lawful right of way over that patch of green; but she had settled it in her own mind that she had, and it was all the same to her. The one great outrage of her life, demanding to be constantly avenged, was the passage of a donkey over that immaculate spot. In whatever occupation she was engaged, however interesting to her the conversation in which she was taking part, a donkey turned the current of her ideas in a moment, and she was upon him straight. Jugs of water, and watering-pots, were kept in secret places ready to be discharged on the offending boys; sticks were laid in ambush behind the door; sallies were made at all hours; and incessant war prevailed. Perhaps this was an agreeable excitement to the donkey-boys; or perhaps the more sagacious of the donkeys, understanding how the case stood, delighted with constitutional obstinacy in coming that way. I only know that there were three alarms before the bath was ready; and that on the occasion of the last and most desperate of all, I saw my aunt engage, single-handed, with a sandy-headed lad of fifteen, and bump his sandy head against her own gate, before he seemed to comprehend what was the matter. These interruptions were of the more ridiculous to me, because she was giving me broth out of a table-spoon at the time (having firmly persuaded herself that I was actually starving, and must receive nourishment at first in very small quantities), and, while my mouth was yet open to receive the spoon, she would put it back into the basin, cry "Janet! Donkeys!" and go out to the assault.

The bath was a great comfort. For I began to be sensible of acute pains in my limbs from lying out in the fields, and was now so tired and low that I could hardly keep myself awake for five minutes together. When I had bathed, they (I mean my aunt and Janet) enrobed me in a shirt and a pair of trousers belonging to Mr Dick, and tied me up in two or three great shawls. What sort of bundle I looked like, I don't know, but I felt a very hot one. Feeling also very faint and drowsy, I soon lay down on the sofa again and fell asleep.

It might have been a dream, originating in the fancy which had occupied my mind so long, but I awoke with the impression that my aunt had come and bent over me, and had put my hair away from my face, and laid my head more comfortably, and had then stood looking at me. The words, "Pretty fellow," or "Poor fellow," seemed to be in my ears, too; but certainly there was nothing else, when I awoke, to lead me to believe that they had been uttered by my aunt, who sat in the bow-window gazing at the sea from behind the green fan, which was mounted on a kind of swivel, and turned any way.

We dined soon after I awoke, off a roast fowl and a pudding; I sitting at table, not unlike a trussed bird myself, and moving my arms with considerable difficulty. But as my aunt had swathed me up, I made no complaint of being inconvenienced. All this time I was deeply anxious to know what she was going to do with me; but she took her dinner in profound silence, except when she occasionally fixed her eyes on me sitting opposite, and said, "Mercy upon us!" which did not by any means relieve my anxiety.

The cloth being drawn, and some sherry put upon the table (of which I had a glass), my aunt sent up for Mr Dick again, who joined us, and looked as wise as he could when she requested him to attend to my story, which she elicited from me, gradually, by a course of questions. During my recital, she kept her eyes on Mr Dick, who I thought would have gone to sleep but for that, and who, whensoever he lapsed into a smile, was checked by a frown from my aunt.

"Whatever possessed that poor unfortunate Baby, that she must go and be married again," said my aunt, when I had finished, "I can't conceive."

"Perhaps she fell in love with her second husband," Mr Dick suggested.

"Fell in love!" repeated my aunt. "What do you mean? What business had she to do it?"

"Perhaps," Mr Dick simpered, after thinking a little, "she did it for pleasure."

"Pleasure, indeed!" replied my aunt. "A mighty pleasure for the poor Baby to fix her simple faith upon any dog of a fellow, certain to ill-use her in some way or other. What did she propose to herself, I should like to know! She had had one husband. She had seen David Copperfield out of the world, who was always running after wax dolls from his cradle. She had got a baby—oh, there were a pair of babies when she gave birth to this child sitting here, that Friday night!—and what more did she want?"

Mr Dick secretly shook his head at me, as if he thought there was no getting over this.

"She couldn't even have a baby like anybody else," said my aunt. "Where was this child's sister, Betsey Trotwood? Not forthcoming. Don't tell me!"

Mr Dick seemed quite frightened.

"That little man of a doctor, with his head on one side," said my aunt, "Jellips, or whatever his name was, what was *he* about? All he could do, was to say to me, like a robin redbreast—as he *is*—'It's a boy.' A boy! Yah, the imbecility of the whole set of 'em!"

The heartiness of the ejaculation startled Mr Dick exceedingly; and me, too, if I am to tell the truth.

"And then, as if this was not enough, and she had not stood sufficiently in the light of this child's sister, Betsey Trotwood," said my aunt, "she marries a second time—goes and marries a Murderer—or a man with a name like it—and stands in *this* child's light! And the natural consequence is, as anybody but a baby might have foreseen, that he prowls and wanders. He's as like Cain before he was grown up, as he can be."

Mr Dick looked hard at me, as if to identify me in this character.

"And then there's that woman with the Pagan name," said my aunt, "that Peggotty, *she* goes and gets married next. Because she has not seen enough of the evil attending such things, *she* goes and gets married next, as the child relates. I only hope," said my aunt, shaking her head, "that her husband is one of those Poker husbands who abound in the newspapers, and will beat her well with one."

I could not bear to hear my old nurse so decried, and made the subject of such a wish. I told my aunt that indeed she was mistaken. That Peggotty was the best, the truest, the most faithful, most devoted, and most self-denying friend and servant in the world; who had ever loved me dearly, who had ever loved my mother dearly; who had held my mother's dying head upon her arm, on whose face my mother had imprinted her last grateful kiss. And my remembrance of them both, choking me, I broke down as I was trying to say that her home was my home, and that all she had was mine, and that I would have gone to her for shelter, but for her humble station, which made me fear that I might bring some trouble on her—I broke down, I say, as I was trying to say so, and laid my face in my hands upon the table.

"Well, well!" said my aunt, "the child is right to stand by those who have stood by him—Janet! Donkeys!"

I thoroughly believe that but for those unfortunate donkeys, we should have come to a good understanding; for my aunt had laid her hand on my shoulder, and the impulse was upon me, thus emboldened, to embrace her and beseech her protection. But the interruption, and the disorder she was thrown into by the struggle outside, put an end to all softer ideas for the present, and kept my aunt indignantly declaiming to Mr Dick about her determination to appeal for redress to the laws of her country, and to bring actions for trespass against the whole donkey proprietorship of Dover, until tea-time.

After tea, we sat at the window—on the look-out, as I imagined, from my aunt's sharp expression of face, for more invaders—until dusk, when Janet set candles, and a back-gammon-board, on the table, and pulled down the blinds.

"Now, Mr Dick," said my aunt, with her grave look, and her forefinger up as before, "I am going to ask you another question. Look at this child."

"David's son?" said Mr Dick, with an attentive, puzzled face.

"Exactly so," returned my aunt. "What would you do with him, now?"

"Do with David's son?" said Mr Dick.

"Ay," replied my aunt, "with David's son."

"Oh!" said Mr Dick. "Yes. Do with—I should put him to bed."

"Janet!" cried my aunt, with the same complacent triumph that I had remarked before. "Mr Dick sets us all right. If the bed is ready, we'll take him up to it."

Janet reporting it to be quite ready, I was taken up to it; kindly, but in some sort like a prisoner; my aunt going in front and Janet bringing up the rear. The only circumstance which gave me any new hope, was my aunt's stopping on the stairs to inquire about a smell of fire that was prevalent there; and Janet's replying that she had been making tinder down in the kitchen, of my old shirt. But there were no other clothes in my room than the odd heap of things I wore; and when I was left there, with a little taper which my aunt forewarned me would burn exactly five minutes, I heard them lock my door on the outside. Turning these things over in my mind I deemed it possible that my aunt, who could know nothing of me, might suspect I had a habit of running away, and took precautions, on that account, to have me in safe keeping.

The room was a pleasant one, at the top of the house, overlooking the sea, on which the moon was shining brilliantly. After I had said my prayers, and the candle had burnt out, I remember how I still sat looking at the moonlight on the water, as if I could hope to read my fortune in it, as in a bright book; or to see my mother with her child, coming from Heaven, along that shining path, to look upon me as she had looked when I last saw her sweet face. I remember how the solemn feeling with which at length I turned my eyes away, yielded to the sensation of gratitude and rest which the sight of the white-curtained bed—and how much more the lying softly down upon it, nestling in the snow-white sheets!—inspired. I remember how I thought of all the solitary places under the night sky where I had slept, and how I prayed that I never might be houseless any more, and never might forget the houseless. I remember how I seemed to float, then, down the melancholy glory of that track upon the sea, away into the world of dreams.

Chapter XIV

MY AUNT MAKES UP HER MIND ABOUT ME

ON going down in the morning, I found my aunt musing so profoundly over the breakfast table, with her elbow on the tray, that the contents of the urn had overflowed the teapot and were laying the whole table-cloth under water, when my entrance put her meditations to flight. I felt sure that I had been the subject of her reflections, and was more than ever anxious to know her intentions towards me. Yet I dared not express my anxiety, lest it should give her offence.

My eyes, however, not being so much under control as my tongue, were attracted towards my aunt very often during breakfast. I never could look at her for a few moments together but I found her looking at me—in an odd thoughtful manner, as if I were an immense way off, instead of being on the other side of the small round table. When she had finished her breakfast, my aunt very deliberately leaned back in her chair, knitted her brows, folded her arms, and contemplated me at her leisure, with such a fixedness of attention that I was quite overpowered by embarrassment. Not having as yet finished my own breakfast, I attempted to hide my confusion by proceeding with it; but my knife tumbled over my fork, my fork tripped up my knife, I chipped bits of bacon a surprising height into the air instead of cutting them for my own eating, and choked myself with my tea, which persisted in going the wrong way instead of the right one, until I gave in altogether, and sat blushing under my aunt's close scrutiny.

"Hallo!" said my aunt, after a long time.

I looked up, and met her sharp bright glance respectfully.

"I have written to him," said my aunt.

"To——?"

"To your father-in-law," said my aunt. "I have sent him a letter that I'll trouble him to attend to, or he and I will fall out, I can tell him!"

"Does he know where I am, aunt?" I inquired, alarmed.

"I have told him," said my aunt, with a nod.

"Shall I—be—given up to him?" I faltered.

"I don't know," said my aunt. "We shall see."

"Oh! I can't think what I shall do," I exclaimed, "if I have to go back to Mr Murdstone!"

"I don't know anything about it," said my aunt, shaking her head. "I can't say, I am sure. We shall see."

My spirits sank under these words, and I became very downcast and heavy of heart. My aunt, without appearing to take much heed of me, put on a coarse apron with a bib, which she took out of the press; washed up the teacups with her own hands; and, when everything was washed and set in the tray again, and the cloth folded and put on the top of the whole, rang for Janet to remove it. She next swept up the crumbs with a little broom (putting on a pair of gloves first), until there did not appear to be one microscopic speck left on the carpet; next dusted and arranged the room, which was dusted and arranged to a hair's-breadth already. When all these tasks were performed to her satisfaction, she took off the gloves and apron, folded them up, put them in the particular corner of the press from which they had been taken, brought out her work-box to her own table in the open window, and sat down, with the green fan between her and the light, to work.

"I wish you'd go upstairs," said my aunt, as she threaded her needle, "and give my compliments to Mr Dick, and I'll be glad to know how he gets on with his Memorial."

I rose with all alacrity, to acquit myself of this commission.

"I suppose," said my aunt, eyeing me as narrowly as she had eyed the needle in threading it, "you think Mr Dick a short name, eh?"

"I thought it was rather a short name, yesterday," I confessed.

"You are not to suppose that he hasn't got a longer name, if he chose to use it," said my aunt, with a loftier air. "Babley—Mr Richard Babley—that's the gentleman's true name."

I was going to suggest, with a modest sense of my youth and familiarity I had been already guilty of, that I had better give him the full benefit of that name, when my aunt went on to say:

"But don't you call him by it, whatever you do. He can't bear his name. That's a peculiarity of his. Though I don't know that it's much of a peculiarity, either; for he has been ill-used enough, by some that bear it, to have a mortal antipathy for it, Heaven knows. Mr Dick is his name here, and everywhere else, now—if he ever went anywhere else, which he don't. So take care, child, you don't call him anything *but* Mr Dick."

I promised to obey, and went upstairs with my message; thinking, as I went, that if Mr Dick had been working at his Memorial long, at the same rate as I had seen him working at it, through the open door, when I came down, he was probably getting on very well indeed. I found him still driving at it with a long pen, and his head almost laid upon the paper. He was so intent upon it, that I had ample leisure to observe the large paper kite in a corner, the confusion of bundles of manuscript, the number of pens, and, above all, the quantity of ink (which he seemed to have in, in half-gallon jars by the dozen), before he observed my being present.

"Ha! Phoebus!" said Mr Dick, laying down his pen. "How does the world go? I'll tell you what," he added, in a lower tone, "I shouldn't wish it to be mentioned, but it's a—" here he beckoned to me, and put his lips close to my ear—"it's a mad world. Mad as Bedlam, boy!" said Mr Dick, taking snuff from a round box on the table, and laughing heartily.

Without presuming to give my opinion on this question, I delivered my message.

"Well," said Mr Dick, in answer, "my compliments to her, and I—I believe I have made a start. I think I have made a start," said Mr Dick, passing his hand among his grey hair, and casting anything but a confident look at his manuscript. "You have been to school?"

"Yes, sir," I answered; "for a short time."

"Do you recollect the date," said Mr Dick, looking earnestly at me, and taking up his pen to note it down, "when King Charles the First had his head cut off?"

I said I believed it happened in the year sixteen hundred and forty-nine.

"Well," returned Mr Dick, scratching his ear with his pen, and looking dubiously at me. "So the books say; but I don't see how that can be. Because, if it was so long ago, how could the people about him have made that mistake of putting some of the trouble out of *his* head, after it was taken off, into *mine?*"

I was very much surprised by the inquiry; but could give no information on this point.

"It's very strange," said Mr Dick, with a despondent look upon his papers, and with his hand among his hair again, "that I never can get that quite right. I never can make that perfectly clear. But no matter, no matter!" he said cheerfully, and rousing himself, "there's time enough! My compliments to Miss Trotwood, I am getting on very well indeed."

I was going away, when he directed my attention to the kite.

"What do you think of that for a kite?" he said.

I answered that it was a beautiful one. I should think it must have been as much as seven feet high.

"I made it. We'll go and fly it, you and I," said Mr Dick. "Do you see this?"

He showed me that it was covered with manuscript, very closely and laboriously written; but so plainly, that as I looked along the lines, I thought I saw some allusion to King Charles the First's head again, in one or two places.

"There's plenty of string," said Mr Dick, "and when it flies high, it takes the facts a long way. That's my manner of diffusing 'em. I don't know where they may come down. It's according to circumstances, and the wind, and so forth; but I take my chance of that."

His face was so very mild and pleasant, and had something so reverend in it, though it was hale and hearty, that I was not sure but that he was having a good-humoured jest with me. So I laughed, and he laughed, and we parted the best friends possible.

"Well, child," said my aunt, when I went downstairs. "And what of Mr Dick, this morning?"

I informed her that he sent his compliments, and was getting on very well indeed.

"What do you think of him?" said my aunt.

I had some shadowy idea of endeavouring to evade the question, by replying that I thought him a very nice gentleman; but my aunt was not to be so put off, for she laid her work down in her lap, and said, folding her hands upon it:

"Come! Your sister Betsey Trotwood would have told me what she thought of anyone, directly. Be as like your sister as you can, and speak out!"

"Is he—is Mr Dick—I ask because I don't know, aunt—is he at all out of his mind, then?" I stammered; for I felt I was on dangerous mood.

"Not a morsel," said my aunt.

"Oh, indeed!" I observed faintly.

"If there is anything in the world," said my aunt, with great decision and force of manner, "that Mr Dick is not, it's that."

I had nothing better to offer, than another timid, "Oh, indeed!"

"He has been *called* mad," said my aunt. "I have a selfish pleasure in saying he has been called mad, or I should not have had the benefit of his society and advice for these last ten years and upwards—in fact, ever since your sister, Betsey Trotwood, disappointed me."

"So long as that?" I said.

"And nice people they were, who had the audacity to call him mad," pursued my aunt. "Mr Dick is a sort of distant connexion of mine—it doesn't matter how; I needn't enter into that. If it hadn't been for me, his own brother would have shut him up for life. That's all."

I am afraid it was hypocritical in me, but seeing that my aunt felt strongly on the subject, I tried to look as if I felt strongly too.

"A proud fool!" said my aunt. "Because his brother was a little eccentric—though he is not half so eccentric as a good many people—he didn't like to have him visible about his house, and sent him away to some private asylum-place: though he had been left to his particular care by their deceased father, who thought him almost a natural. And a wise man *he* must have been to think so! Mad himself, no doubt."

Again, as my aunt looked quite convinced, I endeavoured to look quite convinced also.

"So I stepped in," said my aunt, "and made him an offer. I said, 'Your brother's sane—a great deal more sane than you are, or ever will be, it is to be hoped. Let him have his little income, and come and live with me. *I* am not afraid of him, *I* am not proud, *I* am ready to take care of him, and shall not ill-treat him as some people (besides the asylum-folks) have done.' After a good deal of squabbling," said my aunt, "I got him; and he has been here ever since. He is the most friendly and amenable creature in existence; and as for advice!—But nobody knows what that man's mind is, except myself."

My aunt smoothed her dress and shook her head, as if she smoothed defiance of the whole world out of the one, and shook it out of the other.

"He had a favourite sister," said my aunt, "a good creature, and very kind to him. But she did what they all do—took a husband. And *he* did what they all do—made her wretched. It had such an effect upon the mind of Mr Dick (*that's* not madness, I hope!) that, combined with his fear of his brother, and his sense of his unkindness, it threw him into a fever. That was before he came to me, but the recollection of it is oppressive to him even now. Did he say anything to you about King Charles the First, child?"

"Yes, aunt."

"Ah!" said my aunt, rubbing her nose as if she were a little vexed. "That's his allegorical way of expressing it. He connects his illness with great disturbance and agitation, naturally, and that's the figure, or the simile, or whatever it's called, which he chooses to use. And why shouldn't he, if he thinks proper!"

I said: "Certainly, aunt."

"It's not a business-like way of speaking," said my aunt, "nor a worldly way. I am aware of that; and that's the reason why I insist upon it, and there shan't be a word about it in his Memorial."

"Is it a Memorial about his own history that he is writing, aunt?"

"Yes, child," said my aunt, rubbing her nose again. "He is memorializing the Lord Chancellor, or the Lord Somebody or other—one of those people, at all events, who are paid to *be* memorialized—about his affairs. I suppose it will go in, one of these days. He hasn't been able to draw it up yet, without introducing that mode of expressing himself; but it don't signify; it keeps him employed."

In fact, I found out afterwards that Mr Dick had been for upwards of ten years endeavouring to keep King Charles the First out of the Memorial; but he had been constantly getting into it, and was there now.

"I say again," said my aunt, "nobody knows what that man's mind is except myself; and he's the most amenable and friendly creature in existence. If he likes to fly a kite sometimes, what of that! Franklin used to fly a kite. He was a Quaker, or something of that sort, if I am not mistaken. And a Quaker flying a kite is a much more ridiculous object than anybody else."

If I could have supposed that my aunt had recounted these particulars for my especial behoof, and as a piece of confidence in me, I should have felt very much distinguished, and should have augured favourably from such a mark of her good opinion. But I could hardly help observing that she had launched into them, chiefly because the question was raised in her own mind, and with very little reference to me, though she had addressed herself to me in the absence of anybody else.

At the same time, I must say that the generosity of her championship of poor harmless Mr Dick, not only inspired my young breast with some selfish hope for myself, but, warmed it unselfishly towards her. I believe that I began to know that there was something about my aunt, notwithstanding her many eccentricities and odd humours, to be honoured and trusted in. Though she was just as sharp that day as on the day before, and was in and out about the donkeys just as often, and was thrown into a tremendous state of indignation, when a young man, going by, ogled Janet at a window (which was one of the gravest misdemeanours that could be committed against my aunt's dignity), she seemed to me to command more of my respect, if not less of my fear.

The anxiety I underwent, in the interval which necessarily elapsed before a reply could be received to her letter to Mr Murdstone, was extreme; but I made an endeavour to suppress it, and to be as agreeable as I could in a quiet way, both to my aunt and Mr Dick. The latter and I would have gone out to fly the great kite; but that I had still no other clothes than the anything but ornamental garments with which I had been decorated on the first day, and which confined me to the house, except for an hour after dark, when my aunt, for my health's sake, paraded me up and down on the cliff outside, before going to bed. At length the reply from Mr Murdstone came, and my aunt informed me, to my infinite terror, that he was coming to speak to her himself on the next day. On the next day, still bundled up in my curious habiliments, I sat counting the time, flushed and heated by the conflict of sinking hopes and rising fears within me; and waiting to be startled by the sight of the gloomy face, whose non-arrival startled me every minute.

My aunt was a little more imperious and stern than usual, but I observed no other token of her preparing herself to receive the visitor so much dreaded by me. She sat at work in the window, and I sat by, with my thoughts running astray on all possible and impossible results of Mr Murdstone's visit, until pretty late in the afternoon. Our dinner had been indefinitely postponed; but it was growing so late, that my aunt had ordered it to be got ready, when she gave a sudden alarm of donkeys, and to my consternation and amazement, I beheld Miss Murdstone, on a side-saddle, ride deliberately over the sacred piece of green, and stop in front of the house, looking about her.

"Go along with you!" cried my aunt, shaking her head and her fist at the window. "You have no business there. How dare you trespass? Go along! Oh! you bold-faced thing!"

My aunt was so exasperated by the coolness with which Miss Murdstone looked about her, that I really believe she was motionless, and unable for the moment to dart out according to custom. I seized the opportunity to inform her who it was; and that the gentleman now coming near the offender (for the way up was very steep, and he had dropped behind), was Mr Murdstone himself.

"I don't care who it is!" cried my aunt, still shaking her head and gesticulating anything but welcome from the bow-window. "I won't be trespassed upon. I won't allow it. Go away! Janet, turn him round. Lead him off!" and I saw, from behind my aunt, a sort of hurried battle-piece, in which the donkey stood resisting everybody, with all his four legs planted different ways, while Janet tried to pull him round by the bridle, Mr Murdstone tried to lead him on, Miss Murdstone struck at Janet with a parasol, and several boys, who had come to see the engagement, shouted vigorously. But my aunt, suddenly descrying among them the young malefactor who was the donkey's guardian, and who was one of the most inveterate offenders against her, though hardly in his teens, rushed out to the scene of action, pounced upon him, captured him, dragged him, with his jacket over his head, and his heels grinding the ground, into the garden, and, calling upon Janet to fetch the constables and justices, that he might be taken, tried, and executed on the spot, held him at bay there. This part of the business, however, did not last long; for the young rascal, being expert at a variety of feints and dodges, of which my aunt had no conception, soon went whooping away, leaving some deep impressions of his nailed boots in the flower-beds, and taking his donkey in triumph with him.

Miss Murdstone, during the latter portion of the contest, had dismounted, and was now waiting with her brother at the bottom of the steps, until my aunt should be at leisure to receive them. My aunt, a little ruffled by the combat, marched past them into the house, with great dignity, and took no notice of their presence, until they were announced by Janet.

"Shall I go away, aunt?" I asked, trembling.

"No, sir." said my aunt. "Certainly not!" With which she pushed me into a corner near her, and fenced me in with a chair, as if it were a prison or a bar of justice. This position I continued to occupy during the whole interview, and from it I now saw Mr and Miss Murdstone enter the room.

"Oh!" said my aunt, "I was not aware at first to whom I had the pleasure of objecting. But I don't allow anybody to ride over that turf. I make no exceptions. I don't allow anybody to do it."

"Your regulation is rather awkward to strangers," said Miss Murdstone.

"Is it!" said my aunt.

Mr Murdstone seemed afraid of a renewal of hostilities, and interposing began:

"Miss Trotwood!"

"I beg your pardon," observed my aunt with a keen look. "You are the Mr Murdstone who married the widow of my late nephew, David Copperfield, of Blunderstone Rookery!—Though why Rookery, *I* don't know!"

"I am," said Mr Murdstone.

"You'll excuse my saying, sir," returned my aunt, "that I think it would have been a much better and happier thing if you had left that poor child alone."

"I so far agree with what Miss Trotwood has remarked," observed Miss Murdstone, bridling, "that I consider our lamented Clara to have been, in all essential respects, a mere child."

"It is a comfort to you and me, ma'am," said my aunt, "who are getting on in life, and are not likely to be made unhappy by our personal attractions, that nobody can say the same of us."

"No doubt!" returned Miss Murdstone, though, I thought, not with a very ready or gracious assent. "And it certainly might have been, as you say, a better and happier thing for my brother if he had never entered into such a marriage. I have always been of that opinion."

"I have no doubt you have," said my aunt. "Janet," ringing the bell, "my compliments to Mr Dick, and beg him to come down."

Until he came, my aunt sat perfectly upright and stiff, frowning at the wall. When he came, my aunt performed the ceremony of introduction.

"Mr Dick. An old and intimate friend. On whose judgement," said my aunt, with emphasis, as an admonition to Mr Dick, who was biting his forefinger and looking rather foolish, "I rely."

Mr Dick took his finger out of his mouth, on this hint, and stood among the group, with a grave and attentive expression of face. My aunt inclined her head to Mr Murdstone, who went on:

"Miss Trotwood: on the receipt of your letter, I considered it an act of greater justice to myself, and perhaps of more respect to you—"

"Thank you," said my aunt, still eyeing him keenly. "You needn't mind me."

"To answer it in person, however inconvenient the journey," pursued Mr Murdstone, "rather than by letter. This unhappy boy who has run away from his friends and his occupation—"

"And whose appearance," interposed his sister, directing general attention to me in my indefinable costume, "is perfectly scandalous and disgraceful."

"Jane Murdstone," said her brother, "have the goodness not to interrupt me. This unhappy boy, Miss Trotwood, has been the occasion of much domestic trouble and uneasiness; both during the lifetime of my late dear wife, and since. He has a sullen, rebellious spirit; a violent temper; and an untoward, intractable disposition. Both my sister and myself have endeavoured to correct his vices, but ineffectually. And I have felt—we both have felt, I may say; my sister being fully in my confidence—that it is right you should receive this grave and dispassionate assurance from our lips."

"It can hardly be necessary for me to confirm anything stated by my brother," said Miss Murdstone; "but I beg to observe, that, of all the boys in the world, I believe this is the worst boy."

"Strong!" said my aunt, shortly.

"But not at all too strong for the facts," returned Miss Murdstone.

"Ha!" said my aunt. "Well, sir?"

"I have my own opinions," resumed Mr Murdstone, whose face darkened more and more, the more he and my aunt observed each other, which they did very narrowly, "as to the best mode of bringing him up; they are founded, in part, on my knowledge of him, and in part on my knowledge of my own means and resources. I am responsible for them to myself, I act upon them, and I say no more about them. It is enough that I place this boy under the eye of a friend of my own, in a respectable business; that it does not please him; that he runs away from it; makes himself a common vagabond about the country; and comes here, in rags, to appeal to you, Miss Trotwood. I wish to set before you, honourably, the exact consequences—so far as they are within my knowledge—of your abetting him in this appeal."

"But about the respectable business first," said my aunt. "If he had been your own boy, you would have put him to it, just the same, I suppose?"

"If he had been my brother's own boy," returned Miss Murdstone, striking in, "his character, I trust, would have been altogether different."

"Or if the poor child, his mother, had been alive, he would still have gone into the respectable business, would he?" said my aunt.

"I believe," said Mr Murdstone, with an inclination of his head, "that Clara would have disputed nothing which myself and my sister Jane Murdstone were agreed was for the best."

Miss Murdstone confirmed this with an audible murmur.

"Humph!" said my aunt. "Unfortunate baby!"

Mr Dick, who had been rattling his money all this time, was rattling it so loudly now, that my aunt felt it necessary to check him with a look, before saying:

"The poor child's annuity died with her?"

"Died with her," replied Mr Murdstone.

"And there was no settlement of the little property—the house and garden—the what's-its-name Rookery without any rooks in it—upon her boy?"

"It had been left to her, unconditionally, by her first husband," Mr Murdstone began, when my aunt caught him up with the greatest irascibility and impatience.

"Good Lord, man, there's no occasion to say that. Left to her unconditionally! I think I see David Copperfield looking forward to any condition of any sort or kind, though it stared him point-blank in the face! Of course it was left to her unconditionally. But when she married again—when she took that most disastrous step of marrying you, in short," said my aunt, "to be plain—did no one put in a word for the boy at that time?"

"My late wife loved her second husband, ma'am," said Mr Murdstone, "and trusted implicitly in him."

"Your late wife, sir, was a most unworldly, most unhappy, most unfortunate baby," returned my aunt, shaking her head at him. "That's what *she* was. And now, what have you got to say next?"

"Merely this, Miss Trotwood," he returned. "I am here to take David back—to take him back unconditionally, to dispose of him as I think proper, and to deal with him as I think right. I am not here to make any promise, or give any pledge to anybody. You may possibly have some idea, Miss Trotwood, of abetting him in his running away, and in his complaints to you. Your manner, which I must say does not seem intended to propitiate, induces me to think it possible. Now I must caution you that if you abet him once, you abet him for good and all; if you step in between him and me, now, you must step in, Miss Trotwood, for ever. I cannot trifle, or be trifled with. I am here, for the first and last time, to take him away. Is he ready to go? If he is not—and you tell me he is not; on any pretence; it is indifferent to me what—my doors are shut against him henceforth, and yours, I take it for granted, are open to him."

To this address, my aunt had listened with the closest attention, sitting perfectly upright, with her hands folded on one knee, and looking grimly on the speaker. When he had finished, she turned her eyes so as to command Miss Murdstone, without otherwise disturbing her attitude, and said:

"Well, ma'am, have *you* got anything to remark?"

"Indeed, Miss Trotwood," said Miss Murdstone, "all that I could say has been so well said by my brother, and all that I know to be the fact has been so plainly stated by him, that I have nothing to add except my thanks for your politeness. For your very great politeness, I am sure," said Miss Murdstone; with an irony which no more affected my aunt, than it discomposed the cannon I had slept by at Chatham.

"And what does the boy say?" said my aunt. "Are you ready to go, David?"

I answered no, and entreated her not to let me go. I said that neither Mr nor Miss Murdstone had ever liked me, or had ever been kind to me. That they had made my mama, who always loved me dearly, unhappy about me, and that I knew it well, and that Peggotty knew it. I said that I had been more miserable than I thought anybody could believe, who only knew how young I was. And I begged and prayed my aunt—I forget in what terms now, but I remember that they affected me very much then—to befriend and protect me, for my father's sake.

"Mr Dick," said my aunt, "what shall I do with this child?"

Mr Dick considered, hesitated, brightened, and rejoined, "Have him measured for a suit of clothes directly."

"Mr Dick," said my aunt triumphantly, "give me your hand, for your common sense is invaluable." Having shaken it with great cordiality, she pulled me towards her and said to Mr Murdstone:

"You can go when you like; I'll take my chance with the boy. If he's all you say he is, at least I can do as much for him then, as you have done. But I don't believe a word of it."

"Miss Trotwood," rejoined Mr Murdstone, shrugging his shoulders, as he rose, "if you were a gentleman—"

"Bah! Stuff and nonsense!" said my aunt. "Don't talk to me!"

"How exquisitely polite!" exclaimed Miss Murdstone, rising. "Overpowering, really!"

"Do you think I don't know," said my aunt, turning a deaf ear to the sister, and continuing to address the brother, and to shake her head at him with infinite expression, "what kind of life you must have led that poor, unhappy, misdirected baby? Do you think I don't know what a woeful day it was for the soft little creature when *you* first came in her way—smirking and making great eyes at her, I'll be bound, as if you couldn't say boh! to a goose!"

"I never heard anything so elegant!" said Miss Murdstone.

"Do you think I can't understand you as well as if I had seen you," pursued my aunt, "now that I *do* see and hear you—which, I tell you candidly, is anything but a pleasure to me? Oh yes, bless us! who so smooth and silky as Mr Murdstone at first! The poor, benighted innocent had never seen such a man. He was made of sweetness. He worshipped her. He doted on her boy—tenderly doted on him! He was to be another father to him, and they were all to live together in a garden of roses, weren't they? Ugh! Get along with you, do!" said my aunt.

"I never heard anything like this person in my life!" exclaimed Miss Murdstone.

"And when you had made sure of the poor little fool," said my aunt—"God forgive me that I should call her so, and she gone where *you* won't go in a hurry—because you had not done wrong enough to her and hers, you must begin to train her, must you? begin to break her, like a poor caged bird, and wear her deluded life away, in teaching her to sing *your* notes?"

"This is either insanity or intoxication," said Miss Murdstone, in a perfect agony at not being able to turn the current of my aunt's address towards herself; "and my suspicion is that it's intoxication."

Miss Betsey, without taking the least notice of the interruption, continued to address herself to Mr Murdstone as if there had been no such thing.

"Mr Murdstone," she said, shaking her finger at him, "you were a tyrant to the simple baby, and you broke her heart. She was a loving baby—I know that; I knew it, years before *you* ever saw her—and through the best part of her weakness you gave her the wounds she died of. There is the truth for your comfort, however you like it. And you and your instruments may make the most of it."

"Allow me to inquire, Miss Trotwood," interposed Miss Murdstone, "whom you are pleased to call, in a choice of words in which I am not experienced, my brother's instruments?"

"It was clear enough, as I have told you, years before *you* ever saw her—and why, in the mysterious dispensations of Providence, you ever did see her, is more than humanity can comprehend—it was clear enough that the poor soft little thing would marry somebody, at some time or other; but I did hope it wouldn't have been as bad as it has turned out. That was the time, Mr Murdstone, when she gave birth to her boy here," said my aunt; "to the poor child you sometimes tormented her through afterwards, which is a disagreeable remembrance and makes the sight of him odious now. Aye, aye! you needn't wince!" said my aunt. "I know it's true without that."

He had stood by the door, all this while, observant of her with a smile upon his face, though his black eyebrows were heavily contracted. I remarked now, that, though the smile was on his face still, his colour had gone in a moment, and he seemed to breathe as if he had been running.

"Good day, sir," said my aunt, "and good-bye! Good day to you, too, ma'am," said my aunt, turning suddenly upon his sister. "Let me see you ride a donkey over *my* green again, and as sure as you have a head upon your shoulders, I'll knock your bonnet off, and tread upon it!"

It would require a painter, and no common painter too, to depict my aunt's face as she delivered herself of this very unexpected sentiment, and Miss Murdstone's face as she heard it. But the manner of the speech, no less than the matter, was so fiery, that Miss Murdstone, without a word in answer, discreetly put her arm through her brother's, and walked haughtily out of the cottage; my aunt remaining in the window looking after them; prepared, I have no doubt, in case of the donkey's reappearance, to carry her threat into instant execution.

No attempt at defiance being made, however, her face gradually relaxed, and became so pleasant, that I was emboldened to kiss and thank her; which I did with great heartiness, and with both my arms clasped round her neck. I then shook hands with Mr Dick, who shook hands with me a great many times, and hailed this happy close of the proceedings with repeated bursts of laughter.

"You'll consider yourself guardian, jointly with me, of this child, Mr Dick," said my aunt.

"I shall be delighted," said Mr Dick, "to be the guardian of David's son."

"Very good," returned my aunt, 'that's settled. I have been thinking, do you know, Mr Dick, that I might call him Trotwood?"

"Certainly, certainly. Call him Trotwood, certainly," said Mr Dick. "David's son's Trotwood."

"Trotwood Copperfield, you mean," returned my aunt.

"Yes, to be sure. Yes. Trotwood Copperfield," said Mr Dick, a little abashed.

My aunt took so kindly to the notion, that some ready-made clothes, which were purchased for me that afternoon, were marked "Trotwood Copperfield," in her own handwriting, and in indelible marking-ink, before I put them on; and it was settled that all the other clothes which were ordered to be made for me (a complete outfit was bespoke that afternoon) should be marked in the same way.

Thus I began my new life, in a new name, and with everything new about me. Now that the state of doubt was over, I felt, for many days, like one in a dream. I never thought that I had a curious couple of guardians, in my aunt and Mr Dick. I never thought of anything about myself, distinctly. The two things clearest in my mind were, that a remoteness had come upon the old Blunderstone life—which seemed to lie in the haze of an immeasurable distance; and that a curtain had for ever fallen on my life at Murdstone and Grinby's. No one has ever raised that curtain since. I have lifted it for a moment, even in this narrative, with a reluctant hand, and dropped it gladly. The remembrance of that life is fraught with so much pain to me, with so much mental suffering and want of hope, that I have never had the courage even to examine how long I was doomed to lead it. Whether it lasted for a year, or more, or less, I do not know. I only know that it was, and ceased to be; and that I have written, and there I leave it.

Chapter XV

I MAKE ANOTHER BEGINNING

MR DICK and I soon became the best of friends, and very often, when his day's work was done, went out together to fly the great kite. Every day of his life he had a long sitting at the Memorial, which never made the least progress, however hard he laboured, for King Charles the First always strayed into it, sooner or later, and then it was thrown aside, and another one begun. The patience and hope with which he bore these perpetual disappointments, the mild perception he had that there was something wrong about King Charles the First, the feeble efforts he made to keep him out, and the certainty with which he came in, and tumbled the Memorial out of all shape, made a deep impression on me. What Mr Dick supposed would come of the Memorial, if it were completed; where he thought it was to go, or what he thought it was to do; he knew no more than anybody else, I believe. Nor was it at all necessary that he should trouble himself with such questions, for if anything were certain under the sun, it was certain that the Memorial never would be finished.

It was quite an affecting sight, I used to think, to see him with the kite when it was up a great height in the air. What he had told me, in his room, about his belief in its disseminating the statements pasted on it, which were nothing but old leaves of abortive Memorials, might have been a fancy with him sometimes; but not when he was out, looking up at the kite in the sky, and feeling it pull and tug at his hand. He never looked so serene as he did then. I used to fancy, as I sat by him of an evening, on a green slope, and saw him watch the kite high in the quiet air, that it lifted his mind out of its confusion, and bore it (such was my boyish thought) into the skies. As he wound the string in and it came lower and lower down out of the beautiful light, until it fluttered to the ground, and lay there like a dead thing, he seemed to wake gradually out of a dream; and I remember to have seen him take it up, and look about him in a lost way, as if they had both come down together, so that I pitied him with all my heart.

While I advanced in friendship and intimacy with Mr Dick, I did not go backward in the favour of his staunch friend, my aunt. She took so kindly to me, that, in the course of a few weeks, she shortened my adopted name of Trotwood into Trot; and even encouraged me to hope, that if I went on as I had begun, I might take equal rank in her affections with my sister Betsey Trotwood.

"Trot," said my aunt one evening, when the back-gammon-board was placed as usual for herself and Mr Dick, "we must not forget your education."

This was my only subject of anxiety, and I felt quite delighted by her referring to it.

"Should you like to go to school at Canterbury?" said my aunt.

I replied that I should like it very much, as it was so near her.

"Good," said my aunt. "Should you like to go tomorrow?"

Being already no stranger to the general rapidity of my aunt's evolutions, I was not surprised by the suddenness of the proposal, and said: "Yes."

"Good," said my aunt again. "Janet, hire the grey pony and chaise tomorrow morning at ten o'clock, and pack up Master Trotwood's clothes tonight."

I was greatly elated by these orders; but my heart smote me for my selfishness, when I witnessed their effect on Mr Dick, who was so low-spirited at the prospect of our separation, and played so ill in consequence, that my aunt, after giving him several admonitory raps on the knuckles with her dice-box, shut up the board, and declined to play with him any more. But, on hearing from my aunt that I should sometimes come over on a Saturday, and that he could sometimes come and see me on a Wednesday, he revived; and vowed to make another kite for those occasions, of proportions greatly surpassing the present one. In the morning he was downhearted again, and would have sustained himself by giving me all the money he had in his possession, gold and silver too, if my aunt had not interposed, and limited the gift to five shillings, which, at his earnest petition, were afterwards increased to ten. We parted at the garden-gate in a most affectionate manner, and Mr Dick did not go into the house until my aunt had driven me out of sight of it.

My aunt, who was perfectly indifferent to public opinion, drove the grey pony through Dover in a masterly manner; sitting high and stiff like a state coachman, keeping a steady eye upon him wherever he went, and making a point of not letting him have his own way in any respect. When we came into the country road, she permitted him to relax a little, however; and looking at me down in a valley of cushion by her side, asked me whether I was happy?

"Very happy indeed, thank you, aunt," I said.

She was much gratified; and both her hands being occupied, patted me on the head with her whip.

"Is it a large school, aunt?" I asked.

"Why, I don't know," said my aunt. "We are going to Mr Wickfield's first."

"Does *he* keep a school?" I asked.

"No, Trot," said my aunt. "He keeps an office."

I asked for no more information about Mr Wickfield, as she offered none, and we conversed on other subjects until we came to Canterbury, where, as it was market-day, my aunt had a great opportunity of insinuating the grey pony among carts, baskets, vegetables, and huckster's goods. The hair-breadth turns and twists we made, drew down upon us a variety of speeches from the people standing about, which were not always complimentary; but my aunt drove on with perfect indifference, and I dare say would have taken her own way with as much coolness through an enemy's country.

At length we stopped before a very old house bulging out over the road; a house with long low lattice-windows bulging out still farther, and beams with carved heads on the ends bulging out too, so that I fancied the whole house was leaning forward, trying to see who was passing on the narrow pavement below. It was quite spotless in its cleanliness. The old-fashioned brass knocker on the low arched door, ornamented with carved garlands of fruit and flowers, twinkled like a star; the two stone steps descending to the door were as white as if they had been covered with fair linen; and all the angles and corners, and carvings and mouldings, and quaint little panes of glass, and quainter little windows, though as old as the hills, were as pure as any snow that ever fell upon the hills.

When the pony-chaise stopped at the door, and my eyes were intent upon the house, I saw a cadaverous face appear at a small window on the ground floor (in a little round tower that formed one side of the house), and quickly disappear. The low arched door then opened, and the face came out. It was quite as cadaverous as it had looked in the window, though in the grain of it there was that tinge of red which is sometimes to be observed in the skins of red-haired people. It belonged to a red-haired person—a youth of fifteen, as I take it now, but looking much older—whose hair was cropped as close as the closest stubble; who had hardly any eyebrows, and no eyelashes, and eyes of a red-brown, so unsheltered and unshaded, that I remember wondering how he went to sleep. He was high-shouldered and bony; dressed in decent black, with a white wisp of a neckcloth; buttoned up to the throat; and had a long, lank, skeleton hand, which particularly attracted my attention, as he stood at the pony's head, rubbing his chin with it, and looking up at us in the chaise.

"Is Mr Wickfield at home, Uriah Heep?" said my aunt.

"Mr Wickfield's at home, ma'am," said Uriah Heep, "if you'll please to walk in there"—pointing with his long hand to the room he meant.

We got out; and leaving him to hold the pony, went into a long low parlour looking towards the street, from the window of which I caught a glimpse, as I went in, of Uriah Heep breathing into the pony's nostrils, and immediately covering them with his hand, as if he were putting some spell upon him. Opposite to the tall old chimney-piece were two portraits: one of a gentleman with grey hair (though not by any means an old man) and black eyebrows, who was looking over some papers tied together with red tape; the other, of a lady, with a very placid and sweet expression of face, who was looking at me.

I believe I was turning about in search of Uriah's picture, when, a door at the farther end of the room opening, a gentleman entered, at sight of whom I turned to the first-mentioned portrait again, to make quite sure that it had not come out of its frame. But it was stationary; and as the gentleman advanced into the light, I saw that he was some years older than when he had had his picture painted.

"Miss Betsey Trotwood," said the gentleman, "pray walk in. I was engaged for a moment, but you'll excuse my being busy. You know my motive. I have but one in life."

Miss Betsey thanked him, and we went into his room, which was furnished as an office, with books, papers, tin boxes, and so forth. It looked into a garden, and had an iron safe let into the wall; so immediately over the mantelshelf, that I wondered, as I sat down, how the sweeps got round it when they swept the chimney.

"Well, Miss Trotwood," said Mr Wickfield; for I soon found that it was he, and that he was a lawyer, and steward of the estates of a rich gentleman of the county; "what wind blows you here? Not an ill wind, I hope?"

"No," replied my aunt. "I have not come for any law."

"That's right, ma'am," said Mr Wickfield. "You had better come for anything else."

His hair was quite white now, though his eyebrows were still black. He had a very agreeable face, and, I thought, was handsome. There was a certain richness in his complexion, which I had been long accustomed, under Peggotty's tuition, to connect with port wine; and I fancied it was in his voice too, and referred his growing corpulency to the same cause. He was very cleanly dressed, in a blue coat, striped waistcoat, and nankeen trousers; and his fine frilled shirt and cambric neckcloth looked unusually soft and white, reminding my strolling fancy (I call to mind) of the plumage on the breast of a swan.

"This is my nephew," said my aunt.

"Wasn't aware you had one, Miss Trotwood," said Mr Wickfield.

"My grand-nephew, that is to say," observed my aunt.

"Wasn't aware you had a grand-nephew, I give you my word," said Mr Wickfield.

"I have adopted him," said my aunt, with a wave of her hand, importing that his knowledge and his ignorance were all one to her, "and I have brought him here, to put to a school where he may be thoroughly well taught, and well treated. Now tell me where that school is, and what it is, and all about it."

"Before I can advise you properly," said Mr Wickfield—"the old question, you know. What's your motive in this?"

"Deuce take the man!" exclaimed my aunt. "Always fishing for motives, when they're on the surface! Why, to make the child happy and useful."

"It must be a mixed motive, I think," said Mr Wickfield, shaking his head and smiling incredulously.

"A mixed fiddlestick," returned my aunt. "You claim to have one plain motive in all you do yourself. You don't suppose, I hope, that you are the only plain dealer in the world?"

"Ay, but I have only one motive in life, Miss Trotwood," he rejoined, smiling. "Other people have dozens, scores, hundreds. I have only one. There's the difference. However, that's beside the question. The best school? Whatever the motive, you want the best?"

My aunt nodded assent.

"At the best we have," said Mr Wickfield, considering, "your nephew couldn't board just now."

"But he could board somewhere else, I suppose?" suggested my aunt.

Mr Wickfield thought I could. After a little discussion, he proposed to take my aunt to the school, that she might see it and judge for herself; also, to take her, with the same object, to two or three houses where he thought I could be boarded. My aunt embracing the proposal, we were all three going out together, when he stopped and said:

"Our little friend here might have some motive, perhaps, for objecting to the arrangements. I think we had better leave him behind?"

My aunt seemed disposed to contest the point; but to facilitate matters I said I would gladly remain behind, if they pleased; and returned into Mr Wickfield's office, where I sat down again, in the chair I had first occupied, to await their return.

It so happened that this chair was opposite a narrow passage, which ended in the little circular room where I had seen Uriah Heep's pale face looking out of [the] window. Uriah, having taken the pony to a neighbouring stable, was at work at a desk in this room, which had a brass frame on the top to hang paper upon, and on which the writing he was making a copy of was then hanging. Though his face was towards me, I thought, for some time, the writing being between us, that he could not see me; but looking that way more attentively, it made me uncomfortable to observe that, every now and then, his sleepless eyes would come below the writing, like two red suns, and stealthily stare at me for I dare say a whole minute at a time, during which his pen went, or pretended to go, as cleverly as ever. I made several attempts to get out of their way—such as standing on a chair to look at a map on the other side of the room, and poring over the columns of a Kentish newspaper—but they always attracted me back again; and whenever I looked towards those two red suns, I was sure to find them, either just rising or just setting.

At length, much to my relief, my aunt and Mr Wickfield came back, after a pretty long absence. They were not so successful as I could have wished; for though the advantages of the school were undeniable, my aunt had not approved of any of the boarding-houses proposed for me.

"It's very unfortunate," said my aunt. "I don't know what to do, Trot."

"It *does* happen unfortunately," said Mr Wickfield. "But I'll tell you what you can do, Miss Trotwood."

"What's that?" inquired my aunt.

"Leave your nephew here, for the present. He's a quiet fellow. He won't disturb me at all. It's a capital house for study. As quiet as a monastery, and almost as roomy. Leave him here."

My aunt evidently liked the offer, though she was delicate of accepting it. So did I.

"Come, Miss Trotwood," said Mr Wickfield. "This is the way out of the difficulty. It's only a temporary arrangement, you know. If it don't act well, or don't quite accord with our mutual convenience, he can easily go to the right-about. There will be time to find some better place for him in the meanwhile. You had better determine to leave him here for the present!"

"I am very much obliged to you," said my aunt; "and so is he, I see; but—"

"Come! I know what you mean," cried Mr Wickfield. "You shall not be oppressed by the receipt of favours, Miss Trotwood. You may pay for him, if you like. We won't be hard about terms, but you shall pay if you will."

"On that understanding," said my aunt, "though it doesn't lessen the real obligation, I shall be very glad to leave him."

"Then come and see my little housekeeper," said Mr Wickfield.

We accordingly went up a wonderful old staircase; with a balustrade so broad that we might have gone up that, almost as easily; and into a shady old drawing-room, lighted by some three or four of the quaint windows I had looked up at from the street: which had old oak seats in them, that seemed to have come of the same trees as the shining oak floor, and the great beams in the ceiling. It was a prettily furnished room, with a piano and some lively furniture in red and green, and some flowers. It seemed to be all old nooks and corners; and in every nook and corner there was some queer little table, or cupboard, or bookcase, or seat, or something or other, that made me think there was not such another good corner in the room; until I looked at the next one, and found it equal to it, if not better. On everything there was the same air of retirement and cleanliness that marked the house outside.

Mr Wickfield tapped at a door in a corner of the panelled wall, and a girl of about my own age came quickly out and kissed him. On her face, I saw immediately the placid and sweet expression of the lady whose picture had looked at me downstairs. It seemed to my imagination as if the portrait had grown womanly, and the original remained a child. Although her face was quite bright and happy, there was a tranquillity about it, and about her—a quiet, good, calm spirit—that I never have forgotten; that I shall never forget.

This was his little housekeeper, his daughter Agnes, Mr Wickfield said. When I heard how he said it, and saw how he held her hand, I guessed what the one motive of his life was.

She had a little basket-trifle hanging at her side, with keys in it; and she looked as staid and as discreet a housekeeper as the old house could have. She listened to her father as he told her about me, with a pleasant face; and when he had concluded, proposed to my aunt that we should go upstairs and see my room. We all went together, she before us: and a glorious old room it was, with more oak beams, and diamond panes; and the broad balustrade going all the way up to it.

I cannot call to mind where or when, in my childhood, I had seen a stained glass window in a church. Nor do I recollect its subject. But I know that when I saw her turn round, in the grave light of the old staircase, and wait for us, above, I thought of that window; and I associated something of its tranquil brightness with Agnes Wickfield ever afterwards.

My aunt was as happy as I was, in the arrangement made for me; and we went down to the drawing-room again, well pleased and gratified. As she would not hear of staying to dinner, lest she should by any chance fail to arrive at home with the grey pony before dark; and as I apprehend Mr Wickfield knew her too well, to argue any point with her; some lunch was provided for her there, and Agnes went back to her governess, and Mr

Wickfield to his office. So we were left to take leave of one another without any restraint.

She told me that everything would be arranged for me by Mr Wickfield, and that I should want for nothing, and gave me the kindest words and the best advice.

"Trot," said my aunt in conclusion, "be a credit to yourself, to me, and Mr Dick, and Heaven be with you!"

I was greatly overcome, and could only thank her, again and again, and send my love to Mr Dick.

"Never," said my aunt, "be mean in anything; never be false; never be cruel. Avoid those three vices, Trot, and I can always be hopeful of you."

I promised, as well as I could, that I would not abuse her kindness or forget her admonition.

"The pony's at the door," said my aunt, "and I am off! Stay here."

With these words she embraced me hastily, and went out of the room, shutting the door after her. At first I was startled by so abrupt a departure, and almost feared I had displeased her; but when I looked into the street, and saw how dejectedly she got into the chaise, and drove away without looking up, I understood her better and did not do her that injustice.

By five o'clock, which was Mr Wickfield's dinner-hour, I had mustered up my spirits again, and was ready for my knife and fork. The cloth was only laid for us two; but Agnes was waiting in the drawing-room before dinner, went down with her father, and sat opposite to him at table. I doubted whether he could have dined without her.

We did not stay there, after dinner, but came upstairs into the drawing-room again: in one snug corner of which, Agnes set glasses for her father, and a decanter of port wine. I thought he would have missed its usual flavour, if it had been put there for him by any other hands.

There he sat, taking his wine, and taking a good deal of it, for two hours; while Agnes played on the piano, worked, and talked to him and me. He was, for the most part, gay and cheerful with us; but sometimes his eyes rested on her, and he fell into a brooding state, and was silent. She always observed this quickly, I thought, and always roused him with a question or caress. Then he came out of his meditation, and drank more wine.

Agnes made the tea, and presided over it; and the time passed away after it, as after dinner, until she went to bed; when her father took her in his arms and kissed her, and, she being gone, ordered candles in his office. Then I went to bed too.

But in the course of the evening I had rambled down to the door, and a little way along the street, that I might have another peep at the old houses, and the grey Cathedral; and might think of my coming through that old city on my journey, and of my passing the very house I lived in, without knowing it. As I came back, I saw Uriah Heep shutting up the office; and feeling friendly towards everybody, went in and spoke to him, and at parting, gave him my hand. But oh, what a clammy hand his was! as ghostly to the touch as to the sight! I rubbed mine afterwards, to warm it, *and to rub his off.*

It was such an uncomfortable hand, that, when I went to my room, it was still cold and wet upon my memory. Leaning out of [the] window, and seeing one of the faces on the beam-ends looking at me sideways, I fancied it was Uriah Heep got up there somehow, and shut him out in a hurry.

Chapter XVI

I AM A NEW BOY IN MORE SENSES THAN ONE

NEXT morning, after breakfast, I entered on school life again. I went, accompanied by Mr Wickfield, to the scene of my future studies—a grave building in a court-yard, with a learned air about it that seemed very well suited to the stray rooks and jackdaws who came down from the Cathedral towers to walk with a clerkly bearing on the grass-plot—and was introduced to my new master, Doctor Strong.

Doctor Strong looked almost as rusty, to my thinking, as the tall iron rails and gates outside the house; and almost as stiff and heavy as the great stone urns that flanked them, and were set up, on the top of the red-brick wall, at regular distances all round the court, like sublimated skittles, for Time to play at. He was in his library (I mean Doctor Strong was), with his clothes not particularly well brushed, and his hair not particularly well combed; his knee-smalls unbraced; his long black gaiters unbuttoned; and his shoes yawning like two caverns on the hearth-rug. Turning upon me a lustreless eye, that reminded me of a long-forgotten blind old horse who once used to crop the grass, and tumble over the graves, in Blunderstone churchyard, he said he was glad to see me: and then he gave me his hand; which I didn't know what to do with, as it did nothing for itself.

But, sitting at work, not far from Doctor Strong, was a very pretty young lady—whom he called Annie, and who was his daughter, I supposed—who got me out of my difficulty by kneeling down to put Doctor Strong's shoes on, and button his gaiters, which she did with great cheerfulness and quickness. When she had finished, and we were going out to the schoolroom, I was much surprised to hear Mr Wickfield, in bidding her good morning, address her as "Mrs Strong"; and I was wondering could she be Doctor Strong's son's wife, or could she be Mrs Doctor Strong, when Doctor Strong himself unconsciously enlightened me.

"By the by, Wickfield," he said, stopping in a passage with his hand on my shoulder; "you have not found any suitable provision for my wife's cousin yet?"

"No," said Mr Wickfield. "No. Not yet."

"I could wish it done as soon as it *can* be done, Wickfield," said Doctor Strong, "for Jack Maldon is needy, and idle; and of those two bad things, worse things sometimes come. What does Doctor Watts say," he added, looking at me, and moving his head to the time of his quotation, " 'Satan finds some mischief still, for idle hands to do.' "

"Egad, Doctor," returned Mr Wickfield, "if Doctor Watts knew mankind, he might have written, with as much truth, 'Satan finds some mischief still, for busy hands to do.' The busy people achieve their full share of mischief in the world, you may rely upon it. What have the people been about, who have been the busiest in getting money, and in getting power, this century or two? No mischief?"

"Jack Maldon will never be very busy in getting either, I expect," said Doctor Strong, rubbing his chin thoughtfully.

"Perhaps not," said Mr Wickfield; "and you bring me back to the question, with an apology for digressing. No, I have not been able to dispose of Mr Jack Maldon yet. I believe," he said this with some hesitation, "I penetrate your motive, and it makes the thing more difficult."

"My motive," returned Doctor Strong, "is to make some suitable provision for a cousin, and an old playfellow, of Annie's."

"Yes, I know," said Mr Wickfield; "at home or abroad."

"Aye!" replied the Doctor, apparently wondering why he emphasized those words so much. "At home or abroad."

"Your own expression, you know," said Mr Wickfield. "Or abroad."

"Surely," the Doctor answered. "Surely. One or other."

"One or other? Have you no choice?" asked Mr Wickfield.

"No," returned the Doctor.

"No?" with astonishment.

"Not the least."

"No motive," said Mr Wickfield, "for meaning abroad, and not at home?"

"No," returned the Doctor.

"I am bound to believe you, and of course I do believe you," said Mr Wickfield. "It might have simplified my office very much, if I had known it before. But I confess I entertained another impression."

Doctor Strong regarded him with a puzzled and doubting look, which almost immediately subsided into a smile that gave me great encouragement; for it was full of amiability and sweetness, and there was a simplicity in it, and indeed in his whole manner, when the studious, pondering frost upon it was got through, very attractive and hopeful to a young scholar like me. Repeating "no," and "not the least," and other short assurances to the same purport, Doctor Strong jogged on before us, at a queer, uneven pace; and we followed: Mr Wickfield, looking grave, I observed, and shaking his head to himself, without knowing that I saw him.

The schoolroom was a pretty large hall, on the quietest side of the house, confronted by the stately stare of some half-dozen of the great urns, and commanding a peep of an old secluded garden belonging to the Doctor, where the peaches were ripening on the sunny south wall. There were two great aloes, in tubs, on the turf outside the windows; the broad hard leaves of which plant (looking as if they were made of painted tin) have ever since, by association, been symbolical to me of silence and retirement. About five-and-twenty boys were studiously engaged at their books when we went in, but they rose to give the Doctor good morning, and remained standing when they saw Mr Wickfield and me.

"A new boy, young gentlemen," said the Doctor; "Trotwood Copperfield."

One Adams, who was the head-boy, then stepped out of his place and welcomed me. He looked like a young clergyman, in his white cravat, but he was very affable and good-humoured; and he showed me my place, and presented me to the masters, in a gentlemanly way that would have put me at my ease, if anything could.

It seemed to me so long, however, since I had been among such boys, or among any companions of my own age, except Mick Walker and Mealy Potatoes, that I felt as strange as ever I have done in my life. I was so conscious of having passed through scenes of which they could have no knowledge, and of having acquired experiences foreign to my age, appearance, and condition as one of them, that I half believed it was an imposture to come there as an ordinary little schoolboy. I had become, in the Murdstone and Grinby time, however short or long it may have been, so unused to the sports and games of boys, that I knew I was awkward and inexperienced in the commonest things belonging to them. Whatever I had learnt, had so slipped away from me in the sordid cares of my life from day to night, that now, when I was examined about what I knew, I knew nothing, and was put into the lowest form of the school. But, troubled as I was, by my want of boyish skill, and of book-learning too, I was made infinitely more uncomfortable by the consideration, that, in what I did know, I was much farther removed from my companions than in what I did not. My mind ran upon what they would think, if they knew of my familiar acquaintance with the King's Bench Prison? Was there anything about me which would reveal my proceedings in connexion with the Micawber family—all those pawnings, and sellings, and suppers—in spite of myself? Suppose some of the boys had seen me coming through Canterbury, wayworn and ragged, and should find me out? What would they say, who made so light of money, if they could know how I had scraped my halfpence together, for the purchase of my daily saveloy and beer, or my slices of pudding? How would it affect them, who were so innocent of London life, and London streets, to discover how knowing I was (and was ashamed to be) in some of the meanest phases of both? All this ran in my head so much, on that first day at Doctor Strong's, that I felt distrustful of my slightest look and gesture; shrunk within myself whensoever I was approached by one of my new schoolfellows; and hurried off the minute school was over, afraid of committing myself in my response to any friendly notice or advance.

But there was such an influence in Mr Wickfield's old house, that when I knocked at it, with my new school-books under my arm, I began to feel my uneasiness softening away. As I went up to my airy old room, the grave shadow of the staircase seemed to fall upon my doubts and fears, and to make the past more indistinct. I sat there, sturdily conning my books, until dinner-time (we were out of school for good at three); and went down, hopeful of becoming a passable sort of boy yet.

Agnes was in the drawing-room, waiting for her father, who was detained by someone in his office. She met me with her pleasant smile, and asked me how I liked the school. I told her I should like it very much, I hoped; but I was a little strange to it at first.

"*You* have never been to school," I said, "have you?"

"Oh yes! Every day."

"Ah, but you mean here, at your own home?"

"Papa couldn't spare me to go anywhere else," she answered, smiling and shaking her head. "His housekeeper must be in his house, you know."

"He is very fond of you, I am sure," I said.

She nodded "Yes," and went to the door to listen for his coming up, that she might meet him on the stairs. But, as he was not there, she came back again.

"Mama has been dead ever since I was born," she said, in her quiet way. "I only know her picture, downstairs. I saw you looking at it yesterday. Did you think whose it was?"

I told her yes, because it was so like herself.

"Papa says so, too," said Agnes, pleased. "Hark! That's papa now!"

Her bright calm face lighted up with pleasure as she went to meet him, and as they came in, hand in hand. He greeted me cordially; and told me I should certainly be happy under Doctor Strong, who was one of the gentlest of men.

"There may be some, perhaps—I don't know that there are—who abuse his kindness," said Mr Wickfield. "Never be one of those, Trotwood, in anything. He is the least suspicious of mankind; and whether that's a merit, or whether it's a blemish, it deserves consideration in all dealings with the Doctor, great or small."

He spoke, I thought, as if he were weary, or dissatisfied with something; but I did not pursue the question in my mind, for dinner was just then announced, and we went down and took the same seats as before.

We had scarcely done so, when Uriah Heep put in his red head and his lank hand at the door, and said:

"Here's Mr Maldon begs the favour of a word, sir."

"I am but this moment quit of Mr Maldon," said his master.

"Yes, sir," returned Uriah; "but Mr Maldon has come back, and he begs the favour of a word."

As he held the door open with his hand, Uriah looked at me, and looked at Agnes, and looked at the dishes, and looked at the plates, and looked at every object in the room, I thought,—yet seemed to look at nothing; he made such an appearance all the while of keeping his red eyes dutifully on his master.

"I beg your pardon. It's only to say, on reflection," observed a voice behind Uriah, as Uriah's head was pushed away, and the speaker's substituted—"pray excuse me for this intrusion—that as it seems I have no choice in the matter, the sooner I go abroad the better. My cousin Annie did say, when we talked of it, that she liked to have her friends within reach rather than to have them banished, and the old Doctor—"

"Doctor Strong, was that?" Mr Wickfield interposed, gravely.

"Doctor Strong, of course," returned the other; "I call him the old Doctor; it's all the same, you know."

"I *don't* know," returned Mr Wickfield.

"Well, Doctor Strong," said the other—"Doctor Strong was of the same mind, I believed. But as it appears from the course you take with me he has changed his mind, why there's no more to be said, except that the sooner I am off, the better. Therefore, I thought I'd come back and say, that the sooner I am off the better. When a plunge is to be made into the water, it's of no use lingering on the bank."

"There shall be as little lingering as possible, in your case, Mr Maldon, you may depend upon it," said Mr Wickfield.

"Thank'ee," said the other. "Much obliged. I don't want to look a gift-horse in the mouth, which is not a gracious thing to do; otherwise, I dare say, my cousin Annie could easily arrange it in her own way. I suppose Annie would only have to say to the old Doctor—"

"Meaning that Mrs Strong would only have to say to her husband—do I follow you?" said Mr Wickfield.

"Quite so," returned the other, "—would only have to say, that she wanted such and such a thing to be so and so; and it would be so and so, as a matter of course."

"And why as a matter of course, Mr Maldon?" asked Mr Wickfield, sedately eating his dinner.

"Why, because Annie's a charming young girl, and the old Doctor—Doctor Strong, I mean—is not quite a charming young boy," said Mr Jack Maldon, laughing. "No offence to anybody, Mr Wickfield. I only mean that I suppose some compensation is fair and reasonable in that sort of marriage."

"Compensation to the lady, sir?" asked Mr Wickfield gravely.

"To the lady, sir," Mr Jack Maldon answered, laughing. But appearing to remark that Mr Wickfield went on with his dinner in the same sedate, immovable manner, and that there was no hope of making him relax a muscle of his face, he added:

"However, I have said what I came to say, and, with another apology for this intrusion, I may take myself off. Of course I shall observe your directions, in considering the matter as one to be arranged between you and me solely, and not to be referred to, up at the Doctor's."

"Have you dined?" asked Mr Wickfield, with a motion of his hand towards the table.

"Thank'ee. I am going to dine," said Mr Maldon, "with my cousin Annie. Good-bye!"

Mr Wickfield, without rising, looked after him thoughtfully as he went out. He was rather a shallow sort of young gentleman, I thought, with a handsome face, a rapid utterance, and a confident, bold air. And this was the first I ever saw of Mr Jack Maldon; whom I had not expected to see so soon, when I heard the Doctor speak of him that morning.

When we had dined, we went upstairs again, where everything went on exactly as on the previous day. Agnes set the glasses and decanters in the same corner, and Mr Wickfield sat down to drink, and drank a good deal. Agnes played the piano to him, sat by him, and worked and talked, and played some games at dominoes with me. In good time she made tea; and afterwards, when I brought down my books, looked into them, and showed me what she knew of them (which was no slight matter, though she said it was), and what was the best way to learn and understand them. I see her, with her modest, orderly, placid manner, and I hear her beautiful calm voice, as I write these words. The influence for all good, which she came to exercise over me at a later time, begins already to descend upon my breast. I love little Em'ly, and I don't love Agnes— no, not at all in that way—but I feel that there are goodness, peace, and truth, wherever Agnes is; and that the soft light of the coloured window in the church, seen long ago, falls on her always, and on me when I am near her, and on everything around.

The time having come for her withdrawal for the night, and she having left us, I gave Mr Wickfield my hand, preparatory to going away myself. But he checked me and said: "Should you like to stay with us, Trotwood, or to go elsewhere?"

"To stay," I answered, quickly.

"You are sure?"

"If you please. If I may!"

"Why, it's but a dull life that we lead here, boy, I am afraid," he said.

"Not more dull for me than Agnes, sir. Not dull at all!"

"Than Agnes," he repeated, walking slowly to the great chimneypiece, and leaning against it. "Than Agnes!"

He had drank wine that evening (or I fancied it), until his eyes were bloodshot. Not that I could see them now, for they were cast down, and shaded by his hand; but I had noticed them a little while before.

"Now I wonder," he muttered, "whether my Agnes tires of me. When should I ever tire of her! But that's different, that's quite different."

He was musing, not speaking to me; so I remained quiet.

"A dull old house," he said, "and a monotonous life; but I must have her near me. I must keep her near me. If the thought that I may die and leave my darling, or that my darling may die and leave me, comes like a spectre, to distress my happiest hours, and is only to be drowned in—"

He did not supply the word; but pacing slowly to the place where he had sat, and mechanically going through the action of pouring wine from the empty decanter, set it down and paced back again.

"If it is miserable to bear, when she is here," he said, "what would it be, and she away? No, no, no. I cannot try that."

He leaned against the chimney-piece, brooding so long that I could not decide whether to run the risk of disturbing him by going, or to remain quietly where I was, until he should come out of his reverie. At length he aroused himself, and looked about the room until his eyes encountered mine.

"Stay with us, Trotwood, eh?" he said in his usual manner, and as if he were answering something I had just said. "I am glad of it. You are company to us both. It is wholesome to have you here. Wholesome for me, wholesome for Agnes, wholesome perhaps for all of us."

"I am sure it is for me, sir," I said. "I am so glad to be here."

"That's a fine fellow!" said Mr Wickfield. "As long as you are glad to be here, you shall stay here." He shook hands with me upon it, and clapped me on the back; and told me that when I had anything to do at night after Agnes had left us, or when I wished to read for my own pleasure, I was free to come down to his room, if he were there and if I desired it for company's sake, and to sit with him. I thanked him for his consideration; and, as he went down soon afterwards, and I was not tired, went down too, with a book in my hand, to avail myself, for half-an-hour, of his permission.

But, seeing a light in the little round office, and immediately feeling myself attracted towards Uriah Heep, who had a sort of fascination for me, I went in there instead. I found Uriah reading a great fat book, with such demonstrative attention, that his lank forefinger followed up every line as he read, and made clammy tracks along the page (or so I fully believed) like a snail.

"You are working late tonight, Uriah," says I.

"Yes, Master Copperfield," says Uriah.

As I was getting on the stool opposite, to talk to him more conveniently, I observed that he had not such a thing as a smile about him, and that he could only widen his mouth and make two hard creases down his cheeks, one on each side, to stand for one.

"I am not doing office-work, Master Copperfield," said Uriah.

"What work, then?" I asked.

"I am improving my legal knowledge, Master Copperfield," said Uriah. "I am going through Tidd's *Practice*. Oh, what a writer Mr Tidd is, Master Copperfield!"

My stool was such a tower of observation, that as I watched him reading on again, after this rapturous exclamation, and following up the lines with his forefinger, I observed that his nostrils, which were thin and pointed, with sharp dints in them, had a singular and most uncomfortable way of expanding and contracting themselves—that they seemed to twinkle instead of his eyes, which hardly ever twinkled at all.

"I suppose you are quite a great lawyer?" I said, after looking at him for some time.

"Me, Master Copperfield?" said Uriah. "Oh, no! I'm a very umble person."

It was no fancy of mine about his hands, I observed; for he frequently ground the palms against each other as if to squeeze them dry and warm, besides often wiping them, in a stealthy way, on his pocket-handkerchief.

"I am well aware that I am the umblest person going," said Uriah Heep, modestly; "let the other be where he may. My mother is likewise a very umble person. We live in a umble abode, Master Copperfield, but have much to be thankful for. My father's former calling was umble. He was a sexton."

"What is he now?" I asked.

"He is a partaker of glory at present, Master Copperfield," said Uriah Heep. "But we have much to be thankful for. How much have I to be thankful for in living with Mr Wickfield!"

I asked Uriah if he had been with Mr Wickfield long?

"I have been with him, going on four year, Master Copperfield," said Uriah; shutting up his book, after carefully marking the place where he had left off. "Since a year after my father's death. How much have I to be thankful for, in that! How much have I to be thankful for, in Mr Wickfield's kind intention to give me my articles, which would otherwise not lay within the umble means of mother and self!"

"Then, when your articled time is over, you'll be a regular lawyer, I suppose?" said I.

"With the blessing of Providence, Master Copperfield," returned Uriah.

"Perhaps you'll be a partner in Mr Wickfield's business, one of these days," I said, to make myself agreeable; "and it will be Wickfield and Heep, or Heep late Wickfield."

"Oh no, Master Copperfield," returned Uriah, shaking his head, "I am much too umble for that!"

He certainly did look uncommonly like the carved face on the beam outside my window, as he sat, in his humility, eyeing me sideways, with his mouth widened, and the creases in his cheeks.

"Mr Wickfield is a most excellent man, Master Copperfield," said Uriah. "If you have known him long, you know it, I am sure, much better than I can inform you."

I replied that I was certain he was; but that I had not known him long myself, though he was a friend of my aunt's.

"Oh, indeed, Master Copperfield," said Uriah. "Your aunt is a sweet lady, Master Copperfield!"

He had a way of writhing when he wanted to express enthusiasm, which was very ugly; and which diverted my attention from the compliment he had paid my relation, to the snaky twistings of his throat and body.

"A sweet lady, Master Copperfield!" said Uriah Heep. "She has a great admiration for Miss Agnes, Master Copperfield, I believe?"

I said, "Yes," boldly; not that I knew anything about it, Heaven forgive me!

"I hope you have, too, Master Copperfield," said Uriah. "But I am sure you must have."

"Everybody must have," I returned.

"Oh, thank you, Master Copperfield," said Uriah Heep, "for that remark! It is so true! Umble as I am, I know it is *so* true! Oh, thank you, Master Copperfield!"

He writhed himself quite off his stool in the excitement of his feelings, and, being off, began to make arrangements for going home.

"Mother will be expecting me," he said, referring to a pale, inexpressive-faced watch in his pocket, "and getting uneasy; for though we are very umble, Master Copperfield, we are much attached to one another. If you would come and see us, any afternoon, and take a cup of tea at our lowly dwelling, mother would be as proud of your company as I should be."

I said I should be glad to come.

"Thank you, Master Copperfield," returned Uriah, putting his book away upon the shelf.—"I suppose you stop here, some time, Master Copperfield?"

I said I was going to be brought up there, I believed, as long as I remained at school.

"Oh, indeed!" exclaimed Uriah. "I should think *you* would come into the business at last, Master Copperfield!"

I protested that I had no views of that sort, and that no such scheme was entertained in my behalf by anybody; but Uriah insisted on blandly replying to all my assurances, "Oh, yes, Master Copperfield, I should think you would, indeed!" and, "Oh, indeed, Master Copperfield, I should think you would, certainly!" over and over again. Being, at last, ready to leave the office for the night, he asked me if it would suit my convenience to have the light put out; and on my answering "Yes," instantly extinguished it. After shaking hands with me—his hand felt like a fish, in the dark—he opened the door into the street a very little, and crept out, and shut it, leaving me to grope my way back into the house: which cost me some trouble and a fall over his stool. This was the proximate

cause, I suppose, of my dreaming about him, for what appeared to me to be half the
night; and dreaming, among other things, that he had launched Mr Peggotty's house on
a piratical expedition, with a black flag at the masthead, bearing the inscription "Tidd's
Practice," under which diabolical ensign he was carrying me and little Em'ly to the
Spanish Main, to be drowned.

I got a little the better of my uneasiness when I went to school next day, and a good
deal the better next day, and so shook it off by degrees, that in less than a fortnight I was
quite at home, and happy, among my new companions. I was awkward enough in their
games, and backward enough in their studies; but custom would improve me in the first
respect, I hoped, and hard work in the second. Accordingly, I went to work very hard,
both in play and in earnest, and gained great commendation. And, in a very little while,
the Murdstone and Grinby life became so strange to me that I hardly believed in it, while
my present life grew so familiar, that I seemed to have been leading it a long time.

Doctor Strong's was an excellent school; as different from Mr Creakle's as good is
from evil. It was very gravely and decorously ordered, and on a sound system; with an
appeal, in everything, to the honour and good faith of the boys, and an avowed intention
to rely on their possession of those qualities unless they proved themselves unworthy of
it, which worked wonders. We all felt that we had a part in the management of the place,
and in sustaining its character and dignity. Hence, we soon became warmly attached to
it—I am sure I did for one, and I never knew, in all my time, of any other boy being
otherwise—and learnt with a good will, desiring to do it credit. We had noble games out
of hours, and plenty of liberty; but even then, as I remember, we were well spoken of
in the town, and rarely did any disgrace, by our appearance or manner, to the reputation
of Doctor Strong and Doctor Strong's boys.

Some of the higher scholars boarded in the Doctor's house, and through them I
learned, at second hand, some particulars of the Doctor's history—as, how he had not
yet been married twelve months to the beautiful young lady I had seen in the study,
whom he had married for love; for she had not a sixpence, and had a world of poor
relations (so our fellows said) ready to swarm the Doctor out of house and home. Also,
how the Doctor's cogitating manner was attributable to his being always engaged in
looking out for Greek roots; which, in my innocence and ignorance, I supposed to be
a botanical furor on the Doctor's part, especially as he always looked at the ground when
he walked about, until I understood that they were roots of words, with a view to a new
Dictionary which he had in contemplation. Adams, our head-boy, who had a turn for
mathematics, had made a calculation, I was informed, of the time this Dictionary would
take in completing, on the Doctor's plan, and at the Doctor's rate of going. He considered
that it might be done in one thousand six hundred and forty-nine years, counting from
the Doctor's last, or sixty-second, birthday.

But the Doctor himself was the idol of the whole school: and it must have been a
badly composed school if he had been anything else, for he was the kindest of men; with
a simple faith in him that might have touched the stone hearts of the very turns upon the
wall. As he walked up and down that part of the courtyard which was at the side of the
house, with the stray rooks and jackdaws looking after him with their heads cocked slyly,
as if they knew how much more knowing they were in worldly affairs than he, if any sort
of vagabond could only get near enough to his creaking shoes to attract his attention to
one sentence of a tale of distress, that vagabond was made for the next two days. It was
so notorious in the house, that the masters and head-boys took pains to cut these
marauders off at angles, and to get out of windows, and turn them out of the courtyard,
before they could make the Doctor aware of their presence; which was sometimes

happily effected within a few yards of him, without his knowing anything of the matter, as he jogged to and fro. Outside his own domain, and unprotected, he was a very sheep for the shearers. He would have taken his gaiters off his legs, to give away. In fact, there was a story current among us (I have no idea, and never had, on what authority, but I have believed it for so many years that I feel quite certain it is true), that on a frosty day, one winter-time, he actually did bestow his gaiters on a beggar-woman, who occasioned some scandal in the neighbourhood by exhibiting a fine infant from door to door, wrapped in those garments, which were universally recognized, being as well known in the vicinity as the Cathedral. The legend added that the only person who did not identify them was the Doctor himself, who, when they were shortly afterwards displayed at the door of a little second-hand shop of no very good repute, where such things were taken in exchange for gin, was more than once observed to handle them approvingly, as if admiring some curious novelty in the pattern, and considering them an improvement on his own.

It was very pleasant to see the Doctor with his pretty young wife. He had a fatherly, benignant way of showing his fondness for her, which seemed in itself to express a good man. I often saw them walking in the garden where the peaches were, and I sometimes had a nearer observation of them in the study or the parlour. She appeared to me to take great care of the Doctor, and to like him very much, though I never thought her vitally interested in the Dictionary: some cumbrous fragments of which work the Doctor always carried in his pockets, and in the lining of his hat, and generally seemed to be expounding to her as they walked about.

I saw a good deal of Mrs Strong, both because she had taken a liking for me on the morning of my introduction to the Doctor, and was always afterwards kind to me, and interested in me; and because she was very fond of Agnes, and was often backwards and forwards at our house. There was a curious constraint between her and Mr Wickfield, I thought (of whom she seemed to be afraid), that never wore off. When she came there of an evening, she always shrunk from accepting his escort home, and ran away with me instead. And sometimes, as we were running gaily across the Cathedral yard together, expecting to meet nobody, we would meet Mr Jack Maldon, who was always surprised to see us.

Mrs Strong's mama was a lady I took great delight in. Her name was Mrs Markleham; but our boys used to call her the Old Soldier, on account of her generalship, and the skill with which she marshalled great forces of relations against the Doctor. She was a little, sharp-eyed woman, who used to wear, when she was dressed, one unchangeable cap, ornamented with some artificial flowers, and two artificial butterflies supposed to be hovering above the flowers. There was a superstition among us that this cap had come from France, and could only originate in the workmanship of that ingenious nation: but all I certainly know about it, is, that it always made its appearance of an evening, wheresoever Mrs Markleham made *her* appearance; that it was carried about to friendly meetings in a Hindoo basket; that the butterflies had the gift of trembling constantly; and that they improved the shining hours at Doctor Strong's expense, like busy bees.

I observed the Old Soldier—not to adopt the name disrespectfully—to pretty good advantage, on a night which is made memorable to me by something else I shall relate. It was the night of a little party at the Doctor's, which was given on the occasion of Mr Jack Maldon's departure for India, whither he was going as a cadet, or something of that kind: Mr Wickfield having at length arranged the business. It happened to be the Doctor's birthday, too. We had had a holiday, had made presents to him in the morning, had made a speech to him through the head-boy, and had cheered him until we were hoarse, and until he had shed tears. And now, in the evening, Mr Wickfield, Agnes, and I, went to have tea with him in his private capacity.

Mr Jack Maldon was there, before us. Mrs Strong, dressed in white, with cherry-coloured ribbons, was playing the piano, when we went in; and he was leaning over her to turn the leaves. The clear red and white of her complexion was not so blooming and flower-like as usual, I thought, when she turned round; but she looked very pretty, wonderfully pretty.

"I have forgotten, Doctor," said Mrs Strong's mama, when we were seated, "to pay you the compliments of the day—though they are, as you may suppose, very far from being mere compliments in my case. Allow me to wish you many happy returns."

"I thank you, ma'am," replied the Doctor.

"Many, many, many, happy returns," said the Old Soldier. "Not only for your own sake, but for Annie's, and John Maldon's, and many other people's. It seems but yesterday to me, John, when you were a little creature, a head shorter than Master Copperfield, making baby love to Annie behind the gooseberry bushes in the back-garden."

"My dear mama," said Mrs Strong, "never mind that now."

"Annie, don't be absurd," returned her mother. "If you are to blush to hear of such things now you are an old married woman, when are you not to blush to hear of them?"

"Old?" exclaimed Mr Jack Maldon. "Annie? Come!"

"Yes, John," returned the Soldier. "Virtually, an old married woman. Although not old by years—for when did you ever hear me say, or who has ever heard me say, that a girl of twenty was old by years!—your cousin is the wife of the Doctor, and, as such, what I have described her. It is well for you, John, that your cousin *is* the wife of the Doctor. You have found in him an influential and kind friend, who will be kinder yet, I venture to predict, if you deserve it. I have no false pride. I never hesitate to admit, frankly, that there are some members of our family who want a friend. You were one yourself, before your cousin's influence raised up one for you."

The Doctor, in the goodness of his heart, waved his hand as if to make light of it, and save Mr Jack Maldon from any further reminder. But Mrs Markleham changed her chair for one next the Doctor's, and putting her fan on his coat-sleeve, said:

"No, really, my dear Doctor, you must excuse me if I appear to dwell on this rather, because I feel so very strongly. I call it quite my monomania, it is such a subject of mine. You are a blessing to us. You really are a Boon, you know."

"Nonsense, nonsense," said the Doctor.

"No, no, I beg your pardon," retorted the Old Soldier. "With nobody present, but our dear and confidential friend Mr Wickfield, I cannot consent to be put down. I shall begin to assert the privileges of a mother-in-law, if you go on like that, and scold you. I am perfectly honest and outspoken. What I am saying is, what I said when you first overpowered me with surprise—you remember how surprised I was?—by proposing for Annie. Not that there was anything so very much out of the way, in the mere fact of the proposal—it would be ridiculous to say that!—but because, you having known her poor father, and having known her from a baby six months old, I hadn't thought of you in such a light at all, or indeed as a marrying man in any way,—simply that, you know."

"Aye, aye," returned the Doctor, good-humouredly. "Never mind."

"But I *do* mind," said the Old Soldier, laying her fan upon his lips. "I mind very much. I recall these things that I may be contradicted if I am wrong. Well! Then I spoke to Annie, and I told her what had happened. I said, 'My dear, here's Doctor Strong has positively been and made you the subject of a handsome declaration and an offer.' Did I press it in the least? No. I said, 'Now, Annie, tell me the truth this moment; is your heart free?' 'Mama,' she said crying, 'I am extremely young'—which was perfectly true—'and I hardly know if I have a heart at all.' 'Then, my dear,' I said, 'you may rely upon it, it's free. At all events, my love,' said I, 'Doctor Strong is in an agitated state of mind, and must be answered. He cannot be kept in his present state of suspense.' 'Mama,' said Annie, still crying, 'would he be unhappy without me? If he would, I honour and respect him so much, that I think I will have him.' So it was settled. And then, and not till then, I said to Annie, 'Annie, Doctor Strong will not only be your husband, but he will represent your late father: he will represent the head of our family, he will represent the wisdom and station, and I may say the means, of our family; and will be, in short, a Boon to it.' I used the word at the time, and I have used it again, today. If I have any merit it is consistency."

The daughter had sat quite silent and still during this speech, with her eyes fixed on the ground; her cousin standing near her, and looking on the ground too. She now said very softly, in a trembling voice:

"Mama, I hope you have finished?"

"No, my dear Annie," returned the Old Soldier, "I have not quite finished. Since you ask me, my love, I reply that I have *not*. I complain that you really are a little unnatural towards your own family; and, as it is of no use complaining to you, I mean to complain to your husband. Now, my dear Doctor, do look at that silly wife of yours."

As the Doctor turned his kind face, with its smile of simplicity and gentleness, towards her, she drooped her head more. I noticed that Mr Wickfield looked at her steadily.

"When I happened to say to that naughty thing, the other day," pursued her mother, shaking her head and her fan at her, playfully, "that there was a family circumstance she might mention to you—indeed, I think, was bound to mention—she said, that to mention it was to ask a favour; and that, as you were too generous, and as for her to ask was always to have, she wouldn't."

"Annie, my dear," said the Doctor. "That was wrong. It robbed me of a pleasure."

"Almost the very words I said to her!" exclaimed her mother. "Now really, another time, when I know what she would tell you but for this reason, and won't, I have a great mind, my dear Doctor, to tell you myself."

"I shall be glad if you will," returned the Doctor.

"Shall I?"

"Certainly."

"Well, then, I will!" said the Old Soldier. "That's a bargain." And having, I suppose, carried her point, she tapped the Doctor's hand several times with her fan (which she kissed first), and returned triumphantly to her former station.

Some more company coming in, among whom were the two masters and Adams, the talk became general; and it naturally turned on Mr Jack Maldon, and his voyage, and the country he was going to, and his various plans and prospects. He was to leave that night, after supper, in a post-chaise, for Gravesend; where the ship, in which he was to make the voyage, lay; and was to be gone—unless he came home on leave, or for his health—I don't know how many years. I recollect it was settled by general consent that India was quite a misrepresented country, and had nothing objectionable in it, but a tiger or two, and a little heat in the warm part of the day. For my own part, I looked on Mr Jack Maldon as a modern Sinbad, and pictured him the bosom friend of all the Rajahs in the East, sitting under canopies, smoking curly golden pipes—a mile long, if they could be straightened out.

Mrs Strong was a very pretty singer: as I knew, who often heard her singing by herself. But, whether she was afraid of singing before people, or was out of voice that evening, it was certain that she couldn't sing at all. She tried a duet, once, with her cousin Maldon, but could not so much as begin; and afterwards, when she tried to sing by herself, although she began sweetly, her voice died away on a sudden, and left her quite distressed, with her head hanging down over the keys. The good Doctor said she was nervous, and, to relieve her, proposed a round game at cards; of which he knew as much as of the art of playing the trombone. But I remarked that the Old Soldier took him into custody directly, for her partner; and instructed him, as the first preliminary of initiation, to give her all the silver he had in his pocket.

We had a merry game, not made the less merry by the Doctor's mistakes, of which he committed an innumerable quantity, in spite of the watchfulness of the butterflies, and to their great aggravation. Mrs Strong had declined to play, on the ground of not feeling very well; and her cousin Maldon had excused himself because he had some packing to do. When he had done it, however, he returned, and they sat together, talking, on the sofa. From time to time she came and looked over the Doctor's hand, and told him what to play. She was very pale, as she bent over him, and I thought her finger trembled as she pointed out the cards; but the Doctor was quite happy in her attention, and took no notice of this, if it were so.

At supper, we were hardly so gay. Everyone appeared to feel that a parting of that sort was an awkward thing, and that the nearer it approached, the more awkward it was. Mr Jack Maldon tried to be very talkative, but was not at his ease, and made matters worse. And they were not improved, as it appeared to me, by the Old Soldier: who continually recalled passages of Mr Jack Maldon's youth.

The Doctor, however, who felt, I am sure, that he was making everybody happy, was well pleased, and had no suspicion but that we were all at the utmost height of enjoyment.

"Annie, my dear," said he, looking at his watch, and filling his glass, "it is past your cousin Jack's time, and we must not detain him, since time and tide—both concerned in this case—wait for no man. Mr Jack Maldon, you have a long voyage, and a strange country, before you; but many men have had both, and many men will have both, to the end of time. The winds you are going to tempt, have wafted thousands upon thousands to fortune, and brought thousands upon thousands happily back."

"It's an affecting thing," said Mrs Markleham—"however it's viewed, it's affecting, to see a fine young man one has known from an infant, going away to the other end of the world, leaving all he knows behind, and not knowing what's before him. A young man really well deserves constant support and patronage," looking at the Doctor, "who makes such sacrifices."

"Time will go fast with you, Mr Jack Maldon," pursued the Doctor, "and fast with all of us. Some of us can hardly expect, perhaps, in the natural course of things, to greet you on your return. The next best thing is to hope to do it, and that's my case. I shall not weary you with good advice. You have long had a good model before you, in your cousin Annie. Imitate her virtues as nearly as you can."

Mrs Markleham fanned herself, and shook her head.

"Farewell, Mr Jack," said the Doctor, standing up; on which we all stood up. "A prosperous voyage out, a thriving career abroad, and a happy return home!"

We all drank the toast, and all shook hands with Mr Jack Maldon; after which he hastily took leave of the ladies who were there, and hurried to the door, where he was received, as he got into the chaise, with a tremendous broadside of cheers discharged by our boys, who had assembled on the lawn for the purpose. Running in among them to swell the ranks, I was very near the chaise when it rolled away; and I had a lively impression made upon me, in the midst of the noise and dust, of having seen Mr Jack Maldon rattle past with an agitated face, and something cherry-coloured in his hand.

After another broadside for the Doctor, and another for the Doctor's wife, the boys dispersed, and I went back into the house, where I found the guests all standing in a group about the Doctor, discussing how Mr Jack Maldon had gone away, and how he had borne it, and how he had felt it, and all the rest of it. In the midst of these remarks, Mrs Markleham cried: "Where's Annie?"

No Annie was there; and when they called to her, no Annie replied. But all pressing out of the room, in a crowd, to see what was the matter, we found her lying on the hall floor. There was great alarm at first, until it was found that she was in a swoon, and that the swoon was yielding to the usual means of recovery; when the Doctor, who had lifted her head upon his knee, put her curls aside with his hand, and said, looking around:

"Poor Annie! She's so faithful and tender-hearted! It's the parting from her old playfellow and friend—her favourite cousin—that has done this. Ah! It's a pity! I am very sorry!"

When she opened her eyes, and saw where she was, and that we were all standing about her, she arose with assistance: turning her head, as she did so, to lay it on the Doctor's shoulder—or to hide it, I don't know which. We went into the drawing-room, to leave her with the Doctor and her mother; but she said, it seemed, that she was better than she had been since morning, and that she would rather be brought among us; so they brought her in, looking very white and weak, I thought, and sat her on a sofa.

"Annie, my dear," said her mother, doing something to her dress. "See here! You have lost a bow. Will anybody be so good as find a ribbon; a cherry-coloured ribbon?"

It was the one she had worn at her bosom. We all looked for it; I myself looked everywhere, I am certain—but nobody could find it.

"Do you recollect where you had it last, Annie?" said her mother.

I wondered how I could have thought she looked white, or anything but burning red, when she answered that she had had it safe, a little while ago, she thought, but it was not worth looking for.

Nevertheless, it was looked for again, and still not found. She entreated that there might be no more searching; but it was still sought for, in a desultory way, until she was quite well, and the company took their departure.

We walked very slowly home, Mr Wickfield, Agnes, and I—Agnes and I admiring the moonlight, and Mr Wickfield scarcely raising his eyes from the ground. When we, at last, reached our own door, Agnes discovered that she had left her little reticule behind. Delighted to be of any service to her, I ran back to fetch it.

I went into the supper-room where it had been left, which was deserted and dark. But a door of communication between that and the Doctor's study, where there was a light, being open, I passed on there, to say what I wanted, and to get a candle.

The Doctor was sitting in his easy-chair by the fireside, and his young wife was on a stool at his feet. The Doctor, with a complacent smile, was reading aloud some manuscript explanation or statement of a theory out of that interminable Dictionary, and she was looking up at him. But with such a face as I never saw. It was so beautiful in its form, it was so ashy pale, it was so fixed in its abstraction, it was so full of a wild, sleep-walking, dreamy horror of I don't know what. The eyes were wide open, and her brown hair fell in two rich clusters on her shoulders, and on her white dress, disordered by the want of the lost ribbon. Distinctly as I recollect her look, I cannot say of what it was expressive, I cannot even say of what it is expressive to me now, rising again before my older judgement. Penitence, humiliation, shame, pride, love, and trustfulness—I see them all; and in them all, I see that horror of I don't know what.

My entrance, and my saying what I wanted, roused her. It disturbed the Doctor too, for when I went back to replace the candle I had taken from the table, he was patting her head, in his fatherly way, and saying he was a merciless drone to let her tempt him into reading on; and he would have her go to bed.

But she asked him, in a rapid, urgent manner, to let her stay—to let her feel assured (I heard her murmur some broken words to this effect) that she was in his confidence that night. And, as she turned again towards him, after glancing at me as I left the room and went out at the door, I saw her cross her hands upon his knee, and look up at him with the same face, something quieted, as he resumed his reading.

It made a great impression on me, and I remembered it a long time afterwards; as I shall have occasion to narrate when the time comes.

Chapter XVII

SOMEBODY TURNS UP

IT has not occurred to me to mention Peggotty since I ran away; but, of course, I wrote her a letter almost as soon as I was housed at Dover, and another, and a longer letter, containing all particulars fully related, when my aunt took me formally under her protection. On my being settled at Doctor Strong's I wrote to her again, detailing my happy condition and prospects. I never could have derived anything like the pleasure from spending the money Mr Dick had given me, that I felt in sending a gold half-guinea to Peggotty, per post, enclosed in this last letter, to discharge the sum I had borrowed of her: in which epistle, not before, I mentioned about the young man with the donkey-cart.

To these communications Peggotty replied as promptly, if not as concisely, as a merchant's clerk. Her utmost powers of expression (which were certainly not great in ink) were exhausted in the attempt to write what she felt on the subject of my journey. Four sides of incoherent and interjectional beginnings of sentences, that had no end, except blots, were inadequate to afford her any relief. But the blots were more expressive to me than the best composition; for they showed me that Peggotty had been crying all over the paper, and what could I have desired more?

I made out, without much difficulty, that she could not take quite kindly to my aunt yet. The notice was too short after so long a prepossession the other way. We never knew a person, she wrote; but to think that Miss Betsey should seem to be so different from what she had been thought to be, was a Moral!—that was her word. She was evidently still afraid of Miss Betsey, for she sent her grateful duty to her but timidly; and she was evidently afraid of me, too, and entertained the probability of my running away again soon: if I might judge from the repeated hints she threw out, that the coach-fare to Yarmouth was always to be had of her for the asking.

She gave me one piece of intelligence which affected me very much, namely, that there had been a sale of the furniture at our old home, and that Mr and Miss Murdstone were gone away, and the house was shut up, to be let or sold. God knows I had no part in it while they remained there, but it pained me to think of the dear old place as altogether abandoned; of the weeds growing tall in the garden, and the fallen leaves lying thick and wet upon the paths. I imagined how the winds of winter would howl round it, how the cold rain would beat upon the window-glass, how the moon would make ghosts on the walls of the empty rooms, watching their solitude all night. I thought afresh of the grave in the churchyard, underneath the tree: and it seemed as if the house were dead too, now, and all connected with my father and mother were faded away.

There was no other news in Peggotty's letters. Mr Barkis was an excellent husband, she said, though still a little near; but we all had our faults, and she had plenty (though I am sure I don't know what they were); and he sent his duty, and my little bedroom was always ready for me. Mr Peggotty was well, and Ham was well, and Mrs Gummidge was but poorly, and little Em'ly wouldn't send her love, but said that Peggotty might send it, if she liked.

All this intelligence I dutifully imparted to my aunt, only reserving to myself the mention of little Em'ly, to whom I instinctively felt that she would not very tenderly incline. While I was yet new at Doctor Strong's, she made several excursions over to Canterbury to see me, and always at unseasonable hours: with the view, I suppose, of taking me by surprise. But, finding me well employed, and bearing a good character, and hearing on all hands that I rose fast in the school, she soon discontinued these visits. I saw her on a Saturday, every third or fourth week, when I went over to Dover for a treat; and I saw Mr Dick every alternate Wednesday, when he arrived by stage-coach at noon, to stay until next morning.

On these occasions Mr Dick never travelled without a leathern writing-desk, containing a supply of stationery and the Memorial; in relation to which document he had a notion that time was beginning to press now, and that it really must be got out of hand.

Mr Dick was very partial to gingerbread. To render his visits the more agreeable, my aunt had instructed me to open a credit for him at a cake shop, which was hampered with the stipulation that he should not be served with more than one shilling's-worth in the course of any one day. This, and the reference of all his little bills at the county inn where he slept, to my aunt, before they were paid, induced me to suspect that he was only allowed to rattle his money, and not to spend it. I found on further investigation that this was so, or at least there was an agreement between him and my aunt that he should account to her for all his disbursements. As he had no idea of deceiving her, and always desired to please her, he was thus made chary of launching into expense. On this point, as well as on all other possible points, Mr Dick was convinced that my aunt was the wisest and most wonderful of women; as he repeatedly told me with infinite secrecy, and always in a whisper.

"Trotwood," said Mr Dick, with an air of mystery, after imparting this confidence to me, one Wednesday; "who's the man that hides near our house and frightens her?"

"Frightens my aunt, sir?"

Mr Dick nodded. "I thought nothing would have frightened her," he said, "for she's—" here he whispered softly, "don't mention it—the wisest and most wonderful of women." Having said which, he drew back, to observe the effect which this description of her made upon me.

"The first time he came," said Mr Dick, "was—let me see—sixteen hundred and forty-nine was the date of King Charles's execution. I think you said sixteen hundred and forty-nine?"

"Yes, sir."

"I don't know how it can be," said Mr Dick, sorely puzzled and shaking his head. "I don't think I am as old as that."

"Was it in that year that the man appeared, sir?" I asked.

"Why, really" said Mr Dick, "I don't see how it can have been in that year, Trotwood. Did you get that date out of history?"

"Yes, sir."

"I suppose history never lies, does it?" said Mr Dick, with a gleam of hope.

"Oh dear, no, sir!" I replied, most decisively. I was ingenuous and young, and I thought so.

"I can't make it out," said Mr Dick, shaking his head. "There's something wrong, somewhere. However, it was very soon after the mistake was made of putting some of the trouble out of King Charles's head into my head, that the man first came. I was walking out with Miss Trotwood after tea, just at dark, and there he was, close to our house."

"Walking about?" I inquired.

"Walking about?" repeated Mr Dick. "Let me see, I must recollect a bit. N—no, no; he was not walking about."

I asked, as the shortest way to get at it, what he *was* doing.

"Well, he wasn't there at all," said Mr Dick, "until he came up behind her, and whispered. Then she turned round and fainted, and I stood still and looked at him, and he walked away; but that he should have been hiding ever since (in the ground or somewhere), is the most extraordinary thing!"

"*Has* he been hiding ever since?" I asked.

"To be sure he has," retorted Mr Dick, nodding his head gravely. "Never came out, till last night! We were walking last night, and he came up behind her again, and I knew him again."

"And did he frighten my aunt again?"

"All of a shiver," said Mr Dick, counterfeiting that affection and making his teeth chatter. "Held by the palings. Cried. But, Trotwood, come here," getting me close to him, that he might whisper very softly; "why did she give him money, boy, in the moonlight?"

"He was a beggar, perhaps."

Mr Dick shook his head, as utterly renouncing the suggestion; and having replied a great many times, and with great confidence, "No beggar, no beggar, no beggar, sir!" went on to say, that from his window he had afterwards, and late at night, seen my aunt give this person money outside the garden rails in the moonlight, who then slunk away—into the ground again, as he thought probable—and was seen no more: while my aunt came hurriedly and secretly back into the house, and had, even that morning, been quite different from her usual self; which preyed on Mr Dick's mind.

I had not the least belief, in the outset of this story, that the unknown was anything but a delusion of Mr Dick's, and one of the line of that ill-fated Prince who occasioned him so much difficulty; but after some reflection I began to entertain the question whether an attempt, or threat of an attempt, might have been twice made to take poor Mr Dick himself from under my aunt's protection, and whether my aunt, the strength of whose kind feeling towards him I knew from herself, might have been induced to pay a price for his peace and quiet. As I was already much attached to Mr Dick, and very solicitous for his welfare, my fears favoured this supposition; and for a long time his Wednesday hardly ever came round, without my entertaining a misgiving that he would not be on the coach-box as usual. There he always appeared, however, grey-headed, laughing, and happy; and he never had anything more to tell of the man who could frighten my aunt.

These Wednesdays were the happiest days of Mr Dick's life; they were far from being the least happy of mine. He soon became known to every boy in the school; and though he never took an active part in any game but kite-flying, was as deeply interested in all our sports as anyone among us. How often have I seen him, intent upon a match at marbles or pegtop, looking on with a face of unutterable interest, and hardly breathing at the critical times! How often, at hare and hounds, have I seen him mounted on a little knoll, cheering the whole field on to action, and waving his hat above his grey head, oblivious of King Charles the Martyr's head, and all belonging to it! How many a summer hour have I known to be but blissful minutes to him in the cricket-field! How many winter days have I seen him, standing blue-nosed, in the snow and east wind, looking at the boys going down the long slide, and clapping his worsted gloves in rapture!

He was an universal favourite, and his ingenuity in little things was transcendent. He could cut oranges into such devices as none of us had an idea of. He could make a boat out of anything, from a skewer upwards. He could turn cramp-bones into chessmen; fashion Roman chariots from old court cards; make spoked wheels out of cotton reels, and bird-cages of old wire. But he was greatest of all, perhaps, in the articles of string and straw; with which we were all persuaded he could do anything that could be done by hands.

Mr Dick's renown was not long confined to us. After a few Wednesdays, Doctor Strong himself made some inquiries of me about him, and I told him all my aunt had told me; which interested the Doctor so much that he requested, on the occasion of his next visit, to be presented to him. This ceremony I performed; and the Doctor begging Mr Dick, whensoever he should not find me at the coach office, to come on there, and rest himself until our morning's work was over, it soon passed into a custom for Mr Dick to come on as a matter of course, and, if we were a little late, as often happened on a Wednesday, to walk about the courtyard, waiting for me. Here he made the acquaintance of the Doctor's beautiful young wife (paler than formerly, all this time; more rarely seen by me or anyone, I think; and not so gay, but not less beautiful), and so became more and more familiar by degrees, until, at last, he would come into the school and wait. He always sat in a particular corner, on a particular stool, which was called "Dick," after him; here he would sit, with his grey head bent forward, attentively listening to whatever might be going on, with a profound veneration for the learning he had never been able to acquire.

This veneration Mr Dick extended to the Doctor, whom he thought the most subtle and accomplished philosopher of any age. It was long before Mr Dick ever spoke to him otherwise than bareheaded; and even when he and the Doctor had struck up quite a friendship, and would walk together by the hour, on that side of the courtyard which was known among us as The Doctor's Walk, Mr Dick would pull off his hat at intervals to show his respect for wisdom and knowledge. How it ever came about that the Doctor began to read out scraps of the famous Dictionary, in these walks, I never knew; perhaps he felt it all the same, at first, as reading to himself. However, it passed into a custom too; and Mr Dick, listening with a face shining with pride and pleasure, in his heart of hearts believed the Dictionary to be the most delightful book in the world.

As I think of them going up and down before those schoolroom windows—the Doctor reading with his complacent smile, an occasional flourish of the manuscript, or grave motion of his head; and Mr Dick listening, enchained by interest, with his poor wits calmly wandering God knows where, upon the wings of hard words—I think of it as one of the pleasantest things, in a quiet way, that I have ever seen. I feel as if they might go walking to and fro for ever, and the world might somehow be the better for it—as if a thousand things it makes a noise about, were not one half so good for it, or me.

Agnes was one of Mr Dick's friends, very soon; and in often coming to the house, he made acquaintance with Uriah. The friendship between himself and me increased continually, and it was maintained on this odd footing: that, while Mr Dick came professedly to look after me as my guardian, he always consulted me in any little matter of doubt that arose, and invariably guided himself by my advice; not only having a high respect for my native sagacity, but considering that I inherited a good deal from my aunt.

One Thursday morning, when I was about to walk with Mr Dick from the hotel to the coach office before going back to school (for we had an hour's school before breakfast), I met Uriah in the street, who reminded me of the promise I had made to take tea with himself and his mother: adding, with a writhe, "But I didn't expect you to keep it, Master Copperfield, we're so very umble."

I really had not yet been able to make up my mind whether I liked Uriah or detested him; and I was very doubtful about it still, as I stood looking him in the face in the street. But I felt it quite an affront to be supposed proud, and said I only wanted to be asked.

"Oh, if that's all, Master Copperfield," said Uriah, "and it really isn't our umbleness that prevents you, will you come this evening? But if it is our umbleness, I hope you won't mind owning to it, Master Copperfield; for we are well aware of our condition."

I said I would mention it to Mr Wickfield, and if he approved, as I had no doubt he would, I could come with pleasure. So, at six o'clock that evening, which was one of the early office evenings, I announced myself as ready, to Uriah.

"Mother, will be proud, indeed," he said, as we walked away together. "Or she would be proud, if it wasn't sinful, Master Copperfield."

"Yet you didn't mind supposing *I* was proud this morning," I returned.

"Oh dear, no, Master Copperfield!" returned Uriah. "Oh, believe me, no! Such a thought never came into my head! I shouldn't have deemed it at all proud if you had thought *us* too umble for you. Because we are so very umble."

"Have you been studying much law lately?" I asked, to change the subject.

"Oh, Master Copperfield," he said, with an air of self-denial, "my reading is hardly to be called study. I have passed an hour or two in the evening, sometimes, with Mr Tidd."

"Rather hard, I suppose?" said I.

"He is hard to *me* sometimes," returned Uriah. "But I don't know what he might be to a gifted person."

After beating a little tune on his chin as he walked on, with the two forefingers of his skeleton right hand, he added:

"There are expressions, you see, Master Copperfield—Latin words and terms—in Mr Tidd, that are trying to a reader of my umble attainments."

"Would you like to be taught Latin?" I said briskly. "I will teach it you with pleasure, as I learn it."

"Oh, thank you, Master Copperfield," he answered, shaking his head. "I am sure it's very kind of you to make the offer, but I am much too umble to accept it."

"What nonsense, Uriah!"

"Oh, indeed you must excuse me, Master Copperfield! I am greatly obliged, and I should like it of all things, I assure you; but I am far too umble. There are people enough to tread upon me in my lowly state, without my doing outrage to their feelings by possessing learning. Learning ain't for me. A person like myself had better not aspire. If he is to get on in life, he must get on umbly, Master Copperfield!"

I never saw his mouth so wide, or the creases in his cheeks so deep, as when he delivered himself of these sentiments: shaking his head all the time, and writhing modestly.

"I think you are wrong, Uriah," I said. "I dare say there are several things that I could teach you, if you would like to learn them."

"Oh, I don't doubt that, Master Copperfield," he answered; "not in the least. But not being umble yourself, you don't judge well, perhaps, for them that are. I won't provoke my betters with knowledge, thank you. I'm much too umble. Here is my umble dwelling, Master Copperfield!"

We entered a low, old-fashioned room, walked straight into from the street, and found there, Mrs Heep, who was the dead image of Uriah, only short. She received me with the utmost humility, and apologized to me for giving her son a kiss, observing that, lowly as they were, they had their natural affections, which they hoped would give no offence to anyone. It was a perfectly decent room, half parlour and half kitchen, but not at all a snug room. The tea-things were set upon the table, and the kettle was boiling on the hob. There was a chest of drawers with an escritoire top, for Uriah to read or write at of an evening; there was Uriah's blue bag lying down and vomiting papers; there was a company of Uriah's books commanded by Mr Tidd; there was a corner cupboard: and there were the usual articles of furniture. I don't remember that any individual object had a bare, pinched, spare look; but I do remember that the whole place had.

It was perhaps a part of Mrs Heep's humility, that she still wore weeds. Notwithstanding the lapse of time that had occurred since Mr Heep's decease, she still wore weeds. I think there was some compromise in the cap; but otherwise she was as weedy as in the early days of her mourning.

"This is a day to be remembered, my Uriah, I am sure," said Mrs Heep, making the tea, "when Master Copperfield pays us a visit."

"I said you'd think so, mother," said Uriah.

"If I could have wished father to remain among us for any reason," said Mrs Heep, "it would have been, that he might have known his company this afternoon."

I felt embarrassed by these compliments; but I was sensible, too, of being entertained as an honoured guest, and I thought Mrs Heep an agreeable woman.

"My Uriah," said Mrs Heep, "has looked forward to this, sir, a long while. He had his fears that our umbleness stood in the way, and I joined in them myself. Umble we are, umble we have been, umble we shall ever be," said Mrs Heep.

"I am sure you have no occasion to be so, ma'am," I said, "unless you like."

"Thank you, sir," retorted Mrs Heep. "We know our station and are thankful in it."

I found that Mrs Heep gradually got nearer to me, and that Uriah gradually got opposite to me, and that they respectfully plied me with the choicest of the eatables on the table. There was nothing particularly choice there, to be sure; but I took the will for the deed, and felt that they were very attentive. Presently they began to talk about aunts, and then I told them about mine; and about fathers and mothers, and then I told them about mine; and then Mrs Heep began to talk about fathers-in-law, and then I began to tell her about mine—but stopped, because my aunt had advised me to observe a silence on that subject. A tender young cork, however, would have had no more chance against a pair of corkscrews, or a tender young tooth against a pair of dentists, or a little shuttlecock against two battledores, than I had against Uriah and Mrs Heep. They did just what they liked with me; and wormed things out of me that I had no desire to tell, with a certainty I blush to think of: the more especially, as in my juvenile frankness, I took some credit to myself for being so confidential and felt that I was quite the patron of my two respectful entertainers.

They were very fond of one another: that was certain. I take it, that had its effect upon me, as a touch of nature; but the skill with which the one followed up whatever the other said, was a touch of art which I was still less proof against. When there was nothing more to be got out of me about myself (for on the Murdstone and Grinby life, and on my journey, I was dumb), they began about Mr Wickfield and Agnes. Uriah threw the ball to Mrs Heep, Mrs Heep caught it and threw it back to Uriah, Uriah kept it up a little while, then sent it back to Mrs Heep, and so they went on tossing it about until I had no idea who had got it, and was quite bewildered. The ball itself was always changing too. Now it was Mr Wickfield, now Agnes, now the excellence of Mr Wickfield, now my admiration of Agnes; now the extent of Mr Wickfield's business and resources, now our domestic life after dinner; now, the wine that Mr Wickfield took, the reason why he took it, and the pity that it was he took so much; now one thing, now another, then everything at once; and all the time, without appearing to speak very often, or to do anything but sometimes encourage them a little, for fear they should be overcome by their humility and the honour of my company, I found myself perpetually letting out something or other that I had no business to let out and seeing the effect of it in the twinkling of Uriah's dinted nostrils.

I had begun to be a little uncomfortable, and to wish myself well out of the visit, when a figure coming down the street passed the door—it stood open to air the room, which was warm, the weather being close for the time of year—came back again, looked in, and walked in, exclaiming loudly, "Copperfield! Is it possible?"

It was Mr Micawber! It was Mr Micawber, with his eye-glass, and his walking-stick, and his shirt-collar, and his genteel air, and the condescending roll in his voice, all complete!

"My dear Copperfield," said Mr Micawber, putting out his hand, "this is indeed a meeting which is calculated to impress the mind with a sense of the instability and uncertainty of all human—in short, it is a most extraordinary meeting. Walking along the street, reflecting upon the probability of something turning up (of which I am at present rather sanguine), I find a young but valued friend turn up, who is connected with the most eventful period of my life; I may say, with the turning-point of my existence. Copperfield, my dear fellow, how do you do?"

I cannot say—I really can*not* say—that I was glad to see Mr Micawber there; but I was glad to see him too, and shook hands with him, heartily, inquiring how Mrs Micawber was.

"Thank you," said Mr Micawber, waving his hand as of old, and settling his chin in his shirt-collar. "She is tolerably convalescent. The twins no longer derive their sustenance from Nature's founts—in short," said Mr Micawber, in one of his bursts of confidence, "they are weaned—and Mrs Micawber is, at present, my travelling companion. She will be rejoiced, Copperfield, to renew her acquaintance with one who has proved himself in all respects a worthy minister at the sacred altar of friendship."

I said I should be delighted to see her.

"You are very good," said Mr Micawber.

Mr Micawber then smiled, settled his chin again, and looked about him.

"I have discovered my friend Copperfield," said Mr Micawber genteelly, and without addressing himself particularly to anyone, "not in solitude, but partaking of a social meal in company with a widow lady, and one who is apparently her offspring—in short," said Mr Micawber, in another of his bursts of confidence, "her son. I shall esteem it an honour to be presented."

I could do no less, under these circumstances, than make Mr Micawber known to Uriah Heep and his mother; which I accordingly did. As they abased themselves before him, Mr Micawber took a seat, and waved his hand in his most courtly manner.

"Any friend of my friend Copperfield's," said Mr Micawber, "has a personal claim upon myself."

"We are too umble, sir," said Mrs Heep, "my son and me, to be the friends of Master Copperfield. He has been so good as take his tea with us, and we are thankful to him for his company, also to you, sir, for your notice."

"Ma'am," returned Mr Micawber, with a bow, "you are very obliging: and what are you doing, Copperfield? Still in the wine trade?"

I was excessively anxious to get Mr Micawber away; and replied, with my hat in my hand, and a very red face, I have no doubt, that I was a pupil at Doctor Strong's.

"A pupil?" said Mr Micawber, raising his eyebrows. "I am extremely happy to hear it. Although a mind like my friend Copperfield's"—to Uriah and Mrs Heep—"does not require that cultivation which, without his knowledge of men and things, it would require, still it is a rich soil teeming with latent vegetation—in short," said Mr Micawber, smiling, in another burst of confidence, "it is an intellect capable of getting up the classics to any extent."

Uriah, with his long hands slowly twining over one another, made a ghastly writhe from the waist upwards, to express his concurrence in this estimation of me.

"Shall we go and see Mrs Micawber, sir?" I said, to get Mr Micawber away.

"If you will do her that favour, Copperfield," replied Mr Micawber, rising. "I have no scruple in saying, in the presence of our friends here, that I am a man who has, for some years, contended against the pressure of pecuniary difficulties." I knew he was certain to say something of this kind; he always would be so boastful about his difficulties. "Sometimes I have risen superior to my difficulties. Sometimes my difficulties have—in short, have floored me. There have been times when I have administered a succession of facers to them; there have been times when they have been too many for me, and I have given in, and said to Mrs Micawber, in the words of Cato, 'Plato, thou reasonest well. It's all up now. I can show fight no more.' But at no time of my life," said Mr Micawber, "have I enjoyed a higher degree of satisfaction than in pouring my griefs (if I may describe difficulties, chiefly arising out of warrants of attorney and promissory notes at two and four months, by that word) into the bosom of my friend Copperfield."

Mr Micawber closed this handsome tribute by saying, "Mr Heep! Good evening. Mrs Heep! Your servant," and then walking out with me in his most fashionable manner, making a good deal of noise on the pavement with his shoes, and humming a tune as we went.

It was a little inn where Mr Micawber put up, and he occupied a little room in it, partitioned off from the commercial room, and strongly flavoured with tobacco-smoke. I think it was over the kitchen, because a warm greasy smell appeared to come up through the chinks in the floor, and there was a flabby perspiration on the walls. I know it was near the bar, on account of the smell of spirits and jingling of glasses. Here, recumbent on a small sofa, underneath a picture of a race-horse, with her head close to the fire, and her feet pushing the mustard off the dumb-waiter at the other end of the room, was Mrs Micawber, to whom Mr Micawber entered first, saying, "My dear, allow me to introduce to you a pupil of Doctor Strong's."

I noticed, by the by, that although Mr Micawber was just as much confused as ever about my age and standing, he always remembered, as a genteel thing, that I was a pupil of Doctor Strong's.

Mrs Micawber was amazed, but very glad to see me. I was very glad to see her too, and, after an affectionate greeting on both sides, sat down on the small sofa near her.

"My dear," said Mr Micawber, "if you will mention to Copperfield what our present position is, which I have no doubt he will like to know, I will go and look at the paper the while, and see whether anything turns up among the advertisements."

"I thought you were at Plymouth, ma'am," I said to Mrs Micawber, as he went out.

"My dear Master Copperfield," she replied, "we went to Plymouth."

"To be on the spot," I hinted.

"Just so," said Mrs Micawber. "To be on the spot. But, the truth is, talent is not wanted in the Custom House. The local influence of my family was quite unavailing to obtain any employment in that department, for a man of Mr Micawber's abilities. They would rather *not* have a man of Mr Micawber's abilities. He would only show the deficiency of the others. Apart from which," said Mrs Micawber, "I will not disguise from you, my dear Master Copperfield, that when that branch of my family which is settled in Plymouth, became aware that Mr Micawber was accompanied by myself, and by little Wilkins and his sister, and by the twins, they did not receive him with that ardour which he might have expected, being so newly released from captivity. In fact," said Mrs Micawber, lowering her voice,—"this is between ourselves—our reception was cool."

"Dear me!" I said.

"Yes," said Mrs Micawber. "It is truly painful to contemplate mankind in such an aspect, Master Copperfield, but our reception was, decidedly, cool. There is no doubt about it. In fact, that branch of my family which is settled in Plymouth became quite personal to Mr Micawber, before we had been there a week."

I said, and thought, that they ought to be ashamed of themselves.

"Still, so it was," continued Mrs Micawber. "Under such circumstances, what could a man of Mr Micawber's spirit do? But one obvious course was left. To borrow, of that branch of my family, the money to return to London, and to return at any sacrifice."

"Then you all came back again, ma'am?" I said.

"We all came back again," replied Mrs Micawber. "Since then, I have consulted other branches of my family on the course which it is most expedient for Mr Micawber to take—for I maintain that he must take some course, Master Copperfield," said Mrs Micawber, argumentatively. "It is clear that a family of six, not including a domestic, cannot live upon air."

"Certainly, ma'am," said I.

"The opinion of those other branches of my family," pursued Mrs Micawber, "is, that Mr Micawber should immediately turn his attention to coals."

"To what, ma'am?"

"To coals," said Mrs Micawber. "To the coal trade. Mr Micawber was induced to think, on inquiry, that there might be an opening for a man of his talent in the Medway Coal Trade. Then, as Mr Micawber very properly said, the first step to be taken clearly was, to come and *see* the Medway. Which we came and saw. I say 'we,' Master Copperfield; for I never will," said Mrs Micawber with emotion, "I never will desert Mr Micawber."

I murmured my admiration and approbation.

"We came," repeated Mrs Micawber, "and saw the Medway. My opinion of the coal trade on that river is, that it may require talent, but that it certainly requires capital. Talent,

Mr Micawber has; capital, Mr Micawber has not. We saw, I think, the greater part of the Medway; and that is my individual conclusion. Being so near here, Mr Micawber was of opinion that it would be rash not to come on, and see the Cathedral. Firstly, on account of its being so well worth seeing, and our never having seen it; and secondly, on account of the great probability of something turning up in a cathedral town. We have been here," said Mrs Micawber, "three days. Nothing has, as yet, turned up; and it may not surprise you, my dear Master Copperfield, so much as it would a stranger, to know that we are at present waiting for a remittance from London, to discharge our pecuniary obligations at this hotel. Until the arrival of that remittance," said Mrs Micawber with much feeling, "I am cut off from my home (I allude to lodgings in Pentonville), from my boy and girl, and from my twins."

I felt the utmost sympathy for Mr and Mrs Micawber in this anxious extremity, and said as much to Mr Micawber, who now returned: adding that I only wished I had money enough, to lend them the amount they needed. Mr Micawber's answer expressed the disturbance of his mind. He said, shaking hands with me, "Copperfield, you are a true friend; but when the worst comes to the worst, no man is without a friend who is possessed of shaving materials." At this dreadful hint Mrs Micawber threw her arms round Mr Micawber's neck and entreated him to be calm. He wept; but so far recovered, almost immediately, as to ring the bell for the waiter, and bespeak a hot kidney pudding and a plate of shrimps for breakfast in the morning.

When I took my leave of them, they both pressed me so much to come and dine before they went away, that I could not refuse. But, as I knew I could not come next day, when I should have a good deal to prepare in the evening, Mr Micawber arranged that he would call at Doctor Strong's in the course of the morning (having a presentiment that the remittance would arrive by that post), and propose the day after, if it would suit me better. Accordingly I was called out of school next forenoon, and found Mr Micawber in the parlour; who had called to say that the dinner would take place as proposed. When I asked him if the remittance had come, he pressed my hand and departed.

As I was looking out of window that same evening, it surprised me, and made me rather uneasy, to see Mr Micawber and Uriah Heep walk past, arm in arm: Uriah humbly sensible of the honour that was done him, and Mr Micawber taking a bland delight in extending his patronage to Uriah. But I was still more surprised, when I went to the little hotel next day at the appointed dinner-hour, which was four o'clock, to find, from what Mr Micawber said, that he had gone home with Uriah, and had drunk brandy-and-water at Mrs Heep's.

"And I'll tell you what, my dear Copperfield," said Mr Micawber, "your friend Heep is a young fellow who might be attorney-general. If I had known that young man, at the period when my difficulties came to a crisis, all I can say is, that I believe my creditors would have been a great deal better managed than they were."

I hardly understood how this could have been, seeing that Mr Micawber had paid them nothing at all as it was; but I did not like to ask. Neither did I like to say, that I hoped he had not been too communicative to Uriah; or to inquire if they had talked much about me. I was afraid of hurting Mr Micawber's feelings, or, at all events, Mrs Micawber's, she being very sensitive; but I was uncomfortable about it, too, and often thought about it afterwards.

We had a beautiful little dinner. Quite an elegant dish of fish; the kidney-end of a loin of veal, roasted; fried sausage-meat; a partridge, and a pudding. There was wine, and there was strong ale; and after dinner Mrs Micawber made us a bowl of hot punch with her own hands.

Mr Micawber was uncommonly convivial. I never saw him such good company. He made his face shine with the punch, so that it looked as if it had been varnished all over. He got cheerfully sentimental about the town, and proposed success to it; observing that Mrs Micawber and himself had been made extremely snug and comfortable there and that he never should forget the agreeable hours they had passed in Canterbury. He proposed me afterwards; and he, and Mrs Micawber, and I, took a review of our past acquaintance, in the course of which we sold the property all over again. Then I proposed Mrs Micawber: or, at least, said, modestly, "If you'll allow me, Mrs Micawber, I shall now have the pleasure of drinking *your* health, ma'am." On which Mr Micawber delivered an eulogium on Mrs Micawber's character, and said she had ever been his guide, philosopher, and friend, and that he would recommend me, when I came to a marrying time of life, to marry such another woman, if such another woman could be found.

As the punch disappeared, Mr Micawber became still more friendly and convivial. Mrs Micawber's spirits becoming elevated, too, we sang "Auld Lang Syne." When we came to "Here's a hand, my trusty frere," we all joined hands round the table; and when we declared we would "take a right gude Willie Waught," and hadn't the least idea what it meant, we were really affected.

In a word, I never saw anybody so thoroughly jovial as Mr Micawber was, down to the very last moment of the evening, when I took a hearty farewell of himself and his amiable wife. Consequently, I was not prepared, at seven o'clock next morning, to receive the following communication, dated half past nine in the evening; a quarter of an hour after I had left him.

"MY DEAR YOUNG FRIEND,

"The die is cast—all is over. Hiding the ravages of care with a sickly mask of mirth, I have not informed you, this evening, that there is no hope of the remittance! Under these circumstances, alike humiliating to endure, humiliating to contemplate, and humiliating to relate, I have discharged the pecuniary liability contracted at this establishment, by giving a note of hand, made payable fourteen days after date, at my residence, Pentonville, London. When it becomes due, it will not be taken up. The result is destruction. The bolt is impending, and the tree must fall.

"Let the wretched man who now addresses you, my dear Copperfield, be a beacon to you through life. He writes with that intention, and in that hope. If he could think himself of so much use, one gleam of day might, by possibility, penetrate into the cheerless dungeon of his remaining existence—though his longevity is, at present (to say the least of it), extremely problematical.

"This is the last communication, my dear Copperfield, you will ever receive

"From

"The

"Beggared Outcast,

"WILKINS MICAWBER."

I was so shocked by the contents of this heart-rending letter, that I ran off directly towards the little hotel with the intention of taking it on my way to Doctor Strong's, and trying to soothe Mr Micawber with a word of comfort. But, half-way there, I met the London coach with Mr and Mrs Micawber up behind; Mr Micawber, the very picture of tranquil enjoyment, smiling at Mrs Micawber's conversation, eating walnuts out of a paper bag, with a bottle sticking out of his breast pocket. As they did not see me, I thought it best, all things considered, not to see them. So, with a great weight taken off my mind, I turned into a by-street that was the nearest way to school, and felt, upon the whole, relieved that they were gone; though I still liked them very much, nevertheless.

Chapter XVIII

A RETROSPECT

MY school-days! The silent gliding on of my existence—the unseen, unfelt progress of my life—from childhood up to youth! Let me think, as I look back upon that flowing water, now a dry channel overgrown with leaves, whether there are any marks along its course, by which I can remember how it ran.

A moment, and I occupy my place in the Cathedral, where we all went together, every Sunday morning, assembling first at school for that purpose. The earthy smell, the sunless air, the sensation of the world being shut out, the resounding of the organ through the black and white arched galleries and aisles, are wings that take me back, and hold me hovering above those days, in a half-sleeping and half-waking dream.

I am not the last boy in the school. I have risen in a few months, over several heads. But the first boy seems to me a mighty creature, dwelling afar off, whose giddy height is unattainable. Agnes says "No," but I say "Yes," and tell her that she little thinks what stores of knowledge have been mastered by the wonderful Being, at whose place she thinks I, even I, weak aspirant, may arrive in time. He is not my private friend and public patron, as Steerforth was, but I hold him in a reverential respect. I chiefly wonder what he'll be, when he leaves Doctor Strong's, and what mankind will do to maintain any place against him.

But who is this that breaks upon me? This is Miss Shepherd, whom I love.

Miss Shepherd is a boarder at the Misses Nettingalls' establishment. I adore Miss Shepherd. She is a little girl, in a spencer, with a round face and curly flaxen hair. The Misses Nettingalls' young ladies come to the Cathedral too. I cannot look upon my book, for I must look upon Miss Shepherd. When the choristers chaunt, I hear Miss Shepherd. In the service I mentally insert Miss Shepherd's name—I put her in among the Royal Family. At home, in my own room, I am sometimes moved to cry out, "Oh, Miss Shepherd!" in a transport of love.

For some time, I am doubtful of Miss Shepherd's feelings, but, at length, Fate being propitious, we meet at the dancing-school. I have Miss Shepherd for my partner. I touch Miss Shepherd's glove, and feel a thrill go up the right arm of my jacket, and come out at my hair. I say nothing to Miss Shepherd, but we understand each other. Miss Shepherd and myself live but to be united.

Why do I secretly give Miss Shepherd twelve Brazil nuts for a present, I wonder? They are not expressive of affection, they are difficult to pack into a parcel of any regular shape, they are hard to crack, even in room doors, and they are oily when cracked; yet I feel that they are appropriate to Miss Shepherd. Soft, seedy biscuits, also, I bestow upon

Miss Shepherd; and oranges innumerable. Once, I kiss Miss Shepherd in the cloak-room. Ecstasy! What are my agony and indignation next day, when I hear a flying rumour that the Misses Nettingall have stood Miss Shepherd in the stocks for turning in her toes!

Miss Shepherd being the one pervading theme and vision of my life, how do I ever come to break with her? I can't conceive. And yet a coolness grows between Miss Shepherd and myself. Whispers reach me of Miss Shepherd having said she wished I wouldn't stare so, and having avowed a preference for Master Jones—for Jones! a boy of no merit whatever! The gulf between me and Miss Shepherd widens. At last, one day, I meet the Misses Nettingalls' establishment out walking. Miss Shepherd makes a face as she goes by, and laughs to her companion. All is over. The devotion of a life—it seems a life, it is all the same—is at an end; Miss Shepherd comes out of the morning service, and the Royal Family know her no more.

I am higher in the school, and no one breaks my peace. I am not at all polite, now, to the Misses Nettingalls' young ladies, and shouldn't dote on any of them, if they were twice as many and twenty times as beautiful. I think the dancing-school a tiresome affair, and wonder why the girls can't dance by themselves and leave us alone. I am growing great in Latin verses, and neglect the laces of my boots. Doctor Strong refers to me in public as a promising young scholar. Mr Dick is wild with joy, and my aunt remits me a guinea by the next post.

The shade of a young butcher rises, like the apparition of an armed head in Macbeth. Who is this young butcher? He is the terror of the youth of Canterbury. There is a vague belief abroad, that the beef suet with which he anoints his hair gives him unnatural strength, and that he is a match for a man. He is a broad-faced, bull-necked, young butcher, with rough red cheeks, an ill-conditioned mind, and an injurious tongue. His main use of this tongue, is, to disparage Doctor Strong's young gentlemen. He says, publicly, that if they want anything he'll give it 'em. He names individuals among them (myself included), whom he could undertake to settle with one hand, and the other tied behind him. He waylays the smaller boys to punch their unprotected heads, and calls challenges after me in the open streets. For these sufficient reasons I resolve to fight the butcher.

It is a summer evening, down in a green hollow, at the corner of a wall. I meet the butcher by appointment. I am attended by a select body of our boys; the butcher, by two other butchers, a young publican, and a sweep. The preliminaries are adjusted, and the butcher and myself stand face to face. In a moment the butcher lights ten thousand candles out of my left eyebrow. In another moment, I don't know where the wall is, or where I am, or where anybody is. I hardly know which is myself and which the butcher, we are always in such a tangle and tussle, knocking about upon the trodden grass. Sometimes I see the butcher, bloody but confident; sometimes I see nothing, and sit gasping on my second's knee; sometimes I go in at the butcher madly, and cut my knuckles open against his face, without appearing to discompose him at all. At last I awake, very queer about the head, as from a giddy sleep, and see the butcher walking off, congratulated by the two other butchers and the sweep and publican, and putting on his coat as he goes; from which I augur, justly, that the victory is his.

I am taken home in a sad plight, and I have beef-steaks put to my eyes, and am rubbed with vinegar and brandy, and find a great puffy place bursting out on my upper lip, which swells immoderately. For three or four days I remain at home, a very ill-looking subject, with a green shade over my eyes; and I should be very dull, but that Agnes is a sister to me, and condoles with me, and reads to me, and makes the time light and happy. Agnes has my confidence completely, always; I tell her all about the butcher, and the wrongs he has heaped upon me; she thinks I couldn't have done otherwise than fight the butcher, while she shrinks and trembles at my having fought him.

Time has stolen on unobserved, for Adams is not the headboy in the days that are come now, nor has he been this many and many a day. Adams has left the school so long, that when he comes back, on a visit to Doctor Strong, there are not many there, besides myself, who know him. Adams is going to be called to the bar almost directly, and is to be an advocate, and to wear a wig. I am surprised to find him a meeker man than I had thought, and less imposing in appearance. He has not staggered the world yet, either; for it goes on (as well as I can make out) pretty much the same as if he had never joined it.

A blank, through which the warriors of poetry and history march on in stately hosts that seem to have no end—and what comes next! *I* am the head-boy, now! I look down on the line of boys below me, with a condescending interest in such of them as bring to my mind the boy I was myself, when I first came there. That little fellow seems to be no part of me; I remember him as something left behind upon the road of life—as something I have passed, rather than have actually been—and almost think of him as of someone else.

And the little girl I saw on that first day at Mr Wickfield's, where is she? Gone also. In her stead, the perfect likeness of the picture, a child likeness no more, moves about the house; and Agnes—my sweet sister, as I call her in my thoughts, my counsellor and friend, the better angel of the lives of all who come within her calm, good, self-denying influence—is quite a woman.

What other changes have come upon me, besides the changes in my growth and looks, and in the knowledge I have garnered all this while? I wear a gold watch and chain, a ring upon my little finger, and a long-tailed coat; and I use a great deal of bear's grease—which, taken in conjunction with the ring, looks bad. Am I in love again? I am. I worship the eldest Miss Larkins.

The eldest Miss Larkins is not a little girl. She is a tall, dark, black-eyed, fine figure of a woman. The eldest Miss Larkins is not a chicken; for the youngest Miss Larkins is not that, and the eldest must be three or four years older. Perhaps the eldest Miss Larkins may be about thirty. My passion for her is beyond all bounds.

The eldest Miss Larkins knows officers. It is an awful thing to bear. I see them speaking to her in the street. I see them cross the way to meet her, when her bonnet (she has a bright taste in bonnets) is seen coming down the pavement, accompanied by her sister's bonnet. She laughs and talks, and seems to like it. I spend a good deal of my own spare time in walking up and down to meet her. If I can bow to her once in the day (I know her to bow to, knowing Mr Larkins), I am happier. I deserve a bow now and then. The raging agonies I suffer on the night of the Race Ball, where I know the eldest Miss Larkins will be dancing with the military, ought to have some compensation, if there be even-handed justice in the world.

My passion takes away my appetite, and makes me wear my newest silk neckerchief continually. I have no relief but in putting on my best clothes, and having my boots cleaned over and over again. I seem, then, to be worthier of the eldest Miss Larkins. Everything that belongs to her, or is connected with her, is precious to me. Mr Larkins (a gruff old gentleman with a double chin, and one of his eyes immovable in his head) is fraught with interest to me. When I can't meet his daughter, I go where I am likely to meet him. To say "How do you do, Mr Larkins? Are the young ladies and all the family quite well?" seems so pointed, that I blush.

I think continually about my age. Say I am seventeen, and say that seventeen is young for the eldest Miss Larkins, what of that? Besides, I shall be one-and-twenty in no time almost. I regularly take walks outside Mr Larkins's house in the evening, though it cuts me to the heart to see the officers go in, or to hear them up in the drawing-room, where the eldest Miss Larkins plays the harp. I even walk, on two or three occasions, in a sickly, spoony manner, round and round the house after the family are gone to bed, wondering which is the eldest Miss Larkins's chamber (and pitching, I dare say now, on Mr Larkins's instead); wishing that a fire would burst out; that the assembled crowd would stand appalled; that I, dashing through them with a ladder, might rear it against her window, save her in my arms, go back for something she had left behind, and perish in the flames. For I am generally disinterested in my love, and think I could be content to make a figure before Miss Larkins, and expire.

Generally, but not always. Sometimes brighter visions rise before me. When I dress (the occupation of two hours), for a great ball given at the Larkins's (the anticipation of three weeks), I indulge my fancy with pleasing images. I picture myself taking courage to make a declaration to Miss Larkins. I picture Miss Larkins sinking her head upon my shoulder, and saying, "Oh, Mr Copperfield, can I believe my ears!" I picture Mr Larkins waiting on me next morning, and saying, "My dear Copperfield, my daughter has told me all. Youth is no objection. Here are twenty thousand pounds. Be happy!" I picture my aunt relenting, and blessing us; and Mr Dick and Doctor Strong being present at the marriage ceremony. I am a sensible fellow, I believe—I believe, on looking back, I mean—and modest I am sure; but all this goes on notwithstanding.

I repair to the enchanted house, where there are lights, chattering, music, flowers, officers (I am sorry to see), and the eldest Miss Larkins, a blaze of beauty. She is dressed in blue, with blue flowers in her hair—forget-me-nots—as if *she* had any need to wear forget-me-nots. It is the first really grown-up party that I have ever been invited to, and I am a little uncomfortable; for I appear not to belong to anybody, and nobody appears to have anything to say to me, except Mr Larkins, who asks me how my schoolfellows are, which he needn't do, as I have not come there to be insulted.

But after I have stood in the doorway for some time, and feasted my eyes upon the goddess of my heart, she approaches me—she, the eldest Miss Larkins!—and asks me pleasantly, if I dance?

I stammer, with a bow, "With you, Miss Larkins."

"With no one else?" inquires Miss Larkins.

"I should have no pleasure in dancing with anyone else."

Miss Larkins laughs and blushes (or I think she blushes), and says, "Next time but one, I shall be very glad."

The time arrives. "It is a waltz, I think," Miss Larkins doubtfully observes, when I present myself. "Do you waltz? If not, Captain Bailey—"

But I do waltz (pretty well, too, as it happens), and I take Miss Larkins out. I take her sternly from the side of Captain Bailey. He is wretched, I have no doubt; but he is nothing to me. I have been wretched, too. I waltz with the eldest Miss Larkins! I don't know where, among whom, or how long. I only know that I swim about in space, with a blue angel, in a state of blissful delirium, until I find myself alone with her in a little room, resting on a sofa. She admires a flower (pink camellia japonica, price half-a-crown), in my button-hole. I give it her, and say:

"I ask an inestimable price for it, Miss Larkins."

"Indeed! What is that?" returns Miss Larkins.

"A flower of yours, that I may treasure it as a miser does gold."

"You're a bold boy," says Miss Larkins. "There."

She gives it me, not displeased; and I put it to my lips, and then into my breast. Miss Larkins, laughing, draws her hand through my arm, and says, "Now take me back to Captain Bailey."

I am lost in the recollection of this delicious interview, and the waltz, when she comes to me again, with a plain elderly gentleman who has been playing whist all night, upon her arm, and says:

"Oh! here is my bold friend! Mr Chestle wants to know you, Mr Copperfield."

I feel at once that he is a friend of the family, and am much gratified.

"I admire your taste, sir," says Mr Chestle. "It does you credit. I suppose you don't take much interest in hops; but I am a pretty large grower myself; and if you ever like to come over to our neighbourhood—neighbourhood of Ashford—and take a run about our place, we shall be glad for you to stop as long as you like."

I thank Mr Chestle warmly, and shake hands. I think I am in a happy dream. I waltz with the eldest Miss Larkins once again. She says I waltz so well! I go home in a state of unspeakable bliss, and waltz in imagination, all night long, with my arm round the blue waist of my dear divinity. For some days afterwards, I am lost in rapturous reflections; but I neither see her in the street, nor when I call. I am imperfectly consoled for this disappointment by the sacred pledge, the perished flower.

"Trotwood," says Agnes, one day after dinner. "Who do you think is going to be married tomorrow? Someone you admire."

"Not you, I suppose, Agnes?"

"Not me!" raising her cheerful face from the music she is copying. "Do you hear him, Papa?—The eldest Miss Larkins."

"To—to Captain Bailey?" I have just enough power to ask.

"No; to no Captain. To Mr Chestle, a hop-grower."

I am terribly dejected for about a week or two. I take off my ring, I wear my worst clothes, I use no bear's grease, and I frequently lament over the late Miss Larkins's faded flower. Being, by that time, rather tired of this kind of life, and having received new provocation from the butcher, I throw the flower away, go out with the butcher, and gloriously defeat him.

This, and the resumption of my ring, as well as of the bear's grease in moderation, are the last marks I can discern, now, in my progress to seventeen.

Chapter XIX

I LOOK ABOUT ME, AND MAKE A DISCOVERY

I AM doubtful whether I was at heart glad or sorry, when my school-days drew to an end, and the time came for my leaving Doctor Strong's. I had been very happy there, I had a great attachment for the Doctor, and I was eminent and distinguished in that little world. For these reasons I was sorry to go; but for other reasons, unsubstantial enough, I was glad. Misty ideas of being a young man at my own disposal, of the importance attaching to a young man at his own disposal, of the wonderful things to be seen and done by that magnificent animal, and the wonderful effects he could not fail to make upon society, lured me away. So powerful were these visionary considerations in my boyish mind, that I seem, according to my present way of thinking, to have left school without natural regret. The separation has not made the impression on me, that other separations have. I try in vain to recall how I felt about it, and what its circumstances were; but it is not momentous in my recollection. I suppose the opening prospect confused me. I know that my juvenile experiences went for little or nothing then; and that life was more like a great fairy story, which I was just about to begin to read, than anything else.

My aunt and I had held many grave deliberations on the calling to which I should be devoted. For a year or more I had endeavoured to find a satisfactory answer to her often-repeated question, "What I would like to be?" But I had no particular liking, that I could discover, for anything. If I could have been inspired with a knowledge of the science of navigation, taken the command of a fast-sailing expedition, and gone round the world on a triumphant voyage of discovery, I think I might have considered myself completely suited. But, in the absence of any such miraculous provision, my desire was to apply myself to some pursuit that would not lie too heavily upon her purse; and to do my duty in it, whatever it might be.

Mr Dick had regularly assisted at our councils, with a meditative and sage demeanour. He never made a suggestion but once; and on that occasion (I don't know what put it in his head), he suddenly proposed that I should be "a Brazier." My aunt received this proposal so very ungraciously, that he never ventured on a second; but ever afterwards confined himself to looking watchfully at her for her suggestions, and rattling his money.

"Trot, I tell you what, my dear," said my aunt, one morning in the Christmas season when I left school: "as this knotty point is still unsettled, and as we must not make a mistake in our decision if we can help it, I think we had better take a little breathing-time. In the meanwhile, you must try to look at it from a new point of view, and not as a schoolboy."

"I will, aunt."

"It has occurred to me," pursued my aunt, "that a little change, and a glimpse of life out of doors, may be useful in helping you to know your own mind, and form a cooler judgement. Suppose you were to go down into the old part of the country again, for instance, and see that——that out-of-the-way woman with the savagest of names," said my aunt, rubbing her nose, for she could never thoroughly forgive Peggotty for being so called.

"Of all things in the world, aunt, I should like it best!"

"Well," said my aunt, "that's lucky, for I should like it too. But it's natural and rational that you should like it. And I am very well persuaded that whatever you do, Trot, will always be natural and rational."

"I hope so, aunt."

"Your sister, Betsey Trotwood," said my aunt, "would have been as natural and rational a girl as ever breathed. You'll be worthy of her, won't you?"

"I hope I shall be worthy of *you,* aunt. That will be enough for me."

"It's a mercy that poor dear baby of a mother of yours didn't live," said my aunt, looking at me approvingly. "or she'd have been so vain of her boy by this time, that her soft little head would have been completely turned, if there was anything of it left to turn." (My aunt always excused any weakness of her own in my behalf, by transferring it in this way to my poor mother.) "Bless me, Trotwood, how you do remind me of her!"

"Pleasantly, I hope, aunt?" said I.

"He's as like her, Dick," said my aunt, emphatically, "he's as like her, as she was that afternoon before she began to fret—bless my heart, he's as like her, as he can look at me out of his two eyes!"

"Is he indeed?" said Mr Dick.

"And he's like David, too," said my aunt, decisively.

"He is very like David!" said Mr Dick.

"But what I want you to be, Trot," resumed my aunt, "—I don't mean physically, but morally; you are very well physically—is, a firm fellow. A fine firm fellow, with a will of your own. With resolution," said my aunt, shaking her cap at me, and clenching her hand. "With determination. With character, Trot—with strength of character that is not to be influenced, except on good reason, by anybody, or by anything. That's what I want you to be. That's what your father and mother might both have been, Heaven knows, and been the better for it."

I intimated that I hoped I should be what she described.

"That you may begin, in a small way, to have a reliance upon yourself, and to act for yourself," said my aunt, "I shall send you upon your trip, alone. I did think, once, of Mr Dick's going with you; but, on second thoughts, I shall keep him to take care of me."

Mr Dick, for a moment, looked a little disappointed; until the honour and dignity of having to take care of the most wonderful woman in the world, restored the sunshine to his face.

"Besides," said my aunt, "there's the Memorial—"

"Oh, certainly," said Mr Dick, in a hurry, "I intend, Trotwood, to get that done immediately—it really must be done immediately! And then it will go in, you know—and then—" said Mr Dick, after checking himself, and pausing a long time, "there'll be a pretty kettle of fish!"

In pursuance of my aunt's kind scheme, I was shortly afterwards fitted out with a handsome purse of money, and portmanteau, and tenderly dismissed upon my expedition. At parting, my aunt gave me some good advice, and a good many kisses; and said that as her object was that I should look about me, and should think a little, she would recommend me to stay a few days in London, if I liked it, either on my way down into Suffolk, or in coming back. In a word, I was at liberty to do what I would, for three weeks or a month; and no other conditions were imposed upon my freedom than the before-mentioned thinking and looking about me, and a pledge to write three times a week and faithfully report myself.

I went to Canterbury first, that I might take leave of Agnes and Mr Wickfield (my old room in whose house I had not yet relinquished), and also of the good Doctor. Agnes was very glad to see me, and told me that the house had not been like itself since I had left it.

"I am sure I am not like myself when I am away," said I. "I seem to want my right hand, when I miss you. Though that's not saying much; for there's no head in my right hand, and no heart. Everyone who knows you, consults with you, and is guided by you, Agnes."

"Everyone who knows me, spoils me, I believe," she answered, smiling.

"No. It's because you are like no one else. You are so good, and so sweet-tempered. You have such a gentle nature, and you are always right."

"You talk," said Agnes, breaking into a pleasant laugh, as she sat at work, "as if I were the late Miss Larkins."

"Come! It's not fair to abuse my confidence," I answered, reddening at the recollection of my blue enslaver. "But I shall confide in you, just the same, Agnes. I can never grow out of that. Whenever I fall into trouble, or fall in love, I shall always tell you, if you'll let me—even when I come to fall in love in earnest."

"Why, you have always been in earnest!" said Agnes, laughing again.

"Oh! that was as a child, or a schoolboy," said I, laughing in my turn, not without being a little shame-faced. "Times are altering now, and I suppose I shall be in a terrible state of earnestness one day or other. My wonder is, that you are not in earnest yourself, by this time, Agnes."

Agnes laughed again, and shook her head.

"Oh, I know you are not!" said I, "because if you had been you would have told me. Or at least"—for I saw a faint blush in her face, "you would have let me find it out for myself. But there is no one that I know of, who deserves to love *you,* Agnes. Someone of a nobler character, and more worthy altogether than anyone I have ever seen here, must rise up, before I give *my* consent. In the time to come, I shall have a wary eye on all admirers; and shall exact a great deal from the successful one, I assure you."

We had gone on, so far, in a mixture of confidential jest and earnest, that had long grown naturally out of our familiar relations, begun as mere children. But Agnes, now suddenly lifting up her eyes to mine, and speaking in a different manner, said:

"Trotwood, there is something that I want to ask you, and that I may not have another opportunity of asking for a long time, perhaps—something I would ask, I think, of no one else. Have you observed any gradual alteration in Papa?"

I had observed it, and had often wondered whether she had too. I must have shown as much, now, in my face; for her eyes were in a moment cast down, and I saw tears in them.

"Tell me what it is," she said, in a low voice.

"I think—shall I be quite plain, Agnes, liking him so much?"

"Yes," she said.

"I think he does himself no good by the habit that has increased upon him since I first came here. He is often very nervous—or I fancy so."

"It is not fancy," said Agnes, shaking her head.

"His hand trembles, his speech is not plain, and his eyes look wild. I have remarked that at those times, and when he is least like himself, he is most certain to be wanted on some business."

"By Uriah," said Agnes.

"Yes; and the sense of being unfit for it, or of not having understood it, or of having shown his condition in spite of himself, seems to make him so uneasy, that next day he is worse, and next day worse, and so he becomes jaded and haggard. Do not be alarmed by what I say, Agnes, but in this state I saw him, only the other evening, lay down his head upon his desk, and shed tears like a child."

Her hand passed softly before my lips while I was yet speaking, and in a moment she had met her father at the door of the room, and was hanging on his shoulder. The expression of her face, as they both looked towards me, I felt to be very touching. There was such deep fondness for him, and gratitude to him for all his love and care, in her beautiful look; and there was such a fervent appeal to me to deal tenderly by him, even in my inmost thoughts, and to let no harsh construction find any place against him; she was, at once, so proud of him and devoted to him, yet so compassionate and sorry, and so reliant upon me to be so, too; that nothing she could have said would have expressed more to me, or moved me more.

We were to drink tea at the Doctor's. We went there at the usual hour; and round the study fireside found the Doctor, and his young wife, and her mother. The Doctor, who made as much of my going away as if I were going to China, received me as an honoured guest; and called for a log of wood to be thrown on the fire, that he might see the face of his old pupil reddening in the blaze.

"I shall not see many more new faces in Trotwood's stead, Wickfield," said the Doctor, warming his hands; "I am getting lazy, and want ease. I shall relinquish all my young people in another six months, and lead a quieter life."

"You have said so, any time these ten years, Doctor," Mr Wickfield answered.

"But now I mean to do it," returned the Doctor. "My first master will succeed me—I am in earnest at last—so you'll soon have to arrange our contracts, and to bind us firmly to them, like a couple of knaves."

"And to take care," said Mr Wickfield, "that you're not imposed on, eh? As you certainly would be, in any contract you should make for yourself. Well! I am ready. There are worse tasks than that, in my calling."

"I shall have nothing to think of then," said the Doctor, with a smile, "but my Dictionary; and this other contract-bargain—Annie."

As Mr Wickfield glanced towards her, sitting at the tea table by Agnes, she seemed to me to avoid his look with such unwonted hesitation and timidity, that his attention became fixed upon her, as if something were suggested to his thoughts.

"There is a post come in from India, I observe," he said, after a short silence.

"By the by! and letters from Mr Jack Maldon!" said the Doctor.

"Indeed!"

"Poor dear Jack!" said Mrs Markleham, shaking her head. "That trying climate?—like living, they tell me, on a sand-heap, underneath a burning-glass! He looked strong, but he wasn't. My dear Doctor, it was his spirit, not his constitution, that he ventured on so boldly. Annie, my dear, I am sure you must perfectly recollect that your cousin never was strong—not what can be called *robust,* you know," said Mrs Markleham, with emphasis, and looking round upon us generally, "—from the time when my daughter and himself were children together, and walking about, arm-in-arm, the livelong day."

Annie, thus addressed, made no reply.

"Do I gather from what you say, ma'am, that Mr Maldon is ill?" asked Mr Wickfield.

"Ill!" replied the Old Soldier. "My dear sir, he's all sorts of things."

"Except well?" said Mr Wickfield.

"Except well, indeed!" said the Old Soldier. "He has had dreadful strokes of the sun, no doubt, and jungle fevers and agues, and every kind of thing you can mention. As to his liver," said the Old Soldier resignedly, "that, of course, he gave up altogether, when he first went out!"

"Does he say all this?" asked Mr Wickfield.

"Say? My dear sir," returned Mrs Markleham, shaking her head and her fan, "you little know my poor Jack Maldon when you ask that question. Say? Not he. You might drag him at the heels of four wild horses first."

"Mama!" said Mrs Strong.

"Annie, my dear," returned her mother, "once for all, I must really beg that you will not interfere with me, unless it is to confirm what I say. You know as well as I do that your cousin Maldon would be dragged at the heels of any number of wild horses—why should I confine myself to four! I *won't* confine myself to four—eight, sixteen, two-and-thirty, rather than say anything calculated to overturn the Doctor's plans."

"Wickfield's plans," said the Doctor, stroking his face, and looking penitently at his adviser. "That is to say, our joint plans for him. I said myself, abroad or at home."

"And I said" added Mr Wickfield gravely, "abroad. I was the means of sending him abroad. It's my responsibility."

"Oh! Responsibility!" said the Old Soldier. "Everything was done for the best, my dear Mr Wickfield; everything was done for the kindest and best, we know. But if the dear fellow can't live there, he can't live there. And if he can't live there, he'll die there, sooner than he'll overturn the Doctor's plans. I know him," said the Old Soldier, fanning herself, in a sort of calm prophetic agony, "and I know he'll die there, sooner than he'll overturn the Doctor's plans."

"Well, well, ma'am," said the Doctor cheerfully, "I am not bigoted to my plans, and I can overturn them myself. I can substitute some other plans. If Mr Jack Maldon comes home on account of ill health, he must not be allowed to go back, and we must endeavour to make some more suitable and fortunate provision for him in this country."

Mrs Markleham was so overcome by this generous speech—which, I need not say, she had not at all expected or led up to—that she could only tell the Doctor it was like himself, and go several times through that operation of kissing the sticks of her fan, and then tapping his hand with it. After which she gently chid her daughter Annie, for not being more demonstrative when such kindnesses were showered, for her sake, on her old playfellow; and entertained us with some particulars concerning other deserving members of her family, whom it was desirable to set on their deserving legs.

All this time, her daughter Annie never once spoke, or lifted up her eyes. All this time, Mr Wickfield had his glance upon her as she sat by his own daughter's side. It appeared to me that he never thought of being observed by anyone; but was so intent upon her, and upon his own thoughts in connexion with her, as to be quite absorbed. He now asked what Mr Jack Maldon had actually written in reference to himself, and to whom he had written?

"Why, here," said Mrs Markleham, taking a letter from the chimney-piece above the Doctor's head, "the dear fellow says to the Doctor himself—where is it? Oh!—'I am sorry to inform you that my health is suffering severely, and that I fear I may be reduced to the necessity of returning home for a time, as the only hope of restoration.' That's pretty plain, poor fellow! His only hope of restoration! But Annie's letter is plainer still. Annie, show me that letter again."

"Not now, mama," she pleaded in a low tone.

"My dear, you absolutely are, on some subjects, one of the most ridiculous persons in the world," returned her mother, "and perhaps the most unnatural to the claims of your own family. We never should have heard of the letter at all, I believe, unless I had asked for it myself. Do you call that confidence, my love, towards Doctor Strong? I am surprised. You ought to know better."

The letter was reluctantly produced; and as I handed it to the old lady, I saw how the unwilling hand from which I took it, trembled.

"Now let us see," said Mrs Markleham, putting her glass to her eye, "where the passage is. 'The remembrance of old times, my dearest Annie'—and so forth—it's not there. 'The amiable old Proctor'—who's he? Dear me, Annie, how illegibly your cousin Maldon writes, and how stupid I am! 'Doctor,' of course. Ah! amiable indeed!" Here she left off, to kiss her fan again, and shake it at the Doctor, who was looking at us in a state of placid satisfaction. "Now I have found it. 'You may not be surprised to hear, Annie,'— no, to be sure, knowing that he never was really strong; what did I say just now?—'that I have undergone so much in this distant place, as to have decided to leave it at all hazards; on sick leave, if I can; on total resignation, if that is not to be obtained. What

I have endured, and do endure here, is insupportable.' And but for the promptitude of that best of creatures," said Mrs Markleham, telegraphing the Doctor as before, and refolding the letter, "it would be insupportable to me to think of."

Mr Wickfield said not one word, though the old lady looked to him as if for his commentary on this intelligence; but sat severely silent, with his eyes fixed on the ground. Long after the subject was dismissed, and other topics occupied us, he remained so; seldom raising his eyes, unless to rest them for a moment, with a thoughtful frown, upon the Doctor, or his wife or both.

The Doctor was very fond of music. Agnes sang with great sweetness and expression, and so did Mrs Strong. They sang together, and played duets together, and we had quite a little concert. But I remarked two things: first, that though Annie soon recovered her composure, and was quite herself, there was a blank between her and Mr Wickfield which separated them wholly from each other; secondly, that Mr Wickfield seemed to dislike the intimacy between her and Agnes, and to watch it with uneasiness. And now, I must confess, the recollection of what I had seen on that night when Mr Maldon went away, first began to return upon me with a meaning it had never had, and to trouble me. The innocent beauty of her face was not as innocent to me as it had been; I mistrusted the natural grace and charm of her manner; and when I looked at Agnes by her side, and thought how good and true Agnes was, suspicions arose within me that it was an ill-assorted friendship.

She was so happy in it herself, however, and the other was so happy too, that they made the evening fly away as if it were but an hour. It closed in an incident which I well remember. They were taking leave of each other, and Agnes was going to embrace her and kiss her, when Mr Wickfield stepped between them, as if by accident, and drew Agnes quickly away. Then I saw, as though all the intervening time had been cancelled, and I were still standing in the doorway on the night of the departure, the expression of that night in the face of Mrs Strong, as it confronted his.

I cannot say what an impression this made upon me, or how impossible I found it, when I thought of her afterwards, to separate her from this look, and remember her face in its innocent loveliness again. It haunted me when I got home. I seemed to have left the Doctor's roof with a dark cloud lowering on it. The reverence that I had for his grey head, was mingled with commiseration for his faith in those who were treacherous to him, and with resentment against those who injured him. The impending shadow of a great affliction, and a great disgrace that had no distinct form in it yet, fell like a stain upon the quiet place where I had worked and played as a boy, and did it a cruel wrong. I had no pleasure in thinking, any more, of the grave old broad-leaved aloe-trees, which remained shut up in themselves a hundred years together, and of the trim smooth grass-plot, and the stone urns, and the Doctor's walk, and the congenial sound of the Cathedral bell hovering above them all. It was as if the tranquil sanctuary of my boyhood had been sacked before my face, and its peace and honour given to the winds.

But morning brought with it my parting from the old house, which Agnes had filled with her influence; and that occupied my mind sufficiently. I should be there again soon, no doubt; I might sleep again—perhaps often—in my old room; but the days of my inhabiting there were gone, and the old time was past. I was heavier at heart when I packed up such of my books and clothes as still remained there to be sent to Dover, than I cared to show to Uriah Heep; who was so officious to help me, that I uncharitably thought him mighty glad that I was going.

I got away from Agnes and her father, somehow, with an indifferent show of being very manly, and took my seat upon the box of the London coach. I was so softened and forgiving, going through the town, that I had half a mind to nod to my old enemy the butcher, and throw him five shillings to drink. But he looked such a very obdurate butcher as he stood scraping the great block in the shop, and moreover, his appearance was so little improved by the loss of a front tooth which I had knocked out, that I thought it best to make no advances.

The main object on my mind, I remember, when we got fairly on the road, was to appear as old as possible to the coachman, and to speak extremely gruff. The latter point I achieved at great personal inconvenience; but I stuck to it, because I felt it was a grown-up sort of thing.

"You are going through, sir?" said the coachman.

"Yes, William," I said, condescendingly (I knew him); "I am going to London. I shall go down into Suffolk afterwards."

"Shooting, sir?" said the coachman.

He knew as well as I did that it was just as likely, at that time of year, I was going down there whaling; but I felt complimented, too.

"I don't know," I said, pretending to be undecided, "whether I shall take a shot or not."

"Birds is got wery shy, I'm told," said William.

"So I understand," said I.

"Is Suffolk your county, sir?" asked William.

"Yes," I said, with some importance. "Suffolk's my county."

"I'm told the dumplings is uncommon fine down there," said William.

I was not aware of it myself, but I felt it necessary to uphold the institutions of my county, and to evince a familiarity with them; so I shook my head, as much as to say, "I believe you!"

"And the Punches," said William. "There's cattle! A Suffolk Punch, when he's a good un, is worth his weight in gold. Did you ever breed any Suffolk Punches yourself, sir?"

"N—no," I said, "not exactly."

"Here's a gen'lm'n behind me, I'll pound it," said William, "as has bred 'em by wholesale."

The gentleman spoken of was a gentleman with a very unpromising squint, and a prominent chin, who had a tall white hat on with a narrow flat brim, and whose close-fitting drab trousers seemed to button all the way up outside his legs from his boots to his hips. His chin was cocked over the coachman's shoulder, so near to me, that his breath quite tickled the back of my head; and as I looked at him, he leered at the leaders with the eye with which he didn't squint, in a very knowing manner.

"Ain't you?" asked William.

"Ain't I what?" said the gentleman behind.

"Bred them Suffolk Punches by wholesale?"

"I should think so," said the gentleman. "There ain't no sort of orse that I ain't bred, and no sort of dorg. Orses and dorgs is some men's fancy. They're wittles and drink to me—lodging, wife, and children—reading, writing, and 'rithmetic—snuff, tobacker, and sleep."

"That ain't a sort of man to see sitting behind a coach-box, is it though?" said William in my ear, as he handled the reins.

I construed this remark into an indication of a wish that he should have my place, so I blushingly offered to resign it.

"Well, if you don't mind, sir," said William, "I think it *would* be more correct."

I have always considered this as the first fall I had in life. When I booked my place at the coach office I had had "Box Seat" written against the entry, and had given the book-keeper half-a-crown. I was got up in a special great-coat and shawl, expressly to do honour to that distinguished eminence; had glorified myself upon it a good deal; and had felt that I was a credit to the coach. And here, in the very first stage, I was supplanted by a shabby man with a squint, who had no other merit than smelling like a livery-stables, and being able to walk across me, more like a fly than a human being, while the horses were at a canter!

A distrust of myself, which has often beset me in life on small occasions, when it would have been better away, was assuredly not stopped in its growth by this little incident outside the Canterbury coach. It was in vain to take refuge in gruffness of speech. I spoke from the pit of my stomach for the rest of the journey, but I felt completely extinguished, and dreadfully young.

It was curious and interesting, nevertheless, to be sitting up there behind four horses: well educated, well dressed, and with plenty of money in my pocket; and to look out for the places where I had slept on my weary journey. I had abundant occupation for my thoughts, in every conspicuous landmark on the road. When I looked down at the trampers whom we passed, and saw that well-remembered style of face turned up, I felt as if the tinker's blackened hand were in the bosom of my shirt again. When we clattered through the narrow street of Chatham, and I caught a glimpse, in passing, of the lane where the old monster lived who had bought my jacket, I stretched my neck eagerly to look for the place where I had sat, in the sun and in the shade, waiting for my money. When we came, at last, within a stage of London, and passed the veritable Salem House where Mr Creakle had laid about him with a heavy hand, I would have given all I had, for lawful permission to get down and thrash him, and let all the boys out like so many caged sparrows.

We went to the Golden Cross at Charing Cross, then a mouldy sort of establishment in a close neighbourhood. A waiter showed me into the coffee-room; and a chamber-maid introduced me to my small bedchamber, which smelt like a hackney-coach, and was shut up like a family vault. I was still painfully conscious of my youth, for nobody stood in any awe of me at all: the chambermaid being utterly indifferent to my opinions on any subject, and the waiter being familiar with me, and offering advice to my inexperience.

"Well now," said the waiter, in a tone of confidence, "what would you like for dinner? Young gentlemen likes poultry in general: have a fowl!"

I told him, as majestically as I could, that I wasn't in the humour for a fowl.

"Ain't you?" said the waiter. "Young gentlemen is generally tired of beef and mutton: have a weal cutlet!"

I assented to this proposal, in default of being able to suggest anything else.

"Do you care for taters?" said the waiter, with an insinuating smile, and his head on one side. "Young gentlemen generally has been overdosed with taters."

I commanded him, in my deepest voice, to order a veal cutlet and potatoes, and all things fitting; and to inquire at the bar if there were any letters for Trotwood Copperfield, Esquire—which I knew there were not, and couldn't be, but thought it manly to appear to expect.

He soon came back to say that there were none (at which I was much surprised) and began to lay the cloth for my dinner in a box by the fire. While he was so engaged, he asked me what I would take with it; and on my replying "Half a pint of sherry," thought it a favourable opportunity, I am afraid, to extract that measure of wine from the stale leavings at the bottoms of several small decanters. I am of this opinion, because, while I was reading the newspaper, I observed him behind a low wooden partition, which was his private apartment, very busy pouring out of a number of those vessels into one, like a chemist and druggist making up a prescription. When the wine came, too, I thought it flat; and it certainly had more English crumbs in it, than were to be expected in a foreign wine in anything like a pure state, but I was bashful enough to drink it, and say nothing.

Being then in a pleasant frame of mind (from which I infer that poisoning is not always disagreeable in some stages of the process), I resolved to go to the play. It was Covent Garden Theatre that I chose; and there, from the back of a centre box, I saw *Julius Caesar* and the new Pantomime. To have all those noble Romans alive before me, and walking in and out for my entertainment, instead of being the stern taskmasters they had been at school, was a most novel and delightful effect. But the mingled reality and mystery of the whole show, the influence upon me of the poetry, the lights, the music, the company, the smooth stupendous changes of glittering and brilliant scenery, were so dazzling, and opened up such illimitable regions of delight, that when I came out into the rainy street, at twelve o'clock at night, I felt as if I had come from the clouds, where I had been leading a romantic life for ages, to a bawling, splashing, link-lighted, umbrella-struggling, hackney-coach-jostling, patten-clinking, muddy, miserable world.

I had emerged by another door, and stood in the street for a little while, as if I really were a stranger upon earth; but the unceremonious pushing and hustling that I received, soon recalled me to myself, and put me in the road back to the hotel; whither I went, revolving the glorious vision all the way; and where, after some porter and oysters, I sat revolving it still, at past one o'clock, with my eyes on the coffee-room fire.

I was so filled with the play, and with the past—for it was, in a manner, like a shining transparency, through which I saw my earlier life moving along—that I don't know when the figure of a handsome well-formed young man dressed with a tasteful easy negligence which I have reason to remember very well, became a real presence to me. But I recollect being conscious of his company without having noticed his coming in—and my still sitting, musing, over the coffee-room fire.

At last I rose to go to bed, much to the relief of the sleepy waiter, who had got the fidgets in his legs, and was twisting them, and hitting them, and putting them through all kinds of contortions in his small pantry. In going towards the door, I passed the person who had come in, and saw him plainly. I turned directly, came back, and looked again. He did not know me, but I knew him in a moment.

At another time I might have wanted the confidence or the decision to speak to him, and might have put it off until next day, and might have lost him. But, in the then condition of my mind, where the play was still running high, his former protection of me appeared so deserving of my gratitude, and my old love for him overflowed my breast so freshly and spontaneously, that I went up to him at once, with a fast-beating heart, and said:

"Steerforth! won't you speak to me?"

He looked at me—just as he used to look, sometimes—but I saw no recognition in his face.

"You don't remember me, I am afraid," said I.

"My God!" he suddenly exclaimed. "It's little Copperfield!"

I grasped him by both hands, and could not let them go. But for very shame, and the fear that it might displease him, I could have held him round the neck and cried.

"I never, never, never was so glad! My dear Steerforth, I am so overjoyed to see you!"

"And I am rejoiced to see you, too!" he said, shaking my hands heartily. "Why,

Copperfield, old boy, don't be overpowered!" And yet he was glad, too, I thought, to see how the delight I had in meeting him affected me.

I brushed away the tears that my utmost resolution had not been able to keep back, and I made a clumsy laugh of it, and we sat down together, side by side.

"Why, how do you come to be here?" said Steerforth, clapping me on the shoulder.

"I came here by the Canterbury coach, today. I have been adopted by an aunt down in that part of the country, and have just finished my education there. How do *you* come to be here, Steerforth?"

"Well, I am what they call an Oxford man," he returned; "that is to say, I get bored to death down there, periodically—and I am on my way now to my mother's. You're a devilish amiable-looking fellow, Copperfield. Just what you used to be, now I look at you! Not altered in the least!"

"I knew *you* immediately," I said; "but you are more easily remembered."

He laughed as he ran his hand through the clustering curls of his hair, and said gaily:

"Yes, I am on an expedition of duty. My mother lives a little way out of town; and the roads being in a beastly condition, and our house tedious enough, I remained here tonight instead of going on. I have not been in town half-a-dozen hours, and those I have been dozing and grumbling away at the play."

"I have been at the play, too," said I. "At Covent Garden. What a delightful and magnificent entertainment, Steerforth!"

Steerforth laughed heartily.

—"My dear young Davy," he said, clapping me on the shoulder again, "you are a very Daisy. The daisy of the field, at sunrise, is not fresher than you are. I have been at Covent Garden, too, and there never was a more miserable business. Holloa, you sir!"

This was addressed to the waiter, who had been very attentive to our recognition, at a distance, and now came forward deferentially.

"Where have you put my friend, Mr Copperfield?" said Steerforth.

"Beg your pardon, sir?"

"Where does he sleep? What's his number? You know what I mean," said Steerforth.

"Well, sir," said the waiter, with an apologetic air. "Mr Copperfield is at present in forty-four, sir."

"And what the devil do you mean," retorted Steerforth, "by putting Mr Copperfield into a little loft over a stable?"

"Why, you see we wasn't aware, sir," returned the waiter, still apologetically, "as Mr Copperfield was anyways particular. We can give Mr Copperfield seventy-two, sir, if it would be preferred. Next you, sir."

"Of course it would be preferred," said Steerforth. "And do it at once."

The waiter immediately withdrew to make the exchange. Steerforth, very much amused at my having been put into forty-four, laughed again, and clapped me on the shoulder again, and invited me to breakfast with him next morning at ten o'clock—an invitation I was only too proud and happy to accept. It being now pretty late, we took our candles and went upstairs, where we parted with friendly heartiness at his door, and where I found my new room a great improvement on my old one, it not being at all musty, and having an immense four-post bedstead in it, which was quite a little landed estate. Here, among pillows enough for six, I soon fell asleep in a blissful condition, and dreamed of ancient Rome, Steerforth, and friendship, until the early morning coaches, rumbling out of the archway underneath, made me dream of thunder and the gods.

Chapter XX

STEERFORTH'S HOME

WHEN the chambermaid tapped at my door at eight o'clock, and informed me that my shaving-water was outside, I felt severely the having no occasion for it, and blushed in my bed. The suspicion that she laughed too, when she said it, preyed upon my mind all the time I was dressing; and gave me, I was conscious, a sneaking and guilty air when I passed her on the staircase, as I was going down to breakfast. I was so sensitively aware, indeed, of being younger than I could have wished, that for some time I could not make up my mind to pass her at all, under the ignoble circumstances of the case; but, hearing her there with a broom, stood peeping out of window at King Charles on horseback, surrounded by a maze of hackney-coaches, and looking anything but regal in a drizzling rain and a dark-brown fog, until I was admonished by the waiter that the gentleman was waiting for me.

It was not in the coffee-room that I found Steerforth expecting me, but in a snug private apartment, red-curtained and Turkey-carpeted, where the fire burnt bright, and a fine hot breakfast was set forth on a table covered with a clean cloth; and a cheerful miniature of the room, the fire, the breakfast, Steerforth, and all, was shining in the little round mirror over the sideboard. I was rather bashful at first, Steerforth being so self-possessed, and elegant, and superior to me in all respects (age included); but his easy patronage soon put that to rights, and made me quite at home. I could not enough admire the change he had wrought in the Golden Cross; or compare the dull forlorn state I had held yesterday, with this morning's comfort and this morning's entertainment. As to the waiter's familiarity, it was quenched as if it had never been. He attended on us, as I may say, in sackcloth and ashes.

"Now, Copperfield," said Steerforth, when we were alone, "I should like to hear what you are doing, and where you are going, and all about you. I feel as if you were my property."

Glowing with pleasure to find that he had still this interest in me, I told him how my aunt had proposed the little expedition that I had before me, and whither it tended.

"As you are in no hurry, then," said Steerforth, "come home with me to Highgate, and stay a day or two. You will be pleased with my mother—she is a little vain and prosy about me, but that you can forgive her—and she will be pleased with you."

"I should like to be as sure of that, as you are kind enough to say you are," I answered, smiling.

"Oh!" said Steerforth, "everyone who likes me, has a claim on her that is sure to be acknowledged."

"Then I think I shall be a favourite," said I.

"Good!" said Steerforth. "Come and prove it. We will go and see the lions for an hour or two—it's something to have a fresh fellow like you to show them to, Copperfield—and then we'll journey out to Highgate by the coach."

I could hardly believe but that I was in a dream, and that I should wake presently in number forty-four, to the solitary box in the coffee-room and the familiar waiter again. After I had written to my aunt and told her of my fortunate meeting with my admired old schoolfellow, and my acceptance of his invitation, we went out in a hackney-chariot,

and saw a Panorama and some other sights, and took a walk through the Museum, where
I could not help observing how much Steerforth knew, on an infinite variety of subjects,
and of how little account he seemed to make his knowledge.

"You'll take a high degree at college, Steerforth," said I, "if you have not done so
already; and they will have good reason to be proud of you."

"*I* take a degree!" cried Steerforth. "Not I! my dear Daisy—will you mind my calling
you Daisy?"

"Not at all!" said I.

"That's a good fellow! My dear Daisy," said Steerforth, laughing. "I have not the least
desire or intention to distinguish myself in that way. I have done quite sufficient for my
purpose. I find that I am heavy company enough for myself as I am."

"But the fame—" I was beginning.

"You romantic Daisy!" said Steerforth, laughing still more heartily: "why should I
trouble myself, that a parcel of heavy-headed fellows may gape and hold up their hands?
Let them do it at some other man. There's fame for him, and he's welcome to it."

I was abashed at having made so great a mistake, and was glad to change the
subject. Fortunately it was not difficult to do, for Steerforth could always pass from one
subject to another with a carelessness and lightness that were his own.

Lunch succeeded to our sight-seeing, and the short winter day wore away so fast,
that it was dusk when the stage-coach stopped with us at an old brick house at Highgate
on the summit of the hill. An elderly lady, though not very far advanced in years, with
a proud carriage and a handsome face, was in the doorway as we alighted; and greeting
Steerforth as "My dearest James," folded him in her arms. To this lady he presented me
as his mother, and she gave me a stately welcome.

It was a genteel old-fashioned house, very quiet and orderly. From the windows of
my room I saw all London lying in the distance like a great vapour, with here and there
some lights twinkling through it. I had only time, in dressing, to glance at the solid
furniture, the framed pieces of work (done, I supposed, by Steerforth's mother when she
was a girl), and some pictures in crayons of ladies with powdered hair and bodices,
coming and going on the walls, as the newly-kindled fire crackled and sputtered, when
I was called to dinner.

There was a second lady in the dining-room, of a slight short figure, dark, and not
agreeable to look at, but with some appearance of good looks too, who attracted my
attention: perhaps because I had not expected to see her; perhaps because I found
myself sitting opposite to her; perhaps because of something really remarkable in her.
She had black hair and eager black eyes, and was thin, and had a scar upon her lip. It
was an old scar—I should rather call it seam, for it was not discoloured, and had healed
years ago—which had once cut through her mouth, downward towards the chin, but
was now barely visible across the table, except above and on her upper lip, the shape
of which it had altered. I concluded in my own mind that she was about thirty years of
age, and that she wished to be married. She was a little dilapidated—like a house—with
having been so long to let; yet had, as I have said, an appearance of good looks. Her
thinness seemed to be the effect of some wasting fire within her, which found a vent in
her gaunt eyes.

She was introduced as Miss Dartle, and both Steerforth and his mother called her
Rosa. I found that she lived there, and had been for a long time Mrs Steerforth's companion. It appeared to me that she never said anything she wanted to say, outright; but
hinted it, and made a great deal more of it by this practice. For example, when Mrs

Steerforth observed, more in jest than earnest, that she feared her son led but a wild life at college, Miss Dartle put in thus:

"Oh, really? You know how ignorant I am, and that I only ask for information, but isn't it always so? I thought that kind of life was on all hands understood to be—eh?"

"It is education for a very grave profession, if you mean that, Rosa," Mrs Steerforth answered with some coldness.

"Oh! Yes! That's very true," returned Miss Dartle. "But isn't it, though?—I want to be put right, if I am wrong—isn't it, really?"

"Really what?" said Mrs Steerforth.

"Oh! You mean it's *not!*" returned Miss Dartle. "Well, I'm very glad to hear it! Now, I know what to do! That's the advantage of asking. I shall never allow people to talk before me about wastefulness and profligacy, and so forth, in connexion with that life, any more."

"And you will be right," said Mrs Steerforth. "My son's tutor is a conscientious gentleman; and if I had not implicit reliance on my son, I should have reliance on him."

"Should you?" said Miss Dartle. "Dear me! Conscientious, is he? Really conscientious, now?"

"Yes, I am convinced of it," said Mrs Steerforth.

"How very nice!" exclaimed Miss Dartle. "What a comfort! Really conscientious? Then he's not—but of course he can't be, if he's really conscientious. Well, I shall be quite happy in my opinion of him, from this time. You can't think how it elevates him in my opinion, to know for certain that he's really conscientious!"

Her own views of every question, and her correction of everything that was said to which she was opposed, Miss Dartle insinuated in the same way: sometimes, I could not conceal from myself with great power, though in contradiction even of Steerforth. An instance happened before dinner was done. Mrs Steerforth speaking to me about my intention of going down into Suffolk, I said at hazard how glad I should be, if Steerforth would only go there with me; and explaining to him that I was going to see my old nurse, and Mr Peggotty's family, I reminded him of the boatman whom he had seen at school.

"Oh! That bluff fellow!" said Steerforth. "He had a son with him, hadn't he?"

"No. That was his nephew," I replied; "whom he adopted, though, as a son. He has a very pretty little niece too, whom he adopted as a daughter. In short, his house—or rather his boat, for he lives in one, on dry land—is full of people who are objects of his generosity and kindness. You would be delighted to see that household."

"Should I?" said Steerforth. "Well, I think I should. I must see what can be done. It would be worth a journey (not to mention the pleasure of a journey with you, Daisy), to see that sort of people together, and to make one of 'em."

My heart leaped with a new hope of pleasure. But it was in reference to the tone in which he had spoken of "that sort of people," that Miss Dartle, whose sparkling eyes had been watchful of us, now broke in again.

"Oh, but, really? Do tell me. Are they, though?" she said.

"Are they what? And are who what?" said Steerforth.

"That sort of people.—Are they really animals and clods, and beings of another order? I want to know *so* much."

"Why, there's a pretty wide separation between them and us," said Steerforth, with indifference. "They are not to be expected to be as sensitive as we are. Their delicacy is not to be shocked, or hurt easily. They are wonderfully virtuous, I dare say—some people contend for that, at least; and I am sure I don't want to contradict them—but they have not very fine natures, and they may be thankful that, like their coarse rough skins, they are not easily wounded."

"Really!" said Miss Dartle. "Well, I don't know, now, when I have been better pleased than to hear that. It's so consoling! It's such a delight to know that, when they suffer, they don't feel! Sometimes I have been quite uneasy for that sort of people; but now I shall just dismiss the idea of them, altogether. Live and learn. I had my doubts, I confess, but now they're cleared up. I didn't know, and now I do know, and that shows the advantage of asking—don't it?"

I believed that Steerforth had said what he had, in jest, or to draw Miss Dartle out; and I expected him to say as much when she was gone, and we two were sitting before the fire. But he merely asked me what I thought of her.

"She is very clever, is she not?" I asked.

"Clever! She brings everything to a grindstone," said Steerforth, "and sharpens it, as she has sharpened her own face and figure these years past. She has worn herself away by constant sharpening. She is all edge."

"What a remarkable scar that is upon her lip!" I said.

Steerforth's face fell, and he paused a moment.

"Why, the fact is," he returned, "*I* did that."

"By an unfortunate accident!"

"No. I was a young boy, and she exasperated me, and I threw a hammer at her. A promising young angel I must have been!"

I was deeply sorry to have touched on such a painful theme, but that was useless now.

"She has borne the mark ever since, as you see," said Steerforth; "and she'll bear it to her grave, if she ever rests in one—though I can hardly believe she will ever rest anywhere. She was the motherless child of a sort of cousin of my father's. He died one day. My mother, who was then a widow, brought her here to be company to her. She has a couple of thousand pounds of her own, and saves the interest of it every year, to add to the principal. There's the history of Miss Rosa Dartle for you."

"And I have no doubt she loves you like a brother?" said I.

"Humph!" retorted Steerforth, looking at the fire. "Some brothers are not loved over much; and some love—but help yourself, Copperfield! We'll drink the daisies of the field, in compliment to you; and the lilies of the valley that toil not, neither do they spin, in compliment to me—the more shame for me!" A moody smile that had overspread his features cleared off as he said this merrily, and he was his own frank, winning self again.

I could not help glancing at the scar with a painful interest when we went in to tea. It was not long before I observed that it was the most susceptible part of her face, and that, when she turned pale, that mark altered first, and became a dull, lead-coloured streak, lengthening out to its full extent, like a mark in invisible ink brought to the fire. There was a little altercation between her and Steerforth about a cast of the dice at back-gammon—when I thought her, for one moment, in a storm of rage; and then I saw it start forth like the old writing on the wall.

It was no matter of wonder to me to find Mrs Steerforth devoted to her son. She seemed to be able to speak or think about nothing else. She showed me his picture as an infant, in a locket, with some of his baby-hair in it; she showed me his picture as he had been when I first knew him; and she wore at her breast his picture as he was now. All the letters he had ever written to her, she kept in a cabinet near her own chair by the fire; and she would have read me some of them, and I should have been very glad to hear them too, if he had not interposed, and coaxed her out of the design.

"It was at Mr Creakle's, my son tells me, that you first became acquainted," said Mrs Steerforth, as she and I were talking at one table, while they played back-gammon at another. "Indeed, I recollect his speaking, at that time, of a pupil younger than himself who had taken his fancy there; but your name, as you may suppose, has not lived in my memory."

"He was very generous and noble to me in those days, I assure you, ma'am," said I, "and I stood in need of such a friend. I should have been quite crushed without him."

"He is always generous and noble," said Mrs Steerforth, proudly.

I subscribed to this with all my heart, God knows. She knew I did; for the stateliness of her manner already abated towards me, except when she spoke in praise of him, and then her air was always lofty.

"It was not a fit school generally for my son," said she; "far from it; but there were particular circumstances to be considered at the time, of more importance even than that selection. My son's high spirit made it desirable that he should be placed with some man who felt its superiority, and would be content to bow himself before it; and we found such a man there."

I knew that, knowing the fellow. And yet I did not despise him the more for it, but thought it a redeeming quality in him if he could be allowed any grace for not resisting one so irresistible as Steerforth.

"My son's great capacity was tempted on, there, by a feeling of voluntary emulation and conscious pride," the fond lady went on to say. "He would have risen against all constraint; but he found himself the monarch of the place, and he haughtily determined to be worthy of his station. It was like himself."

I echoed, with all my heart and soul, that it was like himself.

"So my son took, of his own will, and on no compulsion, to the course in which he can always, when it is his pleasure, outstrip every competitor," she pursued. "My son informs me, Mr Copperfield, that you were quite devoted to him, and that when you met yesterday you made yourself known to him with tears of joy. I should be an affected woman if I made any pretence of being surprised by my son's inspiring such emotions; but I cannot be indifferent to anyone who is so sensible of his merit, and I am very glad to see you here, and can assure you that he feels an unusual friendship for you, and that you may rely on his protection."

Miss Dartle played back-gammon as eagerly as she did everything else. If I had seen her, first, at the board, I should have fancied that her figure had got thin, and her eyes had got large, over that pursuit, and no other in the world. But I am very much mistaken if she missed a word of this, or lost a look of mine as I received it with the utmost pleasure, and honoured by Mrs Steerforth's confidence, felt older than I had done since I left Canterbury.

When the evening was pretty far spent, and a tray of glasses and decanters came in, Steerforth promised, over the fire, that he would seriously think of going down into the country with me. There was no hurry, he said; a week hence would do; and his mother hospitably said the same. While we were talking, he more than once called me Daisy; which brought Miss Dartle out again.

"But really, Mr Copperfield," she asked, "is it a nick-name? And why does he give it you? Is it—eh?—because he thinks you young and innocent? I am so stupid in these things."

I coloured in replying that I believed it was.

"Oh!" said Miss Dartle. "Now I am glad to know that! I ask for information, and I am glad to know it. He thinks you young and innocent; and so you are his friend. Well, that's quite delightful!"

She went to bed soon after this, and Mrs Steerforth retired too. Steerforth and I, after lingering for half-an-hour over the fire, talking about Traddles and all the rest of them at old Salem House, went upstairs together. Steerforth's room was next to mine, and I went in to look at it. It was a picture of comfort, full of easy-chairs, cushions and footstools, worked by his mother's hand, and with no sort of thing omitted that could help to render it complete. Finally, her handsome features looked down on her darling from a portrait on the wall, as if it were even something to her that her likeness should watch him while he slept.

I found the fire burning clear enough in my room by this time, and the curtains drawn before the windows and round the bed, giving it a very snug appearance. I sat down in a great chair upon the hearth to meditate on my happiness; and had enjoyed the contemplation of it for some time, when I found a likeness of Miss Dartle looking eagerly at me from above the chimney-piece.

It was a startling likeness, and necessarily had a startling look. The painter hadn't made the scar, but *I* made it; and there it was, coming and going, now confined to the upper lip as I had seen it at dinner, and now showing the whole extent of the wound inflicted by the hammer, as I had seen it when she was passionate.

I wondered peevishly why they couldn't put her anywhere else instead of quartering her on me. To get rid of her, I undressed quickly, extinguished my light, and went to bed. But, as I fell asleep, I could not forget that she was still there looking, "Is it really, though? I want to know"; and when I awoke in the night, I found that I was uneasily asking all sorts of people in my dreams whether it really was or not—without knowing what I meant.

Chapter XXI

LITTLE EM'LY

THERE was a servant in that house, a man who, I understood, was usually with Steerforth, and had come into his service at the University, who was in appearance a pattern of respectability. I believe there never existed in his station a more respectable-looking man. He was taciturn, soft-footed, very quiet in his manner, deferential, observant, always at hand when wanted and never near when not wanted; but his great claim to consideration was his respectability. He had not a pliant face, he had rather a stiff neck, rather a tight smooth head with short hair clinging to it at the sides, a soft way of speaking, with a peculiar habit of whispering the letter S so distinctly, that he seemed to use it oftener than any other man; but every peculiarity that he had he made respectable. If his nose had been upside-down, he would have made that respectable. He surrounded himself with an atmosphere of respectability, and walked secure in it. It would have been next to impossible to suspect him of anything wrong, he was so thoroughly respectable. Nobody could have thought of putting him in a livery, he was so highly respectable. To have imposed any derogatory work upon him, would have been to inflict a wanton insult on the feelings of a most respectable man. And of this, I noticed the women-servants in the household were so intuitively conscious, that they always did such work themselves, and generally while he read the paper by the pantry fire.

Such a self-contained man I never saw. But in that quality, as in every other he possessed, he only seemed to be the more respectable. Even the fact that no one knew his Christian name, seemed to form a part of his respectability. Nothing could be objected against his surname, Littimer, by which he was known. Peter might have been hanged, or Tom transported; but Littimer was perfectly respectable.

It was occasioned, I suppose, by the reverend nature of respectability in the abstract, but I felt particularly young in this man's presence. How old he was himself, I could not guess—and that again went to his credit on the same score; for in the calmness of respectability he might have numbered fifty years as well as thirty.

Littimer was in my room in the morning before I was up, to bring me that reproach-ful shaving-water, and to put out my clothes. When I undrew the curtains and looked out of bed, I saw him, in an equable temperature of respectability, unaffected by the east wind of January, and not even breathing frostily, standing my boots right and left in the first dancing position, and blowing specks of dust off my coat as he laid it down like a baby.

I gave him good morning, and asked him what o'clock it was. He took out of his pocket the most respectable hunting-watch I ever saw, and preventing the spring with his thumb from opening far, looked in at the face as if he were consulting an oracular oyster, shut it up again, and said, if I pleased, it was half past eight.

"Mr Steerforth will be glad to hear how you have rested, sir."

"Thank you," said I, "very well indeed. Is Mr Steerforth quite well?"

"Thank you, sir, Mr Steerforth is tolerably well." Another of his characteristics—no use of superlatives. A cool calm medium always.

"Is there anything more I can have the honour of doing for you, sir? The warning-bell will ring at nine; the family take breakfast at half past nine."

"Nothing, I thank you."

"I thank *you,* sir, if you please"; and with that, and with a little inclination of his head when he passed the bed-side, as an apology for correcting me, he went out, shutting the door as delicately as if I had just fallen into a sweet sleep on which my life depended.

Every morning we held exactly this conversation: never any more, and never any less: and yet, invariably, however far I might have been lifted out of myself over-night, and advanced towards maturer years, by Steerforth's companionship, or Mrs Steerforth's confidence, or Miss Dartle's conversation, in the presence of this most respectable man I became, as our smaller poets sing, "a boy again."

He got horses for us; and Steerforth, who knew everything, gave me lessons in riding. He provided foils for us, and Steerforth gave me lessons in fencing—gloves, and I began, of the same master, to improve in boxing. It gave me no manner of concern that Steerforth should find me a novice in these sciences, but I never could bear to show my want of skill before the respectable Littimer. I had no reason to believe that Littimer understood such arts himself; he never led me to suppose anything of the kind, by so much as the vibration of one of his respectable eyelashes; yet whenever he was by, while we were practising, I felt myself the greenest and most inexperienced of mortals.

I am particular about this man, because he made a particular effect on me at that time, and because of what took place thereafter.

The week passed away in a most delightful manner. It passed rapidly, as may be supposed, to one entranced as I was; and yet it gave me so many occasions for knowing Steerforth better, and admiring him more in a thousand respects, that at its close I seemed to have been with him for a much longer time. A dashing way he had of treating me like a plaything, was more agreeable to me than any behaviour he could have adopted. It reminded me of our old acquaintance; it seemed the natural sequel of it; it showed me that he was unchanged; it relieved me of any uneasiness I might have felt, in comparing my merits with his, and measuring my claims upon his friendship by any equal standard; above all, it was a familiar, unrestrained, affectionate demeanour that he used towards no one else. As he had treated me at school differently from all the rest, I joyfully believed that he treated me in life unlike any other friend he had. I believed that I was nearer to his heart than any other friend, and my own heart warmed with attachment to him.

He made up his mind to go with me into the country, and the day arrived for our departure. He had been doubtful at first whether to take Littimer or not, but decided to leave him at home. The respectable creature, satisfied with his lot whatever it was, arranged our portmanteaux on the little carriage that was to take us into London, as if they were intended to defy the shocks of ages; and received my modestly proffered donation with perfect tranquillity.

We bade adieu to Mrs Steerforth and Miss Dartle, with many thanks on my part, and much kindness on the devoted mother's. The last thing I saw was Littimer's unruffled eye; fraught, as I fancied, with the silent conviction that I was very young indeed.

What I felt, in returning so auspiciously to the old familiar places, I shall not endeavour to describe. We went down by the Mail. I was so concerned, I recollect, even for the honour of Yarmouth, that when Steerforth said, as we drove through its dark streets to the inn, that, as well as he could make out, it was a good, queer, out-of-the-way kind of hole, I was highly pleased. We went to bed on our arrival (I observed a pair of dirty shoes and gaiters in connexion with my old friend the Dolphin as we passed that door), and breakfasted late in the morning. Steerforth, who was in great spirits, had been strolling about the beach before I was up, and had made acquaintance, he said, with half the boatmen in the place. Moreover, he had seen, in the distance, what he was sure must be the identical house of Mr Peggotty, with smoke coming out of the chimney; and had had a great mind, he told me, to walk in and swear he was myself grown out of knowledge.

"When do you propose to introduce me there, Daisy?" he said. "I am at your disposal. Make your own arrangements."

"Why, I was thinking that this evening would be a good time, Steerforth, when they are all sitting round the fire. I should like you to see it when it's snug, it's such a curious place."

"So be it!" returned Steerforth. "This evening."

"I shall not give them any notice that we are here, you know," said I, delighted. "We must take them by surprise."

"Oh, of course! It's no fun," said Steerforth, "unless we take them by surprise. Let us see the natives in their aboriginal condition."

"Though they *are* that sort of people that you mentioned," I returned.

"Aha! What! you recollect my skirmishes with Rosa, do you?" he exclaimed with a quick look. "Confound the girl, I am half afraid of her. She's like a goblin to me. But never mind her. Now what are you going to do? You are going to see your nurse, I suppose?"

"Why, yes," I said, "I must see Peggotty first of all."

"Well," replied Steerforth, looking at his watch. "Suppose I deliver you up to be cried over for a couple of hours. Is that long enough?"

I answered, laughing, that I thought we might get through it in that time, but that he must come also; for he would find that his renown had preceded him, and that he was almost as great a personage as I was.

"I'll come anywhere you like," said Steerforth, "or do anything you like. Tell me where to come to; and in two hours I'll produce myself in any state you please, sentimental or comical."

I gave him minute directions for finding the residence of Mr Barkis, carrier to Blunderstone and elsewhere; and, on this understanding, went out alone. There was a sharp bracing air; the ground was dry; the sea was crisp and clear; the sun was diffusing abundance of light, if not much warmth; and everything was fresh and lively. I was so fresh and lively myself, in the pleasure of being there, that I could have stopped the people in the streets and shaken hands with them.

The streets looked small, of course. The streets that we have only seen as children always do, I believe, when we go back to them. But I had forgotten nothing in them, and found nothing changed, until I came to Mr Omer's shop. OMER AND JORAM was now written up, where OMER used to be; but the inscription, DRAPER, TAILOR, HABERDASHER, FUNERAL FURNISHER, &c., remained as it was.

My footsteps seemed to tend so naturally to the shop door, after I had read these words from over the way, that I went across the road and looked in. There was a pretty woman at the back of the shop, dancing a little child in her arms, while another little fellow clung to her apron. I had no difficulty in recognizing either Minnie or Minnie's children. The glass door of the parlour was not open; but in the workshop across the yard I could faintly hear the old tune playing, as if it had never left off.

"Is Mr Omer at home?" said I, entering. "I should like to see him, for a moment, if he is."

"Oh yes, sir, he is at home," said Minnie; "the weather don't suit his asthma out of doors. Joe, call your grandfather!"

The little fellow, who was holding her apron, gave such a lusty shout, that the sound of it made him bashful, and he buried his face in her skirts, to her great admiration. I heard a heavy puffing and blowing coming towards us, and soon Mr Omer, shorter-winded than of yore, but not much older-looking, stood before me.

"Servant, sir," said Mr Omer. "What can I do for you, sir?"

"You can shake hands with me, Mr Omer, if you please," said I, putting out my own. "You were very good-natured to me once, when I am afraid I didn't show that I thought so."

"Was I though?" returned the old man. "I'm glad to hear it, but I don't remember when. Are you sure it was me?"

"Quite."

"I think my memory has got as short as my breath," said Mr Omer, looking at me and shaking his head; "for I don't remember you."

"Don't you remember your coming to the coach to meet me, and my having breakfast here, and our riding out to Blunderstone together: you, and I, and Mrs Joram, and Mr Joram too—who wasn't her husband then?"

"Why, Lord bless my soul!" exclaimed Mr Omer, after being thrown by his surprise into a fit of coughing, "you don't say so! Minnie, my dear, you recollect? Dear me, yes; the party was a lady, I think?"

"My mother," I rejoined.

"To——be——sure," said Mr Omer, touching my waistcoat with his forefinger, "and there was a little child too! There was two parties. The little party was laid along with the other party. Over at Blunderstone it was, of course. Dear me! And how have you been since?"

Very well, I thanked him, as I hoped he had been too.

"Oh! nothing to grumble at, you know," said Mr Omer. "I find my breath gets short, but it seldom gets longer as a man gets older. I take it as it comes, and make the most of it. That's the best way, ain't it?"

Mr Omer coughed again, in consequence of laughing, and was assisted out of his fit by his daughter, who now stood close beside us, dancing her smallest child on the counter.

"Dear me!" said Mr Omer. "Yes, to be sure. Two parties! Why, in that very ride, if you'll believe me, the day was named for my Minnie to marry Joram. 'Do name it, sir,' says Joram. 'Yes, do, father,' says Minnie. And now he's come into the business. And look here! The youngest!"

Minnie laughed, and stroked her banded hair upon her temples, as her father put one of his fat fingers into the hand of the child she was dancing on the counter.

"Two parties, of course!" said Mr Omer, nodding his head retrospectively. "Ex-actly so! And Joram's at work, at this minute, on a grey one with silver nails, not this measure-ment"—the measurement of the dancing child upon the counter—"by a good two inches.—Will you take something?"

I thanked him, but declined.

"Let me see," said Mr Omer. "Barkis's the carrier's wife—Peggotty's the boatman's sister—she had something to do with your family? She was in service there, sure?"

My answering in the affirmative gave him great satisfaction.

"I believe my breath will get long next, my memory's getting so much so," said Mr Omer. "Well, sir, we've got a young relation of hers here, under articles to us, that has as elegant a taste in the dress-making business—I assure you I don't believe there's a Duchess in England can touch her."

"Not little Em'ly?" said I, involuntarily.

"Em'ly's her name," said Mr Omer, "and she's little too. But if you'll believe me, she has such a face of her own that half the women in this town are mad against her."

"Nonsense, father!" cried Minnie.

"My dear," said Mr Omer, "I don't say it's the case with you," winking at me, "but I say that half the women in Yarmouth—ah! and in five mile round—are mad against that girl."

"Then she should have kept to her own station in life, father," said Minnie, "and not have given them any hold to talk about her, and then they couldn't have done it."

"Couldn't have done it, my dear!" retorted Mr Omer. "Couldn't have done it! Is that *your* knowledge of life? What is there that any woman couldn't do, that she shouldn't do—especially on the subject of another woman's good looks?"

I really thought it was all over with Mr Omer, after he had uttered this libellous pleasantry. He coughed to that extent, and his breath eluded all his attempts to recover it with that obstinacy, that I fully expected to see his head go down behind the counter, and his little black breeches, with the rusty little bunches of ribbons at the knees, come quivering up in a last ineffectual struggle. At length, however, he got better, though he still panted hard, and was so exhausted that he was obliged to sit on the stool of the shop-desk.

"You see," he said, wiping his head, and breathing with difficulty, "she hasn't taken much to any companions here; she hasn't taken kindly to any particular acquaintances and friends, not to mention sweethearts. In consequence, an ill-natured story got about, that Em'ly wanted to be a lady. Now my opinion is, that it came into circulation principally on account of her sometimes saying, at the school, that if she was a lady she would like to do so-and-so for her uncle—don't you see?—and buy him such-and-such fine things."

"I assure you, Mr Omer, she has said so to me," so I returned eagerly, "when we were both children."

Mr Omer nodded his head and rubbed his chin. "Just so. Then out of a very little, she could dress herself, you see, better than most others could out of a deal, and *that* made things unpleasant. Moreover, she was rather what might be called wayward—I'll go so far as to say what I should call wayward myself," said Mr Omer; "—didn't know her own mind quite—a little spoiled—and couldn't, at first, exactly bind herself down. No more than that was ever said against her, Minnie?"

"No, father," said Mrs Joram. "That's the worst, I believe."

"So when she got a situation," said Mr Omer, "to keep a fractious old lady company, they didn't very well agree, and she didn't stop. At last she came here, apprenticed for three years. Nearly two of 'em are over, and she has been as good a girl as ever was. Worth any six! Minnie, is she worth any six, now?"

"Yes, father," replied Minnie. "Never say *I* detracted from her!"

"Very good," said Mr Omer. "That's right. And so, young gentleman," he added, after a few moments' further rubbing of his chin, "that you may not consider me long-winded as well as short-breathed, I believe that's all about it."

As they had spoken in a subdued tone, while speaking of Em'ly, I had no doubt that she was near. On my asking now, if that were not so, Mr Omer nodded yes, and nodded towards the door of the parlour. My hurried inquiry if I might peep in, was answered with a free permission; and, looking through the glass, I saw her sitting at her work. I saw her, a most beautiful little creature, with the cloudless blue eyes, that had looked into my childish heart, turned laughingly upon another child of Minnie's who was playing near her; with enough of wilfulness in her bright face to justify what I had heard; with much of the old capricious coyness lurking in it; but with nothing in her pretty looks, I am sure, but what was meant for goodness and for happiness, and what was on a good and happy course.

The tune across the yard that seemed as if it never had left off—alas! it was the tune that never *does* leave off—was beating, softly, all the while.

"Wouldn't you like to step in," said Mr Omer, "and speak to her? Walk in and speak to her, sir! Make yourself at home!"

I was too bashful to do so then—I was afraid of confusing her, and I was no less afraid of confusing myself: but I informed myself of the hour at which she left of an evening, in order that our visit might be timed accordingly; and taking leave of Mr Omer, and his pretty daughter, and her little children, went away to my dear old Peggotty's.

Here she was, in the tiled kitchen, cooking dinner! The moment I knocked at the door she opened it, and asked me what I pleased to want. I looked at her with a smile, but she gave me no smile in return. I had never ceased to write to her, but it must have been seven years since we had met.

"Is Mr Barkis at home, ma'am?" I said, feigning to speak roughly to her.

"He's at home, sir," returned Peggotty, "but he's bad abed with the rheumatics."

"Don't he go over to Blunderstone now?" I asked.

"When he's well he do," she answered.

"Do *you* ever go there, Mrs Barkis?"

She looked at me more attentively, and I noticed a quick movement of her hands towards each other.

"Because I want to ask a question about a house there, that they call the——what is it?——the Rookery," said I.

She took a step backward, and put out her hands in an undecided frightened way, as if to keep me off.

"Peggotty!" I cried to her.

She cried, "My darling boy!" and we both burst into tears, and were locked in one another's arms.

What extravagances she committed; what laughing and crying over me; what pride she showed, what joy, what sorrow that she whose pride and joy I might have been, could never hold me in a fond embrace; I have not the heart to tell. I was troubled with no misgiving that it was young in me to respond to her emotions. I had never laughed and cried in all my life, I dare say——not even to her——more freely than I did that morning.

"Barkis will be so glad," said Peggotty, wiping her eyes with her apron, "that it'll do him more good than pints of liniment. May I go and tell him you are here? Will you come up and see him, my dear?"

Of course I would. But Peggotty could not get out of the room as easily as she meant to, for as often as she got to the door and looked round at me, she came back again to have another laugh and another cry upon my shoulder. At last, to make the matter easier, I went upstairs with her; and having waited outside for a minute, while she said a word of preparation to Mr Barkis, presented myself before that invalid.

He received me with absolute enthusiasm. He was too rheumatic to be shaken hands with, but he begged me to shake the tassel on the top of his nightcap, which I did most cordially. When I sat down by the side of the bed, he said that it did him a world of good to feel as if he was driving me on the Blunderstone road again. As he lay in bed, face upward, and so covered, with that exception, that he seemed to be nothing but a face——like a conventional cherubim——he looked the queerest object I ever beheld.

"What name was it, as I wrote up in the cart, sir?" said Mr Barkis, with a slow rheumatic smile.

"Ah! Mr Barkis, we had some grave talks about that matter, hadn't we?"

"I was willin' a long time, sir?" said Mr Barkis.

"A long time," said I.

"And I don't regret it," said Mr Barkis. "Do you remember what you told me once, about her making all the apple parsties and doing all the cooking?"

"Yes, very well," I returned.

"It was as true," said Mr Barkis, "as turnips is. It was as true," said Mr Barkis, nodding his nightcap, which was his only means of emphasis, "as taxes is. And nothing's truer than them."

Mr Barkis turned his eyes upon me, as if for my assent to this result of his reflections in bed; and I gave it.

"Nothing's truer than them," repeated Mr Barkis; "a man as poor as I am, finds that out in his mind when he's laid up. I'm a very poor man, sir!"

"I am sorry to hear it, Mr Barkis."

"A very poor man, indeed I am," said Mr Barkis.

Here his right hand came slowly and feebly from under the bed-clothes, and with a purposeless uncertain grasp took hold of a stick which was loosely tied to the side of the bed. After some poking about with this instrument, in the course of which his face assumed a variety of distracted expressions, Mr Barkis poked it against a box, an end of which had been visible to me all the time. Then his face became composed.

"Old clothes," said Mr Barkis.

"Oh!" said I.

"I wish it was Money, sir," said Mr Barkis.

"I wish it was, indeed," said I.

"But it AIN'T," said Mr Barkis, opening both his eyes as wide as he possibly could.

I expressed myself quite sure of that, and Mr Barkis, turning his eyes more gently to his wife, said:

"She's the usefullest and best of women, C. P. Barkis. All the praise that anyone can give to C. P. Barkis, she deserves, and more! My dear, you'll get a dinner today, for company; something good to eat and drink, will you?"

I should have protested against this unnecessary demonstration in my honour, but that I saw Peggotty, on the opposite side of the bed, extremely anxious I should not. So I held my peace.

"I have got a trifle of money somewhere about me, my dear," said Mr Barkis, "but I'm a little tired. If you and Mr David will leave me for a short nap, I'll try and find it when I wake."

We left the room, in compliance with this request. When we got outside the door, Peggotty informed me that Mr Barkis, being now "a little nearer" than he used to be, always resorted to this same device before producing a single coin from his store; and that he endured unheard-of agonies in crawling out of bed alone, and taking it from that unlucky box. In effect, we presently heard him uttering suppressed groans of the most dismal nature, as this magpie proceeding racked him in every joint; but while Peggotty's eyes were full of compassion for him, she said his generous impulse would do him good, and it was better not to check it. So he groaned on, until he had got into bed again, suffering, I have no doubt, a martyrdom; and then called us in, pretending to have just woke up from a refreshing sleep, and to produce a guinea from under his pillow. His satisfaction in which happy imposition on us, and in having preserved the impenetrable secret of the box, appeared to be a sufficient compensation to him for all his tortures.

I prepared Peggotty for Steerforth's arrival and it was not long before he came. I am persuaded she knew no difference between his having been a personal benefactor of hers, and a kind friend to me, and that she would have received him with the utmost gratitude and devotion in any case. But his easy, spirited good humour; his genial manner, his handsome looks, his natural gift of adapting himself to whomsoever he pleased, and making direct, when he cared to do it, to the main point of interest in anybody's heart; bound her to him wholly in five minutes. His manner to me, alone, would have won her. But, through all these causes combined, I sincerely believe she had a kind of adoration for him before he left the house that night.

He stayed there with me to dinner—if I were to say willingly, I should not half express how readily and gaily. He went into Mr Barkis's room like light and air, brightening and refreshing it as if he were healthy weather. There was no noise, no effort, no consciousness, in anything he did; but in everything an indescribable lightness, a seeming impossibility of doing anything else, or doing anything better, which was so graceful, so natural, and agreeable, that it overcomes me, even now, in the remembrance.

We made merry in the little parlour, where the *Book of Martyrs,* unthumbed since my time, was laid out upon the desk as of old, and where I now turned over its terrific pictures, remembering the old sensations they had awakened, but not feeling them.

When Peggotty spoke of what she called my room, and of its being ready for me at night, and of her hoping I would occupy it, before I could so much as look at Steerforth, hesitating, he was possessed of the whole case.

"Of course," he said. "You'll sleep here, while we stay, and I shall sleep at the hotel."

"But to bring you so far," I returned, "and to separate, seems bad companionship, Steerforth."

"Why, in the name of Heaven, where do you naturally belong?" he said. "What is 'seems,' compared to that?" It was settled at once.

He maintained all his delightful qualities to the last, until we started forth, at eight o'clock, for Mr Peggotty's boat. Indeed, they were more and more brightly exhibited as the hours went on; for I thought even then, and I have no doubt now, that the consciousness of success in his determination to please, inspired him with a new delicacy of perception, and made it, subtle as it was, more easy to him. If anyone had told me, then, that all this was a brilliant game, played for the excitement of the moment, for the employment of high spirits, in the thoughtless love of superiority, in a mere wasteful careless course of winning what was worthless to him, and next minute thrown away—I say, if anyone had told me such a lie that night, I wonder in what manner of receiving it my indignation would have found a vent!

Probably only in an increase, had that been possible, of the romantic feelings of fidelity and friendship with which I walked beside him, over the dark wintry sands towards the old boat; the wind sighing around us even more mournfully, than it had sighed and moaned upon the night when I first darkened Mr Peggotty's door.

"This is a wild kind of place, Steerforth, is it not?"

"Dismal enough in the dark," he said: "and the sea roars as if it were hungry for us. Is that the boat, where I see a light yonder?"

"That's the boat," said I.

"And it's the same I saw this morning," he returned. "I came straight to it, by instinct, I suppose."

We said no more as we approached the light, but made softly for the door. I laid my hand upon the latch; and whispering Steerforth to keep close to me, went in.

A murmur of voices had been audible on the outside, and, at the moment of our entrance, a clapping of hands: which latter noise, I was surprised to see, proceeded from the generally disconsolate Mrs Gummidge. But Mrs Gummidge was not the only person there who was unusually excited. Mr Peggotty, his face lighted up with uncommon satisfaction, and laughing with all his might, held his rough arms wide open, as if for little Em'ly to run into them; Ham, with a mixed expression in his face of admiration, exultation, and a lumbering sort of bashfulness that sat upon him very well, held little Em'ly by the hand, as if he were presenting her to Mr Peggotty; little Em'ly herself, blushing and shy, but delighted with Mr Peggotty's delight, as her joyous eyes expressed, was stopped by our entrance (for she saw us first) in the very act of springing from Ham to nestle in Mr Peggotty's embrace. In the first glimpse we had of them all, and at the moment of our passing from the dark cold night into the warm light room, this was the way in which they were all employed: Mrs Gummidge in the background, clapping her hands like a madwoman.

The little picture was so instantaneously dissolved by our going in, that one might have doubted whether it had ever been. I was in the midst of the astonished family, face to face with Mr Peggotty, and holding out my hand to him, when Ham shouted:

"Mas'r Davy! It's Mas'r Davy!"

In a moment we were all shaking hands with one another, and asking one another how we did, and telling one another how glad we were to meet, and all talking at once. Mr Peggotty was so proud and overjoyed to see us, that he did not know what to say or do, but kept over and over again shaking hands with me, and then with Steerforth, and then with me, and then ruffling his shaggy hair all over his head, and laughing with such glee and triumph, that it was a treat to see him.

"Why, that you two gent'lmen—gent'lmen growed—should come to this here roof tonight, of all nights in my life," said Mr Peggotty, "is such a thing as never happened afore, I do rightly believe! Em'ly, my darling, come here! Come here, my little witch! There's Mas'r Davy's friend, my dear! There's the gent'lman as you've heerd on, Em'ly. He comes to see you, along with Mas'r Davy, on the brightest night of your uncle's life as ever was or will be, Gorm the t'other one, and horroar for it!"

After delivering this speech all in a breath, and with extraordinary animation and pleasure, Mr Peggotty put one of his large hands rapturously on each side of his niece's face, and kissing it a dozen times, laid it with a gentle pride and love upon his broad chest, and patted it as if his hand had been a lady's. Then he let her go; and as she ran into the little chamber where I used to sleep, looked round upon us, quite hot and out of breath with his uncommon satisfaction.

"If you two gent'lmen—gent'lmen growed now, and such gent'lmen—" said Mr Peggotty.

"So th' are, so th' are!" cried Ham. "Well said! So th' are. Mas'r Davy bor'—gent'lmen growed—so th' are!"

"If you two gent'lmen, gent'lmen growed," said Mr Peggotty, "don't ex-cuse me for being in a state of mind, when you understand matters, I'll arks your pardon. Em'ly, my dear!—She knows I'm a going to tell," here his delight broke out again, "and has made off. Would you be so good as look arter her, Mawther, for a minute?"

Mrs Gummidge nodded and disappeared.

"If this ain't," said Mr Peggotty, sitting down among us by the fire, "the brightest night o' my life, I'm a shellfish—biled too—and more I can't say. This here little Em'ly, sir," in a low voice to Steerforth, "—her as you see a blushing here just now—"

Steerforth only nodded; but with such a pleased expression of interest, and of participation in Mr Peggotty's feelings, that the latter answered him as if he had spoken.

"To be sure," said Mr Peggotty. "That's her, and so she is. Thankee, sir."

Ham nodded to me several times, as if he would have said so too.

"This here little Em'ly of ours," said Mr Peggotty, "has been, in our house, what I suppose (I'm a ignorant man, but that's my belief) no one but a little bright-eyed creetur *can* be in a house. She ain't my child; I never had one; but I couldn't love her more. You understand! I couldn't do it!"

"I quite understand," said Steerforth.

"I know you do, sir," returned Mr Peggotty, "and thankee again. Mas'r Davy, he can remember what she was; you may judge for your own self what she is; but neither of you can't fully know what she has been, is, and will be, to my loving art. I am rough, sir," said Mr Peggotty, "I am as rough as a Sea Porkypine; but no one, unless, mayhap, it is a woman, can know, I think, what our little Em'ly is to me. And betwixt ourselves," sinking his voice lower yet, "*that* woman's name ain't Missis Gummidge neither, though she has a world of merits."

Mr Peggotty ruffled his hair again, with both hands, as a further preparation for what he was going to say, and went on, with a hand upon each of his knees:

"There was a certain person as had know'd our Em'ly, from the time when her father was drownded; as had seen her constant; when a babby, when a young gal, when a woman. Not much of a person to look at, he warn't," said Mr Peggotty, "something o' my own build—rough—a good deal o' the sou'-wester in him—wery salt—but, on the whole, a honest sort of a chap, with his art in the right place."

I thought I had never seen Ham grin to anything like the extent to which he sat grinning at us now.

"What does this here blessed tarpaulin go and do," said Mr Peggotty, with his face one high noon of enjoyment, "but he loses that there art of his to our little Em'ly. He follers her about, he makes hisself a sort o' servant to her, he loses in a great measure his relish for his wittles, and in the long-run he makes it clear to me wot's amiss. Now I could wish myself, you see, that our little Em'ly was in a fair way of being married. I could wish to see her, at all ewents, under articles to a honest man as had a right to defend her. I don't know how long I may live, or how soon I may die; but I know that if I was capsized, any night, in a gale of wind in Yarmouth Roads here, and was to see the town-lights shining for the last time over the rollers as I couldn't make no head against, I could go down quieter for thinking 'There's a man ashore there, iron-true to my little Em'ly, God bless her, and no wrong can touch my Em'ly while so be as that man lives.' "

Mr Peggotty, in simple earnestness, waved his right arm, as if he were waving it at the town-lights for the last time, and then, exchanging a nod with Ham, whose eye he caught, proceeded as before.

"Well! I counsels him to speak to Em'ly. He's big enough, but he's bashfuller than a little un, and he don't like. So *I* speak. 'What! *Him!*' says Em'ly. *'Him* that I've know'd so intimate so many years, and like so much. Oh, Uncle! I never can have *him*. He's such a good fellow!' I gives her a kiss, and I says no more to her than, 'My dear, you're right to speak out, you're to choose for yourself, you're as free as a little bird.' Then I aways to him, and I says, 'I wish it could have been so, but it can't. But you can both be as you was, and wot I say to you is, Be as you was with her, like a man.' He says to me, a-shaking of my hand, 'I will!' he says. And he was—honourable and manful—for two year going on, and we was just the same at home here as afore."

Mr Peggotty's face, which had varied in its expression with the various stages of his narrative, now resumed all its former triumphant delight, as he laid a hand upon my knee and a hand upon Steerforth's (previously wetting them both, for the greater emphasis of the action), and divided the following speech between us:

"All of a sudden, one evening—as it might be tonight—comes little Em'ly from her work, and him with her! There ain't so much in *that,* you'll say. No, because he takes care on her, like a brother, arter dark, and indeed afore dark, and at all times. But this tarpaulin chap, he takes hold of her hand, and he cries out to me, joyful, 'Look here! This is to be my little wife!' And she says, half bold and half shy, and half a laughing and half a crying, 'Yes, Uncle! If you please.'—If I please!" cried Mr Peggotty, rolling his head in an ecstasy at the idea; "Lord, as if I should do anythink else!—'If you please, I am steadier now, and I have thought better of it, and I'll be as good a little wife as I can to him, for he's a dear, good fellow!' Then Missis Gummidge, she claps her hands like a play, and you come in. Theer! the murder's out!" said Mr Peggotty—"You come in! It took place this here present hour; and here's the man that'll marry her, the minute she's out of her time."

Ham staggered, as well he might, under the blow Mr Peggotty dealt him in his unbounded joy, as a mark of confidence and friendship; but feeling called upon to say something to us, he said, with much faltering and great difficulty:

"She warn't no higher than you was, Mas'r Davy—when you first come—when I thought what she'd grow up to be. I see her grown up—gent'lmen—like a flower. I'd lay down my life for her—Mas'r Davy—Oh! most content and cheerful! She's more to me—gent'lmen—than—she's all to me that ever I can want, and more than ever I—than ever I could say. I—I love her true. There ain't a gent'lman in all the land—nor yet sailing upon all the sea—that can love his lady more than I love her, though there's many a common man—would say better—what he meant."

I thought it affecting to see such a sturdy fellow as Ham was now, trembling in the strength of what he felt for the pretty little creature who had won his heart. I thought the simple confidence reposed in us by Mr Peggotty and by himself, was, in itself affecting. I was affected by the story altogether. How far my emotions were influenced by the recollections of my childhood, I don't know. Whether I had come there with any lingering fancy that I was still to love little Em'ly, I don't know. I know that I was filled with pleasure by all this; but, at first, with an indescribably sensitive pleasure, that a very little would have changed to pain.

Therefore, if it had depended upon me to touch the prevailing chord among them with any skill, I should have made a poor hand of it. But it depended upon Steerforth; and he did it with such address, that in a few minutes we were all as easy and as happy as it was possible to be.

"Mr Peggotty," he said, "you are a thoroughly good fellow, and deserve to be as happy as you are tonight. My hand upon it! Ham, I give you joy, my boy. My hand upon that, too! Daisy, stir the fire, and make it a brisk one! and Mr Peggotty, unless you can induce your gentle niece to come back (for whom I vacate this seat in the corner), I shall go. Any gap at your fireside on such a night—such a gap least of all—I wouldn't make, for the wealth of the Indies!"

So Mr Peggotty went into my old room to fetch little Em'ly. At first little Em'ly didn't like to come, and then Ham went. Presently they brought her to the fireside, very much confused, and very shy,—but she soon became more assured when she found how gently and respectfully Steerforth spoke to her; how skilfully he avoided anything that would embarrass her; how he talked to Mr Peggotty of boats, and ships, and tides, and fish; how he referred to me about the time when he had seen Mr Peggotty at Salem House; how delighted he was with the boat and all belonging to it; how lightly and easily he carried on, until he brought us, by degrees, into a charmed circle, and we were all talking away without any reserve.

Em'ly, indeed, said little all the evening; but she looked, and listened, and her face got animated, and she was charming. Steerforth told a story of a dismal shipwreck (which arose out of his talk with Mr Peggotty), as if he saw it all before him—and little Em'ly's eyes were fastened on him all the time, as if she saw it too. He told us a merry adventure of his own, as a relief to that, with as much gaiety as if the narrative were as fresh to him as it was to us—and little Em'ly laughed until the boat rang with the musical sounds, and we all laughed (Steerforth too), in irresistible sympathy with what was so pleasant and light-hearted. He got Mr Peggotty to sing, or rather to roar, "When the stormy winds do blow, do blow, do blow": and he sang a sailor's song himself, so pathetically and beautifully, that I could have almost fancied that the real wind creeping sorrowfully round the house, and murmuring low through our unbroken silence, was there to listen.

As to Mrs Gummidge, he roused that victim of despondency with a success never attained by anyone else (so Mr Peggotty informed me), since the decease of the old one. He left her so little leisure for being miserable, that she said next day she thought she must have been bewitched.

But he set up no monopoly of the general attention, or the conversation. When little

Em'ly grew more courageous, and talked (but still bashfully) across the fire to me, of our old wanderings upon the beach, to pick up shells and pebbles; and when I asked her if she recollected how I used to be devoted to her; and when we both laughed and reddened, casting these looks back on the pleasant old times, so unreal to look at now; he was silent and attentive, and observed us thoughtfully. She sat, at this time, and all the evening, on the old locker in her old little corner by the fire—Ham beside her, where I used to sit. I could not satisfy myself whether it was in her own little tormenting way, or in a maidenly reserve before us, that she kept quite close to the wall, and away from him; but I observed that she did so, all the evening.

As I remember, it was almost midnight when we took our leave. We had had some biscuit and dried fish for supper, and Steerforth had produced from his pocket a full flask of Hollands, which we men (I may say we men, now, without a blush) had emptied. We parted merrily; and as they all stood crowded round the door to light us as far as they could upon our road, I saw the sweet blue eyes of little Em'ly peeping after us, from behind Ham, and heard her soft voice calling to us to be careful how we went.

"A most engaging little Beauty!" said Steerforth, taking my arm. "Well! It's a quaint place, and they are quaint company, and it's quite a new sensation to mix with them."

"How fortunate we are, too," I returned, "to have arrived to witness their happiness in that intended marriage! I never saw people so happy. How delightful to see it, and to be made the sharers in their honest joy, as we have been!"

"That's rather a chuckle-headed fellow for the girl; isn't he?" said Steerforth.

He had been so hearty with him, and with them all, that I felt a shock in this unexpected and cold reply. But turning quickly upon him, and seeing a laugh in his eyes, I answered, much relieved:

"Ah, Steerforth! It's well for you to joke about the poor! You may skirmish with Miss Dartle, or try to hide your sympathies in jest from me, but I know better. When I see how perfectly you understand them, how exquisitely you can enter into happiness like this plain fisherman's, or humour a love like my old nurse's, I know that there is not a joy or sorrow, not an emotion, of such people, that can be indifferent to you. And I admire and love you for it, Steerforth, twenty times the more!"

He stopped, and, looking in my face, said, "Daisy, I believe you are in earnest, and are good. I wish we all were!" Next moment he was gaily singing Mr Peggotty's song, as we walked at a round pace back to Yarmouth.

Chapter XXII

SOME OLD SCENES, AND SOME NEW PEOPLE

S TEERFORTH and I stayed for more than a fortnight in that part of the country. We were very much together, I need not say; but occasionally we were asunder for some hours at a time. He was a good sailor, and I was but an indifferent one; and when he went out boating with Mr Peggotty, which was a favourite amusement of his, I generally remained ashore. My occupation of Peggotty's spare-room put a constraint upon me, from which he was free: for, knowing how assiduously she attended on Mr Barkis all day, I did not like to remain out late at night; whereas Steerforth, lying at the Inn, had nothing to consult but his own humour. Thus it came about, that I heard of his making little treats for the fishermen at Mr Peggotty's house of call, "The Willing Mind," after I was in bed, and of his being afloat, wrapped in fishermen's clothes, whole moonlight nights, and coming back when the morning tide was at flood. By this time, however, I knew that his restless nature and bold spirits delighted to find a vent in rough toil and hard weather, as in any other means of excitement that presented itself freshly to him; so none of his proceedings surprised me.

Another cause of our being sometimes apart, was, that I had naturally an interest in going over to Blunderstone, and revisiting the old familiar scenes of my childhood; while Steerforth, after being there once, had naturally no great interest in going there again. Hence, on three or four days that I can at once recall, we went our several ways after an early breakfast, and met again at a late dinner. I had no idea how he employed his time in the interval, beyond a general knowledge that he was very popular in the place, and had twenty means of actively diverting himself where another man might not have found one.

For my own part, my occupation in my solitary pilgrimages was to recall every yard of the old road as I went along it, and to haunt the old spots, of which I never tired. I haunted them, as my memory had often done, and lingered among them as my younger thoughts had lingered when I was far away. The grave beneath the tree, where both my parents lay—on which I had looked out, when it was my father's only, with such curious feelings of compassion, and by which I had stood, so desolate, when it was opened to receive my pretty mother and her baby—the grave which Peggotty's own faithful care had ever since kept neat, and made a garden of, I walked near, by the hour. It lay a little off the churchyard path, in a quiet corner, not so far removed but I could read the names upon the stone as I walked to and fro, startled by the sound of the church-bell when it struck the hour, for it was like a departed voice to me. My reflections at these times were always associated with the figure I was to make in life, and the distinguished things I was to do. My echoing footsteps went to no other tune, but were as constant to that as if I had come home to build my castles in the air at a living mother's side.

There were great changes in my old home. The ragged nests, so long deserted by the rooks, were gone; and the trees were lopped and topped out of their remembered shapes. The garden had run wild, and half the windows of the house were shut up. It was occupied, but only by a poor lunatic gentleman, and the people who took care of him. He was always sitting at my little window, looking out into the churchyard; and I wondered whether his rambling thoughts ever went upon any of the fancies that used to occupy mine, on the rosy mornings when I peeped out of that same little window in my night-clothes, and saw the sheep quietly feeding in the light of the rising sun.

Our old neighbours, Mr and Mrs Grayper, were gone to South America, and the rain had made its way through the roof of their empty house, and stained the outer walls. Mr Chillip was married again to a tall, raw-boned, high-nosed wife, and they had a weazen little baby, with a heavy head that it couldn't hold up, and two weak staring eyes, with which it seemed to be always wondering why it had ever been born.

It was with a singular jumble of sadness and pleasure that I used to linger about my native place, until the reddening winter sun admonished me that it was time to start on my returning walk. But, when the place was left behind, and especially when Steerforth and I were happily seated over our dinner by a blazing fire, it was delicious to think of having been there. So it was, though in a softened degree, when I went to my neat room at night; and, turning over the leaves of the crocodile-book (which was always there upon a little table), remembered with a grateful heart how blest I was in having such a friend as Steerforth, such a friend as Peggotty, and such a substitute for what I had lost as my excellent and generous aunt.

My nearest way to Yarmouth, in coming back from these long walks, was by a ferry. It landed me on the flat between the town and the sea, which I could make straight across, and so save myself a considerable circuit by the high road. Mr Peggotty's house being on that waste-place, and not a hundred yards out of my track, I always looked in as I went by. Steerforth was pretty sure to be there expecting me, and we went on together through the frosty air and gathering fog towards the twinkling lights of the town.

One dark evening, when I was later than usual—for I had, that day, been making my parting visit to Blunderstone, as we were now about to return home—I found him alone in Mr Peggotty's house, sitting thoughtfully before the fire. He was so intent upon his own reflections that he was quite unconscious of my approach. This, indeed, he might easily have been if he had been less absorbed, for footsteps fell noiselessly on the sandy ground outside; but even my entrance failed to rouse him. I was standing close to him, looking at him; and still, with a heavy brow, he was lost in his meditations.

He gave such a start when I put my hand upon his shoulder, that he made me start too.

"You come upon me," he said, almost angrily, "like a reproachful ghost!"

"I was obliged to announce myself, somehow," I replied. "Have I called you down from the stars?"

"No," he answered. "No."

"Up from anywhere, then?" said I, taking my seat near him.

"I was looking at the pictures in the fire," he returned.

"But you are spoiling them for me," said I, as he stirred it quickly with a piece of burning wood, striking out of it a train of red-hot sparks that went careering up the little chimney, and roaring out into the air.

"You would not have seen them," he returned. "I detest this mongrel time, neither day nor night. How late you are! Where have you been?"

"I have been taking leave of my usual walk," said I.

"And I have been sitting here," said Steerforth, glancing round the room, "thinking that all the people we found so glad on the night of our coming down, might—to judge from the present wasted air of the place—be dispersed, or dead, or come to I don't know what harm. David, I wish to God I had had a judicious father these last twenty years!"

"My dear Steerforth, what is the matter?"

"I wish with all my soul I had been better guided!" he exclaimed. "I wish with all my soul I could guide myself better!"

There was a passionate dejection in his manner that quite amazed me. He was more unlike himself than I could have supposed possible.

"It would be better to be this poor Peggotty, or his lout of a nephew," he said, getting up and leaning moodily against the chimney-piece, with his face towards the fire, "than to be myself, twenty times richer and twenty times wiser, and be the torment to myself that I have been, in this Devil's bark of a boat, within the last half-hour!"

I was so confounded by the alteration in him, that at first I could only observe him in silence, as he stood leaning his head upon his hand, and looking gloomily down at the fire. At length I begged him, with all the earnestness I felt, to tell me what had occurred to cross him so unusually, and to let me sympathize with him, if I could not hope to advise him. Before I had well concluded, he began to laugh—fretfully at first, but soon with returning gaiety.

"Tut, it's nothing, Daisy! nothing!" he replied. "I told you at the inn in London, I am heavy company for myself, sometimes. I have been a nightmare to myself, just now— must have had one, I think. At odd dull times, nursery tales come up into the memory, unrecognized for what they are. I believe I have been confounding myself with the bad boy who 'didn't care', and became food for lions—a grander kind of going to the dogs, I suppose. What old women call the horrors, have been creeping over me from head to foot. I have been afraid of myself."

"You are afraid of nothing else, I think," said I.

"Perhaps not, and yet may have enough to be afraid of too," he answered. "Well! So it goes by! I am not about to be hipped again, David; but I tell you, my good fellow, once more, that it would have been well for me (and for more than me) if I had had a steadfast and judicious father!"

His face was always full of expression, but I never saw it express such a dark kind of earnestness as when he said these words, with his glance bent on the fire.

"So much for that!" he said, making as if he tossed something light into the air, with his hand.

" 'Why, being gone, I am a man again,'

like Macbeth. And now for dinner! If I have not (Macbeth-like) broken up the feast with most admired disorder, Daisy."

"But where are they all, I wonder!" said I.

"God knows," said Steerforth. "After strolling to the ferry looking for you, I strolled in here and found the place deserted. That set me thinking, and you found me thinking."

The advent of Mrs Gummidge with a basket, explained how the house had happened to be empty. She had hurried out to buy something that was needed, against Mr Peggotty's return with the tide; and had left the door open in the meanwhile, lest Ham and little Em'ly, with whom it was an early night, should come home while she was gone. Steerforth, after very much improving Mrs Gummidge's spirits by a cheerful salutation and a jocose embrace, took my arm, and hurried me away.

He had improved his own spirits, no less than Mrs Gummidge's, for they were again at their usual flow, and he was full of vivacious conversation as we went along.

"And so," he said, gaily, "we abandon this buccaneer life tomorrow, do we?"

"So we agreed," I returned. "And our places by the coach are taken, you know."

"Ay! there's no help for it, I suppose," said Steerforth. "I have almost forgotten that there is anything to do in the world but to go out tossing on the sea here. I wish there was not."

"As long as the novelty should last," said I, laughing.

"Like enough," he returned; "though there's a sarcastic meaning in that observation for an amiable piece of innocence like my young friend. Well! I dare say I am a capricious fellow, David. I know I am; but while the iron *is* hot, I can strike it vigorously too. I could pass a reasonably good examination already, as a pilot in these waters, I think."

"Mr Peggotty says you are a wonder," I returned.

"A nautical phenomenon, eh?" laughed Steerforth.

"Indeed he does, and you know how truly; know how ardent you are in any pursuit you follow, and how easily you can master it. And that amazes me most in you,

Steerforth—that you should be contented with such fitful uses of your powers."

"Contented?" he answered, merrily. "I am never contented, except with your fresh-ness, my gentle Daisy. As to fitfulness, I have never learnt the art of binding myself to any of the wheels on which the Ixions of these days are turning round and round. I missed it somehow in a bad apprenticeship, and now don't care about it.—You know I have bought a boat down here?"

"What an extraordinary fellow you are, Steerforth!" I exclaimed, stopping—for this was the first I had heard of it. "When you may never care to come near the place again!"

"I don't know that," he returned. "I have taken a fancy to the place. At all events," walking me briskly on, "I have bought a boat that was for sale—a clipper, Mr Peggotty says, and so she is—and Mr Peggotty will be master of her in my absence."

"Now I understand you, Steerforth!" said I, exultingly. "You pretend to have bought it for yourself, but you have really done so to confer a benefit on him. I might have known as much at first, knowing you. My dear kind Steerforth, how can I tell you what I think of your generosity?"

"Tush!" he answered, turning red. "The less said, the better."

"Didn't I know?" cried I, "didn't I say that there was not a joy, or sorrow, or any emotion of such honest hearts that was indifferent to you?"

"Aye, aye," he answered, "you told me all that. There let it rest. We have said enough!"

Afraid of offending him by pursuing the subject when he made so light of it, I only pursued it in my thoughts as we went on at even a quicker pace than before.

"She must be newly rigged," said Steerforth, "and I shall leave Littimer behind to see it done, that I may know she is quite complete. Did I tell you Littimer had come down?"

"No."

"Oh yes! came down this morning, with a letter from my mother."

As our looks met, I observed that he was pale even to his lips, though he looked very steadily at me. I feared that some difference between him and his mother might have led to his being in the frame of mind in which I had found him at the solitary fireside. I hinted so.

"Oh no!" he said, shaking his head, and giving a slight laugh. "Nothing of the sort! Yes. He is come down, that man of mine."

"The same as ever?" said I.

"The same as ever," said Steerforth. "Distant and quiet as the North Pole. He shall see to the boat being fresh named. She's the 'Stormy Petrel' now. What does Mr Peggotty care for Stormy Petrels! I'll have her christened again."

"By what name?" I asked.

"The 'Little Em'ly'."

As he had continued to look steadily at me, I took it as a reminder that he objected to being extolled for his consideration. I could not help showing in my face how much it pleased me, but I said little, and he resumed his usual smile, and seemed relieved.

"But see here," he said, looking before us, "where the original little Em'ly comes! And that fellow with her, eh? Upon my soul, he's a true knight. He never leaves her!"

Ham was a boat-builder in these days, having improved a natural ingenuity in that handicraft, until he had become a skilled workman. He was in his working-dress, and looked rugged enough, but manly withal, and a very fit protector for the blooming little creature at his side. Indeed, there was a frankness in his face, an honesty, and an undisguised show of his pride in her, and his love for her, which were, to me, the best of good looks. I thought, as they came towards us, that they were well matched even in that particular.

She withdrew her hand timidly from his arm as we stopped to speak to them, and blushed as she gave it to Steerforth and to me. When they passed on, after we had exchanged a few words, she did not like to replace that hand, but, still appearing timid and constrained, walked by herself. I thought all this very pretty and engaging, and Steerforth seemed to think so too, as we looked after them fading away in the light of a young moon.

Suddenly there passed us—evidently following them—a young woman whose approach we had not observed, but whose face I saw as she went by, and thought I had a faint remembrance of. She was lightly dressed; looked bold, and haggard, and flaunting, and poor: but seemed, for the time, to have given all that to the wind which was blowing, and to have nothing in her mind but going after them. As the dark distant level, absorbing their figures into itself, left but itself visible between us and the sea and clouds, her figure disappeared in like manner, still no nearer to them than before.

"That is a black shadow to be following the girl," said Steerforth, standing still; "what does it mean?"

He spoke in a low voice that sounded almost strange to me.

"She must have it in her mind to beg of them, I think," said I.

"A beggar would be no novelty," said Steerforth; "but it is a strange thing that the beggar should take that shape tonight."

"Why?" I asked.

"For no better reason, truly, than because I was thinking," he said, after a pause, "of something like it, when it came by. Where the Devil did it come from, I wonder!"

"From the shadow of this wall, I think," said I, as we emerged upon a road on which a wall abutted.

"It's gone!" he returned, looking over his shoulder. "And all ill go with it. Now for our dinner!"

But, he looked again over his shoulder towards the sea-line glimmering afar off; and yet again. And he wondered about it, in some broken expressions, several times, in the short remainder of our walk; and only seemed to forget it when the light of fire and candle shone upon us, seated warm and merry, at table.

Littimer was there, and had his usual effect upon me. When I said to him that I hoped Mrs Steerforth and Miss Dartle were well, he answered respectfully (and of course respectably), that they were tolerably well, he thanked me, and had sent their compliments. This was all, and yet he seemed to me to say as plainly as a man could say: "You are very young, sir; you are exceedingly young."

We had almost finished dinner, when taking a step or two towards the table, from the corner where he kept watch upon us, or rather upon me, as I felt, he said to his master:

"I beg your pardon, sir. Miss Mowcher is down here."

"Who?" cried Steerforth, much astonished.

"Miss Mowcher, sir."

"Why, what on earth does *she* do here?" said Steerforth.

"It appears to be her native part of the country, sir. She informs me that she makes one of her professional visits here, every year, sir. I met her in the street this afternoon, and she wished to know if she might have the honour of waiting on you after dinner, sir."

"Do you know the Giantess in question, Daisy?" inquired Steerforth.

I was obliged to confess—I felt ashamed, even of being at this disadvantage before Littimer—that Miss Mowcher and I were wholly unacquainted.

"Then you shall know her," said Steerforth, "for she is one of the seven wonders of the world. When Miss Mowcher comes, show her in."

I felt some curiosity and excitement about this lady, especially as Steerforth burst into a fit of laughing when I referred to her, and positively refused to answer any question of which I made her the subject. I remained, therefore, in a state of considerable expectation until the cloth had been removed some half an hour, and we were sitting over our decanter of wine before the fire, when the door opened, and Littimer, with his habitual serenity quite undisturbed, announced:

"Miss Mowcher!"

I looked at the doorway and saw nothing. I was still looking at the doorway, thinking that Miss Mowcher was a long while making her appearance, when, to my infinite astonishment, there came waddling round a sofa which stood between me and it, a pursy dwarf, of about forty or forty-five, with a very large head and face, a pair of roguish grey eyes, and such extremely little arms, that, to enable herself to lay a finger archly against her snub nose, as she ogled Steerforth, she was obliged to meet the finger half-way, and lay her nose against it. Her chin, which was what is called a double chin, was so fat that it entirely swallowed up the strings of her bonnet, bow and all. Throat she had none; waist she had none; legs she had none, worth mentioning; for though she was more than full-sized down to where her waist would have been, if she had had any, and though she terminated, as human beings generally do, in a pair of feet, she was so short that she stood at a common-sized chair as at a table, resting a bag she carried on the seat. This lady; dressed in an off-hand, easy style; bringing her nose and her forefinger together, with the difficulty I have described; standing with her head necessarily on one side, and, with one of her sharp eyes shut up, making an uncommonly knowing face; after ogling Steerforth for a few moments, broke into a torrent of words.

"What! My flower!" she pleasantly began, shaking her large head at him. "You're there, are you! Oh, you naughty boy, fie for shame, what do you do so far away from home? Up to mischief, I'll be bound. Oh, you're a downy fellow, Steerforth, so you are, and I'm another, ain't I? Ha, ha, ha! You'd have betted a hundred pound to five, now, that you wouldn't have seen me here, wouldn't you? Bless you, man alive, I'm everywhere. I'm here and there, and where not, like the conjurer's half-crown in the lady's handkercher. Talking of handkerchers—*and* talking of ladies—what a comfort you are to your blessed mother, ain't you, my dear boy, over one of my shoulders, and I don't say which!"

Miss Mowcher untied her bonnet, at this passage of her discourse, threw back the strings, and sat down, panting, on a footstool in front of the fire—making a kind of arbour of the dining table, which spread its mahogany shelter above her head.

"Oh my stars and what's-their-names!" she went on, clapping a hand on each of her little knees, and glancing shrewdly at me, "I'm of too full a habit, that's the fact, Steerforth. After a flight of stairs, it gives me as much trouble to draw every breath I want, as if it was a bucket of water. If you saw me looking out of an upper window, you'd think I was a fine woman, wouldn't you?"

"I should think that, wherever I saw you," replied Steerforth.

"Go along, you dog, do!" cried the little creature, making a whisk at him with the handkerchief with which she was wiping her face, "and don't be impudent! But I give you my word and honour I was at Lady Mithers's last week—*there's* a woman! How *she* wears!—and Mithers himself came into the room where I was waiting for her—*there's* a man! How *he* wears! and his wig too, for he's had it these ten years—and he went on at that rate in the complimentary line, that I began to think I should be obliged to ring the bell. Ha! ha! ha! He's a pleasant wretch, but he wants principle."

"What were you doing for Lady Mithers?" asked Steerforth.

"That's tellings, my blessed infant," she retorted, tapping her nose again, screwing up her face, and twinkling her eyes like an imp of supernatural intelligence. "Never *you* mind! You'd like to know whether I stop her hair from falling off, or dye it, or touch up her complexion, or improve her eyebrows, wouldn't you? And so you shall, my darling— when I tell you! Do you know what my great grandfather's name was?"

"No," said Steerforth.

"It was Walker, my sweet pet," replied Miss Mowcher, "and he came of a long line of Walkers, that I inherit all the Hookey estates from."

I never beheld anything approaching to Miss Mowcher's wink except Miss Mowcher's self-possession. She had a wonderful way too, when listening to what was said to her, or when waiting for an answer to what she had said herself, of pausing with her head cunningly on one side, and one eye turned up like a magpie's. Altogether I was lost in amazement, and sat staring at her, quite oblivious, I am afraid, of the laws of politeness.

She had by this time drawn the chair to her side, and was busily engaged in producing from the bag (plunging in her short arm to the shoulder, at every dive) a number of small bottles, sponges, combs, brushes, bits of flannel, little pairs of curling-irons, and other instruments, which she tumbled in a heap upon the chair. From this employment she suddenly desisted, and said to Steerforth, much to my confusion:

"Who's your friend?"

"Mr Copperfield," said Steerforth; "he wants to know you."

"Well, then, he shall! I thought he looked as if he did!" returned Miss Mowcher, waddling up to me, bag in hand, and laughing on me as she came. "Face like a peach!" standing on tiptoe to pinch my cheek as I sat. "Quite tempting! I'm very fond of peaches. Happy to make your acquaintance, Mr Copperfield, I'm sure."

I said that I congratulated myself on having the honour to make hers, and that the happiness was mutual.

"Oh, my goodness, how polite we are!" exclaimed Miss Mowcher, making a preposterous attempt to cover her large face with her morsel of a hand. "What a world of gammon and spinnage it is, though, ain't it!"

This was addressed confidentially to both of us, as the morsel of a hand came away from the face, and buried itself, arm and all, in the bag again.

"What do you mean, Miss Mowcher?" said Steerforth.

"Ha! ha! ha! What a refreshing set of humbugs we are, to be sure, ain't we, my sweet child?" replied that morsel of a woman, feeling in the bag with her head on one side and her eye in the air. "Look here!" taking something out. "Scraps of the Russian Prince's nails. Prince Alphabet turned topsy-turvy, *I* call him, for his name's got all the letters in it, higgledy-piggledy."

"The Russian Prince is a client of yours, is he?" said Steerforth.

"I believe you, my pet," replied Miss Mowcher. "I keep his nails in order for him. Twice a week! Fingers *and* toes."

"He pays well, I hope?" said Steerforth.

"Pays, as he speaks, my dear child—through the nose," replied Miss Mowcher. "None of your close shavers the Prince ain't. You'd say so, if you saw his moustachios. Red by nature, black by art."

"By your art, of course," said Steerforth.

Miss Mowcher winked assent. "Forced to send for me. Couldn't help it. The climate affected *his* dye; it did very well in Russia, but it was no go here. You never saw such a rusty Prince in all your born days as he was. Like old iron!"

"Is that why you called him a humbug, just now?" inquired Steerforth.

"Oh, you're a broth of a boy, ain't you?" returned Miss Mowcher, shaking her head violently. "I said, what a set of humbugs we were in general, and I showed you the scraps of the Prince's nails to prove it. The Prince's nails do more for me in private families of the genteel sort, than all my talents put together. I always carry 'em about. They're the best introduction. If Miss Mowcher cuts the Prince's nails, she *must* be all right. I give 'em away to the young ladies. They put 'em in albums, I believe. Ha! ha! ha! Upon my life, 'the whole social system' (as the men call it when they make speeches in Parliament) is a system of Prince's nails!" said this least of women, trying to fold her short arms, and nodding her large head.

Steerforth laughed heartily, and I laughed too. Miss Mowcher continuing all the time to shake her head (which was very much on one side), and to look into the air with one eye, and to wink with the other.

"Well, well!" she said, smiting her small knees, and rising, "this is not business. Come, Steerforth, let's explore the polar regions, and have it over."

She then selected two or three of the little instruments, and a little bottle, and asked (to my surprise) if the table would bear. On Steerforth's replying in the affirmative, she pushed a chair against it, and begging the assistance of my hand, mounted up, pretty nimbly, to the top, as if it were a stage.

"If either of you saw my ankles," she said, when she was safely elevated, "say so, and I'll go home and destroy myself."

"*I* did not," said Steerforth.

"*I* did not," said I.

"Well then," cried Miss Mowcher, "I'll consent to live. Now, ducky, ducky, ducky, come to Mrs Bond and be killed."

This was an invocation to Steerforth to place himself under her hands; who, accordingly, sat himself down, with his back to the table, and his laughing face towards me, and submitted his head to her inspection, evidently for no other purpose than our entertainment. To see Miss Mowcher standing over him, looking at his rich profusion of brown hair through a large round magnifying glass, which she took out of her pocket, was a most amazing spectacle.

"*You're* a pretty fellow!" said Miss Mowcher, after a brief inspection. "You'd be as bald as a friar on the top of your head in twelve months, but for me. Just half a minute, my young friend, and we'll give you a polishing that shall keep your curls on for the next ten years!"

With this, she tilted some of the contents of the little bottle on to one of the little bits of flannel, and, again imparting some of the virtues of that preparation to one of the little brushes, began rubbing and scraping away with both on the crown of Steerforth's head in the busiest manner I ever witnessed, talking all the time.

"There's Charley Pyegrave, the duke's son," she said. "You know Charley?" peeping round into his face.

"A little," said Steerforth.

"What a man *he* is! *There's* a whisker! As to Charley's legs, if they were only a pair (which they ain't), they'd defy competition. Would you believe he tried to do without me—in the Life-Guards, too?"

"Mad!" said Steerforth.

"It looks like it. However, mad or sane, he tried," returned Miss Mowcher. "What does he do, but, lo and behold you, he goes into a perfumer's shop, and wants to buy a bottle of the Madagascar Liquid."

"Charley does?" said Steerforth.

"Charley does. But they haven't got any of the Madagascar Liquid."

"What is it? Something to drink?" asked Steerforth.

"To drink?" returned Miss Mowcher, stopping to slap his cheek. "To doctor his own moustachios with, you *know*. There was a woman in the shop—elderly female—quite a Griffin—who had never even heard of it by name. 'Begging pardon, sir,' said the Griffin to Charley, 'it's not—not—not ROUGE, is it?' 'Rouge,' said Charley to the Griffin. 'What the unmentionable to ears polite, do you think I want with rouge?' 'No offence, sir,' said the Griffin; 'we have it asked for by so many names, I thought it might be.' Now that, my child," continued Miss Mowcher, rubbing all the time as busily as ever, "is another instance of the refreshing humbug I was speaking of. *I* do something in that way myself—perhaps a good deal—perhaps a little—sharp's the word, my dear boy—never mind!"

"In what way do you mean? In the rouge way?" said Steerforth.

"Put this and that together, my tender pupil," returned the wary Mowcher, touching her nose, "work it by the rule of Secrets in all trades, and the product will give you the desired result. I say *I* do a little in that way myself. One Dowager, *she* calls it lip-salve. Another, *she* calls it gloves. Another, *she* calls it tucker-edging. Another, *she* calls it a fan. *I* call it whatever *they* call it. I supply it for 'em, but we keep up the trick so, to one another, and make believe with such a face, that they'd as soon think of laying it on, before a whole drawing-room, as before me. And when I wait upon 'em, they'll say to me sometimes—*with it on*—thick, and no mistake—'How am I looking, Mowcher? Am I pale?' Ha! ha! ha! ha! Isn't *that* refreshing, my young friend!"

I never did in my days behold anything like Mowcher as she stood upon the dining table, intensely enjoying this refreshment, rubbing busily at Steerforth's head, and winking at me over it.

"Ah!" she said. "Such things are not much in demand hereabouts. That sets me off again! I haven't seen a pretty woman since I've been here, Jemmy."

"No?" said Steerforth.

"Not the ghost of one," replied Miss Mowcher.

"We could show her the substance of one, I think?" said Steerforth, addressing his eyes to mine. "Eh, Daisy?"

"Yes, indeed," said I.

"Aha?" cried the little creature, glancing sharply at my face, and then peeping round at Steerforth's. "Umph?"

The first exclamation sounded like a question put to both of us, and the second like a question put to Steerforth only. She seemed to have found no answer to either, but continued to rub, with her head on one side and her eye turned up, as if she were looking for an answer in the air and were confident of its appearing presently.

"A sister of yours, Mr Copperfield?" she cried, after a pause, and still keeping the same look-out. "Aye, aye?"

"No," said Steerforth, before I could reply. "Nothing of the sort. On the contrary, Mr

Copperfield used—or I am much mistaken—to have a great admiration for her."

"Why, hasn't he now?" returned Miss Mowcher. "Is he fickle? oh, for shame! Did he sip every flower, and change every hour, until Polly his passion requited?—Is her name Polly?"

The Elfin suddenness with which she pounced upon me with this question, and a searching look, quite disconcerted me for a moment.

"No, Miss Mowcher," I replied. "Her name is Emily."

"Aha?" she cried exactly as before. "Umph? What a rattle I am! Mr Copperfield, ain't I volatile?"

Her tone and look implied something that was not agreeable to me in connexion with the subject. So I said, in a graver manner than any of us had yet assumed:

"She is as virtuous as she is pretty. She is engaged to be married to a most worthy and deserving man in her own station of life. I esteem her for her good sense, as much as I admire her for her good looks."

"Well said!" cried Steerforth. "Hear, hear, hear! Now I'll quench the curiosity of this little Fatima, my dear Daisy, by leaving her nothing to guess at. She is at present apprenticed, Miss Mowcher, or articled, or whatever it may be, to Omer and Joram, Haberdashers, Milliners, and so forth, in this town. Do you observe? Omer and Joram. The promise of which my friend has spoken, is made and entered into with her cousin; Christian name, Ham; surname, Peggotty; occupation, boat-builder; also of this town. She lives with a relative; Christian name, unknown; surname, Peggotty; occupation, seafaring; also of this town. She is the prettiest and most engaging little fairy in the world. I admire her—as my friend does—exceedingly. If it were not that I might appear to disparage her Intended, which I know my friend would not like, I would add, that to *me* she seems to be throwing herself away; that I am sure she might do better; and that I swear she was born to be a lady."

Miss Mowcher listened to these words, which were very slowly and distinctly spoken, with her head on one side, and her eye in the air as if she were still looking for that answer. When he ceased she became brisk again in an instant, and rattled away with surprising volubility.

"Oh! And that's all about it, is it?" she exclaimed, trimming his whiskers with a little restless pair of scissors, that went glancing round his head in all directions. "Very well: *very* well! Quite a long story. Ought to end 'and they lived happy ever afterwards'; oughtn't it? Ah! What's that game at forfeits? I love my love with an E, because she's enticing; I hate her with an E, because she's engaged. I took her to the sign of the exquisite, and treated her with an elopement, her name's Emily, and she lives in the east? Ha! ha! ha! Mr Copperfield, ain't I volatile?"

Merely looking at me with extravagant slyness, and not waiting for any reply, she continued, without drawing breath:

"There! If ever any scapegrace was trimmed and touched up to perfection, you are, Steerforth. If I understand any noddle in the world, I understand yours. Do you hear me when I tell you that, my darling? I understand yours," peeping down into his face. "Now you may mizzle, Jemmy (as we say at Court), and if Mr Copperfield will take the chair I'll operate on him."

"What do you say, Daisy?" inquired Steerforth, laughing, and resigning his seat. "Will you be improved?"

"Thank you, Miss Mowcher, not this evening."

"Don't say no," returned the little woman, looking at me with the aspect of a connoisseur; "a little bit more eyebrow?"

"Thank you," I returned, "some other time."

"Have it carried half a quarter of an inch towards the temple," said Miss Mowcher. "We can do it in a fortnight."

"No, I thank you. Not at present."

"Go in for a tip," she urged. "No? Let's get the scaffolding up, then, for a pair of whiskers. Come!"

I could not help blushing as I declined, for I felt we were on my weak point, now. But Miss Mowcher, finding that I was not at present disposed for any decoration within the range of her art, and that I was, for the time being, proof against the blandishments of the small bottle which she held up before one eye to enforce her persuasions, said we would make a beginning on an early day, and requested the aid of my hand to descend from her elevated station. Thus, assisted, she skipped down with much agility, and began to tie her double chin into her bonnet.

"The fee," said Steerforth, "is—"

"Five bob," replied Miss Mowcher, "and dirt cheap, my chicken. Ain't I volatile, Mr Copperfield?"

I replied politely: "Not at all." But I thought she was rather so, when she tossed up his two half-crowns like a goblin pieman, caught them, dropped them in her pocket, and gave it a loud slap.

"That's the Till!" observed Miss Mowcher, standing at the chair again, and replacing in the bag a miscellaneous collection of little objects she had emptied out of it. "Have I got all my traps? It seems so. It won't do to be like long Ned Beadwood, when they took him to church 'to marry him to somebody,' as he says, and left the bride behind. Ha! ha! ha! A wicked rascal, Ned, but droll! Now, I know I'm going to break your hearts, but I am forced to leave you. You must call up all your fortitude, and try to bear it. Good-bye, Mr Copperfield! Take care of yourself, Jockey of Norfolk! How I *have* been rattling on! It's all the fault of you two wretches. *I* forgive you! 'Bob swore!'—as the Englishman said for 'Good night,' when he first learnt French, and thought it so like English. 'Bob swore,' my ducks!"

With the bag slung over her arm, and rattling as she waddled away, she waddled to the door, where she stopped to inquire if she should leave us a lock of her hair. "Ain't I volatile?" she added, as a commentary on this offer, and, with her finger on her nose, departed.

Steerforth laughed to that degree, that it was impossible for me to help laughing too; though I am not sure I should have done so, but for this inducement. When we had had our laugh quite out, which was after some time, he told me that Miss Mowcher had quite an extensive connexion, and made herself useful to a variety of people in a variety of ways. Some people trifled with her as a mere oddity, he said; but she was as shrewdly and sharply observant as anyone he knew, and as long-headed as she was short-armed. He told me that what she had said of being here, and there, and everywhere, was true enough; for she made little darts into the provinces, and seemed to pick up customers everywhere, and to know everybody. I asked him what her disposition was: whether it was at all mischievous, and if her sympathies were generally on the right side of things: but, not succeeding in attracting his attention to these questions after two or three attempts, I forebore or forgot to repeat them. He told me instead, with much rapidity, a good deal about her skill, and her profits; and about her being a scientific cupper, if I should ever have occasion for her service in that capacity.

She was the principal theme of our conversation during the evening: and when we parted for the night Steerforth called after me over the banisters, "Bob swore!" as I went downstairs.

I was surprised, when I came to Mr Barkis's house, to find Ham walking up and down in front of it, and still more surprised to learn from him that little Em'ly was inside. I naturally inquired why he was not there too, instead of pacing the streets by himself?

"Why, you see, Mas'r Davy," he rejoined, in a hesitating manner, "Em'ly, she's talking to some 'un in here."

"I should have thought," said I, smiling, "that that was a reason for your being in here too, Ham."

"Well, Mas'r Davy, in a general way, so 't would be," he returned; "but look'ee here, Mas'r Davy," lowering his voice, and speaking very gravely. "It's a young woman, sir—a young woman, that Em'ly knowed once, and doen't ought to know no more."

When I heard these words, a light began to fall upon the figure I had seen following them, some hours ago.

"It's a poor wurem, Mas'r Davy," said Ham, "as is trod under foot by all the town. Up street and down street. The mowld o' the churchyard don't hold any that the folk shrink away from, more."

"Did I see her tonight, Ham, on the sand, after we met you?"

"Keeping us in sight?" said Ham. "It's like you did, Mas'r Davy. Not that I know'd then, she was theer, sir, but along of her creeping soon arterwards under Em'ly's little winder, when she see the light come, and whisp'ring 'Em'ly, Em'ly, for Christ's sake, have a woman's heart towards me. I was once like you!' Those was solemn words, Mas'r Davy, fur to hear!"

"They were indeed, Ham. What did Em'ly do?"

"Says Em'ly, 'Martha, is it you? Oh, Martha, can it be you?'—for they had sat at work together, many a day, at Mr Omer's."

"I recollect her now!" cried I, recalling one of the two girls I had seen when I first went there. "I recollect her quite well!"

"Martha Endell," said Ham. "Two or three year older than Em'ly, but was at the school with her."

"I never heard her name," said I. "I didn't mean to interrupt you."

"For the matter o' that, Mas'r Davy," replied Ham, "all's told a'most in them words, 'Em'ly, Em'ly, for Christ's sake, have a woman's heart towards me. I was once like you!' She wanted to speak to Em'ly. Em'ly couldn't speak to her theer, for her loving uncle was come home, and he wouldn't—no, Mas'r Davy," said Ham, with great earnestness, "he couldn't, kind-natur'd, tender-hearted as he is, see them two together, side by side, for all the treasures that's wrecked in the sea."

I felt how true this was. I knew it, on the instant, quite as well as Ham.

"So Em'ly writes in pencil on a bit of paper," he pursued, "and gives it to her out o' winder to bring here. 'Show that,' she says, 'to my aunt, Mrs Barkis, and she'll set you down by her fire, for the love of me, till uncle is gone out, and I can come.' By and by she tells me what I tell you, Mas'r Davy, and asks me to bring her. What can I do? She doen't ought to know any such, but I can't deny her, when the tears is on her face."

He put his hand into the breast of his shaggy jacket, and took out with great care a pretty little purse.

"And if I could deny her when the tears was on her face, Mas'r Davy," said Ham, tenderly adjusting it on the rough palm of his hand, "how could I deny her when she give me this to carry for her—knowing what she brought it for? Such a toy as it is!" said Ham, thoughtfully looking on it. "With such a little money in it, Em'ly my dear."

I shook him warmly by the hand when he had put it away again—for that was more satisfactory to me than saying anything—and we walked up and down, for a minute or two, in silence. The door opened then, and Peggotty appeared, beckoning to Ham to come in. I would have kept away, but she came after me, entreating me to come in too. Even then, I would have avoided the room where they all were, but for its being the neat-tiled kitchen I have mentioned more than once. The door opening immediately into it, I found myself among them before I considered whither I was going.

The girl—the same I had seen upon the sands—was near the fire. She was sitting on the ground, with her head and one arm lying on a chair. I fancied, from the disposition of her figure, that Em'ly had but newly risen from the chair, and that the forlorn head might perhaps have been lying on her lap. I saw but little of the girl's face, over which her hair fell loose and scattered, as if she had been disordering it with her own hands; but I saw that she was young, and of a fair complexion. Peggotty had been crying. So had little Em'ly. Not a word was spoken when we first went in; and the Dutch clock by the dresser seemed, in the silence, to tick twice as loud as usual.

Em'ly spoke first.

"Martha wants," she said to Ham, "to go to London."

"Why to London?" returned Ham.

He stood between them, looking on the prostrate girl with a mixture of compassion for her, and of jealousy of her holding any companionship with her whom he loved so well, which I have always remembered distinctly. They both spoke as if she were ill; in a soft, suppressed tone that was plainly heard, although it hardly rose above a whisper.

"Better there than here," said a third voice aloud—Martha's, though she did not move. "No one knows me there. Everybody knows me here."

"What will she do there?" inquired Ham.

She lifted up her head, and looked darkly round at him for a moment; then laid it down again, and curved her right arm about her neck, as a woman in a fever, or in an agony of pain from a shot might twist herself.

"She will try to do well," said little Em'ly. "You don't know what she has said to us. Does he—do they—aunt?"

Peggotty shook her head compassionately.

"I'll try," said Martha, "if you'll help me away. I never can do worse than I have done here. I may do better. Oh!" with a dreadful shiver, "take me out of these streets, where the whole town knows me from a child!"

As Em'ly held out her hand to Ham, I saw him put in it a little canvas bag. She took it, as if she thought it were her purse, and made a step or two forward; but finding her mistake, came back to where he had retired near me, and showed it to him.

"It's all yourn, Em'ly," I could hear him say. "I haven't nowt in all the wureld that ain't yourn, my dear. It ain't of no delight to me, except for you!"

The tears rose freshly in her eyes, but she turned away and went to Martha. What she gave her, I don't know. I saw her stooping over her, and putting money in her bosom. She whispered something, as she asked was that enough? "More than enough," the other said, and took her hand and kissed it.

Then Martha arose, and gathering her shawl about her, covering her face with it, and weeping aloud, went slowly to the door. She stopped a moment before going out, as if she would have uttered something or turned back; but no word passed her lips. Making the same low, dreary, wretched moaning in her shawl, she went away.

As the door closed, little Em'ly looked at us three in a hurried manner, and then hid her face in her hands, and fell to sobbing.

"Doen't, Em'ly!" said Ham, tapping her gently on the shoulder. "Doen't, my dear! You doen't ought to cry so, pretty!"

"Oh, Ham!" she exclaimed, still weeping pitifully, "I am not so good a girl as I ought to be! I know I have not the thankful heart, sometimes, I ought to have!"

"Yes, yes, you have, I'm sure," said Ham.

"No! no! no!" cried little Em'ly, sobbing, and shaking her head. "I am not as good a girl as I ought to be. Not near! not near!"

And still she cried, as if her heart would break.

"I try your love too much. I know I do!" she sobbed. "I'm often cross to you, and changeable with you, when I ought to be far different. You are never so to me. Why am I ever so to you, when I should think of nothing but how to be grateful, and to make you happy!"

"You always make me so," said Ham, "my dear! I am happy in the sight of you. I am happy, all day long, in the thoughts of you."

"Ah! that's not enough!" she cried. "That is because you are good; not because I am! Oh, my dear, it might have been a better fortune for you, if you had been fond of someone else—of someone steadier and much worthier than me, who was all bound up in you, and never vain and changeable like me!"

"Poor little tender-heart," said Ham, in a low voice. "Martha has overset her, altogether."

"Please, aunt," sobbed Em'ly, "come here, and let me lay my head upon you. Oh, I am very miserable tonight, aunt! Oh, I am not as good a girl as I ought to be. I am not, I know!"

Peggotty had hastened to the chair before the fire. Em'ly, with her arms around her neck, kneeled by her, looking up most earnestly into her face.

"Oh, pray, aunt, try to help me! Ham, dear, try to help me! Mr David, for the sake of old times, do, please, try to help me! I want to be a better girl than I am. I want to feel a hundred times more thankful than I do. I want to feel more, what a blessed thing it is to be the wife of a good man, and to lead a peaceful life. Oh me, oh me! Oh my heart, my heart!"

She dropped her face on my old nurse's breast, and, ceasing this supplication, which in its agony and grief was half a woman's, half a child's, as all her manner was (being, in that, more natural, and better suited to her beauty, as I thought, than any other manner could have been), wept silently, while my old nurse hushed her like an infant.

She got calmer by degrees, and then we soothed her; now talking encouragingly, and now jesting a little with her, until she began to raise her head and speak to us. So we got on, until she was able to smile, and then to laugh, and then to sit up, half ashamed; while Peggotty recalled her stray ringlets, dried her eyes, and made her neat again, lest her uncle should wonder, when she got home, why his darling had been crying.

I saw her do, that night, what I had never seen her do before. I saw her innocently kiss her chosen husband on the cheek, and creep close to his bluff form as if it were her best support. When they went away together, in the waning moonlight, and I looked after them, comparing their departure in my mind with Martha's, I saw that she held his arm with both her hands, and still kept close to him.

Chapter XXIII

I CORROBORATE MR DICK, AND CHOOSE A PROFESSION

WHEN I awoke in the morning I thought very much of little Em'ly, and her emotion last night, after Martha had left. I felt as if I had come into the knowledge of those domestic weaknesses and tendernesses in a sacred confidence, and that to disclose them, even to Steerforth, would be wrong. I had no gentler feeling towards anyone than towards the pretty creature who had been my playmate, and whom I have always been persuaded, and shall always be persuaded, to my dying day, I then devotedly loved. The repetition to any ears—even to Steerforth's—of what she had been unable to repress when her heart lay open to me by an accident, I felt would be a rough deed, unworthy of myself, unworthy of the light of our pure childhood, which I always saw encircling her head. I made a resolution, therefore, to keep it in my own breast; and there it gave her image a new grace.

While we were at breakfast, a letter was delivered to me from my aunt. As it contained matter on which I thought Steerforth could advise me as well as anyone, and on which I knew I should be delighted to consult him, I resolved to make it a subject of discussion on our journey home. For the present we had enough to do, in taking leave of all our friends. Mr Barkis was far from being the last among them, in his regret at our departure; and I believe would even have opened the box again, and sacrificed another guinea, if it would have kept us eight-and-forty hours in Yarmouth. Peggotty and all her family were full of grief at our going. The whole house of Omer and Joram turned out to bid us good-bye; and there were so many seafaring volunteers in attendance on Steerforth, when our portmanteaux went to the coach, that if we had had the baggage of a regiment with us, we should hardly have wanted porters to carry it. In a word, we departed to the regret and admiration of all concerned, and left a great many people very sorry behind us.

"Do you stay long here, Littimer?" said I, as he stood waiting to see the coach start.

"No, sir," he replied; "probably not very long, sir."

"He can hardly say, just now," observed Steerforth, carelessly. "He knows what he has to do, and he'll do it."

"That I am sure he will," said I.

Littimer touched his hat in acknowledgement of my good opinion, and I felt about eight years old. He touched it once more, wishing us a good journey; and we left him standing on the pavement, as respectable a mystery as any pyramid in Egypt.

For some little time we held no conversation, Steerforth being unusually silent, and I being sufficiently engaged in wondering, within myself, when I should see the old places again, and what new changes might happen to me or them in the meanwhile. At length Steerforth, becoming gay and talkative in a moment, as he could become anything he liked at any moment, pulled me by the arm:

"Find a voice, David. What about that letter you were speaking of at breakfast?"

"Oh!" said I, taking it out of my pocket. "It's from my aunt."

"And what does she say, requiring consideration?"

"Why, she reminds me, Steerforth," said I, "that I came out on this expedition to look about me, and to think a little."

"Which, of course, you have done?"

"Indeed I can't say I have, particularly. To tell you the truth, I am afraid I have forgotten it."

"Well! look about you now, and make up for your negligence," said Steerforth. "Look to the right, and you'll see a flat country, with a good deal of marsh in it; look to the left, and you'll see the same. Look to the front, and you'll find no difference; look to the rear, and there it is still."

I laughed, and replied that I saw no suitable profession in the whole prospect; which was perhaps to be attributed to its flatness.

"What says our aunt on the subject?" inquired Steerforth, glancing at the letter in my hand. "Does she suggest anything?"

"Why, yes," said I. "She asks me, here, if I think I should like to be a proctor? What do you think of it?"

"Well, I don't know," replied Steerforth, coolly. "You may as well do that as anything else, I suppose?"

I could not help laughing again, at his balancing all callings and professions so equally; and I told him so.

"What *is* a proctor, Steerforth?" said I.

"Why, he is a sort of monkish attorney," replied Steerforth. "He is, to some faded courts held in Doctors' Commons—a lazy old nook near St Paul's Churchyard—what solicitors are to the courts of law and equity. He is a functionary whose existence, in the natural course of things, would have terminated about two hundred years ago. I can tell you best what he is, by telling you what Doctors' Commons is. It's a little out-of-the-way place, where they administer what is called ecclesiastical law, and play all kinds of tricks with obsolete old monsters of acts of Parliament, which three-fourths of the world know nothing about, and the other fourth supposes to have been dug up, in a fossil state, in the days of the Edwards. It's a place that has an ancient monopoly in suits about people's wills and people's marriages, and disputes among ships and boats."

"Nonsense, Steerforth!" I exclaimed. "You don't mean to say that there is any affinity between nautical matters and ecclesiastical matters?"

"I don't, indeed, my dear boy," he returned; "but I mean to say that they are managed and decided by the same set of people, down in that same Doctors' Commons. You shall go there one day, and find them blundering through half the nautical terms in Young's Dictionary, apropos of the 'Nancy' having run down the 'Sarah Jane,' or Mr Peggotty and the Yarmouth boatmen having put off in a gale of wind with an anchor and cable to the 'Nelson' Indiaman in distress; and you shall go there another day, and find them deep in the evidence, pro and con, respecting a clergyman who has misbehaved himself; and you shall find the judge in the nautical case, the advocate in the clergyman's case, or contrariwise. They are like actors: now a man's a judge, and now he is not a judge; now he's one thing, now he's another; now he's something else, change and change about; but it's always a very pleasant, profitable little affair of private theatricals, presented to an uncommonly select audience."

"But advocates and proctors are not one and the same?" said I, a little puzzled. "Are they?"

"No," returned Steerforth, "the advocates are civilians—men who have taken a doctor's degree at college—which is the first reason of my knowing anything about it. The proctors employ the advocates. Both get very comfortable fees, and altogether they make a mighty snug little party. On the whole, I would recommend you to take to

Doctors' Commons kindly, David. They plume themselves on their gentility there, I can tell you, if that's any satisfaction."

I made allowance for Steerforth's light way of treating the subject, and, considering it with reference to the staid air of gravity and antiquity which I associated with that "lazy old nook near St Paul's Churchyard," did not feel indisposed towards my aunt's suggestion; which she left to my free decision, making no scruple of telling me that it had occurred to her, on her lately visiting her own proctor in Doctors' Commons for the purpose of settling her will in my favour.

"That's a laudable proceeding on the part of our aunt, at all events," said Steerforth, when I mentioned it; "and one deserving of all encouragement. Daisy, my advice is that you take kindly to Doctors' Commons."

I quite made up my mind to do so. I then told Steerforth that my aunt was in town awaiting me (as I found from her letter), and that she had taken lodgings for a week at a kind of private hotel at Lincoln's Inn Fields, where there was a stone staircase, and a convenient door in the roof; my aunt being firmly persuaded that every house in London was going to be burnt down every night.

We achieved the rest of our journey pleasantly, sometimes recurring to Doctors' Commons, and anticipating the distant days when I should be a proctor there, which Steerforth pictured in a variety of humorous and whimsical lights, that made us both merry. When we came to our journey's end, he went home, engaging to call upon me next day but one; and I drove to Lincoln's Inn Fields, where I found my aunt up, and waiting supper.

If I had been round the world since we parted, we could hardly have been better pleased to meet again. My aunt cried outright as she embraced me; and said, pretending to laugh, that if my poor mother had been alive, that silly little creature would have shed tears, she had no doubt.

"So you have left Mr Dick behind, aunt?" said I. "I am sorry for that. Ah, Janet, how do you do?"

As Janet curtsied, hoping I was well, I observed my aunt's visage lengthen very much.

"I am sorry for it, too," said my aunt, rubbing her nose. "I have had no peace of mind, Trot, since I have been here."

Before I could ask why, she told me.

"I am convinced," said my aunt, laying her hand with melancholy firmness on the table, "that Dick's character is not a character to keep the donkeys off. I am confident he wants strength of purpose. I ought to have left Janet at home, instead, and then my mind might perhaps have been at ease. If ever there was a donkey trespassing on my green," said my aunt, with emphasis, "there was one this afternoon at four o'clock. A cold feeling came over me from head to foot, and I *know* it was a donkey!"

I tried to comfort her on this point, but she rejected consolation.

"It was a donkey," said my aunt; "and it was the one with the stumpy tail which that Murdering sister of a woman rode, when she came to my house." This had been, ever since, the only name my aunt knew for Miss Murdstone. "If there is any Donkey in Dover, whose audacity it is harder to me to bear than another's, that," said my aunt, striking the table, "is the animal!"

Janet ventured to suggest that my aunt might be disturbing herself unnecessarily, and that she believed the donkey in question was then engaged in the sand-and-gravel line of business, and was not available for purposes of trespass. But my aunt wouldn't hear of it.

Supper was comfortably served and hot, though my aunt's rooms were very high up—whether that she might have more stone stairs for her money, or might be nearer to the door in the roof, I don't know—and consisted of a roast fowl, a steak, and some vegetables, to all of which I did ample justice, and which were all excellent. But my aunt had her own ideas concerning London provision, and ate but little.

"I suppose this unfortunate fowl was born and brought up in a cellar," said my aunt, "and never took the air except on a hackney coach-stand. I *hope* the steak may be beef, but I don't believe it. Nothing's genuine in the place, in my opinion, but the dirt."

"Don't you think the fowl may have come out of the country, aunt?" I hinted.

"Certainly not," returned my aunt. "It would be no pleasure to a London tradesman to sell anything which was what he pretended it was."

I did not venture to controvert this opinion, but I made a good supper, which it greatly satisfied her to see me do. When the table was cleared, Janet assisted her to arrange her hair, to put on her nightcap, which was of a smarter construction than usual ("in case of fire," my aunt said), and to fold her gown back over her knees, these being her usual preparations for warming herself before going to bed. I then made her, according to certain established regulations from which no deviation, however slight, could ever be permitted, a glass of hot wine and water, and a slice of toast cut into long thin strips. With these accompaniments we were left alone to finish the evening, my aunt sitting opposite to me drinking her wine and water; soaking her strips of toast in it, one by one, before eating them; and looking benignantly on me, from among the borders of her nightcap.

"Well, Trot," she began, "what do you think of the proctor plan? Or have you not begun to think about it yet?"

"I have thought a good deal about it, my dear aunt, and I have talked a good deal about it with Steerforth. I like it very much indeed. I like it exceedingly."

"Come!" said my aunt. "That's cheering!"

"I have only one difficulty, aunt."

"Say what it is, Trot," she returned.

"Why, I want to ask, aunt, as this seems, from what I understand, to be a limited profession, whether my entrance into it would not be very expensive?"

"It will cost," returned my aunt, "to article you, just a thousand pounds."

"Now, my dear aunt," said I, drawing my chair nearer, "I am uneasy in my mind about that. It's a large sum of money. You have expended a great deal on my education, and have always been as liberal to me in all things as it was possible to be. You have been the soul of generosity. Surely there are some ways in which I might begin life with hardly any outlay, and yet begin with a good hope of getting on by resolution and exertion. Are you sure that it would not be better to try that course? Are you certain that you can afford to part with so much money, and that it is right that it should be so expended? I only ask you, my second mother, to consider. Are you certain?"

My aunt finished eating the piece of toast on which she was then engaged, looking me full in the face all the while; and then setting her glass on the chimney-piece, and folding her hands upon her folded skirts, replied as follows:

"Trot, my child, if I have any object in life, it is to provide for your being a good, a sensible, and a happy man. I am bent upon it—so is Dick. I should like some people that I know to hear Dick's conversation on the subject. Its sagacity is wonderful. But no one knows the resources of that man's intellect, except myself!"

She stopped for a moment to take my hand between hers, and went on:

"It's in vain, Trot, to recall the past, unless it works some influence upon the present. Perhaps I might have been better friends with your poor father. Perhaps I might have been better friends with that poor child your mother, even after your sister Betsey Trotwood disappointed me. When you came to me, a little runaway boy, all dusty and way-worn, perhaps I thought so. From that time until now, Trot, you have ever been a credit to me and a pride and a pleasure. I have no other claim upon my means; at least"—here to my surprise she hesitated, and was confused—"no, I have *no* other claim upon my means—and you are my adopted child. Only be a loving child to me in my age, and bear with my whims and fancies; and you will do more for an old woman whose prime of life was not so happy or conciliating as it might have been, than ever that old woman did for you."

It was the first time I had heard my aunt refer to her past history. There was a magnanimity in her quiet way of doing so, and of dismissing it, which would have exalted her in my respect and affection, if anything could.

"All is agreed and understood between us, now, Trot," said my aunt, "and we need talk of this no more. Give me a kiss, and we'll go to the Commons after breakfast tomorrow."

We had a long chat by the fire before we went to bed. I slept in a room on the same floor with my aunt's, and was a little disturbed in the course of the night by her knocking at my door as often as she was agitated by a distant sound of hackney-coaches or market-carts, and inquiring, "if I heard the engines?" But towards morning she slept better, and suffered me to do so too.

At about mid-day, we set out for the office of Messrs. Spenlow and Jorkins, in Doctors' Commons. My aunt, who had this other general opinion in reference to London, that every man she saw was a pickpocket, gave me her purse to carry for her, which had ten guineas in it and some silver.

We made a pause at the toy shop in Fleet Street, to see the giants of Saint Dunstan's strike upon the bells—we had timed our going, so as to catch them at it, at twelve o'clock—and then went on towards Ludgate Hill, and St Paul's Churchyard. We were crossing to the former place, when I found that my aunt greatly accelerated her speed, and looked frightened. I observed, at the same time, that a lowering ill-dressed man who had stopped and stared at us in passing, a little before, was coming so close after us as to brush against her.

"Trot! My dear Trot!" cried my aunt, in a terrified whisper, and pressing my arm. "I don't know what I am to do."

"Don't be alarmed," said I. "There's nothing to be afraid of. Step into a shop, and I'll soon get rid of this fellow."

"No, no, child!" she returned. "Don't speak to him for the world. I entreat, I order you!"

"Good Heaven, aunt!" said I. "He is nothing but a sturdy beggar."

"You don't know what he is!" replied my aunt. "You don't know who he is! You don't know what you say!"

We had stopped in an empty doorway, while this was passing, and he had stopped too.

"Don't look at him!" said my aunt, as I turned my head indignantly, "but get me a coach, my dear, and wait for me in St Paul's Churchyard."

"Wait for you?" I replied.

"Yes," rejoined my aunt. "I must go alone. I must go with him."

"With him, aunt? This man?"

"I am in my senses," she replied, "and I tell you I *must*. Get me a coach!"

However much astonished I might be, I was sensible that I had no right to refuse compliance with such a peremptory command. I hurried away a few paces, and called a hackney-chariot which was passing empty. Almost before I could let down the steps, my aunt sprang in, I don't know how, and the man followed. She waved her hand to me to go away, so earnestly, that, all confounded as I was, I turned from them at once. In doing so, I heard her say to the coachman, "Drive anywhere! Drive straight on!" and presently the chariot passed me, going up the hill.

What Mr Dick had told me, and what I had supposed to be a delusion of his, now came into my mind. I could not doubt that this person was the person of whom he had made such mysterious mention, though what the nature of his hold upon my aunt could possibly be, I was quite unable to imagine. After half an hour's cooling in the churchyard, I saw the chariot coming back. The driver stopped beside me, and my aunt was sitting in it alone.

She had not yet sufficiently recovered from her agitation to be quite prepared for the visit we had to make. She desired me to get into the chariot, and to tell the coachman to drive slowly up and down a little while. She said no more, except, "My dear child, never ask me what it was, and don't refer to it," until she had perfectly regained her composure, when she told me she was quite herself now, and we might get out. On her giving me her purse to pay the driver, I found that all the guineas were gone, and only the loose silver remained.

Doctors' Commons was approached by a little low archway. Before we had taken many paces down the street beyond it, the noise of the city seemed to melt, as if by magic, into a softened distance. A few dull courts and narrow ways brought us to the skylighted offices of Spenlow and Jorkins; in the vestibule of which temple, accessible to pilgrims without the ceremony of knocking, three or four clerks were at work as copyists. One of these, a little dry man, sitting by himself, who wore a stiff brown wig that looked as if it were made of gingerbread, rose to receive my aunt, and show us into Mr Spenlow's room.

"Mr Spenlow's in Court, ma'am," said the dry man; "it's an Arches day; but it's close by, and I'll send for him directly."

As we were left to look about us while Mr Spenlow was fetched, I availed myself of the opportunity. The furniture of the room was old-fashioned and dusty; and the green baize on the top of the writing-table had lost all its colour, and was as withered and pale as an old pauper. There were a great many bundles of papers on it, some endorsed as Allegations, and some (to my surprise) as Libels, and some as being in the Consistory Court, and some in the Arches Court, and some in the Prerogative Court, and some in the Admiralty Court, and some in the Delegates' Court; giving me occasion to wonder much, how many Courts there might be in the gross, and how long it would take to understand them all. Besides these, there were sundry immense manuscript Books of Evidence taken on affidavit, strongly bound, and tied together in massive sets, a set to each cause, as if every cause were a history in ten or twenty volumes. All this looked tolerably expensive, I thought, and gave me an agreeable notion of a proctor's business. I was casting my eyes with increasing complacency over these and many similar objects, when hasty footsteps were heard in the room outside, and Mr Spenlow, in a black gown trimmed with white fur, came hurrying in, taking off his hat as he came.

He was a little light-haired gentleman, with undeniable boots, and the stiffest of white cravats and shirt-collars. He was buttoned up, mighty trim and tight, and must have taken a great deal of pains with his whiskers, which were accurately curled. His gold watch-chain was so massive, that a fancy came across me, that he ought to have a sinewy golden arm, to draw it out with, like those which are put up over the goldbeaters' shops. He was got up with such care, and was so stiff, that he could hardly bend himself; being obliged, when he glanced at some papers on his desk, after sitting down in his chair, to move his whole body, from the bottom of his spine, like Punch.

I had previously been presented by my aunt, and had been courteously received. He now said:

"And so, Mr Copperfield, you think of entering into our profession? I casually mentioned to Miss Trotwood, when I had the pleasure of an interview with her the other day,"—with another inclination of his body—Punch again—"that there was a vacancy here. Miss Trotwood was good enough to mention that she had a nephew who was her peculiar care, and for whom she was seeking to provide genteelly in life. That nephew, I believe, I have now the pleasure of"—Punch again.

I bowed my acknowledgements, and said, my aunt had mentioned to me that there was that opening, and that I believed I should like it very much. That I was strongly inclined to like it, and had taken immediately to the proposal. That I could not absolutely pledge myself to like it, until I knew something more about it. That although it was little else than a matter of form, I presumed I should have an opportunity of trying how I liked it, before I bound myself to it irrevocably.

"Oh surely! surely!" said Mr Spenlow. "We always, in this house, propose a month— an initiatory month. I should be happy, myself, to propose two months—three—an indefinite period, in fact—but I have a partner. Mr Jorkins."

"And the premium, sir," I returned, "is a thousand pounds?"

"And the premium, Stamp included, is a thousand pounds," said Mr Spenlow. "As I have mentioned to Miss Trotwood, I am actuated by no mercenary considerations; few men are less so, I believe; but Mr Jorkins has his opinions on these subjects, and I am bound to respect Mr Jorkins's opinions. Mr Jorkins thinks a thousand pounds too little, in short."

"I suppose, sir," said I, still desiring to spare my aunt, "that it is not the custom here, if an articled clerk were particularly useful, and made himself a perfect master of his profession"—I could not help blushing, this looked so like praising myself—"I suppose it is not the custom, in the later years of his time, to allow him any—"

Mr Spenlow, by a great effort, just lifted his head far enough out of his cravat to shake it, and answered, anticipating the word "salary":

"No. I will not say what consideration I might give to that point myself, Mr Copperfield, if I were unfettered. Mr Jorkins is immovable."

I was quite dismayed by the idea of this terrible Jorkins. But I found out afterwards that he was a mild man of a heavy temperament, whose place in the business was to keep himself in the background, and be constantly exhibited by name as the most obdurate and ruthless of men. If a clerk wanted his salary raised, Mr Jorkins wouldn't listen to such a proposition. If a client were slow to settle his bill of costs, Mr Jorkins was resolved to have it paid; and however painful these things might be (and always were) to the feelings of Mr Spenlow, Mr Jorkins would have his bond. The heart and hand of the good angel Spenlow would have been always open, but for the restraining demon Jorkins. As I have grown older, I think I have had experience of some other houses doing business on the principle of Spenlow and Jorkins!

It was settled that I should begin my month's probation as soon as I pleased, and that my aunt need neither remain in town nor return at its expiration, as the articles of agreement, of which I was to be the subject, could easily be sent to her at home for her signature. When we had got so far, Mr Spenlow offered to take me into Court then and there, and show me what sort of place it was. As I was willing enough to know, we went out with this object, leaving my aunt behind; who would trust herself, she said, in no such place, and who, I think, regarded all Courts of Law as a sort of powder-mills that might blow up at any time.

Mr Spenlow conducted me through a paved courtyard formed of grave brick houses, which I inferred, from the Doctors' names upon the doors, to be the official abiding places of the learned advocates of whom Steerforth had told me; and into a large dull room, not unlike a chapel to my thinking, on the left hand. The upper part of this room was fenced off from the rest; and there, on the two sides of a raised platform of the horse-shoe form, sitting on easy old-fashioned dining-room chairs, were sundry gentlemen in red gowns and grey wigs, whom I found to be the Doctors aforesaid. Blinking over a little desk like a pulpit-desk, in the curve of the horse-shoe, was an old gentleman, whom, if I had seen him in an aviary, I should certainly have taken for an owl, but who, I learned, was the presiding judge. In the space within the horse-shoe, lower than these, that is to say, on about the level of the floor, were sundry other gentlemen, of Mr Spenlow's rank, and dressed like him in black gowns with white fur upon them, sitting at a long green table. Their cravats were in general stiff, I thought, and their looks haughty; but in this last respect I presently conceived I had done them an injustice, for when two or three of them had to rise and answer a question of the presiding dignitary, I never saw anything more sheepish. The public, represented by a boy with a comforter, and a shabby-genteel man secretly eating crumbs out of his coat pockets, was warming itself at a stove in the centre of the Court. The languid stillness of the place was only broken by the chirping of this fire and by the voice of one of the Doctors, who was wandering slowly through a perfect library of evidence, and stopping to put up, from time to time, at little roadside inns of argument on the journey. Altogether, I have never, on any occasion, made one at such a cosey, dosey, old-fashioned, time-forgotten, sleepy-headed little family-party in all my life; and I felt it would be quite a soothing opiate to belong to it in any character—except perhaps as a suitor.

Very well satisfied with the dreamy nature of this retreat, I informed Mr Spenlow that I had seen enough for that time, and we rejoined my aunt; in company with whom I presently departed from the Commons, feeling very young when I went out of Spenlow and Jorkins's, on account of the clerks poking one another with their pens to point me out.

We arrived at Lincoln's Inn Fields without any new adventures, except encountering an unlucky donkey in a costermonger's cart, who suggested painful associations to my aunt. We had another long talk about my plans, when we were safely housed; and as I knew she was anxious to get home, and, between fire, food, and pickpockets, could never be considered at her ease for half-an-hour in London, I urged her not to be uncomfortable on my account, but to leave me to take care of myself.

"I have not been here a week tomorrow, without considering that too, my dear," she returned. "There is a furnished little set of chambers to be let in the Adelphi, Trot, which ought to suit you to a marvel."

With this brief introduction, she produced from her pocket an advertisement, carefully cut out of a newspaper, setting forth that in Buckingham Street in the Adelphi there was to be let furnished, with a view of the river, a singularly desirable, and compact set of chambers, forming a genteel residence for a young gentleman, a member of one of the Inns of Court, or otherwise, with immediate possession. Terms moderate, and could be taken for a month only, if required.

"Why, this is the very thing, aunt!" said I, flushed with the possible dignity of living in chambers.

"Then come," replied my aunt, immediately resuming the bonnet she had a minute before laid aside. "We'll go and look at 'em."

Away we went. The advertisement directed us to apply to Mrs Crupp on the premises, and we rung the area bell, which we supposed to communicate with Mrs Crupp. It was not until we had rung three or four times that we could prevail on Mrs Crupp to communicate with us, but at last she appeared, being a stout lady with a flounce of flannel petticoat below a nankeen gown.

"Let us see these chambers of yours, if you please, ma'am," said my aunt.

"For this gentleman?" said Mrs Crupp, feeling in her pocket for her keys.

"Yes, for my nephew," said my aunt.

"And a sweet set they is for sich!" said Mrs Crupp.

So we went upstairs.

They were on the top of the house—a great point with my aunt, being near the fire-escape—and consisted of a little half-blind entry where you could see hardly anything, a little stone-blind pantry where you could see nothing at all, a sitting-room, and a bedroom. The furniture was rather faded, but quite good enough for me; and, sure enough, the river was outside the windows.

As I was delighted with the place, my aunt and Mrs Crupp withdrew into the pantry to discuss the terms, while I remained on the sitting-room sofa, hardly daring to think it possible that I could be destined to live in such a noble residence. After a single combat of some duration they returned, and I saw, to my joy, both in Mrs Crupp's countenance and in my aunt's, that the deed was done.

"Is it the last occupant's furniture?" inquired my aunt.

"Yes, it is, ma'am," said Mrs Crupp.

"What's become of him?" asked my aunt.

Mrs Crupp was taken with a troublesome cough, in the midst of which she articulated with much difficulty. "He was took ill here, ma'am, and—ugh! ugh! ugh! dear me!—and he died!"

"Hey! What did he die of?" asked my aunt.

"Well, ma'am, he died of drink," said Mrs Crupp, in confidence. "And smoke."

"Smoke? You don't mean chimneys?" said my aunt.

"No, ma'am," returned Mrs Crupp. "Cigars and pipes."

"That's not catching, Trot, at any rate," remarked my aunt, turning to me.

"No, indeed," said I.

In short, my aunt, seeing how enraptured I was with the premises, took them for a month, with leave to remain for twelve months when that time was out. Mrs Crupp was to find linen, and to cook; every other necessary was already provided; and Mrs Crupp expressly intimated that she should always yearn towards me as a son. I was to take possession the day after tomorrow, and Mrs Crupp said, thank Heaven she had now found summun she could care for!

On our way back, my aunt informed me how she confidently trusted that the life I was now to lead would make me firm and self-reliant, which was all I wanted. She repeated this several times next day, in the intervals of our arranging for the transmission of my clothes and books from Mr Wickfield's; relative to which, and to all my late holiday, I wrote a long letter to Agnes, of which my aunt took charge, as she was to leave on the succeeding day. Not to lengthen these particulars, I need only add, that she made a handsome provision for all my possible wants during my month of trial; that Steerforth, to my great disappointment and hers too, did not make his appearance before she went away; that I saw her safely seated in the Dover coach, exulting in the coming discomfiture of the vagrant donkeys, with Janet at her side; and that when the coach was gone, I turned my face to the Adelphi, pondering on the old days when I used to roam about its subterranean arches, and on the happy changes which had brought me to the surface.

Chapter XXIV

MY FIRST DISSIPATION

IT was a wonderfully fine thing to have that lofty castle to myself, and to feel, when I shut my outer door, like Robinson Crusoe, when he had got into his fortification, and pulled his ladder up after him. It was a wonderfully fine thing to walk about town with the key of my house in my pocket, and to know that I could ask any fellow to come home, and make quite sure of its being inconvenient to nobody, if it were not so to me. It was a wonderfully fine thing to let myself in and out, and to come and go without a word to anyone, and to ring Mrs Crupp up, gasping, from the depths of the earth, when I wanted her—and when she was disposed to come. All this, I say, was wonderfully fine; but I must say, too, that there were times when it was very dreary.

It was fine in the morning, particularly in the fine mornings. It looked a very fresh, free life, by daylight: still fresher, and more free, by sunlight. But as the day declined, the life seemed to go down too. I don't know how it was; it seldom looked well by candle-light. I wanted somebody to talk to, then. I missed Agnes. I found a tremendous blank, in the place of that smiling repository of my confidence. Mrs Crupp appeared to be a long way off. I thought about my predecessor, who had died of drink and smoke; and I could have wished he had been so good as to live, and not bother me with his decease.

After two days and nights, I felt as if I had lived there for a year, and yet I was not an hour older, but was quite as much tormented by my own youthfulness as ever.

Steerforth not yet appearing, which induced me to apprehend that he must be ill, I left the Commons early on the third day, and walked out to Highgate. Mrs Steerforth was very glad to see me, and said that he had gone away with one of his Oxford friends to see another who lived near St Albans, but that she expected him to return tomorrow. I was so fond of him, that I felt quite jealous of his Oxford friends.

As she pressed me to stay to dinner, I remained, and I believe we talked about nothing but him all day. I told her how much the people liked him at Yarmouth, and what a delightful companion he had been. Miss Dartle was full of hints and mysterious questions, but took a great interest in all our proceedings there, and said, "Was it really though?" and so forth, so often, that she got everything out of me she wanted to know.

Her appearance was exactly what I have described it, when I first saw her; but the society of the two ladies was so agreeable, and came so natural to me, that I felt myself falling a little in love with her. I could not help thinking, several times in the course of the evening, and particularly when I walked home at night, what delightful company she would be in Buckingham Street.

I was taking my coffee and roll in the morning, before going to the Commons—and I may observe in this place that it is surprising how much coffee Mrs Crupp used, and how weak it was, considering—when Steerforth himself walked in, to my unbounded joy.

"My dear Steerforth," cried I, "I began to think I should never see you again!"

"I was carried off, by force of arms," said Steerforth, "the very next morning after I got home. Why, Daisy, what a rare old bachelor you are here!"

I showed him over the establishment, not omitting the pantry, with no little pride, and he commended it highly. "I tell you what, old boy," he added, "I shall make quite a town-house of this place, unless you give me notice to quit."

This was a delightful hearing. I told him if he waited for that, he would have to wait till doomsday.

"But you shall have some breakfast!" said I, with my hand on the bell-rope, "and Mrs Crupp shall make you some fresh coffee, and I'll toast you some bacon in a bachelor's Dutch-oven that I have got here."

"No, no!" said Steerforth. "Don't ring! I can't! I am going to breakfast with one of these fellows who is at the Piazza Hotel, in Covent Garden."

"But you'll come back to dinner?" said I.

"I can't, upon my life. There's nothing I should like better, but I *must* remain with these two fellows. We are all three off together tomorrow morning."

"Then bring them here to dinner," I returned. "Do you think they would come?"

"Oh! they would come fast enough," said Steerforth; "but we should inconvenience you. You had better come and dine with us somewhere."

I would not by any means consent to this, for it occurred to me that I really ought to have a little house-warming, and that there never could be a better opportunity. I had a new pride in my rooms after his approval of them, and burned with a desire to develop their utmost resources. I therefore made him promise positively in the names of his two friends, and we appointed six o'clock as the dinner-hour.

When he was gone, I rang for Mrs Crupp, and acquainted her with my desperate design. Mrs Crupp said, in the first place, of course it was well known she couldn't be expected to wait, but she knew a handy young man, who she thought could be prevailed upon to do it, and whose terms would be five shillings, and what I pleased. I said, certainly we would have him. Next Mrs Crupp said it was clear she couldn't be in two places at once (which I felt to be reasonable), and that "a young gal" stationed in the pantry with a bedroom candle, there never to desist from washing plates, would be indispensable. I said, what would be the expense of this young female? and Mrs Crupp said she supposed eighteenpence would neither make me nor break me. I said I supposed not; and *that* was settled. Then Mrs Crupp said, Now about the dinner.

It was a remarkable instance of want of forethought on the part of the ironmonger who had made Mrs Crupp's kitchen fireplace, that it was capable of cooking nothing but chops and mashed potatoes. As to a fish-kittle, Mrs Crupp said, well! would I only come and look at the range? She couldn't say fairer than that. Would I come and look at it? As I should not have been much the wiser if I *had* looked at it, I declined, and said, "Never mind fish." But Mrs Crupp said, Don't say that; oysters was in, why not them? So *that* was settled. Mrs Crupp then said what she would recommend would be this. A pair of hot roast fowls—from the pastrycook's; a dish of stewed beef, with vegetables—from the pastrycook's; two little corner things, as a raised pie and a dish of kidneys—from the pastrycook's; a tart, and (if I liked) a shape of jelly—from the pastrycook's. This, Mrs Crupp said, would leave her at full liberty to concentrate her mind on the potatoes, and to serve up the cheese and celery as she could wish to see it done.

I acted on Mrs Crupp's opinion, and gave the order at the pastrycook's myself. Walking along the Strand, afterwards, and observing a hard mottled substance in the window of a ham and beef shop, which resembled marble, but was labelled "Mock Turtle," I went in and bought a slab of it, which I have since seen reason to believe would have sufficed for fifteen people. This preparation, Mrs Crupp, after some difficulty, consented to warm up; and it shrunk so much in a liquid state, that we found it what Steerforth called "rather a tight fit" for four.

These preparations happily completed, I bought a little dessert in Covent Garden Market, and gave a rather extensive order at a retail wine-merchant's in that vicinity. When I came home in the afternoon, and saw the bottles drawn up in a square on the pantry floor, they looked so numerous (though there were two missing, which made Mrs Crupp very uncomfortable), that I was absolutely frightened at them.

One of Steerforth's friends was named Grainger, and the other Markham. They were both very gay and lively fellows; Grainger, something older than Steerforth; Markham, youthful-looking, and I should say not more than twenty. I observed that the latter always spoke of himself indefinitely, as "a man," and seldom or never in the first person singular.

"A man might get on very well here, Mr Copperfield," said Markham—meaning himself.

"It's not a bad situation," said I, "and the rooms are really commodious."

"I hope you have both brought appetites with you?" said Steerforth.

"Upon my honour," returned Markham, "town seems to sharpen a man's appetite. A man is hungry all day long. A man is perpetually eating."

Being a little embarrassed at first, and feeling much too young to preside, I made Steerforth take the head of the table when dinner was announced, and seated myself opposite to him. Everything was very good; we did not spare the wine; and he exerted himself so brilliantly to make the thing pass off well, that there was no pause in our festivity. I was not quite such good company during dinner as I could have wished to be, for my chair was opposite the door, and my attention was distracted by observing that the handy young man went out of the room very often, and that his shadow always presented itself, immediately afterwards, on the wall of the entry, with a bottle at its mouth. The "young gal" likewise occasioned me some uneasiness: not so much by neglecting to wash the plates, as by breaking them. For being of an inquisitive disposition, and unable to confine herself (as her positive instructions were) to the pantry, she was constantly peering in at us, and constantly imagining herself detected; in which belief, she several times retired upon the plates (with which she had carefully paved the floor), and did a great deal of destruction.

These, however, were small drawbacks, and easily forgotten when the cloth was cleared, and the dessert put on the table; at which period of the entertainment the handy young man was discovered to be speechless. Giving him private directions to seek the society of Mrs Crupp, and to remove the "young gal" to the basement also, I abandoned myself to enjoyment.

I began, by being singularly cheerful and light-hearted; all sorts of half-forgotten things to talk about, came rushing into my mind, and made me hold forth in a most unwonted manner. I laughed heartily at my own jokes, and everybody else's; called Steerforth to order for not passing the wine; made several engagements to go to Oxford; announced that I meant to have a dinner-party exactly like that, once a week, until further notice; and madly took so much snuff out of Grainger's box, that I was obliged to go into the pantry, and have a private fit of sneezing ten minutes long.

I went on, by passing the wine faster and faster yet, and continually starting up with a corkscrew to open more wine, long before any was needed. I proposed Steerforth's health. I said he was my dearest friend, the protector of my boyhood, and the companion of my prime. I said I was delighted to propose his health. I said I owed him more obligations than I could ever repay, and held him in a higher admiration than I could ever express. I finished by saying, "I'll give you Steerforth! God bless him! Hurrah!" We gave him three times three, and another, and a good one to finish with. I broke my glass in going round the table to shake hands with him, and I said (in two words) "Steerforth— you'retheguidingstarofmyexist-ence."

I went on, by finding suddenly that somebody was in the middle of a song. Markham was the singer, and he sang "When the heart of a man is depressed with care". He said, when he had sung it, he would give us "Woman!" I took objection to that, and I couldn't allow it. I said it was not a respectful way of proposing the toast, and I would never permit that toast to be drunk in my house otherwise than as "The Ladies!" I was very high with him, mainly I think because I saw Steerforth and Grainger laughing at me—or at him—or at both of us. He said a man was not to be dictated to. I said a man *was*. He said a man was not to be insulted, then. I said he was right there—never under my roof, where the Lares were sacred, and the laws of hospitality paramount. He said it was no derogation from a man's dignity to confess that I was a devilish good fellow. I instantly proposed his health.

Somebody was smoking. We were all smoking. *I* was smoking, and trying to suppress a rising tendency to shudder. Steerforth had made a speech about me, in the course of which I had been affected almost to tears. I returned thanks, and hoped the present company would dine with me tomorrow, and the day after—each day at five o'clock, that we might enjoy the pleasures of conversation and society through a long evening. I felt called upon to propose an individual. I would give them my aunt. Miss Betsey Trotwood, the best of her sex!

Somebody was leaning out of my bedroom window, refreshing his forehead against the cool stone of the parapet, and feeling the air upon his face. It was myself. I was addressing myself as "Copperfield," and saying, "Why did you try to smoke? You might have known you couldn't do it." Now, somebody was unsteadily contemplating his features in the looking-glass. That was I too. I was very pale in the looking-glass; my eyes had a vacant appearance; and my hair—only my hair, nothing else—looked drunk.

Somebody said to me, "Let us go to the theatre, Copperfield!" There was no bedroom before me, but again the jingling table covered with glasses; the lamp; Grainger on my right hand, Markham on my left, and Steerforth opposite—all sitting in a mist, and a long way off. The theatre? To be sure. The very thing. Come along! But they must excuse me if I saw everybody out first, and turned the lamp off—in case of fire.

Owing to some confusion in the dark, the door was gone. I was feeling for it in the window-curtains, when Steerforth, laughing, took me by the arm and led me out. We went downstairs, one behind another. Near the bottom, somebody fell, and rolled down.

Somebody else said it was Copperfield. I was angry at that false report, until, finding myself on my back in the passage, I began to think there might be some foundation for it.

A very foggy night, with great rings round the lamps in the streets! There was an indistinct talk of its being wet. *I* considered it frosty. Steerforth dusted me under a lamp-post, and put my hat into shape, which somebody produced from somewhere in a most extraordinary manner, for I hadn't had it on before. Steerforth then said, "You are all right, Copperfield, are you not?" and I told him, "Neverberrer."

A man, sitting in a pigeon-hole-place, looked out of the fog, and took money from somebody, inquiring if I was one of the gentlemen paid for, and appearing rather doubtful (as I remember in the glimpse I had of him) whether to take the money for me or not. Shortly afterwards, we were very high up in a very hot theatre, looking down into a large pit, that seemed to me to smoke; the people with whom it was crammed were so indistinct. There was a great stage, too, looking very clean and smooth after the streets; and there were people upon it, talking about something or other, but not at all intelligibly. There was an abundance of bright lights, and there was music, and there were ladies down in the boxes, and I don't know what more. The whole building looked to me as if it were learning to swim; it conducted itself in such an unaccountable manner, when I tried to steady it.

On somebody's motion, we resolved to go downstairs to the dress-boxes, where the ladies were. A gentleman lounging, full dressed, on a sofa, with an opera-glass in his hand, passed before my view, and also my own figure at full length in a glass. Then I was being ushered into one of these boxes, and found myself saying something as I sat down, and people about me crying "Silence!" to somebody, and ladies casting indignant glances at me, and—what! yes!—Agnes, sitting on the seat before me, in the same box, with a lady and gentleman beside her, whom I didn't know. I see her face now, better than I did then, I dare say, with its indelible look of regret and wonder turned upon me.

"Agnes!" I said, thickly, "Lorblessmer! Agnes!"

"Hush! Pray!" she answered, I could not conceive why. "You disturb the company. Look at the stage!"

I tried, on her injunction, to fix it, and to hear something of what was going on there, but quite in vain. I looked at her again by and by, and saw her shrink into her corner, and put her gloved hand to her forehead.

"Agnes!" I said. "I'mafraidyou'renorwell."

"Yes, yes. Do not mind me, Trotwood," she returned. "Listen! Are you going away soon?"

"Amigoarawaysoo?" I repeated.

"Yes."

I had a stupid intention of replying that I was going to wait, to hand her downstairs. I suppose I expressed it, somehow; for after she had looked at me attentively for a little while, she appeared to understand, and replied in a low tone:

"I know you will do as I ask you, if I tell you I am very earnest in it. Go away now, Trotwood, for my sake, and ask your friends to take you home."

She had so far improved me, for the time, that though I was angry with her, I felt ashamed, and with a short "Goori!" (which I intended for "Good night!") got up and went away. They followed, and I stepped at once out of the box-door into my bedroom, where only Steerforth was with me, helping me to undress, and where I was by turns telling him that Agnes was my sister, and adjuring him to bring the corkscrew, that I might open another bottle of wine.

How somebody, lying in my bed, lay saying and doing all this over again, at cross purposes, in a feverish dream all night—the bed a rocking sea that was never still! How, as that somebody slowly settled down into myself, did I begin to parch, and feel as if my outer covering of skin were a hard board; my tongue the bottom of an empty kettle, furred with long service, and burning up over a slow fire; the palms of my hands, hot plates of metal which no ice could cool!

But the agony of mind, the remorse, and shame I felt when I became conscious next day! My horror of having committed a thousand offences I had forgotten, and which nothing could ever expiate—my recollection of that indelible look which Agnes had given me—the torturing impossibility of communicating with her, not knowing, Beast that I was, how she came to be in London, or where she stayed—my disgust of the very sight of the room where the revel had been held—my racking head—the smell of smoke, the sight of glasses, the impossibility of going out, or even getting up! Oh, what a day it was!

Oh, what an evening, when I sat down by my fire to a basin of mutton broth, dimpled all over with fat, and thought I was going the way of my predecessor, and should succeed to his dismal story as well as to his chambers, and had half a mind to rush express to Dover and reveal all! What an evening, when Mrs Crupp, coming in to take away the broth-basin, produced one kidney on a cheeseplate as the entire remains of yesterday's feast, and I was really inclined to fall upon her nankeen breast and say, in heartfelt penitence, "Oh, Mrs Crupp, Mrs Crupp, never mind the broken meats! I am very miserable!"—only that I doubted, even at that pass, if Mrs Crupp were quite the sort of woman to confide in!

Chapter XXV

GOOD AND BAD ANGELS

I WAS going out at my door on the morning after that deplorable day of headache, sickness, and repentance, with an odd confusion in my mind relative to the date of my dinner-party, as if a body of Titans had taken an enormous lever and pushed the day before yesterday some months back, when I saw a ticket-porter coming upstairs, with a letter in his hand. He was taking his time about his errand, then; but when he saw me on the top of the staircase, looking at him over the banisters, he swung into a trot, and came up panting as if he had run himself into a state of exhaustion.

"T. Copperfield, Esquire," said the ticket-porter, touching his hat with his little cane.

I could scarcely lay claim to the name: I was so disturbed by the conviction that the letter came from Agnes. However, I told him I was T. Copperfield, Esquire, and he believed it, and gave me the letter, which he said required an answer. I shut him out on the landing to wait for the answer, and went into my chambers again, in such a nervous state that I was fain to lay the letter down on my breakfast table, and familiarize myself with the outside of it a little, before I could resolve to break the seal.

I found, when I did open it, that it was a very kind note, containing no reference to my condition at the theatre. All it said was, "My dear Trotwood. I am staying at the house of papa's agent, Mr Waterbrook, in Ely Place, Holborn. Will you come and see me today, at any time you like to appoint? Ever yours affectionately, AGNES."

It took me such a long time to write an answer at all to my satisfaction, that I don't know what the ticket-porter can have thought, unless he thought I was learning to write. I must have written half-a-dozen answers at least. I began one, "How can I ever hope, my dear Agnes, to efface from your remembrance the disgusting impression"—there I didn't like it, and then I tore it up. I began another, "Shakespeare has observed, my dear Agnes, how strange it is that a man should put an enemy into his mouth"—that reminded me of Markham, and it got no farther. I even tried poetry. I began one note, in a six-syllable line, "Oh, do not remember"—but that associated itself with the fifth of November, and became an absurdity. After many attempts, I wrote, "My dear Agnes. Your letter is like you, and what could I say of it that would be higher praise than that? I will come at four o'clock. Affectionately and sorrowfully, T.C." With this missive (which I was in twenty minds at once about recalling, as soon as it was out of my hands), the ticket-porter at last departed.

If the day were half as tremendous to any other professional gentleman in Doctors' Commons as it was to me, I sincerely believe he made some expiation for his share in that rotten old ecclesiastical cheese. Although I left the office at half past three, and was prowling about the place of appointment within a few minutes afterwards, the appointed time was exceeded by a full quarter of an hour, according to the clock of St Andrew's, Holborn, before I could muster up sufficient desperation to pull the private bell-handle let into the left-hand door-post of Mr Waterbrook's house.

The professional business of Mr Waterbrook's establishment was done on the ground-floor, and the genteel business (of which there was a good deal) in the upper part of the building. I was shown into a pretty but rather close drawing-room, and there sat Agnes, netting a purse.

She looked so quiet and good, and reminded me so strongly of my airy fresh school days at Canterbury, and the sodden, smoky, stupid wretch I had been the other night, that, nobody being by, I yielded to my self-reproach and shame, and—in short, made a fool of myself. I cannot deny that I shed tears. To this hour I am undecided whether it was upon the whole the wisest thing I could have done, or the most ridiculous.

"If it had been anyone but you, Agnes," said I, turning away my head, "I should not have minded it half so much. But that it should have been you who saw me! I almost wish I had been dead, first."

She put her hand—its touch was like no other hand—upon my arm for a moment; and I felt so befriended and comforted, that I could not help moving it to my lips, and gratefully kissing it.

"Sit down," said Agnes, cheerfully. "Don't be unhappy, Trotwood. If you cannot confidently trust me, whom will you trust?"

"Ah, Agnes!" I returned. "You are my good Angel!"

She smiled rather sadly, I thought, and shook her head.

"Yes, Agnes, my good Angel! Always my good Angel!"

"If I were, indeed, Trotwood," she returned, "there is one thing that I should set my heart on very much."

I looked at her inquiringly; but already with a foreknowledge of her meaning.

"On warning you," said Agnes, with a steady glance, "against your bad Angel."

"My dear Agnes," I began, "if you mean Steerforth—"

"I do, Trotwood," she returned.

"Then, Agnes, you wrong him very much. He my bad Angel, or anyone's! He, anything but a guide, a support, and a friend to me! My dear Agnes! Now, is it not unjust, and unlike you, to judge him from what you saw of me the other night?"

"I do not judge him from what I saw of you the other night," she quietly replied.

"From what, then?"

"From many things—trifles in themselves, but they do not seem to me to be so, when they are put together. I judge him, partly from your account of him, Trotwood, and your character, and the influence he has over you."

There was always something in her modest voice that seemed to touch a chord within me, answering to that sound alone. It was always earnest; but when it was very earnest, as it was now, there was a thrill in it that quite subdued me. I sat looking at her as she cast her eyes down on her work; I sat seeming still to listen to her; and Steerforth, in spite of all my attachment to him, darkened in that tone.

"It is very bold in me," said Agnes, looking up again, "who have lived in such seclusion, and can know so little of the world, to give you my advice so confidently, or even to have this strong opinion. But I know in what it is engendered, Trotwood,—in how true a remembrance of our having grown up together, and in how true an interest in all relating to you. It is that which makes me bold. I am certain that what I say is right. I am quite sure it is. I feel as if it were someone else speaking to you, and not I, when I caution you that you have made a dangerous friend."

Again I looked at her, again I listened to her after she was silent, and again his image, though it was still fixed in my heart, darkened.

"I am not so unreasonable as to expect," said Agnes, resuming her usual tone, after a little while, "that you will, or that you can, at once, change any sentiment that has become a conviction to you; least of all a sentiment that is rooted in your trusting disposition. You ought not hastily to do that. I only ask you, Trotwood, if you ever think of me—I mean," with a quiet smile, for I was going to interrupt her, and she knew why, "as often as you think of me—to think of what I have said. Do you forgive me for all this?"

"I will forgive you, Agnes," I replied, "when you come to do Steerforth justice, and to like him as well as I do."

"Not until then?" said Agnes.

I saw a passing shadow on her face when I made this mention of him, but she returned my smile, and we were again as unreserved in our mutual confidence as of old.

"And when, Agnes," said I, "will you forgive me the other night?"

"When I recall it," said Agnes.

She would have dismissed the subject so, but I was too full of it to allow that, and insisted on telling her how it happened that I had disgraced myself, and what chain of accidental circumstances had had the theatre for its final link. It was a great relief to me to do this, and to enlarge on the obligation that I owed to Steerforth for his care of me when I was unable to take care of myself.

"You must not forget," said Agnes, calmly changing the conversation as soon as I had concluded, "that you are always to tell me, not only when you fall into trouble, but when you fall in love. Who has succeeded to Miss Larkins, Trotwood?"

"No one, Agnes."

"Someone, Trotwood," said Agnes, laughing, and holding up her finger.

"No, Agnes, upon my word! There is a lady, certainly, at Mrs Steerforth's house, who is very clever, and whom I like to talk to—Miss Dartle—but I don't adore her."

Agnes laughed again at her own penetration, and told me that if I were faithful to her in my confidence she thought she should keep a little register of my violent attachments, with the date, duration, and termination of each, like the table of the reigns of the kings and queens, in the History of England. Then she asked me if I had seen Uriah.

"Uriah Heep?" said I. "No. Is he in London?"

"He comes to the office downstairs, every day," returned Agnes. "He was in London a week before me. I am afraid on disagreeable business, Trotwood."

"On some business that makes you uneasy, Agnes, I see," said I. "What can that be?"

Agnes laid aside her work, and replied, folding her hands upon one another, and looking pensively at me out of those beautiful soft eyes of hers:

"I believe he is going to enter into partnership with papa."

"What? Uriah? That mean, fawning fellow, worm himself into such promotion!" I cried, indignantly. "Have you made no remonstrance about it, Agnes? Consider what a connexion it is likely to be. You must speak out. You must not allow your father to take such a mad step. You must prevent it, Agnes, while there's time."

Still looking at me, Agnes shook her head while I was speaking, with a faint smile at my warmth: and then replied:

"You remember our last conversation about papa? It was not long after that—not more than two or three days—when he gave me the first intimation of what I tell you. It was sad to see him struggling between his desire to represent it to me as a matter of choice on his part, and his inability to conceal that it was forced upon him. I felt very sorry."

"Forced upon him, Agnes! Who forces it upon him?"

"Uriah," she replied, after a moment's hesitation, "has made himself indispensable to papa. He is subtle and watchful. He has mastered papa's weaknesses, fostered them, and taken advantage of them, until—to say all that I mean in a word, Trotwood,—until papa is afraid of him."

There was more that she might have said; more that she knew, or that she suspected; I clearly saw. I could not give her pain by asking what it was, for I knew that she withheld it from me, to spare her father. It had long been going on to this, I was sensible: yes, I could not but feel, on the least reflection, that it had been going on to this for a long time. I remained silent.

"His ascendancy over papa," said Agnes, "is very great. He professes humility and gratitude—with truth, perhaps: I hope so—but his position is really one of power, and I fear he makes a hard use of his power."

I said he was a hound, which, at the moment, was a great satisfaction to me.

"At the time I speak of, as the time when papa spoke to me," pursued Agnes, "he had told papa that he was going away; that he was very sorry, and unwilling to leave, but that he had better prospects. Papa was very much depressed then, and more bowed down by care than ever you or I have seen him; but he seemed relieved by this expedient of the partnership, though at the same time he seemed hurt by it and ashamed of it."

"And how did you receive it, Agnes?"

"I did, Trotwood," she replied, "what I hope was right. Feeling sure that it was necessary for papa's peace that the sacrifice should be made, I entreated him to make it. I said it would lighten the load of his life—I hope it will!—and that it would give me increased opportunities of being his companion. Oh, Trotwood!" cried Agnes, putting her hands before her face, as her tears started on it, "I almost feel as if I had been papa's enemy, instead of his loving child. For I know how he has altered, in his devotion to me. I know how he has narrowed the circle of his sympathies and duties, in the concentration of his whole mind upon me. I know what a multitude of things he has shut out for my sake, and how his anxious thoughts of me have shadowed his life, and weakened his strength and energy, by turning them always upon one idea. If I could ever set this right! If I could ever work out his restoration, as I have so innocently been the cause of his decline!"

I had never before seen Agnes cry. I had seen tears in her eyes when I had brought new honours home from school, and I had seen them there when we last spoke about her father, and I had seen her turn her gentle head aside when we took leave of one another; but I had never seen her grieve like this. It made me so sorry that I could only say, in a foolish, helpless manner, "Pray, Agnes, don't! Don't, my dear sister!"

But Agnes was too superior to me in character and purpose, as I know well now, whatever I might know or not know then, to be long in need of my entreaties. The beautiful, calm manner, which makes her so different in my remembrance from every-body else, came back again, as if a cloud had passed from a serene sky.

"We are not likely to remain alone much longer," said Agnes, "and while I have an opportunity, let me earnestly entreat you, Trotwood, to be friendly to Uriah. Don't repel him. Don't resent (as I think you have a general disposition to do) what may be uncongenial to you in him. He may not deserve it, for we know no certain ill of him. In any case, think first of papa and me!"

Agnes had no time to say more, for the room door opened, and Mrs Waterbrook, who was a large lady—or who wore a large dress: I don't exactly know which, for I don't know which was dress and which was lady—came sailing in. I had a dim recollection of having seen her at the theatre, as if I had seen her in a pale magic lantern; but she appeared to remember me perfectly, and still to suspect me of being in a state of intoxication.

Finding by degrees, however, that I was sober, and (I hope) that I was a modest young gentleman, Mrs Waterbrook softened towards me considerably, and inquired, firstly, if I went much into the parks, and secondly, if I went much into society. On my replying to both these questions in the negative, it occurred to me that I fell again in her good opinion; but she concealed the fact gracefully, and invited me to dinner next day. I accepted the invitation, and took my leave, making a call on Uriah in the office as I went out, and leaving a card for him in his absence.

When I went to dinner next day, and on the street door being opened, plunged into a vapour-bath of haunch of mutton, I divined that I was not the only guest, for I immediately identified the ticket-porter in disguise, assisting the family servant, and waiting at the foot of the stairs to carry up my name. He looked, to the best of his ability, when he asked me for it confidentially, as if he had never seen me before; but well did I know him, and well did he know me. Conscience made cowards of us both.

I found Mr Waterbrook to be a middle-aged gentleman, with a short throat, and a good deal of shirt-collar, who only wanted a black nose to be the portrait of a pug-dog. He told me he was happy to have the honour of making my acquaintance; and when I had paid my homage to Mrs Waterbrook, presented me, with much ceremony, to a very awful lady in a black velvet dress, and a great black velvet hat, whom I remember as looking like a near relation of Hamlet's—say his aunt.

Mrs Henry Spiker was this lady's name; and her husband was there too: so cold a man, that his head, instead of being grey, seemed to be sprinkled with hoar-frost. Immense deference was shown to the Henry Spikers, male and female; which Agnes told me was on account of Mr Henry Spiker being solicitor to something or to somebody, I forget what or which, remotely connected with the Treasury.

I found Uriah Heep among the company, in a suit of black, and in deep humility. He told me, when I shook hands with him, that he was proud to be noticed by me, and that he really felt obliged to me for my condescension. I could have wished he had been less obliged to me, for he hovered about me in his gratitude all the rest of the evening; and whenever I said a word to Agnes, was sure, with his shadowless eyes and cadaverous face, to be looking gauntly down upon us from behind.

There were other guests—all iced for the occasion, as it struck me, like the wine. But there was one who attracted my attention before he came in, on account of my hearing him announced as Mr Traddles! My mind flew back to Salem House; and could it be Tommy, I thought, who used to draw the skeletons!

I looked for Mr Traddles with unusual interest. He was a sober, steady-looking young man of retiring manners, with a comic head of hair, and eyes that were rather wide open; and he got into an obscure corner so soon, that I had some difficulty in making him out. At length I had a good view of him, and either my vision deceived me, or it was the old unfortunate Tommy.

I made my way to Mr Waterbrook, and said, that I believed I had the pleasure of seeing an old schoolfellow there.

"Indeed!" said Mr Waterbrook, surprised. "You are too young to have been at school with Mr Henry Spiker?"

"Oh, I don't mean him!" I returned. "I mean the gentleman named Traddles."

"Oh! Aye, aye! Indeed!" said my host, with much diminished interest. "Possibly."

"If it's really the same person," said I, glancing towards him, "it was at a place called Salem House where we were together, and he was an excellent fellow."

"Oh yes. Traddles is a good fellow," returned my host nodding his head with an air of toleration. "Traddles is quite a good fellow."

"It's a curious coincidence," said I.

"It is really," returned my host, "quite a coincidence, that Traddles should be here at all: as Traddles was only invited this morning, when the place at table, intended to be occupied by Mrs Henry Spiker's brother, became vacant, in consequence of his indisposition. A very gentlemanly man, Mrs Henry Spiker's brother, Mr Copperfield."

I murmured an assent, which was full of feeling, considering that I knew nothing at all about him; and I inquired what Mr Traddles was by profession.

"Traddles," returned Mr Waterbrook, "is a young man reading for the bar. Yes. He is quite a good fellow—nobody's enemy but his own."

"Is he his own enemy?" said I, sorry to hear this.

"Well," returned Mr Waterbrook, pursing up his mouth, and playing with his watch-chain, in a comfortable, prosperous sort of way. "I should say he was one of those men who stand in their own light. Yes, I should say he would never, for example, be worth five hundred pound. Traddles was recommended to me by a professional friend. Oh yes. Yes. He has a kind of talent for drawing briefs, and stating a case in writing, plainly. I am able to throw something in Traddles's way, in the course of the year; something—for him—considerable. Oh yes. Yes."

I was much impressed by the extremely comfortable and satisfied manner in which Mr Waterbrook delivered himself of this little word "Yes," every now and then. There was wonderful expression in it. It completely conveyed the idea of a man who had been born, not to say with a silver spoon, but with a scaling-ladder, and had gone on mounting all the heights of life one after another, until now he looked, from the top of the fortifications, with the eye of a philosopher and a patron, on the people down in the trenches.

My reflections on this theme were still in progress when dinner was announced. Mr Waterbrook went down with Hamlet's aunt. Mr Henry Spiker took Mrs Waterbrook. Agnes, whom I should have liked to take myself, was given to a simpering fellow with weak legs. Uriah, Traddles, and I, as the junior part of the company, went down last, how we could. I was not so vexed at losing Agnes as I might have been, since it gave me an opportunity of making myself known to Traddles on the stairs, who greeted me with great fervour; while Uriah writhed with such obtrusive satisfaction and self-abasement, that I could gladly have pitched him over the banisters.

Traddles and I were separated at table, being billeted in two remote corners: he in the glare of a red velvet lady; I, in the gloom of Hamlet's aunt. The dinner was very long, and the conversation was about the Aristocracy—and Blood. Mrs Waterbrook repeatedly told us, that if she had a weakness, it was Blood.

It occurred to me several times that we should have got on better, if we had not been quite so genteel. We were so exceedingly genteel, that our scope was very limited. A Mr and Mrs Gulpidge were of the party, who had something to do at second-hand (at least, Mr Gulpidge had) with the law business of the Bank; and what with the Bank, and what with the Treasury, we were as exclusive as the Court Circular. To mend the matter, Hamlet's aunt had the family failing of indulging in soliloquy, and held forth in a desultory manner, by herself, on every topic that was introduced. These were few enough, to be sure; but as we always fell back upon Blood, she had as wide a field for abstract speculation as her nephew himself.

We might have been a party of Ogres, the conversation assumed such a sanguine complexion.

"I confess I am of Mrs Waterbrook's opinion," said Mr Waterbrook, with his wineglass at his eye. "Other things are all very well in their way, but give me Blood!"

"Oh! There is nothing," observed Hamlet's aunt, "so satisfactory to one! There is nothing that is so much one's *beau-ideal* of—of all that sort of thing, speaking generally. There are some low minds (not many, I am happy to believe, but there are *some*) that would prefer to do what *I* should call bow down before idols. Positively Idols! Before service, intellect, and so on. But these are intangible points. Blood is not so. We see Blood in a nose, and we know it. We meet with it in a chin, and we say, 'There it is! That's Blood!' It is an actual matter of fact. We point it out. It admits of no doubt."

The simpering fellow with the weak legs, who had taken Agnes down, stated the question more decisively yet, I thought.

"Oh, you know, deuce take it," said this gentleman, looking round the board with an imbecile smile, "we can't forego Blood, you know. We must have Blood, you know. Some young fellows, you know, may be a little behind their station, perhaps, in point of education and behaviour, and may go a little wrong, you know, and get themselves and other people into a variety of fixes—and all that—but deuce take it, it's delightful to reflect that they've got Blood in 'em! Myself, I'd rather at any time be knocked down by a man who had got Blood in him, than I'd be picked up by a man who hadn't!"

This sentiment, as compressing the general question into a nutshell, gave the utmost satisfaction, and brought the gentleman into great notice until the ladies retired. After that, I observed that Mr Gulpidge and Mr Henry Spiker, who had hitherto been very distant, entered into a defensive alliance against us, the common enemy, and exchanged a mysterious dialogue across the table for our defeat and overthrow.

"That affair of the first bond for four thousand five hundred pounds has not taken the course that was expected, Spiker," said Mr Gulpidge.

"Do you mean the D. of A's?" said Mr Spiker.

"The C. of B's!" said Mr Gulpidge.

Mr Spiker raised his eyebrows, and looked much concerned.

"When the question was referred to Lord—I needn't name him," said Mr Gulpidge, checking himself—

"I understand," said Mr Spiker, "N."

Mr Gulpidge darkly nodded—"was referred to him, his answer was, 'Money, or no release.' "

"Lord bless my soul!" cried Mr Spiker.

" 'Money, or no release,' " repeated Mr Gulpidge, firmly. "The next in reversion—you understand me?"

"K.," said Mr Spiker, with an ominous look.

"—K. then positively refused to sign. He was attended at Newmarket for that purpose, and he point-blank refused to do it."

Mr Spiker was so interested, that he became quite stony.

"So the matter rests at this hour," said Mr Gulpidge, throwing himself back in his chair. "Our friend Waterbrook will excuse me if I forbear to explain myself generally, on account of the magnitude of the interests involved."

Mr Waterbrook was only too happy, as it appeared to me, to have such interests, and such names, even hinted at, across his table. He assumed an expression of gloomy intelligence (though I am persuaded he knew no more about the discussion than I did), and highly approved of the discretion that had been observed. Mr Spiker, after the receipt of such a confidence, naturally desired to favour his friend with a confidence of his own; therefore the foregoing dialogue was succeeded by another, in which it was Mr Gulpidge's turn to be surprised, and that by another in which the surprise came round to Mr Spiker's turn again, and so on, turn and turn about. All this time we, the outsiders, remained oppressed by the tremendous interests involved in the conversation; and our host regarded us with pride, as the victims of a salutary awe and astonishment.

I was very glad indeed to get upstairs to Agnes, and to talk with her in a corner, and to introduce Traddles to her, who was shy, but agreeable, and the same good-natured creature still. As he was obliged to leave early, on account of going away next morning for a month, I had not nearly so much conversation with him as I could have wished; but we exchanged addresses, and promised ourselves the pleasure of another meeting when he should come back to town. He was greatly interested to hear that I knew Steerforth, and spoke of him with such warmth that I made him tell Agnes what he thought of him. But Agnes only looked at me the while, and very slightly shook her head when only I observed her.

As she was not among people with whom I believed she could be very much at home, I was almost glad to hear that she was going away within a few days, though I was sorry at the prospect of parting from her again so soon. This caused me to remain until all the company were gone. Conversing with her, and hearing her sing, was such a delightful reminder to me of my happy life in the grave old house she had made so beautiful, that I could have remained there half the night; but, having no excuse for staying any longer, when the lights of Mr Waterbrook's society were all snuffed out, I took my leave very much against my inclination. I felt then, more than ever, that she was my better Angel; and if I thought of her sweet face and placid smile, as though they had shone on me from some removed being, like an Angel, I hope I thought no harm.

I have said that the company were all gone; but I ought to have excepted Uriah, whom I don't include in that denomination, and who had never ceased to hover near us. He was close behind me when I went downstairs. He was close beside me, when I walked away from the house, slowly fitting his long skeleton fingers into the still longer fingers of a great Guy Fawkes pair of gloves.

It was in no disposition for Uriah's company, but in remembrance of the entreaty Agnes had made to me, that I asked him if he would come home to my rooms, and have some coffee.

"Oh, really, Master Copperfield," he rejoined—"I beg your pardon, Mister Copperfield, but the other comes so natural, I don't like that you should put a constraint upon yourself to ask a numble person like me to your ouse."

"There is no constraint in the case," said I. "Will you come?"

"I should like to, very much," replied Uriah, with a writhe.

"Well, then, come along!" said I.

I could not help being rather short with him, but he appeared not to mind it. We went the nearest way, without conversing much upon the road; and he was so humble in respect of those scarecrow gloves, that he was still putting them on, and seemed to have made no advance in that labour, when we got to my place.

I led him up the dark stairs, to prevent his knocking his head against anything, and really his damp cold hand felt so like a frog in mine, that I was tempted to drop it and run away. Agnes and hospitality prevailed, however, and I conducted him to my fireside. When I lighted my candles, he fell into meek transports with the room that was revealed to him; and when I heated the coffee in an unassuming block-tin vessel in which Mrs Crupp delighted to prepare it (chiefly, I believe, because it was not intended for the purpose, being a shaving-pot, and because there was a patent invention of great price mouldering away in the pantry), he professed so much emotion, that I could joyfully have scalded him.

"Oh, really, Master Copperfield,—I mean Mister Copperfield," said Uriah, "to see you waiting upon me is what I never could have expected! But, one way and another, so many things happen to me which I never could have expected, I am sure, in my umble station, that it seems to rain blessings on my ed. You have heard something, I des-say, of a change in my expectations, Master Copperfield—I should say, Mister Copperfield?"

As he sat on my sofa, with his long knees drawn up under his coffee-cup, his hat and gloves upon the ground close to him, his spoon going softly round and round, his shadowless red eyes, which looked as if they had scorched their lashes off, turned towards me without looking at me, the disagreeable dints I have formerly described in his nostrils coming and going with his breath, and a snaky undulation pervading his frame from his chin to his boots, I decided in my own mind that I disliked him intensely. It made me very uncomfortable to have him for a guest, for I was young then, and unused to disguise what I so strongly felt.

"You have heard something, I des-say, of a change in my expectations, Master Copperfield,—I should say, Mister Copperfield?" observed Uriah.

"Yes," said I, "something."

"Ah! I thought Miss Agnes would know of it!" he quietly returned. "I'm glad to find Miss Agnes knows of it. Oh, thank you, Master—Mister Copperfield!"

I could have thrown my bootjack at him (it lay ready on the rug), for having entrapped me into the disclosure of anything concerning Agnes, however immaterial. But I only drank my coffee.

"What a prophet you have shown yourself, Mister Copperfield!" pursued Uriah. "Dear me, what a prophet you have proved yourself to be! Don't you remember saying to me once, that perhaps I should be a partner in Mr Wickfield's business, and perhaps it might be Wickfield and Heep? *You* may not recollect it; but when a person is umble, Master Copperfield, a person treasures such things up!"

"I recollect talking about it," said I, "though I certainly did not think it very likely then."

"Oh! who *would* have thought it likely, Mister Copperfield!" returned Uriah, enthusiastically. "I am sure I didn't myself. I recollect saying with my own lips that I was much too umble. So I considered myself really and truly."

He sat, with that carved grin on his face, looking at the fire, as I looked at him.

"But the umblest persons, Master Copperfield," he presently resumed, "may be the instruments of good. I am glad to think I have been the instrument of good to Mr Wickfield, and that I may be more so. Oh what a worthy man he is, Mister Copperfield, but how imprudent he has been!"

"I am sorry to hear it," said I. I could not help adding, rather pointedly, "on all accounts."

"Decidedly so, Mister Copperfield," replied Uriah. "On all accounts. Miss Agnes's above all! You don't remember your own eloquent expressions, Master Copperfield; but *I* remember how you said one day that everybody must admire her, and how I thanked you for it! You have forgot that, I have no doubt, Master Copperfield?"

"No," said I, drily.

"Oh how glad I am you have not!" exclaimed Uriah. "To think that you should be the first to kindle the sparks of ambition in my umble breast, and that you've not forgot it! Oh!—Would you excuse me asking for a cup more coffee?"

Something in the emphasis he laid upon the kindling of those sparks, and something in the glance he directed at me as he said it, had made me start as if I had seen him illuminated by a blaze of light. Recalled by his request, preferred in quite another tone of voice, I did the honours of the shaving-pot; but I did them with an unsteadiness of hand, a sudden sense of being no match for him, and a perplexed suspicious anxiety as to what he might be going to say next, which I felt could not escape his observation.

He said nothing at all. He stirred his coffee round and round, he sipped it, he felt his chin softly with his grisly hand, he looked at the fire, he looked about the room, he gasped rather than smiled at me, he writhed and undulated about, in his deferential servility, he stirred and sipped again, but he left the renewal of the conversation to me.

"So, Mr Wickfield," said I, at last, "who is worth five hundred of you—or me"; for my life, I think, I could not have helped dividing that part of the sentence with an awkward jerk; "has been imprudent, has he, Mr Heep?"

"Oh, very imprudent indeed, Master Copperfield," returned Uriah, sighing modestly. "Oh, very much so! But I wish you'd call me Uriah, if you please. It's like old times."

"Well! Uriah," said I, bolting it out with some difficulty.

"Thank you," he returned, with fervour. "Thank you, Master Copperfield! It's like the blowing of old breezes or the ringing of old bellses to hear *you* say Uriah. I beg your pardon. Was I making any observation?"

"About Mr Wickfield," I suggested.

"Oh! Yes, truly," said Uriah. "Ah! Great imprudence, Master Copperfield. It's a topic that I wouldn't touch upon, to any soul but you. Even to you I can only touch upon it, and no more. If anyone else had been in my place during the last few years, by this time he would have had Mr Wickfield (oh, what a worthy man he is, Master Copperfield, too!) under his thumb. Un—der—his thumb," said Uriah, very slowly, as he stretched out his cruel-looking hand above my table, and pressed his own thumb upon it, until it shook, and shook the room.

If I had been obliged to look at him with his splay foot on Mr Wickfield's head, I think I could scarcely have hated him more.

"Oh, dear, yes, Master Copperfield," he proceeded, in a soft voice, most remarkably contrasting with the action of his thumb, which did not diminish its hard pressure in the least degree, "there's no doubt of it. There would have been loss, disgrace, I don't know what at all. Mr Wickfield knows it. I am the umble instrument of umbly serving him, and he puts me on an eminence I hardly could have hoped to reach. How thankful should I be!" With his face turned towards me, as he finished, but without looking at me, he took his crooked thumb off the spot where he had planted it, and slowly and thoughtfully scraped his lank jaw with it, as if he were shaving himself.

I recollect well how indignantly my heart beat, as I saw his crafty face, with the appropriately red light of the fire upon it, preparing for something else.

"Master Copperfield," he began—"but am I keeping you up?"

"You are not keeping me up. I generally go to bed late."

"Thank you, Master Copperfield! I have risen from my umble station since first you used to address me, it is true; but I am umble still. I hope I never shall be otherwise than umble. You will not think the worse of my umbleness, if I make a little confidence to you, Master Copperfield? Will you?"

"Oh no," said I, with an effort.

"Thank you!" He took out his pocket-handkerchief, and began wiping the palms of his hands. "Miss Agnes, Master Copperfield—"

"Well, Uriah?"

"Oh, how pleasant to be called Uriah, spontaneously!" he cried; and gave himself a jerk, like a convulsive fish. "You thought her looking very beautiful tonight, Master Copperfield?"

"I thought her looking as she always does: superior, in all respects, to everyone around her," I returned.

"Oh, thank you! It's so true!" he cried. "Oh, thank you very much for that!"

"Not at all," I said, loftily. "There is no reason why you should thank me."

"Why that, Master Copperfield," said Uriah, "is, in fact, the confidence that I am going to take the liberty of reposing. Umble as I am," he wiped his hands harder, and looked at them and at the fire by turns, "umble as my mother is, and lowly as our poor but honest roof has ever been, the image of Miss Agnes (I don't mind trusting you with my secret, Master Copperfield, for I have always overflowed towards you since the first moment I had the pleasure of beholding you in a pony-shay) has been in my breast for years. Oh, Master Copperfield, with what a pure affection do I love the ground my Agnes walks on!"

I believe I had a delirious idea of seizing the red-hot poker out of the fire, and running him through with it. It went from me with a shock, like a ball fired from a rifle: but the image of Agnes, outraged by so much as a thought of this red-headed animal's, remained in my mind when I looked at him, sitting all awry as if his mean soul griped his body, and made me giddy. He seemed to swell and grow before my eyes; the room seemed full of the echoes of his voice; and the strange feeling (to which, perhaps, no one is quite a stranger) that all this had occurred before, at some indefinite time, and that I knew what he was going to say next, took possession of me.

A timely observation of the sense of power that there was in his face, did more to bring back to my remembrance the entreaty of Agnes, in its full force, than any effort I could have made. I asked him, with a better appearance of composure than I could have thought possible a minute before, whether he had made his feelings known to Agnes.

"Oh no, Master Copperfield!" he returned; "oh dear, no! Not to anyone but you. You see I am only just emerging from my lowly station. I rest a good deal of hope on her observing how useful I am to her father (for I trust to be very useful to him indeed, Master Copperfield), and how I smooth the way for him, and keep him straight. She's so much attached to her father, Master Copperfield (oh, what a lovely thing it is in a daughter!), that I think she may come, on his account, to be kind to me."

I fathomed the depth of the rascal's whole scheme, and understood why he laid it bare.

"If you'll have the goodness to keep my secret, Master Copperfield," he pursued, "and not, in general, to go against me, I shall take it as a particular favour. You wouldn't wish to make unpleasantness. I know what a friendly heart you've got; but having only known me on my umble footing (on my umblest I should say, for I am very umble still), you might, unbeknown, go against me rather, with my Agnes. I call her mine, you see, Master Copperfield. There's a song that says, 'I'd crowns resign, to call her mine!' I hope to do it, one of these days."

Dear Agnes! So much too loving and too good for anyone that I could think of, was it possible that she was reserved to be the wife of such a wretch as this!

"There's no hurry at present, you know, Master Copperfield," Uriah proceeded, in his slimy way, as I sat gazing at him, with this thought in my mind. "My Agnes is very young still; and mother and me will have to work our way upwards, and make a good many new arrangements, before it would be quite convenient. So I shall have time gradually to make her familiar with my hopes, as opportunities offer. Oh, I'm so much obliged to you for this confidence! Oh, it's such a relief, you can't think, to know that you understand our situation, and are certain (as you wouldn't wish to make unpleasantness in the family) not to go against me!"

He took the hand which I dared not withhold, and having given it a damp squeeze, referred to his pale-faced watch.

"Dear me!" he said, "it's past one. The moments slip away so, in the confidence of old times, Master Copperfield, that it's almost half past one!"

I answered that I had thought it was later. Not that I had really thought so, but because my conversational powers were effectually scattered.

"Dear me!" he said, considering. "The ouse that I am stopping at—a sort of a private hotel and boarding ouse, Master Copperfield, near the New River ed—will have gone to bed these two hours."

"I am sorry," I returned, "that there is only one bed here, and that I—"

"Oh, don't think of mentioning beds, Master Copperfield!" he rejoined ecstatically, drawing up one leg. "But *would* you have any objections to my laying down before the fire?"

"If it comes to that," I said, "pray take my bed, and I'll lie down before the fire."

His repudiation of this offer was almost shrill enough, in the excess of its surprise and humility, to have penetrated to the ears of Mrs Crupp, then sleeping, I suppose, in a distant chamber, situated at about the level of low-water mark, soothed in her slumbers by the ticking of an incorrigible clock, to which she always referred me when we had any little difference on the score of punctuality, and which was never less than three-quarters of an hour too slow, and had always been put right in the morning by the best authorities. As no arguments I could urge, in my bewildered condition, had the least effect upon his modesty in inducing him to accept my bedroom, I was obliged to make the best arrangements I could, for his repose before the fire. The mattress of the sofa (which was a great deal too short for his lank figure), the sofa pillows, a blanket, the table-cover, a clean breakfast-cloth, and a great-coat, made him a bed and covering, for which he was more than thankful. Having lent him a night-cap, which he put on at once, and in which he made such an awful figure, that I have never worn one since, I left him to his rest.

I never shall forget that night. I never shall forget how I turned and tumbled; how I wearied myself with thinking about Agnes and this creature; how I considered what could I do, and what ought I to do; how I could come to no other conclusion than that the best course for her peace was to do nothing, and to keep to myself what I had heard. If I went to sleep for a few moments, the image of Agnes with her tender eyes, and of her father looking fondly on her, as I had so often seen him look, arose before me with appealing faces, and filled me with vague terrors. When I awoke, the recollection that Uriah was lying in the next room, sat heavy on me like a waking nightmare; and oppressed me with a leaden dread, as if I had had some meaner quality of devil for a lodger.

The poker got into my dozing thoughts besides, and wouldn't come out. I thought, between sleeping and waking, that it was still red hot, and I had snatched it out of the fire, and run him through the body. I was so haunted at last by the idea, though I knew there was nothing in it, that I stole into the next room to look at him. There I saw him, lying on his back, with his legs extending to I don't know where, gurglings taking place in his throat, stoppages in his nose, and his mouth open like a post-office. He was so much worse in reality than in my distempered fancy, that afterwards I was attracted to him in very repulsion, and could not help wandering in and out every half-hour or so, and taking another look at him. Still, the long, long night seemed heavy and hopeless as ever, and no promise of day was in the murky sky.

When I saw him going downstairs early in the morning (for, thank Heaven! he would not stay to breakfast), it appeared to me as if the night was going away in his person. When I went out to the Commons, I charged Mrs Crupp with particular directions to leave the windows open, that my sitting-room might be aired, and purged of his presence.

Chapter XXVI

I FALL INTO CAPTIVITY

I SAW no more of Uriah Heep, until the day when Agnes left town. I was at the coach office to take leave of her and see her go; and there was he, returning to Canterbury by the same conveyance. It was some small satisfaction to me to observe his spare, short-waisted, high-shouldered, mulberry-coloured great-coat perched up, in company with an umbrella like a small tent, on the edge of the back seat on the roof, while Agnes was, of course, inside; but what I underwent in my efforts to be friendly with him, while Agnes looked on, perhaps deserved that little recompense. At the coach window, as at the dinner-party, he hovered about us without a moment's intermission, like a great vulture: gorging himself on every syllable that I said to Agnes, or Agnes said to me.

In the state of trouble into which his disclosure by my fire had thrown me, I had thought very much of the words Agnes had used in reference to the partnership. "I did what I hope was right. Feeling sure that it was necessary for papa's peace that the sacrifice should be made, I entreated him to make it." A miserable foreboding that she would yield to, and sustain herself by, the same feeling in reference to any sacrifice for his sake, had oppressed me ever since. I knew how she loved him. I knew what the devotion of her nature was. I knew from her own lips that she regarded herself as the innocent cause of his errors, and as owing him a great debt she ardently desired to pay. I had no consolation in seeing how different she was from this detestable Rufus with the mulberry-coloured great-coat, for I felt that in the very difference between them, in the self-denial of her pure soul and the sordid baseness of his, the greatest danger lay. All this, doubtless, he knew thoroughly, and had, in his cunning, considered well.

Yet I was so certain that the prospect of such a sacrifice afar off, must destroy the happiness of Agnes; and I was so sure, from her manner, of its being unseen by her then, and having cast no shadow on her yet; that I could as soon have injured her, as given her any warning of what impended. Thus it was that we parted without explanation: she waving her hand and smiling farewell from the coach window; her evil genius writhing on the roof, as if he had her in his clutches and triumphed.

I could not get over this farewell glimpse of them for a long time. When Agnes wrote to tell me of her safe arrival, I was as miserable as when I saw her going away. Whenever I fell into a thoughtful state, this subject was sure to present itself, and all my uneasiness was sure to be redoubled. Hardly a night passed without my dreaming of it. It became a part of my life, and as inseparable from my life as my own head.

I had ample leisure to refine upon my uneasiness: for Steerforth was at Oxford, as he wrote to me, and when I was not at the Commons, I was very much alone. I believe I had at this time some lurking distrust of Steerforth. I wrote to him most affectionately in reply to his, but I think I was glad, upon the whole, that he could not come to London just then. I suspect the truth to be, that the influence of Agnes was upon me, undisturbed by the sight of him; and that it was the more powerful with me, because she had so large a share in my thoughts and interest.

In the meantime, days and weeks slipped away. I was articled to Spenlow and Jorkins. I had ninety pounds a year (exclusive of my house-rent and sundry collateral matters) from my aunt. My rooms were engaged for twelve months certain: and though I still found them dreary of an evening, and the evenings long, I could settle down into a state of equable low spirits, and resign myself to coffee; which I seem, on looking back, to have taken by the gallon at about this period of my existence. At about this time, too, I made three discoveries: first, that Mrs Crupp was a martyr to a curious disorder called "the spazzums," which was generally accompanied with inflammation of the nose, and required to be constantly treated with peppermint; secondly, that something peculiar in the temperature of my pantry, made the brandy-bottles burst; thirdly, that I was alone in the world, and much given to record that circumstance in fragments of English versification.

On the day when I was articled, no festivity took place, beyond my having sandwiches and sherry into the office for the clerks, and going alone to the theatre at night. I went to see *The Stranger* as a Doctors' Commons sort of play, and was so dreadfully cut up, that I hardly knew myself in my own glass when I got home. Mr Spenlow remarked, on this occasion, when we concluded our business, that he should have been happy to have seen me at his house at Norwood to celebrate our becoming connected, but for his domestic arrangements being in some disorder, on account of the expected return of his daughter from finishing her education at Paris. But, he intimated that when she came home he should hope to have the pleasure of entertaining me. I knew that he was a widower with one daughter, and expressed my acknowledgements.

Mr Spenlow was as good as his word. In a week or two, he referred to this engagement, and said, that if I would do him the favour to come down next Saturday, and stay till Monday, he would be extremely happy. Of course I said I *would* do him the favour; and he was to drive me down in his phaeton, and to bring me back.

When the day arrived, my very carpet-bag was an object of veneration to the stipendiary clerks, to whom the house at Norwood was a sacred mystery. One of them informed me that he had heard that Mr Spenlow ate entirely off plate and china; and another hinted at champagne being constantly on draught, after the usual custom of table-beer. The old clerk with the wig, whose name was Mr Tiffey, had been down on business several times in the course of his career, and had on each occasion penetrated to the breakfast-parlour. He described it as an apartment of the most sumptuous nature, and said that he had drunk brown East India sherry there, of a quality so precious as to make a man wink.

We had an adjourned cause in the Consistory that day—about excommunicating a baker who had been objecting in a vestry to a paving-rate—and as the evidence was just twice the length of Robinson Crusoe, according to a calculation I made, it was rather late in the day before we finished. However, we got him excommunicated for six weeks, and sentenced in no end of costs; and then the baker's proctor, and the judge, and the advocates on both sides (who were all nearly related), went out of town together, and Mr Spenlow and I drove away in the phaeton.

The phaeton was a very handsome affair; the horses arched their necks and lifted up their legs as if they knew they belonged to Doctors' Commons. There was a good deal of competition in the Commons on all points of display, and it turned out some very choice equipages then; though I always have considered, and always shall consider, that in my time the great article of competition there was starch: which I think was worn among the proctors to as great an extent as it is in the nature of man to bear.

We were very pleasant, going down, and Mr Spenlow gave me some hints in reference to my profession. He said it was the genteelest profession in the world, and must on no account be confounded with the profession of a solicitor: being quite another sort of thing, infinitely more exclusive, less mechanical, and more profitable. We took things much more easily in the Commons than they could be taken anywhere else, he observed, and that set us, as a privileged class, apart. He said it was impossible to conceal the disagreeable fact, that we were chiefly employed by solicitors; but he gave me to understand that they were an inferior race of men, universally looked down upon by all proctors of any pretensions.

I asked Mr Spenlow what he considered the best sort of professional business? He replied, that a good case of a disputed will, where there was a neat little estate of thirty or forty thousand pounds, was, perhaps, the best of all. In such a case, he said, not only were there very pretty pickings, in the way of arguments at every stage of the proceedings, and mountains upon mountains of evidence on interrogatory and counter-interrogatory (to say nothing of an appeal lying, first to the Delegates, and then to the Lords), but, the costs being pretty sure to come out of the estate at last, both sides went at it in a lively and spirited manner, and expense was no consideration. Then, he launched into a general eulogium on the Commons. What was to be particularly admired (he said) in the Commons, was its compactness. It was the most conveniently organized place in the world. It was the complete idea of snugness. It lay in a nut-shell. For example: You brought a divorce case, or a restitution case, into the Consistory. Very good. You tried it in the Consistory. You made a quiet little round game of it, among a family group, and you played it out at leisure. Suppose you were not satisfied with the Consistory, what did you do then? Why, you went into the Arches. What was the Arches? The same court, in the same room, with the same bar, and the same practitioners, but another judge, for there the Consistory judge could plead any court-day as an advocate. Well, you played your round game out again. Still you were not satisfied. Very good. What did you do then? Why, you went to the Delegates. Who were the Delegates? Why, the Ecclesiastical Delegates were the advocates without any business, who had looked on at the round game when it was playing in both courts, and had seen the cards shuffled, and cut, and played, and had talked to all the players about it, and now came fresh, as judges, to settle the matter to the satisfaction of everybody! Discontented people might talk of corruption in the Commons, closeness in the Commons, and the necessity of reforming the Commons, said Mr Spenlow solemnly, in conclusion; but when the price of wheat per bushel had been highest, the Commons had been busiest; and a man might lay his hand upon his heart, and say this to the whole world,—"Touch the Commons, and down comes the country!"

I listened to all this with attention; and though, I must say, I had my doubts whether the country was quite as much obliged to the Commons as Mr Spenlow made out, I respectfully deferred to his opinion. That about the price of wheat per bushel, I modestly felt was too much for my strength, and quite settled the question. I have never, to this hour, got the better of that bushel of wheat. It has re-appeared to annihilate me, all through my life, in connexion with all kinds of subjects. I don't know now, exactly, what it has to do with me, or what right it has to crush me, on an infinite variety of occasions; but whenever I see my old friend the bushel brought in by the head and shoulders (as he always is, I observe), I give up a subject for lost.

This is a digression. *I* was not the man to touch the Commons, and bring down the country. I submissively expressed, by my silence, my acquiescence in all I had heard from my superior in years and knowledge; and we talked about *The Stranger* and the Drama, and the pairs of horses, until we came to Mr Spenlow's gate.

There was a lovely garden to Mr Spenlow's house; and though that was not the best time of the year for seeing a garden, it was so beautifully kept, that I was quite enchanted. There was a charming lawn, there were clusters of trees, and there were perspective walks that I could just distinguish in the dark, arched over with trellis-work, on which shrubs and flowers grew in the growing season. "Here Miss Spenlow walks by herself," I thought. "Dear me!"

We went into the house, which was cheerfully lighted up, and into a hall where there were all sorts of hats, caps, great-coats, plaids, gloves, whips, and walking-sticks. "Where is Miss Dora?" said Mr Spenlow to the servant. "Dora!" I thought. "What a beautiful name!"

We turned into a room near at hand (I think it was the identical breakfast-room, made memorable by the brown East Indian sherry), and I heard a voice say, "Mr Copperfield, my daughter Dora, and my daughter Dora's confidential friend!" It was, no doubt, Mr Spenlow's voice, but I didn't know it, and I didn't care whose it was. All was

over in a moment. I had fulfilled my destiny. I was a captive and a slave. I loved Dora
Spenlow to distraction!

She was more than human to me. She was a Fairy, a Sylph, I don't know what she
was—anything that no one ever saw, and everything that everybody ever wanted. I was
swallowed up in an abyss of love in an instant. There was no pausing on the brink; no
looking down, or looking back; I was gone, headlong, before I had sense to say a word
to her.

"*I,*" observed a well-remembered voice, when I had bowed and murmured something, "have seen Mr Copperfield before."

The speaker was not Dora. No; the confidential friend, Miss Murdstone!

I don't think I was much astonished. To the best of my judgement, no capacity of
astonishment was left in me. There was nothing worth mentioning in the material world,
but Dora Spenlow, to be astonished about. I said, "How do you do, Miss Murdstone? I
hope you are well." She answered, "Very well." I said, "How is Mr Murdstone?" She
replied, "My brother is robust, I am obliged to you."

Mr Spenlow, who, I suppose, had been surprised to see us recognize each other,
then put in his word.

"I am glad to find," he said, "Copperfield, that you and Miss Murdstone are already
acquainted."

"Mr Copperfield and myself," said Miss Murdstone, with severe composure, "are
connexions. We were once slightly acquainted. It was in his childish days. Circumstances
have separated us since. I should not have known him."

I replied that I should have known her, anywhere. Which was true enough.

"Miss Murdstone has had the goodness," said Mr Spenlow to me, "to accept the
office—if I may so describe it—of my daughter Dora's confidential friend. My daughter
Dora having, unhappily, no mother, Miss Murdstone is obliging enough to become her
companion and protector."

A passing thought occurred to me that Miss Murdstone, like the pocket instrument
called a life-preserver, was not so much designed for purposes of protection as of assault.
But as I had none but passing thoughts for any subject save Dora, I glanced at her,
directly afterwards, and was thinking that I saw, in her prettily pettish manner, that she
was not very much inclined to be particularly confidential to her companion and protector, when a bell rang, which Mr Spenlow said was the first dinner-bell, and so carried
me off to dress.

The idea of dressing one's self, or doing anything in the way of action, in that state
of love, was a little too ridiculous. I could only sit down before my fire, biting the key
of my carpet-bag, and think of the captivating, girlish, bright-eyed lovely Dora. What a
form she had, what a face she had, what a graceful, variable, enchanting manner!

The bell rang again so soon that I made a mere scramble of my dressing, instead of
the careful operation I could have wished under the circumstances, and went downstairs. There was some company. Dora was talking to an old gentleman with a grey head.
Grey as he was—and a great-grandfather into the bargain, for he said so—I was madly
jealous of him.

What a state of mind I was in! I was jealous of everybody. I couldn't bear the idea
of anybody knowing Mr Spenlow better than I did. It was torturing to me to hear them
talk of occurrences in which I had had no share. When a most amiable person, with a
highly polished bald head, asked me across the dinner table, if that were the first

occasion of my seeing the grounds, I could have done anything to him that was savage and revengeful.

I don't remember who was there, except Dora. I have not the least idea what we had for dinner, besides Dora. My impression is, that I dined off Dora, entirely, and sent away half-a-dozen plates untouched. I sat next to her. I talked to her. She had the most delightful little voice, the gayest little laugh, the pleasantest and most fascinating little ways, that ever led a lost youth into hopeless slavery. She was rather diminutive altogether. So much the more precious, I thought.

When she went out of the room with Miss Murdstone (no other ladies were of the party), I fell into a reverie, only disturbed by the cruel apprehension that Miss Murdstone would disparage me to her. The amiable creature with the polished head told me a long story, which I think was about gardening. I think I heard him say, "my gardener," several times. I seemed to pay the deepest attention to him, but I was wandering in a garden of Eden all the while, with Dora.

My apprehensions of being disparaged to the object of my engrossing affection were revived when we went into the drawing-room, by the grim and distant aspect of Miss Murdstone. But I was relieved of them in an unexpected manner.

"David Copperfield," said Miss Murdstone, beckoning me aside into a window. "A word."

I confronted Miss Murdstone alone.

"David Copperfield," said Miss Murdstone, "I need not enlarge upon family circumstances. They are not a tempting subject."

"Far from it, ma'am," I returned.

"Far from it," assented Miss Murdstone. "I do not wish to revive the memory of past differences, or of past outrages. I have received outrages from a person—a female I am sorry to say, for the credit of my sex—who is not to be mentioned without scorn and disgust; and therefore I would rather not mention her."

I felt very fiery on my aunt's account; but I said it would certainly be better, if Miss Murdstone pleased, *not* to mention her. I could not hear her disrespectfully mentioned, I added, without expressing my opinion in a decided tone.

Miss Murdstone shut her eyes, and disdainfully inclined her head; then, slowly opening her eyes, resumed:

"David Copperfield, I shall not attempt to disguise the fact, that I formed an unfavourable opinion of you in your childhood. It may have been a mistaken one, or you may have ceased to justify it. That is not in question between us now. I belong to a family remarkable, I believe, for some firmness; and I am not the creature of circumstance or change. I may have my opinion of you. You may have your opinion of me."

I inclined my head, in my turn.

"But it is not necessary," said Miss Murdstone, "that these opinions should come into collision here. Under existing circumstances, it is as well on all accounts that they should not. As the chances of life have brought us together again, and may bring us together on other occasions, I would say, let us meet here as distant acquaintances. Family circumstances are a sufficient reason for our only meeting on that footing, and it is quite unnecessary that either of us should make the other the subject of remark. Do you approve of this?"

"Miss Murdstone," I returned, "I think you and Mr Murdstone used me very cruelly, and treated my mother with great unkindness. I shall always think so, as long as I live. But I quite agree in what you propose."

Miss Murdstone shut her eyes again, and bent her head. Then, just touching the back of my hand with the tips of her cold, stiff fingers, she walked away, arranging the little fetters on her wrists and round her neck; which seemed to be the same set, in exactly the same state, as when I had seen her last. These reminded me, in reference to Miss Murdstone's nature, of the fetters over a jail door; suggesting on the outside, to all beholders, what was to be expected within.

All I know of the rest of the evening is, that I heard the empress of my heart sing enchanted ballads in the French language, generally to the effect that, whatever was the matter, we ought always to dance, Ta ra la, Ta ra la! accompanying herself on a glorified instrument, resembling a guitar. That I was lost in blissful delirium. That I refused refreshment. That my soul recoiled from punch particularly. That when Miss Murdstone took her into custody and led her away, she smiled and gave me her delicious hand. That I caught a view of myself in a mirror, looking perfectly imbecile and idiotic. That I retired to bed in a most maudlin state of mind, and got up in a crisis of feeble infatuation.

It was a fine morning, and early, and I thought I would go and take a stroll down one of those wire-arched walks, and indulge my passion by dwelling on her image. On my way through the hall, I encountered her little dog, who was called Jip—short for Gipsy. I approached him tenderly, for I loved even him; but he showed his whole set of teeth, got under a chair expressly to snarl, and wouldn't hear of the least familiarity.

The garden was cool and solitary. I walked about, wondering what my feelings of happiness would be, if I could ever become engaged to this dear wonder. As to marriage, and fortune, and all that, I believe I was almost as innocently undesigning then, as when I loved little Em'ly. To be allowed to call her "Dora," to write to her, to dote upon and worship her, to have reason to think that when she was with other people she was yet mindful of me, seemed to me the summit of human ambition—I am sure it was the summit of mine. There is no doubt whatever that I was a lackadaisical young spooney; but there was a purity of heart in all this, that prevents my having quite a contemptuous recollection of it, let me laugh as I may.

I had not been walking long, when I turned a corner, and met her. I tingle again from head to foot as my recollection turns that corner, and my pen shakes in my hand.

"You—are—out early, Miss Spenlow," said I.

"It's so stupid at home," she replied, "and Miss Murdstone is so absurd! She talks such nonsense about its being necessary for the day to be aired, before I come out. Aired!" (She laughed, here, in the most melodious manner.) "On a Sunday morning, when I don't practise, I must do something. So I told papa last night I *must* come out. Besides, it's the brightest time of the whole day. Don't you think so?"

I hazarded a bold flight, and said (not without stammering) that it was very bright to me then, though it had been very dark to me a minute before.

"Do you mean a compliment?" said Dora, "or that the weather has really changed?"

I stammered worse than before, in replying that I meant no compliment, but the plain truth; though I was not aware of any change having taken place in the weather. It was in the state of my own feelings, I added bashfully: to clench the explanation.

I never saw such curls—how could I, for there never were such curls!—as those she shook out to hide her blushes. As to the straw hat and blue ribbons which was on the top of the curls, if I could only have hung it up in my room in Buckingham Street, what a priceless possession it would have been!

"You have just come home from Paris," said I.

"Yes," said she. "Have you ever been there?"

"No."

"Oh! I hope you'll go soon! You would like it so much!"

Traces of deep-seated anguish appeared in my countenance. That she should hope I would go, that she should think it possible I *could* go, was insupportable. I depreciated Paris; I depreciated France. I said I wouldn't leave England, under existing circumstances, for any earthly consideration. Nothing should induce me. In short, she was shaking the curls again, when the little dog came running along the walk to our relief.

He was mortally jealous of me, and persisted in barking at me. She took him up in her arms—oh my goodness!—and caressed him, but he persisted upon barking still. He wouldn't let me touch him, when I tried; and then she beat him. It increased my sufferings greatly to see the pats she gave him for punishment on the bridge of his blunt nose, while he winked his eyes, and licked her hand, and still growled within himself like a little double-bass. At length he was quiet—well he might be with her dimpled chin upon his head!—and we walked away to look at a greenhouse.

"You are not very intimate with Miss Murdstone, are you?" said Dora.—"My pet." (The two last words were to the dog. Oh, if they had only been to me!)

"No," I replied. "Not at all so."

"She is a tiresome creature," said Dora, pouting. "I can't think what papa can have been about, when he chose such a vexatious thing to be my companion. Who wants a protector? I am sure *I* don't want a protector. Jip can protect me a great deal better than Miss Murdstone,—can't you, Jip, dear?"

He only winked lazily, when she kissed his ball of a head.

"Papa calls her my confidential friend, but I am sure she is no such thing—is she, Jip? We are not going to confide in any such cross people, Jip and I. We mean to bestow our confidence where we like, and to find out our own friends, instead of having them found out for us—don't we, Jip?"

Jip made a comfortable noise, in answer, a little like a tea-kettle when it sings. As for me, every word was a new heap of fetters, riveted above the last.

"It is very hard, because we have not a kind Mama, that we are to have, instead, a sulky, gloomy old thing like Miss Murdstone, always following us about—isn't it, Jip? Never mind, Jip. We won't be confidential, and we'll make ourselves as happy as we can in spite of her, and we'll tease her, and not please her—won't we, Jip?"

If it had lasted any longer, I think I must have gone down on my knees on the gravel, with the probability before me of grazing them, and of being presently ejected from the premises besides. But, by good fortune the greenhouse was not far off, and these words brought us to it.

It contained quite a show of beautiful geraniums. We loitered along in front of them, and Dora often stopped to admire this one or that one, and I stopped to admire the same one, and Dora, laughing, held the dog up childishly, to smell the flowers; and if we were not all three in Fairyland, certainly *I* was. The scent of a geranium leaf, at this day, strikes me with a half comical half serious wonder as to what change has come over me in a moment; and then I see a straw hat and blue ribbons, and a quantity of curls, and a little black dog being held up, in two slender arms, against a bank of blossoms and bright leaves.

Miss Murdstone had been looking for us. She found us here; and presented her uncongenial cheek, the little wrinkles in it filled with hair powder, to Dora to be kissed. Then she took Dora's arm in hers, and marched us into breakfast as if it were a soldier's funeral.

How many cups of tea I drank, because Dora made it, I don't know. But, I perfectly remember that I sat swilling tea until my whole nervous system, if I had had any in those days, must have gone by the board. By and by we went to church. Miss Murdstone was between Dora and me in the pew; but I heard her sing, and the congregation vanished. A sermon was delivered—about Dora, of course—and I am afraid that is all I know of the service.

We had a quiet day. No company, a walk, a family dinner of four, and an evening of looking over books and pictures; Miss Murdstone with a homily before her, and her eye upon us, keeping guard vigilantly. Ah! little did Mr Spenlow imagine, when he sat opposite to me after dinner that day, with his pocket-handkerchief over his head, how fervently I was embracing him, in my fancy, as his son-in-law! Little did he think, when I took leave of him at night, that he had just given his full consent to my being engaged to Dora, and that I was invoking blessings on his head!

We departed early in the morning, for we had a Salvage case coming on in the Admiralty Court, requiring a rather accurate knowledge of the whole science of navigation, in which (as we couldn't be expected to know much about those matters in the Commons) the judge had entreated two old Trinity Masters, for charity's sake, to come and help him out. Dora was at the breakfast-table to make the tea again, however; and I had the melancholy pleasure of taking off my hat to her in the phaeton, as she stood on the door-step with Jip in her arms.

What the Admiralty was to me that day; what nonsense I made of our case in my mind, as I listened to it; how I saw "DORA' engraved upon the blade of the silver oar which they lay upon the table, as the emblem of that high jurisdiction; and how I felt when Mr Spenlow went home without me (I had had an insane hope that he might take me back again), as if I were a mariner myself, and the ship to which I belonged had sailed away and left me on a desert island; I shall make no fruitless effort to describe. If that sleepy old court could rouse itself, and present in any visible form the daydreams I have had in it about Dora, it would reveal my truth.

I don't mean the dreams that I dreamed on that day alone, but day after day, from week to week, and term to term. I went there, not to attend to what was going on, but to think about Dora. If ever I bestowed a thought upon the cases, as they dragged their slow length before me, it was only to wonder, in the matrimonial cases (remembering Dora), how it was that married people could ever be otherwise than happy; and, in the Prerogative cases, to consider, if the money in question had been left to me, what were the foremost steps I should immediately have taken in regard to Dora. Within the first week of my passion, I bought four sumptuous waistcoats—not for myself; I had no pride in them; for Dora—and took to wearing straw-coloured kid gloves in the streets, and laid the foundations of all the corns I have ever had. If the boots I wore at that period could only be produced and compared with the natural size of my feet, they would show what the state of my heart was, in a most affecting manner.

And yet, wretched cripple as I made myself by this act of homage to Dora, I walked miles upon miles daily in the hope of seeing her. Not only was I soon as well known on the Norwood Road as the postmen on that beat, but I pervaded London likewise. I walked about the streets where the best shops for ladies were, I haunted the Bazaar like an unquiet spirit, I fagged through the Park again and again, long after I was quite knocked up. Sometimes, at long intervals and on rare occasions, I saw her. Perhaps I saw her glove waved in a carriage window; perhaps I met her, walked with her and Miss Murdstone a little way, and spoke to her. In the latter case I was always very miserable afterwards, to think that I had said nothing to the purpose; or that she had no idea of the extent of my devotion, or that she cared nothing about me. I was always looking out, as may be supposed, for another invitation to Mr Spenlow's house. I was always being disappointed, for I got none.

Mrs Crupp must have been a woman of penetration; for when this attachment was but a few weeks old, and I had not had the courage to write more explicitly even to Agnes, than that I had been to Mr Spenlow's house, "whose family," I added, "consists of one daughter";—I say Mrs Crupp must have been a woman of penetration, for, even in that early stage, she found it out. She came up to me one evening, when I was very low, to ask (she being then afflicted with the disorder I have mentioned) if I could oblige her with a little tincture of cardamums mixed with rhubarb, and flavoured with seven drops of the essence of cloves, which was the best remedy for her complaint;—or, if I had not such a thing by me, with a little brandy, which was the next best. It was not, she remarked, so palatable to her, but it was the next best. As I had never even heard of the first remedy, and always had the second in the closet, I gave Mrs Crupp a glass of the second, which (that I might have no suspicion of its being devoted to any improper use) she began to take in my presence.

"Cheer up, sir," said Mrs Crupp. "I can't abear to see you so, sir: I'm a mother myself."

I did not quite perceive the application of this fact to *my*self, but I smiled on Mrs Crupp, as benignly as was in my power.

"Come, sir," said Mrs Crupp. "Excuse me. I know what it is, sir. There's a lady in the case."

"Mrs Crupp?" I returned, reddening.

"Oh, bless you! Keep a good heart, sir!" said Mrs Crupp, nodding encouragement. "Never say die, sir! If She don't smile upon you, there's a many as will. You are a young gentleman to *be* smiled on, Mr Copperfull, and you must learn your walue, sir."

Mrs Crupp always called me Mr Copperfull: firstly, no doubt, because it was not my name; and secondly, I am inclined to think, in some indistinct association with a washing-day.

"What makes you suppose there is any young lady in the case, Mrs Crupp?" said I.

"Mr Copperfull," said Mrs Crupp, with a great deal of feeling, "I'm a mother myself."

For some time Mrs Crupp could only lay her hand upon her nankeen bosom, and fortify herself against returning pain with sips of her medicine. At length she spoke again.

"When the present set were took for you by your dear aunt, Mr Copperfull," said Mrs Crupp, "my remark were, I had now found summun I could care for. 'Thank Ev'in!' were the expression, 'I have now found summun I can care for!'—You don't eat enough, sir, nor yet drink."

"Is that what you found your supposition on, Mrs Crupp?" said I.

"Sir," said Mrs Crupp, in a tone approaching to severity, "I've laundressed other young gentlemen besides yourself. A young gentleman may be over-careful of himself, or he may be under-careful of himself. He may brush his hair too regular, or too unregular. He may wear his boots much too large for him, or much too small. That is according as the young gentleman has his original character formed. But let him go to which extreme he may, sir, there's a young lady in both of 'em."

Mrs Crupp shook her head in such a determined manner, that I had not an inch of vantage-ground left.

"It was but the gentleman which died here before yourself," said Mrs Crupp, "that fell in love—with a barmaid—and had his waistcoats took in directly, though much swelled by drinking."

"Mrs Crupp," said I, "I must beg you not to connect the young lady in my case with a barmaid, or anything of that sort, if you please."

"Mr Copperfull," returned Mrs Crupp, "I'm a mother myself, and not likely. I ask your pardon, sir, if I intrude. I should never wish to intrude where I were not welcome. But you are a young gentleman, Mr Copperfull, and my advice to you is, to cheer up, sir, to keep a good heart, and to know your own walue. If you was to take to something, sir," said Mrs Crupp, "if you was to take to skittles, now, which is healthy, you might find it divert your mind, and do you good."

With these words, Mrs Crupp, affecting to be very careful of the brandy—which was all gone—thanked me with a majestic curtsey, and retired. As her figure disappeared into the gloom of the entry, this counsel certainly presented itself to my mind in the light of a slight liberty on Mrs Crupp's part; but, at the same time, I was content to receive it, in another point of view, as a word to the wise, and a warning in future to keep my secret better.

Chapter XXVII

TOMMY TRADDLES

IT may have been in consequence of Mrs Crupp's advice, and, perhaps, for no better reason than because there was a certain similarity in the sound of the word skittles and Traddles, that it came into my head, next day, to go and look after Traddles. The time he had mentioned was more than out, and he lived in a little street near the Veterinary College at Camden Town, which was principally tenanted, as one of our clerks who lived in that direction informed me, by gentlemen students, who bought live donkeys, and made experiments on those quadrupeds in their private apartments. Having obtained from this clerk a direction to the academic grove in question, I set out, the same afternoon, to visit my old school-fellow.

I found that the street was not as desirable a one as I could have wished it to be, for the sake of Traddles. The inhabitants appeared to have a propensity to throw any little trifles they were not in want of, into the road: which not only made it rank and sloppy, but untidy too, on account of the cabbage-leaves. The refuse was not wholly vegetable either, for I myself saw a shoe, a doubled-up saucepan, a black bonnet, and an umbrella, in various stages of decomposition, as I was looking out for the number I wanted.

The general air of the place reminded me forcibly of the days when I lived with Mr and Mrs Micawber. An indescribable character of faded gentility that attached to the house I sought, and made it unlike all the other houses in the street—though they were all built on one monotonous pattern, and looked like the early copies of a blundering boy who was learning to make houses, and had not yet got out of his cramped brick-and-mortar pothooks—reminded me still more of Mr and Mrs Micawber. Happening to arrive at the door as it was opened to the afternoon milkman, I was reminded of Mr and Mrs Micawber more forcibly yet.

"Now," said the milkman to a very youthful servant girl. "Has that there little bill of mine been heerd on?"

"Oh, master says he'll attend to it immediate," was the reply.

"Because," said the milkman, going on as if he had received no answer, and speaking, as I judged from his tone, rather for the edification of somebody within the house, than of the youthful servant—an impression which was strengthened by his manner of glaring down the passage—"because that there little bill has been running so long, that I begin to believe it's run away altogether, and never won't be heerd of. Now, I'm not a going to stand it, you know!" said the milkman, still throwing his voice into the house, and glaring down the passage.

As to his dealing in the mild article of milk, by the by, there never was a greater anomaly. His deportment would have been fierce in a butcher or a brandy-merchant.

The voice of the youthful servant became faint, but she seemed to me, from the action of her lips, again to murmur that it would be attended to immediate.

"I tell you what," said the milkman, looking hard at her for the first time, and taking her by the chin, "are you fond of milk?"

"Yes, I likes it," she replied.

"Good," said the milkman. "Then you won't have none tomorrow. D'ye hear? Not a fragment of milk you won't have tomorrow."

I thought she seemed, upon the whole, relieved by the prospect of having any today. The milkman, after shaking his head at her darkly, released her chin, and with anything rather than good-will opened his can, and deposited the usual quantity in the family jug. This done, he went away, muttering, and uttered the cry of his trade next door, in a vindictive shriek.

"Does Mr Traddles live here?" I then inquired.

A mysterious voice from the end of the passage replied "Yes." Upon which the youthful servant replied "Yes."

"Is he at home?" said I.

Again the mysterious voice replied in the affirmative, and again the servant echoed it. Upon this, I walked in, and in pursuance of the servant's directions walked upstairs; conscious, as I passed the back parlour-door, that I was surveyed by a mysterious eye, probably belonging to the mysterious voice.

When I got to the top of the stairs—the house was only a story high above the ground floor—Traddles was on the landing to meet me. He was delighted to see me, and gave me welcome, with great heartiness, to his little room. It was in the front of the house, and extremely neat, though sparely furnished. It was his only room, I saw; for there was a sofa-bedstead in it, and his blacking-brushes and blacking were among his books—on the top shelf, behind a dictionary. His table was covered with papers, and he was hard at work in an old coat. I looked at nothing, that I know of, but I saw everything, even to the prospect of a church upon his china ink-stand, as I sat down— and this, too, was a faculty confirmed in me in the old Micawber times. Various ingenious arrangements he had made, for the disguise of his chest of drawers, and the accommodation of his boots, his shaving-glass, and so forth, particularly impressed themselves upon me, as evidences of the same Traddles who used to make models of elephants' dens in writing-paper to put flies in; and to comfort himself under ill usage, with the memorable works of art I have so often mentioned.

In a corner of the room was something neatly covered up with a large white cloth. I could not make out what that was.

"Traddles," said I, shaking hands with him again, after I had sat down, "I am delighted to see you."

"I am delighted to see *you*, Copperfield," he returned. "I am very glad indeed to see you. It was because I was thoroughly glad to see you when we met in Ely Place, and was sure you were thoroughly glad to see me, that I gave you this address instead of my address at chambers."

"Oh! You have chambers?" said I.

"Why, I have the fourth of a room and a passage, and the fourth of a clerk," returned Traddles. "Three others and myself unite to have a set of chambers—to look business-like—and we quarter the clerk too. Half-a-crown a week he costs me."

His old simple character and good temper, and something of his old unlucky fortune also, I thought, smiled at me in the smile with which he made this explanation.

"It's not because I have the least pride, Copperfield, you understand," said Traddles, "that I don't usually give my address here. It's only on account of those who come to me, who might not like to come here. For myself, I am fighting my way on in the world against difficulties, and it would be ridiculous if I made a pretence of doing anything else."

"You are reading for the bar, Mr Waterbrook informed me?" said I.

"Why, yes," said Traddles, rubbing his hands slowly over one another. "I am reading for the bar. The fact is, I have just begun to keep my terms, after rather a long delay. It's some time since I was articled, but the payment of that hundred pounds was a great pull. A great pull!" said Traddles, with a wince, as if he had had a tooth out.

"Do you know what I can't help thinking of, Traddles, as I sit here looking at you?" I asked him.

"No," said he.

"That sky-blue suit you used to wear."

"Lord, to be sure!" cried Traddles, laughing. "Tight in the arms and legs, you know? Dear me! Well! Those were happy times, weren't they?"

"I think our schoolmaster might have made them happier, without doing any harm to any of us, I acknowledge," I returned.

"Perhaps he might," said Traddles. "But dear me, there was a good deal of fun going on. Do you remember the nights in the bedroom? When we used to have the suppers? And when you used to tell the stories? Ha, ha, ha! And do you remember when I got caned for crying about Mr Mell? Old Creakle! I should like to see him again, too!"

"He was a brute to you, Traddles," said I, indignantly; for his good humour made me feel as if I had seen him beaten but yesterday.

"Do you think so?" returned Traddles. "Really? Perhaps he was rather. But it's all over, a long while. Old Creakle!"

"You were brought up by an uncle, then?" said I.

"Of course I was!" said Traddles. "The one I was always going to write to. And always didn't, eh! Ha, ha, ha! Yes, I had an uncle then. He died soon after I left school."

"Indeed!"

"Yes. He was a retired—what do you call it!—draper—cloth-merchant—and had made me his heir. But he didn't like me when I grew up."

"Do you really mean that?" said I. He was so composed, that I fancied he must have some other meaning.

"Oh dear, yes, Copperfield! I mean it," replied Traddles. "It was an unfortunate thing, but he didn't like me at all. He said I wasn't at all what he expected, and so he married his housekeeper."

"And what did you do?" I asked.

"I didn't do anything in particular," said Traddles. "I lived with them, waiting to be put out in the world, until his gout unfortunately flew to his stomach—and so he died, and so she married a young man, and so I wasn't provided for."

"Did you get nothing, Traddles, after all?"

"Oh dear, yes!" said Traddles. "I got fifty pounds. I had never been brought up to any profession, and at first I was at a loss what to do for myself. However, I began, with the assistance of the son of a professional man, who had been to Salem House—Yawler, with his nose on one side. Do you recollect him?"

No. He had not been there with me; all the noses were straight in my day.

"It don't matter," said Traddles. "I began, by means of his assistance, to copy law writings. That didn't answer very well; and then I began to state cases for them, and make abstracts, and that sort of work. For I am a plodding kind of fellow, Copperfield, and had learnt the way of doing such things pithily. Well! That put it in my head to enter myself as a law student; and that ran away with all that was left of the fifty pounds. Yawler recommended me to one or two other offices, however—Mr Waterbrook's for one— and I got a good many jobs. I was fortunate enough, too, to become acquainted with a person in the publishing way, who was getting up an Encyclopaedia, and he set me to work; and, indeed" (glancing at his table), "I am at work for him at this minute. I am not a bad compiler, Copperfield," said Traddles, preserving the same air of cheerful confidence in all he said, "but I have no invention at all; not a particle. I suppose there never was a young man with less originality than I have."

As Traddles seemed to expect that I should assent to this as a matter of course, I nodded; and he went on, with the same sprightly patience—I can find no better expression—as before.

"So, by little and little, and not living high, I managed to scrape up the hundred pounds at last," said Traddles; "and thank Heaven that's paid—though it was—though it certainly was," said Traddles, wincing again as if he had had another tooth out, "a pull. I am living by the sort of work I have mentioned, still, and I hope, one of these days, to get connected with some newspaper: which would almost be the making of my fortune. Now, Copperfield, you are so exactly what you used to be, with that agreeable face, and it's so pleasant to see you, that I sha'n't conceal anything. Therefore you must know that I am engaged."

Engaged! Oh, Dora!

"She is a curate's daughter," said Traddles; "one of ten, down in Devonshire. Yes!" For he saw me glance, involuntarily, at the prospect on the inkstand. "That's the church! You come round here to the left, out of this gate," tracing his finger along the inkstand, "and exactly where I hold this pen, there stands the house—facing, you understand, towards the church."

The delight with which he entered into these particulars, did not fully present itself to me until afterwards; for my selfish thoughts were making a ground-plan of Mr Spenlow's house and garden at the same moment.

"She is such a dear girl!" said Traddles; "a little older than me, but the dearest girl! I told you I was going out of town? I have been down there. I walked there, and I walked back, and I had the most delightful time! I dare say ours is likely to be a rather long engagement, but our motto is 'Wait and hope!' We always say that. 'Wait and hope,' we always say. And she would wait, Copperfield, till she was sixty—any age you can mention—for me!"

Traddles rose from his chair, and, with a triumphant smile, put his hand upon the white cloth I had observed.

"However," he said, "it's not that we haven't made a beginning towards housekeeping. No, no; we have begun. We must get on by degrees, but we have begun. Here," drawing the cloth off with great pride and care, "are two pieces of furniture to commence with. This flower-pot and stand, she bought herself. You put that in a parlour window," said Traddles, falling a little back from it to survey it with the greater admiration, "with a plant in it, and—and there you are! This little round table with the marble top (it's two feet ten in circumference), *I* bought. You want to lay a book down, you know, or somebody comes to see you or your wife, and wants a place to stand a cup of tea upon, and—and there you are again!" said Traddles. "It's an admirable piece of workmanship—firm as a rock!"

I praised them both, highly, and Traddles replaced the covering as carefully as he had removed it.

"It's not a great deal towards the furnishing," said Traddles, "but it's something. The table-cloths, and pillow-cases, and articles of that kind, are what discourage me most, Copperfield. So does the ironmongery—candle-boxes, and gridirons, and that sort of necessaries—because those things tell, and mount up. However, 'wait and hope!' And I assure you she's the dearest girl!"

"I am quite certain of it," said I.

"In the meantime," said Traddles, coming back to his chair; "and this is the end of my proposing about myself, I get on as well as I can. I don't make much, but I don't spend much. In general, I board with the people downstairs, who are very agreeable people indeed. Both Mr and Mrs Micawber have seen a good deal of life, and are excellent company."

"My dear Traddles!" I quickly exclaimed. "What are you talking about?"

Traddles looked at me, as if he wondered what *I* was talking about.

"Mr and Mrs Micawber!" I repeated. "Why, I am intimately acquainted with them!"

An opportune double knock at the door, which I knew well from old experience in Windsor Terrace, and which nobody but Mr Micawber could ever have knocked at that door, resolved any doubt in my mind as to their being my old friends. I begged Traddles to ask his landlord to walk up. Traddles accordingly did so, over the banister; and Mr Micawber, not a bit changed—his tights, his stick, his shirt-collar, and his eye-glass, all the same as ever—came into the room with a genteel and youthful air.

"I beg your pardon, Mr Traddles," said Mr Micawber, with the old roll in his voice, as he checked himself in humming a soft tune. "I was not aware that there was any individual, alien to this tenement, in your sanctum."

Mr Micawber slightly bowed to me, and pulled up his shirt-collar.

"How do you do, Mr Micawber?" said I.

"Sir," said Mr Micawber, "you are exceedingly obliging. I am *in statu quo.*"

"And Mrs Micawber?" I pursued.

"Sir," said Mr Micawber, "she is also, thank God, *in statu quo.*"

"And the children, Mr Micawber?"

"Sir," said Mr Micawber, "I rejoice to reply that they are, likewise, in the enjoyment of salubrity."

All this time, Mr Micawber had not known me in the least, though he had stood face to face with me. But now, seeing me smile, he examined my features with more attention, fell back, cried, "Is it possible! Have I the pleasure of again beholding Copperfield!" and shook me by both hands with the utmost fervour.

"Good Heaven, Mr Traddles!" said Mr Micawber, "to think that I should find you acquainted with the friend of my youth, the companion of earlier days! My dear!" calling over the banisters to Mrs Micawber, while Traddles looked (with reason) not a little amazed at this description of me. "Here is a gentleman in Mr Traddles's apartment, whom he wishes to have the pleasure of presenting to you, my love!"

Mr Micawber immediately reappeared, and shook hands with me again.

"And how is our good friend the Doctor, Copperfield?" said Mr Micawber, "and all the circle at Canterbury?"

"I have none but good accounts of them," said I.

"I am most delighted to hear it," said Mr Micawber. "It was at Canterbury where we last met. Within the shadow, I may figuratively say, of that religious edifice immortalized by Chaucer, which was anciently the resort of Pilgrims from the remotest corners of—in short," said Mr Micawber, "in the immediate neighbourhood of the Cathedral."

I replied that it was. Mr Micawber continued talking as volubly as he could; but not, I thought, without showing, by some marks of concern in his countenance, that he was sensible of sounds in the next room, as of Mrs Micawber washing her hands, and hurriedly opening and shutting drawers that were uneasy in their action.

"You find us, Copperfield," said Mr Micawber, with one eye on Traddles, "at present established, on what may be designated as a small and unassuming scale; but, you are aware that I have, in the course of my career, surmounted difficulties, and conquered obstacles. You are no stranger to the fact, that there have been periods of my life, when it has been requisite that I should pause, until certain expected events should turn up; when it has been necessary that I should fall back, before making what I trust I shall not be accused of presumption in terming—a spring. The present is one of those momentous stages in the life of man. You find me, fallen back, *for* a spring; and I have every reason to believe that a vigorous leap will shortly be the result."

I was expressing my satisfaction, when Mrs Micawber came in; a little more slatternly than she used to be, or so she seemed now, to my unaccustomed eyes, but still with some preparation of herself for company, and with a pair of brown gloves on.

"My dear," said Mr Micawber, leading her towards me, "here is a gentleman of the name of Copperfield, who wishes to renew his acquaintance with you."

It would have been better, as it turned out, to have led gently up to this announcement, for Mrs Micawber, being in a delicate state of health, was overcome by it, and was taken so unwell, that Mr Micawber was obliged, in great trepidation, to run down to the water-butt in the backyard, and draw a basinful to lave her brow with. She presently revived, however, and was really pleased to see me. We had half-an-hour's talk, all together; and I asked her about the twins, who, she said, were "grown great creatures"; and after Master and Miss Micawber, whom she described as "absolute giants," but they were not produced on that occasion.

Mr Micawber was very anxious that I should stay to dinner. I should not have been averse to do so, but that I imagined I detected trouble, and calculation relative to the extent of the cold meat, in Mrs Micawber's eye. I therefore pleaded another engagement; and observing that Mrs Micawber's spirits were immediately lightened, I resisted all persuasion to forego it.

But I told Traddles, and Mr and Mrs Micawber, that before I could think of leaving, they must appoint a day when they would come and dine with me. The occupations to which Traddles stood pledged, rendered it necessary to fix a somewhat distant one; but an appointment was made for the purpose, that suited us all, and then I took my leave.

Mr Micawber, under pretence of showing me a nearer way than that by which I had come, accompanied me to the corner of the street; being anxious (he explained to me) to say a few words to an old friend, in confidence.

"My dear Copperfield," said Mr Micawber, "I need hardly tell you that to have beneath our roof, under existing circumstances, a mind like that which gleams—if I may be allowed the expression—which gleams—in your friend Traddles, is an unspeakable comfort. With a washerwoman, who exposes hard-bake for sale in her parlour-window, dwelling next door, and a Bow-street officer residing over the way, you may imagine that his society is a source of consolation to myself and to Mrs Micawber. I am at present, my dear Copperfield, engaged in the sale of corn upon commission. It is not an avocation of a remunerative description—in other words, it does *not* pay—and some temporary embarrassments of a pecuniary nature have been the consequence. I am, however, delighted to add that I have now an immediate prospect of something turning up (I am not at liberty to say in what direction), which I trust will enable me to provide, permanently, both for myself and for your friend Traddles, in whom I have an unaffected interest. You may, perhaps, be prepared to hear that Mrs Micawber is in a state of health which renders it not wholly improbable that an addition may be ultimately made to those pledges of affection which—in short, to the infantine group. Mrs Micawber's family have been so good as to express their dissatisfaction at this state of things. I have merely to observe, that I am not aware that it is any business of theirs, and that I repel that exhibition of feeling with scorn, and with defiance!"

Mr Micawber then shook hands with me again, and left me.

Chapter XXVIII

MR MICAWBER'S GAUNTLET

UNTIL the day arrived on which I was to entertain my newly-found old friends, I lived principally on Dora and coffee. In my love-lorn condition, my appetite languished; and I was glad of it, for I felt as though it would have been an act of perfidy towards Dora to have a natural relish for my dinner. The quantity of walking exercise I took, was not in this respect attended with its usual consequence, as the disappointment counteracted the fresh air. I have my doubts, too, founded on the acute experience acquired at this period of my life, whether a sound enjoyment of animal food can develop itself freely in any human subject who is always in torment from tight boots. I think the extremities require to be at peace before the stomach will conduct itself with vigour.

On the occasion of this domestic little party, I did not repeat my former extensive preparations. I merely provided a pair of soles, a small leg of mutton, and a pigeon-pie. Mrs Crupp broke out into rebellion on my first bashful hint in reference to the cooking of the fish and joint, and said, with a dignified sense of injury, "No! No, sir! You will not ask me sich a thing, for you are better acquainted with me than to suppose me capable of doing what I cannot do with ampial satisfaction to my own feelings!" But, in the end, a compromise was effected; and Mrs Crupp consented to achieve this feat, on condition that I dined from home for a fortnight afterwards.

And here I may remark, that what I underwent from Mrs Crupp, in consequence of the tyranny she established over me, was dreadful. I never was so much afraid of anyone. We made a compromise of everything. If I hesitated, she was taken with that wonderful disorder which was always lying in ambush in her system, ready, at the shortest notice, to prey upon her vitals. If I rang the bell impatiently, after half-a-dozen unavailing modest pulls, and she appeared at last—which was not by any means to be relied upon—she would appear with a reproachful aspect, sink breathless on a chair near the door, lay her hand upon her nankeen bosom, and become so ill, that I was glad, at any sacrifice of brandy or anything else, to get rid of her. If I objected to having my bed made at five o'clock in the afternoon—which I *do* still think an uncomfortable arrangement—one motion of her hand towards the same nankeen region of wounded sensibility was enough to make me falter an apology. In short, I would have done anything in an honourable way rather than give Mrs Crupp offence; and she was the terror of my life.

I bought a second-hand dumb-waiter for this dinner-party, in preference to re-engaging the handy young man; against whom I had conceived a prejudice, in consequence of meeting him in the Strand, one Sunday morning, in a waistcoat remarkably like one of mine, which had been missing since the former occasion. The "young gal" was re-engaged; but on the stipulation that she should only bring in the dishes, and then withdraw to the landing-place, beyond the outer door; where a habit of sniffing she had contracted would be lost upon the guests, and where her retiring on the plates would be a physical impossibility.

Having laid in the materials for a bowl of punch, to be compounded by Mr Micawber; having provided a bottle of lavender-water, two wax-candles, a paper of mixed pins, and a pincushion, to assist Mrs Micawber in her toilette at my dressing-table; having also caused the fire in my bedroom to be lighted for Mrs Micawber's convenience; and having laid the cloth with my own hands, I awaited the result with composure.

At the appointed time, my three visitors arrived together. Mr Micawber with more shirt-collar than usual, and a new ribbon to his eye-glass; Mrs Micawber with her cap in a whitey-brown paper parcel; Traddles carrying the parcel, and supporting Mrs Micawber on his arm. They were all delighted with my residence. When I conducted Mrs Micawber to my dressing-table, and she saw the scale on which it was prepared for her, she was in such raptures, that she called Mr Micawber to come in and look.

"My dear Copperfield," said Mr Micawber, "this is luxurious. This is a way of life which reminds me of the period when I was myself in a state of celibacy, and Mrs Micawber had not yet been solicited to plight her faith at the Hymeneal altar."

"He means, solicited by him, Mr Copperfield," said Mrs Micawber, archly. "He cannot answer for others."

"My dear," returned Mr Micawber with sudden seriousness, "I have no desire to answer for others. I am too well aware that when, in the inscrutable decrees of Fate, you were reserved for me, it is possible you may have been reserved for one, destined, after a protracted struggle, at length to fall a victim to pecuniary involvements of a complicated nature. I understand your allusion, my love. I regret it, but I can bear it."

"Micawber!" exclaimed Mrs Micawber, in tears. "Have I deserved this! I, who never have deserted you; who never *will* desert you, Micawber!"

"My love," said Mr Micawber, much affected, "you will forgive, and our old and tried friend Copperfield will, I am sure, forgive, the momentary laceration of a wounded spirit, made sensitive by a recent collision with the Minion of Power—in other words, with a ribald Turncock attached to the water-works—and will pity, not condemn, its excesses."

Mr Micawber then embraced Mrs Micawber, and pressed my hand; leaving me to infer from this broken allusion that his domestic supply of water had been cut off that afternoon, in consequence of default in the payment of the company's rates.

To divert his thoughts from this melancholy subject, I informed Mr Micawber that

I relied upon him for a bowl of punch, and led him to the lemons. His recent despondency, not to say despair, was gone in a moment. I never saw a man so thoroughly enjoy himself amid the fragrance of lemon-peel and sugar, the odour of burning rum, and the steam of boiling water, as Mr Micawber did that afternoon. It was wonderful to see his face shining at us out of a thin cloud of these delicate fumes, as he stirred, and mixed, and tasted, and looked as if he were making, instead of punch, a fortune for his family down to the latest posterity. As to Mrs Micawber, I don't know whether it was the effect of the cap, or the lavender-water, or the pins, or the fire, or the wax-candles, but she came out of my room, comparatively speaking, lovely. And the lark was never gayer than that excellent woman.

I suppose—I never ventured to inquire, but I suppose—that Mrs Crupp, after frying the soles, was taken ill. Because we broke down at that point. The leg of mutton came up very red within, and very pale without: besides having a foreign substance of a gritty nature sprinkled over it, as if it had had a fall into the ashes of that remarkable kitchen fireplace. But we were not in condition to judge of this fact from the appearance of the gravy, forasmuch as the "young gal" had dropped it all upon the stairs—where it remained, by the by, in a long train, until it was worn out. The pigeon-pie was not bad, but it was a delusive pie: the crust being like a disappointing head, phrenologically speaking: full of lumps and bumps, with nothing particular underneath. In short, the banquet was such a failure that I should have been quite unhappy—about the failure, I mean, for I was always unhappy about Dora—if I had not been relieved by the great good humour of my company, and by a bright suggestion from Mr Micawber.

"My dear friend Copperfield," said Mr Micawber, "accidents will occur in the best-regulated families; and in families not regulated by that pervading influence which sanctifies while it enhances the—a—I would say, in short, by the influence of Woman, in the lofty character of Wife, they may be expected with confidence, and must be borne with philosophy. If you will allow me to take the liberty of remarking that there are few comestibles better, in their way, than a Devil, and that I believe, with a little division of labour, we could accomplish a good one if the young person in attendance could produce a gridiron, I would put it to you, that this little misfortune may be easily repaired."

There was a gridiron in the pantry, on which my morning rasher of bacon was cooked. We had it in, in a twinkling, and immediately applied ourselves to carrying Mr Micawber's idea into effect. The division of labour to which he had referred was this:— Traddles cut the mutton into slices; Mr Micawber (who could do anything of this sort to perfection) covered them with pepper, mustard, salt, and cayenne; I put them on the gridiron, turned them with a fork, and took them off, under Mr Micawber's direction; and Mrs Micawber heated, and continually stirred, some mushroom ketchup in a little sauce-pan. When we had slices enough done to begin upon, we fell-to, with our sleeves still tucked up at the wrist, more slices sputtering and blazing on the fire, and our attention divided between the mutton on our plates, and the mutton then preparing.

What with the novelty of this cookery, the excellence of it, the bustle of it, the frequent starting up to look after it, the frequent sitting down to dispose of it as the crisp slices came off the gridiron hot and hot, the being so busy, so flushed with the fire, so amused, and in the midst of such a tempting noise and savour, we reduced the leg of mutton to the bone. My own appetite came back miraculously. I am ashamed to record it, but I really believe I forgot Dora for a little while. I am satisfied that Mr and Mrs Micawber could not have enjoyed the feast more, if they had sold a bed to provide it. Traddles laughed as heartily, almost the whole time, as he ate and worked. Indeed we all did, all at once; and I dare say there was never a greater success.

We were at the height of our enjoyment, and were all busily engaged, in our several departments, endeavouring to bring the last batch of slices to a state of perfection that should crown the feast, when I was aware of a strange presence in the room, and my eyes encountered those of the staid Littimer, standing hat in hand before me.

"What's the matter?" I involuntarily asked.

"I beg your pardon, sir, I was directed to come in. Is my master not here, sir?"

"No."

"Have you not seen him, sir?"

"No; don't you come from him?"

"Not immediately so, sir."

"Did he tell you you would find him here?"

"Not exactly so, sir. But I should think he might be here tomorrow, as he has not been here today."

"Is he coming up from Oxford?"

"I beg, sir," he returned respectfully, "that you will be seated, and allow me to do this." With which he took the fork from my unresisting hand, and bent over the gridiron, as if his whole attention were concentrated on it.

We should not have been much discomposed, I dare say, by the appearance of Steerforth himself, but we became in a moment the meekest of the meek before his respectable serving-man. Mr Micawber, humming a tune, to show that he was quite at ease, subsided into his chair, with the handle of a hastily concealed fork sticking out of the bosom of his coat, as if he had stabbed himself. Mrs Micawber put on her brown gloves, and assumed a genteel languor. Traddles ran his greasy hands through his hair, and stood it bolt upright, and stared in confusion on the table-cloth. As for me, I was a mere infant at the head of my own table; and hardly ventured to glance at the respectable phenomenon, who had come from Heaven knows where, to put my establishment to rights.

Meanwhile he took the mutton off the gridiron, and gravely handed it round. We all took some, but our appreciation of it was gone, and we merely made a show of eating it. As we severally pushed away our plates, he noiselessly removed them, and set on the cheese. He took that off, too, when it was done with; cleared the table; piled everything on the dumb-waiter; gave us our wine-glasses; and, of his own accord, wheeled the dumb-waiter into the pantry. All this was done in a perfect manner, and he never raised his eyes from what he was about. Yet his very elbows, when he had his back towards me, seemed to teem with the expression of his fixed opinion that I was extremely young.

"Can I do anything more, sir?"

I thanked him and said, No; but would he take no dinner himself?

"None, I am obliged to you, sir."

"Is Mr Steerforth coming from Oxford?"

"I beg your pardon, sir?"

"Is Mr Steerforth coming from Oxford?"

"I should imagine that he might be here tomorrow, sir. I rather thought he might have been here today, sir. The mistake is mine, no doubt, sir."

"If you should see him first—" said I.

"If you'll excuse me, sir, I don't think I shall see him first."

"In case you do," said I, "pray say that I am sorry he was not here today, as an old schoolfellow of his was here."

"Indeed, sir!" and he divided a bow between me and Traddles, with a glance at the latter.

He was moving softly to the door, when, in a forlorn hope of saying something naturally—which I never could, to this man—I said:

"Oh! Littimer!"

"Sir!"

"Did you remain long at Yarmouth, that time?"

"Not particularly so, sir."

"You saw the boat completed?"

"Yes, sir. I remained behind on purpose to see the boat completed."

"I know!" He raised his eyes to mine respectfully. "Mr Steerforth has not seen it yet, I suppose?"

"I really can't say, sir. I think—but I really can't say, sir. I wish you good night, sir."

He comprehended everybody present, in the respectful bow with which he followed these words, and disappeared. My visitors seemed to breathe more freely when he was gone; but my own relief was very great, for besides the constraint, arising from that extraordinary sense of being at a disadvantage which I always had in this man's presence, my conscience had embarrassed me with whispers that I had mistrusted his master, and I could not repress a vague uneasy dread that he might find it out. How was it, having so little in reality to conceal, that I always *did* feel as if this man were finding me out?

Mr Micawber roused me from this reflection, which was blended with a certain remorseful apprehension of seeing Steerforth himself, by bestowing many encomiums on the absent Littimer as a most respectable fellow, and a thoroughly admirable servant. Mr Micawber, I may remark, had taken his full share of the general bow, and had received it with infinite condescension.

"But punch, my dear Copperfield," said Mr Micawber, tasting it, "like time and tide, waits for no man. Ah! it is at the present moment in high flavour. My love, will you give me your opinion?"

Mrs Micawber pronounced it excellent.

"Then I will drink," said Mr Micawber, "if my friend Copperfield will permit me to take that social liberty, to the days when my friend Copperfield and myself were younger, and fought our way in the world side by side. I may say, of myself and Copperfield, in words we have sung together before now, that

We twa hae run about the braes
And pu'd the gowans fine

—in a figurative point of view—on several occasions. I am not exactly aware," said Mr Micawber, with the old roll in his voice, and the old indescribable air of saying something genteel, "what gowans may be, but I have no doubt that Copperfield and myself would frequently have taken a pull at them, if it had been feasible."

Mr Micawber, at the then present moment, took a pull at his punch. So we all did: Traddles evidently lost in wondering at what distant time Mr Micawber and I could have been comrades in the battle of the world.

"Ahem!" said Mr Micawber, clearing his throat, and warming with the punch and with the fire. "My dear, another glass?"

Mrs Micawber said it must be very little; but we couldn't allow that, so it was a glassful.

"As we are quite confidential here, Mr Copperfield," said Mrs Micawber, sipping her punch, "Mr Traddles being a part of our domesticity, I should much like to have your opinion on Mr Micawber's prospects. For corn," said Mrs Micawber argumentatively, "as I have repeatedly said to Mr Micawber, may be gentlemanly, but it is not remunerative. Commission to the extent of two and ninepence in a fortnight cannot, however limited our ideas, be considered remunerative."

We were all agreed upon that.

"Then," said Mrs Micawber, who prided herself on taking a clear view of things, and keeping Mr Micawber straight by her woman's wisdom, when he might otherwise go a little crooked, "then I ask myself this question. If corn is not to be relied upon, what is? Are coals to be relied upon? Not at all. We have turned our attention to that experiment, on the suggestion of my family, and we find it fallacious."

Mr Micawber, leaning back in his chair with his hands in his pockets, eyed us aside, and nodded his head, as much as to say that the case was very clearly put.

"The articles of corn and coals," said Mrs Micawber, still more argumentatively, "being equally out of the question, Mr Copperfield, I naturally look round the world, and say, 'What is there in which a person of Mr Micawber's talent is likely to succeed?' And I exclude the doing anything on commission, because commission is not a certainty. What is best suited to a person of Mr Micawber's peculiar temperament is, I am convinced, a certainty."

Traddles and I both expressed, by a feeling murmur, that this great discovery was no doubt true of Mr Micawber, and that it did him much credit.

"I will not conceal from you, my dear Mr Copperfield," said Mrs Micawber, "that I have long felt the Brewing business to be particularly adapted to Mr Micawber. Look at Barclay and Perkins! Look at Truman, Hanbury, and Buxton! It is on that extensive footing that Mr Micawber, I know from my own knowledge of him, is calculated to shine; and the profits, I am told, are e-NOR—mous! But if Mr Micawber cannot get into those firms—which decline to answer his letters, when he offers his services even in an inferior capacity—what is the use of dwelling upon that idea? None. I may have a conviction that Mr Micawber's manners—"

"Hem! Really, my dear," interposed Mr Micawber.

"My love, be silent," said Mrs Micawber, laying her brown glove on his hand. "I may have a conviction, Mr Copperfield, that Mr Micawber's manners peculiarly qualify him for the Banking business. I may argue within myself, that if I had a deposit at a banking-house, the manners of Mr Micawber, as representing that banking-house, would inspire confidence, and must extend the connexion. But if the various banking-houses refuse to avail themselves of Mr Micawber's abilities, or receive the offer of them with contumely, what is the use of dwelling upon *that* idea? None. As to originating a banking-business, I may know that there are members of my family who, if they chose to place their money in Mr Micawber's hands, might found an establishment of that description. But if they do *not* choose to place their money in Mr Micawber's hands—which they don't—what is the use of that? Again I contend that we are no farther advanced than we were before."

I shook my head, and said, "Not a bit." Traddles also shook his head, and said, "Not a bit."

"What do I deduce from this?" Mrs Micawber went on to say, still with the same air of putting a case lucidly. "What is the conclusion, my dear Mr Copperfield, to which I am irresistibly brought? Am I wrong in saying, it is clear that we must live?"

I answered "Not at all!" and Traddles answered "Not at all!" and I found myself afterwards sagely adding, alone, that a person must either live or die.

"Just so," returned Mrs Micawber, "It is precisely that. And the fact is, my dear Mr Copperfield, that we can *not* live without something widely different from existing circumstances shortly turning up. Now I am convinced, myself, and this I have pointed out to Mr Micawber several times of late, that things cannot be expected to turn up of themselves. We must, in a measure, assist to turn them up. I may be wrong, but I have formed that opinion."

Both Traddles and I applauded it highly.

"Very well," said Mrs Micawber. "Then what do I recommend? Here is Mr Micawber with a variety of qualifications—with great talent—"

"Really, my love," said Mr Micawber.

"Pray, my dear, allow me to conclude. Here is Mr Micawber, with a variety of qualifications, with great talent—*I* should say, with genius, but that may be the partiality of a wife—"

Traddles and I both murmured "No."

"And here is Mr Micawber without any suitable position or employment. Where does that responsibility rest? Clearly on society. Then I would make a fact so disgraceful known, and boldly challenge society to set it right. It appears to me, my dear Mr Copperfield," said Mrs Micawber, forcibly, "that what Mr Micawber has to do, is to throw down the gauntlet to society, and say, in effect, 'Show me who will take that up. Let the party immediately step forward.' "

I ventured to ask Mrs Micawber how this was to be done.

"By advertising," said Mrs Micawber—"in all the papers. It appears to me, that what Mr Micawber has to do, in justice to himself, in justice to his family, and I will even go so far as to say in justice to society, by which he has been hitherto overlooked, is to advertise in all the papers; to describe himself plainly as so-and-so, with such and such qualifications and to put it thus: *'Now* employ me, on remunerative terms, and address, post-paid, to *W.M.,* Post Office, Camden Town.' "

"This idea of Mrs Micawber's, my dear Copperfield," said Mr Micawber, making his shirt-collar meet in front of his chin, and glancing at me sideways, "is, in fact, the Leap to which I alluded, when I last had the pleasure of seeing you."

"Advertising is rather expensive," I remarked, dubiously.

"Exactly so!" said Mrs Micawber, preserving the same logical air. "Quite true, my dear Mr Copperfield! I have made the identical observation to Mr Micawber. It is for that reason especially, that I think Mr Micawber ought (as I have already said, in justice to himself, in justice to his family, and in justice to society) to raise a certain sum of money—on a bill."

Mr Micawber, leaning back in his chair, trifled with his eye-glass and cast his eyes up at the ceiling; but I thought him observant of Traddles, too, who was looking at the fire.

"If no member of my family," said Mrs Micawber, "is possessed of sufficient natural feeling to negotiate that bill—I believe there is a better business-term to express what I mean—"

Mr Micawber, with his eyes still cast up at the ceiling, suggested "Discount."

"To discount that bill," said Mrs Micawber, "then my opinion is, that Mr Micawber should go into the City, should take that bill into the Money Market, and should dispose of it for what he can get. If the individuals in the Money Market oblige Mr Micawber to sustain a great sacrifice, that is between themselves and their consciences. I view it, steadily, as an investment. I recommend Mr Micawber, my dear Mr Copperfield, to do the same; to regard it as an investment which is sure of return, and to make up his mind to *any* sacrifice."

I felt, but I am sure I don't know why, that this was self-denying and devoted in Mrs Micawber, and I uttered a murmur to that effect. Traddles, who took his tone from me, did likewise, still looking at the fire.

"I will not," said Mrs Micawber, finishing her punch, and gathering her scarf about her shoulders, preparatory to her withdrawal to my bedroom: "I will not protract these remarks on the subject of Mr Micawber's pecuniary affairs. At your fireside, my dear Mr Copperfield, and in the presence of Mr Traddles, who, though not so old a friend, is quite one of ourselves, I could not refrain from making you acquainted with the course *I* advise Mr Micawber to take. I feel that the time is arrived when Mr Micawber should exert himself and—I will add—assert himself, and it appears to me that these are the means. I am aware that I am merely a female, and that a masculine judgement is usually considered more competent to the discussion of such questions; still I must not forget that, when I lived at home with my papa and mama, my papa was in the habit of saying, 'Emma's form is fragile, but her grasp of a subject is inferior to none.' That my papa was too partial, I well know; but that he was an observer of character in some degree, my duty and my reason equally forbid me to doubt."

With these words, and resisting our entreaties that she would grace the remaining circulation of the punch with her presence, Mrs Micawber retired to my bedroom. And really I felt that she was a noble woman—the sort of woman who might have been a Roman matron, and done all manner of heroic things, in times of public trouble.

In the fervour of this impression, I congratulated Mr Micawber on the treasure he possessed. So did Traddles. Mr Micawber extended his hand to each of us in succession, and then covered his face with his pocket-handkerchief, which I think had more snuff upon it than he was aware of. He then returned to the punch, in the highest state of exhilaration.

He was full of eloquence. He gave us to understand that in our children we lived again, and that, under the pressure of pecuniary difficulties, any accession to their number was doubly welcome. He said that Mrs Micawber had latterly had her doubts on this point, but that he had dispelled them, and reassured her. As to her family, they were totally unworthy of her, and their sentiments were utterly indifferent to him, and they might—I quote his own expression—go to the Devil.

Mr Micawber then delivered a warm eulogy on Traddles. He said Traddles's was a character, to the steady virtues of which he (Mr Micawber) could lay no claim, but which, he thanked Heaven, he could admire. He feelingly alluded to the young lady, unknown, whom Traddles had honoured with his affection, and who had reciprocated that affection by honouring and blessing Traddles with *her* affection. Mr Micawber pledged her. So did I. Traddles thanked us both, by saying, with a simplicity and honesty I had sense enough to be quite charmed with, "I am very much obliged to you indeed. And I do assure you, she's the dearest girl!—"

Mr Micawber took an early opportunity, after that, of hinting, with the utmost delicacy and ceremony, at the state of *my* affections. Nothing but the serious assurance of his friend Copperfield to the contrary, he observed, could deprive him of the impression that his friend Copperfield loved and was beloved. After feeling very hot and uncomfortable for some time, and after a good deal of blushing, stammering, and denying, I said, having my glass in my hand, "Well! I would give them D.!" which so excited and gratified Mr Micawber, that he ran with a glass of punch into my bedroom, in order that Mrs Micawber might drink D., who drank it with enthusiasm, crying from within, in a shrill voice, "Hear, hear! My dear Mr Copperfield, I am delighted. Hear!" and tapping at the wall, by way of applause.

Our conversation, afterwards, took a more worldly turn; Mr Micawber telling us that he found Camden Town inconvenient, and that the first thing he contemplated doing, when the advertisement should have been the cause of something satisfactory turning up, was to move. He mentioned a terrace at the western end of Oxford Street, fronting Hyde Park, on which he had always had his eye, but which he did not expect to attain immediately, as it would require a large establishment. There would probably be an interval, he explained, in which he should content himself with the upper part of a house, over some respectable place of business—say in Piccadilly,—which would be a cheerful situation for Mrs Micawber; and where, by throwing out a bow-window, or carrying up the roof another story, or making some little alteration of that sort, they might live, comfortably and reputably, for a few years. Whatever was reserved for him, he expressly said, or wherever his abode might be, we might rely on this—there would always be a room for Traddles, and a knife and fork for me. We acknowledged his kindness; and he begged us to forgive his having launched into these practical and business-like details, and to excuse it as natural in one who was making entirely new arrangements in life.

Mrs Micawber, tapping at the wall again to know if tea were ready, broke up this particular phase of our friendly conversation. She made tea for us in a most agreeable manner; and, whenever I went near her, in handing about the tea-cups and bread-and-butter, asked me, in a whisper, whether D. was fair, or dark, or whether she was short, or tall: or something of that kind; which I think I liked. After tea, we discussed a variety of topics before the fire; and Mrs Micawber was good enough to sing us (in a small, thin, flat voice, which I remembered to have considered, when I first knew her, the very table-beer of acoustics) the favourite ballads of "The Dashing White Sergeant," and "Little Tafflin." For both of these songs Mrs Micawber had been famous when she lived at home with her papa and mama. Mr Micawber told us, that when he heard her sing the first one, on the first occasion of his seeing her beneath the parental roof, she had attracted his attention in an extraordinary degree; but that when it came to Little Tafflin, he had resolved to win that woman or perish in the attempt.

It was between ten and eleven o'clock when Mrs Micawber rose to replace her cap in the whitey-brown paper parcel, and to put on her bonnet. Mr Micawber took the opportunity of Traddles putting on his great-coat, to slip a letter into my hand, with a whispered request that I would read it at my leisure. I also took the opportunity of my holding a candle over the banisters to light them down, when Mr Micawber was going first, leading Mrs Micawber, and Traddles was following with the cap, to detain Traddles for a moment on the top of the stairs.

"Traddles," said I, "Mr Micawber don't mean any harm, poor fellow: but, if I were you, I wouldn't lend him anything."

"My dear Copperfield," returned Traddles, smiling, "I haven't got anything to lend."

"You have got a name, you know," said I.

"Oh! You call *that* something to lend?" returned Traddles, with a thoughtful look.

"Certainly."

"Oh!" said Traddles. "Yes, to be sure! I am very much obliged to you, Copperfield; but—I am afraid I have lent him that already."

"For the bill that is to be a certain investment?" I inquired.

"No," said Traddles. "Not for that one. This is the first I have heard of that one. I have been thinking that he will most likely propose that one, on the way home. Mine's another."

"I hope there will be nothing wrong about it," said I.

"I hope not," said Traddles. "I should think not, though, because he told me, only the other day, that it was provided for. That was Mr Micawber's expression, 'Provided for.' "

Mr Micawber looking up at this juncture to where we were standing, I had only time to repeat my caution. Traddles thanked me, and descended. But I was much afraid, when I observed the good-natured manner in which he went down with the cap in his hand, and gave Mrs Micawber his arm, that he would be carried into the Money Market neck and heels.

I returned to my fireside, and was musing, half gravely and half laughing, on the character of Mr Micawber and the old relations between us, when I heard a quick step ascending the stairs. At first, I thought it was Traddles coming back for something Mrs Micawber had left behind; but as the step approached, I knew it, and felt my heart beat high, and the blood rush to my face, for it was Steerforth's.

I was never unmindful of Agnes, and she never left that sanctuary in my thoughts— if I may call it so—where I had placed her from the first. But when he entered, and stood before me with his hand out, the darkness that had fallen on him changed to light, and I felt confounded and ashamed of having doubted one I loved so heartily. I loved her none the less; I thought of her as the same benignant, gentle angel in my life; I reproached myself, not her, with having done him an injury; and I would have made him any atonement if I had known what to make, and how to make it.

"Why, Daisy, old boy, dumb-foundered!" laughed Steerforth, shaking my hand heartily, and throwing it gaily away. "Have I detected you in another feast, you Sybarite! These Doctors' Commons fellows are the gayest men in town, I believe, and beat us sober Oxford people all to nothing!" His bright glance went merrily round the room, as he took the seat on the sofa opposite to me, which Mrs Micawber had recently vacated, and stirred the fire into a blaze.

"I was so surprised at first," said I, giving him welcome with all the cordiality I felt, "that I had hardly breath to greet you with, Steerforth."

"Well, the sight of me *is* good for sore eyes, as the Scotch say," replied Steerforth, "and so is the sight of you, Daisy, in full bloom. How are you, my Bacchanal?"

"I am very well," said I; "and not at all Bacchanalian tonight, though I confess to another party of three."

"All of whom I met in the street, talking loud in your praise," returned Steerforth. "Who's our friend in the tights?"

I gave him the best idea I could, in a few words, of Mr Micawber. He laughed heartily at my feeble portrait of that gentleman, and said he was a man to know, and he must know him.

"But who do you suppose our other friend is?" said I, in my turn.

"Heaven knows," said Steerforth. "Not a bore, I hope? I thought he looked a little like one."

"Traddles!" I replied, triumphantly.

"Who's he?" asked Steerforth, in his careless way.

"Don't you remember Traddles? Traddles in our room at Salem House?"

"Oh! That fellow!" said Steerforth, beating a lump of coal on the top of the fire, with the poker. "Is he as soft as ever? And where the deuce did you pick *him* up?"

I extolled Traddles in reply, as highly as I could; for I felt that Steerforth rather slighted him. Steerforth, dismissing the subject with a light nod, and a smile, and the remark that he would be glad to see the old fellow too, for he had always been an odd fish, inquired if I could give him anything to eat? During most of this short dialogue, when he had not been speaking in a wild vivacious manner, he had sat idly beating on the lump of coal with the poker. I observed that he did the same thing while I was getting out the remains of the pigeon-pie, and so forth.

"Why, Daisy, here's a supper for a king!" he exclaimed, starting out of his silence with a burst, and taking his seat at the table. "I shall do it justice, for I have come from Yarmouth."

"I thought you came from Oxford?" I returned.

"Not I," said Steerforth. "I have been seafaring—better employed."

"Littimer was here today, to inquire for you," I remarked, "and I understood him that you were at Oxford; though, now I think of it, he certainly did not say so."

"Littimer is a greater fool than I thought him, to have been inquiring for me at all," said Steerforth, jovially pouring out a glass of wine, and drinking to me. "As to understanding him, you are a cleverer fellow than most of us, Daisy, if you can do that."

"That's true, indeed," said I, moving my chair to the table. "So you have been at Yarmouth, Steerforth!" interested to know all about it. "Have you been there long?"

"No," he returned. "An *escapade* of a week or so."

"And how are they all? Of course, little Emily is not married yet?"

"Not yet. Going to be, I believe—in so many weeks, or months, or something or other. I have not seen much of 'em. By the by"; he laid down his knife and fork, which he had been using with great diligence, and began feeling in his pockets; "I have a letter for you."

"From whom?"

"Why, from your old nurse," he returned, taking some papers out of his breast pocket. " 'J. Steerforth, Esquire, debtor, to The Willing Mind'; that's not it. Patience, and we'll find it presently. Old what's-his-name's in a bad way, and it's about that, I believe."

"Barkis, do you mean?"

"Yes!" still feeling in his pockets, and looking over their contents: "it's all over with poor Barkis, I am afraid. I saw a little apothecary there—surgeon, or whatever he is—who brought your worship into the world. He was mighty learned about the case, to me; but the upshot of his opinion was, that the carrier was making his last journey rather fast.—Put your hand into the breast pocket of my great-coat on the chair yonder, and I think you'll find the letter. Is it there?"

"Here it is!" said I.

"That's right!"

It was from Peggotty, something less legible than usual, and brief. It informed me of her husband's hopeless state, and hinted at his being "a little nearer" than heretofore, and consequently more difficult to manage for his own comfort. It said nothing of her weariness and watching, and praised him highly. It was written with a plain, unaffected, homely piety that I knew to be genuine, and ended with "my duty to my ever darling"— meaning myself.

While I deciphered it, Steerforth continued to eat and drink.

"It's a bad job," he said, when I had done; "but the sun sets every day, and people die every minute, and we mustn't be scared by the common lot. If we failed to hold our own, because that equal foot at all men's doors was heard knocking somewhere, every object in this world would slip from us. No! Ride on! Rough-shod if need be, smooth-shod if that will do, but ride on! Ride on over all obstacles, and win the race!"

"And win what race?" said I.

"The race that one has started in," said he. "Ride on!"

I noticed, I remember, as he paused, looking at me with his handsome head a little thrown back, and his glass raised in his hand, that, though the freshness of the sea-wind was on his face, and it was ruddy, there were traces in it, made since I last saw it, as if he had applied himself to some habitual strain of the fervent energy which, when roused, was so passionately roused within him. I had it in my thoughts to remonstrate with him upon his desperate way of pursuing any fancy that he took—such as this buffeting of rough seas, and braving of hard weather, for example—when my mind glanced off to the immediate subject of our conversation again, and pursued that instead.

"I tell you what, Steerforth," said I, "if your high spirits will listen to me—"

"They are potent spirits, and will do whatever you like," he answered, moving from the table to the fireside again.

"Then I tell you what, Steerforth. I think I will go down and see my old nurse. It is not that I can do her any good, or render her any real service; but she is so attached to me that my visit will have as much effect on her, as if I could do both. She will take it so kindly that it will be a comfort and support to her. It is no great effort to make, I am sure, for such a friend as she has been to me. Wouldn't you go a day's journey, if you were in my place?"

His face was thoughtful, and he sat considering a little before he answered, in a low voice, "Well! Go. You can do no harm."

"You have just come back," said I, "and it would be in vain to ask you to go with me?"

"Quite," he returned. "I am for Highgate tonight. I have not seen my mother this long time, and it lies upon my conscience, for it's something to be loved as she loves her prodigal son.—Bah! Nonsense!—You mean to go tomorrow, I suppose?" he said, holding me out at arm's length, with a hand on each of my shoulders.

"Yes, I think so."

"Well, then, don't go till next day. I wanted you to come and stay a few days with us. Here I am, on purpose to bid you, and you fly off to Yarmouth!"

"You are a nice fellow to talk of flying off, Steerforth, who are always running wild on some unknown expedition or other!"

He looked at me for a moment without speaking, and then rejoined, still holding me as before, and giving me a shake:

"Come! Say the next day, and pass as much of tomorrow as you can with us! Who knows when we may meet again, else? Come! Say the next day! I want you to stand between Rosa Dartle and me, and keep us asunder."

"Would you love each other too much, without me?"

"Yes; or hate," laughed Steerforth; "no matter which. Come! Say the next day!"

I said the next day; and he put on his great-coat and lighted his cigar, and set off to walk home. Finding him in this intention, I put on my own great-coat (but did not light my own cigar, having had enough of that for one while) and walked with him as far as the open road: a dull road, then, at night. He was in great spirits all the way; and when we parted, and I looked after him going so gallantly and airily homeward, I thought of his saying, "Ride on over all obstacles, and win the race!" and wished, for the first time, that he had some worthy race to run.

I was undressing in my own room, when Mr Micawber's letter tumbled on the floor. Thus reminded of it, I broke the seal and read as follows. It was dated an hour and a half before dinner. I am not sure whether I have mentioned that, when Mr Micawber was at any particularly desperate crisis, he used a sort of legal phraseology: which he seemed to think equivalent to winding up his affairs.

> "SIR—for I dare not say my dear Copperfield,
>
> "It is expedient that I should inform you that the undersigned is Crushed. Some flickering efforts to spare you the premature knowledge of his calamitous position, you may observe in him this day; but hope has sunk beneath the horizon, and the undersigned is Crushed.
>
> "The present communication is penned within the personal range (I cannot call it the society) of an individual, in a state closely bordering on intoxication, employed by a broker. That individual is in legal possession of the premises, under a distress for rent. His inventory includes, not only the chattels and effects of every description belonging to the undersigned, as yearly tenant of this habitation, but also those appertaining to Mr Thomas Traddles, lodger, a member of the Honourable Society of the Inner Temple.
>
> "If any drop of gloom were wanting in the overflowing cup, which is now 'commended' (in the language of an immortal Writer) to the lips of the undersigned, it would be found in the fact, that a friendly acceptance granted to the undersigned, by the before-mentioned Mr Thomas Traddles, for the sum of £23 4s.. 9½d. is over due, and is NOT provided for. Also, in the fact that the living responsibilities clinging to the undersigned will, in the course of nature, be increased by the sum of one more helpless victim; whose miserable appearance may be looked for—in round numbers—at the expiration of a period not exceeding six lunar months from the present date.
>
> "After premising thus much, it would be a work of supererogation to add, that dust and ashes are for ever scattered
>
> > "On
> > "The
> > "Head
> > "Of
> > "WILKINS MICAWBER."

Poor Traddles! I knew enough of Mr Micawber by this time, to foresee that *he* might be expected to recover the blow; but my night's rest was sorely distressed by thoughts of Traddles, and of the curate's daughter, who was one of ten, down in Devonshire, and who was such a dear girl, and who would wait for Traddles (ominous praise!) until she was sixty, or any age that could be mentioned.

Chapter XXIX

I VISIT STEERFORTH AT HIS HOME, AGAIN

I MENTIONED to Mr Spenlow in the morning, that I wanted leave of absence for a short time; and as I was not in the receipt of any salary, and consequently was not obnoxious to the implacable Jorkins, there was no difficulty about it. I took that opportunity, with my voice sticking in my throat, and my sight failing as I uttered the words, to express my hope that Miss Spenlow was quite well; to which Mr Spenlow replied, with no more emotion than if he had been speaking of an ordinary human being, that he was much obliged to me, and she was very well.

We articled clerks, as germs of the patrician order of proctors, were treated with so much consideration, that I was almost my own master at all times. As I did not care, however, to get to Highgate before one or two o'clock in the day, and as we had another little excommunication case in court that morning, which was called The office of the Judge promoted by Tipkins against Bullock for his soul's correction, I passed an hour or two in attendance on it with Mr Spenlow very agreeably. It arose out of a scuffle between two churchwardens, one of whom was alleged to have pushed the other against a pump; the handle of which pump projecting into a school-house, which school-house was under a gable of the church-roof, made the push an ecclesiastical offence. It was an amusing case; and sent me up to Highgate, on the box of the stage-coach, thinking about the Commons, and what Mr Spenlow had said about touching the Commons and bringing down the country.

Mrs Steerforth was pleased to see me, and so was Rosa Dartle. I was agreeably surprised to find that Littimer was not there, and that we were attended by a modest little parlour-maid, with blue ribbons in her cap, whose eye it was much more pleasant, and much less disconcerting, to catch by accident, than the eye of that respectable man. But what I particularly observed, before I had been half-an-hour in the house, was the close and attentive watch Miss Dartle kept upon me; and the lurking manner in which she seemed to compare my face with Steerforth's, and Steerforth's with mine, and to lie in wait for something to come out between the two. So surely as I looked towards her, did I see that eager visage, with its gaunt black eyes and searching brow, intent on mine; or passing suddenly from mine to Steerforth's; or comprehending both of us at once. In this lynx-like scrutiny she was so far from faltering when she saw I observed it, that at such a time she only fixed her piercing look upon me with a more intent expression still. Blameless as I was, and knew that I was, in reference to any wrong she could possibly suspect me of, I shrunk before her strange eyes, quite unable to endure their hungry lustre.

All day, she seemed to pervade the whole house. If I talked to Steerforth in his room, I heard her dress rustle in the little gallery outside. When he and I engaged in some of our old exercises on the lawn behind the house, I saw her face pass from window to window, like a wandering light, until it fixed itself in one, and watched us. When we all four went out walking in the afternoon, she closed her thin hand on my arm like a spring, to keep me back, while Steerforth and his mother went on out of hearing: and then spoke to me.

"You have been a long time," she said, "without coming here. Is your profession really so engaging and interesting as to absorb your whole attention? I ask because I always want to be informed, when I am ignorant. Is it really, though?"

I replied that I liked it well enough, but that I certainly could not claim so much for it.

"Oh! I am glad to know that, because I always like to be put right when I am wrong," said Rosa Dartle. "You mean it is a little dry, perhaps?"

"Well," I replied; "perhaps it *was* a little dry."

"Oh! and that's a reason why you want relief and change—excitement and all that?" said she. "Ah! very true! But isn't it a little—Eh?—for him; I don't mean you?"

A quick glance of her eye towards the spot where Steerforth was walking, with his mother leaning on his arm, showed me whom she meant; but beyond that, I was quite lost. And I looked so, I have no doubt.

"Don't it—I don't say that it *does,* mind I want to know—don't it rather engross him? Don't it make him, perhaps, a little more remiss than usual in his visits to his blindly-doting—eh?" With another quick glance at them, and such a glance at me as seemed to look into my innermost thoughts.

"Miss Dartle," I returned, "pray do not think—"

"I don't!" she said. "Oh dear me, don't suppose that I think anything! I am not suspicious. I only ask a question. I don't state any opinion. I want to found an opinion on what you tell me. Then, it's not so? Well! I am very glad to know it."

"It certainly is not the fact," said I, perplexed, "that I am accountable for Steerforth's having been away from home longer than usual—if he has been: which I really don't know at this moment, unless I understand it from you. I have not seen him this long while, until last night."

"No?"

"Indeed, Miss Dartle, no!"

As she looked full at me, I saw her face grow sharper and paler, and the marks of the old wound lengthen out until it cut through the disfigured lip, and deep into the nether lip, and slanted down the face. There was something positively awful to me in this, and in the brightness of her eyes, as she said, looking fixedly at me:

"What is he doing?"

I repeated the words, more to myself than her, being so amazed.

"What is he doing?" she said, with an eagerness that seemed enough to consume her like a fire. "In what is that man assisting him, who never looks at me without an inscrutable falsehood in his eyes? If you are honourable and faithful, I don't ask you to betray your friend. I ask you only to tell me, is it anger, is it hatred, is it pride, is it restlessness, is it some wild fancy, is it love, *what is it,* that is leading him?"

"Miss Dartle," I returned, "how shall I tell you, so that you will believe me, that I know of nothing in Steerforth different from what there was when I first came here? I can think of nothing. I firmly believe there is nothing. I hardly understand even what you mean."

As she still stood looking fixedly at me, a twitching or throbbing, from which I could not dissociate the idea of pain, came into that cruel mark; and lifted up the corner of her lip as if with scorn, or with a pity that despised its object. She put her hand upon it hurriedly—a hand so thin and delicate, that when I had seen her hold it up before the fire to shade her face, I had compared it in my thoughts to fine porcelain—and saying, in a quick, fierce, passionate way, "I swear you to secrecy about this!" said not a word more.

Mrs Steerforth was particularly happy in her son's society, and Steerforth was, on this occasion, particularly attentive and respectful to her. It was very interesting to me to see them together, not only on account of their mutual affection, but because of the strong personal resemblance between them, and the manner in which what was haughty or impetuous in him was softened by age and sex, in her, to a gracious dignity. I thought, more than once, that it was well no serious cause of division had ever come between them; or two such natures—I ought rather to express it, two such shades of the same nature—might have been harder to reconcile than the two extremest opposites in creation. The idea did not originate in my own discernment, I am bound to confess, but in a speech of Rosa Dartle's.

She said at dinner:

"Oh, but do tell me, though, somebody, because I have been thinking about it all day, and I want to know."

"You want to know what, Rosa?" returned Mrs Steerforth. "Pray, pray, Rosa, do not be mysterious."

"Mysterious!" she cried. "Oh! really? Do you consider me so?"

"Do I constantly entreat you," said Mrs Steerforth, "to speak plainly, in your own natural manner?"

"Oh! then this is *not* my natural manner?" she rejoined. "Now you must really bear with me, because I ask for information. We never know ourselves."

"It has become a second nature," said Mrs Steerforth, without any displeasure; "but I remember,—and so must you, I think,—when your manner was different, Rosa; when it was not so guarded, and was more trustful."

"I am sure you are right," she returned; "and so it is that bad habits grow upon one! Really? Less guarded and more trustful? How *can* I, imperceptibly, have changed, I wonder! Well, that's very odd! I must study to regain my former self."

"I wish you would," said Mrs Steerforth, with a smile.

"Oh! I really will, you know!" she answered. "I will learn frankness from—let me see—from James."

"You cannot learn frankness, Rosa," said Mrs Steerforth quickly—for there was always some effect of sarcasm in what Rosa Dartle said, though it was said, as this was, in the most unconscious manner in the world—"in a better school."

"That I am sure of," she answered, with uncommon fervour. "If I am sure of anything, of course, you know, I am sure of that."

Mrs Steerforth appeared to me to regret having been a little nettled; for she presently said, in a kind tone:

"Well, my dear Rosa, we have not heard what it is that you want to be satisfied about?"

"That I want to be satisfied about?" she replied, with provoking coldness. "Oh! It was only whether people, who are like each other in their moral constitution—is that the phrase?"

"It's as good a phrase as another," said Steerforth.

"Thank you:—whether people, who are like each other in their moral constitution, are in greater danger than people not so circumstanced, supposing any serious cause of variance to arise between them, of being divided angrily and deeply?"

"I should say yes," said Steerforth.

"Should you?" she retorted. "Dear me! Supposing then, for instance—any unlikely thing will do for a supposition—that you and your mother were to have a serious quarrel."

"My dear Rosa," interposed Mrs Steerforth, laughing good-naturedly, "suggest some other supposition! James and I know our duty to each other better, I pray Heaven!"

"Oh!" said Miss Dartle, nodding her head thoughtfully. "To be sure. *That* would prevent it? Why, of course it would. Exactly. Now, I am glad I have been so foolish as to put the case, for it is so very good to know that your duty to each other would prevent it! Thank you very much."

One other little circumstance connected with Miss Dartle I must not omit; for I had reason to remember it thereafter, when all the irremediable past was rendered plain. During the whole of this day, but especially from this period of it, Steerforth exerted himself with his utmost skill, and that was with his utmost ease, to charm this singular creature into a pleasant and pleased companion. That he should succeed, was no matter of surprise to me. That she should struggle against the fascinating influence of his delightful art—delightful nature I thought it then—did not surprise me either; for I knew that she was sometimes jaundiced and perverse. I saw her features and her manner slowly change; I saw her look at him with growing admiration; I saw her try, more and more faintly, but always angrily, as if she condemned a weakness in herself, to resist the captivating power that he possessed; and finally, I saw her sharp glance soften, and her smile become quite gentle, and I ceased to be afraid of her as I had really been all day, and we all sat about the fire, talking and laughing together, with as little reserve as if we had been children.

Whether it was because we had sat there so long, or because Steerforth was resolved not to lose the advantage he had gained, I do not know; but we did not remain in the dining-room more than five minutes after her departure. "She is playing her harp," said Steerforth, softly, at the drawing-room door, "and nobody but my mother has heard her do that, I believe, these three years." He said it with a curious smile, which was gone directly; and we went into the room and found her alone.

"Don't get up," said Steerforth (which she had already done) "my dear Rosa, don't! Be kind for once, and sing us an Irish song."

"What do you care for an Irish song?" she returned.

"Much!" said Steerforth. "Much more than for any other. Here is Daisy, too, loves music from his soul. Sing us an Irish song, Rosa! and let me sit and listen as I used to do."

He did not touch her, or the chair from which she had risen, but sat himself near the harp. She stood beside it for some little while, in a curious way, going through the motion of playing it with her right hand, but not sounding it. At length she sat down, and drew it to her with one sudden action, and played and sang.

I don't know what it was, in her touch or voice, that made that song the most unearthly I have ever heard in my life, or can imagine. There was something fearful in the reality of it. It was as if it had never been written, or set to music, but sprung out of passion within her; which found imperfect utterance in the low sounds of her voice, and crouched again when all was still. I was dumb when she leaned beside the harp again, playing it, but not sounding it, with her right hand.

A minute more, and this had roused me from my trance:—Steerforth had left his seat, and gone to her, and had put his arm laughingly about her, and had said, "Come, Rosa, for the future we will love each other very much!" And she had struck him, and had thrown him off with the fury of a wild cat, and had burst out of the room.

"What is the matter with Rosa?" said Mrs Steerforth, coming in.

"She has been an angel, mother," returned Steerforth, "for a little while; and has run into the opposite extreme, since, by way of compensation."

"You should be careful not to irritate her, James. Her temper has been soured, remember, and ought not to be tried."

Rosa did not come back; and no other mention was made of her, until I went with Steerforth into his room to say Good night. Then he laughed about her, and asked me if I had ever seen such a fierce little piece of incomprehensibility.

I expressed as much of my astonishment as was then capable of expression, and asked if he could guess what it was that she had taken so much amiss, so suddenly.

"Oh, Heaven knows," said Steerforth. "Anything you like—or nothing! I told you she took everything, herself included, to a grindstone, and sharpened it. She is an edge-tool, and requires great care in dealing with. She is always dangerous. Good night!"

"Good night!" said I, "my dear Steerforth! I shall be gone before you wake in the morning. Good night!"

He was unwilling to let me go; and stood, holding me out, with a hand on each of my shoulders, as he had done in my own room.

"Daisy," he said, with a smile—"for though that's not the name your godfathers and godmothers gave you, it's the name I like best to call you by—and I wish, I wish, I wish, you could give it to me!"

"Why so I can, if I choose," said I.

"Daisy, if anything should ever separate us, you must think of me at my best, old boy. Come! Let us make that bargain. Think of me at my best, if circumstances should ever part us!"

"You have no best to me, Steerforth," said I, "and no worst. You are always equally loved, and cherished in my heart."

So much compunction for having ever wronged him, even by a shapeless thought, did I feel within me, that the confession of having done so was rising to my lips. But for the reluctance I had to betray the confidence of Agnes, but for my uncertainty how to approach the subject with no risk of doing so, it would have reached them before he said, "God bless you, Daisy, and good night!" In my doubt, it did *not* reach them; and we shook hands, and we parted.

I was up with the dull dawn, and, having dressed as quietly as I could, looked into his room. He was fast asleep; lying, easily, with his head upon his arm, as I had often seen him lie at school.

The time came in its season, and that was very soon, when I almost wondered that nothing troubled his repose, as I looked at him. But he slept—let me think of him so again—as I had often seen him sleep at school; and thus, in this silent hour, I left him.

—Never more, oh God forgive you, Steerforth! to touch that passive hand in love and friendship. Never, never, more!

Chapter XXX

A LOSS

I GOT down to Yarmouth in the evening, and went to the inn. I knew that Peggotty's spare room—my room—was likely to have occupation enough in a little while, if that great Visitor, before whose presence all the living must give place, were not already in the house; so I betook myself to the inn, and dined there, and engaged my bed.

It was ten o'clock when I went out. Many of the shops were shut, and the town was dull. When I came to Omer and Joram's, I found the shutters up, but the shop door standing open. As I could obtain a perspective view of Mr Omer inside, smoking his pipe by the parlour door, I entered, and asked him how he was.

"Why, bless my life and soul!" said Mr Omer, "how do you find yourself? Take a seat.—Smoke not disagreeable, I hope?"

"By no means," said I. "I like it—in somebody else's pipe."

"What, not in your own, eh?" Mr Omer returned, laughing. "All the better, sir. Bad habit for a young man. Take a seat. I smoke, myself, for the asthma."

Mr Omer had made room for me, and placed a chair. He now sat down again very much out of breath, gasping at his pipe as if it contained a supply of that necessary, without which he must perish.

"I am sorry to have heard bad news of Mr Barkis," said I.

Mr Omer looked at me, with a steady countenance, and shook his head.

"Do you know how he is tonight?" I asked.

"The very question I should have put to you, sir," returned Mr Omer, "but on account of delicacy. It's one of the drawbacks of our line of business. When a party's ill, we *can't* ask how the party is."

The difficulty had not occurred to me; though I had had my apprehensions too, when I went in, of hearing the old tune. On its being mentioned, I recognized it, however, and said as much.

"Yes, yes, you understand," said Mr Omer, nodding his head. "We dursn't do it. Bless, you, it would be a shock that the generality of parties mightn't recover, to say 'Omer and Joram's compliments, and how do you find yourself this morning?'—or this afternoon—as it may be.'

Mr Omer and I nodded at each other, and Mr Omer recruited his wind by the aid of his pipe.

"It's one of the things that cut the trade off from attentions they could often wish to show," said Mr Omer. "Take myself. If I have known Barkis a year, to move to as he went by, I have known him forty years. But *I* can't go and say, 'how is he?'"

I felt it was rather hard on Mr Omer, and I told him so.

"I'm not more self-interested, I hope, than another man," said Mr Omer. "Look at me! My wind may fail me at any moment, and it ain't likely that, to my own knowledge, I'd be self-interested under such circumstances. I say it ain't likely, in a man who knows his wind will go, when it *does* go, as if a pair of bellows was cut open; and that man a grandfather," said Mr Omer.

I said, "Not at all."

"It ain't that I complain of my line of business," said Mr Omer. "It ain't that. Some good and some bad goes, no doubt, to all callings. What I wish is, that parties was brought up stronger-minded."

Mr Omer, with a very complacent and amiable face, took several puffs in silence; and then said, resuming his first point:

"Accordingly we're obleeged, in ascertaining how Barkis goes on, to limit ourselves to Em'ly. She knows what our real objects are, and she don't have any more alarms or suspicions about us, than if we was so many lambs. Minnie and Joram have just stepped down to the house, in fact (she's there, after hours, helping her aunt a bit), to ask her how he is tonight; and if you was to please to wait till they come back, they'd give you full partic'lers. Will you take something? A glass of srub and water, now? I smoke on srub and water, myself," said Mr Omer, taking up his glass, "because it's considered softening to the passages, by which this troublesome breath of mine gets into action. But, Lord bless you," said Mr Omer, huskily, "it ain't the passages that's out of order! 'Give me breath enough,' said I to my daughter Minnie, 'and I'll find passages, my dear.' "

He really had no breath to spare, and it was very alarming to see him laugh. When he was again in a condition to be talked to, I thanked him for the proffered refreshment, which I declined, as I had just had dinner; and, observing that I would wait, since he was so good as to invite me, until his daughter and his son-in-law came back, I inquired how little Emily was?

"Well, sir," said Mr Omer, removing his pipe, that he might rub his chin: "I tell you truly, I shall be glad when her marriage has taken place."

"Why so?" I inquired.

"Well, she's unsettled at present," said Mr Omer. "It ain't that she's not as pretty as ever, for she's prettier—I do assure you, she is prettier. It ain't that she don't work as well as ever, for she does. She *was* worth any six, and she *is* worth any six. But somehow she wants heart. If you understand," said Mr Omer, after rubbing his chin again, and smoking a little, "what I mean in a general way by the expression, 'A long pull, and a strong pull, and a pull altogether, my hearties, hurrah!' I should say to you, that *that* was—in a general way—what I miss in Em'ly."

Mr Omer's face and manner went for so much, that I could conscientiously nod my head, as divining his meaning. My quickness of apprehension seemed to please him, and he went on:

"Now I consider this is principally on account of her being in an unsettled state, you see. We have talked it over a good deal, her uncle and myself, and her sweetheart and myself, after business; and I consider it is principally on account of her being unsettled. You must always recollect of Em'ly," said Mr Omer, shaking his head gently, "that she's a most extraordinary affectionate little thing. The proverb says, 'You can't make a silk purse out of a sow's ear.' Well, I don't know about that. I rather think you may, if you begin early in life. She has made a home out of that old boat, sir, that stone and marble couldn't beat."

"I am sure she has!" said I.

"To see the clinging of that pretty little thing to her uncle," said Mr Omer; "to see the way she holds on to him, tighter and tighter, and closer and closer, every day, is to see a sight. Now, you know, there's a struggle going on when that's the case. Why should it be made a longer one than is needful?"

I listened attentively to the good old fellow, and acquiesced, with all my heart, in what he said.

"Therefore, I mentioned to them," said Mr Omer, in a comfortable, easy-going tone, "this. I said, 'Now, don't consider Em'ly nailed down in point of time, at all. Make it your own time. Her services have been more valuable than was supposed; her learning has been quicker than was supposed; Omer and Joram can run their pen through what remains; and she's free when you wish. If she likes to make any little arrangement, afterwards, in the way of doing any little thing for us at home, very well. If she don't, very well still. We're no losers, anyhow.' For—don't you see," said Mr Omer, touching me with his pipe, "it ain't likely that a man so short of breath as myself, and a grandfather too, would go and strain points with a little bit of a blue-eyed blossom, like *her?*"

"Not at all, I am certain," said I.

"Not at all! You're right!" said Mr Omer. "Well, sir, her cousin—you know it's a cousin she's going to be married to?"

"Oh yes," I replied. "I know him well."

"Of course you do," said Mr Omer. "Well, sir! Her cousin being, as it appears, in good work, and well to do, thanked me in a very manly sort of manner for this (conducting himself altogether, I must say, in a way that gives me a high opinion of him), and went and took as comfortable a little house as you or I could wish to clap eyes on. That little house is now furnished right through, as neat and complete as a doll's parlour; and but for Barkis's illness having taken this bad turn, poor fellow, they would have been man and wife—I dare say, by this time. As it is, there's a postponement."

"And Emily, Mr Omer?" I inquired. "Has she become more settled?"

"Why that, you know," he returned, rubbing his double chin again, "can't naturally be expected. The prospect of the change and separation, and all that, is, as one may say, close to her and far away from her, both at once. Barkis's death needn't put it off much, but his lingering might. Anyway, it's an uncertain state of matters, you see."

"I see," said I.

"Consequently," pursued Mr Omer, "Em'ly's still a little down, and a little fluttered; perhaps, upon the whole, she's more so than she was. Every day she seems to get fonder and fonder of her uncle, and more loth to part from all of us. A kind word from me brings the tears into her eyes: and if you was to see her with my daughter Minnie's little girl, you'd never forget it. Bless my heart alive!" said Mr Omer, pondering, "how she loves that child!"

Having so favourable an opportunity, it occurred to me to ask Mr Omer, before our conversation should be interrupted by the return of his daughter and her husband, whether he knew anything of Martha.

"Ah!" he rejoined, shaking his head, and looking very much dejected. "No good. A sad story, sir, however you come to know it. I never thought there was harm in the girl. I wouldn't wish to mention it before my daughter Minnie—for she'd take me up directly—but I never did. None of us ever did."

Mr Omer, hearing his daughter's footstep before I heard it, touched me with his pipe, and shut up one eye, as a caution. She and her husband came in immediately afterwards.

Their report was, that Mr Barkis was "as bad as bad could be"; that he was quite unconscious; and that Mr Chillip had mournfully said in the kitchen, on going away just now, that the College of Physicians, the College of Surgeons, and Apothecaries' Hall, if they were all called in together, couldn't help him. He was past both Colleges, Mr Chillip said, and the Hall could only poison him.

Hearing this, and learning that Mr Peggotty was there, I determined to go to the house at once. I bade good night to Mr Omer, and to Mr and Mrs Joram; and directed my steps thither, with a solemn feeling, which made Mr Barkis quite a new and different creature.

My low tap at the door was answered by Mr Peggotty. He was not so much surprised to see me as I had expected. I remarked this in Peggotty, too, when she came down; and I have seen it since; and I think, in the expectation of that dread surprise, all other changes and surprises dwindle into nothing.

I shook hands with Mr Peggotty, and passed into the kitchen, while he softly closed the door. Little Emily was sitting by the fire, with her hands before her face. Ham was standing near her.

We spoke in whispers; listening, between whiles, for any sound in the room above. I had not thought of it on the occasion of my last visit, but how strange it was to me, now, to miss Mr Barkis out of the kitchen!

"This is very kind of you, Mas'r Davy," said Mr Peggotty.

"It's oncommon kind," said Ham.

"Em'ly, my dear," cried Mr Peggotty. "See here! Here's Mas'r Davy come! What, cheer up, pretty! Not a wured to Mas'r Davy?"

There was a trembling upon her, that I can see now. The coldness of her hand when I touched it, I can feel yet. Its only sign of animation was to shrink from mine; and then she glided from the chair, and creeping to the other side of her uncle, bowed herself, silently and trembling still, upon his breast.

"It's such a loving art," said Mr Peggotty, smoothing her rich hair with his great hard hand, "that it can't abear the sorrer of this. It's nat'ral in young folk, Mas'r Davy, when they're new to these here trials, and timid, like my little bird,—it's nat'ral."

She clung the closer to him, but neither lifted up her face, nor spoke a word.

"It's getting late, my dear," said Mr Peggotty, "and here's Ham come fur to take you home. Theer! Go along with t'other loving art! What, Em'ly? Eh, my pretty?"

The sound of her voice had not reached me, but he bent his head as if he listened to her, and then said:

"Let you stay with your uncle? Why, you doen't mean to ask me that! Stay with your uncle, Moppet? When your husband that'll be so soon, is here fur to take you home? Now a person wouldn't think it, fur to see this little thing alongside a rough-weather chap like me," said Mr Peggotty, looking round at both of us, with infinite pride; "but the sea ain't more salt in it than she has fondness in her for her uncle—a foolish little Em'ly!"

"Em'ly's in the right in that, Mas'r Davy!" said Ham. "Lookee here! As Em'ly wishes of it, and as she's hurried and frightened, like, besides, I'll leave her till morning. Let me stay too!"

"No, no," said Mr Peggotty. "You doen't ought—a married man like you—or what's as good—to take and hull away a day's work. And you doen't ought to watch and work both. That won't do. You go home and turn in. You ain't afeerd of Em'ly not being took good care on, *I* know."

Ham yielded to this persuasion, and took his hat to go. Even when he kissed her—and I never saw him approach her, but I felt that nature had given him the soul of a gentleman—she seemed to cling closer to her uncle, even to the avoidance of her chosen husband. I shut the door after him, that it might cause no disturbance of the quiet that prevailed; and when I turned back, I found Mr Peggotty still talking to her.

"Now, I'm a going upstairs to tell your aunt as Mas'r Davy's here, and that'll cheer her up a bit," he said. "Sit ye down by the fire, the while, my dear, and warm those mortal cold hands. You doen't need to be so fearsome, and take on so much. What? You'll go along with me?—Well! come along with me—come! If her uncle was turned out of house and home, and forced to lay down in a dyke, Mas'r Davy," said Mr Peggotty, with no less pride than before, "it's my belief she'd go along with him, now! But there'll be someone else, soon,—someone else, soon, Em'ly!"

Afterwards, when I went upstairs, as I passed the door of my little chamber, which was dark, I had an indistinct impression of her being within it, cast down upon the floor. But, whether it was really she, or whether it was a confusion of the shadows in the room, I don't know now.

I had leisure to think, before the kitchen fire, of pretty little Emily's dread of death—which, added to what Mr Omer had told me, I took to be the cause of her being so unlike herself—and I had leisure, before Peggotty came down, even to think more leniently of the weakness of it: as I sat counting the ticking of the clock, and deepening my sense of the solemn hush around me. Peggotty took me in her arms, and blessed and thanked me over and over again for being such a comfort to her (that was what she said) in her distress. She then entreated me to come upstairs, sobbing that Mr Barkis had always liked me and admired me; that he had often talked of me, before he fell into a stupor; and that she believed, in case of his coming to himself again, he would brighten up at sight of me, if he could brighten up at any earthly thing.

The probability of his ever doing so, appeared to me, when I saw him, to be very small. He was lying with his head and shoulders out of bed, in an uncomfortable attitude, half resting on the box which had cost him so much pain and trouble. I learned, that, when he was past creeping out of bed to open it, and past assuring himself of its safety by means of the divining rod I had seen him use, he had required to have it placed on the chair at the bed-side, where he had ever since embraced it, night and day. His arm lay on it now. Time and the world were slipping from beneath him, but the box was there; and the last words he had uttered were (in an explanatory tone) "Old clothes!"

"Barkis, my dear!" said Peggotty, almost cheerfully: bending over him, while her brother and I stood at the bed's foot. "Here's my dear boy—my dear boy, Master Davy, who brought us together, Barkis! That you sent messages by, you know! Won't you speak to Master Davy?"

He was as mute and senseless as the box, from which his form derived the only expression it had.

"He's a going out with the tide," said Mr Peggotty to me, behind his hand.

My eyes were dim and so were Mr Peggotty's; but I repeated in a whisper, "With the tide?"

"People can't die, along the coast," said Mr Peggotty, "except when the tide's pretty nigh out. They can't be born, unless it's pretty nigh in—not properly born, till flood. He's a going out with the tide. It's ebb at half-arter three, slack water half an hour. If he lives till it turns, he'll hold his own till past the flood, and go out with the next tide."

We remained there, watching him, a long time—hours. What mysterious influence my presence had upon him in that state of his senses, I shall not pretend to say; but when he at last began to wander feebly, it is certain he was muttering about driving me to school.

"He's coming to himself," said Peggotty.

Mr Peggotty touched me, and whispered with much awe and reverence. "They are both a-going out fast."

"Barkis, my dear!" said Peggotty.

"C. P. Barkis," he cried faintly. "No better woman anywhere!"

"Look! Here's Master Davy!" said Peggotty. For he now opened his eyes.

I was on the point of asking him if he knew me, when he tried to stretch out his arm, and said to me, distinctly, with a pleasant smile:

"Barkis is willin'!"

And, it being low water, he went out with the tide.

Chapter XXXI

A GREATER LOSS

IT was not difficult for me, on Peggotty's solicitation, to resolve to stay where I was, until after the remains of the poor carrier should have made their last journey to Blunderstone. She had long ago bought, out of her own savings, a little piece of ground in our old churchyard near the grave of "her sweet girl," as she always called my mother; and there they were to rest.

In keeping Peggotty company, and doing all I could for her (little enough at the utmost), I was as grateful, I rejoice to think, as even now I could wish myself to have been. But I am afraid I had a supreme satisfaction, of a personal and professional nature, in taking charge of Mr Barkis's will, and expounding its contents.

I may claim the merit of having originated the suggestion that the will should be looked for in the box. After some search, it was found in the box, at the bottom of a horse's nose-bag; wherein (besides hay) there was discovered an old gold watch, with chain and seals, which Mr Barkis had worn on his wedding-day, and which had never been seen before or since; a silver tobacco-stopper, in the form of a leg; an imitation lemon, full of minute cups and saucers, which I have some idea Mr Barkis must have purchased to present to me when I was a child, and afterwards found himself unable to part with; eighty-seven guineas and a half, in guineas and half-guineas; two hundred and ten pounds, in perfectly clean Bank notes; certain receipts for Bank of England stock; an old horseshoe, a bad shilling, a piece of camphor, and an oyster-shell. From the circumstance of the latter article having been much polished, and displaying prismatic colours on the inside, I conclude that Mr Barkis had some general ideas about pearls, which never resolved themselves into anything definite.

For years and years, Mr Barkis had carried this box, on all his journeys, every day. That it might the better escape notice, he had invented a fiction that it belonged to "Mr Blackboy," and was "to be left with Barkis till called for"; a fable he had elaborately written on the lid, in characters now scarcely legible.

He had hoarded, all these years, I found, to good purpose. His property in money amounted to nearly three thousand pounds. Of this he bequeathed the interest of one thousand to Mr Peggotty for his life; on his decease, the principal to be equally divided between Peggotty, little Emily, and me, or the survivor or survivors of us, share and share alike. All the rest he died possessed of, he bequeathed to Peggotty; whom he left residuary legatee, and sole executrix of that his last will and testament.

I felt myself quite a proctor when I read this document aloud with all possible ceremony, and set forth its provisions, any number of times, to those whom they concerned. I began to think there was more in the Commons than I had supposed. I examined the will with the deepest attention, pronounced it perfectly formal in all respects, made a pencil-mark or so in the margin, and thought it rather extraordinary that I knew so much.

In this abstruse pursuit; in making an account for Peggotty, of all the property into which she had come; in arranging all the affairs in an orderly manner; and in being her referee and adviser on every point, to our joint delight; I passed the week before the funeral. I did not see little Emily in that interval, but they told me she was to be quietly married in a fortnight.

I did not attend the funeral in character, if I may venture to say so. I mean I was not dressed up in a black coat and a streamer, to frighten the birds; but I walked over to Blunderstone early in the morning, and was in the churchyard when it came, attended only by Peggotty and her brother. The mad gentleman looked on, out of my little window; Mr Chillip's baby wagged its heavy head, and rolled its goggle eyes, at the clergyman, over its nurse's shoulder; Mr Omer breathed short in the background; no one else was there; and it was very quiet. We walked about the churchyard for an hour, after all was over; and pulled some young leaves from the tree above my mother's grave.

A dread falls on me here. A cloud is lowering on the distant town, towards which I retraced my solitary steps. I fear to approach it. I cannot bear to think of what did come, upon that memorable night; of what must come again, if I go on.

It is no worse, because I write of it. It would be no better, if I stopped my most unwilling hand. It is done. Nothing can undo it; nothing can make it otherwise than as it was.

My old nurse was to go to London with me next day, on the business of the will. Little Emily was passing that day at Mr Omer's. We were all to meet in the old boathouse that night. Ham would bring Emily at the usual hour. I would walk back at my leisure. The brother and sister would return as they had come, and be expecting us, when the day closed in, at the fireside.

I parted from them at the wicket-gate, where visionary Strap had rested with Roderick Random's knapsack in the days of yore; and, instead of going straight back, walked a little distance on the road to Lowestoft. Then I turned, and walked back towards Yarmouth. I stayed to dine at a decent alehouse, some mile or two from the Ferry I have mentioned before; and thus the day wore away, and it was evening when I reached it. Rain was falling heavily by that time, and it was a wild night; but there was a moon behind the clouds, and it was not dark.

I was soon within sight of Mr Peggotty's house, and of the light within it shining through the window. A little floundering across the sand, which was heavy, brought me to the door, and I went in.

It looked very comfortable indeed. Mr Peggotty had smoked his evening pipe and there were preparations for some supper by and by. The fire was bright, the ashes were thrown up, the locker was ready for little Emily in her old place. In her own old place sat Peggotty, once more, looking (but for her dress) as if she had never left it. She had fallen back, already, on the society of the work-box with St Paul's upon the lid, the yard-measure in the cottage, and the bit of wax-candle; and there they all were, just as if they had never been disturbed. Mrs Gummidge appeared to be fretting a little, in her old corner; and consequently looked quite natural, too.

"You're first of the lot, Mas'r Davy!" said Mr Peggotty with a happy face. "Doen't keep in that coat sir, if it's wet."

"Thank you, Mr Peggotty," said I, giving him my other coat to hang up. "It's quite dry."

"So 'tis!" said Mr Peggotty, feeling my shoulders. "As a chip! Sit ye down, sir. It ain't o' no use saying welcome to you, but you're welcome, kind and hearty."

"Thank you, Mr Peggotty, I am sure of that. Well, Peggotty!" said I, giving her a kiss. "And how are you, old woman?"

"Ha, ha!" laughed Mr Peggotty, sitting down beside us, and rubbing his hands in his sense of relief from recent trouble, and in the genuine heartiness of his nature; "there's not a woman in the wureld, sir—as I tell her—that need to feel more easy in her mind than her! She done her dooty by the departed, and the departed know'd it; and the departed done what was right by her, as she done what was right by the departed;—and—and—and it's *all* right!"

Mrs Gummidge groaned.

"Cheer up, my pritty mawther!" said Mr Peggotty. (But he shook his head aside at us, evidently sensible of the tendency of the late occurrences to recall the memory of the old one.) "Doen't be down! Cheer up, for your own self, on'y a little bit, and see if a good deal more doen't come nat'ral!"

"Not to me, Dan'l," returned Mrs Gummidge. "Nothink's nat'ral to me but to be lone and lorn."

"No, no," said Mr Peggotty, soothing her sorrows.

"Yes, yes, Dan'l!" said Mrs Gummidge. "I ain't a person to live with them as has had money left. Thinks go too contrairy with me. I had better be a riddance."

"Why, how should I ever spend it without you?" said Mr Peggotty, with an air of serious remonstrance. "What are you a talking on? Don't I want you more now, than ever I did?"

"I know'd I was never wanted before!" cried Mrs Gummidge, with a pitiable whimper, "and now I'm told so! How could I expect to be wanted, being so lone and lorn, and so contrairy!"

Mr Peggotty seemed very much shocked at himself for having made a speech capable of this unfeeling construction, but was prevented from replying, by Peggotty's pulling his sleeve, and shaking her head. After looking at Mrs Gummidge for some moments, in sore distress of mind, he glanced at the Dutch clock, rose, snuffed the candle, and put it in the window.

"Theer!" said Mr Peggotty, cheerily. "Theer we are, Missis Gummidge!" Mrs Gummidge slightly groaned. "Lighted up, accordin' to custom! You're a wonderin' what that's fur, sir! Well, it's fur our little Em'ly. You see, the path ain't over light or cheerful arter dark; and when I'm here at the hour as she's a comin' home, I puts the light in the winder. That, you see," said Mr Peggotty, bending over me with great glee, "meets two objects. She says, says Em'ly, 'Theer's home!' she says. And likewise, says Em'ly, 'My uncle's theer!' Fur if I ain't theer, I never have no light showed."

"You're a baby!" said Peggotty; very fond of him for it, if she thought so.

"Well," returned Mr Peggotty, standing with his legs pretty wide apart, and rubbing his hands up and down them in his comfortable satisfaction, as he looked alternately at us and at the fire, "I doen't know but I am. Not, you see, to look at."

"Not azackly," observed Peggotty.

"No," laughed Mr Peggotty, "not to look at, but to—to consider on, you know. *I* doen't care, bless you! Now I tell you. When I go a looking and looking about that theer pritty house of our Em'ly's, I'm—I'm Gormed," said Mr Peggotty, with sudden emphasis—"theer! I can't say more—if I doen't feel as if the littlest things was her, a'most. I takes 'em up and I put 'em down, and I touches of 'em as delicate as if they was our Em'ly. So 'tis with her little bonnets and that. I couldn't see one on 'em rough used a purpose—not fur the whole wureld. There's a babby fur you, in the form of a great Sea Porkypine!" said Mr Peggotty, relieving his earnestness with a roar of laughter.

Peggotty and I both laughed, but not so loud.

"It's my opinion, you see," said Mr Peggotty, with a delighted face, after some further rubbing of his legs, "as this is along of my havin' played with her so much, and made believe as we was Turks, and French, and sharks, and every wariety of forinners— bless you, yes; and lions and whales, and I doen't know what all!—when she warn't no higher than my knee. I've got into the way on it, you know. Why, this here candle, now!" said Mr Peggotty, gleefully holding out his hand towards it, *"I* know wery well that arter she's married and gone, I shall put that candle theer, just the same as now. *I* know very well that when I'm here o' nights (and where else should *I* live, bless your arts, whatever fortun' I come into!) and she ain't here or I ain't theer, I shall put the candle in the winder, and sit afore the fire, pretending I'm expecting of her, like I'm doing now. *There's* a babby for you," said Mr Peggotty, with another roar, "in the form of a Sea Porkypine! Why, at the present minute, when I see the candle sparkle up, I says to myself, 'She's a looking at it! Em'ly's a coming!' *There's* a babby, for you, in the form of a Sea Porkypine! Right for all that," said Mr Peggotty, stopping in his roar, and smiting his hands together; "fur here she is!"

It was only Ham. The night should have turned more wet since I came in, for he had a large sou'wester hat on, slouched over his face.

"Wheer's Em'ly?" said Mr Peggotty.

Ham made a motion with his head, as if she were outside. Mr Peggotty took the light from the window, trimmed it, put it on the table, and was busily stirring the fire, when Ham, who had not moved, said:

"Mas'r Davy, will you come out a minute, and see what Em'ly and me has got to show you?"

We went out. As I passed him at the door, I saw, to my astonishment and fright, that he was deadly pale. He pushed me hastily into the open air, and closed the door upon us. Only upon us two.

"Ham! what's the matter?"

"Mas'r Davy!—" Oh, for his broken heart, how dreadfully he wept!

I was paralysed by the sight of such grief. I don't know what I thought, or what I dreaded. I could only look at him.

"Ham! Poor good fellow! For Heaven's sake, tell me what's the matter!"

"My love, Mas'r Davy—the pride and hope of my art—her that I'd have died for, and would die for now—she's gone!"

"Gone!"

"Em'ly's run away! Oh, Mas'r Davy, think *how* she's run away, when I pray my good and gracious God to kill her (her that is so dear above all things) sooner than let her come to ruin and disgrace!"

The face he turned up to the troubled sky, the quivering of his clasped hands, the agony of his figure, remain associated with the lonely waste, in my remembrance, to this hour. It is always night there, and he is the only object in the scene.

"You're a scholar," he said, hurriedly, "and know what's right and best. What am I to say, in-doors? How am I ever to break it to him, Mas'r Davy?"

I saw the door move, and instinctively tried to hold the latch on the outside, to gain a moment's time. It was too late. Mr Peggotty thrust forth his face; and never could I forget the change that came upon it when he saw us, if I were to live five hundred years.

I remember a great wail and cry, and the women hanging about him, and we all standing in the room; I with a paper in my hand, which Ham had given me; Mr Peggotty, with his vest torn open, his hair wild, his face and lips quite white, and blood trickling down his bosom (it had sprung from his mouth, I think), looking fixedly at me.

"Read it, sir," he said, in a low shivering voice. "Slow, please I doesn't know as I can understand."

In the midst of the silence of death, I read thus, from a blotted letter:

> " 'When you, who love me so much better than I ever have deserved, even when my mind was innocent, see this, I shall be far away.' "

"I shall be fur away," he repeated slowly. "Stop! Em'ly fur away. Well!"

> " 'When I leave my dear home—my dear home—oh, my dear home!—in the morning,' "

the letter bore date on the previous night:

> " '—it will be never to come back, unless he brings me back a lady. This will be found at night, many hours after, instead of me. Oh, if you knew how my heart is torn. If even you, that I have wronged so much, that never can forgive me, could only know what I suffer! I am too wicked to write about myself. Oh, take comfort in thinking that I am so bad. Oh, for mercy's sake, tell uncle that I never loved him half so dear as now. Oh, don't remember how affectionate and kind you have all been to me—don't remember we were ever to be married—but try to think as if I died when I was little, and was buried somewhere. Pray Heaven that I am going away from, have compassion on my uncle! Tell him that I never loved him half so dear. Be his comfort. Love some good girl that will be what I was once to uncle, and be true to you, and worthy of you, and know no shame but me. God bless all! I'll pray for all, often, on my knees. If he don't bring me back a lady, and I don't pray for my own self, I'll pray for all. My parting love to uncle. My last tears, and my last thanks, for uncle!' "

That was all.

He stood, long after I had ceased to read, still looking at me. At length I ventured to take his hand, and to entreat him, as well as I could, to endeavour to get some command of himself. He replied, "I thankee, sir, I thankee!" without moving.

Ham spoke to him. Mr Peggotty was so far sensible of *his* affliction, that he wrung his hand; but, otherwise, he remained in the same state, and no one dared to disturb him.

Slowly, at last, he moved his eyes from my face, as if he were waking from a vision, and cast them round the room. Then he said, in a low voice:

"Who's the man? I want to know his name."

Ham glanced at me, and suddenly I felt a shock that struck me back.

"There's a man suspected," said Mr Peggotty. "Who is it?"

"Mas'r Davy!" implored Ham. "Go out a bit, and let me tell him what I must. You doesn't ought to hear it, sir."

I felt the shock again. I sank down in a chair, and tried to utter some reply; but my tongue was fettered, and my sight was weak.

"I want to know his name!" I heard said once more.

"For some time past," Ham faltered, "there's been a servant about here, at odd times.

There's been a gen'lm'n too. Both of 'em belonged to one another."

Mr Peggotty stood fixed as before, but now looking at him.

"The servant," pursued Ham, "was seen along with—our poor girl—last night. He's been in hiding about here, this week or over. He was thought to have gone, but he was hiding. Doen't stay, Mas'r Davy, doen't!"

I felt Peggotty's arm round my neck, but I could not have moved if the house had been about to fall upon me.

"A strange chay and hosses was outside town, this morning, on the Norwich road, a'most afore the day broke," Ham went on. "The servant went to it, and come from it, and went to it again. When he went to it again, Em'ly was nigh him. The t'other was inside. He's the man."

"For the Lord's love," said Mr Peggotty, falling back, and putting out his hand, as if to keep off what he dreaded. "Doen't tell me his name's Steerforth!"

"Mas'r Davy," exclaimed Ham, in a broken voice, "it ain't no fault of yourn—and I am far from laying of it to you—but his name is Steerforth, and he's a damned villain!"

Mr Peggotty uttered no cry, and shed no tear, and moved no more, until he seemed to wake again, all at once, and pulled down his rough coat from its peg in a corner.

"Bear a hand with this! I'm struck of a heap, and can't do it," he said, impatiently. "Bear a hand and help me. Well!" when somebody had done so. "Now give me that theer hat!"

Ham asked him whither he was going.

"I'm a going to seek my niece. I'm a going to seek my Em'ly. I'm a going, first, to stave in that theer boat, and sink it where I would have drownded *him*, as I'm a living soul, if I had had one thought of what was in him! As he sat afore me," he said, wildly, holding out his clenched right hand, "as he sat afore me, face to face, strike me down dead, but I'd have drownded him, and thought it right!—I'm a going to seek my niece."

"Where?" cried Ham, interposing himself before the door.

"Anywhere! I'm a going to seek my niece through the wureld. I'm a going to find my poor niece in her shame, and bring her back. No one stop me! I tell you I'm a going to seek my niece!"

"No, no!" cried Mrs Gummidge, coming between them, in a fit of crying. "No, no, Dan'l, not as you are now. Seek her in a little while, my lone lorn Dan'l, and that'll be but right! but not as you are now. Sit ye down, and give me your forgiveness for having ever been a worrit to you, Dan'l—what have *my* contrairies ever been to this!—and let us speak a word about them times when she was first an orphan, and when Ham was too, and when I was a poor widder woman, and you took me in. It'll soften your poor heart, Dan'l," laying her head upon his shoulder, "and you'll bear your sorrow better; for you know the promise, Dan'l, 'As you have done it unto one of the least of these, you have done it unto me'; and that can never fail under this roof, that's been our shelter for so many, many year!"

He was quite passive now; and when I heard him crying, the impulse that had been upon me to go down upon my knees, and ask their pardon for the desolation I had caused, and curse Steerforth, yielded to a better feeling. My overcharged heart found the same relief, and I cried too.

Chapter XXXII

THE BEGINNING OF A LONG JOURNEY

WHAT is natural in me, is natural in many other men, I infer, and so I am not afraid to write that I never had loved Steerforth better than when the ties that bound me to him were broken. In the keen distress of the discovery of his unworthiness, I thought more of all that was brilliant in him, I softened more towards all that was good in him, I did more justice to the qualities that might have made him a man of a noble nature and a great name, than ever I had done in the height of my devotion to him. Deeply as I felt my own unconscious part in his pollution of an honest home, I believed that if I had been brought face to face with him, I could not have uttered one reproach. I should have loved him so well still—though he fascinated me no longer—I should have held in so much tenderness the memory of my affection for him, that I think I should have been as weak as a spirit-wounded child, in all but the entertainment of a thought that we could ever be re-united. That thought I never had. I felt, as he had felt, that all was at an end between us. What his remembrances of me were, I have never known—they were light enough, perhaps, and easily dismissed—but mine of him were as the remembrances of a cherished friend, who was dead.

Yes, Steerforth, long removed from the scenes of this poor history! My sorrow may bear involuntary witness against you at the Judgement Throne; but my angry thoughts or my reproaches never will, I know!

The news of what had happened soon spread through the town; insomuch that as I passed along the streets next morning, I overheard the people speaking of it at their doors. Many were hard upon her, some few were hard upon him, but towards her second father and her lover there was but one sentiment. Among all kinds of people a respect for them in their distress prevailed, which was full of gentleness and delicacy. The seafaring men kept apart, when those two were seen early, walking with slow steps on the beach; and stood in knots, talking compassionately among themselves.

It was on the beach, close down by the sea, that I found them. It would have been easy to perceive that they had not slept all last night, even if Peggotty had failed to tell me of their still sitting just as I left them, when it was broad day. They looked worn; and I thought Mr Peggotty's head was bowed in one night more than in all the years I had known him. But they were both as grave and steady as the sea itself: then lying beneath a dark sky, waveless—yet with a heavy roll upon it, as if it breathed in its rest—and touched, on the horizon, with a strip of silvery light from the unseen sun.

"We have had a mort of talk, sir," said Mr Peggotty to me, when we had all three walked a little while in silence, "of what we ought and doen't ought to do. But we see our course now."

I happened to glance at Ham, then looking out to sea upon the distant light, and a frightful thought came into my mind—not that his face was angry, for it was not; I recall nothing but an expression of stern determination in it—that if ever he encountered Steerforth, he would kill him.

"My dooty here, sir," said Mr Peggotty, "is done. I'm a going to seek my—" he stopped, and went on in a firmer voice: "I'm a going to seek her. That's my dooty evermore."

He shook his head when I asked him where he would seek her, and inquired if I were going to London tomorrow? I told him I had not gone today, fearing to lose the chance of being of any service to him; but that I was ready to go when he would.

"I'll go along with you, sir," he rejoined, "if you're agreeable, tomorrow."

We walked again, for a while, in silence.

"Ham," he presently resumed, "he'll hold to his present work, and go and live along with my sister. The old boat yonder—"

"Will you desert the old boat, Mr Peggotty?" I gently interposed.

"My station, Mas'r Davy," he returned, "ain't there no longer; and if ever a boat foundered, since there was darkness on the face of the deep, that one's gone down. But no, sir, no; I doen't mean as it should be deserted. Fur from that."

We walked again for a while, as before, until he explained:

"My wishes is, sir, as it shall look, day and night, winter and summer, as it has always looked, since she fust know'd it. If ever she should come a wandering back, I wouldn't have the old place seem to cast her off, you understand, but seem to tempt her to draw nigher to 't, and to peep in, maybe, like a ghost, out of the wind and rain, through the old winder, at the old seat by the fire. Then, maybe, Mas'r Davy, seein' none but Missis Gummidge there, she might take heart to creep in, trembling; and might come to be laid down in her old bed, and rest her weary head where it was once so gay."

I could not speak to him in reply, though I tried.

"Every night," said Mr Peggotty, "as reg'lar as the night comes, the candle must be stood in its old pane of glass, that if ever she should see it, it may seem to say 'Come back, my child, come back!' If ever there's a knock, Ham (partic'ler a soft knock), after dark, at your aunt's door, doen't you go nigh it. Let it be her—not you—that sees my fallen child!"

He walked a little in front of us, and kept before us for some minutes. During this interval, I glanced at Ham again, and observing the same expression on his face, and his eyes still directed to the distant light, I touched his arm.

Twice I called him by his name, in the tone in which I might have tried to rouse a sleeper, before he heeded me. When I at last inquired on what his thoughts were so bent, he replied:

"On what's afore me, Mas'r Davy; and over yon."

"On the life before you, do you mean?" He had pointed confusedly out to sea.

"Ay, Mas'r Davy. I doen't rightly know how 'tis, but from over yon there seemed to me to come—the end of it like," looking at me as if he were waking, but with the same determined face.

"What end?" I asked, possessed by my former fear.

"I doen't know," he said, thoughtfully; "I was calling to mind that the beginning of it all did take place here—and then the end come. But it's gone! Mas'r Davy," he added; answering, as I think, my look; "you han't no call to be afeerd of me: but I'm kiender muddled; I don't fare to feel no matters,"—which was as much as to say that he was not himself, and quite confounded.

Mr Peggotty stopping for us to join him: we did so, and said no more. The remembrance of this, in connexion with my former thought, however, haunted me at intervals, even until the inexorable end came at its appointed time.

We insensibly approached the old boat, and entered. Mrs Gummidge, no longer moping in her especial corner, was busy preparing breakfast. She took Mr Peggotty's hat, and placed his seat for him, and spoke so comfortably and softly, that I hardly knew her.

"Dan'l, my good man," said she, "you must eat and drink, and keep up your strength, for without it you'll do nowt. Try, that's a dear soul! And if I disturb you with my clicketten," she meant her chattering, "tell me so, Dan'l, and I won't."

When she had served us all, she withdrew to the window, where she sedulously employed herself in repairing some shirts and other clothes belonging to Mr Peggotty, and neatly folding and packing them in an old oilskin bag, such as sailors carry. Meanwhile, she continued talking, in the same quiet manner:

"All times and seasons, you know, Dan'l," said Mrs Gummidge, "I shall be allus here, and everythink will look accordin' to your wishes. I'm a poor scholar, but I shall write to you, odd times, when you're away, and send my letters to Mas'r Davy. Maybe you'll write to me too, Dan'l, odd times, and tell me how you fare to feel upon your lone lorn journies."

"You'll be a solitary woman heer, I'm afeerd!" said Mr Peggotty.

"No, no, Dan'l," she returned, "I shan't be that. Doen't you mind me. I shall have enough to do to keep a Beein for you" (Mrs Gummidge meant a home), "again you come back—to keep a Beein here for any that may hap to come back, Dan'l. In the fine time, I shall set outside the door as I used to do. If any *should* come nigh, they shall see the old widder woman true to 'em, a long way off."

What a change in Mrs Gummidge in a little time! She was another woman. She was so devoted, she had such a quick perception of what it would be well to say, and what it would be well to leave unsaid; she was so forgetful of herself, and so regardful of the sorrow about her, that I held her in a sort of veneration. The work she did that day! There were many things to be brought up from the beach and stored in the outhouse—as oars, nets, sails, cordage, spars, lobster-pots, bags of ballast, and the like; and though there was abundance of assistance rendered, there being not a pair of working hands on all that shore but would have laboured hard for Mr Peggotty, and been well paid in being asked to do it, yet she persisted, all day long, in toiling under weights that she was quite unequal to, and fagging to and fro on all sorts of unnecessary errands. As to deploring her misfortunes, she appeared to have entirely lost the recollection of ever having had any. She preserved an equable cheerfulness in the midst of her sympathy, which was not the least astonishing part of the change that had come over her. Querulousness was out of the question. I did not even observe her voice to falter, or a tear to escape from her eyes, the whole day through, until twilight; when she and I and Mr Peggotty being alone together, and he having fallen asleep in perfect exhaustion, she broke into a half-suppressed fit of sobbing and crying, and taking me to the door, said, "Ever bless you, Mas'r Davy, be a friend to him, poor dear!" Then, she immediately ran out of the house to wash her face, in order that she might sit quietly beside him, and be found at work there, when he should awake. In short I left her, when I went away at night, the prop and staff of Mr Peggotty's affliction; and I could not meditate enough upon the lesson that I read in Mrs Gummidge, and the new experience she unfolded to me.

It was between nine and ten o'clock when, strolling in a melancholy manner through the town, I stopped at Mr Omer's door. Mr Omer had taken it so much to heart, his daughter told me, that he had been very low and poorly all day, and had gone to bed without his pipe.

"A deceitful, bad-hearted girl," said Mrs Joram. "There was no good in her, ever!"

"Don't say so," I returned. "You don't think so."

"Yes, I do!" cried Mrs Joram, angrily.

"No, no," said I.

Mrs Joram tossed her head, endeavouring to be very stern and cross; but she could not command her softer self, and began to cry. I was young, to be sure; but I thought much the better of her for this sympathy, and fancied it became her, as a virtuous wife and mother, very well indeed.

"What will she ever do!" sobbed Minnie. "Where will she go! What will become of her! Oh, how could she be so cruel, to herself and him!"

I remembered the time when Minnie was a young and pretty girl; and I was glad she remembered it too, so feelingly.

"My little Minnie," said Mrs Joram, "has only just now been got to sleep. Even in her sleep she is sobbing for Em'ly. All day long, little Minnie has cried for her, and asked me, over and over again, whether Em'ly was wicked? What can I say to her, when Em'ly tied a ribbon off her own neck round little Minnie's the last night she was here, and laid her head down on the pillow beside her till she was fast asleep! The ribbon's round my little Minnie's neck now. It ought not to be, perhaps, but what can I do? Em'ly is very bad, but they were fond of one another. And the child knows nothing!"

Mrs Joram was so unhappy that her husband came out to take care of her. Leaving them together, I went home to Peggotty's; more melancholy myself, if possible, than I had been yet.

That good creature—I mean Peggotty—all untired by her late anxieties and sleepless nights, was at her brother's, where she meant to stay till morning. An old woman, who had been employed about the house for some weeks past, while Peggotty had been unable to attend to it, was the house's only other occupant besides myself. As I had no occasion for her services, I sent her to bed, by no means against her will; and sat down before the kitchen fire a little while, to think about all this.

I was blending it with the deathbed of the late Mr Barkis, and was driving out with the tide towards the distance at which Ham had looked so singularly in the morning, when I was recalled from my wanderings by a knock at the door. There was a knocker upon the door, but it was not that which made the sound. The tap was from a hand, and low down upon the door, as if it were given by a child.

It made me start as much as if it had been the knock of a footman to a person of distinction. I opened the door; and at first looked down, to my amazement, on nothing but a great umbrella that appeared to be walking about of itself. But presently I discovered underneath it, Miss Mowcher.

I might not have been prepared to give the little creature a very kind reception, if, on her removing the umbrella, which her utmost efforts were unable to shut up, she had shown me the "volatile" expression of face which had made so great an impression on me at our first and last meeting. But her face, as she turned it up to mine, was so earnest; and when I relieved her of the umbrella (which would have been an inconvenient one for the Irish Giant), she wrung her little hands in such an afflicted manner; that I rather inclined towards her.

"Miss Mowcher!" said I, after glancing up and down the empty street, without distinctly knowing what I expected to see besides; "how do you come here? What is the matter?"

She motioned to me with her short right arm, to shut the umbrella for her; and passing me hurriedly, went into the kitchen. When I had closed the door, and followed, with the umbrella in my hand, I found her sitting on the corner of the fender—it was a low iron one, with two flat bars at top to stand plates upon—in the shadow of the boiler, swaying herself backwards and forwards, and chafing her hands upon her knees like a person in pain.

Quite alarmed at being the only recipient of this untimely visit, and the only spectator of this portentous behaviour, I exclaimed again, "Pray tell me, Miss Mowcher, what is the matter! are you ill?"

"My dear young soul," returned Miss Mowcher, squeezing her hands upon her heart one over the other. "I am ill here, I am very ill. To think that it should come to this, when I might have known it and perhaps prevented it, if I hadn't been a thoughtless fool!"

Again her large bonnet (very disproportionate to the figure) went backwards and forwards, in her swaying of her little body to and fro; while a most gigantic bonnet rocked, in unison with it, upon the wall.

"I am surprised," I began, "to see you so distressed and serious"—when she interrupted me.

"Yes, it's always so!" she said. "They are all surprised, these inconsiderate young people, fairly and full grown, to see any natural feeling in a little thing like me! They make a plaything of me, use me for their amusement, throw me away when they are tired, and wonder that I feel more than a toy horse or a wooden soldier! Yes, yes, that's the way. The old way!"

"It may be, with others," I returned, "but I do assure you it is not with me. Perhaps I ought not to be at all surprised to see you as you are now: I know so little of you. I said, without consideration, what I thought."

"What can I do?" returned the little woman, standing up, and holding out her arms to show herself. "See! What I am, my father was; and my sister is; and my brother is. I have worked for sister and brother these many years—hard, Mr Copperfield—all day. I must live. I do no harm. If there are people so unreflecting or so cruel, as to make a jest of me, what is left for me to do but to make a jest of myself, them, and everything? If I do so, for the time, whose fault is that? Mine?"

No. Not Miss Mowcher's, I perceived.

"If I had shown myself a sensitive dwarf to your false friend," pursued the little woman, shaking her head at me, with reproachful earnestness, "how much of his help or good will do you think *I* should ever have had? If little Mowcher (who had no hand, young gentleman, in the making of herself) addressed herself to him, or the like of him, because of her misfortunes, when do you suppose her small voice would have been heard? Little Mowcher would have as much need to live, if she was the bitterest and dullest of pigmies; but she couldn't do it. No. She might whistle for her bread and butter till she died of Air."

Miss Mowcher sat down on the fender again, and took out her handkerchief, and wiped her eyes.

"Be thankful for me, if you have a kind heart, as I think you have," she said, "that while I know well what I am, I can be cheerful and endure it all. I am thankful for myself, at any rate, that I can find my tiny way through the world, without being beholden to anyone; and that in return for all that is thrown at me, in folly or vanity, as I go along, I can throw bubbles back. If I don't brood over all I want, it is the better for me, and not the worse for anyone. If I am a plaything for you giants, be gentle with me."

Miss Mowcher replaced her handkerchief in her pocket, looking at me with very intent expression all the while, and pursued:

"I saw you in the street just now. You may suppose I am not able to walk as fast as you, with my short legs and short breath, and I couldn't overtake you; but I guessed where you came, and came after you. I have been here before, today, but the good woman wasn't at home."

"Do you know her?" I demanded.

"I know *of* her, and about her," she replied, "from Omer and Joram. I was there at seven o'clock this morning. Do you remember what Steerforth said to me about this unfortunate girl, that time when I saw you both at the inn?"

The great bonnet on Miss Mowcher's head, and the greater bonnet on the wall, began to go backwards and forwards again when she asked this question.

I remembered very well what she referred to, having had it in my thoughts many times that day. I told her so.

"May the Father of all Evil confound him," said the little woman, holding up her forefinger between me and her sparkling eyes, "and ten times more confound that wicked servant; but I believed it was *you* who had a boyish passion for her!"

"I?" I repeated.

"Child, child! In the name of blind ill-fortune," cried Miss Mowcher, wringing her hands impatiently, as she went to and fro again upon the fender, "why did you praise her so, and blush, and look disturbed?"

I could not conceal from myself that I had done this, though for a reason very different from her supposition.

"What did I know?" said Miss Mowcher, taking out her handkerchief again, and giving one little stamp on the ground whenever, at short intervals, she applied it to her eyes with both hands at once. "He was crossing you and wheedling you, I saw; and you were soft wax in his hands, I saw. Had I left the room a minute, when his man told me that 'Young Innocence' (so he called you, and you may call him 'Old Guilt' all the days of your life) had set his heart upon her, and she was giddy and liked him, but his master was resolved that no harm should come of it—more for your sake than for hers—and that that was their business here? How could I *but* believe him? I saw Steerforth soothe and please you by his praise of her! You were the first to mention her name. You owned to an old admiration of her. You were hot and cold, and red and white, all at once when I spoke to you of her. What could I think—what *did* I think—but that you were a young libertine in everything but experience, and had fallen into hands that had experience enough, and could manage you (having the fancy) for your own good? Oh! oh! oh! They were afraid of my finding out the truth," exclaimed Miss Mowcher, getting off the fender, and trotting up and down the kitchen with her two short arms distressfully lifted up, "because I am a sharp little thing—I need be, to get through the world at all!—and they deceived me altogether, and I gave the poor unfortunate girl a letter, which I fully believe was the beginning of her ever speaking to Littimer, who was left behind on purpose!"

I stood amazed at the revelation of all this perfidy, looking at Miss Mowcher as she walked up and down the kitchen until she was out of breath: when she sat upon the fender again, and, drying her face with her handkerchief, shook her head for a long time, without otherwise moving, and without breaking silence.

"My country rounds," she added at length, "brought me to Norwich, Mr Copperfield, the night before last. What I happened to find there, about their secret way of coming and going, without you—which was strange—led to my suspecting something wrong. I got into the coach from London last night, as it came through Norwich, and was here this morning. Oh, oh, oh! too late!"

Poor little Mowcher turned so chilly after all her crying and fretting, that she turned round on the fender, putting her poor little wet feet in among the ashes to warm them, and sat looking at the fire, like a large doll. I sat in a chair on the other side of the hearth, lost in unhappy reflections, and looking at the fire too, and sometimes at her.

"I must go," she said at last, rising as she spoke. "It's late. You don't mistrust me?"

Meeting her sharp glance, which was as sharp as ever when she asked me, I could not on that short challenge answer no, quite frankly.

"Come!" said she, accepting the offer of my hand to help her over the fender, and looking wistfully up into my face, "you know you wouldn't mistrust me, if I was a full-sized woman!"

I felt that there was much truth in this; and I felt rather ashamed of myself.

"You are a young man," she said, nodding. "Take a word of advice, even from three foot nothing. Try not to associate bodily defects with mental, my good friend, except for a solid reason."

She had got over the fender now, and I had got over my suspicion. I told her that I believed she had given me a faithful account of herself, and that we had both been hapless instruments in designing hands. She thanked me, and said I was a good fellow.

"Now, mind!" she exclaimed, turning back on her way to the door, and looking shrewdly at me, with her forefinger up again. "I have some reason to suspect, from what I have heard—my ears are always open; I can't afford to spare what powers I have—that they are gone abroad. But if ever they return, if ever any one of them returns, while I am alive, I am more likely than another, going about as I do, to find it out soon. Whatever I know, you shall know. If ever I can do anything to serve the poor betrayed girl, I will do it faithfully, please Heaven! And Littimer had better have a bloodhound at his back, than little Mowcher!"

I placed implicit faith in this last statement, when I marked the look with which it was accompanied.

"Trust me no more, but trust me no less, than you would trust a full-sized woman," said the little creature, touching me appealingly on the wrist. "If ever you see me again, unlike what I am now, and like what I was when you first saw me, observe what company I am in. Call to mind that I am a very helpless and defenceless little thing. Think of me at home with my brother like myself and sister like myself, when my day's work is done. Perhaps you won't, then, be very hard upon me, or surprised if I can be distressed and serious. Good night!"

I gave Miss Mowcher my hand, with a very different opinion of her from that which I had hitherto entertained, and opened the door to let her out. It was not a trifling business to get the great umbrella up, and properly balanced in her grasp; but at last I successfully accomplished this, and saw it go bobbing down the street through the rain, without the least appearance of having anybody underneath it, except when a heavier fall than usual from some over-charged water-spout sent it toppling over, on one side, and discovered Miss Mowcher struggling violently to get it right. After making one or two sallies to her relief, which were rendered futile by the umbrella's hopping on again, like an immense bird, before I could reach it, I came in, went to bed, and slept till morning.

In the morning I was joined by Mr Peggotty and by my old nurse, and we went at an early hour to the coach office, where Mrs Gummidge and Ham were waiting to take leave of us.

"Mas'r Davy," Ham whispered, drawing me aside, while Mr Peggotty was stowing his bag among the luggage, "his life is quite broke up. He doen't know wheer he's going; he doen't know what's afore him; he's bound upon a voyage that'll last, on and off, all the rest of his days, take my wured for 't, unless he finds what he's a seeking of. I am sure you'll be a friend to him, Mas'r Davy?"

"Trust me, I will indeed," said I, shaking hands with Ham earnestly.

"Thankee. Thankee, very kind, sir. One thing furder. I'm in good employ, you know,

Mas'r Davy, and I han't no way now of spending what I gets. Money's of no use to me no more, except to live. If you can lay it out for him, I shall do my work with a better art. Though as to that, sir," and he spoke very steadily and mildly, "you're not to think but I shall work at all times, like a man, and act the best that lays in my power!"

I told him I was well convinced of it; and I hinted that I hoped the time might even come, when he would cease to lead the lonely life he naturally contemplated now.

"No, sir," he said, shaking his head, "all that's past and over with me, sir. No one can never fill the place that's empty. But you'll bear in mind about the money, as theer's at all times some laying by for him?"

Reminding him of the fact, that Mr Peggotty derived a steady, though certainly a very moderate income from the bequest of his late brother-in-law, I promised to do so. We then took leave of each other. I cannot leave him even now, without remembering with a pang, at once his modest fortitude and his great sorrow.

As to Mrs Gummidge, if I were to endeavour to describe how she ran down the street by the side of the coach, seeing nothing but Mr Peggotty on the roof, through the tears she tried to repress, and dashing herself against the people who were coming in the opposite direction, I should enter on a task of some difficulty. Therefore I had better leave her sitting on a baker's door-step, out of breath, with no shape at all remaining in her bonnet, and one of her shoes off, lying on the pavement at a considerable distance.

When we got to our journey's end, our first pursuit was to look about for a little lodging for Peggotty, where her brother could have a bed. We were so fortunate as to find one, of a very clean and cheap description, over a chandler's shop, only two streets removed from me. When we had engaged this domicile, I bought some cold meat at an eating-house, and took my fellow-travellers home to tea; a proceeding, I regret to state, which did not meet with Mrs Crupp's approval, but quite the contrary. I ought to observe, however, in explanation of that lady's state of mind, that she was much offended by Peggotty's tucking up her widow's gown before she had been ten minutes in the place, and setting to work to dust my bedroom. This Mrs Crupp regarded in the light of a liberty, and a liberty, she said, was a thing she never allowed.

Mr Peggotty had made a communication to me on the way to London for which I was not unprepared. It was, that he purposed first seeing Mrs Steerforth. As I felt bound to assist him in this, and also to mediate between them; with the view of sparing the mother's feelings as much as possible, I wrote to her that night. I told her as mildly as I could what his wrong was, and what my own share in his injury. I said he was a man in very common life, but of a most gentle and upright character; and that I ventured to express a hope that she would not refuse to see him in his heavy trouble. I mentioned two o'clock in the afternoon as the hour of our coming, and I sent the letter myself by the first coach in the morning.

At the appointed time, we stood at the door—the door of that house where I had been, a few days since, so happy: where my youthful confidence and warmth of heart had been yielded up so freely: which was closed against me henceforth: which was now a waste, a ruin.

No Littimer appeared. The pleasanter face which had replaced his, on the occasion of my last visit, answered to our summons, and went before us to the drawing-room. Mrs Steerforth was sitting there. Rosa Dartle glided, as we went in, from another part of the room and stood behind her chair.

I saw, directly, in his mother's face, that she knew from himself what he had done. It was very pale; and bore the traces of deeper emotion than my letter alone, weakened by the doubts her fondness would have raised upon it, would have been likely to create.

I thought her more like him than ever I had thought her; and I felt, rather than saw, that the resemblance was not lost on my companion.

She sat upright in her arm-chair, with a stately, immovable, passionless air, that it seemed as if nothing could disturb. She looked very steadfastly at Mr Peggotty when he stood before her; and he looked quite as steadfastly at her. Rosa Dartle's keen glance comprehended all of us. For some moments not a word was spoken.

She motioned to Mr Peggotty to be seated. He said, in a low voice, "I shouldn't feel it nat'ral, ma'am, to sit down in this house. I'd sooner stand." And this was succeeded by another silence, which she broke thus:

"I know, with deep regret, what has brought you here. What do you want of me? What do you ask me to do?"

He put his hat under his arm, and feeling in his breast for Emily's letter, took it out, unfolded it, and gave it to her.

"Please to read that, ma'am. That's my niece's hand!"

She read it, in the same stately and impassive way,—untouched by its contents, as far as I could see,—and returned it to him.

" 'Unless he brings me back a lady,' " said Mr Peggotty, tracing out that part with his finger. "I come to know, ma'am, whether he will keep his wured?"

"No," she returned.

"Why not?" said Mr Peggotty.

"It is impossible. He would disgrace himself. You cannot fail to know that she is far below him."

"Raise her up!" said Mr Peggotty.

"She is uneducated and ignorant."

"Maybe she's not; maybe she is," said Mr Peggotty. "*I* think not, ma'am; but I'm no judge of them things. Teach her better!"

"Since you oblige me to speak more plainly, which I am very unwilling to do, her humble connexions would render such a thing impossible, if nothing else did."

"Hark to this, ma'am," he returned, slowly and quietly. "You know what it is to love your child. So do I. If she was a hundred times my child, I couldn't love her more. You doen't know what it is to lose your child. I do. All the heaps of riches in the wureld would be nowt to me (if they was mine) to buy her back! But, save her from this disgrace, and she shall never be disgraced by us. Not one of us that she's growed up among, not one of us that's lived along with her and had her for their all in all, these many year, will ever look upon her pritty face again. We'll be content to let her be; we'll be content to think of her, far off, as if she was underneath another sun and sky; we'll be content to trust her to her husband,—to her little children, p'raps,—and bide the time when all of us shall be alike in quality afore our God!"

The rugged eloquence with which he spoke, was not devoid of all effect. She still preserved her proud manner, but there was a touch of softness in her voice, as she answered:

"I justify nothing. I make no counter-accusations. But I am sorry to repeat, it is impossible. Such a marriage would irretrievably blight my son's career, and ruin his prospects. Nothing is more certain than that it never can take place, and never will. If there is any other compensation—"

"I am looking at the likeness of the face," interrupted Mr Peggotty, with a steady but a kindling eye, "that has looked at me, in my home, at my fireside, in my boat—wheer not?—smiling and friendly, when it was so treacherous, that I go half wild when I think of it. If the likeness of that face don't turn to burning fire, at the thought of offering money to me for my child's blight and ruin, it's as bad. I doen't know, being a lady's, but what it's worse."

She changed now, in a moment. An angry flush overspread her features; and she said, in an intolerant manner, grasping the armchair tightly with her hands:

"What compensation can you make to *me* for opening such a pit between me and my son? What is your love to mine? What is your separation to ours?"

Miss Dartle softly touched her, and bent down her head to whisper, but she would not hear a word.

"No, Rosa, not a word! Let the man listen to what I say! My son, who has been the object of my life, to whom its every thought has been devoted, whom I have gratified from a child in every wish, from whom I have had no separate existence since his birth,—to take up in a moment with a miserable girl, and avoid me! To repay my confidence with systematic deception, for her sake, and quit me for her! To set this wretched fancy, against his mother's claims upon his duty, love, respect, gratitude— claims that every day and hour of his life should have strengthened into ties that nothing could be proof against! Is this no injury?"

Again Rosa Dartle tried to soothe her; again ineffectually.

"I say, Rosa, not a word! If he can stake his all upon the lightest object, I can stake my all upon a greater purpose. Let him go where he will, with the means that my love has secured to him! Does he think to reduce me by long absence? He knows his mother very little if he does. Let him put away his whim now, and he is welcome back. Let him not put her away now, and he never shall come near me, living or dying, while I can raise my hand to make a sign against it, unless, being rid of her for ever, he comes humbly to me and begs for my forgiveness. This is my right. This is the acknowledgement I *will have.* This is the separation that there is between us! And is this," she added, looking at her visitor with the proud intolerant air with which she had begun, "no injury?"

While I heard and saw the mother as she said these words, I seemed to hear and see the son, defying them. All that I had ever seen in him of an unyielding, wilful spirit, I saw in her. All the understanding that I had now of his misdirected energy, became an understanding of her character too, and a perception that it was, in its strongest springs, the same.

She now observed to me, aloud, resuming her former restraint, that it was useless to hear more, or to say more, and that she begged to put an end to the interview. She rose with an air of dignity to leave the room, when Mr Peggotty signified that it was needless.

"Doen't fear me being any hindrance to you, I have no more to say, ma'am," he remarked, as he moved towards the door. "I come heer with no hope, and I take away no hope. I have done what I thowt should be done, but I never looked fur any good to come of my stan'ning where I do. This has been too evil a house fur me and mine, fur me to be in my right senses and expect it."

With this, we departed; leaving her standing by her elbowchair, a picture of a noble presence and a handsome face.

We had, on our way out, to cross a paved hall, with glass sides and roof, over which a vine was trained. Its leaves and shoots were green then, and the day being sunny, a pair of glass doors leading to the garden were thrown open. Rosa Dartle, entering this way with a noiseless step, when we were close to them, addressed herself to me:

"You do well," she said, "indeed, to bring this fellow here!"

Such a concentration of rage and scorn as darkened her face, and flashed in her jet-black eyes, I could not have thought compressible even into that face. The scar made by the hammer was, as usual in this excited state of her features, strongly marked. When the throbbing I had seen before, came into it as I looked at her, she absolutely lifted up her hand, and struck it.

"This is a fellow," she said, "to champion and bring here, is he not? You are a true man!"

"Miss Dartle," I returned, "you are surely not so unjust as to condemn *me!*"

"Why do you bring division between these two mad creatures?" she returned. "Don't you know that they are both mad with their own self-will and pride?"

"Is it my doing?" I returned.

"Is it your doing!" she retorted. "Why do you bring this man here?"

"He is a deeply-injured man, Miss Dartle," I replied. "You may not know it."

"I know that James Steerforth," she said, with her hand on her bosom, as if to prevent the storm that was raging there, from being loud, "has a false, corrupt heart, and is a traitor. But what need I know or care about this fellow, and his common niece?"

"Miss Dartle," I returned, "you deepen the injury. It is sufficient already. I will only say, at parting, that you do him a great wrong."

"I do him no wrong," she returned. "They are a depraved, worthless set. I would have her whipped!"

Mr Peggotty passed on, without a word, and went out at the door.

"Oh, shame, Miss Dartle! shame!" I said indignantly. "How can you bear to trample on his undeserved affliction!"

"I would trample on them all," she answered. "I would have his house pulled down. I would have her branded on the face, dressed in rags, and cast out in the streets to starve. If I had the power to sit in judgement on her, I would see it done. See it done? I would do it! I detest her. If I ever could reproach her with her infamous condition, I would go anywhere to do so. If I could hunt her to her grave, I would. If there was any word of comfort that would be a solace to her in her dying hour, and only I possessed it, I wouldn't part with it for Life itself."

The mere vehemence of her words can convey, I am sensible, but a weak impression of the passion by which she was possessed, and which made itself articulate in her whole figure, though her voice, instead of being raised, was lower than usual. No description I could give of her would do justice to my recollection of her, or to her entire deliverance of herself to her anger. I have seen passion in many forms, but I have never seen it in such a form as that.

When I joined Mr Peggotty, he was walking slowly and thoughtfully down the hill. He told me, as soon as I came up with him, that having now discharged his mind of what he had purposed doing in London, he meant "to set out on his travels," that night. I asked him where he meant to go? He only answered, "I'm a going, sir, to seek my niece."

We went back to the little lodging over the chandler's shop, and there I found an opportunity of repeating to Peggotty what he had said to me. She informed me, in return, that he had said the same to her that morning. She knew no more than I did, where he was going, but she thought he had some project shaped out in his mind.

I did not like to leave him, under such circumstances, and we all three dined together off a beefsteak pie—which was one of the many good things for which Peggotty was famous—and which was curiously flavoured on this occasion, I recollect well, by a miscellaneous taste of tea, coffee, butter, bacon, cheese, new loaves, firewood, candles, and walnut ketchup, continually ascending from the shop. After dinner we sat for an hour or so near the window, without talking much; and then Mr Peggotty got up, and brought his oilskin bag and his stout stick, and laid them on the table.

He accepted, from his sister's stock of ready money, a small sum on account of his legacy; barely enough, I should have thought, to keep him for a month. He promised to communicate with me, when anything befell him; and he slung his bag about him, took his hat and stick, and bade us both "Good-bye!"

"All good attend you, dear old woman," he said, embracing Peggotty, "and you too, Mas'r Davy!" shaking hands with me. "I'm a-going to seek her, fur and wide. If she should come home while I'm away—but ah, that ain't like to be!—or if I should bring her back, my meaning is, that she and me shall live and die where no one can't reproach her. If any hurt should come to me, remember that the last words I left for her was, 'My unchanged love is with my darling child, and I forgive her!' "

He said this solemnly, bare-headed; then, putting on his hat, he went down the stairs, and away. We followed to the door. It was a warm, dusty evening, just the time when, in the great main thoroughfare out of which that by-way turned, there was a temporary lull in the eternal tread of feet upon the pavement, and a strong red sunshine. He turned, alone, at the corner of our shady street, into a glow of light, in which we lost him.

Rarely did that hour of the evening come, rarely did I wake at night, rarely did I look up at the moon, or stars, or watch the falling rain, or hear the wind, but I thought of his solitary figure toiling on, poor pilgrim, and recalled the words:

"I'm a going to seek her, fur and wide. If any hurt should come to me, remember that the last words I left for her was, 'My unchanged love is with my darling child, and I forgive her!' "

Chapter XXXIII

BLISSFUL

ALL this time, I had gone on loving Dora, harder than ever. Her idea was my refuge in disappointment and distress, and made some amends to me, even for the loss of my friend. The more I pitied myself, or pitied others, the more I sought for consolation in the image of Dora. The greater the accumulation of deceit and trouble in the world, the brighter and the purer shone the star of Dora high above the world. I don't think I had any definite idea where Dora came from, or in what degree she was related to a higher order of beings; but I am quite sure I should have scouted the notion of her being simply human, like any other young lady, with indignation and contempt.

If I may so express it, I was steeped in Dora. I was not merely over head and ears in love with her, but I was saturated through and through. Enough love might have been wrung out of me, metaphorically speaking, to drown anybody in; and yet there would have remained enough within me, and all over me, to pervade my entire existence.

The first thing I did, on my own account, when I came back, was to take a night-walk to Norwood, and, like the subject of a venerable riddle of my childhood, to go "round and round the house, without ever touching the house," thinking about Dora.

I believe the theme of this incomprehensible conundrum was the moon. No matter what it was, I, the moon-struck slave of Dora, perambulated round and round the house and garden for two hours, looking through crevices in the palings, getting my chin by dint of violent exertion above the rusty nails on the top, blowing kisses at the lights in the windows, and romantically calling on the night, at intervals, to shield my Dora—I don't exactly know what from, I suppose from fire. Perhaps from mice, to which she had a great objection.

My love was so much in my mind and it was so natural to me to confide in Peggotty, when I found her again by my side of an evening with the old set of industrial implements, busily making the tour of my wardrobe, that I imparted to her, in a sufficiently roundabout way, my great secret. Peggotty was strongly interested, but I could not get her into my view of the case at all. She was audaciously prejudiced in my favour, and quite unable to understand why I should have any misgivings, or be low-spirited about it. "The young lady might think herself well off," she observed, "to have such a beau. And as to her Pa," she said, "what *did* the gentleman expect, for gracious sake!"

I observed, however, that Mr Spenlow's proctorial gown and stiff cravat took Peggotty down a little, and inspired her with a greater reverence for the man who was gradually becoming more and more etherealized in my eyes every day, and about whom a reflected radiance seemed to me to beam when he sat erect in Court among his papers, like a little light-house in a sea of stationery. And by the by, it used to be uncommonly strange to me to consider, I remember, as I sat in Court too, how those dim old judges and doctors wouldn't have cared for Dora, if they had known her; how they wouldn't have gone out of their senses with rapture, if marriage with Dora had been proposed to them; how Dora might have sung, and played upon that glorified guitar, until she led *me* to the verge of madness, yet not have tempted one of those slow-goers an inch out of his road!

I despised them, to a man. Frozen-out old gardeners in the flower-beds of the heart, I took a personal offence against them all. The Bench was nothing to me but an insensible blunderer. The Bar had no more tenderness or poetry in it, than the bar of a public-house.

Taking the management of Peggotty's affairs into my own hands, with no little pride, I proved the will, and came to a settlement with the Legacy Duty-office, and took her to the Bank, and soon got everything into an orderly train. We varied the legal character of these proceedings by going to see some perspiring Wax-work, in Fleet Street (melted, I should hope, these twenty years); and by visiting Miss Linwood's Exhibition, which I remember as a Mausoleum of needlework, favourable to self-examination and repentance; and by inspecting the Tower of London; and going to the top of St Paul's. All these wonders afforded Peggotty as much pleasure as she was able to enjoy, under existing circumstances: except, I think, St Paul's, which, from her long attachment to her work-box, became a rival of the picture on the lid, and was, in some particulars, vanquished, she considered, by that work of art.

Peggotty's business, which was what we used to call "common-form business" in the Commons (and very light and lucrative the common-form business was), being settled, I took her down to the office one morning to pay her bill. Mr Spenlow had stepped out, old Tiffey said, to get a gentleman sworn for a marriage licence; but as I knew he would be back directly, our place lying close to the Surrogate's, and to the Vicar-General's office too, I told Peggotty to wait.

We were a little like undertakers in the Commons, as regarded Probate transactions; generally making it a rule to look more or less cut up, when we had to deal with clients in mourning. In a similar feeling of delicacy, we were always blithe and light-hearted with the licence clients. Therefore I hinted to Peggotty that she would find Mr Spenlow much recovered from the shock of Mr Barkis's decease; and indeed he came in like a bridegroom.

But neither Peggotty nor I had eyes for him, when we saw, in company with him, Mr Murdstone. He was very little changed. His hair looked as thick, and was certainly as black, as ever; and his glance was as little to be trusted as of old.

"Ah, Copperfield?" said Mr Spenlow. "You know this gentleman, I believe?"

I made my gentleman a distant bow, and Peggotty barely recognized him. He was, at first, somewhat disconcerted to meet us two together; but quickly decided what to do, and came up to me.

"I hope," he said, "that you are doing well?"

"It can hardly be interesting to you," said I. "Yes, if you wish to know."

We looked at each other, and he addressed himself to Peggotty.

"And you," said he. "I am sorry to observe that you have lost your husband."

"It's not the first loss I have had in my life, Mr Murdstone," replied Peggotty, trembling from head to foot. "I am glad to hope that there is nobody to blame for this one,—nobody to answer for it."

"Ha!" said he; "that's a comfortable reflection. You have done your duty?"

"I have not worn anybody's life away," said Peggotty, "I am thankful to think! No, Mr Murdstone, I have not worrited and frightened any sweet creetur to an early grave!"

He eyed her gloomily—remorsefully I thought—for an instant; and said, turning his head towards me, but looking at my feet instead of my face:

"We are not likely to encounter soon again;—a source of satisfaction to us both, no doubt, for such meetings as this can never be agreeable. I do not expect that you, who always rebelled against my just authority, exerted for your benefit and reformation, should owe me any good-will now. There is an antipathy between us—"

"An old one, I believe?" said I, interrupting him.

He smiled, and shot as evil a glance at me as could come from his dark eyes.

"It rankled in your baby breast," he said. "It embittered the life of your poor mother. You are right. I hope you may do better, yet; I hope you may correct yourself."

Here he ended the dialogue, which had been carried on in a low voice, in a corner of the outer office, by passing into Mr Spenlow's room, and saying aloud, in his smooth-est manner:

"Gentlemen of Mr Spenlow's profession are accustomed to family differences, and know how complicated and difficult they always are!" With that, he paid the money for his licence; and, receiving it neatly folded from Mr Spenlow, together with a shake of the hand, and a polite wish for his happiness and the lady's went out of the office.

I might have had more difficulty in constraining myself to be silent under his words, if I had had less difficulty in impressing upon Peggotty (who was only angry on my account, good creature!) that we were not in a place for recrimination, and that I besought her to hold her peace. She was so unusually roused, that I was glad to compound for an affectionate hug, elicited by this revival in her mind of our old injuries, and to make the best I could of it, before Mr Spenlow and the clerks.

Mr Spenlow did not appear to know what the connexion between Mr Murdstone and myself was; which I was glad of, for I could not bear to acknowledge him, even in my own breast, remembering what I did of the history of my poor mother. Mr Spenlow seemed to think, if he thought anything about the matter, that my aunt was the leader of the state party in our family, and that there was a rebel party commanded by somebody else—so I gathered at least from what he said, while we were waiting for Mr Tiffey to make out Peggotty's bill of costs.

"Miss Trotwood," he remarked, "is very firm, no doubt, and not likely to give way to opposition. I have an admiration for her character, and I may congratulate you, Copperfield, on being on the right side. Differences between relations are much to be deplored—but they are extremely general—and the great thing is, to be on the right side" meaning, I take it, on the side of the moneyed interest.

"Rather a good marriage this, I believe?" said Mr Spenlow.

I explained that I knew nothing about it.

"Indeed!" he said. "Speaking from the few words Mr Murdstone dropped—as a man frequently does on these occasions—and from what Miss Murdstone let fall, I should say it was rather a good marriage."

"Do you mean that there is money, sir?" I asked.

"Yes," said Mr Spenlow, "I understand there's money. Beauty too, I am told."

"Indeed! Is his new wife young?"

"Just of age," said Mr Spenlow. "So lately, that I should think they had been waiting for that."

"Lord deliver her!" said Peggotty. So very emphatically and unexpectedly, that we were all three discomposed; until Tiffey came in with the bill.

Old Tiffey soon appeared, however, and handed it to Mr Spenlow, to look over. Mr Spenlow, settling his chin in his cravat and rubbing it softly, went over the items with a deprecatory air—as if it were all Jorkins's doing—and handed it back to Tiffey with a bland sigh.

"Yes," he said. "That's right. Quite right. I should have been extremely happy, Copperfield, to have limited these charges to the actual expenditure out of pocket, but it is an irksome incident in my professional life, that I am not at liberty to consult my own wishes. I have a partner—Mr Jorkins."

As he said this with a gentle melancholy, which was the next thing to making no charge at all, I expressed my acknowledgements on Peggotty's behalf, and paid Tiffey in banknotes. Peggotty then retired to her lodging, and Mr Spenlow and I went into Court, where we had a divorce-suit coming on, under an ingenious little statute (repealed now, I believe, but in virtue of which I have seen several marriages annulled), of which the merits were these. The husband, whose name was Thomas Benjamin, had taken out his marriage licence as Thomas only; suppressing the Benjamin, in case he should not find himself as comfortable as he expected. *Not* finding himself as comfortable as he expected, or being a little fatigued with his wife, poor fellow, he now came forward, by a friend, after being married a year or two, and declared that his name was Thomas Benjamin, and therefore he was not married at all. Which the Court confirmed, to his great satisfaction.

I must say that I had my doubts about the strict justice of this, and was not even frightened out of them by the bushel of wheat which reconciles all anomalies. But Mr Spenlow argued the matter with me. He said, Look at the world, there was good and evil in that; look at the ecclesiastical law, there was good and evil in *that*. It was all part of a system. Very good. There you were!

I had not the hardihood to suggest to Dora's father that possibly we might even improve the world a little, if we got up early in the morning, and took off our coats to the work; but I confessed that I thought we might improve the Commons. Mr Spenlow replied that he would particularly advise me to dismiss that idea from my mind, as not being worthy of my gentlemanly character; but that he would be glad to hear from me of what improvement I thought the Commons susceptible?

Taking that part of the Commons which happened to be nearest to us—for our man was unmarried by this time, and we were out of Court, and strolling past the Prerogative Office—I submitted that I thought the Prerogative Office rather a queerly managed institution. Mr Spenlow inquired in what respect? I replied, with all due deference to his experience (but with more deference, I am afraid, to his being Dora's father), that perhaps it was a little nonsensical that the Registry of that Court, containing the original wills of all persons leaving effects within the immense province of Canterbury, for three whole centuries, should be an accidental building, never designed for the purpose, leased by the registrars for their own private emolument, unsafe, not even ascertained to be fire-proof, choked with the important documents it held, and positively, from the roof to the basement, a mercenary speculation of the registrars, who took great fees from the public, and crammed the public's wills away anyhow and anywhere, having no other object than to get rid of them cheaply. That, perhaps, it was a little unreasonable that these registrars in the receipt of profits amounting to eight or nine thousand pounds a year (to say nothing of the profits of the deputy registrars, and clerks of seats), should not be obliged to spend a little of that money, in finding a reasonably safe place for the important documents which all classes of people were compelled to hand over to them, whether they would or no. That, perhaps, it was a little unjust, that all the great offices in this great office should be magnificent sinecures, while the unfortunate working-clerks in the cold dark room upstairs were the worst rewarded, and the least considered men, doing important services, in London. That perhaps it was a little indecent that the principal registrar of all, whose duty it was to find the public, constantly resorting to this place, all needful accommodation, should be an enormous sinecurist in virtue of that post (and might be, besides, a clergyman, a pluralist, the holder of a stall in a cathedral, and what not),—while the public was put to the inconvenience of which we had a specimen every afternoon when the office was busy, and which we knew to be quite monstrous. That, perhaps, in short, this Prerogative Office of the diocese of Canterbury was altogether such a pestilent job, and such a pernicious absurdity, that but for its being squeezed away in a corner of St Paul's Churchyard, which few people knew, it must have been turned completely inside out, and upside down, long ago.

Mr Spenlow smiled as I became modestly warm on the subject, and then argued this question with me as he had argued the other. He said, what was it after all? It was a question of feeling. If the public felt that their wills were in safe keeping, and took it for granted that the office was not to be made better, who was the worse for it? Nobody. Who was the better for it? All the Sinecurists. Very well. Then the good predominated. It might not be a perfect system; nothing *was* perfect; but what he objected to, was, the insertion of the wedge. Under the Prerogative Office, the country had been glorious. Insert the wedge into the Prerogative Office, and the country would cease to be glorious. He considered it the principle of a gentleman to take things as he found them; and he had no doubt the Prerogative Office would last our time. I deferred to his opinion, though I had great doubts of it myself. I find he was right, however; for it has not only lasted to the present moment, but has done so in the teeth of a great parliamentary report made (not too willingly) eighteen years ago, when all these objections of mine were set forth in detail, and when the existing stowage for wills was described as equal to the accumulation of only two years and a half more. What they have done with them since; whether they have lost many, or whether they sell any, now and then, to the butter shops; I don't know. I am glad mine is not there, and I hope it may not go there, yet awhile.

I have set all this down, in my present blissful chapter, because here it comes into its natural place. Mr Spenlow and I falling into this conversation, prolonged it and our saunter to and fro, until we diverged into general topics. And so it came about, in the end, that Mr Spenlow told me this day week was Dora's birthday, and he would be glad if I would come down and join a little picnic on the occasion. I went out of my senses immediately; became a mere driveller next day, on receipt of a little lace-edged sheet of notepaper, "Favoured by papa. To remind"; and passed the intervening period in a state of dotage.

I think I committed every possible absurdity in the way of preparation for this blessed event. I turn hot when I remember the cravat I bought. My boots might be placed in any collection of instruments of torture. I provided, and sent down by the Norwood coach the night before, a delicate little hamper, amounting in itself, I thought, almost to a declaration. There were crackers in it with the tenderest mottoes that could be got for money. At six in the morning, I was in Covent Garden Market, buying a bouquet for Dora. At ten I was on horseback (I hired a gallant grey, for the occasion), with the bouquet in my hat, to keep it fresh, trotting down to Norwood.

I suppose that when I saw Dora in the garden and pretended not to see her, and rode past the house pretending to be anxiously looking for it, I committed two small fooleries which other young gentlemen in my circumstances might have committed— because they came so very natural to me. But oh! when I *did* find the house, and *did* dismount at the garden-gate, and drag those stony-hearted boots across the lawn to Dora sitting on a garden-seat under a lilac tree, what a spectacle she was, upon that beautiful morning, among the butterflies, in a white chip bonnet and a dress of celestial blue!

There was a young lady with her—comparatively stricken in years—almost twenty, I should say. Her name was Miss Mills, and Dora called her Julia. She was the bosom friend of Dora. Happy Miss Mills!

Jip was there, and Jip *would* bark at me again. When I presented my bouquet, he gnashed his teeth with jealousy. Well he might. If he had the least idea how I adored his mistress, well he might!

"Oh, thank you, Mr Copperfield! What dear flowers!" said Dora.

I had had an intention of saying (and had been studying the best form of words for three miles) that I thought them beautiful before I saw them so near *her*. But I couldn't manage it. She was too bewildering. To see her lay the flowers against her little dimpled chin, was to lose all presence of mind and power of language in a feeble ecstasy. I wonder I didn't say, "Kill me, if you have a heart, Miss Mills. Let me die here!"

Then Dora held my flowers to Jip to smell. Then Jip growled, and wouldn't smell them. Then Dora laughed, and held them a little closer to Jip, to make him. Then Jip laid hold of a bit of geranium with his teeth, and worried imaginary cats in it. Then Dora beat him, and pouted, and said, "My poor beautiful flowers!" as compassionately, I thought, as if Jip had laid hold of me. I wished he had!

"You'll be so glad to hear, Mr Copperfield," said Dora, "that that cross Miss Murdstone is not here. She has gone to her brother's marriage, and will be away at least three weeks. Isn't that delightful?"

I said I was sure it must be delightful to her, and all that was delightful to her was delightful to me. Miss Mills, with an air of superior wisdom and benevolence, smiled upon us.

"She is the most disagreeable thing I ever saw," said Dora. "You can't believe how ill-tempered and shocking she is, Julia."

"Yes, I can, my dear!" said Julia.

"*You* can, perhaps, love," returned Dora, with her hand on Julia's. "Forgive my not excepting you, my dear, at first."

I learnt, from this, that Miss Mills had had her trials in the course of a chequered existence; and that to these, perhaps, I might refer that wise benignity of manner which I had already noticed. I found, in the course of the day, that this was the case: Miss Mills having been unhappy in a misplaced affection, and being understood to have retired from the world on her awful stock of experience, but still to take a calm interest in the unblighted hopes and loves of youth.

But now Mr Spenlow came out of the house, and Dora went to him, saying, "Look, papa, what beautiful flowers!" And Miss Mills smiled thoughtfully, as who should say, "Ye Mayflies, enjoy your brief existence in the bright morning of life!" And we all walked from the lawn towards the carriage, which was getting ready.

I shall never have such a ride again. I have never had such another. There were only those three, their hamper, my hamper, and the guitar-case, in the phaeton; and, of course, the phaeton was open; and I rode behind it, and Dora sat with her back to the horses, looking towards me. She kept the bouquet close to her on the cushion, and wouldn't allow Jip to sit on that side of her at all, for fear he should crush it. She often carried it in her hand, often refreshed herself with its fragrance. Our eyes at those times often met; and my great astonishment is that I didn't go over the head of my gallant grey into the carriage.

There was dust, I believe. There was a good deal of dust, I believe. I have a faint impression that Mr Spenlow remonstrated with me for riding in it; but I knew of none. I was sensible of a mist of love and beauty about Dora, but of nothing else. He stood up sometimes, and asked me what I thought of the prospect. I said it was delightful, and I dare say it was; but it was all Dora to me. The sun shone Dora, and the birds sang Dora. The south wind blew Dora, and the wild flowers in the hedges were all Doras, to a bud. My comfort is, Miss Mills understood me. Miss Mills alone could enter into my feelings thoroughly.

I don't know how long we were going, and to this hour I know as little where we went. Perhaps it was near Guildford. Perhaps some Arabian-night magician, opened up the place for the day, and shut it up for ever when we came away. It was a green spot, on a hill, carpeted with soft turf. There were shady trees, and heather, and, as far as the eye could see, a rich landscape.

It was a trying thing to find people here, waiting for us; and my jealousy, even of the ladies, knew no bounds. But all of my own sex—especially one imposter, three or four years my elder, with a red whisker, on which he established an amount of presumption not to be endured—were my mortal foes.

We all unpacked our baskets, and employed ourselves in getting dinner ready. Red Whisker pretended he could make a salad (which I don't believe), and obtruded himself on public notice. Some of the young ladies washed the lettuces for him, and sliced them under his directions. Dora was among these. I felt that fate had pitted me against this man, and one of us must fall.

Red Whisker made his salad (I wondered how they could eat it. Nothing should have induced *me* to touch it!) and voted himself into the charge of the wine-cellar, which he constructed, being an ingenious beast, in the hollow trunk of a tree. By and by, I saw him, with the majority of a lobster on his plate, eating his dinner at the feet of Dora!

I have but an indistinct idea of what happened for some time after this baleful object presented itself to my view. I was very merry, I know; but it was hollow merriment. I attached myself to a young creature in pink, with little eyes, and flirted with her desper-

ately. She received my attentions with favour; but whether on my account solely, or
because she had any designs on Red Whisker, I can't say. Dora's health was drunk. When
I drank it, I affected to interrupt my conversation for that purpose, and to resume it
immediately afterwards. I caught Dora's eye as I bowed to her, and I thought it looked
appealing. But it looked at me over the head of Red Whisker, and I was adamant.

The young creature in pink had a mother in green; and I rather think the latter
separated us from motives of policy. Howbeit, there was a general breaking up of the
party, while the remnants of the dinner were being put away; and I strolled off by myself
among the trees, in a raging and remorseful state. I was debating whether I should
pretend that I was not well, and fly—I don't know where—upon my gallant grey, when
Dora and Miss Mills met me.

"Mr Copperfield," said Miss Mills, "you are dull."

I begged her pardon. Not at all.

"And Dora," said Miss Mills, "*you* are dull."

Oh dear no! Not in the least.

"Mr Copperfield and Dora," said Miss Mills, with an almost venerable air. "Enough
of this. Do not allow a trivial misunderstanding to wither the blossoms of spring, which,
once put forth and blighted, cannot be renewed. I speak," said Miss Mills, "from experience of the past—the remote, irrevocable past. The gushing fountains which sparkle in
the sun, must not be stopped in mere caprice; the oasis in the desert of Sahara must not
be plucked up idly."

I hardly knew what I did, I was burning all over to that extraordinary extent; but I
took Dora's little hand and kissed it—and she let me! I kissed Miss Mills's hand; and we
all seemed, to my thinking, to go straight up to the seventh heaven.

We did not come down again. We stayed up there all the evening. At first we strayed
to and fro among the trees: I with Dora's shy arm drawn through mine: and Heaven
knows, folly as it all was, it would have been a happy fate to have been struck immortal
with those foolish feelings, and have stayed among the trees for ever!

But, much too soon, we heard the others laughing and talking, and calling "where's
Dora?" So we went back, and they wanted Dora to sing. Red Whisker would have got
the guitar-case out of the carriage, but Dora told him nobody knew where it was, but
I. So Red Whisker was done for in a moment; and *I* got it, and *I* unlocked it, and *I* took
the guitar out, and *I* sat by her, and *I* held her handkerchief and gloves, and *I* drank in
every note of her dear voice, and she sang to *me* who loved her, and all the others might
applaud as much as they liked, but they had nothing to do with it!

I was intoxicated with joy. I was afraid it was too happy to be real, and that I should
wake in Buckingham Street presently, and hear Mrs Crupp clinking the teacups in getting
breakfast ready. But Dora sang, and others sang, and Miss Mills sang—about the slumbering echoes in the caverns of Memory; as if she were a hundred years old—and the
evening came on; and we had tea, with the kettle boiling gipsy-fashion; and I was still
as happy as ever.

I was happier than ever when the party broke up, and the other people, defeated
Red Whisker and all, went their several ways, and we went ours through the still evening
and the dying light, with sweet scents rising up around us. Mr Spenlow being a little
drowsy after the champagne—honour to the soil that grew the grape, to the grape that
made the wine, to the sun that ripened it, and to the merchant who adulterated it!—and
being fast asleep in a corner of the carriage, I rode by the side and talked to Dora. She
admired my horse and patted him—oh, what a dear little hand it looked upon a
horse!—and her shawl would not keep right, and now and then I drew it round her with

my arm; and I even fancied that Jip began to see how it was, and to understand that he must make up his mind to be friends with me.

That sagacious Miss Mills, too; that amiable, though quite used up, recluse; that little patriarch of something less than twenty, who had done with the world, and mustn't on any account have the slumbering echoes in the caverns of Memory awakened; what a kind thing *she* did!

"Mr Copperfield," said Miss Mills, "come to this side of the carriage a moment—if you can spare a moment. I want to speak to you."

Behold me, on my gallant grey, bending at the side of Miss Mills, with my hand upon the carriage door!

"Dora is coming to stay with me. She is coming home with me the day after tomorrow. If you would like to call, I am sure papa would be happy to see you."

What could I do but invoke a silent blessing on Miss Mills's head, and store Miss Mills's address in the securest corner of my memory! What could I do but tell Miss Mills, with grateful looks and fervent words, how much I appreciated her good offices, and what an inestimable value I set upon her friendship!

Then Miss Mills benignantly dismissed me, saying, "Go back to Dora!" and I went; and Dora leaned out of the carriage to talk to me, and we talked all the rest of the way; and I rode my gallant grey so close to the wheel that I grazed his near fore leg against it, and "took the bark off," as his owner told me, "to the tune of three pun' sivin"—which I paid, and thought extremely cheap for so much joy. What time Miss Mills sat looking at the moon, murmuring verses and recalling, I suppose, the ancient days when she and earth had anything in common.

Norwood was many miles too near, and we reached it many hours too soon; but Mr Spenlow came to himself a little short of it, and said, "You must come in, Copperfield, and rest!" and I consenting, we had sandwiches and wine-and-water. In the light room, Dora blushing looked so lovely, that I could not tear myself away, but sat there staring, in a dream, until the snoring of Mr Spenlow inspired me with sufficient consciousness to take my leave. So we parted; I riding all the way to London with the farewell touch of Dora's hand still light on mine, recalling every incident and word ten thousand times; lying down in my own bed at last, as enraptured a young noodle as ever was carried out of his five wits by love.

When I awoke next morning, I was resolute to declare my passion to Dora, and know my fate. Happiness or misery was now the question. There was no other question that I knew of in the world, and only Dora could give the answer to it. I passed three days in a luxury of wretchedness, torturing myself by putting every conceivable variety of discouraging construction on all that ever had taken place between Dora and me. At last, arrayed for the purpose at a vast expense, I went to Miss Mills's, fraught with a declaration.

How many times I went up and down the street, and round the square—painfully aware of being a much better answer to the old riddle than the original one—before I could persuade myself to go up the steps and knock, is no matter now. Even when, at last, I had knocked, and was waiting at the door, I had some flurried thought of asking if that were Mr Blackboy's (in imitation of poor Barkis), begging pardon, and retreating. But I kept my ground.

Mr Mills was not at home. I did not expect he would be. Nobody wanted *him*. Miss Mills was at home. Miss Mills would do.

I was shown into a room upstairs, where Miss Mills and Dora were. Jip was there. Miss Mills was copying music (I recollect, it was a new song, called "Affection's Dirge"), and Dora was painting flowers. What were my feelings, when I recognized my own flowers; the identical Covent Garden Market purchase! I cannot say that they were very like, or that they particularly resembled any flowers that have ever come under my observation; but I knew from the paper round them which was accurately copied, what the composition was.

Miss Mills was very glad to see me, and very sorry her papa was not at home: though I thought we all bore that with fortitude. Miss Mills was conversational for a few minutes, and then, laying down her pen upon "Affection's Dirge," got up, and left the room.

I began to think I would put it off till tomorrow.

"I hope your poor horse was not tired, when he got home at night," said Dora, lifting up her beautiful eyes. "It was a long way for him."

I began to think I would do it today.

"It was a long way for *him*," said I, "for *he* had nothing to uphold him on the journey."

"Wasn't he fed, poor thing?" asked Dora.

I began to think I would put it off till tomorrow.

"Ye-yes," I said, "he was well taken care of. I mean he had not the unutterable happiness that I had in being so near you."

Dora bent her head over her drawing and said, after a little while—I had sat, in the interval, in a burning fever, and with my legs in a very rigid state—

"You didn't seem to be sensible of that happiness yourself, at one time of the day."

I saw now that I was in for it, and it must be done on the spot.

"You didn't care for that happiness in the least," said Dora, slightly raising her eyebrows, and shaking her head, "when you were sitting by Miss Kitt."

Kitt, I should observe, was the name of the creature in pink, with the little eyes.

"Though certainly I don't know why you should," said Dora, "or why you should call it a happiness at all. But of course you don't mean what you say. And I am sure no one doubts your being at liberty to do whatever you like. Jip, you naughty boy, come here!"

I don't know how I did it. I did it in a moment. I intercepted Jip. I had Dora in my arms. I was full of eloquence. I never stopped for a word. I told her how I loved her. I told her I should die without her. I told her that I idolized and worshipped her. Jip barked madly all the time.

When Dora hung her head and cried, and trembled, my eloquence increased so much the more. If she would like me to die for her, she had but to say the word, and I was ready. Life without Dora's love was not a thing to have on any terms. I couldn't bear it, and I wouldn't. I had loved her every minute, day and night, since I first saw her. I loved her at that minute to distraction. I should always love her, every minute, to distraction. Lovers had loved before, and lovers would love again; but no lover had ever loved, might, could, would, or should ever love, as I loved Dora. The more I raved, the more Jip barked. Each of us, in his own way, got more mad every moment.

Well, well! Dora and I were sitting on the sofa by and by, quiet enough, and Jip was lying in her lap, winking peacefully at me. It was off my mind. I was in a state of perfect rapture. Dora and I were engaged.

I suppose we had some notion that this was to end in marriage. We must have had some, because Dora stipulated that we were never to be married without her papa's consent. But, in our youthful ecstasy, I don't think that we really looked before us or behind us; or had any aspiration beyond the ignorant present. We were to keep our secret from Mr Spenlow; but I am sure the idea never entered my head, then, that there was anything dishonourable in that.

Miss Mills was more than usually pensive when Dora, going to find her, brought her back;—I apprehend, because there was a tendency in what had passed to awaken the slumbering echoes in the caverns of Memory. But she gave us her blessing, and the assurance of her lasting friendship, and spoke to us, generally, as became a Voice from the Cloister.

What an idle time it was! What an insubstantial, happy, foolish time it was!

When I measured Dora's finger for a ring that was to be made of Forget-me-nots, and when the jeweller, to whom I took the measure, found me out, and laughed over his order-book, and charged me anything he liked for the pretty little toy, with its blue stones—so associated in my remembrance with Dora's hand, that yesterday, when I saw such another, by chance, on the finger of my own daughter, there was a momentary stirring in my heart, like pain!

When I walked about, exalted with my secret, and full of my own interest, and felt the dignity of loving Dora, and of being beloved, so much, that if I had walked the air, I could not have been more above the people not so situated, who were creeping on the earth!

When we had those meetings in the garden of the square, and sat within the dingy summer-house, so happy, that I love the London sparrows to this hour, for nothing else, and see the plumage of the tropics in their smoky feathers!

When we had our first great quarrel (within a week of our betrothal), and when Dora sent me back the ring, enclosed in a despairing cocked-hat note, wherein she used the terrible expression that "our love had begun in folly, and ended in madness!" which dreadful words occasioned me to tear my hair, and cry that all was over!

When, under cover of the night, I flew to Miss Mills, whom I saw by stealth in a back kitchen where there was a mangle, and implored Miss Mills to interpose between us and avert insanity. When Miss Mills undertook the office and returned with Dora, exhorting us, from the pulpit of her own bitter youth, to mutual concession, and the avoidance of the Desert of Sahara!

When we cried, and made it up, and were so blest again, that the back kitchen, mangle and all, changed to Love's own temple, where we arranged a plan of correspondence through Miss Mills, always to comprehend at least one letter on each side every day!

What an idle time! What an insubstantial, happy, foolish time! Of all the times of mine that Time has in his grip, there is none that in one retrospect I can smile at half so much, and think of half so tenderly.

Chapter XXXIV

MY AUNT ASTONISHES ME

I WROTE to Agnes as soon as Dora and I were engaged. I wrote her a long letter, in which I tried to make her comprehend how blest I was, and what a darling Dora was. I entreated Agnes not to regard this as a thoughtless passion which could ever yield to any other, or had the least resemblance to the boyish fancies that we used to joke about. I assured her that its profundity was quite unfathomable, and expressed my belief that nothing like it had ever been known.

Somehow, as I wrote to Agnes on a fine evening by my open window, and the remembrance of her clear calm eyes and gentle face came stealing over me, it shed such a peaceful influence upon the hurry and agitation in which I had been living lately, and of which my very happiness partook in some degree, that it soothed me into tears. I remember that I sat resting my head upon my hand, when the letter was half done, cherishing a general fancy as if Agnes were one of the elements of my natural home. As if, in the retirement of the house made almost sacred to me by her presence, Dora and I must be happier than anywhere. As if, in love, joy, sorrow, hope, or disappointment; in all emotions; my heart turned naturally there, and found its refuge and best friend.

Of Steerforth I said nothing. I only told her there had been sad grief at Yarmouth, on account of Emily's flight; and that on me it made a double wound, by reason of the circumstances attending it. I knew how quick she always was to divine the truth, and that she would never be the first to breathe his name.

To this letter, I received an answer by return of post. As I read it, I seemed to hear Agnes speaking to me. It was like her cordial voice in my ears. What can I say more!

While I had been away from home lately, Traddles had called twice or thrice. Finding Peggotty within, and being informed by Peggotty (who always volunteered that information to whomsoever would receive it), that she was my old nurse, he had established a good-humoured acquaintance with her, and had stayed to have a little chat with her about me. So Peggotty said; but I am afraid the chat was all on her own side, and of immoderate length, as she was very difficult indeed to stop, God bless her! when she had me for her theme.

This reminds me, not only that I expected Traddles on a certain afternoon of his own appointing, which was now come, but that Mrs Crupp had resigned everything appertaining to her office (the salary excepted) until Peggotty should cease to present herself. Mrs Crupp, after holding divers conversations respecting Peggotty, in a very high-pitched voice, on the staircase—with some invisible Familiar it would appear, for corporeally speaking she was quite alone at those times—addressed a letter to me, developing her views. Beginning it with that statement of universal application, which fitted every occurrence of her life, namely, that she was a mother herself, she went on to inform me that she had once seen very different days, but that at all periods of her existence she had had a constitutional objection to spies, intruders, and informers. She named no names, she said; let them the cap fitted, wear it; but spies, intruders, and informers, especially in widders' weeds (this clause was underlined), she had ever accustomed herself to look down upon. If a gentleman was the victim of spies, intruders, and informers (but still naming no names), that was his own pleasure. He had a right to please himself; so let him do. All that she, Mrs Crupp, stipulated for, was, that she should not be "brought in contract" with such persons. Therefore she begged to be excused from any further attendance on the top set, until things were as they formerly was, and as they could be wished to be; and further mentioned that her little book would be found upon the breakfast-table every Saturday morning, when she requested an immediate settlement of the same, with the benevolent view of saving trouble "and an ill-conwenience" to all parties.

After this, Mrs Crupp confined herself to making pitfalls on the stairs, principally with pitchers, and endeavouring to delude Peggotty into breaking her legs. I found it rather harassing to live in this state of siege, but was too much afraid of Mrs Crupp to see any way out of it.

"My dear Copperfield," cried Traddles, punctually appearing at my door, in spite of all these obstacles, "how do you do?"

"My dear Traddles," said I, "I am delighted to see you at last, and very sorry I have not been at home before. But I have been so much engaged——"

"Yes, yes, I know," said Traddles, "of course. Yours lives in London, I think."

"What did you say?"

"She—excuse me—Miss D, you know," said Traddles, colouring in his great delicacy, "lives in London, I believe?"

"Oh yes. Near London."

"Mine, perhaps you recollect," said Traddles, with a serious look, "lives down in Devonshire—one of ten. Consequently, I am not so much engaged as you—in that sense."

"I wonder you can bear," I returned, "to see her so seldom."

"Hah!" said Traddles, thoughtfully. "It does seem a wonder. I suppose it is, Copperfield, because there is no help for it?"

"I suppose so," I replied with a smile, and not without a blush. "And because you have so much constancy and patience, Traddles."

"Dear me!" said Traddles, considering about it, "do I strike you in that way, Copperfield? Really I didn't know that I had. But she is such an extraordinarily dear girl herself, that it's possible she may have imparted something of those virtues to me. Now you mention it, Copperfield, I shouldn't wonder at all. I assure you she is always forgetting herself, and taking care of the other nine."

"Is she the eldest?" I inquired.

"Oh dear, no," said Traddles. "The eldest is a Beauty."

He saw, I suppose, that I could not help smiling at the simplicity of this reply; and added, with a smile upon his own ingenuous face:

"Not, of course, but that my Sophy—pretty name, Copperfield, I always think?"

"Very pretty!" said I.

"Not, of course, but that Sophy is beautiful too in my eyes, and would be one of the dearest girls that ever was, in anybody's eyes (I should think). But when I say the eldest is a Beauty, I mean she really is a——" he seemed to be describing clouds about himself, with both hands: "Splendid, you know," said Traddles, energetically.

"Indeed!" said I.

"Oh, I assure you," said Traddles, "something very uncommon, indeed! Then, you know, being formed for society and admiration, and not being able to enjoy much of it in consequence of their limited means, she naturally gets a little irritable and exacting, sometimes. Sophy puts her in good humour!"

"Is Sophy the youngest?" I hazarded.

"Oh dear, no!" said Traddles, stroking his chin. "The two youngest are only nine and ten. Sophy educates 'em."

"The second daughter, perhaps?" I hazarded.

"No," said Traddles. "Sarah's the second. Sarah has something the matter with her spine, poor girl. The malady will wear out by and by, the doctors say, but in the meantime she has to lie down for a twelvemonth. Sophy nurses her. Sophy's the fourth."

"Is the mother living?" I inquired.

"Oh yes," said Traddles, "she is alive. She is a very superior woman indeed, but the damp country is not adapted to her constitution, and—in fact, she has lost the use of her limbs."

"Dear me!" said I.

"Very sad, is it not?" returned Traddles. "But in a merely domestic view it is not so bad as it might be, because Sophy takes her place. She is quite as much a mother *to* her mother, as she is to the other nine."

I felt the greatest admiration for the virtues of this young lady; and, honestly with the view of doing my best to prevent the good-nature of Traddles from being imposed upon, to the detriment of their joint prospects in life, inquired how Mr Micawber was?

"He is quite well, Copperfield, thank you," said Traddles. "I am not living with him at present."

"No?"

"No. You see the truth is," said Traddles, in a whisper, "he has changed his name to Mortimer, in consequence of his temporary embarrassments; and he don't come out till after dark—and then in spectacles. There was an execution put into our house, for rent. Mrs Micawber was in such a dreadful state that I really couldn't resist giving my name to that second bill we spoke of here. You may imagine how delightful it was to my feelings, Copperfield, to see the matter settled with it, and Mrs Micawber recover her spirits."

"Hum!" said I.

"Not that her happiness was of long duration," pursued Traddles, "for, unfortunately, within a week another execution came in. It broke up the establishment. I have been living in a furnished apartment since then, and the Mortimers have been very private indeed. I hope you won't think it selfish, Copperfield, if I mention that the broker carried off my little round table with the marble top, and Sophy's flower-pot and stand?"

"What a hard thing!" I exclaimed indignantly.

"It was a—it was a pull," said Traddles, with his usual wince at that expression. "I don't mention it reproachfully, however, but with a motive. The fact is, Copperfield, I was unable to repurchase them at the time of their seizure; in the first place, because the broker, having an idea that I wanted them, ran the price up to an extravagant extent; and, in the second place, because I—hadn't any money. Now, I have kept my eye since, upon the broker's shop," said Traddles, with a great enjoyment of his mystery, "which is up at the top of Tottenham Court Road, and, at last, today I find them put out for sale. I have only noticed them from over the way, because if the broker saw *me*, bless you, he'd ask any price for them! What has occurred to me, having now the money, is, that perhaps you wouldn't object to ask that good nurse of yours to come with me to the shop—I can show it her from round the corner of the next street—and make the best bargain for them, as if they were for herself, that she can!"

The delight with which Traddles propounded this plan to me, and the sense he had of its uncommon artfulness, are among the freshest things in my remembrance.

I told him that my old nurse would be delighted to assist him, and that we would all three take the field together, but on one condition. That condition was, that he should make a solemn resolution to grant no more loans of his name, or anything else, to Mr Micawber.

"My dear Copperfield," said Traddles, "I have already done so, because I begin to feel that I have not only been inconsiderate, but that I have been positively unjust to Sophy. My word being passed to myself, there is no longer any apprehension; but I pledge it to you, too, with the greatest readiness. That first unlucky obligation, I have paid. I have no doubt Mr Micawber would have paid it if he could, but he could not. One thing I ought to mention, which I like very much in Mr Micawber, Copperfield. It refers to the second obligation, which is not yet due. He don't tell me that it *is* provided for, but he says it *will be*. Now, I think there is something very fair and honest about that!"

I was unwilling to damp my good friend's confidence, and therefore assented. After a little further conversation, we went round to the chandler's shop, to enlist Peggotty; Traddles declining to pass the evening with me, both because he endured the liveliest apprehensions that his property would be bought by somebody else before he could re-purchase it, and because it was the evening he always devoted to writing to the dearest girl in the world.

I never shall forget him peeping round the corner of the street in Tottenham Court Road, while Peggotty was bargaining for the precious articles; or his agitation when she came slowly towards us after vainly offering a price, and was hailed by the relenting broker, and went back again. The end of the negotiation was, that she bought the property on tolerably easy terms, and Traddles was transported with pleasure.

"I am very much obliged to you, indeed," said Traddles, on hearing it was to be sent to where he lived, that night. "If I might ask one other favour, I hope you would not think it absurd, Copperfield?"

I said beforehand, certainly not.

"Then if you *would* be good enough," said Traddles to Peggotty, "to get the flower-pot now, I think I should like (it being Sophy's, Copperfield) to carry it home myself!"

Peggotty was glad to get it for him, and he overwhelmed her with thanks, and went his way up Tottenham Court Road, carrying the flower-pot affectionately in his arms, with one of the most delighted expressions of countenance I ever saw.

We then turned back towards my chambers. As the shops had charms for Peggotty which I never knew them possess in the same degree for anybody else, I sauntered easily along, amused by her staring in at the windows, and waiting for her as often as she chose. We were thus a good while in getting to the Adelphi.

On our way upstairs, I called her attention to the sudden disappearance of Mrs Crupp's pitfalls, and also to the prints of recent footsteps. We were both very much surprised, coming higher up, to find my outer door standing open (which I had shut) and to hear voices inside.

We looked at one another, without knowing what to make of this, and went into the sitting-room. What was my amazement to find, of all people upon earth, my aunt there, and Mr Dick! My aunt sitting on a quantity of luggage, with her two birds before her, and her cat on her knee, like a female Robinson Crusoe, drinking tea. Mr Dick leaning thoughtfully on a great kite, such as we had often been out together to fly, with more luggage piled about him!

"My dear aunt!" cried I. "Why, what an unexpected pleasure!"

We cordially embraced; and Mr Dick and I cordially shook hands; and Mrs Crupp, who was busy making tea, and could not be too attentive, cordially said she had knowed well as Mr Copperfull would have his heart in his mouth, when he see his dear relations.

"Holloa!" said my aunt to Peggotty, who quailed before her awful presence. "How are *you?*"

"You remember my aunt, Peggotty?" said I.

"For the love of goodness, child," exclaimed my aunt, "don't call the woman by that South Sea Island name! If she married and got rid of it, which was the best thing she could do, why don't you give her the benefit of the change? What's your name now,—P?" said my aunt, as a compromise for the obnoxious appellation.

"Barkis, ma'am," said Peggotty, with a curtsey.

"Well! That's human," said my aunt. "It sounds less as if you wanted a missionary. How d'ye do, Barkis? I hope you're well?"

Encouraged by these gracious words, and by my aunt's extending her hand, Barkis came forward, and took the hand, and curtseyed her acknowledgements.

"We are older than we were, I see," said my aunt. "We have only met each other once before, you know. A nice business we made of it then! Trot, my dear, another cup."

I handed it dutifully to my aunt, who was in her usual inflexible state of figure; and ventured a remonstrance with her on the subject of her sitting on a box.

"Let me draw the sofa here, or the easy-chair, aunt," said I. "Why should you be so uncomfortable?"

"Thank you, Trot," replied my aunt, "I prefer to sit upon my property." Here my aunt looked hard at Mrs Crupp, and observed, "We needn't trouble you to wait, ma'am."

"Shall I put a little more tea in the pot afore I go, ma'am?" said Mrs Crupp.

"No, I thank you, ma'am," replied my aunt.

"Would you let me fetch another pat of butter, ma'am?" said Mrs Crupp. "Or would you be persuaded to try a new-laid hegg? or should I brile a rasher? Ain't there nothing I could do for your dear aunt, Mr Copperfull?"

"Nothing, ma'am," returned my aunt. "I shall do very well, I thank you."

Mrs Crupp, who had been incessantly smiling to express sweet temper, and incessantly holding her head on one side, to express a general feebleness of constitution, and incessantly rubbing her hands, to express a desire to be of service to all deserving objects, gradually smiled herself, one-sided herself, and rubbed herself, out of the room.

"Dick!" said my aunt. "You know what I told you about timeservers and wealthworshippers?"

Mr Dick—with rather a scared look, as if he had forgotten it—returned a hasty answer in the affirmative.

"Mrs Crupp is one of them," said my aunt. "Barkis, I'll trouble you to look after the tea, and let me have another cup, for I don't fancy that woman's pouring-out!"

I knew my aunt sufficiently well to know that she had something of importance on her mind, and that there was far more matter in this arrival than a stranger might have supposed. I noticed how her eye lighted on me, when she thought my attention otherwise occupied; and what a curious process of hesitation appeared to be going on within her, while she preserved her outward stiffness and composure. I began to reflect whether I had done anything to offend her; and my conscience whispered me that I had not yet told her about Dora. Could it by any means be that, I wondered!

As I knew she would only speak in her own good time, I sat down near her, and spoke to the birds, and played with the cat, and was as easy as I could be. But I was very far from being really easy; and I should still have been so, even if Mr Dick, leaning over the great kite behind my aunt, had not taken every secret opportunity of shaking his head darkly at me, and pointing at her.

"Trot," said my aunt at last, when she had finished her tea, and carefully smoothed down her dress, and wiped her lips—"you needn't go, Barkis!—Trot, have you got to be firm and self-reliant?"

"I hope so, aunt."

"What do you think?" inquired Miss Betsey.

"I think so, aunt."

"Then why, my love," said my aunt, looking earnestly at me, "why do you think I prefer to sit upon this property of mine tonight?"

I shook my head, unable to guess.

"Because," said my aunt, "it's all I have. Because I'm ruined, my dear!"

If the house, and every one of us, had tumbled out into the river together, I could hardly have received a greater shock.

"Dick knows it," said my aunt, laying her hand calmly on my shoulder. "I am ruined, my dear Trot! All I have in the world is in this room, except the cottage; and that I have left Janet to let. Barkis, I want to get a bed for this gentleman tonight. To save expense, perhaps you can make up something here for myself. Anything will do. It's only for tonight. We'll talk about this, more, tomorrow."

I was roused from my amazement, and concern for her—I am sure, for her—by her falling on my neck, for a moment, and crying that she only grieved for me. In another moment she suppressed this emotion; and said with an aspect more triumphant than dejected:

"We must meet reverses boldly, and not suffer them to frighten us, my dear. We must learn to act the play out. We must live misfortune down, Trot!"

Chapter XXXV

DEPRESSION

AS soon as I could recover my presence of mind, which quite deserted me in the first overpowering shock of my aunt's intelligence, I proposed to Mr Dick to come round to the chandler's shop, and take possession of the bed which Mr Peggotty had lately vacated. The chandler's shop being in Hungerford Market, and Hungerford Market being a very different place in those days, there was a low wooden colonnade before the door (not very unlike that before the house where the little man and woman used to live, in the old weather-glass), which pleased Mr Dick mightily. The glory of lodging over this structure would have compensated him, I dare say, for many inconveniences; but, as there were really few to bear, beyond the compound of flavours I have already mentioned, and perhaps the want of a little more elbow-room, he was perfectly charmed with his accommodation. Mrs Crupp had indignantly assured him that there wasn't room to swing a cat there; but, as Mr Dick justly observed to me, sitting down on the foot of the bed, nursing his leg, "You know, Trotwood, I don't want to swing a cat. I never do swing a cat. Therefore, what does that signify to *me!*"

I tried to ascertain whether Mr Dick had any understanding of the causes of this sudden and great change in my aunt's affairs. As I might have expected, he had none at all. The only account he could give of it was, that my aunt had said to him, the day before yesterday, "Now, Dick, are you really and truly the philosopher I take you for?" That then he had said, Yes, he hoped so. That then my aunt had said, "Dick, I am ruined." That then he had said, "Oh, indeed!" That then my aunt had praised him highly, which he was glad of. And that then they had come to me, and had had bottled porter and sandwiches on the road.

Mr Dick was so very complacent, sitting on the foot of the bed, nursing his leg, and telling me this, with his eyes wide open and a surprised smile, that I am sorry to say I was provoked into explaining to him that ruin meant distress, want, and starvation; but, I was soon bitterly reproved for this harshness, by seeing his face turn pale, and tears course down his lengthened cheeks, while he fixed upon me a look of such unutterable woe, that it might have softened a far harder heart than mine. I took infinitely greater pains to cheer him up again than I had taken to depress him; and I soon understood (as I ought to have known at first) that he had been so confident, merely because of his faith in the wisest and most wonderful of women, and his unbounded reliance on my intellectual resources. The latter, I believe, he considered a match for any kind of disaster not absolutely mortal.

"What can we do, Trotwood?" said Mr Dick. "There's the Memorial—"

"To be sure there is," said I. "But all we can do just now, Mr Dick, is to keep a cheerful countenance, and not let my aunt see that we are thinking about it."

He assented to this in the most earnest manner; and implored me, if I should see him wandering an inch out of the right course, to recall him by some of those superior methods which were always at my command. But I regret to state that the fright I had given him proved too much for his best attempts at concealment. All the evening his eyes wandered to my aunt's face, with an expression of the most dismal apprehension, as if he saw her growing thin on the spot. He was conscious of this, and put a constraint upon his head; but his keeping that immovable, and sitting rolling his eyes like a piece of machinery, did not mend the matter at all. I saw him look at the loaf at supper (which happened to be a small one), as if nothing else stood between us and famine; and when my aunt insisted on his making his customary repast, I detected him in the act of pocketing fragments of his bread and cheese; I have no doubt for the purpose of reviving us with those savings, when we should have reached an advanced stage of attenuation.

My aunt, on the other hand, was in a composed frame of mind, which was a lesson to all of us—to me, I am sure. She was extremely gracious to Peggotty, except when I inadvertently called her by that name; and, strange as I knew she felt in London, appeared quite at home. She was to have my bed, and I was to lie in the sitting-room, to keep guard over her. She made a great point of being so near the river, in case of a conflagration; and I suppose really did find some satisfaction in that circumstance.

"Trot, my dear," said my aunt, when she saw me making preparations for compounding her usual night-draught, "No!"

"Nothing, aunt?"

"Not wine, my dear. Ale."

"But there is wine here, aunt. And you always have it made of wine."

"Keep that, in case of sickness," said my aunt. "We mustn't use it carelessly, Trot. Ale for me. Half a pint."

I thought Mr Dick would have fallen, insensible. My aunt being resolute, I went out and got the ale myself. As it was growing late, Peggotty and Mr Dick took that opportunity of repairing to the chandler's shop together. I parted from him, poor fellow, at the corner of the street, with his great kite at his back, a very monument of human misery.

My aunt was walking up and down the room when I returned, crimping the borders of her nightcap with her fingers. I warmed the ale and made the toast on the usual infallible principles. When it was ready for her, she was ready for it, with her nightcap on, and the skirt of her gown turned back on her knees.

"My dear," said my aunt, after taking a spoonful of it; "it's a great deal better than wine. Not half so bilious."

I suppose I looked doubtful, for she added:

"Tut, tut, child. If nothing worse than Ale happens to us, we are well off."

"I should think so myself, aunt, I am sure," said I.

"Well, then, why *don't* you think so?" said my aunt.

"Because you and I are very different people," I returned.

"Stuff and nonsense, Trot!" replied my aunt.

My aunt went on with a quiet enjoyment, in which there was very little affectation, if any; drinking the warm ale with a teaspoon, and soaking her strips of toast in it.

"Trot," said she, "I don't care for strange faces in general, but I rather like that Barkis of yours, do you know!"

"It's better than a hundred pounds to hear you say so!" said I.

"It's a most extraordinary world," observed my aunt, rubbing her nose; "how that woman ever got into it with that name, is unaccountable to me. It would be much more easy to be born a Jackson, or something of that sort, one would think."

"Perhaps she thinks so, too; it's not her fault," said I.

"I suppose not," returned my aunt, rather grudging the admission; "but it's very aggravating. However, she's Barkis *now*. That's some comfort. Barkis is uncommonly fond of you, Trot."

"There is nothing she would leave undone to prove it," said I.

"Nothing, I believe," returned my aunt. "Here, the poor fool has been begging and praying about handing over some of her money—because she has got too much of it. A simpleton!"

My aunt's tears of pleasure were positively trickling down into the warm ale.

"She's the most ridiculous creature that ever was born," said my aunt. "I knew, from the first moment when I saw her with that poor dear blessed baby of a mother of yours, that she was the most ridiculous of mortals. But there are good points in Barkis!"

Affecting to laugh, she got an opportunity of putting her hand to her eyes. Having availed herself of it, she resumed her toast and her discourse together.

"Ah! Mercy upon us!" sighed my aunt. "I know all about it, Trot! Barkis and myself had quite a gossip while you were out with Dick. I know all about it. I don't know where these wretched girls expect to go to, for my part. I wonder they don't knock out their brains against—against mantelpieces," said my aunt; an idea which was probably suggested to her by her contemplation of mine.

"Poor Emily!" said I.

"Oh, don't talk to me about poor," returned my aunt. "She should have thought of that, before she caused so much misery! Give me a kiss, Trot. I am sorry for your early experience."

As I bent forward, she put her tumbler on my knee to detain me, and said:

"Oh, Trot, Trot! And so you fancy yourself in love! Do you?"

"Fancy, aunt!" I exclaimed, as red as I could be. "I adore her with my whole soul!"

"Dora, indeed!" returned my aunt. "And you mean to say the little thing is very fascinating, I suppose?"

"My dear aunt," I replied, "no one can form the least idea what she is!"

"Ah! And not silly?" said my aunt.

"Silly, aunt!"

I seriously believe it had never once entered my head for a single moment, to consider whether she was or not. I resented the idea, of course; but I was in a manner struck by it, as a new one altogether.

"Not light-headed?" said my aunt.

"Light-headed, aunt!" I could only repeat this daring speculation with the same kind of feeling with which I had repeated the preceding question.

"Well, well!" said my aunt. "I only ask. I don't depreciate her. Poor little couple! And so you think you were formed for one another, and are to go through a party-supper-table kind of life, like two pretty pieces of confectionery, do you, Trot?"

She asked me this so kindly, and with such a gentle air, half playful and half sorrowful, that I was quite touched.

"We are young and inexperienced, aunt, I know," I replied; "and I dare say we say and think a good deal that is rather foolish. But we love one another truly, I am sure. If I thought Dora could ever love anybody else, or cease to love me; or that I could ever love anybody else, or cease to love her; I don't know what I should do—go out of my mind, I think!"

"Ah, Trot!" said my aunt, shaking her head, and smiling gravely; "blind, blind blind!"

"Someone that I know, Trot," my aunt pursued, after a pause, "though of a very pliant disposition, has an earnestness of affection in him that reminds me of poor Baby. Earnestness is what that somebody must look for, to sustain him and improve him, Trot. Deep, downright, faithful earnestness."

"If you only knew the earnestness of Dora, aunt!" I cried.

"Oh, Trot!" she said again; "blind, blind!" and without knowing why, I felt a vague unhappy loss or want of something overshadow me like a cloud.

"However," said my aunt, "I don't want to put two young creatures out of conceit, with themselves, or to make them unhappy; so, though it is a girl and boy attachment, and girl and boy attachments very often—mind! I don't say always!—come to nothing, still we'll be serious about it, and hope for a prosperous issue one of these days. There's time enough for it to come to anything!"

This was not upon the whole very comforting to a rapturous lover; but I was glad to have my aunt in my confidence, and I was mindful of her being fatigued. So I thanked her ardently for this mark of her affection, and for all her other kindnesses towards me; and after a tender good night, she took her nightcap into my bedroom.

How miserable I was, when I lay down! How I thought and thought about my being poor, in Mr Spenlow's eyes; about my not being what I thought I was, when I proposed to Dora; about the chivalrous necessity of telling Dora what my worldly condition was, and releasing her from her engagement if she thought fit; about how I should contrive to live, during the long term of my articles, when I was earning nothing; about doing something to assist my aunt, and seeing no way of doing anything; about coming down to have no money in my pocket, and to wear a shabby coat, and to be able to carry Dora no little presents, and to ride no gallant greys, and to show myself in no agreeable light! Sordid and selfish as I knew it was, and as I tortured myself by knowing that it was, to let my mind run on my own distress so much, I was so devoted to Dora that I could not help it. I knew that it was base in me not to think more of my aunt, and less of myself; but, so far, selfishness was inseparable from Dora, and I could not put Dora on one side for any mortal creature. How exceedingly miserable I was, that night!

As to sleep, I had dreams of poverty in all sorts of shapes, but I seemed to dream without the previous ceremony of going to sleep. Now I was ragged, wanting to sell Dora matches, six bundles for a halfpenny; now I was at the office in a nightgown and boots, remonstrated with by Mr Spenlow on appearing before the clients in that airy attire; now I was hungrily picking up the crumbs that fell from old Tiffey's daily biscuit, regularly eaten when St Paul's struck one; now I was hopelessly endeavouring to get a licence to marry Dora, having nothing but one of Uriah Heep's gloves to offer in exchange, which the whole Commons rejected; and still, more or less conscious of my own room, I was always tossing about like a distressed ship in a sea of bed-clothes.

My aunt was restless, too, for I frequently heard her walking to and fro. Two or three times in the course of the night, attired in a long flannel wrapper in which she looked seven feet high, she appeared, like a disturbed ghost, in my room, and came to the side of the sofa on which I lay. On the first occasion I started up in alarm, to learn that she inferred from a particular light in the sky, that Westminster Abbey was on fire; and to be consulted in reference to the probability of its igniting Buckingham Street, in case the wind changed. Lying still, after that, I found that she sat down near me, whispering to herself "Poor boy!" And then it made me twenty times more wretched, to know how unselfishly mindful she was of me, and how selfishly mindful I was of myself.

It was difficult to believe that a night so long to me, could be short to anybody else. This consideration set me thinking and thinking of an imaginary party where people were dancing the hours away, until that became a dream too, and I heard the music incessantly playing one tune, and saw Dora incessantly dancing one dance, without taking the least notice of me. The man who had been playing the harp all night, was trying in vain to cover it with an ordinary-sized nightcap, when I awoke; or I should rather say, when I left off trying to go to sleep, and saw the sun shining in through the window at last.

There was an old Roman bath in those days at the bottom of one of the streets out of the Strand—it may be there still—in which I have had many a cold plunge. Dressing myself as quietly as I could, and leaving Peggotty to look after my aunt, I tumbled head foremost into it, and then went for a walk to Hampstead. I had a hope that this brisk treatment might freshen my wits a little; and I think it did them good, for I soon came to the conclusion that the first step I ought to take was, to try if my articles could be cancelled and the premium recovered. I got some breakfast on the Heath, and walked back to Doctors' Commons, along the watered roads and through a pleasant smell of summer flowers, growing in gardens and carried into town on hucksters' heads, intent on this first effort to meet our altered circumstances.

I arrived at the office so soon, after all, that I had half an hour's loitering about the Commons, before old Tiffey, who was always first, appeared with his key. Then I sat down in my shady corner, looking up at the sunlight on the opposite chimney-pots, and thinking about Dora; until Mr Spenlow came in, crisp and curly.

"How are you, Copperfield?" said he. "Fine morning!"

"Beautiful morning, sir," said I. "Could I say a word to you before you go into Court?"

"By all means," said he. "Come into my room."

I followed him into his room, and he began putting on his gown, and touching himself up before a little glass he had, hanging inside a closet door.

"I am sorry to say," said I, "that I have some rather disheartening intelligence from my aunt."

"No!" said he. "Dear me! Not paralysis, I hope?"

"It has no reference to her health, sir," I replied. "She has met with some large losses. In fact, she has very little left, indeed."

"You as-tound me, Copperfield!" cried Mr Spenlow.

I shook my head. "Indeed, sir," said I, "her affairs are so changed, that I wished to ask you whether it would be possible—at a sacrifice on our part of some portion of the premium, of course," I put in this, on the spur of the moment, warned by the blank expression of his face—"to cancel my articles?"

What it cost me to make this proposal, nobody knows. It was like asking, as a favour, to be sentenced to transportation from Dora.

"To cancel your articles, Copperfield? Cancel?"

I explained with tolerable firmness, that I really did not know where my means of subsistence were to come from, unless I could earn them for myself. I had no fear for the future, I said—and I laid great emphasis on that, as if to imply that I should still be decidedly eligible for a son-in-law one of these days—but, for the present, I was thrown upon my own resources.

"I am extremely sorry to hear this, Copperfield," said Mr Spenlow. "Extremely sorry. It is not usual to cancel articles for any such reason. It is not a professional course of proceeding. It is not a convenient precedent at all. Far from it. At the same time—"

"You are very good, sir," I murmured, anticipating a concession.

"Not at all. Don't mention it," said Mr Spenlow. "At the same time, I was going to say, if it had been my lot to have my hands unfettered—if I had not a partner—Mr Jorkins—"

My hopes were dashed in a moment, but I made another effort.

"Do you think, sir," said I, "if I were to mention it to Mr Jorkins—"

Mr Spenlow shook his head discouragingly. "Heaven forbid, Copperfield," he replied, "that I should do any man an injustice: still less, Mr Jorkins. But I know my partner, Copperfield. Mr Jorkins is *not* a man to respond to a proposition of this peculiar nature. Mr Jorkins is very difficult to move from the beaten track. You know what he is!"

I am sure I knew nothing about him, except that he had originally been alone in the business, and now lived by himself in a house near Montagu Square, which was fearfully in want of painting; that he came very late of a day, and went away very early; that he never appeared to be consulted about anything; and that he had a dingy little black-hole of his own upstairs, where no business was ever done, and where there was a yellow old cartridge-paper pad upon his desk, unsoiled by ink, and reported to be twenty years of age.

"Would you object to my mentioning it to him, sir?" I asked.

"By no means," said Mr Spenlow. "But I have some experience of Mr Jorkins, Copperfield. I wish it were otherwise, for I should be happy to meet your views in any respect. I cannot have the objection to your mentioning it to Mr Jorkins, Copperfield, if you think it worth while."

Availing myself of this permission, which was given with a warm shake of the hand, I sat thinking about Dora, and looking at the sunlight stealing from the chimney-pots down the wall of the opposite house, until Mr Jorkins came. I then went up to Mr Jorkins's room, and evidently astonished Mr Jorkins very much by making my appearance there.

"Come in, Mr Copperfield," said Mr Jorkins. "Come in!"

I went in, and sat down; and stated my case to Mr Jorkins pretty much as I had stated it to Mr Spenlow. Mr Jorkins was not by any means the awful creature one might have expected, but a large, mild, smooth-faced man of sixty, who took so much snuff that there was a tradition in the Commons that he lived principally on that stimulant, having little room in his system for any other article of diet.

"You have mentioned this to Mr Spenlow, I suppose?" said Mr Jorkins; when he had heard me, very restlessly, to an end.

I answered Yes, and told him that Mr Spenlow had introduced his name.

"He said I should object?" asked Mr Jorkins.

I was obliged to admit that Mr Spenlow had considered it probable.

"I am sorry to say, Mr Copperfield, I can't advance your object," said Mr Jorkins, nervously. "The fact is—but I have an appointment at the Bank, if you'll have the goodness to excuse me."

With that he rose in a great hurry, and was going out of the room, when I made bold to say that I feared, then, there was no way of arranging the matter?

"No!" said Mr Jorkins, stopping at the door to shake his head. "Oh, no! I object, you know," which he said very rapidly, and went out. "You must be aware, Mr Copperfield," he added, looking restlessly in at the door again, "if Mr Spenlow objects—"

"Personally, he does not object, sir," said I.

"Oh! Personally!" repeated Mr Jorkins, in an impatient manner. "I assure you there's an objection, Mr Copperfield. Hopeless! What you wish to be done, can't be done. I—I really have got an appointment at the Bank." With that he fairly ran away; and to the best of my knowledge, it was three days before he showed himself in the Commons again.

Being very anxious to leave no stone unturned, I waited until Mr Spenlow came in, and then described what had passed; giving him to understand that I was not hopeless of his being able to soften the adamantine Jorkins, if he would undertake the task.

"Copperfield," returned Mr Spenlow, with a gracious smile, "you have not known my partner, Mr Jorkins, as long as I have. Nothing is farther from my thoughts than to attribute any degree of artifice to Mr Jorkins. But Mr Jorkins has a way of stating his objections which often deceives people. No, Copperfield!" shaking his head. "Mr Jorkins is not to be moved, believe me!"

I was completely bewildered between Mr Spenlow and Mr Jorkins, as to which of them really was the objecting partner; but I saw with sufficient clearness that there was obduracy somewhere in the firm, and that the recovery of my aunt's thousand pounds was out of the question. In a state of despondency, which I remember with anything but satisfaction, for I know it still had too much reference to myself (though always in connexion with Dora), I left the office, and went homeward.

I was trying to familiarize my mind with the worst, and to present to myself the arrangements we should have to make for the future in their sternest aspect, when a hackney-chariot coming after me, and stopping at my very feet, occasioned me to look up. A fair hand was stretched forth to me from the window; and the face I had never seen without a feeling of serenity and happiness, from the moment when it first turned back on the old oak staircase with the great broad balustrade, and when I associated its softened beauty with the stained-glass window in the church, was smiling on me.

"Agnes!" I joyfully exclaimed. "Oh, my dear Agnes, of all people in the world, what a pleasure to see you!"

"Is it, indeed?" she said, in her cordial voice.

"I want to talk to you so much!" said I. "It's such a lightening of my heart, only to look at you! If I had had a conjuror's cap, there is no one I should have wished for but you!"

"What?" returned Agnes.

"Well! perhaps Dora first," I admitted, with a blush.

"Certainly, Dora first, I hope," said Agnes, laughing.

"But you next!" said I. "Where are you going?"

She was going to my rooms to see my aunt. The day being very fine, she was glad to come out of the chariot, which smelt (I had my head in it all this time) like a stable put under a cucumber-frame. I dismissed the coachman, and she took my arm, and we walked on together. She was like Hope embodied, to me. How different I felt in one short minute, having Agnes at my side!

My aunt had written her one of the odd, abrupt notes—very little longer than a Bank note—to which her epistolary efforts were usually limited. She had stated therein that she had fallen into adversity, and was leaving Dover for good, but had quite made up her mind to it, and was so well that nobody need be uncomfortable about her. Agnes had come to London to see my aunt, between whom and herself there had been a mutual liking these many years: indeed, it dated from the time of my taking up my residence in Mr Wickfield's house. She was not alone, she said. Her papa was with her—and Uriah Heep.

"And now they are partners," said I. "Confound him!"

"Yes," said Agnes. "They have some business here; and I took advantage of their coming, to come too. You must not think my visit all friendly and disinterested, Trotwood, for—I am afraid I may be cruelly prejudiced—I do not like to let papa go away alone, with him."

"Does he exercise the same influence over Mr Wickfield still, Agnes?"

Agnes shook her head. "There is such a change at home," said she, "that you would scarcely know the dear old house. They live with us now."

"They?" said I.

"Mr Heep and his mother. He sleeps in your old room," said Agnes, looking up into my face.

"I wish I had the ordering of his dreams," said I. "He wouldn't sleep there long."

"I keep my own little room," said Agnes, "where I used to learn my lessons. How the time goes! You remember? The little panelled room that opens from the drawing-room?"

"Remember, Agnes? When I saw you, for the first time, coming out at the door, with your quaint little basket of keys hanging at your side?"

"It is just the same," said Agnes, smiling. "I am glad you think of it so pleasantly. We were very happy."

"We were, indeed," said I.

"I keep that room to myself still; but I cannot always desert Mrs Heep, you know. And so," said Agnes, quietly, "I feel obliged to bear her company, when I might prefer to be alone. But I have no other reason to complain of her. If she tires me, sometimes, by her praises of her son, it is only natural in a mother. He is a very good son to her."

I looked at Agnes when she said these words, without detecting in her any consciousness of Uriah's design. Her mild but earnest eyes met mine with their own beautiful frankness, and there was no change in her gentle face.

"The chief evil of their presence in the house," said Agnes, "is that I cannot be as near papa as I could wish—Uriah Heep being so much between us—and cannot watch over him, if that is not too bold a thing to say, as closely as I would. But if any fraud or treachery is practising against him, I hope that simple love and truth will be strong in the end. I hope that real love and truth are stronger in the end than any evil or misfortune in the world."

A certain bright smile, which I never saw on any other face, died away, even while I thought how good it was, and how familiar it had once been to me; and she asked me, with a quick change of expression (we were drawing very near my street), if I knew how the reverse in my aunt's circumstances had been brought about. On my replying no, she had not told me yet, Agnes became thoughtful, and I fancied I felt her arm tremble in mine.

We found my aunt alone, in a state of some excitement. A difference of opinion had arisen between herself and Mrs Crupp, on an abstract question (the propriety of chambers being inhabited by the gentler sex); and my aunt, utterly indifferent to spasms on the part of Mrs Crupp, had cut the dispute short, by informing that lady that she smelt of my brandy, and that she would trouble her to walk out. Both of these expressions Mrs Crupp considered actionable, and had expressed her intention of bringing before a "British Judy"—meaning, it was supposed, the bulwark of our national liberties.

My aunt, however, having had time to cool, while Peggotty was out showing Mr Dick the soldiers at the Horse Guards—and being, besides, greatly pleased to see Agnes—rather plumed herself on the affair than otherwise, and received us with unimpaired good humour. When Agnes laid her bonnet on the table, and sat down beside her, I could not but think, looking on her mild eyes and her radiant forehead, how natural it seemed to have her there; how trustfully, although she was so young and inexperienced, my aunt confided in her; how strong she was, indeed, in simple love and truth.

We began to talk about my aunt's losses, and I told them what I had tried to do that morning.

"Which was injudicious, Trot," said my aunt, "but well meant. You are a generous boy—I suppose I must say, young man, now—and I am proud of you, my dear. So far, so good. Now, Trot and Agnes, let us look the case of Betsey Trotwood in the face, and see how it stands."

I observed Agnes turn pale, as she looked very attentively at my aunt. My aunt, patting her cat, looked very attentively at Agnes.

"Betsey Trotwood," said my aunt, who had always kept her money matters to herself: "—I don't mean your sister, Trot, my dear, but myself—had a certain property. It don't matter how much; enough to live on. More; for she had saved a little, and added to it. Betsey funded her property for some time, and then, by the advice of her man of business, laid it out on landed security. That did very well, and returned very good interest, till Betsey was paid off. I am talking of Betsey as if she was a man-of-war. Well! Then, Betsey had to look about her, for a new investment. She thought she was wiser, now, than her man of business, who was not such a good man of business by this time, as he used to be—I am alluding to your father, Agnes—and she took it into her head to lay it out for herself. So she took her pigs," said my aunt, "to a foreign market; and a very bad market it turned out to be. First, she lost in the mining way, and then she lost in the diving way—fishing up treasure, or some such Tom Tiddler nonsense," explained my aunt, rubbing her nose; "and then she lost in the mining way again, and, last of all, to set the thing entirely to rights, she lost in the banking way. I don't know what the Bank shares were worth for a little while," said my aunt; "cent per cent was the lowest of it, I believe; but the Bank was at the other end of the world, and tumbled into space, for what I know; anyhow, it fell to pieces, and never will and never can pay sixpence; and Betsey's sixpences were all there, and there's an end of them. Least said, soonest mended!"

My aunt concluded this philosophical summary, by fixing her eyes with a kind of triumph on Agnes, whose colour was gradually returning.

"Dear Miss Trotwood, is that all the history?" said Agnes.

"I hope it's enough, child," said my aunt. "If there had been more money to lose, it wouldn't have been all, I dare say. Betsey would have contrived to throw that after the rest, and make another chapter, I have little doubt. But there was no more money, and there's no more story."

Agnes had listened at first with suspended breath. Her colour still came and went, but she breathed more freely. I thought I knew why. I thought she had had some fear that her unhappy father might be in some way to blame for what had happened. My aunt took her hand in hers, and laughed.

"Is that all?" repeated my aunt. "Why, yes, that's all, except, 'And she lived happy ever afterwards.' Perhaps I may add that of Betsey yet, one of these days. Now, Agnes, you have a wise head. So have you, Trot, in some things, though I can't compliment you always"; and here my aunt shook her own at me, with an energy peculiar to herself. "What's to be done? Here's the cottage, taking one time with another, will produce say seventy pounds a year. I think we may safely put it down at that. Well!—That's all we've got," said my aunt; with whom it was an idiosyncrasy, as it is with some horses, to stop very short when she appeared to be in a fair way of going on for a long while.

"Then," said my aunt, after a rest, "there's Dick. He's good for a hundred a year, but of course that must be expended on himself. I would sooner send him away, though I know I am the only person who appreciates him, than have him, and not spend his money on himself. How can Trot and I do best, upon our means? What do you say, Agnes?"

"I say, aunt," I interposed, "that I must do something!"

"Go for a soldier, do you mean?" returned my aunt, alarmed; "or go to sea? I won't hear of it. You are to be a proctor. We're not going to have any knockings on the head in *this* family, if you please, sir."

I was about to explain that I was not desirous of introducing that mode of provision into the family, when Agnes inquired if my rooms were held for any long term?

"You come to the point, my dear," said my aunt. "They are not to be got rid of, for six months at least, unless they could be underlet, and that I don't believe. The last man died here. Five people out of six *would* die—of course—of that woman in nankeen with the flannel petticoat. I have a little ready money; and I agree with you, the best thing we can do, is, to live the term out here, and get a bedroom hard by."

I thought it my duty to hint at the discomfort my aunt would sustain, from living in a continual state of guerilla warfare with Mrs Crupp; but she disposed of that objection summarily by declaring that, on the first demonstration of hostilities, she was prepared to astonish Mrs Crupp for the whole remainder of her natural life.

"I have been thinking, Trotwood," said Agnes, diffidently, "that if you had time—"

"I have a good deal of time, Agnes. I am always disengaged after four or five o'clock, and I have time early in the morning. In one way and another," said I, conscious of reddening a little as I thought of the hours and hours I had devoted to fagging about town, and to and fro upon the Norwood Road, "I have abundance of time."

"I know you would not mind," said Agnes, coming to me, and speaking in a low voice, so full of sweet and hopeful consideration that I hear it now, "the duties of a secretary."

"Mind, my dear Agnes?"

"Because," continued Agnes, "Doctor Strong has acted on his intention of retiring, and has come to live in London; and he asked papa, I know, if he could recommend him one. Don't you think he would rather have his favourite old pupil near him, than anybody else?"

"Dear Agnes!" said I. "What should I do without you! You are always my good angel. I told you so. I never think of you in any other light."

Agnes answered with her pleasant laugh, that one good Angel (meaning Dora) was enough; and went on to remind me that the Doctor had been used to occupy himself in his study, early in the morning, and in the evening—and that probably my leisure would suit his requirements very well. I was scarcely more delighted with the prospect of earning my own bread, than with the hope of earning it under my old master; in short, acting on the advice of Agnes, I sat down and wrote a letter to the Doctor, stating my object, and appointing to call on him next day at ten in the forenoon. This I addressed to Highgate—for in that place, so memorable to me, he lived—and went and posted, myself, without losing a minute.

Wherever Agnes was, some agreeable token of her noiseless presence seemed inseparable from the place. When I came back, I found my aunt's birds hanging, just as they had hung so long in the parlour window of the cottage; and my easy-chair imitating my aunt's much easier chair in its position at the open window; and even the round green fan, which my aunt had brought away with her, screwed on to the window-sill. I knew who had done all this, by its seeming to have quietly done itself; and I should have known in a moment who had arranged my neglected books in the old order of my school days, even if I had supposed Agnes to be miles away, instead of seeing her busy with them, and smiling at the disorder into which they had fallen.

My aunt was quite gracious on the subject of the Thames (it really did look very well with the sun upon it, though not like the sea before the cottage), but she could not relent towards the London smoke, which, she said, "peppered everything." A complete revolution, in which Peggotty bore a prominent part, was being effected in every corner of my rooms, in regard of this pepper; and I was looking on, thinking how little even Peggotty seemed to do with a good deal of bustle, and how much Agnes did without any bustle at all, when a knock came at the door.

"I think," said Agnes, turning pale, "it's papa. He promised me that he would come."

I opened the door, and admitted, not only Mr Wickfield, but Uriah Heep. I had not seen Mr Wickfield for some time. I was prepared for a great change in him, after what I had heard from Agnes, but his appearance shocked me.

It was not that he looked many years older, though still dressed with the old scrupulous cleanliness; or that there was an unwholesome ruddiness upon his face; or that his eyes were full and bloodshot; or that there was a nervous trembling in his hand, the cause of which I knew, and had for some years seen at work. It was not that he had lost his good looks, or his old bearing of a gentleman—for that he had not—but the thing that struck me most, was, that with the evidences of his native superiority still upon him, he should submit himself to that crawling impersonation of meanness, Uriah Heep. The reversal of the two natures, in their relative positions, Uriah's of power and Mr Wickfield's of dependence, was a sight more painful to me than I can express. If I had seen an Ape taking command of a Man, I should hardly have thought it a more degrading spectacle.

He appeared to be only too conscious of it himself. When he came in, he stood still; and with his head bowed, as if he felt it. This was only for a moment; for Agnes softly said to him, "Papa! Here is Miss Trotwood—and Trotwood, whom you have not seen for a long while!" and then he approached, and constrainedly gave my aunt his hand, and shook hands more cordially with me. In the moment's pause I speak of, I saw Uriah's countenance form itself into a most ill-favoured smile. Agnes saw it too, I think, for she shrank from him.

What my aunt saw, or did not see, I defy the science of physiognomy to have made out, without her own consent. I believe there never was anybody with such an imperturbable countenance when she chose. Her face might have been a dead-wall on the occasion in question, for any light it threw upon her thoughts; until she broke silence with her usual abruptness.

"Well, Wickfield!" said my aunt; and he looked up at her for the first time. "I have been telling your daughter how well I have been disposing of my money for myself, because I couldn't trust it to you, as you were growing rusty in business matters. We have been taking counsel together, and getting on very well, all things considered. Agnes is worth the whole firm, in my opinion."

"If I may umbly make the remark," said Uriah Heep, with a writhe, "I fully agree with Miss Betsey Trotwood, and should be only too appy if Miss Agnes was a partner."

"You're a partner yourself, you know," returned my aunt, "and that's about enough for you, I expect. How do you find yourself, sir?"

In acknowledgment of this question, addressed to him with extraordinary curtness, Mr Heep, uncomfortably clutching the blue bag he carried, replied that he was pretty well, he thanked my aunt, and hoped she was the same.

"And you, Master—I should say, Mister Copperfield," pursued Uriah. "I hope I see you well! I am rejoiced to see you, Mister Copperfield, even under present circumstances." I believed that; for he seemed to relish them very much. "Present circumstances is not what your friends would wish for you, Mister Copperfield, but it isn't money makes the man: it's—I am really unequal with my umble powers to express what it is," said Uriah, with a fawning jerk, "but it isn't money!"

Here he shook hands with me: not in the common way, but standing at a good distance from me, and lifting my hand up and down like a pump handle, that he was a little afraid of.

"And how do you think we are looking, Master Copperfield,—I should say, Mister?" fawned Uriah. "Don't you find Mr Wickfield blooming, sir? Years don't tell much in our firm, Master Copperfield, except in raising up the umble, namely, mother and self—and in developing," he added, as an afterthought, "the beautiful, namely, Miss Agnes."

He jerked himself about, after this compliment, in such an intolerable manner, that my aunt, who had sat looking straight at him, lost all patience.

"Deuce take the man!" said my aunt, sternly, "what's he about? Don't be galvanic, sir!"

"I ask your pardon, Miss Trotwood," returned Uriah; "I'm aware you're nervous."

"Go along with you, sir!" said my aunt, anything but appeased. "Don't presume to say so! I am nothing of the sort. If you're an eel, sir, conduct yourself like one. If you're a man, control your limbs, sir! Good God!" said my aunt, with great indignation, "I am not going to be serpentined and corkscrewed out of my senses!"

Mr Heep was rather abashed, as most people might have been, by this explosion;

which derived great additional force from the indignant manner in which my aunt afterwards moved in her chair, and shook her head as if she were making snaps or bounces at him. But he said to me aside in a meek voice:

"I am well aware, Master Copperfield, that Miss Trotwood, though an excellent lady, has a quick temper (indeed I think I had the pleasure of knowing her, when I was a numble clerk, before you did, Master Copperfield), and it's only natural, I am sure, that it should be made quicker by present circumstances. The wonder is, that it isn't much worse! I only called to say that if there was anything we could do, in present circumstances, mother or self, or Wickfield and Heep, we should be really glad. I may go so far?" said Uriah, with a sickly smile at his partner.

"Uriah Heep," said Mr Wickfield, in a monotonous forced way, "is active in the business, Trotwood. What he says, I quite concur in. You know I had an old interest in you. Apart from that, what Uriah says I quite concur in!"

"Oh, what a reward it is," said Uriah, drawing up one leg, at the risk of bringing down upon himself another visitation from my aunt, "to be so trusted in! But I hope I am able to do something to relieve him from the fatigues of business, Master Copperfield!"

"Uriah Heep is a great relief to me," said Mr Wickfield, in the same dull voice. "It's a load off my mind, Trotwood, to have such a partner."

The red fox made him say all this, I knew, to exhibit him to me in the light he had indicated on the night when he poisoned my rest. I saw the same ill-favoured smile upon his face again, and saw how he watched me.

"You are not going, papa?" said Agnes, anxiously. "Will you not walk back with Trotwood and me?"

He would have looked to Uriah, I believe, before replying, if that worthy had not anticipated him.

"I am bespoke myself," said Uriah, "on business; otherwise I should have been appy to have kept with my friends. But I leave my partner to represent the firm. Miss Agnes, ever yours! I wish you good-day, Master Copperfield, and leave my umble respects for Miss Betsey Trotwood."

With those words, he retired, kissing his great hand, and leering at us like a mask.

We sat there, talking about our pleasant old Canterbury days, an hour or two. Mr Wickfield, left to Agnes, soon became more like his former self; though there was a settled depression upon him, which he never shook off. For all that, he brightened; and had an evident pleasure in hearing us recall the little incidents of our old life, many of which he remembered very well. He said it was like those times, to be alone with Agnes and me again; and he wished to Heaven they had never changed. I am sure there was an influence in the placid face of Agnes, and in the very touch of her hand upon his arm, that did wonders for him.

My aunt (who was busy nearly all this while with Peggotty, in the inner room) would not accompany us to the place where they were staying, but insisted on my going; and I went. We dined together. After dinner, Agnes sat beside him, as of old, and poured out his wine. He took what she gave him, and no more—like a child—and we all three sat together at a window as the evening gathered in. When it was almost dark, he lay down on a sofa, Agnes pillowing his head and bending over him a little while; and when she came back to the window, it was not so dark but I could see tears glittering in her eyes.

I pray Heaven that I never may forget the dear girl in her love and truth, at that time of my life; for if I should, I must be drawing near the end, and then I would desire to remember her best! She filled my heart with such good resolutions, strengthened my weakness so, by her example, so directed—I know not how, she was too modest and gentle to advise me in many words—the wandering ardour and unsettled purpose within me, that all the little good I have done, and all the harm I have forborne, I solemnly believe I may refer to her.

And how she spoke to me of Dora, sitting at the window in the dark; listened to my praises of her; praised again; and round the little fairy-figure shed some glimpses of her own pure light, that made it yet more precious and more innocent to me! Oh, Agnes, sister of my boyhood, if I had known then, what I knew long afterwards!—

There was a beggar in the street, when I went down; and as I turned my head towards the window, thinking of her calm seraphic eyes, he made me start by muttering, as if he were an echo of the morning:

"Blind! Blind! Blind!"

Chapter XXXVI

ENTHUSIASM

I BEGAN the next day with another dive into the Roman bath, and then started for Highgate. I was not dispirited now. I was not afraid of the shabby coat, and had no yearnings after gallant greys. My whole manner of thinking of our late misfortune was changed. What I had to do, was, to show my aunt that her past goodness to me had not been thrown away on an insensible, ungrateful object. What I had to do, was, to turn the painful discipline of my younger days to account, by going to work with a resolute and steady heart. What I had to do, was, to take my woodman's axe in my hand, and clear my own way through the forest of difficulty, by cutting down the trees until I came to Dora. And I went on at a mighty rate, as if it could be done by walking.

When I found myself on the familiar Highgate road, pursuing such a different errand from that old one of pleasure, with which it was associated, it seemed as if a complete change had come on my whole life. But that did not discourage me. With the new life, came new purpose, new intention. Great was the labour; priceless the reward. Dora was the reward, and Dora must be won.

I got into such a transport, that I felt quiie sorry my coat was not a little shabby already. I wanted to be cutting at those trees in the forest of difficulty, under circumstances that should prove my strength. I had a good mind to ask an old man, in wire spectacles, who was breaking stones upon the road, to lend me his hammer for a little while, and let me begin to beat a path to Dora out of granite. I stimulated myself into such a heat, and got so out of breath, that I felt as if I had been earning I don't know how much. In this state, I went into a cottage that I saw was to let, and examined it narrowly,—for I felt it necessary to be practical. It would do for me and Dora admirably: with a little front garden for Jip to run about in, and bark at the tradespeople through the railings, and a capital room upstairs for my aunt. I came out again, hotter and faster than ever, and dashed up to Highgate, at such a rate that I was there an hour too early; and, though I had not been, should have been obliged to stroll about to cool myself, before I was at all presentable.

My first care, after putting myself under this necessary course of preparation, was to find the Doctor's house. It was not in that part of Highgate where Mrs Steerforth lived, but quite on the opposite side of the little town. When I had made this discovery, I went back, in an attraction I could not resist, to a lane by Mrs Steerforth's, and looked over the corner of the garden wall. His room was shut up close. The conservatory doors were standing open, and Rosa Dartle was walking, bareheaded, with a quick, impetuous step, up and down a gravel walk on one side of the lawn. She gave me the idea of some fierce thing, that was dragging the length of its chain to and fro upon a beaten track, and wearing its heart out.

I came softly away from my place of observation, and avoiding that part of the neighbourhood, and wishing I had not gone near it, strolled about until it was ten o'clock. The church with the slender spire, that stands on the top of the hill now, was not there then to tell me the time. An old red-brick mansion, used as a school, was in its place; and a fine old house it must have been to go to school at, as I recollect it.

When I approached the Doctor's cottage—a pretty old place, on which he seemed to have expended some money, if I might judge from the embellishments and repairs that had the look of being just completed—I saw him walking in the garden at the side, gaiters and all, as if he had never left off walking since the days of my pupilage. He had his old companions about him, too; for there were plenty of high trees in the neighbour-hood, and two or three rooks were on the grass, looking after him, as if they had been written to about him by the Canterbury rooks and were observing him closely in consequence.

Knowing the utter hopelessness of attracting his attention from that distance, I made bold to open the gate, and walk after him, so as to meet him when he should turn round. When he did, and came towards me, he looked at me thoughtfully for a few moments, evidently without thinking about me at all; and then his benevolent face expressed extraordinary pleasure, and he took me by both hands.

"Why, my dear Copperfield," said the Doctor, "you are a man! How do you do? I am delighted to see you. My dear Copperfield, how very much you have improved! You are quite—yes—dear me!"

I hoped he was well, and Mrs Strong too.

"Oh dear, yes!" said the Doctor; "Annie's quite well, and she'll be delighted to see you. You were always her favourite. She said so, last night, when I showed her your letter. And—yes, to be sure—you recollect Mr Jack Maldon, Copperfield?"

"Perfectly, sir."

"Of course," said the Doctor. "To be sure. *He's* pretty well, too."

"Has he come home, sir?" I inquired.

"From India?" said the Doctor. "Yes. Mr Jack Maldon couldn't bear the climate, my dear. Mrs Markleham—you have not forgotten Mrs Markleham?"

Forgotten the Old Soldier! And in that short time!

"Mrs Markleham," said the Doctor, "was quite vexed about him, poor thing; so we have got him at home again; and we have bought him a little Patent place, which agrees with him much better."

I knew enough of Mr Jack Maldon to suspect from this account that it was a place where there was not much to do, and which was pretty well paid. The Doctor, walking up and down with his hand on my shoulder, and his kind face turned encouragingly to mine, went on:

"Now, my dear Copperfield, in reference to this proposal of yours. It's very gratifying and agreeable to me, I am sure; but don't you think you could do better? You achieved distinction, you know, when you were with us. You are qualified for many good things. You have laid a foundation that any edifice may be raised upon; and is it not a pity that you should devote the springtime of your life to such a poor pursuit as I can offer?"

I became very glowing again, and, expressing myself in a rhapsodical style, I am afraid, urged my request strongly; reminding the Doctor that I had already a profession.

"Well, well," said the Doctor, "that's true. Certainly, your having a profession, and being actually engaged in studying it, makes a difference. But, my good young friend, what's seventy pounds a year?"

"It doubles our income, Doctor Strong," said I.

"Dear me!" replied the Doctor. "To think of that! Not that I mean to say it's rigidly limited to seventy pounds a year, because I have always contemplated making any young friend I might thus employ, a present too. Undoubtedly," said the Doctor, still walking me up and down with his hand on my shoulder. "I have always taken an annual present into account."

"My dear tutor," said I (now, really, without any nonsense), "to whom I owe more obligations already than I ever can acknowledge——"

"No, no," interposed the Doctor. "Pardon me!"

"If you will take such time as I have, and that is my mornings and evenings, and can think it worth seventy pounds a year, you will do me such a service as I cannot express."

"Dear me!" said the Doctor, innocently. "To think that so little should go for so much! Dear, dear! And when you can do better, you will? On your word, now?" said the Doctor,—which he had always made a very grave appeal to the honour of us boys.

"On my word, sir!" I returned, answering in our old school manner.

"Then be it so," said the Doctor, clapping me on the shoulder, and still keeping his hand there, as we still walked up and down.

"And I shall be twenty times happier, sir," said I, with a little—I hope innocent—flattery, "if my employment is to be on the Dictionary."

The Doctor stopped, smilingly clapped me on the shoulder again, and exclaimed, with a triumph most delightful to behold, as if I had penetrated to the profoundest depths of mortal sagacity, "My dear young friend, you have hit it. It is the Dictionary!"

How could it be anything else! His pockets were as full of it as his head. It was sticking out of him in all directions. He told me that since his retirement from scholastic life, he had been advancing with it wonderfully; and that nothing could suit him better than the proposed arrangements for morning and evening work, as it was his custom to walk about in the daytime with his considering cap on. His papers were in a little confusion, in consequence of Mr Jack Maldon having lately proffered his occasional services as an amanuensis, and not being accustomed to that occupation; but we should soon put right what was amiss, and go on swimmingly. Afterwards, when we were fairly at our work, I found Mr Jack Maldon's efforts more troublesome to me than I had expected, as he had not confined himself to making numerous mistakes, but had sketched so many soldiers, and ladies' heads, over the Doctor's manuscript, that I often became involved in labyrinths of obscurity.

The Doctor was quite happy in the prospect of our going to work together on that wonderful performance, and we settled to begin next morning at seven o'clock. We were to work two hours every morning, and two or three hours every night, except on Saturdays, when I was to rest. On Sundays, of course, I was to rest also, and I considered these very easy terms.

Our plans being thus arranged to our mutual satisfaction, the Doctor took me into the house to present me to Mrs Strong, whom we found in the Doctor's new study, dusting his books,—a freedom which he never permitted anybody else to take with those sacred favourites.

They had postponed their breakfast on my account, and we sat down to table together. We had not been seated long, when I saw an approaching arrival in Mrs Strong's face, before I heard any sound of it. A gentleman on horseback came to the gate, and leading his horse into the little court, with the bridle over his arm, as if he were quite at home, tied him to a ring in the empty coach-house wall, and came into the breakfast parlour, whip in hand. It was Mr Jack Maldon; and Mr Jack Maldon was not at all improved by India, I thought. I was in a state of ferocious virtue, however, as to young men who were not cutting down trees in the forest of difficulty; and my impression must be received with due allowance.

"Mr Jack!" said the Doctor. "Copperfield!"

Mr Jack Maldon shook hands with me; but not very warmly, I believed; and with an air of languid patronage, at which I secretly took great umbrage. But his languor altogether was quite a wonderful sight; except when he addressed himself to his cousin Annie.

"Have you breakfasted this morning, Mr Jack?" said the Doctor.

"I hardly ever take breakfast, sir," he replied, with his head thrown back in an easy-chair. "I find it bores me."

"Is there any news today?" inquired the Doctor.

"Nothing at all, sir," replied Mr Maldon. "There's an account about the people being hungry and discontented down in the North, but they are always being hungry and discontented somewhere."

The Doctor looked grave, and said, as though he wished to change the subject, "Then there's no news at all; and no news, they say, is good news."

"There's a long statement in the papers, sir, about a murder," observed Mr Maldon. "But somebody is always being murdered, and I didn't read it."

A display of indifference to all the actions and passions of mankind was not supposed to be such a distinguished quality at that time, I think, as I have observed it to be considered since. I have known it very fashionable indeed. I have seen it displayed with such success, that I have encountered some fine ladies and gentlemen who might as well have been born caterpillars. Perhaps it impressed me the more then, because it was new to me, but it certainly did not tend to exalt my opinion of, or to strengthen my confidence in, Mr Jack Maldon.

"I came out to inquire whether Annie would like to go to the opera tonight," said Mr Maldon, turning to her. "It's the last good night there will be, this season; and there's a singer there, whom she really ought to hear. She is perfectly exquisite. Besides which, she is so charmingly ugly," relapsing into languor.

The Doctor, ever pleased with what was likely to please his young wife, turned to her and said:

"You must go, Annie. You must go."

"I would rather not," she said to the Doctor. "I prefer to remain at home. I would much rather remain at home."

Without looking at her cousin, she then addressed me, and asked me about Agnes, and whether she should see her, and whether she was not likely to come that day; and was so much disturbed, that I wondered how even the Doctor, buttering his toast, could be blind to what was so obvious.

But he saw nothing. He told her, good-naturedly, that she was young and ought to be amused and entertained, and must not allow herself to be made dull by a dull old fellow. Moreover, he said, he wanted to hear her sing all the new singer's songs to him; and how could she do that well, unless she went? So the Doctor persisted in making the engagement for her, and Mr Jack Maldon was to come back to dinner. This concluded, he went to his Patent place, I suppose; but at all events went away on his horse, looking very idle.

I was curious to find out next morning, whether she had been. She had not, but had sent into London to put her cousin off; and had gone out in the afternoon to see Agnes, and had prevailed upon the Doctor to go with her; and they had walked home by the fields, the Doctor told me, the evening being delightful. I wondered then, whether she would have gone if Agnes had not been in town, and whether Agnes had some good influence over her too!

She did not look very happy, I thought; but it was a good face, or a very false one. I often glanced at it, for she sat in the window all the time we were at work; and made our breakfast, which we took by snatches as we were employed. When I left, at nine o'clock, she was kneeling on the ground at the Doctor's feet, putting on his shoes and gaiters for him. There was a softened shade upon her face, thrown from some green leaves overhanging the open window of the low room; and I thought all the way to Doctors' Commons, of the night when I had seen it looking at him as he read.

I was pretty busy now; up at five in the morning, and home at nine or ten at night. But I had infinite satisfaction in being so closely engaged, and never walked slowly on any account, and felt enthusiastically that the more I tired myself, the more I was doing to deserve Dora. I had not revealed myself in my altered character to Dora yet, because she was coming to see Miss Mills in a few days, and I deferred all I had to tell her until then; merely informing her in my letters (all our communications were secretly forwarded through Miss Mills), that I had much to tell her. In the meantime, I put myself on a short allowance of bear's grease, wholly abandoned scented soap and lavender water, and sold off three waistcoats at a prodigious sacrifice, as being too luxurious for my stern career.

Not satisfied with all these proceedings, but burning with impatience to do something more, I went to see Traddles, now lodging up behind the parapet of a house in Castle Street, Holborn. Mr Dick, who had been with me to Highgate twice already, and had resumed his companionship with the Doctor, I took with me.

I took Mr Dick with me, because, acutely sensitive to my aunt's reverses, and sincerely believing that no galley-slave or convict worked as I did, he had begun to fret and worry himself out of spirits and appetite, as having nothing useful to do. In this condition, he felt more incapable of finishing the Memorial than ever; and the harder he worked at it, the oftener that unlucky head of King Charles the First got into it. Seriously apprehending that his malady would increase, unless we put some innocent deception upon him and caused him to believe that he was useful, or unless we could put him in the way of being really useful (which would be better), I made up my mind to try if Traddles could help us. Before we went, I wrote Traddles a full statement of all that had happened, and Traddles wrote me back a capital answer, expressive of his sympathy and friendship.

We found him hard at work with his inkstand and papers, refreshed by the sight of the flower-pot stand and the little round table in a corner of the small apartment. He received us cordially, and made friends with Mr Dick in a moment. Mr Dick professed an absolute certainty of having seen him before, and we both said, "Very likely."

The first subject on which I had to consult Traddles was this.—I had heard that many men distinguished in various pursuits had begun life by reporting the debates in Parliament. Traddles having mentioned newspapers to me, as one of his hopes, I had put the two things together, and told Traddles in my letter that I wished to know how I could qualify myself for this pursuit. Traddles now informed me, as the result of his inquiries, that the mere mechanical acquisition necessary, except in rare cases, for thorough excellence in it, that is to say, a perfect and entire command of the mystery of short-hand writing and reading, was about equal in difficulty to the mastery of six languages; and that it might perhaps be attained, by dint of perseverance, in the course of a few years. Traddles reasonably supposed that this would settle the business; but I, only feeling that here indeed were a few tall trees to be hewn down, immediately resolved to work my way on to Dora through this thicket, axe in hand.

"I am very much obliged to you, my dear Traddles!" said I. "I'll begin tomorrow."

Traddles looked astonished, as he well might; but he had no notion as yet of my rapturous condition.

"I'll buy a book," said I, "with a good scheme of this art in it; I'll work at it at the Commons, where I haven't half enough to do; I'll take down the speeches in our court for practice—Traddles, my dear fellow, I'll master it!"

"Dear me," said Traddles, opening his eyes, "I had no idea you were such a determined character, Copperfield!"

I don't know how he should have had, for it was new enough to me. I passed that off, and brought Mr Dick on the carpet.

"You see," said Mr Dick, wistfully, "if I could exert myself, Mr Traddles—if I could beat a drum—or blow anything!"

Poor fellow! I have little doubt he would have preferred such an employment in his heart to all others. Traddles, who would not have smiled for the world, replied composedly:

"But you are a very good penman, sir. You told me so, Copperfield?"

"Excellent!" said I. And indeed he was. He wrote with extraordinary neatness.

"Don't you think," said Traddles, "you could copy writings, sir, if I got them for you?"

Mr Dick looked doubtfully at me. "Eh, Trotwood?"

I shook my head. Mr Dick shook his, and sighed. "Tell him about the Memorial," said Mr Dick.

I explained to Traddles that there was a difficulty in keeping King Charles the First out of Mr Dick's manuscripts; Mr Dick in the meanwhile looking very deferentially and seriously at Traddles, and sucking his thumb.

"But these writings, you know, that I speak of, are already drawn up and finished," said Traddles after a little consideration. "Mr Dick has nothing to do with them. Wouldn't that make a difference, Copperfield? At all events, wouldn't it be well to try?"

This gave us new hope. Traddles and I laying our heads together apart, while Mr Dick anxiously watched us from his chair, we concocted a scheme in virtue of which we got him to work next day, with triumphant success.

On a table by the window in Buckingham Street, we set out the work Traddles procured for him—which was to make, I forget how many copies of a legal document about some right of way—and on another table we spread the last unfinished original of the great Memorial. Our instructions to Mr Dick were that he should copy exactly what he had before him, without the least departure from the original; and that when he felt it necessary to make the slightest allusion to King Charles the First, he should fly to the Memorial. We exhorted him to be resolute in this, and left my aunt to observe him. My aunt reported to us, afterwards, that, at first, he was like a man playing the kettle-drums, and constantly divided his attentions between the two; but that, finding this confuse and fatigue him, and having his copy there, plainly before his eyes, he soon sat at it in an orderly business-like manner, and postponed the Memorial to a more convenient time. In a word, although we took great care that he should have no more to do than was good for him, and although he did not begin with the beginning of a week, he earned by the following Saturday night ten shillings and ninepence; and never, while I live, shall I forget his going about to all the shops in the neighbourhood to change this treasure into sixpences, or his bringing them to my aunt arranged in the form of a heart upon a waiter, with tears of joy and pride in his eyes. He was like one under the propitious influence of a charm, from the moment of his being usefully employed; and if there were a happy man in the world, that Saturday night, it was the grateful creature who thought my aunt the most wonderful woman in existence, and me the most wonderful young man.

"No starving now, Trotwood," said Mr Dick, shaking hands with me in a corner. "I'll provide for her, sir!" and he flourished his ten fingers in the air, as if they were ten banks.

I hardly know which was the better pleased, Traddles or I. "It really," said Traddles, suddenly, taking a letter out of his pocket, and giving it to me, "put Mr Micawber quite out of my head!"

The letter (Mr Micawber never missed any possible opportunity of writing a letter) was addressed to me, "By the kindness of T. Traddles, Esquire, of the Inner Temple." It ran thus:—

"MY DEAR COPPERFIELD,

"You may possibly not be unprepared to receive the intimation that something has turned up. I may have mentioned to you on a former occasion that I was in expectation of such an event.

"I am about to establish myself in one of the provincial towns of our favoured island (where the society may be described as a happy admixture of the agricultural and the clerical), in immediate connexion with one of the learned professions. Mrs Micawber and our offspring will accompany me. Our ashes, at a future period, will probably be found commingled in the cemetery attached to a venerable pile, for which the spot to which I refer has acquired a reputation, shall I say from China to Peru?

"In bidding adieu to the modern Babylon, where we have undergone many vicissitudes, I trust not ignobly, Mrs Micawber and myself cannot disguise from our minds that we part, it may be for years and it may be for ever, with an individual linked by strong associations to the altar of our domestic life. If, on the eve of such a departure, you will accompany our mutual friend, Mr Thomas Traddles, to our present abode, and there reciprocate the wishes natural to the occasion, you will confer a Boon

"On
"One
"Who
"Is
"Ever yours,
"WILKINS MICAWBER."

I was glad to find that Mr Micawber had got rid of his dust and ashes, and that something really had turned up at last. Learning from Traddles that the invitation referred to the evening then wearing away, I expressed my readiness to do honour to it; and we went off together to the lodging which Mr Micawber occupied as Mr Mortimer, and which was situated near the top of the Gray's Inn Road.

The resources of this lodging were so limited, that we found the twins, now some eight or nine years old, reposing in a turn-up bedstead in the family sitting-room, where Mr Micawber had prepared, in a wash-hand-stand jug, what he called "a Brew" of the agreeable beverage for which he was famous. I had the pleasure, on this occasion, of renewing the acquaintance of Master Micawber, whom I found a promising boy of about twelve or thirteen, very subject to that restlessness of limb which is not an unfrequent phenomenon in youths of his age. I also became once more known to his sister, Miss Micawber, in whom, as Mr Micawber told us, "her mother renewed her youth, like the Phœnix."

"My dear Copperfield," said Mr Micawber, "yourself and Mr Traddles find us on the brink of migration, and will excuse any little discomforts incidental to that position."

Glancing round as I made a suitable reply, I observed that the family effects were already packed and that the amount of luggage was by no means overwhelming. I congratulated Mrs Micawber on the approaching change.

"My dear Mr Copperfield," said Mrs Micawber, "of your friendly interest in all our affairs, I am well assured. My family may consider it banishment, if they please; but I am a wife and mother, and I never will desert Mr Micawber."

Traddles, appealed to by Mrs Micawber's eye, feelingly acquiesced.

"That," said Mrs Micawber, "that, at least, is my view, my dear Mr Copperfield and Mr Traddles, of the obligation which I took upon myself when I repeated the irrevocable words, 'I, Emma, take thee, Wilkins.' I read the service over with a flat-candle on the previous night, and the conclusion I derived from it was, that I never could desert Mr Micawber. And,' said Mrs Micawber, "though it is possible I may be mistaken in my view of the ceremony, I never will!"

"My dear," said Mr Micawber, a little impatiently, "I am not conscious that you are expected to do anything of the sort."

"I am aware, my dear Mr Copperfield," pursued Mrs Micawber, "that I am now about to cast my lot among strangers; and I am also aware that the various members of my family, to whom Mr Micawber has written in the most gentlemanly terms, announcing that fact, have not taken the least notice of Mr Micawber's communication. Indeed I may be superstitious," said Mrs Micawber, "but it appears to me that Mr Micawber is destined never to receive any answers whatever to the great majority of the communications he writes. I may augur, from the silence of my family, that they object to the resolution I have taken; but I should not allow myself to be swerved from the path of duty, Mr Copperfield, even by my papa and mama, were they still living."

I expressed my opinion that this was going in the right direction.

"It may be a sacrifice," said Mrs Micawber, "to immure one's-self in a Cathedral town; but surely, Mr Copperfield, if it is a sacrifice in me, it is much more a sacrifice in a man of Mr Micawber's abilities."

"Oh! You are going to a Cathedral town?" said I.

Mr Micawber, who had been helping us all, out of the washhand-stand jug, replied:

"To Canterbury. In fact, my dear Copperfield, I have entered into arrangements, by virtue of which I stand pledged and contracted to our friend Heep, to assist and serve him in the capacity of—and to be—his confidential clerk."

I stared at Mr Micawber, who greatly enjoyed my surprise.

"I am bound to state to you," he said, with an official air, "that the business habits, and the prudent suggestions, of Mrs Micawber, have in a great measure conduced to this result. The gauntlet, to which Mrs Micawber referred upon a former occasion, being thrown down in the form of an advertisement, was taken up by my friend Heep, and led to a mutual recognition. Of my friend Heep," said Mr Micawber, "who is a man of remarkable shrewdness, I desire to speak with all possible respect. My friend Heep has not fixed the positive remuneration at too high a figure, but he has made a great deal, in the way of extrication from the pressure of pecuniary difficulties, contingent on the value of my services; and on the value of those services I pin my faith. Such address and intelligence as I chance to possess," said Mr Micawber, boastfully disparaging himself, with the old genteel air, "will be devoted to my friend Heep's service. I have already some acquaintance with the law—as a defendant on civil process—and I shall immediately apply myself to the Commentaries of one of the most eminent and remarkable of our English Jurists. I believe it is unnecessary to add that I allude to Mr Justice Blackstone."

These observations, and indeed the greater part of the observations made that evening, were interrupted by Mrs Micawber's discovering that Master Micawber was sitting on his boots, or holding his head on with both arms as if he felt it loose, or accidentally kicking Traddles under the table, or shuffling his feet over one another, or producing them at distances from himself apparently outrageous to nature, or lying sideways with his hair among the wine-glasses, or developing his restlessness of limb in some other form incompatible with the general interests of society; and by Master Micawber's receiving those discoveries in a resentful spirit. I sat all the while, amazed by Mr Micawber's disclosure, and wondering what it meant; until Mrs Micawber resumed the thread of the discourse, and claimed my attention.

"What I particularly request Mr Micawber to be careful of, is," said Mrs Micawber, "that he does not, my dear Mr Copperfield, in applying himself to this subordinate branch of the law, place it out of his power to rise, ultimately, to the top of the tree. I am convinced that Mr Micawber, giving his mind to a profession so adapted to his fertile resources, and his flow of language, *must* distinguish himself. Now, for example, Mr Traddles," said Mrs Micawber, assuming a profound air, "a Judge, or even say a Chancellor. Does an individual place himself beyond the pale of those preferments by entering on such an office as Mr Micawber has accepted?"

"My dear," observed Mr Micawber—but glancing inquisitively at Traddles, too; "we have time enough before us, for the consideration of those questions."

"Micawber," she returned, "no! Your mistake in life is, that you do not look forward far enough. You are bound, in justice to your family, if not to yourself, to take in at a comprehensive glance the extremest point in the horizon to which your abilities may lead you."

Mr Micawber coughed, and drank his punch with an air of exceeding satisfaction—still glancing at Traddles, as if he desired to have his opinion.

"Why, the plain state of the case, Mrs Micawber," said Traddles, mildly breaking the truth to her. "I mean the real prosaic fact, you know—"

"Just so," said Mrs Micawber, "my dear Mr Traddles, I wish to be prosaic and literal as possible on a subject of so much importance."

"—Is," said Traddles, "that this branch of the law, even if Mr Micawber were a regular solicitor—"

"Exactly so," returned Mrs Micawber. ("Wilkins, you are squinting, and will not be able to get your eyes back.")

"—Has nothing," pursued Traddles, "to do with that. Only a barrister is eligible for such preferments; and Mr Micawber could not be a barrister, without being entered at an inn of court as a student, for five years."

"Do I follow you?" said Mrs Micawber, with her most affable air of business. "Do I understand, my dear Mr Traddles, that, at the expiration of that period, Mr Micawber would be eligible as a Judge or Chancellor?"

"He would be *eligible*," returned Traddles, with a strong emphasis on that word.

"Thank you," said Mrs Micawber. "That is quite sufficient. If such is the case, and Mr Micawber forfeits no privilege by entering on these duties, my anxiety is set at rest. I speak," said Mrs Micawber, "as a female, necessarily; but I have always been of opinion that Mr Micawber possesses what I have heard my papa call, when I lived at home, the judicial mind; and I hope Mr Micawber is now entering on a field where that mind will develop itself, and take a commanding station."

I quite believe that Mr Micawber saw himself, in his judicial mind's eye, on the woolsack. He passed his hand complacently over his bald head, and said with ostentatious resignation:

"My dear, we will not anticipate the decrees of fortune. If I am reserved to wear a wig, I am at least prepared, externally," in allusion to his baldness, "for that distinction. I do not," said Mr Micawber, "regret my hair, and I may have been deprived of it for a specific purpose. I cannot say. It is my intention, my dear Copperfield, to educate my son for the Church; I will not deny that I should be happy, on his account, to attain to eminence."

"For the Church?" said I, still pondering, between whiles, on Uriah Heep.

"Yes," said Mr Micawber. "He has a remarkable head-voice, and will commence as a chorister. Our residence at Canterbury, and our local connexion, will, no doubt, enable him to take advantage of any vacancy that may arise in the Cathedral corps."

On looking at Master Micawber again, I saw that he had a certain expression of face, as if his voice were behind his eyebrows; where it presently appeared to be, on his singing us (as an alternative between that and bed) "The Wood-Pecker tapping." After many compliments on this performance, we fell into some general conversation; and as I was too full of my desperate intentions to keep my altered circumstances to myself, I made them known to Mr and Mrs Micawber. I cannot express how extremely delighted they both were, by the idea of my aunt's being in difficulties; and how comfortable and friendly it made them.

When we were nearly come to the last round of the punch, I addressed myself to Traddles, and reminded him that we must not separate, without wishing our friends health, happiness, and success in their new career. I begged Mr Micawber to fill us bumpers, and proposed the toast in due form: shaking hands with him across the table, and kissing Mrs Micawber, to commemorate that eventful occasion. Traddles imitated me in the first particular, but did not consider himself a sufficiently old friend to venture on the second.

"My dear Copperfield," said Mr Micawber, rising with one of his thumbs in each of his waistcoat pockets, "the companion of my youth: if I may be allowed the expression—and my esteemed friend Traddles: if I may be permitted to call him so—will allow me, on the part of Mrs Micawber, myself, and our offspring, to thank them in the warmest and most uncompromising terms for their good wishes. It may be expected that on the eve of a migration which will consign us to a perfectly new existence," Mr Micawber spoke as if they were going five hundred thousand miles, "I should offer a few valedictory remarks to two such friends as I see before me. But all that I have to say in this way,

I have said. Whatever station in society I may attain, through the medium of the learned profession of which I am about to become an unworthy member, I shall endeavour not to disgrace, and Mrs Micawber will be safe to adorn. Under the temporary pressure of pecuniary liabilities, contracted with a view to their immediate liquidation, but remaining unliquidated through a combination of circumstances, I have been under the necessity of assuming a garb from which my natural instincts recoil—I allude to spectacles—and possessing myself of a cognomen, to which I can establish no legitimate pretensions. All I have to say on that score is, that the cloud has passed from the dreary scene, and the God of Day is once more high upon the mountain tops. On Monday next, on the arrival of the four o'clock afternoon coach at Canterbury, my foot will be on my native heath— my name, Micawber!"

Mr Micawber resumed his seat on the close of these remarks, and drank two glasses of punch in grave succession. He then said with much solemnity:

"One thing more I have to do, before this separation is complete, and that is to perform an act of justice. My friend Mr Thomas Traddles has, on two several occasions, 'put his name,' if I may use a common expression, to bills of exchange for my accommodation. On the first occasion Mr Thomas Traddles was left—let me say, in short, in the lurch. The fulfilment of the second has not yet arrived. The amount of the first obligation," here Mr Micawber carefully referred to papers, "was, I believe, twenty-three, four, nine and a half; of the second, according to my entry of that transaction, eighteen, six, two. These sums, united, make a total, if my calculation is correct, amounting to forty-one, ten, eleven and a half. My friend Copperfield will perhaps do me the favour to check that total?"

I did so and found it correct.

"To leave this metropolis," said Mr Micawber, "and my friend Mr Thomas Traddles, without acquitting myself of the pecuniary part of this obligation, would weigh upon my mind to an insupportable extent. I have, therefore, prepared for my friend Mr Thomas Traddles, and I now hold in my hand, a document, which accomplishes the desired object. I beg to hand to my friend Mr Thomas Traddles my I.O.U. for forty-one, ten, eleven and a half, and I am happy to recover my moral dignity, and to know that I can once more walk erect before my fellow man!"

With this introduction (which greatly affected him), Mr Micawber placed his I.O.U. in the hands of Traddles, and said he wished him well in every relation of life. I am persuaded, not only that this was quite the same to Mr Micawber as paying the money, but that Traddles himself hardly knew the difference until he had had time to think about it.

Mr Micawber walked so erect before his fellow man, on the strength of this virtuous action, that his chest looked half as broad again when he lighted us downstairs. We parted with great heartiness on both sides; and when I had seen Traddles to his own door, and was going home alone, I thought, among the other odd and contradictory things I mused upon, that, slippery as Mr Micawber was, I was probably indebted to some compassionate recollection he retained of me as his boy-lodger, for never having been asked by him for money. I certainly should not have had the moral courage to refuse it; and I have no doubt he knew that (to his credit be it written), quite as well as I did.

Chapter XXXVII

A LITTLE COLD WATER

MY new life had lasted for more than a week, and I was stronger than ever in those tremendous practical resolutions that I felt the crisis required. I continued to walk extremely fast, and to have a general idea that I was getting on. I made it a rule to take as much out of myself as I possibly could, in my way of doing everything to which I applied my energies. I made a perfect victim of myself. I even entertained some idea of putting myself on a vegetable diet, vaguely conceiving that, in becoming a graminivorous animal, I should sacrifice to Dora.

As yet, little Dora was quite unconscious of my desperate firmness, otherwise than as my letters darkly shadowed it forth. But, another Saturday came, and on that Saturday evening she was to be at Miss Mills's; and when Mr Mills had gone to his whist-club (telegraphed to me in the street, by a bird-cage in the drawing-room middle window), I was to go there to tea.

By this time, we were quite settled down in Buckingham Street, where Mr Dick continued his copying in a state of absolute felicity. My aunt had obtained a signal victory over Mrs Crupp, by paying her off, throwing the first pitcher she planted on the stairs out of window, and protecting in person, up and down the staircase, a supernumerary whom she engaged from the outer world. These vigorous measures struck such terror to the breast of Mrs Crupp, that she subsided into her own kitchen, under the impression that my aunt was mad. My aunt being supremely indifferent to Mrs Crupp's opinion and everybody else's, and rather favouring than discouraging the idea, Mrs Crupp, of late the bold, became within a few days so faint-hearted, that rather than encounter my aunt upon the staircase, she would endeavour to hide her portly form behind doors—leaving visible, however, a wide margin of flannel petticoat—or would shrink into dark corners. This gave my aunt such unspeakable satisfaction, that I believe she took a delight in prowling up and down, with her bonnet insanely perched on the top of her head, at times when Mrs Crupp was likely to be in the way.

My aunt, being uncommonly neat and ingenious, made so many little improvements in our domestic arrangements, that I seemed to be richer instead of poorer. Among the rest, she converted the pantry into a dressing-room for me; and purchased and embellished a bedstead for my occupation, which looked as like a bookcase in the daytime as a bedstead could. I was the object of her constant solicitude; and my poor mother herself could not have loved me better, or studied more how to make me happy.

Peggotty had considered herself highly privileged in being allowed to participate in these labours; and, although she still retained something of her old sentiment of awe in reference to my aunt, had received so many marks of encouragement and confidence, that they were the best friends possible. But the time had now come (I am speaking of the Saturday when I was to take tea at Miss Mills's) when it was necessary for her to return home, and enter on the discharge of the duties she had undertaken in behalf of Ham. "So good-bye, Barkis," said my aunt, "and take care of yourself! I am sure I never thought I could be sorry to lose you!"

I took Peggotty to the coach office and saw her off. She cried at parting, and confided her brother to my friendship as Ham had done. We had heard nothing of him since he went away, that sunny afternoon.

"And now, my own dear Davy," said Peggotty, "if, while you're a prentice, you should want any money to spend; or if, when you're out of your time, my dear, you should want any to set you up (and you must do one or other, or both, my darling); who has such a good right to ask leave to lend it you, as my sweet girl's own old stupid me!"

I was not so savagely independent as to say anything in reply, but that if ever I borrowed money of anyone, I would borrow it of her. Next to accepting a large sum on the spot, I believe this gave Peggotty more comfort than anything I could have done.

"And, my dear!" whispered Peggotty, "tell the pretty little angel that I should so have liked to see her, only for a minute! And tell her that before she marries my boy, I'll come and make your house so beautiful for you, if you'll let me!"

I declared that nobody else should touch it; and this gave Peggotty such delight that she went away in good spirits.

I fatigued myself as much as I possibly could in the Commons all day, by a variety of devices, and at the appointed time in the evening repaired to Mr Mills's street. Mr Mills, who was a terrible fellow to fall asleep after dinner, had not yet gone out, and there was no bird-cage in the middle window.

He kept me waiting so long, that I fervently hoped the Club would fine him for being late. At last he came out; and then I saw my own Dora hang up the bird-cage, and peep into the balcony to look for me, and run in again when she saw I was there, while Jip remained behind, to bark injuriously at an immense butcher's dog in the street, who could have taken him like a pill.

Dora came to the drawing-room door to meet me; and Jip came scrambling out, tumbling over his own growls, under the impression that I was a Bandit; and we all three went in, as happy and loving as could be. I soon carried desolation into the bosom of our joys—not that I meant to do it, but that I was so full of the subject—by asking Dora, without the smallest preparation, if she could love a beggar?

My pretty, little, startled Dora! Her only association with the word was a yellow face and a nightcap, or a pair of crutches, or a wooden leg, or a dog with a decanter-stand in his mouth, or something of that kind; and she stared at me with the most delightful wonder.

"How can you ask me anything so foolish?" pouted Dora. "Love a beggar!"

"Dora, my own dearest!" said I. *"I* am a beggar!"

"How can you be such a silly thing," replied Dora, slapping my hand, "as to sit there, telling such stories? I'll make Jip bite you!"

Her childish way was the most delicious way in the world to me, but it was necessary to be explicit, and I solemnly repeated:

"Dora, my own life, I am your ruined David!"

"I declare I'll make Jip bite you!" said Dora, shaking her curls, "if you are so ridiculous."

But I looked so serious, that Dora left off shaking her curls, and laid her trembling little hand upon my shoulder, and first looked scared and anxious, then began to cry. That was dreadful. I fell upon my knees before the sofa, caressing her, and imploring her not to rend my heart; but, for some time, poor little Dora did nothing but exclaim Oh dear! Oh dear! And oh, she was so frightened! And where was Julia Mills! And oh, take her to Julia Mills, and go away, please! until I was almost beside myself.

At last, after an agony of supplication and protestation, I got Dora to look at me, with a horrified expression of face, which I gradually soothed until it was only loving, and her soft, pretty cheek was lying against mine. Then I told her, with my arms clasped round her, how I loved her, so dearly, and so dearly; how I felt it right to offer to release her from her engagement, because now I was poor; how I never could bear it, or recover it, if I lost her; how I had no fears of poverty, if she had none, my arm being nerved and my heart inspired by her; how I was already working with a courage such as none but lovers knew; how I had begun to be practical, and look into the future; how a crust well earned was sweeter far than a feast inherited; and much more to the same purpose, which I delivered in a burst of passionate eloquence quite surprising to myself, though I had been thinking about it, day and night, ever since my aunt had astonished me.

"Is your heart mine still, dear Dora?" said I, rapturously, for I knew by her clinging to me that it was.

"Oh, yes!" cried Dora. "Oh, yes, it's all yours. Oh, don't be dreadful!"

I dreadful! To Dora!

"Don't talk about being poor, and working hard!" said Dora, nestling closer to me. "Oh, don't, don't!"

"My dearest love," said I, "the crust well-earned——"

"Oh, yes; but I don't want to hear any more about crusts!" said Dora. "And Jip must have a mutton-chop every day at twelve, or he'll die."

I was charmed with her childish, winning way. I fondly explained to Dora that Jip should have his mutton-chop with his accustomed regularity. I drew a picture of our frugal home, made independent by my labour—sketching-in the little house I had seen at Highgate, and my aunt in her room upstairs.

"I am not dreadful now, Dora?" said I, tenderly.

"Oh, no, no!" cried Dora. "But I hope your aunt will keep in her own room a good deal. And I hope she's not a scolding old thing!"

If it were possible for me to love Dora more than ever, I am sure I did. But I felt she was a little impracticable. It damped my new-born ardour, to find that ardour so difficult of communication to her. I made another trial. When she was quite herself again, and was curling Jip's ears, as he lay upon her lap, I became grave, and said:

"My own! May I mention something?"

"Oh, please don't be practical!" said Dora, coaxingly. "Because it frightens me so!"

"Sweetheart!" I returned; "there is nothing to alarm you in all this. I want you to think of it quite differently. I want to make it nerve you, and inspire you, Dora!"

"Oh, but that's so shocking!" cried Dora.

"My love, no. Perseverance and strength of character will enable us to bear much worse things."

"But I haven't got any strength at all," said Dora, shaking her curls. "Have I, Jip? Oh, do kiss Jip, and be agreeable!"

It was impossible to resist kissing Jip, when she held him up to me for that purpose, putting her own bright, rosy little mouth into kissing form, as she directed the operation, which she insisted should be performed symmetrically, on the centre of his nose. I did as she bade me—rewarding myself afterwards for my obedience—and she charmed me out of my graver character for I don't know how long.

"But, Dora, my beloved!" said I, at last resuming it; "I was going to mention something."

The Judge of the Prerogative Court might have fallen in love with her, to see her fold her little hands and hold them up, begging and praying me not to be dreadful any more.

"Indeed I am not going to be, my darling!" I assured her. "But, Dora, my love, if you will sometimes think,—not despondingly, you know; far from that!—but if you will sometimes think—just to encourage yourself—that you are engaged to a poor man—"

"Don't, don't! Pray don't!" cried Dora. "It's so very dreadful!"

"My soul, not at all!" said I, cheerfully. "If you will sometimes think of that, and look about now and then at your papa's housekeeping, and endeavour to acquire a little habit—of accounts, for instance—"

Poor little Dora received this suggestion with something that was half a sob and half a scream.

"—It would be so useful to us afterwards," I went on. "And if you would promise me to read a little—a little Cookery Book that I would send you, it would be so excellent for both of us. For our path in life, my Dora," said I, warming with the subject, "is stony and rugged now, and it rests with us to smooth it. We must fight our way onward. We must be brave. There are obstacles to be met, and we must meet, and crush them!"

I was going on at a great rate, with a clenched hand, and a most enthusiastic countenance; but it was quite unnecessary to proceed. I had said enough. I had done it again. Oh, she was so frightened! Oh, where was Julia Mills! Oh, take her to Julia Mills, and go away, please! So that, in short, I was quite distracted, and raved about the drawing-room.

I thought I had killed her, this time. I sprinkled water on her face. I went down on my knees. I plucked at my hair. I denounced myself as a remorseless brute and a ruthless beast. I implored her forgiveness. I besought her to look up. I ravaged Miss Mills's workbox for a smelling-bottle, and in my agony of mind applied an ivory needle-case instead, and dropped all the needles over Dora. I shook my fists at Jip, who was as frantic as myself. I did every wild extravagance that could be done, and was a long way beyond the end of my wits when Miss Mills came into the room.

"Who has done this?" exclaimed Miss Mills, succouring her friend.

I replied, "I, Miss Mills! I have done it! Behold the destroyer!"—or words to that effect—and hid my face from the light, in the sofa cushion.

At first Miss Mills thought it was a quarrel, and that we were verging on the Desert of Sahara; but she soon found out how matters stood, for my dear affectionate little Dora, embracing her, began exclaiming that I was "a poor labourer"; and then cried for me, and embraced me, and asked me would I let her give me all her money to keep, and then fell on Miss Mills's neck, sobbing as if her tender heart were broken.

Miss Mills must have been born to be a blessing to us. She ascertained from me in a few words what it was all about, comforted Dora, and gradually convinced her that I was not a labourer—from my manner of stating the case I believe Dora concluded that I was a navigator, and went balancing myself up and down a plank all day with a wheelbarrow—and so brought us together in peace. When we were quite composed, and Dora had gone upstairs to put some rose-water to her eyes, Miss Mills rang for tea. In the ensuing interval, I told Miss Mills that she was evermore my friend, and that my heart must cease to vibrate ere I could forget her sympathy.

I then expounded to Miss Mills what I had endeavoured, so very unsuccessfully, to expound to Dora. Miss Mills replied, on general principles, that the Cottage of content was better than the Palace of cold splendour, and that where love was, all was.

I said to Miss Mills that this was very true, and who should know it better than I, who loved Dora with a love that never mortal had experienced yet? But on Miss Mills observing, with despondency, that it were well indeed for some hearts if this were so, I explained that I begged leave to restrict the observation to mortals of the masculine gender.

I then put it to Miss Mills, to say whether she considered that there was or was not any practical merit in the suggestion I had been anxious to make, concerning the accounts, the housekeeping, and the Cookery Book?

Miss Mills, after some consideration, thus replied:

"Mr Copperfield, I will be plain with you. Mental suffering and trial supply, in some natures, the place of years, and I will be as plain with you as if I were a Lady Abbess. No. The suggestion is not appropriate to our Dora. Our dearest Dora is a favourite child of nature. She is a thing of light, and airiness, and joy. I am free to confess that if it could be done, it might be well,' but—" And Miss Mills shook her head.

I was encouraged by this closing admission on the part of Miss Mills to ask her, whether, for Dora's sake, if she had any opportunity of luring her attention to such preparations for an earnest life, she would avail herself of it? Miss Mills replied in the affirmative so readily, that I further asked her if she would take charge of the Cookery Book; and, if she ever could insinuate it upon Dora's acceptance, without frightening her, undertake to do me that crowning service. Miss Mills accepted this trust, too; but was not sanguine.

And Dora returned, looking such a lovely little creature, that I really doubted whether she ought to be troubled with anything so ordinary. And she loved me so much, and was so captivating (particularly when she made Jip stand on his hind legs for toast, and when she pretended to hold that nose of his against the hot teapot for punishment because he wouldn't), that I felt like a sort of Monster who had got into a Fairy's bower, when I thought of having frightened her, and made her cry.

After tea we had the guitar; and Dora sang those same dear old French songs about the impossibility of ever on any account leaving off dancing, La ra la, La ra la, until I felt a much greater Monster than before.

We had only one check to our pleasure, and that happened a little while before I took my leave, when, Miss Mills chancing to make some allusion to tomorrow morning, I unluckily let out that, being obliged to exert myself now, I got up at five o'clock. Whether Dora had any idea that I was a Private Watchman, I am unable to say; but it made a great impression on her, and she neither played nor sang any more.

It was still on her mind when I bade her adieu; and she said to me, in her pretty coaxing way—as if I were a doll, I used to think!

"Now don't get up at five o'clock, you naughty boy. It's so nonsensical!"

"My love," said I, "I have work to do."

"But don't do it!" returned Dora. "Why should you?"

It was impossible to say to that sweet little surprised face, otherwise than lightly and playfully, that we must work to live.

"Oh! How ridiculous!" cried Dora.

"How shall we live without, Dora?" said I.

"How? Any how!" said Dora.

She seemed to think she had quite settled the question, and gave me such a triumphant little kiss, direct from her innocent heart, that I would hardly have put her out of conceit with her answer, for a fortune.

Well! I loved her, and I went on loving her, most absorbingly, entirely, and completely. But going on, too, working pretty hard, and busily keeping red-hot all the irons I now had in the fire, I would sit sometimes of a night, opposite my aunt, thinking how I had frightened Dora that time, and how I could best make my way with a guitar-case through the forest of difficulty, until I used to fancy that my head was turning quite grey.

Chapter XXXVIII

A DISSOLUTION OF PARTNERSHIP

I DID not allow my resolution, with respect to the Parliamentary Debates, to cool. It was one of the irons I began to heat immediately, and one of the irons I kept hot, and hammered at, with a perseverance I may honestly admire. I bought an approved scheme of the noble art and mystery of stenography (which cost me ten and sixpence); and plunged into a sea of perplexity that brought me, in a few weeks, to the confines of distraction. The changes that were rung upon dots, which in such a position meant such a thing, and in such another position something else, entirely different; the wonderful vagaries that were played by circles; the unaccountable consequences that resulted from marks like flies' legs; the tremendous effects of a curve in a wrong place; not only troubled my waking hours, but reappeared before me in my sleep. When I had groped my way, blindly, through these difficulties, and had mastered the alphabet, which was an Egyptian Temple in itself, there then appeared a procession of new horrors, called arbitrary characters; the most despotic characters I have ever known; who insisted, for instance, that a thing like the beginning of a cobweb, meant expectation, and that a pen-and-ink skyrocket stood for disadvantageous. When I had fixed these wretches in my mind, I found that they had driven everything else out of it; then, beginning again, I forgot them; while I was picking them up, I dropped the other fragments of the system; in short, it was almost heart-breaking.

It might have been quite heart-breaking, but for Dora, who was the stay and anchor of my tempest-driven bark. Every scratch in the scheme was a gnarled oak in the forest of difficulty, and I went on cutting them down, one after another, with such vigour, that in three or four months I was in a condition to make an experiment on one of our crack speakers in the Commons. Shall I ever forget how the crack speaker walked off from me before I began, and left my imbecile pencil staggering about the paper as if it were in a fit!

This would not do, it was quite clear. I was flying too high, and should never get on, so. I resorted to Traddles for advice; who suggested that he should dictate speeches to me, at a pace, and with occasional stoppages, adapted to my weakness. Very grateful for this friendly aid, I accepted the proposal; and night after night, almost every night, for a long time, we had a sort of Private Parliament in Buckingham Street, after I came home from the Doctor's.

I should like to see such a Parliament anywhere else! My aunt and Mr Dick represented the Government or the Opposition (as the case might be), and Traddles, with the assistance of Enfield's Speaker or a volume of parliamentary orations, thundered astonishing invectives against them. Standing by the table, with his finger in the page to keep the place, and his right arm flourishing above his head, Traddles, as Mr Pitt, Mr Fox, Mr Sheridan, Mr Burke, Lord Castlereagh, Viscount Sidmouth, or Mr Canning, would work himself into the most violent heats, and deliver the most withering denunciations of the profligacy and corruption of my aunt and Mr Dick; while I used to sit, at a little distance, with my notebook on my knee, fagging after him with all my might and main. The inconsistency and recklessness of Traddles were not to be exceeded by any real politician. He was for any description of policy, in the compass of a week; and nailed all sorts of colours to every denomination of mast. My aunt, looking very like an immovable Chancellor of the Exchequer, would occasionally throw in an interruption or two, as "Hear!" or "No!" or "Oh!" when the text seemed to require it: which was always a signal to Mr Dick (a perfect country gentleman) to follow lustily with the same cry. But Mr Dick got taxed with such things in the course of his Parliamentary career, and was made responsible for such awful consequences, that he became uncomfortable in his mind sometimes. I believe he actually began to be afraid he really had been doing something, tending to the annihilation of the British constitution, and the ruin of the country.

Often and often we pursued these debates until the clock pointed to midnight, and the candles were burning down. The result of so much good practice was, that by and by I began to keep pace with Traddles pretty well, and should have been quite triumphant if I had had the least idea what my notes were about. But, as to reading them after I had got them, I might as well have copied the Chinese inscriptions of an immense collection of tea-chests, or the golden characters on all the great red and green bottles in the chemists' shops!

There was nothing for it, but to turn back and begin all over again. It was very hard, but I turned back, though with a heavy heart, and began laboriously and methodically to plod over the same tedious ground at a snail's pace; stopping to examine minutely every speck in the way, on all sides, and making the most desperate efforts to know these elusive characters by sight wherever I met them. I was always punctual at the office; at the Doctor's too: and I really did work, as the common expression is, like a cart-horse.

One day, when I went to the Commons as usual, I found Mr Spenlow in the doorway looking extremely grave, and talking to himself. As he was in the habit of complaining of pains in his head—he had naturally a short throat, and I do seriously believe he over-starched himself—I was at first alarmed by the idea that he was not quite right in that direction; but he soon relieved my uneasiness.

Instead of returning my "Good morning" with his usual affability, he looked at me in a distant, ceremonious manner, and coldly requested me to accompany him to a certain coffee-house, which, in those days, had a door opening into the Commons, just within the little archway in St Paul's Churchyard. I complied, in a very uncomfortable state, and with a warm shooting all over me, as if my apprehensions were breaking out into buds. When I allowed him to go on a little before, on account of the narrowness of the way, I observed that he carried his head with a lofty air that was particularly unpromising; and my mind misgave me that he had found out about my darling Dora.

If I had not guessed this, on the way to the coffee-house, I could hardly have failed to know what was the matter when I followed him into an upstairs room, and found Miss Murdstone there, supported by a background of sideboard, on which were several inverted tumblers sustaining lemons, and two of those extraordinary boxes, all corners and flutings, for sticking knives and forks in, which, happily for mankind, are now obsolete.

Miss Murdstone gave me her chilly finger-nails, and sat severely rigid. Mr Spenlow shut the door, motioned me to a chair, and stood on the hearth-rug in front of the fire-place.

"Have the goodness to show Mr Copperfield," said Mr Spenlow, "what you have in your reticule, Miss Murdstone."

I believe it was the old identical steel-clasped reticule of my childhood, that shut up like a bite. Compressing her lips, in sympathy with the snap, Miss Murdstone opened it—opening her mouth a little at the same time—and produced my last letter to Dora, teeming with expressions of devoted affection.

"I believe that is your writing, Mr Copperfield?" said Mr Spenlow.

I was very hot, and the voice I heard was very unlike mine, when I said, "It is, sir!"

"If I am not mistaken," said Mr Spenlow, as Miss Murdstone brought a parcel of letters out of her reticule, tied round with the dearest bit of blue ribbon, "those are also from your pen, Mr Copperfield?"

I took them from her with a most desolate sensation; and, glancing at such phrases at the top, as "My ever dearest and own Dora," "My best beloved angel," "My blessed one for ever," and the like, blushed deeply, and inclined my head.

"No, thank you!" said Mr Spenlow, coldly, as I mechanically offered them back to him. "I will not deprive you of them. Miss Murdstone, be so good as to proceed!"

That gentle creature, after a moment's thoughtful survey of the carpet, delivered herself with much dry unction as follows.

"I must confess to having entertained my suspicions of Miss Spenlow, in reference to David Copperfield, for some time. I observed Miss Spenlow and David Copperfield, when they first met; and the impression made upon me then was not agreeable. The depravity of the human heart is such—"

"You will oblige me, ma'am," interrupted Mr Spenlow, "by confining yourself to facts."

Miss Murdstone cast down her eyes, shook her head as if protesting against this unseemly interruption, and with frowning dignity resumed:

"Since I am to confine myself to facts, I will state them as dryly as I can. Perhaps that will be considered an acceptable course of proceeding. I have already said, sir, that I have had my suspicions of Miss Spenlow, in reference to David Copperfield, for some time. I have frequently endeavoured to find decisive corroboration of those suspicions, but without effect. I have therefore forborne to mention them to Miss Spenlow's father"; looking severely at him; "knowing how little disposition there usually is in such cases, to acknowledge the conscientious discharge of duty."

Mr Spenlow seemed quite cowed by the gentlemanly sterness of Miss Murdstone's manner, and deprecated her severity with a conciliatory little wave of his hand.

"On my return to Norwood, after the period of absence occasioned by my brother's marriage," pursued Miss Murdstone in a disdainful voice, "and on the return of Miss Spenlow from her visit to her friend Miss Mills, I imagined that the manner of Miss Spenlow gave me greater occasion for suspicion than before. Therefore I watched Miss Spenlow closely."

Dear, tender little Dora, so unconscious of this Dragon's eye!

"Still," resumed Miss Murdstone, "I found no proof until last night. It appeared to me that Miss Spenlow received too many letters from her friend Miss Mills; but Miss Mills being her friend with her father's full concurrence," another telling blow at Mr Spenlow, "it was not for me to interfere. If I may not be permitted to allude to the natural depravity of the human heart, at least I may—I must—be permitted, so far to refer to misplaced confidence."

Mr Spenlow apologetically murmured his assent.

"Last evening after tea," pursued Miss Murdstone, "I observed the little dog starting, rolling, and growling about the drawing-room, worrying something. I said to Miss Spenlow, 'Dora, what is that the dog has in his mouth? It's paper.' Miss Spenlow immediately put her hand to her frock, gave a sudden cry, and ran to the dog. I interposed, and said, 'Dora, my love, you must permit me.'"

Oh Jip, miserable Spaniel, this wretchedness, then, was your work!

"Miss Spenlow endeavoured," said Miss Murdstone, "to bribe me with kisses, work-boxes, and small articles of jewellery—that, of course, I pass over. The little dog retreated under the sofa on my approaching him, and was with great difficulty dislodged by the fire-irons. Even when dislodged, he still kept the letter in his mouth; and on my en-deavouring to take it from him, at the imminent risk of being bitten, he kept it between his teeth so pertinaciously as to suffer himself to be held suspended in the air by means of the document. At length I obtained possession of it. After perusing it, I taxed Miss Spenlow with having many such letters in her possession; and ultimately obtained from her the packet which is now in David Copperfield's hand."

Here she ceased; and snapping her reticule again, and shutting her mouth, looked as if she might be broken, but could never be bent.

"You have heard Miss Murdstone," said Mr Spenlow, turning to me. "I beg to ask, Mr Copperfield, if you have anything to say in reply?"

The picture I had before me, of the beautiful little treasure of my heart, sobbing and crying all night—of her being alone, frightened, and wretched, then—of her hav-ing so piteously begged and prayed that stony-hearted woman to forgive her—of her having vainly offered her those kisses, work-boxes, and trinkets—of her being in such grievous distress, and all for me—very much impaired the little dignity I had been able to muster. I am afraid I was in a tremulous state for a minute or so, though I did my best to disguise it.

"There is nothing I can say, sir," I returned, "except that all the blame is mine. Dora—"

"Miss Spenlow, if you please," said her father, majestically.

"—was induced and persuaded by me," I went on, swallowing that colder designa-tion, "to consent to this concealment, and I bitterly regret it."

"You are very much to blame, sir," said Mr Spenlow, walking to and fro upon the hearth-rug, and emphasizing what he said with his whole body instead of his head, on account of the stiffness of his cravat and spine. "You have done a stealthy and unbecom-ing action, Mr Copperfield. When I take a gentleman to my house, no matter whether he is nineteen, twenty-nine, or ninety, I take him there in a spirit of confidence. If he abuses my confidence, he commits a dishonourable action, Mr Copperfield."

"I feel it, sir, I assure you," I returned. "But I never thought so, before. Sincerely, honestly, indeed, Mr Spenlow, I never thought so, before. I love Miss Spenlow to that extent—"

"Pooh! nonsense!" said Mr Spenlow, reddening. "Pray don't tell me to my face that you love my daughter, Mr Copperfield!"

"Could I defend my conduct if I did not, sir?" I returned, with all humility.

"Can you defend your conduct if you do, sir?" said Mr Spenlow, stopping short upon the hearth-rug. "Have you considered your years, and my daughter's years, Mr Copper-field? Have you considered what it is to undermine the confidence that should subsist between my daughter and myself? Have you considered my daughter's station in life, the projects I may contemplate for her advancement, the testamentary intentions I may have with reference to her? Have you considered anything, Mr Copperfield?"

"Very little, sir, I am afraid"; I answered, speaking to him as respectfully and sorrowfully as I felt; "but pray believe me, I have considered my own worldly position. When I explained it to you, we were already engaged—"

"I BEG," said Mr Spenlow, more like Punch than I had ever seen him, as he energeti-cally struck one hand upon the other—I could not help noticing that even in my despair;

"that you will NOT talk to me of engagements, Mr Copperfield!"

The otherwise immovable Miss Murdstone laughed contemptuously in one short syllable.

"When I explained my altered position to you, sir," I began again, substituting a new form of expression for what was so unpalatable to him, "this concealment, into which I am so unhappy as to have led Miss Spenlow, had begun. Since I have been in that altered position, I have strained every nerve, I have exerted every energy, to improve it. I am sure I shall improve it in time. Will you grant me time—any length of time? We are both so young, sir,—"

"You are right," interrupted Mr Spenlow, nodding his head a great many times, and frowning very much, "you are both very young. It's all nonsense. Let there be an end of the nonsense. Take away those letters, and throw them in the fire. Give me Miss Spenlow's letters to throw in the fire; and although our future intercourse must, you are aware, be restricted to the Commons here, we will agree to make no further mention of the past. Come, Mr Copperfield, you don't want sense; and this is the sensible course."

No. I couldn't think of agreeing to it. I was very sorry, but there was a higher consideration than sense. Love was above all earthly considerations, and I loved Dora to idolatry, and Dora loved me. I didn't exactly say so; I softened it down as much as I could; but I implied it, and I was resolute upon it. I don't think I made myself very ridiculous, but I know I was resolute.

"Very well, Mr Copperfield," said Mr Spenlow, "I must try my influence with my daughter."

Miss Murdstone, by an expressive sound, a long drawn respiration, which was neither a sigh nor a moan, but was like both, gave it as her opinion that he should have done this at first.

"I must try," said Mr Spenlow, confirmed by this support, "my influence with my daughter. Do you decline to take those letters, Mr Copperfield?" For I had laid them on the table.

Yes. I told him I hoped he would not think it wrong, but I couldn't possibly take them from Miss Murdstone.

"Nor from me?" said Mr Spenlow.

No, I replied with the profoundest respect; nor from him.

"Very well!" said Mr Spenlow.

A silence succeeding, I was undecided whether to go or stay. At length I was moving quietly towards the door, with the intention of saying that perhaps I should consult his feelings best by withdrawing: when he said, with his hands in his coat pockets, into which it was as much as he could do to get them; and with what I should call, upon the whole, a decidedly pious air:

"You are probably aware, Mr Copperfield, that I am not altogether destitute of worldly possessions, and that my daughter is my nearest and dearest relative?"

I hurriedly made him a reply to the effect, that I hoped the error into which I had been betrayed by the desperate nature of my love, did not induce him to think me mercenary too?

"I don't allude to the matter in that light," said Mr Spenlow. "It would be better for yourself, and all of us, if you *were* mercenary, Mr Copperfield—I mean, if you were more discreet and less influenced by all this youthful nonsense. No. I merely say, with quite another view, you are probably aware I have some property to bequeath to my child?"

I certainly supposed so.

"And you can hardly think," said Mr Spenlow, "having experience of what we see, in the Commons here, every day, of the various unaccountable and negligent proceedings of men, in respect of their testamentary arrangements—of all subjects, the one on which perhaps the strangest revelations of human inconsistency are to be met with—but that mine are made?"

I inclined my head in acquiescence.

"I should not allow," said Mr Spenlow, with an evident increase of pious sentiment, and slowly shaking his head as he poised himself upon his toes and heels alternately, "my suitable provision for my child to be influenced by a piece of youthful folly like the present. It is mere folly. Mere nonsense. In a little while, it will weigh lighter than any feather. But I might—I might—if this silly business were not completely relinquished altogether, be induced in some anxious moment to guard her from, and surround her with protections against, the consequences of, any foolish step in the way of marriage. Now, Mr Copperfield, I hope that you will not render it necessary for me to open, even for a quarter of an hour, that closed page in the book of life, and unsettle, even for a quarter of an hour, grave affairs long since composed."

There was a serenity, a tranquillity, a calm-sunset air about him, which quite affected me. He was so peaceful and resigned—clearly had his affairs in such perfect train, and so systematically wound up—that he was a man to feel touched in the contemplation of. I really think I saw tears rise to his eyes, from the depth of his own feeling of all this.

But what could I do? I could not deny Dora and my own heart. When he told me I had better take a week to consider of what he had said, how could I say I wouldn't take a week, yet how could I fail to know that no amount of weeks could influence such love as mine?

"In the meantime, confer with Miss Trotwood, or with any person with any knowledge of life," said Mr Spenlow, adjusting his cravat with both hands. "Take a week, Mr Copperfield."

I submitted; and, with a countenance as expressive as I was able to make it of dejected and despairing constancy, came out of the room. Miss Murdstone's heavy eyebrows followed me to the door—I say her eyebrows rather than her eyes, because they were much more important in her face—and she looked so exactly as she used to look, at about that hour of the morning, in our parlour at Blunderstone, that I could have fancied I had been breaking down in my lessons again, and that the dead weight on my mind was that horrible old spelling-book, with oval woodcuts, shaped, to my youthful fancy, like the glasses out of spectacles.

When I got to the office, and, shutting out old Tiffey and the rest of them with my hands, sat at my desk, in my own particular nook, thinking of this earthquake that had taken place so unexpectedly, and in the bitterness of my spirit cursing Jip, I fell into such a state of torment about Dora, that I wonder I did not take up my hat and rush insanely to Norwood. The idea of their frightening her, and making her cry, and of my not being there to comfort her, was so excruciating, that it impelled me to write a wild letter to Mr Spenlow, beseeching him not to visit upon her the consequences of my awful destiny. I implored him to spare her gentle nature—not to crush a fragile flower—and addressed him generally, to the best of my remembrance, as if, instead of being her father, he had been an Ogre, or the Dragon of Wantley. This letter I sealed and laid upon his desk before he returned; and when he came in, I saw him, through the half-opened door of his room, take it up and read it.

He said nothing about it all the morning; but before he went away in the afternoon he called me in, and told me that I need not make myself at all uneasy about his daughter's happiness. He had assured her, he said, that it was all nonsense; and he had nothing more to say to her. He believed he was an indulgent father (as indeed he was), and I might spare myself any solicitude on her account.

"You may make it necessary, if you are foolish or obstinate, Mr Copperfield," he observed, "for me to send my daughter abroad again, for a term; but I have a better opinion of you. I hope you will be wiser than that, in a few days. As to Miss Murdstone," for I had alluded to her in the letter, "I respect that lady's vigilance, and feel obliged to her; but she has strict charge to avoid the subject. All I desire, Mr Copperfield, is, that it should be forgotten. All you have got to do, Mr Copperfield, is to forget it."

All! In the note I wrote to Miss Mills, I bitterly quoted this sentiment. All I had to do, I said, with gloomy sarcasm, was to forget Dora. That was all, and what was that! I entreated Miss Mills to see me, that evening. If it could not be done with Mr Mills's sanction and concurrence, I besought a clandestine interview in the back kitchen where the Mangle was. I informed her that my reason was tottering on its throne, and only she, Miss Mills, could prevent its being deposed. I signed myself, hers distractedly; and I couldn't help feeling, while I read this composition over, before sending it by a porter, that it was something in the style of Mr Micawber.

However, I sent it. At night I repaired to Miss Mills's street, and walked up and down, until I was stealthily fetched in by Miss Mills's maid, and taken the area way to the back kitchen. I have since seen reason to believe that there was nothing on earth to prevent my going in at the front door, and being shown up into the drawing-room, except Miss Mills's love of the romantic and mysterious.

In the back kitchen, I raved as became me. I went there, I suppose, to make a fool of myself, and I am quite sure I did it. Miss Mills had received a hasty note from Dora, telling her that all was discovered, and saying. "Oh pray come to me, Julia, do, do!" But Miss Mills, mistrusting the acceptability of her presence to the higher powers, had not yet gone; and we were all benighted in the Desert of Sahara.

Miss Mills had a wonderful flow of words, and liked to pour them out. I could not help feeling, though she mingled her tears with mine, that she had a dreadful luxury in our afflictions. She petted them, as I may say, and made the most of them. A deep gulf, she observed, had opened between Dora and me, and Love could only span it with its rainbow. Love must suffer in this stern world; it ever had been so, it ever would be so. No matter, Miss Mills remarked. Hearts confined by cobwebs would burst at last, and then Love was avenged.

This was small consolation, but Miss Mills wouldn't encourage fallacious hopes. She made me much more wretched than I was before, and I felt (and told her with the deepest gratitude) that she was indeed a friend. We resolved that she should go to Dora the first thing in the morning, and find some means of assuring her, either by looks or words, of my devotion and misery. We parted, overwhelmed with grief; and I think Miss Mills enjoyed herself completely.

I confided all to my aunt when I got home; and in spite of all she could say to me, went to bed despairing. I got up despairing, and went out despairing. It was Saturday morning, and I went straight to the Commons.

I was surprised, when I came within sight of our office-door, to see the ticket-porters standing outside talking together, and some half-dozen stragglers gazing at the windows which were shut up. I quickened my pace, and, passing among them, wondering at their looks, went hurriedly in.

The clerks were there, but nobody was doing anything. Old Tiffey, for the first time in his life I should think, was sitting on somebody else's stool, and had not hung up his hat.

"This is a dreadful calamity, Mr Copperfield," said he, as I entered.

"What is?" I exclaimed. "What's the matter?"

"Don't you know?" cried Tiffey, and all the rest of them, coming round me.

"No!" said I, looking from face to face.

"Mr Spenlow," said Tiffey.

"What about him!"

"Dead!"

I thought it was the office reeling, and not I, as one of the clerks caught hold of me. They sat me down in a chair, untied my neckcloth, and brought me some water. I have no idea whether this took any time.

"Dead?" said I.

"He dined in town yesterday, and drove down in the phaeton by himself," said Tiffey, "having sent his own groom home by the coach, as he sometimes did, you know——"

"Well?"

"The phaeton went home without him. The horses stopped at the stable-gate. The man went out with a lantern. Nobody in the carriage."

"Had they run away?"

"They were not hot," said Tiffey, putting on his glasses; "no hotter, I understand, than they would have been, going down at the usual pace. The reins were broken, but they had been dragging on the ground. The house was roused up directly, and three of them went out along the road. They found him a mile off."

"More than a mile off, Mr Tiffey," interposed a junior.

"Was it? I believe you are right," said Tiffey,——"*more* than a mile off—not far from the church—lying partly on the roadside, and partly on the path, upon his face. Whether he fell out in a fit, or got out, feeling ill before the fit came on—or even whether he was quite dead then, though there is no doubt he was quite insensible—no one appears to know. If he breathed, certainly he never spoke. Medical assistance was got as soon as possible, but it was quite useless."

I cannot describe the state of mind into which I was thrown by this intelligence. The shock of such an event happening so suddenly, and happening to one with whom I had been in any respect at variance—the appalling vacancy in the room he had occupied so lately, where his chair and table seemed to wait for him, and his handwriting of yesterday was like a ghost—the indefinable impossibility of separating him from the place, and feeling, when the door opened, as if he might come in—the lazy hush and rest there was in the office, and the insatiable relish with which our people talked about it, and other people came in and out all day, and gorged themselves with the subject—this is easily intelligible to anyone. What I cannot describe is, how, in the innermost recesses of my own heart, I had a lurking jealousy even of Death. How I felt as if its might would push me from my ground in Dora's thoughts. How I was, in a grudging way I have no words for, envious of her grief. How it made me restless to think of her weeping to others, or being consoled by others. How I had a grasping, avaricious wish to shut out everybody from her but myself, and to be all in all to her, at that unseasonable time of all times.

In the trouble of this state of mind—not exclusively my own, I hope, but known to others—I went down to Norwood that night; and finding from one of the servants, when I made my inquiries at the door, that Miss Mills was there, got my aunt to direct a letter to her, which I wrote. I deplored the untimely death of Mr Spenlow, most sincerely, and shed tears in doing so. I entreated her to tell Dora, if Dora were in a state to hear it, that he had spoken to me with the utmost kindness and consideration; and had coupled nothing but tenderness, not a single or reproachful word, with her name. I know I did this selfishly, to have my name brought before her; but I tried to believe it was an act of justice to his memory. Perhaps I did believe it.

My aunt received a few lines next day in reply; addressed, outside, to her; within, to me. Dora was overcome by grief; and when her friend had asked her should she send her love to me, had only cried, as she was always crying, "Oh, dear papa! oh, poor papa!" But she had not said No, and that I made the most of.

Mr Jorkins, who had been at Norwood since the occurrence, came to the office a few days afterwards. He and Tiffey were closeted together for some few moments, and then Tiffey looked out at the door and beckoned me in.

"Oh!" said Mr Jorkins. "Mr Tiffey and myself, Mr Copperfield, are about to examine the desks, the drawers, and other such repositories of the deceased, with the view of sealing up his private papers, and searching for a Will. There is no trace of any, elsewhere. It may be as well for you to assist us, if you please."

I had been in agony to obtain some knowledge of the circumstances in which my Dora would be placed—as, in whose guardianship, and so forth—and this was something towards it. We began the search at once; Mr Jorkins unlocking the drawers and desks, and we all taking out the papers. The office-papers we placed on one side, and the private papers (which were not numerous) on the other. We were very grave; and when we came to a stray seal, or pencil-case, or ring, or any little article of that kind which we associated personally with him, we spoke very low.

We had sealed up several packets; and were still going on dustily and quietly, when Mr Jorkins said to us, applying exactly the same words to his late partner as his late partner had applied to him:

"Mr Spenlow was very difficult to move from the beaten track. You know what he was! I am disposed to think he had made no will."

"Oh, I know he had!" said I.

They both stopped and looked at me.

"On the very day when I last saw him," said I, "he told me that he had, and that his affairs were long since settled."

Mr Jorkins and old Tiffey shook their heads with one accord.

"That looks unpromising," said Tiffey.

"Very unpromising," said Mr Jorkins.

"Surely you don't doubt—" I began.

"My good Mr Copperfield!" said Tiffey, laying his hand upon my arm, and shutting up both his eyes as he shook his head: "if you had been in the Commons as long as I have, you would know that there is no subject on which men are so inconsistent, and so little to be trusted."

"Why, bless my soul, he made that very remark!" I replied persistently.

"I should call that almost final," observed Tiffey. "My opinion is—no will."

It appeared a wonderful thing to me, but it turned out that there *was* no will. He had never so much as thought of making one, so far as his papers afforded any evidence; for there was no kind of hint, sketch, or memorandum, of any testamentary intention whatever. What was scarcely less astonishing to me, was, that his affairs were in a most disordered state. It was extremely difficult, I heard, to make out what he owed, or what he had paid, or of what he died possessed. It was considered likely that for years he could have had no clear opinion on these subjects himself. By little and little it came out, that, in the competition on all points of appearance and gentility then running high in the Commons, he had spent more than his professional income, which was not a very large one, and had reduced his private means, if they ever had been great (which was exceedingly doubtful), to a very low ebb indeed. There was a sale of the furniture and lease, at Norwood; and Tiffey told me, little thinking how interested I was in the story, that, paying all the just debts of the deceased, and deducting his share of outstanding bad and doubtful debts due to the firm, he wouldn't give a thousand pounds for all the assets remaining.

This was at the expiration of about six weeks. I had suffered tortures all the time; and thought I really must have laid violent hands upon myself, when Miss Mills still reported to me, that my broken-hearted little Dora would say nothing, when I was mentioned, but "Oh, poor papa! Oh, dear papa!" Also, that she had no other relations than two aunts, maiden sisters of Mr Spenlow, who lived at Putney, and who had not held any other than chance communication with their brother for many years. Not that they had ever quarrelled (Miss Mills informed me); but that having been, on the occasion of Dora's christening, invited to tea, when they considered themselves privileged to be invited to dinner, they had expressed their opinion in writing, that it was "better for the happiness of all parties" that they should stay away. Since which they had gone their road, and their brother had gone his.

These two ladies now emerged from their retirement, and proposed to take Dora to live at Putney. Dora, clinging to them both, and weeping, exclaimed, "O yes, aunts! Please take Julia Mills and me and Jip to Putney!" So they went, very soon after the funeral.

How I found time to haunt Putney, I am sure I don't know; but I contrived, by some means or other, to prowl about the neighbourhood pretty often. Miss Mills, for the more exact discharge of the duties of friendship, kept a journal; and she used to meet me sometimes, on the Common, and read it, or (if she had not time to do that) lend it to me. How I treasured up the entries, of which I subjoin a sample!—

"Monday. My sweet D. still much depressed. Headache. Called attention to J. as being beautifully sleek. D. fondled J. Associations thus awakened, opened floodgates of sorrow. Rush of grief admitted. (Are tears the dewdrops of the heart? J. M.)

"Tuesday. D. weak and nervous. Beautiful in pallor. (Do we not remark this in moon likewise? J. M.) D., J. M. and J. took airing in carriage. J. looking out of window, and barking violently at dustman, occasioned smile to overspread features of D. (Of such slight links is chain of life composed! J. M.)

"Wednesday. D. comparatively cheerful. Sang to her, as congenial melody, 'Evening Bells.' Effect not soothing, but reverse. D. inexpressibly affected. Found sobbing afterwards, in own room. Quoted verses respecting self and young Gazelle. Ineffectually. Also referred to Patience on Monument. (Qy. Why on monument? J. M.)

"Thursday. D. certainly improved. Better night. Slight tinge of damask revisiting cheek. Resolved to mention name of D. C. Introduced same, cautiously, in course of airing. D. immediately overcome. 'Oh, dear, dear Julia! Oh, I have been a naughty and undutiful child!' Soothed and caressed. Drew ideal picture of D. C. on verge of tomb. D. again overcome. 'Oh, what shall I do, what shall I do? Oh, take me somewhere!' Much alarmed. Fainting of D. and glass of water from public-house. (Poetical affinity. Chequered sign on door-post; chequered human life. Alas! J. M.)

"Friday. Day of incident. Man appears in kitchen, with blue bag, 'for lady's boots left out to heel.' Cook replies, 'No such orders.' Man argues point. Cook withdraws to inquire, leaving man alone with J. On Cook's return, man still argues point, but ultimately goes. J. missing. D. distracted. Information sent to police. Man to be identified by broad nose, and legs like balustrades of bridge. Search made in every direction. No J. D. weeping bitterly, and inconsolable. Renewed reference to young Gazelle. Appropriate, but unavailing. Towards evening, strange boy calls. Brought into parlour. Broad nose, but no balustrades. Says he wants a pound, and knows a dog. Declines to explain further, though much pressed. Pound being produced by D. takes Cook to little house, where J. alone tied up to leg of table. Joy of D. who dances round J. while he eats his supper. Emboldened by this happy change, mention D. C. upstairs. D. weeps afresh, cries piteously, 'Oh, don't, don't, don't! It is so wicked to think of anything but poor papa!'— embraces J, and sobs herself to sleep. (Must not D. C. confine himself to the broad pinions of Time? J. M.)"

Miss Mills and her journal were my sole consolation at this period. To see her, who had seen Dora but a little while before—to trace the initial letter of Dora's name through her sympathetic pages—to be made more and more miserable by her—were my only comforts. I felt as if I had been living in a palace of cards, which had tumbled down, leaving only Miss Mills and me among the ruins; I felt as if some grim enchanter had drawn a magic circle round the innocent goddess of my heart, which nothing indeed but those same strong pinions, capable of carrying so many people over so much, would enable me to enter!

Chapter XXXIX

WICKFIELD AND HEEP

M Y aunt, beginning, I imagine, to be made seriously uncomfortable by my pro-
longed dejection, made a pretence of being anxious that I should go to Dover, to see that all was working well at the cottage, which was let; and to conclude an agree- ment, with the same tenant, for a longer term of occupation. Janet was drafted into the service of Mrs Strong, where I saw her every day. She had been undecided, on leaving Dover, whether or no to give the finishing touch to that renunciation of mankind in which she had been educated, by marrying a pilot; but she decided against that venture. Not so much for the sake of principle, I believe, as because she happened not to like him.

Although it required an effort to leave Miss Mills, I fell rather willingly into my aunt's pretence, as a means of enabling me to pass a few tranquil hours with Agnes. I consulted the good Doctor relative to an absence of three days; and the Doctor wishing me to take that relaxation,—he wished me to take more; but my energy could not bear that,—I made up my mind to go.

As to the Commons, I had no great occasion to be particular about my duties in that quarter. To say the truth, we were getting in no very good odour among the tip-top proctors, and were rapidly sliding down to but a doubtful position. The business had been indifferent under Mr Jorkins, before Mr Spenlow's time; and although it had been quickened by the infusion of new blood, and by the display which Mr Spenlow made, still it was not established on a sufficiently strong basis to bear, without being shaken, such a blow as the sudden loss of its active manager. It fell off very much. Mr Jorkins, notwithstanding his reputation in the firm, was an easy-going, incapable, sort of man, whose reputation out of doors was not calculated to back it up. I was turned over to him now, and when I saw him take his snuff and let the business go, I regretted my aunt's thousand pounds more than ever.

But this was not the worst of it. There were a number of hangers-on and outsiders about the Commons, who, without being proctors themselves, dabbled in common-form business, and got it done by real proctors, who lent their names in consideration of a share in the spoil;—and there were a good many of these too. As our house now wanted business on any terms, we joined this noble band; and threw out lures to the hangers-on and outsiders, to bring their business to us. Marriage licences and small probates were what we all looked for, and what paid us best; and the competition for these ran very high indeed. Kidnappers and inveiglers were planted in all the avenues of entrance to the Commons, with instructions to do their utmost to cut off all persons in mourning, and all gentlemen with anything bashful in their appearance, and entice them to the offices in which their respective employers were interested; which instructions were so well observed, that I myself, before I was known by sight, was twice hustled into the premises of our principal opponent. The conflicting interests of these touting gentlemen being of a nature to irritate their feelings, personal collisions took place; and the Commons was even scandalized by our principal inveigler (who had formerly been in the wine trade, and afterwards in the sworn brokery line) walking about for some days with a black eye. Any one of these scouts used to think nothing of politely assisting an old lady in black out of a vehicle, killing any proctor whom she inquired for, representing his employer as the lawful successor and representative of that proctor, and bearing the old lady off (sometimes greatly affected) to his employer's office. Many captives were brought to me in this way. As to marriage licences, the competition rose to such a pitch, that a shy gentleman in want of one, had nothing to do but submit himself to the first inveigler, or be fought for, and become the prey of the strongest. One of our clerks, who was an outsider, used, in the height of this contest, to sit with his hat on, that he might be ready to rush out and swear before a surrogate any victim who was brought in. The system of inveigling continues, I believe, to this day. The last time I was in the Commons, a civil able-bodied person in a white apron pounced out upon me from a doorway, and whispering the word "Marriage-licence" in my ear, was with great difficulty prevented from taking me up in his arms and lifting me into a proctor's.

From this digression, let me proceed to Dover.

I found everything in a satisfactory state at the cottage; and was enabled to gratify my aunt exceedingly by reporting that the tenant inherited her feud, and waged incessant war against donkeys. Having settled the little business I had to transact there, and slept there one night. I walked on to Canterbury early in the morning. It was now winter again; and the fresh, cold windy day, and the sweeping downland, brightened up my hopes a little.

Coming into Canterbury, I loitered through the old streets with a sober pleasure that calmed my spirits, and eased my heart. There were the old signs, the old names over the shops, the old people serving in them. It appeared so long, since I had been a schoolboy there, that I wondered the place was so little changed, until I reflected how little I was changed myself. Strange to say, that quiet influence which was inseparable in my mind from Agnes, seemed to pervade even the city where she dwelt. The venerable cathedral towers, and the old jackdaws and rooks whose airy voices made them more retired than perfect silence would have done; the battered gateways, one stuck full with statues, long thrown down, and crumbled away, like the reverential pilgrims who had gazed upon them; the still nooks, where the ivied growth of centuries crept over gabled ends and ruined walls; the ancient houses, the pastoral landscape of field, orchard, and garden; everywhere—on everything—I felt the same serener air, the same calm, thoughtful, softening spirit.

Arrived at Mr Wickfield's house, I found, in the little lower room on the ground floor, where Uriah Heep had been of old accustomed to sit, Mr Micawber plying his pen with great assiduity. He was dressed in a legal-looking suit of black, and loomed, burly and large, in that small office.

Mr Micawber was extremely glad to see me, but a little confused too. He would have conducted me immediately into the presence of Uriah, but I declined.

"I know the house of old, you recollect," said I, "and will find my way upstairs. How do you like the law, Mr Micawber?"

"My dear Copperfield," he replied. "To a man possessed of the higher imaginative powers, the objection to legal studies is the amount of detail which they involve. Even in our professional correspondence," said Mr Micawber, glancing at some letters he was writing, "the mind is not at liberty to soar to any exalted form of expression. Still, it is a great pursuit. A great pursuit!"

He then told me that he had become the tenant of Uriah Heep's old house; and that Mrs Micawber would be delighted to receive me, once more, under her own roof.

"It is humble," said Mr Micawber, "—to quote a favourite expression of my friend Heep; but it may prove the stepping-stone to more ambitious domiciliary accommodation."

I asked him whether he had reason, so far, to be satisfied with his friend Heep's treatment of him? He got up to ascertain if the door were close shut, before he replied, in a lower voice:

"My dear Copperfield, a man who labours under the pressure of pecuniary embarrassments, is, with the generality of people, at a disadvantage. That disadvantage is not diminished, when that pressure necessitates the drawing of stipendiary emoluments, before those emoluments are strictly due and payable. All I can say is, that my friend Heep has responded to appeals to which I need not more particularly refer, in a manner calculated to redound equally to the honour of his head, and of his heart."

"I should not have supposed him to be very free with his money either," I observed.

"Pardon me!" said Mr Micawber, with an air of constraint, "I speak of my friend Heep as I have experience."

"I am glad your experience is so favourable," I returned.

"You are very obliging, my dear Copperfield," said Mr Micawber; and hummed a tune.

"Do you see much of Mr Wickfield?" I asked, to change the subject.

"Not much," said Mr Micawber, slightingly. "Mr Wickfield is, I dare say, a man of very excellent intentions; but he is—in short, he is obsolete."

"I am afraid his partner seeks to make him so," said I.

"My dear Copperfield!" returned Mr Micawber, after some uneasy evolutions on his stool, "allow me to offer a remark! I am here, in a capacity of confidence. I am here, in a position of trust. The discussion of some topics, even with Mrs Micawber herself (so long the partner of my various vicissitudes, and a woman of a remarkable lucidity of intellect), is, I am led to consider, incompatible with the functions now devolving on me.

I would therefore take the liberty of suggesting that in our friendly intercourse—which I trust will never be disturbed!—we draw a line. On one side of this line," said Mr Micawber, representing it on the desk with the office ruler, "is the whole range of the human intellect, with a trifling exception; on the other, *is* that exception; that is to say, the affairs of Messrs. Wickfield and Heep, with all belonging and appertaining thereunto. I trust I give no offence to the companion of my youth, in submitting this proposition to his cooler judgement?"

Though I saw an uneasy change in Mr Micawber, which sat tightly on him, as if his new duties were a misfit, I felt I had no right to be offended. My telling him so, appeared to relieve him; and he shook hands with me.

"I am charmed, Copperfield," said Mr Micawber, "let me assure you, with Miss Wickfield. She is a very superior young lady, of very remarkable attractions, graces, and virtues. Upon my honour," said Mr Micawber, indefinitely kissing his hand and bowing with his genteelest air, "I do Homage to Miss Wickfield! Hem!"

"I am glad of that, at least," said I.

"If you had not assured us, my dear Copperfield, on the occasion of that agreeable afternoon we had the happiness of passing with you, that D. was your favourite letter," said Mr Micawber, "I should unquestionably have supposed that A. had been so."

We have all some experience of a feeling, that comes over us occasionally, of what we are saying and doing having been said and done before, in a remote time—of our having been surrounded, dim ages ago, by the same faces, objects, and circumstances— of our knowing perfectly what will be said next, as if we suddenly remembered it! I never had this mysterious impression more strongly in my life, than before he uttered those words.

I took my leave of Mr Micawber, for the time, charging him with my best remembrances to all at home. As I left him, resuming his stool and his pen, and rolling his head in his stock, to get it into easier writing order, I clearly perceived that there was something interposed between him and me, since he had come into his new functions, which prevented our getting at each other as we used to do, and quite altered the character of our intercourse.

There was no one in the quaint old drawing-room, though it presented tokens of Mrs Heep's whereabout. I looked into the room still belonging to Agnes, and saw her sitting by the fire, at a pretty old-fashioned desk she had, writing.

My darkening the light made her look up. What a pleasure to be the cause of that bright change in her attentive face, and the object of that sweet regard and welcome!

"Ah, Agnes!" said I, when we were sitting together, side by side; "I have missed you so much, lately!"

"Indeed?" she replied. "Again! And so soon?"

I shook my head.

"I don't know how it is, Agnes; I seem to want some faculty of mind that I ought to have. You were so much in the habit of thinking for me, in the happy old days here, and I came so naturally to you for counsel and support, that I really think I have missed acquiring it."

"And what is it?" said Agnes, cheerfully.

"I don't know what to call it," I replied. "I think I am earnest and persevering?"

"I am sure of it," said Agnes.

"And patient, Agnes?" I inquired, with a little hesitation.

"Yes," returned Agnes, laughing. "Pretty well."

"And yet," said I, "I get so miserable and worried, and am so unsteady and irresolute in my power of assuring myself, that I know I must want—shall I call it—reliance, of some kind?"

"Call it so, if you will," said Agnes.

"Well!" I returned. "See here! You come to London, I rely on you, and I have an object and a course at once. I am driven out of it, I come here, and in a moment I feel an altered person. The circumstances that distressed me are not changed, since I came into this room; but an influence comes over me in that short interval that alters me, oh, how much for the better! What is it? What is your secret, Agnes?"

Her head was bent down, looking at the fire.

"It's the old story," said I. "Don't laugh, when I say it was always the same in little things as it is in greater ones. My old troubles were nonsense, and now they are serious; but whenever I have gone away from my adopted sister—"

Agnes looked up—with such a Heavenly face!—and gave me her hand, which I kissed.

"Whenever I have not had you, Agnes, to advise and approve in the beginning, I have seemed to go wild, and to get into all sorts of difficulty. When I have come to you, at last (as I have always done), I have come to peace and happiness. I come home, now, like a tired traveller, and find such a blessed sense of rest!"

I felt so deeply what I said, it affected me so sincerely, that my voice failed, and I covered my face with my hand, and broke into tears. I write the truth. Whatever contradictions and inconsistencies there were within me, as there are within so many of us; whatever might have been so different, and so much better; whatever I had done, in which I had perversely wandered away from the voice of my own heart; I knew nothing of. I only knew that I was fervently in earnest, when I felt the rest and peace of having Agnes near me.

In her placid sisterly manner; with her beaming eyes; with her tender voice; and with that sweet composure, which had long ago made the house that held her quite a sacred place to me; she soon won me from this weakness, and led me on to tell all that had happened since our last meeting.

"And there is not another word to tell, Agnes," said I, when I had made an end of my confidence. "Now, my reliance is on you."

"But it must not be on me, Trotwood," returned Agnes, with a pleasant smile. "It must be on someone else."

"On Dora?" said I.

"Assuredly."

"Why, I have not mentioned, Agnes," said I, a little embarrassed, "that Dora is rather difficult to—I would not, for the world, say, to rely upon, because she is the soul of purity and truth—but rather difficult to—I hardly know how to express it, really, Agnes. She is a timid little thing, and easily disturbed and frightened. Some time ago, before her father's death, when I thought it right to mention to her—but I'll tell you, if you will bear with me, how it was."

Accordingly, I told Agnes about my declaration of poverty, about the cookery-book, the housekeeping accounts, and all the rest of it.

"Oh, Trotwood!" she remonstrated, with a smile. "Just your old headlong way! You might have been in earnest in striving to get on in the world, without being so very sudden with a timid, loving, inexperienced girl. Poor Dora!"

I never heard such sweet forbearing kindness expressed in a voice, as she expressed in making this reply. It was as if I had seen her admiringly and tenderly embracing Dora, and tacitly reproving me, by her considerate protection, for my hot haste in fluttering that little heart. It was as if I had seen Dora, in all her fascinating artlessness, caressing Agnes, and thanking her, and coaxingly appealing against me, and loving me with all her childish innocence.

I felt so grateful to Agnes, and admired her so! I saw those two together, in a bright perspective, such well-associated friends, each adorning the other so much!

"What ought I to do then, Agnes?" I inquired, after looking at the fire a little while. "What would it be right to do?"

"I think," said Agnes, "that the honourable course to take, would be to write to those two ladies. Don't you think that any secret course is an unworthy one?"

"Yes. If *you* think so," said I.

"I am poorly qualified to judge of such matters," replied Agnes, with a modest hesitation, "but I certainly feel—in short, I feel that your being secret and clandestine, is not being like yourself."

"Like myself, in the too high opinion you have of me, Agnes, I am afraid," said I.

"Like yourself, in the candour of your nature," she returned; "and therefore I would write to those two ladies. I would relate, as plainly and as openly as possible, all that has taken place; and I would ask their permission to visit sometimes, at their house. Considering that you are young, and striving for a place in life, I think it would be well to say that you would readily abide by any conditions they might impose upon you. I would entreat them not to dismiss your request, without a reference to Dora; and to discuss it with her when they should think the time suitable. I would not be too vehement," said Agnes, gently, "or propose too much. I would trust to my fidelity and perseverance— and to Dora."

"But if they were to frighten Dora again, Agnes, by speaking to her," said I. "And if Dora were to cry, and say nothing about me!"

"Is that likely?" inquired Agnes, with the same sweet consideration in her face.

"God bless her, she is as easily scared as a bird," said I. "It might be! Or if the two Miss Spenlows (elderly ladies of that sort are odd characters sometimes) should not be likely persons to address in that way!"

"I don't think, Trotwood," returned Agnes, raising her soft eyes to mine, "I would consider that. Perhaps it would be better only to consider whether it is right to do this; and, if it is, to do it."

I had no longer any doubt on the subject. With a lightened heart, though with a profound sense of the weighty importance of my task, I devoted the whole afternoon to the composition of the draft of this letter; for which great purpose, Agnes relinquished her desk to me. But first I went downstairs to see Mr Wickfield and Uriah Heep.

I found Uriah in possession of a new, plaster-smelling office, built out in the garden; looking extraordinarily mean, in the midst of a quantity of books and papers. He received me in his usual fawning way, and pretended not to have heard of my arrival from Mr Micawber; a pretence I took the liberty of disbelieving. He accompanied me into Mr Wickfield's room, which was the shadow of its former self—having been divested of a variety of conveniences, for the accommodation of the new partner—and stood before the fire, warming his back, and shaving his chin with his bony hand, while Mr Wickfield and I exchanged greetings.

"You stay with us, Trotwood, while you remain in Canterbury?" said Mr Wickfield, not without a glance at Uriah for his approval.

"Is there room for me?" said I.

"I am sure, Master Copperfield—I should say Mister, but the other comes so natural," said Uriah,—"I would turn out of your old room with pleasure, if it would be agreeable."

"No, no," said Mr Wickfield. "Why should *you* be inconvenienced? There's another room. There's another room."

"Oh, but you know," returned Uriah, with a grin, "I should really be delighted!"

To cut the matter short, I said I would have the other room or none at all; so it was settled that I should have the other room; and, taking my leave of the firm until dinner, I went upstairs again.

I had hoped to have no other companion than Agnes. But Mrs Heep had asked permission to bring herself and her knitting near the fire, in that room; on pretence of its having an aspect more favourable for her rheumatics, as the wind then was, than the drawing-room or dining-parlour. Though I could almost have consigned her to the mercies of the wind on the topmost pinnacle of the Cathedral, without remorse, I made a virtue of necessity, and gave her a friendly salutation.

"I'm umbly thankful to you, sir," said Mrs Heep, in acknowledgement of my inquiries concerning her health, "but I'm only pretty well. I haven't much to boast of. If I could see my Uriah well settled in life, I couldn't expect much more I think. How do you think my Ury looking, sir?"

I thought him looking as villainous as ever, and I replied that I saw no change in him.

"Oh, don't you think he's changed?" said Mrs Heep. "There I must umbly beg leave to differ from you. Don't you see a thinness in him?"

"Not more than usual," I replied.

"*Don't* you though!" said Mrs Heep. "But you don't take notice of him with a mother's eye!"

His mother's eye was an evil eye to the rest of the world, I thought as it met mine, howsoever affectionate to him; and I believe she and her son were devoted to one another. It passed me, and went on to Agnes.

"Don't *you* see a wasting and a wearing in him, Miss Wickfield?" inquired Mrs Heep.

"No," said Agnes, quietly pursuing the work on which she was engaged. "You are too solicitious about him. He is very well."

Mrs Heep, with a prodigious sniff, resumed her knitting.

She never left off, or left us for a moment. I had arrived early in the day, and we had still three or four hours before dinner; but she sat there, plying her knitting-needles as monotonously as an hour-glass might have poured out its sands. She sat on one side of the fire; I sat at the desk in front of it; a little beyond me, on the other side, sat Agnes. Whensoever, slowly pondering over my letter, I lifted up my eyes, and meeting the thoughtful face of Agnes, saw it clear, and beam encouragement upon me, with its own angelic expression, I was conscious presently of the evil eye passing me, and going on to her, and coming back to me again, and dropping furtively upon the knitting. What the knitting was, I don't know, not being learned in that art; but it looked like a net; and as she worked away with those Chinese chopsticks of knitting-needles, she showed in the firelight like an ill-looking enchantress, baulked as yet by the radiant goodness opposite, but getting ready for a cast of her net by and by.

At dinner she maintained her watch, with the same unwinking eyes. After dinner, her son took his turn; and when Mr Wickfield, himself, and I were left alone together, leered at me, and writhed until I could hardly bear it. In the drawing-room, there was the mother knitting and watching again. All the time that Agnes sang and played, the mother sat at the piano. Once she asked for a particular ballad, which she said her Ury (who was yawning in a great chair) doted on; and at intervals she looked round at him, and reported to Agnes that he was in raptures with the music. But she hardly ever spoke—I question if she ever did—without making some mention of him. It was evident to me that this was the duty assigned to her.

This lasted until bedtime. To have seen the mother and son, like two great bats hanging over the whole house, and darkening it with their ugly forms, made me so uncomfortable, that I would rather have remained downstairs, knitting and all, than gone to bed. I hardly got any sleep. Next day the knitting and watching began again, and lasted all day.

I had not an opportunity of speaking to Agnes, for ten minutes. I could barely show her my letter. I proposed to her to walk out with me; but Mrs Heep repeatedly complaining that she was worse, Agnes charitably remained within, to bear her company. Towards the twilight I went out by myself, musing on what I ought to do, and whether I was justified in withholding from Agnes, any longer, what Uriah Heep had told me in London; for that began to trouble me again, very much.

I had not walked out far enough to be quite clear of the town, upon the Ramsgate road, where there was a good path, when I was hailed, through the dust, by somebody behind me. The shambling figure, and the scanty great-coat, were not to be mistaken. I stopped, and Uriah Heep came up.

"Well?" said I.

"How fast you walk!" said he. "My legs are pretty long, but you've given 'em quite a job."

"Where are you going?" said I.

"I am going with you, Master Copperfield, if you'll allow me the pleasure of a walk with an old acquaintance." Saying this, with a jerk of his body, which might have been either propitiatory or derisive, he fell into step beside me.

"Uriah!" said I, as civilly as I could, after a silence.

"Master Copperfield!" said Uriah.

"To tell you the truth (at which you will not be offended), I came out to walk alone, because I have had so much company."

He looked at me sideways, and said with his hardest grin, "You mean mother."

"Why yes, I do," said I.

"Ah! But you know we're so very umble," he returned. "And having such a knowledge of our own umbleness, we must really take care that we're not pushed to the wall by them as isn't umble. All stratagems are fair in love, sir."

Raising his great hands until they touched his chin, he rubbed them softly, and softly chuckled; looking as like a malevolent baboon, I thought, as anything human could look.

"You see," he said, still hugging himself in that unpleasant way, and shaking his head at me, "you're quite a dangerous rival, Master Copperfield. You always was, you know."

"Do you set a watch upon Miss Wickfield, and make her home no home, because of me?" said I.

"Oh! Master Copperfield! Those are very arsh words," he replied.

"Put my meaning into any words you like," said I. "You know what it is, Uriah, as well as I do."

"Oh no! You must put it into words," he said. "Oh, really! I couldn't myself."

"Do you suppose," said I, constraining myself to be very temperate and quiet with him, on account of Agnes, "that I regard Miss Wickfield otherwise than as a very dear sister?"

"Well, Master Copperfield," he replied, "you perceive I am not bound to answer that question. You may not, you know. But then, you see, you may!"

Anything to equal the low cunning of his visage, and of his shadowless eyes without the ghost of an eyelash, I never saw.

"Come then!" said I. "For the sake of Miss Wickfield——"

"My Agnes!" he exclaimed, with a sickly, angular contortion of himself. "Would you be so good as call her Agnes, Master Copperfield!"

"For the sake of Agnes Wickfield—Heaven bless her!"

"Thank you for that blessing, Master Copperfield!" he interposed.

"I will tell you what I should, under any other circumstances, as soon have thought of telling to—Jack Ketch."

"To who, sir?" said Uriah, stretching out his neck, and shading his ear with his hand.

"To the hangman," I returned. "The most unlikely person I could think of,"—though his own face had suggested the allusion quite as a natural sequence. "I am engaged to another young lady. I hope that contents you."

"Upon your soul?" said Uriah.

I was about indignantly to give my assertion the confirmation he required, when he caught hold of my hand, and gave it a squeeze.

"Oh, Master Copperfield!" he said. "If you had only had the condescension to return my confidence when I poured out the fulness of my art, the night I put you so much out of the way by sleeping before your sitting-room fire, I never should have doubted you. As it is, I'm sure I'll take off mother directly, and only too appy. I know you'll excuse the precautions of affection, won't you? What a pity, Master Copperfield, that you didn't condescend to return my confidence! I'm sure I gave you every opportunity. But you never have condescended to me, as much as I could have wished. I know you have never liked me, as I have liked you!"

All this time he was squeezing my hand with his damp fishy fingers, while I made every effort I decently could to get it away. But I was quite unsuccessful. He drew it under the sleeve of his mulberry-coloured great-coat, and I walked on, almost upon compulsion, arm-in-arm with him.

"Shall we turn?" said Uriah, by and by wheeling me face about towards the town, on which the early moon was now shining, silvering the distant windows.

"Before we leave the subject, you ought to understand," said I, breaking a pretty long silence, "that I believe Agnes Wickfield to be as far above *you,* and as far removed from all *your* aspirations, as that moon herself!"

"Peaceful! Ain't she!" said Uriah. "Very! Now confess, Master Copperfield, that you haven't liked me quite as I have liked you. All along you've thought me too umble now, I shouldn't wonder?"

"I am not fond of professions of humility," I returned, "or professions of anything else."

"There now!" said Uriah, looking flabby and lead-coloured in the moonlight. "Didn't I know it! But how little you think of the rightful umbleness of a person in my station, Master Copperfield! Father and me was both brought up at a foundation school for boys; and mother, she was likewise brought up at a public, sort of charitable, establishment. They taught us all a deal of umbleness—not much else that I know of, from morning to night. We was to be umble to this person, and umble to that; and to pull off our caps here, and to make bows there; and always to know our place, and abase ourselves before our betters. And we had such a lot of betters! Father got the monitor-medal by being umble. So did I. Father got made a sexton by being umble. He had the character, among the gentlefolks, of being such a well-behaved man, that they were determined to bring him in. 'Be umble, Uriah,' says father to me, 'and you'll get on. It was what was always being dinned into you and me at school: it's what goes down best. Be umble,' says father, 'and you'll do!' And really it ain't done bad!"

It was the first time it had ever occurred to me, that this detestable cant of false humility might have originated out of the Heep family. I had seen the harvest, but had never thought of the seed.

"When I was quite a young boy," said Uriah, "I got to know what umbleness did, and I took to it. I ate umble pie with an appetite. I stopped at the umble point of my learning, and says I, 'Hold hard!' When you offered to teach me Latin, I knew better. 'People like to be above you,' says father, 'keep yourself down.' I am very umble to the present moment, Master Copperfield, but I've got a little power!"

And he said all this—I knew, as I saw his face in the moonlight—that I might understand he was resolved to recompense himself by using his power. I had never doubted his meanness, his craft and malice; but I fully comprehended now, for the first time, what a base, unrelenting, and revengeful spirit, must have been engendered by this early, and this long, suppression.

His account of himself was so far attended with an agreeable result, that it led to his withdrawing his hand in order that he might have another hug of himself under the chin. Once apart from him, I was determined to keep apart; and we walked back, side by side, saying very little more by the way.

Whether his spirits were elevated by the communication I had made to him, or by his having indulged in this retrospect, I don't know; but they were raised by some influence. He talked more at dinner than was usual with him; asked his mother (off duty, from the moment of our re-entering the house) whether he was not growing too old for a bachelor; and once looked at Agnes so, that I would have given all I had, for leave to knock him down.

When we three males were left alone after dinner, he got into a more adventurous state. He had taken little or no wine; and I presume it was the mere insolence of triumph that was upon him, flushed perhaps by the temptation my presence furnished to its exhibition.

I had observed yesterday, that he tried to entice Mr Wickfield to drink; and, inter-preting the look which Agnes had given me as she went out, had limited myself to one glass, and then proposed that we should follow her. I would have done so again today; but Uriah was too quick for me.

"We seldom see our present visitor, sir," he said, addressing Mr Wickfield, sitting, such a contrast to him, at the end of the table, "and I should propose to give him welcome in another glass or two of wine, if you have no objections. Mr Copperfield, your elth and appiness!"

I was obliged to make a show of taking the hand he stretched across to me; and then, with very different emotions, I took the hand of the broken gentleman, his partner.

"Come, fellow-partner," said Uriah, "if I may take the liberty,—now, suppose you give us something or another appropriate to Copperfield!"

I pass over Mr Wickfield's proposing my aunt, his proposing Mr Dick, his proposing Doctors' Commons, his proposing Uriah, his drinking everything twice; his conscious-ness of his own weakness, the ineffectual effort that he made against it; the struggle between his shame in Uriah's deportment, and his desire to conciliate him; the manifest exultation with which Uriah twisted and turned, and held him up before me. It made me sick at heart to see, and my hand recoils from writing it.

"Come, fellow-partner!" said Uriah, at last, "I'll give you another one, and I umbly ask for bumpers, seeing I intend to make it the divinest of her sex."

Her father had his empty glass in his hand. I saw him set it down, look at the picture she was so like, put his hand to his forehead, and shrink back in his elbow-chair.

"I'm an umble individual to give you her elth," proceeded Uriah, "but I admire—adore her."

No physical pain that her father's grey head could have borne, I think, could have been more terrible to me, than the mental endurance I saw compressed now within both his hands.

"Agnes," said Uriah, either not regarding him, or not knowing what the nature of his action was, "Agnes Wickfield is, I am safe to say, the divinest of her sex. May I speak out, among friends? To be her father is a proud distinction, but to be her usband—"

Spare me from ever again hearing such a cry, as that with which her father rose up from the table!

"What's the matter?" said Uriah, turning of a deadly colour. "You are not gone mad, after all, Mr Wickfield, I hope? If I say I've an ambition to make your Agnes my Agnes, I have as good a right to it as another man. I have a better right to it than any other man!"

I had my arms round Mr Wickfield, imploring him by everything that I could think of, oftenest of all by his love for Agnes, to calm himself a little. He was mad for the moment; tearing out his hair, beating his head, trying to force me from him, and to force himself from me, not answering a word, not looking at or seeing anyone; blindly striving for he knew not what, his face all staring and distorted—a frightful spectacle.

I conjured him, incoherently, but in the most impassioned manner, not to abandon himself to this wildness, but to hear me. I besought him to think of Agnes, to connect me with Agnes, to recollect how Agnes and I had grown up together, how I honoured her and loved her, how she was his pride and joy. I tried to bring her idea before him in any form; I even reproached him with not having firmness to spare her the knowledge of such a scene as this. I may have effected something, or his wildness may have spent itself; but by degrees he struggled less, and began to look at me—strangely at first, then with recognition in his eyes. At length he said, "I know, Trotwood! My darling child and you—I know! But look at him!"

He pointed to Uriah, pale and glowering in a corner, evidently very much out in his calculations, and taken by surprise.

"Look at my torturer," he replied. "Before him I have step by step abandoned name and reputation, peace and quiet, house and home."

"I have kept your name and reputation for you, and your peace and quiet, and your house and home too," said Uriah, with a sulky, hurried, defeated air of compromise. "Don't be foolish, Mr Wickfield. If I have gone a little beyond what you were prepared for, I can go back, I suppose? There's no harm done."

"I looked for single motives in everyone," said Mr Wickfield, "and I was satisfied I had bound him to me by motives of interest. But see what he is—oh, see what he is!"

"You had better stop him, Copperfield, if you can," cried Uriah, with his long forefinger pointing towards me. "He'll say something presently—mind you!—he'll be sorry to have said afterwards, and you'll be sorry to have heard!"

"I'll say anything!" cried Mr Wickfield, with a desperate air. "Why should I not be in all the world's power if I am in yours?"

"Mind! I tell you!" said Uriah, continuing to warn me. "If you don't stop his mouth, you're not his friend! Why shouldn't you be in all the world's power, Mr Wickfield? Because you have got a daughter. You and me know what we know, don't we? Let sleeping dogs lie—who wants to rouse 'em? I don't. Can't you see I am as umble as I can be? I tell you, if I've gone too far, I'm sorry. What would you have, sir?"

"Oh, Trotwood, Trotwood!" exclaimed Mr Wickfield, wringing his hands. "What I have come down to be, since I first saw you in this house! I was on my downward way then, but the dreary, dreary, road I have traversed since! Weak indulgence has ruined me. Indulgence in remembrance, and indulgence in forgetfulness. My natural grief for my child's mother turned to disease; my natural love for my child turned to disease. I have infected everything I touched. I have brought misery on what I dearly love, I know—*you* know! I thought it possible that I could truly love one creature in the world, and not love the rest; I thought it possible that I could truly mourn for one creature gone out of the world, and not have some part in the grief of all who mourned. Thus the lessons of my life have been perverted! I have preyed on my own morbid coward heart, and it has preyed on me. Sordid in my grief, sordid in my love, sordid in my miserable escape from the darker side of both, oh see the ruin I am, and hate me, shun me!"

He dropped into a chair, and weakly sobbed. The excitement into which he had been roused was leaving him. Uriah came out of his corner.

"I don't know all I have done, in my fatuity," said Mr Wickfield, putting out his hands, as if to deprecate my condemnation. "*He* knows best," meaning Uriah Heep, "for he has always been at my elbow, whispering me. You see the millstone that he is about my neck. You find him in my house, you find him in my business. You heard him, but a little time ago. What need have I to say more!"

"You haven't need to say so much, nor half so much, nor anything at all," observed Uriah, half defiant, and half fawning. "You wouldn't have took it up so, if it hadn't been for the wine. You'll think better of it tomorrow, sir. If I have said too much, or more than I meant, what of it? I haven't stood by it!"

The door opened, and Agnes, gliding in, without a vestige of colour in her face, put her arm round his neck, and steadily said, "Papa, you are not well. Come with me!" He laid his head upon her shoulder, as if he were oppressed with heavy shame, and went out with her. Her eyes met mine for but an instant, yet I saw how much she knew of what had passed.

"I didn't expect he'd cut up so rough, Master Copperfield," said Uriah. "But it's nothing. I'll be friends with him tomorrow. It's for his good. I'm umbly anxious for his good."

I gave him no answer, and went upstairs into the quiet room where Agnes had so often sat beside me at my books. Nobody came near me until late at night. I took up a book, and tried to read. I heard the clocks strike twelve, and was still reading, without knowing what I read, when Agnes touched me.

"You will be going early in the morning, Trotwood! Let us say good-bye, now!"

She had been weeping, but her face then was so calm and beautiful!

"Heaven bless you!" she said, giving me her hand.

"Dearest Agnes!" I returned, "I see you ask me not to speak of tonight—but is there nothing to be done?"

"There is God to trust in!" she replied.

"Can *I* do nothing—*I*, who come to you with *my* poor sorrows?"

"And make mine so much lighter," she replied. "Dear Trotwood, no!"

"Dear Agnes," I said, "it is presumptuous for me, who am so poor in all in which you are so rich—goodness, resolution, all noble qualities—to doubt or direct you; but you know how much I love you, and how much I owe you. You will never sacrifice yourself to a mistaken sense of duty, Agnes?"

More agitated for a moment than I had ever seen her, she took her hands from me, and moved a step back.

"Say you have no such thought, dear Agnes! Much more than sister! Think of the priceless gift of such a heart as yours, of such a love as yours!"

Oh! long, long afterwards, I saw that face rise up before me, with its momentary look, not wondering, not accusing, not regretting. Oh, long, long afterwards, I saw that look subside, as it did now, into the lovely smile, with which she told me she had no fear for herself—I need have none for her—and parted from me by the name of Brother, and was gone!

It was dark in the morning, when I got upon the coach at the inn door. The day was just breaking when we were about to start, and then, as I sat thinking of her, came struggling up the coach side, through the mingled day and night, Uriah's head.

"Copperfield!" said he, in a croaking whisper, as he hung by the iron on the roof, "I thought you'd be glad to hear before you went off, that there are no squares broke between us. I've been into his room already, and we've made it all smooth. Why, though I'm umble, I'm useful to him, you know; and he understands his interest when he isn't in liquor! What an agreeable man he is, after all, Master Copperfield!"

I obliged myself to say that I was glad he had made his apology.

"Oh, to be sure!" said Uriah. "When a person's umble, you know, what's an apology? So easy! I say! I suppose," with a jerk, "you have sometimes plucked a pear before it was ripe, Master Copperfield?"

"I suppose I have," I replied.

"I did that last night," said Uriah; "but it'll ripen yet! It only wants attending to. I can wait!"

Profuse in his farewells, he got down again as the coachman got up. For anything I know, he was eating something to keep the raw morning air out; but he made motions with his mouth as if the pear were ripe already, and he were smacking his lips over it.

Chapter XL

THE WANDERER

WE had a very serious conversation in Buckingham Street that night, about the domestic occurrences I have detailed in the last chapter. My aunt was deeply interested in them, and walked up and down the room with her arms folded, for more than two hours afterwards. Whenever she was particularly discomposed, she always performed one of these pedestrian feats; and the amount of her discomposure might always be estimated by the duration of her walk. On this occasion she was so much disturbed in mind as to find it necessary to open the bedroom door, and make a course for herself, comprising the full extent of the bedrooms from wall to wall; and while Mr

Dick and I sat quietly by the fire, she kept passing in and out, along this measured track, at an unchanging pace, with the regularity of a clock-pendulum.

When my aunt and I were left to ourselves by Mr Dick's going out to bed, I sat down to write my letter to the two old ladies. By that time she was tired of walking, and sat by the fire with her dress tucked up as usual. But instead of sitting in her usual manner, holding her glass upon her knee, she suffered it to stand neglected on the chimney-piece; and, resting her left elbow on her right arm, and her chin on her left hand, looked thoughtfully at me. As often as I raised my eyes from what I was about, I met hers. "I am in the lovingest of tempers, my dear," she would assure me with a nod, "but I am fidgeted and sorry!"

I had been too busy to observe, until after she was gone to bed, that she had left her night-mixture, as she always called it, untasted on the chimney-piece. She came to her door, with even more than her usual affection of manner, when I knocked to acquaint her with this discovery; but only said, "I have not the heart to take it, Trot, tonight," and shook her head, and went in again.

She read my letter to the two old ladies, in the morning, and approved of it. I posted it, and had nothing to do then, but wait, as patiently as I could, for the reply. I was still in this state of expectation, and had been, for nearly a week; when I left the Doctor's one snowy night, to walk home.

It had been a bitter day, and a cutting north-east wind had blown for some time. The wind had gone down with the light, and so the snow had come on. It was a heavy, settled fall, I recollect, in great flakes; and it lay thick. The noise of wheels and tread of people were as hushed, as if the streets had been strewn that depth with feathers.

My shortest way home,—and I naturally took the shortest way on such a night— was through St Martin's Lane. Now, the church which gives its name to the lane, stood in a less free situation at that time; there being no open space before it, and the lane winding down to the Strand. As I passed the steps of the portico, I encountered, at the corner, a woman's face. It looked in mine, passed across the narrow lane, and disappeared. I knew it. I had seen it somewhere. But I could not remember where. I had some association with it, that struck upon my heart directly; but I was thinking of anything else when it came upon me, and was confused.

On the steps of the church, there was the stooping figure of a man, who had put down some burden on the smooth snow, to adjust it; my seeing the face, and my seeing him, were simultaneous. I don't think I had stopped in my surprise; but, in any case, as I went on, he rose, turned, and came down towards me. I stood face to face with Mr Peggotty!

Then I remembered the woman. It was Martha, to whom Emily had given the money that night in the kitchen. Martha Endell—side by side with whom, he would not have seen his dear niece, Ham had told me, for all the treasures wrecked in the sea.

We shook hands heartily. At first, neither of us could speak a word.

"Mas'r Davy!" he said, gripping me tight, "it do my art good to see you, sir. Well met, well met!"

"Well met, my dear old friend!" said I.

"I had my thowts o' coming to make inquiration for you, sir, tonight," he said, "but knowing as your aunt was living along wi' you—fur I've been down yonder—Yarmouth way—I was afeerd it was too late. I should have come early in the morning, sir, afore going away."

"Again?" said I.

"Yes, sir," he replied, patiently shaking his head, "I'm away tomorrow."

"Where were you going now?" I asked.

"Well!" he replied, shaking the snow out of his long hair, "I was a-going to turn in somewheers."

In those days there was a side-entrance to the stable-yard of the Golden Cross, the inn so memorable to me in connexion with his misfortune, nearly opposite to where we stood. I pointed out the gateway, put my arm through his, and we went across. Two or three public-rooms opened out of the stable-yard; and looking into one of them, and finding it empty, and a good fire burning, I took him in there.

When I saw him in the light, I observed, not only that his hair was long and ragged, but that his face was burnt dark by the sun. He was greyer, the lines in his face and forehead were deeper, and he had every appearance of having toiled and wandered through all varieties of weather; but he looked very strong, and like a man upheld by steadfastness of purpose, whom nothing could tire out. He shook the snow from his hat and clothes, and brushed it away from his face, while I was inwardly making these remarks. As he sat down opposite to me at a table, with his back to the door by which we had entered, he put out his rough hand again, and grasped mine warmly.

"I'll tell you, Mas'r Davy," he said,—"wheer all I've been, and what-all we've heerd. I've been fur, and we've heerd little; but I'll tell you!"

I rang the bell for something hot to drink. He would have nothing stronger than ale; and while it was being brought, and being warmed at the fire, he sat thinking. There was a fine, massive gravity in his face, I did not venture to disturb.

"When she was a child," he said, lifting up his head soon after we were left alone, "she used to talk to me a deal about the sea, and about them coasts where the sea got to be dark blue, and to lay a-shining and a-shining in the sun. I thowt, odd times, as her father being drownded made her think on it so much. I doen't know, you see, but maybe she believed—or hoped—he had drifted out to them parts, where the flowers is always a-blowing, and the country bright."

"It is likely to have been a childish fancy," I replied.

"When she was—lost," said Mr Peggotty, "I know'd in my mind, as he would take her to them countries. I know'd in my mind, as he'd have told her wonders of 'em, and how she was to be a lady theer, and how he got her to listen to him fust, along o' sech like. When we see his mother, I know'd quite well as I was right. I went across-channel to France, and landed theer, as if I'd fell down from the sky."

I saw the door move, and the snow drift in. I saw it move a little more, and a hand softly interpose to keep it open.

"I found out an English gen'leman as was in authority," said Mr Peggotty, "and told him I was a-going to seek my niece. He got me them papers as I wanted fur to carry me through—I doen't rightly know how they're called—and he would have give me money, but that I was thankful to have no need on. I thank him kind, for all he done, I'm sure! 'I've wrote afore you,' he says to me, 'and I shall speak to many as will come that way, and many will know you, fur distant from here, when you're a travelling alone.' I told him, best as I was able, what my gratitoode was, and went away through France."

"Alone, and on foot?" said I.

"Mostly a-foot," he rejoined; "sometimes in carts along with people going to market; sometimes in empty coaches. Many mile a day a-foot, and often with some poor soldier or another, travelling to see his friends. I couldn't talk to him," said Mr Peggotty, "nor he to me; but we was company for one another, too, along the dusty roads."

I should have known that by his friendly tone.

"When I come to any town," he pursued, "I found the inn, and waited about the yard till someone turned up (someone mostly did) as know'd English. Then I told how that I was on my way to seek my niece, and they told me what manner of gentlefolks was in the house, and I waited to see any as seemed like her, going in or out. When it warn't Em'ly, I went on agen. By little and little, when I come to a new village or that, among the poor people, I found they know'd about me. They would set me down at their cottage doors, and give me what-not fur to eat and drink, and show me where to sleep; and many a woman, Mas'r Davy, as has had a daughter of about Em'ly's age, I've found a-waiting fur me, at Our Saviour's Cross outside the village, fur to do me sim'lar kindnesses. Some has had daughters as was dead. And God only knows how good them mothers was to me!"

It was Martha at the door. I saw her haggard, listening face distinctly. My dread was lest he should turn his head, and see her too.

"They would often put their children—partic'lar their little girls," said Mr Peggotty, "upon my knee; and many a time you might have seen me sitting at their doors, when night was coming in, a'most as if they'd been my Darling's children. Oh, my Darling!"

Overpowered by sudden grief, he sobbed aloud. I laid my trembling hand upon the hand he put before his face. "Thankee, sir," he said, "doen't take no notice."

In a very little while he took his hand away and put it on his breast, and went on with his story.

"They often walked with me," he said, "in the morning, maybe a mile or two upon my road; and when we parted, and I said, 'I m very thankful to you! God bless you!' they always seemed to understand, and answered pleasant. At last I come to the sea. It warn't hard, you may suppose, for a seafaring man like me to work his way over to Italy. When I got theer, I wandered on as I had done afore. The people was just as good to me, and I should have gone from town to town, maybe the country through, but that I got news of her being seen among them Swiss mountains yonder. One as know'd his servant see 'em there, all three, and told me how they travelled, and where they was. I made fur them mountains, Mas'r Davy, day and night. Ever so fur as I went, ever so fur the mountains seemed to shift away from me. But I come up with 'em, and I crossed 'em. When I got nigh the place as I had been told of, I began to think within my own self, 'What shall I do when I see her?' "

The listening face, insensible to the inclement night, still drooped at the door, and the hands begged me—prayed me—not to cast it forth.

"I never doubted her," said Mr Peggotty. "No! Not a bit! On'y let her see my face—on'y let her heer my voice—on'y let my stanning still afore her bring to her thoughts the home she had fled away from, and the child she had been—and if she had growed to be a royal lady, she'd have fell down at my feet! I know'd it well! Many a time in my sleep had I heerd her cry out, 'Uncle!' and seen her fall like death afore me. Many a time in my sleep had I raised her up, and whispered to her, 'Em'ly, my dear, I am come fur to bring forgiveness, and to take you home!' "

He stopped and shook his head, and went on with a sigh.

"*He* was nowt to me now. Em'ly was all. I bought a country dress to put upon her; and I know'd that, once found, she would walk beside me over them stony roads, go where I would, and never, never, leave me more. To put that dress upon her, and to cast off what she wore—to take her on my arm again, and wander towards home—to stop sometimes upon the road, and heal her bruised feet and her worse-bruised heart—was all that I thowt of now. I doen't believe I should have done so much as look at him. But,

Mas'r Davy, it warn't to be—not yet! I was too late, and they was gone. Wheer, I couldn't learn. Some said heer, some said theer. I travelled heer, and I travelled theer, but I found no Em'ly, and I travelled home."

"How long ago?" I asked.

"A matter o' fower days," said Mr Peggotty. "I sighted the old boat arter dark, and the light a-shining in the winder. When I come nigh and looked in through the glass, I see the faithful creetur Missis Gummidge sittin' by the fire, as we had fixed upon, alone. I called out, 'Doen't be afeerd! It's Dan'l!' and I went in. I never could have thowt the old boat would have been so strange!"

From some pocket in his breast, he took out, with a very careful hand a small paper bundle containing two or three letters or little packets, which he laid upon the table.

"This fust one come," he said, selecting it from the rest, "afore I had been gone a week. A fifty pound Bank note, in a sheet of paper, directed to me, and put underneath the door in the night. She tried to hide her writing, but she couldn't hide it from Me!"

He folded up the note again, with great patience and care, in exactly the same form, and laid it on one side.

"This come to Missis Gummidge," he said, opening another, "two or three months ago." After looking at it for some moments, he gave it to me, and added in a low voice, "Be so good as read it, sir."

I read as follows:

"Oh what will you feel when you see this writing, and know it comes from my wicked hand! But try, try—not for my sake, but for uncle's goodness, try to let your heart soften to me, only for a little little time! Try, pray do, to relent towards a miserable girl, and write down on a bit of paper whether he is well, and what he said about me before you left off ever naming me among yourselves—and whether, of a night, when it is my old time of coming home, you ever see him look as if he thought of one he used to love so dear. Oh, my heart is breaking when I think about it! I am kneeling down to you, begging and praying you not to be as hard with me as I deserve—as I well, well, know I deserve—but to be so gentle and so good, as to write down something of him, and to send it to me. You need not call me Little, you need not call me by the name I have disgraced; but oh, listen to my agony, and have mercy on me so far as to write me some word of uncle, never, never to be seen in this world by my eyes again!

"Dear, if your heart is hard towards me—justly hard, I know—but, listen, if it is hard, dear, ask him I have wronged the most—him whose wife I was to have been—before you quite decide against my poor poor prayer! If he should be so compassionate as to say that you might write something for me to read—I think he would, oh, I think he would, if you would only ask him, for he always was so brave and so forgiving—tell him then (but not else), that when I hear the wind blowing at night, I feel as if it was passing angrily from seeing him and uncle, and was going up to God against me. Tell him that if I was to die tomorrow (and oh, if I was fit, I would be so glad to die!) I would bless him and uncle with my last words, and pray for his happy home with my last breath!"

Some money was enclosed in this letter also. Five pounds. It was untouched like the previous sum, and he refolded it in the same way. Detailed instructions were added relative to the address of a reply, which, although they betrayed the intervention of several hands, and made it difficult to arrive at any very probable conclusion in reference to her place of concealment, made it at least not unlikely that she had written from that spot where she was stated to have been seen.

"What answer was sent?" I inquired of Mr Peggotty.

"Missis Gummidge," he returned, "not being a good scholar, sir, Ham kindly drawed it out, and she made a copy on it. They told her I was gone to seek her, and what my parting words was."

"Is that another letter in your hand?" said I.

"It's money, sir," said Mr Peggotty, unfolding it a little way. "Ten pound, you see. And wrote inside, 'From a true friend,' like the fust. But the fust was put underneath the door, and this come by the post, day afore yesterday. I'm a-going to seek her at the post-mark."

He showed it to me. It was a town on the Upper Rhine. He had found out, at Yarmouth, some foreign dealers who knew that country, and they had drawn him a rude map on paper, which he could very well understand. He laid it between us on the table; and, with his chin resting on one hand, tracked his course upon it with the other.

I asked him how Ham was? He shook his head.

"He works," he said, "as bold as a man can. His name's as good, in all that part, as any man's is, anywheres in the wureld. Anyone's hand is ready to help him, you understand, and his is ready to help them. He's never been heerd fur to complain. But my sister's belief is ('twixt ourselves) as it has cut him deep."

"Poor fellow, I can believe it!"

"He ain't no care, Mas'r Davy," said Mr Peggotty in a solemn whisper—"keinder no care no-how for his life. When a man's wanted for rough service in rough weather, he's theer. When there's hard duty to be done with danger in it, he steps for'ard afore all his mates. And yet he's as gentle as any child. There ain't a child in Yarmouth that doen't know him."

He gathered up the letters thoughtfully, smoothing them with his hand; put them into their little bundle; and placed it tenderly in his breast again. The face was gone from the door. I still saw the snow drifting in; but nothing else was there.

"Well!" he said, looking to his bag, "having seen you tonight, Mas'r Davy (and that doos me good!), I shall away betimes tomorrow morning. You have seen what I've got heer"; putting his hand on where the little packet lay; "all that troubles me is, to think that any harm might come to me, afore that money was give back. If I was to die, and it was lost, or stole, or elseways made away with, and it was never know'd by him but what I'd took it, I believe the t'other wureld wouldn't hold me! I believe I must come back!"

He rose, and I rose too; we grasped each other by the hand again, before going out.

"I'd go ten thousand mile," he said, "I'd go till I dropped dead, to lay that money down afore him. If I do that, and find my Em'ly, I'm content. If I doen't find her, maybe she'll come to hear, sometime, as her loving uncle only ended his search for her when he ended his life; and if I know her, even that will turn her home at last!"

As he went out into the rigorous night, I saw the lonely figure flit away before us. I turned him hastily on some pretence, and held him in conversation until it was gone.

He spoke of a traveller's house on the Dover Road, where he knew he could find a clean, plain lodging for the night. I went with him over Westminster Bridge, and parted from him on the Surrey shore. Everything seemed, to my imagination, to be hushed in reverence for him, as he resumed his solitary journey through the snow.

I returned to the inn yard, and, impressed by my remembrance of the face, looked awfully around for it. It was not there. The snow had covered our late footprints; my new track was the only one to be seen; and even that began to die away (it snowed so fast) as I looked back over my shoulder.

Chapter XLI

DORA'S AUNTS

AT last, an answer came from the two old ladies. They presented their compliments to Mr Copperfield, and informed him that they had given his letter their best consideration, "with a view to the happiness of both parties"—which I thought rather an alarming expression, not only because of the use they had made of it in relation to the family difference before-mentioned, but because I had (and have all my life) observed that conventional phrases are a sort of fireworks, easily let off, and liable to take a great variety of shapes and colours not at all suggested by their original form. The Misses Spenlow added that they begged to forbear expressing, "through the medium of correspondence," an opinion on the subject of Mr Copperfield's communication; but that if Mr Copperfield would do them the favour to call, upon a certain day (accompanied, if he thought proper, by a confidential friend), they would be happy to hold some conversation on the subject.

To this favour, Mr Copperfield immediately replied, with his respectful compliments, that he would have the honour of waiting on the Misses Spenlow, at the time appointed; accompanied, in accordance with their kind permission, by his friend Mr Thomas Traddles of the Inner Temple. Having dispatched which missive, Mr Copperfield fell into a condition of strong nervous agitation; and so remained until the day arrived.

It was a great augmentation of my uneasiness to be bereaved, at this eventful crisis, of the inestimable services of Miss Mills. But Mr Mills, who was always doing something or other to annoy me—or I felt as if he were, which was the same thing—had brought his conduct to a climax, by taking it into his head that he would go to India. Why should he go to India, except to harass me? To be sure he had nothing to do with any other part of the world, and had a good deal to do with that part; being entirely in the India trade, whatever that was (I had floating dreams myself concerning golden shawls and elephants' teeth); having been at Calcutta in his youth; and designing now to go out there again, in the capacity of resident partner. But this was nothing to me. However, it was so much to him that for India he was bound, and Julia with him; and Julia went into the country to take leave of her relations; and the house was put into a perfect suit of bills, announcing that it was to be let or sold, and that the furniture (Mangle and all) was to be taken at a valuation. So, here was another earthquake of which I became the sport, before I had recovered from the shock of its predecessor!

I was in several minds how to dress myself on the important day; being divided between my desire to appear to advantage, and my apprehensions of putting on anything that might impair my severely practical character in the eyes of the Misses Spenlow. I endeavoured to hit a happy medium between these two extremes; my aunt approved the result; and Mr Dick threw one of his shoes after Traddles and me, for luck, as we went downstairs.

Excellent fellow as I knew Traddles to be, and warmly attached to him as I was, I could not help wishing, on that delicate occasion, that he had never contracted the habit of brushing his hair so very upright. It gave him a surprised look—not to say a hearth-broomy kind of expression—which, my apprehensions whispered, might be fatal to us.

I took the liberty of mentioning it to Traddles, as we were walking to Putney; and saying that if he *would* smooth it down a little—

"My dear Copperfield," said Traddles, lifting off his hat, and rubbing his hair all kinds of ways, "nothing would give me greater pleasure. But it won't."

"Won't be smoothed down?" said I.

"No," said Traddles. "Nothing will induce it. If I was to carry a half-hundred-weight upon it, all the way to Putney, it would be up again the moment the weight was taken off. You have no idea what obstinate hair mine is, Copperfield. I am quite a fretful porcupine."

I was a little disappointed, I must confess, but thoroughly charmed by his good-nature too. I told him how I esteemed his good-nature; and said that his hair must have taken all the obstinacy out of his character, for *he* had none.

"Oh!" returned Traddles, laughing. "I assure you, it's quite an old story, my unfortunate hair. My uncle's wife couldn't bear it. She said it exasperated her. It stood very much in my way, too, when I first fell in love with Sophy. Very much!"

"Did she object to it?"

"*She* didn't," rejoined Traddles; "but her eldest sister—the one that's the Beauty—quite made game of it, I understand. In fact, all the sisters laugh at it."

"Agreeable!" said I.

"Yes," returned Traddles with perfect innocence, "it's a joke for us. They pretend that Sophy has a lock of it in her desk, and is obliged to shut it in a clasped book, to keep it down. We laugh about it."

"By the by, my dear Traddles," said I, "your experience may suggest something to me. When you became engaged to the young lady whom you have just mentioned, did you make a regular proposal to her family? Was there anything like—what we are going through today, for instance?" I added, nervously.

"Why," replied Traddles, on whose attentive face a thoughtful shade had stolen, "it was rather a painful transaction, Copperfield, in my case. You see, Sophy being of so much use in the family, none of them could endure the thought of her ever being married. Indeed, they had quite settled among themselves that she never was to be married, and they called her the old maid. Accordingly, when I mentioned it, with the greatest precaution, to Mrs Crewler—"

"The mama?" said I.

"The mama," said Traddles—"Reverend Horace Crewler—when I mentioned it with every possible precaution to Mrs Crewler, the effect upon her was such that she gave a scream and became insensible. I couldn't approach the subject again, for months."

"You did at last?" said I.

"Well, the Reverend Horace did," said Traddles. "He is an excellent man, most exemplary in every way; and he pointed out to her that she ought, as a Christian, to reconcile herself to the sacrifice (especially as it was so uncertain), and to bear no uncharitable feeling towards me. As to myself, Copperfield, I give you my word, I felt a perfect bird of prey towards the family."

"The sisters took your part, I hope, Traddles?"

"Why, I can't say they did," he returned. "When we had comparatively reconciled Mrs Crewler to it, we had to break it to Sarah. You recollect my mentioning Sarah, as the one that has something the matter with her spine?"

"Perfectly!"

"She clenched both her hands," said Traddles, looking at me in dismay; "shut her eyes; turned lead-colour; became perfectly stiff; and took nothing for two days but toast-and-water, administered with a tea-spoon."

"What a very unpleasant girl, Traddles!" I remarked.

"Oh, I beg your pardon, Copperfield!" said Traddles. "She is a very charming girl, but she has a great deal of feeling. In fact, they all have. Sophy told me afterwards, that the self-reproach she underwent while she was in attendance upon Sarah, no words could describe. I know it must have been severe, by my own feelings, Copperfield; which were like a criminal's. After Sarah was restored, we still had to break it to the other eight; and it produced various effects upon them of a most pathetic nature. The two little ones, whom Sophy educates, have only just left off de-testing me."

"At any rate, they are all reconciled to it now, I hope?" said I.

"Ye-yes, I should say they were, on the whole, resigned to it," said Traddles, doubtfully. "The fact is, we avoid mentioning the subject; and my unsettled prospects and indifferent circumstances are a great consolation to them. There will be a deplorable scene, whenever we are married. It will be much more like a funeral, than a wedding. And they'll all hate me for taking her away!"

His honest face, as he looked at me with a serio-comic shake of his head, impresses me more in the remembrance than it did in the reality, for I was by this time in a state of such excessive trepidation and wandering of mind, as to be quite unable to fix my attention on anything. On our approaching the house where the Misses Spenlow lived, I was at such a discount in respect of my personal looks and presence of mind, that Traddles proposed a gentle stimulant in the form of a glass of ale. This having been administered at a neighbouring public-house, he conducted me, with tottering steps, to the Misses Spenlow's door.

I had a vague sensation of being, as it were, on view, when the maid opened it; and of wavering, somehow, across a hall with a weather-glass in it, into a quiet little drawing-room on the ground-floor, commanding a neat garden. Also of sitting down here, on a sofa, and seeing Traddles's hair start up, now his hat was removed, like one of those obtrusive little figures made of springs, that fly out of fictitious snuff-boxes when the lid is taken off. Also of hearing an old-fashioned clock ticking away on the chimney-piece, and trying to make it keep time to the jerking of my heart,—which it wouldn't. Also of looking round the room for any sign of Dora, and seeing none. Also of thinking that Jip once barked in the distance, and was instantly choked by somebody. Ultimately I found myself backing Traddles into the fire-place, and bowing in great confusion to two dry little elderly ladies, dressed in black, and each looking wonderfully like a preparation in chip or tan of the late Mr Spenlow.

"Pray," said one of the two little ladies, "be seated."

When I had done tumbling over Traddles, and had sat upon something which was not a cat—my first seat was—I so far recovered my sight, as to perceive that Mr Spenlow had evidently been the youngest of the family; that there was a disparity of six or eight years between the two sisters; and that the younger appeared to be the manager of the conference, inasmuch as she had my letter in her hand—so familiar as it looked to me, and yet so odd!—and was referring to it through an eye-glass. They were dressed alike, but this sister wore her dress with a more youthful air than the other; and perhaps had a trifle more frill, or tucker, or brooch, or bracelet, or some little thing of that kind, which made her look more lively. They were both upright in their carriage, formal, precise, composed, and quiet. The sister who had not my letter, had her arms crossed on her breast, and resting on each other, like an Idol.

"Mr Copperfield, I believe," said the sister who had got my letter, addressing herself to Traddles.

This was a frightful beginning. Traddles had to indicate that I was Mr Copperfield, and I had to lay claim to myself, and they had to divest themselves of a preconceived opinion that Traddles was Mr Copperfield, and altogether we were in a nice condition. To improve it, we all distinctly heard Jip give two short barks, and receive another choke.

"Mr Copperfield!" said the sister with the letter.

I did something—bowed, I suppose—and was all attention, when the other sister struck in.

"My sister Lavinia," said she "being conversant with matters of this nature, will state what we consider most calculated to promote the happiness of both parties."

I discovered afterwards that Miss Lavinia was an authority in affairs of the heart, by reason of there having anciently existed a certain Mr Pidger, who played short whist, and was supposed to have been enamoured of her. My private opinion is, that this was entirely a gratuitous assumption, and that Pidger was altogether innocent of any such sentiments—to which he had never given any sort of expression that I could ever hear of. Both Miss Lavinia and Miss Clarissa had a superstition, however, that he would have declared his passion, if he had not been cut short in his youth (at about sixty) by over-drinking his constitution, and over-doing an attempt to set it right again by swilling Bath water. They had a lurking suspicion even, that he died of secret love; though I must say there was a picture of him in the house with a damask nose, which concealment did not appear to have ever preyed upon.

"We will not," said Miss Lavinia, "enter on the past history of this matter. Our poor brother Francis's death has cancelled that."

"We had not," said Miss Clarissa, "been in the habit of frequent association with our brother Francis; but there was no decided division or disunion between us. Francis took his road; we took ours. We considered it conducive to the happiness of all parties that it should be so. And it was so."

Each of the sisters leaned a little forward to speak, shook her head after speaking, and became upright again when silent. Miss Clarissa never moved her arms. She sometimes played tunes upon them with her fingers—minuets and marches I should think—but never moved them.

"Our niece's position, or supposed position, is much changed by our brother Francis's death," said Miss Lavinia; "and therefore we consider our brother's opinions as regarded her position as being changed too. We have no reason to doubt, Mr Copperfield, that you are a young gentleman possessed of good qualities and honourable character; or that you have an affection—or are fully persuaded that you have an affection—for our niece."

I replied, as I usually did whenever I had a chance, that nobody had ever loved anybody else as I loved Dora. Traddles came to my assistance with a confirmatory murmur.

Miss Lavinia was going on to make some rejoinder, when Miss Clarissa, who appeared to be incessantly beset by a desire to refer to her brother Francis, struck in again:

"If Dora's mama," she said, "when she married our brother Francis, had at once said that there was not room for the family at the dinner-table, it would have been better for the happiness of all parties."

"Sister Clarissa," said Miss Lavinia. "Perhaps we needn't mind that now."

"Sister Lavinia," said Miss Clarissa, "it belongs to the subject. With your branch of the subject, on which alone you are competent to speak, I should not think of interfering. On this branch of the subject I have a voice and an opinion. It would have been better for the happiness of all parties, if Dora's mama, when she married our brother Francis, had mentioned plainly what her intentions were. We should then have known what we had to expect. We should have said 'Pray do not invite us, at any time'; and all possibility of misunderstanding would have been avoided."

When Miss Clarissa had shaken her head, Miss Lavinia resumed: again referring to my letter through her eye-glass. They both had little bright round twinkling eyes, by the way, which were like birds' eyes. They were not unlike birds, altogether; having a sharp, brisk, sudden manner, and a little short, spruce way of adjusting themselves, like canaries.

Miss Lavinia, as I have said, resumed:

"You ask permission of my sister Clarissa and myself, Mr Copperfield, to visit here, as the accepted suitor of our niece."

"If our brother Francis," said Miss Clarissa, breaking out again, if I may call anything so calm a breaking out, "wished to surround himself with an atmosphere of Doctors' Commons, and of Doctors' Commons only, what right or desire had we to object? None, I am sure. We have ever been far from wishing to obtrude ourselves on anyone. But why not say so? Let our brother Francis and his wife have their society. Let my sister Lavinia and myself have our society. We can find it for ourselves, I hope."

As this appeared to be addressed to Traddles and me, both Traddles and I made some sort of reply. Traddles was inaudible. I think I observed, myself, that it was highly creditable to all concerned. I don't in the least know what I meant.

"Sister Lavinia," said Miss Clarissa, having now relieved her mind, "you can go on, my dear."

Miss Lavinia proceeded:

"Mr Copperfield, my sister Clarissa and I have been very careful indeed in consider- ing this letter; and we have not considered it without finally showing it to our niece, and discussing it with our niece. We have no doubt that you think you like her very much."

"Think, ma'am," I rapturously began, "oh!—"

But Miss Clarissa giving me a look (just like a sharp canary), as requesting that I would not interrupt the oracle, I begged pardon.

"Affection," said Miss Lavinia, glancing at her sister for corroboration, which she gave in the form of a little nod to every clause, "mature affection, homage, devotion, does not easily express itself. Its voice is low. It is modest and retiring, it lies in ambush, waits and waits. Such is the mature fruit. Sometimes a life glides away, and finds it still ripening in the shade."

Of course I did not understand then that this was an allusion to her supposed experience of the stricken Pidger; but I saw, from the gravity with which Miss Clarissa nodded her head, that great weight was attached to these words.

"The light—for I call them, in comparison with such sentiments, the light—inclina- tions of very young people," pursued Miss Lavinia, "are dust, compared to rocks. It is owing to the difficulty of knowing whether they are likely to endure or have any real foundation, that my sister Clarissa and myself have been very undecided how to act, Mr Copperfield, and Mr—"

"Traddles," said my friend, finding himself looked at.

"I beg pardon. Of the Inner Temple, I believe?" said Miss Clarissa, again glancing at my letter.

Traddles said "Exactly so," and became pretty red in the face.

Now, although I had not received any express encouragement as yet, I fancied that I saw in the two little sisters, and particularly in Miss Lavinia, an intensified enjoyment of this new and fruitful subject of domestic interest, a settling down to make the most of it, a disposition to pet it, in which there was a good bright ray of hope. I thought I perceived that Miss Lavinia would have uncommon satisfaction in superintending two young lovers, like Dora and me; and that Miss Clarissa would have hardly less satisfaction in seeing her superintend us, and in chiming in with her own particular department of the subject whenever that impulse was strong upon her. This gave me courage to protest most vehemently that I loved Dora better than I could tell, or anyone believe; that all my friends knew how I loved her; that my aunt, Agnes, Traddles, everyone who knew me, knew how I loved her, and how earnest my love had made me. For the truth of this, I appealed to Traddles. And Traddles, firing up as if he were plunging into a Parliamentary Debate, really did come out nobly: confirming me in good round terms, and in a plain sensible practical manner, that evidently made a favourable impression.

"I speak, if I may presume to say so, as one who has some little experience of such things," said Traddles, "being myself engaged to a young lady—one of ten, down in Devonshire—and seeing no probability, at present, of our engagement coming to a termination."

"You may be able to confirm what I have said, Mr Traddles," observed Miss Lavinia, evidently taking a new interest in him, "of the affection that is modest and retiring; that waits and waits?"

"Entirely, ma'am," said Traddles.

Miss Clarissa looked at Miss Lavinia, and shook her head gravely. Miss Lavinia looked consciously at Miss Clarissa, and heaved a little sigh.

"Sister Lavinia," said Miss Clarissa, "take my smelling-bottle."

Miss Lavinia revived herself with a few whiffs of aromatic vinegar—Traddles and I looking on with great solicitude the while; and then went on to say, rather faintly:

"My sister and myself have been in great doubt, Mr Traddles, what course we ought to take in reference to the likings, or imaginary likings, of such very young people as your friend Mr Copperfield and our niece."

"Our brother Francis's child," remarked Miss Clarissa. "If our brother Francis's wife had found it convenient in her lifetime (though she had an unquestionable right to act as she thought best) to invite the family to her dinner-table, we might have known our brother Francis's child better at the present moment. Sister Lavinia, proceed."

Miss Lavinia turned my letter, so as to bring the superscription towards herself, and referred through her eye-glass to some orderly-looking notes she had made on that part of it.

"It seems to us," said she, "prudent, Mr Traddles, to bring these feelings to the test of our own observation. At present we know nothing of them, and are not in a situation to judge how much reality there may be in them. Therefore we are inclined so far to accede to Mr Copperfield's proposal, as to admit his visits here."

"I shall never, dear ladies," I exclaimed, relieved of an immense load of apprehension, "forget your kindness!"

"But," pursued Miss Lavinia,—"but, we would prefer to regard those visits, Mr Traddles, as made, at present, to us. We must guard ourselves from recognizing any positive engagement between Mr Copperfield and our niece, until we have had an opportunity—"

"Until *you* have had an opportunity, sister Lavinia," said Miss Clarissa.

"Be it so," assented Miss Lavinia, with a sigh—"until I have had an opportunity of observing them."

"Copperfield," said Traddles, turning to me, "you feel, I am sure, that nothing could be more reasonable or considerate."

"Nothing!" cried I. "I am deeply sensible of it."

"In this position of affairs," said Miss Lavinia, again referring to her notes, "and admitting his visits on this understanding only, we must require from Mr Copperfield a distinct assurance, on his word of honour, that no communication of any kind shall take place between him and our niece without our knowledge. That no project whatever shall be entertained with regard to our niece, without being first submitted to us—"

"To you, sister Lavinia," Miss Clarissa interposed.

"Be it so, Clarissa!" assented Miss Lavinia resignedly—"to me—and receiving our concurrence. We must make this a most express and serious stipulation, not to be broken on any account. We wished Mr Copperfield to be accompanied by some confidential friend today," with an inclination of her head towards Traddles, who bowed, "in order that there might be no doubt or misconception on this subject. If Mr Copperfield, or if you, Mr Traddles, feel the least scruple, in giving this promise, I beg you to take time to consider it."

I exclaimed, in a state of high ecstatic fervour, that not a moment's consideration could be necessary. I bound myself by the required promise, in a most impassioned manner; called upon Traddles to witness it; and denounced myself as the most atrocious of characters if I ever swerved from it in the least degree.

"Stay!" said Miss Lavinia, holding up her hand; "we resolved, before we had the pleasure of receiving you two gentlemen, to leave you alone for a quarter of an hour, to consider this point. You will allow us to retire."

It was in vain for me to say that no consideration was necessary. They persisted in withdrawing for the specified time. Accordingly, these little birds hopped out with great dignity; leaving me to receive the congratulations of Traddles, and to feel as if I were translated to regions of exquisite happiness. Exactly at the expiration of the quarter of an hour, they reappeared with no less dignity than they had disappeared. They had gone rustling away as if their little dresses were made of autumn-leaves: and they came rustling back, in like manner.

I then bound myself once more to the prescribed conditions.

"Sister Clarissa," said Miss Lavinia, "the rest is with you."

Miss Clarissa, unfolding her arms for the first time, took the notes and glanced at them.

"We shall be happy," said Miss Clarissa, "to see Mr Copperfield to dinner, every Sunday, if it should suit his convenience. Our hour is three."

I bowed.

"In the course of the week," said Miss Clarissa, "we shall be happy to see Mr Copperfield to tea. Our hour is half-past six."

I bowed again.

"Twice in the week," said Miss Clarissa, "but, as a rule, not oftener."

I bowed again.

"Miss Trotwood," said Miss Clarissa, "mentioned in Mr Copperfield's letter, will perhaps call upon us. When visiting is better for the happiness of all parties, we are glad to receive visits, and return them. When it is better for the happiness of all parties that no visiting should take place, (as in the case of our brother Francis, and his establishment) that is quite different."

I intimated that my aunt would be proud and delighted to make their acquaintance; though I must say I was not quite sure of their getting on very satisfactorily together. The conditions being now closed, I expressed my acknowledgements in the warmest manner; and, taking the hand, first of Miss Clarissa, and then of Miss Lavinia, pressed it, in each case, to my lips.

Miss Lavinia then arose, and begging Mr Traddles to excuse us for a minute, requested me to follow her. I obeyed, all in a tremble, and was conducted into another room. There I found my blessed darling stopping her ears behind the door, with her dear little face against the wall; and Jip in the plate-warmer with his head tied up in a towel.

Oh! How beautiful she was in her black frock, and how she sobbed and cried at first, and wouldn't come out from behind the door! How fond we were of one another, when she did come out at last; and what a state of bliss I was in, when we took Jip out of the plate-warmer, and restored him to the light, sneezing very much, and were all three reunited!

"My dearest Dora! Now, indeed, my own for ever!"

"Oh, DON'T!" pleaded Dora. "Please!"

"Are you not my own for ever, Dora?"

"Oh yes, of course I am!" cried Dora, "but I am so frightened!"

"Frightened, my own?"

"Oh yes! I don't like him," said Dora. "Why don't he go?"

"Who, my life?"

"Your friend," said Dora. "It isn't any business of his. What a stupid he must be!"

"My love!" (There never was anything so coaxing as her childish ways.) "He is the best creature!"

"Oh, but we don't want any best creatures!" pouted Dora.

"My dear," I argued, "you will soon know him well, and like him of all things. And here is my aunt coming soon; and you'll like her of all things too, when you know her."

"No, please don't bring her!" said Dora, giving me a horrified little kiss, and folding her hands. "Don't. I know she's a naughty, mischief-making old thing! Don't let her come here, Doady!" which was a corruption of David.

Remonstrance was of no use, then; so I laughed, and admired, and was very much in love and very happy; and she showed me Jip's new trick of standing on his hind legs in a corner—which he did for about the space of a flash of lightning, and then fell down—and I don't know how long I should have stayed there, oblivious of Traddles, if Miss Lavinia had not come in to take me away. Miss Lavinia was very fond of Dora (she told me Dora was exactly like what she had been herself at her age—she must have altered a good deal), and she treated Dora just as if she had been a toy. I wanted to persuade Dora to come and see Traddles, but on my proposing it she ran off to her own room and locked herself in; so I went to Traddles without her, and walked away with him on air.

"Nothing could be more satisfactory," said Traddles; "and they are very agreeable old ladies, I am sure. I shouldn't be at all surprised if you were to be married years before me, Copperfield."

"Does your Sophy play on any instrument, Traddles?" I inquired, in the pride of my heart.

"She knows enough of the piano to teach it to her little sisters," said Traddles.

"Does she sing at all?" I asked.

"Why, she sings ballads, sometimes, to freshen up the others a little when they're out of spirits," said Traddles. "Nothing scientific."

"She doesn't sing to the guitar?" said I.

"Oh dear no!" said Traddles.

"Paint at all?"

"Not at all," said Traddles.

I promised Traddles that he should hear Dora sing, and see some of her flower-painting. He said he should like it very much, and we went home arm in arm in great good humour and delight. I encouraged him to talk about Sophy, on the way; which he did with a loving reliance on her that I very much admired. I compared her in my mind with Dora, with considerable inward satisfaction; but I candidly admitted to myself that she seemed to be an excellent kind of girl for Traddles, too.

Of course my aunt was immediately made acquainted with the successful issue of the conference, and with all that had been said and done in the course of it. She was happy to see me so happy, and promised to call on Dora's aunts without loss of time. But she took such a long walk up and down our rooms that night, while I was writing to Agnes, that I began to think she meant to walk till morning.

My letter to Agnes was a fervent and grateful one, narrating all the good effects that had resulted from my following her advice. She wrote, by return of post, to me. Her letter was hopeful, earnest, and cheerful. She was always cheerful from that time.

I had my hands more full than ever, now. My daily journeys to Highgate considered, Putney was a long way off; and I naturally wanted to go there as often as I could. The proposed tea-drinkings being quite impracticable, I compounded with Miss Lavinia for permission to visit every Saturday afternoon, without detriment to my privileged Sundays. So, the close of every week was a delicious time for me; and I got through the rest of the week by looking forward to it.

I was wonderfully relieved to find that my aunt and Dora's aunts rubbed on, all things considered, much more smoothly than I could have expected. My aunt made her promised visit within a few days of the conference; and within a few more days, Dora's aunts called upon her, in due state and form. Similar but more friendly exchanges took place afterwards, usually at intervals of three or four weeks. I know that my aunt distressed Dora's aunts very much, by utterly setting at naught the dignity of fly-convey-ance, and walking out to Putney at extraordinary times, as shortly after breakfast or just before tea; likewise by wearing her bonnet in any manner that happened to be comfort-able to her head, without at all deferring to the prejudices of civilization on that subject. But Dora's aunts soon agreed to regard my aunt as an eccentric and somewhat masculine lady, with a strong understanding; and although my aunt occasionally ruffled the feath-ers of Dora's aunts, by expressing heretical opinions on various points of ceremony, she loved me too well not to sacrifice some of her little peculiarities to the general harmony.

The only member of our small society who positively refused to adapt himself to circumstances, was Jip. He never saw my aunt without immediately displaying every tooth in his head, retiring under a chair, and growling incessantly: with now and then a doleful howl, as if she really were too much for his feelings. All kinds of treatment were tried with him, coaxing, scolding, slapping, bringing him to Buckingham Street (where he instantly dashed at the two cats, to the terror of all beholders); but he never could prevail upon himself to bear my aunt's society. He would sometimes think he had got the better of his objection, and be amiable for a few minutes; and then would put up his snub nose, and howl to that extent, that there was nothing for it but to blind him and put him in the plate-warmer. At length, Dora regularly muffled him in a towel and shut him up there, whenever my aunt was reported at the door.

One thing troubled me much, after we had fallen into this quiet train. It was, that

Dora seemed by one consent to be regarded like a pretty toy or plaything. My aunt, with whom she gradually became familiar, always called her Little Blossom; and the pleasure of Miss Lavinia's life was to wait upon her, curl her hair, make ornaments for her, and treat her like a pet child. What Miss Lavinia did, her sister did as a matter of course. It was very odd to me; but they all seemed to treat Dora, in her degree, much as Dora treated Jip in his.

I made up my mind to speak to Dora about this; and one day when we were out walking (for we were licensed by Miss Lavinia, after a while, to go out walking by ourselves), I said to her that I wished she could get them to behave towards her differently.

"Because you know, my darling," I remonstrated, "you are not a child."

"There!" said Dora. "Now you're going to be cross!"

"Cross, my love?"

"I am sure they're very kind to me," said Dora, "and I am very happy."

"Well! But my dearest life!" said I, "you might be very happy, and yet be treated rationally."

Dora gave me a reproachful look—the prettiest look!—and then began to sob, saying, if I didn't like her, why had I ever wanted so much to be engaged to her? And why didn't I go away, now, if I couldn't bear her?

What could I do, but kiss away her tears, and tell her how I doted on her, after that!

"I am sure I am very affectionate," said Dora; "you oughtn't to be cruel to me, Doady!"

"Cruel, my precious love! As if I would—or could—be cruel to you, for the world!"

"Then don't find fault with me," said Dora, making a rose-bud of her mouth; "and I'll be good."

I was charmed by her presently asking me, of her own accord, to give her that cookery-book I had once spoken of, and to show her how to keep accounts as I had once promised I would. I brought the volume with me on my next visit (I got it prettily bound, first, to make it look less dry and more inviting); and as we strolled about the Common, I showed her an old housekeeping-book of my aunt's, and gave her a set of tablets, and a pretty little pencil-case and box of leads, to practise housekeeping with.

But the cookery-book made Dora's head ache, and the figures made her cry. They wouldn't add up, she said. So she rubbed them out, and drew little nosegays and likenesses of me and Jip, all over the tablets.

Then I playfully tried verbal instruction in domestic matters, as we walked about on a Saturday afternoon. Sometimes, for example, when we passed a butcher's shop, I would say:

"Now suppose, my pet, that we were married, and you were going to buy a shoulder of mutton for dinner, would you know how to buy it?"

My pretty little Dora's face would fall, and she would make her mouth into a bud again, as if she would very much prefer to shut mine with a kiss.

"Would you know how to buy it, my darling?" I would repeat, perhaps, if I were very inflexible.

Dora would think a little, and then reply, perhaps, with great triumph:

"Why, the butcher would know how to sell it, and what need I know? Oh, you silly boy!"

So, when I once asked Dora, with an eye to the cookery-book, what she would do, if we were married, and I were to say I should like a nice Irish stew, she replied that she would tell the servant to make it; and then clapped her little hands together across my arm, and laughed in such a charming manner that she was more delightful than ever.

Consequently, the principal use to which the cookery-book was devoted, was being put down in the corner for Jip to stand upon. But Dora was so pleased, when she had trained him to stand upon it without offering to come off, and at the same time to hold the pencil-case in his mouth, that I was very glad I had bought it.

And we fell back on the guitar-case, and the flower-painting, and the songs about never leaving off dancing, Ta ra la! and were as happy as the week was long. I occasionally wished I could venture to hint to Miss Lavinia, that she treated the darling of my heart a little too much like a plaything; and I sometimes awoke, as it were, wondering to find that I had fallen into the general fault, and treated her like a plaything too—but not often.

Chapter XLII

MISCHIEF

I FEEL as if it were not for me to record, even though this manuscript is intended for no eyes but mine, how hard I worked at that tremendous short-hand, and all improvement appertaining to it, in my sense of responsibility to Dora and her aunts. I will only add, to what I have already written of my perseverance at this time of my life, and of a patient and continuous energy which then began to be matured within me, and which I know to be the strong part of my character, if it have any strength at all, that there, on looking back, I find the source of my success. I have been very fortunate in worldly matters; many men have worked much harder, and not succeeded half so well; but I never could have done what I have done, without the habits of punctuality, order, and diligence, without the determination to concentrate myself on one object at a time, no matter how quickly its successor should come upon its heels, which I then formed. Heaven knows I write this, in no spirit of self-laudation. The man who reviews his own life, as I do mine, in going on here, from page to page, had need to have been a good man indeed, if he would be spared the sharp consciousness of many talents neglected, many opportunities wasted, many erratic and perverted feelings constantly at war within his breast, and defeating him. I do not hold one natural gift, I dare say, that I have not abused. My meaning simply is, that whatever I have tried to do in life, I have tried with all my heart to do well; that whatever I have devoted myself to, I have devoted myself to completely; that in great aims and in small, I have always been thoroughly in earnest. I have never believed it possible that any natural or improved ability can claim immunity from the companionship of the steady, plain, hard-working qualities, and hope to gain its end. There is no such thing as such fulfilment on this earth. Some happy talent, and some fortunate opportunity, may form the two sides of the ladder on which some men mount, but the rounds of that ladder must be made of stuff to stand wear and tear; and there is no substitute for thorough-going, ardent, and sincere earnestness. Never to put one hand to anything, on which I could throw my whole self; and never to affect depreciation of my work, whatever it was; I find, now, to have been my golden rules.

How much of the practice I have just reduced to precept, I owe to Agnes, I will not repeat here. My narrative proceeds to Agnes, with a thankful love.

She came on a visit of a fortnight to the Doctor's. Mr Wickfield was the Doctor's old friend, and the Doctor wished to talk with him, and do him good. It had been matter of conversation with Agnes when she was last in town, and this visit was the result. She and her father came together. I was not much surprised to hear from her that she had engaged to find a lodging in the neighbourhood for Mrs Heep, whose rheumatic complaint required change of air, and who would be charmed to have it in such company. Neither was I surprised when, on the very next day, Uriah, like a dutiful son, brought his worthy mother to take possession.

"You see, Master Copperfield," said he, as he forced himself upon my company for a turn in the Doctor's garden, "where a person loves, a person is a little jealous—leastways, anxious to keep an eye on the beloved one."

"Of whom are you jealous, now?" said I.

"Thanks to you, Master Copperfield," he returned, "of no one in particular just at present—no male person, at least."

"Do you mean that you are jealous of a female person?"

He gave me a sidelong glance out of his sinister red eyes, and laughed.

"Really, Master Copperfield," he said, "—I should say Mister, but I know you'll excuse the abit I've got into—you're so insinuating, that you draw me like a corkscrew! Well, I don't mind telling you," putting his fish-like hand on mine, "I'm not a lady's man in general, sir, and I never was, with Mrs Strong."

His eyes looked green now, as they watched mine with a rascally cunning.

"What do you mean?" said I.

"Why, though I am a lawyer, Master Copperfield," he replied, with a dry grin, "I mean, just at present, what I say."

"And what do you mean by your look?" I retorted, quietly.

"By my look? Dear me, Copperfield, that's sharp practice! What do I mean by my look?"

"Yes," said I. "By your look."

He seemed very much amused, and laughed as heartily as it was in his nature to laugh. After some scraping of his chin with his hand, he went on to say, with his eyes cast downward—still scraping, very slowly:

"When I was but an umble clerk, she always looked down upon me. She was for ever having my Agnes backwards and forwards at her ouse, and she was for ever being a friend to you, Master Copperfield; but I was too far beneath her, myself, to be noticed."

"Well?" said I; "suppose you were!"

"—And beneath him too," pursued Uriah, very distinctly, and in a meditative tone of voice, as he continued to scrape his chin.

"Don't you know the Doctor better," said I, "than to suppose him conscious of your existence, when you were not before him?"

He directed his eyes at me in that sidelong glance again, and he made his face very lantern-jawed, for the greater convenience of scraping, as he answered:

"Oh dear, I am not referring to the Doctor! Oh no, poor man! I mean Mr Maldon!"

My heart quite died within me. All my old doubts and apprehensions on that subject, all the Doctor's happiness and peace, all the mingled possibilities of innocence and compromise, that I could not unravel, I saw, in a moment, at the mercy of this fellow's twisting.

"He never could come into the office, without ordering and shoving me about," said

Uriah. "One of your fine gentlemen he was! I was very meek and umble—and I am. But I didn't like that sort of thing—and I don't!"

He left off scraping his chin, and sucked in his cheeks until they seemed to meet inside; keeping his sidelong glance upon me all the while.

"She is one of your lovely women, she is," he pursued, when he had slowly restored his face to its natural form; "and ready to be no friend to such as me, *I* know. She's just the person as would put my Agnes up to higher sort of game. Now, I ain't one of your lady's men, Master Copperfield; but I've had eyes in my ed, a pretty long time back. We umble ones have got eyes, mostly speaking—and we look out of 'em."

I endeavoured to appear unconscious and not disquieted, but, I saw in his face, with poor success.

"Now, I'm not a-going to let myself be run down, Copperfield," he continued, raising that part of his countenance, where his red eyebrows would have been if he had had any, with malignant triumph, "and I shall do what I can to put a stop to this friendship. I don't approve of it. I don't mind acknowledging to you that I've got rather a grudging disposition, and want to keep off all intruders. I ain't a-going, if I know it, to run the risk of being plotted against."

"You are always plotting, and delude yourself into the belief that everybody else is doing the like, I think," said I.

"Perhaps so, Master Copperfield," he replied. "But I've got a motive, as my fellow-partner used to say; and I go at it tooth and nail. I mustn't be put upon, as a numble person, too much. I can't allow people in my way. Really they must come out of the cart, Master Copperfield!"

"I don't understand you," said I.

"Don't you, though?" he returned, with one of his jerks. "I'm astonished at that, Master Copperfield, you being usually so quick! I'll try to be plainer, another time.—Is that Mr Maldon a-horse-back, ringing at the gate, sir?"

"It looks like him," I replied, as carelessly as I could.

Uriah stopped short, put his hands between his great knobs of knees, and doubled himself up with laughter. With perfectly silent laughter. Not a sound escaped from him. I was so repelled by his odious behaviour, particularly by this concluding instance, that I turned away without any ceremony; and left him doubled up in the middle of the garden, like a scarecrow in want of support.

It was not on that evening; but, as I well remember, on the next evening but one, which was a Sunday; that I took Agnes to see Dora. I had arranged the visit, beforehand, with Miss Lavinia; and Agnes was expected to tea.

I was in a flutter of pride and anxiety; pride in my dear little betrothed, and anxiety that Agnes should like her. All the way to Putney, Agnes being inside the stage-coach, and I outside, I pictured Dora to myself in every one of the pretty looks I knew so well; now making up my mind that I should like her to look exactly as she looked at such a time, and then doubting whether I should not prefer her looking as she looked at such another time; and almost worrying myself into a fever about it.

I was troubled by no doubt of her being very pretty, in any case; but it fell out that I had never seen her look so well. She was not in the drawing-room when I presented Agnes to her little aunts, but was shyly keeping out of the way. I knew where to look for her now; and sure enough I found her stopping her ears again, behind the same dull old door.

At first she wouldn't come at all; and then she pleaded for five minutes by my watch. When at length she put her arm through mine, to be taken to the drawing-room, her charming little face was flushed, and had never been so pretty. But, when we went into the room, and it turned pale, she was ten thousand times prettier yet.

Dora was afraid of Agnes. She had told me that she knew Agnes was "too clever." But when she saw her looking at once so cheerful and so earnest, and so thoughtful, and so good, she gave a faint little cry of pleased surprise, and just put her affectionate arms round Agnes's neck, and laid her innocent cheek against her face.

I never was so happy. I never was so pleased as when I saw those two sit down together, side by side. As when I saw my little darling looking up so naturally to those cordial eyes. As when I saw the tender, beautiful regard which Agnes cast upon her.

Miss Lavinia and Miss Clarissa partook, in their way, of my joy. It was the pleasantest tea-table in the world. Miss Clarissa presided. I cut and handed the sweet seed-cake—the little sisters had a bird-like fondness for picking up seeds and pecking at sugar; Miss Lavinia looked on with benignant patronage, as if our happy love were all her work; and we were perfectly contented with ourselves and one another.

The gentle cheerfulness of Agnes went to all their hearts. Her quiet interest in everything that interested Dora; her manner of making acquaintance with Jip (who responded instantly); her pleasant way, when Dora was ashamed to come over to her usual seat by me; her modest grace and ease, eliciting a crowd of blushing little marks of confidence from Dora; seemed to make our circle quite complete.

"I am so glad," said Dora, after tea, "that you like me. I didn't think you would; and I want, more than ever, to be liked, now Julia Mills is gone."

I have omitted to mention it, by the by. Miss Mills had sailed, and Dora and I had gone aboard a great East Indiaman at Gravesend to see her; and we had had preserved ginger, and guava, and other delicacies of that sort for lunch; and we had left Miss Mills weeping on a camp-stool on the quarter-deck, with a large new diary under her arm, in which the original reflections awakened by the contemplation of Ocean were to be recorded under lock and key.

Agnes said, she was afraid I must have given her an unpromising character; but Dora corrected that directly.

"Oh no!" she said, shaking her curls at me; "it was all praise. He thinks so much of your opinion, that I was quite afraid of it."

"My good opinion cannot strengthen his attachment to some people whom he knows," said Agnes, with a smile; "it is not worth their having."

"But please let me have it," said Dora, in her coaxing way, "if you can!"

We made merry about Dora's wanting to be liked, and Dora said I was a goose, and she didn't like me at any rate, and the short evening flew away on gossamer-wings. The time was at hand when the coach was to call for us. I was standing alone before the fire, when Dora came stealing softly in, to give me that usual precious little kiss before I went.

"Don't you think, if I had had her for a friend a long time ago, Doady," said Dora, her bright eyes shining very brightly, and her little right hand idly busying itself with one of the buttons of my coat, "I might have been more clever perhaps?"

"My love!" said I, "what nonsense!"

"Do you think it is nonsense?" returned Dora, without looking at me. "Are you sure it is?"

"Of course I am!"

"I have forgotten," said Dora, still turning the button round and round, "what relation Agnes is to you, you dear bad boy."

"No blood-relation," I replied; "but we were brought up together, like brother and sister."

"I wonder why you ever fell in love with me?" said Dora, beginning on another button of my coat.

"Perhaps because I couldn't see you, and not love you, Dora!"

"Suppose you had never seen me at all," said Dora, going to another button.

"Suppose we had never been born!" said I, gaily.

I wondered what she was thinking about, as I glanced in admiring silence at the little soft hand travelling up the row of buttons on my coat, and at the clustering hair that lay against my breast, and at the lashes of her downcast eyes, slightly rising as they followed her idle fingers. At length her eyes were lifted up to mine, and she stood on tiptoe to give me, more thoughtfully than usual, that precious little kiss—once, twice, three times—and went out of the room.

They all came back together within five minutes afterwards, and Dora's unusual thoughtfulness was quite gone then. She was laughingly resolved to put Jip through the whole of his performances, before the coach came. They took some time (not so much on account of their variety, as Jip's reluctance), and were still unfinished when it was heard at the door. There was a hurried but affectionate parting between Agnes and herself; and Dora was to write to Agnes (who was not to mind her letters being foolish, she said), and Agnes was to write to Dora; and they had a second parting at the coach door, and a third when Dora, in spite of the remonstrances of Miss Lavinia, would come running out once more to remind Agnes at the coach window about writing, and to shake her curls at me on the box.

The stage-coach was to put us down near Covent Garden, where we were to take another stage-coach for Highgate. I was impatient for the short walk in the interval, that Agnes might praise Dora to me. Ah! what praise it was! How lovingly and fervently did it commend the pretty creature I had won, with all her artless graces best displayed, to my most gentle care! How thoughtfully remind me, yet with no pretence of doing so, of the trust in which I held the orphan child!

Never, never, had I loved Dora so deeply and truly, as I loved her that night. When we had again alighted, and were walking in the starlight along the quiet road that led to the Doctor's house, I told Agnes it was her doing.

"When you were sitting by her," said I, "you seemed to be no less *her* guardian angel than mine; and you seem so now, Agnes."

"A poor angel," she returned, "but faithful."

The clear tone of her voice, going straight to my heart, made it natural to me to say:

"The cheerfulness that belongs to you, Agnes (and to no one else that ever I have seen), is so restored, I have observed today, that I have begun to hope you are happier at home?"

"I am happier in myself," she said; "I am quite cheerful and light-hearted."

I glanced at the serene face looking upward, and thought it was the stars that made it seem so noble.

"There has been no change at home," said Agnes, after a few moments.

"No fresh reference," said I, "to—I wouldn't distress you, Agnes, but I cannot help asking—to what we spoke of, when we parted last?"

"No, none," she answered.

"I have thought so much about it."

"You must think less about it. Remember that I confide in simple love and truth at last. Have no apprehensions for me, Trotwood," she added, after a moment; "the step you dread my taking, I shall never take."

Although I think I had never really feared it, in any season of cool reflection, it was an unspeakable relief to me to have this assurance from her own truthful lips. I told her so, earnestly.

"And when this visit is over," said I,—"for we may not be alone another time,—how long is it likely to be, my dear Agnes, before you come to London again?"

"Probably a long time," she replied; "I think it will be best—for papa's sake—to remain at home. We are not likely to meet often, for some time to come; but I shall be a good correspondent of Dora's, and we shall frequently hear of one another that way."

We were now within the little courtyard of the Doctor's cottage. It was growing late. There was a light in the window of Mrs Strong's chamber, and Agnes, pointing to it, bade me good night.

"Do not be troubled," she said, giving me her hand, "by our misfortunes and anxieties. I can be happier in nothing than in your happiness. If you can ever give me help, rely upon it I will ask you for it. God bless you always!"

In her beaming smile, and in these last tones of her cheerful voice, I seemed again to see and hear my little Dora in her company. I stood awhile, looking through the porch at the stars, with a heart full of love and gratitude, and then walked slowly forth. I had engaged a bed at a decent alehouse close by, and was going out at the gate, when, happening to turn my head, I saw a light in the Doctor's study. A half-reproachful fancy came into my mind, that he had been working at the Dictionary without my help. With the view of seeing if this were so, and, in any case, of bidding him good night, if he were yet sitting among his books, I turned back, and going softly across the hall, and gently opening the door, looked in.

The first person whom I saw, to my surprise, by the sober light of the shaded lamp, was Uriah. He was standing close beside it, with one of his skeleton hands over his mouth, and the other resting on the Doctor's table. The Doctor sat in his study chair, covering his face with his hands. Mr Wickfield, sorely troubled and distressed, was leaning forward, irresolutely touching the Doctor's arm.

For an instant, I supposed that the Doctor was ill. I hastily advanced a step under that impression, when I met Uriah's eye, and saw what was the matter. I would have withdrawn, but the Doctor made a gesture to detain me, and I remained.

"At any rate," observed Uriah, with a writhe of his ungainly person, "we may keep the door shut. We needn't make it known to ALL the town."

Saying which, he went on his toes to the door, which I had left open, and carefully closed it. He then came back, and took up his former position. There was an obtrusive show of compassionate zeal in his voice and manner, more intolerable—at least to me—than any demeanour he could have assumed.

"I have felt it incumbent upon me, Master Copperfield," said Uriah, "to point out to Doctor Strong what you and me have already talked about. You didn't exactly understand me, though?"

I gave him a look, but no other answer; and, going to my good old master, said a few words that I meant to be words of comfort and encouragement. He put his hand upon my shoulder, as it had been his custom to do when I was quite a little fellow, but did not lift his grey head.

"As you didn't understand me, Master Copperfield," resumed Uriah in the same officious manner, "I may take the liberty of umbly mentioning, being among friends, that I have called Doctor Strong's attention to the goings-on of Mrs Strong. It's much against the grain with me, I assure you, Copperfield, to be concerned in anything so unpleasant; but really, as it is, we're all mixing ourselves up with what oughtn't to be. That was what my meaning was, sir, when you didn't understand me."

I wonder now, when I recall his leer, that I did not collar him, and try to shake the breath out of his body.

"I dare say I didn't make myself very clear," he went on, "nor you neither. Naturally, we was both of us inclined to give such a subject a wide berth. Hows'ever, at last I have made up my mind to speak plain; and I have mentioned to Doctor Strong that—did you speak, sir?"

This was to the Doctor, who had moaned. The sound might have touched any heart, I thought, but it had no effect upon Uriah's.

"—mentioned to Doctor Strong," he proceeded, "that anyone may see that Mr Maldon, and the lovely and agreeable lady as is Doctor Strong's wife, are too sweet on one another. Really the time is come (we being at present all mixing ourselves up with what oughtn't to be), when Doctor Strong must be told that this was full as plain to everybody as the sun, before Mr Maldon went to India; that Mr Maldon made excuses to come back, for nothing else; and that he's always here, for nothing else. When you come in, sir, I was just putting it to my fellow-partner," towards whom he turned, "to say to Doctor Strong upon his word and honour, whether he'd ever been of this opinion long ago, or not. Come, Mr Wickfield, sir! Would you be so good as tell us? Yes or no, sir? Come, partner!"

"For God's sake, my dear Doctor," said Mr Wickfield again laying his irresolute hand upon the Doctor's arm, "don't attach too much weight to any suspicions I may have entertained."

"There!" cried Uriah, shaking his head. "What a melancholy confirmation: ain't it? Him! Such an old friend! Bless your soul, when I was nothing but a clerk in his office, Copperfield, I've seen him twenty times, if I've seen him once, quite in a taking about it—quite put out, you know (and very proper in him as a father; I'm sure *I* can't blame him), to think that Miss Agnes was mixing herself up with what oughtn't to be."

"My dear Strong," said Mr Wickfield in a tremulous voice, "my good friend, I needn't tell you that it has been my vice to look for some one master motive in everybody, and to try all actions by one narrow test. I may have fallen into such doubts as I have had, through this mistake."

"You have had doubts, Wickfield," said the Doctor, without lifting up his head. "You have had doubts."

"Speak up, fellow-partner," urged Uriah.

"I had, at one time, certainly," said Mr Wickfield. "I—God forgive me—I thought *you* had."

"No, no, no!" returned the Doctor, in a tone of most pathetic grief.

"I thought, at one time," said Mr Wickfield, "that you wished to send Maldon abroad to effect a desirable separation."

"No, no, no!" returned the Doctor. "To give Annie pleasure, by making some provision for the companion of her childhood. Nothing else."

"So I found," said Mr Wickfield. "I couldn't doubt it, when you told me so. But I thought—I implore you to remember the narrow construction which has been my besetting sin—that, in a case where there was so much disparity in point of years—"

"That's the way to put it, you see, Master Copperfield!" observed Uriah, with fawning and offensive pity.

"—a lady of such youth, and such attractions, however real her respect for you, might have been influenced in marrying, by worldly considerations only. I make no allowance for innumerable feelings and circumstances that may have all tended to good. For Heaven's sake remember that!"

"How kind he puts it!" said Uriah, shaking his head.

"Always observing her from one point of view," said Mr Wickfield; "but by all that is dear to you, my old friend, I entreat you to consider what it was; I am forced to confess now, having no escape—"

"No! There's no way out of it, Mr Wickfield, sir," observed Uriah, "when it's got to this."

"—that I did," said Mr Wickfield, glancing helplessly and distractedly at his partner, "that I did doubt her, and think her wanting in her duty to you; and that I did sometimes, if I must say all, feel averse to Agnes being in such a familiar relation towards her, as to see what I saw, or in my diseased theory fancied that I saw. I never mentioned this to anyone. I never meant it to be known to anyone. And though it is terrible to you to hear," said Mr Wickfield, quite subdued, "if you knew how terrible it is for me to tell, you would feel compassion for me!"

The Doctor, in the perfect goodness of his nature, put out his hand. Mr Wickfield held it for a little while in his, with his head bowed down.

"I am sure," said Uriah, writhing himself into the silence like a Conger-eel, "that this is a subject full of unpleasantness to everybody. But since we have got so far, I ought to take the liberty of mentioning that Copperfield has noticed it too."

I turned upon him, and asked him how he dared refer to me!

"Oh! it's very kind of you, Copperfield," returned Uriah, undulating all over, "and we all know what an amiable character yours is; but you know that the moment I spoke to you the other night, you knew what I meant. You know you knew what I meant, Copperfield. Don't deny it! You deny it with the best intentions; but don't do it, Copperfield."

I saw the mild eye of the good old Doctor turned upon me for a moment, and I felt that the confession of my old misgivings and remembrances was too plainly written in my face to be overlooked. It was of no use raging. I could not undo that. Say what I would, I could not unsay it.

We were silent again, and remained so, until the Doctor rose and walked twice or thrice across the room. Presently he returned to where his chair stood; and, leaning on the back of it, and occasionally putting his handkerchief to his eyes, with a simple honesty that did him more honour, to my thinking, than any disguise he could have effected, said:

"I have been much to blame. I believe I have been very much to blame. I have exposed one whom I hold in my heart, to trials and aspersions—I call them aspersions, even to have been conceived in anybody's inmost mind—of which she never, but for me, could have been the object."

Uriah Heep gave a kind of snivel. I think to express sympathy.

"Of which my Annie," said the Doctor, "never, but for me, could have been the object. Gentlemen, I am old now, as you know; I do not feel, tonight, that I have much to live for. But my life—my Life—upon the truth and honour of the dear lady who has been the subject of this conversation!"

I do not think that the best embodiment of chivalry, the realization of the handsomest and most romantic figure ever imagined by painter, could have said this, with a more impressive and affecting dignity than the plain old Doctor did.

"But I am not prepared," he went on, "to deny—perhaps I may have been, without knowing it, in some degree prepared to admit—that I may have unwittingly ensnared that lady into an unhappy marriage. I am a man quite unaccustomed to observe; and I cannot but believe that the observation of several people, of different ages and positions, all too plainly tending in one direction (and that so natural), is better than mine."

I had often admired, as I have elsewhere described, his benignant manner towards his youthful wife; but the respectful tenderness he manifested in every reference to her on this occasion, and the almost reverential manner in which he put away from him the lightest doubt of her integrity, exalted him, in my eyes, beyond description.

"I married that lady," said the Doctor, "when she was extremely young. I took her to myself when her character was scarcely formed. So far as it was developed, it had been my happiness to form it. I knew her father well. I knew her well. I had taught her what I could, for the love of all her beautiful and virtuous qualities. If I did her wrong; as I fear I did, in taking advantage (but I never meant it) of her gratitude and her affection; I ask pardon of that lady, in my heart!"

He walked across the room, and came back to the same place; holding the chair with a grasp that trembled, like his subdued voice, in its earnestness.

"I regarded myself as a refuge, for her, from the dangers and vicissitudes of life. I persuaded myself that, unequal though we were in years, she would live tranquilly and contentedly with me. I did not shut out of my consideration the time when I should leave her free, and still young and still beautiful, but with her judgement more matured—no, gentlemen—upon my truth!"

His homely figure seemed to be lightened up by his fidelity and generosity. Every word he uttered had a force that no other grace could have imparted to it.

"My life with this lady has been very happy. Until tonight, I have had uninterrupted occasion to bless the day on which I did her great injustice."

His voice, more and more faltering in the utterance of these words, stopped for a few moments; then he went on:

"Once awakened from my dream—I have been a poor dreamer, in one way or other, all my life—I see how natural it is that she should have some regretful feeling towards her old companion and her equal. That she does regard him with some innocent regret, with some blameless thoughts of what might have been, but for me, is, I fear, too true. Much that I have seen, but not noted, has come back upon me with new meaning, during this last trying hour. But, beyond this, gentlemen, the dear lady's name never must be coupled with a word, a breath, of doubt."

For a little while, his eye kindled and his voice was firm; for a little while he was again silent. Presently, he proceeded as before:

"It only remains for me, to bear the knowledge of the unhappiness I have occasioned, as submissively as I can. It is she who should reproach; not I. To save her from misconstruction, cruel misconstruction, that even my friends have not been able to avoid, becomes my duty. The more retired we live, the better I shall discharge it. And when the time comes—may it come soon, if it be His merciful pleasure!—when my death shall release her from constraint, I shall close my eyes upon her honoured face, with unbounded confidence and love; and leave her, with no sorrow then, to happier and brighter days."

I could not see him for the tears which his earnestness and goodness, so adorned by, and so adorning, the perfect simplicity of his manner, brought into my eyes. He had moved to the door, when he added:

"Gentlemen, I have shown you my heart. I am sure you will respect it. What we have said tonight is never to be said more. Wickfield, give me an old friend's arm upstairs!"

Mr Wickfield hastened to him. Without interchanging a word they went slowly out of the room together, Uriah looking after them.

"Well, Master Copperfield!" said Uriah, meekly turning to me. "The thing hasn't took quite the turn that might have been expected, for the old Scholar—what an excellent man!—is as blind as a brickbat; but *this* family's out of the cart, I think!"

I needed but the sound of his voice to be so madly enraged as I never was before, and never have been since.

"You villain," said I, "what do you mean by entrapping me into your schemes? How dare you appeal to me just now, you false rascal, as if we had been in discussion together?"

As we stood, front to front, I saw so plainly, in the stealthy exultation of his face, what I already so plainly knew; I mean that he forced his confidence upon me, expressly to make me miserable, and had set a deliberate trap for me in this very matter; that I couldn't bear it. The whole of his lank cheek was invitingly before me, and I struck it with my open hand with that force that my fingers tingled as if I had burnt them.

He caught the hand in his, and we stood in that connexion, looking at each other. We stood so, a long time; long enough for me to see the white marks of my fingers die out of the deep red of his cheek, and leave it a deeper red.

"Copperfield," he said at length, in a breathless voice, "have you taken leave of your senses?"

"I have taken leave of you," said I, wresting my hand away. "You dog, I'll know no more of you."

"Won't you?" said he, constrained by the pain of his cheek to put his hand there. "Perhaps you won't be able to help it. Isn't this ungrateful of you, now?"

"I have shown you often enough," said I, "that I despise you. I have shown you now, more plainly, that I do. Why should I dread your doing your worst to all about you? What else do you ever do?"

He perfectly understood this allusion to the considerations that had hitherto restrained me in my communications with him. I rather think that neither the blow, nor the allusion, would have escaped me, but for the assurance I had had from Agnes that night. It is no matter.

There was another long pause. His eyes, as he looked at me, seemed to take every shade of colour that could make eyes ugly.

"Copperfield," he said, removing his hand from his cheek, "you have always gone against me. I know you always used to be against me at Mr Wickfield's."

"You may think what you like," said I, still in a towering rage. "If it is not true, so much the worthier you."

"And yet I always liked you, Copperfield!" he rejoined.

I deigned to make him no reply; and, taking up my hat, was going out to bed, when he came between me and the door.

"Copperfield," he said, "there must be two parties to a quarrel. I won't be one."

"You may go to the devil!" said I.

"Don't say that!" he replied. "I know you'll be sorry afterwards. How can you make yourself so inferior to me, as to show such a bad spirit? But I forgive you."

"You forgive me!" I repeated disdainfully.

"I do, and you can't help yourself," replied Uriah. "To think of your going and attacking *me,* that have always been a friend to you! But there can't be a quarrel without two parties, and I won't be one. I will be a friend to you, in spite of you. So now you know what you've got to expect."

The necessity of carrying on this dialogue (his part in which was very slow; mine very quick) in a low tone, that the house might not be disturbed at an unseasonable hour, did not improve my temper; though my passion was cooling down. Merely telling him that I should expect from him what I always had expected, and had never yet been disappointed in, I opened the door upon him, as if he had been a great walnut put there to be cracked, and went out of the house. But he slept out of the house too, at his mother's lodging; and before I had gone many hundred yards, came up with me.

"You know, Copperfield," he said, in my ear (I did not turn my head), "you're in quite a wrong position"; which I felt to be true, and that made me chafe the more; "you can't make this a brave thing, and you can't help being forgiven. I don't intend to mention it to mother, nor to any living soul. I'm determined to forgive you. But I do wonder that you should lift your hand against a person that you knew to be so umble!"

I felt only less mean than he. He knew me better than I knew myself. If he had retorted or openly exasperated me, it would have been a relief and a justification; but he had put me on a slow fire, on which I lay tormented half the night.

In the morning, when I came out, the early church-bell was ringing, and he was walking up and down with his mother. He addressed me as if nothing had happened, and I could do no less than reply. I had struck him hard enough to give him the toothache, I suppose. At all events his face was tied up in a black silk handkerchief, which, with his hat perched on the top of it, was far from improving his appearance. I heard that he went to a dentist's in London on the Monday morning, and had a tooth out. I hope it was a double one.

The Doctor gave out that he was not quite well; and remained alone, for a considerable part of every day, during the remainder of the visit. Agnes and her father had been gone a week, before we resumed our usual work. On the day preceding its resumption, the Doctor gave me with his own hands a folded note not sealed. It was addressed to myself; and laid an injunction on me, in a few affectionate words, never to refer to the subject of that evening. I had confided it to my aunt, but to no one else. It was not a subject I could discuss with Agnes, and Agnes certainly had not the least suspicion of what had passed.

Neither, I felt convinced, had Mrs Strong then. Several weeks elapsed before I saw the least change in her. It came on slowly, like a cloud when there is no wind. At first, she seemed to wonder at the gentle compassion with which the Doctor spoke to her, and at his wish that she should have her mother with her, to relieve the dull monotony of her life. Often, when we were at work, and she was sitting by, I would see her pausing and looking at him with that memorable face. Afterwards, I sometimes observed her rise, with her eyes full of tears, and go out of the room. Gradually an unhappy shadow fell upon her beauty, and deepened every day. Mrs Markleham was a regular inmate of the cottage then; but she talked and talked, and saw nothing.

As this change stole on Annie, once like sunshine in the Doctor's house, the Doctor became older in appearance, and more grave; but the sweetness of his temper, the placid kindness of his manner, and his benevolent solicitude for her, if they were capable of any increase, were increased. I saw him once, early on the morning of her birthday, when she came to sit in the window while we were at work (which she had always done, but now began to do with a timid and uncertain air that I thought very touching), take her forehead between his hands, kiss it, and go hurriedly away, too much moved to remain. I saw her stand where he had left her, like a statue; and then bend down her head, and clasp her hands, and weep, I cannot say how sorrowfully.

Sometimes, after that, I fancied that she tried to speak even to me, in intervals when we were left alone. But she never uttered a word. The Doctor always had some new project for her participating in amusements away from home, with her mother; and Mrs

Markleham, who was very fond of amusements, and very easily dissatisfied with anything else, entered into them with great good-will, and was loud in her commendations. But Annie, in a spiritless unhappy way, only went whither she was led, and seemed to have no care for anything.

I did not know what to think. Neither did my aunt; who must have walked, at various times, a hundred miles in her uncertainty. What was strangest of all was, that the only real relief which seemed to make its way into the secret region of this domestic unhappiness, made its way there in the person of Mr Dick.

What his thoughts were on the subject, or what his observation was, I am as unable to explain, as I dare say he would have been to assist me in the task. But, as I have recorded in the narrative of my school days, his veneration for the Doctor was unbounded; and there is a subtlety of perception in real attachment, even when it is borne towards man by one of the lower animals, which leaves the highest intellect behind. To this mind of the heart, if I may call it so, in Mr Dick, some bright ray of the truth shot straight.

He had proudly resumed his privilege, in many of his spare hours, of walking up and down the garden with the Doctor; as he had been accustomed to pace up and down The Doctor's Walk at Canterbury. But matters were no sooner in this state, than he devoted all his spare time (and got up earlier to make it more) to these perambulations. If he had never been so happy as when the Doctor read that marvellous performance, the Dictionary, to him; he was now quite miserable unless the Doctor pulled it out of his pocket, and began. When the Doctor and I were engaged, he now fell into the custom of walking up and down with Mrs Strong, and helping her to trim her favourite flowers, or weed the beds. I dare say he rarely spoke a dozen words in an hour: but his quiet interest, and his wistful face, found immediate response in both their breasts; each knew that the other liked him, and that he loved both; and he became what no one else could be—a link between them.

When I think of him, with his impenetrably wise face, walking up and down with the Doctor, delighted to be battered by the hard words in the Dictionary; when I think of him carrying huge watering-pots after Annie; kneeling down, in very paws of gloves, at patient microscopic work among the little leaves; expressing as no philosopher could have expressed, in everything he did, a delicate desire to be her friend; showering sympathy, trustfulness, and affection, out of every hole in the watering-pot; when I think of him never wandering in that better mind of his to which unhappiness addressed itself, never bringing the unfortunate King Charles into the garden, never wavering in his grateful service, never diverted from his knowledge that there was something wrong, or from his wish to set it right—I really feel almost ashamed of having known that he was not quite in his wits, taking account of the utmost I have done with mine.

"Nobody but myself, Trot, knows what that man is!" my aunt would proudly remark, when we conversed about it. "Dick will distinguish himself yet!"

I must refer to one other topic before I close this chapter. While the visit at the Doctor's was still in progress, I observed that the postman brought two or three letters every morning for Uriah Heep, who remained at Highgate until the rest went back, it being a leisure time; and that these were always directed in a business-like manner by Mr Micawber, who now assumed a round legal hand. I was glad to infer, from these slight premises, that Mr Micawber was doing well; and consequently was much surprised to receive, about this time, the following letter from his amiable wife.

"CANTERBURY, *Monday Evening.*

"You will doubtless be surprised, my dear Mr Copperfield, to receive this communication. Still more so, by its contents. Still more so, by the stipulation of implicit confidence which I beg to impose. But my feelings as a wife and mother require relief; and as I do not wish to consult my family (already obnoxious to the feelings of Mr Micawber), I know no one of whom I can better ask advice than my friend and former lodger.

"You may be aware, my dear Mr Copperfield, that between myself and Mr Micawber (whom I will never desert), there has always been preserved a spirit of mutual confidence. Mr Micawber may have occasionally given a bill without consulting me, or he may have misled me as to the period when that obligation would become due. This has actually happened. But, in general, Mr Micawber has had no secrets from the bosom of affection—I allude to his wife—and has invariably, on our retirement to rest, recalled the events of the day.

"You will picture to yourself, my dear Mr Copperfield, what the poignancy of my feelings must be, when I inform you that Mr Micawber is entirely changed. He is reserved. He is secret. His life is a mystery to the partner of his joys and sorrows—I again allude to his wife—and if I should assure you that beyond knowing that it is passed from morning to night at the office, I now know less of it than I do of the man in the south, connected with whose mouth the thoughtless children repeat an idle tale respecting cold plum porridge, I should adopt a popular fallacy to express an actual fact.

"But this is not all. Mr Micawber is morose. He is severe. He is estranged from our eldest son and daughter, he has no pride in his twins, he looks with an eye of coldness even on the unoffending stranger who last became a member of our circle. The pecuniary means of meeting our expenses, kept down to the utmost farthing, are obtained from him with great difficulty, and even under fearful threats that he will Settle himself (the exact expression); and he inexorably refuses to give any explanation whatever of this distracting policy.

"This is hard to bear. This is heart-breaking. If you will advise me, knowing my feeble powers such as they are, how you think it will be best to exert them in a dilemma so unwonted, you will add another friendly obligation to the many you have already rendered me. With loves from the children, and a smile from the happily-unconscious stranger, I remain, dear Mr Copperfield,

"Your afflicted,

"EMMA MICAWBER."

I did not feel justified in giving a wife of Mrs Micawber's experience any other recommendation, than that she should try to reclaim Mr Micawber by patience and kindness (as I knew she would in any case); but the letter set me thinking about him very much.

Chapter XLIII

ANOTHER RETROSPECT

ONCE again, let me pause upon a memorable period of my life. Let me stand aside, to see the phantoms of those days go by me, accompanying the shadow of myself, in dim procession.

Weeks, months, seasons, pass along. They seem little more than a summer day and a winter evening. Now, the Common where I walk with Dora is all in bloom, a field of bright gold; and now the unseen heather lies in mounds and bunches underneath a covering of snow. In a breath, the river that flows through our Sunday walks is sparkling in the summer sun, is ruffled by the winter wind, or thickened with drifting heaps of ice. Faster than ever river ran towards the sea, it flashes, darkens, and rolls away.

Not a thread changes, in the house of the two little bird-like ladies. The clock ticks over the fireplace, the weather-glass hangs in the hall. Neither clock nor weather-glass is ever right; but we believe in both, devoutly.

I have come legally to man's estate. I have attained the dignity of twenty-one. But this is a sort of dignity that may be thrust upon one. Let me think what I have achieved.

I have tamed that savage stenographic mystery. I make a respectable income by it. I am in high repute for my accomplishment in all pertaining to the art, and am joined with eleven others in reporting the debates in Parliament for a Morning Newspaper. Night after night, I record predictions that never come to pass, professions that are never fulfilled, explanations that are only meant to mystify. I wallow in words. Britannia, that unfortunate female, is always before me, like a trussed fowl: skewered through and through with office-pens, and bound hand and foot with red tape. I am sufficiently behind the scenes to know the worth of political life. I am quite an Infidel about it, and shall never be converted.

My dear old Traddles has tried his hand at the same pursuit, but it is not in Traddles's way. He is perfectly good-humoured respecting his failure, and reminds me that he always did consider himself slow. He has occasional employment on the same newspaper, in getting up the facts of dry subjects, to be written about and embellished by more fertile minds. He is called to the bar; and with admirable industry and self-denial has scraped another hundred pounds together, to fee a Conveyancer whose chambers he attends. A great deal of very hot port wine was consumed at his call; and, considering the figure, I should think the Inner Temple must have made a profit by it.

I have come out in another way. I have taken with fear and trembling to authorship. I wrote a little something, in secret, and sent it to a magazine, and it was published in the magazine. Since then, I have taken heart to write a good many trifling pieces. Now, I am regularly paid for them. Altogether, I am well off; when I tell my income on the fingers of my left hand, I pass the third finger and take in the fourth to the middle joint.

We have removed, from Buckingham Street, to a pleasant little cottage very near the one I looked at, when my enthusiasm first came on. My aunt, however (who has sold the house at Dover, to good advantage), is not going to remain here, but intends removing herself to a still more tiny cottage close at hand. What does this portend? My marriage? Yes!

Yes! I am going to be married to Dora! Miss Lavinia and Miss Clarissa have given their consent; and if ever canary birds were in a flutter, they are. Miss Lavinia, self-charged with the superintendence of my darling's wardrobe, is constantly cutting out brown-paper cuirasses, and differing in opinion from a highly respectable young man, with a long bundle, and a yard measure under his arm. A dressmaker, always stabbed in the breast with a needle and thread, boards and lodges in the house; and seems to me, eating, drinking, or sleeping, never to take her thimble off. They make a lay-figure of my dear. They are always sending for her to come and try something on. We can't be happy together for five minutes in the evening, but some intrusive female knocks at the door, and says, "Oh, if you please, Miss Dora, would you step upstairs!"

Miss Clarissa and my aunt roam all over London, to find out articles of furniture for Dora and me to look at. It would be better for them to buy the goods at once, without this ceremony of inspection; for, when we go to see a kitchen fender and meat-screen, Dora sees a Chinese house for Jip, with little bells on the top, and prefers that. And it takes a long time to accustom Jip to his new residence, after we have bought it; whenever he goes in or out, he makes all the little bells ring, and is horribly frightened.

Peggotty comes up to make herself useful, and falls to work immediately. Her department appears to be, to clean everything over and over again. She rubs everything that can be rubbed, until it shines, like her own honest forehead, with perpetual friction. And now it is, that I begin to see her solitary brother passing through the dark streets at night, and looking, as he goes, among the wandering faces. I never speak to him at such an hour. I know too well, as his grave figure passes onward, what he seeks, and what he dreads.

Why does Traddles look so important when he calls upon me this afternoon in the Commons—where I still occasionally attend, for form's sake, when I have time? The realization of my boyish day-dreams is at hand. I am going to take out the licence.

It is a little document to do so much; and Traddles contemplates it, as it lies upon my desk, half in admiration, half in awe. There are the names, in the sweet old visionary connexion, David Copperfield and Dora Spenlow; and there, in the corner, is that Parental Institution, the Stamp Office, which is so benignantly interested in the various transactions of human life, looking down upon our Union; and there is the Archbishop of Canterbury invoking a blessing on us in print, and doing it as cheap as could possibly be expected.

Nevertheless, I am in a dream, a flustered, happy, hurried dream. I can't believe that it is going to be; and yet I can't believe but that everyone I pass in the street, must have some kind of perception, that I am to be married the day after tomorrow. The Surrogate knows me, when I go down to be sworn; and disposes of me easily, as if there were a Masonic understanding between us. Traddles is not at all wanted, but is in attendance as my general backer.

"I hope the next time you come here, my dear fellow," I say to Traddles, "it will be on the same errand for yourself. And I hope it will be soon."

"Thank you for your good wishes, my dear Copperfield," he replies. "I hope so too. It's a satisfaction to know that she'll wait for me any length of time, and that she really is the dearest girl—"

"When are you to meet her at the coach?" I ask.

"At seven," says Traddles, looking at his plain old silver watch—the very watch he once took a wheel out of, at school, to make a water-mill. "That is about Miss Wickfield's time, is it not?"

"A little earlier. Her time is half past eight."

"I assure you, my dear boy," says Traddles, "I am almost as pleased as if I were going to be married myself, to think that this event is coming to such a happy termination. And really the great friendship and consideration of personally associating Sophy with the joyful occasion, and inviting her to be a bridesmaid in conjunction with Miss Wickfield, demands my warmest thanks. I am extremely sensible of it."

I hear him, and shake hands with him; and we talk, and walk, and dine, and so on; but I don't believe it. Nothing is real.

Sophy arrives at the house of Dora's aunts, in due course. She has the most agreeable of faces,—not absolutely beautiful, but extraordinarily pleasant,—and is one of the most genial, unaffected, frank, engaging creatures I have ever seen. Traddles presents her to us with great pride; and rubs his hands for ten minutes by the clock, with every individual hair upon his head standing on tiptoe, when I congratulate him in a corner on his choice.

I have brought Agnes from the Canterbury coach, and her cheerful and beautiful face is among us for the second time. Agnes has a great liking for Traddles, and it is capital to see them meet, and to observe the glory of Traddles as he commends the dearest girl in the world to her acquaintance.

Still I don't believe it. We have a delightful evening, and are supremely happy; but I don't believe it yet. I can't collect myself. I can't check off my happiness as it takes place. I feel in a misty and unsettled kind of state; as if I had got up very early in the morning a week or two ago, and had never been to bed since. I can't make out when yesterday was. I seem to have been carrying the licence about, in my pocket, many months.

Next day, too, when we all go in a flock to see the house—our house—Dora's and mine—I am quite unable to regard myself as its master. I seem to be there, by permission of somebody else. I half expect the real master to come home presently, and say he is glad to see me. Such a beautiful little house as it is, with everything so bright and new; with the flowers on the carpets looking as if freshly gathered, and the green leaves on the paper as if they had just come out; with the spotless muslin curtains, and the blushing rose-coloured furniture, and Dora's garden hat with the blue ribbon—do I remember, now, how I loved her in such another hat when I first knew her!—already hanging on its little peg; the guitar-case quite at home on its heels in a corner; and everybody tumbling over Jip's pagoda, which is much too big for the establishment.

Another happy evening, quite as unreal as all the rest of it, and I steal into the usual room before going away. Dora is not there. I suppose they have not done trying on yet. Miss Lavinia peeps in, and tells me mysteriously that she will not be long. She is rather long, notwithstanding; but by and by I hear a rustling at the door, and someone taps.

I say, "Come in!" but someone taps again.

I go to the door, wondering who it is; there, I meet a pair of bright eyes, and a blushing face; they are Dora's eyes and face, and Miss Lavinia has dressed her in tomorrow's dress, bonnet and all, for me to see. I take my little wife to my heart; and Miss Lavinia gives a little scream because I tumble the bonnet, and Dora laughs and cries at once, because I am so pleased; and I believe it less than ever.

"Do you think it pretty, Doady?" says Dora.

Pretty! I should rather think I did.

"And are you sure you like me very much?" says Dora.

The topic is fraught with such danger to the bonnet, that Miss Lavinia gives another little scream, and begs me to understand that Dora is only to be looked at, and on no account to be touched. So Dora stands in a delightful state of confusion for a minute or two, to be admired; and then takes off her bonnet—looking so natural without it!—and runs away with it in her hand; and comes dancing down again in her own familiar dress, and asks Jip if I have got a beautiful little wife, and whether he'll forgive her for being married, and kneels down to make him stand upon the cookery-book, for the last time in her single life.

I go home, more incredulous than ever, to a lodging that I have hard by; and get up very early in the morning, to ride to the Highgate road and fetch my aunt.

I have never seen my aunt in such state. She is dressed in lavender-coloured silk, and has a white bonnet on, and is amazing. Janet has dressed her, and is there to look at me. Peggotty is ready to go to church, intending to behold the ceremony from the gallery. Mr Dick, who is to give my darling to me at the altar, has had his hair curled. Traddles, whom I have taken up by appointment at the turnpike, presents a dazzling combination of cream colour and light blue; and both he and Mr Dick have a general effect about them of being all gloves.

No doubt I see this, because I know it is so; but I am astray, and seem to see nothing. Nor do I believe anything whatever. Still, as we drive along in an open carriage, this fairy marriage is real enough to fill me with a sort of wondering pity for the unfortunate people who have no part in it, but are sweeping out the shops, and going to their daily occupations.

My aunt sits with my hand in hers all the way. When we stop a little way short of the church, to put down Peggotty, whom we have brought on the box, she gives it a squeeze, and me a kiss.

"God bless you, Trot! My own boy never could be dearer. I think of poor dear Baby this morning."

"So do I. And of all I owe to you, dear aunt."

"Tut, child!" says my aunt; and gives her hand in overflowing cordiality to Traddles, who then gives his to Mr Dick, who then gives his to me, who then gives mine to Traddles, and then we come to the church door.

The church is calm enough, I am sure; but it might be a steam-power loom in full action, for any sedative effect it has on me. I am too far gone for that.

The rest is all a more or less incoherent dream.

A dream of their coming in with Dora; of the pew-opener arranging us, like a drill-sergeant, before the altar rails; of my wondering, even then, why pew-openers must always be the most disagreeable females procurable, and whether there is any religious dread of a disastrous infection of good-humour which renders it indispensable to set those vessels of vinegar upon the road to Heaven.

Of the clergyman and clerk appearing; of a few boatmen and some other people strolling in; of an ancient mariner behind me, strongly flavouring the church with rum; of the service beginning in a deep voice, and our all being very attentive.

Of Miss Lavinia, who acts as a semi-auxiliary bridesmaid, being the first to cry, and of her doing homage (as I take it) to the memory of Pidger, in sobs; of Miss Clarissa applying a smelling-bottle; of Agnes taking care of Dora; of my aunt endeavouring to represent herself as a model of sternness, with tears rolling down her face; of little Dora trembling very much, and making her responses in faint whispers.

Of our kneeling down together, side by side; of Dora's trembling less and less, but always clasping Agnes by the hand; of the service being got through, quietly and gravely; of our all looking at each other in an April state of smiles and tears, when it is over; of my young wife being hysterical in the vestry, and crying for her poor papa, her dear papa.

Of her soon cheering up again, and our signing the register all round. Of my going into the gallery for Peggotty to bring *her* to sign it; of Peggotty's hugging me in a corner, and telling me she saw my own dear mother married; of its being over, and our going away.

Of my walking so proudly and lovingly down the aisle with my sweet wife upon my arm, through a mist of half-seen people, pulpits, monuments, pews, fonts, organs, and church windows, in which there flutter faint airs of association with my childish church at home, so long ago.

Of their whispering, as we pass, what a youthful couple we are, and what a pretty little wife she is. Of our all being so merry and talkative in the carriage going back. Of Sophy telling us that when she saw Traddles (whom I had entrusted with the licence) asked for it, she almost fainted, having been convinced that he would contrive to lose it, or to have his pocket picked. Of Agnes laughing gaily; and of Dora being so fond of Agnes that she will not be separated from her, but still keeps her hand.

Of there being a breakfast, with abundance of things, pretty and substantial, to eat and drink, whereof I partake, as I should do in any other dream, without the least perception of their flavour; eating and drinking, as I may say, nothing but love and marriage, and no more believing in the viands than in anything else.

Of my making a speech in the same dreamy fashion, without having an idea of what I want to say, beyond such as may be comprehended in the full conviction that I haven't said it. Of our being very sociably and simply happy (always in a dream though); and of Jip's having wedding cake, and its not agreeing with him afterwards.

Of the pair of hired post-horses being ready, and of Dora's going away to change her dress. Of my aunt and Miss Clarissa remaining with us; and our walking in the garden; and my aunt, who has made quite a speech at breakfast touching Dora's aunts, being mightily amused with herself, but a little proud of it too.

Of Dora's being ready, and of Miss Lavinia's hovering about her, loth to lose the pretty toy that has given her so much pleasant occupation. Of Dora's making a long series of surprised discoveries that she has forgotten all sorts of little things; and of everybody's running everywhere to fetch them.

Of their all closing about Dora, when at last she begins to say good-bye, looking, with their bright colours and ribbons, like a bed of flowers. Of my darling being almost smothered among the flowers, and coming out, laughing and crying both together, to my jealous arms.

Of my wanting to carry Jip (who is to go along with us), and Dora's saying no, that she must carry him, or else he'll think she don't like him any more, now she is married, and will break his heart. Of our going, arm in arm, and Dora stopping and looking back, and saying, "If I have ever been cross or ungrateful to anybody, don't remember it!" and bursting into tears.

Of her waving her little hand, and our going away once more. Of her once more stopping, and looking back, and hurrying to Agnes, and giving Agnes, above all the others, her last kisses and farewells.

We drive away together, and I awake from the dream. I believe it at last. It is my dear, dear, little wife beside me, whom I love so well!

"Are you happy now, you foolish boy?" says Dora, "and sure you don't repent?"

I have stood aside to see the phantoms of those days go by me. They are gone, and I resume the journey of my story.

Chapter XLIV

OUR HOUSEKEEPING

IT was a strange condition of things, the honey-moon being over, and the bridesmaids gone home, when I found myself sitting down in my own small house with Dora; quite thrown out of employment, as I may say, in respect of the delicious old occupation of making love.

It seemed such an extraordinary thing to have Dora always there. It was so unaccountable not to be obliged to go out to see her, not to have any occasion to be tormenting myself about her, not to have to write to her, not to be scheming and devising opportunities of being alone with her. Sometimes of an evening, when I looked up from my writing, and saw her seated opposite, I would lean back in my chair, and think how queer it was that there we were, alone together as a matter of course—nobody's business any more—all the romance of our engagement put away upon a shelf, to rust—no one to please but one another—one another to please, for life.

When there was a debate, and I was kept out very late, it seemed so strange to me, as I was walking home, to think that Dora was at home! It was such a wonderful thing, at first, to have her coming softly down to talk to me as I ate my supper. It was such a stupendous thing to know for certain that she put her hair in papers. It was altogether such an astonishing event to see her do it!

I doubt whether two young birds could have known less about keeping house, than I and my pretty Dora did. We had a servant, of course. She kept house for us. I have still a latent belief that she must have been Mrs Crupp's daughter in disguise, we had such an awful time of it with Mary Anne.

Her name was Paragon. Her nature was represented to us, when we engaged her, as being feebly expressed in her name. She had a written character, as large as a proclamation; and, according to this document, could do everything of a domestic nature that ever I heard of, and a great many things that I never did hear of. She was a woman in the prime of life; of a severe countenance; and subject (particularly in the arms) to a sort of perpetual measles or fiery rash. She had a cousin in the Life-Guards, with such long legs that he looked like the afternoon shadow of somebody else. His shell-jacket was as much too little for him as he was too big for the premises. He made the cottage smaller than it need have been, by being so very much out of proportion to it. Besides which, the walls were not thick, and whenever he passed the evening at our house, we always knew of it by hearing one continual growl in the kitchen.

Our treasure was warranted sober and honest. I am therefore willing to believe that she was in a fit when we found her under the boiler; and that the deficient tea-spoons were attributable to the dustman.

But she preyed upon our minds dreadfully. We felt our inexperience, and were unable to help ourselves. We should have been at her mercy, if she had had any; but she was a remorseless woman, and had none. She was the cause of our first little quarrel.

"My dearest life," I said one day to Dora, "do you think Mary Anne has any idea of time?"

"Why, Doady?" inquired Dora, looking up, innocently, from her drawing.

"My love, because it's five, and we were to have dined at four."

Dora glanced wistfully at the clock, and hinted that she thought it was too fast.

"On the contrary, my love," said I, referring to my watch, "it's a few minutes too slow."

My little wife came and sat upon my knee, to coax me to be quiet, and drew a line with her pencil down the middle of my nose; but I couldn't dine off that, though it was very agreeable.

"Don't you think, my dear," said I, "it would be better for you to remonstrate with Mary Anne?"

"Oh no, please! I couldn't, Doady!" said Dora.

"Why not, my love?" I gently asked.

"Oh, because I am such a little goose," said Dora, "and she knows I am!"

I thought this sentiment so incompatible with the establishment of any system of check on Mary Anne, that I frowned a little.

"Oh, what ugly wrinkles in my bad boy's forehead!" said Dora, and still being on my knee, she traced them with her pencil; putting it to her rosy lips to make it mark blacker, and working at my forehead with a quaint little mockery of being industrious, that quite delighted me in spite of myself.

"There's a good child," said Dora, "it makes its face so much prettier to laugh."

"But, my love," said I.

"No, no! please!" cried Dora, with a kiss, "don't be a naughty Blue Beard! Don't be serious!"

"My precious wife," said I, "we must be serious sometimes. Come! Sit down on this chair, close beside me! Give me the pencil! There! Now let us talk sensibly. You know, dear"; what a little hand it was to hold, and what a tiny wedding-ring it was to see! "You know, my love, it is not exactly comfortable to have to go out without one's dinner. Now, is it?"

"N-n-no!" replied Dora, faintly.

"My love, how you tremble!"

"Because I KNOW you're going to scold me," exclaimed Dora, in a piteous voice.

"My sweet, I am only going to reason."

"Oh, but reasoning is worse than scolding!" exclaimed Dora, in despair. "I didn't marry to be reasoned with. If you meant to reason with such a poor little thing as I am, you ought to have told me so, you cruel boy!"

I tried to pacify Dora, but she turned away her face, and shook her curls from side to side, and said, "You cruel, cruel boy!" so many times, that I really did not exactly know what to do: so I took a few turns up and down the room in my uncertainty, and came back again.

"Dora, my darling!"

"No, I am not your darling. Because you *must* be sorry that you married me, or else you wouldn't reason with me!" returned Dora.

I felt so injured by the inconsequential nature of this charge, that it gave me courage to be grave.

"Now, my own Dora," said I, "you are very childish, and are talking nonsense. You must remember, I am sure, that I was obliged to go out yesterday when dinner was half over; and that, the day before, I was made quite unwell by being obliged to eat underdone veal in a hurry; today, I don't dine at all—and I am afraid to say how long we waited for breakfast—and *then* the water didn't boil. I don't mean to reproach you, my dear, but this is not comfortable."

"Oh, you cruel, cruel boy, to say I am a disagreeable wife!" cried Dora.

"Now, my dear Dora, you must know that I never said that!"

"You said I wasn't comfortable!" said Dora.

"I said the housekeeping was not comfortable!"

"It's exactly the same thing!" cried Dora. And she evidently thought so, for she wept most grievously.

I took another turn across the room, full of love for my pretty wife, and distracted by self-accusatory inclinations to knock my head against the door. I sat down again, and said:

"I am not blaming you, Dora. We have both a great deal to learn. I am only trying to show you, my dear, that you must—you really must" (I was resolved not to give this up)—"accustom yourself to look after Mary Anne. Likewise to act a little for yourself, and me."

"I wonder, I do, at your making such ungrateful speeches," sobbed Dora. "When you know that the other day, when you said you would like a little bit of fish, I went out myself, miles and miles, and ordered it, to surprise you."

"And it was very kind of you, my own darling," said I. "I felt it so much that I wouldn't on any account have even mentioned that you bought a Salmon—which was too much for two. Or that it cost one pound six—which was more than we can afford."

"You enjoyed it very much," sobbed Dora. "And you said I was a Mouse."

"And I'll say so again, my love," I returned, "a thousand times!"

But I had wounded Dora's soft little heart, and she was not to be comforted. She was so pathetic in her sobbing and bewailing, that I felt as if I had said I don't know what to hurt her. I was obliged to hurry away; I was kept out late; and I felt all night such pangs of remorse as made me miserable. I had the conscience of an assassin, and was haunted by a vague sense of enormous wickedness.

It was two or three hours past midnight when I got home. I found my aunt, in our house, sitting up for me.

"Is anything the matter, aunt?" said I, alarmed.

"Nothing, Trot," she replied. "Sit down, sit down. Little Blossom has been rather out of spirits, and I have been keeping her company. That's all."

I leaned my head upon my hand; and felt more sorry and downcast, as I sat looking at the fire, than I could have supposed possible so soon after the fulfilment of my brightest hopes. As I sat thinking, I happened to meet my aunt's eyes, which were resting on my face. There was an anxious expression in them, but it cleared directly.

"I assure you, aunt," said I, "I have been quite unhappy myself all night, to think of Dora's being so. But I had no other intention than to speak to her tenderly and lovingly about our home-affairs."

My aunt nodded encouragement.

"You must have patience, Trot," said she.

"Of course. Heaven knows I don't mean to be unreasonable, aunt!"

"No, no," said my aunt. "But Little Blossom is a very tender little blossom, and the wind must be gentle with her."

I thanked my good aunt, in my heart, for her tenderness towards my wife; and I was sure that she knew I did.

"Don't you think, aunt," said I, after some further contemplation of the fire, "that you could advise and counsel Dora a little, for our mutual advantage, now, and then?"

"Trot," returned my aunt, with some emotion, "no! Don't ask me such a thing."

Her tone was so very earnest that I raised my eyes in surprise.

"I look back on my life, child," said my aunt, "and I think of some who are in their graves, with whom I might have been on kinder terms. If I judged harshly of other people's mistakes in marriage, it may have been because I had bitter reason to judge harshly of my own. Let that pass. I have been a grumpy, frumpy, wayward sort of a woman, a good many years. I am still, and I always shall be. But you and I have done one another some good, Trot,—at all events, you have done me good, my dear; and division must not come between us, at this time of day."

"Division between *us!*" cried I.

"Child, child!" said my aunt, smoothing her dress, "how soon it might come between us, or how unhappy I might make our Little Blossom, if I meddled in anything, a prophet couldn't say. I want our pet to like me, and be as gay as a butterfly. Remember your own home, in that second marriage; and never do both me and her the injury you have hinted at!"

I comprehended, at once, that my aunt was right; and I comprehended the full extent of her generous feeling towards my dear wife.

"These are early days, Trot," she pursued, "and Rome was not built in a day, nor in a year. You have chosen freely for yourself"; a cloud passed over her face for a moment, I thought; "and you have chosen a very pretty and a very affectionate creature. It will be your duty, and it will be your pleasure too—of course I know that; I am not delivering a lecture—to estimate her (as you chose her) by the qualities she has, and not by the qualities she may not have. The latter you must develop in her, if you can. And if you cannot, child," here my aunt rubbed her nose, "you must just accustom yourself to do without 'em. But remember, my dear, your future is between you two. No one can assist you; you are to work it out for yourselves. This is marriage, Trot; and Heaven bless you both, in it, for a pair of babes in the wood as you are!"

My aunt said this in a sprightly way, and gave me a kiss to ratify the blessing.

"Now," said she, "light my little lantern, and see me into my bandbox by the garden path"; for there was a communication between our cottages in that direction. "Give Betsey Trotwood's love to Blossom, when you come back; and whatever you do, Trot, never dream of setting Betsey up as a scarecrow, for if *I* ever saw her in the glass, she's quite grim enough and gaunt enough in her private capacity!"

With this my aunt tied her head up in a handkerchief, with which she was accustomed to make a bundle of it on such occasions; and I escorted her home. As she stood in her garden, holding up her little lantern to light me back, I thought her observation of me had an anxious air again; but I was too much occupied in pondering on what she had said, and too much impressed—for the first time, in reality—by the conviction that Dora and I had indeed to work out our future for ourselves, and that no one could assist us, to take much notice of it.

Dora came stealing down in her little slippers, to meet me, now that I was alone; and cried upon my shoulder, and said I had been hard-hearted and she had been naughty; and I said much the same thing in effect, I believe; and we made it up, and agreed that our first little difference was to be our last, and that we were never to have another if we lived a hundred years.

The next domestic trial we went through, was the Ordeal of Servants. Mary Anne's cousin deserted into our coal-hole, and was brought out, to our great amazement, by a piquet of his companions in arms, who took him away handcuffed in a procession that covered our front-garden with ignominy. This nerved me to get rid of Mary Anne, who went so mildly, on receipt of wages, that I was surprised, until I found out about the tea-spoons, and also about the little sums she had borrowed in my name of the tradespeople without authority. After an interval of Mrs Kidgerbury—the oldest inhabitant of

Kentish Town, I believe, who went out charing, but was too feeble to execute her conceptions of that art—we found another treasure, who was one of the most amiable of women, but who generally made a point of falling either up or down the kitchen stairs with the tray, and almost plunged into the parlour, as into a bath, with the tea-things. The ravages committed by this unfortunate, rendering her dismissal necessary, she was succeeded (with intervals of Mrs Kidgerbury) by a long line of Incapables; terminating in a young person of genteel appearance, who went to Greenwich Fair in Dora's bonnet. After whom I remember nothing but an average equality of failure.

Everybody we had anything to do with seemed to cheat us. Our appearance in a shop was a signal for the damaged goods to be brought out immediately. If we bought a lobster, it was full of water. All our meat turned out to be tough, and there was hardly any crust to our loaves. In search of the principle on which joints ought to be roasted, to be roasted enough, and not too much, I myself referred to the Cookery Book, and found it there established as the allowance of a quarter of an hour to every pound, and say a quarter over. But the principle always failed us by some curious fatality, and we never could hit any medium between redness and cinders.

I had reason to believe that in accomplishing these failures we incurred a far greater expense than if we had achieved a series of triumphs. It appeared to me, on looking over the tradesmen's books, as if we might have kept the basement storey paved with butter, such was the extensive scale of our consumption of that article. I don't know whether the Excise returns of the period may have exhibited any increase in the demand for pepper; but if our performances did not affect the market, I should say several families must have left off using it. And the most wonderful fact of all was, that we never had anything in the house.

As to the washerwoman pawning the clothes, and coming in a state of penitent intoxication to apologize, I suppose that might have happened several times to anybody. Also the chimney on fire, the parish engine, and perjury on the part of the Beadle. But I apprehend that we were personally fortunate in engaging a servant with a taste for cordials, who swelled our running account for porter at the public-house by such inexplicable items as "quartern rum shrub (Mrs C.)"; "Half-quartern gin and cloves (Mrs C.)"; "Glass rum and peppermint (Mrs C.)"—the parentheses always referring to Dora, who was supposed, it appeared on explanation, to have imbibed the whole of these refreshments.

One of our first feats in the housekeeping way was a little dinner to Traddles. I met him in town, and asked him to walk out with me that afternoon. He readily consenting, I wrote to Dora, saying I would bring him home. It was pleasant weather, and on the road we made my domestic happiness the theme of conversation. Traddles was very full of it; and said, that, picturing himself with such a home, and Sophy waiting and preparing for him, he could think of nothing wanting to complete his bliss.

I could not have wished for a prettier little wife at the opposite end of the table, but I certainly could have wished, when we sat down, for a little more room. I did not know how it was, but though there were only two of us, we were at once always cramped for room, and yet had always room enough to lose everything in. I suspect it may have been because nothing had a place of its own, except Jip's pagoda, which invariably blocked up the main thoroughfare. On the present occasion, Traddles was so hemmed in by the pagoda and the guitar-case, and Dora's flower-painting, and my writing-table, that I had serious doubts of the possibility of his using his knife and fork; but he protested, with his own good-humour, "Oceans of room, Copperfield! I assure you, Oceans!"

There was another thing I could have wished, namely, that Jip had never been encouraged to walk about the table-cloth during dinner. I began to think there was something disorderly in his being there at all, even if he had not been in the habit of putting his foot in the salt or the melted butter. On this occasion he seemed to think he was introduced expressly to keep Traddles at bay; and he barked at my old friend, and made short runs at his plate, with such undaunted pertinacity, that he may be said to have engrossed the conversation.

However, as I knew how tender-hearted my dear Dora was, and how sensitive she would be to any slight upon her favourite, I hinted no objection. For similar reasons I made no allusion to the skirmishing plates upon the floor; or to the disreputable appearance of the castors, which were all at sixes and sevens, and looked drunk; or to the further blockade of Traddles by wandering vegetable dishes and jugs. I could not help wondering in my own mind, as I contemplated the boiled leg of mutton before me, previous to carving it, how it came to pass that our joints of meat were of such extraordinary shapes—and whether our butcher contracted for all the deformed sheep that came into the world; but I kept my reflections to myself.

"My love," said I to Dora, "what have you got in that dish?"

I could not imagine why Dora had been making tempting little faces at me, as if she wanted to kiss me.

"Oysters, dear," said Dora, timidly.

"Was that *your* thought?" said I, delighted.

"Ye-yes, Doady," said Dora.

"There never was a happier one!" I exclaimed, laying down the carving-knife and fork. "There is nothing Traddles likes so much!"

"Ye-yes, Doady," said Dora, "and so I bought a beautiful little barrel of them, and the man said they were very good. But I—I am afraid there's something the matter with them. They don't seem right." Here Dora shook her head, and diamonds twinkled in her eyes.

"They are only opened in both shells," said I. "Take the top one off, my love."

"But it won't come off," said Dora, trying very hard, and looking very much distressed.

"Do you know, Copperfield," said Traddles, cheerfully examining the dish, "I think it is in consequence—they are capital oysters, but I *think* it is in consequence—of their never having been opened."

They never had been opened; and we had no oyster-knives—and couldn't have used them if we had; so we looked at the oysters and ate the mutton. At least we ate as much of it as was done, and made up with capers. If I had permitted him, I am satisfied that Traddles would have made a perfect savage of himself, and eaten a plateful of raw meat, to express enjoyment of the repast; but I would hear of no such immolation on the altar of friendship, and we had a course of bacon instead; there happening, by good fortune, to be cold bacon in the larder.

My poor little wife was in such affliction when she thought I should be annoyed, and in such a state of joy when she found I was not, that the discomfiture I had subdued, very soon vanished, and we passed a happy evening; Dora sitting with her arm on my chair while Traddles and I discussed a glass of wine, and taking every opportunity of whispering in my ear that it was so good of me not to be a cruel, cross old boy. By and by she made tea for us; which it was so pretty to see her do, as if she was busying herself with a set of doll's tea-things, that I was not particular about the quality of the beverage. Then Traddles and I played a game or two at cribbage; and Dora singing to the guitar the while, it seemed to me as if our courtship and marriage were a tender dream of mine, and the night when I first listened to her voice were not yet over.

When Traddles went away, and I came back into the parlour from seeing him out, my wife planted her chair close to mine, and sat down by my side.

"I am very sorry," she said. "Will you try to teach me, Doady?"

"I must teach myself first, Dora," said I. "I am as bad as you, love."

"Ah! But you can learn," she returned; "and you are a clever, clever man!"

"Nonsense, mouse!" said I.

"I wish," resumed my wife, after a long silence, "that I could have gone down into the country for a whole year, and lived with Agnes!"

Her hands were clasped upon my shoulder, and her chin rested on them, and her blue eyes looked quietly into mine.

"Why so?" I asked.

"I think she might have improved me, and I think I might have learned from *her*," said Dora.

"All in good time, my love. Agnes has had her father to take care of for these many years, you should remember. Even when she was quite a child, she was the Agnes whom we know," said I.

"Will you call me a name I want you to call me?" inquired Dora, without moving.

"What is it?" I asked with a smile.

"It's a stupid name," she said, shaking her curls for a moment. "Child-wife."

I laughingly asked my child-wife what her fancy was in desiring to be so called. She answered without moving, otherwise than as the arm I twined about her may have brought her blue eyes nearer to me:

"I don't mean, you silly fellow, that you should use the name instead of Dora. I only mean that you should think of me that way. When you are going to be angry with me, say to yourself, 'it's only my child-wife!' When I am very disappointing, say, 'I knew, a long time ago, that she would make but a child-wife!' When you miss what I should like to be, and I think can never be, say, 'still my foolish child-wife loves me!' For indeed I do."

I had not been serious with her; having no idea, until now, that she was serious herself. But her affectionate nature was so happy in what I now said to her with my whole heart, that her face became a laughing one before her glittering eyes were dry. She was soon my child-wife indeed; sitting down on the floor outside the Chinese House, ringing all the little bells one after another, to punish Jip for his recent bad behaviour; while Jip lay blinking in the doorway with his head out, even too lazy to be teased.

This appeal of Dora's made a strong impression on me. I look back on the time I write of; I invoke the innocent figure that I dearly loved, to come out from the mists and shadows of the past, and turn its gentle head towards me once again; and I can still declare that this one little speech was constantly in my memory. I may not have used it to the best account; I was young and inexperienced; but I never turned a deaf ear to its artless pleading.

Dora told me, shortly afterwards, that she was going to be a wonderful house-keeper. Accordingly, she polished the tablets, pointed the pencil, bought an immense account-book, carefully stitched up with a needle and thread all the leaves of the Cookery Book which Jip had torn, and made quite a desperate little attempt "to be good," as she called it. But the figures had the old obstinate propensity—they *would not* add up. When she had entered two or three laborious items in the account-book, Jip would walk over the page, wagging his tail, and smear them all out. Her own little right-hand middle finger got steeped to the very bone in ink; and I think that was the only decided result obtained.

Sometimes, of an evening, when I was at home and at work—for I wrote a good deal now, and was beginning in a small way to be known as a writer—I would lay down my pen, and watch my child-wife trying to be good. First of all, she would bring out the immense account-book, and lay it down upon the table, with a deep sigh. Then she would open it at the place where Jip had made it illegible last night, and call Jip up, to look at his misdeeds. This would occasion a diversion in Jip's favour, and some inking of his nose, perhaps, as a penalty. Then she would tell Jip to lie down on the table instantly, "like a lion"—which was one of his tricks, though I cannot say the likeness was striking—and, if he were in an obedient humour, he would obey. Then she would take up a pen, and begin to write, and find a hair in it. Then she would take up another pen, and begin to write, and find that it spluttered. Then she would take up another pen, and begin to write, and say in a low voice, "Oh, it's a talking pen, and will disturb Doady!" And then she would give it up as a bad job, and put the account-book away, after pretending to crush the lion with it.

Or, if she were in a very sedate and serious state of mind, she would sit down with the tablets, and a little basket of bills and other documents, which looked more like curl-papers than anything else, and endeavour to get some result out of them. After severely comparing one with another, and making entries on the tablets, and blotting them out, and counting all the fingers of her left hand over and over again, backwards and forwards, she would be so vexed and discouraged, and would look so unhappy, that it gave me pain to see her bright face clouded—and for me!—and I would go softly to her, and say:

"What's the matter, Dora?"

Dora would look up hopelessly, and reply, "They won't come right. They make my head ache so. And they won't do anything I want!"

Then I would say, "Now let us try together. Let me show you, Dora."

Then I would commence a practical demonstration, to which Dora would pay profound attention, perhaps for five minutes; when she would begin to be dreadfully tired, and would lighten the subject by curling my hair, or trying the effect of my face with my shirt-collar turned down. If I tacitly checked this playfulness, and persisted, she would look so scared and disconsolate, as she became more and more bewildered, that the remembrance of her natural gaiety when I first strayed into her path, and of her being my child-wife, would come reproachfully upon me; and I would lay the pencil down, and call for the guitar.

I had a great deal of work to do, and had many anxieties, but the same considerations made me keep them to myself. I am far from sure, now, that it was right to do this, but I did it for my child-wife's sake. I search my breast, and I commit its secrets, if I know them, without any reservation to this paper. The old unhappy loss or want of something had, I am conscious, some place in my heart; but not to the embitterment of my life. When I walked alone in the fine weather, and thought of the summer days when all the air had been filled with my boyish enchantment, I did miss something of the realization of my dreams; but I thought it was a softened glory of the Past, which nothing could have thrown upon the present time. I did feel, sometimes, for a little while, that I could have wished my wife had been my counsellor; had had more character and purpose, to sustain me and improve me by; had been endowed with power to fill up the void which somewhere seemed to be about me; but I felt as if this were an unearthly consummation of my happiness, that never had been meant to be, and never could have been.

I was a boyish husband as to years. I had known the softening influence of no other sorrows or experiences than those recorded in these leaves. If I did any wrong, as I may have done much, I did it in mistaken love, and in my want of wisdom. I write the exact truth. It would avail me nothing to extenuate it now.

Thus it was that I took upon myself the toils and cares of our life, and had no partner in them. We lived much as before, in reference to our scrambling household arrangements; but I had got used to those, and Dora I was pleased to see was seldom vexed now. She was bright and cheerful in the old childish way, loved me dearly, and was happy with her old trifles.

When the debates were heavy—I mean as to length, not quality, for in the last respect they were not often otherwise—and I went home late, Dora would never rest when she heard my footsteps, but would always come downstairs to meet me. When my evenings were unoccupied by the pursuit for which I had qualified myself with so much pains, and I was engaged in writing at home, she would sit quietly near me, however late the hour, and be so mute, that I would often think she had dropped asleep. But generally, when I raised my head, I saw her blue eyes looking at me with the quiet attention of which I have already spoken.

"Oh, what a weary boy!" said Dora one night, when I met her eyes as I was shutting up my desk.

"What a weary girl!" said I. "That's more to the purpose. You must go to bed another time, my love. It's far too late for you."

"No, don't send me to bed!" pleaded Dora, coming to my side. "Pray, don't do that!"

"Dora!"

To my amazement she was sobbing on my neck.

"Not well, my dear! not happy!"

"Yes! quite well, and very happy!" said Dora. "But say you'll let me stop, and see you write."

"Why, what a sight for such bright eyes at midnight!" I replied.

"Are they bright, though?" returned Dora, laughing. "I'm so glad they're bright."

"Little Vanity!" said I.

But it was not vanity; it was only harmless delight in my admiration. I knew that very well, before she told me so.

"If you think them pretty, say I may always stop, and see you write!" said Dora. "Do you think them pretty?"

"Very pretty."

"Then let me always stop and see you write."

"I am afraid that won't improve their brightness, Dora."

"Yes, it will! Because, you clever boy, you'll not forget me then, while you are full of silent fancies. Will you mind it, if I say something very, very silly?—more than usual?" inquired Dora, peeping over my shoulder into my face.

"What wonderful thing is that?" said I.

"Please let me hold the pens," said Dora. "I want to have something to do with all those many hours when you are so industrious. May I hold the pens?"

The remembrance of her pretty joy when I said yes, brings tears into my eyes. The next time I sat down to write, and regularly afterwards, she sat in her old place, with a spare bundle of pens at her side. Her triumph in this connexion with my work, and her delight when I wanted a new pen—which I very often feigned to do—suggested to me a new way of pleasing my child-wife. I occasionally made a pretence of wanting a page or two of manuscript copied. Then Dora was in her glory. The preparations she made for this great work, the aprons she put on, the bibs she borrowed from the kitchen to keep off the ink, the time she took, the innumerable stoppages she made to have a laugh with Jip as if he understood it all, her conviction that her work was incomplete unless she signed her name at the end, and the way in which she would bring it to me, like a school-copy, and then, when I praised it, clasp me round the neck, are touching recollections to me, simple as they might appear to other men.

She took possession of the keys soon after this, and went jingling about the house with the whole bunch in a little basket, tied to her slender waist. I seldom found that the places to which they belonged were locked, or that they were of any use except as a plaything for Jip—but Dora was pleased, and that pleased me. She was quite satisfied that a good deal was effected by this make-believe of housekeeping; and was as merry as if we had been keeping a baby-house, for a joke.

So we went on. Dora was hardly less affectionate to my aunt than to me, and often told her of the time when she was afraid she was "a cross old thing," I never saw my aunt unbend more systematically to anyone. She courted Jip, though Jip never responded; listened, day after day, to the guitar, though I am afraid she had no taste for music; never attacked the Incapables, though the temptation must have been severe; went wonderful distances on foot to purchase, as surprises, any trifles that she found out Dora wanted; and never came in by the garden, and missed her from the room, but she would call out, at the foot of the stairs, in a voice that sounded cheerfully all over the house:

"Where's Little Blossom?"

Chapter XLV

MR DICK FULFILS MY AUNT'S PREDICTIONS

I T was some time now, since I had left the Doctor. Living in his neighbourhood, I saw him frequently; and we all went to his house on two or three occasions to dinner or tea. The Old Soldier was in permanent quarters under the Doctor's roof. She was exactly the same as ever, and the same immortal butterflies hovered over her cap.

Like some other mothers, whom I have known in the course of my life, Mrs Markleham was far more fond of pleasure than her daughter was. She required a great deal of amusement, and, like a deep old soldier, pretended, in consulting her own inclinations, to be devoting herself to her child. The Doctor's desire that Annie should be entertained, was therefore particularly acceptable to this excellent parent; who expressed unqualified approval of his discretion.

I have no doubt, indeed, that she probed the Doctor's wound without knowing it. Meaning nothing but a certain matured frivolity and selfishness, not always inseparable from full-blown years, I think she confirmed him in his fear that he was a constraint upon his young wife, and that there was no congeniality of feeling between them, by so strongly commending his design of lightening the load of her life.

"My dear soul," she said to him one day when I was present, "you know there is no doubt it would be a little pokey for Annie to be always shut up here."

The Doctor nodded his benevolent head.

"When she comes to her mother's age," said Mrs Markleham, with a flourish of her fan, "then it'll be another thing. You might put ME into a Jail, with genteel society and a rubber, and I should never care to come out. But I am not Annie, you know; and Annie is not her mother."

"Surely, surely," said the Doctor.

"You are the best of creatures—no, I beg your pardon!" for the Doctor made a gesture of deprecation, "I must say before your face, as I always say behind your back, you are the best of creatures; but of course you don't—now do you?—enter into the same pursuits and fancies as Annie?"

"No," said the Doctor, in a sorrowful tone.

"No, of course not," retorted the Old Soldier. "Take your Dictionary, for example. What a useful work a Dictionary is! What a necessary work! The meanings of words! Without Doctor Johnson, or somebody of that sort, we might have been at this present moment calling an Italian-iron a bedstead. But we can't expect a Dictionary—especially when it's making—to interest Annie, can we?"

The Doctor shook his head.

"And that's why I so much approve," said Mrs Markleham, tapping him on the shoulder with her shut-up fan, "of your thoughtfulness. It shows that you don't expect, as many elderly people do expect, old heads on young shoulders. You have studied Annie's character, and you understand it. That's what I find so charming!"

Even the calm and patient face of Doctor Strong expressed some little sense of pain, I thought, under the infliction of these compliments.

"Therefore, my dear Doctor," said the Old Soldier, giving him several affectionate taps, "you may command me, at all times and seasons. Now, do understand that I am entirely at your service. I am ready to go with Annie to operas, concerts, exhibitions, all kinds of places; and you shall never find that I am tired. Duty, my dear Doctor, before every consideration in the universe!"

She was as good as her word. She was one of those people who can bear a great deal of pleasure, and she never flinched in her perseverance in the cause. She seldom got hold of the newspaper (which she settled herself down in the softest chair in the house to read through an eye-glass, every day, for two hours), but she found out something that she was certain Annie would like to see. It was in vain for Annie to protest that she was weary of such things. Her mother's remonstrance always was, "Now, my dear Annie, I am sure you know better; and I must tell you, my love, that you are not making a proper return for the kindness of Doctor Strong."

This was usually said in the Doctor's presence, and appeared to me to constitute Annie's principal inducement for withdrawing her objections when she made any. But in general she resigned herself to her mother, and went where the Old Soldier would.

It rarely happened now that Mr Maldon accompanied them. Sometimes my aunt and Dora were invited to do so, and accepted the invitation. Sometimes Dora only was asked. The time had been, when I should have been uneasy in her going; but reflection on what had passed that former night in the Doctor's study, had made a change in my mistrust. I believed that the Doctor was right, and I had no worse suspicions.

My aunt rubbed her nose sometimes when she happened to be alone with me, and said she couldn't make it out; she wished they were happier; she didn't think our military friend (so she always called the Old Soldier) mended the matter at all. My aunt further expressed her opinion, "that if our military friend would cut off those butterflies, and give 'em to the chimney-sweepers for May-day, it would look like the beginning of something sensible on her part."

But her abiding reliance was on Mr Dick. That man had evidently an idea in his head, she said; and if he could only once pen it up into a corner, which was his great difficulty, he would distinguish himself in some extraordinary manner.

Unconscious of this prediction, Mr Dick continued to occupy precisely the same ground in reference to the Doctor and to Mrs Strong. He seemed neither to advance nor to recede. He appeared to have settled into his original foundation, like a building; and I must confess that my faith in his ever moving, was not much greater than if he had been a building.

But one night, when I had been married some months, Mr Dick put his head into the parlour, where I was writing alone (Dora having gone out with my aunt to take tea with the two little birds), and said, with a significant cough:

"You couldn't speak to me without inconveniencing yourself, Trotwood, I am afraid?"

"Certainly, Mr Dick," said I; "come in!"

"Trotwood," said Mr Dick, laying his finger on the side of his nose, after he had shaken hands with me. "Before I sit down, I wish to make an observation. You know your aunt?"

"A little," I replied.

"She is the most wonderful woman in the world, sir!"

After the delivery of this communication, which he shot out of himself as if he were loaded with it, Mr Dick sat down with greater gravity than usual, and looked at me.

"Now, boy," said Mr Dick, "I am going to put a question to you."

"As many as you please," said I.

"What do you consider me, sir?" asked Mr Dick, folding his arms.

"A dear old friend," said I.

"Thank you, Trotwood," returned Mr Dick, laughing, and reaching across in high glee to shake hands with me. "But I mean, boy," resuming his gravity, "what do you consider me in this respect?" touching his forehead.

I was puzzled how to answer, but he helped me with a word.

"Weak?" said Mr Dick.

"Well," I replied, dubiously. "Rather so."

"Exactly!" cried Mr Dick, who seemed quite enchanted by my reply. "That is, Trotwood, when they took some of the trouble out of you-know-who's head, and put it you know where, there was a—" Mr Dick made his two hands revolve very fast about each other a great number of times, and then brought them into collision, and rolled them over and over one another, to express confusion. "There was that sort of thing done to me somehow Eh?"

I nodded at him, and he nodded back again.

"In short, boy," said Mr Dick, dropping his voice to a whisper, "I am simple."

I would have qualified that conclusion, but he stopped me.

"Yes, I am! She pretends I am not. She won't hear of it; but I am. I know I am. If she hadn't stood my friend, sir, I should have been shut up, to lead a dismal life these many years. But I'll provide for her! I never spend the copying money. I put it in a box. I have made a will. I'll leave it all to her. She shall be rich—noble!"

Mr Dick took out his pocket-handkerchief, and wiped his eyes. He then folded it up with great care, pressed it smooth between his two hands, put it in his pocket, and seemed to put my aunt away with it.

"Now you are a scholar, Trotwood," said Mr Dick. "You are a fine scholar. You know what a learned man, what a great man, the Doctor is. You know what honour he has always done me. Not proud in his wisdom. Humble, humble—condescending even to poor Dick, who is simple and knows nothing. I have sent his name up, on a scrap of paper, to the kite, along the string, when it has been in the sky, among the larks. The kite has been glad to receive it, sir, and the sky has been brighter with it."

I delighted him by saying, most heartily, that the Doctor was deserving of our best respect and highest esteem.

"And his beautiful wife is a star," said Mr Dick. "A shining star. I have seen her shine, sir. But," bringing his chair nearer, and laying one hand upon my knee—"clouds, sir—clouds."

I answered the solicitude which his face expressed, by conveying the same expression into my own, and shaking my head.

"What clouds?" said Mr Dick.

He looked so wistfully into my face, and was so anxious to understand, that I took great pains to answer him slowly and distinctly, as I might have entered on an explanation to a child.

"There is some unfortunate division between them," I replied. "Some unhappy cause of separation. A secret. It may be inseparable from the discrepancy in their years. It may have grown up out of almost nothing."

Mr Dick, who had told off every sentence with a thoughtful nod, paused when I had done, and sat considering, with his eyes upon my face, and his hand upon my knee.

"Doctor not angry with her, Trotwood?" he said, after some time.

"No. Devoted to her."

"Then, I have got it, boy!" said Mr Dick.

The sudden exultation with which he slapped me on the knee, and leaned back in his chair, with his eyebrows lifted up as high as he could possibly lift them, made me think him farther out of his wits than ever. He became as suddenly grave again, and leaning forward as before, said—first respectfully taking out his pocket-handkerchief, as if it really did represent my aunt:

"Most wonderful woman in the world, Trotwood. Why has *she* done nothing to set things right?"

"Too delicate and difficult a subject for such interference," I replied.

"Fine scholar," said Mr Dick, touching me with his finger. "Why has *he* done nothing?"

"For the same reason," I returned.

"Then, I have got it, boy!" said Mr Dick. And he stood up before me, more exultingly than before, nodding his head, and striking himself repeatedly upon the breast, until one might have supposed that he had nearly nodded and struck all the breath out of his body.

"A poor fellow with a craze, sir," said Mr Dick, "a simpleton, a weak-minded person—present company, you know!" striking himself again, "may do what wonderful people may not do. I'll bring them together, boy. I'll try. They'll not blame *me*. They'll not object to *me*. They'll not mind what *I* do, if it's wrong. I'm only Mr Dick. And who minds Dick? Dick's nobody! Whoo!" He blew a slight, contemptuous breath, as if he blew himself away.

It was fortunate he had proceeded so far with his mystery, for we heard the coach stop at the little garden gate, which brought my aunt and Dora home.

"Not a word, boy!" he pursued in a whisper; "leave all the blame with Dick—simple Dick—mad Dick. I have been thinking, sir, for some time, that I was getting it, and now I have got it. After what you have said to me, I am sure I have got it. All right!"

Not another word did Mr Dick utter on the subject; but he made a very telegraph of himself for the next half-hour (to the great disturbance of my aunt's mind), to enjoin inviolable secrecy on me.

To my surprise, I heard no more about it for some two or three weeks, though I was sufficiently interested in the result of his endeavours; descrying a strange gleam of good sense—I say nothing of good feeling, for that he always exhibited—in the conclusion to which he had come. At last I began to believe, that, in the flighty and unsettled state of his mind, he had either forgotten his intention or abandoned it.

One fair evening, when Dora was not inclined to go out, my aunt and I strolled up to the Doctor's cottage. It was autumn, when there were no debates to vex the evening air; and I remember how the leaves smelt like our garden at Blunderstone as we trod them under foot, and how the old, unhappy feeling, seemed to go by, on the sighing wind.

It was twilight when we reached the cottage. Mrs Strong was just coming out of the garden, where Mr Dick yet lingered, busy with his knife, helping the gardener to point some stakes. The Doctor was engaged with someone in his study; but the visitor would be gone directly, Mrs Strong said, and begged us to remain and see him. We went into the drawing-room with her, and sat down by the darkening window. There was never any ceremony about the visits of such old friends and neighbours as we were.

We had not sat here many minutes, when Mrs Markleham, who usually contrived to be in a fuss about something, came bustling in, with her newspaper in her hand, and said, out of breath, "My goodness gracious, Annie, why didn't you tell me there was someone in the Study!"

"My dear mama," she quietly returned, "how could I know that you desired the information?"

"Desired the information!" said Mrs Markleham, sinking on the sofa. "I never had such a turn in all my life!"

"Have you been to the Study, then, mama?" asked Annie.

"*Been* to the Study, my dear!" she returned emphatically. "Indeed I have! I came upon the amiable creature—if you'll imagine my feelings, Miss Trotwood and David—in the act of making his will."

Her daughter looked round from the window quickly.

"In the act, my dear Annie," repeated Mrs Markleham, spreading the newspaper on her lap like a table-cloth, and patting her hands upon it, "of making his last Will and Testament. The foresight and affection of the dear! I must tell you how it was. I really must, in justice to the darling—for he is nothing less!—tell you how it was. Perhaps you know, Miss Trotwood, that there is never a candle lighted in this house, until one's eyes are literally falling out of one's head with being stretched to read the paper. And that there is not a chair in this house, in which a paper can be what *I* call, read, except one in the Study. This took me to the Study, where I saw a light. I opened the door. In company with the dear Doctor were two professional people, evidently connected with the law, and they were all three standing at the table: the darling Doctor pen in hand. 'This simply expresses then,' said the Doctor—Annie, my love, attend to the very words—'this simply expresses then, gentlemen, the confidence I have in Mrs Strong, and gives her all unconditionally?' One of the professional people replied, 'And gives her all unconditionally.' Upon that, with the natural feelings of a mother, I said, 'Good God, I beg your pardon!' fell over the door-step, and came away through the little back passage where the pantry is."

Mrs Strong opened the window, and went out into the verandah, where she stood leaning against a pillar.

"But now isn't it, Miss Trotwood, isn't it, David, invigorating," said Mrs Markleham, mechanically following her with her eyes, "to find a man at Doctor Strong's time of life, with the strength of mind to do this kind of thing? It only shows how right I was. I said to Annie, when Doctor Strong paid a very flattering visit to myself, and made her the subject of a declaration and an offer, I said, 'My dear, there is no doubt whatever, in my opinion, with reference to a suitable provision for you, that Doctor Strong will do more than he binds himself to do.' "

Here the bell rang, and we heard the sound of the visitors' feet as they went out.

"It's all over, no doubt," said the Old Soldier, after listening; "the dear creature has signed, sealed, and delivered, and his mind's at rest. Well it may be! What a mind! Annie, my love, I am going to the Study with my paper, for I am a poor creature without news. Miss Trotwood, David, pray come and see the Doctor."

I was conscious of Mr Dick's standing in the shadow of the room, shutting up his knife, when we accompanied her to the Study; and of my aunt's rubbing her nose violently, by the way, as a mild vent for her intolerance of our military friend; but who got first into the Study, or how Mrs Markleham settled herself in a moment in her easy-chair, or how my aunt and I came to be left together near the door (unless her eyes were quicker than mine, and she held me back), I have forgotten, if I ever knew. But this I know,—that we saw the Doctor before he saw us, sitting at his table, among the folio volumes in which he delighted, resting his head calmly on his hand. That, in the same moment, we saw Mrs Strong glide in, pale and trembling. That Mr Dick supported her on his arm. That he laid his other hand upon the Doctor's arm, causing him to look up with an abstracted air. That, as the Doctor moved his head, his wife dropped down on one knee at his feet, and, with her hands imploringly lifted, fixed upon his face the memorable look I had never forgotten. That at this sight Mrs Markleham dropped the newspaper, and stared more like a figure-head intended for a ship to be called The Astonishment, than anything else I can think of.

The gentleness of the Doctor's manner and surprise, the dignity that mingled with the supplicating attitude of his wife, the amiable concern of Mr Dick, and the earnestness with which my aunt said to herself, *"That* man mad!" (triumphantly expressive of the misery from which she had saved him)—I see and hear, rather than remember, as I write about it.

"Doctor!" said Mr Dick. "What is it that's amiss? Look here!"

"Annie!" cried the Doctor. "Not at my feet, my dear!"

"Yes!" she said. "I beg and pray that no one will leave the room! Oh, my husband and father, break this long silence. Let us both know what it is that has come between us!"

Mrs Markleham, by this time recovering the power of speech, and seeming to swell with family pride and motherly indignation, here exclaimed, "Annie, get up immediately, and don't disgrace everybody belonging to you by humbling yourself like that, unless you wish to see me go out of my mind on the spot!"

"Mama!" returned Annie. "Waste no words on me, for my appeal is to my husband, and even you are nothing here."

"Nothing!" exclaimed Mrs Markleham. "Me, nothing! The child has taken leave of her senses. Please to get me a glass of water!"

I was too attentive to the Doctor and his wife, to give any heed to this request; and it made no impression on anybody else; so Mrs Markleham panted, stared, and fanned herself.

"Annie!" said the Doctor, tenderly taking her in his hands. "My dear! If any unavoidable change has come, in the sequence of time, upon our married life, you are not to blame. The fault is mine, and only mine. There is no change in my affection, admiration, and respect. I wish to make you happy. I truly love and honour you. Rise, Annie, pray!"

But she did not rise. After looking at him for a little while, she sank down closer to him, laid her arm across his knee, and dropping her head upon it, said:

"If I have any friend here, who can speak one word for me, or for my husband in this matter; if I have any friend here, who can give a voice to any suspicion that my heart has sometimes whispered to me; if I have any friend here, who honours my husband, or has ever cared for me, and has anything within his knowledge, no matter what it is, that may help to mediate between us, I implore that friend to speak!"

There was a profound silence. After a few moments of painful hesitation, I broke the silence.

"Mrs Strong," I said, "there is something within my knowledge, which I have been earnestly entreated by Doctor Strong to conceal, and have concealed until tonight. But, I believe the time has come when it would be mistaken faith and delicacy to conceal it any longer, and when your appeal absolves me from his injunction."

She turned her face towards me for a moment, and I knew that I was right. I could not have resisted its entreaty, if the assurance that it gave me had been less convincing.

"Our future peace," she said, "may be in your hands. I trust it confidently to your not suppressing anything. I know beforehand that nothing you, or anyone, can tell me, will show my husband's noble heart in any other light than one. Howsoever it may seem to you to touch me, disregard that. I will speak for myself, before him, and before God afterwards."

Thus earnestly besought, I made no reference to the Doctor for his permission, but, without any other compromise of the truth than a little softening of the coarseness of Uriah Heep, related plainly what had passed in that same room that night. The staring of Mrs Markleham during the whole narration, and the shrill, sharp interjections with which she occasionally interrupted it, defy description.

When I had finished, Annie remained, for some few moments, silent, with her head bent down, as I have described. Then, she took the Doctor's hand (he was sitting in the same attitude as when we had entered the room), and pressed it to her breast, and kissed it. Mr Dick softly raised her; and she stood, when she began to speak, leaning on him, and looking down upon her husband—from whom she never turned her eyes.

"All that has ever been in my mind, since I was married," she said in a low, submissive, tender voice, "I will lay bare before you. I could not live and have one reservation, knowing what I know now."

"Nay, Annie," said the Doctor, mildly, "I have never doubted you, my child. There is no need; indeed there is no need, my dear."

"There is great need," she answered, in the same way, "that I should open my whole heart before the soul of generosity and truth, whom, year by year, and day by day, I have loved and venerated more and more, as Heaven knows!"

"Really," interrupted Mrs Markleham, "if I have any discretion at all—"

("Which you haven't, you Marplot," observed my aunt, in an indignant whisper.)

—"I must be permitted to observe that it cannot be requisite to enter into these details."

"No one but my husband can judge of that, mama," said Annie without removing her eyes from his face, "and he will hear me. If I say anything to give you pain, mama, forgive me. I have borne pain first, often and long, myself."

"Upon my word!" gasped Mrs Markleham.

"When I was very young," said Annie, "quite a little child, my first associations with knowledge of any kind were inseparable from a patient friend and teacher—the friend of my dead father—who was always dear to me. I can remember nothing that I know, without remembering him. He stored my mind with its first treasures, and stamped his character upon them all. They never could have been, I think, as good as they have been to me, if I had taken them from any other hands."

"Makes her mother nothing!" exclaimed Mrs Markleham.

"Not so mama," said Annie; "but I make him what he was. I must do that. As I grew up, he occupied the same place still. I was proud of his interest: deeply, fondly, gratefully attached to him. I looked up to him, I can hardly describe how—as a father, as a guide, as one whose praise was different from all other praise, as one in whom I could have trusted and confided, if I had doubted all the world. You know, mama, how young and inexperienced I was, when you presented him before me, of a sudden, as a lover."

"I have mentioned the fact, fifty times at least, to everybody here!" said Mrs Markleham.

("Then hold your tongue, for the Lord's sake, and don't mention it any more!" muttered my aunt.)

"It was so great a change: so great a loss, I felt it, at first," said Annie, still preserving the same look and tone, "that I was agitated and distressed. I was but a girl; and when so great a change came in the character in which I had so long looked up to him, I think I was sorry. But nothing could have made him what he used to be again; and I was proud that he should think me so worthy, and we were married."

"—At Saint Alphage, Canterbury," observed Mrs Markleham.

("Confound the woman!" said my aunt, "she *won't* be quiet!")

"I never thought," proceeded Annie, with a heightened colour, "of any worldly gain that my husband would bring to me. My young heart had no room in its homage for any such poor reference. Mama, forgive me when I say that it was *you* who first presented to my mind the thought that anyone could wrong me, and wrong him, by such a cruel suspicion."

"Me!" cried Mrs Markleham.

("Ah! You, to be sure!" observed my aunt, "and you can't fan it away, my military friend!")

"It was the first unhappiness of my new life," said Annie. "It was the first occasion of every unhappy moment I have known. These moments have been more, of late, than I can count; but not—my generous husband!—not for the reason you suppose; for in my heart there is not a thought, a recollection, or a hope, that any power could separate from you!"

She raised her eyes, and clasped her hands, and looked as beautiful and true, I thought, as any Spirit. The Doctor looked on her, henceforth, as steadfastly as she on him.

"Mama is blameless," she went on, "of having ever urged you for herself, and she is blameless in intention every way, I am sure,—but when I saw how many importunate claims were pressed upon you in my name; how you were traded on in my name; how generous you were, and how Mr Wickfield, who had your welfare very much at heart, resented it; the first sense of my exposure to the mean suspicion that my tenderness was bought—and sold to you, of all men on earth—fell upon me like unmerited disgrace, in which I forced you to participate. I cannot tell you what it was—mama cannot imagine what it was—to have this dread and trouble always on my mind, yet know in my own soul that on my marriage-day I crowned the love and honour of my life!"

"A specimen of the thanks one gets," cried Mrs Markleham, in tears, "for taking care of one's family! I wish I was a Turk!"

("I wish you were, with all my heart—and in your native country!" said my aunt.)

"It was at that time that mama was most solicitous about my Cousin Maldon. I had liked him": she spoke softly, but without any hesitation: "very much. We had been little lovers once. If circumstances had not happened otherwise, I might have come to persuade myself that I really loved him, and might have married him, and been most wretched. There can be no disparity in marriage like unsuitability of mind and purpose."

I pondered on those words, even while I was studiously attending to what followed, as if they had some particular interest, or some strange application that I could not divine. "There can be no disparity in marriage like unsuitability of mind and purpose"—"no disparity in marriage like unsuitability of mind and purpose."

"There is nothing," said Annie, "that we have in common. I have long found that there is nothing. If I were thankful to my husband for no more, instead of for so much, I should be thankful to him for having saved me from the first mistaken impulse of my undisciplined heart."

She stood quite still, before the Doctor, and spoke with an earnestness that thrilled me. Yet her voice was just as quiet as before.

"When he was waiting to be the object of your munificence, so freely bestowed for my sake, and when I was unhappy in the mercenary shape I was made to wear, I thought it would have become him better to have worked his own way on. I thought that if I had been he, I would have tried to do it, at the cost of almost any hardship. But I thought no worse of him, until the night of his departure for India. That night I knew he had a false and thankless heart. I saw a double meaning, then, in Mr Wickfield's scrutiny of me. I perceived, for the first time, the dark suspicion that shadowed my life."

"Suspicion, Annie!" said the Doctor. "No, no, no!"

"In your mind there was none, I know, my husband!" she returned. "And when I came to you, that night, to lay down all my load of shame and grief, and knew that I had to tell that, underneath your roof, one of my own kindred, to whom you had been a benefactor, for the love of me, had spoken to me words that should have found no utterance, even if I had been the weak and mercenary wretch he thought me—my mind revolted from the taint the very tale conveyed. It died upon my lips, and from that hour till now has never passed them."

Mrs Markleham, with a short groan, leaned back in her easy-chair; and retired behind her fan, as if she were never coming out any more.

"I have never, but in your presence, interchanged a word with him from that time; then, only when it has been necessary for the avoidance of this explanation. Years have passed since he knew, from me, what his situation here was. The kindnesses you have secretly done for his advancement, and then disclosed to me, for my surprise and pleasure, have been, you will believe, but aggravations of the unhappiness and burden of my secret."

She sunk down gently at the Doctor's feet, though he did his utmost to prevent her; and said, looking up, tearfully, into his face:

"Do not speak to me yet! Let me say a little more! Right or wrong, if this were to be done again, I think I should do just the same. You never can know what it was to be devoted to you, with those old associations; to find that anyone could be so hard as to suppose that the truth of my heart was bartered away, and to be surrounded by appearances confirming that belief. I was very young, and had no adviser. Between mama and me, in all relating to you, there was a wide division. If I shrunk into myself, hiding the disrespect I had undergone, it was because I honoured you so much, and so much wished that you should honour me!"

"Annie, my pure heart!" said the Doctor, "my dear girl!"

"A little more! a very few words more! I used to think there were so many whom you might have married, who would not have brought such charge and trouble on you, and who would have made your home a worthier home. I used to be afraid that I had better have remained your pupil, and almost your child. I used to fear that I was so unsuited to your learning and wisdom. If all this made me shrink within myself (as indeed it did), when I had that to tell, it was still because I honoured you so much, and hoped that you might one day honour me."

"That day has shone this long time, Annie," said the Doctor, "and can have but one long night, my dear."

"Another word! I afterwards meant—steadfastly meant, and purposed to myself— to bear the whole weight of knowing the unworthiness of one to whom you had been so good. And now a last word, dearest and best of friends! The cause of the late change in you, which I have seen with so much pain and sorrow, and have sometimes referred to my old apprehension—at other times to lingering suppositions nearer to the truth— has been made clear tonight; and by an accident I have also come to know, tonight, the full measure of your noble trust in me, even under that mistake. I do not hope that any love and duty I may render in return, will ever make me worthy of your priceless confidence; but with all this knowledge fresh upon me, I can lift my eyes to this dear face, revered as a father's, loved as a husband's, sacred to me in my childhood as a friend's, and solemnly declare that in my lightest thought I have never wronged you; never wavered in the love and the fidelity I owe you!"

She had her arms around the Doctor's neck, and he leant his head down over her, mingling his grey hair with her dark brown tresses.

"Oh, hold me to your heart, my husband! Never cast me out! Do not think or speak of disparity between us, for there is none, except in all my many imperfections. Every succeeding year I have known this better, as I have esteemed you more and more. Oh, take me to your heart, my husband, for my love was founded on a rock, and it endures!"

In the silence that ensued, my aunt walked gravely up to Mr Dick, without at all hurrying herself, and gave him a hug and a sounding kiss. And it was very fortunate, with a view to his credit, that she did so; for I am confident that I detected him at that moment in the act of making preparations to stand on one leg, as an appropriate expression of delight.

"You are a very remarkable man, Dick!" said my aunt, with an air of unqualified approbation; "and never pretend to be anything else, for I know better!"

With that, my aunt pulled him by the sleeve, and nodded to me; and we three stole quietly out of the room, and came away.

"That's a settler for our military friend, at any rate," said my aunt, on the way home. "I should sleep the better for that, if there was nothing else to be glad of!"

"She was quite overcome, I am afraid," said Mr Dick, with great commiseration.

"What! Did you ever see a crocodile overcome?" inquired my aunt.

"I don't think I ever saw a crocodile," returned Mr Dick, mildly.

"There never would have been anything the matter, if it hadn't been for that old Animal," said my aunt, with strong emphasis. "It's very much to be wished that some mothers would leave their daughters alone after marriage, and not be so violently affectionate. They seem to think the only return that can be made them for bringing an unfortunate young woman into the world—God bless my soul, as if she asked to be brought, or wanted to come!—is full liberty to worry her out of it again. What are you thinking of, Trot?"

I was thinking of all that had been said. My mind was still running on some of the expressions used. "There can be no disparity in marriage like unsuitability of mind and purpose." "The first mistaken impulse of an undisciplined heart." "My love was founded on a rock." But we were at home; and the trodden leaves were lying under-foot, and the autumn wind was blowing.

Chapter XLVI

INTELLIGENCE

I MUST have been married, if I may trust to my imperfect memory for dates, about a year or so, when one evening, as I was returning from a solitary walk, thinking of the book I was then writing—for my success had steadily increased with my steady application, and I was engaged at that time upon my first work of fiction—I came past Mrs Steerforth's house. I had often passed it before, during my residence in that neighbourhood, though never when I could choose another road. Howbeit, it did sometimes happen that it was not easy to find another, without making a long circuit; and so I had passed that way, upon the whole, pretty often.

I had never done more than glance at the house, as I went by with a quickened step. It had been uniformly gloomy and dull. None of the best rooms abutted on the road; and the narrow, heavily-framed old-fashioned windows, never cheerful under any circumstances, looked very dismal, close shut, and with their blinds always drawn down. There was a covered way across a little paved court, to an entrance that was never used; and there was one round staircase window, at odds with all the rest, and the only one unshaded by a blind, which had the same unoccupied blank look. I do not remember that I ever saw a light in all the house. If I had been a casual passer-by, I should have probably supposed that some childless person lay dead in it. If I had happily possessed no knowledge of the place, and had seen it often in that changeless state, I should have pleased my fancy with many ingenious speculations, I dare say.

As it was, I thought as little of it as I might. But my mind could not go by it and leave it, as my body did; and it usually awakened a long train of meditations. Coming before me, on this particular evening that I mention, mingled with the childish recollections and later fancies, the ghosts of half-formed hopes, the broken shadows of disappointments dimly seen and understood, the blending of experience and imagination, incidental to the occupation with which my thoughts had been busy, it was more than commonly suggestive. I fell into a brown study as I walked on, and a voice at my side made me start.

It was a woman's voice, too. I was not long in recollecting Mrs Steerforth's little parlour-maid, who had formerly worn blue ribbons in her cap. She had taken them out now, to adapt herself I suppose, to the altered character of the house; and wore but one or two disconsolate bows of sober brown.

"If you please, sir, would you have the goodness to walk in, and speak to Miss Dartle?"

"Has Miss Dartle sent you for me?" I inquired.

"Not tonight, sir, but it's just the same. Miss Dartle saw you pass a night or two ago; and I was to sit at work on the staircase, and when I saw you pass again, to ask you to step in and speak to her."

I turned back, and inquired of my conductor, as we went along, how Mrs Steerforth was. She said her lady was but poorly, and kept her own room a good deal.

When we arrived at the house, I was directed to Miss Dartle in the garden, and left to make my presence known to her myself. She was sitting on a seat at one end of a kind of terrace, overlooking the great city. It was a sombre evening, with a lurid light in the sky; and as I saw the prospect scowling in the distance, with here and there some larger object starting up into the sullen glare, I fancied it was no inapt companion to the memory of this fierce woman.

She saw me as I advanced, and rose for a moment to receive me. I thought her, then, still more colourless and thin than when I had seen her last; the flashing eyes still brighter, and the scar still plainer.

Our meeting was not cordial. We had parted angrily on the last occasion; and there was an air of disdain about her, which she took no pains to conceal.

"I am told you wish to speak to me, Miss Dartle," said I, standing near her, with my hand upon the back of the seat, and declining her gesture of invitation to sit down.

"If you please," said she. "Pray has this girl been found?"

"No."

"And yet she has run away!"

I saw her thin lips working while she looked at me, as if they were eager to load her with reproaches.

"Run away?" I repeated.

"Yes! From him," she said, with a laugh. "If she is not found, perhaps she never will be found. She may be dead!"

The vaunting cruelty with which she met my glance, I never saw expressed in any other face that ever I have seen.

"To wish her dead," said I, "may be the kindest wish that one of her own sex could bestow upon her. I am glad that time has softened you so much, Miss Dartle."

She condescended to make no reply, but, turning on me with another scornful laugh, said:

"The friends of this excellent and much-injured young lady are friends of yours. You are their champion, and assert their rights. Do you wish to know what is known of her?"

"Yes," said I.

She rose with an ill-favoured smile, and taking a few steps towards a wall of holly that was near at hand, dividing the lawn from a kitchen-garden, said, in a louder voice, "Come here!"—as if she were calling to some unclean beast.

"You will restrain any demonstrative championship or vengeance in this place, of course, Mr Copperfield?" said she, looking over her shoulder at me with the same expression.

I inclined my head, without knowing what she meant; and she said, "Come here!" again; and returned, followed by the respectable Mr Littimer, who, with undiminished respectability, made me a bow, and took up his position behind her. The air of wicked grace: of triumph, in which, strange to say, there was yet something feminine and alluring: with which she reclined upon the seat between us, and looked at me, was worthy of a cruel Princess in a Legend.

"Now," said she, imperiously, without glancing at him, and touching the old wound as it throbbed: perhaps, in this instance, with pleasure rather than pain. "Tell Mr Copperfield about the flight."

"Mr James and myself, ma'am—"

"Don't address yourself to me!" she interrupted with a frown.

"Mr James and myself, sir—"

"Nor to me, if you please," said I.

Mr Littimer, without being at all discomposed, signified by a slight obeisance, that anything that was most agreeable to us was most agreeable to him; and began again.

"Mr James and myself have been abroad with the young woman, ever since she left Yarmouth under Mr James's protection. We have been in a variety of places, and seen a deal of foreign country. We have been in France, Switzerland, Italy, in fact, almost all parts."

He looked at the back of the seat, as if he were addressing himself to that; and softly played upon it with his hands, as if he were striking chords upon a dumb piano.

"Mr James took quite uncommonly to the young woman; and was more settled, for a length of time, than I have known him to be since I have been in his service. The young woman was very improvable, and spoke the languages; and wouldn't have been known for the same country-person. I noticed that she was much admired wherever we went."

Miss Dartle put her hand upon her side. I saw him steal a glance at her, and slightly smile to himself.

"Very much admired, indeed, the young woman was. What with her dress; what with the air and sun; what with being made so much of; what with, this, that, and the other; her merits really attracted general notice."

He made a short pause. Her eyes wandered restlessly over the distant prospect, and she bit her nether lip to stop that busy mouth.

Taking his hands from the seat, and placing one of them within the other, as he settled himself on one leg, Mr Littimer proceeded, with his eyes cast down, and his respectable head a little advanced, and a little on one side:

"The young woman went on in this manner for some time, being occasionally low in her spirits, until I think she began to weary Mr James by giving way to her low spirits and tempers of that kind; and things were not so comfortable. Mr James he began to be restless again. The more restless he got, the worse she got; and I must say, for myself, that I had a very difficult time of it indeed between the two. Still matters were patched up here, and made good there, over and over again; and altogether lasted, I am sure, for a longer time than anybody could have expected."

Recalling her eyes from the distance, she looked at me again now, with her former air. Mr Littimer, clearing his throat behind his hand with a respectable short cough, changed legs, and went on:

"At last, when there had been, upon the whole, a good many words and reproaches,

Mr James he set off one morning, from the neighbourhood of Naples, where we had a villa (the young woman being very partial to the sea), and, under pretence of coming back in a day or so, left it in charge with me to break it out, that, for the general happiness of all concerned, he was"—here an interruption of the short cough—"gone. But Mr James, I must say, certainly did behave extremely honourable; for he proposed that the young woman should marry a very respectable person, who was fully prepared to overlook the past, and who was, at least, as good as anybody the young woman could have aspired to in a regular way: her connexions being very common."

He changed legs again, and wetted his lips. I was convinced that the scoundrel spoke of himself, and I saw my conviction reflected in Miss Dartle's face.

"This I also had it in charge to communicate. I was willing to do anything to relieve Mr James from his difficulty, and to restore harmony between himself and an affectionate parent, who has undergone so much on his account. Therefore I undertook the commission. The young woman's violence when she came to, after I broke the fact of his departure, was beyond all expectations. She was quite mad, and had to be held by force; or, if she couldn't have got to a knife, or got to the sea, she'd have beaten her head against the marble floor."

Miss Dartle, leaning back upon the seat, with a light of exultation in her face, seemed almost to caress the sounds this fellow had uttered.

"But when I came to the second part of what had been entrusted to me," said Mr Littimer, rubbing his hands uneasily, "which anybody might have supposed would have been, at all events, appreciated as a kind intention, then the young woman came out in her true colours. A more outrageous person I never did see. Her conduct was surprisingly bad. She had no more gratitude, no more feeling, no more patience, no more reason in her, than a stock or a stone. If I hadn't been upon my guard, I am convinced she would have had my blood."

"I think the better of her for it," said I, indignantly.

Mr Littimer bent his head, as much as to say, "Indeed, sir? But you're young!" and resumed his narrative.

"It was necessary, in short, for a time, to take away everything nigh her, that she could do herself, or anybody else, an injury with, and to shut her up close. Notwithstanding which, she got out in the night; forced the lattice of a window, that I had nailed up myself; dropped on a vine that was trailed below; and never has been seen or heard of, to my knowledge, since."

"She is dead, perhaps," said Miss Dartle, with a smile, as if she could have spurned the body of the ruined girl.

"She may have drowned herself, miss," returned Mr Littimer, catching at an excuse for addressing himself to somebody. "It's very possible. Or, she may have had assistance from the boatmen, and the boatmen's wives and children. Being given to low company, she was very much in the habit of talking to them on the beach, Miss Dartle, and sitting by their boats. I have known her do it, when Mr James has been away, whole days. Mr James was far from pleased to find out, once, that she had told the children she was a boatman's daughter, and that in her own country, long ago, she had roamed about the beach, like them."

Oh, Emily! Unhappy beauty! What a picture rose before me of her sitting on the far-off shore, among the children like herself when she was innocent, listening to little voices such as might have called her Mother had she been a poor man's wife; and to the great voice of the sea, with its eternal "Never more!"

"When it was clear that nothing could be done, Miss Dartle—"

"Did I tell you not to speak to me?" she said, with stern contempt.

"You spoke to me, miss," he replied. "I beg your pardon. But it is my service to obey."

"Do your service," she returned. "Finish your story, and go!"

"When it was clear," he said, with infinite respectability and an obedient bow, "that she was not to be found, I went to Mr James, at the place where it had been agreed that I should write to him, and informed him of what had occurred. Words passed between us in consequence, and I felt it due to my character to leave him. I could bear, and I have borne, a great deal from Mr James; but he insulted me too far. He hurt me. Knowing the unfortunate difference between himself and his mother, and what her anxiety of mind was likely to be, I took the liberty of coming home to England, and relating—"

"For money which I paid him," said Miss Dartle to me.

"Just so, ma'am—and relating what I knew. I am not aware," said Mr Littimer, after a moment's reflection, "that there is anything else. I am at present out of employment, and should be happy to meet with a respectable situation."

Miss Dartle glanced at me, as though she would inquire if there were anything that I desired to ask. As there was something which had occurred to my mind, I said in reply:

"I could wish to know from this—creature," I could not bring myself to utter any more conciliatory word, "whether they intercepted a letter that was written to her from home, or whether he supposes that she received it."

He remained calm and silent, with his eyes fixed on the ground, and the tip of every finger of his right hand delicately poised against the tip of every finger of his left.

Miss Dartle turned her head disdainfully towards him.

"I beg your pardon, miss," he said, awakening from his abstraction, "but, however submissive to you, I have my position, though a servant. Mr Copperfield and you, miss, are different people. If Mr Copperfield wishes to know anything from me, I take the liberty of reminding Mr Copperfield that he can put a question to me. I have a character to maintain."

After a momentary struggle with myself, I turned my eyes upon him, and said, "You have heard my question. Consider it addressed to yourself, if you choose. What answer do you make?"

"Sir," he rejoined, with an occasional separation and reunion of those delicate tips, "my answer must be qualified; because, to betray Mr James's confidence to his mother, and to betray it to you, are two different actions. It is not probable, I consider, that Mr James would encourage the receipt of letters likely to increase low spirits and unpleasantness; but further than that, sir, I should wish to avoid going."

"Is that all?" inquired Miss Dartle of me.

I indicated that I had nothing more to say. "Except," I added, as I saw him moving off, "that I understand this fellow's part in the wicked story, and that, as I shall make it known to the honest man who has been her father from her childhood, I would recommend him to avoid going too much into public."

He had stopped the moment I began, and had listened with his usual repose of manner.

"Thank you, sir. But you'll excuse me if I say, sir, that there are neither slaves nor slave-drivers in this country, and that people are not allowed to take the law into their own hands. If they do, it is more to their own peril, I believe, than to other people's. Consequently speaking, I am not at all afraid of going wherever I may wish, sir."

With that, he made a polite bow; and, with another to Miss Dartle, went away through the arch in the wall of holly by which he had come. Miss Dartle and I regarded each other for a little while in silence; her manner being exactly what it was, when she had produced the man.

"He says besides," she observed, with a slow curling of her lip, "that his master, as he hears, is coasting Spain; and this done, is away to gratify his seafaring tastes till he is weary. But this is of no interest to you. Between these two proud persons, mother and son, there is a wider breach than before, and little hope of its healing, for they are one at heart, and time makes each more obstinate and imperious. Neither is this of any interest to you; but it introduces what I wish to say. This devil whom you make an angel of, I mean this low girl whom he picked out of the tide-mud," with her black eyes full upon me, and her passionate finger up, "may be alive,—for I believe some common things are hard to die. If she is, you will desire to have a pearl of such price found and taken care of. We desire that, too; that he may not by any chance be made her prey again. So far, we are united in one interest; and that is why I, who would do her any mischief that so coarse a wretch is capable of feeling, have sent for you to hear what you have heard."

I saw, by the change in her face, that someone was advancing behind me. It was Mrs Steerforth, who gave me her hand more coldly than of yore, and with an augmentation of her former stateliness of manner; but still, I perceived—and I was touched by it—with an ineffaceable remembrance of my old love for her son. She was greatly altered. Her fine figure was far less upright, her handsome face was deeply marked, and her hair was almost white. But when she sat down on the seat, she was a handsome lady still; and well I knew the bright eye with its lofty look, that had been a light in my very dreams at school.

"Is Mr Copperfield informed of everything, Rosa?"

"Yes."

"And has he heard Littimer himself?"

"Yes; I have told him why you wished it."

"You are a good girl. I have had some slight correspondence with your former friend, sir," addressing me, "but it has not restored his sense of duty or natural obligation. Therefore I have no other object in this, than what Rosa has mentioned. If, by the course which may relieve the mind of the decent man you brought here (for whom I am sorry—I can say no more), my son may be saved from again falling into the snares of a designing enemy, well!"

She drew herself up, and sat looking straight before her, far away.

"Madam," I said respectfully, "I understand. I assure you I am in no danger of putting any strained construction on your motives. But I must say, even to you, having known this injured family from childhood, that if you suppose the girl, so deeply wronged, has not been cruelly deluded, and would not rather die a hundred deaths than take a cup of water from your son's hand now, you cherish a terrible mistake."

"Well, Rosa, well!" said Mrs Steerforth, as the other was about to interpose, "it is no matter. Let it be. You are married, sir, I am told?"

I answered that I had been some time married.

"And are doing well? I hear little in the quiet life I lead, but I understand you are beginning to be famous."

"I have been very fortunate," I said, "and find my name connected with some praise."

"You have no mother?"—in a softened voice.

"No."

"It is a pity," she returned. "She would have been proud of you. Good night!"

I took the hand she held out with a dignified, unbending air, and it was as calm in mine as if her breast had been at peace. Her pride could still its very pulses, it appeared, and draw the placid veil before her face, through which she sat looking straight before her on the far distance.

As I moved away from them along the terrace, I could not help observing how steadily they both sat gazing on the prospect, and how it thickened and closed around them. Here and there, some early lamps were seen to twinkle in the distant city; and in the eastern quarter of the sky the lurid light still hovered. But, from the greater part of the broad valley interposed, a mist was rising like a sea, which, mingling with the darkness, made it seem as if the gathering waters would encompass them. I have reason to remember this, and think of it with awe; for before I looked upon those two again, a stormy sea had risen to their feet.

Reflecting on what had been thus told me, I felt it right that it should be communicated to Mr Peggotty. On the following evening I went into London in quest of him. He was always wandering about from place to place, with his one object of recovering his niece before him; but was more in London than elsewhere. Often and often, now, had I seen him in the dead of night passing along the streets, searching, among the few who loitered out of doors at those untimely hours, for what he dreaded to find.

He kept a lodging over the little chandler's shop in Hungerford Market, which I have had occasion to mention more than once, and from which he first went forth upon his errand of mercy. Hither I directed my walk. On making inquiry for him, I learned from the people of the house that he had not gone out yet, and I should find him in his room upstairs.

He was sitting reading by a window in which he kept a few plants. The room was very neat and orderly. I saw in a moment that it was always kept prepared for her reception, and that he never went out but he thought it possible he might bring her home. He had not heard my tap at the door, and only raised his eyes when I laid my hand upon his shoulder.

"Mas'r Davy! Thankee, sir! thankee hearty, for this visit! Sit ye down. You're kindly welcome, sir!"

"Mr Peggotty," said I, taking the chair he handed me, "don't expect much! I have heard some news."

"Of Em'ly!"

He put his hand, in a nervous manner, on his mouth, and turned pale, as he fixed his eyes on mine.

"It gives no clue to where she is; but she is not with him."

He sat down, looking intently at me, and listened in profound silence to all I had to tell. I well remember the sense of dignity, beauty even, with which the patient gravity of his face impressed me, when, having gradually removed his eyes from mine, he sat looking downward, leaning his forehead on his hand. He offered no interruption, but remained throughout perfectly still. He seemed to pursue her figure through the narrative, and to let every other shape go by him, as if it were nothing.

When I had done, he shaded his face, and continued silent. I looked out of the window for a little while, and occupied myself with the plants.

"How do you fare to feel about it, Mas'r Davy?" he inquired at length.

"I think that she is living," I replied.

"I doen't know. Maybe the first shock was too rough, and in the wildness of her art—! That there blue water as she used to speak on. Could she have thowt o' that so many year, because it was to be her grave!"

He said this, musing, in a low, frightened voice; and walked across the little room.

"And yet," he added, "Mas'r Davy, I have felt so sure as she was living—I have know'd, awake and sleeping, as it was so trew that I should find her—I have been so led on by it, and held up by it—that I doen't believe I can have been deceived. No! Em'ly's alive!"

He put his hand down firmly on the table, and set his sunburnt face into a resolute expression.

"My niece, Em'ly, is alive, sir!" he said, steadfastly. "I doen't know wheer it comes from, or how 'tis, but *I am told* as she's alive!"

He looked almost like a man inspired, as he said it. I waited for a few moments, until he could give me his undivided attention; and then proceeded to explain the precaution, that, it had occurred to me last night, it would be wise to take.

"Now, my dear friend—" I began.

"Thankee, thankee, kind sir," he said, grasping my hand in both of his.

"If she should make her way to London, which is likely—for where could she lose herself so readily as in this vast city; and what would she wish to do, but lose and hide herself, if she does not go home?—"

"And she won't go home," he interposed, shaking his head mournfully. "If she had left of her own accord, she might; not as 'twas, sir."

"If she should come here," said I, "I believe there is one person, here, more likely to discover her than any other in the world. Do you remember—hear what I say, with fortitude—think of your great object!—do you remember Martha?"

"Of our town?"

I needed no other answer than his face.

"Do you know that she is in London?"

"I have seen her in the streets," he answered, with a shiver.

"But you don't know," said I, "that Emily was charitable to her, with Ham's help, long before she fled from home. Nor, that, when we met one night, and spoke together in the room yonder, over the way, she listened at the door."

"Mas'r Davy!" he replied in astonishment. "That night when it snew so hard?"

"That night. I have never seen her since. I went back, after parting from you, to speak to her, but she was gone. I was unwilling to mention her to you then, and I am now; but she is the person of whom I speak, and with whom I think we should communicate. Do you understand?"

"Too well, sir," he replied. We had sunk our voices, almost to a whisper, and continued to speak in that tone.

"You say you have seen her. Do you think that you could find her? I could only hope to do so by chance."

"I think, Mas'r Davy, I know wheer to look."

"It is dark. Being together, shall we go out now, and try to find her tonight?"

He assented, and prepared to accompany me. Without appearing to observe what he was doing, I saw how carefully he adjusted the little room, put a candle ready and the means of lighting it, arranged the bed, and finally took out of a drawer one of her dresses (I remember to have seen her wear it), neatly folded with some other garments, and a bonnet, which he placed upon a chair. He made no allusion to these clothes, neither did I. There they had been waiting for her, many and many a night, no doubt.

"The time was, Mas'r Davy," he said, as we came downstairs, "when I thowt this girl, Martha, a'most like the dirt underneath my Em'ly's feet. God forgive me, theer's a difference now!"

As we went along, partly to hold him in conversation, and partly to satisfy myself, I asked him about Ham. He said, almost in the same words as formerly, that Ham was just the same, "wearing away his life with kiender no care nohow for 't; but never murmuring, and liked by all."

I asked him what he thought Ham's state of mind was, in reference to the cause of their misfortunes? Whether he believed it was dangerous? What he supposed, for example, Ham would do, if he and Steerforth ever should encounter?

"I doen't know, sir," he replied. "I have thowt of it oftentimes, but I can't awize myself of it, no matters."

I recalled to his remembrance the morning after her departure, when we were all three on the beach. "Do you recollect," said I, "a certain wild way in which he looked out to sea, and spoke about 'the end of it'?"

"Sure I do!" said he.

"What do you suppose he meant?"

"Mas'r Davy," he replied, "I've put the question to myself a mort o' times, and never found no answer. And theer's one curious thing—that, though he is so pleasant, I wouldn't fare to feel comfortable to try and get his mind upon 't. He never said a wured to me as warn't as dootiful as dootiful could be, and it ain't likely as he'd begin to speak any other ways now; but it's fur from being fleet water in his mind, where them thowts lays. It's deep, sir, and I can't see down."

"You are right," said I, "and that has sometimes made me anxious."

"And me too, Mas'r Davy," he rejoined. "Even more so, I do assure you, than his ventersome ways, though both belongs to the alteration in him. I doen't know as he'd do violence under any circumstances, but I hope as them two may be kep asunders."

We had come, through Temple Bar, into the city. Conversing no more now, and walking at my side, he yielded himself up to the one aim of his devoted life, and went on, with that hushed concentration of his faculties which would have made his figure solitary in a multitude. We were not far from Blackfriars Bridge, when he turned his head and pointed to a solitary female figure flitting along the opposite side of the street. I knew it, readily, to be the figure that we sought.

We crossed the road, and were pressing on towards her, when it occurred to me that she might be more disposed to feel a woman's interest in the lost girl, if we spoke to her in a quieter place, aloof from the crowd, and where we should be less observed. I advised my companion therefore, that we should not address her yet, but follow her; consulting in this, likewise, an indistinct desire I had, to know where she went.

He acquiescing, we followed at a distance: never losing sight of her, but never caring to come very near, as she frequently looked about. Once, she stopped to listen to a band of music; and then we stopped too.

She went on a long way. Still we went on. It was evident, from the manner in which she held her course, that she was going to some fixed destination; and this, and her keeping in the busy streets, and I suppose the strange fascination in the secrecy and mystery of so following anyone, made me adhere to my first purpose. At length she turned into a dull, dark street, where the noise and crowd were lost; and I said, "We may speak to her now"; and, mending our pace, we went after her.

Chapter XLVII

MARTHA

W E were now down in Westminster. We had turned back to follow her, having encountered her coming towards us; and Westminster Abbey was the point at which she passed from the lights and noise of the leading streets. She proceeded so quickly, when she got free of the two currents of passengers setting towards and from the bridge, that, between this and the advance she had of us when she struck off, we were in the narrow water-side street by Millbank before we came up with her. At that moment she crossed the road, as if to avoid the footsteps that she heard so close behind; and, without looking back, passed on even more rapidly.

A glimpse of the river through a dull gateway, where some waggons were housed for the night, seemed to arrest my feet. I touched my companion without speaking, and we both forbore to cross after her, and both followed on that opposite side of the way; keeping as quietly as we could in the shadow of the houses, but keeping very near her.

There was, and is when I write, at the end of that low-lying street, a dilapidated little wooden building, probably an obsolete old ferry-house. Its position is just at that point where the street ceases, and the road begins to lie between a row of houses and the river. As soon as she came here, and saw the water, she stopped as if she had come to her destination; and presently went slowly along by the brink of the river, looking intently at it.

All the way here, I had supposed that she was going to some house; indeed, I had vaguely entertained the hope that the house might be in some way associated with the lost girl. But, that one dark glimpse of the river, through the gateway, had instinctively prepared me for her going no farther.

The neighbourhood was a dreary one at that time; as oppressive, sad, and solitary by night, as any about London. There were neither wharves nor houses on the melancholy waste of road near the great blank Prison. A sluggish ditch deposited its mud at the prison walls. Coarse grass and rank weeds straggled over all the marshy land in the vicinity. In one part, carcases of houses, inauspiciously begun and never finished, rotted away. In another, the ground was cumbered with rusty iron monsters of steam-boilers, wheels, cranks, pipes, furnaces, paddles, anchors, diving-bells, windmill-sails, and I know not what strange objects, accumulated by some speculator, and grovelling in the dust, underneath which—having sunk into the soil of their own weight in wet weather—they had the appearance of vainly trying to hide themselves. The clash and glare of sundry fiery Works upon the river-side, arose by night to disturb everything except the heavy and unbroken smoke that poured out of their chimneys. Slimy gaps and causeways, winding among old wooden piles, with a sickly substance clinging to the latter, like green hair, and the rags of last year's handbills offering rewards for drowned men fluttering above high-water mark, led down through the ooze and slush to the ebb-tide. There was a story that one of the pits dug for the dead in the time of the Great Plague was hereabout; and a blighting influence seemed to have proceeded from it over the whole place. Or else it looked as if it had gradually decomposed into that nightmare condition, out of the overflowings of the polluted stream.

As if she were a part of the refuse it had cast out, and left to corruption and decay, the girl we had followed strayed down to the river's brink, and stood in the midst of this night-picture, lonely and still, looking at the water.

There were some boats and barges astrand in the mud, and these enabled us to come within a few yards of her without being seen. I then signed to Mr Peggotty to remain where he was, and emerged from their shade to speak to her. I did not approach her solitary figure without trembling; for this gloomy end to her determined walk, and the way in which she stood, almost within the cavernous shadow of the iron bridge, looking at the lights crookedly reflected in the strong tide, inspired a dread within me.

I think she was talking to herself. I am sure, although absorbed in gazing at the water, that her shawl was off her shoulders, and that she was muffling her hands in it, in an unsettled and bewildered way, more like the action of a sleep-walker than a waking person. I know, and never can forget, that there was that in her wild manner which gave me no assurance but that she would sink before my eyes, until I had her arm within my grasp.

At the same moment I said "Martha!"

She uttered a terrified scream, and struggled with me with such strength that I doubt if I could have held her alone. But a stronger hand than mine was laid upon her; and when she raised her frightened eyes and saw whose it was, she made but one more effort and dropped down between us. We carried her away from the water to where there were some dry stones, and there laid her down, crying and moaning. In a little while she sat among the stones, holding her wretched head with both her hands.

"Oh, the river!" she cried passionately. "Oh, the river!"

"Hush, hush!" said I. "Calm yourself."

But she still repeated the same words, continually exclaiming, "Oh, the river!" over and over again.

"I know it's like me!" she exclaimed. "I know that I belong to it. I know that it's the natural company of such as I am! It comes from country places, where there was once no harm in it—and it creeps through the dismal streets, defiled and miserable—and it goes away, like my life, to a great sea, that is always troubled—and I feel that I must go with it!"

I have never known what despair was, except in the tone of those words.

"I can't keep away from it. I can't forget it. It haunts me day and night. It's the only thing in all the world that I am fit for, or that's fit for me. Oh, the dreadful river!"

The thought passed through my mind that in the face of my companion, as he looked upon her without speech or motion, I might have read his niece's history, if I had known nothing of it. I never saw, in any painting or reality, horror and compassion so impressively blended. He shook as if he would have fallen; and his hand—I touched it with my own, for his appearance alarmed me—was deadly cold.

"She is in a state of frenzy," I whispered to him. "She will speak differently in a little time."

I don't know what he would have said in answer. He made some motion with his mouth, and seemed to think he had spoken; but he had only pointed to her with his outstretched hand.

A new burst of crying came upon her now, in which she once more hid her face among the stones, and lay before us, a prostrate image of humiliation and ruin. Knowing that this state must pass, before we could speak to her with any hope, I ventured to restrain him when he would have raised her, and we stood by in silence until she became more tranquil.

"Martha," said I then, leaning down, and helping her to rise—she seemed to want to rise as if with the intention of going away, but she was weak, and leaned against a boat. "Do you know who this is, who is with me?"

She said faintly, "Yes."

"Do you know that we have followed you a long way tonight?"

She shook her head. She looked neither at him nor at me, but stood in a humble attitude, holding her bonnet and shawl in one hand, without appearing conscious of them, and pressing the other, clenched, against her forehead.

"Are you composed enough," said I, "to speak on the subject which so interested you—I hope Heaven may remember it!—that snowy night?"

Her sobs broke out afresh, and she murmured some inarticulate thanks to me for not having driven her away from the door.

"I want to say nothing for myself," she said, after a few moments. "I am bad, I am lost. I have no hope at all. But tell him, sir," she had shrunk away from him, "if you don't feel too hard to me to do it, that I never was in any way the cause of his misfortune."

"It has never been attributed to you," I returned, earnestly responding to her earnestness.

"It was you, if I don't deceive myself," she said, in a broken voice, "that came into the kitchen, the night she took such pity on me; was so gentle to me; didn't shrink away from me like all the rest, and gave me such kind help! Was it you, sir?"

"It was," said I.

"I should have been in the river long ago," she said, glancing at it with a terrible expression, "if any wrong to her had been upon my mind. I never could have kept out of it a single winter's night, if I had not been free of any share in that!"

"The cause of her flight is too well understood," I said. "You are innocent of any part in it, we thoroughly believe,—we know."

"Oh, I might have been much the better for her, if I had had a better heart!" exclaimed the girl, with most forlorn regret; "for she was always good to me! She never spoke a word to me but what was pleasant and right. Is it likely I would try to make her what I am myself, knowing what I am myself, so well? When I lost everything that makes life dear, the worst of all my thoughts was that I was parted for ever from her!"

Mr Peggotty, standing with one hand on the gunwale of the boat, and his eyes cast down, put his disengaged hand before his face.

"And when I heard what had happened before that snowy night, from some belonging to our town," cried Martha, "the bitterest thought in all my mind was, that the people would remember she once kept company with me, and would say I had corrupted her! When, Heaven knows, I would have died to have brought back her good name!"

Long unused to any self-control, the piercing agony of her remorse and grief was terrible.

"To have died, would not have been much—what can I say?—I would have lived!" she cried. "I would have lived to be old, in the wretched streets—and to wander about, avoided, in the dark—and to see the day break on the ghastly line of houses, and remember how the same sun used to shine into my room, and wake me once—I would have done even that, to save her!"

Sinking on the stones, she took some in each hand, and clenched them up, as if she would have ground them. She writhed into some new posture constantly: stiffening her arms, twisting them before her face, as though to shut out from her eyes the little light there was, and drooping her head, as if it were heavy with insupportable recollections.

"What shall I ever do!" she said, fighting thus with her despair. "How can I go on as I am, a solitary curse to myself, a living disgrace to everyone I come near!" Suddenly she turned to my companion. "Stamp upon me, kill me! When she was your pride, you would have thought I had done her harm if I had brushed against her in the street. You can't believe—why should you?—a syllable that comes out of my lips. It would be a burning shame upon you, even now, if she and I exchanged a word. I don't complain. I don't say she and I are alike—I know there is a long, long way between us. I only say, with all my guilt and wretchedness upon my head, that I am grateful to her from my soul, and love her. Oh don't think that all the power I had of loving anything, is quite worn out! Throw me away, as all the world does. Kill me for being what I am, and having ever known her; but don't think that of me!"

He looked upon her, while she made this supplication, in a wild distracted manner; and, when she was silent, gently raised her.

"Martha," said Mr Peggotty, "God forbid as I should judge you. Forbid as I, of all men, should do that, my girl! You doen't know half the change that's come, in course of time, upon me, when you think it likely. Well!" he paused a moment, then went on. "You doen't understand how 'tis that this here gentleman and me has wished to speak to you. You doen't understand what 'tis we has afore us. Listen now!"

His influence upon her was complete. She stood, shrinkingly, before him, as if she were afraid to meet his eyes; but her passionate sorrow was quite hushed and mute.

"If you heerd," said Mr Peggotty, "owt of what passed between Mas'r Davy and me, th' night when it snew so hard, you know as I have been—wheer not—fur to seek my dear niece. My dear niece," he repeated steadily. "Fur she's more dear to me now, Martha, than she was dear afore."

She put her hands before her face; but otherwise remained quiet.

"I have heerd her tell," said Mr Peggotty, "as you was early left fatherless and motherless, with no friend fur to take, in a rough seafaring-way, their place. Maybe you can guess that if you'd had such a friend, you'd have got into a way of being fond of him in course of time, and that my niece was kiender daughter-like to me."

As she was silently trembling, he put her shawl carefully about her, taking it up from the ground for that purpose.

"Whereby," said he, "I know, both as she would go to the wureld's furdest end with me, if she could once see me again; and that she would fly to the wureld's furdest end to keep off seeing me. For though she ain't no call to doubt my love, and doen't—and doen't," he repeated, with a quiet assurance of the truth of what he said, "there's shame steps in, and keeps betwixt us."

I read, in every word of his plain impressive way of delivering himself, new evidence of his having thought of this one topic, in every feature it presented.

"According to our reckoning," he proceeded, "Mas'r Davy's here, and mine, she is like, one day, to make her own poor solitary course to London. We believe—Mas'r Davy, me, and all of us—that you are as innocent of everything that has befell her, as the unborn child. You've spoke of her being pleasant, kind, and gentle to you. Bless her, I knew she was! I knew she always was, to all. You're thankful to her, and you love her. Help us all you can to find her, and may Heaven reward you!"

She looked at him hastily, and for the first time, as if she were doubtful of what he had said.

"Will you trust me?" she asked, in a low voice of astonishment.

"Full and free!" said Mr Peggotty.

"To speak to her, if I should ever find her; shelter her, if I have any shelter to divide with her; and then, without her knowledge, come to you, and bring you to her?" she asked hurriedly.

We both replied together, "Yes!"

She lifted up her eyes, and solemnly declared that she would devote herself to this task, fervently and faithfully. That she would never waver in it, never be diverted from it, never relinquish it, while there was any chance of hope. If she were not true to it, might the object she now had in life, which bound her to something devoid of evil, in its passing away from her, leave her more forlorn and more despairing, if that were possible, than she had been upon the river's brink that night; and then might all help, human and Divine, renounce her evermore!

She did not raise her voice above her breath, or address us, but said this to the night sky; then stood profoundly quiet, looking at the gloomy water.

We judged it expedient, now, to tell her all we knew; which I recounted at length. She listened with great attention, and with a face that often changed, but had the same purpose in all its varying expressions. Her eyes occasionally filled with tears, but those she repressed. It seemed as if her spirit were quite altered, and she could not be too quiet.

She asked, when all was told, where we were to be communicated with, if occasion should arise. Under a dull lamp in the road, I wrote our two addresses on a leaf of my pocket-book, which I tore out and gave to her, and which she put in her poor bosom. I asked her where she lived herself. She said, after a pause, in no place long. It were better not to know.

Mr Peggotty suggesting to me, in a whisper, what had already occurred to myself, I took out my purse; but I could not prevail upon her to accept any money, nor could I exact any promise from her that she would do so at another time. I represented to her that Mr Peggotty could not be called, for one in his condition, poor; and that the idea of her engaging in this search, while depending on her own resources, shocked us both. She continued steadfast. In this particular, his influence upon her was equally powerless with mine. She gratefully thanked him but remained inexorable.

"There may be work to be got," she said. "I'll try."

"At least take some assistance," I returned, "until you have tried."

"I could not do what I have promised, for money," she replied. "I could not take it, if I was starving. To give me money would be to take away your trust, to take away the object that you have given me, to take away the only certain thing that saves me from the river."

"In the name of the great Judge," said I, "before whom you and all of us must stand at His dread time, dismiss that terrible idea! We can all do some good, if we will."

She trembled, and her lip shook, and her face was paler, as she answered:

"It has been put into your hearts, perhaps, to save a wretched creature for repent- ance. I am afraid to think so; it seems too bold. If any good should come of me, I might begin to hope; for nothing but harm has ever come of my deeds yet. I am to be trusted, for the first time in a long while, with my miserable life, on account of what you have given me to try for. I know no more, and I can say no more."

Again she repressed the tears that had begun to flow; and, putting out her trembling hand, and touching Mr Peggotty, as if there was some healing virtue in him, went away along the desolate road. She had been ill, probably for a long time. I observed, upon that closer opportunity of observation, that she was worn and haggard, and that her sunken eyes expressed privation and endurance.

We followed her at a short distance, our way lying in the same direction, until we came back into the lighted and populous streets. I had such implicit confidence in her declaration, that I then put it to Mr Peggotty, whether it would not seem, in the onset, like distrusting her, to follow her any farther. He being of the same mind, and equally reliant on her, we suffered her to take her own road, and took ours, which was towards Highgate. He accompanied me a good part of the way; and when we parted, with a prayer for the success of this fresh effort, there was a new and thoughtful compassion in him that I was at no loss to interpret.

It was midnight when I arrived at home. I had reached my own gate, and was standing listening for the deep bell of St Paul's, the sound of which I thought had been borne towards me among the multitude of striking clocks, when I was rather surprised to see that the door of my aunt's cottage was open, and that a faint light in the entry was shining out across the road.

Thinking that my aunt might have relapsed into one of her old alarms, and might be watching the progress of some imaginary conflagration in the distance, I went to speak to her. It was with very great surprise that I saw a man standing in her little garden.

He had a glass and bottle in his hand, and was in the act of drinking. I stopped short, among the thick foliage outside for the moon was up now, though obscured; and I recognized the man whom I had once supposed to be a delusion of Mr Dick's, and had once encountered with my aunt in the streets of the city.

He was eating as well as drinking, and seemed to eat with a hungry appetite. He seemed curious regarding the cottage, too, as if it were the first time he had seen it. After stooping to put the bottle on the ground, he looked up at the windows, and looked about; though with a covert and impatient air, as if he was anxious to be gone.

The light in the passage was obscured for a moment, and my aunt came out. She was agitated, and told some money into his hand. I heard it chink.

"What's the use of this?" he demanded.

"I can spare no more," returned my aunt.

"Then I can't go," said he. "Here! You may take it back!"

"You bad man," returned my aunt, with great emotion; "how can you use me so? But why do I ask? It is because you know how weak I am! What have I to do, to free myself for ever of your visits, but to abandon you to your deserts?"

"And why don't you abandon me to my deserts?" said he.

"*You* ask me why!" returned my aunt. "What a heart you must have!"

He stood moodily rattling the money, and shaking his head, until at length he said:

"Is this all you mean to give me, then?"

"It is all I *can* give you," said my aunt. "You know I have had losses, and am poorer than I used to be. I have told you so. Having got it, why do you give me the pain of looking at you for another moment, and seeing what you have become?"

"I have become shabby enough, if you mean that," he said. "I lead the life of an owl."

"You stripped me of the greater part of all I ever had," said my aunt. "You closed my heart against the whole world, years and years. You treated me falsely, ungratefully, and cruelly. Go, and repent of it. Don't add new injuries to the long, long list of injuries you have done me!"

"Aye!" he returned. "It's all very fine—Well! I must do the best I can, for the present, I suppose."

In spite of himself, he appeared abashed by my aunt's indignant tears, and came slouching out of the garden. Taking two or three quick steps, as if I had just come up, I met him at the gate, and went in as he came out. We eyed one another narrowly in passing, and with no favour.

"Aunt," said I, hurriedly. "This man alarming you again! Let me speak to him. Who is he?"

"Child," returned my aunt, taking my arm, "come in, and don't speak to me for ten minutes."

We sat down in her little parlour. My aunt retired behind the round green fan of former days, which was screwed on the back of a chair, and occasionally wiped her eyes, for about a quarter of an hour. Then she came out, and took a seat beside me.

"Trot," said my aunt, calmly, "it's my husband."

"Your husband, aunt? I thought he had been dead!"

"Dead to me," returned my aunt, "but living."

I sat in silent amazement.

"Betsey Trotwood don't look a likely subject for the tender passion," said my aunt, composedly, "but the time, was, Trot, when she believed in that man most entirely. When she loved him, Trot, right well. When there was no proof of attachment and affection that she would not have given him. He repaid her by breaking her fortune, and nearly breaking her heart. So she put all that sort of sentiment, once and for ever, in a grave, and filled it up, and flattened it down."

"My dear, good aunt!"

"I left him," my aunt proceeded, laying her hand as usual on the back of mine, "generously. I may say at this distance of time, Trot, that I left him generously. He had been so cruel to me, that I might have effected a separation on easy terms for myself; but I did not. He soon made ducks and drakes of what I gave him, sank lower and lower, married another woman, I believe, became an adventurer, a gambler, and a cheat. What he is now, you see. But he was a fine-looking man when I married him," said my aunt, with an echo of her old pride and admiration in her tone; "and I believed him—I was a fool!—to be the soul of honour!"

She gave my hand a squeeze, and shook her head.

"He is nothing to me now, Trot—less than nothing. But, sooner than have him punished for his offences (as he would be if he prowled about in this country), I give him more money than I can afford, at intervals when he reappears, to go away. I was a fool when I married him; and I am so far an incurable fool on that subject, that, for the sake of what I once believed him to be, I wouldn't have even this shadow of my idle fancy hardly dealt with. For I was in earnest, Trot, if ever a woman was."

My aunt dismissed the matter with a heavy sigh, and smoothed her dress.

"There, my dear!" she said. "Now you know the beginning, middle, and end, and all about it. We won't mention the subject to one another any more; neither, of course, will you mention it to anybody else. This is my grumpy, frumpy story, and we'll keep it to ourselves, Trot!"

Chapter XLVIII

DOMESTIC

I LABOURED hard at my book, without allowing it to interfere with the punctual discharge of my newspaper duties; and it came out and was very successful. I was not stunned by the praise which sounded in my ears, notwithstanding that I was keenly alive to it, and thought better of my own performance, I have little doubt, than anybody else did. It has always been in my observation of human nature, that a man who has any good reason to believe in himself never flourishes himself before the faces of other people in order that they may believe in him. For this reason, I retained my modesty in very self-respect; and the more praise I got, the more I tried to deserve.

It is not my purpose, in this record, though in all other essentials it is my written memory, to pursue the history of my own fictions. They express themselves, and I leave them to themselves. When I refer to them, incidentally, it is only as a part of my progress.

Having some foundation for believing, by this time, that nature and accident had made me an author, I pursued my vocation with confidence. Without such assurance I should certainly have left it alone, and bestowed my energy on some other endeavour. I should have tried to find out what nature and accident really had made me, and to be that, and nothing else.

I had been writing, in the newspaper and elsewhere, so prosperously, that when my new success was achieved, I considered myself reasonably entitled to escape from the dreary debates. One joyful night, therefore, I noted down the music of the parliamentary bagpipes for the last time, and I have never heard it since; though I still recognize the old drone in the newspapers, without any substantial variation (except, perhaps, that there is more of it), all the livelong session.

I now write of the time when I had been married, I suppose, about a year and a half. After several varieties of experiment, we had given up the housekeeping as a bad job. The house kept itself, and we kept a page. The principal function of this retainer was to quarrel with the cook; in which respect he was a perfect Whittington, without his cat, or the remotest chance of being made Lord Mayor.

He appears to me to have lived in a hail of saucepan-lids. His whole existence was a scuffle. He would shriek for help on the most improper occasions,—as when we had a little dinner-party, or a few friends in the evening,—and would come tumbling out of the kitchen, with iron missiles flying after him. We wanted to get rid of him, but he was very much attached to us, and wouldn't go. He was a tearful boy, and broke into such deplorable lamentations, when a cessation of our connexion was hinted at, that we were obliged to keep him. He had no mother—no anything in the way of a relative, that I could discover, except a sister, who fled to America the moment we had taken him off her hands; and he became quartered on us like a horrible young changeling. He had a lively perception of his own unfortunate state, and was always rubbing his eyes with the sleeve of his jacket, or stooping to blow his nose on the extreme corner of a little pocket-handkerchief, which he never *would* take completely out of his pocket, but always economized and secreted.

This unlucky page, engaged in an evil hour at six pounds ten per annum, was a source of continual trouble to me. I watched him as he grew—and he grew like scarlet beans—with painful apprehensions of the time when he would begin to shave; even of the days when he would be bald or grey. I saw no prospect of ever getting rid of him; and, projecting myself into the future, used to think what an inconvenience he would be when he was an old man.

I never expected anything less, than this unfortunate's manner of getting me out of my difficulty. He stole Dora's watch, which, like everything else belonging to us, had no particular place of its own; and, converting it into money, spent the produce (he was always a weak-minded boy) in incessantly riding up and down between London and Uxbridge outside the coach. He was taken to Bow Street, as well as I remember, on the completion of his fifteenth journey; when four-and-sixpence, and a second-hand fife which he couldn't play, were found upon his person.

The surprise and its consequences would have been much less disagreeable to me if he had not been penitent. But he was very penitent indeed, and in a peculiar way—not in the lump, but by instalments. For example: the day after that on which I was obliged to appear against him, he made certain revelations touching a hamper in the cellar, which we believed to be full of wine, but which had nothing in it except bottles and corks. We supposed he had now eased his mind, and told the worst he knew of the cook; but, a day or two afterwards, his conscience sustained a new twinge, and he disclosed how she had a little girl, who, early every morning, took away our bread; and also how he himself had been suborned to maintain the milkman in coals. In two or three days more, I was informed by the authorities of his having led to the discovery of sirloins of beef among the kitchen-stuff, and sheets in the rag-bag. A little while afterwards, he broke out in an entirely new direction, and confessed to a knowledge of burglarious intentions as to our premises, on the part of the pot-boy, who was immediately taken up. I got to be so ashamed of being such a victim, that I would have given him any money to hold his tongue, or would have offered a round bribe for his being permitted to run away. It was an aggravating circumstance in the case that he had no idea of this, but conceived that he was making me amends in every new discovery: not to say, heaping obligations on my head.

At last I ran away myself, whenever I saw an emissary of the police approaching with some new intelligence; and lived a stealthy life until he was tried and ordered to be transported. Even then he couldn't be quiet, but was always writing us letters; and wanted so much to see Dora before he went away, that Dora went to visit him, and fainted when she found herself inside the iron bars. In short, I had no peace of my life until he was expatriated, and made (as I afterwards heard) a shepherd of, "up the country" somewhere; I have no geographical idea where.

All this led me into some serious reflections, and presented our mistakes in a new aspect; as I could not help communicating to Dora one evening, in spite of my tenderness for her.

"My love," said, I, "it is very painful to me to think that our want of system and management, involves not only ourselves (which we have got used to), but other people."

"You have been silent for a long time, and now you are going to be cross!" said Dora.

"No, my dear, indeed! Let me explain to you what I mean."

"I think I don't want to know," said Dora.

"But I want you to know, my love. Put Jip down."

Dora put his nose to mine, and said "Boh!" to drive my seriousness away; but, not succeeding, ordered him into his Pagoda, and sat looking at me, with her hands folded, and a most resigned little expression of countenance.

"The fact is, my dear," I began, "there is contagion in us. We infect everyone about us."

I might have gone on in this figurative manner, if Dora's face had not admonished me that she was wondering with all her might whether I was going to propose any new kind of vaccination, or other medical remedy, for this unwholesome state of ours. Therefore I checked myself, and made my meaning plainer.

"It is not merely, my pet," said I, "that we lose money and comfort, and even temper sometimes, by not learning to be more careful; but that we incur the serious responsibility of spoiling everyone who comes into our service, or has any dealings with us. I begin to be afraid that the fault is not entirely on one side, but that these people all turn out ill because we don't turn out very well ourselves."

"Oh, what an accusation," exclaimed Dora, opening her eyes wide; "to say that you ever saw me take gold watches! Oh!"

"My dearest." I remonstrated, "don't talk preposterous nonsense! Who has made the least allusion to gold watches?"

"You did," returned Dora. "You know you did. You said I hadn't turned out well, and compared me to him."

"To whom?" I asked.

"To the page," sobbed Dora. "Oh, you cruel fellow, to compare your affectionate wife to a transported page! Why didn't you tell me your opinion of me before we were married? Why didn't you say, you hard-hearted thing, that you were convinced I was worse than a transported page? Oh, what a dreadful opinion to have of me! Oh, my goodness!"

"Now, Dora, my love," I returned, gently trying to remove the handkerchief she pressed to her eyes, "this is not only very ridiculous of you, but very wrong. In the first place, it's not true."

"You always said he was a story-teller," sobbed Dora. "And now you say the same of me! Oh, what shall I do! What shall I do!"

"My darling girl," I retorted, "I really must entreat you to be reasonable, and listen to what I did say, and do say. My dear Dora, unless we learn to do our duty to those whom we employ, they will never learn to do their duty to us. I am afraid we present opportunities to people to do wrong, that never ought to be presented. Even if we were as lax as we are, in all our arrangements, by choice—which we are not—even if we liked it, and found it agreeable to be so—which we don't—I am persuaded we should have no right to go on in this way. We are positively corrupting people. We are bound to think of that. I can't help thinking of it, Dora. It is a reflection I am unable to dismiss, and it sometimes makes me very uneasy. There, dear, that's all. Come now. Don't be foolish!"

Dora would not allow me, for a long time, to remove the handkerchief. She sat sobbing and murmuring behind it, that, if I was uneasy, why had I ever been married? Why hadn't I said, even the day before we went to church, that I knew I should be uneasy, and I would rather not? If I couldn't bear her, why didn't I send her away to her aunts at Putney, or to Julia Mills in India? Julia would be glad to see her, and would not call her a transported page; Julia never had called her anything of the sort. In short, Dora was so afflicted, and so afflicted me by being in that condition, that I felt it was of no use repeating this kind of effort, though never so mildly, and I must take some other course.

What other course was left to take? To "form her mind"? This was a common phrase of words which had a fair and promising sound, and I resolved to form Dora's mind.

I began immediately. When Dora was very childish, and I would have infinitely preferred to humour her, I tried to be grave—and disconcerted her, and myself too. I talked to her on the subjects which occupied my thoughts; and I read Shakespeare to her—and fatigued her to the last degree. I accustomed myself to giving her, as it were quite casually, little scraps of useful information, or sound opinion—and she started from them when I let them off, as if they had been crackers. No matter how incidentally or naturally I endeavoured to form my little wife's mind, I could not help seeing that she always had an instinctive perception of what I was about, and became a prey to the keenest apprehensions. In particular, it was clear to me, that she thought Shakespeare a terrible fellow. The formation went on very slowly.

I pressed Traddles into the service without his knowledge; and whenever he came to see us, exploded my mines upon him for the edification of Dora at second hand. The amount of practical wisdom I bestowed upon Traddles in this manner was immense, and of the best quality; but it had no other effect upon Dora than to depress her spirits, and make her always nervous with the dread that it would be her turn next. I found myself in the condition of a schoolmaster, a trap, a pitfall; of always playing spider to Dora's fly, and always pouncing out of my hole to her infinite disturbance.

Still, looking forward through this intermediate stage, to the time when there should be a perfect sympathy between Dora and me, and when I should have "formed her mind" to my entire satisfaction, I persevered, even for months. Finding at last, however, that, although I had been all this time a very porcupine or hedgehog, bristling all over with determination, I had effected nothing, it began to occur to me that perhaps Dora's mind was already formed.

On further consideration this appeared so likely, that I abandoned my scheme, which had had a more promising appearance in words than in action; resolving henceforth to be satisfied with my child-wife, and to try to change her into nothing else by any process. I was heartily tired of being sagacious and prudent by myself, and of seeing my darling under restraint; so I bought a pretty pair of ear-rings for her, and a collar for Jip, and went home one day to make myself agreeable.

Dora was delighted with the little presents, and kissed me joyfully; but, there was a shadow between us, however slight, and I had made up my mind that it should not be there. If there must be such a shadow anywhere, I would keep it for the future in my own breast.

I sat down by my wife on the sofa, and put the ear-rings in her ears; and then I told her that I feared we had not been quite as good company lately, as we used to be, and that the fault was mine. Which I sincerely felt, and which indeed it was.

"The truth is, Dora, my life," I said; "I have been trying to be wise."

"And to make me wise too," said Dora, timidly. "Haven't you, Doady?"

I nodded assent to the pretty inquiry of the raised eyebrows, and kissed the parted lips.

"It's of not a bit of use," said Dora, shaking her head, until the ear-rings rang again. "You know what a little thing I am, and what I wanted you to call me from the first. If you can't do so, I am afraid you'll never like me. Are you sure you don't think, sometimes, it would have been better to have—"

"Done what, my dear?" For she made no effort to proceed.

"Nothing!" said Dora.

"Nothing?" I repeated.

She put her arms round my neck, and laughed, and called herself by her favourite name of a goose, and hid her face on my shoulder in such a profusion of curls that it was quite a task to clear them away and see it.

"Don't I think it would have been better to have done nothing, than to have tried to form my little wife's mind?" said I, laughing at myself. "Is that the question? Yes, indeed, I do."

"Is that what you have been trying?" cried Dora. "Oh what a shocking boy!"

"But I shall never try any more," said I. "For I love her dearly as she is."

"Without a story—really?" inquired Dora, creeping closer to me.

"Why should I seek to change," said I, "what has been so precious to me for so long! You never can show better than as your own natural self, my sweet Dora; and we'll try no conceited experiments, but go back to our old way, and be happy."

"And be happy!" returned Dora. "Yes! All day! And you won't mind things going a tiny morsel wrong, sometimes?"

"No, no," said I. "We must do the best we can."

"And you won't tell me, any more, that we make other people bad," coaxed Dora; "will you? Because you know it's so dreadfully cross!"

"No, no," said I.

"It's better for me to be stupid than uncomfortable, isn't it?" said Dora.

"Better to be naturally Dora than anything else in the world."

"In the world! Ah, Doady, it's a large place!"

She shook her head, turned her delighted bright eyes up to mine, kissed me, broke into a merry laugh, and sprang away to put on Jip's new collar.

So ended my last attempt to make any change in Dora. I had been unhappy in trying it; I could not endure my own solitary wisdom; I could not reconcile it with her former appeal to me as my child-wife. I resolved to do what I could, in a quiet way, to improve our proceedings myself; but, I foresaw that my utmost would be very little, or I must degenerate into the spider again, and be for ever lying in wait.

And the shadow I have mentioned, that was not to be between us any more, but was to rest wholly on my own heart? How did that fall?

The old unhappy feeling pervaded my life. It was deepened, if it were changed at all; but it was as undefined as ever, and addressed me like a strain of sorrowful music faintly heard in the night. I loved my wife dearly, and I was happy; but the happiness I had vaguely anticipated, once, was not the happiness I enjoyed, and there was always something wanting.

In fulfilment of the compact I have made with myself, to reflect my mind on this paper, I again examine it, closely, and bring its secrets to the light. What I missed, I still regarded—I always regarded—as something that had been a dream of my youthful fancy; that was incapable of realization; that I was now discovering to be so, with some natural pain, as all men did. But that it would have been better for me if my wife could have helped me more, and shared the many thoughts in which I had no partner; and that this might have been, I knew.

Between these two irreconcilable conclusions: the one, that what I felt was general and unavoidable; the other, that it was particular to me, and might have been different: I balanced curiously, with no distinct sense of their opposition to each other. When I thought of the airy dreams of youth that are incapable of realization, I thought of the better state preceding manhood that I had outgrown; and then the contented days with Agnes, in the dear old house, arose before me, like spectres of the dead, that might have some renewal in another world, but never more could be reanimated here.

Sometimes, the speculation came into my thoughts, What might have happened, or what would have happened, if Dora and I had never known each other? But she was so incorporated with my existence, that it was the idlest of all fancies, and would soon rise out of my reach and sight, like gossamer floating in the air.

I always loved her. What I am describing, slumbered, and half awoke, and slept again, in the innermost recesses of my mind. There was no evidence of it in me; I know of no influence it had in anything I said or did. I bore the weight of all our little cares, and all my projects; Dora held the pens; and we both felt that our shares were adjusted as the case required. She was truly fond of me, and proud of me; and when Agnes wrote a few earnest words in her letters to Dora, of the pride and interest with which my old friends heard of my growing reputation, and read my book as if they heard me speaking its contents, Dora read them out to me with tears of joy in her bright eyes, and said I was a dear old clever, famous boy.

"The first mistaken impulse of an undisciplined heart." Those words of Mrs Strong's were constantly recurring to me, at this time; were almost always present to my mind. I awoke with them, often, in the night; I remember to have even read them, in dreams, inscribed upon the walls of houses. For I knew, now, that my own heart was undisciplined when it first loved Dora; and that if it had been disciplined, it never could have felt, when we were married, what it had felt in its secret experience.

"There can be no disparity in marriage, like unsuitability of mind and purpose." Those words I remembered too. I had endeavoured to adapt Dora to myself, and found it impracticable. It remained for me to adapt myself to Dora; to share with her what I could, and be happy; to bear on my own shoulders what I must, and be happy still. This was the discipline to which I tried to bring my heart, when I began to think. It made my second year much happier than my first; and, what was better still, made Dora's life all sunshine.

But, as that year wore on, Dora was not strong. I had hoped that lighter hands than mine would help to mould her character, and that a baby-smile upon her breast might change my child-wife to a woman. It was not to be. The spirit fluttered for a moment on the threshold of its little prison, and, unconscious of captivity, took wing.

"When I can run about again, as I used to do, aunt," said Dora, "I shall make Jip race. He is getting quite slow and lazy."

"I suspect, my dear," said my aunt quietly working by her side, "he has a worse disorder than that. Age, Dora."

"Do you think he is old?" said Dora, astonished. "Oh, how strange it seems that Jip should be old!"

"It's a complaint we are all liable to, Little One, as we get on in life," said my aunt, cheerfully; "I don't feel more free from it than I used to be, I assure you."

"But Jip," said Dora, looking at him with compassion, "even little Jip! Oh, poor fellow!"

"I dare say he'll last a long time yet, Blossom," said my aunt, patting Dora on the cheek, as she leaned out of her couch to look at Jip, who responded by standing on his hind legs, and baulking himself in various asthmatic attempts to scramble up by the head and shoulders. "He must have a piece of flannel in his house this winter, and I shouldn't wonder if he came out quite fresh again, with the flowers in the spring. Bless the little dog!" exclaimed my aunt, "if he had as many lives as a cat, and was on the point of losing 'em all, he'd bark at me with his last breath, I believe!"

Dora had helped him up on the sofa; where he really was defying my aunt to such a furious extent, that he couldn't keep straight, but barked himself sideways. The more my aunt looked at him, the more he reproached her; for, she had lately taken to spectacles, and for some inscrutable reason he considered the glasses personal.

Dora made him lie down by her, with a good deal of persuasion; and when he was quiet, drew one of his long ears through and through her hand, repeating thoughtfully, "Even little Jip! Oh, poor fellow!"

"His lungs are good enough," said my aunt, gaily, "and his dislikes are not at all feeble. He has a good many years before him, no doubt. But if you want a dog to race with, Little Blossom, he has lived too well for that, and I'll give you one."

"Thank you, aunt," said Dora, faintly. "But don't, please!"

"No?" said my aunt, taking off her spectacles.

"I couldn't have any other dog but Jip," said Dora. "It would be so unkind to Jip! Besides, I couldn't be such friends with any other dog but Jip; because he wouldn't have known me before I was married, and wouldn't have barked at Doady when he first came to our house. I couldn't care for any other dog but Jip, I am afraid, aunt."

"To be sure!" said my aunt, patting her cheek again. "You are right."

"You are not offended," said Dora. "Are you?"

"Why, what a sensitive pet it is!" cried my aunt, bending over her affectionately. "To think that I could be offended!"

"No, no, I didn't really think so," returned Dora; "but I am a little tired, and it made me silly for a moment—I am always a silly little thing, you know, but it made me more silly—to talk about Jip. He has known me in all that has happened to me, haven't you, Jip? And I couldn't bear to slight him, because he was a little altered—could I, Jip?"

Jip nestled closer to his mistress, and lazily licked her hand.

"You are not so old, Jip, are you, that you'll leave your mistress yet?" said Dora. "We may keep one another company a little longer!"

My pretty Dora! When she came down to dinner on the ensuing Sunday, and was so glad to see old Traddles (who always dined with us on Sunday), we thought she would be "running about as she used to do," in a few days. But they said, wait a few days more; and then, wait a few days more; and still she neither ran nor walked. She looked very pretty, and was very merry; but the little feet that used to be so nimble when they danced round Jip, were dull and motionless.

I began to carry her downstairs every morning, and upstairs every night. She would clasp me round the neck and laugh, the while, as if I did it for a wager. Jip would bark and caper round us, and go on before, and look back on the landing, breathing short, to see that we were coming. My aunt, the best and most cheerful of nurses, would trudge after us, a moving mass of shawls and pillows. Mr Dick would not have relinquished his post of candle-bearer to anyone alive. Traddles would be often at the bottom of the staircase, looking on, and taking charge of sportive messages from Dora to the dearest girl in the world. We made quite a gay procession of it, and my child-wife was the gayest there.

But, sometimes, when I took her up, and felt that she was lighter in my arms, a dead blank feeling came upon me, as if I were approaching to some frozen region yet unseen, that numbed my life. I avoided the recognition of this feeling by any name, or by any communing with myself; until one night, when it was very strong upon me, and my aunt had left her with a parting cry of "Good night, Little Blossom," I sat down at my desk alone, and cried to think, Oh what a fatal name it was, and how the blossom withered in its bloom upon the tree!

Chapter XLIX

I AM INVOLVED IN MYSTERY

I RECEIVED one morning by the post, the following letter, dated Canterbury, and addressed to me at Doctor's Commons; which I read with some surprise:

MY DEAR SIR,

"Circumstances beyond my individual control have, for a considerable lapse of time, effected a severance of that intimacy which, in the limited opportunities conceded to me in the midst of my professional duties, of contemplating the scenes and events of the past, tinged by the prismatic hues of memory, has ever afforded me, as it ever must continue to afford, gratifying emotions of no common description. This fact, my dear sir, combined with the distinguished elevation to which your talents have raised you, deters me from presuming to aspire to the liberty of addressing the companion of my youth, by the familiar appellation of Copperfield! It is sufficient to know that the name to which I do myself the honour to refer, will ever be treasured among the muniments of our house (I allude to the archives connected with our former lodgers, preserved by Mrs Micawber), with sentiments of personal esteem amounting to affection.

"It is not for one, situated, through his original errors and a fortuitous combination of unpropitious events, as is the foundered Bark (if he may be allowed to assume so maritime a denomination), who now takes up the pen to address you—it is not, I repeat, for one so circumstanced, to adopt the language of compliment, or of congratulation. That he leaves to abler and to purer hands.

"If your more important avocations should admit of your ever tracing these imperfect characters thus far—which may be, or may not be, as circumstances arise—you will naturally inquire by what object am I influenced, then, in inditing the present missive? Allow me to say that I fully defer to the reasonable character of that inquiry, and proceed to develop it; premising that it is *not* an object of a pecuniary nature.

"Without more directly referring to any latent ability that may possibly exist on my part, of wielding the thunderbolt, or directing the devouring and avenging flame in any quarter, I may be permitted to observe, in passing, that my brightest visions are for ever dispelled—that my peace is shattered and my power of enjoyment destroyed—that my heart is no longer in the right place—and that I no more walk erect before my fellow man. The canker is in the flower. The cup is bitter to the brim. The worm is at his work, and will soon dispose of his victim. The sooner the better. But I will not digress.

"Placed in a mental position of peculiar painfulness, beyond the assuaging reach even of Mrs Micawber's influence, though exercised in the tripartite character of woman, wife, and mother, it is my intention to fly from myself for a short period, and devote a respite of eight-and-forty hours to revisiting some metropolitan scenes of past enjoyment. Among other havens of domestic tranquillity and peace of mind, my feet will naturally tend towards the King's Bench Prison. In stating that I shall be (D. V.) on the outside of the south wall of that place of incarceration on civil process, the day after tomorrow, at seven in the evening, precisely, my object in this epistolary communication is accomplished.

"I do not feel warranted in soliciting my former friend Mr Copperfield, or my former friend Mr Thomas Traddles of the Inner Temple, if that gentleman is still existent and forthcoming, to condescend to meet me, and renew (so far as may be) our past relations of the olden time. I confine myself to throwing out the observation, that, at the hour and place I have indicated, may be found such ruined vestiges as yet

"Remain,

"Of

"A

"Fallen Tower,

"WILKINS MICAWBER.

"P.S. It may be advisable to superadd to the above, the statement that Mrs Micawber is *not* in confidential possession of my intentions."

I read the letter over several times. Making due allowance for Mr Micawber's lofty style of composition, and for the extraordinary relish with which he sat down and wrote long letters on all possible and impossible occasions, I still believed that something important lay hidden at the bottom of this roundabout communication. I put it down, to think about it; and took it up again, to read it once more; and was still pursuing it, when Traddles found me in the height of my perplexity.

"My dear fellow," said I, "I never was better pleased to see you. You come to give me the benefit of your sober judgment at a most opportune time. I have received a very singular letter, Traddles, from Mr Micawber."

"No?" cried Traddles. "You don't say so? And I have received one from Mrs Micawber!"

With that, Traddles, who was flushed with walking, and whose hair, under the combined effects of exercise and excitement, stood on end as if he saw a cheerful ghost, produced his letter and made an exchange with me. I watched him into the heart of Mr Micawber's letter, and returned the elevation of eyebrows with which he said " 'Wielding the thunderbolt, or directing the devouring and avenging flame!' Bless me, Copperfield!"—and then entered on the perusal of Mrs Micawber's epistle.

It ran thus:

"My best regards to Mr Thomas Traddles, and if he should still remember one who formerly had the happiness of being well acquainted with him, may I beg a few moments of his leisure time? I assure Mr T. T. that I would not intrude upon his kindness, were I in any other position than on the confines of distraction.

"Though harrowing to myself to mention, the alienation of Mr Micawber (formerly so domesticated) from his wife and family, is the cause of my addressing my unhappy appeal to Mr Traddles, and soliciting his best indulgence. Mr T. can form no adequate idea of the change in Mr Micawber's conduct, of his wildness, of his violence. It has gradually augmented, until it assumes the appearance of aberration of intellect. Scarcely a day passes, I assure Mr Traddles, on which some paroxysm does not take place. Mr T. will not require me to depict my feelings, when I inform him that I have become accustomed to hear Mr Micawber assert that he has sold himself to the D. Mystery and secrecy have long been his principal characteristic, have long replaced unlimited confidence. The slightest provocation, even being asked if there is anything he would prefer for dinner, causes him to express a wish for a separation. Last night, on being childishly solicited for two-pence, to buy "lemon-stunners"—a local sweetmeat—he presented an oyster-knife at the twins!

"I entreat Mr Traddles to bear with me in entering into these details. Without them, Mr T. would indeed find it difficult to form the faintest conception of my heart-rending situation.

"May I now venture to confide to Mr T. the purport of my letter? Will he now allow me to throw myself on his friendly consideration? Oh yes, for I know his heart!

"The quick eye of affection is not easily blinded, when of the female sex. Mr Micawber is going to London. Though he studiously concealed his hand, this morning before breakfast, in writing the direction-card which he attached to the little brown valise of happier days, the eagle-glance of matrimonial anxiety detected, d, o, n, distinctly traced. The West-End destination of the coach, is the Golden Cross. Dare I fervently implore Mr T. to see my misguided husband, and to reason with him? Dare I ask Mr T. to endeavour to step in between Mr Micawber and his agonized family? Oh no, for that would be too much!

"If Mr Copperfield should yet remember one unknown to fame, will Mr T. take charge of my unalterable regards and similar entreaties? In any case, he will have the benevolence *to consider this communication strictly private, and on no account whatever to be alluded to, however distantly, in the presence of Mr Micawber.* If Mr T. should ever reply to it (which I cannot but feel to be *most* improbable), a letter addressed to M. E., Post Office, Canterbury, will be fraught with less painful consequences than any addressed immediately to one, who subscribes herself, in extreme distress,

"Mr Thomas Traddles's respectful friend and suppliant,

"EMMA MICAWBER."

"What do you think of that letter?" said Traddles, casting his eyes upon me, when I had read it twice.

"What do you think of the other?" said I. For he was still reading it with knitted brows.

"I think that the two together, Copperfield," replied Traddles, "mean more than Mr and Mrs Micawber usually mean in their correspondence—but I don't know what. They are both written in good faith, I have no doubt, and without any collusion. Poor thing!" he was now alluding to Mrs Micawber's letter, and we were standing side by side comparing the two; "it will be a charity to write to her, at all events, and tell her that we will not fail to see Mr Micawber."

I acceded to this the more readily, because I now reproached myself with having treated her former letter rather lightly. It had set me thinking a good deal at the time, as I have mentioned in its place; but my absorption in my own affairs, my experience of the family, and my hearing nothing more, had gradually ended in my dismissing the subject. I had often thought of the Micawbers, but chiefly to wonder what "pecuniary liabilities" they were establishing in Canterbury, and to recall how shy Mr Micawber was of me when he became clerk to Uriah Heep.

However, I now wrote a comforting letter to Mrs Micawber, in our joint names, and we both signed it. As we walked into town to post it, Traddles and I held a long conference, and launched into a number of speculations, which I need not repeat. We took my aunt into our counsels in the afternoon; but our only decided conclusion was, that we would be very punctual in keeping Mr Micawber's appointment.

Although we appeared at the stipulated place a quarter of an hour before the time, we found Mr Micawber already there. He was standing with his arms folded, over against the wall, looking at the spikes on the top, with a sentimental expression, as if they were the interlacing boughs of trees that had shaded him in his youth.

When we accosted him, his manner was something more confused, and something less genteel, than of yore. He had relinquished his legal suit of black for the purposes of this excursion, and wore the old surtout and tights, but not quite with the old air. He gradually picked up more and more of it as we conversed with him; but, his very eye-glass seemed to hang less easily, and his shirt-collar, though still of the old formidable dimensions, rather drooped.

"Gentlemen!" said Mr Micawber, after the first salutations, "you are friends in need, and friends indeed. Allow me to offer my inquiries with reference to the physical welfare of Mrs Copperfield *in esse,* and Mrs Traddles *in posse,*—presuming, that is to say, that my friend Mr Traddles is not yet united to the object of his affections, for weal and for woe."

We acknowledged his politeness, and made suitable replies. He then directed our attention to the wall, and was beginning, "I assure you, gentlemen," when I ventured to object to that ceremonious form of address, and to beg that he would speak to us in the old way.

"My dear Copperfield," he returned, pressing my hand, "your cordiality overpowers me. This reception of a shattered fragment of the Temple once called Man—if I may be permitted so to express myself—bespeaks a heart that is an honour to our common nature. I was about to observe that I again behold the serene spot where some of the happiest hours of my existence fleeted by."

"Made so, I am sure, by Mrs Micawber," said I. "I hope she is well?"

"Thank you," returned Mr Micawber, whose face clouded at this reference, "she is but so-so. And this," said Mr Micawber, nodding his head sorrowfully, "is the Bench! Where, for the first time in many revolving years, the overwhelming pressure of pecuniary liabilities was not proclaimed, from day to day, by importune voices declining to vacate the passage; where there was no knocker on the door for any creditor to appeal to; where personal service of process was not required, and detainers were merely lodged at the gate! Gentlemen," said Mr Micawber, "when the shadow of that iron-work on the summit of the brick structure has been reflected on the gravel of the Parade, I have seen my children thread the mazes of the intricate pattern, avoiding the dark marks. I have been familiar with every stone in the place. If I betray weakness, you will know how to excuse me."

"We have all got on in life since then, Mr Micawber," said I.

"Mr Copperfield," returned Mr Micawber, bitterly, "when I was an inmate of that retreat I could look my fellow-man in the face, and punch his head if he offended me. My fellow-man and myself are no longer on those glorious terms!"

Turning from the building in a downcast manner, Mr Micawber accepted my proffered arm on one side, and the proffered arm of Traddles on the other, and walked away between us.

"There are some landmarks," observed Mr Micawber, looking fondly back over his shoulder, "on the road to the tomb, which, but for the impiety of the aspiration, a man would wish never to have passed. Such is the Bench in my chequered career."

"Oh, you are in low spirits, Mr Micawber," said Traddles.

"I am, sir," interposed Mr Micawber.

"I hope," said Traddles, "it is not because you have conceived a dislike to the law—for I am a lawyer myself, you know."

Mr Micawber answered not a word.

"How is our friend Heep, Mr Micawber?" said I, after a silence.

"My dear Copperfield," returned Mr Micawber, bursting into a state of much excitement, and turning pale, "if you ask after my employer as *your* friend, I am sorry for it; if you ask after him as *my* friend, I sardonically smile at it. In whatever capacity you ask after my employer, I beg, without offence to you, to limit my reply to this—that whatever his state of health may be, his appearance is foxy: not to say diabolical. You will allow me, as a private individual, to decline pursuing a subject which has lashed me to the utmost verge of desperation in my professional capacity."

I expressed my regret for having innocently touched upon a theme that roused him so much. "May I ask," said I, "without any hazard of repeating the mistake, how my old friends Mr and Miss Wickfield are?"

"Miss Wickfield," said Mr Micawber, now turning red, "is, as she always is, a pattern, and a bright example. My dear Copperfield, she is the only starry spot in a miserable existence. My respect for that young lady, my admiration of her character, my devotion to her for her love and truth, and goodness!—Take me," said Mr Micawber, "down a turning, for, upon my soul, in my present state of mind I am not equal to this!"

We wheeled him off into a narrow street, where he took out his pocket-handkerchief, and stood with his back to a wall. If I looked as gravely at him as Traddles did, he must have found our company by no means inspiriting.

"It is my fate," said Mr Micawber, unfeignedly sobbing, but doing even that, with a shadow of the old expression of doing something genteel; "it is my fate, gentlemen, that the finer feelings of our nature have become reproaches to me. My homage to Miss Wickfield, is a flight of arrows in my bosom. You had better leave me, if you please, to walk the earth as a vagabond. The worm will settle *my* business in double-quick time."

Without attending to this invocation, we stood by, until he put up his pocket-handkerchief, pulled up his shirt-collar, and, to delude any person in the neighbourhood who might have been observing him, hummed a tune with his hat very much on one side. I then mentioned—not knowing what might be lost if we lost sight of him yet—that it would give me great pleasure to introduce him to my aunt, if he would ride out to Highgate, where a bed was at his service.

"You shall make us a glass of your own punch, Mr Micawber," said I, "and forget whatever you have on your mind, in pleasanter reminiscences."

"Or, if confiding anything to friends will be more likely to relieve you, you shall impart it to us, Mr Micawber," said Traddles, prudently.

"Gentlemen," returned Mr Micawber, "do with me as you will! I am a straw upon the surface of the deep, and am tossed in all directions by the elephants—I beg your pardon; I should have said the elements."

We walked on, arm-in-arm, again; found the coach in the act of starting; and arrived at Highgate without encountering any difficulties by the way. I was very uneasy and very uncertain in my mind what to say or do for the best—so was Traddles, evidently. Mr Micawber was for the most part plunged into deep gloom. He occasionally made an attempt to smarten himself, and hum the fag-end of a tune; but his relapses into profound melancholy were only made the more impressive by the mockery of a hat exceedingly on one side, and a shirt-collar pulled up to his eyes.

We went to my aunt's house rather than to mine, because of Dora's not being well. My aunt presented herself on being sent for, and welcomed Mr Micawber with gracious cordiality. Mr Micawber kissed her hand, retired to the window, and pulling out his pocket-handkerchief, had a mental wrestle with himself.

Mr Dick was at home. He was by nature so exceedingly compassionate of anyone who seemed to be ill at ease, and was so quick to find any such person out, that he shook hands with Mr Micawber, at least half-a-dozen times in five minutes. To Mr Micawber, in his trouble, this warmth, on the part of a stranger, was so extremely touching, that he could only say, on the occasion of each successive shake, "My dear sir, you overpower me!" Which gratified Mr Dick so much, that he went at it again with greater vigour than before.

"The friendliness of this gentleman," said Mr Micawber to my aunt, "if you will allow me, ma'am, to cull a figure of speech from the vocabulary of our coarser national sports—floors me. To a man who is struggling with a complicated burden of perplexity and disquiet, such a reception is trying, I assure you."

"My friend Mr Dick," replied my aunt proudly, "is not a common man."

"That I am convinced of," said Mr Micawber. "My dear sir!" for Mr Dick was shaking hands with him again; "I am deeply sensible of your cordiality!"

"How do you find yourself?" said Mr Dick, with an anxious look.

"Indifferent, my dear sir," returned Mr Micawber, sighing.

"You must keep up your spirits," said Mr Dick, "and make yourself as comfortable as possible."

Mr Micawber was quite overcome by these friendly words, and by finding Mr Dick's hand again within his own. "It has been my lot," he observed, "to meet, in the diversified panorama of human existence, with an occasional oasis, but never with one so green, so gushing, as the present!"

At another time I should have been amused by this; but I felt that we were all constrained and uneasy, and I watched Mr Micawber so anxiously, in his vacillations between an evident disposition to reveal something, and a counter-disposition to reveal nothing, that I was in a perfect fever. Traddles, sitting on the edge of his chair, with his eyes wide open, and his hair more emphatically erect than ever, stared by turns at the ground and at Mr Micawber, without so much as attempting to put in a word. My aunt, though I saw that her shrewdest observation was concentrated on her new guest, had more useful possession of her wits than either of us; for she held him in conversation, and made it necessary for him to talk, whether he liked it or not.

"You are a very old friend of my nephew's, Mr Micawber," said my aunt. "I wish I had had the pleasure of seeing you before."

"Madam," returned Mr Micawber, "I wish I had had the honour of knowing you at an earlier period. I was not always the wreck you at present behold."

"I hope Mrs Micawber and your family are well, sir," said my aunt.

Mr Micawber inclined his head. "They are as well, ma'am," he desperately observed after a pause, "as Aliens and Outcasts can ever hope to be."

"Lord, bless you, sir!" exclaimed my aunt, in her abrupt way. "What are you talking about?"

"The subsistence of my family, ma'am," returned Mr Micawber, "trembles in the balance. My employer—"

Here Mr Micawber provokingly left off; and began to peel the lemons that had been under my directions set before him, together with all the other appliances he used in making punch.

"Your employer, you know," said Mr Dick, jogging his arm as a gentle reminder.

"My good sir," returned Mr Micawber, "you recall me, I am obliged to you." They shook hands again. "My employer, ma'am—Mr Heep—once did me the favour to observe to me, that if I were not in the receipt of the stipendiary emoluments appertaining to my engagement with him, I should probably be a mountebank about the country, swallowing a sword-blade, and eating the devouring element. For anything that I can perceive to the contrary, it is still probable that my children may be reduced to seek a livelihood by personal contortion, while Mrs Micawber abets their unnatural feats by playing the barrel-organ."

Mr Micawber, with a random but expressive flourish of his knife, signified that these performances might be expected to take place after he was no more; then resumed his peeling with a desperate air.

My aunt leaned her elbow on the little round table that she usually kept beside her, and eyed him attentively. Notwithstanding the aversion with which I regarded the idea of entrapping him into any disclosure he was not prepared to make voluntarily, I should have taken him up at this point, but for the strange proceedings in which I saw him engaged; whereof his putting the lemon-peel into the kettle, the sugar into the snuffer-tray, the spirit into the empty jug, and confidently attempting to pour boiling water out of a candlestick, were among the most remarkable. I saw that a crisis was at hand, and it came. He clattered all his means and implements together, rose from his chair, pulled out his pocket-handkerchief, and burst into tears.

"My dear Copperfield," said Mr Micawber, behind his handkerchief, "this is an occupation, of all others, requiring an untroubled mind, and self-respect. I cannot perform it. It is out of the question."

"Mr Micawber," said I, "what is the matter? Pray speak out. You are among friends."

"Among friends, sir!" repeated Mr Micawber; and all he had reserved came breaking out of him. "Good heavens, it is principally because I *am* among friends that my state of mind is what it is. What is the matter, gentlemen? What is *not* the matter? Villainy is the matter; baseness is the matter; deception, fraud, conspiracy, are the matter; and the name of the whole atrocious mass is—HEEP!"

My aunt clapped her hands, and we all started up as if we were possessed.

"The struggle is over!" said Mr Micawber, violently gesticulating with his pocket-handkerchief, and fairly striking out from time to time with both arms, as if he were swimming under superhuman difficulties. "I will lead this life no longer. I am a wretched being, cut off from everything that makes life tolerable. I have been under a Taboo in that infernal scoundrel's service. Give me back my wife, give me back my family, substitute Micawber for the petty wretch who walks about in the boots at present on my feet, and call upon me to swallow a sword tomorrow, and I'll do it. With an appetite!"

I never saw a man so hot in my life. I tried to calm him, that we might come to something rational; but he got hotter and hotter, and wouldn't hear a word.

"I'll put my hand in no man's hand," said Mr Micawber, gasping, puffing, and sobbing, to that degree that he was like a man fighting with cold water, "until I have—blown to fragments—the—a—detestable—serpent—HEEP! I'll partake of no one's hospitality, until I have—a—moved Mount Vesuvius—to eruption—on—a—the abandoned rascal—HEEP! Refreshment—a—underneath this roof—particularly punch—would—a—choke me—unless—I had—previously—choked the eyes—out of the head—a—of—interminable cheat, and liar—HEEP! I—a—I'll know nobody—and—a—say nothing—and—a—live nowhere—until I have crushed—to—a—undiscoverable atoms—the—transcendent and immortal hypocrite and perjurer—HEEP!"

I really had some fear of Mr Micawber's dying on the spot. The manner in which he struggled through these inarticulate sentences, and, whenever he found himself getting near the name of Heep, fought his way on to it, dashed at it in a fainting state, and brought it out with a vehemence little less than marvellous, was frightful; but now, when he sank into a chair, steaming, and looked at us, with every possible colour in his face that had no business there, and an endless procession of lumps following one another in hot haste up his throat, whence they seemed to shoot into his forehead, he had the appearance of being in the last extremity. I would have gone to his assistance, but he waved me off, and wouldn't hear a word.

"No, Copperfield!—No communication—a—until—Miss Wickfield—a—redress from wrongs inflicted by consummate scoundrel—HEEP!" (I am quite convinced he could not have uttered three words, but for the amazing energy with which this word inspired him when he felt it coming.) "Inviolable secret—a—from the whole world—a—no exceptions—this day week—a—at breakfast-time—a—everybody present—including aunt—a—and extremely friendly gentleman—to be at the hotel at Canterbury—a—where—Mrs Micawber and myself—Auld Lang Syne in chorus—and—a—will expose intolerable ruffian—HEEP! No more to say—a—or listen to persuasion—go immediately—not capable—a—bear society—upon the track of devoted and doomed traitor—HEEP!"

With this last repetition of the magic word that had kept him going at all, and in which he surpassed all his previous efforts, Mr Micawber rushed out of the house; leaving us in a state of excitement, hope, and wonder, that reduced us to a condition little better than his own. But even then his passion for writing letters was too strong to be resisted; for while we were yet in the height of our excitement, hope, and wonder, the following pastoral note was brought to me from a neighbouring tavern, at which he had called to write it:—

"Most secret and confidential.

"MY DEAR SIR,

"I beg to be allowed to convey, through you, my apologies to your excellent aunt for my late excitement. An explosion of a smouldering volcano long suppressed, was the result of an internal contest more easily conceived than described.

"I trust I rendered tolerably intelligible my appointment for the morning of this day week, at the house of public entertainment at Canterbury, where Mrs Micawber and myself had once the honour of uniting our voices to yours, in the well-known strain of the Immortal exciseman nurtured beyond the Tweed.

"The duty done, and act of reparation performed, which can alone enable me to contemplate my fellow mortal, I shall be known no more. I shall simply require to be deposited in that place of universal resort, where

" 'Each in his narrow cell for ever laid,

" 'The rude forefathers of the hamlet sleep,'

"—With the plain Inscription,

"WILKINS MICAWBER."

Chapter L

MR PEGGOTTY'S DREAM COMES TRUE

BY this time, some months had passed since our interview on the bank of the river with Martha. I had never seen her since, but she had communicated with Mr Peggotty on several occasions. Nothing had come of her zealous intervention; nor could I infer, from what he told me, that any clue had been obtained, for a moment, to Emily's fate. I confess that I began to despair of her recovery, and gradually to sink deeper and deeper into the belief that she was dead.

His conviction remained unchanged. So far as I know—and I believe his honest heart was transparent to me—he never wavered again, in his solemn certainty of finding her. His patience never tired. And, although I trembled for the agony it might one day be to him to have his strong assurance shivered at a blow, there was something so religious in it, so affectingly expressive of its anchor being in the purest depths of his fine nature, that the respect and honour in which I held him were exalted every day.

His was not a lazy trustfulness that hoped, and did no more. He had been a man of sturdy action all his life, and he knew that in all things wherein he wanted help he must do his own part faithfully, and help himself. I have known him set out in the night, on a misgiving that the light might not be, by some accident, in the window of the old boat, and walk to Yarmouth. I have known him, on reading something in the newspaper that might apply to her, take up his stick, and go forth on a journey of three- or four-score miles. He made his way by sea to Naples, and back, after hearing the narrative to which Miss Dartle had assisted me. All his journeys were ruggedly performed; for he was always steadfast in a purpose of saving money for Emily's sake, when she should be found. In all this long pursuit, I never heard him repine; I never heard him say he was fatigued, or out of heart.

Dora had often seen him since our marriage, and was quite fond of him. I fancy his figure before me now, standing near her sofa, with his rough cap in his hand, and the blue eyes of my child-wife raised, with a timid wonder, to his face. Sometimes of an evening, about twilight, when he came to talk with me, I would induce him to smoke his pipe in the garden, as we slowly paced to and fro together; and then, the picture of his deserted home, and the comfortable air it used to have in my childish eyes of an evening when the fire was burning, and the wind moaning round it, came most vividly into my mind.

One evening, at this hour, he told me that he had found Martha waiting near his lodging on the preceding night when he came out, and that she had asked him not to leave London on any account, until he should have seen her again.

"Did she tell you why?" I inquired.

"I asked her, Mas'r Davy," he replied, "but it is but few words as she ever says, and she on'y got my promise and so went away."

"Did she say when you might expect to see her again?" I demanded.

"No, Mas'r Davy," he returned, drawing his hand thoughtfully down his face. "I asked that too; but it was more (she said) than she could tell."

As I had long forborne to encourage him with hopes that hung on threads, I made no other comment on this information than that I supposed he would see her soon. Such speculations as it engendered within me I kept to myself, and those were faint enough.

I was walking alone in the garden, one evening, about a fortnight afterwards. I remember that evening well. It was the second in Mr Micawber's week of suspense. There had been rain all day, and there was a damp feeling in the air. The leaves were thick upon the trees, and heavy with wet; but the rain had ceased, though the sky was still dark; and the hopeful birds were singing cheerfully. As I walked to and fro in the garden, and the twilight began to close around me, their little voices were hushed; and that peculiar silence which belongs to such an evening in the country when the lightest trees are quite still, save for the occasional droppings from their boughs, prevailed.

There was a little green perspective of trellis-work and ivy at the side of our cottage, through which I could see, from the garden where I was walking, into the road before the house. I happened to turn my eyes towards this place, as I was thinking of many things; and I saw a figure beyond, dressed in a plain cloak. It was bending eagerly towards me, and beckoning.

"Martha!" said I, going to it.

"Can you come with me?" she inquired, in an agitated whisper. "I have been to him, and he is not at home. I wrote down where he was to come, and left it on his table with my own hand. They said he would not be out long. I have tidings for him. Can you come directly?"

My answer was, to pass out at the gate immediately. She made a hasty gesture with her hand, as if to entreat my patience and my silence, and turned towards London, whence, as her dress betokened, she had come expeditiously on foot.

I asked her if that were not our destination? On her motioning Yes, with the same hasty gesture as before, I stopped an empty coach that was coming by, and we got into it. When I asked her where the coachman was to drive, she answered, "Anywhere near Golden Square! And quick!"—then shrunk into a corner, with one trembling hand before her face, and the other making the former gesture, as if she could not bear a voice.

Now much disturbed, and dazzled with conflicting gleams of hope and dread, I looked at her for some explanation. But seeing how strongly she desired to remain quiet, and feeling that it was my own natural inclination too, at such a time, I did not attempt to break the silence. We proceeded without a word being spoken. Sometimes she glanced out of the window, as though she thought we were going slowly, though indeed we were going fast; but otherwise remained exactly as at first.

We alighted at one of the entrances to the Square she had mentioned, where I directed the coach to wait, not knowing but that we might have some occasion for it. She laid her hand on my arm, and hurried me on to one of the sombre streets, of which there are several in that part, where the houses were once fair dwellings in the occupation of single families, but have, and had, long degenerated into poor lodgings let off in rooms. Entering at the open door of one of these, and releasing my arm, she beckoned me to follow her up the common staircase, which was like a tributary channel to the street.

The house swarmed with inmates. As we went up, doors of rooms were opened and people's heads put out; and we passed other people on the stairs, who were coming down. In glancing up from the outside, before we entered, I had seen women and children lolling at the windows over flower-pots; and we seemed to have attracted their curiosity, for these were principally the observers who looked out of their doors. It was a broad panelled staircase, with massive balustrades of some dark wood; cornices above the doors, ornamented with carved fruit and flowers; and broad seats in the windows. But all these tokens of past grandeur were miserably decayed and dirty; rot, damp, and age, had weakened the flooring, which in many places was unsound and even unsafe. Some attempts had been made, I noticed, to infuse new blood into this dwindling frame, by repairing the costly old wood-work here and there with common deal; but it was like the marriage of a reduced old noble to a plebeian pauper, and each party to the ill-assorted union shrunk away from the other. Several of the back windows on the staircase had been darkened or wholly blocked up. In those that remained, there was scarcely any glass; and, through the crumbling frames by which the bad air seemed always to come in, and never to go out, I saw, through other glassless windows, into other houses in a similar condition, and looked giddily down into a wretched yard, which was the common dust-heap of the mansion.

We proceeded to the top-storey of the house. Two or three times, by the way, I thought I observed in the indistinct light the skirts of a female figure going up before us. As we turned to ascend the last flight of stairs between us and the roof, we caught a full view of this figure pausing for a moment, at a door. Then it turned the handle, and went in.

"What's this!" said Martha, in a whisper. "She has gone into my room. I don't know her!"

I knew her. I had recognized her with amazement, for Miss Dartle.

I said something to the effect that it was a lady whom I had seen before, in a few words, to my conductress; and had scarcely done so, when we heard her voice in the room, though not, from where we stood, what she was saying. Martha, with an astonished look, repeated her former action, and softly led me up the stairs; and then, by a little back-door which seemed to have no lock, and which she pushed open with a touch, into a small empty garret with a low sloping roof: little better than a cupboard. Between this, and the room she had called hers, there was a small door of communication, standing partly open. Here we stopped, breathless with our ascent, and she placed her hand lightly on my lips. I could only see, of the room beyond, that it was pretty large; that there was a bed in it; and that there were some common pictures of ships upon the walls. I could not see Miss Dartle, or the person whom we had heard her address. Certainly, my companion could not, for my position was the best.

A dead silence prevailed for some moments. Martha kept one hand on my lips, and raised the other in a listening attitude.

"It matters little to me her not being at home," said Rosa Dartle haughtily, "I know nothing of her. It is you I come to see."

"Me?" replied a soft voice.

At the sound of it, a thrill went through my frame. For it was Emily's!

"Yes," returned Miss Dartle, "I have come to look at you. What? You are not ashamed of the face that has done so much?"

The resolute and unrelenting hatred of her tone, its cold stern sharpness, and its mastered rage, presented her before me, as if I had seen her standing in the light. I saw the flashing black eyes, and the passion-wasted figure; and I saw the scar, with its white track cutting through her lips, quivering and throbbing as she spoke.

"I have come to see," she said, "James Steerforth's fancy; the girl who ran away with him, and is the town-talk of the commonest people of her native place; the bold, flaunting, practised companion of persons like James Steerforth. I want to know what such a thing is like."

There was a rustle, as if the unhappy girl, on whom she heaped these taunts, ran towards the door, and the speaker swiftly interposed herself before it. It was succeeded by a moment's pause.

When Miss Dartle spoke again, it was through her set teeth, and with a stamp upon the ground.

"Stay there!" she said, "or I'll proclaim you to the house, and the whole street! If you try to evade *me,* I'll stop you, if it's by the hair, and raise the very stones against you!"

A frightened murmur was the only reply that reached my ears. A silence succeeded. I did not know what to do. Much as I desired to put an end to the interview, I felt that I had no right to present myself; that it was for Mr Peggotty alone to see her and recover her. Would he never come? I thought impatiently.

"So!" said Rosa Dartle, with a contemptuous laugh, "I see her at last! Why, he was a poor creature to be taken by that delicate mock-modesty, and that hanging head!"

"Oh, for Heaven's sake, spare me!" exclaimed Emily. "Whoever you are, you know my pitiable story, and for Heaven's sake spare me, if you would be spared yourself!"

"If *I* would be spared!" returned the other fiercely; "what is there in common between *us,* do you think!"

"Nothing but our sex," said Emily, with a burst of tears.

"And that," said Rosa Dartle, "is so strong a claim, preferred by one so infamous, that if I had any feeling in my breast but scorn and abhorrence of you, it would freeze it up. Our sex! You are an honour to our sex!"

"I have deserved this," said Emily, "but it's dreadful! Dear, dear lady, think what I have suffered, and how I am fallen! Oh, Martha, come back! Oh, home, home!"

Miss Dartle placed herself in a chair, within view of the door, and looked downward, as if Emily were crouching on the floor before her. Being now between me and the light, I could see her curled lip, and her cruel eyes intently fixed on one place, with a greedy triumph.

"Listen to what I say!" she said; "and reserve your false arts for your dupes. Do you hope to move *me* by your tears? No more than you could charm me by your smiles, you purchased slave."

"Oh, have some mercy on me!" cried Emily. "Show me some compassion, or I shall die mad!"

"It would be no great penance," said Rosa Dartle, "for your crimes. Do you know what you have done? Do you ever think of the home you have laid waste?"

"Oh, is there ever night or day, when I don't think of it!" cried Emily; and now I could just see her, on her knees, with her head thrown back, her pale face looking upward, her hands wildly clasped and held out, and her hair streaming about her. "Has there ever been a single minute, waking or sleeping, when it hasn't been before me, just as it used to be in the lost days when I turned my back upon it for ever and for ever! Oh, home, home! Oh dear, dear uncle, if you ever could have known the agony your love would cause me when I fell away from good, you never would have shown it to me so constant, much as you felt it; but would have been angry to me, at least once in my life, that I might have had some comfort! I have none, none, no comfort upon earth, for all of them were always fond of me!" She dropped on her face, before the imperious figure in the chair, with an imploring effort to clasp the skirt of her dress.

Rosa Dartle sat looking down upon her, as inflexible as a figure of brass. Her lips were tightly compressed, as if she knew that she must keep a strong constraint upon herself—I write what I sincerely believe—or she would be tempted to strike the beautiful form with her foot. I saw her, distinctly, and the whole power of her face and character seemed forced into that expression.—Would he never come?

"The miserable vanity of these earth-worms!" she said, when she had so far controlled the angry heavings of her breast, that she could trust herself to speak. "*Your* home! Do you imagine that I bestow a thought on it, or suppose you could do any harm to that low place, which money would not pay for, and handsomely? *Your* home! You were a part of the trade of your home, and were bought and sold like any other vendible thing your people dealt in."

"Oh, not that!" cried Emily. "Say anything of me; but don't visit my disgrace and shame, more than I have done, on folks who are as honourable as you! Have some respect for them, as you are a lady, if you have no mercy for me."

"I speak," she said, not deigning to take any heed of this appeal, and drawing away her dress from the contamination of Emily's touch, "I speak of *his* home—where I live. Here," she said, stretching out her hand with her contemptuous laugh, and looking down upon the prostrate girl, "is a worthy cause of division between lady-mother and gentleman-son; of grief in a house where she wouldn't have been admitted as a kitchen-girl; of anger, and repining, and reproach. This piece of pollution, picked up from the water-side, to be made much of for an hour, and then tossed back to her original place!"

"No! no!" cried Emily, clasping her hands together. "When he first came into my way—that the day had never dawned upon me, and he had met me being carried to my grave!—I had been brought up as virtuous as you or any lady, and was going to be the wife of as good a man as you or any lady in the world can ever marry. If you live in his home and know him, you know, perhaps, what his power with a weak, vain girl might be. I don't defend myself, but I know well, and he knows well, or he will know when he comes to die, and his mind is troubled with it, that he used all his power to deceive me, and that I believed him, trusted him, and loved him!"

Rosa Dartle sprang up from her seat; recoiled; and in recoiling struck at her, with a face of such malignity, so darkened and disfigured by passion, that I had almost thrown myself between them. The blow, which had no aim, fell upon the air. As she now stood panting, looking at her with the utmost detestation that she was capable of expressing, and trembling from head to foot with rage and scorn, I thought I had never seen such a sight, and never could see such another.

"You love him? *You?"* she cried, with her clenched hand, quivering as if it only wanted a weapon to stab the object of her wrath.

Emily had shrunk out of my view. There was no reply.

"And tell that to *me,"* she added, "with your shameful lips? Why don't they whip these creatures? If I could order it to be done, I would have this girl whipped to death."

And so she would, I have no doubt. I would not have trusted her with the rack itself, while that furious look lasted.

She slowly, very slowly, broke into a laugh, and pointed at Emily with her hand, as if she were a sight of shame for gods and men.

"She love!" she said. "That carrion! And he ever cared for her, she'd tell me. Ha, ha! The liars that these traders are!"

Her mockery was worse than her undisguised rage. Of the two, I would have much preferred to be the object of the latter. But, when she suffered it to break loose, it was only for a moment. She had chained it up again, and however it might tear her within, she subdued it to herself.

"I came here, you pure fountain of love," she said, "to see—as I began by telling you—what such a thing as you was like. I was curious. I am satisfied. Also to tell you, that you had best seek that home of yours, with all speed, and hide your head among those excellent people who are expecting you, and whom your money will console. When it's all gone, you can believe, and trust, and love again, you know! I thought you a broken toy that had lasted its time; a worthless spangle that was tarnished, and thrown away. But, finding you true gold, a very lady, and an ill-used innocent, with a fresh heart full of love and trustfulness—which you look like, and is quite consistent with your story!—I have something more to say. Attend to it; for what I say I'll do. Do you hear me, you fairy spirit? What I say, I mean to do!"

Her rage got the better of her again, for a moment; but it passed over her face like a spasm, and left her smiling.

"Hide yourself," she pursued, "if not at home, somewhere. Let it be somewhere beyond reach; in some obscure life—or, better still, in some obscure death. I wonder, if your loving heart will not break, you have found no way of helping it to be still! I have heard of such means sometimes. I believe they may be easily found."

A low crying, on the part of Emily, interrupted her here. She stopped, and listened to it as if it were music.

"I am of a strange nature, perhaps," Rose Dartle went on; "but I can't breathe freely in the air you breathe. I find it sickly. Therefore, I will have it cleared; I will have it purified of you. If you live here tomorrow, I'll have your story and your character proclaimed on the common stair. There are decent women in the house, I am told; and it is a pity such a light as you should be among them, and concealed. If, leaving here, you seek any refuge in this town in any character but your true one (which you are welcome to bear, without molestation from me), the same service shall be done you, if I hear of your retreat. Being assisted by a gentleman who not long ago aspired to the favour of your hand, I am sanguine as to that."

Would he never, never come? How long was I to bear this? How long could I bear it?

"Oh me, oh me!" exclaimed the wretched Emily, in a tone that might have touched the hardest heart, I should have thought; but there was no relenting in Rosa Dartle's smile. "What, what, shall I do!"

"Do?" returned the other. "Live happy in your own reflections! Consecrate your existence to the recollection of James Steerforth's tenderness—he would have made you his serving-man's wife, would he not?—or to feeling grateful to the upright and deserving creature who would have taken you as his gift. Or, if those proud remembrances, and the consciousness of your own virtues, and the honourable position to which they have raised you in the eyes of everything that wears the human shape, will not sustain you, marry that good man, and be happy in his condescension. If this will not do either, die! There are doorways and dust-heaps for such deaths, and such despair—find one, and take your flight to Heaven!"

I heard a distant foot upon the stairs. I knew it, I was certain. It was his, thank God!

She moved slowly from before the door when she said this, and passed out of my sight.

"But mark!" she added, slowly and sternly, opening the other door to go away, "I am resolved, for reasons that I have and hatreds that I entertain, to cast you out, unless you withdraw from my reach altogether, or drop your pretty mask. This is what I had to say; and what I say, I mean to do!"

The foot upon the stairs came nearer—nearer—passed her as she went down—rushed into the room!

"Uncle!"

A fearful cry followed the word. I paused a moment, and looking in, saw him supporting her insensible figure in his arms. He gazed for a few seconds in the face; then stooped to kiss it—oh, how tenderly!—and drew a handkerchief before it.

"Mas'r Davy," he said, in a low tremulous voice, when it was covered, "I thank my Heav'nly Father as my dream's come true! I thank Him hearty for having guided of me, in His own ways, to my darling!"

With those words he took her up in his arms; and, with the veiled face lying on his bosom, and addressed towards his own, carried her, motionless and unconscious, down the stairs.

Chapter LI

THE BEGINNING OF A LONGER JOURNEY

IT was yet early in the morning of the following day, when, as I was walking in my garden with my aunt (who took little other exercise now, being so much in attendance on my dear Dora), I was told that Mr Peggotty desired to speak with me. He came into the garden to meet me half-way, on my going towards the gate; and bared his head, as it was always his custom to do when he saw my aunt, for whom he had a high respect. I had been telling her all that had happened overnight. Without saying a word, she walked up with a cordial face, shook hands with him, and patted him on the arm. It was so expressively done, that she had no need to say a word. Mr Peggotty understood her quite as well as if she had said a thousand.

"I'll go in now, Trot," said my aunt, "and look after Little Blossom, who will be getting up presently."

"Not along of my being heer, ma'am, I hope?" said Mr Peggotty. "Unless my wits is gone a bahd's neezing"—by which Mr Peggotty meant to say, bird's-nesting—"this morning, 'tis along of me as you're a-going to quit us?"

"You have something to say, my good friend," returned my aunt, "and will do better without me."

"By your leave, ma'am," returned Mr Peggotty, "I should take it kind, pervising you doen't mind my clicketten, if you'd bide heer."

"Would you?" said my aunt, with short good-nature. "Then I am sure I will!"

So, she drew her arm through Mr Peggotty's, and walked with him to a leafy little summer-house there was at the bottom of the garden, where she sat down on a bench, and I beside her. There was a seat for Mr Peggotty too, but he preferred to stand, leaning his hand on the small rustic table. As he stood, looking at his cap for a little while before beginning to speak, I could not help observing what power and force of character his sinewy hand expressed, and what a good and trusty companion it was to his honest brow and iron-grey hair.

"I took my dear child away last night," Mr Peggotty began, as he raised his eyes to ours, "to my lodging, wheer I have a long time been expecting of her and preparing fur her. It was hours afore she knowed me right; and when she did, she kneeled down at my feet, and kiender said to me, as if it was her prayers, how it all come to be. You may believe me, when I heerd her voice, as I had heerd at home so playful—and see her humbled, as it might be in the dust our Saviour wrote in with his blessed hand—I felt a wownd go to my 'art, in the midst of all its thankfulness."

He drew his sleeve across his face, without any pretence of concealing why; and then cleared his voice.

"It warn't for long as I felt that; for she was found. I had on'y to think as she was found, and it was gone. I doen't know why I do so much as mention of it now, I'm sure. I didn't have it in my mind a minute ago, to say a word about myself; but it come up so nat'ral, that I yielded to it afore I was aweer."

"You are a self-denying soul," said my aunt, "and will have your reward."

Mr Peggotty, with the shadows of the leaves playing athwart his face, made a surprised inclination of the head towards my aunt, as an acknowledgement of her good opinion; then took up the thread he had relinquished.

"When my Em'ly took flight," he said, in stern wrath for the moment, "from the house wheer she was made a pris'ner by that theer spotted snake as Mas'r Davy see,—and his story's trew, and may GOD confound him!—she took flight in the night. It was a dark night, with a many stars a-shining. She was wild. She ran along the sea beach, believing the old boat was theer; and calling out to us to turn away our faces, for she was a-coming by. She heerd herself a-crying out, like as if it was another person; and cut herself on them sharp-pinted stones and rocks, and felt it no more than if she had been rock herself. Ever so fur she run, and there was fire afore her eyes, and roarings in her ears. Of a sudden—or so she thowt, you unnerstand—the day broke, wet and windy, and she was lying b'low a heap of stone upon the shore, and a woman was a-speaking to her, saying, in the language of that country, what was it as had gone so much amiss?"

He saw everything he related. It passed before him, as he spoke, so vividly, that, in the intensity of his earnestness, he presented what he described to me, with greater distinctness than I can express. I can hardly believe, writing now long afterwards, but that I was actually present in these scenes; they are impressed upon me with such an astonishing air of fidelity.

"As Em'ly's eyes—which was heavy—see this woman better," Mr Peggotty went on, "she know'd as she was one of them as she had often talked to on the beach. Fur, though she had run (as I have said) ever so fur in the night, she had oftentimes wandered long ways, partly afoot, partly in boats and carriages, and know'd all that country, 'long the coast, miles and miles. She hadn't no children of her own, this woman, being a young wife; but she was a-looking to have one afore long. And may my prayers go up to Heaven that 'twill be a happ'ness to her, and a comfort, and a honour, all her life! May it love her and be dootiful to her, in her old age; helpful of her at the last; a Angel to her heer, and heerafter!"

"Amen!" said my aunt.

"She had been summat timorous and down," said Mr Peggotty, "and had sat, at first, a little way off, at her spinning, or such work as it was, when Em'ly talked to the children. But Em'ly had took notice of her, and had gone and spoke to her; and as the young woman was partial to the children herself, they had soon made friends. Sermuchser, that when Em'ly went that way, she always giv Em'ly flowers. This was her as now asked what it was that had gone so much amiss. Em'ly told her, and she—took her home. She did indeed. She took her home," said Mr Peggotty, covering his face.

He was more affected by this act of kindness, than I had ever seen him affected by anything since the night she went away. My aunt and I did not attempt to disturb him.

"It was a little cottage, you may suppose," he said, presently, "but she found space for Em'ly in it,—her husband was away at sea,—and she kep it secret, and prevailed upon such neighbours as she had (they was not many near) to keep it secret too. Em'ly was took bad with fever, and, what is very strange to me is,—maybe 'tis not so strange to scholars,—the language of that country went out of her head, and she could only speak her own, that no one unnerstood. She recollects, as if she had dreamed it, that she lay there always a-talking her own tongue, always believing as the old boat was round the next pint in the bay, and begging and imploring of 'em to send theer and tell how she was dying, and bring back a message of forgiveness, if it was on'y a wured. A'most the whole time, she thowt,—now, that him as I made mention on just now was lurking for her unnerneath the winder; now that him as had brought her to this was in the room,—and cried to the good young woman not to give her up, and know'd, at the same time, that she couldn't unnerstand, and dreaded that she must be took away. Likewise the fire was afore her eyes, and the roarings in her ears; and theer was no today, nor yesterday, nor yet tomorrow; but everything in her life as ever had been, or as ever could be, and everything as never had been, and as never could be, was a crowding on her all at once, and nothing clear nor welcome, and yet she sang and laughed about it! How long this lasted, I doen't know; but then theer come a sleep; and in that sleep, from being a many times stronger than her own self, she fell into the weakness of the littlest child."

Here he stopped, as if for relief from the terrors of his own description. After being silent for a few moments, he pursued his story.

"It was a pleasant arternoon when she awoke; and so quiet, that there warn't a sound but the rippling of that blue sea without a tide, upon the shore. It was her belief, at first, that she was at home upon a Sunday morning; but the vine leaves as she see at the winder, and the hills beyond, warn't home, and contradicted of her. Then, come in her friend to watch alongside of her bed; and then she know'd as the old boat warn't round that next pint in the bay no more, but was fur off; and know'd where she was, and why; and broke out a-crying on that good young woman's bosom, wheer I hope her baby is a-lying now, a-cheering of her with its pretty eyes!"

He could not speak of this good friend of Emily's without a flow of tears. It was in vain to try. He broke down again, endeavouring to bless her!

"That done my Em'ly good," he resumed, after such emotion as I could not behold without sharing in; and as to my aunt, she wept with all her heart; "that done Em'ly good, and she begun to mend. But, the language of that country was quite gone from her, and she was forced to make signs. So she went on, getting better from day to day, slow, but sure, and trying to learn the names of common things—names as she seemed never to have heerd in all her life—till one evening come, when she was a-setting at her window, looking at a little girl at play upon the beach. And of a sudden this child held out her hand, and said, what would be in English, 'Fisherman's daughter, here's a shell!'—for you are to unnerstand that they used at first to call her 'Pretty lady,' as the general way in that country is, and that she had taught 'em to call her 'Fisherman's daughter' instead. The child says of a sudden, 'Fisherman's daughter, here's a shell!' Then Em'ly unnerstands her; and she answers, bursting out a-crying; and it all comes back!

"When Em'ly got strong again," said Mr Peggotty, after another short interval of silence, "she cast about to leave that good young creetur, and get to her own country. The husband was come home, then; and the two together put her aboard a small trader bound to Leghorn, and from that to France. She had a little money, but it was less than little as they would take for all they done. I'm a'most glad on it, though they was so poor! What they done, is laid up wheer neither moth or rust doth corrupt, and wheer thieves do not break through nor steal. Mas'r Davy, it'll outlast all the treasure in the wureld.

"Em'ly got to France, and took service to wait on travelling ladies at a inn in the port. Theer, theer come, one day, that snake.—Let him never come nigh me. I doen't know what hurt I might do him!—Soon as she see him, without him seeing her, all her fear and wildness returned upon her, and she fled afore the very breath he draw'd. She come to England, and was set ashore at Dover.

"I doen't know," said Mr Peggotty, "for sure, when her 'art begun to fail her; but all the way to England she had thowt to come to her dear home. Soon as she got to England she turned her face tow'rds it. But, fear of not being forgiv, fear of being pinted at, fear of some of us being dead along of her, fear of many things, turned her from it, kiender by force, upon the road: 'Uncle, uncle,' she says to me, 'the fear of not being worthy to do, what my torn and bleeding breast so longed to do, was the most fright'ning fear of all! I turned back, when my 'art was full of prayers that I might crawl to the old door-step, in the night, kiss it, lay my wicked face upon it, and theer be found dead in the morning.'

"She come," said Mr Peggotty, dropping his voice to an awe-stricken whisper, "to London. She—as had never seen it in her life—alone—without a penny—young—so pretty—come to London. A'most the moment as she lighted heer, all so desolate, she found (as she believed) a friend; a decent woman as spoke to her about the needle-work as she had been brought up to do, about finding plenty of it fur her, about a lodging fur the night, and making secret inquiration concerning of me and all at home, tomorrow. When my child," he said aloud, and with an energy of gratitude that shook him from head to foot, "stood upon the brink of more than I can say or think on—Martha, trew to her promise, saved her."

I could not repress a cry of joy.

"Mas'r Davy!" said he, gripping my hand in that strong hand of his, "it was you as first made mention of her to me. I thankee, sir! She was arnest. She had know'd of her bitter knowledge wheer to watch and what to do. She had done it. And the Lord was above all! She come, white and hurried, upon Em'ly in her sleep. She says to her, 'Rise up from worse than death, and come with me!' Them belonging to the house would have stopped her, but they might as soon have stopped the sea. 'Stand away from me,' she says, 'I am a ghost that calls her from beside her open grave!' She told Em'ly she had seen me, and know'd I loved her, and forgive her. She wrapped her, hasty, in her clothes. She took her, faint and trembling, on her arm. She heeded no more what they said, than if she had had no ears. She walked among 'em with my child, minding only her; and brought her safe out, in the dead of the night, from that black pit of ruin!

"She attended on Em'ly," said Mr Peggotty, who had released my hand, and put his own hand on his heaving chest; "she attended to my Em'ly, lying wearied out, and wandering betwixt whiles, till late next day. Then she went in search of me; then in search of you, Mas'r Davy. She didn't tell Em'ly what she come out fur, lest her 'art should fail, and she should think of hiding of herself. How the cruel lady know'd of her being theer, I can't say. Whether him as I have spoke so much of, chanced to see 'em going theer, or whether (which is most like, to my thinking) he had heerd it from the woman, I doen't greatly ask myself. My niece is found.

"All night long," said Mr Peggotty, "we have been together, Em'ly and me. 'Tis little (considering the time) as she has said, in wureds, through them broken-hearted tears; 'tis less as I have seen of her dear face, as grow'd into a woman's at my hearth. But, all night long, her arms has been about my neck; and her head has laid heer; and we knows full well, as we can put our trust in one another, ever more."

He ceased to speak, and his hand upon the table rested there in perfect repose, with a resolution in it that might have conquered lions.

"It was a gleam of light upon me, Trot," said my aunt, drying her eyes, "when I formed the resolution of being godmother to your sister Betsey Trotwood, who disappointed me; but, next to that, hardly anything would have given me greater pleasure, than to be godmother to that good young creature's baby!"

Mr Peggotty nodded his understanding of my aunt's feelings, but could not trust himself with any verbal reference to the subject of her commendation. We all remained silent, and occupied with our own reflections (my aunt drying her eyes, and now sobbing convulsively, and now laughing and calling herself a fool); until I spoke.

"You have quite made up your mind," said I to Mr Peggotty, "as to the future, good friend? I need scarcely ask you."

"Quite, Mas'r Davy," he returned; "and told Em'ly. Theer's mighty countries, fur from heer. Our future life lays over the sea."

"They will emigrate together, aunt," said I.

"Yes!" said Mr Peggotty, with a hopeful smile. "No one can't reproach my darling in Australia. We will begin a new life over theer!"

I asked him if he yet proposed to himself any time for going away.

"I was down at the Docks early this morning, sir," he returned, "to get information concerning of them ships. In about six weeks or two months from now, there'll be one sailing—I see her this morning—went aboard—and we shall take our passage in her."

"Quite alone?" I asked.

"Aye, Mas'r Davy!" he returned. "My sister, you see, she's that fond of you and yourn, and that accustomed to think on'y of her own country, that it wouldn't be hardly fair to let her go. Besides which, theer's one she has in charge, Mas'r Davy, as doen't ought to be forgot."

"Poor Ham!" said I.

"My good sister takes care of his house, you see, ma'am, and he takes kindly to her," Mr Peggotty explained for my aunt's better information. "He'll set and talk to her, with a calm spirit, wen it's like he couldn't bring himself to open his lips to another. Poor fellow!" said Mr Peggotty, shaking his head, "theer's not so much left him, that he could spare the little as he has!"

"And Mrs Gummidge?" said I.

"Well, I've had a mort of con-sideration, I do tell you," returned Mr Peggotty, with a perplexed look which gradually cleared as he went on, "concerning of Missis Gum-midge. You see, wen Missis Gummidge falls a-thinking of the old 'un, she an't what you may call good company. Betwixt you and me, Mas'r Davy—and you, ma'am—wen Mrs Gummidge takes to wimicking,—our old country word for crying,—she's liable to be considered to be, by them as didn't know the old 'un, peevish-like. Now I *did* know the old 'un," said Mr Peggotty, "and I know'd his merits, so I unnerstan' her; but 'tan't entirely so, you see, with others—nat'rally can't be!"

My aunt and I both acquiesced.

"Wheerby," said Mr Peggotty, "my sister might—I doen't say she would, but might—find Missis Gummidge give her a leetle trouble now-and-again. Theerfur 'tan't my intentions to moor Missis Gummidge 'long with them, but to find a Beein' fur her wheer she can fisherate for herself." (A Beein' signifies, in that dialect, a home, and to fisherate is to provide.) "Fur which purpose," said Mr Peggotty, "I means to make her a 'lowance afore I go, as'll leave her pretty comfort'ble. She's the faithfullest of creeturs. 'Tan't to be expected, of course, at her time of life, and being lone and lorn, as the good old Mawther is to be knocked about aboardship, and in the woods and wilds of a new and fur-away country. So that's what I'm a-going to do with *her*."

He forgot nobody. He thought of everybody's claims and strivings, but his own.

"Em'ly," he continued, "will keep along with me—poor child, she's sore in need of peace and rest!—until such time as we goes upon our voyage. She'll work at them clothes, as must be made; and I hope her troubles will begin to seem longer ago than they was, wen she finds herself once more by her rough but loving uncle."

My aunt nodded confirmation of this hope, and imparted great satisfaction to Mr Peggotty.

"Theer's one thing furder, Mas'r Davy," said he, putting his hand in his breast-pocket, and gravely taking out the little paper bundle I had seen before, which he unrolled on the table. "Theer's these here banknotes—fifty pound, and ten. To them I wish to add the money as she come away with. I've asked her about that (but not saying why), and have added of it up. I an't a scholar. Would you be so kind as see how 'tis?"

He handed me, apologetically for his scholarship, a piece of paper, and observed me while I looked it over. It was quite right.

"Thankee, sir," he said, taking it back. "This money, if you doen't see objections, Mas'r Davy, I shall put up jest afore I go, in a cover d'rected to him; and put that up in another, d'rected to his mother. I shall tell her, in no more wureds than I speak to you, what it's the price on; and that I'm gone, and past receiving of it back."

I told him that I thought it would be right to do so—that I was thoroughly convinced it would be, since he felt it to be right.

"I said that theer was on'y one thing furder," he proceeded with a grave smile, when he had made up his little bundle again, and put it in his pocket; "but theer was two. I warn't sure in my mind, wen I come out this morning, as I could go and break to Ham, of my own self, what had so thankfully happened. So I writ a letter while I was out, and put it in the post-office, telling of 'em how all was as 'tis; and that I should come down tomorrow to unload my mind of what little needs a-doing of down theer, and, most-like, take my farewell leave of Yarmouth."

"And do you wish me to go with you?" said I, seeing that he left something unsaid.

"If you could do me that kind favour, Mas'r Davy," he replied. "I know the sight on you would cheer 'em up a bit."

My little Dora being in good spirits, and very desirous that I should go—as I found on talking it over with her—I readily pledged myself to accompany him in accordance with his wish. Next morning, consequently, we were on the Yarmouth coach, and again travelling over the old ground.

As we passed along the familiar street at night—Mr Peggotty, in despite of all my remonstrances, carrying my bag—I glanced into Omer and Joram's shop, and saw my old friend Mr Omer there, smoking his pipe. I felt reluctant to be present, when Mr Peggotty first met his sister and Ham; and made Mr Omer my excuse for lingering behind.

"How is Mr Omer, after this long time?" said I, going in.

He fanned away the smoke of his pipe, that he might get a better view of me, and soon recognized me with great delight.

"I should get up, sir, to acknowledge such an honour as this visit," said he, "only my limbs are rather out of sorts, and I am wheeled about. With the exception of my limbs and my breath. hows'ever, I am as hearty as a man can be, I'm thankful to say."

I congratulated him on his contented looks and his good spirits, and saw, now, that his easy-chair went on wheels.

"It's an ingenious thing, ain't it?" he inquired, following the direction of my glance, and polishing the elbow with his arm. "It runs as light as a feather, and tracks as true as a mail-coach. Bless you, my little Minnie—my grand-daughter you know, Minnie's child—puts her little strength against the back, gives it a shove, and away we go, as clever and merry as ever you see anything! And I tell you what—it's a most uncommon chair to smoke a pipe in."

I never saw such a good old fellow to make the best of a thing, and find out the enjoyment of it, as Mr Omer. He was as radiant, as if his chair, his asthma, and the failure of his limbs, were the various branches of a great invention for enhancing the luxury of a pipe.

"I see more of the world, I can assure you," said Mr Omer. "in this chair, than ever I see out of it. You'd be surprised at the number of people that looks in of a day to have a chat. You really would! There's twice as much in the newspaper, since I've taken to this chair, as there used to be. As to general reading, dear me, what a lot of it I do get through! That's what I feel so strong, you know! If it had been my eyes, what should I have done? If it had been my ears, what should I have done? Being my limbs, what does it signify? Why, my limbs only made my breath shorter when I used 'em. And now, if I want to go out into the street or down to the sands, I've only got to call Dick, Joram's youngest 'prentice, and away I go in my own carriage, like the Lord Mayor of London."

He half suffocated himself with laughing here.

"Lord bless you!" said Mr Omer, resuming his pipe, "a man must take the fat with the lean; that's what he must make up his mind to, in this life. Joram does a fine business. Ex-cellent business!"

"I am very glad to hear it," said I.

"I knew you would be," said Mr Omer. "And Joram and Minnie are like Valentines. What more can a man expect? What's his limbs to *that!*"

His supreme contempt for his limbs, as he sat smoking, was one of the pleasantest oddities I have ever encountered.

"And since I've took to general reading, you've took to general writing, eh, sir?" said Mr Omer, surveying me admiringly. "What a lovely work that was of yours! What expressions in it! I read it every word—every word. And as to feeling sleepy! Not at all!"

I laughingly expressed my satisfaction, but I must confess that I thought this association of ideas significant.

"I give you my word and honour, sir," said Mr Omer, "that when I lay that book upon the table, and look at it outside; compact in three separate and indiwidual wol-lumes—one, two, three; I am as proud as Punch to think that I once had the honour of being connected with your family. And dear me, it's a long time ago, now, ain't it? Over at Blunderstone. With a pretty little party laid along with the other party. And you quite a small party then, yourself. Dear, dear!"

I changed the subject by referring to Emily. After assuring him that I did not forget how interested he had always been in her, and how kindly he had always treated her, I gave him a general account of her restoration to her uncle by the aid of Martha; which I knew would please the old man. He listened with the utmost attention, and said, feelingly, when I had done:

"I am rejoiced at it, sir! It's the best news I have heard for many a day. Dear, dear, dear! And what's going to be undertook for that unfortunate young woman, Martha, now?"

"You touch a point that my thoughts have been dwelling on since yesterday," said I, "but on which I can give you no information yet, Mr Omer. Mr Peggotty has not alluded to it, and I have a delicacy in doing so. I am sure he has not forgotten it. He forgets nothing that is disinterested and good."

"Because you know," said Mr Omer, taking himself up, where he had left off, "whatever *is* done, I should wish to be a member of. Put me down for anything you may consider right, and let me know. I never could think the girl all bad, and I am glad to find she's not. So will my daughter Minnie be. Young women are contradictory creatures in some things—her mother was just the same as her—but their hearts are soft and kind. It's all show with Minnie, about Martha. Why she should consider it necessary to make any show, I don't undertake to tell you. But it's all show, bless you. She'd do her any kindness in private. So, put me down for whatever you may consider right, will you be so good? and drop me a line where to forward it. Dear me!" said Mr Omer, "when a man is drawing on to a time of life, where the two ends of life meet; when he finds himself, however hearty he is, being wheeled about for the second time, in a speeches of go-cart; he should be over-rejoiced to do a kindness if he can. He wants plenty. And I don't speak of myself, particular," said Mr Omer, "because, sir, the way I look at it is, that we are all drawing on to the bottom of the hill, whatever age we are, on account of time never standing still for a single moment. So let us always do a kindness, and be over-rejoiced. To be sure!"

He knocked the ashes out of his pipe, and put it on a ledge in the back of his chair, expressly made for its reception.

"There's Em'ly's cousin, him that she was to have been married to," said Mr Omer, rubbing his hands feebly, "as fine a fellow as there is in Yarmouth! He'll come and talk or read to me, in the evening, for an hour together sometimes. That's a kindness, I should call it! All his life's a kindness."

"I am going to see him now," said I.

"Are you?" said Mr Omer. "Tell him I was hearty, and sent my respects. Minnie and Joram's at a ball. They would be as proud to see you as I am, if they was at home. Minnie won't hardly go out at all, you see, 'on account of father,' as she says. So I swore tonight, that if she didn't go, I'd go to bed at six. In consequence of which," Mr Omer shook himself and his chair with laughter at the success of his device, "she and Joram's at a ball."

I shook hands with him, and wished him good night.

"Half a minute, sir," said Mr Omer. "If you was to go without seeing my little elephant, you'd lose the best of sights. You never see such a sight! Minnie!"

A musical little voice answered, from somewhere upstairs, "I am coming, grandfather!" and a pretty little girl with long, flaxen, curling hair, soon came running into the shop.

"This is my little elephant, sir," said Mr Omer, fondling the child. "Siamese breed, sir. Now, little elephant!"

The little elephant set the door of the parlour open, enabling me to see that, in these latter days, it was converted into a bedroom for Mr Omer who could not be easily conveyed upstairs; and then hid her pretty forehead, and tumbled her long hair, against the back of Mr Omer's chair.

"The elephant butts, you know, sir," said Mr Omer, winking, "when he goes at a object. Once, elephant. Twice. Three times!"

At this signal, the little elephant, with a dexterity that was next to marvellous in so small an animal whisked the chair round with Mr Omer in it, and rattled it off, pell-mell, into the parlour, without touching the doorpost: Mr Omer indescribably enjoying the performance, and looking back at me on the road as if it were the triumphant issue of his life's exertions.

After a stroll about the town I went to Ham's house. Peggotty had now removed here for good; and had let her own house to the successor of Mr Barkis in the carrying business, who had paid her very well for the goodwill, cart, and horse. I believe the very same slow horse that Mr Barkis drove was still at work.

I found them in the neat kitchen, accompanied by Mrs Gummidge, who had been fetched from the old boat by Mr Peggotty himself. I doubt if she could have been induced to desert her post, by any one else. He had evidently told them all. Both Peggotty and Mrs Gummidge had their aprons to their eyes, and Ham had just stepped out "to take a turn on the beach." He presently came home, very glad to see me; and I hope they were all the better for my being there. We spoke, with some approach to cheerfulness, of Mr Peggotty's growing rich in a new country, and of the wonders he would describe in his letters. We said nothing of Emily by name, but distantly referred to her more than once. Ham was the serenest of the party.

But, Peggotty told me, when she lighted me to a little chamber where the Crocodile book was lying ready for me on the table, that he always was the same. She believed (she told me, crying) that he was broken-hearted; though he was as full of courage as of sweetness, and worked harder and better than any boat-builder in any yard in all that part. There were times, she said, of an evening, when he talked of their old life in the boat-house; and then he mentioned Emily as a child. But, he never mentioned her as a woman.

I thought I had read in his face that he would like to speak to me alone. I therefore resolved to put myself in his way next evening, as he came home from his work. Having settled this with myself, I fell asleep. That night, for the first time in all those many nights, the candle was taken out of the window, Mr Peggotty swung in his old hammock in the old boat, and the wind murmured with the old sound round his head.

All next day, he was occupied in disposing of his fishing-boat and tackle; in packing up, and sending to London by waggon, such of his little domestic possessions as he thought would be useful to him; and in parting with the rest, or bestowing them on Mrs Gummidge. She was with him all day. As I had a sorrowful wish to see the old place once more, before it was locked up, I engaged to meet them there in the evening. But I so arranged it, as that I should meet Ham first.

It was easy to come in his way, as I knew where he worked. I met him at a retired part of the sands, which I knew he would cross, and turned back with him, that he might have leisure to speak to me if he really wished. I had not mistaken the expression of his face. We had walked but a little way together, when he said, without looking at me:

"Mas'r Davy, have you seen her?"

"Only for a moment, when she was in a swoon," I softly answered.

We walked a little farther, and he said:

"Mas'r Davy, shall you see her, d'ye think?"

"It would be too painful to her, perhaps," said I.

"I have thowt of that," he replied. "So 'twould, sir, so 'twould."

"But, Ham," said I, gently, "if there is anything that I could write to her, for you, in case I could not tell it; if there is anything you would wish to make known to her through me; I should consider it a sacred trust."

"I am sure on't. I thankee, sir, most kind! I think theer is something I could wish said or wrote."

"What is it?"

We walked a little farther in silence, and then he spoke.

" 'Tan't that I forgive her. 'Tan't that so much. 'Tis more as I beg of her to forgive me, for having pressed my affections upon her. Odd times, I think that if I hadn't had her promise fur to marry me, sir, she was that trustful of me, in a friendly way, that she'd have told me what was struggling in her mind, and would have counselled with me, and I might have saved her."

I pressed his hand. "Is that all?"

"Theer's yet a something else," he returned, "if I can say it, Mas'r Davy."

We walked on, farther than we had walked yet, before he spoke again. He was not crying when he made the pauses I shall express by lines. He was merely collecting himself to speak very plainly.

"I loved her—and I love the mem'ry of her—too deep—to be able to lead her to believe of my own self as I'm a happy man. I could only be happy—by forgetting of her—and I'm afeerd I couldn't hardly bear as she should be told I done that. But if you, being so full of learning, Mas'r Davy, could think of anything to say as might bring her to believe I wasn't greatly hurt: still loving of her, and mourning for her; anything as might bring her to believe as I was not tired of my life, and yet was hoping fur to see her without blame, wheer the wicked cease from troubling and the weary are at rest— anything as would ease her sorrowful mind, and yet not make her think as I could ever marry, or as 'twas possible that anyone could ever be to me what she was—I should ask of you to say that—with my prayers for her—that was so dear.'

I pressed his manly hand again, and told him I would charge myself to do this as well as I could.

"I thankee, sir," he answered. " 'Twas kind of you to meet me. 'Twas kind of you to bear him company down. Mas'r Davy, I unnerstan' very well, though my aunt will come to Lon'on afore they sail, and they'll unite once more, that I am not like to see him agen. I fare to feel sure on't. We doen't say so, but so 'twill be, and better so. The last you see on him—the very last—will you give him the lovingest duty and thanks of the orphan, as he was ever more than a father to?"

This I also promised, faithfully.

"I thankee agen, sir," he said, heartily shaking hands. "I know wheer you're a-going. Good-bye!"

With a slight wave of his hand, as though to explain to me that he could not enter the old place, he turned away. As I looked after his figure, crossing the waste in the moonlight, I saw him turn his face towards a strip of silvery light upon the sea, and pass on, looking at it, until he was a shadow in the distance.

The door of the boat-house stood open when I approached; and, on entering, I found it emptied of all its furniture, saving one of the old lockers, on which Mrs Gummidge, with a basket on her knee, was seated, looking at Mr Peggotty. He leaned his elbow on the rough chimney-piece, and gazed upon a few expiring embers in the grate; but he raised his head, hopefully, on my coming in, and spoke in a cheery manner.

"Come, according to promise, to bid farewell to 't, eh, Mas'r Davy" he said, taking up the candle. 'Bare enough, now, an't it?"

"Indeed you have made good use of the time," said I.

"Why, we have not been idle, sir. Missis Gummidge has worked like a—I doen't know what Missis Gummidge an't worked like," said Mr Peggotty, looking at her, at a loss for a sufficiently approving smile.

Mrs Gummidge, leaning on her basket, made no observation.

"Theer's the very locker that you used to sit on, 'long with Em'ly!" said Mr Peggotty, in a whisper. "I'm a-going to carry it away with me, last of all. And heer's your old little bedroom, see, Mas'r Davy! A'most as bleak tonight, as 'art could wish!"

In truth, the wind, though it was low, had a solemn sound, and crept around the deserted house with a whispered wailing that was very mournful. Everything was gone, down to the little mirror with the oyster-shell frame. I thought of myself, lying here, when the first great change was being wrought at home. I thought of the blue-eyed child who had enchanted me. I thought of Steerforth: and a foolish, fearful fancy came upon me of his being near at hand, and liable to be met at any turn.

" 'Tis like to be long," said Mr Peggotty, in a low voice, "afore the boat finds new tenants. They look upon't, down heer, as being unfort'nate now!"

"Does it belong to anybody in the neighbourhood?" I asked.

"To a mast-maker up town," said Mr Peggotty. "I'm a-going to give the key to him tonight."

We looked into the other little room, and came back to Mrs Gummidge, sitting on the locker, whom Mr Peggotty, putting the light on the chimney-piece, requested to rise, that he might carry it outside the door before extinguishing the candle.

"Dan'l," said Mrs Gummidge, suddenly deserting her basket, and clinging to his arm, "my dear Dan'l, the parting words I speak in this house is, I mustn't be left behind. Doen't ye think of leaving me behind, Dan'l! Oh, doen't ye ever do it!"

Mr Peggotty, taken aback, looked from Mrs Gummidge to me, and from me to Mrs Gummidge, as if he had been awakened from a sleep.

"Doen't ye, dearest Dan'l, doen't ye!" cried Mrs Gummidge, fervently. "Take me 'long with you, Dan'l, take me 'long with you and Em'ly! I'll be your servant, constant and trew. If there's slaves in them parts where you're a-going, I'll be bound to you for one, and happy, but doen't ye leave me behind, Dan'l, that's a deary dear!"

"My good soul," said Mr Peggotty, shaking his head, "you doen't know what a long voyage, and what a hard life 'tis!"

"Yes, I do, Dan'l! I can guess!" cried Mrs Gummidge. "But my parting words under this roof is, I shall go into the house and die, if I am not took. I can dig, Dan'l. I can work. I can live hard. I can be loving and patient now—more than you think, Dan'l, if you'll on'y try me. I wouldn't touch the 'lowance, not if I was dying of want, Dan'l Peggotty; but I'll go with you and Em'ly, if you'll on'y let me, to the world's end! I know how 'tis; I know you think that I am lone and lorn; but, deary love, 'tan't so no more! I ain't sat here, so long, a-watching, and a-thinking of your trials, without some good being done me. Mas'r Davy, speak to him for me! I knows his ways, and Em'ly's, and I knows their sorrows, and can be a comfort to 'em, some odd times, and labour for 'em allus! Dan'l, deary Dan'l, let me go 'long with you!"

And Mrs Gummidge took his hand, and kissed it with a homely pathos and affection, in a homely rapture of devotion and gratitude, that he well deserved.

We brought the locker out, extinguished the candle, fastened the door on the outside, and left the old boat close shut up, a dark speck in the cloudy night. Next day, when we were returning to London outside the coach, Mrs Gummidge and her basket were on the seat behind, and Mrs Gummidge was happy.

Chapter LII

I ASSIST AT AN EXPLOSION

W HEN the time Mr Micawber had appointed so mysteriously, was within four-and-twenty hours of being come, my aunt and I consulted how we should proceed; for my aunt was very unwilling to leave Dora. Ah! how easily I carried Dora up and down stairs, now!

We were disposed, notwithstanding Mr Micawber's stipulation for my aunt's attendance, to arrange that she should stay at home, and be represented by Mr Dick and me. In short, we had resolved to take this course, when Dora again unsettled us by declaring that she never would forgive herself, and never would forgive her bad boy, if my aunt remained behind, on any pretence.

"I won't speak to you," said Dora, shaking her curls at my aunt. "I'll be disagreeable! I'll make Jip bark at you all day. I shall be sure that you really are a cross old thing, if you don't go!"

"Tut, Blossom!" laughed my aunt. "You know you can't do without me!"

"Yes, I can," said Dora. "You are no use to me at all. You never run up and down stairs for me, all day long. You never sit and tell me stories about Doady, when his shoes were worn out, and he was covered with dust—oh, what a poor little mite of a fellow! You never do anything at all to please me, do you, dear?" Dora made haste to kiss my aunt, and say, "Yes, you do! I'm only joking!"—lest my aunt should think she really meant it.

"But, aunt," said Dora, coaxingly, "now listen. You must go. I shall tease you, till you let me have my own way about it. I shall lead my naughty boy *such* a life, if he don't make you go. I shall make myself *so* disagreeable—and so will Jip! You'll wish you had gone, like a good thing, for ever and ever so long, if you don't go. Besides," said Dora, putting back her hair, and looking wonderingly at my aunt and me, "why shouldn't you both go? I am not very ill indeed. Am I?"

"Why, what a question!" cried my aunt.

"What a fancy!" said I.

"Yes! I know I am a silly little thing!" said Dora, slowly looking from one of us to the other, and then putting up her pretty lips to kiss us as she lay upon her couch. "Well, then, you must both go, or I shall not believe you; and then I shall cry!"

I saw, in my aunt's face, that she began to give way now, and Dora brightened again, as she saw it too.

"You'll come back with so much to tell me, that it'll take at least a week to make me understand!" said Dora. "Because I *know* I shan't understand, for a length of time, if there's any business in it. And there's sure to be some business in it! If there's anything to add up, besides, I don't know when I shall make it out; and my bad boy will look *so* miserable all the time. There! Now you'll go, won't you? You'll only be gone one night, and Jip will take care of me while you are gone. Doady will carry me upstairs before you go, and I won't come down again till you come back; and you shall take Agnes a dreadfully scolding letter from me, because she had never been to see us!"

We agreed, without any more consultation, that we would both go, and that Dora was a little Impostor, who feigned to be rather unwell, because she liked to be petted. She was greatly pleased, and very merry; and we four, that is to say, my aunt, Mr Dick, Traddles, and I, went down to Canterbury by the Dover mail that night.

At the hotel where Mr Micawber had requested us to await him, which we got into, with some trouble, in the middle of the night, I found a letter, importing that he would appear in the morning punctually at half past nine. After which, we went shivering, at that uncomfortable hour, to our respective beds, through various close passages; which smelt as if they had been steeped, for ages, in a solution of soup and stables.

Early in the morning, I sauntered through the dear old tranquil streets, and again mingled with the shadows of the venerable gateways and churches. The rooks were sailing about the cathedral towers; and the towers themselves, overlooking many a long unaltered mile of the rich country and its pleasant streams, were cutting the bright morning air, as if there were no such thing as change on earth. Yet the bells, when they sounded, told me sorrowfully of change in everything; told me of their own age, and my pretty Dora's youth; and of the many, never old, who had lived and loved and died, while the reverberations of the bells had hummed through the rusty armour of the Black Prince hanging up within, and, motes upon the deep of Time, had lost themselves in air, as circles do in water.

I looked at the old house from the corner of the street, but did not go nearer to it, lest, being observed, I might unwittingly do any harm to the design I had come to aid. The early sun was striking edgewise on its gables and lattice-windows, touching them with gold; and some beams of its old peace seemed to touch my heart.

I strolled into the country for an hour or so, and then returned by the main street, which in the interval had shaken off its last night's sleep. Among those who were stirring in the shops, I saw my ancient enemy, the butcher, now advanced to top-boots and a baby, and in business for himself. He was nursing the baby, and appeared to be a benignant member of society.

We all became very anxious and impatient, when we sat down to breakfast. As it approached nearer and nearer to half past nine o'clock, our restless expectation of Mr Micawber increased. At last we made no more pretence of attending to the meal, which, except with Mr Dick, had been a mere form from the first; but my aunt walked up and down the room, Traddles sat upon the sofa affecting to read the paper with his eyes on the ceiling; and I looked out of the window to give early notice of Mr Micawber's coming. Nor had I long to watch, for, at the first chime of the half hour, he appeared in the street.

"Here he is," said I, "and not in his legal attire!"

My aunt tied the strings of her bonnet (she had come down to breakfast in it), and put on her shawl, as if she were ready for anything that was resolute and uncompromising. Traddles buttoned his coat with a determined air. Mr Dick, disturbed by these formidable appearances, but feeling it necessary to imitate them, pulled his hat, with both hands, as firmly over his ears as he possibly could; and instantly took it off again, to welcome Mr Micawber.

"Gentlemen, and madam," said Mr Micawber, "good morning! My dear sir," to Mr Dick, who shook hands with him violently, "you are extremely good."

"Have you breakfasted?" said Mr Dick. "Have a chop!"

"Not for the world, my good sir!" cried Mr Micawber, stopping him on his way to the bell; "appetite and myself, Mr Dixon, have long been strangers."

Mr Dixon was so well pleased with his new name, and appeared to think it so obliging in Mr Micawber to confer it upon him, that he shook hands with him again, and laughed rather childishly.

"Dick," said my aunt, "attention!"

Mr Dick recovered himself, with a blush.

"Now, sir," said my aunt to Mr Micawber, as she put on her gloves, "we are ready for Mount Vesuvius, or anything else, as soon as *you* please."

"Madam," returned Mr Micawber, "I trust you will shortly witness an eruption. Mr Traddles, I have your permission, I believe, to mention here that we have been in communication together?"

"It is undoubtedly the fact, Copperfield," said Traddles, to whom I looked in surprise. "Mr Micawber has consulted me, in reference to what he has in contemplation; and I have advised him to the best of my judgement."

"Unless I deceive myself, Mr Traddles," pursued Mr Micawber, "what I contemplate is a disclosure of an important nature."

"Highly so," said Traddles.

"Perhaps, under such circumstances, madam and gentlemen," said Mr Micawber, "you will do me the favour to submit yourselves, for the moment, to the direction of one who, however unworthy to be regarded in any other light but as a Waif and Stray upon the shore of human nature, is still your fellow-man, though crushed out of his original form by individual errors, and the accumulative force of a combination of circumstances?"

"We have perfect confidence in you, Mr Micawber," said I, "and will do what you please."

"Mr Copperfield," returned Mr Micawber, "your confidence is not, at the existing juncture, ill-bestowed. I would beg to be allowed a start of five minutes by the clock; and then to receive the present company, inquiring for Miss Wickfield, at the office of Wickfield and Heep, whose Stipendiary I am."

My aunt and I looked at Traddles, who nodded his approval.

"I have no more," observed Mr Micawber, "to say at present."

With which, to my infinite surprise, he included us all in a comprehensive bow, and disappeared; his manner being extremely distant, and his face extremely pale.

Traddles only smiled, and shook his head (with his hair standing upright on the top of it), when I looked to him for an explanation; so I took out my watch, and, as a last resource, counted off the five minutes. My aunt, with her own watch in her hand, did the like. When the time was expired, Traddles gave her his arm; and we all went out together to the old house, without saying one word on the way.

We found Mr Micawber at his desk, in the turret office on the ground floor, either writing, or pretending to write, hard. The large office-ruler was stuck into his waistcoat, and was not so well concealed but that a foot or more of that instrument protruded from his bosom, like a new kind of shirt-frill.

As it appeared to me that I was expected to speak, I said aloud:

"How do you do, Mr Micawber?"

"Mr Copperfield," said Mr Micawber, gravely, "I hope I see you well?"

"Is Miss Wickfield at home?" said I.

"Mr Wickfield is unwell in bed, sir, of a rheumatic fever," he returned; "but Miss Wickfield, I have no doubt, will be happy to see old friends. Will you walk in, sir?"

He preceded us to the dining-room—the first room I had entered in that house—and flinging open the door of Mr Wickfield's former office, said, in a sonorous voice:

"Miss Trotwood, Mr David Copperfield, Mr Thomas Traddles, and Mr Dixon!"

I had not seen Uriah Heep since the time of the blow. Our visit astonished him, evidently; not the less, I dare say, because it astonished ourselves. He did not gather his eyebrows together, for he had none worth mentioning; but he frowned to that degree that he almost closed his small eyes, while the hurried raising of his grisly hand to his chin betrayed some trepidation or surprise. This was only when we were in the act of entering his room, and when I caught a glance at him over my aunt's shoulder. A moment afterwards, he was as fawning and as humble as ever.

"Well, I am sure," he said. "This is indeed an unexpected pleasure! To have, as I may say, all friends round St Paul's, at once, is a treat unlooked for! Mr Copperfield, I hope I see you well, and—if I may umbly express myself so—friendly towards them as is ever your friends, whether or not. Mrs Copperfield, sir, I hope she's getting on. We have been made quite uneasy by the poor accounts we have had of her state, lately, I do assure you."

I felt ashamed to let him take my hand, but I did not know yet what else to do.

"Things are changed in this office, Miss Trotwood, since I was a numble clerk, and held your pony; ain't they?" said Uriah, with his sickliest smile. "But *I* am not changed, Miss Trotwood."

"Well, sir," returned my aunt, "to tell you the truth, I think you are pretty constant to the promise of your youth; if that's any satisfaction to you."

"Thank you, Miss Trotwood," said Uriah, writhing in his ungainly manner, "for your good opinion! Micawber, tell 'em to let Miss Agnes know—and mother. Mother will be quite in a state, when she sees the present company!" said Uriah, setting chairs.

"You are not busy, Mr Heep?" said Traddles, whose eye the cunning red eye accidentally caught, as it at once scrutinized and evaded us.

"No, Mr Traddles," replied Uriah, resuming his official seat, and squeezing his bony hands, laid palm to palm between his bony knees. "Not so much so as I could wish. But lawyers, sharks, and leeches, are not easily satisfied, you know! Not but what myself and Micawber have our hands pretty full, in general, on account of Mr Wickfield's being hardly fit for any occupation, sir. But it's a pleasure as well as a duty, I am sure, to work for *him*. You've not been intimate with Mr Wickfield, I think, Mr Traddles? I believe I've only had the honour of seeing you once myself?"

"No, I have not been intimate with Mr Wickfield," returned Traddles; "or I might perhaps have waited on you long ago, Mr Heep."

There was something in the tone of this reply, which made Uriah look at the speaker again, with a very sinister and suspicious expression. But, seeing only Traddles, with his good-natured face, simple manner, and hair on end, he dismissed it as he replied, with a jerk of his whole body, but especially his throat:

"I am sorry for that, Mr Traddles. You would have admired him as much as we all do. His little failings would only have endeared him to you the more. But if you would like to hear my fellow-partner eloquently spoken of, I should refer you to Copperfield. The family is a subject he's very strong upon, if you never heard him."

I was prevented from disclaiming the compliment (if I should have done so, in any case), by the entrance of Agnes, now ushered in by Mr Micawber. She was not quite so self-possessed as usual, I thought; and had evidently undergone anxiety and fatigue. But her earnest cordiality, and her quiet beauty, shone with the gentler lustre for it.

I saw Uriah watch her while she greeted us; and he reminded me of an ugly and rebellious genie watching a good spirit. In the meanwhile, some slight sign passed between Mr Micawber and Traddles; and Traddles, unobserved except by me, went out.

"Don't wait, Micawber," said Uriah.

Mr Micawber, with his hand upon the ruler in his breast, stood erect before the door, most unmistakably contemplating one of his fellow-men, and that man his employer.

"What are you waiting for?" said Uriah. "Micawber! did you hear me tell you not to wait?"

"Yes!" replied the immovable Mr Micawber.

"Then why *do* you wait?" said Uriah.

"Because I—in short, choose," replied Mr Micawber, with a burst.

Uriah's cheeks lost colour, and an unwholesome paleness, still faintly tinged by his pervading red, overspread them. He looked at Mr Micawber attentively, with his whole face breathing short and quick in every feature.

"You are a dissipated fellow, as all the world knows," he said, with an effort at a smile, "and I am afraid you'll oblige me to get rid of you. Go along! I'll talk to you presently."

"If there is a scoundrel on this earth," said Mr Micawber, suddenly breaking out again with the utmost vehemence, "with whom I have already talked too much, that scoundrel's name is—HEEP!"

Uriah fell back, as if he had been struck or stung. Looking slowly round upon us with the darkest and wickedest expression that his face could wear, he said, in a lower voice:

"Oho! This is a conspiracy! You have met here by appointment! You are playing Booty with my clerk, are you, Copperfield? Now, take care. You'll make nothing of this. We understand each other, you and me. There's no love between us. You were always a puppy with a proud stomach, from your first coming here; and you envy me my rise, do you? None of your plots against me; I'll counterplot you! Micawber, you be off. I'll talk to you presently."

"Mr Micawber," said I, "there is a sudden change in this fellow, in more respects than the extraordinary one of his speaking the truth in one particular, which assures me that he is brought to bay. Deal with him as he deserves!"

"You are a precious set of people, ain't you?" said Uriah, in the same low voice, and breaking out into a clammy heat, which he wiped from his forehead, with his long lean hand, "to buy over my clerk, who is the very scum of society,—as you yourself were, Copperfield, you know it, before anyone had charity on you,—to defame me with his lies? Miss Trotwood, you had better stop this; or I'll stop your husband shorter than will be pleasant to you. I won't know your story professionally, for nothing, old lady! Miss Wickfield, if you have any love for your father, you had better not join that gang. I'll ruin him, if you do. Now, come! I have got some of you under the harrow. Think twice, before it goes over you. Think twice, you, Micawber, if you don't want to be crushed. I recommend you to take yourself off, and be talked to presently, you fool! while there's time to retreat. Where's mother?" he said, suddenly appearing to notice, with alarm, the absence of Traddles, and pulling down the bell-rope. "Fine doings in a person's own house!"

"Mrs Heep is here, sir," said Traddles, returning with that worthy mother of a worthy son. "I have taken the liberty of making myself known to her."

"Who are you to make yourself known?" retorted Uriah. "And what do you want here?"

"I am the agent and friend of Mr Wickfield, sir," said Traddles, in a composed and business-like way. "And I have a power of attorney from him in my pocket, to act for him in all matters."

"The old ass has drunk himself into a state of dotage," said Uriah, turning uglier than before, "and it has been got from him by fraud!"

"Something has been got from him by fraud, I know," returned Traddles quietly; "and so do you, Mr Heep. We will refer that question, if you please, to Mr Micawber."

"Ury——!" Mrs Heep began, with an anxious gesture.

"You hold your tongue, mother," he returned; "least said, soonest mended."

"But, my Ury——"

"Will you hold your tongue, mother, and leave it to me?"

Though I had long known that his servility was false, and all his pretences knavish and hollow, I had had no adequate conception of the extent of his hypocrisy, until I now saw him with his mask off. The suddenness with which he dropped it, when he perceived that it was useless to him; the malice, insolence, and hatred, he revealed; the leer with which he exulted, even at this moment, in the evil he had done—all this time being desperate too, and at his wits' end for the means of getting the better of us—though perfectly consistent with the experience I had of him, at first took even me by surprise, who had known him so long, and disliked him so heartily.

I say nothing of the look he conferred on me, as he stood eyeing us, one after another; for I had always understood that he hated me, and I remembered the marks of my hand upon his cheek. But when his eyes passed on to Agnes, and I saw the rage with which he felt his power over her slipping away, and the exhibition, in their disappoint-ment, of the odious passions that had led him to aspire to one whose virtues he could never appreciate or care for, I was shocked by the mere thought of her having lived, an hour, within sight of such a man.

After some rubbing of the lower part of his face, and some looking at us with those bad eyes, over his grisly fingers, he made one more address to me, half whining, and half abusive.

"You think it justifiable, do you, Copperfield, you who pride yourself so much on your honour and all the rest of it, to sneak about my place, eaves-dropping with my clerk? If it had been *me,* I shouldn't have wondered; for I don't make myself out a gentleman (though I never was in the streets either, as you were, according to Mi-cawber), but being *you!*—And you're not afraid of doing this, either? You don't think at all of what I shall do, in return; or of getting yourself into trouble for conspiracy and so forth? Very well. We shall see! Mr What's-your-name, you were going to refer some question to Micawber. There's your referee. Why don't you make him speak? He has learnt his lesson, I see."

Seeing that what he said had no effect on me or any of us, he sat on the edge of his table with his hands in his pockets, and one of his splay feet twisted round the other leg, waiting doggedly for what might follow.

Mr Micawber, whose impetuosity I had restrained thus far with the greatest diffi-culty, and who had repeatedly interposed with the first syllable of Scoun-drel! without getting to the second, now burst forward, drew the ruler from his breast (apparently as a defensive weapon), and produced from his pocket a foolscap document, folded in the form of a large letter. Opening this packet, with his old flourish, and glancing at the contents, as if he cherished an artistic admiration of their style of composition, he began to read as follows:

" 'Dear Miss Trotwood and gentlemen—' "

"Bless and save the man!" exclaimed my aunt in a low voice. "He'd write letters by the ream, if it was a capital offence!"

Mr Micawber, without hearing her, went on.

" 'In appearing before you to denounce probably the most consummate Villain that has ever existed,' Mr Micawber, without looking off the letter, pointed the ruler, like a ghostly truncheon, at Uriah Heep, " 'I ask no consideration for myself. The victim, from my cradle, of pecuniary liabilities to which I have been unable to respond, I have ever been the sport and toy of debasing circumstances. Ignominy, Want, Despair, and Madness, have, collectively or separately, been the attendants of my career.' "

The relish with which Mr Micawber described himself as a prey to these dismal calamities, was only to be equalled by the emphasis with which he read his letter; and the kind of homage he rendered to it with a roll of his head, when he thought he had hit a sentence very hard indeed.

" 'In an accumulation of Ignominy, Want, Despair, and Madness, I entered the office—or, as our lively neighbour the Gaul would term it, the Bureau—of the Firm, nominally conducted under the appellation of Wickfield and—HEEP, but in reality, wielded by—HEEP alone. HEEP, and only HEEP, is the mainspring of that machine, HEEP, and only HEEP, is the Forger and the Cheat.' "

Uriah, more blue than white at these words, made a dart at the letter, as if to tear it in pieces. Mr Micawber, with a perfect miracle of dexterity or luck, caught his advancing knuckles with the ruler, and disabled his right hand. It dropped at the wrist, as if it were broken. The blow sounded as if it had fallen on wood.

"The Devil take you!" said Uriah, writhing in a new way with pain. "I'll be even with you."

"Approach me again, you—you—you Heep of infamy," gasped Mr Micawber, "and if your head is human, I'll break it. Come on, come on!"

I think I never saw anything more ridiculous—I was sensible of it, even at the time—than Mr Micawber making broad-sword guards with the ruler, and crying, "Come on!" while Traddles and I pushed him back into a corner, from which, as often as we got him into it, he persisted in emerging again.

His enemy, muttering to himself, after wringing his wounded hand for sometime, slowly drew off his neck-kerchief and bound it up; then held it in his other hand, and sat upon his table with his sullen face looking down.

Mr Micawber, when he was sufficiently cool, proceeded with his letter.

> " 'The stipendiary emoluments in consideration of which I entered into the service of—HEEP,' " always pausing before that word and uttering it with astonishing vigour, " 'were not defined, beyond the pittance of twenty-two shillings and six per week. The rest was left contingent on the value of my professional exertions; in other and more expressive words, on the baseness of my nature, the cupidity of my motives, the poverty of my family, the general moral (or rather immoral) resemblance between myself and—HEEP. Need I say, that it soon became necessary for me to solicit from—HEEP—pecuniary advances towards the support of Mrs Micawber, and our blighted but rising family? Need I say that this necessity had been foreseen by—HEEP? That those advances were secured by I.O.U.'s and other similar acknowledgements, known to the legal institutions of this country? And that I thus became immeshed in the web he had spun for my reception?' "

Mr Micawber's enjoyment of his epistolary powers, in describing this unfortunate state of things, really seemed to outweigh any pain or anxiety that the reality could have caused him. He read on:

> " 'Then it was that—HEEP—began to favour me with just so much of his confidence, as was necessary to the discharge of his infernal business. Then it was that I began, if I may so Shakespearianly express myself, to dwindle, peak, and pine. I found that my services were constantly called into requisition for the falsification of business, and the mystification of an individual whom I will designate as Mr W. That Mr W. was imposed upon, kept in ignorance, and deluded, in every possible way; yet, that all this while, the ruffian—HEEP—was professing unbounded gratitude to, and unbounded friendship for, that much-abused gentleman. This was bad enough; but, as the philosophic Dane observes, with that universal applicability which distinguishes the illustrious ornament of the Elizabethan Era, worse remains behind!' "

Mr Micawber was so very much struck by this happy rounding off with a quotation, that he indulged himself, and us, with a second reading of the sentence, under pretence of having lost his place.

" 'It is not my intention,' " he continued reading on, " 'to enter on a detailed list, within the compass of the present epistle (though it is ready elsewhere), of the various malpractices of a minor nature, affecting the individual whom I have denominated Mr W., to which I have been a tacitly consenting party. My object, when the contest within myself between stipend and no stipend, baker and no baker, existence and non-existence, ceased, was to take advantage of my opportunities to discover and expose the major malpractices committed, to that gentleman's grievous wrong and injury, by—HEEP. Stimulated by the silent monitor within, and by a no less touching and appealing monitor without—to whom I will briefly refer as Miss W.—I entered on a not unlaborious task of clandestine investigation, protracted now, to the best of my knowledge, information, and belief, over a period exceeding twelve calendar months.' "

He read this passage as if it were from an Act of Parliament; and appeared majestically refreshed by the sound of the words.

" 'My charges against—HEEP,' " he read on, glancing at him, and drawing the ruler into a convenient position under his left arm, in case of need, " 'are as follows.' "

We all held our breath, I think. I am sure Uriah held his.

" 'First,' " said Mr Micawber, " 'When Mr W.'s faculties and memory for business became, through causes into which it is not necessary or expedient for me to enter, weakened and confused,—HEEP—designedly perplexed and complicated the whole of the official transactions. When Mr W. was least fit to enter on business,—HEEP—was always at hand to force him to enter on it. He obtained Mr W.'s signature under such circumstances to documents of importance, representing them to be other documents of no importance. He induced Mr W. to empower him to draw out, thus, one particular sum of trust-money, amounting to twelve six fourteen, two and nine, and employed it to meet pretended business charges and deficiencies which were either already provided for, or had never really existed. He gave this proceeding, throughout, the appearance of having originated in Mr W.'s own dishonest intention, and of having been accomplished by Mr W.'s own dishonest act; and has used it, ever since, to torture and constrain him.' "

"You shall prove this, you Copperfield!" said Uriah, with a threatening shake of the head. "All in good time!"

"Ask—HEEP—Mr Traddles, who lived in his house after him," said Mr Micawber, breaking off from the letter; "will you?"

"The fool himself—and lives there now," said Uriah, disdainfully.

"Ask—HEEP—if he ever kept a pocket-book in that house," said Mr Micawber; "will you?"

I saw Uriah's lank hand stop, involuntarily, in the scraping of his chin.

"Or ask him," said Mr Micawber, "if he ever burnt one there. If he says yes, and asks you where the ashes are, refer him to Wilkins Micawber, and he will hear of something not at all to his advantage!"

The triumphant flourish with which Mr Micawber delivered himself of these words, had a powerful effect in alarming the mother; who cried out, in much agitation:

"Ury, Ury! Be umble, and make terms, my dear!"

"Mother!" he retorted, "will you keep quiet? You're in a fright, and don't know what you say or mean. Umble!" he repeated, looking at me, with a snarl; "I've umbled some of 'em for a pretty long time back, umble as I was!"

Mr Micawber, genteelly adjusting his chin in his cravat, presently proceeded with his composition.

> " 'Second. HEEP has, on several occasions, to the best of my knowledge, information, and belief—' "

"But *that* won't do," muttered Uriah, relieved. "Mother, you keep quiet."

"We will endeavour to provide something that WILL do, and do for you finally, sir, very shortly," replied Mr Micawber.

> " 'Second. HEEP has, on several occasions, to the best of my knowledge, information, and belief, systematically forged, to various entries, books, and documents, the signature of Mr W.; and has distinctly done so in one instance, capable of proof by me. To wit, in manner following, that is to say:' "

Again, Mr Micawber had a relish in this formal piling up of words, which, however ludicrously displayed in his case, was, I must say, not at all peculiar to him. I have observed it, in the course of my life, in numbers of men. It seems to me to be a general rule. In the taking of legal oaths, for instance, deponents seem to enjoy themselves mightily when they come to several good words in succession, for the expression of one idea; as, that they utterly detest, abominate, and abjure, or so forth; and the old anathemas were made relishing on the same principle. We talk about the tyranny of words, but we like to tyrannize over them too; we are fond of having a large superfluous establishment of words to wait upon us on great occasions; we think it looks important, and sounds well. As we are not particular about the meaning of our liveries on state occasions, if they be but fine and numerous enough, so, the meaning or necessity of our words is a secondary consideration, if there be but a great parade of them. And as individuals get into trouble by making too great a show of liveries, or as slaves when they are too numerous rise against their masters, so I think I could mention a nation that has got into many great difficulties, and will get into many greater, from maintaining too large a retinue of words.

Mr Micawber read on, almost smacking his lips:

> " 'To wit, in manner following, that is to say. Mr W. being infirm, and it being within the bounds of probability that his decease might lead to some discoveries, and to the downfall of—HEEP's—power over the W. family,—as I, Wilkins Micawber, the undersigned, assume—unless the filial affection of his daughter could be secretly influenced from allowing any investigation of the partnership affairs to be ever made, the said—HEEP—deemed it expedient to have a bond ready by him, as from Mr W., for the before-mentioned sum of twelve six fourteen, two and nine, with interest, stated therein to have been advanced by—HEEP—to Mr W. to save Mr W. from dishonour; though really the sum was never advanced by him, and has long been replaced. The signatures to this instrument purporting to be executed by Mr W. and attested by Wilkins Micawber, are forgeries by—HEEP. I have, in my possession, in his hand and pocket-book, several similar imitations of Mr W.'s signature, here and there defaced by fire, but legible to anyone. I never attested any such document. And I have the document itself, in my possession.' "

Uriah Heep, with a start, took out of his pocket a bunch of keys, and opened a certain drawer; then, suddenly bethought himself of what he was about, and turned again towards us, without looking in it.

" 'And I have the document,' " Mr Micawber read again, looking about as if it were the text of a sermon, " 'in my possession,—that is to say, I had, early this morning, when this was written, but have since relinquished it to Mr Traddles.' "

"It is quite true," assented Traddles.

"Ury, Ury!" cried the mother, "be umble and make terms. I know my son will be umble, gentlemen, if you'll give him time to think. Mr Copperfield, I'm sure you know that he was always very umble sir!"

It was singular to see how the mother still held to the old trick, when the son had abandoned it as useless.

"Mother," he said, with an impatient bite at the handkerchief in which his hand was wrapped, "you had better take and fire a loaded gun at me."

"But I love you, Ury," cried Mrs Heep. And I have no doubt she did; or that he loved her, however strange it may appear; though, to be sure, they were a congenial couple. "And I can't bear to hear you provoking the gentlemen, and endangering of yourself more. I told the gentleman at first, when he told me upstairs it was come to light, that I would answer for your being umble, and making amends. Oh, see how umble *I* am, gentlemen, and don't mind him!"

"Why, there's Copperfield, mother," he angrily retorted, pointing his lean finger at me, against whom all his animosity was levelled, as the prime mover in the discovery; and I did not undeceive him; "there's Copperfield, would have given you a hundred pound to say less than you've blurted out!"

"I can't help it, Ury," cried his mother. "I can't see you running into danger, through carrying your head so high. Better be umble, as you always was."

He remained for a little, biting the handkerchief, and then said to me with a scowl:

"What more have you got to bring forward? If anything, go on with it. What do you look at me for?"

Mr Micawber promptly resumed his letter, glad to revert to a performance with which he was so highly satisfied.

" 'Third. And last. I am now in a condition to show, by—HEEP's—false books, and—HEEP's—real memoranda, beginning with the partially destroyed pocket-book (which I was unable to comprehend, at the time of its accidental discovery by Mrs Micawber, on our taking possession of our present abode, in the locker or bin devoted to the reception of the ashes calcined on our domestic hearth), that the weaknesses, the faults, the very virtues, the parental affections, and the sense of honour, of the unhappy Mr W. have been for years acted on by, and warped to the base purposes of—HEEP. That Mr W. has been for years deluded and plundered, in every conceivable manner, to the pecuniary aggrandisement of the avaricious, false, and grasping—HEEP. That the engrossing object of—HEEP—was, next to gain, to subdue Mr and Miss W. (of his ulterior views in reference to the latter I say nothing) entirely to himself. That his last act, completed but a few months since, was to induce Mr W. to execute a relinquishment of his share in the partnership, and even a bill of sale on the very furniture of his house, in consideration of a certain annuity, to be well and truly paid by—HEEP—on the four common quarter-days in each and every year. That these meshes; beginning with alarming and falsified accounts of the estate of which Mr W. is the receiver, at a period when Mr W. had launched into imprudent and ill-judged speculations, and may not have had the money, for which he was morally and legally responsible, in hand; going on with pretended borrowings of money at enormous interest, really coming from—HEEP—and by—HEEP—fraudulently obtained or withheld from Mr W. himself, on pretence of such speculations or otherwise; perpetuated by a miscellaneous catalogue of unscrupulous chicaneries—gradually thickened, until the unhappy Mr W. could see no world beyond. Bankrupt, as he believed, alike in circumstances, in all other hope, and in honour, his sole reliance was upon the monster in the garb of man,' "—Mr Micawber made a good deal of this, as a new turn of expression,—" 'who, by making himself necessary to him, had achieved his destruction. All this I undertake to show. Probably much more!' "

I whispered a few words to Agnes, who was weeping, half joyfully, half sorrowfully, at my side; and there was a movement among us, as if Mr Micawber had finished. He said, with exceeding gravity, "Pardon me," and proceeded, with a mixture of the lowest spirits and the most intense enjoyment, to the peroration of his letter.

" 'I have now concluded. It merely remains for me to substantiate these accusations; and then, with my ill-starred family, to disappear from the landscape on which we appear to be an incumbrance. That is soon done. It may be reasonably inferred that our baby will first expire of inanition, as being the frailest member of our circle; and that our twins will follow next in order. So be it! For myself, my Canterbury Pilgrimage has done much; imprisonment on civil process, and want, will soon do more. I trust that the labour and hazard of an investigation—of which the smallest results have been slowly pieced together, in the pressure of arduous avocations, under grinding penurious apprehensions, at rise of morn, at dewy eve, in the shadows of night, under the watchful eye of one whom it were superfluous to call Demon—combined with the struggle of parental Poverty to turn it, when completed, to the right account, may be as the sprinkling of a few drops of sweet water on my funeral pyre. I ask no more. Let it be, in justice, merely said of me, as of a gallant and eminent naval Hero, with whom I have no pretensions to cope, that what I have done, I did, in despite of mercenary and selfish objects,

For England, home, and Beauty.

" 'Remaining always, &c. &c., WILKINS MICAWBER.' "

Much affected, but still intensely enjoying himself, Mr Micawber folded up his letter, and handed it with a bow to my aunt, as something she might like to keep.

There was, as I had noticed on my first visit long ago, an iron safe in the room. The key was in it. A hasty suspicion seemed to strike Uriah; and, with a glance at Mr Micawber, he went to it, and threw the doors clanking open. It was empty.

"Where are the books?" he cried, with a frightful face. "Some thief has stolen the books!"

Mr Micawber tapped himself with the ruler. "I did, when I got the key from you as usual—but a little earlier—and opened it this morning."

"Don't be uneasy," said Traddles. "They have come into my possession. I will take care of them, under the authority I mentioned."

"You receive stolen goods, do you?" cried Uriah.

"Under such circumstances," answered Traddles, "yes."

What was my astonishment when I beheld my aunt, who had been profoundly quiet and attentive, make a dart at Uriah Heep, and seize him by the collar with both hands!

"You know what I want?" said my aunt.

"A strait-waistcoat," said he.

"No. My property!" returned my aunt. "Agnes, my dear, as long as I believed it had been really made away with by your father, I wouldn't—and, my dear, I didn't, even to

Trot, as he knows—breathe a syllable of its having been placed here for investment. But, now I know this fellow's answerable for it, and I'll have it! Trot, come and take it away from him!"

Whether my aunt supposed, for the moment, that he kept her property in his neck-kerchief, I am sure I don't know; but she certainly pulled at it as if she thought so. I hastened to put myself between them, and to assure her that we would all take care that he should make the utmost restitution of everything he had wrongly got. This, and a few moments' reflection, pacified her; but she was not at all disconcerted by what she had done (though I cannot say as much for her bonnet) and resumed her seat composedly.

During the last few minutes, Mrs Heep had been clamouring to her son to be "numble"; and had been going down on her knees to all of us in succession, and making the wildest promises. Her son sat her down in his chair; and, standing sulkily by her, holding her arm with his hand, but not rudely, said to me, with a ferocious look:

"What do you want done?"

"I will tell you what must be done," said Traddles.

"Has that Copperfield no tongue?" muttered Uriah, "I would do a good deal for you if you could tell me, without lying, that somebody had cut it out."

"My Uriah means to be umble!" cried his mother. "Don't mind what he says, good gentlemen!"

"What must be done," said Traddles, "is this. First, the deed of relinquishment, that we have heard of, must be given over to me now—here."

"Suppose I haven't got it," he interrupted.

"But you have," said Traddles; "therefore, you know, we won't suppose so." And I cannot help avowing that this was the first occasion on which I really did justice to the clear head, and the plain, patient, practical good sense, of my old schoolfellow. "Then," said Traddles, "you must prepare to disgorge all that your rapacity has become possessed of, and to make restoration to the last farthing. All the partnership books and papers must remain in our possession; all your books and papers; all money accounts and securities, of both kinds. In short, everything here."

"Must it? I don't know that," said Uriah. "I must have time to think about that."

"Certainly," replied Traddles; "but, in the meanwhile, and until everything is done to our satisfaction, we shall maintain possession of these things; and beg you—in short, compel you—to keep to your own room, and hold no communication with anyone."

"I won't do it!" said Uriah, with an oath.

"Maidstone Jail is a safer place of detention," observed Traddles; "and though the law may be longer in righting us, and may not be able to right us so completely as you can, there is no doubt of its punishing *you*. Dear me, you know that quite as well as I! Copperfield, will you go round to the Guildhall, and bring a couple of officers?"

Here, Mrs Heep broke out again, crying on her knees to Agnes to interfere in their behalf, exclaiming that he was very humble, and it was all true, and if he didn't do what we wanted, she would, and much more to the same purpose; being half frantic with fears for her darling. To inquire what he might have done, if he had had any boldness, would be like inquiring what a mongrel cur might do, if it had the spirit of a tiger. He was a coward, from head to foot; and showed his dastardly nature through his sullenness and mortification, as much as at any time of his mean life.

"Stop!" he growled to me; and wiped his hot face with his hand. "Mother, hold your noise. Well! Let 'em have that deed. Go and fetch it!"

"Do you help her, Mr Dick," said Traddles, "if you please."

Proud of his commission, and understanding it, Mr Dick accompanied her as a shepherd's dog might accompany a sheep. But, Mrs Heep gave him little trouble; for she not only returned with the deed, but with the box in which it was, where we found a banker's book and some other papers that were afterwards serviceable.

"Good!" said Traddles, when this was brought. "Now, Mr Heep, you can retire to think: particularly observing, if you please, that I declare to you, on the part of all present, that there is only one thing to be done; that it is what I have explained; and that it must be done without delay."

Uriah, without lifting his eyes from the ground, shuffled across the room with his hand to his chin, and pausing at the door, said:

"Copperfield, I have always hated you. You've always been an upstart, and you've always been against me."

"As I think I told you once before," said I, "it is you who have been, in your greed and cunning, against all the world. It may be profitable to you to reflect, in future, that there never were greed and cunning in the world yet, that did not do too much, and overreach themselves. It is as certain as death."

"Or as certain as they used to teach at school (the same school where I picked up so much umbleness), from nine o'clock to eleven, that labour was a curse; and from eleven o'clock to one, that it was a blessing and a cheerfulness, and a dignity, and I don't know what all, eh?" said he with a sneer. "You preach, about as consistent as they did. Won't umbleness go down? I shouldn't have got round my gentleman fellow-partner without it, I think.—Micawber, you old bully, I'll pay *you!*"

Mr Micawber, supremely defiant of him and his extended finger, and making a great deal of his chest until he had slunk out at the door, then addressed himself to me, and proffered me the satisfaction of "witnessing the re-establishment of mutual confidence between himself and Mrs Micawber." After which, he invited the company generally to the contemplation of that affecting spectacle.

"The veil that has long been interposed between Mrs Micawber and myself, is now withdrawn," said Mr Micawber; "and my children and the Author of their Being can once more come in contact on equal terms."

As we were all very grateful to him, and all desirous to show that we were, as well as the hurry and disorder of our spirits would permit, I dare say we should all have gone, but that it was necessary for Agnes to return to her father, as yet unable to bear more than the dawn of hope; and for someone else to hold Uriah in safe keeping. So, Traddles remained for the latter purpose, to be presently relieved by Mr Dick; and Mr Dick, my aunt, and I, went home with Mr Micawber. As I parted hurriedly from the dear girl to whom I owed so much, and thought from what she had been saved, perhaps, that morning—her better resolution notwithstanding—I felt devoutly thankful for the miseries of my younger days which had brought me to the knowledge of Mr Micawber.

His house was not far off; and as the street door opened into the sitting-room, and he bolted in with a precipitation quite his own, we found ourselves at once in the bosom of the family. Mr Micawber exclaiming, "Emma! my life!" rushed into Mrs Micawber's arms. Mrs Micawber shrieked, and folded Mr Micawber in her embrace. Miss Micawber, nursing the unconscious stranger of Mrs Micawber's last letter to me, was sensibly affected. The stranger leaped. The twins testified their joy by several inconvenient but innocent demonstrations. Master Micawber, whose disposition appeared to have been soured by early disappointment, and whose aspect had become morose, yielded to his better feelings, and blubbered.

"Emma!" said Mr Micawber. "The cloud is past from my mind. Mutual confidence, so long preserved between us once, is restored, to know no further interruption. Now, welcome poverty!" cried Mr Micawber, shedding tears. "Welcome misery, welcome houselessness, welcome hunger, rags, tempest, and beggary! Mutual confidence will sustain us to the end!"

With these expressions, Mr Micawber placed Mrs Micawber in a chair, and embraced the family all round; welcoming a variety of bleak prospects, which appeared, to the best of my judgement, to be anything but welcome to them; and calling upon them to come out into Canterbury and sing a chorus, as nothing else was left for their support.

But Mrs Micawber having, in the strength of her emotions, fainted away, the first thing to be done, even before the chorus could be considered complete, was to recover her. This my aunt and Mr Micawber did; and then my aunt was introduced, and Mrs Micawber recognized me.

"Excuse me, dear Mr Copperfield," said the poor lady, giving me her hand, "but I am not strong; and the removal of the late misunderstanding between Mr Micawber and myself was at first too much for me."

"Is this all your family, ma'am?" said my aunt.

"There are no more at present," returned Mrs Micawber.

"Good gracious, I didn't mean that, ma'am," said my aunt. "I mean, are all these yours?"

"Madam," replied Mr Micawber, "it is a true bill."

"And that eldest young gentleman, now," said my aunt, musing, "what has *he* been brought up to?"

"It was my hope when I came here," said Mr Micawber, "to have got Wilkins into the Church: or perhaps I shall express my meaning more strictly, if I say the Choir. But there was no vacancy for a tenor in the venerable Pile for which this city is so justly eminent; and he has—in short, he has contracted a habit of singing in public-houses, rather than in sacred edifices."

"But he means well," said Mrs Micawber, tenderly.

"I dare say, my love," rejoined Mr Micawber, "that he means particularly well; but I have not yet found that he carries out his meaning, in any given direction whatsoever."

Master Micawber's moroseness of aspect returned upon him again, and he demanded, with some temper, what he was to do? Whether he had been born a carpenter, or a coach-painter, any more than he had been born a bird? Whether he could go into the next street, and open a chemist's shop? Whether he could rush to the next assizes, and proclaim himself a lawyer? Whether he could come out by force at the opera, and succeed by violence? Whether he could do anything, without being brought up to something?

My aunt mused a little while, and then said:

"Mr Micawber, I wonder you have never turned your thoughts to emigration."

"Madam," returned Mr Micawber, "it was the dream of my youth, and the fallacious aspiration of my riper years." I am thoroughly persuaded, by the by, that he had never thought of it in his life.

"Aye?" said my aunt, with a glance at me. "Why, what a thing it would be for yourselves and your family, Mr and Mrs Micawber, if you were to emigrate now."

"Capital, madam, capital," urged Mr Micawber, gloomily.

"That is the principal, I may say the only difficulty, my dear Mr Copperfield," assented his wife.

"Capital?" cried my aunt. "But you are doing us a great service—have done us a great service, I may say, for surely much will come out of the fire—and what could we do for you, that would be half so good as to find the capital?"

"I could not receive it as a gift," said Mr Micawber, full of fire and animation, "but if a sufficient sum could be advanced, say at five per cent interest, per annum, upon my personal liability—say my notes of hand, at twelve, eighteen, and twenty-four months, respectively, to allow time for something to turn up—"

"Could be? Can be and shall be, on your own terms," returned my aunt, "if you say the word. Think of this now, both of you. Here are some people David knows, going out to Australia shortly. If you decide to go, why shouldn't you go in the same ship? You may help each other. Think of this now, Mr and Mrs Micawber. Take your time, and weigh it well."

"There is but one question, my dear ma'am, I could wish to ask," said Mrs Micawber. "The climate, I believe, is healthy?"

"Finest in the world!" said my aunt.

"Just so," returned Mrs Micawber. "Then my question arises. Now, *are* the circumstances of the country such, that a man of Mr Micawber's abilities would have a fair chance of rising in the social scale? I will not say, at present, might he aspire to be Governor, or anything of that sort; but would there be a reasonable opening for his talents to develop themselves—that would be amply sufficient—and find their own expansion?"

"No better opening anywhere," said my aunt, "for a man who conducts himself well, and is industrious."

"For a man who conducts himself well," repeated Mrs Micawber, with her clearest business manner, "and is industrious. Precisely. It is evident to me that Australia is the legitimate sphere of action for Mr Micawber!"

"I entertain the conviction, my dear madam," said Mr Micawber, "that it is, under existing circumstances, the land, the only land, for myself and family; and that something of an extraordinary nature will turn up on that shore. It is no distance—comparatively speaking; and though consideration is due to the kindness of your proposal, I assure you that is a mere matter of form."

Shall I ever forget how, in a moment, he was the most sanguine of men, looking on to fortune; or how Mrs Micawber presently discoursed about the habits of the kangaroo! Shall I ever recall that street of Canterbury on a market-day, without recalling him, as he walked back with us; expressing, in the hardy roving manner he assumed, the unsettled habits of a temporary sojourner in the land; and looking at the bullocks, as they came by, with the eye of an Australian farmer!

Chapter LIII

ANOTHER RETROSPECT

I MUST pause yet once again. O, my child-wife, there is a figure in the moving crowd before my memory, quiet and still, saying in its innocent love and childish beauty, Stop to think of me—turn to look upon the Little Blossom, as it flutters to the ground!

I do. All else grows dim, and fades away. I am again with Dora, in our cottage. I do not know how long she has been ill. I am so used to it in feeling, that I cannot count the time. It is not really long, in weeks or months; but, in my usage and experience, it is a weary, weary while.

They have left off telling me to "wait a few days more." I have begun to fear, remotely, that the day may never shine, when I shall see my child-wife running in the sunlight with her old friend Jip.

He is, as it were suddenly, grown very old. It may be that he misses in his mistress, something that enlivened him and made him younger; but he mopes, and his sight is weak, and his limbs are feeble, and my aunt is sorry that he objects to her no more, but creeps near her as he lies on Dora's bed—she sitting at the bedside—and mildly licks her hand.

Dora lies smiling on us, and is beautiful, and utters no hasty or complaining word. She says that we are very good to her; that her dear old careful boy is tiring himself out, she knows; that my aunt has no sleep, yet is always wakeful, active, and kind. Sometimes, the little bird-like ladies come to see her; and then we talk about our wedding-day, and all that happy time.

What a strange rest and pause in my life there seems to be—and in all life, within doors and without—when I sit in the quiet, shaded, orderly room, with the blue eyes of my child-wife turned towards me, and her little fingers twining round my hand! Many and many an hour I sit thus; but, of all those times, three times come the freshest on my mind.

It is morning; and Dora, made so trim by my aunt's hands, shows me how her pretty hair *will* curl upon the pillow yet, and how long and bright it is, and how she likes to have it loosely gathered in that net she wears.

"Not that I am vain of it, now, you mocking boy," she says, when I smile; "but because you used to say you thought it so beautiful; and because, when I first began to think about you, I used to peep in the glass, and wonder whether you would like very much to have a lock of it. Oh what a foolish fellow you were, Doady, when I gave you one!"

"That was on the day when you were painting the flowers I had given you, Dora, and when I told you how much in love I was."

"Ah! but I didn't like to tell *you," says Dora, *"then,* how I had cried over them, because I believed you really liked me! When I can run about again as I used to do, Doady, let us go and see those places where we were such a silly couple, shall we? And take some of the old walks? And not forget poor papa?"

"Yes, we will, and have some happy days. So you must make haste to get well, my dear."

"Oh, I shall soon do that! I am so much better, you don't know!"

It is evening; and I sit in the same chair, by the same bed, with the same face turned towards me. We have been silent, and there is a smile upon her face. I have ceased to carry my light burden up and down stairs now. She lies here all the day.

"Doady!"

"My dear Dora!"

"You won't think what I am going to say, unreasonable, after what you told me, such a little while ago, of Mr Wickfield's not being well? I want to see Agnes. Very much I want to see her."

"I will write to her, my dear."

"Will you?"

"Directly."

"What a good, kind boy! Doady, take me on your arm. Indeed, my dear, it's not a whim. It's not a foolish fancy. I want, very much indeed, to see her!"

"I am certain of it. I have only to tell her so, and she is sure to come."

"You are very lonely when you go downstairs, now?" Dora whispers, with her arm about my neck.

"How can I be otherwise, my own love, when I see your empty chair?"

"My empty chair!" She clings to me for a little while, in silence. "And you really miss me, Doady?" looking up, and brightly smiling. "Even poor, giddy, stupid me?"

"My heart, who is there upon earth that I could miss so much?"

"Oh, husband! I am so glad, yet so sorry!" creeping closer to me, and folding me in both her arms. She laughs and sobs, and then is quiet, and quite happy.

"Quite!" she says. "Only give Agnes my dear love, and tell her that I want very, very, much to see her; and I have nothing left to wish for."

"Except to get well again. Dora."

"Ah, Doady! Sometimes I think—you know I always was a silly little thing!—that that will never be!"

"Don't say so, Dora! Dearest love, don't think so!"

"I won't, if I can help it, Doady. But I am very happy; though my dear boy is so lonely by himself, before his child-wife's empty chair!"

It is night; and I am with her still. Agnes has arrived; has been among us for a whole day and an evening. She, my aunt, and I, have sat with Dora since the morning, all together. We have not talked much, but Dora has been perfectly contented and cheerful. We are now alone.

Do I know, now, that my child-wife will soon leave me? They have told me so; they have told me nothing new to my thoughts; but I am far from sure that I have taken that truth to heart. I cannot master it. I have withdrawn by myself, many times today, to weep. I have remembered Who wept for a parting between the living and the dead. I have bethought me of all that gracious and compassionate history. I have tried to resign myself, and to console myself; and that, I hope, I may have done imperfectly; but what I cannot firmly settle in my mind is, that the end will absolutely come. I hold her hand in mine, I hold her heart in mine, I see her love for me, alive in all its strength. I cannot shut out a pale lingering shadow of belief that she will be spared.

"I am going to speak to you, Doady. I am going to say something I have often thought of saying, lately. You won't mind?" with a gentle look.

"Mind, my darling?"

"Because I don't know what you will think, or what you may have thought sometimes. Perhaps you have often thought the same. Doady, dear, I am afraid I was too young."

I lay my face upon the pillow by her, and she looks into my eyes, and speaks very softly. Gradually, as she goes on, I feel, with a stricken heart, that she is speaking of herself as past.

"I am afraid, dear, I was too young. I don't mean in years only, but in experience, and thoughts, and everything. I was such a silly little creature! I am afraid it would have been better, if we had only loved each other as a boy and girl, and forgotten it. I have begun to think I was not fit to be a wife."

I try to stay my tears, and to reply, "Oh, Dora, love, as fit as I to be a husband!"

"I don't know," with the old shake of her curls. "Perhaps! But if I had been more fit to be married I might have made you more so, too. Besides, you are very clever, and I never was."

"We have been very happy, my sweet Dora."

"I was very happy, very. But, as years went on, my dear boy would have wearied of his child-wife. She would have been less and less a companion for him. He would have been more and more sensible of what was wanting in his home. She wouldn't have improved. It is better as it is."

"Oh, Dora, dearest, dearest, do not speak to me so. Every word seems a reproach!"

"No, not a syllable!" she answers, kissing me. "Oh, my dear, you never deserved it, and I loved you far too well to say a reproachful word to you, in earnest—it was all the merit I had, except being pretty—or you thought me so. Is it lonely, downstairs, Doady?"

"Very! Very!"

"Don't cry! Is my chair there?"

"In its old place."

"Oh, how my poor boy cries! Hush, hush! Now, make me one promise. I want to speak to Agnes. When you go downstairs, tell Agnes so, and send her up to me; and while I speak to her, let no one come—not even aunt. I want to speak to Agnes by herself. I want to speak to Agnes, quite alone."

I promise that she shall, immediately; but I cannot leave her, for my grief.

"I said that it was better as it is!" she whispers, as she holds me in her arms. "Oh, Doady, after more years, you never could have loved your child-wife better than you do; and, after more years, she would so have tried and disappointed you, that you might not have been able to love her half so well! I know I was too young and foolish. It is much better as it is!"

Agnes is downstairs, when I go into the parlour; and I give her the message. She disappears, leaving me alone with Jip.

His Chinese house is by the fire; and he lies within it, on his bed of flannel, querulously trying to sleep. The bright moon is high and clear. As I look out on the night, my tears fall fast, and my undisciplined heart is chastened heavily—heavily.

I sit down by the fire, thinking with a blind remorse of all those secret feelings I have nourished since my marriage. I think of every little trifle between me and Dora, and feel the truth, that trifles make the sum of life. Ever rising from the sea of my remembrance, is the image of the dear child as I knew her first, graced by my young love, and by her own, with every fascination wherein such love is rich. Would it, indeed, have been better if we had loved each other as a boy and a girl, and forgotten it? Undisciplined heart, reply!

How the time wears, I know not; until I am recalled by my child-wife's old companion. More restless than he was, he crawls out of his house, and looks at me, and wanders to the door, and whines to go upstairs.

"Not tonight, Jip! Not tonight!"

He comes very slowly back to me, licks my hand, and lifts his dim eyes to my face.

"Oh, Jip! It may be, never again!"

He lies down at my feet, stretches himself out as if to sleep, and with a plaintive cry, is dead.

"Oh, Agnes! Look, look, here!"

—That face, so full of pity, and of grief, that rain of tears, that awful mute appeal to me, that solemn hand upraised towards Heaven!

"Agnes?"

It is over. Darkness comes before my eyes; and, for a time, all things are blotted out of my remembrance.

Chapter LIV

MR MICAWBER'S TRANSACTIONS

THIS is not the time at which I am to enter on the state of my mind beneath its load of sorrow. I came to think that the Future was walled up before me, that the energy and action of my life were at an end, that I never could find any refuge but in the grave. I came to think so, I say, but not in the first shock of my grief. It slowly grew to that. If the events I go on to relate, had not thickened around me, in the beginning to confuse, and in the end to augment, my affliction, it is possible (though I think not probable), that I might have fallen at once into this condition. As it was, an interval occurred before I fully knew my own distress; an interval, in which I even supposed that its sharpest pangs were past; and when my mind could soothe itself by resting on all that was most innocent and beautiful, in the tender story that was closed for ever.

When it was first proposed that I should go abroad, or how it came to be agreed among us that I was to seek the restoration of my peace in change and travel, I do not, even now, distinctly know. The spirit of Agnes so pervaded all we thought, and said, and did, in that time of sorrow, that I assume I may refer the project to her influence. But her influence was so quiet that I know no more.

And now, indeed, I began to think that in my old association of her with the stained-glass window in the church, a prophetic foreshadowing of what she would be to me, in the calamity that was to happen in the fullness of time, had found a way into my mind. In all that sorrow, from the moment, never to be forgotten, when she stood before me with her upraised hand, she was like a sacred presence in my lonely house. When the Angel of Death alighted there, my child-wife fell asleep—they told me so when I could bear to hear it—on her bosom, with a smile. From my swoon, I first awoke to a consciousness of her compassionate tears, her words of hope and peace, her gentle face bending down as from a purer region nearer Heaven, over my undisciplined heart, and softening its pain.

Let me go on.

I was to go abroad. That seemed to have been determined among us from the first. The ground now covering all that could perish of my departed wife, I waited only for what Mr Micawber called the "final pulverization of Heep"; and for the departure of the emigrants.

At the request of Traddles, most affectionate and devoted of friends in my trouble, we returned to Canterbury: I mean my aunt, Agnes, and I. We proceeded by appointment straight to Mr Micawber's house; where, and at Mr Wickfield's, my friend had been labouring ever since our explosive meeting. When poor Mrs Micawber saw me come in, in my black clothes, she was sensibly affected. There was a great deal of good in Mrs Micawber's heart, which had not been dunned out of it in all those many years.

"Well, Mr and Mrs Micawber," was my aunt's first salutation after we were seated. "Pray, have you thought about that emigration proposal of mine?"

"My dear madam," returned Mr Micawber, "perhaps I cannot better express the conclusion at which Mrs Micawber, your humble servant, and I may add our children, have jointly and severally arrived, than by borrowing the language of an illustrious poet, to reply that our Boat is on the shore, and our Bark is on the sea."

"That's right," said my aunt. "I augur all sort of good from your sensible decision."

"Madam, you do us a great deal of honour," he rejoined. He then referred to a memorandum. "With respect to the pecuniary assistance enabling us to launch our frail canoe on the ocean of enterprise, I have reconsidered that important business-point; and would beg to propose my notes of hand—drawn, it is needless to stipulate, on stamps of the amounts respectively required by the various Acts of Parliament applying to such securities—at eighteen, twenty-four, and thirty months. The proposition I originally submitted, was twelve, eighteen, and twenty-four; but I am apprehensive that such an arrangement might not allow sufficient time for the requisite amount of—Something—to turn up. We might not," said Mr Micawber, looking round the room as if it represented several hundred acres of highly cultivated land, "on the first responsibility becoming due, have been successful in our harvest, or we might not have got our harvest in. Labour, I believe, is sometimes difficult to obtain in that portion of our colonial possessions where it will be our lot to combat with the teeming soil."

"Arrange it in any way you please, sir," said my aunt.

"Madam," he replied, "Mrs Micawber and myself are deeply sensible of the very considerate kindness of our friends and patrons. What I wish is, to be perfectly business-like, and perfectly punctual. Turning over, as we are about to turn over, an entirely new leaf; and falling back, as we are now in the act of falling back, for a Spring of no common magnitude; it is important to my sense of self-respect, besides being an example to my son, that these arrangements should be concluded as between man and man."

I don't know that Mr Micawber attached any meaning to this last phrase; I don't know that anybody ever does, or did; but he appeared to relish it uncommonly, and repeated, with an impressive cough, "as between man and man".

"I propose," said Mr Micawber, "Bills—a convenience to the mercantile world, for which, I believe, we are originally indebted to the Jews, who appear to me to have had a devilish deal too much to do with them ever since—because they are negotiable. But if a Bond, or any other description of security, would be preferred, I should be happy to execute any such instrument. As between man and man."

My aunt observed, that in a case where both parties were willing to agree to anything, she took it for granted there would be no difficulty in settling this point. Mr Micawber was of her opinion.

"In reference to our domestic preparations, madam," said Mr Micawber, with some pride, "for meeting the destiny to which we are now understood to be self-devoted, I beg to report them. My eldest daughter attends at five every morning in a neighbouring establishment, to acquire the process—if process it may be called—of milking cows. My younger children are instructed to observe, as closely as circumstances will permit, the habits of the pigs and poultry maintained in the poorer parts of this city: a pursuit from which they have, on two occasions, been brought home, within an inch of being run over. I have myself directed some attention, during the past week, to the art of baking; and my son Wilkins has issued forth with a walking-stick and driven cattle, when permitted, by the rugged hirelings who had them in charge, to render any voluntary service in that direction—which I regret to say, for the credit of our nature, was not often; he being generally warned, with imprecations, to desist."

"All very right indeed," said my aunt, encouragingly. "Mrs Micawber has been busy, too, I have no doubt."

"My dear madam," returned Mrs Micawber, with her business-like air. "I am free to confess that I have not been actively engaged in pursuits immediately connected with cultivation or with stock, though well aware that both will claim my attention on a foreign shore. Such opportunities as I have been enabled to alienate from my domestic duties, I have devoted to corresponding at some length with my family. For I own it seems to me, my dear Mr Copperfield," said Mrs Micawber, who always fell back on me, I suppose from old habit, to whomsoever else she might address her discourse at starting, "that the time is come when the past should be buried in oblivion; when my family should take Mr Micawber by the hand, and Mr Micawber should take my family by the hand; when the lion should lie down with the lamb, and my family be on terms with Mr Micawber."

I said I thought so too.

"This, at least, is the light, my dear Mr Copperfield," pursued Mrs Micawber, "in which *I* view the subject. When I lived at home with my papa and mama, my papa was accustomed to ask, when any point was under discussion in our limited circle, 'In what light does my Emma view the subject?' That my papa was too partial, I know; still, on such a point as the frigid coldness which has ever subsisted between Mr Micawber and my family, I necessarily have formed an opinion, delusive though it may be."

"No doubt. Of course you have, ma'am," said my aunt.

"Precisely so," assented Mrs Micawber. "Now, I may be wrong in my conclusions; it is very likely that I am, but my individual impression is, that the gulf between my family and Mr Micawber may be traced to an apprehension, on the part of my family, that Mr Micawber would require pecuniary accommodation. I cannot help thinking," said Mrs Micawber, with an air of deep sagacity, "that there are members of my family who have been apprehensive that Mr Micawber would solicit them for their names.—I do not mean to be conferred in Baptism upon our children, but to be inscribed on Bills of Exchange, and negotiated in the Money Market."

The look of penetration with which Mrs Micawber announced this discovery, as if no one had ever thought of it before, seemed rather to astonish my aunt; who abruptly replied, "Well, ma'am, upon the whole, I shouldn't wonder if you were right!"

"Mr Micawber being now on the eve of casting off the pecuniary shackles that have so long enthralled him," said Mrs Micawber, "and of commencing a new career in a country where there is sufficient range for his abilities,—which, in my opinion, is exceedingly important; Mr Micawber's abilities peculiarly requiring space,—it seems to me that my family should signalize the occasion by coming forward. What I could wish to see, would be a meeting between Mr Micawber and my family at a festive entertainment, to be given at my family's expense; where Mr Micawber's health and prosperity being proposed, by some leading member of my family, Mr Micawber might have an opportunity of developing his views."

"My dear," said Mr Micawber, with some heat, "it may be better for me to state distinctly, at once, that if I were to develop my views to that assembled group, they would possibly be found of an offensive nature; my impression being that your family are, in the aggregate, impertinent Snobs; and, in detail, unmitigated Ruffians."

"Micawber," said Mrs Micawber, shaking her head, "no! You have never understood them, and they have never understood you."

Mr Micawber coughed.

"They have never understood you, Micawber," said his wife. "They may be incapable of it. If so, that is their misfortune. I can pity their misfortune."

"I am extremely sorry, my dear Emma," said Mr Micawber, relenting, "to have been betrayed into any expressions that might, even remotely, have the appearance of being strong expressions. All I would say is, that I can go abroad without your family coming forward to favour me,—in short, with a parting Shove of their cold shoulders; and that, upon the whole, I would rather leave England with such impetus as I possess, than derive any acceleration of it from that quarter. At the same time, my dear, if they should condescend to reply to your communications—which our joint experience renders most improbable—far be it from me to be a barrier to your wishes."

The matter being thus amicably settled, Mr Micawber gave Mrs Micawber his arm, and glancing at the heap of books and papers lying before Traddles on the table, said they would leave us to ourselves; which they ceremoniously did.

"My dear Copperfield," said Traddles, leaning back in his chair when they were gone, and looking at me with an affection that made his eyes red, and his hair all kinds of shapes, "I don't make any excuse for troubling you with business, because I know you are deeply interested in it, and it may divert your thoughts. My dear boy, I hope you are not worn out?"

"I am quite myself," said I, after a pause. "We have more cause to think of my aunt than of anyone. You know how much she has done."

"Surely, surely," answered Traddles. "Who can forget it!"

"But even that is not all," said I. "During the last fortnight, some new trouble has vexed her; and she has been in and out of London every day. Several times she has gone out early, and been absent until evening. Last night, Traddles, with this journey before her, it was almost midnight before she came home. You know what her consideration for others is. She will not tell me what had happened to distress her."

My aunt, very pale, and with deep lines in her face, sat immovable until I had finished; when some stray tears found their way to her cheeks, and she put her hand on mine.

"It's nothing, Trot; it's nothing. There will be no more of it. You shall know by and by. Now Agnes, my dear, let us attend to these affairs."

"I must do Mr Micawber the justice to say," Traddles began, "that although he would appear not to have worked to any good account for himself, he is a most untiring man when he works for other people. I never saw such a fellow. If he always goes on in the same way, he must be, virtually, about two hundred years old, at present. The heat into which he has been continually putting himself; and the distracted and impetuous manner in which he has been diving, day and night, among papers and books; to say nothing of the immense number of letters he has written me between this house and Mr Wickfield's, and often across the table when he has been sitting opposite, and might much more easily have spoken; is quite extraordinary."

"Letters!" cried my aunt. "I believe he dreams in letters!"

"There's Mr Dick, too," said Traddles, "has been doing wonders! As soon as he was released from overlooking Uriah Heep, whom he kept in such charge as *I* never saw exceeded, he began to devote himself to Mr Wickfield. And really his anxiety to be of use in the investigations we have been making, and his real usefulness in extracting, and copying, and fetching, and carrying, have been quite stimulating to us."

"Dick is a very remarkable man," exclaimed my aunt; "and I always said he was. Trot, you know it."

"I am happy to say, Miss Wickfield," pursued Traddles, at once with great delicacy and with great earnestness, "that in your absence Mr Wickfield has considerably improved. Relieved of the incubus that had fastened upon him for so long a time, and of the dreadful apprehensions under which he had lived, he is hardly the same person. At times, even his impaired power of concentrating his memory and attention on particular points of business, has recovered itself very much; and he has been able to assist us in making some things clear, that we should have found very difficult indeed, if not hopeless, without him. But, what I have to do is to come to results; which are short enough; not to gossip on all the hopeful circumstances I have observed, or I shall never have done."

His natural manner and agreeable simplicity made it transparent that he said this to put us in good heart, and to enable Agnes to hear her father mentioned with greater confidence; but it was not the less pleasant for that.

"Now, let me see," said Traddles, looking among the papers on the table. "Having counted our funds, and reduced to order a great mass of unintentional confusion in the first place, and of wilful confusion and falsification in the second, we take it to be clear that Mr Wickfield might now wind up his business, and his agency-trust, and exhibit no deficiency or defalcation whatever."

"Oh, thank Heaven!" cried Agnes, fervently.

"But," said Traddles, "the surplus that would be left as his means of support—and I suppose the house to be sold, even in saying this—would be so small, not exceeding in all probability some hundreds of pounds, that perhaps, Miss Wickfield, it would be best to consider whether he might not retain his agency of the estate to which he has so long been receiver. His friends might advise him, you know; now he is free. You yourself, Miss Wickfield—Copperfield—I—"

"I have considered it, Trotwood," said Agnes, looking to me, "and I feel that it ought not to be, and must not be; even on the recommendation of a friend to whom I am so grateful, and owe so much."

"I will not say that I recommend it," observed Traddles. "I think it right to suggest it. No more."

"I am happy to hear you say so," answered Agnes, steadily, "for it gives me hope, almost assurance, that we think alike. Dear Mr Traddles and dear Trotwood, papa once free with honour, what could I wish for! I have always aspired, if I could have released him from the toils in which he was held, to render back some little portion of the love and care I owe him, and to devote my life to him. It has been, for years, the utmost height of my hopes. To take our future on myself, will be the next great happiness—the next to his release from all trust and responsibility—that I can know."

"Have you thought how, Agnes?"

"Often! I am not afraid, dear Trotwood. I am certain of success. So many people know me here, and think kindly of me, that I am certain. Don't mistrust me. Our wants are not many. If I rent the dear old house, and keep a school, I shall be useful and happy."

The calm fervour of her cheerful voice brought back so vividly, first the dear old house itself, and then my solitary home, that my heart was too full for speech. Traddles pretended for a little while to be busily looking among the papers.

"Next, Miss Trotwood," said Traddles, "that property of yours."

"Well, sir," sighed my aunt. "All I have got to say about it is, that if it's gone, I can bear it; and if it's not gone, I shall be glad to get it back."

"It was originally, I think, eight thousand pounds, Consols?" said Traddles.

"Right!" replied my aunt.

"I can't account for more than five," said Traddles, with an air of perplexity.

"—thousand, do you mean?" inquired my aunt, with uncommon composure, "or pounds?"

"Five thousand pounds," said Traddles.

"It was all there was," returned my aunt. "I sold three, myself. One, I paid for your articles, Trot, my dear; and the other two I have by me. When I lost the rest, I thought it wise to say nothing about that sum, but to keep it secretly for a rainy day. I wanted to see how you would come out of the trial, Trot; and you came out nobly—persevering, self-reliant, self-denying! So did Dick. Don't speak to me, for I find my nerves a little shaken!"

Nobody would have thought so, to see her sitting upright, with her arms folded; but she had wonderful self-command.

"Then I am delighted to say," cried Traddles, beaming with joy, "that we have recovered the whole money!"

"Don't congratulate me, anybody!" exclaimed my aunt. "How so, sir?"

"You believed it had been misappropriated by Mr Wickfield?" said Traddles.

"Of course I did," said my aunt, "and was therefore easily silenced. Agnes, not a word!"

"And indeed," said Traddles, "it was sold, by virtue of the power of management he held from you; but I needn't say by whom sold, or on whose actual signature. It was afterwards pretended to Mr Wickfield, by that rascal,—and proved, too, by figures—that he had possessed himself of the money (on general instructions, *he* said) to keep other deficiencies and difficulties from the light. Mr Wickfield, being so weak and helpless in his hands as to pay you, afterwards, several sums of interest on a pretended principal which he knew did not exist, made himself, unhappily, a party to the fraud."

"And at last took the blame upon himself," added my aunt; "and wrote me a mad letter, charging himself with robbery, and wrong unheard of. Upon which I paid him a visit early one morning, called for a candle, burnt the letter, and told him if he ever could right me and himself, to do it; and if he couldn't, to keep his own counsel for his daughter's sake.—If anybody speaks to me, I'll leave the house!"

We all remained quiet; Agnes covering her face.

"Well, my dear friend," said my aunt, after a pause, "and you have really extorted the money back from him?"

"Why, the fact is," returned Traddles, "Mr Micawber had so completely hemmed him in, and was always ready with so many new points if an old one failed, that he could not escape from us. A most remarkable circumstance is, that I really don't think he grasped this sum even so much for the gratification of his avarice, which was inordinate, as in the hatred he felt for Copperfield. He said so to me, plainly. He said he would even have spent as much, to baulk or injure Copperfield."

"Ha!" said my aunt, knitting her brows, thoughtfully, and glancing at Agnes. "And what's become of him?"

"I don't know. He left here," said Traddles, "with his mother, who had been clamouring, and beseeching, and disclosing, the whole time. They went away by one of the London night coaches, and I know no more about him; except that his malevolence to me at parting was audacious. He seemed to consider himself hardly less indebted to me, than to Mr Micawber; which I consider (as I told him) quite a compliment."

"Do you suppose he has any money, Traddles?" I asked.

"Oh dear, yes, I should think so," he replied, shaking his head, seriously. "I should say he must have pocketed a good deal, in one way or other. But, I think you would find, Copperfield, if you had an opportunity of observing his course, that money would never keep that man out of mischief. He is such an incarnate hypocrite, that whatever object he pursues, he must pursue crookedly. It's his only compensation for the outward restraints he puts upon himself. Always creeping along the ground to some small end or other, he will always magnify every object in the way; and consequently will hate and suspect everybody that comes, in the most innocent manner, between him and it. So the crooked courses will become crookeder, at any moment, for the least reason, or for none. It's only necessary to consider his history here," said Traddles, "to know that."

"He's a monster of meanness!" said my aunt.

"Really I don't know about that," observed Traddles thoughtfully. "Many people can be very mean, when they give their minds to it."

"And now, touching Mr Micawber," said my aunt.

"Well, really," said Traddles, cheerfully, "I must, once more, give Mr Micawber high praise. But for his having been so patient and persevering for so long a time, we never could have hoped to do anything worth speaking of. And I think we ought to consider that Mr Micawber did right, for right's sake, when we reflect what terms he might have made with Uriah Heep himself, for his silence."

"I think so too," said I.

"Now, what would you give him?" inquired my aunt.

"Oh! Before you come to that," said Traddles, a little disconcerted, "I am afraid I thought it discreet to omit (not being able to carry everything before me) two points, in making this lawless adjustment—for it's perfectly lawless from beginning to end—of a difficult affair. Those I.O.U.'s, and so forth, which Mr Micawber gave him for the advances he had—"

"Well! They must be paid," said my aunt.

"Yes, but I don't know when they may be proceeded on, or where they are," rejoined Traddles, opening his eyes; "and I anticipate, that, between this time and his departure, Mr Micawber will be constantly arrested, or taken in execution."

"Then he must be constantly set free again, and taken out of execution," said my aunt. "What's the amount altogether?"

"Why, Mr Micawber has entered the transactions—he calls them transactions—with great form, in a book," rejoined Traddles, smiling; "and he makes the amount a hundred and three pounds, five."

"Now, what shall we give him, that sum included?" said my aunt. "Agnes, my dear, you and I can talk about division of it afterwards. What should it be? Five hundred pounds?"

Upon this, Traddles and I both struck in at once. We both recommended a small sum in money, and the payment, without stipulation to Mr Micawber, of the Uriah claims as they came in. We proposed that the family should have their passage and their outfit, and a hundred pounds; and that Mr Micawber's arrangement for the repayment of the advances should be gravely entered into, as it might be wholesome for him to suppose himself under that responsibility. To this, I added the suggestion, that I should give some explanation of his character and history to Mr Peggotty, who I knew could be relied on; and that to Mr Peggotty should be quietly entrusted the discretion of advancing another hundred. I further proposed to interest Mr Micawber in Mr Peggotty, by confiding so much of Mr Peggotty's story to him as I might feel justified in relating, or might think expedient; and to endeavour to bring each of them to bear upon the other, for the common advantage. We all entered warmly into these views; and I may mention at once, that the principals themselves did so, shortly afterwards, with perfect good will and harmony.

Seeing that Traddles now glanced anxiously at my aunt again, I reminded him of the second and last point to which he had adverted.

"You and your aunt will excuse me, Copperfield, if I touch upon a painful theme, as I greatly fear I shall," said Traddles, hesitating; "but I think it necessary to bring it to your recollection. On the day of Mr Micawber's memorable denunciation a threatening allusion was made by Uriah Heep to your aunt's—husband."

My aunt, retaining her stiff position, and apparent composure, assented with a nod.

"Perhaps," observed Traddles, "it was mere purposeless impertinence?"

"No," returned my aunt.

"There was—pardon me—really such a person, and at all in his power?" hinted Traddles.

"Yes, my good friend," said my aunt.

Traddles, with a perceptible lengthening of his face, explained that he had not been able to approach this subject; that it had shared the fate of Mr Micawber's liabilities, in not being comprehended in the terms he had made; that we were no longer of any authority with Uriah Heep; and that if he could do us, or any of us, any injury or annoyance, no doubt he would.

My aunt remained quiet; until again some stray tears found their way to her cheeks.

"You are quite right," she said. "It was very thoughtful to mention it."

"Can I—or Copperfield—do anything?" asked Traddles, gently.

"Nothing," said my aunt. "I thank you many times. Trot, my dear, a vain threat! Let us have Mr and Mrs Micawber back. And don't any of you speak to me!" With that she smoothed her dress, and sat, with her upright carriage, looking at the door.

"Well, Mr and Mrs Micawber!" said my aunt, when they entered. "We have been discussing your emigration, with many apologies to you for keeping you out of the room so long; and I'll tell you what arrangements we propose."

These she explained to the unbounded satisfaction of the family,—children and all being then present,—and so much to the awakening of Mr Micawber's punctual habits in the opening stage of all bill transactions, that he could not be dissuaded from immediately rushing out, in the highest spirits, to buy the stamps for his notes of hand. But, his joy received a sudden check; for within five minutes, he returned in the custody of a sheriff's officer, informing us, in a flood of tears, that all was lost. We, being quite prepared for this event, which was of course a proceeding of Uriah Heep's, soon paid the money; and in five minutes more Mr Micawber was seated at the table, filling up the stamps with an expression of perfect joy, which only that congenial employment, or the making of punch, could impart in full completeness to his shining face. To see him at work on the stamps, with the relish of an artist, touching them like pictures, looking at them sideways, taking weighty notes of dates and amounts in his pocket-book, and contemplating them when finished, with a high sense of their precious value, was a sight indeed.

"Now, the best thing you can do, sir, if you'll allow me to advise you," said my aunt, after silently observing him, "is to abjure that occupation for evermore."

"Madam," replied Mr Micawber, "it is my intention to register such a vow on the virgin page of the future. Mrs Micawber will attest it. I trust," said Mr Micawber, solemnly, "that my son Wilkins will ever bear in mind, that he had infinitely better put his fist in the fire, than use it to handle the serpents that have poisoned the life-blood of his unhappy parent!" Deeply affected, and changed in a moment to the image of despair, Mr Micawber regarded the serpents with a look of gloomy abhorrence (in which his late admiration of them was not quite subdued), folded them up and put them in his pocket.

This closed the proceedings of the evening. We were weary with sorrow and fatigue, and my aunt and I were to return to London on the morrow. It was arranged that the Micawbers should follow us, after effecting a sale of their goods to a broker; that Mr Wickfield's affairs should be brought to a settlement, with all convenient speed, under the direction of Traddles; and that Agnes should also come to London, pending those arrangements. We passed the night at the old house, which, freed from the presence of the Heeps, seemed purged of a disease; and I lay in my old room, like a shipwrecked wanderer come home.

We went back next day to my aunt's house—not to mine; and when she and I sat alone, as of old, before going to bed, she said:

"Trot, do you really wish to know what I have had upon my mind lately?"

"Indeed I do, aunt. If there ever was a time when I felt unwilling that you should have a sorrow or anxiety which I could not share, it is now."

"You have had sorrow enough, child," said my aunt, affectionately, "without the addition of *my* little miseries. I could have no other motive, Trot, in keeping anything from you."

"I know that well," said I. "But tell me now."

"Would you ride with me a little way tomorrow morning?" asked my aunt.

"Of course."

"At nine," said she. "I'll tell you then, my dear."

At nine, accordingly, we went out in a little chariot, and drove to London. We drove a long way through the streets, until we came to one of the large hospitals. Standing hard by the building was a plain hearse. The driver recognized my aunt, and, in obedience to a motion of her hand at the window, drove slowly off; we following.

"You understand it now, Trot," said my aunt. "He is gone!"

"Did he die in the hospital?"

"Yes."

She sat immovable beside me; but, again I saw the stray tears on her face.

"He was there once before," said my aunt presently. "He was ailing a long time—a shattered, broken man, these many years. When he knew his state in this last illness, he asked them to send for me. He was sorry then. Very sorry."

"You went, I know, aunt."

"I went. I was with him a good deal afterwards."

"He died the night before we went to Canterbury?" said I.

My aunt nodded. "No one can harm him now," she said. "It was a vain threat."

We drove away, out of town, to the churchyard at Hornsey. "Better here than in the streets," said my aunt. "He was born here."

We alighted; and followed the plain coffin to a corner I remember well, where the service was read consigning it to the dust.

"Six-and-thirty years ago, this day, my dear," said my aunt, as we walked back to the chariot, "I was married. God forgive us all!"

We took our seats in silence; and so she sat beside me for a long time, holding my hand. At length she suddenly burst into tears, and said:

"He was a fine-looking man when I married him, Trot—and he was sadly changed!"

It did not last long. After the relief of tears, she soon became composed, and even cheerful. Her nerves were a little shaken, she said, or she would not have given way to it. God forgive us all!

So we rode back to her little cottage at Highgate, where we found the following short note, which had arrived by that morning's post from Mr Micawber:

> "CANTERBURY,
> "Friday.

"My dear Madam, and Copperfield,

"The fair land of promise lately looming on the horizon is again enveloped in impenetrable mists, and for ever withdrawn from the eyes of a drifting wretch whose Doom is sealed!

"Another writ has been issued (in His Majesty's High Court of King's Bench at Westminster), in another cause of HEEP *v.* MICAWBER, and the defendant in that cause is the prey of the sheriff having legal jurisdiction in this bailiwick.

> "Now's the day, and now's the hour,
> See the front of battle lower,
> See approach proud EDWARD's power—
> Chains and slavery!"

"Consigned to which, and to a speedy end (for mental torture is not supportable beyond a certain point, and that point I feel I have attained), my course is run. Bless you, bless you! Some future traveller, visiting, from motives of curiosity, not unmingled, let us hope, with sympathy, the place of confinement allotted to debtors in this city, may, and I trust will, Ponder, as he traces on its wall, inscribed with a rusty nail,

> "The obscure initials,
> "W. M.

"P.S. I re-open this to say that our common friend, Mr Thomas Traddles (who has not yet left us, and is looking extremely well), has paid the debt and costs, in the noble name of Miss Trotwood; and that myself and family are at the height of earthly bliss."

Chapter LV

TEMPEST

I NOW approach an event in my life, so indelible, so awful, so bound by an infinite variety of ties to all that has preceded it, in these pages, that, from the beginning of my narrative, I have seen it growing larger and larger as I advanced, like a great tower in a plain, and throwing its fore-cast shadow even on the incidents of my childish days.

For years after it occurred, I dreamed of it often. I have started up so vividly impressed by it, that its fury has yet seemed raging in my quiet room, in the still night. I dream of it sometimes, though at lengthened and uncertain intervals, to this hour. I have an association between it and a stormy wind, or the lightest mention of a sea-shore, as strong as any of which my mind is conscious. As plainly as I behold what happened, I will try to write it down. I do not recall it, but see it done; for it happens again before me.

The time drawing on rapidly for the sailing of the emigrant-ship, my good old nurse (almost broken-hearted for me, when we first met) came up to London. I was constantly with her, and her brother, and the Micawbers (they being very much together); but Emily I never saw.

One evening when the time was close at hand, I was alone with Peggotty and her brother. Our conversation turned on Ham. She described to us how tenderly he had taken leave of her, and how manfully and quietly he had borne himself. Most of all, of late, when she believed he was most tried. It was a subject of which the affectionate creature never tired; and our interest in hearing the many examples which she, who was so much with him, had to relate, was equal to hers in relating them.

My aunt and I were at that time vacating the two cottages at Highgate; I intending to go abroad, and she to return to her house at Dover. We had a temporary lodging in Covent Garden. As I walked home to it, after this evening's conversation, reflecting on what had passed between Ham and myself when I was last at Yarmouth, I wavered in the original purpose I had formed, of leaving a letter for Emily when I should take leave of her uncle on board the ship, and thought it would be better to write to her now. She might desire, I thought, after receiving my communication, to send some parting word by me to her unhappy lover. I ought to give her the opportunity.

I therefore sat down in my room, before going to bed, and wrote to her. I told her that I had seen him, and that he had requested me to tell her what I have already written in its place in these sheets. I faithfully repeated it. I had no need to enlarge upon it, if I had had the right. Its deep fidelity and goodness were not to be adorned by me or any man. I left it out, to be sent round in the morning; with a line to Mr Peggotty, requesting him to give it to her; and went to bed at daybreak.

I was weaker than I knew then; and, not falling asleep until the sun was up, lay late, and unrefreshed, next day. I was roused by the silent presence of my aunt at my bedside. I felt it in my sleep, as I suppose we all do feel such things.

"Trot, my dear," she said, when I opened my eyes, "I couldn't make up my mind to disturb you. Mr Peggotty is here; shall he come up?"

I replied yes, and he soon appeared.

"Mas'r Davy," he said, when we had shaken hands, "I giv Em'ly your letter, sir, and she writ this heer; and begged of me fur to ask you to read it, and if you see no hurt in't, to be so kind as take charge on 't."

"Have you read it?" said I.

He nodded sorrowfully. I opened it, and read as follows:

> "I have got your message. Oh, what can I write, to thank you for your good and blessed kindness to me!
>
> "I have put the words close to my heart. I shall keep them till I die. They are sharp thorns, but they are such comfort. I have prayed over them, oh, I have prayed so much. When I find what you are, and what uncle is, I think what God must be, and can cry to him.
>
> "Good-bye for ever. Now, my dear, my friend, good-bye for ever in this world. In another world, if I am forgiven, I may wake a child and come to you. All thanks and blessings. Farewell, evermore."

This, blotted with tears, was the letter.

"May I tell her as you doen't see no hurt in't, and as you'll be so kind as take charge on't, Mas'r Davy?" said Mr Peggotty, when I had read it.

"Unquestionably," said I—"but I am thinking—"

"Yes, Mas'r Davy?"

"I am thinking," said I, "that I'll go down again to Yarmouth. There's time, and to spare, for me to go and come back before the ship sails. My mind is constantly running on him, in his solitude; to put this letter of her writing in his hand at this time, and to enable you to tell her, in the moment of parting, that he has got it, will be a kindness to both of them. I solemnly accepted his commission, dear good fellow, and cannot discharge it too completely. The journey is nothing to me. I am restless, and shall be better in motion. I'll go down tonight."

Though he anxiously endeavoured to dissuade me, I saw that he was of my mind; and this, if I had required to be confirmed in my intention, would have had the effect. He went round to the coach office, at my request, and took the box-seat for me on the mail. In the evening I started, by that conveyance, down the road I had traversed under so many vicissitudes.

"Don't you think that," I asked the coachman, in the first stage out of London, "a very remarkable sky? I don't remember to have seen one like it."

"Nor I—not equal to it," he replied. "That's wind, sir. There'll be mischief done at sea, I expect, before long."

It was a murky confusion—here and there blotted with a colour like the colour of the smoke from damp fuel—of flying clouds, tossed up into most remarkable heaps, suggesting greater heights in the clouds than there were depths below them to the bottom of the deepest hollows in the earth, through which the wild moon seemed to plunge headlong, as if, in a dread disturbance of the laws of nature, she had lost her way and were frightened. There had been a wind all day; and it was rising then, with an extraordinary great sound. In another hour it had much increased, and the sky was more overcast, and blew hard.

But, as the night advanced, the clouds closing in and densely over-spreading the whole sky, then very dark, it came on to blow, harder and harder. It still increased, until our horses could scarcely face the wind. Many times, in the dark part of the night (it was then late in September, when the nights were not short), the leaders turned about, or came to a dead stop; and we were often in serious apprehension that the coach would be blown over. Sweeping gusts of rain came up before this storm, like showers of steel; and, at those times, when there was any shelter of trees or lee walls to be got, we were fain to stop, in a sheer impossibility of continuing the struggle.

When the day broke, it blew harder and harder. I had been in Yarmouth when the seamen said it blew great guns, but I had never known the like of this, or anything approaching to it. We came to Ipswich—very late, having had to fight every inch of ground since we were ten miles out of London; and found a cluster of people in the market-place, who had risen from their beds in the night, fearful of falling chimneys. Some of these, congregating about the inn-yard while we changed horses, told us of great sheets of lead having been ripped off a high church-tower, and flung into a by-street, which they then blocked up. Others had to tell of country people, coming in from neighbouring villages, who had seen great trees lying torn out of the earth, and whole ricks scattered about the roads and fields. Still, there was no abatement in the storm, but it blew harder.

As we struggled on, nearer and nearer to the sea, from which this mighty wind was blowing dead on shore, its force became more and more terrific. Long before we saw the sea, its spray was on our lips, and showered salt rain upon us. The water was out, over miles and miles of the flat country adjacent to Yarmouth; and every sheet and puddle lashed its banks, and had its stress of little breakers setting heavily towards us. When we came within sight of the sea, the waves on the horizon, caught at intervals above the rolling abyss, were like glimpses of another shore with towers and buildings. When at last we got into the town, the people came out to their doors, all aslant, and with streaming hair, making a wonder of the mail that had come through such a night.

I put up at the old inn, and went down to look at the sea; staggering along the street, which was strewn with sand and seaweed, and with flying blotches of sea-foam; afraid of falling slates and tiles; and holding by people I met, at angry corners. Coming near the beach, I saw, not only the boatmen, but half the people of the town, lurking behind buildings; some, now and then braving the fury of the storm to look away to sea, and blown sheer out of their course in trying to get zigzag back.

Joining these groups, I found bewailing women whose husbands were away in herring or oyster boats, which there was too much reason to think might have foundered before they could run in anywhere for safety. Grizzled old sailors were among the people, shaking their heads, as they looked from water to sky, and muttering to one another; ship-owners, excited and uneasy; children, huddling together, and peering into older faces; even stout mariners, disturbed and anxious, levelling their glasses at the sea from behind places of shelter, as if they were surveying an enemy.

The tremendous sea itself, when I could find sufficient pause to look at it, in the agitation of the blinding wind, the flying stones and sand, and the awful noise, confounded me. As the high watery walls came rolling in, and, at their highest, tumbled into surf, they looked as if the least would engulf the town. As the receding wave swept back with a hoarse roar, it seemed to scoop out deep caves in the beach, as if its purpose were to undermine the earth. When some white-headed billows thundered on, and dashed themselves to pieces before they reached the land, every fragment of the late whole seemed possessed by the full might of its wrath, rushing to be gathered to the composition of another monster. Undulating hills were changed to valleys, undulating valleys (with a solitary storm-bird sometimes skimming through them) were lifted up to hills; masses of water shivered and shook the beach with a booming sound; every shape tumultuously rolled on, as soon as made, to change its shape and place, and beat another shape and place away; the ideal shore on the horizon, with its towers and buildings, rose and fell; the clouds fell fast and thick; I seemed to see a rending and upheaving of all nature.

Not finding Ham among the people whom this memorable wind—for it is still remembered down there, as the greatest ever known to blow upon that coast—had brought together, I made my way to his house. It was shut; and as no one answered to my knocking, I went, by back ways and by-lanes, to the yard where he worked. I learned, there, that he had gone to Lowestoft, to meet some sudden exigency of ship-repairing in which his skill was required; but that he would be back tomorrow morning, in good time.

I went back to the inn; and when I had washed and dressed, and tried to sleep, but in vain, it was five o'clock in the afternoon. I had not sat five minutes by the coffee-room fire, when the waiter, coming to stir it, as an excuse for talking, told me that two colliers had gone down, with all hands, a few miles away; and that some other ships had been seen labouring hard in the Roads, and trying, in great distress, to keep off shore. Mercy on them, and on all poor sailors, said he, if we had another night like the last!

I was very much depressed in spirits; very solitary; and felt an uneasiness in Ham's not being there, disproportionate to the occasion. I was seriously affected, without knowing how much, by late events; and my long exposure to the fierce wind had confused me. There was that jumble in my thoughts and recollections, that I had lost the clear arrangement of time and distance. Thus, if I had gone out into the town, I should not have been surprised, I think, to encounter someone who I knew must be then in London. So to speak, there was in these respects a curious inattention in my mind. Yet it was busy, too, with all the remembrances the place naturally awakened; and they were particularly distinct and vivid.

In this state, the waiter's dismal intelligence about the ships immediately connected itself, without any effort of my volition, with my uneasiness about Ham. I was persuaded that I had an apprehension of his returning from Lowestoft by sea, and being lost. This grew so strong with me, that I resolved to go back to the yard before I took my dinner, and ask the boat-builder if he thought his attempting to return by sea at all likely? If he gave me the least reason to think so, I would go over to Lowestoft and prevent it by bringing him with me.

I hastily ordered my dinner, and went back to the yard. I was none too soon; for the boat-builder, with a lantern in his hand, was locking the yard-gate. He quite laughed when I asked him the question, and said there was no fear; no man in his senses, or out of them, would put off in such a gale of wind, least of all Ham Peggotty, who had been born to seafaring.

So sensible of this, beforehand, that I had really felt ashamed of doing what I was nevertheless impelled to do, I went back to the inn. If such a wind could rise, I think it was rising. The howl and roar, the rattling of the doors and windows, the rumbling in the chimneys, the apparent rocking of the very house that sheltered me, and the prodigious tumult of the sea, were more fearful than in the morning. But there was now a great darkness besides; and that invested the storm with new terrors, real and fanciful.

I could not eat, I could not sit still, I could not continue steadfast to anything. Something within me, faintly answering to the storm without, tossed up the depths of my memory and made a tumult in them. Yet, in all the hurry of my thoughts, wild running with the thundering sea,—the storm, and my uneasiness regarding Ham were always in the fore-ground.

My dinner went away almost untasted, and I tried to refresh myself with a glass or two of wine. In vain. I fell into a dull slumber before the fire, without losing my consciousness, either of the uproar out of doors, or of the place in which I was. Both became overshadowed by a new and indefinable horror; and when I awoke—or rather when I shook off the lethargy that bound me in my chair—my whole frame thrilled with objectless and unintelligible fear.

I walked to and fro, tried to read an old gazetteer, listened to the awful noises: looked at faces, scenes, and figures in the fire. At length, the steady ticking of the undisturbed clock on the wall tormented me to that degree that I resolved to go to bed.

It was reassuring, on such a night, to be told that some of the inn-servants had agreed together to sit up until morning. I went to bed, exceedingly weary and heavy; but, on my lying down, all such sensations vanished, as if by magic, and I was broad awake, with every sense refined.

For hours I lay there, listening to the wind and water; imagining, now, that I heard shrieks out at sea; now, that I distinctly heard the firing of signal guns; and now, the fall of houses in the town. I got up, several times, and looked out; but could see nothing, except the reflection in the window-panes of the faint candle I had left burning, and of my own haggard face looking in at me from the black void.

At length, my restlessness attained to such a pitch, that I hurried on my clothes, and went downstairs. In the large kitchen, where I dimly saw bacon and ropes of onions hanging from the beams, the watchers were clustered together, in various attitudes, about a table, purposely moved away from the great chimney, and brought near the door. A pretty girl, who had her ears stopped with her apron, and her eyes upon the door, screamed when I appeared, supposing me to be a spirit; but the others had more presence of mind, and were glad of an addition to their company. One man, referring to the topic they had been discussing, asked me whether I thought the souls of the collier-crews who had gone down, were out in the storm?

I remained there, I dare say, two hours. Once, I opened the yard-gate, and looked into the empty street. The sand, the seaweed, and the flakes of foam, were driving by; and I was obliged to call for assistance before I could shut the gate again, and make it fast against the wind.

There was a dark gloom in my solitary chamber, when I at length returned to it; but I was tired now, and, getting into bed again, fell—off a tower and down a precipice— into the depths of sleep. I have an impression that for a long time, though I dreamed of being elsewhere and in a variety of scenes, it was always blowing in my dream. At length, I lost that feeble hold upon reality, and was engaged with two dear friends, but who they were I don't know, at the siege of some town in a roar of cannonading.

The thunder of the cannon was so loud and incessant, that I could not hear something I much desired to hear, until I made a great exertion and awoke. It was broad day—eight or nine o'clock; the storm raging, in lieu of the batteries; and someone knocking and calling at my door.

"What is the matter?" I cried.

"A wreck! Close by!"

I sprung out of bed, and asked, what wreck?

"A schooner, from Spain or Portugal, laden with fruit and wine. Make haste, sir, if you want to see her! It's thought, down on the beach, she'll go to pieces every moment."

The excited voice went clamouring along the staircase; and I wrapped myself in my clothes as quickly as I could, and ran into the street.

Numbers of people were there before me, all running in one direction, to the beach. I ran the same way, outstripping a good many, and soon came facing the wild sea.

The wind might by this time have lulled a little, though not more sensibly than if the cannonading I had dreamed of, had been diminished by the silencing of half-a-dozen guns out of hundreds. But, the sea, having upon it the additional agitation of the whole night, was infinitely more terrific than when I had seen it last. Every appearance it had then presented, bore the expression of being *swelled;* and the height to which the breakers rose, and, looking over one another, bore one another down, and rolled in, in interminable hosts, was most appalling.

In the difficulty of hearing anything but wind and waves, and in the crowd, and the unspeakable confusion, and my first breathless efforts to stand against the weather, I was so confused that I looked out to sea for the wreck, and saw nothing but the foaming heads of the great waves. A half-dressed boatman, standing next me, pointed with his bare arm (a tattoo'd arrow on it, pointing in the same direction) to the left. Then, O great Heaven, I saw it, close in upon us!

One mast was broken short off, six or eight feet from the deck, and lay over the side, entangled in a maze of sail and rigging; and all that ruin, as the ship rolled and beat—which she did without a moment's pause, and with a violence quite inconceivable—beat the side as if it would stave it in. Some efforts were even then being made, to cut this portion of the wreck away; for, as the ship, which was broadside on, turned towards us in her rolling, I plainly descried her people at work with axes, especially one active figure with long curling hair, conspicuous among the rest. But, a great cry, which was audible even above the wind and water, rose from the shore at this moment; the sea, sweeping over the rolling wreck, made a clean breach, and carried men, spars, casks, planks, bulwarks, heaps of such toys, into the boiling surge.

The second mast was yet standing, with the rags of a rent sail, and a wild confusion of broken cordage flapping to and fro. The ship had struck once, the same boatman hoarsely said in my ear, and then lifted in and struck again. I understood him to add that she was parting amidships, and I could readily suppose so, for the rolling and beating were too tremendous for any human work to suffer long. As he spoke, there was another great cry of pity from the beach; four men arose with the wreck out of the deep, clinging to the rigging of the remaining mast; uppermost, the active figure with the curling hair.

There was a bell on board; and as the ship rolled and dashed, like a desperate creature driven mad, now showing us the whole sweep of her deck, as she turned on her beam-ends towards the shore, now nothing but her keel, as she sprung wildly over and turned towards the sea, the bell rang; and its sound, the knell of those unhappy men, was borne towards us on the wind. Again we lost her, and again she rose. Two men were gone. The agony on the shore increased. Men groaned, and clasped their hands; women shrieked, and turned away their faces. Some ran wildly up and down along the beach, crying for help where no help could be. I found myself one of these, frantically imploring a knot of sailors whom I knew, not to let those two lost creatures perish before our eyes.

They were making out to me, in an agitated way—I don't know how, for the little I could hear I was scarcely composed enough to understand—that the lifeboat had been bravely manned an hour ago, and could do nothing; and that as no man would be so desperate as to attempt to wade off with a rope, and establish a communication with the shore, there was nothing left to try; when I noticed that some new sensation moved the people on the beach, and saw them part, and Ham come breaking through them to the front.

I ran to him—as well as I know, to repeat my appeal for help. But, distracted though I was, by a sight so new to me and terrible, the determination in his face, and his look out to sea—exactly the same look as I remembered in connexion with the morning after

Emily's flight—awoke me to a knowledge of his danger. I held him back with both arms; and implored the men with whom I had been speaking, not to listen to him, not to do murder, not to let him stir from off that sand!

Another cry arose on shore; and looking to the wreck, we saw the cruel sail, with blow on blow, beat off the lower of the two men, and fly up in triumph round the active figure left alone upon the mast.

Against such a sight, and against such determination as that of the calmly desperate man who was already accustomed to lead half the people present, I might as hopefully have entreated the wind. "Mas'r Davy," he said, cheerily grasping me by both hands, "if my time is come, 'tis come. If 'tan't, I'll bide it. Lord above bless you, and bless all! Mates, make me ready! I'm a-going off!"

I was swept away, but not unkindly, to some distance, where the people around me made me stay; urging, as I confusedly perceived, that he was bent on going, with help or without, and that I should endanger the precautions for his safety by troubling those with whom they rested. I don't know what I answered, or what they rejoined; but, I saw hurry on the beach, and men running with ropes from a capstan that was there, and penetrating into a circle of figures that hid him from me. Then, I saw him standing alone, in a seaman's frock and trousers: a rope in his hand, or slung to his wrist: another round his body: and several of the best men holding, at a little distance, to the latter, which he laid out himself, slack upon the shore, at his feet.

The wreck, even to my unpractised eye, was breaking up. I saw that she was parting in the middle, and that the life of the solitary man upon the mast hung by a thread. Still, he clung to it. He had a singular red cap on,—not like a sailor's cap, but of a finer colour; and as the few yielding planks between him and destruction rolled and bulged, and his anticipative death-knell rung, he was seen by all of us to wave it. I saw him do it now, and thought I was going distracted, when his action brought an old remembrance to my mind of a once dear friend.

Ham watched the sea, standing alone, with the silence of suspended breath behind him, and the storm before, until there was a great retiring wave, when, with a backward glance at those who held the rope which was made fast round his body, he dashed in after it, and in a moment was buffeting with the water; rising with the hills, falling with the valleys, lost beneath the foam; then drawn again to land. They hauled in hastily.

He was hurt. I saw blood on his face, from where I stood; but he took no thought of that. He seemed hurriedly to give them some directions for leaving him more free—or so I judged from the motion of his arm—and was gone as before.

And now he made for the wreck, rising with the hills, falling with the valleys, lost beneath the rugged foam, borne in towards the shore, borne on towards the ship, striving hard and valiantly. The distance was nothing, but the power of the sea and wind made the strife deadly. At length he neared the wreck. He was so near, that with one more of his vigorous strokes he would be clinging to it,—when a high, green, vast hill-side of water, moving on shoreward, from beyond the ship, he seemed to leap up into it with a mighty bound, and the ship was gone!

Some eddying fragments I saw in the sea, as if a mere cask had been broken, in running to the spot where they were hauling in. Consternation was in every face. They drew him to my very feet—insensible—dead. He was carried to the nearest house; and, no one preventing me now, I remained near him, busy, while every means of restoration were tried; but he had been beaten to death by the great wave, and his generous heart was stilled for ever.

As I sat beside the bed, when hope was abandoned and all was done, a fisherman, who had known me when Emily and I were children, and ever since, whispered my name at the door.

"Sir," said he, with tears starting to his weather-beaten face, which, with his trembling lips, was ashy pale, "will you come over yonder?"

The old remembrance that had been recalled to me, was in his look. I asked him, terror-stricken, leaning on the arm he held out to support me:

"Has a body come ashore?"

He said, "Yes."

"Do I know it?" I asked then.

He answered nothing.

But, he led me to the shore. And on that part of it where she and I had looked for shells, two children—on that part of it where some lighter fragments of the old boat, blown down last night, had been scattered by the wind—among the ruins of the home he had wronged—I saw him lying with his head upon his arm, as I had often seen him lie at school.

Chapter LVI

THE NEW WOUND, AND THE OLD

NO need, O Steerforth, to have said, when we last spoke together, in that hour which I so little deemed to be our parting-hour—no need to have said, "Think of me at my best!" I had done that ever; and could I change now, looking on this sight!

They brought a hand-bier, and laid him on it, and covered him with a flag, and took him up and bore him on towards the houses. All the men who carried him had known him, and gone sailing with him, and seen him merry and bold. They carried him through the wild roar, a hush in the midst of all the tumult; and took him to the cottage where Death was already.

But, when they set the bier down on the threshold, they looked at one another, and at me, and whispered. I knew why. They felt as if it were not right to lay him down in the same quiet room.

We went into the town, and took our burden to the inn. So soon as I could at all collect my thoughts, I sent for Joram, and begged him to provide me a conveyance in which it could be got to London in the night. I knew that the care of it, and the hard duty of preparing his mother to receive it, could only rest with me; and I was anxious to discharge that duty as faithfully as I could.

I chose the night for the journey, that there might be less curiosity when I left the town. But, although it was nearly midnight when I came out of the yard in a chaise, followed by what I had in charge, there were many people waiting. At intervals, along the town, and even a little way out upon the road, I saw more: but at length only the bleak night and the open country were around me, and the ashes of my youthful friendship.

Upon a mellow autumn day, about noon, when the ground was perfumed by fallen leaves, and many more, in beautiful tints of yellow, red, and brown, yet hung upon the trees, through which the sun was shining, I arrived at Highgate. I walked the last mile, thinking as I went along of what I had to do; and left the carriage that had followed me all through the night, awaiting orders to advance.

The house, when I came up to it, looked just the same. Not a blind was raised; no sign of life was in the dull paved court, with its covered way leading to the disused door. The wind had quite gone down, and nothing moved.

I had not, at first, the courage to ring at the gate; and when I did ring, my errand seemed to me to be expressed in the very sound of the bell. The little parlour-maid came out, with the key in her hand; and looking earnestly at me as she unlocked the gate, said:

"I beg your pardon, sir. Are you ill?"

"I have been much agitated, and am fatigued."

"Is anything the matter, sir?—Mr James?—"

"Hush!" said I. "Yes, something has happened, that I have to break to Mrs Steerforth. She is at home?"

The girl anxiously replied that her mistress was very seldom out now, even in a carriage; that she kept her room; that she saw no company, but would see me. Her mistress was up, she said, and Miss Dartle was with her. What message should she take upstairs?

Giving her a strict charge to be careful of her manner, and only to carry in my card and say I waited, I sat down in the drawing-room (which we had now reached) until she should come back. Its former pleasant air of occupation was gone, and the shutters were half closed. The harp had not been used for many and many a day. His picture, as a boy, was there. The cabinet in which his mother had kept his letters was there. I wondered if she ever read them now; if she would ever read them more!

The house was so still that I heard the girl's light step upstairs. On her return, she brought a message, to the effect that Mrs Steerforth was an invalid and could not come down; but, that if I would excuse her being in her chamber, she would be glad to see me. In a few moments I stood before her.

She was in his room; not in her own. I felt, of course, that she had taken to occupy it, in remembrance of him; and that the many tokens of his old sports and accomplishments, by which she was surrounded, remained there, just as he had left them, for the same reason. She murmured, however, even in her reception of me, that she was out of her own chamber because its aspect was unsuited to her infirmity; and with her stately look repelled the least suspicion of the truth.

At her chair, as usual, was Rosa Dartle. From the first moment of her dark eyes resting on me, I saw she knew I was the bearer of evil tidings. The scar sprung into view that instant. She withdrew herself a step behind the chair, to keep her own face out of Mrs Steerforth's observation; and scrutinized me with a piercing gaze that never faltered, never shrunk.

"I am sorry to observe you are in mourning, sir," said Mrs Steerforth.

"I am unhappily a widower," said I.

"You are very young to know so great a loss," she returned. "I am grieved to hear it. I am grieved to hear it. I hope Time will be good to you."

"I hope Time," said I, looking at her, "will be good to all of us. Dear Mrs Steerforth, we must all trust to that, in our heaviest misfortunes."

The earnestness of my manner, and the tears in my eyes, alarmed her. The whole course of her thoughts appeared to stop, and change.

I tried to command my voice in gently saying his name, but it trembled. She repeated it to herself, two or three times, in a low tone. Then, addressing me, she said, with enforced calmness:

"My son is ill."

"Very ill."

"You have seen him?"

"I have."

"Are you reconciled?"

I could not say Yes, I could not say No. She slightly turned her head towards the spot where Rosa Dartle had been standing at her elbow, and in that moment I said, by the motion of my lips, to Rosa, "Dead!"

That Mrs Steerforth might not be induced to look behind her, and read, plainly written, what she was not yet prepared to know, I met her look quickly; but I had seen Rosa Dartle throw her hands up in the air with vehemence of despair and horror, and then clasp them on her face.

The handsome lady—so like, oh so like!—regarded me with a fixed look, and put her hand to her forehead. I besought her to be calm, and prepare herself to bear what I had to tell; but I should rather have entreated her to weep, for she sat like a stone figure.

"When I was last here," I faltered, "Miss Dartle told me he was sailing here and there. The night before last was a dreadful one at sea. If he were at sea that night, and near a dangerous coast, as it is said he was; and if the vessel that was seen should really be the ship which—"

"Rosa!" said Mrs Steerforth, "come to me!"

She came, but with no sympathy or gentleness. Her eyes gleamed like fire as she confronted his mother, and broke into a frightful laugh.

"Now," she said, "is your pride appeased, you madwoman? *Now* has he made atonement to you—with his life! Do you hear?—His life!"

Mrs Steerforth, fallen back stiffly in her chair, and making no sound but a moan, cast her eyes upon her with a wide stare.

"Aye!" cried Rosa, smiting herself passionately on the breast, "look at me! Moan, and groan, and look at me! Look here!" striking the scar, "at your dead child's handiwork!"

The moan the mother uttered, from time to time, went to my heart. Always the same. Always inarticulate and stifled. Always accompanied with an incapable motion of the head, but with no change of face. Always proceeding from a rigid mouth and closed teeth, as if the jaw were locked and the face frozen up in pain.

"Do you remember when he did this?" she proceeded. "Do you remember when, in his inheritance of your nature, and in your pampering of his pride and passion, he did this, and disfigured me for life? Look at me, marked until I die with his high displeasure; and moan and groan for what you made him!"

"Miss Dartle," I entreated her. "For Heaven's sake—"

"I *will* speak!" she said, turning on me with her lightning eyes. "Be silent, you! Look at me, I say, proud mother of a proud false son! Moan for your nurture of him, moan for your corruption of him, moan for your loss of him, moan for mine!"

She clenched her hand, and trembled through her spare, worn figure, as if her passion were killing her by inches.

"YOU, resent his self-will!" she exclaimed. "YOU, injured by his haughty temper! YOU, who opposed to both, when your hair was grey, the qualities which made both when you gave him birth! YOU, who from his cradle reared him to be what he was, and stunted what he should have been! Are you rewarded, *now,* for your years of trouble?"

"Oh, Miss Dartle, shame! Oh cruel!"

"I tell you," she returned, "I *will* speak to her. No power on earth should stop me, while I was standing here! Have I been silent all these years, and shall I not speak now? I loved him better than you ever loved him!" turning on her fiercely. "I could have loved him, and asked no return. If I had been his wife, I could have been the slave of his caprices for a word of love a year. I should have been. Who knows it better than I? You were exacting, proud, punctilious, selfish. My love would have been devoted—would have trod your paltry whimpering under foot!"

With flashing eyes, she stamped upon the ground as if she actually did it.

"Look here!" she said, striking the scar again, with a relentless hand. "When he grew into the better understanding of what he had done, he saw it, and repented of it! I could sing to him, and talk to him, and show the ardour that I felt in all he did, and attain with labour to such knowledge as most interested him; and I attracted him. When he was freshest and truest, he loved *me*. Yes, he did! Many a time, when you were put off with a slight word, he has taken Me to his heart!"

She said it with a taunting pride in the midst of her frenzy—for it was little less—yet with an eager remembrance of it, in which the smouldering embers of a gentler feeling kindled for the moment.

"I descended—as I might have known I should, but that he fascinated me with his boyish courtship—into a doll, a trifle for the occupation of an idle hour, to be dropped, and taken up, and trifled with, as the inconstant humour took him. When he grew weary, I grew weary. As his fancy died out, I would no more have tried to strengthen any power I had, than I would have married him on his being forced to take me for his wife. We fell away from one another without a word. Perhaps you saw it, and were not sorry. Since then, I have been a mere disfigured piece of furniture between you both; having no eyes, no ears, no feelings, no remembrances. Moan? Moan for what you made him; not for your love. I tell you that the time was, when I loved him better than you ever did!"

She stood with her bright angry eyes confronting the wide stare, and the set face; and softened no more, when the moaning was repeated, than if the face had been a picture.

"Miss Dartle," said I, "if you can be so obdurate as not to feel for this afflicted mother—"

"Who feels for me?" she sharply retorted. "She has sown this. Let her moan for the harvest that she reaps today!"

"And if his faults—" I began.

"Faults!" she cried, bursting into passionate tears. "Who dares malign him? He had a soul worth millions of the friends to whom he stooped!"

"No one can have loved him better, no one can hold him in dearer remembrance than I," I replied. "I meant to say, if you have no compassion for his mother; or if his faults—you have been bitter on them—"

"It's false," she cried, tearing her black hair; "I loved him!"

"—cannot," I went on, "be banished from your remembrance, in such an hour; look at that figure, even as one you have never seen before, and render it some help!"

All this time, the figure was unchanged, and looked unchangeable. Motionless, rigid, staring; moaning in the same dumb way from time to time, with the same helpless motion of the head; but giving no other sign of life. Miss Dartle suddenly kneeled down before it, and began to loosen the dress.

"A curse upon you!" she said, looking round at me, with a mingled expression of rage and grief. "It was in an evil hour that you ever came here! A curse upon you! Go!"

After passing out of the room, I hurried back to ring the bell, the sooner to alarm the servants. She had then taken the impassive figure in her arms, and, still upon her knees, was weeping over it, kissing it, calling to it, rocking it to and fro upon her bosom like a child, and trying every tender means to rouse the dormant senses. No longer afraid of leaving her, I noiselessly turned back again; and alarmed the house as I went out.

Later in the day, I returned, and we laid him in his mother's room. She was just the same, they told me; Miss Dartle never left her; doctors were in attendance, many things had been tried; but she lay like a statue, except for the low sound now and then.

I went through the dreary house, and darkened the windows. The windows of the chamber where he lay, I darkened last. I lifted up the leaden hand, and held it to my heart; and all the world seemed death and silence, broken only by his mother's moaning.

Chapter LVII

THE EMIGRANTS

ONE thing more, I had to do, before yielding myself to the shock of these emotions. It was, to conceal what had occurred, from those who were going away; and to dismiss them on their voyage in happy ignorance. In this, no time was to be lost.

I took Mr Micawber aside that same night, and confided to him the task of standing between Mr Peggotty and intelligence of the late catastrophe. He zealously undertook to do so, and to intercept any newspaper through which it might, without such precautions, reach him.

"If it penetrates to him, sir," said Mr Micawber, striking himself on the breast, "it shall first pass through this body!"

Mr Micawber, I must observe, in his adaptation of himself to a new state of society, had acquired a bold buccaneering air, not absolutely lawless, but defensive and prompt. One might have supposed him a child of the wilderness, long accustomed to live out of the confines of civilization, and about to return to his native wilds.

He had provided himself, among other things, with a complete suit of oilskin, and a straw hat with a very low crown, pitched or caulked on the outside. In this rough clothing, with a common mariner's telescope under his arm, and a shrewd trick of casting up his eye at the sky as looking out for dirty weather, he was far more nautical, after his manner, than Mr Peggotty. His whole family, if I may so express it, were cleared for action. I found Mrs Micawber in the closest and most uncompromising of bonnets, made fast under the chin; and in a shawl which tied her up (as I had been tied up, when my aunt first received me) like a bundle, and was secured behind at the waist, in a strong knot. Miss Micawber I found made snug for stormy weather, in the same manner; with nothing superfluous about her. Master Micawber was hardly visible in a Guernsey shirt, and the shaggiest suit of slops I ever saw; and the children were done up, like preserved meats, in impervious cases. Both Mr Micawber and his eldest son wore their sleeves loosely turned back at the wrists, as being ready to lend a hand in any direction, and to "tumble up," or sing out, "Yeo—Heave—Yeo!" on the shortest notice.

Thus Traddles and I found them at nightfall, assembled on the wooden steps, at that time known as Hungerford Stairs, watching the departure of a boat with some of their property on board. I had told Traddles of the terrible event, and it had greatly shocked him; but there could be no doubt of the kindness of keeping it a secret, and he had come to help me in this last service. It was here that I took Mr Micawber aside, and received his promise.

The Micawber family were lodged in a little, dirty, tumble-down public-house, which in those days was close to the stairs, and whose protruding wooden rooms overhung the river. The family, as emigrants, being objects of some interest in and about Hungerford, attracted so many beholders, that we were glad to take refuge in their room. It was one of the wooden chambers upstairs, with the tide flowing underneath. My aunt and Agnes were there, busily making some little extra comforts, in the way of dress, for the children. Peggotty was quietly assisting, with the old insensible work-box, yard-measure, and bit of wax-candle before her, that had now outlived so much.

It was not easy to answer her inquiries; still less to whisper Mr Peggotty, when Mr Micawber brought him in, that I had given the letter, and all was well. But I did both, and made them happy. If I showed any trace of what I felt, my own sorrows were sufficient to account for it.

"And when does the ship sail, Mr Micawber?" asked my aunt.

Mr Micawber considered it necessary to prepare either my aunt or his wife, by degrees, and said, sooner than he had expected yesterday.

"The boat brought you word, I suppose?" said my aunt.

"It did, ma'am," he returned.

"Well?" said my aunt. "And she sails—"

"Madam," he replied, "I am informed that we must positively be on board before seven tomorrow morning."

"Heyday!" said my aunt, "that's soon. Is it a sea-going fact, Mr Peggotty?"

" 'Tis so, ma'am. She'll drop down the river with that theer tide. If Mas'r Davy and my sister comes aboard at Gravesen', afternoon o' next day, they'll see the last on us."

"And that we shall do," said I, "be sure!"

"Until then, and until we are at sea," observed Mr Micawber, with a glance of intelligence at me, "Mr Peggotty and myself will constantly keep a double look-out together, on our goods and chattels. Emma, my love," said Mr Micawber, clearing his throat in his magnificent way, "my friend Mr Thomas Traddles is so obliging as to solicit, in my ear, that he should have the privilege of ordering the ingredients necessary to the composition of a moderate portion of that Beverage which is peculiarly associated, in our minds, with the Roast Beef of Old England. I allude to—in short, Punch. Under ordinary circumstances, I should scruple to entreat the indulgence of Miss Trotwood and Miss Wickfield, but—"

"I can only say for myself," said my aunt, "that I will drink all happiness and success to you, Mr Micawber, with the utmost pleasure."

"And I too!" said Agnes, with a smile.

Mr Micawber immediately descended to the bar, where he appeared to be quite at home; and in due time returned with a steaming jug. I could not but observe that he had been peeling the lemons with his own clasp-knife, which, as became the knife of a practical settler, was about a foot long; and which he wiped, not wholly without ostentation, on the sleeve of his coat. Mrs Micawber and the two elder members of the family I now found to be provided with similar formidable instruments, while every child had its own wooden spoon attached to its body by a strong line. In a similar anticipation of life afloat, and in the Bush, Mr Micawber, instead of helping Mrs Micawber and his eldest son and daughter punch, in wine-glasses, which he might easily have done, for there was a shelf-full in the room, served it out to them in a series of villainous little tin pots; and I never saw him enjoy anything so much as drinking out of his own particular pint pot, and putting it in his pocket at the close of the evening.

"The luxuries of the old country," said Mr Micawber, with an intense satisfaction in their renouncement, "we abandon. The denizens of the forest cannot, of course, expect to participate in the refinements of the land of the Free."

Here, a boy came in to say that Mr Micawber was wanted downstairs.

"I have a presentiment," said Mrs Micawber, setting down her tin pot, "that it is a member of my family!"

"If so, my dear," observed Mr Micawber, with his usual suddenness of warmth on that subject, "as the member of your family—whoever he, she, or it, may be—has kept *us* waiting for a considerable period, perhaps the Member may now wait *my* convenience."

"Micawber," said his wife, in a low tone, "at such a time as this—"

" 'It is not meet,' " said Mr Micawber, rising, " 'that every nice offence should bear its comment!' Emma, I stand reproved."

"The loss, Micawber," observed his wife, "has been my family's, not yours. If my family are at length sensible of the deprivation to which their own conduct has, in the past exposed them, and now desire to extend the hand of fellowship, let it not be repulsed."

"My dear," he returned, "so be it!"

"If not for their sakes; for mine, Micawber," said his wife.

"Emma," he returned, "that view of the question is, at such a moment, irresistible. I cannot, even now, distinctly pledge myself to fall upon your family's neck; but the member of your family, who is now in attendance, shall have no genial warmth frozen by me."

Mr Micawber withdrew, and was absent some little time; in the course of which Mrs Micawber was not wholly free from an apprehension that words might have arisen between him and the Member. At length the same boy reappeared, and presented me with a note written in pencil, and headed, in a legal manner, "Heep *v.* Micawber." From this document, I learned that Mr Micawber being again arrested, was in a final paroxysm of despair; and that he begged me to send him his knife and pint pot, by bearer, as they might prove serviceable during the brief remainder of his existence, in jail. He also requested, as a last act of friendship, that I would see his family to the Parish Workhouse, and forget that such a Being ever lived.

Of course I answered this note by going down with the boy to pay the money, where I found Mr Micawber sitting in a corner, looking darkly at the Sheriff's Officer who had effected the capture. On his release, he embraced me with the utmost fervour; and made an entry of the transaction in his pocket-book—being very particular, I recollect, about a halfpenny I inadvertently omitted from my statement of the total.

This momentous pocket-book was a timely reminder to him of another transaction. On our return to the room upstairs (where he accounted for his absence by saying that it had been occasioned by circumstances over which he had no control), he took out of it a large sheet of paper, folded small, and quite covered with long sums, carefully worked. From the glimpse I had of them, I should say that I never saw such sums out of a school ciphering-book. These, it seemed, were calculations of compound interest on what he called "the principal amount of forty-one, ten, eleven and a half," for various periods. After a careful consideration of these, and an elaborate estimate of his resources, he had come to the conclusion to select that sum which represented the amount with compound interest to two years, fifteen calendar months, and fourteen days, from that date. For this he had drawn a note-of-hand with great neatness, which he handed over to Traddles on the spot, a discharge of his debt in full (as between man and man), with many acknowledgements.

"I have still a presentiment," said Mrs Micawber, pensively shaking her head, "that my family will appear on board, before we finally depart."

Mr Micawber evidently had his presentiment on the subject too, but he put it in his tin pot and swallowed it.

"If you have any opportunity of sending letters home, on your passage, Mrs Micawber," said my aunt, "you must let us hear from you, you know."

"My dear Miss Trotwood," she replied, "I shall only be too happy to think that anyone expects to hear from us. I shall not fail to correspond. Mr Copperfield, I trust, as an old and familiar friend, will not object to receive occasional intelligence, himself, from one who knew him when the twins were yet unconscious?"

I said that I should hope to hear, whenever she had an opportunity of writing.

"Please Heaven, there will be many such opportunities," said Mr Micawber. "The ocean, in these times, is a perfect fleet of ships; and we can hardly fail to encounter many, in running over. It is merely crossing," said Mr Micawber, trifling with his eye-glass, "merely crossing. The distance is quite imaginary."

I think, now, how odd it was, but how wonderfully like Mr Micawber, that, when he went from London to Canterbury, he should have talked as if he were going to the farthest limits of the earth; and, when he went from England to Australia, as if he were going for a little trip across the channel.

"On the voyage, I shall endeavour," said Mr Micawber, "occasionally to spin them a yarn; and the melody of my son Wilkins will, I trust, be acceptable at the galley-fire. When Mrs Micawber has her sea-legs on—an expression in which I hope there is no conventional impropriety—she will give them, I dare say, 'Little Tafflin.' Porpoises and dolphins, I believe, will be frequently observed athwart our Bows; and, either on the starboard or the larboard quarter, objects of interest will be continually descried. In short," said Mr Micawber, with the old genteel air, "the probability is, all will be found so exciting, alow and aloft, that when the lookout, stationed in the main-top, cries Land-oh! we shall be very considerably astonished!"

With that he flourished off the contents of his little tin pot, as if he had made the voyage, and had passed a first-class examination before the highest naval authorities.

"What I chiefly hope, my dear Mr Copperfield," said Mrs Micawber, "is, that in some branches of our family we may live again in the old country. Do not frown, Micawber! I do not now refer to my own family, but to our children's children. However vigorous the sapling," said Mrs Micawber, shaking her head, "I cannot forget the parent-tree; and when our race attains to eminence and fortune, I own I should wish that fortune to flow into the coffers of Britannia."

"My dear," said Mr Micawber, "Britannia must take her chance. I am bound to say that she has never done much for me, and that I have no particular wish upon the subject."

"Micawber," returned Mrs Micawber, "there, you are wrong. You are going out, Micawber, to this distant clime, to strengthen, not to weaken, the connexion between yourself and Albion."

"The connexion in question, my love," rejoined Mr Micawber, "has not laid me, I repeat, under that load of personal obligation, that I am at all sensitive as to the formation of another connexion."

"Micawber," returned Mrs Micawber. "There, I again say, you are wrong. You do not know your power, Micawber. It is that which will strengthen, even in this step you are about to take, the connexion between yourself and Albion."

Mr Micawber sat in his elbow-chair, with his eyebrows raised; half receiving and half repudiating Mrs Micawber's views as they were stated, but very sensible of their foresight.

"My dear Mr Copperfield," said Mrs Micawber, "I wish Mr Micawber to feel his position. It appears to me highly important that Mr Micawber should, from the hour of his embarkation, feel his position. Your old knowledge of me, my dear Mr Copperfield, will have told you that I have not the sanguine disposition of Mr Micawber. My disposition is, if I may say so, eminently practical. I know that this is a long voyage. I know that it will involve many privations and inconveniences. I cannot shut my eyes to those facts. But, I also know what Mr Micawber is. I know the latent power of Mr Micawber. And therefore I consider it vitally important that Mr Micawber should feel his position."

"My love," he observed, "perhaps you will allow me to remark that it is barely possible that I *do* feel my position at the present moment."

"I think not, Micawber," she rejoined. "Not fully. My dear Mr Copperfield, Mr Micawber's is not a common case. Mr Micawber is going to a distant country expressly in order that he may be fully understood and appreciated for the first time. I wish Mr Micawber to take his stand upon that vessel's prow, and firmly say, 'This country I am come to conquer! Have you honours? Have you riches? Have you posts of profitable pecuniary emolument? Let them be brought forward. They are mine!' "

Mr Micawber, glancing at us all, seemed to think there was a good deal in this idea.

"I wish Mr Micawber, if I make myself understood," said Mrs Micawber, in her argumentative tone, "to be the Caesar of his own fortunes. That, my dear Mr Copperfield, appears to me to be his true position. From the first moment of this voyage, I wish Mr Micawber to stand upon that vessel's prow and say, 'Enough of delay: enough of disappointment: enough of limited means. That was in the old country. This is the new. Produce your reparation. Bring it forward!' "

Mr Micawber folded his arms in a resolute manner, as if he were then stationed on the figure-head.

"And doing that," said Mrs Micawber, "—feeling his position—am I not right in saying that Mr Micawber will strengthen, and not weaken, his connexion with Britain? An important public character arising in that hemisphere, shall I be told that its influence will not be felt at home? Can I be so weak as to imagine that Mr Micawber, wielding the rod of talent and of power in Australia, will be nothing in England? I am but a woman; but I should be unworthy of myself and of my papa, if I were guilty of such absurd weakness."

Mrs Micawber's conviction that her arguments were unanswerable, gave a moral elevation to her tone which I think I had never heard in it before.

"And therefore it is," said Mrs Micawber, "that I the more wish, that, at a future period, we may live again on the parent soil. Mr Micawber may be—I cannot disguise from myself that the probability is, Mr Micawber will be—a page of History; and he ought then to be represented in the country which gave him birth, and did *not* give him employment!"

"My love," observed Mr Micawber, "it is impossible for me not to be touched by your affection. I am always willing to defer to your good sense. What will be—will be.

Heaven forbid that I should grudge my native country any portion of the wealth that may be accumulated by our descendants!"

"That's well," said my aunt, nodding towards Mr Peggotty, "and I drink my love to you all, and every blessing and success attend you!"

Mr Peggotty put down the two children he had been nursing, one on each knee, to join Mr and Mrs Micawber in drinking to all of us in return; and when he and the Micawbers cordially shook hands as comrades, and his brown face brightened with a smile, I felt that he would make his way, establish a good name, and be beloved, go where he would.

Even the children were instructed, each to dip a wooden spoon into Mr Micawber's pot, and pledge us in its contents. When this was done, my aunt and Agnes rose, and parted from the emigrants. It was a sorrowful farewell. They were all crying; the children hung about Agnes to the last; and we left poor Mrs Micawber in a very distressed condition, sobbing and weeping by a dim candle, that must have made the room look, from the river, like a miserable light-house.

I went down again next morning to see that they were away. They had departed, in a boat, as early as five o'clock. It was a wonderful instance to me of the gap such partings make, that although my association of them with the tumble-down public-house and the wooden stairs dated only from last night, both seemed dreary and deserted, now that they were gone.

In the afternoon of the next day, my old nurse and I went down to Gravesend. We found the ship in the river, surrounded by a crowd of boats; a favourable wind blowing; the signal for sailing at her mast-head. I hired a boat directly, and we put off to her; and getting through the little vortex of confusion of which she was the centre, went on board.

Mr Peggotty was waiting for us on deck. He told me that Mr Micawber had just now been arrested again (and for the last time) at the suit of Heep, and that, in compliance with a request I had made to him, he had paid the money; which I repaid him. He then took us down between decks; and there, any lingering fears I had of his having heard any rumours of what had happened, were dispelled by Mr Micawber's coming out of the gloom, taking his arm with an air of friendship and protection, and telling me that they had scarcely been asunder for a moment, since the night before last.

It was such a strange scene to me, and so confined and dark, that, at first, I could make out hardly anything; but, by degrees, it cleared, as my eyes became more accustomed to the gloom, and I seemed to stand in a picture by OSTADE. Among the great beams, bulks, and ringbolts of the ship, and the emigrant-berths, and chests, and bundles, and barrels, and heaps of miscellaneous baggage—lighted up, here and there, by dangling lanterns; and elsewhere by the yellow daylight straying down a windsail or a hatchway—were crowded groups of people, making new friendships, taking leave of one another, talking, laughing, crying, eating and drinking; some, already settled down into the possession of their few feet of space, with their little households arranged, and tiny children established on stools, or in dwarf elbow-chairs; others, despairing of a resting-place, and wandering disconsolately. From babies who had but a week or two of life behind them, to crooked old men and women who seemed to have but a week or two of life before them; and from ploughmen bodily carrying out soil of England on their boots, to smiths taking away samples of its soot and smoke upon their skins; every age and occupation appeared to be crammed into the narrow compass of the 'tween decks.

As my eye glanced round this place, I thought I saw sitting, by an open port, with one of the Micawber children near her, a figure like Emily's; it first attracted my attention, by another figure parting from it with a kiss; and as it glided calmly away through the disorder, reminding me of——Agnes! But in the rapid motion and confusion, and in the unsettlement of my own thoughts, I lost it again; and only knew that the time was come when all visitors were being warned to leave the ship; that my nurse was crying on a chest beside me; and that Mrs Gummidge, assisted by some younger stooping woman in black, was busily arranging Mr Peggotty's goods.

"Is there any last wured, Mas'r Davy?" said he. "Is there any one forgotten thing afore we parts?"

"One thing!" said I. "Martha!"

He touched the younger woman I have mentioned on the shoulder, and Martha stood before me.

"Heaven bless you, you good man!" cried I. "You take her with you!"

She answered for him, with a burst of tears. I could speak no more at that time, but I wrung his hand; and if ever I have loved and honoured any man, I loved and honoured that man in my soul.

The ship was clearing fast of strangers. The greatest trial that I had, remained. I told him what the noble spirit that was gone, had given me in charge to say at parting. It moved him deeply. But when he charged me, in return, with many messages of affection and regret for those dear ears, he moved me more.

The time was come. I embraced him, took my weeping nurse upon my arm, and hurried away. On deck, I took leave of poor Mrs Micawber. She was looking distractedly about for her family, even then; and her last words to me were, that she never would desert Mr Micawber.

We went over the side into our boat, and lay at a little distance to see the ship wafted on her course. It was then calm, radiant sunset. She lay between us, and the red light; and every taper line and spar was visible against the glow. A sight at once so beautiful, so mournful, and so hopeful, as the glorious ship, lying, still, on the flushed water, with all the life on board her crowded at the bulwarks, and there clustering, for a moment, bare-headed and silent, I never saw.

Silent, only for a moment. As the sails rose to the wind, and the ship began to move, there broke from all the boats three resounding cheers, which those on board took up, and echoed back, and which were echoed and re-echoed. My heart burst out when I heard the sound, and beheld the waving of the hats and handkerchiefs——and then I saw her!

Then, I saw her, at her uncle's side, and trembling on his shoulder. He pointed to us with an eager hand; and she saw us, and waved her last good-bye to me. Aye, Emily, beautiful and drooping, cling to him with the utmost trust of thy bruised heart; for he has clung to thee, with all the might of his great love!

Surrounded by the rosy light, and standing high upon the deck, apart together, she clinging to him, and he holding her, they solemnly passed away. The night had fallen on the Kentish hills when we were rowed ashore——and fallen darkly upon me.

Chapter LVIII

ABSENCE

I T was a long and gloomy night that gathered on me, haunted by the ghosts of many hopes, of many dear remembrances, many errors, many unavailing sorrows and regrets.

I went away from England; not knowing, even then, how great the shock was, that I had to bear. I left all who were dear to me, and went away; and believed that I had borne it, and it was past. As a man upon a field of battle will receive a mortal hurt, and scarcely know that he is struck, so I, when I was left alone with my undisciplined heart, had no conception of the wound with which it had to strive.

The knowledge came upon me, not quickly, but little by little, and grain by grain. The desolate feeling with which I went abroad, deepened and widened hourly. At first it was a heavy sense of loss and sorrow, wherein I could distinguish little else. By imperceptible degrees, it became a hopeless consciousness of all that I had lost—love, friendship, interest; of all that had been shattered—my first trust, my first affection, the whole airy castle of my life; of all that remained—a ruined blank and waste, lying wide around me, unbroken, to the dark horizon.

If my grief were selfish, I did not know it to be so. I mourned for my child-wife, taken from her blooming world, so young. I mourned for him who might have won the love and admiration of thousands, as he had won mine long ago. I mourned for the broken heart that had found rest in the stormy sea; and for the wandering remnants of the simple home, where I had heard the night-wind blowing, when I was a child.

From the accumulated sadness into which I fell, I had at length no hope of ever issuing again. I roamed from place to place, carrying my burden with me everywhere. I felt its whole weight now; and I drooped beneath it, and I said in my heart that it could never be lightened.

When this despondency was at its worst, I believed that I should die. Sometimes, I thought that I would like to die at home; and actually turned back on my road, that I might get there soon. At other times, I passed on farther away, from city to city, seeking I know not what, and trying to leave I know not what behind.

It is not in my power to retrace, one by one, all the weary phases of distress of mind through which I passed. There are some dreams that can only be imperfectly and vaguely described; and when I oblige myself to look back on this time of my life, I seem to be recalling such a dream. I see myself passing on among the novelties of foreign towns, palaces, cathedrals, temples, pictures, castles, tombs, fantastic streets—the old abiding places of History and Fancy—as a dreamer might; bearing my painful load through all, and hardly conscious of the objects as they fade before me. Listlessness to everything, but brooding sorrow, was the night that fell on my undisciplined heart. Let me look up from it—as at last I did, thank Heaven!—and from its long, sad, wretched dream, to dawn.

For many months I travelled with this ever-darkening cloud upon my mind. Some blind reasons that I had for not returning home—reasons then struggling within me, vainly, for more distinct expression—kept me on my pilgrimage. Sometimes, I had proceeded restlessly from place to place, stopping nowhere; sometimes, I had lingered long in one spot. I had had no purpose, no sustaining soul within me, anywhere.

I was in Switzerland. I had come out of Italy, over one of the great passes of the Alps, and had since wandered with a guide among the by-ways of the mountains. If those awful solitudes had spoken to my heart, I did not know it. I had found sublimity and wonder in the dread heights and precipices, in the roaring torrents, and the wastes of ice and snow; but as yet, they had taught me nothing else.

I came, one evening before sunset, down into a valley, where I was to rest. In the course of my descent to it, by the winding track along the mountain-side, from which I saw it shining far below, I think some long-unwonted sense of beauty and tranquillity, some softening influence awakened by its peace, moved faintly in my breast. I remember pausing once, with a kind of sorrow that was not all oppressive, not quite despairing. I remember almost hoping that some better change was possible within me.

I came into the valley, as the evening sun was shining on the remote heights of snow, that closed it in, like eternal clouds. The bases of the mountains forming the gorge in which the little village lay, were richly green; and high above this gentler vegetation, grew forests of dark fir, cleaving the wintry snow-drift, wedge-like, and stemming the avalanche. Above these, were range upon range of craggy steeps, grey rock, bright ice, and smooth verdure-specks of pasture, all gradually blending with the crowning snow. Dotted here and there on the mountain's-side, each tiny dot a home, were lonely wooden cottages, so dwarfed by the towering heights that they appeared too small for toys. So did even the clustered village in the valley, with its wooden bridge across the stream, where the stream tumbled over broken rocks, and roared away among the trees. In the quiet air, there was a sound of distant singing—shepherd voices; but, as one bright evening cloud floated midway along the mountain's-side, I could almost have believed it came from there, and was not earthly music. All at once, in this serenity, great Nature spoke to me; and soothed me to lay down my weary head upon the grass, and weep as I had not wept yet, since Dora died!

I had found a packet of letters awaiting me but a few minutes before, and had strolled out of the village to read them while my supper was making ready. Other packets had missed me, and I had received none for a long time. Beyond a line or two, to say that I was well, and had arrived at such a place, I had not had fortitude or constancy to write a letter since I left home.

The packet was in my hand. I opened it, and read the writing of Agnes.

She was happy and useful, was prospering as she had hoped. That was all she told me of herself. The rest referred to me.

She gave me no advice; she urged no duty on me; she only told me, in her own fervent manner, what her trust in me was. She knew (she said) how such a nature as mine would turn affliction to good. She knew how trial and emotion would exalt and strengthen it. She was sure that in my every purpose I should gain a firmer and a higher tendency, through the grief I had undergone. She, who so gloried in my fame, and so looked forward to its augmentation, well knew that I would labour on. She knew that in me, sorrow could not be weakness, but must be strength. As the endurance of my childish days had done its part to make me what I was, so greater calamities would nerve me on, to be yet better than I was; and so, as they had taught me, would I teach others. She commended me to God, who had taken my innocent darling to His rest; and in her sisterly affection cherished me always, and was always at my side go where I would; proud of what I had done, but infinitely prouder yet of what I was reserved to do.

I put the letter in my breast, and thought what had I been an hour ago! When I heard the voices die away, and saw the quiet evening cloud grow dim, and all the colours in the valley fade, and the golden snow upon the mountain-tops become a remote part of the pale night sky, yet felt that the night was passing from my mind, and all its shadows clearing, there was no name for the love I bore her, dearer to me, henceforward, than ever until then.

I read her letter, many times. I wrote to her before I slept. I told her that I had been in sore need of her help; that without her I was not, and I never had been, what she thought me; but, that she inspired me to be that, and I would try.

I did try. In three months more, a year would have passed since the beginning of my sorrow. I determined to make no resolutions until the expiration of those three months, but to try. I lived in that valley, and its neighbourhood, all the time.

The three months gone, I resolved to remain away from home for some time longer; to settle myself for the present in Switzerland, which was growing dear to me in the remembrance of that evening; to resume my pen; to work.

I resorted humbly whither Agnes had commended me; I sought out Nature, never sought in vain; and I admitted to my breast the human interest I had lately shrunk from. It was not long, before I had almost as many friends in the valley as in Yarmouth: and when I left it, before the winter set in, for Geneva, and came back in the spring, their cordial greetings had a homely sound to me, although they were not conveyed in English words.

I worked early and late, patiently and hard. I wrote a Story, with a purpose growing, not remotely, out of my experience, and sent it to Traddles, and he arranged for its publication very advantageously for me; and the tidings of my growing reputation began to reach me from travellers whom I encountered by chance. After some rest and change, I fell to work, in my old ardent way, on a new fancy, which took strong possession of me. As I advanced in the execution of this task, I felt it more and more, and roused my utmost energies to do it well. This was my third work of fiction. It was not half written, when, in an interval of rest, I thought of returning home.

For a long time, though studying and working patiently, I had accustomed myself to robust exercise. My health, severely impaired when I left England, was quite restored. I had seen much. I had been in many countries, and I hope I had improved my store of knowledge.

I have now recalled all that I think it needful to recall here, of this term of absence—with one reservation. I have made it, thus far, with no purpose of suppressing any of my thoughts; for, as I have elsewhere said, this narrative is my written memory. I have desired to keep the most secret current of my mind apart, and to the last. I enter on it now.

I cannot so completely penetrate the mystery of my own heart, as to know when I began to think that I might have set its earliest and brightest hopes on Agnes. I cannot say at what stage of my grief it first became associated with the reflection, that, in my wayward boyhood, I had thrown away the treasure of her love. I believe I may have heard some whisper of that distant thought, in the old unhappy loss or want of something never to be realized, of which I had been sensible. But the thought came into my mind as a new reproach and new regret, when I was left so sad and lonely in the world.

If, at that time, I had been much with her, I should, in the weakness of my desolation, have betrayed this. It was what I remotely dreaded when I was first impelled to stay away from England. I could not have borne to lose the smallest portion of her sisterly affection; yet, in that betrayal, I should have set a constraint between us hitherto unknown.

I could not forget that the feeling with which she now regarded me had grown up in my own free choice and course. That if she had ever loved me with another love—and

I sometimes thought the time was when she might have done so—I had cast it away. It was nothing, now, that I had accustomed myself to think of her, when we were both mere children, as one who was far removed from my wild fancies. I had bestowed my passionate tenderness upon another object; and what I might have done, I had not done; and what Agnes was to me, I and her own noble heart had made her.

In the beginning of the change that gradually worked in me, when I tried to get a better understanding of myself and be a better man, I did glance, through some indefinite probation, to a period when I might possibly hope to cancel the mistaken past, and to be so blessed as to marry her. But, as time wore on, this shadowy prospect faded, and departed from me. If she had ever loved me, then, I should hold her the more sacred; remembering the confidences I had reposed in her, her knowledge of my errant heart, the sacrifice she must have made to be my friend and sister, and the victory she had won. If she had never loved me, could I believe that she would love me now?

I had always felt my weakness, in comparison with her constancy and fortitude; and now I felt it more and more. Whatever I might have been to her, or she to me, if I had been more worthy of her long ago, I was not now, and she was not. The time was past. I had let it go by, and had deservedly lost her.

That I suffered much in these contentions, that they filled me with unhappiness and remorse, and yet that I had a sustaining sense that it was required of me, in right and honour, to keep away from myself, with shame, the thought of turning to the dear girl in the withering of my hopes, from whom I had frivolously turned when they were bright and fresh—which consideration was at the root of every thought I had concerning her—is all equally true. I made no effort to conceal from myself, now, that I loved her, that I was devoted to her; but I brought the assurance home to myself, that it was now too late, and that our long-subsisting relation must be undisturbed.

I had thought, much and often, of my Dora's shadowing out to me what might have happened, in those years that were destined not to try us; I had considered how the things that never happen, are often as much realities to us, in their effects, as those that are accomplished. The very years she spoke of, were realities now, for my correction; and would have been, one day, a little later perhaps, though we had parted in our earliest folly. I endeavoured to convert what might have been between myself and Agnes, into a means of making me more self-denying, more resolved, more conscious of myself, and my defects and errors. Thus, through the reflection that it might have been, I arrived at the conviction that it could never be.

These, with their perplexities and inconsistencies, were the shifting quicksands of my mind, from the time of my departure to the time of my return home, three years afterwards. Three years had elapsed since the sailing of the emigrant ship; when, at that same hour of sunset, and in the same place, I stood on the deck of the packet vessel that brought me home, looking on the rosy water where I had seen the image of that ship reflected.

Three years. Long in the aggregate, though short as they went by. And home was very dear to me, and Agnes too—but she was not mine—she was never to be mine. She might have been, but that was past!

Chapter LIX

RETURN

I LANDED in London on a wintry autumn evening. It was dark and raining, and I saw more fog and mud in a minute than I had seen in a year. I walked from the Custom House to the Monument before I found a coach; and although the very house-fronts, looking on the swollen gutters, were like old friends to me, I could not but admit that they were very dingy friends.

I have often remarked—I suppose everybody has—that one's going away from a familiar place, would seem to be the signal for change in it. As I looked out of the coach window, and observed that an old house on Fish-street Hill, which had stood untouched by painter, carpenter, or bricklayer, for a century, had been pulled down in my absence; and that a neighbouring street, of time-honoured insalubrity and inconvenience, was being drained and widened; I half expected to find St Paul's Cathedral looking older.

For some changes in the fortunes of my friends, I was prepared. My aunt had long been re-established at Dover, and Traddles had begun to get into some little practice at the Bar, in the very first term after my departure. He had chambers in Gray's Inn, now; and had told me, in his last letters, that he was not without hopes of being soon united to the dearest girl in the world.

They expected me home before Christmas; but had no idea of my returning so soon. I had purposely misled them, that I might have the pleasure of taking them by surprise. And yet, I was perverse enough to feel a chill and disappointment in receiving no welcome, and rattling, alone and silent, through the misty streets.

The well-known shops, however, with their cheerful lights, did something for me; and when I alighted at the door of the Gray's Inn Coffee-house, I had recovered my spirits. It recalled, at first, that so-different time when I had put up at the Golden Cross, and reminded me of the changes that had come to pass since then; but that was natural.

"Do you know where Mr Traddles lives in the Inn?" I asked the waiter, as I warmed myself by the coffee-room fire.

"Holborn Court, sir. Number two."

"Mr Traddles has a rising reputation among the lawyers, I believe?" said I.

"Well, sir," returned the waiter, "probably he has, sir; but I am not aware of it myself."

This waiter, who was middle-aged and spare, looked for help to a waiter of more authority—a stout, potential old man, with a double chin, in black breeches and stockings, who came out of a place like a churchwarden's pew, at the end of the coffee-room, where he kept company with a cash-box, a Directory, a Law-list, and other books and papers.

"Mr Traddles," said the spare waiter. "Number two in the Court."

The potential waiter waved him away, and turned, gravely, to me.

"I was inquiring," said I, "whether Mr Traddles, at number two in the Court, has not a rising reputation among the lawyers?"

"Never heard his name," said the waiter, in a rich husky voice.

I felt quite apologetic for Traddles.

"He's a young man, sure?" said the portentous waiter, fixing his eyes severely on me. "How long has he been in the Inn?"

"Not above three years," said I.

The waiter, who I supposed had lived in his churchwarden's pew for forty years, could not pursue such an insignificant subject. He asked me what I would have for dinner?

I felt I was in England again, and really was quite cast down on Traddles's account. There seemed to be no hope for him. I meekly ordered a bit of fish and a steak, and stood before the fire musing on his obscurity.

As I followed the chief waiter with my eyes, I could not help thinking that the garden in which he had gradually blown to be the flower he was, was an arduous place to rise in. It had such a prescriptive, stiff-necked, long-established, solemn, elderly air. I glanced about the room, which had had its sanded floor sanded, no doubt, in exactly the same manner when the chief waiter was a boy—if he ever was a boy, which appeared improbable; and at the shining tables, where I saw myself reflected, in unruffled depths of old mahogany; and at the lamps, without a flaw in their trimming or cleaning; and at the comfortable green curtains, with their pure brass rods, snugly enclosing the boxes; and at the two large coal fires, brightly burning; and at the rows of decanters, burly as if with the consciousness of pipes of expensive old port wine below; and both England, and the law, appeared to me to be very difficult indeed to be taken by storm. I went up to my bedroom to change my wet clothes; and the vast extent of that old wainscoted apartment (which was over the archway leading to the Inn, I remember), and the sedate immensity of the four-post bedstead, and the indomitable gravity of the chests of drawers, all seemed to unite in sternly frowning on the fortunes of Traddles, or on any such daring youth. I came down again to my dinner; and even the slow comfort of the meal, and the orderly silence of the place—which was bare of guests, the Long Vacation not yet being over—were eloquent on the audacity of Traddles, and his small hopes of a livelihood for twenty years to come.

I had seen nothing like this since I went away, and it quite dashed my hopes for my friend. The chief waiter had had enough of me. He came near me no more; but devoted himself to an old gentleman in long gaiters, to meet whom a pint of special port seemed to come out of the cellar of its own accord, for he gave no order. The second waiter informed me, in a whisper, that this old gentleman was a retired conveyancer living in the Square, and worth a mint of money, which it was expected he would leave to his laundress's daughter; likewise that it was rumoured that he had a service of plate in a bureau, all tarnished with lying by, though more than one spoon and a fork had never yet been beheld in his chambers by mortal vision. By this time, I quite gave Traddles up for lost; and settled in my own mind that there was no hope for him.

Being very anxious to see the dear old fellow, nevertheless, I dispatched my dinner, in a manner not at all calculated to raise me in the opinion of the chief waiter, and hurried out by the back way. Number two in the Court was soon reached; and an inscription on the door-post informing me that Mr Traddles occupied a set of chambers on the top storey, I ascended the staircase. A crazy old staircase I found it to be, feebly lighted on each landing by a club-headed little oil wick, dying away in a little dungeon of dirty glass.

In the course of my stumbling upstairs, I fancied I heard a pleasant sound of laughter; and not the laughter of an attorney or barrister, or attorney's clerk or barrister's clerk, but of two or three merry girls. Happening, however, as I stopped to listen, to put my foot in a hole where the Honourable Society of Gray's Inn had left a plank deficient, I fell down with some noise, and when I recovered my footing all was silent.

Groping my way more carefully, for the rest of the journey, my heart beat high when I found the outer door, which had Mr Traddles painted on it, open. I knocked. A considerable scuffling within ensued, but nothing else. I therefore knocked again.

A small sharp-looking lad, half-footboy and half-clerk, who was very much out of breath, but who looked at me as if he defied me to prove it legally, presented himself.

"Is Mr Traddles within?" I said.

"Yes, sir, but he's engaged."

"I want to see him."

After a moment's survey of me, the sharp-looking lad decided to let me in; and opening the door wider for that purpose, admitted me, first, into a little closet of a hall, and next into a little sitting-room; where I came into the presence of my old friend (also out of breath), seated at a table, and bending over papers.

"Good God!" cried Traddles, looking up. "It's Copperfield!" and rushed into my arms, where I held him tight.

"All well, my dear Traddles?"

"All well, my dear, dear Copperfield, and nothing but good news!"

We cried with pleasure, both of us.

"My dear fellow," said Traddles, rumpling his hair in his excitement, which was a most unnecessary operation, "my dearest Copperfield, my long-lost and most welcome friend, how glad I am to see you! How brown you are! How glad I am! Upon my life and honour, I never was so rejoiced, my beloved Copperfield, never!"

I was equally at a loss to express my emotions. I was quite unable to speak, at first.

"My dear fellow!" said Traddles. "And grown so famous! My glorious Copperfield! Good gracious me, *when* did you come, *where* have you come from, *what* have you been doing?"

Never pausing for an answer to anything he said, Traddles, who had clapped me into an easy-chair by the fire, all this time impetuously stirred the fire with one hand, and pulled at my neckerchief with the other, under some wild delusion that it was a great-coat. Without putting down the poker, he now hugged me again; and I hugged him; and, both laughing, and both wiping our eyes, we both sat down, and shook hands across the hearth.

"To think," said Traddles, "that you should have been so nearly coming home as you must have been, my dear old boy, and not at the ceremony!"

"What ceremony, my dear Traddles?"

"Good gracious me!" cried Traddles, opening his eyes in his old way. "Didn't you get my last letter?"

"Certainly not, if it referred to any ceremony."

"Why, my dear Copperfield," said Traddles, sticking his hair upright with both hands, and then putting his hands on my knees, "I am married!"

"Married!" I cried joyfully.

"Lord bless me, yes!" said Traddles—"by the Reverend Horace—to Sophy—down in Devonshire. Why, my dear boy, she's behind the window curtain! Look here!"

To my amazement, the dearest girl in the world came at that same instant, laughing and blushing, from her place of concealment. And a more cheerful, amiable, honest, happy, bright-looking bride, I believe (as I could not help saying on the spot) the world never saw. I kissed her as an old acquaintance should, and wished them joy with all my might of heart.

"Dear me," said Traddles, "what a delightful re-union this is! You are so extremely brown, my dear Copperfield! God bless my soul, how happy I am!"

"And so am I," said I.

"And I am sure I am!" said the blushing and laughing Sophy.

"We are all as happy as possible!" said Traddles. "Even the girls are happy. Dear me, I declare I forgot them!"

"Forgot?" said I.

"The girls," said Traddles. "Sophy's sisters. They are staying with us. They have come to have a peep at London. The fact is, when—was it you that tumbled upstairs, Copperfield?"

"It was," said I, laughing.

"Well then, when you tumbled upstairs," said Traddles, "I was romping with the girls. In point of fact, we were playing at Puss in the Corner. But as that wouldn't do in Westminster Hall, and as it wouldn't look quite professional if they were seen by a client, they decamped. And they are now—listening, I have no doubt," said Traddles, glancing at the door of another room.

"I am sorry," said I, laughing afresh, "to have occasioned such a dispersion."

"Upon my word," rejoined Traddles, greatly delighted, "if you had seen them running away, and running back again, after you had knocked, to pick up the combs they had dropped out of their hair, and going on in the maddest manner, you wouldn't have said so. My love, will you fetch the girls?"

Sophy tripped away, and we heard her received in the adjoining room with a peal of laughter.

"Really musical, isn't it, my dear Copperfield?" said Traddles. "It's very agreeable to hear. It quite lights up these old rooms. To an unfortunate bachelor of a fellow who has lived alone all his life, you know, it's positively delicious. It's charming. Poor things, they have had a great loss in Sophy—who, I do assure you, Copperfield, is, and ever was, the dearest girl!—and it gratifies me beyond expression to find them in such good spirits. The society of girls is a very delightful thing, Copperfield. It's not professional, but it's very delightful."

Observing that he slightly faltered, and comprehending that in the goodness of his heart he was fearful of giving me some pain by what he had said, I expressed my concurrence with a heartiness that evidently relieved and pleased him greatly.

"But then," said Traddles, "our domestic arrangements are, to say the truth, quite unprofessional altogether, my dear Copperfield. Even Sophy's being here, is unprofessional. And we have no other place of abode. We have put to sea in a cockboat, but we are quite prepared to rough it. And Sophy's an extraordinary manager! You'll be surprised how those girls are stowed away. I am sure I hardly know how it's done!"

"Are many of the young ladies with you?" I inquired.

"The eldest, the Beauty, is here," said Traddles, in a low confidential voice, "Caroline. And Sarah's here—the one I mentioned to you as having something the matter with her spine, you know. Immensely better! And the two youngest that Sophy educated are with us. And Louisa's here."

"Indeed!" cried I.

"Yes," said Traddles. "Now the whole set—I mean the chambers—is only three rooms; but Sophy arranges for the girls in the most wonderful way, and they sleep as comfortably as possible. Three in that room," said Traddles, pointing. "Two in that."

I could not help glancing round, in search of the accommodation remaining for Mr and Mrs Traddles. Traddles understood me.

"Well!" said Traddles, "we are prepared to rough it, as I said just now, and we *did* improvise a bed last week, upon the floor here. But there's a little room in the roof—a very nice room, when you're up there—which Sophy papered herself, to surprise me; and that's our room at present. It's a capital little gipsy sort of place. There's quite a view from it."

"And you are happily married at last, my dear Traddles!" said I. "How rejoiced I am!"

"Thank you, my dear Copperfield," said Traddles, as we shook hands once more. "Yes, I am as happy as it's possible to be. There's your old friend, you see," said Traddles, nodding triumphantly at the flower-pot and stand; "and there's the table with the marble top! All the other furniture is plain and serviceable, you perceive. And as to plate, Lord bless you, we haven't so much as a tea-spoon."

"All to be earned?" said I, cheerfully.

"Exactly so," replied Traddles, "all to be earned. Of course we have something in the shape of tea-spoons, because we stir our tea. But they're Britannia metal."

"The silver will be the brighter when it comes," said I.

"The very thing we say!" cried Traddles. "You see, my dear Copperfield," falling again into the low confidential tone, "after I had delivered my argument in DOE *dem.* JIPES *versus* WIGZELL, which did me great service with the profession, I went down into Devonshire, and had some serious conversation in private with the Reverend Horace. I dwelt upon the fact that Sophy—who I do assure you, Copperfield, is the dearest girl!—"

"I am certain she is!" said I.

"She is, indeed!" rejoined Traddles. "But I am afraid I am wandering from the subject. Did I mention the Reverend Horace?"

"You said that you dwelt upon the fact—"

"True! Upon the fact that Sophy and I had been engaged for a long period, and that Sophy, with the permission of her parents, was more than content to take me—in short," said Traddles, with his old frank smile, "on our present Britannia-metal footing. Very well. I then proposed to the Reverend Horace—who is a most excellent clergyman, Copperfield, and ought to be a Bishop; or at least ought to have enough to live upon, without pinching himself—that if I could turn the corner, say of two hundred and fifty pounds, in one year; and could see my way pretty clearly to that, or something better, next year; and could plainly furnish a little place like this, besides: then, and in that case, Sophy and I should be united. I took the liberty of representing that we had been patient for a good many years; and that the circumstance of Sophy's being extraordinarily useful at home, ought not to operate with her affectionate parents, against her establishment in life—don't you see?"

"Certainly it ought not," said I.

"I am glad you think so, Copperfield," rejoined Traddles, "because, without any imputation on the Reverend Horace, I do think parents, and brothers, and so forth, are sometimes rather selfish in such cases. Well! I also pointed out, that my most earnest desire was, to be useful to the family; and that if I got on in the world, and anything should happen to him—I refer to the Reverend Horace—"

"I understand," said I.

"—Or to Mrs Crewler—it would be the utmost gratification of my wishes, to be a parent to the girls. He replied in a most admirable manner, exceedingly flattering to my feelings, and undertook to obtain the consent of Mrs Crewler to this arrangement. They had a dreadful time of it with her. It mounted from her legs into her chest, and then into her head—"

"What mounted?" I asked.

"Her grief," replied Traddles, with a serious look. "Her feelings generally. As I mentioned on a former occasion, she is a very superior woman, but has lost the use of her limbs. Whatever occurs to harass her, usually settles in her legs; but on this occasion it mounted to the chest, and then to the head, and, in short, pervaded the whole system in a most alarming manner. However, they brought her through it by unremitting and affectionate attention; and we were married yesterday six weeks. You have no idea what a Monster I felt, Copperfield, when I saw the whole family crying and fainting away in every direction! Mrs Crewler couldn't see me before we left—couldn't forgive me, then, for depriving her of her child—but she is a good creature, and has done so since. I had a delightful letter from her, only this morning."

"And in short, my dear friend," said I, "you feel as blest as you deserve to feel!"

"Oh! That's your partiality!" laughed Traddles. "But, indeed, I am in a most enviable state. I work hard, and read Law insatiably. I get up at five every morning, and don't mind it at all. I hide the girls in the daytime, and make merry with them in the evening. And I assure you I am quite sorry that they are going home on Tuesday, which is the day before the first day of Michaelmas Term. But here," said Traddles, breaking off in his confidence, and speaking aloud, *"are* the girls! Mr Copperfield, Miss Crewler—Miss Sarah—Miss Louisa—Margaret and Lucy!"

They were a perfect nest of roses; they looked so wholesome and fresh. They were all pretty, and Miss Caroline was very handsome; but there was a loving, cheerful, fireside quality in Sophy's bright looks, which was better than that, and which assured me that my friend had chosen well. We all sat round the fire; while the sharp boy, who I now divined had lost his breath in putting the papers out, cleared them away again, and produced the tea-things. After that, he retired for the night, shutting the outer door upon us with a bang. Mrs Traddles, with perfect pleasure and composure beaming from her household eyes, having made the tea, then quietly made the toast as she sat in a corner by the fire.

She had seen Agnes, she told me while she was toasting. "Tom" had taken her down into Kent for a wedding trip, and there she had seen my aunt, too; and both my aunt and Agnes were well, and they had all talked of nothing but me. "Tom" had never had me out of his thoughts, she really believed, all the time I had been away. "Tom" was the authority for everything. "Tom" was evidently the idol of her life; never to be shaken on his pedestal by any commotion; always to be believed in, and done homage to with the whole faith of her heart, come what might.

The deference which both she and Traddles showed towards the Beauty, pleased me very much. I don't know that I thought it very reasonable; but I thought it very delightful, and essentially a part of their character. If Traddles ever for an instant missed the tea-spoons that were still to be won, I have no doubt it was when he handed the Beauty her tea. If his sweet-tempered wife could have got up any self-assertion against anyone, I am satisfied it could only have been because she was the Beauty's sister. A few slight indications of a rather petted and capricious manner, which I observed in the Beauty, were manifestly considered, by Traddles and his wife, as her birthright and natural endowment. If she had been born a Queen Bee, and they labouring Bees, they could not have been more satisfied of that.

But their self-forgetfulness charmed me. Their pride in these girls, and their submission of themselves to all their whims, was the pleasantest little testimony to their own worth I could have desired to see. If Traddles were addressed as "a darling," once in the course of that evening; and besought to bring something here, or carry something there, or take something up, or put something down, or find something, or fetch something, he was so addressed, by one or other of his sisters-in-law, at least twelve times in an hour.

Neither could they do anything without Sophy. Somebody's hair fell down, and nobody but Sophy could put it up. Somebody forgot how a particular tune went, and nobody but Sophy could hum that tune right. Somebody wanted to recall the name of a place in Devonshire, and only Sophy knew it. Something was wanted to be written home, and Sophy alone could be trusted to write before breakfast in the morning. Somebody broke down in a piece of knitting, and no one but Sophy was able to put the defaulter in the right direction. They were entire mistresses of the place, and Sophy and Traddles waited on them. How many children Sophy could have taken care of in her time, I can't imagine; but she seemed to be famous for knowing every sort of song that ever was addressed to a child in the English tongue; and she sang dozens to order with the clearest little voice in the world, one after another (every sister issuing directions for a different tune, and the Beauty generally striking in last), so that I was quite fascinated. The best of all was, that, in the midst of their exactions, all the sisters had a great tenderness and respect both for Sophy and Traddles. I am sure, when I took my leave, and Traddles was coming out to walk with me to the coffee-house, I thought I had never seen an obstinate head of hair, or any other head of hair, rolling about in such a shower of kisses.

Altogether, it was a scene I could not help dwelling on with pleasure, for a long time after I got back and had wished Traddles good night. If I had beheld a thousand roses blowing in a top set of chambers, in that withered Gray's Inn, they could not have brightened it half so much. The idea of those Devonshire girls, among the dry law-stationers and the attorneys' offices; and of the tea and toast, and children's songs, in that grim atmosphere of pounce and parchment, red-tape, dusty wafers, ink-jars, brief and draft paper, law reports, writs, declarations, and bills of costs: seemed almost as pleas-antly fanciful as if I had dreamed that the Sultan's famous family had been admitted on the roll of attorneys, and had brought the talking bird, the singing tree, and the golden water into Gray's Inn Hall. Somehow, I found that I had taken leave of Traddles for the night, and come back to the coffee-house, with a great change in my despondency about him. I began to think he would get on, in spite of all the many orders of chief waiters in England.

Drawing a chair before one of the coffee-room fires to think about him at my leisure, I gradually fell from the consideration of his happiness to tracing prospects in the live-coals, and to thinking, as they broke and changed, of the principal vicissitudes and separations that had marked my life. I had not seen a coal fire, since I had left England three years ago: though many a wood fire had I watched, as it crumbled into hoary ashes, and mingled with the feathery heap upon the hearth, which not inaptly figured to me, in my despondency, my own dead hopes.

I could think of the past now, gravely, but not bitterly; and could contemplate the future in a brave spirit. Home, in its best sense, was for me no more. She in whom I might have inspired a dearer love, I had taught to be my sister. She would marry, and would have new claimants on her tenderness; and in doing it, would never know the love for her that had grown up in my heart. It was right that I should pay the forfeit of my headlong passion. What I reaped, I had sown.

I was thinking. And had I truly disciplined my heart to this, and could I resolutely bear it, and calmly hold the place in her home which she had calmly held in mine,—when I found my eyes resting on a countenance that might have arisen out of the fire, in its association with my early remembrances.

Little Mr Chillip the Doctor, to whose good offices I was indebted in the very first chapter of this history, sat reading a newspaper in the shadow of an opposite corner. He was tolerably stricken in years by this time; but, being a mild, meek, calm little man, had worn so easily, that I thought he looked at that moment just as he might have looked when he sat in our parlour, waiting for me to be born.

Mr Chillip had left Blunderstone six or seven years ago, and I had never seen him since. He sat placidly perusing the newspaper, with his little head on one side, and a glass of warm sherry negus at his elbow. He was so extremely conciliatory in his manner that he seemed to apologize to the very newspaper for taking the liberty of reading it.

I walked up to where he was sitting, and said, "How do you do, Mr Chillip?"

He was greatly fluttered by this unexpected address from a stranger, and replied, in his slow way, "I thank you, sir, you are very good. Thank you, sir. I hope *you* are well."

"You don't remember me?" said I.

"Well, sir," returned Mr Chillip, smiling very meekly, and shaking his head as he surveyed me, "I have a kind of an impression that something in your countenance is familiar to me, sir; but I couldn't lay my hand upon your name, really."

"And yet you knew it, long before I knew it myself," I returned.

"Did I indeed, sir?" said Mr Chillip. "Is it possible that I had the honour, sir, of officiating when——?"

"Yes," said I.

"Dear me!" cried Mr Chillip. "But no doubt you are a good deal changed since then, sir?"

"Probably," said I.

"Well, sir," observed Mr Chillip, "I hope you'll excuse me, if I am compelled to ask the favour of your name?"

On my telling him my name, he was really moved. He quite shook hands with me—which was a violent proceeding for him, his usual course being to slide a tepid little fish-slice, an inch or two in advance of his hip, and evince the greatest discomposure when anybody grappled with it. Even now, he put his hand in his coat-pocket as soon as he could disengage it, and seemed relieved when he had got it safe back.

"Dear me, sir!" said Mr Chillip, surveying me with his head on one side. "And it's Mr Copperfield, is it? Well, sir, I think I should have known you, if I had taken the liberty of looking more closely at you. There's a strong resemblance between you and your poor father, sir."

"I never had the happiness of seeing my father," I observed.

"Very true, sir," said Mr Chillip, in a soothing tone. "And very much to be deplored it was, on all accounts! We are not ignorant, sir," said Mr Chillip, slowly shaking his little head again, "down in our part of the country, of your fame. There must be great excitement here, sir," said Mr Chillip, tapping himself on the forehead with his forefinger. "You must find it a trying occupation, sir!"

"What is your part of the country now?" I asked, seating myself near him.

"I am established within a few miles of Bury St Edmund's, sir," said Mr Chillip. "Mrs Chillip, coming into a little property in that neighbourhood, under her father's will, I bought a practice down there, in which you will be glad to hear I am doing well. My daughter is growing quite a tall lass now, sir," said Mr Chillip, giving his little head another little shake. "Her mother let down two tucks in her frocks only last week. Such is time, you see, sir!"

As the little man put his now empty glass to his lips, when he made this reflection, I proposed to him to have it refilled, and I would keep him company with another. "Well, sir," he returned, in his slow way, "it's more than I am accustomed to; but I can't deny myself the pleasure of your conversation. It seems but yesterday that I had the honour of attending you in the measles. You came through them charmingly, sir!"

I acknowledged this compliment, and ordered the negus, which was soon produced. "Quite an uncommon dissipation!" said Mr Chillip, stirring it, "but I can't resist so extraordinary an occasion. You have no family, sir?"

I shook my head.

"I was aware that you sustained a bereavement, sir, some time ago," said Mr Chillip. "I heard it from your father-in-law's sister. Very decided character there, sir?"

"Why, yes," said I, "decided enough. Where did you see her, Mr Chillip?"

"Are you not aware, sir," returned Mr Chillip, with his placidest smile, "that your father-in-law is again a neighbour of mine?"

"No," said I.

"He is indeed, sir!" said Mr Chillip. "Married a young lady of that part, with a very good little property, poor thing.—And this action of the brain now, sir? Don't you find it fatigue you?" said Mr Chillip, looking at me like an admiring Robin.

I waived that question, and returned to the Murdstones. "I was aware of his being married again. Do you attend the family?" I asked.

"Not regularly. I have been called in," he replied. "Strong phrenological development of the organ of firmness, in Mr Murdstone and his sister, sir."

I replied with such an expressive look, that Mr Chillip was emboldened by that, and the negus together, to give his head several short shakes, and thoughtfully exclaim, "Ah, dear me! We remember old times, Mr Copperfield!"

"And the brother and sister are pursuing their old course, are they?" said I.

"Well, sir," replied Mr Chillip, "a medical man, being so much in families, ought to have neither eyes nor ears for anything but his profession. Still, I must say, they are very severe, sir: both as to this life and the next."

"The next will be regulated without much reference to them, I dare say," I returned: "what are they doing as to this?"

Mr Chillip shook his head, stirred his negus, and sipped it.

"She was a charming woman, sir!" he observed in a plaintive manner.

"The present Mrs Murdstone?"

"A charming woman indeed, sir," said Mr Chillip; "as amiable, I am sure, as it was possible to be! Mrs Chillip's opinion is, that her spirit has been entirely broken since her marriage, and that she is all but melancholy mad. And the ladies," observed Mr Chillip, timorously, "are great observers, sir."

"I suppose she was to be subdued and broken to their detestable mould, Heaven help her!" said I. "And she has been."

"Well, sir, there were violent quarrels at first, I assure you," said Mr Chillip; "but she is quite a shadow now. Would it be considered forward if I was to say to you, sir, in confidence, that since the sister came to help, the brother and sister between them have nearly reduced her to a state of imbecility?"

I told him I could easily believe it.

"I have no hesitation in saying," said Mr Chillip, fortifying himself with another sip of negus, "between you and me, sir, that her mother died of it—or that tyranny, gloom, and worry have made Mrs Murdstone nearly imbecile. She was a lively young woman, sir, before marriage, and their gloom and austerity destroyed her. They go about with her, now, more like her keepers than her husband and sister-in-law. That was Mrs Chillip's remark to me, only last week. And I assure you, sir, the ladies are great observers. Mrs Chillip herself is a *great* observer!"

"Does he gloomily profess to be (I am ashamed to use the word in such association) religious still?" I inquired.

"You anticipate, sir," said Mr Chillip, his eyelids getting quite red with the unwonted stimulus in which he was indulging. "One of Mrs Chillip's most impressive remarks. Mrs Chillip," he proceeded, in the calmest and slowest manner, "quite electrified me, by pointing out that Mr Murdstone sets up an image of himself, and calls it the Divine Nature. You might have knocked me down on the flat of my back, sir, with the feather of a pen, I assure you, when Mrs Chillip said so. The ladies are great observers, sir?"

"Intuitively," said I, to his extreme delight.

"I am very happy to receive such support in my opinion, sir," he rejoined. "It is not often that I venture to give a non-medical opinion, I assure you. Mr Murdstone delivers public addresses sometimes, and it is said,—in short, sir, it is said by Mrs Chillip,—that the darker tyrant he has lately been, the more ferocious is his doctrine."

"I believe Mrs Chillip to be perfectly right," said I.

"Mrs Chillip does go so far as to say," pursued the meekest of little men, much encouraged, "that what such people miscall their religion, is a vent for their bad-humours and arrogance. And do you know I must say, sir," he continued, mildly laying his head on one side, "that I *don't* find authority for Mr and Miss Murdstone in the New Testament?"

"I never found it either!" said I.

"In the meantime, sir," said Mr Chillip, "they are much disliked; and as they are very free in consigning everybody who dislikes them to perdition, we really have a good deal of perdition going on in our neighbourhood! However, as Mrs Chillip says, sir, they undergo a continual punishment; for they are turned inward, to feed upon their own hearts, and their own hearts are very bad feeding. Now, sir, about that brain of yours, if you'll excuse my returning to it. Don't you expose it to a good deal of excitement, sir?"

I found it not difficult, in the excitement of Mr Chillip's own brain, under his potations of negus, to divert his attention from this topic to his own affairs, on which, for the next half-hour, he was quite loquacious; giving me to understand, among other pieces of information, that he was then at the Gray's Inn Coffee-house to lay his professional evidence before a Commission of Lunacy, touching the state of mind of a patient who had become deranged from excessive drinking.

"And I assure you, sir," he said, "I am extremely nervous on such occasions. I could not support being what is called Bullied, sir. It would quite unman me. Do you know it was some time before I recovered the conduct of that alarming lady, on the night of your birth, Mr Copperfield?"

I told him that I was going down to my aunt, the Dragon of that night, early, in the morning; and that she was one of the most tender-hearted and excellent of women, as he would know full well if he knew her better. The mere notion of the possibility of his ever seeing her again, appeared to terrify him. He replied with a small pale smile, "Is she so, indeed sir? Really?" and almost immediately called for a candle, and went to bed, as if he were not quite safe anywhere else. He did not actually stagger under the negus; but I should think his placid little pulse must have made two or three more beats in a minute, than it had done since the great night of my aunt's disappointment, when she struck at him with her bonnet.

Thoroughly tired, I went to bed too, at midnight; passed the next day on the Dover coach; burst safe and sound into my aunt's old parlour while she was at tea (she wore spectacles now); and was received by her, and Mr Dick, and dear old Peggotty, who acted as housekeeper, with open arms and tears of joy. My aunt was mightily amused, when we began to talk composedly, by my account of my meeting with Mr Chillip, and of his holding her in such dread remembrance; and both she and Peggotty had a great deal to say about my poor mother's second husband, and "that murdering woman of a sister,"—on whom I think no pain or penalty would have induced my aunt to bestow any Christian or Proper Name, or any other designation.

Chapter LX

AGNES

M Y aunt and I, when we were left alone, talked far into the night. How the emigrants never wrote home, otherwise than cheerfully and hopefully; how Mr Micawber had actually remitted divers small sums of money, on account of those "pecuniary liabilities," in reference to which he had been so business-like as between man and man; how Janet, returning into my aunt's service when she came back to Dover, had finally carried out her renunciation of mankind by entering into wedlock with a thriving tavern-keeper; and how my aunt had finally set *her* seal on the same great principle, by aiding and abetting the bride, and crowning the marriage-ceremony with her presence; were among our topics—already more or less familiar to me through the letters I had had. Mr Dick, as usual, was not forgotten. My aunt informed me how he incessantly occupied himself in copying everything he could lay his hands on, and kept King Charles the First at a respectful distance by that semblance of employment; how it was one of the main joys and rewards of her life that he was free and happy, instead of pining in monotonous restraint; and how (as a novel general conclusion) nobody but she could ever fully know what he was.

"And when, Trot," said my aunt, patting the back of my hand, as we sat in our old way before the fire, "when are you going over to Canterbury?"

"I shall get a horse, and ride over tomorrow morning, aunt, unless you will go with me?"

"No!" said my aunt, in her short abrupt way. "I mean to stay where I am."

Then, I should ride, I said. I could not have come through Canterbury today without stopping, if I had been coming to anyone but her.

She was pleased, but answered, "Tut, Trot? *my* old bones would have kept till tomorrow!" and softly patted my hand again, as I sat looking thoughtfully at the fire.

Thoughtfully, for I could not be here once more, and so near Agnes, without the revival of those regrets with which I had so long been occupied. Softened regrets they might be, teaching me what I had failed to learn when my younger life was all before me, but not the less regrets. "Oh, Trot," I seemed to hear my aunt say once more; and I understood her better now—"Blind, blind, blind!"

We both kept silence for some minutes. When I raised my eyes, I found that she was steadily observant of me. Perhaps she had followed the current of my mind; for it seemed to me an easy one to track now, wilful as it had been once.

"You will find her father a white-haired old man," said my aunt, "though a better man in all other respects—a reclaimed man. Neither will you find him measuring all human interests, and joys, and sorrows, with his one poor little inch-rule now. Trust me, child, such things must shrink very much, before they can be measured off in *that* way."

"Indeed they must," said I.

"You will find her," pursued my aunt, "as good, as beautiful, as earnest, as disinterested, as she has always been. If I knew higher praise, Trot, I would bestow it on her."

There was no higher praise for her; no higher reproach for me. Oh, how had I strayed so far away!

"If she trains the young girls whom she has about her, to be like herself," said my aunt, earnest even to the filling of her eyes with tears, "Heaven knows, her life will be well employed! Useful and happy, as she said that day! How could she be otherwise than useful and happy!"

"Has Agnes any—" I was thinking aloud, rather than speaking.

"Well? Hey? Any what?" said my aunt, sharply.

"Any lover," said I.

"A score," cried my aunt, with a kind of indignant pride. "She might have married twenty times, my dear, since you have been gone!"

"No doubt," said I. "No doubt. But has she any lover who is worthy of her? Agnes could care for no other."

My aunt sat musing for a little while, with her chin upon her hand. Slowly raising her eyes to mine, she said:

"I suspect she has an attachment, Trot."

"A prosperous one?" said I.

"Trot," returned my aunt gravely, "I can't say. I have no right to tell you even so much. She has never confided it to me, but I suspect it."

She looked so attentively and anxiously at me (I even saw her tremble), that I felt now, more than ever, that she had followed my late thoughts. I summoned all the resolutions I had made, in all those many days and nights, and all those many conflicts of my heart.

"If it should be so," I began, "and I hope it is—"

"I don't know that it is," said my aunt curtly. "You must not be ruled by my suspicions. You must keep them secret. They are very slight, perhaps. I have no right to speak."

"If it should be so," I repeated, "Agnes will tell me at her own good time. A sister to whom I have confided so much, aunt, will not be reluctant to confide in me."

My aunt withdrew her eyes from mine, as slowly as she had turned them upon me; and covered them thoughtfully with her hand. By and by she put her other hand on my shoulder; and so we both sat, looking into the past, without saying another word, until we parted for the night.

I rode away, early in the morning, for the scene of my old school days. I cannot say that I was yet quite happy, in the hope that I was gaining a victory over myself; even in the prospect of so soon looking on her face again.

The well-remembered ground was soon traversed, and I came into the quiet streets, where every stone was a boy's book to me. I went on foot to the old house, and went away with a heart too full to enter. I returned; and looking, as I passed, through the low window of the turret-room where first Uriah Heep, and afterwards Mr Micawber, had been wont to sit, saw that it was a little parlour now, and that there was no office. Otherwise the staid old house was, as to its cleanliness and order, still just as it had been when I first saw it. I requested the new maid who admitted me, to tell Miss Wickfield that a gentleman who waited on her from a friend abroad, was there; and I was shown up the grave old staircase (cautioned of the steps I knew so well), into the unchanged drawing-room. The books that Agnes and I had read together, were on their shelves; and the desk where I had laboured at my lessons, many a night, stood yet at the same old corner of the table. All the little changes that had crept in when the Heeps were there, were changed again. Everything was as it used to be, in the happy time.

I stood in a window, and looked across the ancient street at the opposite houses, recalling how I had watched them on wet afternoons, when I first came there; and how I had used to speculate about the people who appeared at any of the windows, and had followed them with my eyes up and down stairs, while women went clicking along the pavement in pattens, and the dull rain fell in slanting lines, and poured out of the water-spout yonder, and flowed into the road. The feeling with which I used to watch the tramps, as they came into the town on those wet evenings, at dusk, and limped past, with their bundles drooping over their shoulders at the ends of sticks, came freshly back to me; fraught, as then, with the smell of damp earth, and wet leaves and briar, and the sensation of the very airs that blew upon me in my own toilsome journey.

The opening of the little door in the panelled wall made me start and turn. Her beautiful serene eyes met mine as she came towards me. She stopped and laid her hand upon her bosom, and I caught her in my arms.

"Agnes! my dear girl! I have come too suddenly upon you."

"No, no! I am so rejoiced to see you, Trotwood!"

"Dear Agnes, the happiness it is to me, to see you once again!"

I folded her to my heart, and, for a little while, we were both silent. Presently we sat down, side by side; and her angel-face was turned upon me with the welcome I had dreamed of, waking and sleeping, for whole years.

She was so true, she was so beautiful, she was so good,—I owed her so much gratitude, she was so dear to me, that I could find no utterance for what I felt. I tried to bless her, tried to thank her, tried to tell her (as I had often done in letters) what an influence she had upon me; but all my efforts were in vain. My love and joy were dumb.

With her own sweet tranquillity, she calmed my agitation; led me back to the time of our parting; spoke to me of Emily, whom she had visited, in secret, many times; spoke to me tenderly of Dora's grave. With the unerring instinct of her noble heart, she touched the chords of my memory so softly and harmoniously, that not one jarred within me; I could listen to the sorrowful, distant music, and desire to shrink from nothing it awoke. How could I, when, blended with it all, was her dear self, the better angel of my life?

"And you, Agnes," I said, by and by. "Tell me of yourself. You have hardly ever told me of your own life, in all this lapse of time!"

"What should I tell?" she answered, with her radiant smile. "Papa is well. You see us here, quiet in our own home; our anxieties set at rest, our home restored to us; and knowing that, dear Trotwood, you know all."

"All, Agnes?" said I.

She looked at me, with some fluttering wonder in her face.

"Is there nothing else, Sister?" I said.

Her colour, which had just now faded, returned, and faded again. She smiled; with a quiet sadness, I thought; and shook her head.

I had sought to lead her to what my aunt had hinted at; for, sharply painful to me as it must be to receive that confidence, I was to discipline my heart, and do my duty to her. I saw, however, that she was uneasy, and I let it pass.

"You have much to do, dear Agnes?"

"With my school?" said she, looking up again, in all her bright composure.

"Yes. It is laborious, is it not?"

"The labour is so pleasant," she returned, "that it is scarcely grateful in me to call it by that name."

"Nothing good is difficult to you," said I.

Her colour came and went once more; and once more, as she bent her head, I saw the same sad smile.

"You will wait and see papa," said Agnes, cheerfully, "and pass the day with us? Perhaps you will sleep in your own room? We always call it yours."

I could not do that, having promised to ride back to my aunt's at night; but I would pass the day there, joyfully.

"I must be a prisoner for a little while," said Agnes, "but here are the old books, Trotwood, and the old music."

"Even the old flowers are here," said I, looking round; "or the old kinds."

"I have found a pleasure," returned Agnes, smiling, "while you have been absent, in keeping everything as it used to be when we were children. For we were very happy then, I think."

"Heaven knows we were!" said I.

"And every little thing that has reminded me of my brother," said Agnes, with her cordial eyes turned cheerfully upon me, "has been a welcome companion. Even this," showing me the basket-trifle, full of keys, still hanging at her side, "seems to jingle a kind of old tune!"

She smiled again, and went out at the door by which she had come.

It was for me to guard this sisterly affection with religious care. It was all that I had left myself, and it was a treasure. If I once shook the foundations of the sacred confidence and usage, in virtue of which it was given to me, it was lost, and could never be recovered. I set this steadily before myself. The better I loved her, the more it behoved me never to forget it.

I walked through the streets; and, once more seeing my old adversary the butcher—now a constable, with his staff hanging up in the shop—went down to look at the place where I had fought him; and there meditated on Miss Shepherd and the eldest Miss Larkins, and all the idle loves and likings, and dislikings, of that time. Nothing seemed to have survived that time but Agnes; and she, ever a star above me, was brighter and higher.

When I returned, Mr Wickfield had come home, from a garden he had, a couple of miles or so out of town, where he now employed himself almost every day. I found him as my aunt had described him. We sat down to dinner, with some half-dozen little girls; and he seemed but the shadow of his handsome picture on the wall.

The tranquillity and peace belonging, of old, to that quiet ground in my memory, pervaded it again. When dinner was done, Mr Wickfield taking no wine, and I desiring none, we went upstairs; where Agnes and her little charges sang and played, and worked. After tea the children left us; and we three sat together, talking of the bygone days.

"My part in them," said Mr Wickfield, shaking his white head, "has much matter for regret—for deep regret, and deep contrition, Trotwood, you well know. But I would not cancel it, if it were in my power."

I could readily believe that, looking at the face beside him.

"I should cancel with it," he pursued, "such patience and devotion, such fidelity, such a child's love, as I must not forget, no! even to forget myself."

"I understand you, sir," I softly said. "I hold it—I have always held it—in veneration."

"But no one knows, not even you," he returned, "how much she has done, how much she has undergone, how hard she has striven. Dear Agnes!"

She had put her hand entreatingly on his arm, to stop him; and was very, very, pale.

"Well, well!" he said with a sigh, dismissing, as I then saw, some trial she had borne, or was yet to bear. in connexion with what my aunt had told me. "Well! I have never told you, Trotwood, of her mother. Has anyone?"

"Never, sir."

"It's not much—though it was much to suffer. She married me in opposition to her father's wish, and he renounced her. She prayed him to forgive her, before my Agnes came into this world. He was a very hard man, and her mother had long been dead. He repulsed her. He broke her heart."

Agnes leaned upon his shoulder, and stole her arm about his neck.

"She had an affectionate and gentle heart," he said; "and it was broken. I knew its tender nature very well. No one could, if I did not. She loved me dearly, but was never happy. She was always labouring, in secret, under this distress; and being delicate and downcast at the time of his last repulse—for it was not the first, by many—pined away and died. She left me Agnes, two weeks old; and the grey hair that you recollect me with, when you first came."

He kissed Agnes on her cheek.

"My love for my dear child was a diseased love, but my mind was all unhealthy then. I say no more of that. I am not speaking of myself, Trotwood, but of her mother, and of her. If I give you any clue to what I am, or to what I have been, you will unravel it, I know. What Agnes is, I need not say. I have always read something of her poor mother's story, in her character; and so I tell it you tonight, when we three are again together, after such great changes. I have told it all."

His bowed head, and her angel-face and filial duty, derived a more pathetic meaning from it than they had had before. If I had wanted anything by which to mark this night of our re-union, I should have found it in this.

Agnes rose up from her father's side, before long; and going softly to her piano, played some of the old airs to which we had often listened in that place.

"Have you any intention of going away again?" Agnes asked me, as I was standing by.

"What does my sister say to that?"

"I hope not."

"Then I have no such intention, Agnes."

"I think you ought not, Trotwood, since you ask me," she said, mildly. "Your growing reputation and success enlarge your power of doing good; and if *I* could spare my brother," with her eyes upon me, "perhaps the time could not."

"What I am, you have made me, Agnes. You should know best."

"*I* made you, Trotwood?"

"Yes! Agnes, my dear girl!" I said, bending over her. "I tried to tell you, when we met today, something that has been in my thoughts since Dora died. You remember, when you came down to me in our little room—pointing upward, Agnes?"

"Oh, Trotwood!" she returned, her eyes filled with tears. "So loving, so confiding, and so young! Can I ever forget?"

"As you were then, my sister, I have often thought since, you have ever been to me.

Ever pointing upward, Agnes; ever leading me to something better; ever directing me to higher things!"

She only shook her head; through her tears I saw the same sad quiet smile.

"And I am so grateful to you for it, Agnes, so bound to you, that there is no name for the affection of my heart. I want you to know, yet don't know how to tell you, that all my life long I shall look up to you, and be guided by you, as I have been through the darkness that is past. Whatever betides, whatever new ties you may form, whatever changes may come between us, I shall always look to you, and love you, as I do now, and have always done. You will always be my solace and resource, as you have always been. Until I die, my dearest sister, I shall see you always before me, pointing upward!"

She put her hand in mine, and told me she was proud of me, and of what I said; although I praised her very far beyond her worth. Then she went on softly playing, but without removing her eyes from me.

"Do you know, what I have heard tonight, Agnes," said I, "strangely seems to be a part of the feeling with which I regarded you when I saw you first—with which I sat beside you in my rough school-days?"

"You knew I had no mother," she replied with a smile, "and felt kindly towards me."

"More than that, Agnes, I knew, almost as if I had known this story, that there was something inexplicably gentle and softened, surrounding you; something that might have been sorrowful in someone else (as I can now understand it was), but was not so in you."

She softly played on, looking at me still.

"Will you laugh at my cherishing such fancies, Agnes?"

"No!"

"Or at my saying that I really believe I felt, even then, that you could be faithfully affectionate against all discouragement, and never cease to be so, until you ceased to live?—Will you laugh at such a dream?"

"Oh, no! Oh, no!"

For an instant, a distressful shadow crossed her face; but, even in the start it gave me, it was gone; and she was playing on, and looking at me with her own calm smile.

As I rode back in the lonely night, the wind going by me like a restless memory, I thought of this, and feared she was not happy. *I* was not happy; but, thus far, I had faithfully set the seal upon the Past, and, thinking of her, pointing upward, thought of her as pointing to that sky above me, where, in the mystery to come, I might yet love her with a love unknown on earth, and tell her what the strife had been within me when I loved her here.

Chapter LXI

I AM SHOWN TWO INTERESTING PENITENTS

F OR a time—at all events until my book should be completed, which would be the
work of several months—I took up my abode in my aunt's house at Dover; and
there, sitting in the window from which I had looked out at the moon upon the sea,
when that roof first gave me shelter, I quietly pursued my task.

In pursuance of my intention of referring to my own fictions only when their course
should incidentally connect itself with the progress of my story, I do not enter on the
aspirations, the delights, anxieties, and triumphs of my art. That I truly devoted myself
to it with my strongest earnestness, and bestowed upon it every energy of my soul, I have
already said. If the books I have written be of any worth, they will supply the rest. I shall
otherwise have written to poor purpose, and the rest will be of interest to no one.

Occasionally, I went to London; to lose myself in the swarm of life there, or to
consult with Traddles on some business point. He had managed for me, in my absence,
with the soundest judgment; and my worldly affairs were prospering. As my notoriety
began to bring upon me an enormous quantity of letters from people of whom I had no
knowledge—chiefly about nothing, and extremely difficult to answer—I agreed with
Traddles to have my name painted up on his door. There, the devoted postman on that
beat delivered bushels of letters for me; and there, at intervals, I laboured through them,
like a Home Secretary of State without the salary.

Among this correspondence, there dropped in, every now and then, an obliging
proposal from one of the numerous outsiders always lurking about the Commons, to
practise under cover of my name (if I would take the necessary steps remaining to make
a proctor of myself), and pay me a percentage on the profits. But I declined these offers;
being already aware that there were plenty of such covert practitioners in existence, and
considering the Commons quite bad enough, without my doing anything to make it
worse.

The girls had gone home, when my name burst into bloom on Traddles's door; and
the sharp boy looked, all day, as if he had never heard of Sophy, shut up in a back room,
glancing down from her work into a sooty little strip of garden with a pump in it. But,
there I always found her, the same bright housewife; often humming her Devonshire
ballads when no strange foot was coming up the stairs, and blunting the sharp boy in
his official closet with melody.

I wondered, at first, why I so often found Sophy writing in a copy-book; and why
she always shut it up when I appeared, and hurried it into the table-drawer. But the
secret soon came out. One day, Traddles (who had just come home through the drizzling
sleet from Court) took a paper out of his desk, and asked me what I thought of that
handwriting?

"Oh, *don't,* Tom!" cried Sophy, who was warming his slippers before the fire.

"My dear," returned Tom, in a delighted state, "why not? What do you say to that
writing, Copperfield?"

"It's extraordinarily legal and formal," said I. "I don't think I ever saw such a stiff
hand."

"Not like a lady's hand, is it?" said Traddles.

"A lady's!" I repeated. "Bricks and mortar are more like a lady's hand!"

Traddles broke into a rapturous laugh, and informed me that it was Sophy's writing; that Sophy had vowed and declared he would need a copying-clerk soon, and she would be that clerk; that she had acquired this hand from a pattern; and that she could throw off—I forget how many folios an hour. Sophy was very much confused by my being told all this, and said that when "Tom" was made a judge he wouldn't be so ready to proclaim it. Which "Tom" denied; averring that he should always be equally proud of it, under all circumstances.

"What a thoroughly good and charming wife she is, my dear Traddles!" said I, when she had gone away, laughing.

"My dear Copperfield," returned Traddles, "she is, without any exception, the dearest girl! The way she manages this place; her punctuality, domestic knowledge, economy, and order; her cheerfulness, Copperfield!"

"Indeed, you have reason to commend her!" I returned. "You are a happy fellow. I believe you make yourselves, and each other, two of the happiest people in the world."

"I am sure we *are* two of the happiest people," returned Traddles. "I admit that, at all events. Bless my soul, when I see her getting up by candle-light on these dark mornings, busying herself in the day's arrangements, going out to market before the clerks come into the Inn, caring for no weather, devising the most capital little dinners out of the plainest materials, making puddings and pies, keeping everything in its right place, always so neat and ornamental herself, sitting up at night with me if it's ever so late, sweet-tempered and encouraging always, and all for me, I positively sometimes can't believe it, Copperfield!"

He was tender of the very slippers she had been warming, as he put them on, and stretched his feet enjoyingly upon the fender.

"I positively sometimes can't believe it," said Traddles. "Then our pleasures! Dear me, they are inexpensive, but they are quite wonderful! When we are at home here, of an evening, and shut the outer door, and draw those curtains—which she made—where could we be more snug? When it's fine, and we go out for a walk in the evening, the streets abound in enjoyment for us. We look into the glittering windows of the jewellers' shops; and I show Sophy which of the diamond-eyed serpents, coiled up on white satin rising grounds, I would give her if I could afford it; and Sophy shows me which of the gold watches that are capped and jewelled and engine-turned, and possessed of the horizontal lever-escape-movement, and all sorts of things, she would buy for me if *she* could afford it; and we pick out the spoons and forks, fish-slices, butter-knives, and sugar-tongs, we should both prefer if we could both afford it; and really we go away as if we had got them! Then, when we stroll into the squares, and great streets, and see a house to let, sometimes we look up at it, and say, how would *that* do, if I was made a judge? And we parcel it out—such a room for us, such rooms for the girls, and so forth; until we settle to our satisfaction that it would do, or it wouldn't do, as the case may be. Sometimes, we go at half-price to the pit of the theatre—the very smell of which is cheap, in my opinion, at the money—and there we thoroughly enjoy the play: which Sophy believes every word of, and so do I. In walking home, perhaps we buy a little bit of something at a cook's-shop, or a little lobster at the fishmonger's, and bring it here, and make a splendid supper, chatting about what we have seen. Now, you know, Copperfield, if I was Lord Chancellor, we couldn't do this!"

"You would do something, whatever you were, my dear Traddles," thought I, "that would be pleasant and amiable. And by the way," I said aloud, "I suppose you never draw any skeletons now?"

"Really," replied Traddles, laughing, and reddening, "I can't wholly deny that I do, my dear Copperfield. For being in one of the back rows of the King's Bench the other day, with a pen in my hand, the fancy came into my head to try how I had preserved that accomplishment. And I am afraid there's a skeleton—in a wig—on the ledge of the desk."

After we had both laughed heartily, Traddles wound up by looking with a smile at the fire, and saying, in his forgiving way, "Old Creakle!"

"I have a letter from that old—Rascal here," said I. For I never was less disposed to forgive him the way he used to batter Traddles, than when I saw Traddles so ready to forgive him himself.

"From Creakle the schoolmaster?" exclaimed Traddles. "No!"

"Among the persons who are attracted to me in my rising fame and fortune," said I, looking over my letters, "and who discover that they were always much attached to me, is the self-same Creakle. He is not a schoolmaster now, Traddles. He is retired. He is a Middlesex Magistrate."

I thought Traddles might be surprised to hear it, but he was not so at all.

"How do you suppose he comes to be a Middlesex Magistrate?" said I.

"Oh dear me!" replied Traddles, "it would be very difficult to answer that question. Perhaps he voted for somebody, or lent money to somebody, or bought something of somebody, or otherwise obliged somebody, or jobbed for somebody, who knew somebody who got the lieutenant of the county to nominate him for the commission."

"On the commission he is, at any rate," said I. "And he writes to me here, that he will be glad to show me, in operation, the only true system of prison discipline; the only unchallengeable way of making sincere and lasting converts and penitents—which, you know, is by solitary confinement. What do you say?"

"To the system?" inquired Traddles, looking grave.

"No. To my accepting the offer, and your going with me?"

"I don't object," said Traddles.

"Then I'll write to say so. You remember (to say nothing of our treatment) this same Creakle turning his son out of doors, I suppose, and the life he used to lead his wife and daughter?"

"Perfectly," said Traddles.

"Yet, if you'll read his letter, you'll find he is the tenderest of men to prisoners convicted of the whole calendar of felonies," said I; "though I can't find that his tenderness extends to any other class of created beings."

Traddles shrugged his shoulders, and was not at all surprised. I had not expected him to be, and was not surprised myself; or my observation of similar practical satires would have been but scanty. We arranged the time of our visit, and I wrote accordingly to Mr Creakle that evening.

On the appointed day—I think it was the next day, but no matter—Traddles and I repaired to the prison where Mr Creakle was powerful. It was an immense and solid building, erected at a vast expense. I could not help thinking, as we approached the gate, what an uproar would have been made in the country, if any deluded man had proposed to spend one half the money it had cost, on the erection of an industrial school for the young, or a house of refuge for the deserving old.

In an office that might have been on the ground-floor of the Tower of Babel, it was so massively constructed, we were presented to our old schoolmaster; who was one of a group, composed of two or three of the busier sort of magistrates, and some visitors they had brought. He received me, like a man who had formed my mind in bygone years, and had always loved me tenderly. On my introducing Traddles, Mr Creakle expressed, in like manner, but in an inferior degree, that he had always been Traddles's guide, philosopher, and friend. Our venerable instructor was a great deal older, and not improved in appearance. His face was as fiery as ever; his eyes were as small, and rather deeper set. The scanty, wet-looking grey hair, by which I remembered him, was almost gone; and the thick veins in his bald head were none the more agreeable to look at.

After some conversation among these gentlemen, from which I might have supposed that there was nothing in the world to be legitimately taken into account but the supreme comfort of prisoners, at any expense, and nothing on the wide earth to be done outside prison-doors, we began our inspection. It being then just dinner-time, we went, first into the great kitchen, where every prisoner's dinner was in course of being set out separately (to be handed to him in his cell), with the regularity and precision of clockwork. I said aside, to Traddles, that I wondered whether it occurred to anybody, that there was a striking contrast between these plentiful repasts of choice quality, and the dinners, not to say of paupers, but of soldiers, sailors, labourers, the great bulk of the honest, working community; of whom not one man in five hundred ever dined half so well. But I learned that the "system" required high living; and, in short, to dispose of the system, once for all, I found that on that head and on all others, "the system" put an end to all doubts, and disposed of all anomalies. Nobody appeared to have the least idea that there was any other system, but *the* system, to be considered.

As we were going through some of the magnificent passages, I inquired of Mr Creakle and his friends what were supposed to be the main advantages of this all-governing and universally overriding system? I found them to be the perfect isolation of prisoners—so that no one man in confinement there, knew anything about another; and the reduction of prisoners to a wholesome state of mind, leading to sincere contrition and repentance.

Now, it struck me, when we began to visit individuals in their cells, and to traverse the passages in which those cells were, and to have the manner of the going to chapel and so forth, explained to us, that there was a strong probability of the prisoners knowing a good deal about each other, and of their carrying on a pretty complete system of intercourse. This, at the time I write, has been proved, I believe, to be the case; but, as it would have been flat blasphemy against the system to have hinted such a doubt then, I looked out for the penitence as diligently as I could.

And here again, I had great misgivings. I found as prevalent a fashion in the form of the penitence, as I had left outside in the forms of the coats and waistcoats in the windows of the tailors' shops. I found a vast amount of profession, varying very little in character: varying very little (which I thought exceedingly suspicious), even in words. I found a great many foxes, disparaging whole vineyards of inaccessible grapes; but I found very few foxes whom I would have trusted within reach of a bunch. Above all, I found that the most professing men were the greatest objects of interest; and that their conceit, their vanity, their want of excitement, and their love of deception (which many of them possessed to an almost incredible extent, as their histories showed), all prompted to these professions, and were all gratified by them.

However, I heard so repeatedly, in the course of our goings to and fro, of a certain Number Twenty Seven, who was the Favourite, and who really appeared to be a Model Prisoner, that I resolved to suspend my judgement until I should see Twenty Seven. Twenty Eight, I understood, was also a bright particular star; but it was his misfortune to have his glory a little dimmed by the extraordinary lustre of Twenty Seven. I heard so much of Twenty Seven, of his pious admonitions to everybody around him, and of the beautiful letters he constantly wrote to his mother (whom he seemed to consider in a very bad way), that I became quite impatient to see him.

I had to restrain my impatience for some time, on account of Twenty Seven being reserved for a concluding effect. But, at last, we came to the door of his cell; and Mr Creakle, looking through a little hole in it, reported to us, in a state of the greatest admiration, that he was reading a Hymn Book.

There was such a rush of heads immediately, to see Number Twenty Seven reading his Hymn Book, that the little hole was blocked up, six or seven heads deep. To remedy this inconvenience, and give us an opportunity of conversing with Twenty Seven in all his purity, Mr Creakle directed the door of the cell to be unlocked, and Twenty Seven to be invited out into the passage. This was done; and whom should Traddles and I then behold, to our amazement, in this converted Number Twenty Seven, but Uriah Heep!

He knew us directly; and said, as he came out—with the old writhe,—

"How do you do, Mr Copperfield? How do you do, Mr Traddles?"

This recognition caused a general admiration in the party. I rather thought that everyone was struck by his not being proud, and taking notice of us.

"Well, Twenty Seven," said Mr Creakle, mournfully admiring him. "How do you find yourself today?"

"I am very umble, sir!" replied Uriah Heep.

"You are always so, Twenty Seven," said Mr Creakle.

Here, another gentleman asked, with extreme anxiety: "Are you quite comfortable?"

"Yes, I thank you, sir!" said Uriah Heep, looking in that direction. "Far more comfortable here, than ever I was outside. I see my follies, now, sir. That's what makes me comfortable."

Several gentlemen were much affected; and a third questioner, forcing himself to the front, inquired with extreme feeling: "How do you find the beef?"

"Thank you, sir," replied Uriah, glancing in the new direction of this voice, "it was tougher yesterday than I could wish; but it's my duty to bear. I have committed follies, gentlemen," said Uriah, looking round with a meek smile, "and I ought to bear the consequences without repining."

A murmur, partly of gratification at Twenty Seven's celestial state of mind, and partly of indignation against the Contractor who had given him any cause of complaint (a note of which was immediately made by Mr Creakle), having subsided, Twenty Seven stood in the midst of us, as if he felt himself the principal object of merit in a highly meritorious museum. That we, the neophytes, might have an excess of light shining upon us all at once, orders were given to let out Twenty Eight.

I had been so much astonished already, that I only felt a kind of resigned wonder when Mr Littimer walked forth, reading a good book!

"Twenty Eight," said a gentleman in spectacles, who had not yet spoken, "you complained last week, my good fellow, of the cocoa. How has it been since?"

"I thank you, sir," said Mr Littimer, "it has been better made. If I might take the liberty of saying so, sir, I don't think the milk which is boiled with it is quite genuine; but I am aware, sir, that there is a great adulteration of milk, in London, and that the article in a pure state is difficult to be obtained."

It appeared to me that the gentleman in spectacles backed his Twenty Eight against Mr Creakle's Twenty Seven, for each of them took his own man in hand.

"What is your state of mind, Twenty Eight?" said the questioner in spectacles.

"I thank you, sir," returned Mr Littimer; "I see my follies now, sir. I am a good deal troubled when I think of the sins of my former companions, sir; but I trust they may find forgiveness."

"You are quite happy yourself?" said the questioner, nodding encouragement.

"I am much obliged to you, sir," returned Mr Littimer. "Perfectly so."

"Is there anything at all on your mind now?" said the questioner. "If so, mention it, Twenty Eight."

"Sir," said Mr Littimer, without looking up, "if my eyes have not deceived me, there is a gentleman present who was acquainted with me in my former life. It may be profitable to that gentleman to know, sir, that I attribute my past follies, entirely to having lived a thoughtless life in the service of young men; and to having allowed myself to be led by them into weaknesses, which I had not the strength to resist. I hope that gentleman will take warning, sir, and will not be offended at my freedom. It is for his good. I am conscious of my own past follies. I hope he may repent of all the wickedness and sin to which he has been a party."

I observed that several gentlemen were shading their eyes, each with one hand, as if they had just come into church.

"This does you credit, Twenty Eight," returned the questioner. "I should have expected it of you. Is there anything else?"

"Sir," returned Mr Littimer, slightly lifting up his eyebrows, but not his eyes, "there was a young woman who fell into dissolute courses, that I endeavoured to save, sir, but could not rescue. I beg that gentleman, if he has it in his power, to inform that young woman from me that I forgive her her bad conduct towards myself; and that I call her to repentance—if he will be so good."

"I have no doubt, Twenty Eight," returned the questioner, "that the gentleman you refer to feels very strongly—as we all must—what you have so properly said. We will not detain you."

"I thank you, sir," said Mr Littimer. "Gentlemen, I wish you a good day, and hoping you and your families will also see your wickedness, and amend!"

With this, Number Twenty Eight retired, after a glance between him and Uriah; as if they were not altogether unknown to each other, through some medium of communication; and a murmur went round the group, as his door shut upon him, that he was a most respectable man, and a beautiful case.

"Now, Twenty Seven," said Mr Creakle, entering on a clear stage with *his* man, "is there anything that anyone can do for you? If so, mention it."

"I would umbly ask, sir," returned Uriah, with a jerk of his malevolent head, "for leave to write again to mother."

"It shall certainly be granted," said Mr Creakle.

"Thank you, sir! I am anxious about mother. I am afraid she ain't safe."

Somebody incautiously asked, what from? But there was a scandalized whisper of "Hush!"

"Immortally safe, sir," returned Uriah, writhing in the direction of the voice. "I should wish mother to be got into my state. I never should have been got into my present state if I hadn't come here. I wish mother had come here. It would be better for everybody, if they got took up, and was brought here."

This sentiment gave unbounded satisfaction—greater satisfaction, I think, than anything that had passed yet.

"Before I come here," said Uriah, stealing a look at us, as if he would have blighted the outer world to which we belonged, if he could, "I was given to follies; but now I am sensible of my follies. There's a deal of sin outside. There's a deal of sin in mother. There's nothing but sin everywhere—except here."

"You are quite changed?" said Mr Creakle.

"Oh dear, yes, sir!" cried this hopeful penitent.

"You wouldn't relapse, if you were going out?" asked somebody else.

"Oh de-ar no, sir!"

"Well!" said Mr Creakle, "this is very gratifying. You have addressed Mr Copperfield, Twenty Seven. Do you wish to say anything further to him?"

"You knew me, a long time before I came here and was changed, Mr Copperfield," said Uriah, looking at me; and a more villainous look I never saw, even on his visage. "You knew me when, in spite of my follies, I was umble among them that was proud, and meek among them that was violent—you was violent to me yourself, Mr Copperfield. Once, you struck me a blow in the face, you know."

General commiseration. Several indignant glances directed at me.

"But I forgive you, Mr Copperfield," said Uriah, making his forgiving nature the subject of a most impious and awful parallel, which I shall not record. "I forgive everybody. It would ill become me to bear malice. I freely forgive you, and I hope you'll curb your passions in future. I hope Mr W. will repent, and Miss W., and all of that sinful lot. You've been visited with affliction, and I hope it may do you good; but you'd better have come here. Mr W. had better have come here, and Miss W. too. The best wish I could give you, Mr Copperfield, and give all of you gentlemen, is, that you could be took up and brought here. When I think of my past follies, and my present state, I am sure it would be best for you. I pity all who ain't brought here!"

He sneaked back into his cell, amidst a little chorus of approbation; and both Traddles and I experienced a great relief when he was locked in.

It was a characteristic feature in this repentance, that I was fain to ask what these two men had done, to be there at all. That appeared to be the last thing about which they had anything to say. I addressed myself to one of the two warders, who, I suspected from certain latent indications in their faces, knew pretty well what all this stir was worth.

"Do you know," said I, as we walked along the passage, "what felony was Number Twenty Seven's last 'folly'?"

The answer was that it was a Bank case.

"A fraud on the Bank of England?" I asked.

"Yes, sir. Fraud, forgery, and conspiracy. He and some others. He set the others on. It was a deep plot for a large sum. Sentence, transportation for life. Twenty Seven was the knowingest bird of the lot, and had very nearly kept himself safe; but not quite. The Bank was just able to put salt upon his tail—and only just."

"Do you know Twenty Eight's offence?"

"Twenty Eight," returned my informant, speaking throughout in a low tone, and looking over his shoulder as we walked along the passage, to guard himself from being overheard, in such an unlawful reference to these Immaculates, by Creakle and the rest; "Twenty Eight (also transportation) got a place, and robbed a young master of a matter of two hundred and fifty pounds in money and valuables, the night before they were going abroad. I particularly recollect his case, from his being took by a dwarf."

"A what?"

"A little woman. I have forgot her name?"

"Not Mowcher?"

"That's it! He had eluded pursuit, and was going to America in a flaxen wig, and whiskers, and such a complete disguise as never you see in all your born days; when the little woman, being in Southampton, met him walking along the street—picked him out with her sharp eye in a moment—ran betwixt his legs to upset him—and held on to him like grim Death."

"Excellent Miss Mowcher!" cried I.

"You'd have said so, if you had seen her, standing on a chair in the witness-box at the trial, as I did," said my friend. "He cut her face right open, and pounded her in the most brutal manner, when she took him; but she never loosed her hold till he was locked up. She held so tight to him, in fact, that the officers were obliged to take 'em both together. She gave her evidence in the gamest way, and was highly complimented by the Bench, and cheered right home to her lodgings. She said in Court that she'd have took him single-handed (on account of what she knew concerning him), if he had been Samson. And it's my belief she would!"

It was mine too, and I highly respected Miss Mowcher for it.

We had now seen all there was to see. It would have been in vain to represent to such a man as the Worshipful Mr Creakle, that Twenty Seven and Twenty Eight were perfectly consistent and unchanged; that exactly what they were then, they had always been; that the hypocritical knaves were just the subjects to make that sort of profession in such a place; that they knew its market-value at least as well as we did, in the immediate service it would do them when they were expatriated; in a word, that it was a rotten, hollow, painfully-suggestive piece of business altogether. We left them to their system and themselves, and went home wondering.

"Perhaps it's a good thing, Traddles," said I, "to have an unsound Hobby ridden hard; for it's the sooner ridden to death."

"I hope so," replied Traddles.

Chapter LXII

A LIGHT SHINES ON MY WAY

THE year came round to Christmas-time, and I had been at home above two months. I had seen Agnes frequently. However loud the general voice might be in giving me encouragement, and however fervent the emotions and endeavours to which it roused me, I heard her lightest word of praise as I heard nothing else.

At least once a week, and sometimes oftener, I rode over there, and passed the evening. I usually rode back at night; for the old unhappy sense was always hovering about me now—most sorrowfully when I left her—and I was glad to be up and out, rather than wandering over the past in weary wakefulness or miserable dreams. I wore away the longest part of many wild sad nights, in those rides; reviving, as I went, the thoughts that had occupied me in my long absence.

Or, if I were to say rather that I listened to the echoes of those thoughts, I should better express the truth. They spoke to me from afar off. I had put them at a distance, and accepted my inevitable place. When I read to Agnes what I wrote; when I saw her listening face; moved her to smiles or tears; and heard her cordial voice so earnest on the shadowy events of that imaginative world in which I lived; I thought what a fate mine might have been—but only thought so, as I had thought after I was married to Dora, what I could have wished my wife to be.

My duty to Agnes, who loved me with a love, which, if I disquieted, I wronged most selfishly and poorly, and could never restore; my matured assurance that I, who had worked out my own destiny, and won what I had impetuously set my heart on, had no right to murmur, and must bear; comprised what I felt and what I had learned. But I loved her: and now it even became some consolation to me, vaguely to conceive a distant day when I might blamelessly avow it; when all this should be over; when I could say "Agnes, so it was when I came home; and now I am old, and I never have loved since!"

She did not once show me any change in herself. What she always had been to me, she still was; wholly unaltered.

Between my aunt and me there had been something, in this connexion, since the night of my return, which I cannot call a restraint, or an avoidance of the subject, so much as an implied understanding that we thought of it together, but did not shape our thoughts into words. When, according to our old custom, we sat before the fire at night, we often fell into this train, as naturally, and as consciously to each other, as if we had unreservedly said so. But we preserved an unbroken silence. I believed that she had read, or partly read, my thoughts that night; and that she fully comprehended why I gave mine no more distinct expression.

This Christmas-time being come, and Agnes having reposed no new confidence in me, a doubt that had several times arisen in my mind—whether she could have that perception of the true state of my breast, which restrained her with the apprehension of giving me pain—began to oppress me heavily. If that were so, my sacrifice was nothing; my plainest obligation to her unfulfilled; and every poor action I had shrunk from, I was hourly doing. I resolved to set this right beyond all doubt;—if such a barrier were between us, to break it down at once with a determined hand.

It was—what lasting reason have I to remember it!—a cold, harsh, winter day. There had been snow, some hours before; and it lay, not deep, but hard-frozen on the ground. Out at sea, beyond my window, the wind blew ruggedly from the north. I had been thinking of it, sweeping over those mountain wastes of snow in Switzerland, then inaccessible to any human foot; and had been speculating which was the lonelier, those solitary regions, or a deserted ocean.

"Riding today, Trot?" said my aunt, putting her head in at the door.

"Yes," said I, "I am going over to Canterbury. It's a good day for a ride."

"I hope your horse may think so too," said my aunt; "but at present he is holding down his head and his ears, standing before the door there, as if he thought his stable preferable."

My aunt, I may observe, allowed my horse on the forbidden ground, but had not at all relented towards the donkeys.

"He will be fresh enough, presently!" said I.

"The ride will do his master good, at all events," observed my aunt, glancing at the papers on my table. "Ah, child, you pass a good many hours here! I never thought, when I used to read books, what work it was to write them."

"It's work enough to read them, sometimes," I returned. "As to the writing, it has its own charms, aunt."

"Ah! I see!" said my aunt. "Ambition, love of approbation, sympathy, and much more, I suppose? Well: go along with you!"

"Do you know anything more," said I, standing composedly before her—she had patted me on the shoulder, and sat down in my chair—"of that attachment of Agnes?"

She looked up in my face a little while, before replying:

"I think I do, Trot."

"Are you confirmed in your impression?" I inquired.

"I think I am, Trot."

She looked so steadfastly at me: with a kind of doubt, or pity, or suspense in her affection: that I summoned the stronger determination to show her a perfectly cheerful face.

"And what is more, Trot—" said my aunt.

"Yes!"

"I think Agnes is going to be married."

"God bless her!" said I, cheerfully.

"God bless her!" said my aunt, "and her husband too!"

I echoed it, parted from my aunt, and went lightly downstairs, mounted, and rode away. There was greater reason than before to do what I had resolved to do.

How well I recollect the wintry ride! The frozen particles of ice, brushed from the blades of grass by the wind, and borne across my face; the hard clatter of the horse's hoofs, beating a tune upon the ground; the stiff-tilled soil; the snowdrift, lightly eddying in the chalk-pit as the breeze ruffled it; the smoking team with the waggon of old hay, stopping to breathe on the hill-top, and shaking their bells musically; the whitened slopes and sweeps of Down-land lying against the dark sky, as if they were drawn on a huge slate!

I found Agnes alone. The little girls had gone to their own homes now, and she was alone by the fire, reading. She put down her book on seeing me come in; and having welcomed me as usual, took her work-basket and sat in one of the old-fashioned windows.

I sat beside her on the window-seat, and we talked of what I was doing, and when it would be done, and of the progress I had made since my last visit. Agnes was very cheerful; and laughingly predicted that I should soon become too famous to be talked to, on such subjects.

"So I make the most of the present time, you see," said Agnes, "and talk to you while I may."

As I looked at her beautiful face, observant of her work, she raised her mild clear eyes, and saw that I was looking at her.

"You are thoughtful today, Trotwood!"

"Agnes, shall I tell you what about? I came to tell you."

She put aside her work, as she was used to do when we were seriously discussing anything; and gave me her whole attention.

"My dear Agnes, do you doubt my being true to you?"

"No!" she answered, with a look of astonishment.

"Do you doubt my being what I always have been to you?"

"No!" she answered, as before.

"Do you remember that I tried to tell you, when I came home, what a debt of gratitude I owed you, dearest Agnes, and how fervently I felt towards you?"

"I remember it," she said, gently, "very well."

"You have a secret," said I. "Let me share it, Agnes."

She cast down her eyes, and trembled.

"I could hardly fail to know, even if I had not heard—but from other lips than yours, Agnes, which seems strange—that there is someone upon whom you have bestowed the treasure of your love. Do not shut me out of what concerns your happiness so nearly! If you can trust me, as you say you can, and as I know you may, let me be your friend, your brother, in this matter, of all others!"

With an appealing, almost a reproachful, glance, she rose from the window; and hurrying across the room as if without knowing where, put her hands before her face, and burst into such tears as smote me to the heart.

And yet they awakened something in me, bringing promise to my heart. Without my knowing why, these tears allied themselves with the quietly sad smile which was so fixed in my remembrance, and shook me more with hope than fear or sorrow.

"Agnes! Sister! Dearest! What have I done?"

"Let me go away, Trotwood. I am not well. I am not myself. I will speak to you by and by—another time. I will write to you. Don't speak to me now. Don't! don't!"

I sought to recollect what she had said, when I had spoken to her on that former night, of her affection needing no return. It seemed a very world that I must search through in a moment.

"Agnes, I cannot bear to see you so, and think that I have been the cause. My dearest girl, dearer to me than anything in life, if you are unhappy, let me share your unhappiness. If you are in need of help or counsel, let me try to give it to you. If you have indeed a burden on your heart, let me try to lighten it. For whom do I live now, Agnes, if it is not for you!"

"Oh, spare me! I am not myself! Another time!" was all I could distinguish.

Was it a selfish error that was leading me away? Or, having once a clue to hope, was there something opening to me that I had not dared to think of?

"I must say more. I cannot let you leave me so! For Heaven's sake, Agnes, let us not mistake each other after all these years, and all that has come and gone with them! I must speak plainly. If you have any lingering thought that I could envy the happiness you will confer; that I could not resign you to a dearer protector, of your own choosing; that I could not, from my removed place, be a contented witness of your joy; dismiss it, for I don't deserve it! I have not suffered quite in vain. You have not taught me quite in vain. There is no alloy of self in what I feel for you."

She was quiet now. In a little time, she turned her pale face towards me, and said in a low voice, broken here and there, but very clear,

"I owe it to your pure friendship for me, Trotwood—which, indeed, I do not doubt—to tell you, you are mistaken. I can do no more. If I have sometimes, in the course of years, wanted help and counsel, they have come to me. If I have sometimes been unhappy, the feeling has passed away. If I have ever had a burden on my heart, it has been lightened for me. If I have any secret, it is—no new one; and is—not what you suppose. I cannot reveal it, or divide it. It has long been mine, and must remain mine."

"Agnes! Stay! A moment!"

She was going away, but I detained her. I clasped my arm about her waist. "In the course of years!" "It is not a new one!" New thoughts and hopes were whirling through my mind, and all the colours of my life were changing.

"Dearest Agnes! Whom I so respect and honour—whom I so devotedly love! When I came here today, I thought that nothing could have wrested this confession from me. I thought I could have kept it in my bosom all our lives, till we were old. But, Agnes, if

I have indeed any new-born hope that I may ever call you something more than Sister, widely different from Sister!—"

Her tears fell fast; but they were not like those she had lately shed, and I saw my hope brighten in them.

"Agnes! Ever my guide, and best support! If you had been more mindful of yourself, and less of me, when we grew up here together, I think my heedless fancy never would have wandered from you. But you were so much better than I, so necessary to me in every boyish hope and disappointment, that to have you to confide in, and rely upon in everything, became a second nature, supplanting for the time the first and greater one of loving you as I do!"

Still weeping, but not sadly—joyfully! And clasped in my arms as she had never been, as I had thought she never was to be!

"When I loved Dora—fondly, Agnes, as you know—"

"Yes!" she cried, earnestly. "I am glad to know it!"

"When I loved her—even then, my love would have been incomplete, without your sympathy. I had it, and it was perfected. And when I lost her, Agnes, what should I have been without you, still!"

Closer in my arms, nearer to my heart, her trembling hand upon my shoulder, her sweet eyes shining through her tears, on mine!

"I went away, dear Agnes, loving you. I stayed away, loving you. I returned home, loving you!"

And now, I tried to tell her of the struggle I had had, and the conclusion I had come to. I tried to lay my mind before her, truly, and entirely. I tried to show her how I had hoped I had come into the better knowledge of myself and of her; how I had resigned myself to what that better knowledge brought; and how I had come there, even that day, in my fidelity to this. If she did so love me (I said) that she could take me for her husband, she could do so, on no deserving of mine, except upon the truth of my love for her, and the trouble in which it had ripened to be what it was; and hence it was that I revealed it. And O, Agnes, even out of thy true eyes, in that same time, the spirit of my child-wife looked upon me, saying it was well; and winning me, through thee, to tenderest recollections of the Blossom that had withered in its bloom!

"I am so blest, Trotwood—my heart is so overcharged—but there is one thing I must say."

"Dearest, what?"

She laid her gentle hands upon my shoulders, and looked calmly in my face.

"Do you know, yet, what it is?"

"I am afraid to speculate on what it is. Tell me, my dear."

"I have loved you all my life!"

O, we were happy, we were happy! Our tears were not for the trials (hers so much the greater) through which we had come to be thus, but for the rapture of being thus, never to be divided more!

We walked, that winter evening, in the fields together; and the blessed calm within us seemed to be partaken by the frosty air. The early stars began to shine while we were lingering on, and looking up to them, we thanked our GOD for having guided us to this tranquillity.

We stood together in the same old-fashioned window at night, when the moon was shining; Agnes with her quiet eyes raised up to it; I following her glance. Long miles of road then opened out before my mind; and, toiling on, I saw a ragged way-worn boy, forsaken and neglected, who should come to call even the heart now beating against mine, his own.

It was nearly dinner-time next day when we appeared before my aunt. She was up in my study, Peggotty said: which it was her pride to keep in readiness and order for me. We found her, in her spectacles, sitting by the fire.

"Goodness me!" said my aunt, peering through the dusk, "who's this you're bringing home?"

"Agnes," said I.

As we had arranged to say nothing at first, my aunt was not a little discomfited. She darted a hopeful glance at me, when I said "Agnes"; but seeing that I looked as usual, she took off her spectacles in despair, and rubbed her nose with them.

She greeted Agnes heartily, nevertheless; and we were soon in the lighted parlour downstairs, at dinner. My aunt put on her spectacles twice or thrice, to take another look at me, but as often took them off again, disappointed, and rubbed her nose with them. Much to the discomfiture of Mr Dick, who knew this to be a bad symptom.

"By the by, aunt," said I, after dinner; "I have been speaking to Agnes about what you told me."

"Then, Trot," said my aunt, turning scarlet, "you did wrong, and broke your promise."

"You are not angry, aunt, I trust? I am sure you won't be, when you learn that Agnes is not unhappy in any attachment."

"Stuff and nonsense!" said my aunt.

As my aunt appeared to be annoyed, I thought the best way was to cut her annoyance short. I took Agnes in my arm to the back of her chair, and we both leaned over her. My aunt, with one clap of her hands, and one look through her spectacles, immediately went into hysterics, for the first and only time in all my knowledge of her.

The hysterics called up Peggotty. The moment my aunt was restored, she flew at Peggotty, and calling her a silly old creature, hugged her with all her might. After that, she hugged Mr Dick (who was highly honoured, but a good deal surprised); and after that, told them why. Then, we were all happy together.

I could not discover whether my aunt, in her last short conversation with me, had fallen on a pious fraud, or had really mistaken the state of my mind. It was quite enough, she said, that she had told me Agnes was going to be married; and that I now knew better than anyone how true it was.

We were married within a fortnight. Traddles and Sophy, and Doctor and Mrs Strong, were the only guests at our quiet wedding. We left them full of joy; and drove away together. Clasped in my embrace, I held the source of every worthy aspiration I had ever had; the centre of myself, the circle of my life, my own, my wife; my love of whom was founded on a rock!

"Dearest husband!" said Agnes. "Now that I may call you by that name, I have one thing more to tell you."

"Let me hear it, love."

"It grows out of the night when Dora died. She sent you for me."

"She did."

"She told me that she left me something. Can you think what it was?"

I believed I could. I drew the wife who had so long loved me, closer to my side.

"She told me that she made a last request to me, and left me a last charge."

"And it was—"

"That only I would occupy this vacant place."

And Agnes laid her head upon my breast, and wept; and I wept with her, though we were so happy.

Chapter LXIII

A VISITOR

WHAT I have purposed to record is nearly finished; but there is yet an incident conspicuous in my memory, on which it often rests with delight, and without which one thread in the web I have spun, would have a ravelled end.

I had advanced in fame and fortune, my domestic joy was perfect, I had been married ten happy years. Agnes and I were sitting by the fire, in our house in London, one night in spring, and three of our children were playing in the room, when I was told that a stranger wished to see me.

He had been asked if he came on business, and had answered No; he had come for the pleasure of seeing me, and had come a long way. He was an old man, my servant said, and looked like a farmer.

As this sounded mysterious to the children, and moreover was like the beginning of a favourite story Agnes used to tell them, introductory to the arrival of a wicked old Fairy in a cloak who hated everybody, it produced some commotion. One of our boys laid his head in his mother's lap to be out of harm's way, and little Agnes (our eldest child) left her doll in a chair to represent her, and thrust out her little heap of golden curls from between the window-curtains, to see what happened next.

"Let him come in here!" said I.

There soon appeared, pausing in the dark doorway as he entered, a hale, grey-haired old man. Little Agnes, attracted by his looks, had run to bring him in, and I had not yet clearly seen his face, when my wife, starting up, cried out to me, in a pleased and agitated voice, that it was Mr Peggotty!

It *was* Mr Peggotty. An old man now, but in a ruddy, hearty, strong old age. When our first emotion was over, and he sat before the fire with the children on his knees, and the blaze shining on his face, he looked, to me, as vigorous and robust, withal as handsome, an old man, as ever I had seen.

"Mas'r Davy," said he. And the old name in the old tone fell so naturally on my ear! "Mas'r Davy, 'tis a joyful hour as I see you, once more, 'long with your own trew wife!"

"A joyful hour indeed, old friend!" cried I.

"And these heer pretty ones," said Mr Peggotty. "To look at these heer flowers! Why, Mas'r Davy, you was but the heighth of the littlest of these, when I first see you! When Em'ly warn't no bigger, and our poor lad were *but* a lad!"

"Time has changed me more than it has changed you since then," said I. "But, let these dear rogues go to bed; and as no house in England but this must hold you, tell me where to send for your luggage (is the old black bag among it, that went so far, I wonder!), and then, over a glass of Yarmouth grog, we will have the tidings of ten years!"

"Are you alone?" asked Agnes.

"Yes, ma'am," he said, kissing her hand, "quite alone."

We sat him between us, not knowing how to give him welcome enough; and as I began to listen to his old familiar voice, I could have fancied he was still pursuing his long journey in search of his darling niece.

"It's a mort of water," said Mr Peggotty, "fur to come across, and on'y stay a matter of fower weeks. But water ('specially when 'tis salt) comes nat'ral to me; and friends is dear, and I am heer.—Which is verse," said Mr Peggotty, surprised to find it out, "though I hadn't such intentions."

"Are you going back those many thousand miles, so soon?" asked Agnes.

"Yes, ma'am," he returned. "I giv the promise to Em'ly, afore I come away. You see, I doen't grow younger as the years comes round, and if I hadn't sailed as 'twas, most like I shouldn't never have done 't. And it's allus been on my mind, as I *must* come and see Mas'r Davy and your own sweet blooming self, in your wedded happiness, afore I got to be too old."

He looked at us, as if he could never feast his eyes on us sufficiently. Agnes laughingly put back some scattered locks of his grey hair, that he might see us better.

"And now tell us," said I, "everything relating to your fortunes."

"Our fortuns, Mas'r Davy," he rejoined, "is soon told. We haven't fared nohows, but fared to thrive. We've allus thrived. We've worked as we ought to 't, and maybe we lived a leetle hard at first or so, but we have allus thrived. What with sheep-farming, and what with stock-farming, and what with one thing and what with t' other, we are as well to do, as well could be. Theer's been kiender a blessing fell upon us," said Mr Peggotty, reverentially inclining his head, "and we've done nowt but prosper. That is, in the long run. If not yesterday, why then today. If not today, why then tomorrow."

"And Emily?" said Agnes and I, both together.

"Em'ly," said he, "arter you left her, ma'am—and I never heerd her saying of her prayers at night, t' other side the canvas screen, when we was settled in the Bush, but what I heerd your name—and arter she and me lost sight of Mas'r Davy, that theer shining sundown—was that low, at first, that, if she had know'd then what Mas'r Davy kep from us so kind and thowtful, 'tis my opinion she'd have drooped away. But theer was some poor folks aboard as had illness among 'em, and she took care of *them;* and theer was the children in our company, and she took care of *them;* and so she got to be busy, and to be doing good, and that helped her."

"When did she first hear of it?" I asked.

"I kep it from her arter I heerd on 't," said Mr Peggotty, "going on nigh a year. We was living then in a solitary place, but among the beautifullest trees, and with the roses a-covering our Beein to the roof. Theer come along one day, when I was out a-working on the land, a traveller from our own Norfolk or Suffolk in England (I doen't rightly mind which), and of course we took him in, and giv him to eat and drink, and made him welcome. We all do that, all the colony over. He'd got an old newspaper with him, and some other account in print of the storm. That's how she know'd it. When I came home at night, I found she know'd it."

He dropped his voice as he said these words, and the gravity I so well remembered overspread his face.

"Did it change her much?" we asked.

"Aye, for a good long time," he said, shaking his head; "if not to this present hour. But I think the solitoode done her good. And she had a deal to mind in the way of poultry and the like, and minded of it, and come through. I wonder," he said thoughtfully, "if you could see my Em'ly now, Mas'r Davy, whether you'd know her!"

"Is she so altered?" I inquired.

"I doen't know. I see her ev'ry day, and doen't know; but, oddtimes, I have thowt so. A slight figure," said Mr Peggotty, looking at the fire, "kiender worn; soft, sorrowful, blue eyes; a delicate face; a pritty head, leaning a little down; a quiet voice and way— timid a'most. That's Em'ly!"

We silently observed him as he sat, still looking at the fire.

"Some thinks," he said, "as her affection was ill-bestowed; some, as her marriage was broken off by death. No one knows how 'tis. She might have married well, a mort of times, 'but, uncle,' she says to me, 'that's gone for ever.' Cheerful along with me; retired when others is by; fond of going any distance fur to teach a child, or fur to tend a sick person, or fur to do some kindness tow'rds a young girl's wedding (and she's done a many, but has never seen one); fondly loving of her uncle; patient; liked by young and old; sowt out by all that has any trouble. That's Em'ly!"

He drew his hand across his face, and with a half-suppressed sigh looked up from the fire.

"Is Martha with you yet?" I asked.

"Martha," he replied, "got married, Mas'r Davy, in the second year. A young man, a farm-labourer, as come by us on his way to market with his mas'r's drays—a journey of over five hundred mile, theer and back—made offers fur to take her fur his wife (wives is very scarce theer), and then to set up fur their two selves in the Bush. She spoke to me fur to tell him her trew story. I did. They was married, and they live fower hundred mile away from any voices but their own and the singing birds."

"Mrs Gummidge?" I suggested.

It was a pleasant key to touch, for Mr Peggotty suddenly burst into a roar of laughter, and rubbed his hands up and down his legs, as he had been accustomed to do when he enjoyed himself in the long-shipwrecked boat.

"Would you believe it!" he said. "Why, someun even made offer fur to marry *her!* If a ship's cook that was turning settler, Mas'r Davy, didn't make offers fur to marry Missis Gummidge, I'm Gormed—and I can't say no fairer than that!"

I never saw Agnes laugh so. This sudden ecstasy on the part of Mr Peggotty was so delightful to her, that she could not leave off laughing; and the more she laughed the more she made me laugh, and the greater Mr Peggotty's ecstasy became, and the more he rubbed his legs.

"And what did Mrs Gummidge say?" I asked, when I was grave enough.

"If you'll believe me," returned Mr Peggotty, "Missis Gummidge, 'stead of saying 'thank you, I'm much obleeged to you, I ain't a-going fur to change my condition at my time of life,' up'd with a bucket as was standing by, and laid it over that theer ship's cook's head 'till he sung out fur help, and I went in and reskied of him."

Mr Peggotty burst into a great roar of laughter, and Agnes and I both kept him company.

"But I must say this, for the good creetur," he resumed, wiping his face, when we were quite exhausted; "she has been all she said she'd be to us, and more. She's the willingest, the trewest, the honestest-helping woman, Mas'r Davy, as ever draw'd the breath of life. I have never know'd her to be lone and lorn, for a single minute, not even when the colony was all afore us, and we was new to it. And thinking of the old 'un is a thing she never done, I do assure you, since she left England!"

"Now, last, not least, Mr Micawber," said I. "He has paid off every obligation he incurred here—even to Traddles's bill, you remember my dear Agnes—and therefore we may take it for granted that he is doing well. But what is the latest news of him?"

Mr Peggotty, with a smile, put his hand in his breast-pocket, and produced a flat-folded, paper parcel, from which he took out, with much care, a little odd-looking newspaper.

"You are to understan', Mas'r Davy," said he, "as we have left the Bush now, being so well to do; and have gone right away round to Port Middlebay Harbour, wheer theer's what *we* call a town."

"Mr Micawber was in the Bush near you?" said I.

"Bless you, yes," said Mr Peggotty, "and turned to with a will. I never wish to meet a better gen'l'man for turning to with a will. I've seen that theer bald head of his a perspiring in the sun, Mas'r Davy, till I a'most thowt it would have melted away. And now he's a Magistrate."

"A Magistrate, eh?" said I.

Mr Peggotty pointed to a certain paragraph in the newspaper, where I read aloud as follows, from the *Port Middlebay Times:*

> "The public dinner to our distinguished fellow-colonist and townsman, WILKINS MICAWBER, ESQUIRE, Port Middlebay District Magistrate, came off yesterday in the large room of the Hotel, which was crowded to suffocation. It is estimated that not fewer than forty-seven persons must have been accommodated with dinner at one time, exclusive of the company in the passage and on the stairs. The beauty, fashion, and exclusiveness of Port Middlebay, flocked to do honour to one so deservedly esteemed, so highly talented, and so widely popular. Doctor Mell (of Colonial Salem-House Grammar School, Port Middlebay) presided, and on his right sat the distinguished guest. After the removal of the cloth, and the singing of Non Nobis (beautifully executed, and in which we were at no loss to distinguish the bell-like notes of that gifted amateur, WILKINS MICAWBER, ESQUIRE, JUNIOR), the usual loyal and patriotic toasts were severally given and rapturously received. Doctor Mell, in a speech replete with feeling, then proposed 'Our distinguished Guest, the ornament of our town. May he never leave us but to better himself, and may his success among us be such as to render his bettering himself impossible!' The cheering with which the toast was received defies description. Again and again it rose and fell, like the waves of ocean. At length all was hushed, and WILKINS MICAWBER, ESQUIRE, presented himself to return thanks. Far be it from us, in the present comparatively imperfect state of the resources of our establishment, to endeavour to follow our distinguished townsman through the smoothly-flowing periods of his polished and highly-ornate address! Suffice it to observe, that it was a masterpiece of eloquence; and that those passages in which he more particularly traced his own successful career to its source, and warned the younger portion of his auditory from the shoals of ever incurring pecuniary liabilities which they were unable to liquidate, brought a tear into the manliest eye present. The remaining toasts were DOCTOR MELL; MRS MICAWBER (who gracefully bowed her acknowledgements from the side-door, where a galaxy of beauty was elevated on chairs, at once to witness and adorn the gratifying scene), MRS RIDGER BEGS (late Miss Micawber); MRS MELL; WILKINS MICAWBER, ESQUIRE, JUNIOR (who convulsed the assembly by humorously remarking that he found himself unable to return thanks in a speech, but would do so, with their permission in a song); MRS MICAWBER's FAMILY (well known, it is needless to remark, in the mother-country), &c. &c. &c. At the conclusion of the proceedings the

tables were cleared as if by art-magic for dancing. Among the votaries of TERPSI-
CHORE, who disported themselves until Sol gave warning for departure, Wilkins
Micawber, Esquire, Junior, and the lovely and accomplished Miss Helena, fourth
daughter of Doctor Mell, were particularly remarkable."

I was looking back to the name of Doctor Mell, pleased to have discovered, in these
happier circumstances, Mr Mell, formerly poor pinched usher to my Middlesex magistrate, when Mr Peggotty pointing to another part of the paper, my eyes rested on my own
name, and I read thus:

"TO DAVID COPPERFIELD, ESQUIRE,
"THE EMINENT AUTHOR.

"My Dear Sir,
   "Years have elapsed, since I had an opportunity of ocularly perusing the lineaments, now familiar to the imaginations of a considerable portion of the civilized
world.
   "But, my dear sir, though estranged (by the force of circumstances over which
I have had no control) from the personal society of the friend and companion of my
youth, I have not been unmindful of his soaring flight. Nor have I been debarred,

Though seas between us braid ha" roared,

(BURNS) from participating in the intellectual feasts he has spread before us.
   "I cannot, therefore, allow of the departure from this place of an individual
whom we mutually respect and esteem, without, my dear sir, taking this public
opportunity of thanking you, on my own behalf, and, I may undertake to add, on that
of the whole of the Inhabitants of Port Middlebay, for the gratification of which you
are the ministering agent.
   "Go on, my dear sir! You are not unknown here, you are not unappreciated.
Though 'remote,' we are neither 'unfriended,' 'melancholy,' nor (I may add) 'slow.'
Go on, my dear sir, in your Eagle course! The inhabitants of Port Middlebay may at
least aspire to watch it, with delight, with entertainment, with instruction!
   "Among the eyes elevated towards you from this portion of the globe, will ever
be found, while it has light and life,

"The
"Eye
"Appertaining to
"WILKINS MICAWBER,
"MAGISTRATE."

I found, on glancing at the remaining contents of the newspaper, that Mr Micawber
was a diligent and esteemed correspondent of that Journal. There was another letter from
him in the same paper, touching a bridge; there was an advertisement of a collection of
similar letters by him, to be shortly republished, in a neat volume, "with considerable
additions"; and, unless I am very much mistaken the Leading Article was his also.
   We talked much of Mr Micawber, on many other evenings while Mr Peggotty
remained with us. He lived with us during the whole term of his stay,—which, I think,
was something less than a month,—and his sister and my aunt came to London to see
him. Agnes and I parted from him aboard-ship, when he sailed; and we shall never part
from him more, on earth.
   But before he left, he went with me to Yarmouth, to see a little tablet I had put up
in the churchyard to the memory of Ham. While I was copying the plain inscription for

him at his request, I saw him stoop, and gather a tuft of grass from the grave and a little earth.

"For Em'ly," he said, as he put it in his breast. "I promised, Mas'r Davy."

Chapter LXIV

A LAST RETROSPECT

A ND now my written story ends. I look back, once more—for the last time—before I close these leaves.

I see myself, with Agnes at my side, journeying along the road of life. I see our children and our friends around us; and I hear the roar of many voices, not indifferent to me as I travel on.

What faces are the most distinct to me in the fleeting crowd? Lo, these; all turning to me as I ask my thoughts the question!

Here is my aunt, in stronger spectacles, an old woman of four-score years and more, but upright yet, and a steady walker of six miles at a stretch in winter weather.

Always with her, here comes Peggotty, my good old nurse, likewise in spectacles, accustomed to do needle-work at night very close to the lamp, but never sitting down to it without a bit of wax-candle, a yard-measure in a little house, and a work-box with a picture of St Paul's upon the lid.

The cheeks and arms of Peggotty, so hard and red in my childish days, when I wondered why the birds didn't peck her in preference to apples, are shrivelled now; and her eyes, that used to darken their whole neighbourhood in her face, are fainter (though they glitter still); but her rough forefinger, which I once associated with a pocket nutmeg-grater, is just the same, and when I see my least child catching at it as it totters from my aunt to her, I think of our little parlour at home, when I could scarcely walk. My aunt's old disappointment is set right, now. She is godmother to a real living Betsey Trotwood; and Dora (the next in order) says she spoils her.

There is something bulky in Peggotty's pocket. It is nothing smaller than the Crocodile Book, which is in rather a dilapidated condition by this time, with divers of the leaves torn and stitched across, but which Peggotty exhibits to the children as a precious relic. I find it very curious to see my own infant face, looking up at me from the crocodile stories; and to be reminded by it of my old acquaintance Brooks of Sheffield.

Among my boys, this summer holiday time, I see an old man making giant kites, and gazing at them in the air, with a delight for which there are no words. He greets me rapturously, and whispers, with many nods and winks, "Trotwood, you will be glad to hear that I shall finish the Memorial when I have nothing else to do, and that your aunt's the most extraordinary woman in the world, sir!"

Who is this bent lady, supporting herself by a stick, and showing me a countenance in which there are some traces of old pride and beauty, feebly contending with a querulous, imbecile, fretful wandering of the mind? She is in a garden; and near her stands a sharp, dark, withered woman, with a white scar on her lip. Let me hear what they say.

"Rosa, I have forgotten this gentleman's name."

Rosa bends over her, and calls to her, "Mr Copperfield."

"I am glad to see you, sir. I am sorry to observe you are in mourning. I hope Time will be good to you."

Her impatient attendant scolds her, tells her I am not in mourning, bids her look again, tries to rouse her.

"You have seen my son, sir," says the elder lady. "Are you reconciled?"

Looking fixedly at me, she puts her hand to her forehead, and moans. Suddenly, she cries, in a terrible voice, "Rosa, come to me. He is dead!" Rosa kneeling at her feet, by turns caresses her, and quarrels with her; now fiercely telling her, "I loved him better than you ever did!"—now soothing her to sleep on her breast, like a sick child. Thus I leave them; thus I always find them; thus they wear their time away, from year to year.

What ship comes sailing home from India, and what English lady is this, married to a growling old Scotch Crœsus with great flaps of ears? Can this be Julia Mills?

Indeed it is Julia Mills, peevish and fine, with a black man to carry cards and letters to her on a golden salver, and a copper-coloured woman in linen, with a bright handkerchief round her head, to serve her Tiffin in her dressing-room. But Julia keeps no diary in these days; never sings Affection's Dirge; eternally quarrels with the old Scotch Crœsus, who is a sort of yellow bear with a tanned hide. Julia is steeped in money to the throat, and talks and thinks of nothing else. I liked her better in the Desert of Sahara.

Or perhaps this *is* the Desert of Sahara! For, though Julia has a stately house, and mighty company, and sumptuous dinners every day, I see no green growth near her; nothing that can ever come to fruit or flower. What Julia calls "society," I see; among it Mr Jack Maldon, from his Patent Place, sneering at the hand that gave it him, and speaking to me of the Doctor as "so charmingly antique." But when society is the name for such hollow gentlemen and ladies, Julia, and when its breeding is professed indifference to everything that can advance or can retard mankind, I think we must have lost ourselves in that same Desert of Sahara, and had better find the way out.

And lo, the Doctor, always our good friend, labouring at his Dictionary (somewhere about the letter D), and happy in his home and wife. Also the Old Soldier, on a considerably reduced footing, and by no means so influential as in days of yore!

Working at his chambers in the Temple, with a busy aspect, and his hair (where he is not bald) made more rebellious than ever by the constant friction of his lawyer's-wig, I come, in a later time, upon my dear old Traddles. His table is covered with thick piles of papers; and I say, as I look around me:

"If Sophy were your clerk, now, Traddles, she would have enough to do!"

"You may say that, my dear Copperfield! But those were capital days, too, in Holborn Court! Were they not?"

"When she told you you would be a Judge? But it was not the town talk *then*!"

"At all events," says Traddles, "if I ever am one—"

"Why, you know you will be."

"Well, my dear Copperfield, *when* I am one, I shall tell the story, as I said I would."

We walk away, arm in arm. I am going to have a family dinner with Traddles. It is Sophy's birthday; and, on our road, Traddles discourses to me of the good fortune he has enjoyed.

"I really have been able, my dear Copperfield, to do all that I had most at heart. There's the Reverend Horace promoted to that living at four hundred and fifty pounds a year; there are our two boys receiving the very best education, and distinguishing themselves as steady scholars and good fellows; there are three of the girls married very comfortably; there are three more living with us; there are three more keeping house for the Reverend Horace since Mrs Crewler's decease; and all of them happy."

"Except—" I suggest.

"Except the Beauty," says Traddles. "Yes. It was very unfortunate that she should marry such a vagabond. But there was a certain dash and glare about him that caught her. However, now we have got her safe at our house, and got rid of him, we must cheer her up again."

Traddles's house is one of the very houses—or it easily may have been—which he and Sophy used to parcel out, in their evening walks. It is a large house; but Traddles keeps his papers in his dressing-room and his boots with his papers; and he and Sophy squeeze themselves into upper rooms, reserving the best bedrooms for the Beauty and the girls. There is no room to spare in the house; for more of "the girls" are here, and always are here, by some accident or other, than I know how to count. Here, when we go in, is a crowd of them, running down to the door, and handing Traddles about to be kissed, until he is out of breath. Here, established in perpetuity, is the poor Beauty, a widow with a little girl; here, at dinner on Sophy's birthday, are the three married girls with their three husbands, and one of the husband's brothers, and another husband's cousin, and another husband's sister, who appears to me to be engaged to the cousin. Traddles, exactly the same simple, unaffected fellow as he ever was, sits at the foot of the large table like a Patriarch; and Sophy beams upon him, from the head, across a cheerful space that is certainly not glittering with Britannia metal.

And now, as I close my task, subduing my desire to linger yet, these faces fade away. But one face, shining on me like a Heavenly light by which I see all other objects, is above them and beyond them all. And that remains.

I turn my head, and see it, in its beautiful serenity, beside me.

My lamp burns low, and I have written far into the night; but the dear presence, without which I were nothing, bears me company.

O Agnes, O my soul, so may thy face be by me when I close my life indeed; so may I, when realities are melting from me, like the shadows which I now dismiss, still find thee near me, pointing upward!

The Old Curiosity Shop

Chapter I

NIGHT is generally my time for walking. In the summer I often leave home early in the morning, and roam about fields and lanes all day, or even escape for days or weeks together, but saving in the country I seldom go out until after dark, though, Heaven be thanked, I love its light and feel the cheerfulness it sheds upon the earth, as much as any creature living.

I have fallen insensibly into this habit, both because it favours my infirmity and because it affords me greater opportunity of speculating on the characters and occupations of those who fill the streets. The glare and hurry of broad noon are not adapted to idle pursuits like mine; a glimpse of passing faces caught by the light of a street-lamp or a shop-window is often better for my purpose than their full revelation in the daylight, and, if I must add the truth, night is kinder in this respect than day, which too often destroys an air-built castle at the moment of its completion, without the smallest ceremony or remorse.

That constant pacing to and fro, that never-ending restlessness, that incessant tread of feet wearing the rough stones smooth and glossy—is it not a wonder how the dwellers in narrow ways can bear to hear it! Think of a sick man in such a place as Saint Martin's Court, listening to the footsteps, and in the midst of pain and weariness obliged, despite himself (as though it were a task he must perform) to detect the child's step from the man's, the slipshod beggar from the booted exquisite, the lounging from the busy, the dull heel of the sauntering outcast from the quick tread of an expectant pleasure-seeker—think of the hum and noise being always present to his senses, and of the stream of life that will not stop, pouring on, on, on, through all his restless dreams, as if he were condemned to lie dead but conscious, in a noisy churchyard, and had no hope of rest for centuries to come.

Then the crowds for ever passing and repassing on the bridges (on those which are free of toll at least) where many stop on fine evenings looking listlessly down upon the water with some vague idea that by and by it runs between green banks which grow wider and wider until at last it joins the broad vast sea—where some halt to rest from heavy loads and think as they look over the parapet that to smoke and lounge away one's life, and lie sleeping in the sun upon a hot tarpaulin, in a dull, slow, sluggish barge, must be happiness unalloyed—and where some, and a very different class, pause with heavier loads than they, remembering to have heard or read in some old time that drowning was not a hard death, but of all means of suicide the easiest and best.

Covent Garden Market at sunrise too, in the spring or summer, when the fragrance of sweet flowers is in the air, overpowering even the unwholesome streams of last night's debauchery, and driving the dusky thrush, whose cage has hung outside a garret window all night long, half mad with joy! Poor bird! the only neighbouring thing at all akin to the other little captives, some of whom, shrinking from the hot hands of drunken purchasers, lie drooping on the path already, while others, soddened by close contact, await the time when they shall be watered and freshened up to please more sober company, and make old clerks who pass them on their road to business, wonder what has filled their breasts with visions of the country.

But my present purpose is not to expatiate upon my walks. An adventure which I am about to relate, and to which I shall recur at intervals, arose out of one of these rambles, and thus I have been led to speak of them by way of preface.

One night I had roamed into the City, and was walking slowly on in my usual way, musing upon a great many things, when I was arrested by an inquiry, the purport of which did not reach me, but which seemed to be addressed to myself, and was preferred in a soft sweet voice that struck me very pleasantly. I turned hastily round and found at my elbow a pretty little girl, who begged to be directed to a certain street at a considerable distance, and indeed in quite another quarter of the town.

"It is a very long way from here," said I, "my child."

"I know that, sir," she replied timidly. "I am afraid it is a very long way, for I came from there to-night."

"Alone?" said I, in some surprise.

"Oh, yes, I don't mind that, but I am a little frightened now, for I had lost my road."

"And what made you ask it of me? Suppose I should tell you wrong."

"I am sure you will not do that," said the little creature, "you are such a very old gentleman, and walk so slow yourself."

I cannot describe how much I was impressed by this appeal and the energy with which it was made, which brought a tear into the child's clear eye, and made her slight figure tremble as she looked up into my face.

"Come," said I, "I'll take you there."

She put her hand in mine as confidingly as if she had known me from her cradle, and we trudged away together: the little creature accommodating her pace to mine, and rather seeming to lead and take care of me than I to be protecting her. I observed that every now and then she stole a curious look at my face, as if to make quite sure that I was not deceiving her, and that these glances (very sharp and keen they were too) seemed to increase her confidence at every repetition.

For my part, my curiosity and interest were at least equal to the child's, for child she certainly was, although I thought it probable from what I could make out, that her very small and delicate frame imparted a peculiar youthfulness to her appearance. Though more scantily attired than she might have been she was dressed with perfect neatness, and betrayed no marks of poverty or neglect.

"Who has sent you so far by yourself?" said I.

"Somebody who is very kind to me, sir."

"And what have you been doing?"

"That, I must not tell," said the child firmly.

There was something in the manner of this reply which caused me to look at the little creature with an involuntary expression of surprise; for I wondered what kind of errand it might be that occasioned her to be prepared for questioning. Her quick eye seemed to read my thoughts, for as it met mine she added that there was no harm in what she had been doing, but it was a great secret—a secret which she did not even know herself.

This was said with no appearance of cunning or deceit, but with an unsuspicious frankness that bore the impress of truth. She walked on as before, growing more familiar with me as we proceeded and talking cheerfully by the way, but she said no more about her home, beyond remarking that we were going quite a new road and asking if it were a short one.

While we were thus engaged, I revolved in my mind a hundred different explanations of the riddle and rejected them every one. I really felt ashamed to take advantage of the ingenuousness or grateful feeling of the child for the purpose of gratifying my curiosity. I love these little people; and it is not a slight thing when they, who are so fresh from God, love us. As I had felt pleased at first by her confidence I determined to deserve it, and to do credit to the nature which had prompted her to repose it in me.

There was no reason, however, why I should refrain from seeing the person who had inconsiderately sent her to so great a distance by night and alone, and as it was not improbable that if she found herself near home she might take farewell of me and deprive me of the opportunity, I avoided the most frequented ways and took the most intricate, and thus it was not until we arrived in the street itself that she knew where we were. Clapping her hands with pleasure and running on before me for a short distance, my little acquaintance stopped at a door and remaining on the step till I came up knocked at it when I joined her.

A part of this door was of glass unprotected by any shutter, which I did not observe at first, for all was very dark and silent within, and I was anxious (as indeed the child was also) for an answer to our summons. When she had knocked twice or thrice there was a noise as if some person were moving inside, and at length a faint light appeared through the glass which, as it approached very slowly, the bearer having to make his way through a great many scattered articles, enabled me to see both what kind of person it was who advanced and what kind of place it was through which he came.

It was a little old man with long grey hair, whose face and figure as he held the light above his head and looked before him as he approached, I could plainly see. Though much altered by age, I fancied I could recognise in his spare and slender form something of that delicate mould which I had noticed in the child. Their bright blue eyes were certainly alike, but his face was so deeply furrowed and so very full of care, that here all resemblance ceased.

The place through which he made his way at leisure was one of those receptacles for old and curious things which seem to crouch in odd corners of this town and to hide their musty treasures from the public eye in jealousy and distrust. There were suits of mail standing like ghosts in armour here and there, fantastic carvings brought from monkish cloisters, rusty weapons of various kinds, distorted figures in china and wood and iron and ivory: tapestry and strange furniture that might have been designed in dreams. The haggard aspect of the little old man was wonderfully suited to the place; he might have groped among old churches and tombs and deserted houses and gathered all the spoils with his own hands. There was nothing in the whole collection but was in keeping with himself: nothing that looked older or more worn than he.

As he turned the key in the lock, he surveyed me with some astonishment which was not diminished when he looked from me to my companion. The door being opened, the child addressed him as grandfather, and told him the little story of our companionship.

"Why, bless thee, child," said the old man, patting her on the head, "how couldst thou miss thy way? What if I had lost thee, Nell!"

"I would have found my way back to *you*, grandfather," said the child boldly; "never fear."

The old man kissed her, then turning to me and begging me to walk in, I did so. The door was closed and locked. Preceding me with the light, he led me through the place I had already seen from without, into a small sitting-room behind, in which was another door opening into a kind of closet, where I saw a little bed that a fairy might have slept in, it looked so very small and was so prettily arranged. The child took a candle and tripped into this little room, leaving the old man and me together.

"You must be tired, sir," said he as he placed a chair near the fire, how can I thank you?"

"By taking more care of your grandchild another time, my good friend," I replied.

"More care!" said the old man in a shrill voice, "more care of Nelly! Why, who ever loved a child as I love Nell?"

He said this with such evident surprise that I was perplexed what answer to make, and the more so because coupled with something feeble and wandering in his manner, there were in his face marks of deep and anxious thought which convinced me that he could not be, as I had been at first inclined to suppose, in a state of dotage or imbecility.

"I don't think you consider——" I began.

"I don't consider!" cried the old man interrupting me, "I don't consider her! Ah, how little you know of the truth! Little Nelly, little Nelly!"

It would be impossible for any man, I care not what his form of speech might be, to express more affection than the dealer in curiosities did, in these four words. I waited for him to speak again, but he rested his chin upon his hand and shaking his head twice or thrice fixed his eyes upon the fire.

While we were sitting thus in silence, the door of the closet opened, and the child returned, her light brown hair hanging loose about her neck, and her face flushed with the haste she had made to rejoin us. She busied herself immediately in preparing supper, and while she was thus engaged I remarked that the old man took an opportunity of observing me more closely than he had done yet. I was surprised to see that all this time everything was done by the child, and that there appeared to be no other persons but ourselves in the house. I took advantage of a moment when she was absent to venture a hint on this point, to which the old man replied that there were few grown persons as trustworthy or as careful as she.

"It always grieves me," I observed, roused by what I took to be his selfishness, "it always grieves me to contemplate the initiation of children into the ways of life, when they are scarcely more than infants. It checks their confidence and simplicity—two of the best qualities that Heaven gives them—and demands that they share our sorrows before they are capable of entering into our enjoyments."

"It will never check hers," said the old man looking steadily at me, "the springs are too deep. Besides, the children of the poor know but few pleasures. Even the cheap delights of childhood must be bought and paid for."

"But—forgive me for saying this—you are surely not so very poor"—said I.

"She is not my child, sir," returned the old man. "Her mother was, and she was poor. I save nothing—not a penny—though I live as you see, but"—he laid his hand upon my arm and leant forward to whisper—"she shall be rich one of these days, and a fine lady. Don't you think ill of me, because I use her help. She gives it cheerfully as you see, and it would break her heart if she knew that I suffered anybody else to do for me what her little hands could undertake. I don't consider!"—he cried with sudden querulousness, "why, God knows that this one child is the thought and object of my life, and yet he never prospers me—no, never!"

At this juncture, the subject of our conversation again returned, and the old man motioning to me to approach the table, broke off, and said no more.

We had scarcely begun our repast when there was a knock at the door by which I had entered, and Nell bursting into a hearty laugh, which I was rejoiced to hear, for it was childlike and full of hilarity, said it was no doubt dear old Kit come back at last.

"Foolish Nell!" said the old man fondling with her hair. "She always laughs at poor Kit."

The child laughed again more heartily than before, and I could not help smiling from pure sympathy. The little old man took up a candle and went to open the door. When he came back, Kit was at his heels.

Kit was a shock-headed, shambling, awkward lad with an uncommonly wide mouth, very red cheeks, a turned-up nose, and certainly the most comical expression of face I ever saw. He stopped short at the door on seeing a stranger, twirled in his hand a perfectly round old hat without any vestige of a brim, and resting himself now on one leg and now on the other and changing them constantly, stood in the doorway, looking into the parlour with the most extraordinary leer I ever beheld. I entertained a grateful feeling towards the boy from that minute, for I felt that he was the comedy of the child's life.

"A long way, wasn't it, Kit?" said the little old man.

"Why, then, it was a goodish stretch, master," returned Kit.

"Did you find the house easily?"

"Why, then, not over and above easy, master," said Kit.

"Of course you have come back hungry?"

"Why, then, I do consider myself rather so, master," was the answer.

The lad had a remarkable manner of standing sideways as he spoke, and thrusting his head forward over his shoulder, as if he could not get at his voice without that accompanying action. I think he would have amused one anywhere, but the child's exquisite enjoyment of his oddity, and the relief it was to find that there was something she associated with merriment in a place that appeared so unsuited to her, were quite irresistible. It was a great point too that Kit himself was flattered by the sensation he created, and after several efforts to preserve his gravity, burst into a loud roar, and so stood with his mouth wide open and his eyes nearly shut, laughing violently.

The old man had again relapsed into his former abstraction and took no notice of what passed, but I remarked that when her laugh was over, the child's bright eyes were dimmed with tears, called forth by the fulness of heart with which she welcomed her uncouth favourite after the little anxiety of the night. As for Kit himself (whose laugh had been all the time one of that sort which very little would change into a cry) he carried a large slice of bread and meat and a mug of beer into a corner, and applied himself to disposing of them with great voracity.

"Ah!" said the old man turning to me with a sigh, as if I had spoken to him but that moment, "you don't know what you say when you tell me that I don't consider her."

"You must not attach too great weight to a remark founded on first appearances, my friend," said I.

"No," returned the old man thoughtfully, "no. Come hither, Nell."

The little girl hastened from her seat, and put her arm about his neck.

"Do I love thee, Nell?" said he. "Say—do I love thee, Nell, or no?"

The child only answered by her caresses, and laid her head upon his breast.

"Why dost thou sob?" said the grandfather, pressing her closer to him and glancing towards me. "Is it because thou know'st I love thee, and dost not like that I should seem to doubt it by my question? Well, well—then let us say I love thee dearly."

"Indeed, indeed you do," replied the child with great earnestness, "Kit knows you do."

Kit, who in despatching his bread and meat had been swallowing two-thirds of his knife at every mouthful with the coolness of a juggler, stopped short in his operations on being thus appealed to, and bawled "Nobody isn't such a fool as to say he doosn't," after which he incapacitated himself for further conversation by taking a most prodigious sandwich at one bite.

"She is poor now"—said the old man, patting the child's cheek, "but I say again that the time is coming when she shall be rich. It has been a long time coming, but it must come at last; a very long time, but it surely must come. It has come to other men who do nothing but waste and riot. When *will* it come to me!"

"I am very happy as I am, grandfather," said the child.

"Tush, tush!" returned the old man, "thou dost not know—how should'st thou!" Then he muttered again between his teeth, "The time must come, I am very sure it must. It will be all the better for coming late"; and then he sighed and fell into his former musing state, and still holding the child between his knees appeared to be insensible to everything around him. By this time it wanted but a few minutes of midnight and I rose to go, which recalled him to himself.

"One moment, sir," he said. "Now, Kit—near midnight, boy, and you still here! Get home, get home, and be true to your time in the morning, for there's work to do. Good night! There, bid him good night, Nell, and let him be gone!"

"Good night, Kit," said the child, her eyes lighting up with merriment and kindness.

"Good night, Miss Nell," returned the boy.

"And thank this gentleman," interposed the old man, "but for whose care I might have lost my little girl to-night."

"No, no, master," said Kit, "that won't do, that won't."

"What do you mean?" cried the old man.

"I'd have found her, master," said Kit, "I'd have found her. I'll bet that I'd find her if she was above ground, I would, as quick as anybody, master. Ha, ha, ha!"

Once more opening his mouth and shutting his eyes, and laughing like a stentor, Kit gradually backed to the door, and roared himself out.

Free of the room, the boy was not slow in taking his departure; when he had gone, and the child was occupied in clearing the table, the old man said:

"I haven't seemed to thank you, sir, enough for what you have done to-night, but I do thank you humbly and heartily, and so does she, and her thanks are better worth than mine. I should be sorry that you went away and thought I was unmindful of your goodness, or careless of her—I am not indeed."

I was sure of that, I said, from what I had seen. "But," I added, "may I ask you a question?"

"Ay, sir," replied the old man, "what is it?"

"This delicate child," said I, "with so much beauty and intelligence—has she nobody to care for her but you? Has she no other companion or adviser?"

"No," he returned, looking anxiously in my face, "no, and she wants no other."

"But are you not fearful," said I, "that you may misunderstand a charge so tender? I am sure you mean well, but are you quite certain that you know how to execute such a trust as this? I am an old man, like you, and I am actuated by an old man's concern in all that is young and promising. Do you not think that what I have seen of you and this little creature to-night must have an interest not wholly free from pain?"

"Sir," rejoined the old man after a moment's silence, "I have no right to feel hurt at what you say. It is true that in many respects I am the child, and she the grown person—that you have seen already. But waking or sleeping, by night or day, in sickness or health, she is the one object of my care, and if you knew of how much care, you would look on me with different eyes, you would indeed. Ah! it's a weary life for an old man—a weary, weary life—but there is a great end to gain and that I keep before me."

Seeing that he was in a state of excitement and impatience, I turned to put on an outer coat which I had thrown off on entering the room, purposing to say no more. I was surprised to see the child standing patiently by with a cloak upon her arm, and in her hand a hat and stick."

"Those are not mine, my dear," said I.

"No," returned the child quietly, "they are grandfather's."

"But he is not going out to-night."

"Oh, yes, he is," said the child, with a smile.

"And what becomes of you, my pretty one?"

"Me! I stay here of course. I always do."

I looked in astonishment towards the old man, but he was, or feigned to be, busied in the arrangement of his dress. From him I looked back to the slight gentle figure of the child. Alone! In that gloomy place all the long, dreary night.

She evinced no consciousness of my surprise, but cheerfully helped the old man with his cloak, and when he was ready took a candle to light us out. Finding that we did not follow as she expected, she looked back with a smile and waited for us. The old man showed by his face that he plainly understood the cause of my hesitation, but he merely signed to me with an inclination of the head to pass out of the room before him, and remained silent. I had no resource but to comply.

When we reached the door, the child setting down the candle, turned to say good night and raised her face to kiss me. Then she ran to the old man, who folded her in his arms and bade God bless her.

"Sleep soundly, Nell," he said in a low voice, "and angels guard thy bed! Do not forget thy prayers, my sweet."

"No, indeed," answered the child fervently, "they make me feel so happy!"

"That's well; I know they do; they should." said the old man. "Bless thee a hundred times! Early in the morning I shall be home."

"You'll not ring twice," returned the child. "The bell wakes me, even in the middle of a dream."

With this, they separated. The child opened the door (now guarded by a shutter which I had heard the boy put up before he left the house) and with another farewell whose clear and tender note I have recalled a thousand times, held it until we had passed out. The old man paused a moment while it was gently closed and fastened on the inside, and, satisfied that this was done, walked on at a slow pace. At the street-corner he stopped, and regarding me with a troubled countenance said that our ways were widely different and that he must take his leave. I would have spoken, but summoning up more alacrity than might have been expected in one of his appearance, he hurried away. I could see that twice or thrice he looked back as if to ascertain if I were still watching him, or perhaps to assure himself that I was not following at a distance. The obscurity of the night favoured his disappearance, and his figure was soon beyond my sight.

I remained standing on the spot where he had left me, unwilling to depart, and yet unknowing why I should loiter there. I looked wistfully into the street we had lately quitted, and after a time directed my steps that way. I passed and repassed the house, and stopped and listened at the door; all was dark, and silent as the grave.

Yet I lingered about, and could not tear myself away, thinking of all possible harm that might happen to the child—of fires and robberies and even murder—and feeling as if some evil must ensue if I turned my back upon the place. The closing of a door or window in the street brought me before the curiosity-dealer's once more; I crossed the road and looked up at the house to assure myself that the noise had not come from there. No, it was black, cold, and lifeless as before.

There were few passengers astir; the street was sad and dismal, and pretty well my own. A few stragglers from the theatres hurried by, and now and then I turned aside to avoid some noisy drunkard as he reeled homewards, but these interruptions were not frequent and soon ceased. The clocks struck one. Still I paced up and down, promising myself that every time should be the last, and breaking faith with myself on some new plea as often as I did so.

The more I thought of what the old man had said, and of his looks and bearing, the less I could account for what I had seen and heard. I had a strong misgiving that his nightly absence was for no good purpose. I had only come to know the fact through the innocence of the child, and though the old man was by at the time, and saw my undisguised surprise, he had preserved a strange mystery upon the subject and offered no word of explanation. These reflections naturally recalled again more strongly than before his haggard face, his wandering manner, his restless anxious looks. His affection for the child might not be inconsistent with villany of the worst kind; even that very affection was in itself an extraordinary contradiction, or how could he leave her thus? Disposed as I was to think badly of him, I never doubted that his love for her was real. I could not admit the thought, remembering what had passed between us, and the tone of voice in which he had called her by her name.

"Stay here of course," the child had said in answer to my question, "I always do!" What could take him from home by night, and every night! I called up all the strange tales I had ever heard of dark and secret deeds committed in great towns and escaping detection for a long series of years; wild as many of these stories were, I could not find one adapted to this mystery, which only became the more impenetrable, in proportion as I sought to solve it.

Occupied with such thoughts as these, and a crowd of others all tending to the same point, I continued to pace the street for two long hours; at length the rain began to descend heavily, and then overpowered by fatigue though no less interested than I had been at first, I engaged the nearest coach and so got home. A cheerful fire was blazing on the hearth, the lamp burnt brightly, my clock received me with its old familiar welcome; everything was quiet, warm and cheering, and in happy contrast to the gloom and darkness I had quitted.

But all that night, waking or in my sleep, the same thoughts recurred and the same images retained possession of my brain. I had ever before me the old dark murky rooms—the gaunt suits of mail with their ghostly silent air—the faces all awry, grinning from wood and stone—the dust and rust and worm that lives in wood—and alone in the midst of all this lumber and decay and ugly age, the beautiful child in her gentle slumber, smiling through her light and sunny dreams.

Chapter II

AFTER combating, for nearly a week, the feeling which impelled me to revisit the place I had quitted under the circumstances already detailed, I yielded to it at length; and determining that this time I would present myself by the light of day, bent my steps thither early in the afternoon.

I walked past the house, and took several turns in the street, with that kind of hesitation which is natural to a man who is conscious that the visit he is about to pay is unexpected, and may not be very acceptable. However, as the door of the shop was shut, and it did not appear likely that I should be recognised by those within, if I continued merely to pass up and down before it, I soon conquered this irresolution, and found myself in the curiosity-dealer's warehouse.

The old man and another person were together in the back part, and there seemed to have been high words between them, for their voices which were raised to a very loud pitch suddenly stopped on my entering, and the old man advancing hastily towards me, said in a tremulous tone that he was very glad I had come.

"You interrupted us at a critical moment," he said, pointing to the man whom I had found in company with him; "this fellow will murder me one of these days. He would have done so, long ago, if he had dared."

"Bah! You would swear away my life if you could," returned the other, after bestowing a stare and a frown on me; "we all know that!"

"I almost think I could," cried the old man, turning feebly upon him. "If oaths, or prayers, or words, could rid me of you, they should. I would be quit of you, and would be relieved if you were dead."

"I know it," returned the other. "I said so, didn't I? But neither oaths, nor prayers, nor words, *will* kill me, and therefore I live, and mean to live."

"And his mother died!" cried the old man, passionately clasping his hands and looking upward; "and this is Heaven's justice!"

The other stood lounging with his foot upon a chair, and regarded him with a contemptuous sneer. He was a young man of one-and-twenty or thereabouts; well made, and certainly handsome, though the expression of his face was far from prepossessing, having in common with his manner and even his dress, a dissipated, insolent air which repelled one.

"Justice or no justice," said the young fellow, "here I am and here I shall stop till such time as I think fit to go, unless you send for assistance to put me out—which you won't do, I know. I tell you again that I want to see my sister."

"*Your* sister!" said the old man bitterly.

"Ah! You can't change the relationship," returned the other. "If you could, you'd have done it long ago. I want to see my sister, that you keep cooped up here, poisoning her mind with your sly secrets and pretending an affection for her that you may work her to death, and add a few scraped shillings every week to the money you can hardly count. I want to see her; and I will."

"Here's a moralist to talk of poisoned minds! Here's a generous spirit to scorn scraped-up shillings!" cried the old man, turning from him to me. "A profligate, sir, who has forfeited every claim not only upon those who have the misfortune to be of his blood, but upon society which knows nothing of him but his misdeeds. A liar too," he added, in a lower voice as he drew closer to me, "who knows how dear she is to me, and seeks to wound me even there, because there is a stranger by."

"Strangers are nothing to me, grandfather," said the young fellow catching at the word, "nor I to them, I hope. The best they can do, is to keep an eye to their business and leave me to mine. There's a friend of mine waiting outside, and as it seems that I may have to wait some time, I'll call him in, with your leave."

Saying this, he stepped to the door, and looking down the street beckoned several times to some unseen person, who, to judge from the air of impatience with which these signals were accompanied, required a great quantity of persuasion to induce him to advance. At length there sauntered up, on the opposite side of the way—with a bad pretence of passing by accident—a figure conspicuous for its dirty smartness, which after a great many frowns and jerks of the head, in resistance of the invitation, ultimately crossed the road and was brought into the shop.

"There. It's Dick Swiveller," said the young fellow, pushing him in. "Sit down, Swiveller."

"But is the old min agreeable?" said Mr Swiveller in an undertone.

"Sit down," repeated his companion.

Mr Swiveller complied, and looking about him with a propitiatory smile, observed that last week was a fine week for the ducks, and this week was a fine week for the dust; he also observed that whilst standing by the post at the street-corner, he had observed a pig with a straw in his mouth issuing out of the tobacco-shop, from which appearance he augured that another fine week for the ducks was approaching, and that rain would certainly ensue. He furthermore took occasion to apologize for any negligence that might be perceptible in his dress, on the ground that last night he had had "the sun very strong in his eyes"; by which expression he was understood to convey to his hearers in the most delicate manner possible, the information that he had been extremely drunk.

"But what," said Mr Swiveller with a sigh, "what is the odds so long as the fire of soul is kindled at the taper of conwiviality, and the wing of friendship never moults a feather! What is the odds so long as the spirit is expanded by means of rosy wine, and the present moment is the least happiest of our existence!"

"You needn't act the chairman here," said his friend, half aside.

"Fred!" cried Mr Swiveller, tapping his nose, "a word to the wise is sufficient for them—we may be good and happy without riches, Fred. Say not another syllable. I know my cue; smart is the word. Only one little whisper, Fred—*is* the old min friendly?"

"Never you mind," replied his friend.

"Right again, quite right," said Mr Swiveller, "caution is the word, and caution is the act." With that, he winked as if in preservation of some deep secret, and folding his arms and leaning back in his chair, looked up at the ceiling with profound gravity.

It was perhaps not very unreasonable to suspect from what had already passed, that Mr Swiveller was not quite recovered from the effects of the powerful sunlight to which he had made allusion; but if no such suspicion had been awakened by his speech, his wiry hair, dull eyes, and sallow face would still have been strong witnesses against him. His attire was not, as he had himself hinted, remarkable for the nicest arrangement, but was in a state of disorder which strongly induced the idea that he had gone to bed in it. It consisted of a brown body-coat with a great many brass buttons up the front and only one behind, a bright check neckerchief, a plaid waistcoat, soiled white trousers, and a very limp hat, worn with the wrong side foremost, to hide a hole in the brim. The breast of his coat was ornamented with an outside pocket from which there peeped forth the cleanest end of a very large and very ill-favoured handkerchief; his dirty wristbands were

pulled down as far as possible and ostentatiously folded back over his cuffs; he displayed
no gloves, and carried a yellow cane having at the top a bone hand with the semblance
of a ring on its little finger and a black ball in its grasp. With all these personal advantages
(to which may be added a strong savour of tobacco-smoke, and a prevailing greasiness
of appearance) Mr Swiveller leant back in his chair with his eyes fixed on the ceiling, and
occasionally pitching his voice to the needful key, obliged the company with a few bars
of an intensely dismal air, and then, in the middle of a note, relapsed into his former
silence.

The old man sat himself down in a chair, and, with folded hands, looked sometimes
at his grandson and sometimes at his strange companion, as if he were utterly powerless
and had no resource but to leave them to do as they pleased. The young man reclined
against a table at no great distance from his friend, in apparent indifference to everything
that had passed; and I—who felt the difficulty of any interference, notwithstanding that
the old man had appealed to me, both by words and looks—made the best feint I could
of being occupied in examining some of the goods that were disposed for sale, and
paying very little attention to the persons before me.

The silence was not of long duration, for Mr Swiveller, after favouring us with several
melodious assurances that his heart was in the Highlands, and that he wanted but his
Arab steed as a preliminary to the achievement of great feats of valour and loyalty,
removed his eyes from the ceiling and subsided into prose again.

"Fred," said Mr Swiveller stopping short, as if the idea had suddenly occurred to
him, and speaking in the same audible whisper as before, "*is* the old min friendly?"

"What does it matter?" returned his friend peevishly.

"No, but *is* he?" said Dick.

"Yes, of course. What do I care whether he is or not?"

Emboldened as it seemed by this reply to enter into a more general conversation,
Mr Swiveller plainly laid himself out to captivate our attention.

He began by remarking that soda-water, though a good thing in the abstract, was
apt to lie cold upon the stomach unless qualified with ginger, or a small infusion of
brandy, which latter article he held to be preferable in all cases, saving for the one
consideration of expense. Nobody venturing to dispute these positions, he proceeded to
observe that the human hair was a great retainer of tobacco-smoke, and that the young
gentlemen of Westminster and Eton, after eating vast quantities of apples to conceal any
scent of cigars from their anxious friends, were usually detected in consequence of their
heads possessing this remarkable property; whence he concluded that if the Royal
Society would turn their attention to the circumstance, and endeavour to find in the
resources of science a means of preventing such untoward revelations, they might
indeed be looked upon as benefactors to mankind. These opinions being equally incon-
trovertible with those he had already pronounced, he went on to inform us that Jamaica
rum, though unquestionably an agreeable spirit of great richness and flavour, had the
drawback of remaining constantly present to the taste next day; and nobody being
venturous enough to argue this point either, he increased in confidence and became yet
more companionable and communicative.

"It's a devil of a thing, gentlemen," said Mr Swiveller, "when relations fall out and
disagree. If the wing of friendship should never moult a feather, the wing of relationship
should never be clipped, but be always expanded and serene. Why should a grandson
and grandfather peg away at each other with mutual wiolence when all might be bliss
and concord? Why not jine hands and forget it?"

"Hold your tongue," said his friend.

"Sir," replied Mr Swiveller, "don't you interrupt the chair. Gentlemen, how does the case stand, upon the present occasion? Here is a jolly old grandfather—I say it with the utmost respect—and here is a wild young grandson. The jolly old grandfather says to the wild young grandson, 'I have brought you up and educated you, Fred; I have put you in the way of getting on in life; you have bolted a little out of the course, as young fellows often do; and you shall never have another chance, nor the ghost of half a one.' The wild young grandson makes answer to this and says, 'You're as rich as rich can be; you have been at no uncommon expense on my account, you're saving up piles of money for my little sister that lives with you in a secret, stealthy, hugger-muggering kind of way and with no manner of enjoyment—why can't you stand a trifle for your grown-up relation?' The jolly old grandfather unto this, retorts, not only that he declines to fork out with that cheerful readiness which is always so agreeable and pleasant in a gentleman of his time of life, but that he will blow up, and call names, and make reflections whenever they meet. Then the plain question is, an't it a pity that this state of things should continue, and how much better would it be for the old gentleman to hand over a reasonable amount of tin, and make it all right and comfortable?"

Having delivered this oration with a great many waves and flourishes of the hand, Mr Swiveller abruptly thrust the head of his cane into his mouth as if to prevent himself from impairing the effect of his speech by adding one other word.

"Why do you hunt and persecute me, God help me!" said the old man turning to his grandson. "Why do you bring your profligate companions here? How often am I to tell you that my life is one of care and self-denial, and that I am poor?"

"How often am I to tell you," returned the other, looking coldly at him, "that I know better?"

"You have chosen your own path," said the old man. "Follow it. Leave Nell and me to toil and work."

"Nell will be a woman soon," returned the other, "and, bred in your faith, she'll forget her brother unless he shows himself sometimes."

"Take care," said the old man with sparkling eyes, "that she does not forget you when you would have her memory keenest. Take care that the day don't come when you walk barefoot in the streets, and she rides by in a gay carriage of her own."

"You mean when she has your money?" retorted the other. "How like a poor man he talks!"

"And yet," said the old man dropping his voice and speaking like one who thinks aloud, "how poor we are, and what a life it is! The cause is a young child's, guiltless of all harm or wrong, but nothing goes well with it! Hope and patience, hope and patience!"

These words were uttered in too low a tone to reach the ears of the young men. Mr Swiveller appeared to think that they implied some mental struggle consequent upon the powerful effect of his address, for he poked his friend with his cane and whispered his conviction that he had administered "a clincher," and that he expected a commission on the profits. Discovering his mistake after a while, he appeared to grow rather sleepy and discontented, and had more than once suggested the propriety of an immediate departure, when the door opened, and the child herself appeared.

Chapter III

T HE child was closely followed by an elderly man of remarkably hard features and forbidding aspect, and so low in stature as to be quite a dwarf, though his head and face were large enough for the body of a giant. His black eyes were restless, sly, and cunning; his mouth and chin, bristly with the stubble of a coarse hard beard; and his complexion was one of that kind which never looks clean or wholesome. But what added most to the grotesque expression of his face was a ghastly smile, which, appearing to be the mere result of habit and to have no connection with any mirthful or complacent feeling, constantly revealed the few discoloured fangs that were yet scattered in his mouth, and gave him the aspect of a panting dog. His dress consisted of a large high-crowned hat, a worn dark suit, a pair of capacious shoes, and a dirty white neckerchief sufficiently limp and crumpled to disclose the greater portion of his wiry throat. Such hair as he had was of a grizzled black, cut short and straight upon his temples, and hanging in a frowzy fringe about his ears. His hands, which were of a rough, coarse grain, were very dirty; his finger-nails were crooked, long, and yellow.

There was ample time to note these particulars, for besides that they were sufficiently obvious without very close observation, some moments elapsed before any one broke silence. The child advanced timidly towards her brother and put her hand in his, the dwarf (if we may call him so) glanced keenly at all present, and the curiosity-dealer, who plainly had not expected his uncouth visitor, seemed disconcerted and embarrassed.

"Ah!" said the dwarf, who with his hand stretched out above his eyes had been surveying the young man attentively, "that should be your grandson, neighbour!"

"Say rather that he should not be," replied the old man. "But he is."

"And that?" said the dwarf, pointing to Dick Swiveller.

"Some friend of his, as welcome here as he," said the old man.

"And that?" inquired the dwarf wheeling round and pointing straight at me.

"A gentleman who was so good as to bring Nell home the other night when she lost her way, coming from your house."

The little man turned to the child as if to chide her or express his wonder, but as she was talking to the young man, held his peace, and bent his head to listen.

"Well, Nelly," said the young fellow aloud. "Do they teach you to hate me, eh?"

"No, no. For shame. Oh, no!" cried the child.

"To love me, perhaps?" pursued her brother with a sneer.

"To do neither," she returned. "They never speak to me about you. Indeed they never do."

"I dare be bound for that," he said, darting a bitter look at the grandfather. "I dare be bound for that, Nell. Oh! I believe you there!"

"But I love you dearly, Fred," said the child.

"No doubt!"

"I do indeed, and always will," the child repeated with great emotion, "but oh! if you would leave off vexing him and making him unhappy, then I could love you more."

"I see!" said the young man, as he stooped carelessly over the child, and having kissed her, pushed her from him: "There—get you away now you have said your lesson. You needn't whimper. We part good friends enough, if that's the matter."

He remained silent, following her with his eyes, until she had gained her little room and closed the door; and then turning to the dwarf, said abruptly,

"Harkee, Mr——"

"Meaning me?" returned the dwarf. "Quilp is my name. You might remember. It's not a long one—Daniel Quilp."

"Harkee, Mr Quilp, then," pursued the other. "You have some influence with my grandfather there."

"Some," said Mr Quilp emphatically.

"And are in a few of his mysteries and secrets."

"A few," replied Quilp, with equal dryness.

"Then let me tell him once for all, through you, that I will come into and go out of this place as often as I like, so long as he keeps Nell here; and that if he wants to be quit of me, he must first be quit of her. What have I done to be made a bugbear of, and to be shunned and dreaded as if I brought the plague? He'll tell you that I have no natural affection; and that I care no more for Nell, for her own sake, than I do for him. Let him say so. I care for the whim, then, of coming to and fro and reminding her of my existence. I *will* see her when I please. That's my point. I came here to-day to maintain it, and I'll come here again fifty times with the same object and always with the same success. I said I would stop till I had gained it. I have done so, and now my visit's ended. Come, Dick."

"Stop!" cried Mr Swiveller, as his companion turned towards the door. "Sir!"

"Sir, I am your humble servant," said Mr Quilp, to whom the monosyllable was addressed.

"Before I leave the gay and festive scene, and halls of dazzling light, sir," said Mr Swiveller, "I will, with your permission, attempt a slight remark. I came here, sir, this day, under the impression that the old min was friendly."

"Proceed, sir," said Daniel Quilp; for the orator had made a sudden stop.

"Inspired by this idea and the sentiments it awakened, sir, and feeling as a mutual friend that badgering, baiting, and bullying, was not the sort of thing calculated to expand the souls and promote the social harmony of the contending parties, I took upon myself to suggest a course which is *the* course to be adopted on the present occasion. Will you allow me to whisper half a syllable, sir?"

Without waiting for the permission he sought, Mr Swiveller stepped up to the dwarf, and leaning on his shoulder and stooping down to get at his ear, said in a voice which was perfectly audible to all present,

"The watch-word to the old min is—fork."

"Is what?" demanded Quilp.

"Is fork, sir, fork," replied Mr Swiveller slapping his pocket. "You are awake, sir?"

The dwarf nodded. Mr Swiveller drew back and nodded likewise, then drew a little further back and nodded again, and so on. By these means he in time reached the door, where he gave a great cough to attract the dwarf's attention and gain an opportunity of expressing in dumb show, the closest confidence and most inviolable secrecy. Having performed the serious pantomime that was necessary for the due conveyance of these ideas, he cast himself upon his friend's track, and vanished.

"Humph!" said the dwarf with a sour look and a shrug of his shoulders, "so much for dear relations. Thank God I acknowledge none! Nor need you either," he added, turning to the old man, "if you were not as weak as a reed, and nearly as senseless."

"What would you have me do?" he retorted in a kind of helpless desperation. "It is easy to talk and sneer. What would you have me do?"

"What would *I* do if I was in your case?" said the dwarf.

"Something violent, no doubt."

"You're right there," returned the little man, highly gratified by the compliment, for such he evidently considered it; and grinning like a devil as he rubbed his dirty hands together. "Ask Mrs Quilp, pretty Mrs Quilp, obedient, timid, loving Mrs. Quilp. But that reminds me—I have left her all alone, and she will be anxious and know not a moment's peace till I return. I know she's always in that condition when I'm away, though she doesn't dare to say so, unless I lead her on and tell her she may speak freely and I won't be angry with her. Oh! well-trained Mrs Quilp!"

The creature appeared quite horrible with his monstrous head and little body, as he rubbed his hands slowly round, and round, and round again—with something fantastic even in his manner of performing this slight action—and, dropping his shaggy brows and cocking his chin in the air, glanced upward with a stealthy look of exultation that an imp might have copied and appropriated to himself.

"Here," he said, putting his hand into his breast and sidling up to the old man as he spoke; "I brought it myself for fear of accidents, as, being in gold, it was something large and heavy for Nell to carry in her bag. She need be accustomed to such loads betimes though, neighbour, for she will carry weight when you are dead."

"Heaven send she may! I hope so," said the old man with something like a groan.

"Hope so!" echoed the dwarf, approaching close to his ear; "neighbour, I would I knew in what good investment all these supplies are sunk. But you are a deep man, and keep your secret close."

"My secret!" said the other with a haggard look. "Yes, you're right—I—I—keep it close—very close."

He said no more, but taking the money turned away with a slow, uncertain step, and pressed his hand upon his head like a weary and dejected man. The dwarf watched him sharply, while he passed into the little sitting-room and locked it in an iron safe above the chimney-piece; and after musing for a short space, prepared to take his leave, observing that unless he made good haste, Mrs Quilp would certainly be in fits on his return.

"And so, neighbour," he added, "I'll turn my face homewards, leaving my love for Nelly and hoping she may never lose her way again, though her doing so *has* procured me an honour I didn't expect." With that he bowed and leered at me, and with a keen glance around which seemed to comprehend every object within his range of vision, however small or trivial, went his way.

I had several times essayed to go myself, but the old man had always opposed it and entreated me to remain. As he renewed his entreaties on our being left alone, and adverted with many thanks to the former occasion of our being together, I willingly yielded to his persuasions, and sat down, pretending to examine some curious minia-tures and a few old medals which he placed before me. It needed no great pressing to induce me to stay, for if my curiosity had been excited on the occasion of my first visit, it certainly was not diminished now.

Nell joined us before long, and bringing some needle-work to the table, sat by the old man's side. It was pleasant to observe the fresh flowers in the room, the pet bird with a green bough shading his little cage, the breath of freshness and youth which seemed to rustle through the old dull house and hover round the child. It was curious, but not so pleasant, to turn from the beauty and grace of the girl, to the stooping figure, care-worn face, and jaded aspect of the old man. As he grew weaker and more feeble, what would become of this lonely little creature; poor protector as he was, say that he died—what would her fate be, then?

The old man almost answered my thoughts, as he laid his hand on hers, and spoke aloud.

"I'll be of better cheer, Nell," he said; "there must be good fortune in store for thee—I do not ask it for myself, but thee. Such miseries must fall on thy innocent head without it, that I cannot believe but that, being tempted, it will come at last!"

She looked cheerfully into his face, but made no answer.

"When I think," said he, "of the many years—many in thy short life—that thou hast lived alone with me; of thy monotonous existence, knowing no companions of thy own age nor any childish pleasures; of the solitude in which thou hast grown to be what thou art, and in which thou hast lived apart from nearly all thy kind but one old man; I sometimes fear I have dealt hardly by thee, Nell."

"Grandfather!" cried the child in unfeigned surprise.

"Not in intention—no no," said he. "I have ever looked forward to the time that should enable thee to mix among the gayest and prettiest, and take thy station with the best. But I still look forward, Nell, I still look forward, and if I should be forced to leave thee, meanwhile, how have I fitted thee for struggles with the world? The poor bird yonder is as well qualified to encounter it, and be turned adrift upon its mercies—Hark! I hear Kit outside. Go to him, Nell, go to him."

She rose, and hurrying away, stopped, turned back, and put her arms about the old man's neck, then left him and hurried away again—but faster this time, to hide her falling tears.

"A word in your ear, sir," said the old man in a hurried whisper. "I have been rendered uneasy by what you said the other night, and can only plead that I have done all for the best—that it is too late to retract, if I could (though I cannot)—and that I hope to triumph yet. All is for her sake. I have borne great poverty myself, and would spare her the sufferings that poverty carries with it. I would spare her the miseries that brought her mother, my own dear child, to an early grave. I would leave her—not with resources which could be easily spent or squandered away, but with what would place her beyond the reach of want for ever. You mark me, sir? She shall have no pittance, but a fortune—Hush! I can say no more than that, now or at any other time, and she is here again!"

The eagerness with which all this was poured into my ear, the trembling of the hand with which he clasped my arm, the strained and starting eyes he fixed upon me, the wild vehemence and agitation of his manner, filled me with amazement. All that I had heard and seen, and a great part of what he had said himself, led me to suppose that he was a wealthy man. I could form no comprehension of his character, unless he were one of those miserable wretches who, having made gain the sole end and object of their lives and having succeeded in amassing great riches, are constantly tortured by the dread of poverty, and beset by fears of loss and ruin. Many things he had said which I had been at a loss to understand, were quite reconcileable with the idea thus presented to me, and at length I concluded that beyond all doubt he was one of this unhappy race.

The opinion was not the result of hasty consideration, for which indeed there was no opportunity at that time, as the child came back directly, and soon occupied herself in preparations for giving Kit a writing lesson, of which it seemed he had a couple every week, and one regularly on that evening, to the great mirth and enjoyment both of himself and his instructress. To relate how it was a long time before his modesty could be so far prevailed upon as to admit of his sitting down in the parlour, in the presence of an unknown gentleman—how, when he did sit down, he tucked up his sleeves and squared his elbows and put his face close to the copy-book and squinted horribly at the lines—how, from the very first moment of having the pen in his hand, he began to wallow in blots, and to daub himself with ink up to the very roots of his hair—how, if he did by accident form a letter properly, he immediately smeared it out again with his arm in his preparations to make another—how, at every fresh mistake, there was a fresh burst of merriment from the child and a louder and not less hearty laugh from poor Kit himself—and how there was all the way through, notwithstanding, a gentle wish on her part to teach, and an anxious desire on his to learn—to relate all these particulars would no doubt occupy more space and time than they deserve. It will be sufficient to say that the lesson was given—that evening passed and night came on—that the old man again grew restless and impatient—that he quitted the house secretly at the same hour as before—and that the child was once more left alone within its gloomy walls.

And now that I have carried this history so far in my own character and introduced these personages to the reader, I shall for the convenience of the narrative detach myself from its further course, and leave those who have prominent and necessary parts in it to speak and act for themselves.

Chapter IV

MR and Mrs Quilp resided on Tower Hill; and in her bower on Tower Hill Mrs Quilp was left to pine the absence of her lord, when he quitted her on the business which he has been already seen to transact.

Mr Quilp could scarcely be said to be of any particular trade or calling, though his pursuits were diversified and his occupations numerous. He collected the rents of whole colonies of filthy streets and alleys by the waterside, advanced money to the seamen and petty officers of merchant vessels, had a share in the ventures of divers mates of East Indiamen, smoked his smuggled cigars under the very nose of the Custom House, and made appointments on 'Change with men in glazed hats and round jackets pretty well every day. On the Surrey side of the river was a small rat-infested dreary yard called "Quilp's Wharf," in which were a little wooden counting-house burrowing all awry in the dust as if it had fallen from the clouds and ploughed into the ground; a few fragments of rusty anchors; several large iron rings; some piles of rotten wood; and two or three heaps of old sheet copper, crumpled, cracked, and battered. On Quilp's Wharf, Daniel Quilp was a ship-breaker, yet to judge from these appearances he must either have been a ship-breaker on a very small scale, or have broken his ships up very small indeed. Neither did the place present any extraordinary aspect of life or activity, as its only human occupant was an amphibious boy in a canvas suit, whose sole change of occupation was from sitting on the head of a pile and throwing stones into the mud when the tide was out, to standing with his hands in his pockets gazing listlessly on the motion and on the bustle of the river at high-water.

The dwarf's lodging on Tower Hill comprised, besides the needful accommodation for himself and Mrs Quilp, a small sleeping-closet for that lady's mother, who resided with the couple and waged perpetual war with Daniel; of whom, notwithstanding, she stood in no slight dread. Indeed, the ugly creature contrived by some means or other—

whether by his ugliness or his ferocity or his natural cunning is no great matter—to impress with a wholesome fear of his anger, most of those with whom he was brought into daily contact and communication. Over nobody had he such complete ascendancy as Mrs Quilp herself—a pretty little, mild-spoken, blue-eyed woman, who having allied herself in wedlock to the dwarf in one of those strange infatuations of which examples are by no means scarce, performed a sound practical penance for her folly, every day of her life.

It has been said that Mrs Quilp was pining in her bower. In her bower she was, but not alone, for besides the old lady her mother of whom mention has recently been made, there were present some half-dozen ladies of the neighbourhood who had happened by a strange accident (and also by a little understanding among themselves) to drop in one after another, just about tea-time. This being a season favourable to conversation, and the room being a cool, shady, lazy kind of place, with some plants at the open window shutting out the dust, and interposing pleasantly enough between the tea table within and the old Tower without, it is no wonder that the ladies felt an inclination to talk and linger, especially when there are taken into account the additional inducements of fresh butter, new bread, shrimps, and watercresses.

Now, the ladies being together under these circumstances, it was extremely natural that the discourse should turn upon the propensity of mankind to tyrannise over the weaker sex, and the duty that developed upon the weaker sex to resist that tyranny and assert their rights and dignity. It was natural for four reasons: firstly, because Mrs Quilp being a young woman and notoriously under the dominion of her husband ought to be excited to rebel; secondly, because Mrs Quilp's parent was known to be laudably shrewish in her disposition and inclined to resist male authority; thirdly, because each visitor wished to show for herself how superior she was in this respect to the generality of her sex; and fourthly, because the company being accustomed to scandalise each other in pairs, were deprived of their usual subject of conversation now that they were all assembled in close friendship, and had consequently no better employment than to attack the common enemy.

Moved by these considerations, a stout lady opened the proceedings by inquiring, with an air of great concern and sympathy, how Mr Quilp was; whereunto Mr Quilp's wife's mother replied sharply, "Oh! he was well enough—nothing much was ever the matter with him—and ill weeds were sure to thrive." All the ladies then sighed in concert, shook their heads gravely, and looked at Mrs Quilp as at a martyr.

"Ah!" said the spokeswoman, "I wish you'd give her a little of your advice, Mrs Jiniwin"—Mrs Quilp had been a Miss Jiniwin it should be observed—"nobody knows better than you, ma'am, what us women owe to ourselves."

"Owe indeed, ma'am!" replied Mrs Jiniwin. "When my poor husband, her dear father, was alive, if he had ever ventur'd a cross word to *me,* I'd have——" The good old lady did not finish the sentence, but she twisted off the head of a shrimp with a vindictiveness which seemed to imply that the action was in some degree a substitute for words. In this light it was clearly understood by the other party, who immediately replied with great approbation, "You quite enter into my feelings, ma'am, and it's jist what I'd do myself."

"But you have no call to do it," said Mrs Jiniwin. "Luckily for you, you have no more occasion to do it than I had."

"No woman need have, if she was true to herself," rejoined the stout lady.

"Do you hear that, Betsy?" said Mrs Jiniwin, in a warning voice. "How often have

I said the very same words to you, and almost gone down on my knees when I spoke 'em!"

Poor Mrs Quilp, who had looked in a state of helplessness from one face of condolence to another, coloured, smiled, and shook her head doubtfully. This was the signal for a general clamour, which beginning in a low murmur gradually swelled into a great noise in which everybody spoke at once, and all said that she being a young woman had no right to set up her opinions against the experiences of those who knew so much better; that it was very wrong of her not to take the advice of people who had nothing at heart but her good; that it was next door to being downright ungrateful to conduct herself in that manner; that if she had no respect for herself she ought to have some for other women, all of whom she compromised by her meekness; and that if she had no respect for other women, the time would come when other women would have no respect for her; and she would be very sorry for that, they could tell her. Having dealt out these admonitions, the ladies fell to a more powerful assault than they had yet made upon the mixed tea, new bread, fresh butter, shrimps, and watercresses, and said that their vexation was so great to see her going on like that, that they could hardly bring themselves to eat a single morsel.

"It's all very fine to talk," said Mrs Quilp with much simplicity, "but I know that if I was to die to-morrow, Quilp could marry anybody he pleased—now that he could, I know!"

There was quite a scream of indignation at this idea. Marry whom he pleased! They would like to see him dare to think of marrying any of them; they would like to see the faintest approach to such a thing. One lady (a widow) was quite certain she should stab him if he hinted at it.

"Very well," said Mrs Quilp, nodding her head, "as I said just now, it's very easy to talk, but I say again that I know—that I'm sure—Quilp has such a way with him when he likes, that the best-looking woman here couldn't refuse him if I was dead, and she was free, and he chose to make love to her. Come!"

Everybody bridled up at this remark, as much as to say "I know you mean me. Let him try—that's all." And yet for some hidden reason they were all angry with the widow, and each lady whispered in her neighbour's ear that it was very plain the said widow thought herself the person referred to, and what a puss she was!

"Mother knows," said Mrs Quilp, "that what I say is quite correct, for she often said so before we were married. Didn't you say so, mother?"

This inquiry involved the respected lady in rather a delicate position, for she certainly had been an active party in making her daughter Mrs Quilp, and, besides, it was not supporting the family credit to encourage the idea that she had married a man whom nobody else would have. On the other hand, to exaggerate the captivating qualities of her son-in-law would be to weaken the cause of revolt, in which all her energies were deeply engaged. Beset by these opposing considerations, Mrs Jiniwin admitted the powers of insinuation, but denied the right to govern, and with a timely compliment to the stout lady brought back the discussion to the point from which it had strayed.

"Oh! It's a sensible and proper thing indeed, what Mrs George has said!" exclaimed the old lady. "If women are only true to themselves!—But Betsy isn't, and more's the shame and pity."

"Before I'd let a man order me about as Quilp orders her," said Mrs. George; "before I'd consent to stand in awe of a man as she does of him, I'd—I'd kill myself, and write a letter first to say he did it!"

This remark being loudly commended and approved of, another lady (from the Minories) put in her word:

"Mr Quilp may be a very nice man," said this lady, "and I suppose there's no doubt he is, because Mrs Quilp says he is, and Mrs Jiniwin says he is, and they ought to know, or nobody does. But still he is not quite a—what one calls a handsome man, nor quite a young man neither, which might be a little excuse for him if anything could be; whereas his wife is young, and is good-looking, and is a woman—which is the great thing after all."

This last clause being delivered with extraordinary pathos, elicited a corresponding murmur from the hearers, stimulated by which the lady went on to remark that if such a husband was cross and unreasonable with such a wife, then——

"If he is!" interposed the mother, putting down her tea-cup and brushing the crumbs out of her lap, preparatory to making a solemn declaration. "If he is! He is the greatest tyrant that ever lived, she daren't call her soul her own, he makes her tremble with a word and even with a look, he frightens her to death, and she hasn't the spirit to give him a word back, no, not a single word."

Notwithstanding that the fact had been notorious beforehand to all the tea-drinkers, and had been discussed and expatiated on at every tea-drinking in the neighbourhood for the last twelve months, this official communication was no sooner made than they all began to talk at once and to vie with each other in vehemence and volubility. Mrs George remarked that people would talk, that people had often said this to her before, that Mrs Simmons then and there present had told her so twenty times, that she had always said, "No, Henrietta Simmons, unless I see it with my own eyes and hear it with my own ears, I never will believe it." Mrs Simmons corroborated this testimony and added strong evidence of her own. The lady from the Minories recounted a successful course of treatment under which she had placed her own husband, who, from manifesting one month after marriage unequivocal symptoms of the tiger, had by this means become subdued into a perfect lamb. Another lady recounted her own personal struggle and final triumph, in the course whereof she had found it necessary to call in her mother and two aunts, and to weep incessantly night and day for six weeks. A third, who in the general confusion could secure no other listener, fastened herself upon a young woman still unmarried who happened to be amongst them, and conjured her as she valued her own peace of mind and happiness to profit by this solemn occasion, to take example from the weakness of Mrs Quilp, and from that time forth to direct her whole thoughts to taming and subduing the rebellious spirit of man. The noise was at its height, and half the company had elevated their voices into a perfect shriek in order to drown the voices of the other half, when Mrs Jiniwin was seen to change colour and shake her forefinger stealthily, as if exhorting them to silence. Then, and not until then, Daniel Quilp himself, the cause and occasion of all this clamour, was observed to be in the room, looking on and listening with profound attention.

"Go on, ladies, go on," said Daniel. "Mrs Quilp, pray ask the ladies to stop to supper, and have a couple of lobsters and something light and palatable."

"I—I—didn't ask them to tea, Quilp," stammered his wife. "It's quite an accident."

"So much the better, Mrs Quilp; these accidental parties are always the pleasantest," said the dwarf, rubbing his hands so hard that he seemed to be engaged in manufacturing, of the dirt with which they were encrusted, little charges for popguns. "What! Not going, ladies, you are not going, surely!"

His fair enemies tossed their heads slightly as they sought their respective bonnets and shawls, but left all verbal contention to Mrs Jiniwin, who finding herself in the position of champion, made a faint struggle to sustain the character.

"And why *not* stop to supper, Quilp," said the old lady, "if my daughter had a mind?"

"To be sure," rejoined Daniel. "Why not?"

"There's nothing dishonest or wrong in a supper, I hope?" said Mrs Jiniwin.

"Surely not," returned the dwarf. "Why should there be? Nor anything unwholesome either, unless there's lobster-salad or prawns, which I'm told are not good for digestion."

"And you wouldn't like *your* wife to be attacked with that, or anything else that would make her uneasy, would you?" said Mrs Jiniwin.

"Not for a score of worlds," replied the dwarf with a grin. "Not even to have a score of mothers-in-law at the same time—and what a blessing that would be!"

"My daughter's your wife, Mr Quilp, certainly," said the old lady with a giggle, meant for satirical and to imply that he needed to be reminded of the fact; "your wedded wife."

"So she is, certainly. So she is," observed the dwarf.

"And she has a right to do as she likes, I hope, Quilp," said the old lady trembling, partly with anger and partly with a secret fear of her impish son-in-law.

"Hope she has!" he replied. "Oh! Don't you know she has? Don't you know she has, Mrs Jiniwin?"

"I know she ought to have, Quilp, and would have, if she was of my way of thinking."

"Why an't you of your mother's way of thinking, my dear?" said the dwarf, turning round and addressing his wife, "why don't you always imitate your mother, my dear? She's the ornament of her sex—your father said so every day of his life. I am sure he did."

"Her father was a blessed creetur, Quilp, and worth twenty thousand of some people," said Mrs Jiniwin; "twenty hundred million thousand."

"I should like to have known him," remarked the dwarf. "I dare say he was a blessed creature then; but I'm sure he is now. It was a happy release. I believe he had suffered a long time?"

The old lady gave a gasp, but nothing came of it; Quilp resumed, with the same malice in his eye and the same sarcastic politeness on his tongue.

"You look ill, Mrs Jiniwin; I know you have been exciting yourself too much—talking perhaps, for it is your weakness. Go to bed. Do go to bed."

"I shall go when I please, Quilp, and not before."

"But please to go now. Do please to go now," said the dwarf.

The old woman looked angrily at him, but retreated as he advanced, and falling back before him, suffered him to shut the door upon her and bolt her out among the guests, who were by this time crowding downstairs. Being left alone with his wife, who sat trembling in a corner with her eyes fixed upon the ground, the little man planted himself before her, and folding his arms looked steadily at her for a long time without speaking.

"Mrs Quilp," he said at last.

"Yes, Quilp," she replied meekly.

Instead of pursuing the theme he had in his mind, Quilp folded his arms again, and looked at her more sternly than before, while she averted her eyes and kept them on the ground.

"Mrs Quilp."

"Yes, Quilp."

"If ever you listen to these beldames again, I'll bite you."

With this laconic threat, which he accompanied with a snarl that gave him the appearance of being particularly in earnest, Mr Quilp bade her clear the teaboard away, and bring the rum. The spirit being set before him in a huge case-bottle, which had originally come out of some ship's locker, he ordered cold water and the box of cigars; and these being supplied, he settled himself in an arm-chair with his large head and face squeezed up against the back, and his little legs planted on the table.

"Now, Mrs Quilp," he said; "I feel in a smoking humour, and shall probably blaze away all night. But sit where you are, if you please, in case I want you."

His wife returned no other reply than the customary "Yes, Quilp," and the small lord of the creation took his first cigar and mixed his first glass of grog. The sun went down and the stars peeped out, the Tower turned from its own proper colours to grey and from grey to black, the room became perfectly dark and the end of the cigar a deep fiery red, but still Mr Quilp went on smoking and drinking in the same position, and staring listlessly out of window with the doglike smile always on his face, save when Mrs Quilp made some involuntary movement of restlessness or fatigue; and then it expanded into a grin of delight.

Chapter V

WHETHER Mr Quilp took any sleep by snatches of a few winks at a time, or whether he sat with his eyes wide open all night long, certain it is that he kept his cigar alight, and kindled every fresh one from the ashes of that which was nearly consumed, without requiring the assistance of a candle. Nor did the striking of the clocks, hour after hour, appear to inspire him with any sense of drowsiness or any natural desire to go to rest, but rather to increase his wakefulness, which he showed, at every such indication of the progress of the night, by a suppressed cackling in his throat, and a motion of his shoulders, like one who laughs heartily but at the same time slily and by stealth.

At length the day broke, and poor Mrs Quilp, shivering with the cold of early morning and harassed by fatigue and want of sleep, was discovered sitting patiently on her chair, raising her eyes at intervals in mute appeal to the compassion and clemency of her lord, and gently reminding him by an occasional cough that she was still unpardoned and that her penance had been of long duration. But her dwarfish spouse still smoked his cigar and drank his rum without heeding her; and it was not until the sun had some time risen, and the activity and noise of city day were rife in the street, that he deigned to recognise her presence by any word or sign. He might not have done so even then, but for certain impatient tappings at the door which seemed to denote that some pretty hard knuckles were actively engaged upon the other side.

"Why dear me!" he said looking round with a malicious grin, "it's day! Open the door, sweet Mrs Quilp!"

His obedient wife withdrew the bolt, and her lady mother entered.

Now, Mrs Jiniwin bounced into the room with great impetuosity; for, supposing her son-in-law to be still a-bed, she had come to relieve her feelings by pronouncing a strong opinion upon his general conduct and character. Seeing that he was up and dressed, and that the room appeared to have been occupied ever since she quitted it on the previous evening, she stopped short, in some embarrassment.

Nothing escaped the hawk's eye of the ugly little man, who, perfectly understanding what passed in the old lady's mind, turned uglier still in the fulness of his satisfaction, and bade her good morning, with a leer of triumph.

"Why, Betsy," said the old woman, "you haven't been a—you don't mean to say you've been a———"

"Sitting up all night?" said Quilp, supplying the conclusion of the sentence. "Yes she has!"

"All night!" cried Mrs Jiniwin.

"Ay, all night. Is the dear old lady deaf?" said Quilp, with a smile of which a frown was part. "Who says man and wife are bad company? Ha ha! The time has flown."

"You're a brute!" exclaimed Mrs Jiniwin.

"Come come," said Quilp, wilfully misunderstanding her, of course, "you mustn't call her names. She's married now, you know. And though she *did* beguile the time and keep me from my bed, you must not be so tenderly careful of me as to be out of humour with her. Bless you for a dear old lady. Here's your health!"

"I am *much* obliged to you," returned the old woman, testifying by a certain restlessness in her hands a vehement desire to shake her matronly fist at her son-in-law. "Oh! I'm very much obliged to you!"

"Grateful soul!" cried the dwarf. "Mrs Quilp."

"Yes, Quilp," said the timid sufferer.

"Help your mother to get breakfast, Mrs Quilp. I am going to the wharf this morning—the earlier, the better, so be quick."

Mrs Jiniwin made a faint demonstration of rebellion by sitting down in a chair near the door and folding her arms as if in a resolute determination to do nothing. But a few whispered words from her daughter, and a kind inquiry from her son-in-law whether she felt faint, with a hint that there was abundance of cold water in the next apartment, routed these symptoms effectually, and she applied herself to the prescribed preparations with sullen diligence.

While they were in progress, Mr Quilp withdrew to the adjoining room, and, turning back his coat-collar, proceeded to smear his countenance with a damp towel of very unwholesome appearance, which made his complexion rather more cloudy than it was before. But, while he was thus engaged, his caution and inquisitiveness did not forsake him, for with a face as sharp and cunning as ever, he often stopped, even in this short process, and stood listening for any conversation in the next room, of which he might be the theme.

"Ah!" he said after a short effort of attention, "it was not the towel over my ears, I thought it wasn't. I'm a little hunchy villain and a monster, am I, Mrs Jiniwin? Oh!"

The pleasure of this discovery called up the old doglike smile in full force. When he had quite done with it, he shook himself in a very doglike manner, and rejoined the ladies.

Mr Quilp now walked up to the front of a looking-glass, and was standing there putting on his neckerchief, when Mrs Jiniwin, happening to be behind him, could not resist the inclination she felt to shake her fist at her tyrant son-in-law. It was the gesture of an instant, but as she did so and accompanied the action with a menacing look, she met his eye in the glass, catching her in the very act. The same glance at the mirror conveyed to her the reflection of a horribly grotesque and distorted face with the tongue lolling out; and the next instant the dwarf, turning about with a perfectly bland and placid look, inquired in a tone of great affection,

"How are you now, my dear old darling?"

Slight and ridiculous as the incident was, it made him appear such a little fiend, and withal such a keen and knowing one, that the old woman felt too much afraid of him to utter a single word, and suffered herself to be led with extraordinary politeness to the breakfast-table. Here he by no means diminished the impression he had just produced, for he ate hard eggs, shell and all, devoured gigantic prawns with the heads and tails on, chewed tobacco and water-cresses at the same time and with extraordinary greediness, drank boiling tea without winking, bit his fork and spoon till they bent again, and in short performed so many horrifying and uncommon acts that the women were nearly frightened out of their wits, and began to doubt if he were really a human creature. At last, having gone through these proceedings and many others which were equally a part of his system, Mr Quilp left them, reduced to a very obedient and humbled state, and betook himself to the river-side, where he took boat for the wharf on which he had bestowed his name.

It was flood tide when Daniel Quilp sat himself down in the wherry to cross to the opposite shore. A fleet of barges were coming lazily on, some sideways, some head first, some stern first; all in a wrong-headed, dogged, obstinate way, bumping up against the larger craft, running under the bows of steamboats, getting into every kind of nook and corner where they had no business, and being crunched on all sides like so many walnut-shells; while each with its pair of long sweeps struggling and splashing in the water looked like some lumbering fish in pain. In some of the vessels at anchor all hands were busily engaged in coiling ropes, spreading out sails to dry, taking in or discharging their cargoes; in others no life was visible but two or three tarry boys, and perhaps a barking dog running to and fro upon the deck or scrambling up to look over the side and bark the louder for the view. Coming slowly on through the forests of masts was a great steamship, beating the water in short impatient strokes with her heavy paddles as though she wanted room to breathe, and advancing in her huge bulk like a sea monster among the minnows of the Thames. On either hand were long black tiers of colliers; between them vessels slowly working out of harbour with sails glistening in the sun, and creaking noise on board, re-echoed from a hundred quarters. The water and all upon it was in active motion, dancing and buoyant and bubbling up; while the old grey Tower and piles of building on the shore, with many a church-spire shooting up between, looked coldly on, and seemed to disdain their chafing, restless neighbour.

Daniel Quilp, who was not much affected by a bright morning save in so far as it spared him the trouble of carrying an umbrella, caused himself to be put ashore hard by the wharf, and proceeded thither through a narrow lane which, partaking of the amphibious character of its frequenters, had as much water as mud in its composition, and a very liberal supply of both. Arrived at his destination, the first object that presented itself to his view was a pair of very imperfectly shod feet elevated in the air with the soles upwards, which remarkable appearance was referable to the boy, who being of an eccentric spirit and having a natural taste for tumbling, was now standing on his head and contemplating the aspect of the river under these uncommon circumstances. He was speedily brought on his heels by the sound of his master's voice, and as soon as his head was in its right position, Mr Quilp, to speak expressively in the absence of a better verb, 'punched it' for him.

"Come, you let me alone," said the boy, parrying Quilp's hand with both his elbows alternately. "You'll get something you won't like if you don't, and so I tell you."

"You dog," snarled Quilp, "I'll beat you with an iron rod, I'll scratch you with a rusty nail, I'll pinch your eyes, if you talk to me—I will."

With these threats he clenched his hand again, and dexterously diving in between the elbows and catching the boy's head as it dodged from side to side, gave it three or four good hard knocks. Having now carried his point and insisted on it, he left off.

"You won't do it again," said the boy, nodding his head and drawing back, with the elbows ready in case of the worst; "now———"

"Stand still, you dog," said Quilp. "I won't do it again, because I've done it as often as I want. Here. Take the key."

"Why don't you hit one of your size?" said the boy approaching very slowly.

"Where is there one of my size, you dog?" returned Quilp. "Take the key, or I'll brain you with it"—indeed he gave him a smart tap with the handle as he spoke. "Now, open the counting-house."

The boy sulkily complied, muttering at first, but desisting when he looked round and saw that Quilp was following him with a steady look. And here it may be remarked, that between this boy and the dwarf there existed a strange kind of mutual liking. How born or bred, or how nourished upon blows and threats on one side, and retorts and defiances on the other, is not to the purpose. Quilp would certainly suffer nobody to contradict him but the boy, and the boy would assuredly not have submitted to be so knocked about by anybody but Quilp, when he had the power to run away at any time he chose.

"Now," said Quilp, passing into the wooden counting-house, "you mind the wharf. Stand upon your head again, and I'll cut one of your feet off."

The boy made no answer, but directly Quilp had shut himself in, stood on his head before the door, then walked on his hands to the back and stood on his head there, and then to the opposite side and repeated the performance. There were indeed four sides to the counting-house, but he avoided that one where the window was, deeming it probable that Quilp would be looking out of it. This was prudent, for in point of fact the dwarf, knowing his disposition, was lying in wait at a little distance from the sash armed with a large piece of wood, which, being rough and jagged and studded in many parts with broken nails, might possibly have hurt him.

It was a dirty little box, this counting-house, with nothing in it but an old ricketty desk and two stools, a hat-peg, an ancient almanack, an inkstand with no ink and the stump of one pen, and an eight-day clock which hadn't gone for eighteen years at least, and of which the minute-hand had been twisted off for a tooth-pick. Daniel Quilp pulled his hat over his brows, climbed on to the desk (which had a flat top), and stretching his short length upon it went to sleep with the ease of an old practitioner; intending, no doubt, to compensate himself for the deprivation of last night's rest, by a long and sound nap.

Sound it might have been, but long it was not, for he had not been asleep a quarter of an hour when the boy opened the door and thrust in his head, which was like a bundle of badly-picked oakum. Quilp was a light sleeper and started up directly.

"Here's somebody for you," said the boy.

"Who?"

"I don't know."

"Ask!" said Quilp, seizing the trifle of wood before mentioned and throwing it at him with such dexterity that it was well the boy disappeared before it reached the spot on which he had stood. "Ask, you dog."

Not caring to venture within range of such missiles again, the boy discreetly sent in his stead the first cause of the interruption, who now presented herself at the door.

"What, Nelly!" cried Quilp.

"Yes," said the child, hesitating whether to enter or retreat, for the dwarf just roused, with his dishevelled hair hanging all about him and a yellow handkerchief over his head, was something fearful to behold; "it's only me, sir."

"Come in," said Quilp, without getting off the desk. "Come in. Stay. Just look out into the yard, and see whether there's a boy standing on his head."

"No, sir," replied Nell. "He's on his feet."

"You're sure he is?" said Quilp. "Well. Now, come in and shut the door. What's your message, Nelly?"

The child handed him a letter; Mr Quilp, without changing his position further than to turn over a little more on his side and rest his chin on his hand, proceeded to make himself acquainted with its contents.

Chapter VI

LITTLE Nell stood timidly by, with her eyes raised to the countenance of Mr Quilp as he read the letter, plainly showing by her looks that while she entertained some fear and distrust of the little man, she was much inclined to laugh at his uncouth appearance and grotesque attitude. And yet there was visible on the part of the child a painful anxiety for his reply, and a consciousness of his power to render it disagreeable or distressing, which was strongly at variance with this impulse and restrained it more effectually than she could possibly have done by any efforts of her own.

That Mr Quilp was himself perplexed, and that in no small degree, by the contents of the letter, was sufficiently obvious. Before he had got through the first two or three lines he began to open his eyes very wide and to frown most horribly, the next two or three caused him to scratch his head in an uncommonly vicious manner, and when he came to the conclusion he gave a long dismal whistle indicative of surprise and dismay. After folding and laying it down beside him, he bit the nails of all his ten fingers with extreme voracity; and taking it up sharply, read it again. The second perusal was to all appearance as unsatisfactory as the first, and plunged him into a profound reverie from which he awakened to another assault upon his nails and a long stare at the child, who with her eyes turned towards the ground awaited his further pleasure.

"Halloa here!" he said at length, in a voice, and with a suddenness, which made the child start as though a gun had been fired off at her ear. "Nelly!"

"Yes, sir."

"Do you know what's inside this letter, Nell?"

"No, sir!"

"Are you sure, quite sure, quite certain, upon your soul?"

"Quite sure, sir."

"Do you wish you may die if you do know, hey?" said the dwarf.

"Indeed I don't know," returned the child.

"Well!" muttered Quilp as he marked her earnest look. "I believe you. Humph! Gone already? Gone in four-and-twenty hours! What the devil has he done with it, that's the mystery!"

This reflection set him scratching his head and biting his nails once more. While he was thus employed his features gradually relaxed into what was with him a cheerful smile, but which in any other man would have been a ghastly grin of pain, and when the child looked up again she found that he was regarding her with extraordinary favour and complacency.

"You look very pretty to-day, Nelly, charmingly pretty. Are you tired, Nelly?"

"No, sir. I'm in a hurry to get back, for he will be anxious while I am away."

"There's no hurry, little Nell, no hurry at all," said Quilp. "How should you like to be my number two, Nelly?"

"To be what, sir?"

"My number two, Nelly, my second, my Mrs Quilp," said the dwarf.

The child looked frightened, but seemed not to understand him, which Mr Quilp observing, hastened to explain his meaning more distinctly.

"To be Mrs Quilp the second, when Mrs Quilp the first is dead, sweet Nell," said Quilp, wrinkling up his eyes and luring her towards him with his bent forefinger, "to be my wife, my little cherry-cheeked, red-lipped wife. Say that Mrs Quilp lives five years, or only four, you'll be just the proper age for me. Ha ha! Be a good girl, Nelly, a very good girl, and see if one of these days you don't come to be Mrs Quilp of Tower Hill."

So far from being sustained and stimulated by this delightful prospect, the child shrank from him in great agitation, and trembled violently. Mr Quilp, either because frightening anybody afforded him a constitutional delight, or because it was pleasant to contemplate the death of Mrs Quilp number one, and the elevation of Mrs. Quilp number two to her post and title, or because he was determined for purposes of his own to be agreeable and good-humoured at that particular time, only laughed and feigned to take no heed of her alarm.

"You shall come with me to Tower Hill, and see Mrs Quilp that is, directly," said the dwarf. "She's very fond of you, Nell, though not so fond as I am. You shall come home with me."

"I must go back indeed," said the child. "He told me to return directly I had the answer."

"But you haven't it, Nelly," retorted the dwarf, "and won't have it, and can't have it, until I have been home, so you see that to do your errand, you must go with me. Reach me yonder hat, my dear, and we'll go directly." With that, Mr Quilp suffered himself to roll gradually off the desk until his short legs touched the ground, when he got upon them and led the way from the counting-house to the wharf outside, when the first objects that presented themselves were the boy who had stood on his head and another young gentleman of about his own stature, rolling in the mud together, locked in a tight embrace, and cuffing each other with mutual heartiness.

"It's Kit!" cried Nelly, clasping her hands, "poor Kit who came with me! oh, pray stop them, Mr Quilp!"

"I'll stop 'em," cried Quilp, diving into the little counting-house and returning with a thick stick, "I'll stop 'em. Now, my boys, fight away. I'll fight you both. I'll take both of you, both together, both together!"

With which defiances the dwarf flourished his cudgel, and dancing round the combatants and treading upon them and skipping over them, in a kind of frenzy, laid about him, now on one and now on the other, in a most desperate manner, always aiming at their heads and dealing such blows as none but the veriest little savage would have inflicted. This being warmer work than they had calculated upon, speedily cooled the courage of the belligerents, who scrambled to their feet and called for quarter.

"I'll beat you to a pulp, you dogs," said Quilp, vainly endeavouring to get near either of them for a parting blow. "I'll bruise you till you're copper-coloured, I'll break your faces till you haven't a profile between you, I will."

"Come, you drop that stick or it'll be worse for you," said his boy, dodging round him and watching an opportunity to rush in; "you drop that stick."

"Come a little nearer, and I'll drop it on your skull, you dog," said Quilp with gleaming eyes; "a little nearer—nearer yet."

But the boy declined the invitation until his master was apparently a little off his guard, when he darted in and seizing the weapon tried to wrest it from his grasp. Quilp, who was as strong as a lion, easily kept his hold until the boy was tugging at it with his utmost power, when he suddenly let it go and sent him reeling backwards, so that he fell violently upon his head. The success of this manœuvre tickled Mr Quilp beyond description, and he laughed and stamped upon the ground as at a most irresistible jest.

"Never mind," said the boy, nodding his head and rubbing it at the same time; "you see if ever I offer to strike anybody again because they say you're a uglier dwarf than can be seen anywheres for a penny, that's all."

"Do you mean to say, I'm not, you dog?" returned Quilp.

"No!" retorted the boy.

"Then what do you fight on my wharf for, you villain?" said Quilp.

"Because he said so," replied the boy, pointing to Kit, "not because you an't."

"Then why did he say," bawled Kit, "that Miss Nelly was ugly, and that she and my master was obliged to do whatever his master liked? Why did he say that?"

"He said what he did because he's a fool, and you said what you did because you're very wise and clever—almost too clever to live, unless you're very careful of yourself, Kit," said Quilp, with great suavity in his manner, but still more of quiet malice about his eyes and mouth. "Here's sixpence for you, Kit. Always speak the truth. At all times, Kit, speak the truth. Lock the counting-house, you dog, and bring me the key."

The other boy, to whom this order was addressed, did as he was told, and was rewarded for his partizanship in behalf of his master, by a dexterous rap on the nose with the key, which brought the water into his eyes. Then Mr Quilp departed with the child and Kit in a boat, and the boy revenged himself by dancing on his head at intervals on the extreme verge of the wharf, during the whole time they crossed the river.

There was only Mrs Quilp at home, and she, little expecting the return of her lord, was just composing herself for a refreshing slumber when the sound of his footsteps roused her. She had barely time to seem to be occupied in some needle-work, when he entered, accompanied by the child; having left Kit downstairs.

"Here's Nelly Trent, dear Mrs Quilp," said her husband. "A glass of wine, my dear, and a biscuit, for she has had a long walk. She'll sit with you, my soul, while I write a letter."

Mrs Quilp looked tremblingly in her spouse's face to know what this unusual courtesy might portend, and obedient to the summons she saw in his gesture, followed him into the next room.

"Mind what I say to you," whispered Quilp. "See if you can get out of her anything about her grandfather, or what they do, or how they live, or what he tells her. I've my reasons for knowing, if I can. You women talk more freely to one another than you do to us, and you have a soft, mild way with you that'll win upon her. Do you hear?"

"Yes, Quilp."

"Go, then. What's the matter now?"

"Dear Quilp." faltered his wife, "I love the child—if you *could* do without making me deceive her———"

The dwarf muttering a terrible oath looked round as if for some weapon with which to inflict condign punishment upon his disobedient wife. The submissive little woman hurriedly entreated him not to be angry, and promised to do as he bade her.

"Do you hear me," whispered Quilp, nipping and pinching her arm; "worm yourself into her secrets; I know you can. I'm listening, recollect. If you're not sharp enough I'll creak the door, and woe betide you if I have to creak it much. Go!"

Mrs Quilp departed according to order, and her amiable husband, ensconcing himself behind the partly opened door, and applying his ear close to it, began to listen with a face of great craftiness and attention.

Poor Mrs Quilp was thinking, however, in what manner to begin or what kind of inquiries she could make; and it was not until the door, creaking in a very urgent manner, warned her to proceed without further consideration, that the sound of her voice was heard.

"How very often you have come backwards and forwards lately to Mr Quilp, my dear."

"I have said so to grandfather, a hundred times," returned Nell innocently.

"And what has he said to that?"

"Only sighed, and dropped his head, and seemed so sad and wretched that if you could have seen him I am sure you must have cried; you could not have helped it more than I, I know. How that door creaks!"

"It often does," returned Mrs Quilp, with an uneasy glance towards it. "But your grandfather—he used not to be so wretched?"

"Oh, no!" said the child eagerly, "so different! we were once so happy and he so cheerful and contented! You cannot think what a sad change has fallen on us since."

"I am very, very sorry, to hear you speak like this, my dear!" said Mrs Quilp. And she spoke the truth.

"Thank you," returned the child, kissing her cheek, "you are always kind to me, and it is a pleasure to talk to you. I can speak to no one else about him, but poor Kit. I am very happy still, I ought to feel happier perhaps than I do, but you cannot think how it grieves me sometimes to see him alter so."

"He'll alter again, Nelly," said Mrs Quilp, "and be what he was before."

"Oh, if God would only let that come about!" said the child with streaming eyes; "but it is a long time now, since he first began to—I thought I saw that door moving!"

"It's the wind," said Mrs Quilp faintly. "Began to———"

"To be so thoughtful and dejected, and to forget our old way of spending the time in the long evenings," said the child. "I used to read to him by the fireside, and he sat listening, and when I stopped and we began to talk, he told me about my mother, and how she once looked and spoke just like me when she was a little child. Then he used to take me on his knee, and try to make me understand that she was not lying in her grave, but had flown to a beautiful country beyond the sky, where nothing died or ever grew old—we were very happy once!"

"Nelly, Nelly!"—said the poor woman, "I can't bear to see one as young as you so sorrowful. Pray don't cry.

"I do so very seldom," said Nell, "but I have kept this to myself a long time, and I am not quite well, I think, for the tears come into my eyes and I cannot keep them back. I don't mind telling you my grief, for I know you will not tell it to any one again."

Mrs Quilp turned away her head and made no answer.

"Then," said the child, "we often walked in the fields and among the green trees, and when we came home at night, we liked it better for being tired, and said what a happy place it was. And if it was dark and rather dull, we used to say, what did it matter to us, for it only made us remember our last walk with greater pleasure, and look forward to our next one. But now we never have these walks, and though it is the same house it is darker and much more gloomy than it used to be, indeed!"

She paused here, but though the door creaked more than once, Mrs Quilp said nothing.

"Mind you don't suppose," said the child earnestly, "that grandfather is less kind to me than he was. I think he loves me better every day, and is kinder and more affectionate than he was the day before. You do not not know how fond he is of me!"

"I am sure he loves you dearly," said Mrs Quilp.

"Indeed, indeed he does!" cried Nell, "as dearly as I love him. But I have not told you the greatest change of all, and this you must never breathe again to any one. He has no sleep or rest, but that which he takes by day in his easy chair; for every night and nearly all night long he is away from home."

"Nelly!"

"Hush!" said the child, laying her finger on her lip and looking round. "When he comes home in the morning, which is generally just before day, I let him in. Last night he was very late, and it was quite light. I saw that his face was deadly pale, that his eyes were bloodshot, and that his legs trembled as he walked. When I had gone to bed again, I heard him groan. I got up and ran back to him, and heard him say, before he knew that I was there, that he could not bear his life much longer, and if it was not for the child, would wish to die. What shall I do! Oh! what shall I do!"

The fountains of her heart were opened; the child, overpowered by the weight of her sorrows and anxieties, by the first confidence she had ever shown, and the sympathy with which her little tale had been received, hid her face in the arms of her helpless friend, and burst into a passion of tears.

In a few moments Mr Quilp returned, and expressed the utmost surprise to find her in this condition, which he did very naturally and with admirable effect, for that kind of acting had been rendered familiar to him by long practice, and he was quite at home in it.

"She's tired you see, Mrs Quilp," said the dwarf, squinting in a hideous manner to imply that his wife was to follow his lead. "It's a long way from her home to the wharf, and then she was alarmed to see a couple of young scoundrels fighting, and was timorous on the water besides. All this together has been too much for her. Poor Nell!"

Mr Quilp unintentionally adopted the very best means he could have devised for the recovery of his young visitor, by patting her on the head. Such an application from any other hand might not have produced a remarkable effect, but the child shrank so quickly from his touch and felt such an instinctive desire to get out of his reach, that she rose directly and declared herself ready to return.

"But you'd better wait, and dine with Mrs Quilp and me," said the dwarf.

"I have been away too long, sir, already," returned Nell, drying her eyes.

"Well," said Mr Quilp, "if you will go, you will, Nelly. Here's the note. It's only to say that I shall see him to-morrow or maybe next day, and that I couldn't do that little business for him this morning. Good-bye, Nelly. Here, you sir; take care of her, d'ye hear?"

Kit, who appeared at the summons, deigned to make no reply to so needless an injunction, and after staring at Quilp in a threatening manner as if he doubted whether he might not have been the cause of Nelly shedding tears, and felt more than half disposed to revenge the fact upon him on the mere suspicion, turned about and followed his young mistress, who had by this time taken her leave of Mrs Quilp and departed.

"You're a keen questioner, an't you, Mrs Quilp?" said the dwarf, turning upon her as soon as they were left alone.

"What more could I do?" returned his wife mildly.

"What more could you do!" sneered Quilp, "couldn't you have done something less? couldn't you have done what you had to do, without appearing in your favourite part of the crocodile, you minx?"

"I am very sorry for the child, Quilp," said his wife. "Surely I've done enough. I've led her on to tell her secret when she supposed we were alone; and you were by, God forgive me."

"You led her on! You did a great deal truly!" said Quilp. "What did I tell you about making me creak the door? It's lucky for you that from what she let fall, I've got the clue I want, for if I hadn't, I'd have visited the failure upon you, I can tell you."

Mrs. Quilp being fully persuaded of this, made no reply. Her husband added with some exultation,

"But you may thank your fortunate stars—the same stars that made you Mrs Quilp—you may thank them that I'm upon the old gentleman's track, and have got a new light. So let me hear no more about this matter now or at any other time, and don't get anything too nice for dinner, for I shan't be home to it."

So saying, Mr Quilp put his hat on and took himself off, and Mrs Quilp, who was afflicted beyond measure by the recollection of the part she had just acted, shut herself up in her chamber, and smothering her head in the bed-clothes bemoaned her fault more bitterly than many less tender-hearted persons would have mourned a much greater offence; for, in the majority of cases, conscience is an elastic and very flexible article, which will bear a deal of stretching and adapt itself to a great variety of circumstances. Some people by prudent management and leaving it off piece by piece like a flannel waistcoat in warm weather, even contrive, in time, to dispense with it altogether; but there be others who can assume the garment and throw it off at pleasure; and this, being the greatest and most convenient improvement, is the one most in vogue.

Chapter VII

F RED," said Mr Swiveller, "remember the once popular melody of *Begone dull care;* fan the sinking flame of hilarity with the wing of friendship; and pass the rosy wine." Mr Richard Swiveller's apartments were in the neighbourhood of Drury Lane, and in addition to this conveniency of situation had the advantage of being over a tobacco-nist's shop, so that he was enabled to procure a refreshing sneeze at any time by merely stepping out upon the staircase, and was saved the trouble and expense of maintaining a snuff-box. It was in these apartments that Mr Swiveller made use of the expressions above recorded for the consolation and encouragement of his desponding friend; and it may not be uninteresting or improper to remark that even these brief observations partook in a double sense of the figurative and poetical character of Mr Swiveller's mind, as the rosy wine was in fact represented by one glass of cold gin-and-water, which was replenished as occasion required from a bottle and jug upon the table, and was passed from one to another, in a scarcity of tumblers which, as Mr Swiveller's was a bachelor's establishment, may be acknowledged without a blush. By a like pleasant fiction his single chamber was always mentioned in the plural number. In its disengaged times, the tobacconist had announced it in his window as "apartments" for a single gentleman, and Mr Swiveller, following up the hint, never failed to speak of it as his rooms, his lodgings, or his chambers, conveying to his hearers a notion of indefinite space, and leaving their imaginations to wander through long suites of lofty halls, at pleasure.

In this flight of fancy, Mr Swiveller was assisted by a deceptive piece of furniture, in reality a bedstead, but in semblance a bookcase, which occupied a prominent situa-tion in his chamber and seemed to defy suspicion and challenge inquiry. There is no doubt that by day Mr Swiveller firmly believed this secret convenience to be a bookcase and nothing more; that he closed his eyes to the bed, resolutely denied the existence of the blankets, and spurned the bolster from his thoughts. No word of its real use, no hint of its nightly service, no allusion to its peculiar properties, had ever passed between him and his most intimate friends. Implicit faith in the deception was the first article of his creed. To be the friend of Swiveller you must reject all circumstantial evidence, all reason, observation, and experience, and repose a blind belief in the bookcase. It was his pet weakness, and he cherished it.

"Fred!" said Mr Swiveller, finding that his former adjuration had been productive of no effect. "Pass the rosy."

Young Trent with an impatient gesture pushed the glass towards him, and fell again into the moody attitude from which he had been unwillingly roused.

"I'll give you, Fred," said his friend, stirring the mixture, "a little sentiment appropri-ate to the occasion. Here's May the——"

"Pshaw!" interposed the other. "You worry me to death with your chattering. You can be merry under any circumstances."

"Why, Mr Trent," returned Dick, "there is a proverb which talks about being merry and wise. There are some people who can be merry and can't be wise, and some who can be wise (or think they can) and can't be merry. I'm one of the first sort. If the proverb's a good 'un, I suppose it's better to keep to half of it than none; at all events I'd rather be merry and not wise, than like you, neither one nor t'other."

"Bah!" muttered his friend, peevishly.

"With all my heart," said Mr Swiveller. "In the polite circles I believe this sort of thing isn't usually said to a gentleman in his own apartments, but never mind that. Make yourself at home." Adding to this retort an observation to the effect that his friend appeared to be rather "cranky" in point of temper, Richard Swiveller finished the rosy and applied himself to the composition of another glassful, in which, after tasting it with great relish, he proposed a toast to an imaginary company.

"Gentlemen, I'll give you, if you please, Success to the ancient family of the Swivell-ers, and good luck to Mr Richard in particular—Mr Richard, gentlemen," said Dick with great emphasis, 'who spends all his money on his friends and is *Bah!'d* for his pains. Hear, hear!"

"Dick!" said the other, returning to his seat after having paced the room twice or thrice, "will you talk seriously for two minutes, if I show you a way to make your fortune with very little trouble?"

"You've shown me so many," returned Dick; "and nothing has come of any one of 'em but empty pockets———"

"You'll tell a different story of this one, before a very long time is over," said his companion, drawing his chair to the table. "You saw my sister Nell?"

"What about her?" returned Dick.

"She has a pretty face, has she not?"

"Why, certainly," replied Dick, "I must say for her that there's not any very strong family likeness between her and you."

"Has she a pretty face?" repeated his friend impatiently.

"Yes," said Dick, "she has a pretty face, a very pretty face. What of that?"

"I'll tell you," returned his friend. "It's very plain that the old man and I will remain at daggers drawn to the end of our lives, and that I have nothing to expect from him. You see that, I suppose?"

"A bat might see that, with the sun shining," said Dick.

"It's equally plain that the money which the old flint—rot him—first taught me to expect that I should share with her at his death, will all be hers, is it not?"

"I should say it was," replied Dick; "unless the way in which I put the case to him, made an impression. It may have done so. It was powerful, Fred. 'Here is a jolly old grandfather'—that was strong, I thought—very friendly and natural. Did it strike you in that way?"

"It didn't strike *him,*" returned the other, "so we needn't discuss it. Now look here. Nell is nearly fourteen."

"Fine girl of her age, but small," observed Richard Swiveller parenthetically.

"If I am to go on, be quiet for one minute," returned Trent, fretting at the very slight interest the other appeared to take in the conversation. "Now I'm coming to the point."

"That's right," said Dick.

"The girl has strong affections, and brought up as she has been, may, at her age, be easily influenced and persuaded. If I take her in hand, I will be bound by a very little coaxing and threatening to bend her to my will. Not to beat about the bush (for the advantages of the scheme would take a week to tell) what's to prevent your marrying her?"

Richard Swiveller, who had been looking over the rim of the tumbler while his companion addressed the foregoing remarks to him with great energy and earnestness of manner, no sooner heard these words than he evinced the utmost consternation, and with difficulty ejaculated the monosyllable:

"What!"

"I say, what's to prevent," repeated the other with a steadiness of manner, of the effect of which upon his companion he was well assured by long experience, "what's to prevent your marrying her?"

"And she 'nearly fourteen'!" cried Dick.

"I don't mean marrying her now"—returned the brother angrily; "say in two years' time, in three, in four. Does the old man look like a long-liver?"

"He don't look like it," said Dick shaking his head, "but these old people—there's no trusting 'em, Fred. There's an aunt of mine down in Dorsetshire that was going to die when I was eight years old, and hasn't kept her word yet. They're so aggravating, so unprincipled, so spiteful—unless there's apoplexy in the family, Fred, you can't calculate upon 'em, and even then they deceive you just as often as not."

"Look at the worst side of the question then," said Trent as steadily as before, and keeping his eyes upon his friend. "Suppose he lives."

"To be sure," said Dick. "There's the rub."

"I say," resumed his friend, "suppose he lives, and I persuaded, or if the word sounds more feasible, forced, Nell to a secret marriage with you. What do you think would come of that?"

"A family and an annual income of nothing, to keep 'em on," said Richard Swiveller after some reflection.

"I tell you," returned the other with an increased earnestness, which, whether it were real or assumed, had the same effect on his companion, "that he lives for her, that his whole energies and thoughts are bound up in her, that he would no more disinherit her for an act of disobedience than he would take me into his favour again for any act of obedience or virtue that I could possibly be guilty of. He could not do it. You or any other man with eyes in his head may see that, if he chooses."

"It seems improbable certainly," said Dick, musing.

"It seems improbable because it is improbable," his friend returned. "If you would furnish him with an additional inducement to forgive you, let there be an irreconcileable breach, a most deadly quarrel, between you and me—let there be a pretence of such a thing, I mean, of course—and he'll do so fast enough. As to Nell, constant dropping will wear away a stone; you know you may trust to me as far as she is concerned. So, whether he lives or dies, what does it come to? That you become the sole inheritor of the wealth of this rich old hunks, that you and I spend it together, and that you get into the bargain a beautiful young wife."

"I suppose there's no doubt about his being rich"—said Dick.

"Doubt! Did you hear what he let fall the other day when we were there? Doubt! What will you doubt next, Dick?"

It would be tedious to pursue the conversation through all its artful windings, or to develop the gradual approaches by which the heart of Richard Swiveller was gained. It is sufficient to know that vanity, interest, poverty, and every spendthrift consideration urged him to look upon the proposal with favour, and that where all other inducements were wanting, the habitual carelessness of his disposition stepped in and still weighed down the scale on the same side. To these impulses must be added the complete ascendancy which his friend had long been accustomed to exercise over him—an ascendancy exerted in the beginning sorely at the expense of the unfortunate Dick's purse and prospects, but still maintained without the slightest relaxation, notwithstanding that Dick suffered for all his friend's vices, and was in nine cases out of ten looked upon as his designing tempter when he was indeed nothing but his thoughtless, light-headed tool.

The motives on the other side were something deeper than any which Richard Swiveller entertained or understood, but these being left to their own development, require no present elucidation. The negotiation was concluded very pleasantly, and Mr Swiveller was in the act of stating in flowery terms that he had no insurmountable objection to marrying anybody plentifully endowed with money or moveables, who could be induced to take him, when he was interrupted in his observations by a knock at the door, and the consequent necessity of crying "Come in."

The door was opened, but nothing came in except a soapy arm and a strong gush of tobacco. The gush of tobacco came from the shop downstairs, and the soapy arm proceeded from the body of a servant-girl, who being then and there engaged in cleaning the stairs had just drawn it out of a warm pail to take in a letter, which letter she now held in her hand, proclaiming aloud with that quick perception of surnames peculiar to her class that it was for Mister Snivelling.

Dick looked rather pale and foolish when he glanced at the direction, and still more so when he came to look at the inside, observing that this was one of the inconveniences of being a lady's man, and that it was very easy to talk as they had been talking, but he had quite forgotten her.

"*Her*. Who?" demanded Trent.

"Sophy Wackles," said Dick.

"Who's she?"

"She's all my fancy painted her, sir, that's what she is," said Mr Swiveller, taking a long pull at "the rosy" and looking gravely at his friend. "She is lovely, she's divine. You know her."

"I remember," said his companion carelessly. "What of her?"

"Why, sir," returned Dick, "between Miss Sophia Wackles and the humble individual who has now the honour to address you, warm and tender sentiments have been engendered, sentiments of the most honourable and inspiring kind. The Goddess Diana, sir, that calls aloud for the chase, is not more particular in her behaviour than Sophia Wackles; I can tell you that."

"Am I to believe there's anything real in what you say?" demanded his friend; "you don't mean to say that any love-making has been going on?"

"Love-making, yes. Promising, no," said Dick. "There can be no action for breach, that's one comfort. I've never committed myself in writing, Fred."

"And what's in the letter, pray?"

"A reminder, Fred, for to-night—a small party of twenty, making two hundred light fantastic toes in all, supposing every lady and gentleman to have the proper complement. I must go, if it's only to begin breaking off the affair—I'll do it, don't you be afraid. I should like to know whether she left this herself. If she did, unconscious of any bar to her happiness, it's affecting, Fred."

To solve this question, Mr Swiveller summoned the handmaid and ascertained that Miss Sophy Wackles had indeed left the letter with her own hands; and that she had come accompanied, for decorum's sake no doubt, by a younger Miss Wackles; and that on learning that Mr Swiveller was at home and being requested to walk upstairs, she was extremely shocked and professed that she would rather die. Mr Swiveller heard this account with a degree of admiration not altogether consistent with the project in which he had just concurred, but his friend attached very little importance to his behaviour in this respect, probably because he knew that he had influence sufficient to control Richard Swiveller's proceedings in this or any other matter, whenever he deemed it necessary, for the advancement of his own purposes, to exert it.

Chapter VIII

BUSINESS disposed of, Mr Swiveller was inwardly reminded of its being nigh dinner-time, and to the intent that his health might not be endangered by longer absti-nence, despatched a message to the nearest eating-house requiring an immediate supply of boiled beef and greens for two. With this demand, however, the eating-house (having experience of its customer) declined to comply, churlishly sending back for answer that if Mr Swiveller stood in need of beef perhaps he would be so obliging as to come there and eat it, bringing with him, as grace before meat, the amount of a certain small account which had been long outstanding. Not at all intimidated by this rebuff, but rather sharpened in wits and appetite, Mr Swiveller forwarded the same message to another and more distant eating-house, adding to it by way of rider that the gentleman was induced to send so far, not only by the great fame and popularity its beef had acquired, but in consequence of the extreme toughness of the beef retailed at the obdurate cook's shop, which rendered it quite unfit not merely for gentlemanly food, but for any human consumption. The good effect of this politic course was demonstrated by the speedy arrival of a small pewter pyramid, curiously constructed of platters and covers, whereof the boiled-beef-plates formed the base, and a foaming quart-pot the apex; the structure being resolved into its component parts afforded all things requisite and necessary for a hearty meal, to which Mr Swiveller and his friend applied themselves with great keenness and enjoyment.

"May the present moment," said Dick, sticking his fork into a large carbuncular potato, "be the worst of our lives! I like this plan of sending 'em with the peel on; there's a charm in drawing a potato from its native element (if I may so express it) to which the rich and powerful are strangers. Ah! 'Man wants but little here below, nor wants that little long!' How true that is!—after dinner."

"I hope the eating-house keeper will want but little and that *he* may not want that little long," returned his companion; "but I suspect you've no means of paying for this!"

"I shall be passing presently, and I'll call," said Dick, winking his eye significantly. "The waiter's quite helpless. The goods are gone, Fred, and there's an end of it."

In point of fact, it would seem that the waiter felt this wholesome truth, for when he returned for the empty plates and dishes and was informed by Mr Swiveller with dignified carelessness that he would call and settle when he should be passing presently, he displayed some perturbation of spirit, and muttered a few remarks about "payment on delivery," and "no trust," and other unpleasant subjects, but was fain to content himself with inquiring at what hour it was likely the gentleman would call, in order that being personally responsible for the beef, greens, and sundries, he might take care to be in the way at the time. Mr Swiveller, after mentally calculating his engagements to a nicety, replied that he should look in at from two minutes before six to seven minutes past; and the man disappearing with this feeble consolation, Richard Swiveller took a greasy memorandum-book from his pocket and made an entry therein.

"Is that a reminder, in case you should forget to call?" said Trent with a sneer.

"Not exactly, Fred," replied the imperturbable Richard, continuing to write with a businesslike air. "I enter in this little book the names of the streets that I can't go down while the shops are open. This dinner to-day closes Long Acre. I bought a pair of boots in Great Queen Street last week, and made that no thoroughfare too. There's only one avenue to the Strand left open now, and I shall have to stop up that to-night with a pair of gloves. The roads are closing so fast in every direction, that in about a month's time, unless my aunt sends me a remittance, I shall have to go three or four miles out of town to get over the way."

"There's no fear of her failing, in the end?" said Trent.

"Why, I hope not," returned Mr Swiveller, "but the average number of letters it takes to soften her is six, and this time we have got as far as eight without any effect at all. I'll write another to-morrow morning. I mean to blot it a good deal and shake some water over it out of the pepper-castor, to make it look penitent. 'I'm in such a state of mind that I hardly know what I write'—blot—'if you could see me at this minute shedding tears for my past misconduct'—pepper-castor—'my hand trembles when I think'—blot again—if that don't produce the effect, it's all over."

By this time Mr Swiveller had finished his entry, and he now replaced his pencil in its little sheath and closed the book, in a perfectly grave and serious frame of mind. His friend discovered that it was time for him to fulfil some other engagement, and Richard Swiveller was accordingly left alone, in company with the rosy wine and his own meditations touching Miss Sophy Wackles.

"It's rather sudden," said Dick shaking his head with a look of infinite wisdom, and running on (as he was accustomed to do) with scraps of verse as if they were only prose in a hurry; "when the heart of a man is depressed with fears, the mist is dispelled when Miss Wackles appears: she's a very nice girl. She's like the red red rose that's newly sprung in June—there's no denying that—she's also like a melody that's sweetly played in tune. It's really very sudden. Not that there's any need, on account of Fred's little sister, to turn cool directly, but it's better not to go too far. If I begin to cool at all I must begin at once, I see that. There's the chance of an action for breach, that's one reason. There's the chance of Sophy's getting another husband, that's another. There's the chance of—no, there's no chance of that, but it's as well to be on the safe side."

This undeveloped consideration was the possibility, which Richard Swiveller sought to conceal even from himself, of his not being proof against the charms of Miss Wackles, and in some unguarded moment, by linking his fortunes to hers for ever, of putting it out of his own power to further the notable scheme to which he had so readily become a party. For all these reasons, he decided to pick a quarrel with Miss Wackles without delay, and casting about for a pretext determined in favour of groundless jealousy. Having made up his mind on this important point, he circulated the glass (from his right hand to his left, and back again) pretty freely, to enable him to act his part with the greater discretion, and then, after making some slight improvements in his toilet, bent his steps towards the spot hallowed by the fair object of his meditations.

This spot was at Chelsea, for there Miss Sophia Wackles resided with her widowed mother and two sisters, in conjunction with whom she maintained a very small day-school for young ladies of proportionate dimensions; a circumstance which was made known to the neighbourhood by an oval board over the front first-floor window, whereon appeared in circumambient flourishes the words "Ladies' Seminary"; and which was further published and proclaimed at intervals between the hours of half-past nine and ten in the morning, by a straggling and solitary young lady of tender years standing on the scraper on the tips of her toes and making futile attempts to reach the knocker with a spelling-book. The several duties of instruction in this establishment were thus discharged. English grammar, composition, geography, and the use of the dumb-bells, by Miss Melissa Wackles; writing, arithmetic, dancing, music, and general fascina-tion, by Miss Sophy Wackles; the art of needle-work, marking, and samplery, by Miss

Jane Wackles; corporal punishment, fasting, and other tortures and terrors, by Mrs Wackles. Miss Melissa Wackles was the eldest daughter, Miss Sophy the next, and Miss Jane the youngest. Miss Melissa might have seen five-and-thirty summers or thereabouts, and verged on the autumnal; Miss Sophy was a fresh, good-humoured, buxom girl of twenty; and Miss Jane numbered scarcely sixteen years. Mrs Wackles was an excellent but rather venomous old lady of three-score.

To this Ladies' Seminary then, Richard Swiveller hied, with designs obnoxious to the peace of the fair Sophia, who, arrayed in virgin white, embellished by no ornament but one blushing rose, received him on his arrival, in the midst of very elegant not to say brilliant preparations; such as the embellishment of the room with the little flower-pots which always stood on the window-sill outside, save in windy weather when they blew into the area; the choice attire of the day-scholars who were allowed to grace the festival; the unwonted curls of Miss Jane Wackles who had kept her head during the whole of the preceding day screwed up tight in a yellow play-bill; and the solemn gentility and stately bearing of the old lady and her eldest daughter, which struck Mr Swiveller as being uncommon but made no further impression upon him.

The truth is—and, as there is no accounting for tastes, even a taste so strange as this may be recorded without being looked upon as a wilful and malicious invention—the truth is that neither Mrs Wackles nor her eldest daughter had at any time greatly favoured the pretensions of Mr Swiveller, being accustomed to make slight mention of him as "a gay young man" and to sigh and shake their heads ominously whenever his name was mentioned. Mr Swiveller's conduct in respect to Miss Sophy having been of that vague and dilatory kind which is usually looked upon as betokening no fixed matrimonial intentions, the young lady herself began in course of time to deem it highly desirable, that it should be brought to an issue one way or other. Hence she had at last consented to play off against Richard Swiveller a stricken market-gardener known to be ready with his offer on the smallest encouragement, and hence—as this occasion had been specially assigned for the purpose—that great anxiety on her part for Richard Swiveller's presence which had occasioned her to leave the note he has been seen to receive. "If he has any expectations at all or any means of keeping a wife well," said Mrs Wackles to her eldest daughter, "he'll state 'em to us now or never."—"If he really cares about me," thought Miss Sophy, "he must tell me so, to-night."

But all these sayings and doings and thinkings being unknown to Mr Swiveller, affected him not in the least; he was debating in his mind how he could best turn jealous, and wishing that Sophy were for that occasion only far less pretty than she was, or that she were her own sister, which would have served his turn as well, when the company came, and among them the market-gardener, whose name was Cheggs. But Mr Cheggs came not alone or unsupported, for he prudently brought along with him his sister, Miss Cheggs, who making straight to Miss Sophy and taking her by both hands, and kissing her on both cheeks, hoped in an audible whisper that they had not come too early.

"Too early, no!" replied Miss Sophy.

"Oh, my dear," rejoined Miss Cheggs in the same whisper as before, "I've been so tormented, so worried, that it's a mercy we were not here at four o'clock in the afternoon. Alick has been in *such* a state of impatience to come! You'd hardly believe that he was dressed before dinner-time and has been looking at the clock and teasing me ever since. It's all your fault, you naughty thing."

Hereupon Miss Sophy blushed, and Mr Cheggs (who was bashful before ladies) blushed too, and Miss Sophy's mother and sisters, to prevent Mr Cheggs from blushing more, lavished civilities and attentions upon him, and left Richard Swiveller to take care of himself. Here was the very thing he wanted, here was good cause reason and foundation for pretending to be angry; but having this cause reason and foundation which he had come expressly to seek, not expecting to find, Richard Swiveller was angry in sound earnest, and wondered what the devil Cheggs meant by his impudence.

However, Mr Swiveller had Miss Sophy's hand for the first quadrille (country-dances being low, were utterly proscribed) and so gained an advantage over his rival, who sat despondingly in a corner and contemplated the glorious figure of the young lady as she moved through the mazy dance. Nor was this the only start Mr Swiveller had of the market-gardener, for determining to show the family what quality of man they trifled with, and influenced perhaps by his late libations, he performed such feats of agility and such spins and twirls as filled the company with astonishment, and in particular caused a very long gentleman who was dancing with a very short scholar, to stand quite transfixed by wonder and admiration. Even Mrs Wackles forgot for the moment to snub three small young ladies who were inclined to be happy, and could not repress a rising thought that to have such a dancer as that in the family would be a pride indeed.

At this momentous crisis, Miss Cheggs proved herself a vigorous and useful ally, for not confining herself to expressing by scornful smiles a contempt for Mr Swiveller's accomplishments, she took every opportunity of whispering into Miss Sophy's ear expressions of condolence and sympathy on her being worried by such a ridiculous creature, declaring that she was frightened to death lest Alick should fall upon, and beat him, in the fulness of his wrath, and entreating Miss Sophy to observe how the eyes of the said Alick gleamed with love and fury; passions, it may be observed, which being too much for his eyes rushed into his nose also, and suffused it with a crimson glow.

"You must dance with Miss Cheggs," said Miss Sophy to Dick Swiveller, after she had herself danced twice with Mr Cheggs and made great show of encouraging his advances. "She's such a nice girl—and her brother's quite delightful."

"Quite delightful is he?" muttered Dick. "Quite delighted too, I should say, from the manner in which he's looking this way."

Here Miss Jane (previously instructed for the purpose) interposed her many curls and whispered her sister to observe how jealous Mr Cheggs was.

"Jealous! Like his impudence!" said Richard Swiveller.

"His impudence, Mr Swiveller!" said Miss Jane, tossing her head. "Take care he don't hear you, sir, or you may be sorry for it."

"Oh, pray, Jane——" said Miss Sophy.

"Nonsense!" replied her sister. "Why shouldn't Mr Cheggs be jealous if he likes? I like that, certainly. Mr Cheggs has as good a right to be jealous as anybody else has, and perhaps he may have a better right soon if he hasn't already. You know best about that, Sophy!"

Though this was a concerted plot between Miss Sophy and her sister, originating in humane intentions and having for its object the inducing Mr Swiveller to declare himself in time, it failed in its effect; for Miss Jane being one of those young ladies who are prematurely shrill and shrewish, gave such undue importance to her part that Mr Swiveller retired in dudgeon, resigning his mistress to Mr Cheggs and conveying a defiance into his looks which that gentleman indignantly returned.

"Did you speak to me, sir?" said Mr Cheggs, following him into a corner. "Have the kindness to smile, sir, in order that we may not be suspected. Did you speak to me, sir?"

Mr Swiveller looked with a supercilious smile at Mr Cheggs's toes, then raised his eyes from them to his ankle, from that to his shin, from that to his knee, and so on very gradually, keeping up his right leg, until he reached his waistcoat, when he raised his eyes from button to button until he reached his chin, and travelling straight up the middle of his nose came at last to his eyes, when he said abruptly,

"No, sir, I didn't."

"Hem!" said Mr Cheggs, glancing over his shoulder, "have the goodness to smile again, sir. Perhaps you wished to speak to me, sir."

"No, sir, I didn't do that, either."

"Perhaps you may have nothing to say to me *now,* sir," said Mr Cheggs fiercely.

At these words Richard Swiveller withdrew his eyes from Mr Cheggs's face, and travelling down the middle of his nose and down his waistcoat and down his right leg, reached his toes again, and carefully surveyed them; this done, he crossed over, and coming up the other leg and thence approaching by the waistcoat as before, said when he had got to his eyes "No, sir, I haven't."

"Oh, indeed, sir!" said Mr Cheggs. "I'm glad to hear it. You know where I'm to be found, I suppose, sir, in case you *should* have anything to say to me?"

"I can easily inquire, sir, when I want to know."

"There's nothing more we need say, I believe, sir?"

"Nothing more, sir"—With that they closed the tremendous dialogue by frowning mutually. Mr Cheggs hastened to tender his hand to Miss Sophy, and Mr Swiveller sat himself down in a corner in a very moody state.

Hard by this corner, Mrs Wackles and Miss Wackles were seated, looking on at the dance; and unto Mrs and Miss Wackles, Miss Cheggs occasionally darted when her partner was occupied with his share of the figure, and made some remark or other which was gall and wormwood to Richard Swiveller's soul. Looking into the eyes of Mrs and Miss Wackles for encouragement, and sitting very upright and uncomfortable on a couple of hard stools, were two of the day-scholars; and when Miss Wackles smiled, and Mrs Wackles smiled, the two little girls on the stools sought to curry favour by smiling likewise, in gracious acknowledgment of which attention the old lady frowned them down instantly, and said that if they dared to be guilty of such an impertinence again, they should be sent under convoy to their respective homes. This threat caused one of the young ladies, she being of a weak and trembling temperament, to shed tears, and for this offence they were both filed off immediately, with a dreadful promptitude that struck terror into the souls of all the pupils.

"I've got such news for you," said Miss Cheggs approaching once more. "Alick has been saying such things to Sophy. Upon my word, you know, it's quite serious and in earnest, that's clear."

"What's he been saying, my dear?" demanded Mrs Wackles.

"All manner of things," replied Miss Cheggs, "you can't think how out he has been speaking!"

Richard Swiveller considered it advisable to hear no more, but taking advantage of a pause in the dancing, and the approach of Mr Cheggs to pay his court to the old lady, swaggered with an extremely careful assumption of extreme carelessness towards the door, passing on the way Miss Jane Wackles, who in all the glory of her curls was holding a flirtation (as good practice when no better was to be had) with a feeble old gentleman who lodged in the parlour. Near the door sat Miss Sophy, still fluttered and confused by the attentions of Mr Cheggs, and by her side Richard Swiveller lingered for a moment to exchange a few parting words.

"My boat is on the shore and my bark is on the sea, but before I pass this door I will say farewell to thee," murmured Dick, looking gloomily upon her.

"Are you going?" said Miss Sophy, whose heart sank within her at the result of her stratagem, but who affected a light indifference notwithstanding.

"Am I going!" echoed Dick bitterly. "Yes, I am. What then?"

"Nothing, except that it's very early," said Miss Sophy; "but you are your own master, of course."

"I would that I had been my own mistress too," said Dick, "before I had ever entertained a thought of you. Miss Wackles, I believed you true, and I was blest in so believing, but now I mourn that e'er I knew, a girl so fair yet so deceiving."

Miss Sophy bit her lip and affected to look with great interest after Mr Cheggs, who was quaffing lemonade in the distance.

"I came here," said Dick, rather oblivious of the purpose with which he had really come, "with my bosom expanded, my heart dilated, and my sentiments of a corresponding description. I go away with feelings that may be conceived but cannot be described, feeling within myself the desolating truth that my best affections have experienced this night a stifler!"

"I am sure I don't know what you mean, Mr Swiveller," said Miss Sophy with downcast eyes. "I'm very sorry if—"

"Sorry, Ma'am!" said Dick, "sorry in the possession of a Cheggs! But I wish you a very good night, concluding with this slight remark, that there is a young lady growing up at this present moment for me, who has not only great personal attractions but great wealth, and who has requested her next of kin to propose for my hand, which, having a regard for some members of her family, I have consented to promise. It's a gratifying circumstance which you'll be glad to hear, that a young and lovely girl is growing into a woman expressly on my account, and is now saving up for me. I thought I'd mention it. I have now merely to apologise for trespassing so long upon your attention. Good night."

"There's one good thing springs out of all this," said Richard Swiveller to himself when he had reached home and was hanging over the candle with the extinguisher in his hand, "which is, that I now go heart and soul, neck and heels, with Fred in all his scheme about little Nelly, and right glad he'll be to find me so strong upon it. He shall know all about that to-morrow, and in the mean time, as it's rather late, I'll try and get a wink or two of the balmy."

"The balmy" came almost as soon as it was courted. In a very few minutes Mr Swiveller was fast asleep, dreaming that he had married Nelly Trent and come into the property, and that his first act of power was to lay waste the market-garden of Mr Cheggs and turn it into a brick-field.

Chapter IX

T HE child, in her confidence with Mrs Quilp, had but feebly described the sadness and sorrow of her thoughts, or the heaviness of the cloud which overhung her home, and cast dark shadows on its hearth. Besides that it was very difficult to impart to any person not intimately acquainted with the life she led, an adequate sense of its gloom and loneliness, a constant fear of in some way committing or injuring the old man to whom she was so tenderly attached, had restrained her even in the midst of her heart's overflowing, and made her timid of allusion to the main cause of her anxiety and distress.

For, it was not the monotonous days unchequered by variety and uncheered by pleasant companionship, it was not the dark dreary evenings or the long solitary nights, it was not the absence of every slight and easy pleasure for which young hearts beat high, or the knowing nothing of childhood but its weakness and its easily wounded spirit, that had wrung such tears from Nell. To see the old man struck down beneath the pressure of some hidden grief, to mark his wavering and unsettled state, to be agitated at times with a dreadful fear that his mind was wandering, and to trace in his words and looks the dawning of despondent madness; to watch and wait and listen for confirmation of these things day after day, and to feel and know that, come what might, they were alone in the world with no one to help or advise or care about them—these were causes of depression and anxiety that might have sat heavily on an older breast with many influences at work to cheer and gladden it, but how heavily on the mind of a young child to whom they were ever present, and who was constantly surrounded by all that could keep such thoughts in restless action!

And yet, to the old man's vision, Nell was still the same. When he could for a moment disengage his mind from the phantom that haunted and brooded on it always, there was his young companion with the same smile for him, the same earnest words, the same merry laugh, the same love and care that sinking deep into his soul seemed to have been present to him through his whole life. And so he went on, content to read the book of her heart from the page first presented to him, little dreaming of the story that lay hidden in its other leaves, and murmuring within himself that at least the child was happy.

She had been once. She had gone singing through the dim rooms, and moving with gay and lightsome step among their dusty treasures, making them older by her young life, and sterner and more grim by her gay and cheerful presence. But now the chambers were cold and gloomy, and when she left her own little room to while away the tedious hours, and sat in one of them, she was still and motionless as their inanimate occupants, and had no heart to startle the echoes—hoarse from their long silence—with her voice.

In one of these rooms was a window looking into the street, where the child sat, many and many a long evening, and often far into the night, alone and thoughtful. None are so anxious as those who watch and wait, and at these times, mournful fancies came flocking on her mind, in crowds.

She would take her station here at dusk, and watch the people as they passed up and down the street, or appeared at the windows of the opposite houses, wondering whether those rooms were as lonesome as that in which she sat, and whether those people felt it company to see her sitting there, as she did only to see them look out and draw in their heads again. There was a crooked stack of chimneys on one of the roofs, in which by often looking at them she had fancied ugly faces that were frowning over at her and trying to peer into the room, and she felt glad when it grew too dark to make them out, though she was sorry too, when the man came to light the lamps in the street, for it made it late, and very dull inside. Then she would draw in her head to look round the room and see that everything was in its place and hadn't moved; and looking out into the street again, would perhaps see a man passing with a coffin on his back, and two or three others silently following him to a house where somebody lay dead, which made her shudder and think of such things until they suggested afresh the old man's altered face and manner, and a new train of fears and speculations. If he were to die—if sudden illness had happened to him, and he were never to come home again, alive—if, one night, he should come home, and kiss and bless her as usual, and after she had gone to bed and had fallen asleep and was perhaps dreaming pleasantly, and smiling in her sleep, he should kill himself and his blood come creeping, creeping, on the ground to her own bedroom door! These thoughts were too terrible to dwell upon, and again she would have recourse to the street, now trodden by fewer feet and darker and more silent than before. The shops were closing fast, and lights began to shine from the upper windows, as the neighbours went to bed. By degrees these dwindled away and disappeared, or were replaced here and there by a feeble rush-candle which was to burn all night. Still there was one late shop at no great distance which sent forth a ruddy glare upon the pavement even yet, and looked bright and companionable. But in a little time this closed, the light was extinguished, and all was gloomy and quiet, except when some stray footsteps sounded on the pavement, or a neighbour, out later than his wont, knocked lustily at his house-door to rouse the sleeping inmates.

When the night had worn away thus far (and seldom now until it had) the child would close the window, and steal softly downstairs, thinking as she went that if one of those hideous faces below, which often mingled with her dreams, were to meet her by the way, rendering itself visible by some strange light of its own, how terrified she would be. But these fears vanished before a well-trimmed lamp and the familiar aspect of her own room. After praying fervently and with many bursting tears for the old man, and the restoration of his peace of mind and the happiness they had once enjoyed, she would lay her head upon the pillow and sob herself to sleep, often starting up again, before the daylight came, to listen for the bell, and respond to the imaginary summons which had roused her from her slumber.

One night, the third after Nelly's interview with Mrs Quilp, the old man, who had been weak and ill all day, said he should not leave home. The child's eyes sparkled at the intelligence, but her joy subsided when they reverted to his worn and sickly face.

"Two days," he said, "two whole, clear, days have passed, and there is no reply. What *did* he tell thee, Nell?"

"Exactly what I told you, dear grandfather, indeed."

"True," said the old man, faintly. "Yes. But tell me again, Nell. My head fails me. What was it that he told thee? Nothing more than that he would see me to-morrow or next day? That was in the note."

"Nothing more," said the child. "Shall I go to him again to-morrow, dear grandfather? Very early? I will be there and back, before breakfast."

The old man shook his head, and sighing mournfully, drew her towards him.

" 'Twould be of no use, my dear, no earthly use. But if he deserts me, Nell, at this moment—if he deserts me now, when I should, with his assistance, be recompensed for all the time and money I have lost, and all the agony of mind I have undergone, which makes me what you see, I am ruined, and—worse, far worse than that—have ruined thee, for whom I ventured all. If we are beggars—!"

"What if we are?" said the child boldly. "Let us be beggars, and be happy."

"Beggars—and happy!" said the old man. "Poor child!"

"Dear grandfather," cried the girl with an energy which shone in her flushed face, trembling voice, and impassioned gesture, "I am not a child in that I think, but even if I am, oh, hear me pray that we may beg, or work in open roads or fields, to earn a scanty living, rather than live as we do now."

"Nelly!" said the old man.

"Yes, yes, rather than live as we do now," the child repeated, more earnestly than before. "If you are sorrowful, let me know why and be sorrowful too; if you waste away and are paler and weaker every day, let me be your nurse and try to comfort you. If you are poor, let us be poor together, but let me be with you, do let me be with you, do not let me see such change and not know why, or I shall break my heart and die. Dear grandfather, let us leave this sad place to-morrow, and beg our way from door to door."

The old man covered his face with his hands, and hid it in the pillow of the couch on which he lay.

"Let us be beggars," said the child passing an arm round his neck, "I have no fear but we shall have enough, I am sure we shall. Let us walk through country places, and sleep in fields and under trees, and never think of money again, or anything that can make you sad, but rest at nights, and have the sun and wind upon our faces in the day, and thank God together. Let us never set foot in dark rooms or melancholy houses any more, but wander up and down wherever we like to go, and when you are tired, you shall stop to rest in the pleasantest place that we can find, and I will go and beg for both."

The child's voice was lost in sobs as she dropped upon the old man's neck; nor did she weep alone.

These were not words for other ears, nor was it a scene for other eyes. And yet other ears and eyes were there and greedily taking in all that passed, and moreover they were the ears and eyes of no less a person than Mr Daniel Quilp, who, having entered unseen when the child first placed herself at the old man's side, refrained—actuated, no doubt, by motives of the purest delicacy—from interrupting the conversation, and stood looking on with his accustomed grin. Standing, however, being a tiresome attitude to a gentleman already fatigued with walking, and the dwarf being one of that kind of persons who usually make themselves at home, he soon cast his eyes upon a chair into which he skipped with uncommon agility, and perching himself on the back with his feet upon the seat, was thus enabled to look on and listen with greater comfort to himself, besides gratifying at the same time that taste for doing something fantastic and monkey-like, which on all occasions had strong possession of him. Here, then, he sat, one leg cocked carelessly over the other, his chin resting on the palm of his hand, his head turned a little on one side, and his ugly features twisted into a complacent grimace. And in this position the old man, happening in course of time to look that way, at length chanced to see him, to his unbounded astonishment.

The child uttered a suppressed shriek on beholding this agreeable figure; in their first surprise both she and the old man, not knowing what to say, and half doubting its reality, looked shrinkingly at it. Not at all disconcerted by this reception, Daniel Quilp preserved the same attitude, merely nodding twice or thrice with great condescension. At length the old man pronounced his name, and inquired how he came there.

"Through the door," said Quilp, pointing over his shoulder with his thumb. "I'm not quite small enough to get through keyholes. I wish I was. I want to have some talk with you, particularly, and in private—with nobody present, neighbour. Good-bye, little Nelly."

Nell looked at the old man, who nodded to her to retire, and kissed her cheek.

"Ah!" said the dwarf, smacking his lips, "what a nice kiss that was—just upon the rosy part. What a capital kiss!"

Nell was none the slower in going away, for this remark. Quilp looked after her with an admiring leer, and when she had closed the door, fell to complimenting the old man upon her charms.

"Such a fresh, blooming, modest little bud, neighbour," said Quilp, nursing his short leg, and making his eyes twinkle very much; "such a chubby, rosy, cosy, little Nell!"

The old man answered by a forced smile, and was plainly struggling with a feeling of the keenest and most exquisite impatience. It was not lost upon Quilp, who delighted in torturing him, or indeed anybody else when he could.

"She's so," said Quilp, speaking very slowly, and feigning to be quite absorbed in the subject, "so small, so compact, so beautifully modelled, so fair, with such blue veins and such a transparent skin, and such little feet, and such winning ways—but bless me, you're nervous! Why neighbour, what's the matter? I swear to you," continued the dwarf, dismounting from the chair and sitting down in it, with a careful slowness of gesture very different from the rapidity with which he had sprung up unheard, "I swear to you that I had no idea old blood ran so fast or kept so warm. I thought it was sluggish in its course, and cool, quite cool. I am pretty sure it ought to be. Yours must be out of order, neighbour."

"I believe it is," groaned the old man, clasping his head with both hands. "There's burning fever here, and something now and then to which I fear to give a name."

The dwarf said never a word, but watched his companion as he paced restlessly up and down the room, and presently returned to his seat. Here he remained, with his head bowed upon his breast for some time, and then suddenly raising it, said:

"Once, and once for all, have you brought me any money?"

"No!" returned Quilp.

"Then," said the old man, clenching his hands desperately, and looking upward, "the child and I are lost!"

"Neighbour," said Quilp glancing sternly at him, and beating his hand twice or thrice upon the table to attract his wandering attention, "let me be plain with you, and play a fairer game than when you held all the cards, and I saw but the backs and nothing more. You have no secret from me now."

The old man looked up, trembling.

"You are surprised," said Quilp. "Well, perhaps that's natural. You have no secret from me now, I say; no, not one. For now I know that all those sums of money, that all those loans, advances, and supplies that you have had from me, have found their way to—shall I say the word?"

"Ay!" replied the old man, "say it, if you will."

"To the gaming-table," rejoined Quilp, "your nightly haunt. This was the precious scheme to make your fortune, was it; this was the secret certain source of wealth in which I was to have sunk my money (if I had been the fool you took me for); this was your inexhaustible mine of gold, your El Dorado, eh?"

"Yes," cried the old man, turning upon him with gleaming eyes, "it was. It is. It will be till I die."

"That I should have been blinded," said Quilp, looking contemptuously at him, "by a mere shallow gambler!"

"I am no gambler," cried the old man fiercely. "I call Heaven to witness that I never played for gain of mine, or love of play; that at every piece I staked, I whispered to myself that orphan's name and called on Heaven to bless the venture, which it never did. Whom did it prosper? Who were those with whom I played? Men who lived by plunder, profligacy, and riot, squandering their gold in doing ill and propagating vice and evil. My winnings would have been from them, my winnings would have been bestowed to the last farthing on a young sinless child whose life they would have sweetened and made happy. What would they have contracted? The means of corruption, wretchedness, and misery. Who would not have hoped in such a cause—tell me that; now who would not have hoped as I did?"

"When did you first begin this mad career?" asked Quilp, his taunting inclination subdued for a moment by the old man's grief and wildness.

"When did I first begin?" he rejoined, passing his hand across his brow. "When *was* it, that I first began? When should it be, but when I began to think how little I had saved, how long a time it took to save at all, how short a time I might have at my age to live, and how she would be left to the rough mercies of the world, with barely enough to keep her from the sorrows that wait on poverty; then it was that I began to think about it."

"After you first came to me to get your precious grandson packed off to sea?" said Quilp.

"Shortly after that," replied the old man. "I thought of it a long time, and had it in my sleep for months. Then I began. I found no pleasure in it, I expected none. What has it ever brought to me but anxious days and sleepless nights, but loss of health and peace of mind, and gain of feebleness and sorrow!"

"You lost what money you had laid by, first, and then came to me. While I thought you were making your fortune (as you said you were) you were making yourself a beggar, eh? Dear me! And so it comes to pass that I hold every security you could scrape together, and a bill of sale upon the—upon the stock and property," said Quilp, standing up and looking about him, as if to assure himself that none of it had been taken away. "But did you never win?"

"Never!" groaned the old man. "Never won back my loss!"

"I thought," sneered the dwarf, "that if a man played long enough he was sure to win at last, or at the worst not to come off a loser."

"And so he is," cried the old man, suddenly rousing himself from his state of despondency, and lashed into the most violent excitement, "so he is; I have felt that from the first, I have always known it, I've seen it, I never felt it half so strongly as I feel it now. Quilp, I have dreamed three nights of winning the same large sum, I never could dream that dream before, though I have often tried. Do not desert me now I have this chance. I have no resource but you, give me some help, let me try this one last hope."

The dwarf shrugged his shoulders and shook his head.

"See, Quilp, good tender-hearted Quilp," said the old man, drawing some scraps of paper from his pocket with a trembling hand, and clasping the dwarf's arm, "only see here. Look at these figures, the result of long calculation, and painful and hard experience. I *must* win. I only want a little help once more, a few pounds, but two score pounds, dear Quilp."

"The last advance was seventy," said the dwarf; "and it went in one night."

"I know it did," answered the old man, "but that was the very worst fortune of all, and the time had not come then. Quilp, consider, consider," the old man cried, trembling so much the while that the papers in his hand fluttered as if they were shaken by the wind, "that orphan child. If I were alone, I could die with gladness—perhaps even anticipate that doom which is dealt out so unequally, coming as it does on the proud and happy in their strength, and shunning the needy and afflicted and all who court it in their despair—but what I have done has been for her. Help me for her sake I implore you—not for mine, for hers!"

"I'm sorry I've got an appointment in the City," said Quilp, looking at his watch with perfect self-possession, "or I should have been very glad to have spent half an hour with you while you composed yourself—very glad."

"Nay, Quilp, good Quilp," gasped the old man, catching at his skirts—"you and I have talked together more than once of her poor mother's story. The fear of her coming to poverty has perhaps been bred in me by that. Do not be hard upon me, but take that into account. You are a great gainer by me. Oh, spare me the money for this one last hope!"

"I couldn't do it really," said Quilp with unusual politeness, "though I tell you what—and this is a circumstance worth bearing in mind as showing how the sharpest among us may be taken in sometimes—I was so deceived by the penurious way in which you lived, alone with Nelly——"

"All done to save money for tempting fortune, and make her triumph greater," cried the old man.

"Yes yes, I understand that now," said Quilp; "but I was going to say, I was so deceived by that, your miserly way, the reputation you had among those who knew you of being rich, and your repeated assurances that you would make of my advances treble and quadruple the interest you paid me, that I'd have advanced you even now what you want, on your simple note of hand, though I had been led to suspect something wrong, if I hadn't unexpectedly become acquainted with your secret way of life."

"Who is it," retorted the old man desperately, "that notwithstanding all my caution, told you that? Come. Let me know the name—the person."

The crafty dwarf, bethinking himself that his giving up the child would lead to the disclosure of the artifice he had employed, which, as nothing was to be gained by it, it was as well to conceal, stopped short in his answer and said, "Now, who do you think?"

"It was Kit, it must have been the boy; he played the spy and you tampered with him?" said the old man.

"How came you to think of him?" said the dwarf in a tone of great commiseration. "Yes, it was Kit. Poor Kit!"

So saying, he nodded in a friendly manner, and took his leave, stopping when he had passed the outer door a little distance, and grinning with extraordinary delight.

"Poor Kit!" muttered Quilp. "I think it was Kit who said I was an uglier dwarf than could be seen anywhere for a penny, wasn't it? Ha, ha, ha! Poor Kit!"

And with that he went his way, still chuckling as he went.

Chapter X

DANIEL Quilp neither entered nor left the old man's house, unobserved. In the shadow of an archway nearly opposite, leading to one of the many passages which diverged from the main street, there lingered one who having taken up his position when the twilight first came on, still maintained it with undiminished patience, and leaning against the wall with the manner of one who had a long time to wait, and being well used to it was quite resigned, scarcely changed his attitude for the hour together.

This patient lounger attracted little attention from any of those who passed, and bestowed as little upon them. His eyes were constantly directed towards one object, the window at which the child was accustomed to sit. If he withdrew them for a moment, it was only to glance at a clock in some neighbouring shop, and then to strain his sight once more in the old quarter with increased earnestness and attention.

It has been remarked that this personage evinced no weariness in his place of concealment, nor did he, long as his waiting was. But as the time went on, he manifested some anxiety and surprise, glancing at the clock more frequently and at the window less hopefully than before. At length the clock was hidden from his sight by some envious shutters, then the church steeples proclaimed eleven at night, then the quarter past, and then the conviction seemed to obtrude itself upon his mind that it was of no use tarrying there any longer.

That the conviction was an unwelcome one, and that he was by no means willing to yield to it, was apparent from his reluctance to quit the spot; from the tardy steps with which he often left it, still looking over his shoulder at the same window; and from the precipitation with which he as often returned, when a fancied noise or the changing and imperfect light induced him to suppose it had been softly raised. At length he gave the matter up as hopeless for that night, and suddenly breaking into a run as though to force himself away, scampered off at his utmost speed, nor once ventured to look behind him lest he should be tempted back again.

Without relaxing his pace or stopping to take breath, this mysterious individual dashed on through a great many alleys and narrow ways until he at length arrived in a square paved court, when he subsided into a walk, and making for a small house from the window of which a light was shining, lifted the latch of the door and passed in.

"Bless us!" cried a woman turning sharply round, "who's that? Oh! It's you, Kit!"

"Yes, mother, it's me."

"Why, how tired you look, my dear!"

"Old master an't gone out to-night," said Kit; "and so she hasn't been at the window at all." With which words, he sat down by the fire and looked very mournful and discontented.

The room in which Kit sat himself down in this condition was an extremely poor and homely place, but with that air of comfort about it, nevertheless, which—or the spot must be a wretched one indeed—cleanliness and order can always impart in some degree. Late as the Dutch clock showed it to be, the poor woman was still hard at work at an ironing-table; a young child lay sleeping in a cradle near the fire; and another, a sturdy boy of two or three years old, very wide awake, with a very tight night-cap on his head, and a night-gown very much too small for him on his body, was sitting bolt upright in a clothes-basket, staring over the rim with his great round eyes, and looking as if he had thoroughly made up his mind never to go to sleep any more; which, as he had already declined to take his natural rest and had been brought out of bed in conse-quence, opened a cheerful prospect for his relations and friends. It was rather a queer-looking family; Kit, his mother, and the children, being all strongly alike.

Kit was disposed to be out of temper, as the best of us are too often—but he looked at the youngest child who was sleeping soundly, and from him to his other brother in the clothes-basket, and from him to their mother, who had been at work without complaint since morning, and thought it would be a better and kinder thing to be good-humoured. So he rocked the cradle with his foot, made a face at the rebel in the clothes-basket, which put him in high good-humour directly, and stoutly determined to be talkative and make himself agreeable.

"Ah, mother!" said Kit, taking out his clasp-knife and falling upon a great piece of bread and meat which she had had ready for him, hours before, "what a one you are! There an't many such as you, I know."

"I hope there are many a great deal better, Kit," said Mrs Nubbles; "and that there are, or ought to be, accordin' to what the parson at chapel says."

"Much *he* knows about it," returned Kit contemptuously. "Wait till he's a widder and works like you do, and gets as little, and does as much, and keeps his spirits up the same, and then I'll ask him what's o'clock and trust him for being right to half a second."

"Well," said Mrs Nubbles, evading the point, "your beer's down there by the fender, Kit."

"I see," replied her son, taking up the porter pot, "my love to you, mother. And the parson's health too if you like. I don't bear him any malice, not I!"

"Did you tell me just now that your master hadn't gone out to-night?" inquired Mrs Nubbles.

"Yes," said Kit, "worse luck."

"You should say better luck, I think," returned his mother, "because Miss Nelly won't have been left alone."

"Ah!" said Kit, "I forgot that. I said worse luck, because I've been watching ever since eight o'clock, and seen nothing of her."

"I wonder what she'd say," cried his mother, stopping in her work and looking round, "if she knew that every night, when she—poor thing—is sitting alone at that window, you are watching in the open street for fear any harm should come to her, and that you never leave the place or come home to your bed though you're ever so tired, till such time as you think she's safe in hers."

"Never mind what she'd say," replied Kit, with something like a blush on his uncouth face; "she'll never know nothing, and consequently, she'll never say nothing."

Mrs Nubbles ironed away in silence for a minute or two, and coming to the fireplace for another iron, glanced stealthily at Kit while she rubbed it on a board and dusted it with a duster, but said nothing until she had returned to her table again, when holding the iron at an alarmingly short distance from her cheek, to test its temperature, and looking round with a smile, she observed:

"I know what some people would say, Kit——"

"Nonsense." interposed Kit with a perfect apprehension of what was to follow.

"No, but they would indeed. Some people would say that you'd fallen in love with her, I know they would."

To this, Kit only replied by bashfully bidding his mother "get out," and forming sundry strange figures with his legs and arms, accompanied by sympathetic contortions of his face. Not deriving from these means the relief which he sought, he bit off an immense mouthful from the bread and meat, and took a quick drink of the porter, by which artificial aids he choked himself and effected a diversion of the subject.

"Speaking seriously though, Kit," said his mother taking up the theme afresh, after a time, "for of course I was only in joke just now, it's very good and thoughtful, and like you, to do this, and never let anybody know it, though some day I hope she may come to know it, for I'm sure she would be very grateful to you, and feel it very much. It's a cruel thing to keep the dear child shut up there. I don't wonder that the old gentleman wants to keep it from you."

"He don't think it's cruel, bless you," said Kit, "and don't mean it to be so, or he wouldn't do it—I do consider, mother, that he wouldn't do it for all the gold and silver in the world. No, no, that he wouldn't. I know him better than that."

"Then what does he do it for, and why does he keep it so close from you?" said Mrs Nubbles.

"That I don't know," returned her son. "If he hadn't tried to keep it so close though, I should never have found it out, for it was his getting me away at night and sending me off so much earlier than he used to, that first made me curious to know what was going on. Hark! What's that?"

"It's only somebody outside."

"It's somebody crossing over here"—said Kit, standing up to listen, "and coming very fast too. He can't have gone out after I left, and the house caught fire, mother!"

The boy stood for a moment, really bereft, by the apprehension he had conjured up, of the power to move. The footsteps drew nearer, the door was opened with a hasty hand, and the child herself, pale and breathless, and hastily wrapped in a few disordered garments, hurried into the room.

"Miss Nelly! What is the matter!" cried mother and son together.

"I must not stay a moment," she returned, "grandfather has been taken very ill. I found him in a fit upon the floor——"

"I'll run for a doctor"—said Kit, seizing his brimless hat. "I'll be there directly, I'll——"

"No, no," cried Nell, "there is one there, you're not wanted, you—you—must never come near us any more!"

"What!" roared Kit.

"Never again," said the child. "Don't ask me why, for I don't know. Pray don't ask me why, pray don't be sorry, pray don't be vexed with me, I have nothing to do with it indeed!"

Kit looked at her with his eyes stretched wide, and opened and shut his mouth a great many times, but couldn't get out one word.

"He complains and raves of you," said the child. "I don't know what you have done, but I hope it's nothing very bad."

"*I* done!" roared Kit.

"He cries that you're the cause of all his misery," returned the child with tearful eyes; "he screamed and called for you, they say you must not come near him or he will die. You must not return to us any more. I came to tell you. I thought it would be better that I should come than somebody quite strange. Oh, Kit, what *have* you done? You, in whom I trusted so much, and who were almost the only friend I had!"

The unfortunate Kit looked at his young mistress harder and harder, and with eyes growing wider and wider, but was perfectly motionless and silent.

"I have brought his money for the week," said the child, looking to the woman and laying it on the table—"and—and—a little more, for he was always good and kind to me. I hope he will be sorry and do well somewhere else and not take this to heart too much. It grieves me very much to part with him like this, but there is no help. It must be done. Good night!"

With the tears streaming down her face, and her slight figure trembling with the agitation of the scene she had left, the shock she had received, the errand she had just discharged, and a thousand painful and affectionate feelings, the child hastened to the door, and disappeared as rapidly as she had come.

The poor woman, who had no cause to doubt her son, but every reason for relying on his honesty and truth, was staggered, notwithstanding, by his not having advanced one word in his defence. Visions of gallantry, knavery, robbery; and of the nightly absences from home for which he had accounted so strangely, having been occasioned by some unlawful pursuit; flocked into her brain and rendered her afraid to question him. She rocked herself upon a chair, wringing her hands and weeping bitterly, but Kit made no attempt to comfort her and remained quite bewildered. The baby in the cradle woke up and cried, the boy in the clothes-basket fell over on his back with the basket upon him and was seen no more, the mother wept louder yet and rocked faster, but Kit, insensible to all the din and tumult, remained in a state of utter stupefaction.

Chapter XI

QUIET and solitude were destined to hold uninterrupted rule no longer, beneath the roof that sheltered the child. Next morning the old man was in a raging fever accompanied with delirium, and sinking under the influence of this disorder he lay for many weeks in imminent peril of his life. There was watching enough now, but it was the watching of strangers who made of it a greedy trade, and who, in the intervals of their attendance upon the sick man huddled together with a ghastly good-fellowship, and ate and drank and made merry; for disease and death were their ordinary household gods.

Yet in all the hurry and crowding of such a time, the child was more alone than she had ever been before; alone in spirit, alone in her devotion to him who was wasting away upon his burning bed; alone in her unfeigned sorrow, and her unpurchased sympathy. Day after day, and night after night, found her still by the pillow of the unconscious sufferer, still anticipating his every want, and still listening to those repetitions of her name and those anxieties and cares for her, which were ever uppermost among his feverish wanderings.

The house was no longer theirs. Even the sick chamber seemed to be retained on the uncertain tenure of Mr Quilp's favour. The old man's illness had not lasted many days when he took formal possession of the premises and all upon them, in virtue of certain legal powers to that effect, which few understood and none presumed to call in question. This important step secured, with the assistance of a man of law whom he brought with him for the purpose, the dwarf proceeded to establish himself and his coadjutor in the house, as an assertion of his claim against all comers; and then set about making his quarters comfortable after his own fashion.

To this end, Mr Quilp encamped in the back parlour, having first put an effectual stop to any further business by shutting up the shop. Having looked out from among the old furniture the handsomest and most commodious chair he could possibly find, which he reserved for his own use, and an especially hideous and uncomfortable one, which he considerately appropriated to the accommodation of his friend, he caused them to be carried into this room and took up his position in great state. The apartment was very far removed from the old man's chamber, but Mr Quilp deemed it prudent, as a precaution against infection from fever, and a means of wholesome fumigation, not only to smoke himself without cessation, but to insist upon it that his legal friend did the like. Moreover, he sent an express to the wharf for the tumbling boy, who arriving with all despatch was enjoined to sit himself down in another chair just inside the door, continually to smoke a great pipe which the dwarf had provided for the purpose, and to take it from his lips under any pretence whatever, were it only for one minute at a time, if he dared. These arrangements completed, Mr Quilp looked round him with chuckling satisfaction, and remarked that he called that comfort.

The legal gentleman, whose melodious name was Brass, might have called it comfort also but for two drawbacks: one was that he could by no exertion sit easily in his chair, the seat of which was very hard, angular, slippery, and sloping; the other that tobacco-smoke always caused him great internal discomposure and annoyance. But as he was quite a creature of Mr Quilp's and had a thousand reasons for conciliating his good opinion, he tried to smile, and nodded his acquiescence with the best grace he could assume.

This Brass was an attorney of no very good repute from Bevis Marks in the City of London; he was a tall, meagre man, with a nose like a wen, a protruding forehead, retreating eyes, and hair of a deep red. He wore a long black surtout reaching nearly to his ankles, short black trousers, high shoes, and cotton stockings of a bluish grey. He had a cringing manner but a very harsh voice, and his blandest smiles were so extremely forbidding, that to have had his company under the least repulsive circumstances, one would have wished him to be out of temper that he might only scowl.

Quilp looked at his legal adviser, and seeing that he was winking very much in the anguish of his pipe, that he sometimes shuddered when he happened to inhale its full flavour, and that he constantly fanned the smoke from him, was quite overjoyed and rubbed his hands with glee.

"Smoke away, you dog," said Quilp turning to the boy; "fill your pipe again and smoke it fast, down to the last whiff, or I'll put the sealing-waxed end of it in the fire and rub it red-hot upon your tongue."

Luckily the boy was case-hardened, and would have smoked a small lime-kiln if anybody had treated him with it. Wherefore he only muttered a brief defiance of his master, and did as he was ordered.

"Is it good, Brass, is it nice, is it fragrant, do you feel like the Grand Turk?" said Quilp.

Mr Brass thought that if he did, the Grand Turk's feelings were by no means to be envied, but he said it was famous, and he had no doubt he felt very like that Potentate.

"This is the way to keep off fever," said Quilp, "this is the way to keep off every calamity of life. We'll never leave off all the time we stop here—smoke away, you dog, or you shall swallow the pipe."

"Shall we stop here long, Mr Quilp?" inquired his legal friend, when the dwarf had given his boy this last gentle admonition.

"We must stop, I suppose, till the old gentleman upstairs is dead," returned Quilp.

"He, he, he!" laughed Mr. Brass, "oh! very good!"

"Smoke away!" cried Quilp. "Never stop! you can talk as you smoke. Don't lose time."

"He, he, he!" cried Brass faintly, as he again applied himself to the odious pipe. "But if he should get better, Mr Quilp?"

"Then we shall stop till he does, and no longer," returned the dwarf.

"How kind it is of you, sir, to wait 'till then!" said Brass. "Some people, sir, would have sold or removed the goods—oh, dear, the very instant the law allowed 'em. Some people, sir, would have been all flintiness and granite. Some people, sir, would have——"

"Some people would have spared themselves the jabbering of such a parrot as you," interposed the dwarf.

"He, he, he!" cried Brass. "You have *such* spirits!"

The smoking sentinel at the door interposed in this place, and without taking his pipe from his lips, growled,

"Here's the gal a comin' down."

"The what, you dog?" said Quilp.

"The gal," returned the boy. "Are you deaf?"

"Oh!" said Quilp, drawing in his breath with great relish as if he were taking soup, "you and I will have such a settling presently; there's such a scratching and bruising in store for you, my dear young friend. Aha! Nelly! How is he now, my duck of diamonds?"

"He's very bad," replied the weeping child.

"What a pretty little Nell!" cried Quilp.

"Oh, beautiful, sir, beautiful indeed," said Brass. "Quite charming!"

"Has she come to sit upon Quilp's knee," said the dwarf, in what he meant to be a soothing tone, "or is she going to bed in her own little room inside here—which is poor Nelly going to do?"

"What a remarkable pleasant way he has with children!" muttered Brass, as if in confidence between himself and the ceiling; "upon my word it's quite a treat to hear him."

"I'm not going to stay at all," faltered Nell. "I want a few things out of that room, and then I—I—won't come down here any more."

"And a very nice little room it is!" said the dwarf looking into it as the child entered. "Quite a bower. You're sure you're not going to use it, you're sure you're not coming back, Nelly?"

"No," replied the child, hurrying away, with the few articles of dress she had come to remove; "never again, never again."

"She's very sensitive," said Quilp, looking after her. "Very sensitive; that's a pity. The bedstead is much about my size. I think I shall make it *my* little room."

Mr Brass encouraging this idea, as he would have encouraged any other emanating from the same source, the dwarf walked in to try the effect, which he did by throwing himself on his back upon the bed with his pipe in his mouth, and then kicking up his legs and smoking violently. Mr Brass applauding this picture very much, and the bed being soft and comfortable, Mr Quilp determined to use it, both as a sleeping place by night and as a kind of divan by day, and in order that it might be converted to the latter purpose at once, remained where he was and smoked his pipe out. The legal gentleman being by this time rather giddy and perplexed in his ideas (for this was one of the operations of the tobacco upon his nervous system), took the opportunity of slinking away into the open air where in course of time he recovered sufficiently to return with a countenance of tolerable composure. He was soon led on by the malicious dwarf to smoke himself into a relapse, and in that state stumbled upon a settee, where he slept till morning.

Such were Mr Quilp's first proceedings on entering upon his new property. He was for some days restrained by business from performing any particular pranks, as his time was pretty well occupied between taking, with the assistance of Mr Brass, a minute inventory of all the goods in the place, and going abroad upon his other concerns, which happily engaged him for several hours at a time. His avarice and caution being now thoroughly awakened, however, he was never absent from the house one night, and his eagerness for some termination, good or bad, to the old man's disorder, increasing rapidly as the time passed by, soon began to vent itself in open murmurs and exclamations of impatience.

Nell shrank timidly from all the dwarf's advances towards conversation and fled from the very sound of his voice, nor were the lawyer's smiles less terrible to her than Quilp's grimaces. She lived in such continual dread and apprehension of meeting one or other of them upon the stairs or in the passages if she stirred from her grandfather's chamber, that she seldom left it for a moment until late at night, when the silence encouraged her to venture forth and breathe the purer air of some empty room.

One night she had stolen to her usual window and was sitting there very sorrowfully, for the old man had been worse that day, when she thought she heard her name pronounced by a voice in the street, and looking down, recognised Kit, whose endeavours to attract her attention had roused her from her sad reflections.

"Miss Nell!" said the boy in a low voice.

"Yes," replied the child, doubtful whether she ought to hold any communication with the supposed culprit, but inclining to her old favourite still, "what do you want?"

"I have wanted to say a word to you for a long time," the boy replied, "but the people below have driven me away and wouldn't let me see you. You don't believe—I hope you don't really believe—that I deserve to be cast off as I have been; do you, Miss?"

"I must believe it," returned the child. "Or why would grandfather have been so angry with you?"

"I don't know," replied Kit. "I'm sure I've never deserved it from him, no, nor from you. I can say that with a true and honest heart any way. And then to be driven from the door, when I only came to ask how old master was——!"

"They never told me that," said the child. "I didn't know it indeed. I wouldn't have had them do it for the world."

"Thank'ee, Miss," returned Kit, "it's comfortable to hear you say that. I said I never would believe that it was your doing."

"That was right!" said the child eagerly.

"Miss Nell," cried the boy, coming under the window and speaking in a lower tone, "there are new masters downstairs. It's a change for you."

"It is indeed," replied the child.

"And so it will be for him when he gets better," said the boy, pointing towards the sick room.

"——If he ever does," added the child, unable to restrain her tears.

"Oh, he'll do that, he'll do that," said Kit, "I'm sure he will. You mustn't be cast down, Miss Nell. Now don't be, pray."

These words of encouragement and consolation were few and roughly said, but they affected the child and made her for the moment weep the more.

"He'll be sure to get better now," said the boy anxiously, "if you don't give way to low spirits and turn ill yourself, which would make him worse and throw him back just as he was recovering. When he does, say a good word—say a kind word for me, Miss Nell."

"They tell me I must not even mention your name to him for a long, long time," rejoined the child, "I dare not; and even if I might, what good would a kind word do you, Kit? We shall be very poor. We shall scarcely have bread to eat."

"It's not that I may be taken back," said the boy, "that I ask the favour of you. It isn't for the sake of food and wages that I've been waiting about so long in hopes to see you. Don't think that I'd come in a time of trouble to talk of such things as them."

The child looked gratefully and kindly at him, but waited that he might speak again.

"No, it's not that," said Kit hesitating, "it's something very different from that. I haven't got much sense I know, but if he could be brought to believe that I'd been a faithful servant to him, doing the best I could, and never meaning harm, perhaps he mightn't——"

Here Kit faltered so long that the child entreated him to speak out, and quickly, for it was very late, and time to shut the window.

"Perhaps he mightn't think it over venturesome of me to say—well, then, to say this"—cried Kit with sudden boldness. "This home is gone from you and him. Mother and I have got a poor one, but that's better than this with all these people here; and why not come there, till he's had time to look about and find a better!"

The child did not speak. Kit, in the relief of having made his proposition, found his tongue loosened, and spoke out in its favour with his utmost eloquence.

"You think," said the boy, "that it's very small and inconvenient. So it is, but it's very clean. Perhaps you think it would be noisy, but there's not a quieter court than ours in all the town. Don't be afraid of the children; the baby hardly ever cries, and the other one is very good—besides I'd mind 'em. They wouldn't vex you much, I'm sure. Do try, Miss Nell, do try. The little front room upstairs is very pleasant. You can see a piece of the church-clock through the chimneys and almost tell the time; mother says it would be just the thing for you, and so it would, and you'd have her to wait upon you both, and me to run of errands. We don't mean money, bless you; you're not to think of that. Will you try him, Miss Nell? Only say you'll try him. Do try to make old master come, and ask him first what I have done—will you only promise that, Miss Nell?"

Before the child could reply to this earnest solicitation, the street-door opened, and Mr Brass thrusting out his night-capped head called in a surly voice, "Who's there!" Kit immediately glided away, and Nell, closing the window softly, drew back into the room.

Before Mr Brass had repeated his inquiry many times, Mr Quilp, also embellished with a night-cap, emerged from the same door and looked carefully up and down the street, and up at all the windows of the house from the opposite side. Finding that there was nobody in sight he presently returned into the house with his legal friend, protesting (as the child heard from the staircase) that there was a league and plot against him, that he was in danger of being robbed and plundered by a band of conspirators who prowled about the house at all seasons, and that he would delay no longer but take immediate steps for disposing of the property and returning to his own peaceful roof. Having growled forth these and a great many other threats of the same nature, he coiled himself once more in the child's little bed, and Nell crept softly up the stairs.

It was natural enough that her short and unfinished dialogue with Kit should leave a strong impression on her mind, and influence her dreams that night and her recollections for a long, long time. Surrounded by unfeeling creditors, and mercenary attendants upon the sick, and meeting in the height of her anxiety and sorrow with little regard or sympathy even from the women about her, it is not surprising that the affectionate heart of the child should have been touched to the quick by one kind and generous spirit, however uncouth the temple in which it dwelt. Thank Heaven that the temples of such spirits are not made with hands, and that they may be more worthily hung with poor patchwork than with purple and fine linen!

Chapter XII

AT length the crisis of the old man's disorder was past, and he began to mend. By very slow and feeble degrees his consciousness came back, but the mind was weakened and its functions were impaired. He was patient, and quiet; often sat brooding, but not despondently, for a long space; was easily amused, even by a sunbeam on the wall or ceiling; made no complaint that the days were long or the nights tedious; and appeared indeed to have lost all count of time and every sense of care or weariness. He would sit for hours together with Nell's small hand in his, playing with the fingers and stopping sometimes to smooth her hair or kiss her brow; and when he saw that tears were glistening in her eyes would look, amazed, about him for the cause, and forget his wonder even while he looked.

The child and he rode out: the old man propped up with pillows, and the child beside him. They were hand in hand as usual. The noise and motion in the streets fatigued his brain at first, but he was not surprised, or curious, or pleased, or irritated. He was asked if he remembered this, or that. "Oh, yes," he said, "quite well—why not?" Sometimes he turned his head and looked with earnest gaze and outstretched neck, after some stranger in the crowd, until he disappeared from sight; but, to the question why he did this, he answered not a word.

He was sitting in his easy-chair one day, and Nell upon a stool beside him, when a man outside the door inquired if he might enter. "Yes," he said without emotion, "it was Quilp, he knew. Quilp was master there. Of course he might come in." And so he did.

"I'm glad to see you well again at last, neighbour," said the dwarf, sitting down opposite to him. "You're quite strong now?"

"Yes," said the old man feebly, "yes."

"I don't want to hurry you, you know, neighbour," said the dwarf, raising his voice, for the old man's senses were duller than they had been; "but, as soon as you *can* arrange your future proceedings, the better."

"Surely," said the old man. "The better for all parties."

"You see," pursued Quilp after a short pause, "the goods being once removed, this house would be uncomfortable; uninhabitable in fact."

"You say true," returned the old man. "Poor Nell too, what would *she* do?"

"Exactly," bawled the dwarf nodding his head; "that's very well observed. Then will you consider about it, neighbour?"

"I will, certainly," replied the old man. "We shall not stop here."

"So I supposed," said the dwarf. "I have sold the things. They have not yielded quite as much as they might have done, but pretty well—pretty well. To-day's Tuesday. When shall they be moved? There's no hurry—shall we say this afternoon?"

"Say Friday morning," returned the old man.

"Very good," said the dwarf. "So be it—with the understanding that I can't go beyond that day, neighbour, on any account."

"Good," returned the old man. "I shall remember it."

"Say Friday morning," returned the old man. "So be it—with the understanding that I can't go beyond that day, neighbour, on any account."

Mr Quilp seemed rather puzzled by the strange, even spiritless way in which all this was said; but as the old man nodded his head and repeated "on Friday morning. I shall remember it," he had no excuse for dwelling upon the subject any further, and so took a friendly leave with many expressions of good-will and many compliments to his friend on his looking so remarkably well; and went below stairs to report progress to Mr Brass.

All that day, and all the next, the old man remained in this state. He wandered up and down the house and into and out of the various rooms, as if with some vague intent of bidding them adieu, but he referred neither by direct allusions nor in any other manner to the interview of the morning or the necessity of finding some other shelter. An indistinct idea he had, that the child was desolate and in want of help, for he often drew her to his bosom and bade her be of good cheer, saying that they would not desert each other; but he seemed unable to contemplate their real position more distinctly, and was still the listless, passionless creature that suffering of mind and body had left him.

We call this a state of childishness, but it is the same poor hollow mockery of it, that death is of sleep. Where, in the dull eyes of doating men, are the laughing light and life of childhood, the gaiety that has known no check, the frankness that has felt no chill, the hope that has never withered, the joys that fade in blossoming? Where, in the sharp lineaments of rigid and unsightly death, is the calm beauty of slumber, telling of rest for the waking hours that are past, and gentle hopes and loves for those which are to come? Lay death and sleep down, side by side, and say who shall find the two akin. Send forth the child and childish man together, and blush for the pride that libels our own old happy state, and gives its title to an ugly and distorted image.

Thursday arrived, and there was no alteration in the old man. But, a change came upon him that evening, as he and the child sat silently together.

In a small dull yard below his window, there was a tree—green and flourishing enough, for such a place—and as the air stirred among its leaves, it threw a rippling shadow on the white wall. The old man sat watching the shadows as they trembled in this patch of light until the sun went down, and when it was night and the moon was slowly rising he still sat in the same spot.

To one who had been tossing on a restless bed so long, even these few green leaves and this tranquil light, although it languished among chimneys and house-tops, were pleasant things. They suggested quiet places afar off, and rest, and peace.

The child thought more than once that he was moved, and had forborne to speak. But now he shed tears—tears that it lightened her aching heart to see—and making as though he would fall upon his knees, besought her to forgive him.

"Forgive you—what?" said Nell, interposing to prevent his purpose. "Oh, grandfather, what should *I* forgive?"

"All that is past, all that has come upon thee, Nell, all that was done in that uneasy dream," returned the old man.

"Do not talk so," said the child. "Pray do not. Let us speak of something else."

"Yes, yes, we will," he rejoined. "And it shall be of what we talked of long ago—many months—months is it, or weeks, or days? which is it, Nell?"

"I do not understand you"—said the child.

"It has come back upon me to-day, it has all come back since we have been sitting here. I bless thee for it, Nell!"

"For what, dear grandfather?"

"For what you said when we were first made beggars, Nell. Let us speak softly. Hush! for if they knew our purpose downstairs, they would cry that I was mad and take thee from me. We will not stop here another day. We will go far away from here."

"Yes, let us go," said the child earnestly. "Let us be gone from this place, and never turn back or think of it again. Let us wander barefoot through the world, rather than linger here."

"We will"—answered the old man, "we will travel afoot through fields and woods, and by the side of rivers, and trust ourselves to God in the places where He dwells. It is far better to lie down at night beneath an open sky like that yonder—see how bright it is—than to rest in close rooms which are always full of care and weary dreams. Thou and I together, Nell, may be cheerful and happy yet, and learn to forget this time, as if it had never been."

"We will be happy," cried the child. "We never can be here."

"No, we never can again—never again—that's truly said," rejoined the old man. "Let us steal away to-morrow morning—early and softly, that we may not be seen or heard—and leave no trace or track for them to follow by. Poor Nell, thy cheek is pale and thy eyes are heavy with watching and weeping—with watching and weeping for me—I know—for me; but thou wilt be well again, and merry too, when we are far away. To-morrow morning, dear, we'll turn our faces from this scene of sorrows, and be as free and happy as the birds."

And then the old man clasped his hands above her head, and said in a few broken words that from that time forth they would wander up and down together, and never part more until Death took one or other of the twain.

The child's heart beat high with hope and confidence. She had no thought of hunger or cold, or thirst, or suffering. She saw in this but a return of the simple pleasures they had once enjoyed, a relief from the gloomy solitude in which she had lived, an escape from the heartless people by whom she had been surrounded in her late time of trial, the restoration of the old man's health and peace, and a life of tranquil happiness. Sun, and stream, and meadow, and summer days, shone brightly in her view, and there was no dark tint in all the sparkling picture.

The old man had slept for some hours soundly in his bed, and she was yet busily engaged in preparing for their flight. There were a few articles of clothing for herself to carry, and a few for him; old garments, such as became their fallen fortunes, laid out to wear; and a staff to support his feeble steps, put ready for his use. But this was not all her task, for now she must visit the old rooms for the last time.

And how different the parting with them was from any she had expected, and most of all from that which she had oftenest pictured to herself. How could she ever have thought of bidding them farewell in triumph, when the recollection of the many hours she had passed among them rose to her swelling heart, and made her feel the wish a cruelty, lonely and sad though many of those hours had been! She sat down at the window where she had spent so many evenings—darker far than this—and every thought of hope or cheerfulness that had occurred to her in that place came vividly upon her mind, and blotted out all its dull and mournful associations in an instant.

Her own little room too, where she had so often knelt down and prayed at night— prayed for the time which she hoped was dawning now—the little room where she had slept so peacefully, and dreamed such pleasant dreams—it was hard not to be able to glance round it once more, and to be forced to leave it without one kind look or grateful tear. There were some trifles there—poor useless things—that she would have liked to take away; but that was impossible.

This brought to mind her bird, her poor bird, who hung there yet. She wept bitterly for the loss of this little creature—until the idea occurred to her—she did not know how or why it came into her head—that it might by some means fall into the hands of Kit, who would keep it for her sake, and think perhaps that she had left it behind in the hope that he might have it, and as an assurance that she was grateful to him. She was calmed and comforted by the thought, and went to rest with a lighter heart.

From many dreams of rambling through light and sunny places, but with some vague object unattained which ran indistinctly through them all, she awoke to find that it was yet night, and that the stars were shining brightly in the sky. At length the day began to glimmer, and the stars to grow pale and dim. As soon as she was sure of this, she arose, and dressed herself for the journey.

The old man was yet asleep, and as she was unwilling to disturb him, she left him to slumber on until the sun rose. He was anxious that they should leave the house without a minute's loss of time, and was soon ready.

The child then took him by the hand, and they trod lightly and cautiously down the stairs, trembling whenever a board creaked, and often stopping to listen. The old man had forgotten a kind of wallet which contained the light burden he had to carry, and the going back a few steps to fetch it seemed an interminable delay.

At last they reached the passage on the ground floor, where the snoring of Mr Quilp and his legal friend sounded more terrible in their ears than the roars of lions. The bolts of the door were rusty, and difficult to unfasten without noise. When they were all drawn back it was found to be locked, and, worst of all, the key was gone. Then the child remembered for the first time one of the nurses having told her that Quilp always locked both the house-doors at night, and kept the keys on the table in his bedroom.

It was not without great fear and trepidation that little Nell slipped off her shoes and gliding through the store-room of old curiosities, where Mr Brass—the ugliest piece of goods in all the stock—lay sleeping on a mattress, passed into her own little chamber.

Here she stood for a few moments quite transfixed with terror at the sight of Mr Quilp, who was hanging so far out of bed that he almost seemed to be standing on his head, and who either from the uneasiness of this posture or in one of his agreeable habits, was gasping and growling with his mouth wide open, and the whites (or rather the dirty yellows) of his eyes distinctly visible. It was no time, however, to ask whether anything ailed him, so possessing herself of the key after one hasty glance about the room, and repassing the prostrate Mr Brass, she rejoined the old man in safety. They got the door open without noise, and passing into the street, stood still.

"Which way?" said the child.

The old man looked, irresolutely and helplessly, first at her, then to the right and left, then at her again, and shook his head. It was plain that she was thenceforth his guide and leader. The child felt it, but had no doubts or misgiving, and putting her hand in his, led him gently away.

It was the beginning of a day in June; the deep blue sky unsullied by a cloud, and teeming with brilliant light. The streets were as yet nearly free from passengers, the houses and shops were closed, and the healthful air of morning fell like breath from angels, on the sleeping town.

The old man and the child passed on through the glad silence, elate with hope and pleasure. They were alone together once again; every object was bright and fresh; nothing reminded them, otherwise than by contrast, of the monotony and constraint they had left behind; church towers and steeples, frowning and dark at other times, now shone and dazzled in the sun; each humble nook and corner rejoiced in light; and the sky, dimmed by excessive distance, shed its placid smile on everything beneath.

Forth from the city, while it yet slumbered, went the two poor adventurers, wandering they knew not whither.

Chapter XIII

DANIEL Quilp of Tower Hill, and Sampson Brass of Bevis Marks in the city of London, Gentleman, one of her Majesty's attornies of the Courts of King's Bench and Common Pleas at Westminster and a solicitor of the High Court of Chancery, slumbered on unconscious and unsuspicious of any mischance, until a knocking at the street door, often repeated and gradually mounting up from a modest single rap into a perfect battery of knocks, fired in long discharges with a very short interval between, caused the said Daniel Quilp to struggle into a horizontal position, and to stare at the ceiling with a drowsy indifference, betokening that he heard the noise and rather wondered at the same, but couldn't be at the trouble of bestowing any further thought upon the subject.

As the knocking, however, instead of accommodating itself to his lazy state, increased in vigour and became more importunate, as if in earnest remonstrance against his falling asleep again now that he had once opened his eyes, Daniel Quilp began by degrees to comprehend the possibility of there being somebody at the door, and thus he gradually came to recollect that it was Friday morning, and he had ordered Mrs Quilp to be in waiting upon him at an early hour.

Mr Brass, after writhing about in a great many strange attitudes, and often twisting his face and eyes into an expression like that which is usually produced by eating gooseberries very early in the season, was by this time awake also, and seeing that Mr Quilp invested himself in his everyday garments, hastened to do the like, putting on his shoes before his stockings, and thrusting his legs into his coat-sleeves, and making such other small mistakes in his toilet as are not uncommon to those who dress in a hurry, and labour under the agitation of having been suddenly roused.

While the attorney was thus engaged, the dwarf was groping under the table, muttering desperate imprecations upon himself and mankind in general and all inanimate objects to boot, which suggested to Mr Brass the question "What's the matter?"

"The key," said the dwarf, looking viciously at him, "the door-key—that's the matter. D'ye know anything of it?"

"How should I know anything of it, sir?" returned Mr Brass.

"How should you?" repeated Quilp with a sneer. "You're a nice lawyer, an't you. Ugh, you idiot!"

Not caring to represent to the dwarf in his present humour, that the loss of a key by another person could scarcely be said to affect his (Brass's) legal knowledge in any material degree, Mr Brass humbly suggested that it must have been forgotten overnight, and was doubtless at that moment in its native keyhole. Notwithstanding that Mr Quilp had a strong conviction to the contrary, founded on his recollection of having carefully taken it out, he was fain to admit that this was possible, and therefore went grumbling to the door where, sure enough, he found it.

Now, just as Mr Quilp laid his hand upon the lock and saw with great astonishment that the fastenings were undone, the knocking came again with most irritating violence, and the daylight which had been shining through the keyhole was intercepted on the outside by a human eye. The dwarf was very much exasperated, and wanting somebody to wreak his ill-humour upon, determined to dart out suddenly and favour Mrs Quilp with a gentle acknowledgment of her attention in making that hideous uproar.

With this view he drew back the lock very silently and softly, and opening the door all at once, pounced out upon the person on the other side, who had at that moment raised the knocker for another application, and at whom the dwarf ran head first, throwing out his hands and feet together, and biting the air in the fulness of his malice.

So far, however, from rushing upon somebody who offered no resistance and implored his mercy, Mr Quilp was no sooner in the arms of the individual whom he had taken for his wife than he found himself complimented with two staggering blows on the head, and two more, of the same quality, in the chest, and closing with his assailant, such a shower of buffets rained down upon his person as sufficed to convince him that he was in skilful and experienced hands. Nothing daunted by this reception, he clung tight to his opponent, and bit and hammered away with such good-will and heartiness, that it was at least a couple of minutes before he was dislodged. Then, and not until then, Daniel Quilp found himself, all flushed and dishevelled, in the middle of the street, with Mr Richard Swiveller performing a kind of dance round him and requiring to know "whether he wanted any more?"

"There's plenty more of it at the same shop," said Mr Swiveller, by turns advancing and retreating in a threatening attitude, "a large and extensive assortment always on hand—country orders executed with promptitude and despatch—will you have a little more, sir—don't say no, if you'd rather not."

"I thought it was somebody else," said Quilp rubbing his shoulders; "why didn't you say who you were?"

"Why didn't you say who *you* were?" returned Dick, "instead of flying out of the house like a Bedlamite?"

"It was you that—that knocked," said the dwarf, getting up with a short groan, "was it?"

"Yes, I am the man," replied Dick. "That lady had begun when I came, but she knocked too soft, so I relieved her." As he said this, he pointed towards Mrs Quilp, who stood trembling at a little distance.

"Humph!" muttered the dwarf, darting an angry look at his wife, "I thought it was your fault! And you, sir—don't you know there has been somebody ill here, that you knock as if you'd beat the door down?"

"Damme!" answered Dick, "that's why I did it. I thought there was somebody dead here."

"You came for some purpose, I suppose," said Quilp. "What is it you want?"

"I want to know how the old gentleman is," rejoined Mr Swiveller, "and to hear from Nell herself, with whom I should like to have a little talk. I'm a friend of the family, sir—at least I'm the friend of one of the family, and that's the same thing."

"You'd better walk in then," said the dwarf. "Go on, sir, go on. Now, Mrs Quilp—after you, ma'am."

Mrs Quilp hesitated, but Mr Quilp insisted. And it was not a contest of politeness, or by any means a matter of form, for she knew very well that her husband wished to enter the house in this order, that he might have a favourable opportunity of inflicting a few pinches on her arms, which were seldom free from impressions of his fingers in black and blue colours. Mr Swiveller, who was not in the secret, was a little surprised to hear a suppressed scream, and, looking round, to see Mrs Quilp following him with a sudden jerk; but he did not remark on these appearances, and soon forgot them.

"Now, Mrs Quilp," said the dwarf when they had entered the shop, "go you upstairs, if you please, to Nelly's room, and tell her that she's wanted."

"You seem to make yourself at home here," said Dick, who was unacquainted with Mr. Quilp's authority.

"I *am* at home, young gentleman," returned the dwarf.

Dick was pondering what these words might mean, and still more what the presence of Mr Brass might mean, when Mrs Quilp came hurrying downstairs, declaring that the rooms above were empty.

"Empty, you fool!" said the dwarf.

"I give you my word, Quilp," answered his trembling wife, "that I have been into every room, and there's not a soul in any of them."

"And that," said Mr Brass, clapping his hands once, with an emphasis, "explains the mystery of the key!"

Quilp looked frowningly at him, and frowningly at his wife and frowningly at Richard Swiveller; but, receiving no enlightenment from any of them, hurried upstairs, whence he soon hurried down again, confirming the report which had been already made.

"It's a strange way of going," he said, glancing at Swiveller, "very strange not to communicate with me who am such a close and intimate friend of his! Ah! he'll write to me no doubt, or he'll bid Nelly write—yes, yes, that's what he'll do. Nelly's very fond of me. Pretty Nell!"

Mr Swiveller looked, as he was, all open-mouthed astonishment. Still glancing furtively at him, Quilp turned to Mr Brass and observed with assumed carelessness, that this need not interfere with the removal of the goods.

"For indeed," he added, "we knew that they'd go away to-day, but not that they'd go so early or so quietly. But they have their reasons, they have their reasons."

"Where in the devil's name are they gone?" said the wondering Dick.

Quilp shook his head and pursed up his lips, in a manner which implied that he knew very well, but was not at liberty to say.

"And what," said Dick, looking at the confusion about him, "what do you mean by moving the goods?"

"That I have bought 'em, sir," rejoined Quilp. "Eh? What then?"

"Has the sly old fox made his fortune then, and gone to live in a tranquil cot in a pleasant spot with a distant view of the changing sea?" said Dick, in great bewilderment.

"Keeping his place of retirement very close, that he may not be visited too often by affectionate grandsons and their devoted friends, eh?" added the dwarf, rubbing his hands hard; "*I* say nothing, but is that your meaning, sir?"

Richard Swiveller was utterly aghast at this unexpected alteration of circumstances, which threatened the complete overthrow of the project in which he bore so conspicuous a part, and seemed to nip his prospects in the bud. Having only received from Frederick Trent, late on the previous night, information of the old man's illness, he had come upon a visit of condolence and enquiry to Nell, prepared with the first instalment of that long train of fascinations which was to fire her heart at last. And here, when he had been thinking of all kinds of graceful and insinuating approaches, and meditating on the fearful retaliation which was slowly working against Sophy Wackles—here were Nell, the old man, and all the money gone, melted away, decamped he knew not whither, as if with a fore-knowledge of the scheme and a resolution to defeat it in the very outset, before a step was taken.

In his secret heart, Daniel Quilp was both surprised and troubled by the flight which had been made. It had not escaped his keen eye that some indispensable articles of clothing were gone with the fugitives, and knowing the old man's weak state of mind, he marvelled what that course of proceeding might be in which he had so readily procured the concurrence of the child. It must not be supposed (or it would be a gross injustice to Mr Quilp) that he was tortured by any disinterested anxiety on behalf of either. His uneasiness arose from a misgiving that the old man had some secret store of money which he had not suspected, and the bare idea of its escaping his clutches, overwhelmed him with mortification and self-reproach.

In this frame of mind, it was some consolation to him to find that Richard Swiveller was, for different reasons, evidently irritated and disappointed by the same cause. It was plain, thought the dwarf, that he had come there on behalf of his friend to cajole or frighten the old man out of some small fraction of that wealth of which they supposed him to have an abundance. Therefore it was a relief to vex his heart with a picture of the riches the old man hoarded, and to expatiate on his cunning in removing himself even beyond the reach of importunity.

"Well," said Dick, with a blank look, "I suppose it's of no use my staying here."

"Not the least in the world," rejoined the dwarf.

"You'll mention that I called, perhaps?" said Dick.

Mr Quilp nodded, and said he certainly would, the very first time he saw them.

"And say," added Mr Swiveller, "say, sir, that I was wafted here upon the pinions of concord; that I came to remove, with the rake of friendship, the seeds of mutual wiolence and heart-burning, and to sow in their place, the germs of social harmony. Will you have the goodness to charge yourself with that commission, sir?"

"Certainly!" rejoined Quilp.

"Will you be kind enough to add to it, sir," said Dick, producing a very small limp card, "that *that* is my address, and that I am to be found at home every morning. Two distinct knocks, sir, will produce the slavey at any time. My particular friends, sir, are accustomed to sneeze when the door is opened, to give her to understand that they *are* my friends and have no interested motives in asking if I'm at home. I beg your pardon; will you allow me to look at that card again?"

"Oh! by all means," rejoined Quilp.

"By a slight and not unnatural mistake, sir," said Dick, substituting another in its stead, "I had handed you the pass-ticket of a select convivial circle called the Glorious Apollers, of which I have the honour to be Perpetual Grand. That is the proper document, sir. Good morning."

Quilp bade him good-day; the Perpetual Grand Master of the Glorious Apollers, elevating his hat in honour of Mrs Quilp, dropped it carelessly on the side of his head again, and disappeared with a flourish.

By this time certain vans had arrived for the conveyance of the goods, and divers strong men in carpet caps were balancing chests of drawers and other trifles of that nature upon their heads, and performing muscular feats which heightened their complexions considerably. Not to be behind-hand in the bustle, Mr Quilp went to work with surprising vigour; hustling and driving the people about, like an evil spirit; setting Mrs Quilp upon all kinds of arduous and impracticable tasks; carrying great weights up and down with no apparent effort; kicking the boy from the wharf whenever he could get near him; and inflicting with his loads a great many sly bumps and blows upon the shoulders of Mr Brass, as he stood upon the door-steps to answer all the enquiries of curious neighbours, which was his department. His presence and example diffused such alacrity among the persons employed, that in a few hours the house was emptied of everything but pieces of matting, empty porter-pots, and scattered fragments of straw.

Seated, like an African chief, on one of these pieces of matting, the dwarf was regaling himself in the parlour with bread and cheese and beer, when he observed, without appearing to do so, that a boy was prying in at the outer door. Assured that it was Kit, though he saw little more than his nose, Mr Quilp hailed him by his name; whereupon Kit came in and demanded what he wanted.

"Come here, you sir," said the dwarf. "Well, so your old master and young mistress have gone?"

"Where?" rejoined Kit, looking round.

"Do you mean to say you don't know where?" answered Quilp sharply. "Where have they gone, eh?"

"I don't know," said Kit.

"Come," retorted Quilp, "let's have no more of this! Do you mean to say that you don't know they went away by stealth, as soon as it was light this morning?"

"No," said the boy, in evident surprise.

"You don't know that?" cried Quilp. "Don't I know that you were hanging about the house the other night, like a thief, eh? Weren't you told then?"

"No," replied the boy.

"You were not?" said Quilp. "What were you told then; what were you talking about?"

Kit, who knew no particular reason why he should keep the matter secret now, related the purpose for which he had come on that occasion, and the proposal he had made.

"Oh!" said the dwarf after a little consideration. "Then, I think they'll come to you yet."

"Do you think they will?" cried Kit eagerly.

"Ay, I think they will," returned the dwarf. "Now, when they do, let me know; d'ye hear? Let me know, and I'll give you something. I want to do 'em a kindness, and I can't do 'em a kindness unless I know where they are. You hear what I say?"

Kit might have returned some answer which would not have been agreeable to his irascible questioner, if the boy from the wharf, who had been skulking about the room in search of anything that might have been left about by accident, had not happened to cry, "Here's a bird! What's to be done with this?"

"Wring its neck," rejoined Quilp.

"Oh, no, don't do that," said Kit, stepping forward. "Give it to me."

"Oh, yes, I dare say," cried the other boy. "Come! You let the cage alone, and let me wring its neck, will you? He said I was to do it. You let the cage alone, will you?"

"Give it here, give it to me, you dogs," roared Quilp. "Fight for it, you dogs, or I'll wring its neck myself!"

Without further persuasion, the two boys fell upon each other tooth and nail, while Quilp, holding up the cage in one hand, and chopping the ground with his knife in an ecstasy, urged them on by his taunts and cries to fight more fiercely. They were a pretty equal match, and rolled about together, exchanging blows which were by no means child's play, until at length Kit, planting a well-directed hit in his adversary's chest, disengaged himself, sprang nimbly up, and snatching the cage from Quilp's hands made off with his prize.

He did not stop once until he reached home, where his bleeding face occasioned great consternation, and caused the elder child to howl dreadfully.

"Goodness gracious, Kit, what is the matter, what have you been doing?" cried Mrs Nubbles.

"Never you mind, mother," answered her son, wiping his face on the jack-towel behind the door. "I'm not hurt, don't you be afraid for me. I've been a fightin' for a bird and won him, that's all. Hold your noise, little Jacob. I never see such a naughty boy in all my days!"

"You have been fighting for a bird!" exclaimed his mother.

"Ah! Fightin' for a bird!" replied Kit, "and here he is—Miss Nelly's bird, mother, that they was a goin' to wring the neck of! I stopped that though—ha, ha, ha! They wouldn't wring his neck and me by, no, no. It wouldn't do, mother, it wouldn't do at all. Ha, ha, ha!"

Kit laughing so heartily, with his swoln and bruised face looking out of the towel, made little Jacob laugh, and then his mother laughed, and then the baby crowed and kicked with great glee, and then they all laughed in concert, partly because of Kit's triumph, and partly because they were very fond of each other. When this fit was over, Kit exhibited the bird to both children, as a great and precious rarity—it was only a poor linnet—and looking about the wall for an old nail, made a scaffolding of a chair and table and twisted it out with great exultation.

"Let me see." said the boy, "I think I'll hang him in the winder, because it's more light and cheerful, and he can see the sky there, if he looks up very much. He's such a one to sing, I can tell you!"

So, the scaffolding was made again, and Kit, climbing up with the poker for a hammer, knocked in the nail and hung up the cage, to the immeasurable delight of the whole family. When it had been adjusted and straightened a great many times, and he had walked backwards into the fireplace in his admiration of it, the arrangement was pronounced to be perfect.

"And now, mother," said the boy, "before I rest any more, I'll go out and see if I can find a horse to hold, and then I can buy some birdseed, and a bit of something nice for you, into the bargain."

Chapter XIV

A S it was very easy for Kit to persuade himself that the old house was in his way, his way being anywhere, he tried to look upon his passing it once more as a matter of imperative and disagreeable necessity, quite apart from any desire of his own, to which he could not choose but yield. It is not uncommon for people who are much better fed and taught than Christopher Nubbles had ever been, to make duties of their inclinations in matters of more doubtful propriety, and to take great credit for the self-denial with which they gratify themselves.

There was no need of any caution this time and no fear of being detained by having to play out a return match with Daniel Quilp's boy. The place was entirely deserted, and looked as dusty and dingy as if it had been so for months. A rusty padlock was fastened on the door, ends of discoloured blinds and curtains flapped drearily against the half-opened upper windows, and the crooked holes cut in the closed shutters below were black with the darkness of the inside. Some of the glass in the window he had so often watched, had been broken in the rough hurry of the morning, and that room looked more deserted and dull than any. A group of idle urchins had taken possession of the door-steps; some were plying the knocker and listening with delighted dread to the hollow sounds it spread through the dismantled house; others were clustered about the keyhole, watching half in jest and half in earnest for "the ghost," which an hour's gloom, added to the mystery that hung about the late inhabitants, had already raised. Standing all alone in the midst of the business and bustle of the street, the house looked a picture of cold desolation; and Kit, who remembered the cheerful fire that used to burn there on a winter's night and the no less cheerful laugh that made the small room ring, turned quite mournfully away.

It must be specially observed in justice to poor Kit that he was by no means of a sentimental turn, and perhaps had never heard that adjective in all his life. He was only a soft-hearted grateful fellow, and had nothing genteel or polite about him; consequently instead of going home again in his grief to kick the children and abuse his mother (for when your finely strung people are out of sorts they must have everybody else unhappy likewise), he turned his thoughts to the vulgar expedient of making them more comfortable if he could.

Bless us, what a number of gentlemen on horseback there were riding up and down, and how few of them wanted their horses held! A good City speculator or a Parliamentary commissioner could have told to a fraction, from the crowds that were cantering about, what sum of money was realised in London in the course of a year, by holding horses alone. And undoubtedly it would have been a very large one, if only a twentieth part of the gentlemen without grooms had had occasion to alight; but they hadn't; and it is often an ill-natured circumstance like this, which spoils the most ingenious estimate in the world.

Kit walked about, now with quick steps and now with slow; now lingering as some rider slackened his horse's pace and looked about him; and now darting at full speed up a bye-street as he caught a glimpse of some distant horseman going lazily up the shady side of the road, and promising to stop, at every door. But on they all went, one after another, and there was not a penny stirring. "I wonder," thought the boy, "if one of these gentlemen knew there was nothing in the cupboard at home, whether he'd stop on purpose, and make believe that he wanted to call somewhere, that I might earn a trifle?"

He was quite tired out with pacing the streets, to say nothing of repeated disappointments, and was sitting down upon a step to rest, when there approached towards him a little clattering jingling four-wheeled chaise, drawn by a little obstinate-looking rough-coated pony, and driven by a little fat placid-faced old gentleman. Beside the little old gentleman sat a little old lady, plump and placid like himself, and the pony was coming along at his own pace and doing exactly as he pleased with the whole concern. If the old gentleman remonstrated by shaking the reins, the pony replied by shaking his head. It was plain that the utmost the pony would consent to do was to go in his own way up any street that the old gentleman particularly wished to traverse, but that it was an understanding between them that he must do this after his own fashion or not at all.

As they passed where he sat, Kit looked so wistfully at the little turn-out that the old gentleman looked at him, and Kit rising and putting his hand to his hat, the old gentleman intimated to the pony that he wished to stop, to which proposal the pony (who seldom objected to that part of his duty) graciously acceded.

"I beg your pardon, sir," said Kit. "I'm sorry you stopped, sir. I only meant did you want your horse minded."

"I'm going to get down in the next street," returned the old gentleman. "If you like to come on after us, you may have the job."

Kit thanked him, and joyfully obeyed. The pony ran off at a sharp angle to inspect a lamp-post on the opposite side of the way, and then went off at a tangent to another lamp-post on the other side. Having satisfied himself that they were of the same pattern and materials, he came to a stop, apparently absorbed in meditation.

"Will you go on, sir," said the old gentleman, gravely, "or are we to wait here for you 'till it's too late for our appointment?"

The pony remained immoveable.

"Oh, you naughty Whisker," said the old lady. "Fie upon you! I'm ashamed of such conduct."

The pony appeared to be touched by this appeal to his feelings, for he trotted on directly, though in a sulky manner, and stopped no more until he came to a door whereon was a brass plate with the words "Witherden—Notary." Here the old gentleman got out and helped out the old lady, and then took from under the seat a nosegay resembling in shape and dimensions a full-sized warming-pan with the handle cut short off. This the old lady carried into the house with a staid and stately air, and the old gentleman (who had a club-foot) followed close upon her.

They went, as it was easy to tell from the sound of their voices, into the front parlour, which seemed to be a kind of office. The day being very warm and the street a quiet one, the windows were wide open, and it was easy to hear through the Venetian blinds all that passed inside.

At first there was a great shaking of hands and shuffling of feet, succeeded by the presentation of the nosegay, for a voice, supposed by the listener to be that of Mr Witherden the Notary, was heard to exclaim a great many times, "Oh, delicious!" "Oh, fragrant, indeed!" and a nose, also supposed to be the property of that gentleman, was heard to inhale the scent with a snuffle of exceeding pleasure.

"I brought it in honour of the occasion, sir," said the old lady.

"Ah! an occasion indeed, ma'am; an occasion which does honour to me, ma'am, honour to me," rejoined Mr Witherden the Notary. "I have had many a gentleman articled to me, ma'am, many a one. Some of them are now rolling in riches, unmindful of their old companion and friend, ma'am, others are in the habit of calling upon me to this day and saying, 'Mr Witherden, some of the pleasantest hours I ever spent in my life were spent in this office—were spent, sir, upon this very stool'; but there was never one among the number, ma'am, attached as I have been to many of them, of whom I augured such bright things as I do of your only son."

"Oh, dear!" said the old lady. "How happy you do make us when you tell us that, to be sure!"

"I tell you, ma'am," said Mr Witherden, "what I think as an honest man, which, as the poet observes, is the noblest work of God. I agree with the poet in every particular, ma'am. The mountainous Alps on the one hand, or a humming-bird on the other, is nothing, in point of workmanship, to an honest man—or woman—or woman."

"Anything that Mr Witherden can say of me," observed a small quiet voice, "I can say with interest of him, I am sure."

"It's a happy circumstance, a truly happy circumstance," said the Notary, "to happen too upon his eight-and-twentieth birthday, and I hope I know how to appreciate it. I trust, Mr. Garland, my dear sir, that we may mutually congratulate each other upon this auspicious occasion."

To this the old gentleman replied that he felt assured they might. There appeared to be another shaking of hands in consequence, and when it was over, the old gentleman said that, though he said it who should not, he believed no son had ever been a greater comfort to his parents than Abel Garland had been to his.

"Marrying as his mother and I did, late in life, sir, after waiting for a great many years, until we were well enough off—coming together when we were no longer young, and then being blessed with one child who has always been dutiful and affectionate—why, it's a source of great happiness to us both, sir."

"Of course it is, I have no doubt of it," returned the Notary in a sympathising voice. "It's the contemplation of this sort of thing, that makes me deplore my fate in being a bachelor. There was a young lady once, sir, the daughter of an outfitting warehouse of the first respectability—but that's a weakness. Chuckster, bring in Mr Abel's articles."

"You see, Mr Witherden," said the old lady, "that Abel has not been brought up like the run of young men. He has always had a pleasure in our society, and always been with us. Abel has never been absent from us, for a day; has he, my dear?"

"Never, my dear," returned the old gentleman, "except when he went to Margate one Saturday with Mr Tomkinley that had been a teacher at that school he went to, and came back upon the Monday; but he was very ill after that, you remember, my dear; it was quite a dissipation."

"He was not used to it, you know," said the old lady, "and he couldn't bear it, that's the truth. Besides he had no comfort in being there without us, and had nobody to talk to or enjoy himself with."

"That was it, you know," interposed the same small quiet voice that had spoken once before. "I was quite abroad, mother, quite desolate, and to think that the sea was between us—oh, I never shall forget what I felt when I first thought that the sea was between us!"

"Very natural under the circumstances," observed the Notary. "Mr Abel's feelings did credit to his nature, and credit to your nature, ma'am, and his father's nature, and human nature. I trace the same current now, flowing through all his quiet and unobtrusive proceedings.—I am about to sign my name, you observe, at the foot of the articles which Mr Chuckster will witness; and, placing my finger upon this blue wafer with the van-dyked corners, I am constrained to remark in a distinct tone of voice—don't be alarmed, ma'am, it is merely a form of law—that I deliver this, as my act and deed. Mr Abel will place his name against the other wafer, repeating the same cabalistic words, and the business is over. Ha, ha, ha! You see how easily these things are done!"

There was a short silence, apparently, while Mr Abel went through the prescribed form, and then the shaking of hands and shuffling of feet were renewed, and shortly afterwards there was a clinking of wine-glasses and a great talkativeness on the part of everybody. In about a quarter of an hour Mr Chuckster (with a pen behind his ear and his face inflamed with wine) appeared at the door, and condescending to address Kit by the jocose appellation of "Young Snob," informed him that the visitors were coming out.

Out they came forthwith; Mr Witherden, who was short, chubby, fresh-coloured, brisk, and pompous, leading the old lady with extreme politeness, and the father and son following them, arm in arm. Mr Abel, who had a quaint old-fashioned air about him, looked nearly of the same age as his father, and bore a wonderful resemblance to him in face and figure, though wanting something of his full, round cheerfulness, and substituting in its place, a timid reserve. In all other respects, in the neatness of the dress, and even in the club-foot, he and the old gentleman were precisely alike.

Having seen the old lady safely in her seat, and assisted in the arrangement of her cloak and a small basket which formed an indispensable portion of her equipage, Mr

Abel got into a little box behind which had evidently been made for his express accommodation, and smiled at everybody present by turns, beginning with his mother and ending with the pony. There was then a great to-do to make the pony hold up his head that the bearing-rein might be fastened; at last even this was effected; and the old gentleman, taking his seat and the reins, put his hand in his pocket to find a sixpence for Kit.

He had no sixpences, neither had the old lady, nor Mr Abel, nor the Notary, nor Mr Chuckster. The old gentleman thought a shilling too much, but there was no shop in the street to get change at, so he gave it to the boy.

"There," he said jokingly, "I'm coming here again next Monday at the same time, and mind you're here, my lad, to work it out."

"Thank you, sir," said Kit. "I'll be sure to be here."

He was quite serious, but they all laughed heartily at his saying so, especially Mr Chuckster, who roared outright and appeared to relish the joke amazingly. As the pony, with a presentiment that he was going home, or a determination that he would not go anywhere else (which was the same thing) trotted away pretty nimbly, Kit had no time to justify himself, and went his way also. Having expended his treasure in such purchases as he knew would be most acceptable at home, not forgetting some seed for the wonderful bird. he hastened back as fast as he could, so elated with his success and great good-fortune, that he more than half expected Nell and the old man would have arrived before him.

Chapter XV

O FTEN, while they were yet pacing the silent streets of the town on the morning of their departure, the child trembled with a mingled sensation of hope and fear as in some far-off figure imperfectly seen in the clear distance, her fancy traced a likeness to honest Kit. But although she would gladly have given him her hand and thanked him for what he had said at their last meeting, it was always a relief to find, when they came nearer to each other, that the person who approached was not he, but a stranger; for even if she had not dreaded the effect which the sight of him might have wrought upon her fellow-traveller, she felt that to bid farewell to anybody now, and most of all to him who had been so faithful and so true, was more than she could bear. It was enough to leave dumb things behind, and objects that were insensible both to her love and sorrow. To have parted from her only other friend upon the threshold of that wild journey, would have wrung her heart indeed.

Why is it that we can better bear to part in spirit than in body, and while we have the fortitude to act farewell have not the nerve to say it? On the eve of long voyages or an absence of many years, friends who are tenderly attached will separate with the usual look, the usual pressure of the hand, planning one final interview for the morrow, while each well knows that it is but a poor feint to save the pain of uttering that one word, and that the meeting will never be. Should possibilities be worse to bear than certainties? We do not shun our dying friends; the not having distinctly taken leave of one among them, whom we left in all kindness and affection, will often embitter the whole remainder of a life.

The town was glad with morning light; places that had shown ugly and distrustful all night long, now wore a smile; and sparkling sunbeams dancing on chamber windows, and twinkling through blind and curtain before sleepers' eyes, shed light even into dreams, and chased away the shadows of the night. Birds in hot rooms, covered up close and dark, felt it was morning, and chafed and grew restless in their little cells; bright-eyed mice crept back to their tiny homes and nestled timidly together; the sleek house-cat, forgetful of her prey, sat winking at the rays of sun starting through keyhole and cranny in the door, and longed for her stealthy run and warm sleek bask outside. The nobler beasts confined in dens stood motionless behind their bars, and gazed on fluttering boughs and sunshine peeping through some little window, with eyes in which old forests gleamed—then trod impatiently the track their prisoned feet had worn—and stopped and gazed again. Men in their dungeons stretched their cramp cold limbs and cursed the stone that no bright sky could warm. The flowers that sleep by night, opened their gentle eyes and turned them to the day. The light, creation's mind, was everywhere, and all things owned its power.

The two pilgrims, often pressing each other's hands, or exchanging a smile or cheerful look, pursued their way in silence. Bright and happy as it was, there was something solemn in the long, deserted streets, from which like bodies without souls all habitual character and expression had departed, leaving but one dead uniform repose, that made them all alike. All was so still at that early hour, that the few pale people whom they met seemed as much unsuited to the scene, as the sickly lamp which had been here and there left burning was powerless and faint in the full glory of the sun.

Before they had penetrated very far into the labyrinth of men's abodes which yet lay between them and the outskirts, this aspect began to melt away, and noise and bustle to usurp its place. Some straggling carts and coaches rumbling by first broke the charm, then others came, then others yet more active, then a crowd. The wonder was at first to see a tradesman's window open, but it was a rare thing soon to see one closed; then smoke rose slowly from the chimneys, and sashes were thrown up to let in air, and doors were opened, and servant-girls, looking lazily in all directions but their brooms, scattered brown clouds of dust into the eyes of shrinking passengers, or listened disconsolately to milkmen who spoke of country fairs, and told of waggons in the mews, with awnings and all things complete and gallant swains to boot, which another hour would see upon their journey.

This quarter passed, they came upon the haunts of commerce and great traffic, where many people were resorting, and business was already rife. The old man looked about him with a startled and bewildered gaze, for these were places that he hoped to shun. He pressed his finger on his lip, and drew the child along by narrow courts and winding ways, nor did he seem at ease until they had left it far behind, often casting a backward look towards it, murmuring that ruin and self-murder were crouching in every street, and would follow if they scented them; and that they could not fly too fast.

Again this quarter passed, they came upon a straggling neighbourhood, where the mean houses parcelled off in rooms, and windows patched with rags and paper, told of the populous poverty that sheltered there. The shops sold goods that only poverty could buy, and sellers and buyers were pinched and griped alike. Here were poor streets where faded gentility essayed with scanty space and shipwrecked means to make its last feeble stand, but tax-gatherer and creditor came there as elsewhere, and the poverty that yet faintly struggled, was hardly less squalid and manifest than that which had long ago submitted and given up the game.

This was a wide, wide track—for the humble followers of the camp of wealth pitch their tents round about it for many a mile—but its character was still the same. Damp rotten houses, many to let, many yet building, many half built and mouldering away—lodgings, where it would be hard to tell which needed pity most, those who let or those who came to take—children, scantily fed and clothed, spread over every street, and sprawling in the dust—scolding mothers, stamping their slipshod feet with noisy threats upon the pavement—shabby fathers, hurrying with dispirited looks to the occupation which brought them "daily bread" and little more—mangling-women washerwomen, cobblers, tailors, chandlers, driving their trades in parlours and kitchens and back rooms and garrets, and sometimes all of them under the same roof—brick-fields, skirting gardens paled with staves of old casks, or timber pillaged from houses burnt down and blackened and blistered by the flames—mounds of dock-weed, nettles, coarse grass and oyster-shells, heaped in rank confusion—small Dissenting chapels to teach, with no lack of illustration, the miseries of Earth, and plenty of new churches, erected with a little superfluous wealth, to show the way to Heaven.

At length these streets, becoming more straggling yet, dwindled and dwindled away, until there were only small garden patches bordering the road, with many a summer-house innocent of paint and built of old timber or some fragments of a boat, green as the tough cabbage-stalks that grew about it, and grottoed at the seams with toad-stools and tight-sticking snails. To these succeeded pert cottages, two and two with plots of ground in front, laid out in angular beds with stiff box borders and narrow paths between, where footstep never strayed to make the gravel rough. Then came the public-house, freshly painted in green and white, with tea-gardens and a bowling-green, spurning its old neighbour with the horse-trough where the waggons stopped; then fields; and then some houses, one by one, of goodly size with lawns, some even with a lodge where dwelt a porter and his wife. Then came a turnpike; then fields again with trees and haystacks; then a hill; and on the top of that the traveller might stop, and—looking back at old Saint Paul's looming through the smoke, its cross peeping above the cloud (if the day were clear), and glittering in the sun; and casting his eyes upon the Babel out of which it grew until he traced it down to the furthest outposts of the invading army of bricks and mortar whose station lay for the present nearly at his feet—might feel at last that he was clear of London.

Near such a spot as this, and in a pleasant field, the old man and his little guide (if guide she were, who knew not whither they were bound) sat down to rest. She had had the precaution to furnish her basket with some slices of bread and meat, and here they made their frugal breakfast.

The freshness of the day, the singing of the birds, the beauty of the waving grass, the deep green leaves, the wild flowers, and the thousand exquisite scents and sounds that floated in the air—deep joys to most of us, but most of all to those whose life is in a crowd or who live solitarily in great cities as in the bucket of a human well—sank into their breasts and made them very glad. The child had repeated her artless prayers once that morning, more earnestly perhaps than she had ever done in all her life, but as she felt all this, they rose to her lips again. The old man took off his hat—he had no memory for the words—but he said amen, and that they were very good.

There had been an old copy of the *Pilgrim's Progress,* with strange plates, upon a shelf at home, over which she had often pored whole evenings, wondering whether it was true in every word, and where those distant countries with the curious names might be. As she looked back upon the place they had left, one part of it came strongly on her mind.

"Dear grandfather," she said, "only that this place is prettier and a great deal better than the real one, if that in the book is like it, I feel as if we were both Christian, and laid down on this grass all the cares and troubles we brought with us; never to take them up again."

"No—never to return—never to return"—replied the old man, waving his hand towards the city. "Thou and I are free of it now, Nell. They shall never lure us back."

"Are you tired?" said the child, "are you sure you don't feel ill from this long walk?"

"I shall never feel ill again, now that we are once away," was his reply. "Let us be stirring, Nell. We must be further away—a long, long way further. We are too near to stop, and be at rest. Come!"

There was a pool of clear water in the field, in which the child laved her hands and face, and cooled her feet before setting forth to walk again. She would have the old man refresh himself in this way too, and making him sit down upon the grass, cast the water on him with her hands, and dried it with her simple dress.

"I can do nothing for myself, my darling," said the grandfather, "I don't know how it is, I could once, but the time's gone. Don't leave me, Nell; say that thou'lt not leave me. I loved thee all the while, indeed I did. If I lose thee too, my dear, I must die!"

He laid his head upon her shoulder and moaned piteously. The time had been, and a very few days before, when the child could not have restrained her tears and must have wept with him. But now she soothed him with gentle and tender words, smiled at his thinking they could ever part, and rallied him cheerfully upon the jest. He was soon calmed and fell asleep, singing to himself in a low voice, like a little child.

He awoke refreshed, and they continued their journey. The road was pleasant, lying between beautiful pastures and fields of corn, above which, poised high in the clear blue sky, the lark trilled out her happy song. The air came laden with the fragrance it caught upon its way, and the bees, upborne upon its scented breath, hummed forth their drowsy satisfaction as they floated by.

They were now in the open country; the houses were very few and scattered at long intervals, often miles apart. Occasionally they came upon a cluster of poor cottages, some with a chair or low board put across the open door to keep the scrambling children from the road, others shut up close while all the family were working in the fields. These were often the commencement of a little village: and after an interval came a wheelwright's shed or perhaps a blacksmith's forge; then a thriving farm with sleepy cows lying about the yard, and horses peering over the low wall and scampering away when harnessed horses passed upon the road, as though in triumph at their freedom. There were dull pigs too, turning up the ground in search of dainty food, and grunting their monotonous grumblings as they prowled about, or crossed each other in their quest; plump pigeons skimming round the roof or strutting on the eaves; and ducks and geese, far more graceful in their own conceit, waddling awkwardly about the edges of the pond or sailing glibly on its surface. The farm-yard passed, then came the little inn; the humbler beer-shop; and the village tradesman's; then the lawyer's and the parson's, at whose dread names the beer-shop trembled; the church then peeped out modestly from a clump of trees; then there were a few more cottages; then the cage, and pound, and not unfrequently, on a bank by the wayside, a deep old dusty well. Then came the trim-hedged fields on either hand, and the open road again.

They walked all day, and slept that night at a small cottage where beds were let to travellers. Next morning they were afoot again, and though jaded at first, and very tired, recovered before long and proceeded briskly forward.

They often stopped to rest, but only for a short space at a time, and still kept on, having had but slight refreshment since the morning. It was nearly five o'clock in the afternoon, when, drawing near another cluster of labourers' huts, the child looked wistfully in each, doubtful at which to ask for permission to rest awhile, and buy a draught of milk.

It was not easy to determine, for she was timid and fearful of being repulsed. Here was a crying child, and there a noisy wife. In this, the people seemed too poor; in that, too many. At length she stopped at one where the family were seated round the table—chiefly because there was an old man sitting in a cushioned chair beside the hearth, and she thought he was a grandfather and would feel for hers.

There were besides, the cottager and his wife, and three young sturdy children, brown as berries. The request was no sooner preferred, than granted. The eldest boy ran out to fetch some milk, the second dragged two stools towards the door, and the youngest crept to his mother's gown, and looked at the strangers from beneath his sunburnt hand.

"God save you, master," said the old cottager in a thin piping voice; "are you travelling far?"

"Yes, sir, a long way"—replied the child; for her grandfather appealed to her.

"From London?" enquired the old man.

The child said yes.

Ah! He had been in London many a time—used to go there often once, with waggons. It was nigh two-and-thirty year since he had been there last, and he did hear say there were great changes. Like enough! He had changed, himself, since then. Two-and-thirty year was a long time and eighty-four a great age, though there was some he had known that had lived to very hard upon a hundred—and not so hearty as he, neither—no, nothing like it.

"Sit thee down, master, in the elbow chair," said the old man, knocking his stick upon the brick floor, and trying to do so sharply. "Take a pinch out o' that box; I don't take much myself, for it comes dear, but I find it wakes me up sometimes, and ye're but a boy to me. I should have a son pretty nigh as old as you if he'd lived, but they listed him for a so'ger—he come back home though, for all he had but one poor leg. He always said he'd be buried near the sundial he used to climb upon when he was a baby, did my poor boy, and his words come true—you can see the place with your own eyes; we've kept the turf up, ever since."

He shook his head, and looking at his daughter with watery eyes, said she needn't be afraid that he was going to talk about that any more. He didn't wish to trouble nobody, and if he had troubled anybody by what he said, he asked pardon, that was all.

The milk arrived, and the child producing her little basket and selecting its best fragments for her grandfather, they made a hearty meal. The furniture of the room was very homely of course—a few rough chairs and a table, a corner cupboard with their little stock of crockery and delf, a gaudy tea-tray, representing a lady in bright red, walking out with a very blue parasol, a few common, coloured Scripture subjects in frames upon the wall and chimney, an old dwarf clothes-press and an eight-day clock, with a few bright saucepans and a kettle, comprised the whole. But everything was clean and neat, and as the child glanced round, she felt a tranquil air of comfort and content to which she had long been unaccustomed.

"How far is it to any town or village?" she asked of the husband.

"A matter of good five mile, my dear," was the reply, "but you're not going on to-night?"

"Yes yes, Nell," said the old man hastily, urging her too by signs. "Further on, further on, darling, further away if we walk 'till midnight."

"There's a good barn hard by, master," said the man, "or there's travellers' lodgings, I know, at the Plow an' Harrer. Excuse me, but you do seem a little tired, and unless you're very anxious to get on———"

"Yes yes, we are," returned the old man fretfully. "Further away, dear Nell, pray further away."

"We must go on, indeed," said the child, yielding to his restless wish. "We thank you very much, but we cannot stop so soon. I'm quite ready, grandfather."

But the woman had observed, from the young wanderer's gait, that one of her little feet was blistered and sore, and being a woman and a mother too, she would not suffer her to go until she had washed the place and applied some simple remedy, which she did so carefully and with such a gentle hand—rough-grained and hard though it was, with work—that the child's heart was too full to admit of her saying more than a fervent "God bless you!" nor could she look back nor trust herself to speak, until they had left the cottage some distance behind. When she turned her head, she saw that the whole family, even the old grandfather, were standing in the road watching them as they went, and so, with many waves of the hand, and cheering nods, and on one side at least not without tears, they parted company.

They trudged forward, more slowly and painfully than they had done yet, for another mile or thereabouts, when they heard the sound of wheels behind them, and looking round observed an empty cart approaching pretty briskly. The driver on coming up to them stopped his horse and looked earnestly at Nell.

"Didn't you stop to rest at a cottage yonder?" he said.

"Yes, sir," replied the child.

"Ah! They asked me to look out for you," said the man. "I'm going your way. Give me your hand—jump up, master."

This was a great relief, for they were very much fatigued and could scarcely crawl along. To them the jolting cart was a luxurious carriage, and the ride the most delicious in the world. Nell had scarcely settled herself on a little heap of straw in one corner, when she fell asleep, for the first time that day.

She was awakened by the stopping of the cart, which was about to turn up a bye-lane. The driver kindly got down to help her out, and pointing to some trees at a very short distance before them, said that the town lay there, and that they had better take the path which they would see, leading through the churchyard. Accordingly, towards this spot, they directed their weary steps.

Chapter XVI

T HE sun was setting when they reached the wicket-gate at which the path began, and, as the rain falls upon the just and unjust alike, it shed its warm tint even upon the resting-places of the dead, and bade them be of good hope for its rising on the morrow. The church was old and grey, with ivy clinging to the walls, and round the porch. Shunning the tombs, it crept about the mounds, beneath which slept poor humble men, twining for them the first wreaths they had ever won, but wreaths less liable to wither and far more lasting in their kind, than some which were graven deep in stone and marble, and told in pompous terms of virtues meekly hidden for many a year, and only revealed at last to executors and mourning legatees.

The clergyman's horse, stumbling with a dull blunt sound among the graves, was cropping the grass; at once deriving orthodox consolation from the dead parishioners, and enforcing last Sunday's text that this was what all flesh came to; a lean ass who had sought to expound it also, without being qualified and ordained, was pricking his ears in an empty pound hard by, and looking with hungry eyes upon his priestly neighbour.

The old man and the child quitted the gravel path, and strayed among the tombs; for there the ground was soft, and easy to their tired feet. As they passed behind the church, they heard voices near at hand, and presently came on those who had spoken.

They were two men who were seated in easy attitudes upon the grass, and so busily engaged as to be at first unconscious of intruders. It was not difficult to divine that they were of a class of itinerant showmen—exhibitors of the freaks of Punch—for, perched cross-legged upon a tombstone behind them, was a figure of that hero himself, his nose and chin as hooked and his face as beaming as usual. Perhaps his imperturbable character was never more strikingly developed, for he preserved his usual equable smile notwithstanding that his body was dangling in a most uncomfortable position, all loose and limp and shapeless, while his long peaked cap, unequally balanced against his exceedingly slight legs, threatened every instant to bring him toppling down.

In part scattered upon the ground at the feet of the two men, and in part jumbled together in a long flat box, were the other persons of the Drama. The hero's wife and one child, the hobby-horse, the doctor, the foreign gentleman who not being familiar with the language is unable in the representation to express his ideas otherwise than by the utterance of the word "Shallabalah" three distinct times, the Radical neighbour who will by no means admit that a tin bell is an organ, the executioner, and the Devil, were all here. Their owners had evidently come to that spot to make some needful repairs in the stage arrangements, for one of them was engaged in binding together a small gallows with thread, while the other was intent upon fixing a new black wig, with the aid of a small hammer and some tacks, upon the head of the Radical neighbour, who had been beaten bald.

They raised their eyes when the old man and his young companion were close upon them, and pausing in their work, returned their looks of curiosity. One of them, the actual exhibitor no doubt, was a little merry-faced man with a twinkling eye and a red nose, who seemed to have unconsciously imbibed something of his hero's character. The other—that was he who took the money—had rather a careful and cautious look, which was perhaps inseparable from his occupation also.

The merry man was the first to greet the strangers with a nod; and following the old man's eyes, he observed that perhaps that was the first time he had ever seen a Punch off the stage. (Punch, it may be remarked, seemed to be pointing with the tip of his cap to a most flourishing epitaph, and to be chuckling over it with all his heart.)

"Why do you come here to do this?" said the old man, sitting down beside them, and looking at the figures with extreme delight.

"Why, you see," rejoined the little man, "we're putting up for tonight at the public-house yonder, and it wouldn't do to let 'em see the present company undergoing repair."

"No!" cried the old man, making signs to Nell to listen, "why not, eh? why not?"

"Because it would destroy all the delusion, and take away all the interest, wouldn't it?" replied the little man. "Would you care a ha'penny for the Lord Chancellor if you know'd him in private and without his wig?—certainly not."

"Good!" said the old man, venturing to touch one of the puppets, and drawing away his hand with a shrill laugh. "Are you going to show 'em to-night? are you?"

"That is the intention, governor," replied the other, "and unless I'm much mistaken, Tommy Codlin is a calculating at this minute what we've lost through your coming upon us. Cheer up, Tommy, it can't be much."

The little man accompanied these latter words with a wink, expressive of the estimate he had formed of the travellers' finances.

To this Mr Codlin, who had a surly, grumbling manner, replied, as he twitched Punch off the tombstone and flung him into the box:

"I don't care if we haven't lost a farden, but you're too free. If you stood in front of the curtain and see the public's faces as I do, you'd know human natur' better."

"Ah! it's been the spoiling of you, Tommy, your taking to that branch," rejoined his companion. "When you played the ghost in the reg'lar drama in the fairs, you believed in everything—except ghosts. But now you're a universal mistruster. *I* never see a man so changed."

"Never mind," said Mr Codlin, with the air of a discontented philosopher. "I know better now, and p'raps I'm sorry for it."

Turning over the figures in the box like one who knew and despised them, Mr. Codlin drew one forth and held it up for the inspection of his friend:

"Look here; here's all this Judy's clothes falling to pieces again. You haven't got a needle and thread I suppose?"

The little man shook his head, and scratched it ruefully as he contemplated this severe indisposition of a principal performer. Seeing that they were at a loss, the child said timidly:

"I have a needle, sir, in my basket, and thread too. Will you let me try to mend it for you? I think I can do it neater than you could."

Even Mr Codlin had nothing to urge against a proposal so seasonable. Nelly, kneeling down beside the box, was soon busily engaged in her task, and accomplishing it to a miracle.

While she was thus engaged, the merry little man looked at her with an interest which did not appear to be diminished when he glanced at her helpless companion. When she had finished her work he thanked her, and enquired whither they were travelling.

"N—no further to-night, I think," said the child, looking towards her grandfather.

"If you're wanting a place to stop at," the man remarked, "I should advise you to take up at the same house with us. That's it—the long, low, white house there. It's very cheap."

The old man, notwithstanding his fatigue, would have remained in the churchyard all night if his new acquaintance had stayed there too. As he yielded to this suggestion a ready and rapturous assent, they all rose and walked away together; he keeping close to the box of puppets in which he was quite absorbed, the merry little man carrying it slung over his arm by a strap attached to it for the purpose, Nelly having hold of her grandfather's hand, and Mr Codlin sauntering slowly behind, casting up at the church tower and neighbouring trees such looks as he was accustomed in town-practice to direct to drawing-room and nursery windows, when seeking for a profitable spot on which to plant the show.

The public-house was kept by a fat old landlord and landlady who made no objection to receiving their new guests, but praised Nelly's beauty and were at once prepossessed in her behalf. There was no other company in the kitchen but the two showmen, and the child felt very thankful that they had fallen upon such good quarters. The landlady was very much astonished to learn that they had come all the way from London, and appeared to have no little curiosity touching their farther destination. The child parried her enquiries as well as she could, and with no great trouble, for finding that they appeared to give her pain, the old lady desisted.

"These two gentlemen have ordered supper in an hour's time," she said, taking her into the bar; "and your best plan will be to sup with them. Meantime you shall have a little taste of something that'll do you good, for I'm sure you must want it after all you've gone through to-day. Now, don't look after the old gentleman, because when you've drunk that, he shall have some too."

As nothing could induce the child to leave him alone, however, or to touch anything in which he was not the first and greatest sharer, the old lady was obliged to help him first. When they had been thus refreshed, the whole house hurried away into an empty stable where the show stood, and where, by the light of a few flaring candles stuck round a hoop which hung by a line from the ceiling, it was to be forthwith exhibited.

And now Mr Thomas Codlin, the misanthrope, after blowing away at the Pan's pipes until he was intensely wretched, took his station on one side of the checked drapery which concealed the mover of the figures, and putting his hands in his pockets prepared to reply to all questions and remarks of Punch, and to make a dismal feint of being his most intimate private friend, of believing in him to the fullest and most unlimited extent, of knowing that he enjoyed day and night a merry and glorious existence in that temple, and that he was at all times and under every circumstance the same intelligent and joyful person that the spectators then beheld him. All this Mr Codlin did with the air of a man who had made up his mind for the worst and was quite resigned; his eye slowly wandering about during the briskest repartee to observe the effect upon the audience, and particularly the impression made upon the landlord and landlady, which might be productive of very important results in connexion with the supper.

Upon this head, however, he had no cause for any anxiety, for the whole performance was applauded to the echo, and voluntary contributions were showered in with a liberality which testified yet more strongly to the general delight. Among the laughter none was more loud and frequent than the old man's. Nell's was unheard, for she, poor child, with her head drooping on his shoulder, had fallen asleep, and slept too soundly to be roused by any of his efforts to awaken her to a participation in his glee.

The supper was very good, but she was too tired to eat, and yet would not leave the old man until she had kissed him in his bed. He, happily insensible to every care and anxiety, sat listening with a vacant smile and admiring face to all that his new friends said; and it was not until they retired yawning to their room, that he followed the child upstairs.

It was but a loft partitioned into two compartments, where they were to rest, but they were well pleased with their lodging and had hoped for none so good. The old man was uneasy when he had lain down, and begged that Nell would come and sit at his bedside as she had done for so many nights. She hastened to him, and sat there till he slept.

There was a little window, hardly more than a chink in the wall, in her room, and when she left him, she opened it, quite wondering at the silence. The sight of the old church and the graves about it in the moonlight, and the dark trees whispering among themselves, made her more thoughtful than before. She closed the window again, and sitting down upon the bed, thought of the life that was before them.

She had a little money, but it was very little, and when that was gone, they must begin to beg. There was one piece of gold among it, and an emergency might come when its worth to them would be increased a hundredfold. It would be best to hide this coin, and never produce it unless their case was absolutely desperate, and no other resource was left them.

Her resolution taken, she sewed the piece of gold into her dress, and going to bed with a lighter heart sank into a deep slumber.

Chapter XVII

ANOTHER bright day shining in through the small casement, and claiming fellowship with the kindred eyes of the child, awoke her. At sight of the strange room and its unaccustomed objects she started up in alarm, wondering how she had been moved from the familiar chamber in which she seemed to have fallen asleep last night, and whither she had been conveyed. But another glance around called to her mind all that had lately passed, and she sprang from her bed, hoping and trustful.

It was yet early, and the old man being still asleep, she walked out into the churchyard, brushing the dew from the long grass with her feet, and often turning aside into places where it grew longer than in others, that she might not tread upon the graves. She felt a curious kind of pleasure in lingering among these houses of the dead, and read the inscriptions on the tombs of the good people (a great number of good people were buried there), passing on from one to another with increasing interest.

It was a very quiet place, as such a place should be, save for the cawing of the rooks who had built their nests among the branches of some tall old trees, and were calling to one another, high up in the air. First one sleek bird, hovering near his ragged house as it swung and dangled in the wind, uttered his hoarse cry, quite by chance as it would seem, and in a sober tone as though he were but talking to himself. Another answered, and he called again, but louder than before; then another spoke and then another; and each time the first, aggravated by contradiction, insisted on his case more strongly. Other voices, silent till now, struck in from boughs lower down and higher up and midway, and to the right and left, and from the tree-tops; and others, arriving hastily from the grey church turrets and old belfry window, joined the clamour which rose and fell, and swelled and dropped again, and still went on; and all this noisy contention amidst a skimming to and fro, and lighting on fresh branches, and frequent change of place, which satirised the old restlessness of those who lay so still beneath the moss and turf below, and the useless strife in which they had worn away their lives.

Frequently raising her eyes to the trees whence these sounds came down, and feeling as though they made the place more quiet than perfect silence would have done, the child loitered from grave to grave, now stopping to replace with careful hands the bramble which had started from some green mound it helped to keep in shape, and now peeping through one of the low latticed windows into the church, with its worm-eaten books upon the desks, and baize of whitened-green mouldering from the pew sides and leaving the naked wood to view. There were the seats where the poor old people sat, worn spare, and yellow like themselves; the rugged font where children had their names, the homely altar where they knelt in after-life, the plain black tressels that bore their weight on their last visit to the cool old shady church. Everything told of long use and quiet slow decay; the very bell-rope in the porch was frayed into a fringe, and hoary with old age.

She was looking at a humble stone which told of a young man who had died at twenty-three years old, fifty-five years ago, when she heard a faltering step approaching, and looking round saw a feeble woman bent with the weight of years, who tottered to the foot of that same grave and asked her to read the writing on the stone. The old woman thanked her when she had done, saying that she had had the words by heart for many a long, long year, but could not see them now.

"Were you his mother?" said the child.

"I was his wife, my dear."

She was the wife of a young man of three-and-twenty! Ah, true! It was fifty-five years ago.

"You wonder to hear me say that," remarked the old woman, shaking her head. "You're not the first. Older folk than you have wondered at the same thing before now. Yes, I was his wife. Death doesn't change us more than life, my dear."

"Do you come here often?" asked the child.

"I sit here very often in the summer-time," she answered; "I used to come here once to cry and mourn, but that was a weary while ago, bless God!"

"I pluck the daisies as they grow, and take them home," said the old woman after a short silence. "I like no flowers so well as these, and haven't for five-and-fifty year. It's a long time, and I'm getting very old!"

Then growing garrulous upon a theme which was new to one listener though it were but a child, she told her how she had wept and moaned and prayed to die herself, when this happened; and how when she first came to that place, a young creature strong in love and grief, she had hoped that her heart was breaking as it seemed to be. But that time passed by, and although she continued to be sad when she came there, still she could bear to come, and so went on until it was pain no longer, but a solemn pleasure, and a duty she had learned to like. And now that five-and-fifty years were gone, she spoke of the dead man as if he had been her son or grandson, with a kind of pity for his youth, growing out of her own old age, and an exalting of his strength and manly beauty as compared with her own weakness and decay; and yet she spoke about him as her husband too, and thinking of herself in connexion with him, as she used to be and not as she was now, talked of their meeting in another world as if he were dead but yesterday, and she, separated from her former self, were thinking of the happiness of that comely girl who seemed to have died with him.

The child left her gathering the flowers that grew upon the grave, and thoughtfully retraced her steps.

The old man was by this time up and dressed. Mr Codlin, still doomed to contemplate the harsh realities of existence, was packing among his linen the candle-ends which had been saved from the previous night's performance; while his companion received the compliments of all the loungers in the stable-yard, who, unable to separate him from the master-mind of Punch, set him down as next in importance to that merry outlaw, and loved him scarcely less. When he had sufficiently acknowledged his popularity he came in to breakfast, at which meal they all sat down together.

"And where are you going to-day?" said the little man, addressing himself to Nell.

"Indeed I hardly know—we have not determined yet," replied the child.

"We're going on to the races," said the little man. "If that's your way and you like to have us for company, let us travel together. If you prefer going alone, only say the word and you'll find that we shan't trouble you."

"We'll go with you," said the old man. "Nell—with them, with them."

The child considered for a moment, and reflecting that she must shortly beg, and could scarcely hope to do so at a better place than where crowds of rich ladies and gentlemen were assembled together for purposes of enjoyment and festivity, determined to accompany these men so far. She therefore thanked the little man for his offer, and said, glancing timidly towards his friend, that if there was no objection to their accompanying them as far as the race town——

"Objection!" said the little man. "Now be gracious for once, Tommy, and say that you'd rather they went with us. I know you would. Be gracious, Tommy."

"Trotters," said Mr Codlin, who talked very slowly and eat very greedily, as is not uncommon with philosophers and misanthropes; "you're too free."

"Why, what harm can it do?" urged the other.

"No harm at all in this particular case, perhaps," replied Mr Codlin; "but the principle's a dangerous one, and you're too free I tell you."

"Well, are they to go with us or not?"

"Yes, they are," said Mr. Codlin; "but you might have made a favour of it, mightn't you?"

The real name of the little man was Harris, but it had gradually merged into the less euphonious one of Trotters, which, with the prefatory adjective Short, had been conferred upon him by reason of the small size of his legs. Short Trotters, however, being a compound name, inconvenient of use in friendly dialogue, the gentleman on whom it had been bestowed was known among his intimates either as "Short," or "Trotters," and was seldom accosted at full length as Short Trotters, except in formal conversations and on occasions of ceremony.

Short, then, or Trotters, as the reader pleases, returned unto the remonstrance of his friend Mr Thomas Codlin a jocose answer calculated to turn aside his discontent; and applying himself with great relish to the cold boiled beef, the tea, and bread and butter, strongly impressed upon his companions that they should do the like. Mr Codlin indeed required no such persuasion, as he had already eat as much as he could possibly carry and was now moistening his clay with strong ale, whereof he took deep draughts with a silent relish and invited nobody to partake—thus again strongly indicating his misanthropical turn of mind.

Breakfast being at length over, Mr Codlin called the bill, and charging the ale to the company generally (a practice also savouring of misanthropy) divided the sum-total into two fair and equal parts, assigning one moiety to himself and friend, and the other to

Nelly and her grandfather. These being duly discharged and all things ready for their departure, they took farewell of the landlord and landlady and resumed their journey.

And here Mr Codlin's false position in society and the effect it wrought upon his wounded spirit were strongly illustrated; for whereas he had been last night accosted by Mr Punch as "master," and had by inference left the audience to understand that he maintained that individual for his own luxurious entertainment and delight, here he was, now, painfully walking beneath the burden of that same Punch's temple, and bearing it bodily upon his shoulders on a sultry day and along a dusty road. In place of enlivening his patron with a constant fire of wit or the cheerful rattle of his quarterstaff on the heads of his relations and acquaintance, here was that beaming Punch utterly devoid of spine, all slack and drooping in a dark box, with his legs doubled up round his neck, and not one of his social qualities remaining.

Mr Codlin trudged heavily on, exchanging a word or two at intervals with Short, and stopping to rest and growl occasionally. Short led the way; with the flat box, the private luggage (which was not extensive) tied up in a bundle, and a brazen trumpet slung from his shoulder-blade. Nell and her grandfather walked next him on either hand, and Thomas Codlin brought up the rear.

When they came to any town or village, or even to a detached house of good appearance, Short blew a blast upon the brazen trumpet and carolled a fragment of a song in that hilarious tone common to Punches and their consorts. If people hurried to the windows, Mr Codlin pitched the temple, and hastily unfurling the drapery and concealing Short therewith, flourished hysterically on the pipes and performed an air. Then the entertainment began as soon as might be; Mr Codlin having the responsibility of deciding on its length and of protracting or expediting the time for the hero's final triumph over the enemy of mankind, according as he judged that the after-crop of halfpence would be plentiful or scant. When it had been gathered in to the last farthing, he resumed his load and on they went again.

Sometimes they played out the toll across a bridge or ferry, and once exhibited by particular desire at a turnpike, where the collector, being drunk in his solitude, paid down a shilling to have it to himself. There was one small place of rich promise in which their hopes were blighted, for a favourite character in the play having gold-lace upon his coat and being a meddling wooden-headed fellow was held to be a libel on the beadle, for which reason the authorities enforced a quick retreat; but they were generally well received, and seldom left a town without a troop of ragged children shouting at their heels.

They made a long day's journey, despite these interruptions, and were yet upon the road when the moon was shining in the sky. Short beguiled the time with songs and jests, and made the best of everything that happened. Mr Codlin on the other hand, cursed his fate, and all the hollow things of earth (but Punch especially), and limped along with the theatre on his back, a prey to the bitterest chagrin.

They had stopped to rest beneath a finger-post where four roads met, and Mr Codlin in his deep misanthropy had let down the drapery and seated himself in the bottom of the show, invisible to mortal eyes and disdainful of the company of his fellow-creatures, when two monstrous shadows were seen stalking towards them from a turning in the road by which they had come. The child was at first quite terrified by the sight of these gaunt giants—for such they looked as they advanced with lofty strides beneath the shadow of the trees—but Short, telling her there was nothing to fear, blew a blast upon the trumpet, which was answered by a cheerful shout.

"It's Grinder's lot, an't it?" cried Mr Short in a loud key.

"Yes," replied a couple of shrill voices.

"Come on then," said Short. "Let's have a look at you. I thought it was you."

Thus invited, "Grinder's lot" approached with redoubled speed and soon came up with the little party. Mr. Grinder's company, familiarly termed a lot, consisted of a young gentleman and a young lady on stilts, and Mr Grinder himself, who used his natural legs for pedestrian purposes and carried at his back a drum. The public costume of the young people was of the Highland kind, but the night being damp and cold, the young gentleman wore over his kilt a man's pea-jacket reaching to his ankles, and a glazed hat; the young lady too was muffled in an old cloth pelisse and had a handkerchief tied about her head. Their Scotch bonnets, ornamented with plumes of jet black feathers, Mr Grinder carried on his instrument.

"Bound for the races, I see," said Mr Grinder, coming up out of breath. "So are we. How are you, Short?" With that they shook hands in a very friendly manner. The young people being too high up for the ordinary salutations, saluted Short after their own fashion. The young gentleman twisted up his right stilt and patted him on the shoulder, and the young lady rattled her tambourine.

"Practice?" said Short, pointing to the stilts.

"No," returned Grinder. "It comes either to walkin' in 'em or carryin' of 'em, and they like walkin' in 'em best. It's wery pleasant for the prospects. Which road are you takin'? We go the nighest."

"Why, the fact is," said Short, "that we were going the longest way, because then we could stop for the night, a mile and a half on. But three or four mile gained to-night is so many saved to-morrow, and if you keep on, I think our best way is to do the same."

"Where's your partner?" inquired Grinder.

"Here he is," cried Mr Thomas Codlin, presenting his head and face in the proscenium of the stage, and exhibiting an expression of countenance not often seen there; "and he'll see *his* partner boiled alive before he'll go on to-night. That's what *he* says."

"Well, don't say such things as them, in a spear which is dewoted to something pleasanter," urged Short. "Respect associations, Tommy, even if you do cut up rough."

"Rough or smooth," said Mr Codlin, beating his hand on the little footboard where Punch, when suddenly struck with the symmetry of his legs and their capacity for silk stockings, is accustomed to exhibit them to popular admiration, "rough or smooth, I won't go further than the mile and a half to-night. I put up at the Jolly Sandboys and nowhere else. If you like to come there, come there. If you like to go on by yourself, go on by yourself, and do without me if you can."

So saying, Mr Codlin disappeared from the scene and immediately presented himself outside the theatre, took it on his shoulders at a jerk, and made off with most remarkable agility.

Any further controversy being now out of the question, Short was fain to part with Mr Grinder and his pupils and to follow his morose companion. After lingering at the finger-post for a few minutes to see the stilts frisking away in the moonlight and the bearer of the drum toiling slowly after them, he blew a few notes upon the trumpet as a parting salute, and hastened with all speed to follow Mr Codlin. With this view he gave his unoccupied hand to Nell, and bidding her be of good cheer as they would soon be at the end of their journey for that night, and stimulating the old man with a similar assurance, led them at a pretty swift pace towards their destination, which he was the less unwilling to make for, as the moon was now overcast and the clouds were threatening rain.

Chapter XVIII

THE Jolly Sandboys was a small roadside inn of pretty ancient date, with a sign representing three Sandboys increasing their jollity with as many jugs of ale and bags of gold, creaking and swinging on its post on the opposite side of the road. As the travellers had observed that day many indications of their drawing nearer and nearer to the race town, such as gipsy camps, carts laden with gambling-booths and their appurtenances, itinerant showmen of various kinds, and beggars and trampers of every degree, all wending their way in the same direction, Mr Codlin was fearful of finding the accommodations forestalled; this fear increasing as he diminished the distance between himself and the hostelry, he quickened his pace, and notwithstanding the burden he had to carry, maintained a round trot until he reached the threshold. Here he had the gratification of finding that his fears were without foundation, for the landlord was leaning against the door-post looking lazily at the rain, which had by this time begun to descend heavily, and no tinkling of cracked bell, nor boisterous shout, nor noisy chorus, gave note of company within.

"All alone?" said Mr Codlin, putting down his burden and wiping his forehead.

"All alone as yet," rejoined the landlord, glancing at the sky, "but we shall have more company to-night I expect. Here, one of you boys, carry that show into the barn. Make haste in out of the wet, Tom; when it came on to rain I told 'em to make the fire up, and there's a glorious blaze in the kitchen, I can tell you."

Mr Codlin followed with a willing mind, and soon found that the landlord had not commended his preparations without good reason. A mighty fire was blazing on the hearth and roaring up the wide chimney with a cheerful sound, which a large iron cauldron, bubbling and simmering in the heat, lent its pleasant aid to swell. There was a deep red ruddy blush upon the room, and when the landlord stirred the fire, sending the flames skipping and leaping up—when he took off the lid of the iron pot and there rushed out a savoury smell, while the bubbling sound grew deeper and more rich, and an unctuous steam came floating out, hanging in a delicious mist above their heads— when he did this, Mr Codlin's heart was touched. He sat down in the chimney-corner and smiled.

Mr Codlin sat smiling in the chimney-corner, eyeing the landlord as with a roguish look he held the cover in his hand, and, feigning that his doing so was needful to the welfare of the cookery, suffered the delightful steam to tickle the nostrils of his guest. The glow of the fire was upon the landlord's bald head, and upon his twinkling eye, and upon his watering mouth, and upon his pimpled face, and upon his round fat figure. Mr Codlin drew his sleeve across his lips, and said in a murmuring voice, "What is it?"

"It's a stew of tripe," said the landlord smacking his lips, "and cow-heel," smacking them again, "and bacon," smacking them once more, "and steak," smacking them for the fourth time, "and peas, cauliflowers, new potatoes, and sparrow-grass, all working up together in one delicious gravy." Having come to the climax, he smacked his lips a great many times, and taking a long hearty sniff of the fragrance that was hovering about, put on the cover again with the air of one whose toils on earth were over.

"At what time will it be ready?" asked Mr Codlin faintly.

"It'll be done to a turn," said the landlord looking up at the clock—and the very clock had a colour in its fat white face, and looked a clock for Jolly Sandboys to consult—"it'll be done to a turn at twenty-two minutes before eleven."

"Then," said Mr Codlin, "fetch me a pint of warm ale, and don't let anybody bring into the room even so much as a biscuit till the time arrives."

Nodding his approval of this decisive and manly course of procedure, the landlord retired to draw the beer, and presently returning with it, applied himself to warm the same in a small tin vessel shaped funnel-wise, for the convenience of sticking it far down in the fire and getting at the bright places. This was soon done, and he handed it over to Mr Codlin with that creamy froth upon the surface which is one of the happy circumstances attendant upon mulled malt.

Greatly softened by this soothing beverage, Mr Codlin now bethought him of his companions, and acquainted mine host of the Sandboys that their arrival might be shortly looked for. The rain was rattling against the windows and pouring down in torrents, and such was Mr Codlin's extreme amiability of mind, that he more than once expressed his earnest hope that they would not be so foolish as to get wet.

At length they arrived, drenched with the rain and presenting a most miserable appearance, notwithstanding that Short had sheltered the child as well as he could under the skirts of his own coat, and they were nearly breathless from the haste they had made. But their steps were no sooner heard upon the road than the landlord, who had been at the outer door anxiously watching for their coming, rushed into the kitchen and took the cover off. The effect was electrical. They all came in with smiling faces, though the wet was dripping from their clothes upon the floor, and Short's first remark was, "What a delicious smell!"

It is not very difficult to forget rain and mud by the side of a cheerful fire, and in a bright room. They were furnished with slippers and such dry garments as the house or their own bundles afforded, and ensconcing themselves, as Mr Codlin had already done, in the warm chimney-corner, soon forgot their late troubles or only remembered them as enhancing the delights of the present time. Overpowered by the warmth and comfort and the fatigue they had undergone, Nelly and the old man had not long taken their seats here, when they fell asleep.

"Who are they?" whispered the landlord.

Short shook his head, and wished he knew himself.

"Don't *you* know?" asked the host, turning to Mr Codlin.

"Not I," he replied. "They're no good, I suppose."

"They're no harm," said Short. "Depend upon that. I tell you what—it's plain that the old man an't in his right mind——"

"If you haven't got anything newer than that to say," growled Mr Codlin, glancing at the clock, "you'd better let us fix our minds upon the supper, and not disturb us."

"Hear me out, won't you?" retorted his friend. "It's very plain to me, besides, that they're not used to this way of life. Don't tell me that that handsome child has been in the habit of prowling about as she's done these last two or three days. I know better."

"Well, who *does* tell you she has?" growled Mr Codlin, again glancing at the clock and from it to the cauldron, "can't you think of anything more suitable to present circumstances than saying things and then contradicting 'em?"

"I wish somebody would give you your supper," returned Short, "for there'll be no peace till you've got it. Have you seen how anxious the old man is to get on—always wanting to be furder away—furder away. Have you seen that?"

"Ah! what then?" muttered Thomas Codlin.

"This, then," said Short. "He has given his friends the slip. Mind what I say—he has given his friends the slip, and persuaded this delicate young creetur all along of her fondness for him to be his guide and travelling companion—where to, he knows no more than the man in the moon. Now, I'm not a-going to stand that."

"*You're* not a-going to stand that!" cried Mr Codlin, glancing at the clock again and pulling his hair with both hands in a kind of frenzy, but whether occasioned by his companion's observation or the tardy pace of Time, it was difficult to determine. "Here's a world to live in!"

"I," repeated Short emphatically and slowly, "am not a-going to stand it. I am not a-going to see this fair young child a-falling into bad hands, and getting among people that she's no more fit for, than they are to get among angels as their ordinary chums. Therefore when they dewelope an intention of parting company from us, I shall take measures for detaining of 'em, and restoring 'em to their friends, who I dare say have had their disconsolation pasted up on every wall in London by this time."

"Short," said Mr Codlin, who with his head upon his hands, and his elbows on his knees, had been shaking himself impatiently from side to side up to this point and occasionally stamping on the ground, but who now looked up with eager eyes; "it's possible that there may be uncommon good sense in what you've said. If there is, and there should be a reward, Short, remember that we're partners in everything!"

His companion had only time to nod a brief assent to this position, for the child awoke at the instant. They had drawn close together during the previous whispering, and now hastily separated and were rather awkwardly endeavouring to exchange some casual remarks in their usual tone, when strange footsteps were heard without, and fresh company entered.

These were no other than four very dismal dogs, who came pattering in one after the other, headed by an old bandy dog of particularly mournful aspect, who, stopping when the last of his followers had got as far as the door, erected himself upon his hind-legs and looked round at his companions, who immediately stood upon their hind-legs, in a grave and melancholy row. Nor was this the only remarkable circumstance about these dogs, for each of them wore a kind of little coat of some gaudy colour trimmed with tarnished spangles, and one of them had a cap upon his head, tied very carefully under his chin, which had fallen down upon his nose and completely obscured one eye; add to this, that the gaudy coats were all wet through and discoloured with rain, and that the wearers were splashed and dirty, and some idea may be formed of the unusual appearance of these new visitors to the Jolly Sandboys.

Neither Short nor the landlord nor Thomas Codlin, however, were the least surprised, merely remarking that these were Jerry's dogs and that Jerry could not be far behind. So there the dogs stood, patiently winking and gaping and looking extremely hard at the boiling pot, until Jerry himself appeared, when they all dropped down at once and walked about the room in their natural manner. This posture it must be confessed did not much improve their appearance, as their own personal tails and their coat-tails— both capital things in their way—did not agree together.

Jerry, the manager of these dancing dogs, was a tall black-whiskered man in a velveteen coat, who seemed well known to the landlord and his guests and accosted them with great cordiality. Disencumbering himself of a barrel-organ which he placed upon a chair, and retaining in his hand a small whip wherewith to awe his company of comedians, he came up to the fire to dry himself, and entered into conversation.

"Your people don't usually travel in character, do they?" said Short, pointing to the dresses of the dogs. "It must come expensive if they do?"

"No," replied Jerry, "no, it's not the custom with us. But we've been playing a little on the road to-day, and we come out with a new wardrobe at the races, so I didn't think it worth while to stop to undress. Down, Pedro!"

This was addressed to the dog with the cap on, who, being a new member of the company and not quite certain of his duty, kept his unobscured eye anxiously on his master, and was perpetually starting upon his hind-legs when there was no occasion, and falling down again.

"I've got a animal here," said Jerry, putting his hand into the capacious pocket of his coat, and diving into one corner as if he were feeling for a small orange or an apple or some such article, "a animal here, wot I think you know something of, Short."

"Ah!" cried Short, "let's have a look at him."

"Here he is," said Jerry, producing a little terrier from his pocket. "He was once a Toby of yours, warn't he!"

In some versions of the great drama of Punch there is a small dog—a modern innovation—supposed to be the private property of that gentleman, whose name is always Toby. This Toby has been stolen in youth from another gentleman, and fraudulently sold to the confiding hero, who having no guile himself has no suspicion that it lurks in others; but Toby, entertaining a grateful recollection of his old master, and scorning to attach himself to any new patrons, not only refuses to smoke a pipe at the bidding of Punch, but to mark his old fidelity more strongly, seizes him by the nose and wrings the same with violence, at which instance of canine attachment the spectators are deeply affected. This was the character which the little terrier in question had once sustained; if there had been any doubt upon the subject he would speedily have resolved it by his conduct; for not only did he, on seeing Short, give the strongest tokens of recognition, but catching sight of the flat-box he barked so furiously at the pasteboard nose which he knew was inside, that his master was obliged to gather him up and put him into his pocket again, to the great relief of the whole company.

The landlord now busied himself in laying the cloth, in which process Mr Codlin obligingly assisted by setting forth his own knife and fork in the most convenient place and establishing himself behind them. When everything was ready, the landlord took off the cover for the last time, and then indeed there burst forth such a goodly promise of supper, that if he had offered to put it on again or had hinted at postponement, he would certainly have been sacrificed on his own hearth.

However, he did nothing of the kind, but instead thereof assisted a stout servant-girl in turning the contents of the cauldron into a large tureen; a proceeding which the dogs, proof against various hot splashes which fell upon their noses, watched with terrible eagerness. At length the dish was lifted on the table, and mugs of ale having been previously set round, little Nell ventured to say grace, and supper began.

At this juncture the poor dogs were standing on their hind-legs quite surprisingly; the child, having pity on them, was about to cast some morsels of food to them before she tasted it herself, hungry though she was, when their master interposed.

"No, my dear, no, not an atom from anybody's hand but mine if you please. That dog," said Jerry, pointing out the old leader of the troop, and speaking in a terrible voice, "lost a halfpenny to-day. *He* goes without his supper."

The unfortunate creature dropped upon his forelegs directly, wagged his tail, and looked imploringly at his master.

"You must be more careful, sir," said Jerry, walking coolly to the chair where he had placed the organ, and setting the stop. "Come here. Now, sir, you play away at that, while we have supper, and leave off if you dare."

The dog immediately began to grind most mournful music. His master having shown him the whip resumed his seat and called up the others, who, at his directions, formed in a row, standing upright as a file of soldiers.

"Now, gentlemen," said Jerry, looking at them attentively. "The dog whose name's called, eats. The dogs whose names an't called, keep quiet. Carlo!"

The lucky individual whose name was called, snapped up the morsel thrown towards him, but none of the others moved a muscle. In this manner they were fed at the discretion of their master. Meanwhile the dog in disgrace ground hard at the organ, sometimes in quick time, sometimes in slow, but never leaving off for an instant. When the knives and forks rattled very much, or any of his fellows got an unusually large piece of fat, he accompanied the music with a short howl, but he immediately checked it on his master looking round, and applied himself with increased diligence to the Old Hundredth.

Chapter XIX

SUPPER was not yet over, when there arrived at the Jolly Sandboys two more travellers bound for the same haven as the rest, who had been walking in the rain for some hours, and came in shining and heavy with water. One of these was the proprietor of a giant, and a little lady without legs or arms, who had jogged forward in a van; the other, a silent gentleman who earned his living by showing tricks upon the cards, and who had rather deranged the natural expression of his countenance by putting small leaden lozenges into his eyes and bringing them out at his mouth, which was one of his professional accomplishments. The name of the first of these new-comers was Vuffin; the other, probably as a pleasant satire upon his ugliness, was called Sweet William. To render them as comfortable as he could, the landlord bestirred himself nimbly, and in a very short time both gentlemen were perfectly at their ease.

"How's the Giant?" said Short, when they all sat smoking round the fire.

"Rather weak upon his legs," returned Mr Vuffin. "I begin to be afraid he's going at the knees."

"That's a bad look-out," said Short.

"Ay! Bad indeed," replied Mr Vuffin, contemplating the fire with a sigh. "Once get a giant shaky on his legs, and the public care no more about him than they do for a dead cabbage-stalk."

"What becomes of the old giants?" said Short, turning to him again after a little reflection.

"They're usually kept in caravans to wait upon the dwarfs," said Mr Vuffin.

"The maintaining of 'em must come expensive, when they can't be shown, eh?" remarked Short, eyeing him doubtfully.

"It's better that, than letting 'em go upon the parish or about the streets," said Mr Vuffin. "Once make a giant common and giants will never draw again. Look at wooden legs. If there was only one man with a wooden leg what a property *he'd* be!"

"So he would!" observed the landlord and Short both together. "That's very true."

"Instead of which," pursued Mr Vuffin, "if you was to advertise Shakespeare played entirely by wooden legs, it's my belief you wouldn't draw a sixpence."

"I don't suppose you would," said Short. And the landlord said so too.

"This shows, you see," said Mr Vuffin, waving his pipe with an argumentative air, "this shows the policy of keeping the used-up giants still in the carawans, where they get food and lodging for nothing, all their lives, and in general very glad they are to stop there. There was one giant—a black 'un—as left his carawan some year ago and took to carrying coach-bills about London, making himself as cheap as crossing-sweepers. He died. I make no insinuation against anybody in particular," said Mr Vuffin, looking solemnly round, "but he was ruining the trade;—and he died."

The landlord drew his breath hard, and looked at the owner of the dogs, who nodded and said gruffly that *he* remembered.

"I know you do, Jerry," said Mr Vuffin with profound meaning. "I know you remember it, Jerry, and the universal opinion was, that it served him right. Why, I remember the time when old Maunders as had three-and-twenty wans—I remember the time when old Maunders had in his cottage in Spa Fields in the winter-time when the season was over, eight male and female dwarfs setting down to dinner every day, who was waited on by eight old giants in green coats, red smalls, blue cotton stockings, and high-lows: and there was one dwarf as had grown elderly and wicious who whenever his giant wasn't quick enough to please him, used to stick pins in his legs, not being able to reach up any higher. I know that's a fact, for Maunders told it me himself."

"What about the dwarfs, when *they* get old?" inquired the landlord.

"The older a dwarf is, the better worth he is," returned Mr Vuffin; "a grey-headed dwarf, well wrinkled, is beyond all suspicion. But a giant weak in the legs and not standing upright!—keep him in the carawan, but never show him, never show him, for any persuasion that can be offered."

While Mr Vuffin and his two friends smoked their pipes and beguiled the time with such conversation as this, the silent gentleman sat in a warm corner, swallowing, or seeming to swallow, sixpennyworth of halfpence for practice, balancing a feather upon his nose, and rehearsing other feats of dexterity of that kind, without paying any regard whatever to the company, who in their turn left him utterly unnoticed. At length the weary child prevailed upon her grandfather to retire, and they withdrew, leaving the company yet seated round the fire, and the dogs fast asleep at a humble distance.

After bidding the old man good night, Nell retired to her poor garret, but had scarcely closed the door, when it was gently tapped at. She opened it directly, and was a little startled by the sight of Mr Thomas Codlin, whom she had left, to all appearance, fast asleep downstairs.

"What is the matter?" said the child.

"Nothing's the matter, my dear," returned her visitor. "I'm your friend. Perhaps you haven't thought so, but it's me that's your friend—not him."

"Not who?" the child enquired.

"Short, my dear. I tell you what," said Codlin, "for all his having a kind of way with him that you'd be very apt to like, I'm the real, open-hearted man. I mayn't look it, but I am indeed."

The child began to be alarmed, considering that the ale had taken effect upon Mr Codlin, and that this commendation of himself was the consequence.

"Short's very well, and seems kind," resumed the misanthrope, "but he overdoes it. Now I don't."

Certainly if there were any fault in Mr Codlin's usual deportment, it was that he rather underdid his kindness to those about him, than overdid it. But the child was puzzled, and could not tell what to say.

"Take my advice," said Codlin; "don't ask me why, but take it. As long as you travel with us, keep as near me as you can. Don't offer to leave us—not on any account—but always stick to me and say that I'm your friend. Will you bear that in mind, my dear, and always say that it was me that was your friend?"

"Say so where—and when?" enquired the child innocently.

"Oh, nowhere in particular," replied Codlin, a little put out as it seemed by the question; "I'm only anxious that you should think me so, and do me justice. You can't think what an interest I have in you. Why didn't you tell me your little history—that about you and the poor old gentleman? I'm the best adviser that ever was, and *so* interested in you—so much more interested than Short. I think they're breaking up downstairs; you needn't tell Short, you know, that we've had this little talk together. God bless you. Recollect the friend. Codlin's the friend, not Short. Short's very well as far as he goes, but the real friend is Codlin—not Short."

Eking out these professions with a number of benevolent and protecting looks and great fervour of manner, Thomas Codlin stole away on tiptoe, leaving the child in a state of extreme surprise. She was still ruminating upon his curious behaviour, when the floor of the crazy stairs and landing cracked beneath the tread of the other travellers who were passing to their beds. When they had all passed, and the sound of their footsteps had died away, one of them returned, and after a little hesitation and rustling in the passage, as if he were doubtful what door to knock at, knocked at hers.

"Yes?" said the child from within.

"It's me—Short"—a voice called through the keyhole. "I only wanted to say that we must be off early to-morrow morning, my dear, because unless we get the start of the dogs and the conjuror, the villages won't be worth a penny. You'll be sure to be stirring early and go with us? I'll call you."

The child answered in the affirmative, and returning his "good night" heard him creep away. She felt some uneasiness at the anxiety of these men, increased by the recollection of their whispering together downstairs and their slight confusion when she awoke, nor was she quite free from a misgiving that they were not the fittest companions she could have stumbled on. Her uneasiness, however, was nothing, weighed against her fatigue; and she soon forgot it in sleep.

Very early next morning Short fulfilled his promise, and knocking softly at her door, entreated that she would get up directly, as the proprietor of the dogs was still snoring, and if they lost no time they might get a good deal in advance both of him and the conjuror, who was talking in his sleep, and from what he could be heard to say, appeared to be balancing a donkey in his dreams. She started from her bed without delay, and roused the old man with so much expedition that they were both ready as soon as Short himself, to that gentleman's unspeakable gratification and relief.

After a very unceremonious and scrambling breakfast, of which the staple commodities were bacon and bread and beer, they took leave of the landlord and issued from the door of the Jolly Sandboys. The morning was fine and warm, the ground cool to the feet after the late rain, the hedges gayer and more green, the air clear, and everything fresh and healthful. Surrounded by these influences, they walked on pleasantly enough.

They had not gone very far, when the child was again struck by the altered behaviour of Mr Thomas Codlin, who instead of plodding on sulkily by himself as he had theretofore done, kept close to her, and when he had an opportunity of looking at her unseen by his companion, warned her by certain wry faces and jerks of the head not to put any trust in Short, but to reserve all confidences for Codlin. Neither did he confine himself to looks and gestures, for when she and her grandfather were walking on beside the aforesaid Short, and that little man was talking with his accustomed cheerfulness on a variety of indifferent subjects, Thomas Codlin testified his jealousy and distrust by following close at her heels, and occasionally admonishing her ankles with the legs of the theatre in a very abrupt and painful manner.

All these proceedings naturally made the child more watchful and suspicious, and she soon observed that whenever they halted to perform outside a village alehouse or other place, Mr Codlin while he went through his share of the entertainments kept his eye steadily upon her and the old man, or with a show of great friendship and consideration invited the latter to lean upon his arm, and so held him tight until the representation was over and they again went forward. Even Short seemed to change in this respect, and to mingle with his good-nature something of a desire to keep them in safe custody. This increased the child's misgivings, and made her yet more anxious and uneasy.

Meanwhile, they were drawing near the town where the races were to begin next day; for, from passing numerous groups of gipsies and trampers on the road, wending their way towards it, and straggling out from every by-way and cross-country lane, they gradually fell into a stream of people, some walking by the side of covered carts, others with horses, others with donkeys, others toiling on with heavy loads upon their backs, but all tending to the same point. The public-houses by the wayside, from being empty and noiseless as those in the remoter parts had been, now sent out boisterous shouts and clouds of smoke; and, from the misty windows, clusters of broad red faces looked down upon the road. On every piece of waste or common ground, some small gambler drove his noisy trade, and bellowed to the idle passers-by to stop and try their chance; the crowd grew thicker and more noisy; gilt gingerbread in blanket-stalls exposed its glories to the dust; and often a four-horse carriage, dashing by, obscured all objects in the gritty cloud it raised, and left them, stunned and blinded, far behind.

It was dark before they reached the town itself, and long indeed the few last miles had been. Here all was tumult and confusion; the streets were filled with throngs of people—many strangers were there, it seemed, by the looks they cast about—the church-bells rang out their noisy peals, and flags streamed from windows and housetops. In the large inn-yards waiters flitted to and fro and ran against each other, horses clattered on the uneven stones, carriage steps fell rattling down, and sickening smells from many dinners came in a heavy lukewarm breath upon the sense. In the smaller public-houses, fiddles with all their might and main were squeaking out the tune to staggering feet; drunken men, oblivious of the burden of their song, joined in a senseless howl, which drowned the tinkling of the feeble bell and made them savage for their drink; vagabond groups assembled round the doors to see the stroller women dance, and add their uproar to the shrill flageolet and deafening drum.

Through this delirious scene the child, frightened and repelled by all she saw, led on her bewildered charge, clinging close to her conductor, and trembling lest in the press she should be separated from him and left to find her way alone. Quickening their steps to get clear of all the roar and riot, they at length passed through the town and made for the race-course, which was upon an open heath, situated on an eminence, a full mile distant from its furthest bounds.

Although there were many people here, none of the best favoured or best clad, busily erecting tents and driving stakes into the ground, and hurrying to and fro with dusty feet and many a grumbled oath—although there were tired children cradled on heaps of straw between the wheels of carts, crying themselves to sleep—and poor lean horses and donkeys just turned loose, grazing among the men and women, and pots and kettles, and half-lighted fires, and ends of candles flaring and wasting in the air—for all this, the child felt it an escape from the town and drew her breath more freely. After a scanty supper, the purchase of which reduced her little stock so low, that she had only a few halfpence with which to buy a breakfast on the morrow, she and the old man lay down to rest in a corner of a tent, and slept, despite the busy preparations that were going on around them all night long.

And now they had come to the time when they must beg their bread. Soon after sunrise in the morning she stole out from the tent, and rambling into some fields at a short distance, plucked a few wild roses and such humble flowers, purposing to make them into little nosegays and offer them to the ladies in the carriages when the company arrived. Her thoughts were not idle while she was thus employed; when she returned and was seated beside the old man in one corner of the tent, tying her flowers together, while the two men lay dozing in another corner, she plucked him by the sleeve, and slightly glancing towards them, said in a low voice:

"Grandfather, don't look at those I talk of, and don't seem as if I spoke of anything but what I am about. What was that you told me before we left the old house? That if they knew what we were going to do, they would say that you were mad, and part us?"

The old man turned to her with an aspect of wild terror; but she checked him by a look, and bidding him hold some flowers while she tied them up, and so bringing her lips closer to his ear, said:

"I know that was what you told me. You needn't speak, dear. I recollect it very well. It was not likely that I should forget it. Grandfather, these men suspect that we have secretly left our friends, and mean to carry us before some gentleman and have us taken care of and sent back. If you let your hand tremble so, we can never get away from them, but if you're only quiet now, we shall do so, easily."

"How?" muttered the old man. "Dear Nelly, how? They will shut me up in a stone room, dark and cold, and chain me up to the wall, Nell—flog me with whips, and never let me see thee more!"

"You're trembling again," said the child. "Keep close to me all day. Never mind them, don't look at them, but me. I shall find a time when we can steal away. When I do, mind you come with me, and do not stop or speak a word. Hush! That's all."

"Halloa! what are you up to, my dear?" said Mr Codlin, raising his head, and yawning. Then observing that his companion was fast asleep, he added in an earnest whisper, "Codlin's the friend, remember—not Short."

"Making some nosegays," the child replied; "I am going to try and sell some, these three days of the races. Will you have one—as a present I mean?"

Mr Codlin would have risen to receive it, but the child hurried towards him and placed it in his hand. He stuck it in his buttonhole with an air of ineffable complacency for a misanthrope, and leering exultingly at the unconscious Short, muttered, as he laid himself down again, "Tom Codlin's the friend by G—!"

As the morning wore on, the tents assumed a gayer and more brilliant appearance, and long lines of carriages came rolling softly on the turf. Men who had lounged about all night in smock-frocks and leather leggings, came out in silken vests and hats and plumes, as jugglers or mountebanks; or in gorgeous liveries as soft-spoken servants at gambling-booths; or in sturdy yeoman dress as decoys at unlawful games. Black-eyed gipsy girls, hooded in showy handkerchiefs, sallied forth to tell fortunes, and pale slender women with consumptive faces lingered upon the footsteps of ventriloquists and conjurors, and counted the sixpences with anxious eyes long before they were gained. As many of the children as could be kept within bounds, were stowed away, with all the other signs of dirt and poverty, among the donkeys, carts, and horses; and as many as could not be thus disposed of ran in and out in all intricate spots, crept between people's legs and carriage wheels, and came forth unharmed from under horses' hoofs. The dancing-dogs, the stilts, the little lady and the tall man, and all the other attractions, with organs out of number and bands innumerable, emerged from the holes and corners in which they had passed the night, and flourished boldly in the sun.

Along the uncleared course, Short led his party, sounding the brazen trumpet and revelling in the voice of Punch; and at his heels went Thomas Codlin, bearing the show as usual, and keeping his eye on Nelly and her grandfather, as they rather lingered in the rear. The child bore upon her arm the little basket with her flowers, and sometimes stopped, with timid and modest looks, to offer them at some gay carriage; but alas! there were many bolder beggars there, gipsies who promised husbands, and other adepts in their trade, and although some ladies smiled gently as they shook their heads, and others cried to the gentlemen beside them "See, what a pretty face!" they let the pretty face pass on, and never thought that it looked tired or hungry.

There was but one lady who seemed to understand the child, and she was one who sat alone in a handsome carriage, while two young men in dashing clothes, who had just dismounted from it, talked and laughed loudly at a little distance, appearing to forget her, quite. There were many ladies all around, but they turned their backs, or looked another way, or at the two young men (not unfavourably at *them*), and left her to herself. She motioned away a gipsy-woman urgent to tell her fortune, saying that it was told already and had been for some years, but called the child towards her, and taking her flowers put money into her trembling hand, and bade her go home and keep at home for God's sake.

Many a time they went up and down those long, long lines, seeing everything but the horses and the race; when the bell rang to clear the course, going back to rest among the carts and donkeys, and not coming out again until the heat was over. Many a time, too, was Punch displayed in the full zenith of his humour, but all this while the eye of Thomas Codlin was upon them, and to escape without notice was impracticable.

At length, late in the day, Mr Codlin pitched the show in a convenient spot, and the spectators were soon in the very triumph of the scene. The child, sitting down with the old man close behind it, had been thinking how strange it was that horses who were such fine honest creatures should seem to make vagabonds of all the men they drew about them, when a loud laugh at some extemporaneous witticism of Mr Short's, having allusion to the circumstances of the day, roused her from her meditation and caused her to look around.

If they were ever to get away unseen, that was the very moment. Short was plying the quarter-staves vigorously and knocking the characters in the fury of the combat against the sides of the show, the people were looking on with laughing faces, and Mr Codlin had relaxed into a grim smile as his roving eye detected hands going into waistcoat pockets and groping secretly for sixpences. If they were ever to get away unseen, that was the very moment. They seized it, and fled.

They made a path through booths and carriages and throngs of people, and never once stopped to look behind. The bell was ringing and the course was cleared by the time they reached the ropes, but they dashed across it insensible to the shouts and screeching that assailed them for breaking in upon its sanctity, and creeping under the brow of the hill at a quick pace, made for the open fields.

Chapter XX

D AY after day as he bent his steps homeward, returning from some new effort to procure employment, Kit raised his eyes to the window of the little room he had so much commended to the child, and hoped to see some indication of her presence. His own earnest wish, coupled with the assurance he had received from Quilp, filled him with the belief that she would yet arrive to claim the humble shelter he had offered, and from the death of each day's hope, another hope sprang up to live to-morrow.

"I think they must certainly come to-morrow, eh, mother?" said Kit, laying aside his hat with a weary air and sighing as he spoke. "They have been gone a week. They surely couldn't stop away more than a week, could they now?"

The mother shook her head, and reminded him how often he had been disappointed already.

"For the matter of that," said Kit, "you speak true and sensible enough, as you always do, mother. Still, I do consider that a week is quite long enough for 'em to be rambling about; don't you say so?"

"Quite long enough, Kit, longer than enough, but they may not come back for all that."

Kit was for a moment disposed to be vexed by this contradiction, and not the less so from having anticipated it in his own mind and knowing how just it was. But the impulse was only momentary, and the vexed look became a kind one before it had crossed the room.

"Then what do you think, mother, has become of 'em? You don't think they've gone to sea, anyhow?"

"Not gone for sailors, certainly," returned the mother with a smile. "But I can't help thinking that they have gone to some foreign country."

"I say," cried Kit with a rueful face, "don't talk like that, mother."

"I am afraid they have, and that's the truth," she said. "It's the talk of all the neighbours, and there are some even that know of their having been seen on board ship, and can tell you the name of the place they've gone to, which is more than I can, my dear, for it's a very hard one."

"I don't believe it," said Kit. "Not a word of it. A set of idle chatterboxes, how should they know!"

"They may be wrong of course," returned the mother. "I can't tell about that, though I don't think it's at all unlikely that they're in the right, for the talk is that the old gentleman had put by a little money that nobody knew of, not even that ugly little man you talk to me about—what's his name—Quilp; and that he and Miss Nell have gone to live abroad where it can't be taken from them, and they will never be disturbed. That don't seem very far out of the way now, do it?"

Kit scratched his head mournfully, in reluctant admission that it did not, and clambering up to the old nail took down the cage and set himself to clean it and to feed the bird. His thoughts reverting from his occupation to the little old gentleman who had given him the shilling, he suddenly recollected that that was the very day—nay, nearly the very hour—at which the little old gentleman had said he should be at the notary's house again. He no sooner remembered this, than he hung up the cage with great precipitation, and hastily explaining the nature of his errand, went off at full speed to the appointed place.

It was some two minutes after the time when he reached the spot, which was a considerable distance from his home, but by great good luck the little old gentleman had not yet arrived; at least there was no pony-chaise to be seen, and it was not likely that he had come and gone again in so short a space. Greatly relieved to find that he was not too late, Kit leant against a lamp-post to take breath, and waited the advent of the pony and his charge.

Sure enough, before long the pony came trotting round the corner of the street, looking as obstinate as a pony might, and picking his steps as if he were spying about for the cleanest places, and would by no means dirty his feet or hurry himself inconveniently. Behind the pony sat the little old gentleman, and by the old gentleman's side sat the little old lady, carrying just such a nosegay as she had brought before.

The old gentleman, the old lady, the pony, and the chaise, came up the street in perfect unanimity, until they arrived within some half a dozen doors of the notary's house, when the pony, deceived by a brass-plate beneath a tailor's knocker, came to a halt, and maintained by a sturdy silence, that that was the house they wanted.

"Now, sir, will you have the goodness to go on; this is *not* the place," said the old gentleman.

The pony looked with great attention into a fire-plug which was near him, and appeared to be quite absorbed in contemplating it.

"Oh, dear, such a naughty Whisker!" cried the old lady. "After being so good too, and coming along so well! I am quite ashamed of him. I don't know what we are to do with him, I really don't."

The pony having thoroughly satisfied himself as to the nature and properties of the fire-plug, looked into the air after his old enemies the flies, and as there happened to be one of them tickling his ear at that moment he shook his head and whisked his tail, after which he appeared full of thought but quite comfortable and collected. The old gentleman having exhausted his powers of persuasion, alighted to lead him; whereupon the pony, perhaps because he held this to be a sufficient concession, perhaps because he happened to catch sight of the other brass-plate, or perhaps because he was in a spiteful humour, darted off with the old lady and stopped at the right house, leaving the old gentleman to come panting on behind.

It was then that Kit presented himself at the pony's head, and touched his hat with a smile.

"Why, bless me," cried the old gentleman, "the lad *is* here! My dear, do you see?"

"I said I'd be here, sir," said Kit, patting Whisker's neck. "I hope you've had a pleasant ride, sir. He's a very nice little pony."

"My dear," said the old gentleman. "This is an uncommon lad; a good lad, I'm sure."

"I'm sure he is," rejoined the old lady. "A very good lad, and I am sure he is a good son."

Kit acknowledged these expressions of confidence by touching his hat again and blushing very much. The old gentleman then handed the old lady out, and after looking at him with an approving smile, they went into the house—talking about him as they went, Kit could not help feeling. Presently Mr Witherden, smelling very hard at the nosegay, came to the window and looked at him, and after that Mr Abel came and looked at him, and after that the old gentleman and lady came and looked at him again, and after that they all came and looked at him together, which Kit, feeling very much embarrassed by, made a pretence of not observing. Therefore he patted the pony more and more; and this liberty the pony most handsomely permitted.

The faces had not disappeared from the window many moments, when Mr Chuckster in his official coat, and with his hat hanging on his head just as it happened to fall from its peg, appeared upon the pavement, and telling him he was wanted inside, bade him go in and he would mind the chaise the while. In giving him this direction Mr Chuckster remarked that he wished he might be blessed if he could make out whether he (Kit) was "precious raw" or "precious deep," but intimated by a distrustful shake of the head, that he inclined to the latter opinion.

Kit entered the office in a great tremor, for he was not used to going among strange ladies and gentleman, and the tin boxes and bundles of dusty papers had in his eyes an awful and venerable air. Mr Witherden too was a bustling gentleman who talked loud and fast, and all eyes were upon him, and he was very shabby.

"Well, boy," said Mr Witherden, "you came to work out that shilling;—not to get another, hey?"

"No indeed, sir," replied Kit, taking courage to look up. "I never thought of such a thing."

"Father alive?"

"Dead, sir."

"Mother?"

"Yes, sir."

"Married again—eh?"

Kit made answer, not without some indignation, that she was a widow with three children, and that as to her marrying again, if the gentleman knew her he wouldn't think of such a thing. At this reply Mr Witherden buried his nose in the flowers again, and whispered behind the nosegay to the old gentleman that he believed the lad was as honest a lad as need be.

"Now," said Mr Garland when they had made some further inquiries of him, "I am not going to give you anything——"

"Thank you, sir," Kit replied; and quite seriously too, for this announcement seemed to free him from the suspicion which the notary had hinted.

"—But," resumed the old gentleman, "perhaps I may want to know something more about you, so tell me where you live and I'll put it down in my pocket-book."

Kit told him, and the old gentleman wrote down the address with his pencil. He had scarcely done so, when there was a great uproar in the street, and the old lady hurrying to the window cried that Whisker had run away, upon which Kit darted out to the rescue, and the others followed.

It seemed that Mr Chuckster had been standing with his hands in his pockets looking carelessly at the pony, and occasionally insulting him with such admonitions as "Stand still"—"Be quiet"—"Woa-a-a," and the like, which by a pony of spirit cannot be borne. Consequently, the pony being deterred by no considerations of duty or obedience, and not having before him the slightest fear of the human eye, had at length started off, and was at that moment rattling down the street—Mr Chuckster, with his hat off and a pen behind his ear, hanging on in the rear of the chaise and making futile attempts to draw it the other way, to the unspeakable admiration of all beholders. Even in running away, however, Whisker was perverse, for he had not gone very far when he suddenly stopped, and before assistance could be rendered, commenced backing at nearly as quick a pace as he had gone forward. By these means Mr Chuckster was pushed and hustled to the office again, in a most inglorious manner, and arrived in a state of great exhaustion and discomfiture.

The old lady then stepped into her seat, and Mr Abel (whom they had come to fetch) into his. The old gentleman, after reasoning with the pony on the extreme impropriety of his conduct, and making the best amends in his power to Mr Chuckster, took his place also, and they drove away, waving a farewell to the notary and his clerk, and more than once turning to nod kindly to Kit as he watched them from the road.

Chapter XXI

K IT turned away and very soon forgot the pony, and the chaise, and the little old lady, and the little old gentleman, and the little young gentleman to boot, in thinking what could have become of his late master and his lovely grandchild, who were the fountain-head of all his meditations. Still casting about for some plausible means of accounting for their non-appearance, and of persuading himself that they must soon return, he bent his steps towards home, intending to finish the task which the sudden recollection of his contract had interrupted, and then to sally forth once more to seek his fortune for the day.

When he came to the corner of the court in which he lived, lo and behold there was the pony again! Yes, there he was, looking more obstinate than ever; and alone in the chaise, keeping a steady watch upon his every wink, sat Mr Abel, who, lifting up his eyes by chance and seeing Kit pass by, nodded to him as though he would have nodded his head off.

Kit wondered to see the pony again, so near his own home too, but it never occurred to him for what purpose the pony might have come there, or where the old lady and the old gentleman had gone, until he lifted the latch of the door, and walking in, found them seated in the room in conversation with his mother, at which unexpected sight he pulled off his hat and made his best bow in some confusion.

"We are here before you, you see, Christopher," said Mr Garland smiling.

"Yes, sir," said Kit; and as he said it he looked towards his mother for an explanation of the visit.

"The gentleman's been kind enough, my dear," said she, in reply to this mute interrogation, "to ask me whether you were in a good place, or in any place at all, and when I told him no, you were not in any, he was so good as to say that——"

"That we wanted a good lad in our house," said the old gentleman and the old lady both together, "and that perhaps we might think of it, if we found everything as we would wish it to be."

As this thinking of it, plainly meant the thinking of engaging Kit, he immediately partook of his mother's anxiety and fell into a great flutter; for the little old couple were very methodical and cautious, and asked so many questions that he began to be afraid there was no chance of his success.

"You see, my good woman," said Mrs Garland to Kit's mother, "that it's necessary to be very careful and particular in such a matter as this, for we're only three in family, and are very quiet regular folks, and it would be a sad thing if we made any kind of mistake, and found things different from what we hoped and expected."

To this, Kit's mother replied, that certainly it was quite true, and quite right, and quite proper, and Heaven forbid that she should shrink, or have cause to shrink, from any inquiry into her character or that of her son, who was a very good son though she was his mother, in which respect, she was bold to say, he took after his father, who was not only a good son to *his* mother, but the best of husbands and the best of fathers besides, which Kit could and would corroborate she knew, and so would little Jacob and the baby likewise if they were old enough, which unfortunately they were not, though as they didn't know what a loss they had had, perhaps it was a great deal better that they should be as young as they were; and so Kit's mother wound up a long story by wiping her eyes with her apron, and patting little Jacob's head, who was rocking the cradle and staring with all his might at the strange lady and gentleman.

When Kit's mother had done speaking, the old lady struck in again, and said that she was quite sure she was a very honest and very respectable person or she never would have expressed herself in that manner, and that certainly the appearance of the children and the cleanliness of the house deserved great praise and did her the utmost credit, whereat Kit's mother dropped a curtsey and became consoled. Then the good woman entered into a long and minute account of Kit's life and history from the earliest period down to that time, not omitting to make mention of his miraculous fall out of a back-parlour window when an infant of tender years, or his uncommon sufferings in a state of measles, which were illustrated by correct imitations of the plaintive manner in which he called for toast and water, day and night, and said "don't cry, mother, I shall soon be better"; for proof of which statements reference was made to Mrs Green, lodger, at the cheesemonger's round the corner, and divers other ladies and gentlemen in various parts of England and Wales (and one Mr Brown who was supposed to be then a corporal in the East Indies, and who could of course be found with very little trouble), within whose personal knowledge the circumstances had occurred. This narration ended, Mr Garland put some questions to Kit respecting his qualifications and general acquirements, while Mrs Garland noticed the children, and hearing from Kit's mother certain remarkable circumstances which had attended the birth of each, related certain other remarkable circumstances which had attended the birth of her own son, Mr Abel, from which it appeared that both Kit's mother and herself had been, above and beyond all other women of what condition or age soever, peculiarly hemmed in with perils and dangers. Lastly, inquiry was made into the nature and extent of Kit's wardrobe, and a small advance being made to improve the same, he was formally hired at an annual income of Six Pounds, over and above his board and lodging, by Mr and Mrs Garland, of Abel Cottage, Finchley.

It would be difficult to say which party appeared most pleased with this arrangement, the conclusion of which was hailed with nothing but pleasant looks and cheerful smiles on both sides. It was settled that Kit should repair to his new abode on the next day but one, in the morning; and finally, the little old couple, after bestowing a bright half-crown on little Jacob and another on the baby, took their leaves; being escorted as far as the street by their new attendant, who held the obdurate pony by the bridle while they took their seats, and saw them drive away with a lightened heart.

"Well, mother," said Kit, hurrying back into the house, "I think my fortune's about made now."

"I should think it was indeed, Kit," rejoined his mother. "Six pound a year! Only think!"

"Ah!" said Kit, trying to maintain the gravity which the consideration of such a sum demanded, but grinning with delight in spite of himself. "There's a property!"

Kit drew a long breath when he had said this, and putting his hands deep into his pockets as if there were one year's wages at least in each, looked at his mother, as though he saw through her, and down an immense perspective of sovereigns beyond.

"Please God we'll make such a lady of you for Sundays, mother! such a scholar of Jacob, such a child of the baby, such a room of the one upstairs! Six pound a year?"

"Hem!" croaked a strange voice. "What's that about six pound a year? What about six pound a year?" And as the voice made this inquiry, Daniel Quilp walked in with Richard Swiveller at his heels.

"Who said he was to have six pound a year?" said Quilp, looking sharply round. "Did the old man say it, or did little Nell say it? And what's he to have it for, and where are they, eh?"

The good woman was so much alarmed by the sudden apparition of this unknown piece of ugliness, that she hastily caught the baby from its cradle and retreated into the furthest corner of the room; while little Jacob, sitting upon his stool with his hands on his knees, looked full at him in a species of fascination, roaring lustily all the time. Richard Swiveller took an easy observation of the family over Mr Quilp's head, and Quilp himself, with his hands in his pockets, smiled in an exquisite enjoyment of the commotion he occasioned.

"Don't be frightened, mistress," said Quilp, after a pause. "Your son knows me; I don't eat babies; I don't like 'em. It will be as well to stop that young screamer though, in case I should be tempted to do him a mischief. Holloa, sir! Will you be quiet?"

Little Jacob stemmed the course of two tears which he was squeezing out of his eyes, and instantly subsided into a silent horror.

"Mind you don't break out again, you villain," said Quilp, looking sternly at him, "or I'll make faces at you and throw you into fits, I will. Now you, sir, why haven't you been to me as you promised?"

"What should I come for?" retorted Kit. "I hadn't any business with you, no more than you had with me."

"Here, mistress," said Quilp, turning quickly away, and appealing from Kit to his mother. "When did his old master come or send here last? Is he here now? If not, where's he gone?"

"He has not been here at all," she replied. "I wish we knew where they have gone, for it would make my son a good deal easier in his mind, and me too. If you're the gentleman named Mr Quilp, I should have thought you'd have known, and so I told him only this very day."

"Humph!" muttered Quilp, evidently disappointed to believe that this was true. "That's what you tell this gentleman too, is it?"

"If the gentleman comes to ask the same question, I can't tell him anything else, sir; and I only wish I could, for our own sakes," was the reply.

Quilp glanced at Richard Swiveller, and observed that having met him on the threshold, he assumed that he had come in search of some intelligence of the fugitives. He supposed he was right?

"Yes," said Dick, "that was the object of the present expedition. I fancied it possible—but let us go ring fancy's knell. *I'll* begin it."

"You seem disappointed," observed Quilp.

"A baffler, sir, a baffler, that's all," returned Dick. "I have entered upon a speculation which has proved a baffler; and a Being of brightness and beauty will be offered up a sacrifice at Cheggs's altar. That's all, sir."

The dwarf eyed Richard with a sarcastic smile, but Richard, who had been taking a rather strong lunch with a friend, observed him not, and continued to deplore his fate with mournful and despondent looks. Quilp plainly discerned that there was some secret reason for this visit and his uncommon disappointment, and, in the hope that there might be means of mischief lurking beneath it, resolved to worm it out. He had no sooner adopted this resolution, than he conveyed as much honesty into his face as it was capable of expressing, and sympathised with Mr Swiveller exceedingly.

"I am disappointed myself," said Quilp, "out of mere friendly feeling for them; but you have real reasons, private reasons I have no doubt, for your disappointment, and therefore it comes heavier than mine."

"Why, of course it does," Dick observed, testily.

"Upon my word, I'm very sorry, very sorry. I'm rather cast down myself. As we are companions in adversity, shall we be companions in the surest way of forgetting it? If you had no particular business, now, to lead you in another direction," urged Quilp, plucking him by the sleeve and looking slyly up into his face out of the corners of his eyes, "there is a house by the water-side where they have some of the noblest Schiedam—reputed to be smuggled, but that's between ourselves—that can be got in all the world. The landlord knows me. There's a little summer-house overlooking the river, where we might take a glass of this delicious liquor with a whiff of the best tobacco—it's in this case, and of the rarest quality, to my certain knowledge—and be perfectly snug and happy, could we possibly contrive it; or is there any very particular engagement that peremptorily takes you another way, Mr Swiveller, eh?"

As the dwarf spoke, Dick's face relaxed into a compliant smile, and his brows slowly unbent. By the time he had finished, Dick was looking down at Quilp in the same sly manner as Quilp was looking up at him, and there remained nothing more to be done but to set out for the house in question. This they did, straightway. The moment their backs were turned, little Jacob thawed, and resumed his crying from the point where Quilp had frozen him.

The summer-house of which Mr Quilp had spoken was a rugged wooden box, rotten and bare to see, which overhung the river's mud, and threatened to slide down into it. The tavern to which it belonged was a crazy building, sapped and undermined by the rats, and only upheld by great bars of wood which were reared against its walls, and had propped it up so long that even they were decaying and yielding with their load, and of a windy night might be heard to creak and crack as if the whole fabric were about to come toppling down. The house stood—if anything so old and feeble could be said to stand—on a piece of waste ground, blighted with the unwholesome smoke of factory chimneys, and echoing the clank of iron wheels and rush of troubled water. Its internal accommodations amply fulfilled the promise of the outside. The rooms were low and damp, the clammy walls were pierced with chinks and holes, the rotten floors had sunk from their level, the very beams started from their places and warned the timid stranger from their neighbourhood.

To this inviting spot, entreating him to observe its beauties as they passed along, Mr Quilp led Richard Swiveller, and on the table of the summer-house, scored deep with many a gallows and initial letter, there soon appeared a wooden keg, full of the vaunted liquor. Drawing it off into the glasses with the skill of a practised hand, and mixing it with about a third part of water, Mr Quilp assigned to Richard Swiveller his portion, and lighting his pipe from an end of a candle in a very old and battered lantern, drew himself together upon a seat and puffed away.

"Is it good?" said Quilp, as Richard Swiveller smacked his lips, "is it strong and fiery? Does it make you wink, and choke, and your eyes water, and your breath come short—does it?"

"Does it?" cried Dick, throwing away part of the contents of his glass, and filling it up with water, "why, man, you don't mean to tell me that you drink such fire as this?"

"No!" rejoined Quilp, "not drink it! Look here. And here. And here again. Not drink it!"

As he spoke, Daniel Quilp drew off and drank three small glassfuls of the raw spirit, and then with a horrible grimace took a great many pulls at his pipe, and swallowing the smoke, discharged it in a heavy cloud from his nose. This feat accomplished he drew himself together in his former position, and laughed excessively.

"Give us a toast!" cried Quilp, rattling on the table in a dexterous manner with his fist and elbow alternately, in a kind of tune, "a woman, a beauty. Let's have a beauty for our toast and empty our glasses to the last drop. Her name, come!"

"If you want a name," said Dick, "here's Sophy Wackles."

"Sophy Wackles," screamed the dwarf, "Miss Sophy Wackles that is—Mrs Richard Swiveller that shall be—that shall be—ha, ha, ha!"

"Ah!" said Dick, "you might have said that a few weeks ago, but it won't do now, my buck. Immolating herself upon the shrine of Cheggs———"

"Poison Cheggs, cut Cheggs's ears off," rejoined Quilp. "I won't hear of Cheggs. Her name is Swiveller or nothing. I'll drink her health again, and her father's, and her mother's; and to all her sisters and brothers—the glorious family of the Wackleses—all the Wackleses in one glass—down with it to the dregs!"

"Well," said Richard Swiveller, stopping short in the act of raising the glass to his lips and looking at the dwarf in a species of stupor as he flourished his arms and legs about: "you're a jolly fellow, but of all the jolly fellows I ever saw or heard of, you have the queerest and most extraordinary way with you, upon my life you have."

This candid declaration tended rather to increase than restrain Mr Quilp's eccentricities, and Richard Swiveller, astonished to see him in such a roystering vein, and drinking not a little himself, for company—began imperceptibly to become more companionable and confiding, so that, being judiciously led on by Mr Quilp, he grew at last very confiding indeed. Having once got him into this mood, and knowing now the keynote to strike whenever he was at a loss, Daniel Quilp's task was comparatively an easy one, and he was soon in possession of the whole details of the scheme contrived between the easy Dick and his more designing friend.

"Stop!" said Quilp. "That's the thing, that's the thing. It can be brought about, it shall be brought about. There's my hand upon it; I am your friend from this minute."

"What! do you think there's still a chance?" enquired Dick, in surprise at this encouragement.

"A chance!" echoed the dwarf, "a certainty! Sophy Wackles may become a Cheggs or anything else she likes, but not a Swiveller. Oh, you lucky dog! He's richer than any Jew alive; you're a made man. I see in you now nothing but Nelly's husband, rolling in gold and silver. I'll help you. It shall be done. Mind my words, it shall be done."

"But how?" said Dick.

"There's plenty of time," rejoined the dwarf, "and it shall be done. We'll sit down and talk it over again all the way through. Fill your glass while I'm gone. I shall be back directly—directly."

With these hasty words, Daniel Quilp withdrew into a dismantled skittle-ground behind the public-house, and, throwing himself upon the ground, actually screamed and rolled about in uncontrollable delight.

"Here's sport!" he cried, "sport ready to my hand, all invented and arranged, and only to be enjoyed. It was this shallow-pated fellow who made my bones ache t'other day, was it? It was his friend and fellow-plotter, Mr Trent, that once made eyes at Mrs Quilp, and leered and looked, was it? After labouring for two or three years in their precious scheme, to find that they've got a beggar at last, and one of them tied for life. Ha, ha, ha! He shall marry Nell. He shall have her, and I'll be the first man, when the knot's tied hard and fast, to tell 'em what they've gained and what I've helped 'em to. Here will be a clearing of old scores, here will be a time to remind 'em what a capital friend I was, and how I helped them to the heiress. Ha, ha, ha!"

In the height of his ecstasy, Mr Quilp had like to have met with a disagreeable check, for, rolling very near a broken dog-kennel, there leapt forth a large fierce dog, who, but that his chain was of the shortest, would have given him a disagreeable salute. As it was, the dwarf remained upon his back in perfect safety, taunting the dog with hideous faces, and triumphing over him in his inability to advance another inch, though there were not a couple of feet between them.

"Why don't you come and bite me, why don't you come and tear me to pieces, you coward?" said Quilp, hissing and worrying the animal till he was nearly mad. "You're afraid, you bully, you're afraid, you know you are."

The dog tore and strained at his chain with starting eyes and furious bark, but there the dwarf lay, snapping his fingers with gestures of defiance and contempt. When he had sufficiently recovered from his delight, he rose, and with his arms a-kimbo, achieved a kind of demon-dance round the kennel, just without the limits of the chain, driving the dog quite wild. Having by this means composed his spirits and put himself in a pleasant train, he returned to his unsuspicious companion, whom he found looking at the tide with exceeding gravity, and thinking of that same gold and silver which Mr Quilp had mentioned.

Chapter XXII

THE remainder of that day and the whole of the next were a busy time for the Nubbles family, to whom everything connected with Kit's outfit and departure was matter of as great moment as if he had been about to penetrate into the interior of Africa, or to take a cruise round the world. It would be difficult to suppose that there ever was a box which was opened and shut so many times within four-and-twenty hours, as that which contained his wardrobe and necessaries; and certainly there never was one which to two small eyes presented such a mine of clothing, as this mighty chest with its three shirts and proportionate allowance of stockings and pocket-handkerchiefs, disclosed to the astonished vision of little Jacob. At last it was conveyed to the carrier's, at whose house at Finchley Kit was to find it next day; and the box being gone, there remained but two questions for consideration: firstly, whether the carrier would lose, or dishonestly feign to lose, the box upon the road; and secondly, whether Kit's mother perfectly understood how to take care of herself in the absence of her son.

"I don't think there's hardly a chance of his really losing it, but carriers are under great temptation to pretend they lose things, no doubt," said Mrs Nubbles apprehensively, in reference to the first point.

"No doubt about it," returned Kit, with a serious look; "upon my word, mother, I don't think it was right to trust it to itself. Somebody ought to have gone with it, I'm afraid."

"We can't help it now," said his mother; "but it was foolish and wrong. People oughtn't to be tempted."

Kit inwardly resolved that he would never tempt a carrier any more, save with an empty box; and having formed this Christian determination, he turned his thoughts to the second question.

"You know you must keep up your spirits, mother, and not be lonesome because I'm not at home. I shall very often be able to look in when I come into town I dare say, and I shall send you a letter sometimes, and when the quarter comes round, I can get a holiday of course; and then see if we don't take little Jacob to the play, and let him know what oysters means."

"I hope plays mayn't be sinful, Kit, but I'm a'most afraid," said Mrs Nubbles.

"I know who has been putting that in your head," rejoined her son disconsolately; "that's Little Bethel again. Now I say, mother, pray don't take to going there regularly, for if I was to see your good-humoured face that has always made home cheerful, turned into a grievous one, and the baby trained to look grievous too, and to call itself a young sinner (bless its heart) and a child of the devil (which is calling its dead father names); if I was to see this, and see little Jacob looking grievous likewise, I should so take it to heart that I'm sure I should go and list for a soldier, and run my head on purpose against the first cannon-ball I saw coming my way."

"Oh, Kit, don't talk like that."

"I would indeed, mother, and unless you want to make me feel very wretched and uncomfortable, you'll keep that bow on your bonnet, which you'd more than half a mind to pull off last week. Can you suppose there's any harm in looking as cheerful and being as cheerful as our poor circumstances will permit? Do I see anything in the way I'm made, which calls upon me to be a snivelling, solemn, whispering chap, sneaking about as if I couldn't help it, and expressing myself in a most unpleasant snuffle? on the contrary, don't I see every reason why I shouldn't? Just hear this! Ha, ha, ha! An't that as nat'ral as walking, and as good for the health? Ha, ha, ha! An't that as nat'ral as a sheep's bleating, or a pig's grunting, or a horse's neighing, or a bird's singing? Ha, ha, ha! Isn't it, mother?"

There was something contagious in Kit's laugh, for his mother, who had looked grave before, first subsided into a smile, and then fell to joining in it heartily, which occasioned Kit to say that he knew it was natural, and to laugh the more. Kit and his mother, laughing together in a pretty loud key, woke the baby, who, finding that there was something very jovial and agreeable in progress, was no sooner in its mother's arms than it began to kick and laugh, most vigorously. This new illustration of his argument so tickled Kit, that he fell backward in his chair in a state of exhaustion, pointing at the baby and shaking his sides till he rocked again. After recovering twice or thrice, and as often relapsing, he wiped his eyes and said grace; and a very cheerful meal their scanty supper was.

With more kisses, and hugs, and tears, than many young gentlemen who start upon their travels, and leave well-stocked homes behind them, would deem within the bounds of probability (if matter so low could be herein set down), Kit left the house at an early hour next morning, and set out to walk to Finchley; feeling a sufficient pride in his appearance to have warranted his excommunication from Little Bethel from that time forth, if he had ever been one of that mournful congregation.

Lest anybody should feel a curiosity to know how Kit was clad, it may be briefly remarked that he wore no livery, but was dressed in a coat of pepper-and-salt with waistcoat of canary colour, and nether garments of iron-grey; besides these glories, he shone in the lustre of a new pair of boots and an extremely stiff and shiny hat, which on being struck anywhere with the knuckles, sounded like a drum. And in this attire, rather wondering that he attracted so little attention, and attributing the circumstance to the insensibility of those who got up early, he made his way towards Abel Cottage.

Without encountering any more remarkable adventure on the road, than meeting a lad in a brimless hat, the exact counterpart of his old one, on whom he bestowed half the sixpence he possessed, Kit arrived in course of time at the carrier's house, where, to the lasting honour of human nature, he found the box in safety. Receiving from the wife of this immaculate man, a direction to Mr Garland's, he took the box upon his shoulder and repaired thither directly.

To be sure, it was a beautiful little cottage with a thatched roof and little spires at the gable-ends, and pieces of stained glass in some of the windows, almost as large as pocket-books. On one side of the house was a little stable, just the size for the pony, with a little room over it, just the size for Kit. White curtains were fluttering, and birds, in cages that looked as bright as if they were made of gold, were singing at the windows; plants were arranged on either side of the path, and clustered about the door; and the garden was bright with flowers in full bloom, which shed a sweet odour all round, and had a charming and elegant appearance. Everything, within the house and without, seemed to be the perfection of neatness and order. In the garden there was not a weed to be seen, and to judge from some dapper gardening-tools, a basket, and a pair of gloves which were lying in one of the walks, old Mr Garland had been at work in it that very morning.

Kit looked about him, and admired, and looked again, and this a great many times before he could make up his mind to turn his head another way and ring the bell. There was abundance of time to look about him again though, when he had rung it, for nobody came, so after ringing twice or thrice he sat down upon his box, and waited.

He rang the bell a great many times, and yet nobody came. But at last, as he was sitting upon the box thinking about giants' castles, and princesses tied up to pegs by the hair of their heads, and dragons bursting out from behind gates, and other incidents of the like nature, common in story-books to youths of low degree on their first visit to strange houses, the door was gently opened, and a little servant-girl, very tidy, modest, and demure, but very pretty too, appeared.

"I suppose you're Christopher, sir," said the servant-girl.

Kit got off the box, and said yes, he was.

"I'm afraid you've rung a good many times perhaps," she rejoined, "but we couldn't hear you, because we've been catching the pony."

Kit rather wondered what this meant, but as he couldn't stop there, asking questions, he shouldered the box again and followed the girl into the hall, where through a back-door he descried Mr Garland leading Whisker in triumph up the garden, after that self-willed pony had (as he afterwards learned) dodged the family round a small paddock in the rear, for one hour and three-quarters.

The old gentleman received him very kindly and so did the old lady, whose previous

good opinion of him was greatly enhanced by his wiping his boots on the mat until the
soles of his feet burnt again. He was then taken into the parlour to be inspected in his
new clothes; and when he had been surveyed several times, and had afforded by his
appearance unlimited satisfaction, he was taken into the stable (where the pony received
him with uncommon complaisance); and thence into the little chamber he had already
observed, which was very clean and comfortable; and thence into the garden, in which
the old gentleman told him he would be taught to employ himself, and where he told
him, besides, what great things he meant to do to make him comfortable, and happy,
if he found he deserved it. All these kindnesses, Kit acknowledged with various expressions of gratitude, and so many touches of the new hat, that the brim suffered considerably. When the old gentleman had said all he had to say in the way of promise and advice,
and Kit had said all he had to say in the way of assurance and thankfulness, he was
handed over again to the old lady, who, summoning the little servant-girl (whose name
was Barbara), instructed her to take him downstairs and give him something to eat and
drink, after his walk.

Downstairs therefore, Kit went; and at the bottom of the stairs there was such a
kitchen as was never before seen or heard of out of a toy-shop window, with everything
in it as bright and glowing, and as precisely ordered too, as Barbara herself. And in this
kitchen, Kit sat himself down at a table as white as a tablecloth, to eat cold meat, and
drink small ale, and use his knife and fork the more awkwardly, because there was an
unknown Barbara looking on and observing him.

It did not appear, however, that there was anything remarkably tremendous about
this strange Barbara, who having lived a very quiet life, blushed very much and was quite
as embarrassed and uncertain what she ought to say or do, as Kit could possibly be.
When he had sat for some little time, attentive to the ticking of the sober clock, he
ventured to glance curiously at the dresser, and there, among the plates and dishes, were
Barbara's little work-box with a sliding lid to shut in the balls of cotton, and Barbara's
prayer-book, and Barbara's hymn-book, and Barbara's Bible. Barbara's little looking-
glass hung in a good light near the window, and Barbara's bonnet was on a nail behind
the door. From all these mute signs and tokens of her presence, he naturally glanced at
Barbara herself, who sat as mute as they, shelling peas into a dish; and just when Kit was
looking at her eyelashes and wondering—quite in the simplicity of his heart—what
colour her eyes might be, it perversely happened that Barbara raised her head a little to
look at him, when both pair of eyes were hastily withdrawn, and Kit leant over his plate,
and Barbara over her pea-shells, each in extreme confusion at having been detected by
the other.

Chapter XXIII

MR Richard Swiveller wending homewards from the wilderness (for such was the appropriate name of Quilp's choice retreat), after a sinuous and corkscrew fashion, with many checks and stumbles; after stopping suddenly and staring about him, then as suddenly running forward for a few paces, and as suddenly halting again and shaking his head; doing everything with a jerk and nothing by premeditation;—Mr Richard Swiveller wending his way homewards after this fashion, which is considered by evil-minded men to be symbolical of intoxication, and is not held by such persons to denote that state of deep wisdom and reflection in which the actor knows himself to be, began to think that possibly he had misplaced his confidence and that the dwarf might not be precisely the sort of person to whom to entrust a secret of such delicacy and importance. And being led and tempted on by this remorseful thought into a condition which the evil-minded class before referred to would term the maudlin state or stage of drunkenness, it occurred to Mr Swiveller to cast his hat upon the ground, and moan, crying aloud that he was an unhappy orphan, and that if he had not been an unhappy orphan things had never come to this.

"Left an infant by my parents, at an early age," said Mr Swiveller, bewailing his hard lot, "cast upon the world in my tenderest period, and thrown upon the mercies of a deluding dwarf, who can wonder at my weakness! Here's a miserable orphan for you. Here," said Mr Swiveller raising his voice to a high pitch, and looking sleepily round, "is a miserable orphan!"

"Then," said somebody hard by, "let me be a father to you."

Mr Swiveller swayed himself to and fro to preserve his balance, and, looking into a kind of haze which seemed to surround him, at last perceived two eyes dimly twinkling through the mist, which he observed after a short time were in the neighbourhood of a nose and mouth. Casting his eyes down towards that quarter in which, with reference to a man's face, his legs are usually to be found, he observed that the face had a body attached; and when he looked more intently he was satisfied that the person was Mr Quilp, who indeed had been in his company all the time, but whom he had some vague idea of having left a mile or two behind.

"You have deceived an orphan, sir," said Mr Swiveller solemnly.

"I! I'm a second father to you," replied Quilp.

"You my father, sir!" retorted Dick. "Being all right myself, sir, I request to be left alone—instantly, sir."

"What a funny fellow you are!" cried Quilp.

"Go, sir," returned Dick, leaning against a post and waving his hand. "Go, deceiver, go; some day, sir, p'r'aps you'll waken, from pleasure's dream to know, the grief of orphans forsaken. Will you go, sir?"

The dwarf taking no heed of this adjuration, Mr Swiveller advanced with the view of inflicting upon him condign chastisement. But forgetting his purpose or changing his mind before he came close to him, he seized his hand and vowed eternal friendship, declaring with an agreeable frankness that from that time forth they were brothers in everything but personal appearance. Then he told his secret all over again, with the addition of being pathetic on the subject of Miss Wackles, who, he gave Mr Quilp to understand, was the occasion of any slight incoherency he might observe in his speech at that moment, which was attributable solely to the strength of his affection and not to rosy wine or other fermented liquor. And then they went on arm in arm, very lovingly together.

"I'm as sharp," said Quilp to him, at parting, "as sharp as a ferret, and as cunning as a weazel. You bring Trent to me; assure him that I'm his friend though I fear he a little distrusts me (I don't know why, I have not deserved it); and you've both of you made your fortunes—in perspective."

"That's the worst of it," returned Dick. "These fortunes in perspective look such a long way off."

"But they look smaller than they really are, on that account," said Quilp pressing his arm. "You'll have no conception of the value of your prize until you draw close to it. Mark that."

"D'ye think not?" said Dick.

"Ay, I do; and I am certain of what I say, that's better," returned the dwarf. "You bring Trent to me. Tell him I am his friend and yours—why shouldn't I be?"

"There's no reason why you shouldn't, certainly," replied Dick, "and perhaps there are a great many why you should—at least there would be nothing strange in your wanting to be my friend, if you were a choice spirit, but then you know you're *not* a choice spirit."

"I not a choice spirit!" cried Quilp.

"Devil a bit, sir," returned Dick. "A man of your appearance couldn't be. If you're any spirit at all, sir, you're an evil spirit. Choice spirits," added Dick, smiting himself on the breast, "are quite a different looking sort of people, you may take your oath of that, sir."

Quilp glanced at his free-spoken friend with a mingled expression of cunning and dislike, and wringing his hand almost at the same moment, declared that he was an uncommon character and had his warmest esteem. With that they parted; Mr Swiveller to make the best of his way home and sleep himself sober; and Quilp to cogitate upon the discovery he had made, and exult in the prospect of the rich field of enjoyment and reprisal it opened to him.

It was not without great reluctance and misgiving that Mr Swiveller, next morning, his head racked by the fumes of the renowned Schiedam, repaired to the lodging of his friend Trent (which was in the roof of an old house in an old ghostly inn), and recounted by very slow degrees what had yesterday taken place between him and Quilp. Nor was it without great surprise and much speculation on Quilp's probable motives, nor without many bitter comments on Dick Swiveller's folly, that his friend received the tale.

"I don't defend myself, Fred," said the penitent Richard; "but the fellow has such a queer way with him and is such an artful dog, that first of all he set me upon thinking whether there was any harm in telling him, and while I was thinking, screwed it out of me. If you had seen him drink and smoke, as I did, you couldn't have kept anything from him. He's a salamander you know, that's what *he* is."

Without inquiring whether salamanders were of necessity good confidential agents, or whether a fire-proof man was as a matter of course trustworthy, Frederick Trent threw himself into a chair, and, burying his head in his hands, endeavoured to fathom the motives which had led Quilp to insinuate himself into Richard Swiveller's confidence;— for that the disclosure was of his seeking, and had not been spontaneously revealed by Dick, was sufficiently plain from Quilp's seeking his company and enticing him away.

The dwarf had twice encountered him when he was endeavouring to obtain intelligence of the fugitives. This, perhaps, as he had not shown any previous anxiety about them, was enough to awaken suspicion in the breast of a creature so jealous and distrustful by nature, setting aside any additional impulse to curiosity that he might have derived from Dick's incautious manner. But knowing the scheme they had planned, why should he offer to assist it? This was a question more difficult of solution; but as knaves generally overreach themselves by imputing their own designs to others, the idea immediately presented itself that some circumstances of irritation between Quilp and the old man, arising out of their secret transactions and not unconnected perhaps with his sudden disappearance, now rendered the former desirous of revenging himself upon him by seeking to entrap the sole object of his love and anxiety into a connexion of which he knew he had a dread and hatred. As Frederick Trent himself, utterly regardless of his sister, had this object at heart, only second to the hope of gain, it seemed to him the more likely to be Quilp's main principle of action. Once investing the dwarf with a design of his own in abetting them, which the attainment of their purpose would serve, it was easy to believe him sincere and hearty in the cause; and as there could be no doubt of his proving a powerful and useful auxiliary, Trent determined to accept his invitation and go to his house that night, and if what he said and did confirmed him in the impression he had formed, to let him share the labour of their plan, but not the profit.

Having revolved these things in his mind and arrived at this conclusion, he communicated to Mr Swiveller as much of his meditations as he thought proper (Dick would have been perfectly satisfied with less), and giving him the day to recover himself from his late salamandering, accompanied him at evening to Mr Quilp's house.

Mightily glad Mr Quilp was to see them, or mightily glad he seemed to be; and fearfully polite Mr Quilp was to Mrs Quilp and Mrs Jiniwin; and very sharp was the look he cast on his wife to observe how she was affected by the recognition of young Trent. Mrs Quilp was as innocent as her own mother of any emotion, painful or pleasant, which the sight of him awakened, but as her husband's glance made her timid and confused, and uncertain what to do or what was required of her, Mr Quilp did not fail to assign her embarrassment to the cause he had in his mind, and while he chuckled at his penetration was secretly exasperated by his jealousy.

Nothing of this appeared, however. On the contrary, Mr Quilp was all blandness and suavity, and presided over the case-bottle of rum with extraordinary open-heartedness.

"Why, let me see," said Quilp. "It must be a matter of nearly two years since we were first acquainted."

"Nearer three, I think," said Trent.

"Nearer three!" cried Quilp. "How fast time flies! Does it seem as long as that to you, Mrs Quilp?"

"Yes, I think it seems full three years, Quilp," was the unfortunate reply.

"Oh, indeed, Ma'am," thought Quilp, "you have been pining, have you? Very good, Ma'am."

"It seems to me but yesterday that you went out to Demerara in the *Mary Anne*," said Quilp; "but yesterday, I declare. Well, I like a little wildness. I was wild myself once."

Mr Quilp accompanied this admission with such an awful wink, indicative of old rovings and backslidings, that Mrs Jiniwin was indignant, and could not forbear from remarking under her breath that he might at least put off his confessions until his wife was absent; for which act of boldness and insubordination Mr Quilp first stared her out of countenance and then drank her health ceremoniously.

"I thought you'd come back directly, Fred. I always thought that," said Quilp setting down his glass. "And when the *Mary Anne* returned with you on board, instead of a letter to say what a contrite heart you had, and how happy you were in the situation that had been provided for you, I was amused—exceedingly amused. Ha, ha, ha!"

The young man smiled, but not as though the theme were the most agreeable one that could have been selected for his entertainment; and for that reason Quilp pursued it.

"I always will say," he resumed, "that when a rich relation having two young people—sisters or brothers, or brother and sister—dependent on him, attaches himself exclusively to one, and casts off the other, he does wrong."

The young man made a movement of impatience, but Quilp went on as calmly as if he were discussing some abstract question in which nobody present had the slightest personal interest.

"It's very true," said Quilp, "that your grandfather urged repeated forgiveness, ingratitude, riot, and extravagance, and all that; but as I told him 'these are common faults.' 'But he's a scoundrel,' said he. 'Granting that,' said I (for the sake of argument of course), 'a great many young noblemen and gentlemen are scoundrels too!' But he wouldn't be convinced."

"I wonder at that, Mr Quilp," said the young man sarcastically.

"Well, so did I at the time," returned Quilp, "but he was always obstinate. He was in a manner a friend of mine, but he was always obstinate and wrong-headed. Little Nell is a nice girl, a charming girl, but you're her brother, Frederick. You're her brother after all; as you told him the last time you met, he can't alter that."

"He would if he could, confound him for that and all other kindnesses," said the young man impatiently. "But nothing can come of this subject now, and let us have done with it in the Devil's name."

"Agreed," returned Quilp, "agreed on my part, readily. Why have I alluded to it? Just to show you, Frederick, that I have always stood your friend. You little knew who was your friend, and who your foe; now did you? You thought I was against you, and so there has been a coolness between us; but it was all on your side, entirely on your side. Let's shake hands again, Fred."

With his head sunk down between his shoulders, and a hideous grin overspreading his face, the dwarf stood up and stretched his short arm across the table. After a moment's hesitation, the young man stretched out his to meet it; Quilp clutched his fingers in a grip that for the moment stopped the current of the blood within them, and pressing his other hand upon his lip and frowning towards the unsuspicious Richard, released them and sat down.

This action was not lost upon Trent, who, knowing that Richard Swiveller was a mere tool in his hands and knew no more of his designs than he thought proper to communicate, saw that the dwarf perfectly understood their relative position, and fully entered into the character of his friend. It is something to be appreciated, even in knavery. This silent homage to his superior abilities, no less than a sense of the power with which the dwarf's quick perception had already invested him, inclined the young man towards that ugly worthy, and determined him to profit by his aid.

It being now Mr Quilp's cue to change the subject with all convenient expedition, lest Richard Swiveller in his heedlessness should reveal anything which it was inexpedient for the women to know, he proposed a game at four-handed cribbage; and partners being cut for, Mrs Quilp fell to Frederick Trent, and Dick himself to Quilp. Mrs Jiniwin being very fond of cards was carefully excluded by her son-in-law from any participation in the game, and had assigned to her the duty of occasionally replenishing the glasses from the case-bottle; Mr Quilp from that moment keeping one eye constantly upon her, lest she should by any means procure a taste of the same, and thereby tantalising the wretched old lady (who was as much attached to the case-bottle as the cards) in a double degree and most ingenious manner.

But it was not to Mrs Jiniwin alone that Mr Quilp's attention was restricted, as several other matters required his constant vigilance. Among his various eccentric habits he had a humorous one of always cheating at cards, which rendered necessary on his part, not only a close observance of the game, and a sleight-of-hand in counting and scoring, but also involved the constant correction, by looks, and frowns, and kicks under the table, of Richard Swiveller, who being bewildered by the rapidity with which his cards were told, and the rate at which the pegs travelled down the board, could not be prevented from sometimes expressing his surprise and incredulity. Mrs Quilp too was the partner of young Trent, and for every look that passed between them, and every word they spoke, and every card they played, the dwarf had eyes and ears; not occupied alone with what was passing above the table, but with signals that might be exchanging beneath it, which he laid all kinds of traps to detect; besides often treading on his wife's toes to see whether she cried out or remained silent under the infliction, in which latter case it would have been quite clear that Trent had been treading on her toes before. Yet, in the most of all these distractions, the one eye was upon the old lady always, and if she so much as stealthily advanced a tea-spoon towards a neighbouring glass (which she often did), for the purpose of abstracting but one sup of its sweet contents, Quilp's hand would overset it in the very moment of her triumph, and Quilp's mocking voice implore her to regard her precious health. And in any one of these his many cares, from first to last, Quilp never flagged nor faltered.

At length, when they had played a great many rubbers and drawn pretty freely upon the case-bottle, Mr Quilp warned his lady to retire to rest, and that submissive wife complying, and being followed by her indignant mother, Mr Swiveller fell asleep. The dwarf beckoning his remaining companion to the other end of the room, held a short conference with him in whispers.

"It's as well not to say more than one can help before our worthy friend," said Quilp, making a grimace towards the slumbering Dick. "Is it a bargain between us, Fred? Shall he marry little rosy Nell by-and-by?"

"You have some end of your own to answer, of course," returned the other.

"Of course I have, dear Fred," said Quilp, grinning to think how little he suspected what the real end was. "It's retaliation perhaps; perhaps whim. I have influence, Fred, to help or oppose. Which way shall I use it? There are a pair of scales, and it goes into one."

"Throw it into mine then," said Trent.

"It's done, Fred," rejoined Quilp, stretching out his clenched hand and opening it as if he had let some weight fall out. "It's in the scale from this time, and turns it, Fred. Mind that."

"Where have they gone?" asked Trent.

Quilp shook his head, and said that point remained to be discovered, which it might be, easily. When it was, they would begin their preliminary advances. He would visit the old man, or even Richard Swiveller might visit him, and by affecting a deep concern in his behalf, and imploring him to settle in some worthy home, lead to the child's remembering him with gratitude and favour. Once impressed to this extent, it would be easy, he said, to win her in a year or two, for she supposed the old man to be poor, as it was a part of his jealous policy (in common with many other misers) to feign to be so, to those about him.

"He has feigned it often enough to me, of late," said Trent.

"Oh! and to me too!" replied the dwarf. "Which is more extraordinary, as I know how rich he really is."

"I suppose you should," said Trent.

"I think I should indeed," rejoined the dwarf; and in that, at least, he spoke the truth.

After a few more whispered words, they returned to the table, and the young man rousing Richard Swiveller informed him that he was waiting to depart. This was welcome news to Dick, who started up directly. After a few words of confidence in the result of their project had been exchanged, they bade the grinning Quilp good night.

Quilp crept to the window as they passed in the street below, and listened. Trent was pronouncing an encomium upon his wife, and they were both wondering by what enchantment she had been brought to marry such a misshapen wretch as he. The dwarf after watching their retreating shadows with a wider grin than his face had yet displayed, stole softly in the dark to bed.

In this hatching of their scheme, neither Trent nor Quilp had had one thought about the happiness or misery of poor innocent Nell. It would have been strange if the careless profligate, who was the butt of both, had been harassed by any such consideration; for his high opinion of his own merits and deserts rendered the project rather a laudable one than otherwise; and if he had been visited by so unwonted a guest as reflection, he would—being a brute only in the gratification of his appetites—have soothed his conscience with the plea that he did not mean to beat or kill his wife, and would therefore, after all said and done, be a very tolerable, average husband.

Chapter XXIV

IT was not until they were quite exhausted and could no longer maintain the pace at which they had fled from the race-ground, that the old man and the child ventured to stop, and sit down to rest upon the borders of a little wood. Here, though the course was hidden from their view, they could yet faintly distinguish the noise of distant shouts, the hum of voices, and the beating of drums. Climbing the eminence which lay between them and the spot they had left, the child could even discern the fluttering flags and white tops of booths; but no person was approaching towards them, and their resting-place was solitary and still.

Some time elapsed before she could reassure her trembling companion, or restore him to a state of moderate tranquillity. His disordered imagination represented to him a crowd of persons stealing towards them beneath the cover of the bushes, lurking in every ditch, and peeping from the boughs of every rustling tree. He was haunted by apprehensions of being led captive to some gloomy place where he would be chained and scourged, and worse than all, where Nell could never come to see him, save through iron bars and gratings in the wall. His terrors affected the child. Separation from her grandfa-ther was the greatest evil she could dread; and feeling for the time as though, go where they would, they were to be hunted down, and could never be safe but in hiding, her heart failed her, and her courage drooped.

In one so young, and so unused to the scenes in which she had lately moved, this sinking of the spirit was not surprising. But Nature often enshrines gallant and noble hearts in weak bosoms—oftenest, God bless her, in female breasts—and when the child, casting her tearful eyes upon the old man, remembered how weak he was, and how destitute and helpless he would be if she failed him, her heart swelled within her, and animated her with new strength and fortitude.

"We are quite safe now, and have nothing to fear indeed, dear grandfather," she said.

"Nothing to fear!" returned the old man. "Nothing to fear if they took me from thee! Nothing to fear if they parted us! Nobody is true to me. No, not one. Not even Nell!"

"Oh! do not say that," replied the child, "for if ever anybody was true at heart, and earnest, I am. I am sure you know I am."

"Then how," said the old man, looking fearfully round, "how can you bear to think that we are safe, when they are searching for me everywhere, and may come here, and steal upon us, even while we're talking?"

"Because I'm sure we have not been followed," said the child. "Judge for yourself, dear grandfather; look round, and see how quiet and still it is. We are alone together, and may ramble where we like. Not safe! Could I feel easy—did I feel at ease—when any danger threatened you?"

"True, true," he answered, pressing her hand, but still looking anxiously about. "What noise was that?"

"A bird," said the child, "flying into the wood, and leading the way for us to follow. You remember that we said we would walk in woods and fields, and by the side of rivers, and how happy we would be—you remember that? But here, while the sun shines above our heads, and everything is bright and happy, we are sitting sadly down, and losing time. See what a pleasant path; and there's the bird—the same bird—now he flies to another tree, and stays to sing. Come!"

When they rose up from the ground, and took the shady track which led them through the wood, she bounded on before, printing her tiny footsteps in the moss, which rose elastic from so light a pressure and gave it back as mirrors throw off breath; and thus she lured the old man on, with many a backward look and merry beck, now pointing stealthily to some lone bird as it perched and twittered on a branch that strayed across their path, now stopping to listen to the songs that broke the happy silence, or watch the sun as it trembled through the leaves, and stealing in among the ivied trunks of stout old trees, opened long paths of light. As they passed onward, parting the boughs that clustered in their way, the serenity which the child had first assumed, stole into her breast in earnest; the old man cast no longer fearful looks behind, but felt at ease and cheerful, for the further they passed into the deep green shade, the more they felt that the tranquil mind of God was there, and shed its peace on them.

At length, the path becoming clearer and less intricate, brought them to the end of the wood, and into a public road. Taking their way along it for a short distance, they came to a lane, so shaded by the trees on either hand that they met together overhead, and arched the narrow way. A broken finger-post announced that this led to a village three miles off; and thither they resolved to bend their steps.

The miles appeared so long that they sometimes thought they must have missed their road. But at last, to their great joy, it led downward in a steep descent, with overhanging banks over which the footpaths led; and the clustered houses of the village peeped out from the woody hollow below.

It was a very small place. The men and boys were playing at cricket on the green; and as the other folks were looking on, they wandered up and down, uncertain where to seek a humble lodging. There was but one old man in the little garden before his cottage, and him they were timid of approaching, for he was the schoolmaster, and had "School" written up over his window in black letters on a white board. He was a pale, simple-looking man, of a spare and meagre habit, and sat among his flowers and beehives, smoking his pipe, in the little porch before his door.

"Speak to him, dear," the old man whispered.

"I am almost afraid to disturb him," said the child timidly. "He does not seem to see us. Perhaps if we wait a little, he may look this way."

They waited, but the schoolmaster cast no look towards them, and still sat, thoughtful and silent, in the little porch. He had a kind face. In his plain old suit of black, he looked pale and meagre. They fancied, too, a lonely air about him and his house, but perhaps that was because the other people formed a merry company upon the green, and he seemed the only solitary man in all the place.

They were very tired, and the child would have been bold enough to address even a schoolmaster, but for something in his manner which seemed to denote that he was uneasy or distressed. As they stood hesitating at a little distance, they saw that he sat for a few minutes at a time like one in a brown study, then laid aside his pipe and took a few turns in his garden, then approached the gate and looked towards the green, then took up his pipe again with a sigh, and sat down thoughtfully as before.

As nobody else appeared and it would soon be dark, Nell at length took courage, and when he had resumed his pipe and seat, ventured to draw near, leading her grandfather by the hand. The slight noise they made in raising the latch of the wicket-gate, caught his attention. He looked at them kindly but seemed disappointed too, and slightly shook his head.

Nell dropped a curtsey, and told him they were poor travellers who sought a shelter for the night which they would gladly pay for, so far as their means allowed. The schoolmaster looked earnestly at her as she spoke, laid aside his pipe, and rose up directly.

"If you could direct us anywhere, sir," said the child, "we should take it very kindly."

"You have been walking a long way," said the schoolmaster.

"A long way, sir," the child replied.

"You're a young traveller, my child," he said, laying his hand gently on her head. "Your grandchild, friend?"

"Ay, sir," cried the old man, "and the stay and comfort of my life."

"Come in," said the schoolmaster.

Without further preface he conducted them into his little schoolroom, which was parlour and kitchen likewise, and told them they were welcome to remain under his roof till morning. Before they had done thanking him, he spread a coarse white cloth upon the table, with knives and platters; and bringing out some bread and cold meat and a jug of beer, besought them to eat and drink.

The child looked round the room as she took her seat. There were a couple of forms, notched and cut and inked all over; a small deal desk perched on four legs, at which no doubt the master sat; a few dog's-eared books upon a high shelf; and beside them a motley collection of peg-tops, balls, kites, fishing-lines, marbles, half-eaten apples, and other confiscated property of idle urchins. Displayed on hooks upon the wall in all their terrors, were the cane and ruler; and near them, on a small shelf of its own, the dunce's cap, made of old newspapers and decorated with glaring wafers of the largest size. But the great ornaments of the walls were certain moral sentences fairly copied in good round text, and well-worked sums in simple addition and multiplication, evidently achieved by the same hand, which were plentifully pasted all round the room: for the double purpose, as it seemed, of bearing testimony to the excellence of the school, and kindling a worthy emulation in the bosoms of the scholars.

"Yes," said the old schoolmaster, observing that her attention was caught by these latter specimens. "That's beautiful writing, my dear."

"Very, sir," replied the child modestly, "is it yours?"

"Mine!" he returned, taking out his spectacles and putting them on, to have a better view of the triumphs so dear to his heart. "I couldn't write like that, now-a-days. No. They're all done by one hand; a little hand it is, not so old as yours, but a very clever one."

As the schoolmaster said this, he saw that a small blot of ink had been thrown on one of the copies, so he took a penknife from his pocket, and going up to the wall, carefully scraped it out. When he had finished, he walked slowly backward from the writing, admiring it as one might contemplate a beautiful picture, but with something of sadness in his voice and manner which quite touched the child, though she was unacquainted with its cause.

"A little hand indeed," said the poor schoolmaster. "Far beyond all his companions, in his learning and his sports too, how did he ever come to be so fond of me! That I should love him is no wonder, but that he should love me——" and there the schoolmaster stopped, and took off his spectacles to wipe them, as though they had grown dim.

"I hope there is nothing the matter, sir," said Nell anxiously.

"Not much, my dear," returned the schoolmaster. "I hoped to have seen him on the green to-night. He was always foremost among them. But he'll be there to-morrow."

"Has he been ill?" asked the child, with a child's quick sympathy.

"Not very. They said he was wandering in his head yesterday, dear boy, and so they said the day before. But that's a part of that kind of disorder; it's not a bad sign—not at all a bad sign."

The child was silent. He walked to the door, and looked wistfully out. The shadows of night were gathering, and all was still.

"If he could lean upon anybody's arm, he would come to me, I know," he said, returning into the room. "He always came into the garden to say good-night. But perhaps his illness has only just taken a favourable turn, and it's too late for him to come out, for it's very damp and there's a heavy dew. It's much better he shouldn't come to-night."

The schoolmaster lighted a candle, fastened the window-shutter, and closed the door. But after he had done this, and sat silent a little time, he took down his hat, and said he would go and satisfy himself, if Nell would sit up till he returned. The child readily complied, and he went out.

She sat there half an hour or more, feeling the place very strange and lonely, for she had prevailed upon the old man to go to bed, and there was nothing to be heard but the ticking of an old clock, and the whistling of the wind among the trees. When he returned, he took his seat in the chimney-corner, but remained silent for a long time. At length he turned to her, and speaking very gently, hoped she would say a prayer that night for a sick child.

"My favourite scholar!" said the poor schoolmaster, smoking a pipe he had forgotten to light, and looking mournfully round about the walls. "It is a little hand to have done all that, and waste away with sickness. It is a very, very little hand!"

Chapter XXV

A FTER a sound night's rest in a chamber in the thatched roof, in which it seemed the sexton had for some years been a lodger, but which he had lately deserted for a wife and a cottage of his own, the child rose early in the morning and descended to the room where she had supped last night. As the schoolmaster had already left his bed and gone out, she bestirred herself to make it neat and comfortable, and had just finished its arrangement when the kind host returned.

He thanked her many times, and said that the old dame who usually did such offices for him had gone to nurse the little scholar whom he had told her of. The child asked how he was, and hoped he was better.

"No," rejoined the schoolmaster shaking his head sorrowfully, "No better. They even say he is worse."

"I am very sorry for that, sir," said the child.

The poor schoolmaster appeared to be gratified by her earnest manner, but yet rendered more uneasy by it, for he added hastily that anxious people often magnified an evil and thought it greater than it was; "for my part," he said, in his quiet, patient way, "I hope it's not so. I don't think he can be worse."

The child asked his leave to prepare breakfast, and her grandfather coming downstairs, they all three partook of it together. While the meal was in progress, their host remarked that the old man seemed much fatigued, and evidently stood in need of rest.

"If the journey you have before you is a long one," he said, "and don't press you for one day, you're very welcome to pass another night here. I should really be glad if you would, friend."

He saw that the old man looked at Nell, uncertain whether to accept or decline his offer; and added:

"I shall be glad to have your young companion with me for one day. If you can do a charity to a lone man, and rest yourself at the same time, do so. If you must proceed upon your journey, I wish you well through it, and will walk a little way with you before school begins."

"What are we to do, Nell?" said the old man irresolutely, "say what we're to do, dear."

It required no great persuasion to induce the child to answer that they had better accept the invitation and remain. She was happy to show her gratitude to the kind schoolmaster by busying herself in the performance of such household duties as his little cottage stood in need of. When these were done, she took some needle-work from her basket, and sat herself down upon a stool beside the lattice, where the honeysuckle and woodbine entwined their tender stems, and stealing into the room filled it with their delicious breath. Her grandfather was basking in the sun outside, breathing the perfume of the flowers, and idly watching the clouds as they floated on before the light summer wind.

As the schoolmaster, after arranging the two forms in due order, took his seat behind his desk and made other preparations for school, the child was apprehensive that she might be in the way, and offered to withdraw to her little bedroom. But this he would not allow, and as he seemed pleased to have her there, she remained, busying herself with her work.

"Have you many scholars, sir?" she asked.

The poor schoolmaster shook his head, and said that they barely filled the two forms.

"Are the others clever, sir?" asked the child, glancing at the trophies on the wall.

"Good boys," returned the schoolmaster, "good boys enough, my dear, but they'll never do like that."

A small white-headed boy with a sunburnt face appeared at the door while he was speaking, and stopping there to make a rustic bow, came in and took his seat upon one of the forms. The white-headed boy then put an open book, astonishingly dog's-eared, upon his knees, and thrusting his hands into his pockets began counting the marbles with which they were filled; displaying in the expression of his face a remarkable capacity of totally abstracting his mind from the spelling on which his eyes were fixed. Soon afterwards another white-headed little boy came straggling in, and after him a red-headed lad, and after him two more with white heads, and then one with a flaxen poll, and so on until the forms were occupied by a dozen boys or thereabouts, with heads of every colour but grey, and ranging in their ages from four years old to fourteen years or more; for the legs of the youngest were a long way from the floor when he sat upon the form. and the eldest was a heavy good-tempered foolish fellow, about half a head taller than the schoolmaster.

At the top of the first form—the post of honour in the school—was the vacant place of the little sick scholar, and at the head of the row of pegs on which those who came in hats or caps were wont to hang them up, one was left empty. No boy attempted to violate the sanctity of seat or peg, but many a one looked from the empty spaces to the schoolmaster, and whispered his idle neighbour behind his hand.

Then began the hum of conning over lessons and getting them by heart, the whispered jest and stealthy game, and all the noise and drawl of school; and in the midst of the din sat the poor schoolmaster, the very image of meekness and simplicity, vainly attempting to fix his mind upon the duties of the day, and to forget his little friend. But the tedium of his office reminded him more strongly of the willing scholar, and his thoughts were rambling from his pupils—it was plain.

None knew this better than the idlest boys, who, growing bolder with impunity, waxed louder and more daring; playing odd-or-even under the master's eye, eating apples openly and without rebuke, pinching each other in sport or malice without the least reserve, and cutting their autographs in the very legs of his desk. The puzzled dunce, who stood beside it to say his lesson out of book, looked no longer at the ceiling for forgotten words, but drew closer to the master's elbow and boldly cast his eye upon the page; the wag of the little troop squinted and made grimaces (at the smallest boy of course), holding no book before his face, and his approving audience knew no constraint in their delight. If the master did chance to rouse himself and seem alive to what was going on, the noise subsided for a moment and no eyes met his but wore a studious and a deeply humble look; but the instant he relapsed again, it broke out afresh, and ten times louder than before.

Oh! how some of those idle fellows longed to be outside, and how they looked at the open door and window, as if they half meditated rushing violently out, plunging into the woods, and being wild boys and savages from that time forth. What rebellious thoughts of the cool river, and some shady bathing-place beneath willow-trees with branches dipping in the water, kept tempting and urging that sturdy boy, who, with his shirt-collar unbuttoned and flung back as far as it could go, sat fanning his flushed face with a spelling-book, wishing himself a whale, or a tittlebat, or a fly, or anything but a boy at school on that hot, broiling day! Heat! ask that other boy, whose seat being nearest to the door gave him opportunities of gliding out into the garden and driving his companions to madness by dipping his face into the bucket of the well and then rolling on the grass—ask him if there were ever such a day as that, when even the bees were diving deep down into the cups of flowers and stopping there, as if they had made up their minds to retire from business and be manufacturers of honey no more. The day was made for laziness, and lying on one's back in green places, and staring at the sky till its brightness forced one to shut one's eyes and go to sleep; and was this a time to be poring over musty books in a dark room, slighted by the very sun itself? Monstrous!

Nell sat by the window occupied with her work, but attentive still to all that passed, though sometimes rather timid of the boisterous boys. The lessons over, writing-time began; and there being but one desk and that the master's, each boy sat at it in turn and laboured at his crooked copy, while the master walked about. This was a quieter time; for he would come and look over the writer's shoulder, and tell him mildly to observe how such a letter was turned in such a copy on the wall, praise such an up-stroke here and such a down-stroke there, and bid him take it for his model. Then he would stop and tell them what the sick child had said last night, and how he had longed to be among them once again; and such was the poor schoolmaster's gentle and affectionate manner, that the boys seemed quite remorseful that they had worried him so much, and were absolutely quiet, eating no apples, cutting no names, inflicting no pinches, and making no grimaces, for full two minutes afterwards.

"I think, boys," said the schoolmaster when the clock struck twelve, "that I shall give an extra half-holiday this afternoon."

At this intelligence, the boys, led on and headed by the tall boy, raised a great shout, in the midst of which the master was seen to speak, but could not be heard. As he held up his hand, however, in token of his wish that they should be silent, they were considerate enough to leave off, as soon as the longest-winded among them were quite out of breath.

"You must promise me first," said the schoolmaster, "that you'll not be noisy, or at least, if you are, that you'll go away and be so—away out of the village I mean. I'm sure you wouldn't disturb your old playmate and companion."

There was a general murmur (and perhaps a very sincere one, for they were but boys) in the negative; and the tall boy, perhaps as sincerely as any of them, called those about him to witness that he had only shouted in a whisper.

"Then pray don't forget, there's my dear scholars," said the schoolmaster, "what I have asked you, and do it as a favour to me. Be as happy as you can, and don't be unmindful that you are blessed with health. Good-bye all!"

"Thank'ee, sir," and "Good-bye, sir," were said a great many times in a variety of voices, and the boys went out very slowly and softly. But there was the sun shining and there were the birds singing, as the sun only shines and the birds only sing on holidays and half-holidays; there were the trees waving to all free boys to climb and nestle among their leafy branches; the hay, entreating them to come and scatter it to the pure air; the green corn, gently beckoning towards wood and stream; the smooth ground, rendered smoother still by blending lights and shadows, inviting to runs and leaps, and long walks God knows whither. It was more than boy could bear, and with a joyous whoop the whole cluster took to their heels and spread themselves about, shouting and laughing as they went.

"It's natural, thank Heaven!" said the poor schoolmaster looking after them. "I'm very glad they didn't mind me!"

It is difficult, however, to please everybody, as most of us would have discovered, even without the fable which bears that moral; and in the course of the afternoon several mothers and aunts of pupils looked in to express their entire disapproval of the school-master's proceeding. A few confined themselves to hints, such as politely inquiring what red-letter day or saint's day the almanack said it was; a few (these were the profound village politicians) argued that it was a slight to the Throne and an affront to Church and State, and savoured of revolutionary principles, to grant a half-holiday upon any lighter occasion than the birthday of the Monarch; but the majority expressed their displeasure on private grounds and in plain terms, arguing that to put the pupils on this short allowance of learning was nothing but an act of downright robbery and fraud: and one old lady, finding that she could not inflame or irritate the peaceable schoolmaster by talking to him, bounced out of his house and talked at him for half-an-hour outside his own window, to another old lady, saying that of course he would deduct this half-holiday from his weekly charge, or of course he would naturally expect to have an opposition started against him; there was no want of idle chaps in that neighbourhood (here the old lady raised her voice), and some chaps who were too idle even to be schoolmasters, might soon find that there were other chaps put over their heads, and so she would have them take care, and look pretty sharp about them. But all these taunts and vexations failed to elicit one word from the meek schoolmaster, who sat with the child by his side,—a little more dejected perhaps, but quite silent and uncomplaining.

Towards night an old woman came tottering up the garden as speedily as she could, and meeting the schoolmaster at the door, said he was to go to Dame West's directly, and had best run on before her. He and the child were on the point of going out together for a walk, and without relinquishing her hand, the schoolmaster hurried away, leaving the messenger to follow as she might.

They stopped at a cottage door, and the schoolmaster knocked softly at it with his hand. It was opened without loss of time. They entered a room where a little group of women were gathered about one, older than the rest, who was crying very bitterly, and sat wringing her hands and rocking herself to and fro.

"Oh, dame!" said the schoolmaster, drawing near her chair, "is it so bad as this?"

"He's going fast," cried the old woman; "my grandson's dying. It's all along of you. You shouldn't see him now, but for his being so earnest on it. This is what his learning has brought him to. Oh, dear, dear, dear, what can I do!"

"Do not say that I am in any fault," urged the gentle schoolmaster. "I am not hurt, dame. No, no. You are in great distress of mind, and don't mean what you say. I am sure you don't."

"I do," returned the old woman. "I mean it all. If he hadn't been poring over his books out of fear of you, he would have been well and merry now, I know he would."

The schoolmaster looked round upon the other women as if to entreat some one among them to say a kind word for him, but they shook their heads, and murmured to each other that they never thought there was much good in learning, and that this convinced them. Without saying a word in reply, or giving them a look of reproach, he followed the old woman who had summoned him (and who had now rejoined them) into another room, where his infant friend, half dressed, lay stretched upon a bed.

He was a very young boy; quite a little child. His hair still hung in curls about his face, and his eyes were very bright; but their light was of Heaven, not earth. The schoolmaster took a seat beside him, and stooping over the pillow, whispered his name. The boy sprang up, stroked his face with his hand, and threw his wasted arms around his neck, crying out that he was his dear kind friend.

"I hope I always was. I meant to be, God knows," said the poor schoolmaster.

"Who is that?" said the boy, seeing Nell. "I am afraid to kiss her, lest I should make her ill. Ask her to shake hands with me."

The sobbing child came closer up, and took the little languid hand in hers. Releasing his again after a time, the sick boy laid him gently down.

"You remember the garden, Harry," whispered the schoolmaster, anxious to rouse him, for a dulness seemed gathering upon the child, "and how pleasant it used to be in the evening time? You must make haste to visit it again, for I think the very flowers have missed you, and are less gay than they used to be. You will come soon, my dear, very soon now—won't you?"

The boy smiled faintly—so very, very faintly—and put his hand upon his friend's grey head. He moved his lips too, but no voice came from them; no, not a sound.

In the silence that ensued, the hum of distant voices borne upon the evening air came floating through the open window. "What's that?" said the sick child, opening his eyes.

"The boys at play upon the green."

He took a handkerchief from his pillow, and tried to wave it above his head. But the feeble arm dropped powerless down.

"Shall I do it?" said the schoolmaster.

"Please wave it at the window," was the faint reply. "Tie it to the lattice. Some of them may see it there. Perhaps they'll think of me, and look this way."

He raised his head, and glanced from the fluttering signal to his idle bat, that lay with slate and book and other boyish property upon a table in the room. And then he laid him softly down once more, and asked if the little girl were there, for he could not see her.

She stepped forward, and pressed the passive hand that lay upon the coverlet. The two old friends and companions—for such they were, though they were man and child—held each other in a long embrace, and then the little scholar turned his face towards the wall, and fell asleep.

The poor schoolmaster sat in the same place, holding the small cold hand in his, and chafing it. It was but the hand of a dead child. He felt that; and yet he chafed it still, and could not lay it down.

Chapter XXVI

ALMOST broken-hearted, Nell withdrew with the schoolmaster from the bedside and returned to his cottage. In the midst of her grief and tears she was yet careful to conceal their real cause from the old man, for the dead boy had been a grandchild, and left but one aged relative to mourn his premature decay.

She stole away to bed as quickly as she could, and when she was alone, gave free vent to the sorrow with which her breast was overcharged. But the sad scene she had witnessed, was not without its lesson of content and gratitude; of content with the lot which left her health and freedom; and gratitude that she was spared to the one relative and friend she loved, and to live and move in a beautiful world, when so many young creatures—as young and full of hope as she—were stricken down and gathered to their graves. How many of the mounds in that old churchyard where she had lately strayed, grew green above the graves of children! And though she thought as a child herself, and did not perhaps sufficiently consider to what a bright and happy existence those who die young are borne, and how in death they lose the pain of seeing others die around them, bearing to the tomb some strong affection of their hearts (which makes the old die many times in one long life), still she thought wisely enough, to draw a plain and easy moral from what she had seen that night, and to store it, deep in her mind.

Her dreams were of the little scholar: not coffined and covered up, but mingling with angels, and smiling happily. The sun darting his cheerful rays into the room, awoke her; and now there remained but to take leave of the poor schoolmaster and wander forth once more.

By the time they were ready to depart, school had begun. In the darkened room, the din of yesterday was going on again: a little sobered and softened down, perhaps, but only a very little, if at all. The schoolmaster rose from his desk and walked with them to the gate.

It was with a trembling and reluctant hand that the child held out to him the money which the lady had given her at the races for her flowers: faltering in her thanks as she thought how small the sum was, and blushing as she offered it. But he bade her put it up, and stooping to kiss her cheek, turned back into his house.

They had not gone half a dozen paces when he was at the door again; the old man retraced his steps to shake hands, and the child did the same.

"Good fortune and happiness go with you!" said the poor schoolmaster. "I am quite a solitary man now. If you ever pass this way again, you'll not forget the little village-school."

"We shall never forget it, sir," rejoined Nell; "nor ever forget to be grateful to you for your kindness to us."

"I have heard such words from the lips of children very often," said the schoolmaster, shaking his head, and smiling thoughtfully, "but they were soon forgotten. I had attached one young friend to me, the better friend for being young—but that's over—God bless you!"

They bade him farewell very many times, and turned away, walking slowly and often looking back, until they could see him no more. At length they had left the village far behind, and even lost sight of the smoke among the trees. They trudged onward now, at a quicker pace, resolving to keep the main road, and go wherever it might lead them.

But main roads stretch a long, long way. With the exception of two or three inconsiderable clusters of cottages which they passed, without stopping, and one lonely roadside public-house where they had some bread and cheese, this highway had led them to nothing—late in the afternoon—and still lengthened out, far in the distance, the same dull, tedious, winding course, that they had been pursuing all day. As they had no resource, however, but to go forward, they still kept on, though at a much slower pace, being very weary and fatigued.

The afternoon had worn away into a beautiful evening, when they arrived at a point where the road made a sharp turn and struck across a common. On the border of this common, and close to the hedge which divided it from the cultivated fields, a caravan was drawn up to rest; upon which, by reason of its situation, they came so suddenly that they could not have avoided it if they would.

It was not a shabby, dingy, dusty cart, but a smart little house upon wheels, with white dimity curtains festooning the windows, and window-shutters of green picked out with panels of a staring red, in which happily contrasted colours the whole concern shone brilliant. Neither was it a poor caravan drawn by a single donkey or emaciated horse, for a pair of horses in pretty good condition were released from the shafts and grazing on the frowzy grass. Neither was it a gipsy caravan, for at the open door (graced with a bright brass knocker) sat a Christian lady, stout and comfortable to look upon, who wore a large bonnet trembling with bows. And that it was not an unprovided or destitute caravan was clear from this lady's occupation, which was the very pleasant and refreshing one of taking tea. The tea-things, including a bottle of rather suspicious character and a cold knuckle of ham, were set forth upon a drum, covered with a white napkin; and there, as if at the most convenient round-table in all the world, sat this roving lady, taking her tea and enjoying the prospect.

It happened that at that moment the lady of the caravan had her cup (which, that everything about her might be of a stout and comfortable kind, was a breakfast cup) to her lips, and that having her eyes lifted to the sky in her enjoyment of the full flavour of the tea, not unmingled possibly with just the slightest dash or gleam of something out of the suspicious bottle—but this is mere speculation and not distinct matter of history—it happened that being thus agreeably engaged, she did not see the travellers when they first came up. It was not until she was in the act of setting down the cup, and drawing a long breath after the exertion of causing its contents to disappear, that the lady of the caravan beheld an old man and a young child walking slowly by, and glancing at her proceedings with eyes of modest but hungry admiration.

"Hey!" cried the lady of the caravan, scooping the crumbs out of her lap and swallowing the same before wiping her lips. "Yes, to be sure—Who won the Helter-Skelter Plate, child?"

"Won what, ma'am?" asked Nell.

"The Helter-Skelter Plate at the races, child—the plate that was run for on the second day."

"On the second day, ma'am?"

"Second day! Yes, second day," repeated the lady with an air of impatience. "Can't you say who won the Helter-Skelter Plate when you're asked the question civilly?"

"I don't know, ma'am."

"Don't know!" repeated the lady of the caravan; "why, you were there. I saw you with my own eyes."

Nell was not a little alarmed to hear this, supposing that the lady might be intimately acquainted with the firm of Short and Codlin; but what followed tended to reassure her.

"And very sorry I was," said the lady of the caravan, "to see you in company with a Punch; a low, practical, wulgar wretch, that people should scorn to look at."

"I was not there by choice," returned the child; "we didn't know our way, and the two men were very kind to us, and let us travel with them. Do you—do you know them, ma'am?"

"Know 'em, child!" cried the lady of the caravan in a sort of shriek. "Know *them!* But you're young and inexperienced, and that's your excuse for asking sich a question. Do I look as if I know'd 'em, does the caravan look as if *it* know'd 'em?"

"No, ma'am, no," said the child, fearing she had committed some grievous fault. "I beg your pardon."

It was granted immediately, though the lady still appeared much ruffled and discomposed by the degrading supposition. The child then explained that they had left the races on the first day, and were travelling to the next town on that road, where they purposed to spend the night. As the countenance of the stout lady began to clear up, she ventured to inquire how far it was. The reply—which the stout lady did not come to, until she had thoroughly explained that she went to the races on the first day in a gig, and as an expedition of pleasure, and that her presence there had no connexion with any matters of business or profit—was, that the town was eight miles off.

This discouraging information a little dashed the child, who could scarcely repress a tear as she glanced along the darkening road. Her grandfather made no complaint, but he sighed heavily as he leaned upon his staff, and vainly tried to pierce the dusty distance.

The lady of the caravan was in the act of gathering her tea equipage together preparatory to clearing the table, but noting the child's anxious manner she hesitated and stopped. The child curtseyed, thanked her for her information, and giving her hand to the old man had already got some fifty yards or so, away, when the lady of the caravan called to her to return.

"Come nearer, nearer still"—said she, beckoning to her to ascend the steps. "Are you hungry, child?"

"Not very, but we are tired, and it's—it *is* a long way———"

"Well, hungry or not, you had better have some tea," rejoined her new acquaintance. "I suppose you are agreeable to that, old gentleman?"

The grandfather humbly pulled off his hat and thanked her. The lady of the caravan then bade him come up the steps likewise, but the drum proving an inconvenient table for two, they descended again, and sat upon the grass, where she handed down to them the tea-tray, the bread and butter, the knuckle of ham, and in short everything of which she had partaken herself, except the bottle which she had already embraced an opportunity of slipping into her pocket.

"Set 'em out near the hind-wheels, child, that's the best place"—said their friend, superintending the arrangements from above. "Now hand up the teapot for a little more hot water, and a pinch of fresh tea, and then both of you eat and drink as much as you can, and don't spare anything; that's all I ask of you."

They might perhaps have carried out the lady's wish, if it had been less freely expressed, or even if it had not been expressed at all. But as this direction relieved them from any shadow of delicacy or uneasiness, they made a hearty meal and enjoyed it to the utmost.

While they were thus engaged, the lady of the caravan alighted on the earth, and with her hands clasped behind her, and her large bonnet trembling excessively, walked up and down in a measured tread and very stately manner, surveying the caravan from time to time with an air of calm delight, and deriving particular gratification from the red panels and the brass knocker. When she had taken this gentle exercise for some time, she sat down upon the steps and called "George"; whereupon a man in a carter's frock, who had been so shrouded in a hedge up to this time as to see everything that passed without being seen himself, parted the twigs that concealed him, and appeared in a sitting attitude, supporting on his legs a baking-dish and a half-gallon stone bottle, and bearing in his right hand a knife, and in his left a fork.

"Yes, Missus"—said George.

"How did you find the cold pie, George?"

"It warn't amiss, Mum."

"And the beer," said the lady of the caravan, with an appearance of being more interested in this question than the last; "is it passable, George?"

"It's more flatterer than it might be," George returned, "but it an't so bad for all that."

To set the mind of his mistress at rest, he took a sip (amounting in quantity to a pint or thereabouts) from the stone bottle, and then smacked his lips, winked his eye, and nodded his head. No doubt with the same amiable desire, he immediately resumed his knife and fork, as a practical assurance that the beer had wrought no bad effect upon his appetite.

The lady of the caravan looked on approvingly for some time, and then said:

"Have you nearly finished?"

"Wery nigh, Mum." And indeed, after scraping the dish all round with his knife and carrying the choice brown morsels to his mouth, and after taking such a scientific pull at the stone bottle that, by degrees almost imperceptible to the sight, his head went further and further back until he lay nearly at his full length upon the ground, this gentleman declared himself quite disengaged, and came forth from his retreat.

"I hope I haven't hurried you, George," said his mistress, who appeared to have a great sympathy with his late pursuit.

"If you have," returned the follower, wisely reserving himself for any favourable contingency that might occur, "we must make up for it next time, that's all."

"We are not a heavy load, George?"

"That's always what the ladies say," replied the man, looking a long way round, as if he were appealing to Nature in general against such monstrous propositions. "If you see a woman a-driving, you'll always perceive that she never will keep her whip still; the horse can't go fast enough for her. If cattle have got their proper load, you never can persuade a woman that they'll not bear something more. What is the cause of this here?"

"Would these two travellers make much difference to the horses, if we took them with us?" asked his mistress, offering no reply to the philosophical inquiry, and pointing to Nell and the old man, who were painfully preparing to resume their journey on foot.

"They'd make a difference in course," said George doggedly.

"Would they make much difference?" repeated his mistress. "They can't be very heavy."

"The weight o' the pair, Mum," said George, eyeing them with the look of a man who was calculating within half an ounce or so, "would be a trifle under that of Oliver Cromwell."

Nell was very much surprised that the man should be so accurately acquainted with the weight of one whom she had read of in books as having lived considerably before their time, but speedily forgot the subject in the joy of hearing that they were to go forward in the caravan, for which she thanked its lady with unaffected earnestness. She helped with great readiness and alacrity to put away the tea-things and other matters that were lying about, and, the horses being by that time harnessed, mounted into the vehicle, followed by her delighted grandfather. Their patroness then shut the door and sat herself down by her drum at an open window; and, the steps being struck by George and stowed under the carriage, away they went, with a great noise of flapping and creaking and straining, and the bright brass knocker, which nobody ever knocked at, knocking one perpetual double knock of its own accord as they jolted heavily along.

Chapter XXVII

WHEN they had travelled slowly forward for some short distance, Nell ventured to steal a look round the caravan and observe it more closely. One half of it—that moiety in which the comfortable proprietress was then seated—was carpeted, and so partitioned off at the further end as to accommodate a sleeping-place, constructed after the fashion of a berth on board ship, which was shaded, like the little windows, with fair white curtains, and looked comfortable enough, though by what kind of gymnastic exercise the lady of the caravan ever contrived to get into it, was an unfathomable mystery. The other half served for a kitchen, and was fitted up with a stove whose small chimney passed through the roof. It held also a closet or larder, several chests, a great pitcher of water, and a few cooking-utensils and articles of crockery. These latter necessaries hung upon the walls, which in that portion of the establishment devoted to the lady of the caravan, were ornamented with such gayer and lighter decorations as a triangle and a couple of well-thumbed tambourines.

The lady of the caravan sat at one window in all the pride and poetry of the musical instruments, and little Nell and her grandfather sat at the other in all the humility of the kettle and sauce-pans, while the machine jogged on and shifted the darkening prospect very slowly. At first the two travellers spoke little, and only in whispers, but as they grew more familiar with the place they ventured to converse with greater freedom, and talked about the country through which they were passing, and the different objects that presented themselves, until the old man fell asleep; which the lady of the caravan observing, invited Nell to come and sit beside her.

"Well, child," she said, "how do you like this way of travelling?"

Nell replied that she thought it was very pleasant indeed, to which the lady assented in the case of people who had their spirits. For herself, she said, she was troubled with a lowness in that respect which required a constant stimulant; though whether the aforesaid stimulant was derived from the suspicious bottle of which mention has been already made, or from other sources, she did not say.

"That's the happiness of you young people," she continued. "You don't know what it is to be low in your feelings. You always have your appetites too, and what a comfort that is."

Nell thought that she could sometimes dispense with her own appetite very conveniently; and thought, moreover, that there was nothing either in the lady's personal appearance or in her manner of taking tea, to lead to the conclusion that her natural relish for meat and drink had at all failed her. She silently assented, however, as in duty bound, to what the lady had said, and waited until she should speak again.

Instead of speaking, however, she sat looking at the child for a long time in silence, and then getting up, brought out from a corner a large roll of canvas about a yard in width, which she laid upon the floor and spread open with her foot until it nearly reached from one end of the caravan to the other.

"There, child," she said, "read that."

Nell walked down it, and read aloud, in enormous black letters, the inscription, "JARLEY'S WAX-WORK."

"Read it again," said the lady complacently.

"Jarley's Wax-work," repeated Nell.

"That's me," said the lady. "I am Mrs Jarley."

Giving the child an encouraging look, intended to reassure her and let her know, that, although she stood in the presence of the original Jarley, she must not allow herself to be utterly overwhelmed and borne down, the lady of the caravan unfolded another scroll, whereon was the inscription, "One hundred figures the full size of life," and then another scroll, on which was written, "The only stupendous collection of real wax-work in the world," and then several smaller scrolls with such inscriptions as "Now exhibiting within"—"The genuine and only Jarley"—"Jarley's unrivalled collection"—"Jarley is the delight of the Nobility and Gentry"—"The Royal Family are the patrons of Jarley." When she had exhibited these leviathans of public announcement to the astonished child, she brought forth specimens of the lesser fry in the shape of handbills, some of which were couched in the form of parodies on popular melodies, as "Believe me if all Jarley's wax-work so rare"—"I saw thy show in youthful prime"—"Over the water to Jarley"; while, to consult all tastes, others were composed with a view to the lighter and more facetious spirits, as a parody on the favourite air of "If I had a donkey," beginning

> If I know'd a donkey wot wouldn't go
> To see MRS JARLEY's wax-work show,
> Do you think I'd acknowledge him?
>   Oh, no, no!
>   Then run to Jarley's—

—besides several compositions in prose, purporting to be dialogues between the Emperor of China and an oyster, or the Archbishop of Canterbury and a Dissenter on the subject of church-rates, but all having the same moral, namely, that the reader must make haste to Jarley's, and that children and servants were admitted at half-price. When she had brought all these testimonials of her important position in society to bear upon her young companion, Mrs Jarley rolled them up, and having put them carefully away, sat down again, and looked at the child in triumph.

"Never go into the company of a filthy Punch any more," said Mrs Jarley, "after this."

"I never saw any wax-work, ma'am," said Nell. "Is it funnier than Punch?"

"Funnier!" said Mrs Jarley in a shrill voice. "It is not funny at all."

"Oh!" said Nell, with all possible humility.

"It isn't funny at all," repeated Mrs Jarley. "It's calm and—what's that word again—critical?—no—classical, that's it—it's calm and classical. No low beatings and knockings about, no jokings and squeakings like your precious Punches, but always the same, with a constantly unchanging air of coldness and gentility; and so like life, that if wax-work only spoke and walked about, you'd hardly know the difference. I won't go so far as to say, that, as it is, I've seen wax-work quite like life, but I've certainly seen some life that was exactly like wax-work."

"Is it here, ma'am?" asked Nell, whose curiosity was awakened by this description.

"Is what here, child?"

"The wax-work, ma'am."

"Why, bless you, child, what are you thinking of? How could such a collection be here, where you see everything except the inside of one little cupboard and a few boxes? It's gone on in the other wans to the assembly rooms, and there it'll be exhibited the day after to-morrow. You are going to the same town, and you'll see it I dare say. It's natural to expect that you'll see it, and I've no doubt you will. I suppose you couldn't stop away if you was to try ever so much."

"I shall not be in the town, I think, ma'am," said the child.

"Not there!" cried Mrs Jarley. "Then where will you be?"

"I—I—don't quite know. I am not certain."

"You don't mean to say that you're travelling about the country without knowing where you're going to?" said the lady of the caravan. "What curious people you are! What line are you in? You looked to me at the races, child, as if you were quite out of your element, and had got there by accident."

"We were there quite by accident," returned Nell, confused by this abrupt questioning. "We are poor people, ma'am, and are only wandering about. We have nothing to do;—I wish we had."

"You amaze me more and more," said Mrs Jarley, after remaining for some time as mute as one of her own figures. "Why, what do you call yourselves? Not beggars?"

"Indeed, ma'am, I don't know what else we are," returned the child.

"Lord bless me," said the lady of the caravan. "I never heard of such a thing. Who'd have thought it!"

She remained so long silent after this exclamation, that Nell feared she felt her having been induced to bestow her protection and conversation upon one so poor, to be an outrage upon her dignity that nothing could repair. This persuasion was rather confirmed than otherwise by the tone in which she at length broke silence and said:

"And yet you can read. And write too, I shouldn't wonder?"

"Yes, ma'am," said the child, fearful of giving new offence by the confession.

"Well, and what a thing that is," returned Mrs Jarley. "*I* can't!"

Nell said "indeed" in a tone which might imply, either that she was reasonably surprised to find the genuine and only Jarley, who was the delight of the Nobility and Gentry and the peculiar pet of the Royal Family, destitute of these familiar arts; or that she presumed so great a lady could scarcely stand in need of such ordinary accomplishments. In whatever way Mrs Jarley received the response, it did not provoke her to further questioning, or tempt her into any more remarks at the time, for she relapsed into a thoughtful silence, and remained in that state so long that Nell withdrew to the other window and rejoined her grandfather, who was now awake.

At length the lady of the caravan shook off her fit of meditation, and, summoning the driver to come under the window at which she was seated, held a long conversation with him in a low tone of voice, as if she were asking his advice on an important point, and discussing the pros and cons of some very weighty matter. This conference at length concluded, she drew in her head again, and beckoned Nell to approach.

"And the old gentleman too," said Mrs Jarley; "for I want to have a word with him. Do you want a good situation for your granddaughter, master? If you do, I can put her in the way of getting one. What do you say?"

"I can't leave her," answered the old man. "We can't separate. What would become of me without her?"

"I should have thought you were old enough to take care of yourself, if you ever will be," retorted Mrs Jarley sharply.

"But he never will be," said the child in an earnest whisper. "I fear he never will be again. Pray do not speak harshly to him. We are very thankful to you," she added aloud; "but neither of us could part from the other if all the wealth of the world were halved between us."

Mrs Jarley was a little disconcerted by this reception of her proposal, and looked at the old man, who tenderly took Nell's hand and detained it in his own, as if she could have very well dispensed with his company or even his earthly existence. After an awkward pause, she thrust her head out of the window again, and had another conference with the driver upon some point on which they did not seem to agree quite so readily as on their former topic of discussion; but they concluded at last, and she addressed the grandfather again.

"If you're really disposed to employ yourself," said Mrs Jarley, "there would be plenty for you to do in the way of helping to dust the figures, and take the checks, and so forth. What I want your granddaughter for, is to point 'em out to the company; they would be soon learnt, and she has a way with her that people wouldn't think unpleasant, though she does come after me; for I've been always accustomed to go round with visitors myself, which I should keep on doing now, only that my spirits make a little ease absolutely necessary. It's not a common offer, bear in mind," said the lady, rising into the tone and manner in which she was accustomed to address her audiences; "it's Jarley's wax-work, remember. The duty's very light and genteel, the company particular select, the exhibition takes place in assembly rooms, town-halls, large rooms at inns, or auction galleries. There is none of your open-air wagrancy at Jarley's, recollect; there is no tarpaulin and sawdust at Jarley's, remember. Every expectation held out in the handbills is realised to the utmost, and the whole forms an effect of imposing brilliancy hitherto unrivalled in this kingdom. Remember that the price of admission is only sixpence, and that this is an opportunity which may never occur again!"

Descending from the sublime when she had reached this point, to the details of common life, Mrs Jarley remarked that with reference to salary she could pledge herself to no specific sum until she had sufficiently tested Nell's abilities, and narrowly watched her in the performance of her duties. But board and lodging, both for her and her grandfather, she bound herself to provide, and she furthermore passed her word that the board should always be good in quality, and in quantity plentiful.

Nell and her grandfather consulted together, and while they were so engaged, Mrs Jarley with her hands behind her walked up and down the caravan, as she had walked after tea on the dull earth, with uncommon dignity and self-esteem. Nor will this appear so slight a circumstance as to be unworthy of mention, when it is remembered that the caravan was in uneasy motion all the time, and that none but a person of great natural stateliness and acquired grace could have forborne to stagger.

"Now, child?" cried Mrs Jarley, coming to a halt as Nell turned towards her.

"We are very much obliged to you, ma'am," said Nell, "and thankfully accept your offer."

"And you'll never be sorry for it," returned Mrs Jarley. "I'm pretty sure of that. So as that's all settled, let us have a bit of supper."

In the meanwhile, the caravan blundered on as if it too had been drinking strong beer and was drowsy, and came at last upon the paved streets of a town which were clear of passengers, and quiet, for it was by this time near midnight, and the townspeople were all abed. As it was too late an hour to repair to the exhibition room, they turned aside into a piece of waste ground that lay just within the old town-gate, and drew up there for the night, near to another caravan, which, notwithstanding that it bore on the lawful panel the great name of Jarley, and was employed besides in conveying from place to place the wax-work which was its country's pride, was designated by a grovelling stamp-office as a "Common Stage Waggon," and numbered too—seven thousand odd hundred—as though its precious freight were mere flour or coals!

This ill-used machine being empty (for it had deposited its burden at the place of exhibition, and lingered here until its services were again required) was assigned to the old man as his sleeping-place for the night; and within its wooden walls, Nell made him up the best bed she could, from the materials at hand. For herself, she was to sleep in Mrs Jarley's own travelling-carriage, as a signal mark of that lady's favour and confidence.

She had taken leave of her grandfather and was returning to the other waggon, when she was tempted by the pleasant coolness of the night to linger for a little while in the air. The moon was shining down upon the old gateway of the town, leaving the low archway very black and dark; and with a mingled sensation of curiosity and fear, she slowly approached the gate, and stood still to look up at it, wondering to see how dark, and grim, and old, and cold, it looked.

There was an empty niche from which some old statue had fallen or been carried away hundreds of years ago, and she was thinking what strange people it must have looked down upon when it stood there, and how many hard struggles might have taken place, and how many murders might have been done, upon that silent spot, when there suddenly emerged from the black shade of the arch, a man. The instant he appeared, she recognized him— Who could have failed to recognize, in that instant, the ugly mis-shapen Quilp!

The street beyond was so narrow, and the shadow of the houses on one side of the way so deep, that he seemed to have risen out of the earth. But there he was. The child withdrew into a dark corner, and saw him pass close to her. He had a stick in his hand, and, when he had got clear of the shadow of the gateway, he leant upon it, looked back—directly, as it seemed, towards where she stood—and beckoned.

To her? oh, no, thank God, not to her; for as she stood, in an extremity of fear, hesitating whether to scream for help, or come from her hiding-place and fly, before he should draw nearer, there issued slowly forth from the arch another figure—that of a boy—who carried on his back a trunk.

"Faster, sirrah!" said Quilp, looking up at the old gateway, and showing in the moonlight like some monstrous image that had come down from its niche and was casting a backward glance at its old house, "faster!"

"It's a dreadful heavy load, sir," the boy pleaded. "I've come on very fast, consider-ing."

"*You* have come fast, considering!" retorted Quilp; "you creep, you dog, you crawl, you measure distance like a worm. There are the chimes now, half-past twelve."

He stopped to listen, and then turning upon the boy with a suddenness and ferocity that made him start, asked at what hour that London coach passed the corner of the road. The boy replied, at one.

"Come on then," said Quilp, "or I shall be too late. Faster—do you hear me? Faster."

The boy made all the speed he could, and Quilp led onward, constantly turning back to threaten him, and urge him to greater haste. Nell did not dare to move until they were out of sight and hearing, and then hurried to where she had left her grandfather, feeling as if the very passing of the dwarf so near him must have filled him with alarm and terror. But he was sleeping soundly, and she softly withdrew.

As she was making her way to her own bed, she determined to say nothing of this adventure, as upon whatever errand the dwarf had come (and she feared it must have been in search of them) it was clear by his enquiry about the London coach that he was on his way homeward, and as he had passed through that place, it was but reasonable to suppose that they were safer from his enquiries there, than they could be elsewhere. These reflections did not remove her own alarm, for she had been too much terrified to be easily composed, and felt as if she were hemmed in by a legion of Quilps, and the very air itself were filled with them.

The delight of the Nobility and Gentry and the patronized of Royalty had, by some process of self-abridgment known only to herself, got into her travelling bed, where she was snoring peacefully, while the large bonnet, carefully disposed upon the drum, was revealing its glories by the light of a dim lamp that swung from the roof. The child's bed was already made upon the floor, and it was a great comfort to her to hear the steps removed as soon as she had entered, and to know that all easy communication between persons outside and the brass knocker was by this means effectually prevented. Certain guttural sounds, too, which from time to time ascended through the floor of the caravan, and a rustling of straw in the same direction, apprised her that the driver was couched upon the ground beneath, and gave her an additional feeling of security.

Notwithstanding these protections, she could get none but broken sleep by fits and starts all night, for fear of Quilp, who throughout her uneasy dreams was somehow connected with the wax-work, or was wax-work himself, or was Mrs Jarley and wax-work too, or was himself, Mrs Jarley, wax-work, and a barrel organ all in one, and yet not exactly any of them either. At length, towards break of day, that deep sleep came upon her which succeeds to weariness and over-watching, and which has no consciousness but one of overpowering and irresistible enjoyment.

Chapter XXVIII

S LEEP hung upon the eyelids of the child so long, that, when she awoke, Mrs Jarley was already decorated with her large bonnet, and actively engaged in preparing breakfast. She received Nell's apology for being so late with perfect good-humour, and said that she should not have roused her if she had slept on until noon.

"Because it does you good," said the lady of the caravan, "when you're tired, to sleep as long as ever you can, and get the fatigue quite off; and that's another blessing of your time of life—you can sleep so very sound."

"Have you had a bad night, ma'am?" asked Nell.

"I seldom have anything else, child," replied Mrs Jarley, with the air of a martyr. "I sometimes wonder how I bear it."

Remembering the snores which had proceeded from that cleft in the caravan in which the proprietress of the wax-work passed the night, Nell rather thought she must have been dreaming of lying awake. However, she expressed herself very sorry to hear such a dismal account of her state of health, and shortly afterwards sat down with her grandfather and Mrs Jarley to breakfast. The meal finished, Nell assisted to wash the cups and saucers, and put them in their proper places, and these household duties performed, Mrs Jarley arrayed herself in an exceedingly bright shawl for the purpose of making a progress through the streets of the town.

"The wan will come on to bring the boxes," said Mrs Jarley, "and you had better come in it, child. I am obliged to walk, very much against my will; but the people expect it of me, and public characters can't be their own masters and mistresses in such matters as these. How do I look, child?"

Nell returned a satisfactory reply, and Mrs Jarley, after sticking a great many pins into various parts of her figure, and making several abortive attempts to obtain a full view of her own back, was at last satisfied with her appearance, and went forth majestically.

The caravan followed at no great distance. As it went jolting through the streets, Nell peeped from the window, curious to see in what kind of place they were, and yet fearful of encountering at every turn the dreaded face of Quilp. It was a pretty large town, with an open square which they were crawling slowly across, and in the middle of which was the Town Hall, with a clock-tower and a weathercock. There were houses of stone, houses of red brick, houses of yellow brick, houses of lath and plaster; and houses of wood, many of them very old, with withered faces carved upon the beams, and staring down into the street. These had very little winking windows, and low-arched doors, and, in some of the narrower ways, quite overhung the pavement. The streets were very clean, very sunny, very empty, and very dull. A few idle men lounged about the two inns, and the empty market-place, and the tradesmen's doors, and some old people were dozing in chairs outside an almshouse wall; but scarcely any passengers who seemed bent on going anywhere, or to have any object in view, went by; and if perchance some straggler did, his footsteps echoed on the hot bright pavement for minutes afterwards. Nothing seemed to be going on but the clocks, and they had such drowsy faces, such heavy lazy hands, and such cracked voices, that they surely must have been too slow. The very dogs were all asleep, and the flies, drunk with moist sugar in the grocer's shop, forgot their wings and briskness, and baked to death in dusty corners of the window.

Rumbling along with most unwonted noise, the caravan stopped at last at the place of exhibition, where Nell dismounted amidst an admiring group of children, who evidently supposed her to be an important item of the curiosities, and were fully impressed with the belief that her grandfather was a cunning device in wax. The chests were taken out with all convenient despatch, and taken in to be unlocked by Mrs Jarley, who, attended by George and another man in velveteen shorts and a drab hat ornamented with turnpike tickets, were waiting to dispose their contents (consisting of red festoons and other ornamental devices in upholstery work) to the best advantage in the decoration of the room.

They all got to work without loss of time, and very busy they were. As the stupendous collection were yet concealed by cloths, lest the envious dust should injure their complexions, Nell bestirred herself to assist in the embellishment of the room, in which her grandfather also was of great service. The two men being well used to it, did a great deal in a short time; and Mrs Jarley served out the tin tacks from a linen pocket like a toll-collector's which she wore for the purpose, and encouraged her assistants to renewed exertion.

While they were thus employed, a tallish gentleman with a hook nose and black hair, dressed in a military surtout very short and tight in the sleeves, and which had once been frogged and braided all over, but was now sadly shorn of its garniture and quite threadbare—dressed too in ancient grey pantaloons fitting tight to the leg, and a pair of pumps in the winter of their existence—looked in at the door, and smiled affably. Mrs Jarley's back being then towards him, the military gentleman shook his forefinger as a sign that her myrmidons were not to apprise her of his presence, and stealing up close behind her, tapped her on the neck, and cried playfully "Boh!"

"What, Mr Slum!" cried the lady of the wax-work. "Lor! who'd have thought of seeing you here!"

" 'Pon my soul and honour," said Mr Slum, "that's a good remark. 'Pon my soul and honour, that's a wise remark. Who *would* have thought it! George, my faithful feller, how are you?"

George received this advance with a surly indifference, observing that he was well enough for the matter of that, and hammering lustily all the time.

"I came here," said the military gentleman turning to Mrs Jarley—" 'pon my soul and honour, I hardly know what I came here for. It would puzzle me to tell you, it would by Gad. I wanted a little inspiration, a little freshening up, a little change of ideas, and—'Pon my soul and honour," said the military gentleman, checking himself and looking round the room, "what a devilish classical thing this is! By Gad, it's quite Minervian!"

"It'll look well enough when it comes to be finished," observed Mrs Jarley.

"Well enough!" said Mr Slum. "Will you believe me when I say it's the delight of my life to have dabbled in poetry, when I think I've exercised my pen upon this charming theme? By the way—any orders? Is there any little thing I can do for you?"

"It comes so very expensive, sir," replied Mrs Jarley, "and I really don't think it does much good."

"Hush! No, no!" returned Mr Slum, elevating his hand. "No fibs. I'll not hear it. Don't say it don't do good. Don't say it. I know better!"

"I don't think it does," said Mrs Jarley.

"Ha, ha!" cried Mr Slum, "you're giving way, you're coming down. Ask the perfumers, ask the blacking-makers, ask the hatters, ask the old lottery-office-keepers—ask any man among 'em what my poetry has done for him, and mark my words, he blesses the name of Slum. If he's an honest man, he raises his eyes to heaven, and blesses the name of Slum—mark that! You are acquainted with Westminster Abbey, Mrs Jarley?"

"Yes, surely."

"Then upon my soul and honour, ma'am, you'll find in a certain angle of that dreary pile, called Poets' Corner, a few smaller names than Slum," retorted that gentleman, tapping himself expressively on the forehead to imply that there was some slight quantity of brains behind it. "I've got a little trifle here, now," said Mr Slum, taking off his hat which was full of scraps of paper, "a little trifle here, thrown off in the heat of the moment, which I should say was exactly the thing you wanted to set this place on fire with. It's an acrostic—the name at this moment is Warren, but the idea's a convertible one, and a positive inspiration for Jarley. Have the acrostic."

"I suppose it's very dear," said Mrs Jarley.

"Five shillings," returned Mr Slum, using his pencil as a tooth-pick. "Cheaper than any prose."

"I couldn't give more than three," said Mrs Jarley.

"—And six," retorted Slum. "Come. Three-and-six."

Mrs Jarley was not proof against the poet's insinuating manner, and Mr Slum entered the order in a small notebook as a three-and-sixpenny one. Mr Slum then withdrew to alter the acrostic, after taking a most affectionate leave of his patroness, and promising to return, as soon as he possibly could, with a fair copy for the printer.

As his presence had not interfered with or interrupted the preparations, they were now far advanced, and were completed shortly after his departure. When the festoons were all put up as tastily as they might be, the stupendous collection was uncovered, and there were displayed, on a raised platform some two feet from the floor, running round the room and parted from the rude public by a crimson rope breast high, divers sprightly effigies of celebrated characters, singly and in groups, clad in glittering dresses of various climes and times, and standing more or less unsteadily upon their legs, with their eyes very wide open, and their nostrils very much inflated, and the muscles of their legs and arms very strongly developed, and all their countenances expressing great surprise. All the gentlemen were very pigeon-breasted and very blue about the beards; and all the ladies were miraculous figures; and all the ladies and all the gentlemen were looking intensely nowhere, and staring with extraordinary earnestness at nothing.

When Nell had exhausted her first raptures at this glorious sight, Mrs Jarley ordered the room to be cleared of all but herself and the child, and, sitting herself down in an armchair in the centre, formally invested her with a willow wand, long used by herself for pointing out the characters, and was at great pains to instruct her in her duty.

"That," said Mrs Jarley in her exhibition tone, as Nell touched a figure at the beginning of the platform, "is an unfortunate Maid of Honour in the Time of Queen Elizabeth, who died from pricking her finger in consequence of working upon a Sunday. Observe the blood which is trickling from her finger; also the gold-eyed needle of the period, with which she is at work."

All this Nell repeated twice or thrice, pointing to the finger and the needle at the right times, and then passed on to the next.

"That, ladies and gentlemen," said Mrs Jarley, "is Jasper Packlemerton of atrocious memory, who courted and married fourteen wives, and destroyed them all by tickling the soles of their feet when they was sleeping in the consciousness of innocence and virtue. On being brought to the scaffold and asked if he was sorry for what he had done, he replied yes, he was sorry for having let 'em off so easy, and hoped all Christian husbands would pardon him the offence. Let this be a warning to all young ladies to be particular in the character of the gentlemen of their choice. Observe that his fingers is curled as if in the act of tickling, and that his face is represented with a wink, as he appeared when committing his barbarous murders."

When Nell knew all about Mr Packlemerton, and could say it without faltering, Mrs Jarley passed on to the fat man, and then to the thin man, the tall man, the short man, the old lady who died of dancing at a hundred and thirty-two, the wild boy of the woods, the woman who poisoned fourteen families with pickled walnuts, and other historical characters and interesting but misguided individuals. And so well did Nell profit by her instructions, and so apt was she to remember them, that by the time they had been shut up together for a couple of hours, she was in full possession of the history of the whole establishment, and perfectly competent to the enlightenment of visitors.

Mrs Jarley was not slow to express her admiration at this happy result, and carried her young friend and pupil to inspect the remaining arrangements within doors, by virtue of which the passage had been already converted into a grove of green-baize hung with the inscriptions she had already seen (Mr Slum's productions), and a highly ornamented table placed at the upper end for Mrs Jarley herself, at which she was to preside and take the money, in company with his Majesty King George the Third, Mr Grimaldi as clown, Mary Queen of Scots, an anonymous gentleman of the Quaker persuasion, and Mr Pitt holding in his hand a correct model of the Bill for the imposition of the window duty. The preparations without doors had not been neglected either; for a nun of great personal attractions was telling her beads on the little portico over the door; and a brigand with the blackest possible head of hair, and the clearest possible complexion, was at that moment going round the town in a cart, consulting the miniature of a lady.

It now only remained that Mr Slum's compositions should be judiciously distributed; that the pathetic effusions should find their way to all private houses and tradespeople; and that the parody commencing "If I know'd a donkey," should be confined to the taverns, and circulated only among the lawyers' clerks and choice spirits of the place. When this had been done, and Mrs Jarley had waited upon the boarding-schools in person, with a handbill composed expressly for them, in which it was distinctly proved that wax-work refined the mind, cultivated the taste, and enlarged the sphere of the human understanding, that indefatigable lady sat down to dinner, and drank out of the suspicious bottle to a flourishing campaign.

Chapter XXIX

U NQUESTIONABLY Mrs Jarley had an inventive genius. In the midst of the various devices for attracting visitors to the exhibition, little Nell was not forgotten. The light cart in which the Brigand usually made his perambulations being gaily dressed with flags and streamers, and the Brigand placed therein, contemplating the miniature of his beloved as usual, Nell was accommodated with a seat beside him, decorated with artificial flowers, and in this state and ceremony rode slowly through the town every morning, dispersing handbills from a basket, to the sound of drum and trumpet. The beauty of the child, coupled with her gentle and timid bearing, produced quite a sensation in the little country place. The Brigand, heretofore a source of exclusive interest in the streets, became a mere secondary consideration, and to be important only as a part of the show of which she was the chief attraction. Grown-up folks began to be interested in the bright-eyed girl, and some score of little boys fell desperately in love, and constantly left inclosures of nuts and apples, directed in small text, at the wax-work door.

This desirable impression was not lost upon Mrs Jarley, who, lest Nell should become too cheap, soon sent the Brigand out alone again, and kept her in the exhibition room, where she described the figures every half-hour to the great satisfaction of admiring audiences. And these audiences were of a very superior description, including a great many young ladies' boarding-schools, whose favour Mrs Jarley had been at great pains to conciliate, by altering the face and costume of Mr Grimaldi as clown to represent Mr Lindley Murray as he appeared when engaged in the composition of his English Grammar, and turning a murderess of great renown into Mrs Hannah More—both of which likenesses were admitted by Miss Monflathers, who was at the head of the head Boarding and Day Establishment in the town, and who condescended to take a Private View with eight chosen young ladies, to be quite startling from their extreme correctness. Mr Pitt in a nightcap and bed-gown, and without his boots, represented the poet Cowper with perfect exactness; and Mary Queen of Scots in a dark wig, white shirt-collar, and male attire, was such a complete image of Lord Byron that the young ladies quite screamed when they saw it. Miss Monflathers, however, rebuked this enthusiasm, and took occasion to reprove Mrs Jarley for not keeping her collection more select, observing that His Lordship had held certain free opinions quite incompatible with wax-work honours, and adding something about a Dean and Chapter, which Mrs Jarley did not understand.

Although her duties were sufficiently laborious, Nell found in the lady of the caravan a very kind and considerate person, who had not only a peculiar relish for being comfortable herself, but for making everybody about her comfortable also; which latter taste, it may be remarked, is, even in persons who live in much finer places than caravans, a far more rare and uncommon one than the first, and is not by any means its necessary consequence. As her popularity procured her various little fees from the visitors on which her patroness never demanded any toll, and as her grandfather too was well treated and useful, she had no cause of anxiety in connexion with the wax-work, beyond that which sprang from her recollection of Quilp, and her fears that he might return and one day suddenly encounter them.

Quilp indeed was a perpetual nightmare to the child, who was constantly haunted by a vision of his ugly face and stunted figure. She slept, for their better security, in the room where the wax-work figures were, and she never retired to this place at night but she tortured herself—she could not help it—with imagining a resemblance, in some one or other of their deathlike faces, to the dwarf, and this fancy would sometimes so gain upon her that she would almost believe he had removed the figure and stood within the clothes. Then there were so many of them with their great glassy eyes—and, as they stood one behind the other all about her bed, they looked so like living creatures, and yet so unlike in their grim stillness and silence, that she had a kind of terror of them for their own sakes, and would often lie watching their dusky figures until she was obliged to rise and light a candle, or go and sit at the open window and feel a companionship in the bright stars. At these times, she would recall the old house and the window at which she used to sit alone; and then she would think of poor Kit and all his kindness, until the tears came into her eyes, and she would weep and smile together.

Often and anxiously at this silent hour, her thoughts reverted to her grandfather, and she would wonder how much he remembered of their former life, and whether he was ever really mindful of the change in their condition and of their late helplessness and destitution. When they were wandering about, she seldom thought of this, but now she could not help considering what would become of them if he fell sick, or her own strength were to fail her. He was very patient and willing, happy to execute any little task, and glad to be of use; but he was in the same listless state, with no prospect of improvement—a mere child—a poor, thoughtless, vacant creature—a harmless fond old man, susceptible of tender love and regard for her, and of pleasant and painful impressions, but alive to nothing more. It made her very sad to know that this was so—so sad to see it that sometimes when he sat idly by, smiling and nodding to her when she looked round, or when he caressed some little child and carried it to and fro, as he was fond of doing by the hour together, perplexed by its simple questions, yet patient under his own infirmity, and seeming almost conscious of it too, and humbled even before the mind of an infant—so sad it made her to see him thus, that she would burst into tears, and, withdrawing into some secret place, fall down upon her knees and pray that he might be restored.

But the bitterness of her grief was not in beholding him in this condition, when he was at least content and tranquil, nor in her solitary meditations on his altered state, though these were trials for a young heart. Cause for deeper and heavier sorrow was yet to come.

One evening, a holiday night with them, Nell and her grandfather went out to walk. They had been rather closely confined for some days, and the weather being warm, they strolled a long distance. Clear of the town, they took a footpath which struck through some pleasant fields, judging that it would terminate in the road they quitted and enable them to return that way. It made, however, a much wider circuit than they had supposed, and thus they were tempted onward until sunset, when they reached the track of which they were in search, and stopped to rest.

It had been gradually getting overcast, and now the sky was dark and lowering, save where the glory of the departing sun piled up masses of gold and burning fire, decaying embers of which gleamed here and there through the black veil, and shone redly down upon the earth. The wind began to moan in hollow murmurs, as the sun went down carrying glad day elsewhere; and a train of dull clouds coming up against it, menaced thunder and lightning. Large drops of rain soon began to fall, and, as the storm clouds came sailing onward, others supplied the void they left behind and spread over all the sky. Then was heard the low rumbling of distant thunder, then the lightning quivered, and then the darkness of an hour seemed to have gathered in an instant.

Fearful of taking shelter beneath a tree or hedge, the old man and the child hurried along the highroad, hoping to find some house in which they could seek a refuge from the storm, which had now burst forth in earnest, and every moment increased in violence. Drenched with the pelting rain, confused by the deafening thunder, and bewildered by the glare of the forked lightning, they would have passed a solitary house without being aware of its vicinity, had not a man, who was standing at the door, called lustily to them to enter.

"Your ears ought to be better than other folks' at any rate, if you make so little of the chance of being struck blind," he said, retreating from the door and shading his eyes with his hands as the jagged lightning came again. "What were you going past for, eh?" he added, as he closed the door and led the way along a passage to a room behind.

"We didn't see the house, sir, till we heard you calling," Nell replied.

"No wonder," said the man, "with this lightning in one's eyes, by the by. You had better stand by the fire here, and dry yourselves a bit. You can call for what you like if you want anything. If you don't want anything, you are not obliged to give an order, don't be afraid of that. This is a public-house, that's all. The Valiant Soldier is pretty well known hereabouts."

"Is this house called the Valiant Soldier, sir?" asked Nell.

"I thought everybody knew that," replied the landlord. "Where have you come from, if you don't know the Valiant Soldier as well as the Church catechism? This is the Valiant Soldier, by James Groves—Jem Groves—honest Jem Groves, as is a man of unblemished moral character, and has a good dry skittle-ground. If any man has got anything to say again Jem Groves, let him say it *to* Jem Groves, and Jem Groves can accommodate him with a customer on any terms from four pound a side to forty."

With these words, the speaker tapped himself on the waistcoat to intimate that he was the Jem Groves so highly eulogized; sparred scientifically at a counterfeit Jem Groves, who was sparring at society in general from a black frame over the chimney-piece; and, applying a half-emptied glass of spirits and water to his lips, drank Jem Groves's health.

The night being warm, there was a large screen drawn across the room, for a barrier against the heat of the fire. It seemed as if somebody on the other side of this screen had been insinuating doubts of Mr Groves's prowess, and had thereby given rise to these egotistical expressions, for Mr Groves wound up his defiance by giving a loud knock upon it with his knuckles and pausing for a reply from the other side.

"There an't many men," said Mr Groves, no answer being returned, "who would ventur' to cross Jem Groves under his own roof. There's only one man, I know, that has nerve enough for that, and that man's not a hundred mile from here neither. But he's worth a dozen men, and I let him say of me whatever he likes in consequence—he knows that."

In return for his complimentary address, a very gruff hoarse voice bade Mr Groves "hold his noise and light a candle." And the same voice remarked that the same gentle-man "needn't waste his breath in brag, for most people knew pretty well what sort of stuff he was made of."

"Nell, they're—they're playing cards," whispered the old man, suddenly interested. "Don't you hear them?"

"Look sharp with that candle," said the voice; "it's as much as I can do to see the pips on the cards as it is; and get this shutter closed as quick as you can, will you? Your beer will be the worse for tonight's thunder I expect.—Game! Seven-and-sixpence to me, old Isaac. Hand over."

"Do you hear, Nell, do you hear them?" whispered the old man again, with in-creased earnestness, as the money chinked upon the table.

"I haven't seen such a storm as this," said a sharp cracked voice of most disagreeable quality, when a tremendous peal of thunder had died away, "since the night when old Luke Withers won thirteen times running, upon the red. We all said he had the Devil's luck and his own, and as it was the kind of night for the Devil to be out and busy, I suppose he *was* looking over his shoulder, if anybody could have seen him."

"Ah!" returned the gruff voice; "for all old Luke's winning through thick and thin of late years, I remember the time when he was the unluckiest and unfortunatest of men. He never took a dice-box in his hand, or held a card, but he was plucked, pigeoned, and cleaned out completely."

"Do you hear what he says?" whispered the old man. "Do you hear that, Nell?"

The child saw with astonishment and alarm that his whole appearance had under-gone a complete change. His face was flushed and eager, his eyes were strained, his teeth set, his breath came short and thick, and the hand he laid upon her arm trembled so violently that she shook beneath its grasp.

"Bear witness," he muttered, looking upward, "that I always said it; that I knew it, dreamed of it, felt it was the truth, and that it must be so! What money have we, Nell? Come! I saw you with money yesterday. What money have we? Give it to me."

"No, no, let me keep it, grandfather," said the frightened child. "Let us go away from here. Do not mind the rain. Pray let us go."

"Give it to me, I say," returned the old man fiercely. "Hush, hush, don't cry, Nell. If I spoke sharply, dear, I didn't mean it. It's for thy good. I have wronged thee, Nell, but I will right thee yet, I will indeed. Where is the money?"

"Do not take it," said the child. "Pray do not take it, dear. For both our sakes let me keep it, or let me throw it away—better let me throw it away, than you take it now. Let us go; do let us go."

"Give me the money," returned the old man, "I must have it. There—there—that's my dear Nell. I'll right thee one day, child, I'll right thee, never fear!"

She took from her pocket a little purse. He seized it with the same rapid impatience which had characterized his speech, and hastily made his way to the other side of the screen. It was impossible to restrain him, and the trembling child followed close behind.

The landlord had placed a light upon the table, and was engaged in drawing the curtain of the window. The speakers whom they had heard were two men, who had a pack of cards and some silver money between them, while upon the screen itself the games they had played were scored in chalk. The man with the rough voice was a burly fellow of middle age, with large black whiskers, broad cheeks, a coarse wide mouth, and bull neck, which was pretty freely displayed as his shirt collar was only confined by a loose red neckerchief. He wore his hat, which was of a brownish-white, and had beside him a thick knotted stick. The other man, whom his companion had called Isaac, was of a more slender figure—stooping, and high in the shoulders—with a very ill-favoured face, and a most sinister and villainous squint.

"Now, old gentleman," said Isaac, looking round. "Do you know either of us? This side of the screen is private, sir."

"No offence, I hope," returned the old man.

"But by G——, sir, there *is* offence," said the other, interrupting him, "when you intrude yourself upon a couple of gentlemen who are particularly engaged."

"I had no intention to offend," said the old man, looking anxiously at the cards, "I thought that——"

"But you had no right to think, sir," retorted the other. "What the devil has a man at your time of life to do with thinking?"

"Now, bully boy," said the stout man, raising his eyes from his cards for the first time, "can't you let him speak?"

The landlord, who had apparently resolved to remain neutral until he knew which side of the question the stout man would espouse, chimed in at this place with "Ah, to be sure, can't you let him speak, Isaac List?"

"Can't I let him speak," sneered Isaac in reply, mimicking as nearly as he could, in his shrill voice, the tones of the landlord. "Yes, I can let him speak, Jemmy Groves."

"Well, then, do it, will you?" said the landlord.

Mr List's squint assumed a portentous character, which seemed to threaten a prolongation of this controversy, when his companion, who had been looking sharply at the old man, put a timely stop to it.

"Who knows," said he, with a cunning look, "but the gentleman may have civilly meant to ask if he might have the honour to take a hand with us!"

"I did mean it," cried the old man. "That is what I mean. That is what I want now!"

"I thought so," returned the same man. "Then who knows but the gentleman, anticipating our objection to play for love, civilly desired to play for money?"

The old man replied by shaking the little purse in his eager hand, and then throwing it down upon the table, and gathering up the cards as a miser would clutch at gold.

"Oh! That indeed——" said Isaac; "if that's what the gentleman meant, I beg the gentleman's pardon. Is this the gentleman's little purse? A very pretty little purse. Rather a light purse," added Isaac, throwing it into the air and catching it dexterously, "but enough to amuse a gentleman for half an hour or so."

"We'll make a four-handed game of it, and take in Groves," said the stout man. "Come, Jemmy."

The landlord, who conducted himself like one who was well used to such little parties, approached the table and took his seat. The child, in a perfect agony, drew her grandfather aside, and implored him, even then, to come away.

"Come; and we may be so happy," said the child.

"We *will* be happy," replied the old man hastily. "Let me go, Nell. The means of happiness are on the cards and in the dice. We must rise from little winnings to great. There's little to be won here; but great will come in time. I shall but win back my own, and it's all for thee, my darling."

"God help us!" cried the child. "Oh! what hard fortune brought us here?"

"Hush!" rejoined the old man laying his hand upon her mouth. "Fortune will not bear chiding. We must not reproach her, or she shuns us; I have found that out."

"Now, mister," said the stout man. "If you're not coming yourself, give us the cards, will you?"

"I am coming," cried the old man. "Sit thee down, Nell, sit thee down and look on. Be of good heart, it's all for thee—all—every penny. I don't tell them, no, no, or else they wouldn't play, dreading the chance that such a cause must give me. Look at them. See what they are and what thou art. Who doubts that we must win!"

"The gentleman has thought better of it, and isn't coming," said Isaac, making as though he would rise from the table. "I'm sorry the gentleman's daunted—nothing venture, nothing have—but the gentleman knows best."

"Why, I am ready. You have all been slow but me," said the old man. "I wonder who's more anxious to begin than I."

As he spoke he drew a chair to the table; and the other three closing round it at the same time, the game commenced.

The child sat by, and watched its progress with a troubled mind. Regardless of the run of luck, and mindful only of the desperate passion which had its hold upon her grandfather, losses and gains were to her alike. Exulting in some brief triumph, or cast down by a defeat, there he sat so wild and restless, so feverishly and intensely anxious, so terribly eager, so ravenous for the paltry stakes, that she could have almost better borne to see him dead. And yet she was the innocent cause of all this torture, and he, gambling with such a savage thirst for gain as the most insatiable gambler never felt, had not one selfish thought!

On the contrary, the other three—knaves and gamesters by their trade—while intent upon their game, were yet as cool and quiet as if every virtue had been centered in their breasts. Sometimes one would look up to smile to another, or to snuff the feeble candle, or to glance at the lightning as it shot through the open window and fluttering curtain, or to listen to some louder peal of thunder than the rest, with a kind of momentary impatience, as if it put him out; but there they sat, with a calm indifference to everything but their cards, perfect philosophers in appearance, and with no greater show of passion or excitement than if they had been made of stone.

The storm had raged for full three hours; the lightning had grown fainter and less frequent; the thunder, from seeming to roll and break above their heads, had gradually died away into a deep hoarse distance; and still the game went on, and still the anxious child was quite forgotten.

Chapter XXX

AT length the play came to an end, and Mr Isaac List rose the only winner. Mat and the landlord bore their losses with professional fortitude. Isaac pocketed his gains with the air of a man who had quite made up his mind to win, all along, and was neither surprised nor pleased.

Nell's little purse was exhausted; but, although it lay empty by his side, and the other players had now risen from the table, the old man sat poring over the cards, dealing them as they had been dealt before, and turning up the different hands to see what each man would have held if they had still been playing. He was quite absorbed in the occupation, when the child drew near and laid her hand upon his shoulder, telling him it was near midnight.

"See the curse of poverty, Nell," he said, pointing to the packs he had spread out upon the table. "If I could have gone on a little longer, only a little longer, the luck would have turned on my side. Yes, it's as plain as the marks upon the cards. See here—and there—and here again."

"Put them away," urged the child. "Try to forget them."

"Try to forget them!" he rejoined, raising his haggard face to hers, and regarding her with an incredulous stare. "To forget them! How are we ever to grow rich if I forget them?"

The child could only shake her head.

"No, no, Nell," said the old man, patting her cheek; "they must not be forgotten. We must make amends for this as soon as we can. Patience—patience, and we'll right thee yet, I promise thee. Lose to-day, win to-morrow. And nothing can be won without anxiety and care—nothing. Come, I am ready."

"Do you know what the time is?" said Mr Groves, who was smoking with his friends. "Past twelve o'clock—"

"—And a rainy night," added the stout man.

"The Valiant Soldier, by James Groves. Good beds. Cheap entertainment for man and beast," said Mr Groves, quoting his signboard. "Half-past twelve o'clock."

"It's very late," said the uneasy child. "I wish we had gone before. What will they think of us! It will be two o'clock by the time we get back. What would it cost, sir, if we stopped here?"

"Two good beds, one-and-sixpence; supper and beer, one shilling; total, two shillings and sixpence," replied the Valiant Soldier.

Now, Nell had still the piece of gold sewn in her dress; and when she came to consider the lateness of the hour, and the somnolent habits of Mrs Jarley, and to imagine the state of consternation in which they would certainly throw that good lady by knocking her up in the middle of the night—and when she reflected, on the other hand, that if they remained where they were, and rose early in the morning, they might get back before she awoke, and could plead the violence of the storm by which they had been overtaken, as a good apology for their absence—she decided, after a great deal of hesitation, to remain. She therefore took her grandfather aside, and telling him that she had still enough left to defray the cost of their lodging, proposed that they should stay there for the night.

"If I had had but that money before—if I had only known of it a few minutes ago!" muttered the old man.

"We will decide to stop here if you please," said Nell, turning hastily to the landlord.

"I think that's prudent," returned Mr Groves. "You shall have your suppers directly."

Accordingly, when Mr Groves had smoked his pipe out, knocked out the ashes, and placed it carefully in a corner of the fireplace, with the bowl downwards, he brought in the bread and cheese, and beer, with many high encomiums upon their excellence, and bade his guests to fall to and make themselves at home. Nell and her grandfather ate sparingly, for both were occupied with their own reflections; the other gentlemen, for whose constitutions beer was too weak and tame a liquid, consoled themselves with spirits and tobacco.

As they would leave the house very early in the morning, the child was anxious to pay for their entertainment before they retired to bed. But as she felt the necessity of concealing her little hoard from her grandfather, and had to change the piece of gold, she took it secretly from its place of concealment, and embraced an opportunity of following the landlord when he went out of the room, and tendered it to him in the little bar.

"Will you give me the change here, if you please?" said the child.

Mr James Groves was evidently surprised, and looked at the money, and rang it, and looked at the child, and at the money again, as though he had a mind to inquire how she came by it. The coin being genuine, however, and changed at his house, he probably felt, like a wise landlord, that it was no business of his. At any rate, he counted out the change, and gave it her. The child was returning to the room where they had passed the evening, when she fancied she saw a figure just gliding in at the door. There was nothing but a long dark passage between this door and the place where she had changed the money, and, being very certain that no person had passed in or out while she stood there, the thought struck her that she had been watched.

But by whom? When she re-entered the room, she found its inmates exactly as she had left them. The stout fellow lay upon two chairs, resting his head on his hand, and the squinting man reposed in a similar attitude on the opposite side of the table. Between them sat her grandfather, looking intently at the winner with a kind of hungry admiration, and hanging upon his words as if he were some superior being. She was puzzled for a moment, and looked round to see if any one else was there. No. Then she asked her grandfather in a whisper whether anybody had left the room while she was absent. "No," he said, "nobody."

It must have been her fancy then; and yet it was strange, that, without anything in her previous thoughts to lead to it, she should have imagined this figure so very distinctly. She was still wondering and thinking of it, when a girl came to light her to bed.

The old man took leave of the company at the same time, and they went upstairs together. It was a great, rambling house, with dull corridors and wide staircases which the flaring candles seemed to make more gloomy. She left her grandfather in his chamber, and followed her guide to another, which was at the end of a passage, and approached by some half-dozen crazy steps. This was prepared for her. The girl lingered a little while to talk, and tell her grievances. She had not a good place, she said; the wages were low, and the work was hard. She was going to leave it in a fortnight; the child couldn't recommend her to another, she supposed? Indeed, she was afraid another would be difficult to get after living there, for the house had a very indifferent character; there was far too much card-playing, and suchlike. She was very much mistaken if some of the people who came there oftenest were quite as honest as they might be, but she wouldn't have it known that she had said so, for the world. Then there were some rambling allusions to a rejected sweetheart, who had threatened to go a-soldiering—a final promise of knocking at the door early in the morning—and "Good night."

The child did not feel comfortable when she was left alone. She could not help thinking of the figure stealing through the passage downstairs; and what the girl had said did not tend to reassure her. The men were very ill-looking. They might get their living by robbing and murdering travellers. Who could tell?

Reasoning herself out of these fears, or losing sight of them for a little while, there came the anxiety to which the adventures of the night gave rise. Here was the old passion awakened again in her grandfather's breast, and to what further distraction it might tempt him Heaven only knew. What fears their absence might have occasioned already! Persons might be seeking for them even then. Would they be forgiven in the morning, or turned adrift again? Oh! why had they stopped in that strange place? It would have been better, under any circumstances, to have gone on!

At last, sleep gradually stole upon her—a broken, fitful sleep, troubled by dreams of falling from high towers, and waking with a start and in great terror. A deeper slumber followed this—and then—What! That figure in the room!

A figure was there. Yes, she had drawn up the blind to admit the light when it should dawn, and there, between the foot of the bed and the dark casement, it crouched and slunk along, groping its way with noiseless hands, and stealing round the bed. She had no voice to cry for help, no power to move, but lay still, watching it.

On it came—on, silently and stealthily, to the bed's head. The breath so near her pillow, that she shrank back into it, lest those wandering hands should light upon her face. Back again it stole to the window—then turned its head towards her.

The dark form was a mere blot upon the lighter darkness of the room, but she saw the turning of the head, and felt and knew how the eyes looked and the ears listened. There it remained, motionless as she. At length, still keeping the face towards her, it busied its hands in something, and she heard the chink of money.

Then, on it came again, silent and stealthy as before, and, replacing the garments it had taken from the bedside, dropped upon its hands and knees, and crawled away. How slowly it seemed to move, now that she could hear but not see it, creeping along the floor! It reached the door at last, and stood upon its feet. The steps creaked beneath its noiseless tread, and it was gone.

The first impulse of the child was to fly from the terror of being by herself in that room—to have somebody by—not to be alone—and then her power of speech would be restored. With no consciousness of having moved, she gained the door.

There was the dreadful shadow, pausing at the bottom of the steps.

She could not pass it; she might have done so, perhaps, in the darkness, without being seized, but her blood curdled at the thought. The figure stood quite still, and so did she; not boldly, but of necessity; for going back into the room was hardly less terrible than going on.

The rain beat fast and furiously without, and ran down in plashing streams from the thatched roof. Some summer insect, with no escape into the air, flew blindly to and fro, beating his body against the walls and ceiling, and filling the silent place with his murmurs. The figure moved again. The child involuntarily did the same. Once in her grandfather's room, she would be safe.

It crept along the passage until it came to the very door she longed so ardently to reach. The child, in the agony of being so near, had almost darted forward with the design of bursting into the room and closing it behind her, when the figure stopped again.

The idea flashed suddenly upon her—what if it entered there, and had a design upon the old man's life! She turned faint and sick. It did. It went in. There was a light inside. The figure was now within the chamber, and she, still dumb—quite dumb, and almost senseless—stood looking on.

The door was partly open. Not knowing what she meant to do, but meaning to preserve him or be killed herself, she staggered forward and looked in. What sight was that which met her view!

The bed had not been lain on, but was smooth and empty. And at a table sat the old man himself, the only living creature there, his white face pinched and sharpened by the greediness which made his eyes unnaturally bright, counting the money of which his hands had robbed her.

Chapter XXXI

WITH steps more faltering and unsteady than those with which she had approached the room, the child withdrew from the door, and groped her way back to her own chamber. The terror she had lately felt was nothing compared with that which now oppressed her. No strange robber, no treacherous host conniving at the plunder of his guests, or stealing to their beds to kill them in their sleep, no nightly prowler, however terrible and cruel, could have awakened in her bosom half the dread which the recognition of her silent visitor inspired. The grey-headed old man gliding like a ghost into her room and acting the thief while he supposed her fast asleep, then bearing off his prize and hanging over it with the ghastly exultation she had witnessed, was worse— immeasurably worse, and far more dreadful, for the moment, to reflect upon—than anything her wildest fancy could have suggested. If he should return—there was no lock or bolt upon the door, and if, distrustful of having left some money yet behind, he should come back to seek for more—a vague awe and horror surrounded the idea of his slinking in again with stealthy tread, and turning his face toward the empty bed, while she shrank down close at his feet to avoid his touch, which was almost insupportable. She sat and listened. Hark! A footstep on the stairs, and now the door was slowly opening. It was but imagination, yet imagination had all the terrors of reality; nay, it was worse, for the reality would have come and gone, and there an end, but in imagination it was always coming, and never went away.

The feeling which beset the child was one of dim uncertain horror. She had no fear of the dear old grandfather, in whose love for her this disease of the brain had been engendered; but the man she had seen that night, wrapt in the game of chance, lurking in her room, and counting the money by the glimmering light, seemed like another creature in his shape, a monstrous distortion of his image, a something to recoil from, and be the more afraid of, because it bore a likeness to him, and kept close about her, as he did. She could scarcely connect her own affectionate companion, save by his loss, with this old man, so like yet so unlike him. She had wept to see him dull and quiet. How much greater cause she had for weeping now!

The child sat watching and thinking of these things, until the phantom in her mind so increased in gloom and terror, that she felt it would be a relief to hear the old man's voice, or, if he were asleep, even to see him, and banish some of the fears that clustered round his image. She stole down the stairs and passage again. The door was still ajar as she had left it, and the candle burning as before.

She had her own candle in her hand, prepared to say, if he were waking, that she was uneasy and could not rest, and had come to see if his were still alight. Looking into the room, she saw him lying calmly on his bed, and so took courage to enter.

Fast asleep—no passion in the face, no avarice, no anxiety, no wild desire; all gentle, tranquil, and at peace. This was not the gambler, or the shadow in her room; this was not even the worn and jaded man whose face had so often met her own in the grey morning light; this was her dear old friend, her harmless fellow-traveller, her good, kind grandfather.

She had no fear as she looked upon his slumbering features, but she had a deep and weighty sorrow, and it found its relief in tears.

"God bless him!" said the child, stooping softly to kiss his placid cheek. "I see too well now, that they would indeed part us if they found us out, and shut him up from the light of the sun and sky. He has only me to help him. God bless us both!"

Lighting her candle, she retreated as silently as she had come, and, gaining her own room once more, sat up during the remainder of that long, long, miserable night.

At last the day turned her waning candle pale, and she fell asleep. She was quickly roused by the girl who had shown her up to bed; and, as soon as she was dressed, prepared to go down to her grandfather. But first she searched her pocket and found that her money was all gone—not a sixpence remained.

The old man was ready, and in a few seconds they were on their road. The child thought he rather avoided her eye, and appeared to expect that she would tell him of her loss. She felt she must do that, or he might suspect the truth.

"Grandfather," she said in a tremulous voice, after they had walked about a mile in silence, "do you think they are honest people at the house yonder?"

"Why?" returned the old man, trembling. "Do I think them honest—yes, they played honestly."

"I'll tell you why I ask," rejoined Nell. "I lost some money last night—out of my bedroom I am sure. Unless it was taken by somebody in jest—only in jest, dear grandfather, which would make me laugh heartily if I could but know it—"

"Who would take money in jest?" returned the old man in a hurried manner. "Those who take money, take it to keep. Don't talk of jest."

"Then it was stolen out of my room, dear," said the child, whose last hope was destroyed by the manner of this reply.

"But is there no more, Nell?" said the old man; "no more anywhere? Was it all taken—every farthing of it—was there nothing left?"

"Nothing," replied the child.

"We must get more," said the old man, "we must earn it, Nell, hoard it up, scrape it together, come by it somehow. Never mind this loss. Tell nobody of it, and perhaps we may regain it. Don't ask how;—we may regain it, and a great deal more;—but tell nobody, or trouble may come of it. And so they took it out of thy room, when thou wert asleep!" he added in a compassionate tone, very different from the secret, cunning way in which he had spoken until now. "Poor Nell, poor little Nell!"

The child hung down her head and wept. The sympathising tone in which he spoke was quite sincere; she was sure of that. It was not the lightest part of her sorrow to know that this was done for her.

"Not a word about it to any one but me," said the old man, "no, not even to me," he added hastily, "for it can do no good. All the losses that ever were, are not worth tears from thy eyes, darling. Why should they be, when we will win them back?"

"Let them go," said the child looking up. "Let them go, once and for ever, and I would never shed another tear if every penny had been a thousand pounds."

"Well, well," returned the old man, checking himself as some impetuous answer rose to his lips, "she knows no better. I ought to be thankful for it."

"But listen to me," said the child earnestly, "will you listen to me?"

"Ay, ay, I'll listen," returned the old man, still without looking at her; "a pretty voice. It has always a sweet sound to me. It always had when it was her mother's, poor child."

"Let me persuade you, then—oh, do let me persuade you," said the child, "to think no more of gains or losses, and to try no fortune but the fortune we pursue together."

"We pursue this aim together," retorted her grandfather, still looking away and seeming to confer with himself. "Whose image sanctifies the game?"

"Have we been worse off," resumed the child, "since you forgot these cares, and we have been travelling on together? Have we not been much better and happier without a home to shelter us, than ever we were in that unhappy house, when they were on your mind?"

"She speaks the truth," murmured the old man in the same tone as before. "It must not turn me, but it is the truth—no doubt it is."

"Only remember what we have been since that bright morning when we turned our backs upon it for the last time," said Nell, "only remember what we have been since we have been free of all those miseries—what peaceful days and quiet nights we have had—what pleasant times we have known—what happiness we have enjoyed. If we have been tired or hungry, we have been soon refreshed, and slept the sounder for it. Think what beautiful things we have seen, and how contented we have felt. And why was this blessed change?"

He stopped her with a motion of his hand, and bade her talk to him no more just then, for he was busy. After a time he kissed her cheek, still motioning her to silence, and walked on, looking far before him, and sometimes stopping and gazing with a puckered brow upon the ground, as if he were painfully trying to collect his disordered thoughts. Once she saw tears in his eyes. When he had gone on thus for some time, he took her hand in his as he was accustomed to do, with nothing of the violence or animation of his late manner; and so, by degrees so fine that the child could not trace them, settled down into his usual quiet way, and suffered her to lead him where she would.

When they presented themselves in the midst of the stupendous collection, they found, as Nell had anticipated, that Mrs Jarley was not yet out of bed, and that, although she had suffered some uneasiness on their account overnight, and had indeed sat up for them until past eleven o'clock, she had retired in the persuasion, that, being overtaken by storm at some distance from home, they had sought the nearest shelter, and would not return before morning. Nell immediately applied herself with great assiduity to the decoration and preparation of the room, and had the satisfaction of completing her task, and dressing herself neatly, before the beloved of the Royal Family came down to breakfast.

"We haven't had," said Mrs Jarley when the meal was over, "more than eight of Miss Monflathers's young ladies all the time we've been here, and there's twenty-six of 'em, as I was told by the cook when I asked her a question or two and put her on the free-list. We must try 'em with a parcel of new bills, and you shall take it, my dear, and see what effect that has upon 'em."

The proposed expedition being one of paramount importance, Mrs Jarley adjusted Nell's bonnet with her own hands, and declaring that she certainly did look very pretty, and reflected credit on the establishment, dismissed her with many commendations, and certain needful directions as to the turnings on the right which she was to take, and the turnings on the left which she was to avoid. Thus instructed, Nell had no difficulty in finding out Miss Monflathers's Boarding and Day Establishment, which was a large house, with a high wall, and a large garden gate with a large brass plate, and a small grating through which Miss Monflathers's parlour-maid inspected all visitors before admitting them; for nothing in the shape of a man—no, not even a milkman—was suffered, without special licence, to pass that gate. Even the tax-gatherer, who was stout, and wore spectacles and a broad-brimmed hat, had the taxes handed through the grating. More obdurate than gate of adamant or brass, this gate of Miss Monflathers's frowned on all mankind. The very butcher respected it as a gate of mystery, and left off whistling when he rang the bell.

As Nell approached the awful door, it turned slowly upon its hinges with a creaking noise, and, forth from the solemn grove beyond, came a long file of young ladies, two and two, all with open books in their hands, and some with parasols likewise. And last of the goodly procession came Miss Monflathers, bearing herself a parasol of lilac silk, and supported by two smiling teachers, each mortally envious of the other, and devoted unto Miss Monflathers.

Confused by the looks and whispers of the girls, Nell stood with downcast eyes and suffered the procession to pass on, until Miss Monflathers, bringing up the rear, approached her, when she curtseyed and presented her little packet; on receipt whereof Miss Monflathers commanded that the line should halt.

"You're the wax-work child, are you not?" said Miss Monflathers.

"Yes, ma'am," replied Nell, colouring deeply, for the young ladies had collected about her, and she was the centre on which all eyes were fixed.

"And don't you think you must be a very wicked little child," said Miss Monflathers, who was of rather uncertain temper, and lost no opportunity of impressing moral truths upon the tender minds of the young ladies, "to be a wax-work child at all?"

Poor Nell had never viewed her position in this light, and not knowing what to say, remained silent, blushing more deeply than before.

"Don't you know," said Miss Monflathers, "that it's very naughty and unfeminine, and a perversion of the properties wisely and benignantly transmitted to us, with expansive powers to be roused from their dormant state through the medium of cultivation?"

The two teachers murmured their respectful approval of this home-thrust, and looked at Nell as though they would have said that there indeed Miss Monflathers had hit her very hard. Then they smiled and glanced at Miss Monflathers, and then, their eyes meeting, they exchanged looks which plainly said that each considered herself smiler in ordinary to Miss Monflathers, and regarded the other as having no right to smile, and that her so doing was an act of presumption and impertinence.

"Don't you feel how naughty it is of you," resumed Miss Monflathers, "to be a wax-work child, when you might have the proud consciousness of assisting, to the extent of your infant powers, the manufactures of your country; of improving your mind by the constant contemplation of the steam-engine; and of earning a comfortable and independent subsistence of from two-and-ninepence to three shillings per week? Don't you know that the harder you are at work, the happier you are?"

" 'How doth the little———' " murmured one of the teachers, in quotation from Doctor Watts.

"Eh?" said Miss Monflathers, turning smartly round. "Who said that?"

Of course the teacher who had not said it indicated the rival who had, whom Miss Monflathers frowningly requested to hold her peace; by that means throwing the informing teacher into raptures of joy.

"The little busy bee," said Miss Monflathers, drawing herself up, "is applicable only to genteel children.

> In books, or work, or healthful play

is quite right as far as they are concerned; and the work means painting on velvet, fancy needle-work, or embroidery. In such cases as these," pointing to Nell, with her parasol, "and in the case of all poor people's children, we should read it thus:

> In work, work, work. In work alway
> Let my first years be past,
> That I may give for ev'ry day
> Some good account at last."

A deep hum of applause rose not only from the two teachers, but from all the pupils, who were equally astonished to hear Miss Monflathers improvising after this brilliant style; for although she had been long known as a politician, she had never appeared before as an original poet. Just then somebody happened to discover that Nell was crying, and all eyes were again turned towards her.

There were indeed tears in her eyes, and drawing out her handkerchief to brush them away, she happened to let it fall. Before she could stoop to pick it up, one young lady of about fifteen or sixteen, who had been standing a little apart from the others, as though she had no recognised place among them, sprang forward and put it in her hand. She was gliding timidly away again, when she was arrested by the governess.

"It was Miss Edwards who did that, I *know,*" said Miss Monflathers predictively. "Now I am sure that was Miss Edwards."

It was Miss Edwards, and everybody said it was Miss Edwards, and Miss Edwards herself admitted that it was.

"Is it not," said Miss Monflathers, putting down her parasol to take a severer view of the offender. "a most remarkable thing, Miss Edwards, that you have an attachment to the lower classes which always draws you to their sides; or, rather, is it not a most extraordinary thing that all I say and do will not wean you from propensities which your original station in life have unhappily rendered habitual to you, you extremely vulgar-minded girl?"

"I really intended no harm, ma'am," said a sweet voice. "It was a momentary impulse, indeed."

"An impulse!" repeated Miss Monflathers scornfully. "I wonder that you presume to speak of impulses to me"—both the teachers assented—"I am astonished"—both the teachers were astonished—"I suppose it is an impulse which induces you to take the part of every grovelling and debased person that comes in your way"—both the teachers supposed so too.

"But I would have you know, Miss Edwards," resumed the governess in a tone of increased severity, "that you cannot be permitted—if it be only for the sake of preserving a proper example and decorum in this establishment—that you cannot be permitted, and that you shall not be permitted, to fly in the face of your superiors in this exceedingly gross manner. If *you* have no reason to feel a becoming pride before wax-work children, there are young ladies here who have, and you must either defer to those young ladies or leave the establishment, Miss Edwards."

This young lady, being motherless and poor, was apprenticed at the school—taught for nothing—teaching others what she learnt, for nothing—boarded for nothing—lodged for nothing—and set down and rated as something immeasurably less than nothing, by all the dwellers in the house. The servant-maids felt her inferiority, for they were better treated; free to come and go, and regarded in their stations with much more respect. The teachers were infinitely superior, for they had paid to go to school in their time, and were paid now. The pupils cared little for a companion who had no grand stories to tell about home; no friends to come with post-horses, and be received in all humility, with cake and wine, by the governess; no deferential servant to attend and bear her home for the holidays; nothing genteel to talk about, and nothing to display. But why was Miss Monflathers always vexed and irritated with the poor apprentice—how did that come to pass?

Why, the gayest feather in Miss Monflathers's cap, and the brightest glory of Miss Monflathers's school, was a baronet's daughter—the real live daughter of a real live baronet—who, by some extraordinary reversal of the Laws of Nature, was not only plain in features but dull in intellect, while the poor apprentice had both a ready wit, and a handsome face and figure. It seems incredible. Here was Miss Edwards, who only paid a small premium which had been spent long ago, every day outshining and excelling the baronet's daughter, who learned all the extras (or was taught them all) and whose half-yearly bill came to double that of any other young lady's in the school, making no account of the honour and reputation of her pupilage. Therefore, and because she was a dependent, Miss Monflathers had a great dislike to Miss Edwards, and was spiteful to her, and aggravated by her, and, when she had compassion on little Nell, verbally fell upon and maltreated her as we have already seen.

"You will not take the air to-day, Miss Edwards," said Miss Monflathers. "Have the goodness to retire to your own room, and not to leave it without permission."

The poor girl was moving hastily away, when she was suddenly, in nautical phrase, 'brought to' by a subdued shriek from Miss Monflathers.

"She has passed me without any salute!" cried the governess, raising her eyes to the sky. "She has actually passed me without the slightest acknowledgment of my presence!"

The young lady turned and curtsied. Nell could see that she raised her dark eyes to the face of her superior, and that their expression, and that of her whole attitude for the instant, was one of mute but most touching appeal against this ungenerous usage. Miss Monflathers only tossed her head in reply, and the great gate closed upon a bursting heart.

"As for you, you wicked child," said Miss Monflathers, turning to Nell, "tell your mistress that if she presumes to take the liberty of sending to me any more, I will write to the legislative authorities and have her put in the stocks, or compelled to do penance in a white sheet; and you may depend upon it that you shall certainly experience the treadmill if you dare to come here again. Now, ladies, on."

The procession filed off, two and two, with the books and parasols, and Miss Monflathers, calling the baronet's daughter to walk with her and smooth her ruffled feelings, discarded the two teachers—who by this time had exchanged their smiles for looks of sympathy—and left them to bring up the rear, and hate each other a little more for being obliged to walk together.

Chapter XXXII

MRS Jarley's wrath on first learning that she had been threatened with the indignity of Stocks and Penance, passed all description. The genuine and only Jarley exposed to public scorn, jeered by children, and flouted by beadles! The delight of the Nobility and Gentry shorn of a bonnet which a Lady Mayoress might have sighed to wear, and arrayed in a white sheet as a spectacle of mortification and humility! And Miss Monflathers, the audacious creature who presumed, even in the dimmest and remotest distance of her imagination, to conjure up the degrading picture. "I am a'most inclined," said Mrs Jarley, bursting with the fulness of her anger and the weakness of her means of revenge, "to turn atheist when I think of it!"

But instead of adopting this course of retaliation, Mrs Jarley, on second thoughts, brought out the suspicious bottle, and ordering glasses to be set forth upon her favourite drum, and sinking into a chair behind it, called her satellites about her, and to them several times recounted, word for word, the affronts she had received. This done, she begged them in a kind of deep despair to drink; then laughed, then cried, then took a little sip herself, then laughed and cried again, and took a little more; and so by degrees the worthy lady went on, increasing in smiles and decreasing in tears, until at last she could not laugh enough at Miss Monflathers, who, from being an object of dire vexation, became one of sheer ridicule and absurdity.

"For which of us is best off, I wonder," quoth Mrs Jarley, "she or me! It's only talking, when all is said and done, and if she talks of me in the stocks, why I can talk of her in the stocks, which is a good deal funnier if we come to that. Lord, what *does* it matter, after all!"

Having arrived at this comfortable frame of mind (to which she had been greatly assisted by certain short interjectional remarks of the philosophic George), Mrs Jarley consoled Nell with many kind words, and requested as a personal favour that whenever she thought of Miss Monflathers she would do nothing else but laugh at her, all the days of her life.

So ended Mrs Jarley's wrath, which subsided long before the going down of the sun. Nell's anxieties, however, were of a deeper kind, and the checks they imposed upon her cheerfulness were not so easily removed.

That evening, as she had dreaded, her grandfather stole away, and did not come back until the night was far spent. Worn out as she was, and fatigued in mind and body, she sat up alone, counting the minutes, until he returned—penniless, broken-spirited, and wretched, but still hotly bent upon his infatuation.

"Get me money," he said wildly, as they parted for the night. "I must have money,

Nell. It shall be paid thee back with gallant interest one day, but all the money that comes unto thy hands must be mine—not for myself, but to use for thee. Remember, Nell, to use for thee!"

What could the child do, with the knowledge she had, but give him every penny that came into her hands, lest he should be tempted on to rob their benefactress? If she told the truth (so thought the child) he would be treated as a madman; if she did not supply him with money, he would supply himself; supplying him, she fed the fire that burnt him up, and put him perhaps beyond recovery. Distracted by these thoughts, borne down by the weight of the sorrow which she dared not tell, tortured by a crowd of apprehensions whenever the old man was absent, and dreading alike his stay and his return, the colour forsook her cheek, her eye grew dim, and her heart was oppressed and heavy. All her old sorrows had come back upon her, augmented by new fears and doubts; by day they were ever present to her mind; by night they hovered round her pillow, and haunted her in dreams.

It was natural that, in the midst of her affliction, she should often revert to that sweet young lady of whom she had only caught a hasty glance, but whose sympathy, expressed in one slight brief action, dwelt in her memory like the kindnesses of years. She would often think, if she had such a friend as that to whom to tell her griefs, how much lighter her heart would be—that if she were but free to hear that voice, she would be happier. Then she would wish that she were something better, that she were not quite so poor and humble, that she dared address her without fearing a repulse; and then feel that there was an immeasurable distance between them, and have no hope that the young lady thought of her any more.

It was now holiday-time at the schools, and the young ladies had gone home, and Miss Monflathers was reported to be flourishing in London and damaging the hearts of middle-aged gentlemen, but nobody said anything about Miss Edwards, whether she had gone home, or whether she had any home to go to, whether she was still at the school, or anything about her. But one evening, as Nell was returning from a lonely walk, she happened to pass the inn where the stagecoaches stopped, just as one drove up, and there was the beautiful girl she so well remembered, pressing forward to embrace a young child whom they were helping down from the roof.

Well, this was her sister, her little sister, much younger than Nell, whom she had not seen (so the story went afterwards) for five years, and to bring whom to that place on a short visit, she had been saving her poor means all that time. Nell felt as if her heart would break when she saw them meet. They went a little apart from the knot of people who had congregated about the coach, and fell upon each other's neck, and sobbed, and wept with joy. Their plain and simple dress, the distance which the child had come alone, their agitation and delight, and the tears they shed, would have told their history by themselves.

They became a little more composed in a short time, and went away, not so much hand in hand as clinging to each other. "Are you sure you're happy, sister?" said the child as they passed where Nell was standing. "Quite happy now," she answered. "But always?" said the child. "Ah, sister, why do you turn away your face?"

Nell could not help following at a little distance. They went to the house of an old nurse, where the elder sister had engaged a bedroom for the child. "I shall come to you early every morning," she said, "and we can be together all the day."—"Why not at night-time too? Dear sister, would they be angry with you for *that?*"

Why were the eyes of little Nell wet, that night, with tears like those of the two sisters? Why did she bear a grateful heart because they had met, and feel it pain to think that they would shortly part? Let us not believe that any selfish reference—unconscious though it might have been—to her own trials awoke this sympathy, but thank God that the innocent joys of others can strongly move us, and that we, even in our fallen nature, have one source of pure emotion which must be prized in Heaven!

By morning's cheerful glow, but oftener still by evening's gentle light, the child, with a respect for the short and happy intercourse of these two sisters which forbade her to approach and say a thankful word, although she yearned to do so, followed them at a distance in their walks and rambles, stopping when they stopped, sitting on the grass when they sat down, rising when they went on, and feeling it a companionship and delight to be so near them. Their evening walk was by the river's side. Here, every night, the child was too, unseen by them, unthought of, unregarded; but feeling as if they were her friends, as if they had confidences and trusts together, as if her load were lightened and less hard to bear; as if they mingled their sorrows, and found mutual consolation. It was a weak fancy perhaps, the childish fancy of a young and lonely creature; but night after night, and still the sisters loitered in the same place, and still the child followed with a mild and softened heart.

She was much startled, on returning home one night, to find that Mrs Jarley had commanded an announcement to be prepared, to the effect that the stupendous collection would only remain in its present quarters one day longer; in fulfilment of which threat (for all announcements connected with public amusements are well known to be irrevocable and most exact), the stupendous collection shut up next day.

"Are we going from this place directly, ma'am?" said Nell.

"Look here, child," returned Mrs Jarley. "That'll inform you." And so saying, Mrs Jarley produced another announcement, wherein it was stated, that, in consequence of numerous inquiries at the wax-work door, and in consequence of crowds having been disappointed in obtaining admission, the Exhibition would be continued for one week longer, and would reopen next day.

"For now that the schools are gone, and the regular sight-seers exhausted," said Mrs Jarley, "we come to the General Public, and they want stimulating."

Upon the following day at noon, Mrs Jarley established herself behind the highly ornamented table, attended by the distinguished effigies before mentioned, and ordered the doors to be thrown open for the readmission of a discerning and enlightened public. But the first day's operations were by no means of a successful character, inasmuch as the general public, though they manifested a lively interest in Mrs Jarley personally, and such of her waxen satellites as were to be seen for nothing, were not affected by any impulses moving them to the payment of sixpence a head. Thus, notwithstanding that a great many people continued to stare at the entry and the figures therein displayed; and remained there with great perseverance, by the hour at a time, to hear the barrel-organ played and to read the bills; and notwithstanding that they were kind enough to recommend their friends to patronise the exhibition in the like manner, until the doorway was regularly blockaded by half the population of the town, who, when they went off duty, were relieved by the other half; it was not found that the treasury was any the richer, or that the prospects of the establishment were at all encouraging.

In this depressed state of the classical market, Mrs Jarley made extraordinary efforts to stimulate the popular taste, and whet the popular curiosity. Certain machinery in the body of the nun on the leads over the door was cleaned up and put in motion, so that the figure shook its head paralytically all day long, to the great admiration of a drunken, but very Protestant barber over the way, who looked upon the said paralytic motion as typical of the degrading effect wrought upon the human mind by the ceremonies of the

Romish Church, and discoursed upon that theme with great eloquence and morality. The two carters constantly passed in and out of the exhibition room, under various disguises, protesting aloud that the sight was better worth the money than anything they had beheld in all their lives, and urging the bystanders, with tears in their eyes, not to neglect such a brilliant gratification. Mrs Jarley sat in the pay-place, chinking silver moneys from noon till night, and solemnly calling upon the crowd to take notice that the price of admission was only sixpence, and that the departure of the whole collection, on a short tour among the Crowned Heads of Europe, was positively fixed for that day week.

"So be in time, be in time, be in time," said Mrs Jarley, at the close of every such address. "Remember that this is Jarley's stupendous collection of upwards of One Hundred Figures, and that it is the only collection in the world; all others being imposters and deceptions. Be in time, be in time, be in time!"

Chapter XXXIII

A S the course of this tale requires that we should become acquainted, somewhere hereabouts, with a few particulars connected with the domestic economy of Mr Sampson Brass, and as a more convenient place than the present is not likely to occur for that purpose, the historian takes the friendly reader by the hand, and springing with him into the air, and cleaving the same at a greater rate than ever Don Cleophas Leandro Perez Zambullo and his familiar travelled through that pleasant region in company, alights with him upon the pavement of Bevis Marks.

The intrepid aeronauts alight before a small dark house, once the residence of Mr Sampson Brass.

In the parlour window of this little habitation, which is so close upon the footway that the passenger who takes the wall brushes the dim glass with his coat sleeve—much to its improvement, for it is very dirty—in this parlour window in the days of its occupation by Sampson Brass, there hung, all awry and slack, and discoloured by the sun, a curtain of faded green, so threadbare from long service as by no means to intercept the view of the little dark room, but rather to afford a favourable medium through which to observe it accurately. There was not much to look at. A rickety table, with spare bundles of papers, yellow and ragged from long carriage in the pocket, ostentatiously displayed upon its top; a couple of stools set face to face on opposite sides of this crazy piece of furniture; a treacherous old chair by the fireplace, whose withered arms had hugged full many a client and helped to squeeze him dry; a second-hand wig-box, used as a depository for blank writs and declarations and other small forms of law, once the sole contents of the head which belonged to the wig which belonged to the box, as they were now of the box itself; two or three common books of practice; a jar of ink, a pounce box, a stunted hearth-broom, a carpet trodden to shreds but still clinging with the tightness of desperation to its tacks—these, with the yellow wainscot of the walls, the smoke-discoloured ceiling, the dust and cobwebs, were among the most prominent decorations of the office of Mr Sampson Brass.

But this was mere still-life, of no greater importance than the plate, "Brass, Solicitor," upon the door, and the bill, "First floor to let to a single gentleman," which was tied to the knocker. The office commonly held two examples of animated nature, more to the purpose of this history, and in whom it has a stronger interest and more particular concern.

Of these, one was Mr Brass himself, who has already appeared in these pages. The other was his clerk, assistant, housekeeper, secretary, confidential plotter, adviser, intriguer, and bill of cost increaser, Miss Brass—a kind of Amazon at common law, of whom it may be desirable to offer a brief description.

Miss Sally Brass, then, was a lady of thirty-five or thereabouts, of a gaunt and bony figure, and a resolute bearing, which if it repressed the softer emotions of love, and kept admirers at a distance, certainly inspired a feeling akin to awe in the breasts of those male strangers who had the happiness to approach her. In face she bore a striking resemblance to her brother, Sampson—so exact, indeed, was the likeness between them, that had it consorted with Miss Brass's maiden modesty and gentle womanhood to have assumed her brother's clothes in a frolic and sat down beside him, it would have been difficult for the oldest friend of the family to determine which was Sampson and which Sally, especially as the lady carried upon her upper lip certain reddish demonstrations, which, if the imagination had been assisted by her attire, might have been mistaken for a beard. These were, however, in all probability, nothing more than eyelashes in a wrong place, as the eyes of Miss Brass were quite free from any such natural impertinencies. In complexion Miss Brass was sallow—rather a dirty sallow, so to speak—but this hue was agreeably relieved by the healthy glow which mantled in the extreme tip of her laughing nose. Her voice was exceedingly impressive—deep and rich in quality, and, once heard, not easily forgotten. Her usual dress was a green gown, in colour not unlike the curtain of the office window, made tight to the figure, and terminating at the throat, where it was fastened behind by a peculiarly large and massive button. Feeling, no doubt, that simplicity and plainness are the soul of elegance, Miss Brass wore no collar or kerchief except upon her head, which was invariably ornamented with a brown gauze scarf, like the wing of the fabled vampire, and which, twisted into any form that happened to suggest itself, formed an easy and graceful headdress.

Such was Miss Brass in person. In mind, she was of a strong and vigorous turn, having from her earliest youth devoted herself with uncommon ardour to the study of the law; not wasting her speculations upon its eagle flights, which are rare, but tracing it attentively through all the slippery and eel-like crawlings in which it commonly pursues its way. Nor had she, like many persons of great intellect, confined herself to theory, or stopped short where practical usefulness begins; inasmuch as she could ingross, fair-copy, fill up printed forms with perfect accuracy, and in short transact any ordinary duty of the office down to pouncing a skin of parchment or mending a pen. It is difficult to understand how, possessed of these combined attractions, she should remain Miss Brass; but whether she had steeled her heart against mankind, or whether those who might have wooed and won her, were deterred by fears that, being learned in the law, she might have too near her fingers' ends those particular statutes which regulate what are familiarly termed actions for breach, certain it is that she was still in a state of celibacy, and still in daily occupation of her old stool opposite to that of her brother Sampson. And equally certain it is, by the way, that between these two stools a great many people had come to the ground.

One morning Mr Sampson Brass sat upon his stool copying some legal process, and viciously digging his pen deep into the paper, as if he were writing upon the very heart of the party against whom it was directed; and Miss Sally Brass sat upon her stool making a new pen preparatory to drawing out a little bill, which was her favourite occupation; and so they sat in silence for a long time, until Miss Brass broke silence.

"Have you nearly done, Sammy?" said Miss Brass; for in her mild and feminine lips, Sampson became Sammy, and all things were softened down.

"No," returned her brother. "It would have been all done though, if you had helped at the right time."

"Oh, yes, indeed," cried Miss Sally; "you want my help, don't you—*you,* too, that are going to keep a clerk!"

"Am I going to keep a clerk for my own pleasure, or because of my own wish, you provoking rascal?" said Mr Brass, putting his pen in his mouth, and grinning spitefully at his sister. "What do you taunt me about going to keep a clerk for?"

It may be observed in this place, lest the fact of Mr Brass calling a lady a rascal, should occasion any wonderment or surprise, that he was so habituated to having her near him in a man's capacity, that he had gradually accustomed himself to talk to her as though she were really a man. And this feeling was so perfectly reciprocal, that not only did Mr Brass often call Miss Brass a rascal, or even put an adjective before the rascal, but Miss Brass looked upon it as quite a matter of course, and was as little moved as any other lady would be by being called an angel.

"What do you taunt me, after three hours' talk last night, with going to keep a clerk for?" repeated Mr Brass, grinning again with the pen in his mouth, like some nobleman's or gentleman's crest. "Is it my fault?"

"All I know is," said Miss Sally, smiling drily, for she delighted in nothing so much as irritating her brother, "that if every one of your clients is to force us to keep a clerk, whether we want to or not, you had better leave off business, strike yourself off the roll, and get taken in execution as soon as you can."

"Have we got any other client like him?" said Brass. "Have we got any other client like him, now—will you answer me that?"

"Do you mean in the face?" said his sister.

"Do I mean in the face!" sneered Sampson Brass, reaching over to take up the bill-book, and fluttering its leaves rapidly. "Look here—Daniel Quilp, Esquire—Daniel Quilp, Esquire—Daniel Quilp, Esquire—all through. Whether should I take a clerk that he recommends, and says 'this is the man for you,' or lose all this—eh?"

Miss Sally deigned to make no reply, but smiled again, and went on with her work.

"But I know what it is," resumed Brass after a short silence. "You're afraid you won't have as long a finger in the business as you've been used to have. Do you think I don't see through that?"

"The business wouldn't go on very long, I expect, without me," returned his sister composedly. "Don't you be a fool and provoke me, Sammy, but mind what you're doing, and do it."

Sampson Brass, who was at heart in great fear of his sister, sulkily bent over his writing again, and listened as she said:

"If I determined that the clerk ought not to come, of course he wouldn't be allowed to come. You know that well enough, so don't talk nonsense."

Mr Brass received this observation with increased meekness, merely remarking, under his breath, that he didn't like that kind of joking, and that Miss Sally would be "a much better fellow" if she forbore to aggravate him. To this compliment Miss Sally replied, that she had a relish for the amusement, and had no intention to forego its gratification. Mr Brass not caring, as it seemed, to pursue the subject any further, they both plied their pens at a great pace, and there the discussion ended.

While they were thus employed, the window was suddenly darkened, as by some person standing close against it. As Mr Brass and Miss Sally looked up to ascertain the cause, the top sash was nimbly lowered from without, and Quilp thrust in his head.

"Hallo!" he said, standing on tiptoe on the window-sill, and looking down into the room. "Is there anybody at home? Is there any of the Devil's ware here? Is Brass at a premium, eh?"

"Ha, ha, ha!" laughed the lawyer in an affected ecstasy. "Oh, very good, sir! Oh, very good indeed! Quite eccentric! Dear me, what humour he has!"

"Is that my Sally?" croaked the dwarf, ogling the fair Miss Brass. "Is it Justice with the bandage off her eyes, and without the sword and scales? Is it the Strong Arm of the Law? Is it the Virgin of Bevis?"

"What an amazing flow of spirits!" cried Brass. "Upon my word, it's quite extraordinary!"

"Open the door," said Quilp, "I've got him here. Such a clerk for you, Brass, such a prize, such an ace of trumps. Be quick and open the door, or, if there's another lawyer near and he should happen to look out of window, he'll snap him up before your eyes, he will."

It is probable that the loss of the phoenix of clerks, even to a rival practitioner, would not have broken Mr Brass's heart; but, pretending great alacrity, he rose from his seat, and going to the door, returned, introducing his client, who led by the hand no less a person than Mr Richard Swiveller.

"There she is," said Quilp, stopping short at the door, and wrinkling up his eyebrows as he looked towards Miss Sally; "there is the woman I ought to have married— there is the beautiful Sarah—there is the female who has all the charms of her sex and none of their weaknesses. Oh, Sally, Sally!"

To this amorous address Miss Brass briefly responded "Bother!"

"Hard-hearted as the metal from which she takes her name," said Quilp. "Why don't she change it—melt down the brass, and take another name?"

"Hold your nonsense, Mr Quilp, do," returned Miss Sally, with a grim smile. "I wonder you're not ashamed of yourself before a strange young man."

"The strange young man," said Mr Quilp, handing Dick Swiveller forward, "is too susceptible himself not to understand me well. This is Mr Swiveller, my intimate friend—a gentleman of good family and great expectations, but who, having rather involved himself by youthful indiscretion, is content for a time to fill the humble station of a clerk—humble, but here most enviable. What a delicious atmosphere!"

If Mr Quilp spoke figuratively, and meant to imply that the air breathed by Miss Sally Brass was sweetened and rarefied by that dainty creature, he had doubtless good reason for what he said. But if he spoke of the delights of the atmosphere of Mr Brass's office in a literal sense, he had certainly a peculiar taste, as it was of a close and earthy kind, and, besides being frequently impregnated with strong whiffs of the second-hand wearing apparel exposed for sale in Duke's Place and Houndsditch, had a decided flavour of rats and mice, and a taint of mouldiness. Perhaps some doubts of its pure delight presented themselves to Mr Swiveller, as he gave vent to one or two short abrupt sniffs, and looked incredulously at the grinning dwarf.

"Mr Swiveller," said Quilp, "being pretty well accustomed to the agricultural pursuits of sowing wild oats, Miss Sally, prudently considers that half a loaf is better than no bread. To be out of harm's way he prudently thinks is something too, and therefore he accepts your brother's offer. Brass, Mr Swiveller is yours."

"I am very glad, sir," said Mr Brass, "very glad indeed. Mr Swiveller, sir, is very fortunate to have your friendship. You may be very proud, sir, to have the friendship of Mr Quilp."

Dick murmured something about never wanting a friend or a bottle to give him, and also gasped forth his favourite allusion to the wing of friendship and its never moulting a feather; but his faculties appeared to be absorbed in the contemplation of Miss Sally Brass, at whom he stared with blank and rueful looks, which delighted the watchful dwarf beyond measure. As to the divine Miss Sally herself, she rubbed her hands as men of business do, and took a few turns up and down the office with her pen behind her ear.

"I suppose," said the dwarf, turning briskly to his legal friend, "that Mr Swiveller enters upon his duties at once? It's Monday morning."

"At once, if you please, sir, by all means," returned Brass.

"Miss Sally will teach him law, the delightful study of the law," said Quilp; "she'll be his guide, his friend, his companion, his Blackstone, his Coke upon Littleton, his Young Lawyer's Best Companion."

"He is exceedingly eloquent," said Brass, like a man abstracted, and looking at the roofs of the opposite houses, with his hands in his pockets; "he has an extraordinary flow of language. Beautiful, really."

"With Miss Sally," Quilp went on, "and the beautiful fictions of the law, his days will pass like minutes. Those charming creations of the poet, John Doe and Richard Roe, when they first dawn upon him, will open a new world for the enlargement of his mind and the improvement of his heart."

"Oh, beautiful, beautiful! Beau-ti-ful indeed!" cried Brass. "It's a treat to hear him!"

"Where will Mr Swiveller sit?" said Quilp, looking round.

"Why, we'll buy another stool, sir," returned Brass. "We hadn't any thoughts of having a gentleman with us, sir, until you were kind enough to suggest it, and our accommodation's not extensive. We'll look about for a second-hand stool, sir. In the meantime, if Mr Swiveller will take my seat, and try his hand at a fair copy of this ejectment, as I shall be out pretty well all the morning—"

"Walk with me," said Quilp. "I have a word or two to say to you on points of business. Can you spare the time?"

"Can I spare the time to walk with *you,* sir? You're joking, sir, you're joking with me," replied the lawyer, putting on his hat. "I'm ready, sir, quite ready. My time must be fully occupied indeed, sir, not to leave me time to walk with you. It's not everybody, sir, who has an opportunity of improving himself by the conversation of Mr Quilp."

The dwarf glanced sarcastically at his brazen friend, and, with a short dry cough, turned upon his heel to bid adieu to Miss Sally. After a very gallant parting on his side, and a very cool and gentlemanly sort of one on hers, he nodded to Dick Swiveller, and withdrew with the attorney.

Dick stood at the desk in a state of utter stupefaction, staring with all his might at the beauteous Sally, as if she had been some curious animal whose like had never lived. When the dwarf got into the street, he mounted again upon the window-sill, and looked into the office for a moment with a grinning face, as a man might peep into a cage. Dick glanced upward at him, but without any token of recognition; and long after he had disappeared, still stood gazing upon Miss Sally Brass, seeing or thinking of nothing else, and rooted to the spot.

Miss Brass being by this time deep in the bill of costs, took no notice whatever of Dick, but went scratching on, with a noisy pen, scoring down the figures with evident delight, and working like a steam-engine. There stood Dick, gazing now at the green gown, now at the brown headdress, now at the face, and now at the rapid pen, in a state of stupid perplexity, wondering how he got into the company of that strange monster, and whether it was a dream and he would ever wake. At last he heaved a deep sigh, and began slowly pulling off his coat.

Mr Swiveller pulled off his coat, and folded it up with great elaboration, staring at Miss Sally all the time; then put on a blue jacket with a double row of gilt buttons, which he had originally ordered for aquatic expeditions, but had brought with him that morning for office purposes; and, still keeping his eye upon her, suffered himself to drop down silently upon Mr Brass's stool. Then he underwent a relapse, and becoming powerless again, rested his chin upon his hand, and opened his eyes so wide, that it appeared quite out of the question that he could ever close them any more.

When he had looked so long that he could see nothing, Dick took his eyes off the fair object of his amazement, turned over the leaves of the draft he was to copy, dipped his pen into the inkstand, and at last, and by slow approaches, began to write. But he had not written half a dozen words when, reaching over to the inkstand to take a fresh dip, he happened to raise his eyes, and there was the intolerable brown headdress—there was the green gown—there, in short, was Miss Sally Brass, arrayed in all her charms, and more tremendous than ever.

This happened so often, that Mr Swiveller by degrees began to feel strange influences creeping over him—horrible desires to annihilate this Sally Brass—mysterious promptings to knock her headdress off and try how she looked without it. There was a very large ruler on the table—a large, black, shining ruler. Mr Swiveller took it up and began to rub his nose with it.

From rubbing his nose with the ruler, to poising it in his hand and giving it an occasional flourish after the tomahawk manner, the transition was easy and natural. In some of these flourishes it went close to Miss Sally's head; the ragged edges of the headdress fluttered with the wind it raised; advance it but an inch, and that great brown knot was on the ground: yet still the unconscious maiden worked away, and never raised her eyes.

Well, this was a great relief. It was a good thing to write doggedly and obstinately until he was desperate, and then snatch up the ruler and whirl it about the brown headdress with the consciousness that he could have it off if he liked. It was a good thing to draw it back, and rub his nose very hard with it, if he thought Miss Sally was going to look up, and to recompense himself with more hardy flourishes when he found she was still absorbed. By these means Mr Swiveller calmed the agitation of his feelings, until his applications to the ruler became less fierce and frequent, and he could even write as many as half a dozen consecutive lines without having recourse to it—which was a great victory.

Chapter XXXIV

I N course of time, that is to say, after a couple of hours or so, of diligent application, Miss Brass arrived at the conclusion of her task, and recorded the fact by wiping her pen upon the green gown, and taking a pinch of snuff from a little round tin box which she carried in her pocket. Having disposed of this temperate refreshment, she arose from her stool, tied her papers into a formal packet with red tape, and taking them under her arm, marched out of the office.

Mr Swiveller had scarcely sprung off his seat and commenced the performance of a maniac hornpipe, when he was interrupted, in the fulness of his joy at being again alone, by the opening of the door, and the reappearance of Miss Sally's head.

"I am going out," said Miss Brass.

"Very good, ma'am," returned Dick. "And don't hurry yourself on my account to come back, ma'am," he added inwardly.

"If anybody comes on office business, take their messages, and say that the gentleman who attends to that matter isn't in at present, will you?" said Miss Brass.

"I will, ma'am," replied Dick.

"I shan't be very long," said Miss Brass, retiring.

"I'm sorry to hear it, ma'am," rejoined Dick when she had shut the door. "I hope you may be unexpectedly detained, ma'am. If you could manage to be run over, ma'am, but not seriously, so much the better."

Uttering these expressions of good-will with extreme gravity, Mr Swiveller sat down in the client's chair and pondered; then took a few turns up and down the room and fell into the chair again.

"So I'm Brass's clerk, am I?" said Dick. "Brass's clerk, eh? And the clerk of Brass's sister—clerk to a female Dragon. Very good, very good! What shall I be next? Shall I be a convict in a felt hat and a grey suit, trotting about a dockyard with my number neatly embroidered on my uniform, and the order of the garter on my leg, restrained from chafing my ankle by a twisted Belcher handkerchief? Shall I be that? Will that do, or is it too genteel? Whatever you please, have it your own way of course."

As he was entirely alone, it may be presumed that, in these remarks, Mr Swiveller addressed himself to his fate or destiny, whom, as we learn by the precedents, it is the custom of heroes to taunt in a very bitter and ironical manner when they find themselves in situations of an unpleasant nature. This is the more probable from the circumstance of Mr Swiveller directing his observations to the ceiling, which these bodily personages are usually supposed to inhabit—except in theatrical cases, when they live in the heart of the great chandelier.

"Quilp offers me this place, which he says he can insure me," resumed Dick after a thoughtful silence, and telling off the circumstances of his position, one by one, upon his fingers; "Fred, who, I could have taken my affidavit, would not have heard of such a thing, backs Quilp to my astonishment, and urges me to take it also—staggerer, number one. My aunt in the country stops the supplies, and writes an affectionate note to say that she has made a new will, and left me out of it—staggerer, number two. No money; no credit; no support from Fred, who seems to turn steady all at once; notice to quit the old lodgings—staggerers three, four, five, and six. Under an accumulation of staggerers, no man can be considered a free agent. No man knocks himself down; if his destiny knocks him down, his destiny must pick him up again. Then I'm very glad that mine has brought all this upon itself, and I shall be as careless as I can, and make myself quite at home to spite it. So go on, my buck," said Mr Swiveller, taking his leave of the ceiling with a significant nod, "and let us see which of us will be tired first!"

Dismissing the subject of his downfall with these reflections, which were no doubt very profound, and are indeed not altogether unknown in certain systems of moral philosophy, Mr Swiveller shook off his despondency and assumed the cheerful ease of an irresponsible clerk.

As a means towards his composure and self-possession, he entered into a more minute examination of the office than he had yet had time to make; looked into the wig box, the books, and ink-bottle; untied and inspected all the papers; carved a few devices on the table with the sharp blade of Mr Brass's penknife; and wrote his name on the inside of the wooden coal-scuttle. Having, as it were, taken formal possession of his clerkship in virtue of these proceedings, he opened the window and leaned negligently out of it until a beer-boy happened to pass, whom he commanded to set down his tray and to serve him with a pint of mild porter, which he drank upon the spot and promptly paid for, with the view of breaking ground for a system of future credit and opening a correspondence tending thereto, without loss of time. Then three or four little boys dropped in, on legal errands from three or four attorneys of the Brass grade: whom Mr Swiveller received and dismissed with about as professional a manner, and as correct and comprehensive an understanding of their business, as would have been shown by a clown in a pantomime under similar circumstances. These things done and over, he got upon his stool again and tried his hand at drawing caricatures of Miss Brass with a pen and ink, whistling very cheerfully all the time.

He was occupied in this diversion when a coach stopped near the door, and presently afterwards there was a loud double-knock. As this was no business of Mr Swiveller's, the person not ringing the office bell, he pursued his diversion with perfect composure, notwithstanding that he rather thought there was nobody else in the house.

In this, however, he was mistaken; for, after the knock had been repeated with increased impatience, the door was opened, and somebody with a very heavy tread went up the stairs and into the room above. Mr Swiveller was wondering whether this might be another Miss Brass, twin sister to the Dragon, when there came a rapping of knuckles at the office door.

"Come in!" said Dick. "Don't stand upon ceremony. The business will get rather complicated if I've many more customers. Come in!"

"Oh, please," said a little voice very low down in the doorway, "will you come and show the lodgings?"

Dick leant over the table, and descried a small slipshod girl in a dirty coarse apron and bib, which left nothing of her visible but her face and feet. She might as well have been dressed in a violin-case.

"Why, who are you?" said Dick.

To which the only reply was, "Oh, please will you come and show the lodgings?"

There never was such an old-fashioned child in her looks and manner. She must have been at work from her cradle. She seemed as much afraid of Dick as Dick was amazed at her.

"I hav'n't got anything to do with the lodgings," said Dick. "Tell 'em to call again."

"Oh, but please will you come and show the lodgings," returned the girl; "it's eighteen shillings a week and us finding plate and linen. Boots and clothes is extra, and fires in winter-time is eightpence a day."

"Why don't you show 'em yourself? You seem to know all about 'em," said Dick.

"Miss Sally said I wasn't to, because people wouldn't believe the attendance was good if they saw how small I was first."

"Well, but they'll see how small you are afterwards, won't they?" said Dick.

"Ah! But then they'll have taken 'em for a fortnight certain," replied the child with a shrewd look; "and people don't like moving when they're once settled."

"This is a queer sort of thing," muttered Dick, rising. "What do you mean to say you are—the cook?"

"Yes, I do plain cooking," replied the child. "I'm housemaid too; I do all the work of the house."

"I suppose Brass and the Dragon and I do the dirtiest part of it," thought Dick. And he might have thought much more, being in a doubtful and hesitating mood, but that the girl again urged her request, and certain mysterious bumping sounds on the passage and staircase seemed to give note of the applicant's impatience. Richard Swiveller, therefore, sticking a pen behind each ear, and carrying another in his mouth as a token of his great importance and devotion to business, hurried out to meet and treat with the single gentleman.

He was a little surprised to perceive that the bumping sounds were occasioned by the progress upstairs of the single gentleman's trunk, which, being nearly twice as wide as the staircase, and exceedingly heavy withal, it was no easy matter for the united exertions of the single gentleman and the coachman to convey up the steep ascent. But there they were, crushing each other, and pushing and pulling with all their might, and getting the trunk tight and fast in all kinds of impossible angles, and to pass them was out of the question; for which sufficient reason, Mr Swiveller followed slowly behind, entering a new protest on every stair against the house of Mr Sampson Brass being thus taken by storm.

To these remonstrances, the single gentleman answered not a word, but when the trunk was at last got into the bedroom, sat down upon it and wiped his bald head and face with his handkerchief. He was very warm, and well he might be; for, not to mention the exertion of getting the trunk upstairs, he was closely muffled up in winter garments, though the thermometer had stood all day at eighty-one in the shade.

"I believe, sir," said Richard Swiveller, taking his pen out of his mouth, "that you desire to look at these apartments. They are very charming apartments, sir. They command an uninterrupted view of—of over the way, and they are within one minute's walk of—of the corner of the street. There is exceedingly mild porter, sir, in the immediate vicinity, and the contingent advantages are extraordinary."

"What's the rent?" said the single gentleman.

"One pound per week," replied Dick, improving on the terms.

"I'll take 'em."

"The boots and clothes are extras," said Dick; "and the fires in winter time are—"

"Are all agreed to," answered the single gentleman.

"Two weeks certain," said Dick, "are the—"

"Two weeks!" cried the single gentleman gruffly, eyeing him from top to toe. "Two years. I shall live here for two years. Here. Ten pounds down. The bargain's made."

"Why, you see," said Dick, "my name is not Brass, and—"

"Who said it was? *My* name's not Brass. What then?"

"The name of the master of the house is," said Dick.

"I'm glad of it," returned the single gentleman; "it's a good name for a lawyer. Coachman, you may go. So may you, sir."

Mr Swiveller was so much confounded by the single gentleman riding rough-shod over him at this rate, that he stood looking at him almost as hard as he had looked at Miss Sally. The single gentleman, however, was not in the slightest degree affected by this circumstance, but proceeded with perfect composure to unwind the shawl which was tied round his neck, and then to pull off his boots. Freed of these encumbrances, he went on to divest himself of his other clothing, which he folded up piece by piece, and ranged in order upon the trunk. Then he pulled down the window-blinds, drew the curtains, wound up his watch, and, quite leisurely and methodically, got into bed.

"Take down the bill," were his parting words, as he looked out from between the curtains; "and let nobody call me till I ring the bell."

With that the curtains closed, and he seemed to snore immediately.

"This is a most remarkable and supernatural sort of house!" said Mr Swiveller, as he walked into the office with the bill in his hand. "She-dragons in the business, conducting themselves like professional gentlemen; plain cooks of three feet high appearing mysteriously from underground; strangers walking in and going to bed without leave or licence in the middle of the day! If he should be one of the miraculous fellows that turn up now and then, and has gone to sleep for two years, I shall be in a pleasant situation. It's my destiny, however, and I hope Brass may like it. I shall be sorry if he don't. But it's no business of mine—I have nothing whatever to do with it!"

Chapter XXXV

M R Brass on returning home received the report of his clerk with much complacency and satisfaction, and was particular in inquiring after the ten-pound note, which, proving on examination to be a good and lawful note of the Governor and Company of the Bank of England, increased his good-humour considerably. Indeed he so overflowed with liberality and condescension, that in the fulness of his heart he invited Mr Swiveller to partake of a bowl of punch with him at that remote and indefinite period which is currently denominated "one of these days," and paid him many handsome compliments on the uncommon aptitude for business which his conduct on the first day of his devotion to it had so plainly evinced.

It was a maxim with Mr Brass that the habit of paying compliments kept a man's tongue oiled without any expense; and, as that useful member ought never to grow rusty or creak in turning on its hinges in the case of a practitioner of the law, in whom it should be always glib and easy, he lost few opportunities of improving himself by the utterance of handsome speeches and eulogistic expressions. And this had passed into such a habit with him, that, if he could not be correctly said to have his tongue at his fingers' ends, he might certainly be said to have it anywhere but in his face: which being, as we have already seen, of a harsh and repulsive character, was not oiled so easily, but frowned above all the smooth speeches—one of nature's beacons, warning off those who navigated the shoals and breakers of the World, or of that dangerous strait the Law, and admonishing them to seek less treacherous harbours and try their fortune elsewhere.

While Mr Brass by turns overwhelmed his clerk with compliments and inspected the ten-pound note, Miss Sally showed little emotion and that of no pleasurable kind, for as the tendency of her legal practice had been to fix her thoughts on small gains and gripings, and to whet and sharpen her natural wisdom, she was not a little disappointed that the single gentleman had obtained the lodgings at such an easy rate, arguing that when he was seen to have set his mind upon them, he should have been at the least charged double or treble the usual terms, and that, in exact proportion as he pressed forward, Mr Swiveller should have hung back. But neither the good opinion of Mr Brass, nor the dissatisfaction of Miss Sally, wrought any impression upon that young gentleman, who, throwing the responsibility of this and all other acts and deeds thereafter to be done by him upon his unlucky destiny, was quite resigned and comfortable: fully prepared for the worst, and philosophically indifferent to the best.

"Good morning, Mr Richard," said Brass, on the second day of Mr Swiveller's clerkship. "Sally found you a second-hand stool, sir, yesterday evening in Whitechapel. She's a rare fellow at a bargain, I can tell you, Mr Richard. You'll find that a first-rate stool, sir, take my word for it."

"It's rather a crazy one to look at," said Dick.

"You'll find it a most amazing stool to sit down upon, you may depend," returned Mr Brass. "It was bought in the open street just opposite the hospital, and as it has been standing there a month or two, it has got rather dusty and a little brown from being in the sun, that's all."

"I hope it hasn't got any fevers or anything of that sort in it," said Dick, sitting himself down discontentedly, between Mr Sampson and the chaste Sally. "One of the legs is longer than the others."

"Then we get a bit of timber in, sir," retorted Brass. "Ha, ha, ha! We get a bit of timber in, sir, and that's another advantage of my sister's going to market for us. Miss Brass, Mr Richard is the—"

"Will you keep quiet?" interrupted the fair subject of these remarks, looking up from her papers. "How am I to work if you keep on chattering?"

"What an uncertain chap you are!" returned the lawyer. "Sometimes you're all for a chat. At another time you're all for work. A man never knows what humour he'll find you in."

"I'm in a working humour now," said Miss Sally, "so don't disturb me, if you please. And don't take him," Miss Sally pointed with the feather of her pen to Richard, "off his business. He won't do more than he can help, I dare say."

Mr Brass had evidently a strong inclination to make an angry reply, but was deterred by prudent or timid considerations, as he only muttered something about aggravation and a vagabond; not associating the terms with any individual, but mentioning them as connected with some abstract ideas which happened to occur to him. They went on writing for a long time in silence after this—in such a dull silence that Mr Swiveller (who required excitement) had several times fallen asleep, and written divers strange words in an unknown character with his eyes shut, when Miss Sally at length broke in upon the monotony of the office by pulling out the little tin box, taking a noisy pinch of snuff, and then expressing her opinion that Mr Richard Swiveller had "done it."

"Done what, ma'am?" said Richard.

"Do you know," returned Miss Brass, "that the lodger isn't up yet—that nothing has been seen or heard of him since he went to bed yesterday afternoon?"

"Well, ma'am," said Dick, "I suppose he may sleep his ten pound out, in peace and quietness, if he likes."

"Ah! I begin to think he'll never wake," observed Miss Sally.

"It's a very remarkable circumstance," said Brass, laying down his pen; "really, very remarkable. Mr Richard, you'll remember, if this gentleman should be found to have hung himself to the bed-post, or any unpleasant accident of that kind should happen— you'll remember, Mr Richard, that this ten-pound note was given to you in part payment of two years' rent? You'll bear that in mind, Mr Richard; you had better make a note of it, sir, in case you should ever be called upon to give evidence."

Mr Swiveller took a large sheet of foolscap, and with a countenance of profound gravity, began to make a very small note in one corner.

"We can never be too cautious," said Mr Brass. "There is a deal of wickedness going about the world, a deal of wickedness. Did the gentleman happen to say, sir——But never mind that at present, sir; finish that little memorandum first."

Dick did so, and handed it to Mr Brass, who had dismounted from his stool and was walking up and down the office.

"Oh, this is the memorandum, is it?" said Brass, running his eye over the document. "Very good. Now, Mr Richard, did the gentleman say anything else?"

"No."

"Are you sure, Mr Richard," said Brass solemnly, "that the gentleman said nothing else?"

"Devil a word, sir," replied Dick.

"Think again, sir," said Brass; "it's my duty, sir, in the position in which I stand, and as an honourable member of the legal profession—the first profession in this country, sir, or in any other country, or in any of the planets that shine above us at night and are supposed to be inhabited—it's my duty, sir, as an honourable member of that profession, not to put to you a leading question in a matter of this delicacy and importance. Did the gentleman, sir, who took the first floor of you yesterday afternoon, and who brought with him a box of property—a box of property—say anything more than is set down in this memorandum?"

"Come, don't be a fool," said Miss Sally.

Dick looked at her, and then at Brass, and then at Miss Sally again, and still said "No."

"Pooh, pooh! Deuce take it, Mr Richard, how dull you are!" cried Brass, relaxing into a smile. "Did he say anything about his property?—there!"

"That's the way to put it," said Miss Sally, nodding to her brother.

"Did he say, for instance," added Brass, in a kind of comfortable, cozy tone—"I don't assert that he did say so, mind; I only ask you, to refresh your memory—did he say, for instance, that he was a stranger in London—that it was not his humour or within his ability to give any references—that he felt we had a right to require them—and that, in case anything should happen to him, at any time, he particularly desired that whatever property he had upon the premises should be considered mine, as some slight recompense for the trouble and annoyance I should sustain—and were you, in short," added Brass, still more comfortably and cozily than before, "were you induced to accept him on my behalf, as a tenant, upon those conditions?"

"Certainly not," replied Dick.

"Why, then, Mr Richard," said Brass, darting at him a supercilious and reproachful look, "it's my opinion that you've mistaken your calling, and will never make a lawyer."

"Not if you live a thousand years," added Miss Sally. Whereupon the brother and sister took each a noisy pinch of snuff from the little tin box, and fell into a gloomy thoughtfulness.

Nothing further passed up to Mr Swiveller's dinner-time, which was at three o'clock, and seemed about three weeks in coming. At the first stroke of the hour, the new clerk disappeared. At the last stroke of five, he reappeared, and the office, as if by magic, became fragrant with the smell of gin and water and lemon-peel.

"Mr Richard," said Brass, "this man's not up yet. Nothing will wake him, sir. What's to be done?"

"I should let him have his sleep out," returned Dick.

"Sleep out!" cried Brass; "why, he has been asleep now six-and-twenty hours. We have been moving chests of drawers over his head, we have knocked double knocks at the street door, we have made the servant-girl fall downstairs several times (she's a light weight, and it don't hurt her much), but nothing wakes him."

"Perhaps a ladder," suggested Dick, "and getting in at the first-floor window—"

"But then there's a door between; besides, the neighbourhood would be up in arms," said Brass.

"What do you say to getting on the roof of the house through the trap-door, and dropping down the chimney?" suggested Dick.

"That would be an excellent plan," said Brass, "if anybody would be"—and here he looked very hard at Mr Swiveller—"would be kind, and friendly, and generous enough, to undertake it. I dare say it would not be anything like as disagreeable as one supposes."

Dick had made the suggestion, thinking that the duty might possibly fall within Miss Sally's department. As he said nothing further, and declined taking the hint, Mr Brass was fain to propose that they should go upstairs together, and make a last effort to awaken the sleeper by some less violent means, which, if they failed on this last trial, must positively be succeeded by stronger measures. Mr Swiveller, assenting, armed himself with his stool and the large ruler, and repaired with his employer to the scene of action, where Miss Brass was already ringing a hand-bell with all her might, and yet without producing the smallest effect upon their mysterious lodger.

"There are his boots, Mr Richard," said Brass.

"Very obstinate-looking articles they are too," quoth Richard Swiveller. And truly they were as sturdy and bluff a pair of boots as one would wish to see; as firmly planted on the ground as if their owner's legs and feet had been in them, and seeming, with their broad soles and blunt toes, to hold possession of their place by main force.

"I can't see anything but the curtain of the bed," said Brass, applying his eye to the keyhole of the door. "Is he a strong man, Mr Richard?"

"Very," answered Dick.

"It would be an extremely unpleasant circumstance if he was to bounce out suddenly," said Brass. "Keep the stairs clear. I should be more than a match for him, of course, but I'm the master of the house, and the laws of hospitality must be respected.— Hallo there! Hallo, hallo!"

While Mr Brass, with his eye curiously twisted into the keyhole, uttered these sounds as a means of attracting the lodger's attention, and while Miss Brass plied the hand-bell, Mr Swiveller put his stool close against the wall by the side of the door, and mounting on the top and standing bolt upright, so that if the lodger did make a rush, he would most probably pass him in its onward fury, began a violent battery with the ruler upon the upper panels of the door. Captivated with his own ingenuity, and confident in the strength of his position, which he had taken up after the method of those hardy individuals who open the pit and gallery doors of theatres on crowded nights, Mr Swiveller rained down such a shower of blows that the noise of the bell was drowned; and the small servant, who lingered on the stairs below, ready to fly at a moment's notice, was obliged to hold her ears lest she should be rendered deaf for life.

Suddenly the door was unlocked on the inside and flung violently open. The small servant fled to the coal-cellar; Miss Sally dived into her own bedroom; Mr Brass, who was not remarkable for personal courage, ran into the next street, and finding that nobody followed him, armed with a poker or other offensive weapon, put his hands in his pockets, walked very slowly all at once, and whistled.

Meanwhile Mr Swiveller, on the top of the stool, drew himself into as flat a shape as possible against the wall and looked, not unconcernedly, down upon the single gentleman, who appeared at the door growling and cursing in a very awful manner, and, with the boots in his hand, seemed to have an intention of hurling them downstairs on speculation. This idea, however, he abandoned, and he was turning into his room again, still growling vengefully, when his eyes met those of the watchful Richard.

"Have *you* been making that horrible noise?" said the single gentleman.

"I have been helping, sir," returned Dick, keeping his eye upon him, and waving the ruler gently in his right hand, as an indication of what the single gentleman had to expect if he attempted any violence.

"How dare you then," said the lodger. "Eh?"

To this, Dick made no other reply than by inquiring whether the lodger held it to be consistent with the conduct and character of a gentleman to go to sleep for six-and-twenty hours at a stretch, and whether the peace of an amiable and virtuous family was to weigh as nothing in the balance.

"Is my peace nothing?" said the single gentleman.

"Is their peace nothing, sir?" returned Dick. "I don't wish to hold out any threats, sir—indeed the law does not allow of threats, for to threaten is an indictable offence—but if ever you do that again, take care you're not sat upon by the coroner and buried in a crossroad before you wake. We have been distracted with fears that you were dead, sir," said Dick, gently sliding to the ground, "and the short and the long of it is, that we cannot allow single gentlemen to come into this establishment and sleep like double gentlemen without paying extra for it."

"Indeed!" cried the lodger.

"Yes, sir, indeed," returned Dick, yielding to his destiny and saying whatever came uppermost; "an equal quantity of slumber was never got out of one bed and bedstead, and if you're going to sleep in that way, you must pay for a double-bedded room."

Instead of being thrown into a greater passion by these remarks, the lodger lapsed into a broad grin and looked at Mr Swiveller, with twinkling eyes. He was a brown-faced, sun-burnt man, and appeared browner and more sun-burnt from having a white night-cap on. As it was clear that he was a choleric fellow in some respects, Mr Swiveller was relieved to find him in such good humour, and, to encourage him in it, smiled himself.

The lodger, in the testiness of being so rudely roused, had pushed his nightcap very much on one side of his bald head. This gave him a rakish eccentric air which, now that he had leisure to observe it, charmed Mr Swiveller exceedingly; therefore, by way of propitiation, he expressed his hope that the gentleman was going to get up, and further that he would never do so any more.

"Come here, you impudent rascal!" was the lodger's answer as he re-entered his room.

Mr Swiveller followed him in, leaving the stool outside, but reserving the ruler in case of a surprise. He rather congratulated himself upon his prudence when the single gentleman, without notice or explanation of any kind, double-locked the door.

"Can you drink anything?" was his next inquiry.

Mr Swiveller replied that he had very recently been assuaging the pangs of thirst, but that he was still open to "a modest quencher," if the materials were at hand. Without another word spoken on either side, the lodger took from his great trunk a kind of temple, shining as of polished silver, and placed it carefully on the table.

Greatly interested in his proceedings, Mr Swiveller observed him closely. Into one little chamber of this temple he dropped an egg, into another some coffee, into a third a compact piece of raw steak from a neat tin case, into a fourth he poured some water. Then, with the aid of a phosphorus-box and some matches, he procured a light and applied it to a spirit-lamp which had a place of its own below the temple; then he shut down the lids of all the little chambers; then he opened them; and then, by some wonderful and unseen agency, the steak was done, the egg was boiled, the coffee was accurately prepared, and his breakfast was ready.

"Hot water—" said the lodger, handing it to Mr Swiveller with as much coolness as if he had a kitchen fire before him—"extraordinary rum—sugar—and a travelling glass. Mix for yourself. And make haste."

Dick complied, his eyes wandering all the time from the temple on the table, which seemed to do everything, to the great trunk, which seemed to hold everything. The lodger took his breakfast like a man who was used to work these miracles, and thought nothing of them.

"The man of the house is a lawyer, is he not?" said the lodger.

Dick nodded. The rum was amazing.

"The woman of the house—what's she?"

"A dragon," said Dick.

The single gentleman, perhaps because he had met with such things in his travels, or perhaps because he *was* a single gentleman, evinced no surprise, but merely inquired "Wife or sister?" "Sister," said Dick.—"So much the better," said the single gentleman; "he can get rid of her when he likes."

"I want to do as I like, young man," he added after a short silence; "to go to bed when I like, get up when I like, come in when I like, go out when I like—to be asked no questions and be surrounded by no spies. In this last respect, servants are the devil. There's only one here."

"And a very little one," said Dick.

"And a very little one," repeated the lodger. "Well, the place will suit me, will it?"

"Yes," said Dick.

"Sharks, I suppose?" said the lodger.

Dick nodded assent, and drained his glass.

"Let them know my humour," said the single gentleman, rising. "If they disturb me, they lose a good tenant. If they know me to be that, they know enough. If they try to know more, it's a notice to quit. It's better to understand these things at once. Good day."

"I beg your pardon," said Dick, halting in his passage to the door, which the lodger prepared to open. "When he who adores thee has left but the name—"

"What do you mean?"

"—But the name," said Dick—"has left but the name—in case of letters or parcels—"

"I never have any," returned the lodger.

"Or in case anybody should call."

"Nobody ever calls on me."

"If any mistake should arise from not having the name, don't say it was my fault, sir," added Dick, still lingering.—"Oh, blame not the bard—"

"I'll blame nobody," said the lodger, with such irascibility that in a moment Dick found himself on the staircase, and the locked door between them.

Mr Brass and Miss Sally were lurking hard by, having been, indeed, only routed from the keyhole by Mr Swiveller's abrupt exit. As their utmost exertions had not enabled them to overhear a word of the interview, however, in consequence of a quarrel for precedence, which, though limited of necessity to pushes and pinches and such quiet pantomime, had lasted the whole time, they hurried him down to the office to hear his account of the conversation.

This Mr Swiveller gave them—faithfully as regarded the wishes and character of the single gentleman, and poetically as concerned the great trunk, of which he gave a description more remarkable for bri'liancy of imagination than a strict adherence to truth; declaring, with many strong asseverations, that it contained a specimen of every kind of rich food and wine known in these times, and in particular that it was of a self-acting kind and served up whatever was required, as he supposed by clock-work. He also gave them to understand that the cooking apparatus roasted a fine piece of sirloin of beef, weighing about six pounds avoirdupois, in two minutes and a quarter, as he had himself witnessed, and proved by his sense of taste; and further that, however the effect was produced, he had distinctly seen water boil and bubble up when the single gentleman winked; from which facts he (Mr Swiveller) was led to infer that the lodger was some great conjuror or chemist, or both, whose residence under that roof could not fail at some future day to shed a great credit and distinction upon the name of Brass, and add a new interest to the history of Bevis Marks.

There was one point which Mr Swiveller deemed it unnecessary to enlarge upon, and that was the fact of the modest quencher, which, by reason of its intrinsic strength and its coming close upon the heels of the temperate beverage he had discussed at dinner, awakened a slight degree of fever, and rendered necessary two or three other modest quenchers at the public-house in the course of the evening.

Chapter XXXVI

AS the single gentleman, after some weeks' occupation of his lodgings, still declined to correspond by word or gesture either with Mr Brass or his sister Sally, but invariably chose Richard Swiveller as his channel of communication; and as he proved himself in all respects a highly desirable inmate, paying for everything beforehand, giving very little trouble, making no noise, and keeping early hours; Mr Richard imperceptibly rose to an important position in the family, as one who had influence over this mysterious lodger, and could negotiate with him, for good or evil, when nobody else durst approach his person.

If the truth must be told, even Mr Swiveller's approaches to the single gentleman were of a very distant kind, and met with small encouragement; but, as he never returned from a monosyllabic conference with the unknown, without quoting such expressions as "Swiveller, I know I can rely upon you"—"I have no hesitation in saying, Swiveller, that I entertain a regard for you"—"Swiveller, you are my friend, and will stand by me I am sure," with many other short speeches of the same familiar and confiding kind, purporting to have been addressed by the single gentleman to himself, and to form the staple of their ordinary discourse, neither Mr Brass nor Miss Sally for a moment questioned the extent of his influence, but accorded to him their fullest and most unqualified belief.

But quite apart from and independent of this source of popularity, Mr Swiveller had another, which promised to be equally enduring, and to lighten his position considerably.

He found favour in the eyes of Miss Sally Brass. Let not the light scorners of female fascination erect their ears to listen to a new tale of love which shall serve them for a jest; for Miss Brass, however accurately formed to be beloved, was not of the loving kind. That amiable virgin, having clung to the skirts of the Law from her earliest youth—having sustained herself by their aid, as it were, in her first running alone, and maintained a firm grasp upon them ever since—had passed her life in a kind of legal childhood. She had been remarkable, when a tender prattler, for an uncommon talent in counterfeiting the walk and manner of a bailiff: in which character she had learned to tap her little playfellows on the shoulder, and to carry them off to imaginary sponging-houses, with a correctness of imitation which was the surprise and delight of all who witnessed her performances, and which was only to be exceeded by her exquisite manner of putting an execution into her doll's house, and taking an exact inventory of the chairs and tables. These artless sports had naturally soothed and cheered the decline of her widowed father: a most exemplary gentleman (called "old Foxey" by his friends from his extreme sagacity), who encouraged them to the utmost, and whose chief regret on finding that he drew near to Houndsditch Churchyard was that his daughter could not take out an attorney's certificate and hold a place upon the roll. Filled with this affectionate and touching sorrow, he had solemnly confided her to his son Sampson as an invaluable auxiliary; and from the old gentleman's decease to the period of which we treat, Miss Sally Brass had been the prop and pillar of his business.

It is obvious that, having devoted herself from infancy to this one pursuit and study, Miss Brass could know but little of the world, otherwise than in connexion with the law; and that from a lady gifted with such high tastes, proficiency in those gentler and softer arts in which women usually excel, was scarcely to be looked for. Miss Sally's accomplishments were all of a masculine and strictly legal kind. They began with the practice of an attorney and they ended with it. She was in a state of lawful innocence, so to speak. The law had been her nurse, and, as bandy-legs or such physical deformities in children are held to be the consequence of bad nursing, so, if in a mind so beautiful any moral twist or bandiness could be found, Miss Sally Brass's nurse was alone to blame.

It was upon this lady, then, that Mr Swiveller burst in full freshness as something new and hitherto undreamed of, lighting up the office with scraps of song and merriment, conjuring with inkstands and boxes of wafers, catching three oranges in one hand, balancing stools upon his chin and penknives on his nose, and constantly performing a hundred other feats of equal ingenuity; for with such unbendings did Richard, in Mr Brass's absence, relieve the tedium of his confinement. These social qualities, which Miss Sally first discovered by accident, gradually made such an impression upon her, that she would entreat Mr Swiveller to relax as though she were not by, which Mr Swiveller, nothing loth, would readily consent to do. By these means a friendship sprang up between them. Mr Swiveller gradually came to look upon her as her brother Sampson did, and as he would have looked upon any other clerk. He imparted to her the mystery of going the odd man or plain Newmarket for fruit, ginger-beer, baked potatoes, or even a modest quencher, of which Miss Brass did not scruple to partake. He would often persuade her to undertake his share of writing in addition to her own; nay, he would sometimes reward her with a hearty slap on the back, and protest that she was a devilish good fellow, a jolly dog, and so forth; all of which compliments Miss Sally would receive in entire good part and with perfect satisfaction.

One circumstance troubled Mr Swiveller's mind very much, and that was that the small servant always remained somewhere in the bowels of the earth under Bevis Marks, and never came to the surface unless the single gentleman rang his bell, when she would answer it and immediately disappear again. She never went out, or came into the office, or had a clean face, or took off the coarse apron, or looked out of any one of the windows, or stood at the street door for a breath of air, or had any rest or enjoyment whatever. Nobody ever came to see her, nobody spoke of her, nobody cared about her. Mr Brass had said once that he believed she was a "love-child" (which means anything but a child of love), and that was all the information Richard Swiveller could obtain.

"It's of no use asking the dragon," thought Dick one day, as he sat contemplating the features of Miss Sally Brass. "I suspect if I asked any questions on that head, our alliance would be at an end. I wonder whether she *is* a dragon by the bye, or something in the mermaid way. She has rather a scaly appearance. But mermaids are fond of looking at themselves in the glass, which she can't be. And they have a habit of combing their hair, which she hasn't. No, she's a dragon."

"Where are you going, old fellow?" said Dick aloud, as Miss Sally wiped her pen as usual on the green dress, and uprose from her seat.

"To dinner," answered the dragon.

"To dinner!" thought Dick, "that's another circumstance. I don't believe that small servant ever has anything to eat."

"Sammy won't be home," said Miss Brass. "Stop till I come back. I shan't be long."

Dick nodded, and followed Miss Brass—with his eyes to the door, and with his ears to a little back parlour, where she and her brother took their meals.

"Now," said Dick, walking up and down with his hands in his pockets, "I'd give something—if I had it—to know how they use that child, and where they keep her. My mother must have been a very inquisitive woman; I have no doubt I'm marked with a note of interrogation somewhere. My feelings I smother, but thou hast been the cause of this anguish, my—upon my word," said Mr Swiveller, checking himself and falling thoughtfully into the client's chair, "I should like to know how they use her!"

After running on in this way for some time, Mr Swiveller softly opened the office door, with the intention of darting across the street for a glass of the mild porter. At that moment he caught a parting glimpse of the brown headdress of Miss Brass flitting down the kitchen stairs. "And by Jove!" thought Dick, "she's going to feed the servant. Now or never!"

First peeping over the handrail and allowing the headdress to disappear in the darkness below, he groped his way down, and arrived at the door of a back kitchen immediately after Miss Brass had entered the same, bearing in her hand a cold leg of mutton. It was a very dark, miserable place, very low and very damp: the walls disfigured by a thousand rents and blotches. The water was trickling out of a leaky butt, and a most wretched cat was lapping up the drops with the sickly eagerness of starvation. The grate,

which was a wide one, was wound and screwed up tight, so as to hold no more than
a little thin sandwich of fire. Everything was locked up; the coal-cellar, the candle-box,
the salt-box, the meat-safe, were all padlocked. There was nothing that a beetle could
have lunched upon. The pinched and meagre aspect of the place would have killed a
chameleon. He would have known at the first mouthful that the air was not eatable, and
must have given up the ghost in despair.—The small servant stood with humility in
presence of Miss Sally, and hung her head.

"Are you there?" said Miss Sally.

"Yes, ma'am," was the answer in a weak voice.

"Go further away from the leg of mutton, or you'll be picking it, I know," said Miss
Sally.

The girl withdrew into a corner, while Miss Brass took a key from her pocket, and
opening the safe, brought from it a dreary waste of cold potatoes, looking as eatable as
Stonehenge. This she placed before the small servant, ordering her to sit down before
it, and then, taking up a great carving-knife, made a mighty show of sharpening it upon
the carving-fork.

"Do you see this?" said Miss Brass, slicing off about two square inches of cold
mutton, after all this preparation, and holding it out on the point of the fork.

The small servant looked hard enough at it with her hungry eyes to see every shred
of it, small as it was, and answered, "Yes."

"Then don't you ever go and say," retorted Miss Sally, "that you hadn't meat here.
There, eat it up."

This was soon done. "Now, do you want any more?" said Miss Sally.

The hungry creature answered with a faint "No." They were evidently going through
an established form.

"You've been helped once to meat," said Miss Brass, summing up the facts; "you
have had as much as you can eat, you're asked if you want any more, and you answer,
'No!' Then don't you ever go and say you were allowanced, mind that."

With those words, Miss Sally put the meat away and locked the safe, and then
drawing near to the small servant, overlooked her while she finished the potatoes.

It was plain that some extraordinary grudge was working in Miss Brass's gentle
breast, and that it was this which impelled her, without the smallest present cause, to rap
the child with the blade of the knife, now on her hand, now on her head, and now on
her back, as if she found it quite impossible to stand so close to her without administering
a few slight knocks. But Mr Swiveller was not a little surprised to see his fellow-clerk,
after walking slowly backwards towards the door, as if she were trying to withdraw
herself from the room but could not accomplish it, dart suddenly forward, and falling on
the small servant give her some hard blows with her clenched hand. The victim cried,
but in a subdued manner as if she feared to raise her voice, and Miss Sally, comforting
herself with a pinch of snuff, ascended the stairs, just as Richard had safely reached the
office.

Chapter XXXVII

T HE single gentleman among his other peculiarities—and he had a very plentiful stock, of which he every day furnished some new specimen—took a most extraordinary and remarkable interest in the exhibition of Punch. If the sound of a Punch's voice, at ever so remote a distance, reached Bevis Marks, the single gentleman, though in bed and asleep, would start up, and, hurrying on his clothes, make for the spot with all speed, and presently return at the head of a long procession of idlers, having in the midst the theatre and its proprietors. Straightway, the stage would be set up in front of Mr Brass's house; the single gentleman would establish himself at the first-floor window; and the entertainment would proceed with all its exciting accompaniments of fife and drum and shout, to the excessive consternation of all sober votaries of business in that silent thoroughfare. It might have been expected that when the play was done, both players and audience would have dispersed; but the epilogue was as bad as the play, for no sooner was the Devil dead, than the manager of the puppets and his partner were summoned by the single gentleman to his chamber, where they were regaled with strong waters from his private store, and where they held with him long conversations, the purport of which no human being could fathom. But the secret of these discussions was of little importance. It was sufficient to know that while they were proceeding, the concourse without still lingered round the house; that boys beat upon the drum with their fists, and imitated Punch with their tender voices; that the office window was rendered opaque by flattened noses, and the keyhole of the street door luminous with eyes; that every time the single gentleman or either of his guests was seen at the upper window, or so much as the end of one of their noses was visible, there was a great shout of execration from the excluded mob, who remained howling and yelling, and refusing consolation, until the exhibitors were delivered up to them to be attended elsewhere. It was sufficient, in short, to know that Bevis Marks was revolutionised by these popular movements, and that peace and quietness fled from its precincts.

Nobody was rendered more indignant by these proceedings than Mr Sampson Brass, who, as he could by no means afford to lose so profitable an inmate, deemed it prudent to pocket his lodger's affront along with his cash, and to annoy the audiences who clustered round his door by such imperfect means of retaliation as were open to him, and which were confined to the trickling down of foul water on their heads from unseen watering-pots, pelting them with fragments of tile and mortar from the roof of the house, and bribing the drivers of hackney cabriolets to come suddenly round the corner and dash in among them precipitately. It may at first sight be matter of surprise to the thoughtless few that Mr Brass, being a professional gentleman, should not have legally indicted some party or parties, active in the promotion of the nuisance; but they will be good enough to remember that as Doctors seldom take their own prescriptions, and Divines do not always practise what they preach, so Lawyers are shy of meddling with the Law on their own account, knowing it to be an edged tool of uncertain application, very expensive in the working, and rather remarkable for its properties of close shaving, than for its always shaving the right person.

"Come," said Mr Brass one afternoon, "this is two days without a Punch. I'm in hopes he has run through 'em all, at last."

"Why are you in hopes?" returned Miss Sally. "What harm do they do?"

"Here's a pretty sort of fellow!" cried Brass, laying down his pen in despair. "Now here's an aggravating animal!"

"Well, what harm do they do?" retorted Sally.

"What harm!" cried Brass. "Is it no harm to have a constant hallooing and hooting under one's very nose, distracting one from business, and making one grind one's teeth with vexation? Is it no harm to be blinded and choked up, and have the King's highway stopped with a set of screamers and roarers whose throats must be made of—of—"

"Brass," suggested Mr Swiveller.

"Ah! of brass," said the lawyer, glancing at his clerk, to assure himself that he had suggested the word in good faith and without any sinister intention. "Is that no harm?"

The lawyer stopped short in his invective, and listening for a moment, and recognising the well-known voice, rested his head upon his hand, raised his eyes to the ceiling and muttered faintly, "There's another!"

Up went the single gentleman's window directly.

"There's another," repeated Brass; "and if I could get a break and four blood horses to cut into the Marks when the crowd is at its thickest, I'd give eighteenpence and never grudge it!"

The distant squeak was heard again. The single gentleman's door burst open. He ran violently down the stairs, out into the street, and so past the window, without any hat, towards the quarter whence the sound proceeded—bent, no doubt, upon securing the strangers' services directly.

"I wish I only knew who his friends were," muttered Sampson, filling his pocket with papers; "if they'd just get up a pretty little Commission *de lunatico* at the Gray's Inn Coffee House and give me the job, I'd be content to have the lodgings empty for one while, at all events."

With which words, and knocking his hat over his eyes as if for the purpose of shutting out even a glimpse of the dreadful visitation, Mr Brass rushed from the house and hurried away.

As Mr Swiveller was decidedly favourable to these performances, upon the ground that looking at a Punch, or indeed looking at anything out of window, was better than working; and as he had been for this reason at some pains to awaken in his fellow-clerk a sense of their beauties and manifold deserts; both he and Miss Sally rose as with one accord and took up their positions at the window: upon the sill whereof, as in a post of honour, sundry young ladies and gentlemen who were employed in the dry nurture of babies, and who made a point of being present, with their young charges, on such occasions, had already established themselves as comfortably as the circumstances would allow.

The glass being dim, Mr Swiveller, agreeably to a friendly custom which he had established between them, hitched off the brown headdress from Miss Sally's head, and dusted it carefully therewith. By the time he had handed it back, and its beautiful wearer had put it on again (which she did with perfect composure and indifference), the lodger returned with the show and showmen at his heels, and a strong addition to the body of spectators. The exhibitor disappeared with all speed behind the drapery, and his partner, stationing himself by the side of the Theatre, surveyed the audience with a remarkable expression of melancholy, which became more remarkable still when he breathed a hornpipe tune into that sweet musical instrument which is popularly termed a mouth-organ, without at all changing the mournful expression of the upper part of his face, though his mouth and chin were, of necessity, in lively spasms.

The drama proceeded to its close, and held the spectators enchained in the customary manner. The sensation which kindles in large assemblies, when they are relieved from a state of breathless suspense and are again free to speak and move, was yet rife, when the lodger, as usual, summoned the men upstairs.

"Both of you," he called from the window; for only the actual exhibitor—a little fat man—prepared to obey the summons. "I want to talk to you. Come, both of you."

"Come, Tommy," said the little man.

"I an't a talker," replied the other. "Tell him so. What should I go and talk for?"

"Don't you see the gentleman's got a bottle and glass up there?" returned the little man.

"And couldn't you have said so, at first?" retorted the other with sudden alacrity. "Now, what are you waiting for? Are you going to keep the gentleman expecting us all day? haven't you *no* manners?"

With this remonstrance, the melancholy man, who was no other than Mr Thomas Codlin, pushed past his friend and brother in the craft, Mr Harris, otherwise Short or Trotters, and hurried before him to the single gentleman's apartment.

"Now, my men," said the single gentleman; "you have done very well. What will you take? Tell that little man behind to shut the door."

"Shut the door, can't you?" said Mr Codlin, turning gruffly to his friend. "You might have knowed that the gentleman wanted the door shut, without being told, I think."

Mr Short obeyed, observing under his breath that his friend seemed unusually "cranky," and expressing a hope that there was no dairy in the neighbourhood, or his temper would certainly spoil its contents.

The gentleman pointed to a couple of chairs, and intimated by an emphatic nod of his head that he expected them to be seated. Messrs Codlin and Short, after looking at each other with considerable doubt and indecision, at length sat down—each on the extreme edge of the chair pointed out to him—and held their hats very tight, while the single gentleman filled a couple of glasses from a bottle on the table beside him, and presented them in due form.

"You're pretty well browned by the sun, both of you," said their entertainer. "Have you been travelling?"

Mr Short replied in the affirmative with a nod and a smile. Mr Codlin added a corroborative nod and a short groan, as if he still felt the weight of the Temple upon his shoulders.

"To fairs, markets, races, and so forth, I suppose?" pursued the single gentleman.

"Yes, sir," returned Short, "pretty nigh all over the West of England."

"I have talked to men of your craft from North, East, and South," returned their host, in rather a hasty manner; "but I never lighted on any from the West before."

"It's our regular summer circuit is the West, master," said Short; "that's where it is. We take the East of London in the spring and winter, and the West of England in the summer-time. Many's the hard day's walking in rain and mud, and with never a penny earned, we've had down in the West."

"Let me fill your glass again."

"Much obleeged to you, sir, I think I will," said Mr Codlin, suddenly thrusting in his own and turning Short's aside. "I'm the sufferer, sir, in all the travelling, and in all the staying at home. In town or country, wet or dry, hot or cold, Tom Codlin suffers. But Tom Codlin isn't to complain for all that. Oh, no! Short may complain, but if Codlin grumbles by so much as a word—oh dear, down with him, down with *him* directly. It isn't *his* place to grumble. That's quite out of the question."

"Codlin an't without his usefulness," observed Short with an arch look, "but he don't always keep his eyes open. He falls asleep sometimes, you know. Remember them last races, Tommy."

"Will you never leave off aggravating a man?" said Codlin. "It's very likely I was asleep when five-and-tenpence was collected, in one round, isn't it? I was attending to my business, and couldn't have my eyes in twenty places at once, like a peacock, no more than you could. If I an't a match for an old man and a young child, you an't neither, so don't throw that out against me, for the cap fits your head quite as correct as it fits mine."

"You may as well drop the subject, Tom," said Short. "It isn't particular agreeable to the gentleman, I dare say."

"Then you shouldn't have brought it up," returned Mr Codlin; "and I ask the gentleman's pardon on your account, as a giddy chap that likes to hear himself talk, and don't much care what he talks about, so that he does talk."

Their entertainer had sat perfectly quiet in the beginning of this dispute, looking first at one man and then at the other, as if he were lying in wait for an opportunity of putting some further question, or reverting to that from which the discourse had strayed. But, from the point where Mr Codlin was charged with sleepiness, he had shown an increasing interest in the discussion: which now attained a very high pitch.

"You are the two men I want," he said, "the two men I have been looking for, and searching after. Where are that old man and that child you speak of?"

"Sir?" said Short, hesitating, and looking towards his friend.

"The old man and his grandchild who travelled with you—where are they? It will be worth your while to speak out, I assure you; much better worth your while than you believe. They left you, you say—at those races, as I understand. They have been traced to that place, and there lost sight of. Have you no clue, can you suggest no clue, to their recovery?"

"Did I always say, Thomas," cried Short, turning with a look of amazement to his friend, "that there was sure to be an inquiry after them two travellers?"

"*You* said!" returned Mr Codlin. "Did I always say that that 'ere blessed child was the most interesting I ever see? Did I always say I loved her, and doted on her? Pretty creetur, I think I hear her now. 'Codlin's my friend,' she says, with a tear of gratitude a-trickling down her little eye; 'Codlin's my friend,'" she says—'not Short. Short's very well,' she says; 'I've no quarrel with Short; he means to be kind, I dare say; but Codlin,' she says, 'has the feelings for my money, though he mayn't look it.' "

Repeating these words with great emotion, Mr Codlin rubbed the bridge of his nose with his coat-sleeve, and shaking his head mournfully from side to side, left the single gentleman to infer that, from the moment when he lost sight of his dear young charge, his peace of mind and happiness had fled.

"Good God!" said the single gentleman, pacing up and down the room, "have I found these men at last, only to discover that they can give me no information or assistance! It would have been better to have lived on in hope from day to day, and never to have lighted on them, than to have my expectations scattered."

"Stay a minute," said Short. "A man of the name of Jerry—you know Jerry, Thomas?"

"Oh, don't talk to me of Jerrys," replied Mr Codlin. "How can I care a pinch of snuff for Jerrys, when I think of that 'ere darling child? 'Codlin's my friend,' she says, 'dear, good, kind Codlin, as is always a devising pleasures for me! I don't object to Short,' she says, 'but I cotton to Codlin.' Once," said that gentleman reflectively, "she called me Father Codlin. I thought I should have bust!"

"A man of the name of Jerry, sir," said Short, turning from his selfish colleague to their new acquaintance, "wot keeps a company of dancing dogs, told me in a accidental sort of way, that he had seen the old gentleman in connexion with a travelling wax-work, unbeknown to him. As they'd given us the slip, and nothing had come of it, and this was down in the country that he'd been seen, I took no measures about it, and asked no questions—But I can, if you like."

"Is this man in town?" said the impatient single gentleman. "Speak faster."

"No he isn't, but he will be to-morrow, for he lodges in our house," replied Mr Short rapidly.

"Then bring him here," said the single gentleman. "Here's a sovereign a-piece. If I can find these people through your means, it is but a prelude to twenty more. Return to me to-morrow, and keep your own counsel upon this subject—though I need hardly tell you that, for you'll do so for your own sakes. Now, give me your address, and leave me."

The address was given, the two men departed, the crowd went with them, and the single gentleman for two mortal hours walked in uncommon agitation up and down his room, over the wondering heads of Mr Swiveller and Miss Sally Brass.

Chapter XXXVIII

K IT —for it happens at this juncture, not only that we have breathing time to follow his fortunes, but that the necessities of these adventures so adapt themselves to our ease and inclination as to call upon us imperatively to pursue the track we most desire to take—Kit, while the matters treated of in the last fifteen chapters were yet in progress, was, as the reader may suppose, gradually familiarising himself more and more with Mr and Mrs Garland, Mr Abel, the pony, and Barbara, and gradually coming to consider them one and all as his particular private friends, and Abel Cottage, Finchley, as his own proper home.

Stay—the words are written, and may go, but if they convey any notion that Kit, in the plentiful board and comfortable lodging of his new abode, began to think slightingly of the poor fare and furniture of his old dwelling, they do their office badly and commit injustice. Who so mindful of those he left at home—albeit they were but a mother and two young babies—as Kit? What boastful father in the fulness of his heart ever related such wonders of his infant prodigy, as Kit never wearied of telling Barbara in the evening time, concerning little Jacob? Was there ever such a mother as Kit's mother, on her son's showing; or was there ever such comfort in poverty as in the poverty of Kit's family, if any correct judgment might be arrived at, from his own glowing account!

And let us linger in this place for an instant to remark that if ever household affections and loves are graceful things, they are graceful in the poor. The ties that bind the wealthy and the proud to home may be forged on earth, but those which link the poor man to his humble hearth are of the true metal and bear the stamp of Heaven. The man of high descent may love the halls and lands of his inheritance as a part of himself, as trophies of his birth and power; his associations with them are associations of pride and wealth and triumph; the poor man's attachment to the tenements he holds, which strangers have held before, and may to-morrow occupy again, has a worthier root, struck deep into a purer soil. His household gods are of flesh and blood, with no alloy of silver, gold, or precious stone; he has no property but in the affections of his own heart; and when they endear bare floors and walls, despite of rags and toil and scanty meals, that man has his love of home from God, and his rude hut becomes a solemn place.

Oh! if those who rule the destinies of nations would but remember this—if they would but think how hard it is for the very poor to have engendered in their hearts that love of home from which all domestic virtues spring, when they live in dense and squalid masses where social decency is lost, or rather never found—if they would but turn aside from the wide thoroughfares and great houses, and strive to improve the wretched dwellings in bye-ways where only Poverty may walk—many low roofs would point more truly to the sky, than the loftiest steeple that now rears proudly up from the midst of guilt, and crime, and horrible disease, to mock them by its contrast. In hollow voices from Workhouse, Hospital, and Jail, this truth is preached from day to day, and has been proclaimed for years. It is no light matter—no outcry from the working vulgar—no mere question of the people's health and comforts that may be whistled down on Wednesday nights. In love of home, the love of country has its rise; and who are the truer patriots or the best in time of need—those who venerate the land, owning its wood, and stream, and earth, and all that they produce? or those who love their country, boasting not a foot of ground in all its wide domain?

Kit knew nothing about such questions, but he knew that his old home was a very poor place and that his new one was very unlike it, and yet he was constantly looking back with grateful satisfaction and affectionate anxiety, and often indited square-folded letters to his mother, inclosing a shilling or eighteen-pence or such other small remittance, which Mr Abel's liberality enabled him to make. Sometimes, being in the neighbourhood, he had leisure to call upon her, and then great was the joy and pride of Kit's mother, and extremely noisy the satisfaction of little Jacob and the baby, and cordial the congratulations of the whole court, who listened with admiring ears to the accounts of Abel Cottage, and could never be told too much of its wonders and magnificence.

Although Kit was in the very highest favour with the old lady and gentleman, and Mr Abel, and Barbara, it is certain that no member of the family evinced such a remarkable partiality for him as the self-willed pony, who, from being the most obstinate and opinionated pony on the face of the earth, was in his hands the meekest and most tractable of animals. It is true that in exact proportion as he became manageable by Kit he became utterly ungovernable by anybody else (as if he had determined to keep him in the family at all risks and hazards), and that, even under the guidance of his favourite, he would sometimes perform a great variety of strange freaks and capers, to the extreme discomposure of the old lady's nerves; but as Kit always represented that this was only his fun, or a way he had of showing his attachment to his employers, Mrs Garland gradually suffered herself to be persuaded into the belief, in which she at last became so strongly confirmed that if in one of these ebullitions he had overturned the chaise, she would have been quite satisfied that he did it with the very best intentions.

Besides becoming in a short time a perfect marvel in all stable matters, Kit soon made himself a very tolerable gardener, a handy fellow within doors, and an indispensable attendant on Mr Abel, who every day gave him some new proof of his confidence and approbation. Mr Witherden the notary, too, regarded him with a friendly eye; and even Mr Chuckster would sometimes condescend to give him a slight nod, or honour him with that peculiar form of recognition which is called "taking a sight," or to favour him with some other salute combining pleasantry with patronage.

One morning Kit drove Mr Abel to the notary's office, as he sometimes did, and having set him down at the house, was about to drive off to a livery stable hard by, when this same Mr Chuckster emerged from the office door, and cried "Woa-a-a-a-a-a!"—dwelling upon the note a long time, for the purpose of striking terror into the pony's heart, and asserting the supremacy of man over the inferior animals.

"Pull up, Snobby," cried Mr Chuckster, addressing himself to Kit. "You're wanted inside here."

"Has Mr Abel forgotten anything, I wonder?" said Kit as he dismounted.

"Ask no questions, Snobby," returned Mr Chuckster, "but go and see. Woa-a-a then, will you? If that pony was mine, I'd break him."

"You must be very gentle with him, if you please," said Kit, "or you'll find him troublesome. You'd better not keep on pulling his ears, please. I know he won't like it."

To this remonstrance Mr Chuckster deigned no other answer, than addressing Kit with a lofty and distant air as "young feller," and requesting him to cut and come again with all speed. The "young feller" complying, Mr Chuckster put his hands in his pockets, and tried to look as if he were not minding the pony, but happened to be lounging there by accident.

Kit scraped his shoes very carefully (for he had not yet lost his reverence for the bundles of papers and the tin boxes), and tapped at the office door, which was quickly opened by the notary himself.

"Oh! come in, Christopher," said Mr Witherden.

"Is that the lad?" asked an elderly gentleman, but of a stout, bluff figure—who was in the room.

"That's the lad," said Mr Witherden. "He fell in with my client, Mr Garland, sir, at this very door. I have reason to think he is a good lad, sir, and that you may believe what he says. Let me introduce Mr Abel Garland, sir—his young master; my articled pupil, sir, and most particular friend. My most particular friend, sir," repeated the notary, drawing out his silk handkerchief and flourishing it about his face.

"Your servant, sir," said the stranger gentleman.

"Yours, sir, I'm sure," replied Mr Abel mildly. "You were wishing to speak to Christopher, sir?"

"Yes, I was. Have I your permission?"

"By all means."

"My business is no secret; or I should rather say it need be no secret *here,*" said the stranger, observing that Mr Abel and the notary were preparing to retire. "It relates to a dealer in curiosities with whom he lived, and in whom I am earnestly and warmly interested. I have been a stranger to this country, gentlemen, for very many years, and if I am deficient in form and ceremony, I hope you will forgive me."

"No forgiveness is necessary, sir;—none whatever," replied the notary, and so said Mr Abel.

"I have been making inquiries in the neighbourhood in which his old master lived," said the stranger, "and I learnt that he had been served by this lad. I found out his mother's house, and was directed by her to this place as the nearest in which I should be likely to find him. That's the cause of my presenting myself here this morning."

"I am very glad of any cause, sir," said the notary, "which procures me the honour of this visit."

"Sir," retorted the stranger, "you speak like a mere man of the world, and I think you something better. Therefore, pray do not sink your real character in paying unmeaning compliments to me."

"Hem!" coughed the notary. "You're a plain speaker, sir."

"And a plain dealer," returned the stranger. "It may be my long absence and inexperience that lead me to the conclusion, but if plain speakers are scarce in this part of the world, I fancy that plain dealers are still scarcer. If my speaking should offend you, sir, my dealing, I hope, will make amends."

Mr Witherden seemed a little disconcerted by the elderly gentleman's mode of conducting the dialogue; and as for Kit, he looked at him in open-mouthed astonishment, wondering what kind of language he would address to him, if he talked in that free and easy way to a notary. It was with no harshness, however, though with something of constitutional irritability and haste, that he turned to Kit and said:

"If you think, my lad, that I am pursuing these inquiries with any other view than that of serving and reclaiming those I am in search of, you do me a very great wrong, and deceive yourself. Don't be deceived, I beg of you, but rely upon my assurance. The fact is, gentlemen," he added, turning again to the Notary and his pupil, "that I am in a very painful and wholly unexpected position. I came to this city with a darling object at my heart, expecting to find no obstacle or difficulty in the way of its attainment. I find myself suddenly checked and stopped short in the execution of my design, by a mystery which I cannot penetrate. Every effort I have made to penetrate it has only served to render it darker and more obscure; and I am afraid to stir openly in the matter, lest those whom I anxiously pursue should fly still farther from me. I assure you that if you could give me any assistance, you would not be sorry to do so, if you knew how greatly I stand in need of it, and what a load it would relieve me from."

There was a simplicity in this confidence which occasioned it to find a quick response in the breast of the good-natured notary, who replied, in the same spirit, that the stranger had not mistaken his desire, and that if he could be of service to him, he would most readily.

Kit was then put under examination and closely questioned by the unknown gentleman touching his old master and the child, their lonely way of life, their retired habits, and strict seclusion. The nightly absence of the old man, the solitary existence of the child at those times, his illness and recovery, Quilp's possession of the house, and their sudden disappearance, were all the subjects of much questioning and answer. Finally, Kit informed the gentleman that the premises were now to let, and that a board upon the door referred all inquirers to Mr Sampson Brass, Solicitor, of Bevis Marks, from whom he might perhaps learn some further particulars.

"Not by inquiry," said the gentleman shaking his head. "I live there."

"Live at Brass's the attorney's!" cried Mr Witherden in some surprise, having professional knowledge of the gentleman in question.

"Ay," was the reply. "I entered upon his lodgings t'other day, chiefly because I had seen this very board. It matters little to me where I live, and I had a desperate hope that some intelligence might be cast in my way there, which would not reach me elsewhere. Yes, I live at Brass's—more shame for me, I suppose?"

"That's a mere matter of opinion," said the notary, shrugging his shoulders. "He is looked upon as rather a doubtful character."

"Doubtful?" echoed the other. "I am glad to hear there's any doubt about it. I supposed that had been thoroughly settled, long ago. But will you let me speak a word or two with you in private?"

Mr Witherden consenting, they walked into that gentleman's private closet, and remained there in close conversation for some quarter of an hour, when they returned into the outer office. The stranger had left his hat in Mr Witherden's room, and seemed to have established himself in this short interval on quite a friendly footing.

"I'll not detain you any longer now," he said, putting a crown into Kit's hand, and looking towards the notary. "You shall hear from me again. Not a word of this, you know, except to your master and mistress."

"Mother, sir, would be glad to know"—said Kit, faltering.

"Glad to know what?"

"Anything—so that it was no harm—about Miss Nell."

"Would she? Well then, you may tell her if she can keep a secret. But mind, not a word of this to anybody else. Don't forget that. Be particular."

"I'll take care, sir," said Kit. "Thankee, sir, and good morning."

Now, it happened that the gentleman, in his anxiety to impress upon Kit that he was not to tell anybody what had passed between them, followed him out to the door to repeat his caution, and it further happened that at that moment the eyes of Mr Richard Swiveller were turned in that direction, and beheld his mysterious friend and Kit together.

It was quite an accident, and the way in which it came about was this. Mr Chuckster, being a gentleman of a cultivated taste and refined spirit, was one of that Lodge of Glorious Apollos whereof Mr Swiveller was Perpetual Grand. Mr Swiveller, passing through the street in the execution of some Brazen errand, and beholding one of his Glorious Brotherhood intently gazing on a pony, crossed over to give him that fraternal greeting with which Perpetual Grands are, by the very constitution of their office, bound to cheer and encourage their disciples. He had scarcely bestowed upon him his blessing, and followed it with a general remark touching the present state and prospects of the weather, when lifting up his eyes he beheld the single gentleman of Bevis Marks in earnest conversation with Christopher Nubbles.

"Hallo!" said Dick, "who *is* that?"

"He called to see my Governor this morning," replied Mr Chuckster; "and beyond that I don't know him from Adam."

"At least you know his name?" said Dick.

To which Mr Chuckster replied, with an elevation of speech becoming a Glorious Apollo, that he was "everlastingly blessed" if he did.

"All I know, my dear feller," said Mr Chuckster, running his fingers through his hair, "is, that he is the cause of my having stood here twenty minutes, for which I hate him with a mortal and undying hatred, and would pursue him to the confines of eternity, if I could afford the time."

While they were thus discoursing, the subject of their conversation (who had not appeared to recognise Mr Richard Swiveller) re-entered the house, and Kit came down the steps and joined them; to whom Mr Swiveller again propounded his inquiry with no better success.

"He is a very nice gentleman, sir," said Kit, "and that's all *I* know about him."

Mr Chuckster waxed wroth at this answer, and without applying the remark to any particular case, mentioned as a general truth that it was expedient to break the heads of Snobs, and to tweak their noses. Without expressing his concurrence in this sentiment, Mr Swiveller after a few moments of abstraction inquired which way Kit was driving, and, being informed, declared it was his way, and that he would trespass on him for a lift. Kit would gladly have declined the proffered honour, but as Mr Swiveller was already established in the seat beside him, he had no means of doing so otherwise than by a forcible ejectment, and therefore drove briskly off—so briskly indeed as to cut short the leave-taking between Mr Chuckster and his Grand Master, and to occasion the former gentleman some inconvenience from having his corns squeezed by the impatient pony.

As Whisker was tired of standing, and Mr Swiveller was kind enough to stimulate him still further by shrill whistles, and various sporting cries, they rattled off at too sharp a pace to admit of much conversation, especially as the pony, incensed by Mr Swiveller's admonitions, took a particular fancy for the lamp-posts and cart-wheels and evinced a strong desire to run on the pavement and rasp himself against brick walls. It was not, therefore, until they had arrived at the stable, and the chaise had been extricated from a very small doorway, into which the pony dragged it under the impression that he would take it along with him into his usual stall, that Mr Swiveller found time to talk.

"It's hard work," said Richard. "What do you say to some beer?"

Kit at first declined, but presently consented, and they adjourned to the neighbouring bar together.

"We'll drink our friend what's-his-name," said Dick, holding up the bright frothy pot; "—that was talking to you this morning, you know—I know him—a good fellow, but eccentric—very—here's what's-his-name!"

Kit pledged him.

"He lives in my house," said Dick; "at least in the house occupied by the firm in which I'm a sort of a—of a managing partner—a difficult fellow to get anything out of, but we like him—we like him."

"I must be going, sir, if you please," said Kit, moving away.

"Don't be in a hurry, Christopher," replied his patron, "we'll drink your mother."

"Thank you, sir."

"An excellent woman that mother of yours, Christopher," said Mr Swiveller. "Who ran to catch me when I fell, and kissed the place to make it well? My mother. A charming woman. He's a liberal sort of fellow. We must get him to do something *for* your mother. Does he know her, Christopher?"

Kit shook his head, and glancing slyly at his questioner, thanked him, and made off before he could say another word.

"Humph!" said Mr Swiveller pondering, "this is queer. Nothing but mysteries in connexion with Brass's house. I'll keep my own counsel, however. Everybody and anybody has been in my confidence as yet, but now I think I'll set up in business for myself. Queer—very queer!"

After pondering deeply and with a face of exceeding wisdom for some time, Mr Swiveller drank some more of the beer, and summoning a small boy who had been watching his proceedings, poured forth the few remaining drops as a libation upon the gravel, and bade him carry the empty vessel to the bar with his compliments, and above all things to lead a sober and temperate life, and abstain from all intoxicating and exciting liquors. Having given him this piece of moral advice for his trouble (which, as he wisely observed, was far better than half-pence), the Perpetual Grand Master of the Glorious Apollos thrust his hands into his pockets and sauntered away; still pondering as he went.

Chapter XXXIX

A LL that day, though he waited for Mr Abel until evening, Kit kept clear of his mother's house, determined not to anticipate by the slightest approach the pleasures of the morrow, but to let them come in their full rush of delight; for to-morrow was the great and long-looked-for epoch in his life—to-morrow was the end of his first quarter—the day of receiving for the first time one fourth part of his annual income of Six Pounds in one vast sum of Thirty Shillings—to-morrow was to be a half-holiday devoted to a whirl of entertainments, and little Jacob was to know what oysters meant, and to see a play.

All manner of incidents combined in favour of the occasion: not only had Mr and Mrs Garland forewarned him that they intended to make no deduction for his outfit from the great amount, but to pay it him unbroken in all its gigantic grandeur; not only had the unknown gentleman increased the stock by the sum of five shillings, which was a perfect godsend and in itself a fortune; not only had these things come to pass which nobody could have calculated upon, or in their wildest dreams have hoped; but it was Barbara's quarter too—Barbara's quarter, that very day—and Barbara had a half-holiday as well as Kit, and Barbara's mother was going to make one of the party, and to take tea with Kit's mother, and cultivate her acquaintance.

To be sure Kit looked out of his window very early that morning to see which way the clouds were flying, and to be sure Barbara would have been at hers too if she had not sat up so late overnight, starching and ironing small pieces of muslin, and crimping them into frills, and sewing them on to other pieces to form magnificent wholes for next day's wear. But they were both up very early for all that, and had small appetites for breakfast and less for dinner, and were in a state of great excitement when Barbara's mother came in with astonishing accounts of the fineness of the weather out of doors (but with a very large umbrella notwithstanding, for people like Barbara's mother seldom make holiday without one), and when the bell rang for them to go upstairs and receive their quarter's money in gold and silver.

Well, wasn't Mr Garland kind when he said, "Christopher, here's your money, and you have earned it well"; and wasn't Mrs Garland kind when she said, "Barbara, here's yours, and I'm much pleased with you"; and didn't Kit sign his name bold to his receipt, and didn't Barbara sign her name all a-trembling to hers; and wasn't it beautiful to see how Mrs Garland poured out Barbara's mother a glass of wine; and didn't Barbara's mother speak up when she said, "Here's blessing you, ma'am, as a good lady, and you, sir, as a good gentleman, and Barbara, my love to you, and here's towards you, Mr Christopher"; and wasn't she as long drinking it as if it had been a tumblerful; and didn't she look genteel, standing there with her gloves on; and wasn't there plenty of laughing and talking among them as they reviewed all these matters upon the top of the coach; and didn't they pity the people who hadn't got a holiday!

But Kit's mother, again—wouldn't anybody have supposed she had come of a good stock and been a lady all her life? There she was, quite ready to receive them, with a display of tea-things that might have warmed the heart of a china-shop; and little Jacob and the baby in such a state of perfection that their clothes looked as good as new, though Heaven knows they were old enough! Didn't she say before they had sat down five minutes that Barbara's mother was exactly the sort of lady she expected, and didn't

Barbara's mother say that Kit's mother was the very picture of what *she* had expected, and didn't Kit's mother compliment Barbara's mother on Barbara, and didn't Barbara's mother compliment Kit's mother on Kit, and wasn't Barbara herself quite fascinated with little Jacob, and did ever a child show off when he was wanted, as that child did, or make such friends as he made?

"And we are both widows too!" said Barbara's mother. "We must have been made to know each other."

"I haven't a doubt about it," returned Mrs Nubbles. "And what a pity it is we didn't know each other sooner."

"But then you know it's such a pleasure," said Barbara's mother, "to have it brought about by one's son and daughter, that it's fully made up for, now, an't it?"

To this, Kit's mother yielded her full assent, and tracing things back from effects to causes, they naturally reverted to their deceased husbands, respecting whose lives, deaths, and burials, they compared notes, and discovered sundry circumstances that tallied with wonderful exactness; such as Barbara's father having been exactly four years and ten months older than Kit's father, and one of them having died on a Wednesday and the other on a Thursday, and both of them having been of a very fine make and remarkably good-looking, with other extraordinary coincidences. These recollections being of a kind calculated to cast a shadow on the brightness of the holiday, Kit diverted the conversation to general topics, and they were soon in great force again, and as merry as before. Among other things, Kit told them about his old place, and the extraordinary beauty of Nell (of whom he had talked to Barbara a thousand times already); but the last-named circumstance failed to interest his hearers to anything like the extent he had supposed, and even his mother said (looking accidentally at Barbara at the same time) that there was no doubt Miss Nell was very pretty, but she was but a child after all, and there were many young women quite as pretty as she; and Barbara mildly observed that she should think so, and that she never could help believing Mr Christopher must be under a mistake—which Kit wondered at very much, not being able to conceive what reason she had for doubting him. Barbara's mother too observed that it was very common for young folks to change at about fourteen or fifteen, and whereas they had been very pretty before, to grow up quite plain; which truth she illustrated by many forcible examples, especially one of a young man, who, being a builder with great prospects, had been particular in his attentions to Barbara, but whom Barbara would have nothing to say to; which (though everything happened for the best) she almost thought was a pity. Kit said he thought so too, and so he did honestly, and he wondered what made Barbara so silent all at once, and why his mother looked at him as if he shouldn't have said it.

However, it was high time now to be thinking of the play; for which great preparation was required in the way of shawls and bonnets, not to mention one handkerchief full of oranges and another of apples, which took some time tying up, in consequence of the fruit having a tendency to roll out at the corners. At length everything was ready, and they went off very fast; Kit's mother carrying the baby, who was dreadfully wide awake, and Kit holding little Jacob in one hand, and escorting Barbara with the other—a state of things which occasioned the two mothers, who walked behind, to declare that they looked quite family folks, and caused Barbara to blush and say, "Now don't, mother!" But Kit said she had no call to mind what they said; and indeed she need not have had, if she had known how very far from Kit's thoughts any love-making was. Poor Barbara!

At last they got to the theatre, which was Astley's: and in some two minutes after they had reached the yet unopened door, little Jacob was squeezed flat, and the baby had received divers concussions, and Barbara's mother's umbrella had been carried several yards off and passed back to her over the shoulders of the people, and Kit had hit a man on the head with the handkerchief of apples for "scrowdging" his parent with unnecessary violence, and there was a great uproar. But when they were once past the pay-place and tearing away for very life with their checks in their hands; and above all, when they were fairly in the theatre, and seated in such places that they couldn't have had better if they had picked them out and taken them beforehand; all this was looked upon as quite a capital joke, and an essential part of the entertainment.

Dear, dear, what a place it looked, that Astley's! with all the paint, gilding, and looking-glass; the vague smell of horses suggestive of coming wonders; the curtain that hid such gorgeous mysteries; the clean white sawdust down in the circus; the company coming in and taking their places; the fiddlers looking carelessly up at them while they tuned their instruments, as if they didn't want the play to begin, and knew it all beforehand! What a glow was that which burst upon them all, when that long, clear, brilliant row of lights came slowly up; and what the feverish excitement when the little bell rang and the music began in good earnest, with strong parts for the drums, and sweet effects for the triangles! Well might Barbara's mother say to Kit's mother that the gallery was the place to see from, and wonder it wasn't much dearer than the boxes; and well might Barbara feel doubtful whether to laugh or cry, in her flutter of delight.

Then the play itself! the horses which little Jacob believed from the first to be alive, and the ladies and gentlemen of whose reality he could be by no means persuaded, having never seen or heard anything at all like them—the firing, which made Barbara wink—the forlorn lady, who made her cry—the tyrant, who made her tremble—the man who sang the song with the lady's-maid and danced the chorus, who made her laugh—the pony who reared up on his hind-legs when he saw the murderer, and wouldn't hear of walking on all fours again until he was taken into custody—the clown who ventured on such familiarities with the military man in boots—the lady who jumped over the nine-and-twenty ribbons and came down safe upon the horse's back—everything was delightful, splendid, and surprising. Little Jacob applauded till his hands were sore; Kit cried "an-kor" at the end of everything, the three-act piece included; and Barbara's mother beat her umbrella on the floor, in her ecstasies, until it was nearly worn down to the gingham.

In the midst of all these fascinations, Barbara's thoughts seemed to have been still running upon what Kit had said at tea-time: for when they were coming out of the play, she asked him, with an hysterical simper, if Miss Nell was as handsome as the lady who jumped over the ribbons.

"As handsome as *her?*" said Kit. "Double as handsome."

"Oh, Christopher! I'm sure she was the beautifullest creature ever was," said Barbara.

"Nonsense!" returned Kit. "She was well enough, I don't deny that; but think how she was dressed and painted, and what a difference that made. Why, *you* are a good deal better-looking than her, Barbara."

"Oh, Christopher!" said Barbara, looking down.

"You are, any day," said Kit—"and so's your mother."

Poor Barbara!

What was all this, though—even all this—to the extraordinary dissipation that ensued, when Kit, walking into an oyster-shop as bold as if he lived there, and not so much as looking at the counter or the man behind it, led his party into a box—a private box, fitted up with red curtains, white table-cloth, and cruet-stand complete—and ordered a fierce gentleman with whiskers, who acted as waiter and called him, him, Christopher Nubbles, "Sir," to bring three dozen of his largest-sized oysters, and to look sharp about it! Yes, Kit told this gentleman to look sharp, and he not only said he would look sharp, but he actually did, and presently came running back with the newest loaves, and the freshest butter, and the largest oysters, ever seen. Then said Kit to this gentleman, "A pot of beer"—just so—and the gentleman, instead of replying, "Sir, did you address that language to me?" only said, "Pot o' beer, sir? Yes, sir," and went off and fetched it, and put it on the table in a small decanter-stand, like those which blind men's dogs carry about the streets in their mouths to catch the halfpence in; and both Kit's mother and Barbara's mother declared as he turned away that he was one of the slimmest and gracefullest young men she had ever looked upon.

Then they fell to work upon the supper in earnest; and there was Barbara, that foolish Barbara, declaring that she couldn't eat more than two, and wanting more pressing than you would believe before she would eat four; though her mother and Kit's mother made up for it pretty well, and ate and laughed and enjoyed themselves so thoroughly that it did Kit good to see them, and made him laugh and eat likewise from strong sympathy. But the greatest miracle of the night was little Jacob, who ate oysters as if he had been born and bred to the business, sprinkled the pepper and the vinegar with a discretion beyond his years, and afterwards built a grotto on the table with the shells. There was the baby too, who had never closed an eye all night, but had sat as good as gold, trying to force a large orange into his mouth, and gazing intently at the lights in the chandelier—there he was, sitting up in his mother's lap, staring at the gas without winking, and making indentations in his soft visage with an oyster-shell, to that degree that a heart of iron must have loved him! In short, there never was a more successful supper; and when Kit ordered in a glass of something hot to finish with, and proposed Mr and Mrs Garland before sending it round, there were not six happier people in all the world.

But all happiness has an end—hence the chief pleasure of its next beginning—and as it was now growing late, they agreed it was time to turn their faces homewards. So, after going a little out of their way to see Barbara and Barbara's mother safe to a friend's house, where they were to pass the night, Kit and his mother left them at the door, with an early appointment for returning to Finchley next morning, and a great many plans for next quarter's enjoyment. Then Kit took little Jacob on his back, and giving his arm to his mother, and a kiss to the baby, they all trudged merrily home together.

Chapter XL

FULL of that vague kind of penitence which holidays awaken next morning, Kit turned out at sunrise, and, with his faith in last night's enjoyments a little shaken by cool daylight and the return to everyday duties and occupations, went to meet Barbara and her mother at the appointed place. And being careful not to awaken any of the little household, who were yet resting from their unusual fatigues, Kit left his money on the chimney-piece, with an inscription in chalk calling his mother's attention to the circumstance, and informing her that it came from her dutiful son; and went his way, with a heart something heavier than his pockets, but free from any very great oppression notwithstanding.

Oh, these holidays! why will they leave us some regret! why cannot we push them back only a week or two in our memories, so as to put them at once at that convenient distance whence they may be regarded either with a calm indifference or a pleasant effort of recollection! why will they hang about us like the flavour of yesterday's wine, suggestive of headaches and lassitude, and those good intentions for the future, which under the earth form the everlasting pavement of a large estate, and upon it usually endure until dinner-time or thereabouts!

Who will wonder that Barbara had a headache, or that Barbara's mother was disposed to be cross, or that she slightly underrated Astley's, and thought the clown was older than they had taken him to be last night? Kit was not surprised to hear her say so—not he. He had already had a misgiving that the inconstant actors in that dazzling vision had been doing the same thing the night before last, and would do it again that night, and the next, and for weeks and months to come, though he would not be there. Such is the difference between yesterday and to-day. We are all going to the play, or coming home from it.

However, the Sun himself is weak when he first rises, and gathers strength and courage as the day gets on. By degrees, they began to recall circumstances more and more pleasant in their nature, until, what between talking, walking, and laughing, they reached Finchley in such good heart, that Barbara's mother declared she never felt less tired or in better spirits, and so said Kit. Barbara had been silent all the way, but she said so too. Poor little Barbara! she was very quiet.

They were at home in such good time that Kit had rubbed down the pony and made him as spruce as a racehorse before Mr Garland came down to breakfast; which punctual and industrious conduct the old lady, and the old gentleman, and Mr Abel, highly extolled. At his usual hour (or rather at his usual minute and second, for he was the soul of punctuality) Mr Abel walked out, to be overtaken by the London coach, and Kit and the old gentleman went to work in the garden.

This was not the least pleasant of Kit's employments, for on a fine day they were quite a family party; the old lady sitting hard by with her work-basket on a little table; the old gentleman digging, or pruning, or clipping about with a large pair of shears, or helping Kit in some way or other with great assiduity; and Whisker looking on from his paddock in placid contemplation of them all. To-day they were to trim the grape-vine, so Kit mounted half-way up a short ladder, and began to snip and hammer away, while the old gentleman, with a great interest in his proceedings, handed up the nails and shreds of cloth as he wanted them. The old lady and Whisker looked on as usual.

"Well, Christopher," said Mr Garland, "and so you have made a new friend, eh?"

"I beg your pardon, sir?" returned Kit, looking down from the ladder.

"You have made a new friend, I hear from Mr Abel," said the old gentleman, "at the office?"

"Oh—yes, sir, yes. He behaved very handsome, sir."

"I'm glad to hear it," returned the old gentleman with a smile. "He is disposed to behave more handsomely still though, Christopher."

"Indeed, sir! It's very kind in him, but I don't want him to, I'm sure," said Kit, hammering stoutly at an obdurate nail.

"He is rather anxious," pursued the old gentleman, "to have you in his own service—take care what you're doing, or you will fall down and hurt yourself."

"To have me in his service, sir!" cried Kit, who had stopped short in his work and faced about upon the ladder like some dexterous tumbler. "Why, sir, I don't think he can be in earnest when he says that."

"Oh! But he is indeed," said Mr Garland. "And he has told Mr Abel so."

"I never heard of such a thing!" muttered Kit, looking ruefully at his master and mistress. "I wonder at him; that I do."

"You see, Christopher," said Mr Garland, "this is a point of much importance to you, and you should understand and consider it in that light. This gentleman is able to give you more money than I—not, I hope, to carry through the various relations of master and servant more kindness and confidence, but certainly, Christopher, to give you more money."

"Well," said Kit, "after that, sir—"

"Wait a moment," interposed Mr Garland. "That is not all. You were a very faithful servant to your old employers, as I understand, and should this gentleman recover them, as it is his purpose to attempt doing by every means in his power, I have no doubt that you, being in his service, would meet with your reward. Besides," added the old gentleman with stronger emphasis, "besides having the pleasure of being again brought into communication with those to whom you seem to be so very strongly and disinterestedly attached. You must think of all this, Christopher, and not be rash or hasty in your choice."

Kit did suffer one twinge, one momentary pang in keeping the resolution he had already formed, when this last argument passed swiftly into his thoughts, and conjured up the realization of all his hopes and fancies. But it was gone in a minute, and he sturdily rejoined that the gentleman must look out for somebody else, as he did think he might have done at first.

"He has no right to think that I'd be led away to go to him, sir," said Kit, turning round again after half a minute's hammering. "Does he think I'm a fool?"

"He may, perhaps, Christopher, if you refuse his offer," said Mr Garland gravely.

"Then let him, sir," retorted Kit; "what do I care, sir, what he thinks? why should I care for his thinking, sir, when I know that I should be a fool, and worse than a fool, sir, to leave the kindest master and mistress that ever was or can be, who took me out of the streets a very poor and hungry lad indeed—poorer and hungrier perhaps than ever you think for, sir—to go to him or anybody? If Miss Nell was to come back, ma'am," added Kit, turning suddenly to his mistress, "why, that would be another thing, and perhaps if *she* wanted me, I might ask you now and then to let me work for her when all was done at home. But when she comes back, I see now that she'll be rich as old master always said she would, and being a rich young lady, what could she want of me? No, no," added Kit, shaking his head sorrowfully, "she'll never want me any more, and bless her, I hope she never may, though I *should* like to see her too!"

Here Kit drove a nail into the wall, very hard—much harder than was necessary—and having done so, faced about again.

"There's the pony, sir," said Kit—"Whisker, ma'am (and he knows so well I'm talking about him that he begins to neigh directly, sir)—would he let anybody come near him but me, ma'am? Here's the garden, sir, and Mr Abel, ma'am. Would Mr Abel part with me, sir, or is there anybody that could be fonder of the garden, ma'am? It would break mother's heart, sir, and even little Jacob would have sense enough to cry his eyes out, ma'am, if he thought that Mr Abel could wish to part with me so soon, after having told me only the other day, that he hoped we might be together for years to come—"

There is no telling how long Kit might have stood upon the ladder, addressing his master and mistress by turns, and generally turning towards the wrong person, if Barbara had not at that moment come running up to say that a messenger from the office had brought a note, which, with an expression of some surprise at Kit's oratorial appearance, she put into her master's hand.

"Oh!" said the old gentleman after reading it, "ask the messenger to walk this way." Barbara tripping off to do as she was bid, he turned to Kit and said that they would not pursue the subject any further, and that Kit could not be more unwilling to part with them, than they would be to part with Kit; a sentiment which the old lady very generously echoed.

"At the same time, Christopher," added Mr Garland, glancing at the note in his hand, "if the gentleman should want to borrow you now and then for an hour or so, or even a day or so, at a time, we must consent to lend you, and you must consent to be lent.—Oh! here is the young gentleman. How do you do, sir?"

This salutation was addressed to Mr Chuckster, who, with his hat extremely on one side, and his hair a long way beyond it, came swaggering up the walk.

"Hope I see you well, sir," returned that gentleman. "Hope I see *you* well, ma'am. Charming box this, sir. Delicious country, to be sure."

"You want to take Kit back with you, I find?" observed Mr Garland.

"I've got a chariot-cab waiting on purpose," replied the clerk. "A very spanking grey in that cab, sir, if you're a judge of horse-flesh."

Declining to inspect the spanking grey, on the plea that he was but poorly acquainted with such matters, and would but imperfectly appreciate his beauties, Mr Garland invited Mr Chuckster to partake of a slight repast in the way of lunch, and that gentleman readily consenting, certain cold viands, flanked with ale and wine, were speedily prepared for his refreshment.

At this repast, Mr Chuckster exerted his utmost abilities to enchant his entertainers, and impress them with a conviction of the mental superiority of those who dwelt in town; with which view he led the discourse to the small scandal of the day, in which he was justly considered by his friends to shine prodigiously. Thus, he was in a condition to relate the exact circumstances of the difference between the Marquis of Mizzler and Lord Bobby, which it appeared originated in a disputed bottle of champagne, and not in a pigeon-pie, as erroneously reported in the newspapers; neither had Lord Bobby said to the Marquis of Mizzler, "Mizzler, one of us two tells a lie, and I'm not the man," as incorrectly stated by the same authorities; but "Mizzler, you know where I'm to be found, and damme, sir, find me if you want me"—which, of course, entirely changed the aspect of this interesting question, and placed it in a very different light. He also acquainted them with the precise amount of the income guaranteed by the Duke of Thigsberry to Violetta Stetta of the Italian Opera, which it appeared was payable quarterly, and not half-yearly, as the public had been given to understand, and which was *ex*clusive, and not *in*clusive (as had been monstrously stated), of jewellery, perfumery, hair-powder for five footmen, and two daily changes of kid-gloves for a page. Having entreated the old lady and gentleman to set their minds at rest upon these absorbing points, for they might rely on his statement being the correct one, Mr Chuckster entertained them with theatrical chit-chat and the Court circular; and so wound up a brilliant and fascinating conversation which he had maintained alone, and without any assistance whatever, for upwards of three-quarters of an hour.

"And now that the nag has got his wind again," said Mr Chuckster, rising in a graceful manner, "I'm afraid I must cut my stick."

Neither Mr nor Mrs Garland offered any opposition to his tearing himself away (feeling, no doubt, that such a man could ill be spared from his proper sphere of action), and therefore Mr Chuckster and Kit were shortly afterwards upon their way to town; Kit being perched upon the box of the cabriolet beside the driver, and Mr Chuckster seated in solitary state inside, with one of his boots sticking out at each of the front windows.

When they reached the notary's house, Kit followed into the office, and was desired by Mr Abel to sit down and wait, for the gentleman who wanted him had gone out, and perhaps might not return for some time. This anticipation was strictly verified, for Kit had had his dinner, and his tea, and had read all the lighter matter in the Law List, and the Post Office Directory, and had fallen asleep a great many times, before the gentleman whom he had seen before came in; which he did at last in a very great hurry.

He was closeted with Mr Witherden for some little time, and Mr Abel had been called in to assist at the conference, before Kit, wondering very much what he was wanted for, was summoned to attend them.

"Christopher," said the gentleman, turning to him directly he entered the room, "I have found your old master and young mistress."

"No, sir! Have you, though?" returned Kit, his eyes sparkling with delight. "Where are they, sir? How are they, sir? Are they—are they near here?"

"A long way from here," returned the gentleman, shaking his head. "But I am going away to-night to bring them back, and I want you to go with me."

"Me, sir?" cried Kit, full of joy and surprise.

"The place," said the strange gentleman, turning thoughtfully to the notary, "indicated by this man of the dogs is—how far from here—sixty miles?"

"From sixty to seventy."

"Humph! If we travel post all night, we shall reach there in good time to-morrow morning. Now, the only question is, as they will not know me, and the child, God bless her, would think that any stranger pursuing them had a design upon her grandfather's liberty—can I do better than take this lad, whom they both know and will readily remember, as an assurance to them of my friendly intentions?"

"Certainly not," replied the notary. "Take Christopher by all means."

"I beg your pardon, sir," said Kit, who had listened to this discourse with a lengthening countenance, "but if that's the reason, I'm afraid I should do more harm than good—Miss Nell, sir, *she* knows me, and would trust in me, I am sure; but old master—I don't know why, gentlemen; nobody does—would not bear me in his sight after he had been ill, and Miss Nell herself told me that I must not go near him or let him see me any more. I should spoil all that you were doing if I went, I'm afraid. I'd give the world to go, but you had better not take me, sir."

"Another difficulty!" cried the impetuous gentleman. "Was ever man so beset as I? Is there nobody else that knew them, nobody else in whom they had any confidence? Solitary as their lives were, is there no one person who would serve my purpose?"

"*Is* there, Christopher?" said the notary.

"Not one, sir," replied Kit.—"Yes, though—there's my mother."

"Did they know her?" said the single gentleman.

"Know her, sir! why, she was always coming backwards and forwards. They were as kind to her as they were to me. Bless you, sir, she expected they'd come back to her house."

"Then where the devil is the woman?" said the impatient gentleman, catching up his hat. "Why isn't she here? Why is that woman always out of the way when she is most wanted?"

In a word, the single gentleman was bursting out of the office, bent upon laying violent hands on Kit's mother, forcing her into a post-chaise, and carrying her off, when this novel kind of abduction was with some difficulty prevented by the joint efforts of Mr Abel and the notary, who restrained him by dint of their remonstrances, and persuaded him to sound Kit upon the probability of her being able and willing to undertake such a journey on so short a notice.

This occasioned some doubts on the part of Kit, and some violent demonstrations on that of the single gentleman, and a great many soothing speeches on that of the notary and Mr Abel. The upshot of the business was that Kit, after weighing the matter in his mind and considering it carefully, promised, on behalf of his mother, that she should be ready within two hours from that time to undertake the expedition, and engaged to produce her in that place, in all respects equipped and prepared for the journey, before the specified period had expired.

Having given this pledge, which was rather a bold one, and not particularly easy of redemption, Kit lost no time in sallying forth, and taking measures for its immediate fulfilment.

Chapter XLI

KIT made his way through the crowded streets, dividing the stream of people, dashing across the busy roadways, diving into lanes and alleys, and stopping or turning aside for nothing, until he came in front of the Old Curiosity Shop, when he came to a stand; partly from habit and partly from being out of breath.

It was a gloomy autumn evening, and he thought the old place had never looked so dismal as in its dreary twilight. The windows broken, the rusty sashes rattling in their frames, the deserted house a dull barrier dividing the glaring lights and bustle of the street into two long lines, and standing in the midst, cold, dark, and empty—presented a cheerless spectacle which mingled harshly with the bright prospects the boy had been building up for its late inmates, and came like a disappointment or misfortune. Kit would have had a good fire roaring up the empty chimneys, lights sparkling and shining through the windows, people moving briskly to and fro, voices in cheerful conversation, something in unison with the new hopes that were astir. He had not expected that the house would wear any different aspect—had known indeed that it could not—but coming upon it in the midst of eager thoughts and expectations, it checked the current in its flow, and darkened it with a mournful shadow.

Kit, however, fortunately for himself, was not learned enough or contemplative enough to be troubled with presages of evil afar off, and, having no mental spectacles to assist his vision in this respect, saw nothing but the dull house, which jarred uncomfortably upon his previous thoughts. So, almost wishing that he had not passed it, though hardly knowing why, he hurried on again, making up by his increased speed for the few moments he had lost.

"Now, if she should be out," thought Kit, as he approached the poor dwelling of his mother, "and I not able to find her, this impatient gentleman would be in a pretty taking. And sure enough there's no light, and the door's fast. Now, God forgive me for saying so, but if this is Little Bethel's doing, I wish Little Bethel was—was farther off," said Kit checking himself, and knocking at the door.

A second knock brought no reply from within the house; but caused a woman over the way to look out and inquire who that was wanting Mrs Nubbles.

"Me," said Kit. "She's at—at Little Bethel, I suppose?"—getting out the name of the obnoxious conventicle with some reluctance, and laying a spiteful emphasis upon the words.

The neighbour nodded assent.

"Then pray tell me where it is," said Kit, "for I have come on a pressing matter, and must fetch her out, even if she was in the pulpit."

It was not very easy to procure a direction to the fold in question, as none of the neighbours were of the flock that resorted thither, and few knew anything more of it than the name. At last a gossip of Mrs Nubbles's, who had accompanied her to chapel on one or two occasions when a comfortable cup of tea had preceded her devotions, furnished the needful information, which Kit had no sooner obtained than he started off again.

Little Bethel might have been nearer, and might have been in a straighter road, though in that case the reverend gentleman who presided over its congregation would have lost his favourite allusion to the crooked ways by which it was approached, and which enabled him to liken it to Paradise itself, in contradistinction to the parish church and the broad thoroughfare leading thereunto. Kit found it at last after some trouble, and pausing at the door to take breath that he might enter with becoming decency, passed into the chapel.

It was not badly named in one respect, being in truth a particularly little Bethel—a Bethel of the smallest dimensions—with a small number of small pews, and a small pulpit, in which a small gentleman (by trade a Shoemaker, and by calling a Divine) was delivering in a by no means small voice, a by no means small sermon, judging of its dimensions by the condition of his audience, which, if their gross amount were but small, comprised a still smaller number of hearers, as the majority were slumbering.

Among these was Kit's mother, who, finding it matter of extreme difficulty to keep her eyes open after the fatigues of last night, and feeling their inclination to close strongly backed and seconded by the arguments of the preacher, had yielded to the drowsiness that overpowered her, and fallen asleep; though not so soundly but that she could from time to time utter a slight and almost inaudible groan, as if in recognition of the orator's doctrines. The baby in her arms was as fast asleep as she; and little Jacob, whose youth prevented him from recognising in this prolonged spiritual nourishment anything half as interesting as oysters, was alternately very fast asleep and very wide awake, as his inclination to slumber, or his terror of being personally alluded to in the discourse, gained the mastery over him.

"And now I'm here," thought Kit, gliding into the nearest empty pew which was opposite his mother's, and on the other side of the little aisle, "how am I ever to get at her, or persuade her to come out! I might as well be twenty miles off. She'll never wake till it's all over, and there goes the clock again! If he would but leave off for a minute, or if they'd only sing—!"

But there was little encouragement to believe that either event would happen for a couple of hours to come. The preacher went on telling them what he meant to convince them of before he had done, and it was clear that if he only kept to one-half of his promises and forgot the other he was good for that time at least.

In his desperation and restlessness Kit cast his eyes about the chapel, and happening to let them fall upon a little seat in front of the clerk's desk, could scarcely believe them when they showed him—Quilp!

He rubbed them twice or thrice, but still they insisted that Quilp was there, and there indeed he was, sitting with his hands upon his knees, and his hat between them on a little wooden bracket, with the accustomed grin upon his dirty face, and his eyes fixed upon the ceiling. He certainly did not glance at Kit or at his mother, and appeared utterly unconscious of their presence; still, Kit could not help feeling directly that the attention of the sly little fiend was fastened upon them, and upon nothing else.

But astounded as he was by the apparition of the dwarf among the Little Bethelites, and not free from a misgiving that it was the forerunner of some trouble or annoyance, he was compelled to subdue his wonder and to take active measures for the withdrawal of his parent, as the evening was now creeping on, and the matter grew serious. Therefore the next time little Jacob woke, Kit set himself to attract his wandering attention, and this not being a very difficult task (one sneeze effected it), he signed to him to rouse his mother.

Ill-luck would have it, however, that just then the preacher, in a forcible exposition of one head of his discourse, leaned over upon the pulpit desk so that very little more of him than his legs remained inside; and, while he made vehement gestures with his right hand, and held on with his left, stared, or seemed to stare, straight into little Jacob's eyes, threatening him by his strained look and attitude—so it appeared to the child— that if he so much as moved a muscle, he, the preacher, would be literally, and not figuratively, "down upon him" that instant. In this fearful state of things, distracted by the sudden appearance of Kit, and fascinated by the eyes of the preacher, the miserable Jacob sat bolt upright, wholly incapable of motion, strongly disposed to cry but afraid to do so, and returning his pastor's gaze until his infant eyes seemed starting from their sockets.

"If I must do it openly, I must," thought Kit. With that, he walked softly out of his pew and into his mother's, and as Mr Swiveller would have observed if he had been present, "collared" the baby without speaking a word.

"Hush, mother!" whispered Kit. "Come along with me, I've got something to tell you."

"Where am I?" said Mrs Nubbles.

"In this blessed Little Bethel," returned her son, peevishly.

"Blessed indeed!" cried Mrs Nubbles, catching at the word. "Oh, Christopher, how have I been edified this night!"

"Yes, yes, I know," said Kit hastily; "but come along, mother, everybody's looking at us. Don't make a noise—bring Jacob—that's right."

"Stay, Satan, stay!" cried the preacher, as Kit was moving off.

"The gentleman says you're to stay, Christopher," whispered his mother.

"Stay, Satan, stay!" roared the preacher again. "Tempt not the woman that doth incline her ear to thee, but hearken to the voice of him that calleth. He hath a lamb from the fold!" cried the preacher, raising his voice still higher and pointing to the baby. "He beareth off a lamb, a precious lamb! He goeth about like a wolf in the night season, and inveigleth the tender lambs!"

Kit was the best-tempered fellow in the world, but considering this strong language, and being somewhat excited by the circumstances in which he was placed, he faced round to the pulpit with the baby in his arms, and replied aloud:

"No, I don't. He's my brother."

"He's *my* brother!" cried the preacher.

"He isn't," said Kit indignantly. "How can you say such a thing?—And don't call me names if you please; what harm have I done? I shouldn't have come to take 'em away unless I was obliged, you may depend upon that; and I wanted to do it very quiet, but you wouldn't let me. Now, you have the goodness to abuse Satan and them as much as you like, sir, and to let me alone if you please."

So saying, Kit marched out of the chapel, followed by his mother and little Jacob, and found himself in the open air, with an indistinct recollection of having seen the people wake up and look surprised, and of Quilp having remained throughout the interruption in his old attitude, without moving his eyes from the ceiling, or appearing to take the smallest notice of anything that passed.

"Oh, Kit!" said his mother, with her handkerchief to her eyes, "what have you done! I never can go there again—never!"

"I'm glad of it, mother. What was there in the little bit of pleasure you took last night that made it necessary for you to be low-spirited and sorrowful to-night? That's the way you do. If you're happy or merry ever, you come here to say, along with that chap, that you're sorry for it. More shame for you, mother, I was going to say."

"Hush, dear!" said Mrs Nubbles; "you don't mean what you say, I know, but you're talking sinfulness."

"Don't mean it? But I do mean it!" retorted Kit. "I don't believe, mother, that harmless cheerfulness and good-humour are thought greater sins in Heaven than shirt-collars are, and that those chaps are just about as right and sensible in putting down the one as in leaving off the other—that's my belief. But I won't say anything more about it, if you'll promise not to cry, that's all; and you take the baby that's a lighter weight, and give me little Jacob; and as we go along (which we must do pretty quick) I'll tell you the news I bring, which will surprise you a little, I can tell you. There—that's right. Now you look as if you'd never seen Little Bethel in all your life, as I hope you never will again; and here's the baby; and little Jacob, you get atop of my back and catch hold of me tight round the neck, and whenever a Little Bethel parson calls you a precious lamb or says your brother's one, you tell him it's the truest thing he's said for a twelvemonth, and that if he'd got a little more of the lamb himself, and less of the mint-sauce—not being quite so sharp and sour over it—I should like him all the better. That's what you've got to say to *him*, Jacob."

Talking on in this way, half in jest and half in earnest, and cheering up his mother, the children, and himself, by the one simple process of determining to be in a good-humour, Kit led them briskly forward; and on the road home he related what had passed at the notary's house, and the purpose with which he had intruded on the solemnities of Little Bethel.

His mother was not a little startled on learning what service was required of her, and presently fell into a confusion of ideas, of which the most prominent were that it was a great honour and dignity to ride in a post-chaise, and that it was a moral impossibility to leave the children behind. But this objection, and a great many others, founded upon certain articles of dress being at the wash, and certain other articles having no existence in the wardrobe of Mrs Nubbles, were overcome by Kit, who opposed to each and every of them, the pleasure of recovering Nell, and the delight it would be to bring her back in triumph.

"There's only ten minutes now, mother"—said Kit when they reached home. "There's a bandbox. Throw in what you want, and we'll be off directly."

To tell how Kit then hustled into the box all sorts of things which could by no remote contingency be wanted, and how he left out everything likely to be of the smallest use; how a neighbour was persuaded to come and stop with the children, and how the children at first cried dismally, and then laughed heartily on being promised all kinds of impossible and unheard-of toys; how Kit's mother wouldn't leave off kissing them, and how Kit couldn't make up his mind to be vexed with her for doing it; would take more time and room than we can spare. So, passing over all such matters, it is sufficient to say that within a few minutes after the two hours had expired, Kit and his mother arrived at the notary's door, where a post-chaise was already waiting.

"With four horses I declare!" said Kit, quite aghast at the preparations. "Well you *are* going to do it, mother! Here she is, sir. Here's my mother. She's quite ready, sir."

"That's well"—returned the gentleman. "Now, don't be in a flutter, ma'am; you'll be taken great care of. Where's the box with the new clothing and necessaries for them?"

"Here it is." said the notary. "In with it, Christopher."

"All right, sir," replied Kit. "Quite ready now, sir."

"Then come along," said the single gentleman. And thereupon he gave his arm to Kit's mother, handed her into the carriage as politely as you please, and took his seat beside her.

Up went the steps, bang went the door, round whirled the wheels, and off they rattled, with Kit's mother hanging out at one window waving a damp pocket-handkerchief and screaming out a great many messages to little Jacob and the baby, of which nobody heard a word.

Kit stood in the middle of the road, and looked after them with tears in his eyes— not brought there by the departure he witnessed, but by the return to which he looked forward. "They went away," he thought, "on foot with nobody to speak to them or say a kind word at parting, and they'll come back, drawn by four horses, with this rich gentleman for their friend, and all their troubles over! She'll forget that she taught me to write—"

Whatever Kit thought about after this took some time to think of, for he stood gazing up the lines of shining lamps, long after the chaise had disappeared, and did not return into the house until the notary and Mr Abel, who had themselves lingered outside till the sound of the wheels was no longer distinguishable, had several times wondered what could possibly detain him.

Chapter XLII

I T behoves us to leave Kit for a while, thoughtful and expectant, and to follow the fortunes of little Nell; resuming the thread of the narrative at the point where it was left, some chapters back.

In one of those wanderings in the evening time, when, following the two sisters at a humble distance, she felt, in her sympathy with them and her recognition in their trials of something akin to her own loneliness of spirit, a comfort and consolation which made such moments a time of deep delight, though the softened pleasure they yielded was of that kind which lives and dies in tears—in one of those wanderings at the quiet hour of twilight, when sky, and earth, and air, and rippling water, and sound of distant bells, claimed kindred with the emotions of the solitary child, and inspired her with soothing thoughts, but not of a child's world or its easy joys—in one of those rambles which had now become her only pleasure or relief from care, light had faded into darkness and evening deepened into night, and still the young creature lingered in the gloom; feeling a companionship in Nature so serene and still, when noise of tongues and glare of garish lights would have been solitude indeed.

The sisters had gone home, and she was alone. She raised her eyes to the bright stars, looking down so mildly from the wide worlds of air, and, gazing on them, found new stars burst upon her view, and more beyond, and more beyond again, until the whole great expanse sparkled with shining spheres, rising higher and higher in im-measurable space, eternal in their numbers as in their changeless and incorruptible existence. She bent over the calm river, and saw them shining in the same majestic order as when the dove beheld them gleaming through the swollen waters, upon the moun-tain-tops down far below, and dead mankind, a million fathoms deep.

The child sat silently beneath a tree, hushed in her very breath by the stillness of the night, and all its attendant wonders. The time and place awoke reflection, and she thought with a quiet hope—less hope, perhaps, than resignation—on the past, and present, and what was yet before her. Between the old man and herself there had come a gradual separation, harder to bear than any former sorrow. Every evening, and often in the daytime too, he was absent, alone; and although she well knew where he went, and why—too well from the constant drain upon her scanty purse and from his haggard looks—he evaded all inquiry, maintained a strict reserve, and even shunned her pres-ence.

She sat meditating sorrowfully upon this change, and mingling it, as it were, with everything about her, when the distant church-clock bell struck nine. Rising at the sound, she retraced her steps, and turned thoughtfully towards the town.

She had gained a little wooden bridge, which, thrown across the stream, led into a meadow in her way, when she came suddenly upon a ruddy light, and looking forward more attentively, discerned that it proceeded from what appeared to be an encampment of gipsies, who had made a fire in one corner at no great distance from the path, and were sitting or lying round it. As she was too poor to have any fear of them, she did not alter her course (which, indeed, she could not have done without going a long way round), but quickened her pace a little, and kept straight on.

A movement of timid curiosity impelled her, when she approached the spot, to glance towards the fire. There was a form between it and her, the outline strongly developed against the light, which caused her to stop abruptly. Then, as if she had reasoned with herself and were assured that it could not be, or had satisfied herself that it was not that of the person she had supposed, she went on again.

But at that instant the conversation, whatever it was, which had been carrying on near this fire was resumed, and the tones of the voice that spoke—she could not distinguish words—sounded as familiar to her as her own.

She turned, and looked back. The person had been seated before, but was now in a standing posture, and leaning forward upon a stick on which he rested both hands. The attitude was no less familiar to her than the tone of voice had been. It *was* her grandfa-ther.

Her first impulse was to call to him; her next to wonder who his associates could be, and for what purpose they were together. Some vague apprehension succeeded, and, yielding to the strong inclination it awakened, she drew nearer to the place; not advancing across the open field, however, but creeping towards it by the hedge.

In this way she advanced within a few feet of the fire, and standing among a few young trees, could both see and hear, without much danger of being observed.

There were no women or children, as she had seen in other gipsy camps they had passed in their wayfaring, and but one gipsy—a tall athletic man, who stood with his arms folded, leaning against a tree at a little distance off, looking now at the fire, and now, under his black eyelashes, at three other men who were there, with a watchful but half-concealed interest in their conversation. Of these her grandfather was one; the others she recognised as the first card-players at the public-house on the eventful night of the storm—the man whom they had called Isaac List and his gruff companion. One of the low, arched gipsy-tents, common to that people, was pitched hard by, but it either was, or appeared to be, empty.

"Well, are you going?" said the stout man, looking up from the ground where he was lying at his ease, into her grandfather's face. "You were in a mighty hurry a minute ago. Go, if you like. You're your own master, I hope?"

"Don't vex him," returned Isaac List, who was squatting like a frog on the other side of the fire, and had so screwed himself up that he seemed to be squinting all over; "he didn't mean any offence."

"You keep me poor, and plunder me, and make a sport and jest of me besides," said the old man, turning from one to the other. "Ye'll drive me mad among ye."

The utter irresolution and feebleness of the grey-haired child, contrasted with the keen and cunning looks of those in whose hands he was, smote upon the little listener's heart. But she constrained herself to attend to all that passed, and to note each look and word.

"Confound you, what do you mean?" said the stout man rising a little, and supporting himself upon his elbow. "Keep you poor! You'd keep us poor if you could, wouldn't you? That's the way with you whining, puny, pitiful players. When you lose, you're martyrs; but I don't find that when you win, you look upon the other losers in that light. As to plunder!" cried the fellow, raising his voice—"damme, what do you mean by such ungentlemanly language as plunder, eh?"

The speaker laid himself down again at full length, and gave one or two short, angry kicks, as if in further expression of his unbounded indignation. It was quite plain that he acted the bully, and his friend the peacemaker, for some particular purpose; or rather, it would have been to any one but the weak old man; for they exchanged glances quite openly, both with each other and with the gipsy, who grinned his approval of the jest until his white teeth shone again.

The old man stood helplessly among them for a little time, and then said, turning to his assailant:

"You yourself were speaking of plunder just now, you know. Don't be so violent with me. You were, were you not?"

"Not of plundering among present company! Honour among—among gentlemen, sir," returned the other, who seemed to have been very near giving an awkward termination to the sentence.

"Don't be hard upon him, Jowl," said Isaac List. "He's very sorry for giving offence. There—go on with what you were saying—go on."

"I'm a jolly old tender-hearted lamb, I am," cried Mr Jowl, "to be sitting here at my time of life giving advice when I know it won't be taken, and that I shall get nothing but abuse for my pains. But that's the way I've gone through life. Experience has never put a chill upon my warm-heartedness."

"I tell you he's very sorry, don't I?" remonstrated Isaac List, "and that he wishes you'd go on."

"*Does* he wish it?" said the other.

"Ay," groaned the old man sitting down, and rocking himself to and fro. "Go on, go on. It's in vain to fight with it; I can't do it; go on."

"I go on then," said Jowl, "where I left off, when you got up so quick. If you're persuaded that it's time for luck to turn, as it certainly is, and find that you haven't means enough to try it (and that's where it is, for you know yourself that you never have the funds to keep on long enough at a sitting), help yourself to what seems put in your way on purpose. Borrow it, I say, and, when you're able, pay it back again."

"Certainly," Isaac List struck in, "if this good lady as keeps the wax-works has money, and does keep it in a tin box when she goes to bed, and doesn't lock her door for fear of fire, it seems a easy thing; quite a Providence, *I* should call it—but then I've been religiously brought up."

"You see, Isaac," said his friend, growing more eager, and drawing himself closer to the old man, while he signed to the gipsy not to come between them; "you see, Isaac, strangers are going in and out every hour of the day; nothing would be more likely than for one of these strangers to get under the good lady's bed, or lock himself in the cupboard; suspicion would be very wide, and would fall a long way from the mark, no doubt. I'd give him his revenge to the last farthing he brought, whatever the amount was."

"But could you?" urged Isaac List. "Is your bank strong enough?"

"Strong enough!" answered the other, with assumed disdain. "Here, you, sir, give me that box out of the straw!"

This was addressed to the gipsy, who crawled into the low tent on all fours, and after some rummaging and rustling returned with a cash-box, which the man who had spoken opened with a key he wore about his person.

"Do you see this?" he said, gathering up the money in his hand and letting it drop back into the box, between his fingers, like water. "Do you hear it? Do you know the sound of gold? There, put it back—and don't talk about banks again, Isaac, till you've got one of your own."

Isaac List, with great apparent humility, protested that he had never doubted the credit of a gentleman so notorious for his honourable dealing as Mr Jowl, and that he had hinted at the production of the box, not for the satisfaction of his doubts, for he could have none, but with a view to being regaled with a sight of so much wealth, which, though it might be deemed by some but an unsubstantial and visionary pleasure, was to one in his circumstances a source of extreme delight, only to be surpassed by its safe depository in his own personal pockets. Although Mr List and Mr Jowl addressed themselves to each other, it was remarkable that they both looked narrowly at the old man, who, with his eyes fixed upon the fire, sat brooding over it, yet listening eagerly—as it seemed from a certain involuntary motion of the head, or twitching of the face from time to time—to all they said.

"My advice," said Jowl, lying down again with a careless air, "is plain—I have given it, in fact. I act as a friend. Why should I help a man to the means perhaps of winning all I have, unless I considered him my friend? It's foolish, I dare say, to be so thoughtful of the welfare of other people, but that's my constitution, and I can't help it; so don't blame me, Isaac List."

"*I* blame you!" returned the person addressed; "not for the world, Mr Jowl. I wish I could afford to be as liberal as you; and as you say, he might pay it back if he won—and if he lost—"

"You're not to take that into consideration at all," said Jowl. "But suppose he did (and nothing's less likely, from all I know of chances), why, it's better to lose other people's money than one's own, I hope?"

"Ah!" cried Isaac List rapturously, "the pleasures of winning! The delight of picking up the money—the bright, shining yellow-boys—and sweeping 'em into one's pocket! The deliciousness of having a triumph at last, and thinking that one didn't stop short and turn back, but went half-way to meet it! The—But you're not going, old gentleman?"

"I'll do it," said the old man, who had risen and taken two or three hurried steps away, and now returned as hurriedly. "I'll have it, every penny."

"Why, that's brave," cried Isaac jumping up and slapping him on the shoulder; "and I respect you for having so much young blood left. Ha, ha, ha! Joe Jowl's half sorry he advised you now. We've got the laugh against him. Ha, ha, ha!"

"He gives me my revenge, mind," said the old man, pointing to him eagerly with his shrivelled hand: "mind—he stakes coin against coin, down to the last one in the box, be there many or few. Remember that!"

"I'm witness," returned Isaac. "I'll see fair between you."

"I have passed my word," said Jowl with feigned reluctance, "and I'll keep it. When does this match come off? I wish it was over.—To-night?"

"I must have the money first." said the old man; "and that I'll have to-morrow———"

"Why not to-night?" urged Jowl.

"It's late now, and I should be flushed and flurried," said the old man. "It must be softly done. No, to-morrow night."

"Then to-morrow be it," said Jowl. "A drop of comfort here. Luck to the best man! Fill!"

The gipsy produced three tin cups, and filled them to the brim with brandy. The old man turned aside and muttered to himself before he drank. Her own name struck upon the listener's ear, coupled with some wish so fervent, that he seemed to breathe it in an agony of supplication.

"God be merciful to us!" cried the child within herself, "and help us in this trying hour! What shall I do to save him!"

The remainder of their conversation was carried on in a lower tone of voice, and was sufficiently concise; relating merely to the execution of the project, and the best precautions for diverting suspicion. The old man then shook hands with his tempters, and withdrew.

They watched his bowed and stooping figure as it retreated slowly, and when he turned his head to look back, which he often did, waved their hands, or shouted some brief encouragement. It was not until they had seen him gradually diminish into a mere speck upon the distant road, that they turned to each other, and ventured to laugh aloud.

"So," said Jowl, warming his hands at the fire, "it's done at last. He wanted more persuading than I expected. It's three weeks ago since we first put this in his head. What'll he bring, do you think?"

"Whatever he brings, it's halved between us," returned Isaac List.

The other man nodded. "We must make quick work of it," he said, "and then cut his acquaintance, or we may be suspected. Sharp's the word."

List and the gipsy acquiesced. When they had all three amused themselves a little with their victim's infatuation, they dismissed the subject as one which had been sufficiently discussed, and began to talk in a jargon which the child did not understand. As their discourse appeared to relate to matters in which they were warmly interested, however, she deemed it the best time for escaping unobserved; and crept away with slow and cautious steps, keeping in the shadow of the hedges, or forcing a path through them or the dry ditches, until she could emerge upon the road at a point beyond their range of vision. Then she fled homewards as quickly as she could, torn and bleeding from the wounds of thorns and briars, but more lacerated in mind, and threw herself upon her bed, distracted.

The first idea that flashed upon her mind was flight, instant flight; dragging him from that place, and rather dying of want upon the roadside, than ever exposing him again to such terrible temptations. Then she remembered that the crime was not to be committed until next night, and there was the intermediate time for thinking, and resolving what to do. Then she was distracted with a horrible fear that he might be committing it at that moment; with a dread of hearing shrieks and cries piercing the silence of the night; with fearful thoughts of what he might be tempted and led on to do, if he were detected in the act, and had but a woman to struggle with. It was impossible to bear such torture. She stole to the room where the money was, opened the door, and looked in. God be praised! He was not there, and she was sleeping soundly.

She went back to her own room, and tried to prepare herself for bed. But who could sleep—sleep! who could lie passively down, distracted by such terrors? They came upon her more and more strongly yet. Half undressed, and with her hair in wild disorder, she flew to the old man's bedside, clasped him by the wrist, and roused him from his sleep.

"What's this!" he cried, starting up in bed, and fixing his eyes upon her spectral face.

"I have had a dreadful dream," said the child, with an energy that nothing but such terrors could have inspired. "A dreadful, horrible dream. I have had it once before. It is a dream of grey-haired men like you, in darkened rooms by night, robbing the sleepers of their gold. Up, up!" The old man shook in every joint, and folded his hands like one who prays.

"Not to me," said the child, "not to me—to Heaven, to save us from such deeds! This dream is too real. I cannot sleep, I cannot stay here, I cannot leave you alone under the roof where such dreams come. Up! We must fly."

He looked at her as if she were a spirit—she might have been, for all the look of earth she had—and trembled more and more.

"There is no time to lose; I will not lose one minute," said the child. "Up! and away with me!"

"To-night!" murmured the old man.

"Yes, to-night," replied the child. "To-morrow night will be too late. The dream will have come again. Nothing but flight can save us. Up!"

The old man rose from his bed, his forehead bedewed with the cold sweat of fear, and, bending before the child as if she had been an angel messenger sent to lead him where she would, made ready to follow her. She took him by the hand and led him on. As they passed the door of the room he had proposed to rob, she shuddered and looked up into his face. What a white face was that, and with what a look did he meet hers!

She took him to her own chamber, and, still holding him by the hand as if she feared to lose him for an instant, gathered together the little stock she had, and hung her basket on her arm. The old man took his wallet from her hands and strapped it on his shoulders—his staff, too, she had brought away—and then she led him forth.

Through the strait streets, and narrow crooked outskirts, their trembling feet passed quickly. Up the steep hill too, crowned by the old grey castle, they toiled with rapid steps, and had not once looked behind.

But as they drew nearer the ruined walls, the moon rose in all her gentle glory, and, from their venerable age, garlanded with ivy, moss, and waving grass, the child looked back upon the sleeping town, deep in the valley's shade, and on the far-off river with its winding track of light, and on the distant hills; and as she did so, she clasped the hand she held, less firmly, and bursting into tears, fell upon the old man's neck.

Chapter XLIII

HER momentary weakness past, the child again summoned the resolution which had until now sustained her, and, endeavouring to keep steadily in her view the one idea that they were flying from disgrace and crime, and that her grandfather's preservation must depend solely upon her firmness, unaided by one word of advice or any helping hand, urged him onward and looked back no more.

While he, subdued and abashed, seemed to crouch before her, and to shrink and cower down as if in the presence of some superior creature, the child herself was sensible of a new feeling within her, which elevated her nature, and inspired her with an energy and confidence she had never known. There was no divided responsibility now; the whole burden of their two lives had fallen upon her, and henceforth she must think and act for both. "I have saved him," she thought. "In all dangers and distresses, I will remember that."

At any other time the recollection of having deserted the friend who had shown them so much homely kindness, without a word of justification—the thought that they were guilty, in appearance, of treachery and ingratitude—even the having parted from the two sisters—would have filled her with sorrow and regret. But now all other considerations were lost in the new uncertainties and anxieties of their wild and wandering life; and the very desperation of their condition roused and stimulated her.

In the pale moonlight, which lent a wanness of its own, the delicate face where thoughtful care already mingled with the winning grace and loveliness of youth, the too bright eye, the spiritual head, the lips that pressed each other with such high resolve and courage of the heart, the slight figure firm in its bearing and yet so very weak, told their silent tale; but told it only to the wind that rustled by, which, taking up its burden, carried, perhaps to some mother's pillow, faint dreams of childhood fading in its bloom, and resting in the sleep that knows no waking.

The night crept on apace, the moon went down, the stars grew pale and dim, and morning, cold as they, slowly approached. Then, from behind a distant hill, the noble sun rose up, driving the mists in phantom shapes before it, and clearing the earth of their ghostly forms till darkness came again. When it had climbed higher into the sky, and there was warmth in its cheerful beams, they laid them down to sleep, upon a bank, hard by some water.

But Nell retained her grasp upon the old man's arm, and long after he was slumbering soundly, watched him with untiring eyes. Fatigue stole over her at last; her grasp relaxed, tightened, relaxed again, and they slept side by side.

A confused sound of voices, mingling with her dreams, awoke her. A man of very uncouth and rough appearance was standing over them, and two of his companions were looking on from a long heavy boat which had come close to the bank while they were sleeping. The boat had neither oar nor sail, but was towed by a couple of horses, who, with the rope to which they were harnessed slack and dripping in the water, were resting on the path.

"Holloa!" said the man roughly. "What's the matter here, eh?"

"We were only asleep, sir," said Nell. "We have been walking all night."

"A pair of queer travellers to be walking all night," observed the man who had first accosted them. "One of you is a trifle too old for that sort of work, and the other a trifle too young. Where are you going?"

Nell faltered, and pointed at hazard towards the west, upon which the man inquired if she meant a certain town which he named. Nell, to avoid further questioning, said, "Yes, that was the place."

"Where have you come from?" was the next question; and this being an easier one to answer, Nell mentioned the name of the village in which their friend the schoolmaster dwelt, as being less likely to be known to the men or to provoke further inquiry.

"I thought somebody had been robbing and ill-using you, might be," said the man. "That's all. Good day."

Returning his salute and feeling greatly relieved by his departure, Nell looked after him as he mounted one of the horses, and the boat went on. It had not gone very far, when it stopped again, and she saw the men beckoning to her.

"Did you call to me?" said Nell, running up to them.

"You may go with us if you like," replied one of those in the boat. "We're going to the same place."

The child hesitated for a moment, and thinking, as she had thought with great trepidation more than once before, that the men whom she had seen with her grandfather might perhaps, in their eagerness for the booty, follow them, and, regaining their influence over him, set hers at nought; and that if they went with these men, all traces of them must surely be lost at that spot; determined to accept the offer. The boat came close to the bank again, and before she had had any time for further consideration, she and her grandfather were on board, and gliding smoothly down the canal.

The sun shone pleasantly upon the bright water, which was sometimes shaded by trees, and sometimes open to a wide extent of country, intersected by running streams, and rich with wooded hills, cultivated land, and sheltered farms. Now and then a village with its modest spire, thatched roofs, and gable-ends, would peep out from among the trees; and more than once a distant town, with great church towers looming through its smoke, and high factories or workshops rising above the mass of houses, would come in view, and, by the length of time it lingered in the distance, show them how slowly they travelled. Their way lay for the most part through the low grounds, and open plains; and except these distant places, and occasionally some men working in the fields, or lounging on the bridges under which they passed, to see them creep along, nothing encroached on their monotonous and secluded track.

Nell was rather disheartened, when they stopped at a kind of wharf late in the afternoon, to learn from one of the men that they would not reach their place of destination until next day, and that if she had no provision with her she had better buy it there. She had but a few pence, having already bargained with them for some bread, but even of these it was necessary to be very careful, as they were on their way to an utterly strange place, with no resource whatever. A small loaf and a morsel of cheese, therefore, were all she could afford, and with these she took her place in the boat again, and, after half an hour's delay during which the men were drinking at the public-house, proceeded on the journey.

They brought some beer and spirits into the boat with them, and what with drinking freely before, and again now, were soon on a fair way of being quarrelsome and intoxicated. Avoiding the small cabin, therefore, which was very dark and filthy, and to which they often invited both her and her grandfather, Nell sat in the open air with the old man by her side, listening to their boisterous hosts with a palpitating heart, and almost wishing herself safe on shore again though she should have to walk all night.

They were in truth very rugged, noisy fellows, and quite brutal among themselves, though civil enough to their two passengers. Thus, when a quarrel arose between the man who was steering and his friend in the cabin, upon the question who had first suggested the propriety of offering Nell some beer, and when the quarrel led to a scuffle in which they beat each other fearfully, to her inexpressible terror, neither visited his displeasure upon her, but each contented himself with venting it on his adversary, on whom, in addition to blows, he bestowed a variety of compliments, which, happily for the child, were conveyed in terms to her quite unintelligible. The difference was finally adjusted, by the man who had come out of the cabin knocking the other into it head first, and taking the helm into his own hands, without evincing the least discomposure himself, or causing any in his friend, who, being of a tolerably strong constitution and perfectly inured to such trifles, went to sleep as he was, with his heels upwards, and in a couple of minutes or so was snoring comfortably.

By this time it was night again, and though the child felt cold, being but poorly clad, her anxious thoughts were far removed from her own suffering or uneasiness, and busily engaged in endeavouring to devise some scheme for their joint subsistence. The same spirit which had supported her on the previous night upheld and sustained her now. Her grandfather lay sleeping safely at her side, and the crime to which his madness urged him was not committed. That was her comfort.

How every circumstance of her short, eventful life, came thronging into her mind as they travelled on! Slight incidents, never thought of or remembered until now; faces seen once and ever since forgotten; words spoken and scarcely heeded at the time; scenes of a year ago and those of yesterday mixing up and linking themselves together; familiar places shaping themselves out in the darkness from things which, when approached, were of all others the most remote and most unlike them; sometimes a strange confusion in her mind relative to the occasion of her being there, and the place to which she was going, and the people she was with; and imagination suggesting remarks and questions which sounded so plainly in her ears, that she would start, and turn, and be almost tempted to reply;—all the fancies and contradictions common in watching and excitement and restless change of place, beset the child.

She happened, while she was thus engaged, to encounter the face of the man on deck, in whom the sentimental stage of drunkenness had now succeeded to the boisterous, and who, taking from his mouth a short pipe, quilted over with string for its longer preservation, requested that she would oblige him with a song.

"You've got a very pretty voice, a very soft eye, and a very strong memory," said this gentleman; "the voice and eye I've got evidence for, and the memory's an opinion of my own. And I'm never wrong. Let me hear a song this minute."

"I don't think I know one, sir," returned Nell.

"You know forty-seven songs," said the man, with a gravity which admitted of no altercation on the subject. "Forty-seven's your number. Let me hear one of 'em—the best. Give me a song this minute."

Not knowing what might be the consequences of irritating her friend, and trembling with the fear of doing so, poor Nell sang him some little ditty which she had learned in happier times, and which was so agreeable to his ear, that on its conclusion he in the same peremptory manner requested to be favoured with another, to which he was so obliging as to roar a chorus to no particular tune, and with no words at all, but which amply made up in its amazing energy for its deficiency in other respects. The noise of this vocal performance awakened the other man, who, staggering upon deck and shaking his late opponent by the hand, swore that singing was his pride and joy and chief delight, and that he desired no better entertainment. With a third call, more imperative than either of the two former, Nell felt obliged to comply, and this time a chorus was maintained not only by the two men together, but also by the third man on horseback, who, being by his position debarred from a nearer participation in the revels of the night, roared when his companions roared, and rent the very air. In this way, with little cessation, and singing the same songs again and again, the tired and exhausted child kept them in good humour all that night; and many a cottager, who was roused from his soundest sleep by the discordant chorus as it floated away upon the wind, hid his head beneath the bedclothes and trembled at the sounds.

At length the morning dawned. It was no sooner light than it began to rain heavily. As the child could not endure the intolerable vapours of the cabin, they covered her, in return for her exertions, with some pieces of sail-cloth and ends of tarpaulin, which sufficed to keep her tolerably dry and to shelter her grandfather besides. As the day advanced the rain increased. At noon it poured down more hopelessly and heavily than ever, without the faintest promise of abatement.

They had for some time been gradually approaching the place for which they were bound. The water had become thicker and dirtier; other barges coming from it passed them frequently; the paths of coal-ash and huts of staring brick, marked the vicinity of some great manufacturing town; while scattered streets and houses, and smoke from distant furnaces, indicated that they were already in the outskirts. Now, the clustered roofs, and piles of buildings trembling with the working of engines, and dimly resounding with their shrieks and throbbings; the tall chimneys vomiting forth a black vapour, which hung in a dense ill-favoured cloud above the housetops and filled the air with gloom; the clank of hammers beating upon iron, the roar of busy streets and noisy crowds, gradually augmenting until all the various sounds blended into one and none was distinguishable for itself, announced the termination of their journey.

The boat floated into the wharf to which it belonged. The men were occupied directly. The child and her grandfather, after waiting in vain to thank them, or ask them whither they should go, passed through a dirty lane into a crowded street, and stood amid its din and tumult, and in the pouring rain, as strange, bewildered, and confused, as if they had lived a thousand years before, and were raised from the dead and placed there by a miracle.

Chapter XLIV

T HE throng of people hurried by, in two opposite streams, with no symptom of cessation or exhaustion; intent upon their own affairs; and undisturbed in their business speculations, by the roar of carts and waggons laden with clashing wares, the slipping of horses' feet upon the wet and greasy pavement, the rattling of the rain on windows and umbrella-tops, the jostling of the more impatient passengers, and all the noise and tumult of a crowded street in the high tide of its occupation: while the two poor strangers, stunned and bewildered by the hurry they beheld but had no part in, looked mournfully on; feeling amidst the crowd a solitude which has no parallel but in the thirst of the shipwrecked mariner, who, tossed to and fro upon the billows of a mighty ocean, his red eyes blinded by looking on the water which hems him in on every side, has not one drop to cool his burning tongue.

They withdrew into a low archway for shelter from the rain, and watched the faces of those who passed, to find in one among them a ray of encouragement or hope. Some frowned, some smiled, some muttered to themselves, some made slight gestures, as if anticipating the conversation in which they would shortly be engaged, some wore the cunning look of bargaining and plotting, some were anxious and eager, some slow and dull; in some countenances were written gain; in others loss. It was like being in the confidence of all these people to stand quietly there, looking into their faces as they flitted past. In busy places, where each man has an object of his own, and feels assured that every other man has his, his character and purpose are written broadly in his face. In the public walks and lounges of a town, people go to see and to be seen, and there the same expression, with little variety, is repeated a hundred times. The working-day faces come nearer to the truth, and let it out more plainly.

Falling into that kind of abstraction which such a solitude awakens, the child continued to gaze upon the passing crowd with a wondering interest, amounting almost to a temporary forgetfulness of her own condition. But cold, wet, hunger, want of rest, and lack of any place in which to lay her aching head, soon brought her thoughts back to the point whence they had strayed. No one passed who seemed to notice them, or to whom she durst appeal. After some time, they left their place of refuge from the weather, and mingled with the concourse.

Evening came on. They were still wandering up and down, with fewer people about them, but with the same sense of solitude in their own breasts, and the same indifference from all around. The lights in the streets and shops made them feel yet more desolate, for with their help, night and darkness seemed to come on faster. Shivering with the cold and damp, ill in body, and sick to death at heart, the child needed her utmost firmness and resolution even to creep along.

Why had they ever come to this noisy town, when there were peaceful country places, in which at least, they might have hungered and thirsted, with less suffering than in its squalid strife! They were but an atom, here, in a mountain heap of misery, the very sight of which increased their hopelessness and suffering.

The child had not only to endure the accumulated hardships of their destitute condition, but to bear the reproaches of her grandfather, who began to murmur at having been led away from their late abode, and demand that they should return to it. Being now penniless, and no relief or prospect of relief appearing, they retraced their steps through the deserted streets, and went back to the wharf, hoping to find the boat in which they had come, and to be allowed to sleep on board that night. But here again they were disappointed, for the gate was closed, and some fierce dogs, barking at their approach, obliged them to retreat.

"We must sleep in the open air to-night, dear," said the child in a weak voice, as they turned away from this last repulse; "and tomorrow we will beg our way to some quiet part of the country, and try to earn our bread in very humble work."

"Why did you bring me here?" returned the old man fiercely. "I cannot bear these close eternal streets. We came from a quiet part. Why did you force me to leave it?"

"Because I must have that dream I told you of, no more," said the child, with a momentary firmness that lost itself in tears; "and we must live among poor people, or it will come again. Dear grandfather, you are old and weak, I know; but look at me. I never will complain if you will not, but I have some suffering indeed."

"Ah, poor, houseless, wandering, motherless child!" cried the old man, clasping his hands and gazing as if for the first time upon her anxious face, her travel-stained dress, and bruised and swollen feet; "has all my agony of care brought her to this at last! Was I a happy man once, and have I lost happiness and all I had, for this!"

"If we were in the country now," said the child, with assumed cheerfulness, as they walked on looking about them for a shelter, "we should find some good old tree, stretching out his green arms as if he loved us, and nodding and rustling as if he would have us fall asleep, thinking of him while he watched. Please God, we shall be there soon—to-morrow or next day at the farthest—and in the meantime let us think, dear, that it was a good thing we came here; for we are lost in the crowd and hurry of this place, and if any cruel people should pursue us, they could surely never trace us further. There's comfort in that. And here's a deep old doorway—very dark, but quite dry, and warm too, for the wind don't blow in here—What's that!"

Uttering a half-shriek, she recoiled from a black figure which came suddenly out of the dark recess in which they were about to take refuge, and stood still looking at them.

"Speak again," it said; "do I know the voice?"

"No," replied the child timidly; "we are strangers, and having no money for a night's lodging, were going to rest here."

There was a feeble lamp at no great distance; the only one in the place, which was a kind of square yard, but sufficient to show how poor and mean it was. To this, the figure beckoned them; at the same time drawing within its rays, as if to show that it had no desire to conceal itself or take them at an advantage.

The form was that of a man, miserably clad and begrimed with smoke, which, perhaps by its contrast with the natural colour of his skin, made him look paler than he really was. That he was naturally of a very wan and pallid aspect, however, his hollow cheeks, sharp features, and sunken eyes, no less than a certain look of patient endurance, sufficiently testified. His voice was harsh by nature, but not brutal; and though his face, besides possessing the characteristics already mentioned, was overshadowed by a quantity of long dark hair, its expression was neither ferocious nor cruel.

"How came you to think of resting there?" he said. "Or how," he added, looking more attentively at the child, "do you come to want a place of rest at this time of night?"

"Our misfortunes," the grandfather answered, "are the cause."

"Do you know," said the man, looking still more earnestly at Nell, "how wet she is, and that the damp streets are not a place for her?"

"I know it well, God help me," he replied. "What can I do!"

The man looked at Nell again, and gently touched her garments, from which the rain was running off in little streams. "I can give you warmth," he said, after a pause; "nothing else. Such lodging as I have is in that house," pointing to the doorway from which he had emerged, "but she is safer and better there than here. The fire is in a rough place, but you can pass the night beside it safely, if you'll trust yourselves to me. You see that red light yonder?"

They raised their eyes, and saw a lurid glare hanging in the dark sky; the dull reflection of some distant fire.

"It's not far," said the man. "Shall I take you there? You were going to sleep upon cold bricks; I can give you a bed of warm ashes—nothing better."

Without waiting for any further reply than he saw in their looks, he took Nell in his arms, and bade the old man follow.

Carrying her as tenderly, and as easily too, as if she had been an infant, and showing himself both swift and sure of foot, he led the way through what appeared to be the poorest and most wretched quarter of the town; not turning aside to avoid the overflowing kennels or running waterspouts, but holding his course, regardless of such obstructions, and making his way straight through them. They had proceeded thus in silence for some quarter of an hour, and had lost sight of the glare to which he had pointed, in the dark and narrow ways by which they had come, when it suddenly burst upon them again, streaming up from the high chimney of a building close before them.

"This is the place," he said, pausing at a door to put Nell down and take her hand. "Don't be afraid. There's nobody here will harm you."

It needed a strong confidence in this assurance to induce them to enter, and what they saw inside did not diminish their apprehension and alarm. In a large and lofty building, supported by pillars of iron, with great black apertures in the upper walls, open to the external air; echoing to the roof with the beating of hammers and roar of furnaces, mingled with the hissing of red-hot metal plunged in water, and a hundred strange unearthly noises never heard elsewhere; in this gloomy place, moving like demons among the flame and smoke, dimly and fitfully seen, flushed and tormented by the burning fires, and wielding great weapons, a faulty blow from any one of which must have crushed some workman's skull, a number of men laboured like giants. Others, reposing upon heaps of coals or ashes with their faces turned to the black vault above, slept or rested from their toil. Others again, opening the white-hot furnace doors, cast fuel on the flames, which came rushing and roaring forth to meet it, and licked it up like oil. Others drew forth, with clashing noise upon the ground, great sheets of glowing steel, emitting an insupportable heat, and a dull deep light like that which reddens in the eyes of savage beasts.

Through these bewildering sights and deafening sounds, their conductor led them to where, in a dark portion of the building, one furnace burnt by night and day—so at least they gathered from the motion of his lips, for as yet they could only see him speak: not hear him. The man who had been watching this fire, and whose task was ended for the present, gladly withdrew, and left them with their friend, who, spreading Nell's little cloak upon a heap of ashes, and showing her where she could hang her outer clothes to dry, signed to her and the old man to lie down and sleep. For himself, he took his station on a rugged mat before the furnace door, and resting his chin upon his hands, watched the flame as it shone through the iron chinks, and the white ashes as they fell into their bright hot grave below.

The warmth of her bed, hard and humble as it was, combined with the great fatigue she had undergone, soon caused the tumult of the place to fall with a gentler sound upon the child's tired ears, and was not long in lulling her to sleep. The old man was stretched beside her, and with her hand upon his neck she lay and dreamed.

It was yet night when she awoke, nor did she know how long, or for how short a time, she had slept. But she found herself protected, both from any cold air that might find its way into the building, and from the scorching heat, by some of the workmen's clothes; and glancing at their friend saw that he sat in exactly the same attitude, looking with a fixed earnestness of attention towards the fire, and keeping so very still that he did not even seem to breathe. She lay in the state between sleeping and waking, looking so long at his motionless figure that at length she almost feared he had died as he sat there; and, softly rising and drawing close to him, ventured to whisper in his ear.

He moved, and glancing from her to the place she had lately occupied, as if to assure himself that it was really the child so near him, looked inquiringly into her face.

"I feared you were ill," she said. "The other men are all in motion, and you are so very quiet."

"They leave me to myself," he replied. "They know my humour. They laugh at me, but don't harm me in it. See yonder there—that's *my* friend."

"The fire?" said the child.

"It has been alive as long as I have," the man made answer. "We talk and think together all night long."

The child glanced quickly at him in her surprise, but he had turned his eyes in their former direction, and was musing as before.

"It's like a book to me," he said—"the only book I ever learned to read; and many an old story it tells me. It's music, for I should know its voice among a thousand, and there are other voices in its roar. It has its pictures too. You don't know how many strange faces and different scenes I trace in the red-hot coals. It's my memory, that fire, and shows me all my life."

The child, bending down to listen to his words, could not help remarking with what brightened eyes he continued to speak and muse.

"Yes," he said, with a faint smile, "it was the same when I was quite a baby, and crawled about it, till I fell asleep. My father watched it then."

"Had you no mother?" asked the child.

"No, she was dead. Women work hard in these parts. She worked herself to death they told me, and, as they said so then, the fire has gone on saying the same thing ever since. I suppose it was true. I have always believed it."

"Were you brought up here, then?" said the child.

"Summer and winter," he replied. "Secretly at first, but when they found it out, they let him keep me here. So the fire nursed me—the same fire. It has never gone out."

"You are fond of it?" said the child.

"Of course I am. He died before it. I saw him fall down—just there, where those ashes are burning now—and wondered, I remember, why it didn't help him."

"Have you been here ever since?" asked the child.

"Ever since I came to watch it; but there was a while between, and a very cold dreary while it was. It burned all the time though, and roared and leaped when I came back, as it used to do in our play-days. You may guess from looking at me what kind of child I was, but for all the difference between us I was a child, and when I saw you in the street to-night, you put me in mind of myself as I was after he died, and made me wish to bring you to the old fire. I thought of those old times again when I saw you sleeping by it. You should be sleeping now. Lie down again, poor child, lie down again."

With that he led her to her rude couch, and covering her with the clothes with which she had found herself enveloped when she woke, returned to his seat, whence he moved no more unless to feed the furnace, but remained motionless as a statue. The child continued to watch him for a little time, but soon yielded to the drowsiness that came upon her, and, in the dark strange place and on the heap of ashes, slept as peacefully as if the room had been a palace chamber, and the bed a bed of down.

When she awoke again, broad day was shining through the lofty openings in the walls, and, stealing in slanting rays but midway down, seemed to make the building darker than it had been at night. The clang and tumult were still going on, and the remorseless fires were burning fiercely as before; for few changes of night and day brought rest or quiet there.

Her friend parted his breakfast—a scanty mess of coffee and some coarse bread—with the child and her grandfather, and inquired whither they were going. She told him that they sought some distant country place remote from towns or even other villages, and with a faltering tongue inquired what road they would do best to take.

"I know little of the country," he said, shaking his head, "for such as I pass all our lives before our furnace doors, and seldom go forth to breathe. But there *are* such places yonder."

"And far from here?" said Nell.

"Ay, surely. How could they be near us, and be green and fresh? The road lies, too, through miles and miles, all lighted up by fires like ours—a strange black road, and one that would frighten you by night."

"We are here and must go on," said the child boldly; for she saw that the old man listened with anxious ears to this account.

"Rough people—paths never made for little feet like yours—a dismal, blighted way—is there no turning back, my child?"

"There is none," cried Nell, pressing forward. "If you can direct us, do. If not, pray do not seek to turn us from our purpose. Indeed, you do not know the danger that we shun, and how right and true we are in flying from it, or you would not try to stop us, I am sure you would not."

"God forbid, if it is so!" said their uncouth protector, glancing from the eager child to her grandfather, who hung his head and bent his eyes upon the ground. "I'll direct you from the door, the best I can. I wish I could do more."

He showed them, then, by which road they must leave the town, and what course they should hold when they had gained it. He lingered so long on these instructions, that the child, with a fervent blessing, tore herself away, and stayed to hear no more.

But before they had reached the corner of the lane, the man came running after them, and, pressing her hand, left something in it—two old, battered, smoke-encrusted penny pieces. Who knows but they shone as brightly in the eyes of angels as golden gifts that have been chronicled on tombs?

And thus they separated; the child to lead her sacred charge farther from guilt and shame; and the labourer to attach a fresh interest to the spot where his guests had slept, and read new histories in his furnace fire.

Chapter XLV

I N all their journeying, they had never longed so ardently, they had never so pined and wearied, for the freedom of pure air and open country, as now. No, not even on that memorable morning, when, deserting their old home, they abandoned themselves to the mercies of a strange world, and left all the dumb and senseless things they had known and loved behind—not even then had they so yearned for the fresh solitudes of wood, hillside, and field, as now; when the noise and dirt and vapour of the great manufacturing town, reeking with lean misery and hungry wretchedness, hemmed them in on every side, and seemed to shut out hope, and render escape impossible.

"Two days and nights!" thought the child. "He said two days and nights we should have to spend among such scenes as these. Oh! if we live to reach the country once again, if we get clear of these dreadful places, though it is only to lie down and die, with what a grateful heart I shall thank God for so much mercy!"

With thoughts like this, and with some vague design of travelling to a great distance among streams and mountains, where only very poor and simple people lived, and where they might maintain themselves by very humble helping work in farms, free from such terrors as that from which they fled—the child, with no resource but the poor man's gift, and no encouragement but that which flowed from her own heart, and its sense of the truth and right of what she did, nerved herself to this last journey and boldly pursued her task.

"We shall be very slow to-day, dear," she said, as they toiled painfully through the streets; "my feet are sore, and I have pains in all my limbs from the wet of yesterday. I saw that he looked at us and thought of that, when he said how long we should be upon the road."

"It was a dreary way he told us of," returned her grandfather piteously. "Is there no other road? Will you not let me go some other way than this?"

"Places lie beyond these," said the child firmly, "where we may live in peace, and be tempted to do no harm. We will take the road that promises to have that end, and we would not turn out of it, if it were a hundred times worse than our fears lead us to expect. We would not, dear, would we?"

"No," replied the old man, wavering in his voice, no less than in his manner. "No. Let us go on. I am ready. I am quite ready, Nell."

The child walked with more difficulty than she had led her companion to expect, for the pains that racked her joints were of no common severity, and every exertion increased them. But they wrung from her no complaint, or look of suffering; and, though the two travellers proceeded very slowly, they did proceed; and clearing the town in course of time, began to feel that they were fairly on their way.

A long suburb of red-brick houses—some with patches of garden-ground, where coal-dust and factory smoke darkened the shrinking leaves and coarse, rank flowers; and where the struggling vegetation sickened and sank under the hot breath of kiln and furnace, making them by its presence seem yet more blighting and unwholesome than in the town itself—a long, flat, straggling suburb passed, they came by slow degrees upon a cheerless region, where not a blade of grass was seen to grow; where not a bud put forth its promise in the spring; where nothing green could live but on the surface of the stagnant pools, which here and there lay idly sweltering by the black roadside.

Advancing more and more into the shadow of this mournful place, its dark depressing influence stole upon their spirits, and filled them with a dismal gloom. On every side, and far as the eye could see into the heavy distance, tall chimneys, crowding on each other, and presenting that endless repetition of the same dull, ugly form, which is the horror of oppressive dreams, poured out their plague of smoke, obscured the light, and made foul the melancholy air. On mounds of ashes by the wayside, sheltered only by a few rough boards, or rotten pent-house roofs, strange engines spun and writhed like tortured creatures; clanking their iron chains, shrieking in their rapid whirl from time to time as though in torment unendurable, and making the ground tremble with their agonies. Dismantled houses here and there appeared, tottering to the earth, propped up by fragments of others that had fallen down, unroofed, windowless, blackened, desolate, but yet inhabited. Men, women, children, wan in their looks and ragged in attire, tended the engines, fed their tributary fires, begged upon the road, or scowled half naked from the doorless houses. Then came more of the wrathful monsters, whose like they almost seemed to be in their wildness and their untamed air, screeching and turning round and round again; and still, before, behind, and to the right and left, was the same interminable perspective of brick towers, never ceasing in their black vomit, blasting all things living or inanimate, shutting out the face of day, and closing in on all these horrors with a dense dark cloud.

But night-time in this dreadful spot!—night, when the smoke was changed to fire; when every chimney spirted up its flame; and places, that had been dark vaults all day, now shone red-hot, with figures moving to and fro within their blazing jaws, and calling to one another with hoarse cries—night, when the noise of every strange machine was aggravated by the darkness; when the people near them looked wilder and more savage; when bands of unemployed labourers paraded in the roads, or clustered by torch-light round their leaders, who told them in stern language of their wrongs, and urged them on to frightful cries and threats; when maddened men, armed with sword and firebrand, spurning the tears and prayers of women who would restrain them, rushed forth on errands of terror and destruction, to work no ruin half so surely as their own—night, when carts came rumbling by, filled with rude coffins (for contagious disease and death had been busy with the living crops); when orphans cried, and distracted women shrieked and followed in their wake—night, when some called for bread, and some for drink to drown their cares; and some with tears, and some with staggering feet, and some with bloodshot eyes, went brooding home—night, which, unlike the night that Heaven sends on earth, brought with it no peace, nor quiet, nor signs of blessed sleep—who shall tell the terrors of the night to that young wandering child!

And yet she lay down, with nothing between her and the sky; and, with no fear for herself, for she was past it now, put up a prayer for the poor old man. So very weak and spent she felt, so very calm and unresisting, that she had no thought of any wants of her own, but prayed that God would raise up some friend for *him*. She tried to recall the way they had come, and to look in the direction where the fire by which they had slept last night was burning. She had forgotten to ask the name of the poor man, their friend, and when she had remembered him in her prayers, it seemed ungrateful not to turn one look towards the spot where he was watching.

A penny loaf was all they had had that day. It was very little, but even hunger was forgotten in the strange tranquillity that crept over her senses. She lay down very gently, and, with a quiet smile upon her face, fell into a slumber. It was not like sleep—and yet it must have been, or why those pleasant dreams of the little scholar all night long!

Morning came. Much weaker, diminished powers even of sight and hearing, and yet the child made no complaint—perhaps would have made none, even if she had not that inducement to be silent, travelling by her side. She felt a hopelessness of their ever being extricated together from that forlorn place, a dull conviction that she was very ill, perhaps dying; but no fear or anxiety.

A loathing of food, that she was not conscious of until they expended their last penny in the purchase of another loaf, prevented her partaking even of this poor repast. Her grandfather ate greedily, which she was glad to see.

Their way lay through the same scenes as yesterday, with no variety or improvement. There was the same thick air, difficult to breathe; the same blighted ground, the same hopeless prospect, the same misery and distress. Objects appeared more dim, the noise less, the path more rugged and uneven, for sometimes she stumbled, and became roused, as it were, in the effort to prevent herself from falling. Poor child! the cause was in her tottering feet.

Towards the afternoon, her grandfather complained bitterly of hunger. She approached one of the wretched hovels by the wayside, and knocked with her hand upon the door.

"What would you have here?" said a gaunt miserable man, opening it.

"Charity. A morsel of bread."

"Do you see that!" returned the man hoarsely, pointing to a kind of bundle on the ground. "That's a dead child. I and five hundred other men were thrown out of work three months ago. That is my third dead child, and last. Do you think I have charity to bestow, or a morsel of bread to spare?"

The child recoiled from the door, and it closed upon her. Impelled by strong necessity, she knocked at another; her neighbouring one, which, yielding to the slight pressure of her hand, flew open.

It seemed that a couple of poor families lived in this hovel, for two women, each among children of her own, occupied different portions of the room. In the centre stood a grave gentleman in black who appeared to have just entered, and who held by the arm a boy.

"Here, woman," he said, "here's your deaf and dumb son. You may thank me for restoring him to you. He was brought before me this morning, charged with theft; and with any other boy it would have gone hard, I assure you. But as I had compassion on his infirmities, and thought he might have learnt no better, I have managed to bring him back to you. Take more care of him for the future."

"And won't you give me back *my* son!" said the other woman, hastily rising and confronting him. "Won't you give me back *my* son, sir, who was transported for the same offense!"

"Was *he* deaf and dumb, woman?" asked the gentleman sternly.

"Was he not, sir?"

"You know he was not."

"He was," cried the woman. "He was deaf, dumb, and blind, to all that was good and right, from his cradle. Her boy may have learnt no better! where did mine learn better? where could he? who was there to teach him better, or where was it to be learnt?"

"Peace, woman," said the gentleman, "your boy was in possession of all his senses."

"He was," cried the mother; "and he was the more easy to be led astray because he had them. If you save this boy because he may not know right from wrong, why did you not save mine who was never taught the difference? You gentlemen have as good a right to punish her boy, that God has kept in ignorance of sound and speech, as you have to punish mine, that you kept in ignorance yourselves. How many of the girls and boys—

ah, men and women too—that are brought before you and you don't pity, are deaf and dumb in their minds, and go wrong in that state, and are punished in that state, body and soul, while you gentlemen are quarrelling among yourselves whether they ought to learn this or that?—Be a just man, sir, and give me back my son."

"You are desperate," said the gentleman, taking out his snuff-box, "and I am sorry for you."

"I *am* desperate," returned the woman, "and you have made me so. Give me back my son, to work for these helpless children. Be a just man, sir, and for God's sake, as you have had mercy upon this boy, give me back my son!"

The child had seen and heard enough to know that this was not a place at which to ask for alms. She led the old man softly from the door, and they pursued their journey.

With less and less of hope or strength, as they went on, but with an undiminished resolution not to betray by any word or sign her sinking state, so long as she had energy to move, the child throughout the remainder of that hard day compelled herself to proceed: not even stopping to rest as frequently as usual, to compensate in some measure for the tardy pace at which she was obliged to walk. Evening was drawing on, but had not closed in, when—still travelling among the same dismal objects—they came to a busy town.

Faint and spiritless as they were, its streets were insupportable. After humbly asking for relief at some few doors and being repulsed, they agreed to make their way out of it as speedily as they could, and try if the inmates of any lone house beyond, would have more pity on their exhausted state.

They were dragging themselves along through the last street, and the child felt that the time was close at hand when her enfeebled powers would bear no more. There appeared before them, at this juncture, going in the same direction as themselves, a traveller on foot, who, with a portmanteau strapped to his back, leant upon a stout stick as he walked, and read from a book which he held in his other hand.

It was not an easy matter to come up with him, and beseech his aid, for he walked fast, and was a little distance in advance. At length he stopped to look more attentively at some passage in his book. Animated with a ray of hope, the child shot on before her grandfather, and, going close to the stranger without rousing him by the sound of her footsteps, began in a few faint words to implore his help.

He turned his head, the child clapped her hands together, uttered a wild shriek, and fell senseless at his feet.

Chapter XLVI

IT was the poor schoolmaster. No other than the poor schoolmaster. Scarcely less moved and surprised by the sight of the child than she had been on recognising him, he stood for a moment silent and confounded by this unexpected apparition, without even the presence of mind to raise her from the ground.

But quickly recovering his self-possession, he threw down his stick and book, and dropping on one knee beside her, endeavoured, by such simple means as occurred to him, to restore her to herself; while her grandfather, standing idly by, wrung his hands, and implored her with many endearing expressions to speak to him, were it only a word.

"She is quite exhausted," said the schoolmaster, glancing upward into his face. "You have taxed her powers too far, friend."

"She is perishing of want," rejoined the old man. "I never thought how weak and ill she was, till now."

Casting a look upon him, half reproachful and half compassionate, the schoolmaster took the child in his arms, and bidding the old man gather up her little basket and follow him directly, bore her away at his utmost speed.

There was a small inn within sight, to which it would seem he had been directing his steps when so unexpectedly overtaken. Towards this place he hurried with his unconscious burden, and rushing into the kitchen, and calling upon the company there assembled to make way for God's sake, deposited it on a chair before the fire.

The company, who rose in confusion upon the schoolmaster's entrance, did as people usually do under such circumstances. Everybody called for his or her favourite remedy, which nobody brought; each cried for more air, at the same time carefully excluding what air there was, by closing round the object of sympathy; and all wondered why somebody else didn't do what it never appeared to occur to them might be done by themselves.

The landlady, however, who possessed more readiness and activity than any of them, and who had withal a quicker perception of the merits of the case, soon came running in, with a little hot brandy and water, followed by her servant-girl, carrying vinegar, hartshorn, smelling-salts, and such other restoratives; which, being duly administered, recovered the child so far as to enable her to thank them in a faint voice, and to extend her hand to the poor schoolmaster, who stood with an anxious face hard by. Without suffering her to speak another word, or so much as to stir a finger any more, the women straightway carried her off to bed; and having covered her up warm, bathed her cold feet, and wrapped them in flannel, they despatched a messenger for the doctor.

The doctor, who was a red-nosed gentleman with a great bunch of seals dangling below a waistcoat of ribbed black satin, arrived with all speed, and taking his seat by the bedside of poor Nell, drew out his watch, and felt her pulse. Then he looked at her tongue, then he felt her pulse again, and while he did so, he eyed the half-emptied wine-glass as if in profound abstraction.

"I should give her"—said the doctor at length, "a teaspoonful, every now and then, of hot brandy and water."

"Why, that's exactly what we've done, sir!" said the delighted landlady.

"I should also," observed the doctor, who had passed the footbath on the stairs, "I should also," said the doctor, in the voice of an oracle, "put her feet in hot water, and wrap them up in flannel. I should likewise," said the doctor with increased solemnity, "give her something light for supper—the wing of a roasted fowl now———"

"Why, goodness gracious me, sir, it's cooking at the kitchen fire this instant!" cried the landlady. And so indeed it was, for the schoolmaster had ordered it to be put down, and it was getting on so well that the doctor might have smelt it if he had tried—perhaps he did.

"You may then," said the doctor, rising gravely, "give her a glass of hot mulled port wine, if she likes wine——"

"And a toast, sir?" suggested the landlady.

"Ay," said the doctor, in the tone of a man who makes a dignified concession. "And a toast—of bread. But be very particular to make it of bread, if you please, ma'am."

With which parting injunction, slowly and portentously delivered, the doctor departed, leaving the whole house in admiration of that wisdom which tallied so closely with their own. Everybody said he was a very shrewd doctor indeed, and knew perfectly what people's constitutions were; which there appears some reason to suppose he did.

While her supper was preparing, the child fell into a refreshing sleep, from which they were obliged to rouse her when it was ready. As she evinced extraordinary uneasiness on learning that her grandfather was below-stairs, and as she was greatly troubled at the thought of their being apart, he took his supper with her. Finding her still very restless on this head, they made him up a bed in an inner room, to which he presently retired. The key of this chamber happened by good fortune to be on that side of the door which was in Nell's room; she turned it on him when the landlady had withdrawn, and crept to bed again with a thankful heart.

The schoolmaster sat for a long time smoking his pipe by the kitchen fire, which was now deserted, thinking, with a very happy face, on the fortunate chance which had brought him so opportunely to the child's assistance, and parrying, as well as in his simple way he could, the inquisitive cross-examination of the landlady, who had a great curiosity to be made acquainted with every particular of Nell's life and history. The poor schoolmaster was so open-hearted, and so little versed in the most ordinary cunning or deceit, that she could not have failed to succeed in the first five minutes, but that he happened to be unacquainted with what she wished to know; and so he told her. The landlady, by no means satisfied with this assurance, which she considered an ingenious evasion of the question, rejoined that he had his reasons of course. Heaven forbid that she should wish to pry into the affairs of her customers, which indeed were no business of hers, who had so many of her own. She had merely asked a civil question, and to be sure she knew it would meet with a civil answer. She was quite satisfied—quite. She had rather perhaps that he would have said at once that he didn't choose to be communicative, because that would have been plain and intelligible. However, she had no right to be offended of course. He was the best judge, and had a perfect right to say what he pleased; nobody could dispute that, for a moment. Oh, dear, no!

"I assure you, my good lady," said the mild schoolmaster, "that I have told you the plain truth—as I hope to be saved, I have told you the truth."

"Why, then, I do believe you are in earnest," rejoined the landlady, with ready good-humour, "and I'm very sorry I have teazed you. But curiosity you know is the curse of our sex, and that's the fact."

The landlord scratched his head, as if he thought the curse sometimes involved the other sex likewise; but he was prevented from making any remark to that effect, if he had it in contemplation to do so, by the schoolmaster's rejoinder.

"You should question me for half a dozen hours at a sitting, and welcome, and I would answer you patiently for the kindness of heart you have shown to-night, if I could," he said. "As it is, please to take care of her in the morning, and let me know early how she is; and to understand that I am paymaster for the three."

So, parting with them on most friendly terms, not the less cordial perhaps for this last direction, the schoolmaster went to his bed, and the host and hostess to theirs.

The report in the morning was, that the child was better, but was extremely weak, and would at least require a day's rest, and careful nursing, before she could proceed upon her journey. The schoolmaster received this communication with perfect cheerfulness, observing that he had a day to spare—two days for that matter—and could very well afford to wait. As the patient was to sit up in the evening, he appointed to visit her in her room at a certain hour, and rambling out with his book, did not return until the hour arrived.

Nell could not help weeping when they were left alone; whereat, and at sight of her pale face and wasted figure, the simple schoolmaster shed a few tears himself, at the same time showing in very energetic language how foolish it was to do so, and how very easily it could be avoided, if one tried.

"It makes me unhappy even in the midst of all this kindness," said the child, "to think that we should be a burden upon you. How can I ever thank you? If I had not met you so far from home, I must have died, and he would have been left alone."

"We'll not talk about dying," said the schoolmaster; "and as to burdens, I have made my fortune since you slept at my cottage.

"Indeed!" cried the child joyfully.

"Oh yes," returned her friend. "I have been appointed clerk and schoolmaster to a village a long way from here—and a long way from the old one as you may suppose—at five-and-thirty pounds a year. Five-and-thirty pounds!"

"I am very glad," said the child—"so very, very glad."

"I am on my way there now," resumed the schoolmaster. "They allowed me the stage-coach hire—outside stage-coach hire all the way. Bless you, they grudge me nothing. But as the time at which I am expected there, left me ample leisure, I determined to walk instead. How glad I am, to think I did so!"

"How glad should we be!"

"Yes, yes," said the schoolmaster, moving restlessly in his chair, "certainly, that's very true. But you—where are you going, where are you coming from, what have you been doing since you left me, what had you been doing before? Now, tell me—do tell me. I know very little of the world, and perhaps you are better fitted to advise me in its affairs than I am qualified to give advice to you; but I am very sincere, and I have a reason (you have not forgotten it) for loving you. I have felt since that time as if my love for him who died, had been transferred to you who stood beside his bed. If this," he added, looking upwards, "is the beautiful creation that springs from ashes, let its peace prosper with me, as I deal tenderly and compassionately by this young child!"

The plain, frank kindness of the honest schoolmaster, the affectionate earnestness of his speech and manner, the truth which was stamped upon his every word and look, gave the child a confidence in him, which the utmost arts of treachery and dissimulation could never have awakened in her breast. She told him all—that they had no friend or relative—that she had fled with the old man, to save him from a madhouse and all the miseries he dreaded—that she was flying now, to save him from himself—and that she sought an asylum in some remote and primitive place, where the temptation before which he fell would never enter, and her late sorrows and distresses could have no place.

The schoolmaster heard her with astonishment. "This child!"—he thought—"Has this child heroically persevered under all doubts and dangers, struggled with poverty and suffering, upheld and sustained by strong affection and the consciousness of rectitude alone! And yet the world is full of such heroism. Have I yet to learn that the hardest and best-borne trials are those which are never chronicled in any earthly record, and are suffered every day! And should I be surprised to hear the story of this child!"

What more he thought or said matters not. It was concluded that Nell and her grandfather should accompany him to the village whither he was bound, and that he should endeavour to find them some humble occupation by which they could subsist. "We shall be sure to succeed," said the schoolmaster heartily. "The cause is too good a one to fail."

They arranged to proceed upon their journey next evening, as a stage-waggon, which travelled for some distance on the same road as they must take, would stop at the inn to change horses, and the driver for a small gratuity would give Nell a place inside. A bargain was soon struck when the waggon came; and in due time it rolled away; with the child comfortably bestowed among the softer packages, her grandfather and the schoolmaster walking on beside the driver, and the landlady and all the good folks of the inn screaming out their good wishes and farewells.

What a soothing, luxurious, drowsy way of travelling, to lie inside that slowly-moving mountain, listening to the tinkling of the horses' bells, the occasional smacking of the carter's whip, the smooth rolling of the great broad wheels, the rattle of the harness, the cheery goodnights of passing travellers jogging past on little short-stepped horses—all made pleasantly indistinct by the thick awning, which seemed made for lazy listening under, till one fell asleep! The very going to sleep, still with an indistinct idea, as the head jogged to and fro upon the pillow, of moving onward with no trouble or fatigue, and hearing all these sounds like dreamy music, lulling to the senses—and the slow waking up, and finding one's self staring out through the breezy curtain half opened in the front, far up into the cold bright sky with its countless stars, and downward at the driver's lantern dancing on like its namesake Jack of the swamps and marshes, and sideways at the dark grim trees, and forward at the long bare road rising up, up, up, until it stopped abruptly at a sharp high ridge as if there were no more road, and all beyond was sky—and the stopping at the inn to bait, and being helped out, and going into a room with fire and candles, and winking very much, and being agreeably reminded that the night was cold, and anxious for very comfort's sake to think it colder than it was!—What a delicious journey was that journey in the waggon!

Then the going on again—so fresh at first, and shortly afterwards so sleepy. The waking from a sound nap as the mail came dashing past like a highway comet, with gleaming lamps and rattling hoofs, and visions of a guard behind, standing up to keep his feet warm, and of a gentleman in a fur cap opening his eyes and looking wild and stupefied—the stopping at the turnpike where the man was gone to bed, and knocking at the door until he answered with a smothered shout from under the bedclothes in the little room above, where the faint light was burning, and presently came down, night-capped and shivering, to throw the gate wide open, and wish all waggons off the road except by day. The cold, sharp interval between night and morning—the distant streak of light widening and spreading, and turning from grey to white, and from white to yellow, and from yellow to burning red—the presence of day, with all its cheerfulness and life—men and horses at the plough—birds in the trees and hedges, and boys in solitary fields, frightening them away with rattles. The coming to a town—people busy in the markets; light carts and chaises round the tavern yard; tradesmen standing at their doors; men running horses up and down the street for sale; pigs plunging and grunting in the dirty distance, getting off with long strings at their legs, running into clean chemists' shops and being dislodged with brooms by 'prentices; the night coach changing horses—the passengers cheerless, cold, ugly, and discontented, with three months' growth of hair in one night—the coachman fresh as from a bandbox, and exquisitely beautiful by contrast:—so much bustle, so many things in motion, such a variety of incidents—when was there a journey with so many delights as that journey in the waggon!

Sometimes walking for a mile or two while her grandfather rode inside, and some-times even prevailing upon the schoolmaster to take her place and lie down to rest, Nell travelled on very happily until they came to a large town, where the waggon stopped, and where they spent a night. They passed a large church; and in the streets were a number of old houses, built of a kind of earth or plaster, crossed and recrossed in a great many directions with black beams, which gave them a remarkable and very ancient look. The doors, too, were arched and low, some with oaken portals and quaint benches, where the former inhabitants had sat on summer evenings. The windows were latticed in little diamond panes, that seemed to wink and blink upon the passengers as if they were dim of sight. They had long since got clear of the smoke and furnaces, except in one or two solitary instances, where a factory planted among fields withered the space about it, like a burning mountain. When they had passed through this town, they entered again upon the country, and began to draw near their place of destination.

It was not so near, however, but that they spent another night upon the road; not that their doing so was quite an act of necessity, but that the schoolmaster, when they approached within a few miles of his village, had a fidgety sense of his dignity as the new clerk, and was unwilling to make his entry in dusty shoes, and travel-disordered dress. It was a fine, clear, autumn morning, when they came upon the scene of his promotion, and stopped to contemplate its beauties.

"See—here's the church!" cried the delighted schoolmaster, in a low voice; "and that old building close beside it is the school-house, I'll be sworn. Five-and-thirty pounds a year in this beautiful place!"

They admired everything—the old grey porch, the mullioned windows, the venerable gravestones dotting the green churchyard, the ancient tower, the very weathercock; the brown thatched roofs of cottage, barn, and homestead, peeping from among the trees; the stream that rippled by the distant watermill; the blue Welsh mountains far away. It was for such a spot the child had wearied in the dense, dark, miserable haunts of labour. Upon her bed of ashes, and amidst the squalid horrors through which they had forced their way, visions of such scenes—beautiful indeed, but not more beautiful than this sweet reality—had been always present to her mind. They had seemed to melt into a dim and airy distance, as the prospect of ever beholding them again grew fainter; but, as they receded, she had loved and panted for them more.

"I must leave you somewhere for a few minutes," said the schoolmaster, at length breaking the silence into which they had fallen in their gladness. "I have a letter to present, and inquiries to make, you know. Where shall I take you? To the little inn yonder?"

"Let us wait here," rejoined Nell. "The gate is open. We will sit in the church porch till you come back."

"A good place too," said the schoolmaster, leading the way towards it, disencumbering himself of his portmanteau, and placing it on the stone seat. "Be sure that I come back with good news, and am not long gone."

So the happy schoolmaster put on a bran-new pair of gloves which he had carried in a little parcel in his pocket all the way, and hurried off, full of ardour and excitement.

The child watched him from the porch until the intervening foliage hid him from her view, and then stepped softly out into the old churchyard—so solemn and quiet, that every rustle of her dress upon the fallen leaves, which strewed the path and made her footsteps noiseless, seemed an invasion of its silence. It was a very aged, ghostly place; the church had been built many hundreds of years ago, and had once had a convent or monastery attached; for arches in ruins, remains of oriel windows, and fragments of blackened walls, were yet standing; while other portions of the old building, which had crumbled away and fallen down, were mingled with the churchyard earth and overgrown with grass, as if they too claimed a burying-place and sought to mix their ashes with the dust of men. Hard by these gravestones of dead years, and forming a part of the ruin which some pains had been taken to render habitable in modern times, were two small dwellings with sunken windows and oaken doors, fast hastening to decay, empty and desolate.

Upon these tenements, the attention of the child became exclusively riveted. She knew not why. The church, the ruin, the antiquated graves, had equal claims at least upon a stranger's thoughts, but from the moment when her eyes first rested on these two dwellings, she could turn to nothing else. Even when she had made the circuit of the inclosure, and, returning to the porch, sat pensively waiting for their friend, she took her station where she could still look upon them, and felt as if fascinated towards that spot.

Chapter XLVII

K IT'S mother and the single gentleman—upon whose track it is expedient to follow with hurried steps, lest this history should be chargeable with inconstancy, and the offence of leaving its characters in situations of uncertainty and doubt—Kit's mother and the single gentleman, speeding onward in the post-chaise-and-four whose departure from the notary's door we have already witnessed, soon left the town behind them, and struck fire from the flints of the broad highway.

The good woman, being not a little embarrassed by the novelty of her situation, and certain maternal apprehensions that perhaps by this time little Jacob, or the baby, or both, had fallen into the fire, or tumbled downstairs, or had been squeezed behind doors, or had scalded their windpipes in endeavouring to allay their thirst at the spouts of tea-kettles, preserved an uneasy silence; and meeting from the window the eyes of turnpike-men, omnibus-drivers, and others, felt in the new dignity of her position like a mourner at a funeral, who, not being greatly afflicted by the loss of the departed, recognizes his every-day acquaintance from the window of the mourning-coach, but is constrained to preserve a decent solemnity, and the appearance of being indifferent to all external objects.

To have been indifferent to the companionship of the single gentleman would have been tantamount to being gifted with nerves of steel. Never did chaise inclose, or horses draw, such a restless gentleman as he. He never sat in the same position for two minutes together, but was perpetually tossing his arms and legs about, pulling up the sashes and letting them violently down, or thrusting his head out of one window to draw it in again and thrust it out of another. He carried in his pocket, too, a fire-box of mysterious and unknown construction; and as sure as ever Kit's mother closed her eyes, so surely— whisk, rattle, fizz—there was the single gentleman consulting his watch by a flame of fire, and letting the sparks fall down among the straw as if there were no such thing as a possibility of himself and Kit's mother being roasted alive before the boys could stop their horses. Whenever they halted to change, there he was—out of the carriage without letting down the steps, bursting about the inn-yard like a lighted cracker, pulling out his watch by lamplight and forgetting to look at it before he put it up again, and in short committing so many extravagances that Kit's mother was quite afraid of him. Then, when the horses were to, in he came like a harlequin, and before they had gone a mile, out came the watch and the fire-box together, and Kit's mother was wide awake again, with no hope of a wink of sleep for that stage.

"Are you comfortable?" the single gentleman would say after one of these exploits, turning sharply round.

"Quite, sir, thank you."

"Are you sure? An't you cold?"

"It is a little chilly, sir," Kit's mother would reply.

"I knew it!" cried the single gentleman, letting down one of the front glasses. "She wants some brandy and water! Of course she does. How could I forget it? Hallo! Stop at the next inn, and call out for a glass of hot brandy and water."

It was in vain for Kit's mother to protest that she stood in need of nothing of the kind. The single gentleman was inexorable; and whenever he had exhausted all other modes and fashions of restlessness, it invariably occurred to him that Kit's mother wanted brandy and water.

In this way they travelled on until near midnight, when they stopped to supper, for which meal the single gentleman ordered everything eatable that the house contained; and because Kit's mother didn't eat everything at once, and eat it all, he took it into his head that she must be ill.

"You're faint," said the single gentleman, who did nothing himself but walk about the room. "I see what's the matter with you, ma'am. You're faint."

"Thank you, sir, I'm not indeed."

"I know you are. I'm sure of it. I drag this poor woman from the bosom of her family at a minute's notice, and she goes on getting fainter and fainter before my eyes. I'm a pretty fellow! How many children have you got, ma'am?"

"Two, sir, besides Kit."

"Boys, ma'am?"

"Yes, sir."

"Are they christened?"

"Only half baptised, as yet, sir."

"I'm godfather to both of 'em. Remember that, if you please, ma'am. You had better have some mulled wine."

"I couldn't touch a drop indeed, sir."

"You must," said the single gentleman. "I see you want it. I ought to have thought of it before."

Immediately flying to the bell, and calling for mulled wine as impetuously as if it had been wanted for instant use in the recovery of some person apparently drowned, the single gentleman made Kit's mother swallow a bumper of it at such a high temperature that the tears ran down her face, and then hustled her off to the chaise again, where—not impossibly from the effects of this agreeable sedative—she soon became insensible to his restlessness, and fell fast asleep. Nor were the happy effects of this prescription of a transitory nature, as, notwithstanding that the distance was greater, and the journey longer, than the single gentleman had anticipated, she did not awake until it was broad day, and they were clattering over the pavement of a town.

"This is the place!" cried her companion, letting down all the glasses. "Drive to the wax-work!"

The boy on the wheeler touched his hat, and setting spurs to his horse, to the end that they might go in brilliantly, all four broke into a smart canter, and dashed through the streets with a noise that brought the good folks wondering to their doors and windows, and drowned the sober voices of the town-clocks as they chimed out half-past eight. They drove up to a door round which a crowd of persons were collected, and there stopped.

"What's this?" said the single gentleman thrusting out his head. "Is anything the matter here?"

"A wedding, sir, a wedding!" cried several voices. "Hurrah!"

The single gentleman, rather bewildered by finding himself the centre of this noisy throng, alighted with the assistance of one of the postilions, and handed out Kit's mother, at sight of whom the populace cried out, "Here's another wedding!" and roared and leaped for joy.

"The world has gone mad, I think," said the single gentleman, pressing through the concourse with his supposed bride. "Stand back here, will you, and let me knock."

Anything that makes a noise is satisfactory to a crowd. A score of dirty hands were raised directly to knock for him, and seldom has a knocker of equal powers been made to produce more deafening sounds than this particular engine on the occasion in question. Having rendered these voluntary services, the throng modestly retired a little, preferring that the single gentleman should bear their consequences alone.

"Now, sir, what do you want?" said a man with a large white bow at his button-hole, opening the door, and confronting him with a very stoical aspect.

"Who has been married here, my friend?" said the single gentleman.

"I have."

"You! and to whom in the devil's name?"

"What right have you to ask?" returned the bridegroom, eyeing him from top to toe.

"What right!" cried the single gentleman, drawing the arm of Kit's mother more tightly through his own, for that good woman evidently had it in contemplation to run away. "A right you little dream of. Mind, good people, if this fellow has been marrying a minor—tut, tut, that can't be. Where is the child you have here, my good fellow? You call her Nell. Where is she?"

As he propounded this question, which Kit's mother echoed, somebody in a room near at hand uttered a great shriek, and a stout lady in a white dress came running to the door, and supported herself upon the bridegroom's arm.

"Where is she!" cried this lady. "What news have you brought me? What has become of her?"

The single gentleman started back, and gazed upon the face of the late Mrs Jarley (that morning wedded to the philosophic George, to the eternal wrath and despair of Mr Slum the poet), with looks of conflicting apprehension, disappointment, and incredulity. At length he stammered out,

"I ask *you* where she is? What do you mean?"

"Oh, sir!" cried the bride, "if you have come here to do her any good, why weren't you here a week ago?"

"She is not—not dead?" said the person to whom she addressed herself, turning very pale.

"No, not so bad as that."

"I thank God!" cried the single gentleman feebly. "Let me come in."

They drew back to admit him, and when he had entered, closed the door.

"You see in me, good people," he said, turning to the newly married couple, "one to whom life itself is not dearer than the two persons whom I seek. They would not know me. My features are strange to them, but if they or either of them are here, take this good woman with you, and let them see her first, for her they both know. If you deny them from any mistaken regard or fear for them, judge of my intentions by their recognition of this person as their old humble friend."

"I always said it!" cried the bride; "I knew she was not a common child! Alas, sir! we have no power to help you, for all that we could do has been tried in vain."

With that, they related to him, without disguise or concealment, all that they knew of Nell and her grandfather, from their first meeting with them, down to the time of their sudden disappearance; adding (which was quite true) that they had made every possible effort to trace them, but without success; having been at first in great alarm for their safety, as well as on account of the suspicions to which they themselves might one day be exposed in consequence of their abrupt departure. They dwelt upon the old man's imbecility of mind, upon the uneasiness the child had always testified when he was absent, upon the company he had been supposed to keep, and upon the increased depression which had gradually crept over her and changed her both in health and spirits. Whether she had missed the old man in the night, and, knowing or conjecturing whither he had bent his steps, had gone in pursuit, or whether they had left the house together, they had no means of determining. Certain they considered it, that there was but slender prospect left of hearing of them again, and that whether their flight originated with the old man, or with the child, there was now no hope of their return.

To all this, the single gentleman listened with the air of a man quite borne down by grief and disappointment. He shed tears when he spoke of the grandfather, and appeared in deep affliction.

Not to protract this portion of our narrative, and to make short work of a long story, let it be briefly written that before the interview came to a close, the single gentleman deemed he had sufficient evidence of having been told the truth, and that he endeavoured to force upon the bride and bridegroom an acknowledgment of their kindness to the unfriended child, which, however, they steadily declined accepting. In the end, the happy couple jolted away in the caravan to spend their honeymoon in a country excursion; and the single gentleman and Kit's mother stood ruefully before their carriage door.

"Where shall we drive you, sir?" said the post-boy.

"You may drive me," said the single gentleman, "to the——" He was not going to add "inn," but he added it for the sake of Kit's mother; and to the inn they went.

Rumours had already got abroad that the little girl who used to show the wax-work, was the child of great people who had been stolen from her parents in infancy, and had only just been traced. Opinion was divided whether she was the daughter of a prince, a duke, an earl, a viscount, or a baron, but all agreed upon the main fact, and that the single gentleman was her father; and all bent forward to catch a glimpse, though it were only of the tip of his noble nose, as he rode away, desponding, in his four-horse chaise.

What would he have given to know, and what sorrow would have been saved if he had only known, that at that moment both child and grandfather were seated in the old church porch, patiently awaiting the schoolmaster's return!

Chapter XLVIII

POPULAR rumour concerning the single gentleman and his errand, travelling from mouth to mouth, and waxing stronger in the marvellous as it was bandied about— for your popular rumour, unlike the rolling stone of the proverb, is one which gathers a deal of moss in its wanderings up and down—occasioned his dismounting at the inn door to be looked upon as an exciting and attractive spectacle, which could scarcely be enough admired; and drew together a large concourse of idlers, who having recently been, as it were, thrown out of employment by the closing of the wax-work and the completion of the nuptial ceremonies, considered his arrival as little else than a special providence, and hailed it with demonstrations of the liveliest joy.

Not at all participating in the general sensation, but wearing the depressed and wearied look of one who sought to meditate on his disappointment in silence and privacy, the single gentleman alighted, and handed out Kit's mother with a gloomy politeness which impressed the lookers-on extremely. That done, he gave her his arm and escorted her into the house, while several active waiters ran on before as a skirmishing party, to clear the way and to show the room which was ready for their reception.

"Any room will do," said the single gentleman. "Let it be near at hand, that's all."

"Close here, sir, if you please to walk this way."

"Would the gentleman like this room?" said a voice, as a little out-of-the-way door at the foot of the well-staircase flew briskly open and a head popped out. "He's quite welcome to it. He's as welcome as flowers in May, or coals in Christmas. *Would* you like this room, sir? Honour me by walking in. Do me the favour, pray."

"Goodness gracious me!" cried Kit's mother, falling back in extreme surprise, "only think of this!"

She had some reason to be astonished, for the person who proffered the gracious invitation was no other than Daniel Quilp. The little door out of which he had thrust his head was close to the inn larder; and there he stood, bowing with grotesque politeness; as much at his ease as if the door were that of his own house; blighting all the legs of mutton and cold roast fowls by his close companionship, and looking like the evil genius of the cellars come from underground upon some work of mischief.

"Would you do me the honour?" said Quilp.

"I prefer being alone," replied the single gentleman.

"Oh!" said Quilp. And with that, he darted in again with one jerk and clapped the little door to, like a figure in a Dutch clock when the hour strikes.

"Why it was only last night, sir," whispered Kit's mother, "that I left him in Little Bethel."

"Indeed!" said her fellow-passenger. "When did that person come here, waiter?"

"Come down by the night-coach this morning, sir."

"Humph! And when is he going?"

"Can't say, sir, really. When the chambermaid asked him just now if he should want a bed, sir, he first made faces at her, and then wanted to kiss her."

"Beg him to walk this way," said the single gentleman. "I should be glad to exchange a word with him, tell him. Beg him to come at once, do you hear?"

The man stared on receiving these instructions, for the single gentleman had not only displayed as much astonishment as Kit's mother at sight of the dwarf, but, standing in no fear of him, had been at less pains to conceal his dislike and repugnance. He departed on his errand, however, and immediately returned, ushering in its object.

"Your servant, sir," said the dwarf. "I encountered your messenger half-way. I thought you'd allow me to pay my compliments to you. I hope you're well. I hope you're very well."

There was a short pause, while the dwarf, with half-shut eyes and puckered face, stood waiting for an answer. Receiving none, he turned towards his more familiar acquaintance.

"Christopher's mother!" he cried. "Such a dear lady, such a worthy woman, so blest in her honest son! How is Christopher's mother? Have change of air and scene improved her? Her little family too, and Christopher? Do they thrive? Do they flourish? Are they growing into worthy citizens, eh?"

Making his voice ascend in the scale with every succeeding question, Mr Quilp finished in a shrill squeak, and subsided into the panting look which was customary with him, and which, whether it were assumed or natural, had equally the effect of banishing all expression from his face, and rendering it, as far as it afforded any index to his mood or meaning, a perfect blank.

"Mr Quilp," said the single gentleman.

The dwarf put his hand to his great flapped ear, and counterfeited the closest attention.

"We two have met before——"

"Surely," cried Quilp, nodding his head. "Oh, surely, sir. Such an honour and pleasure—it's both, Christopher's mother, it's both—is not to be forgotten so soon. By no means!"

"You may remember that the day I arrived in London, and found the house to which I drove, empty and deserted, I was directed by some of the neighbours to you, and waited upon you without stopping for rest or refreshment?"

"How precipitate that was and yet what an earnest and vigorous measure!" said Quilp, conferring with himself, in imitation of his friend Mr Sampson Brass.

"I found," said the single gentleman, "you, most unaccountably, in possession of everything that had so recently belonged to another man, and that other man, who up to the time of your entering upon his property had been looked upon as affluent, reduced to sudden beggary, and driven from house and home."

"We had warrant for what we did, my good sir," rejoined Quilp, "we had our warrant. Don't say driven either. He went of his own accord—vanished in the night, sir."

"No matter," said the single gentleman angrily. "He was gone."

"Yes, he was gone," said Quilp, with the same exasperating composure. "No doubt he was gone. The only question was, where. And it's a question still."

"Now, what am I to think," said the single gentleman, sternly regarding him, "of you, who, plainly indisposed to give me any information then—nay, obviously holding back, and sheltering yourself with all kinds of cunning, trickery, and evasion—are dogging my footsteps now?"

"I dogging!" cried Quilp.

"Why, are you not?" returned his questioner, fretted into a state of the utmost irritation. "Were you not a few hours since, sixty miles off, and in the chapel to which this good woman goes to say her prayers?"

"She was there too, I think?" said Quilp, still perfectly unmoved. "I might say, if I was inclined to be rude, how do I know but you are dogging *my* footsteps. Yes, I was at chapel. What then? I've read in books that pilgrims were used to go to chapel before they went on journeys, to put up petitions for their safe return. Wise men! journeys are very perilous—especially outside the coach. Wheels come off, horses take fright, coachmen drive too fast, coaches overturn. I always go to chapel before I start on journeys. It's the last thing I do on such occasions, indeed."

That Quilp lied most heartily in this speech, it needed no very great penetration to discover, although for anything that he suffered to appear in his face, voice, or manner, he might have been clinging to the truth with the quiet constancy of a martyr.

"In the name of all that's calculated to drive one crazy, man," said the unfortunate single gentleman, "have you not, for some reason of your own, taken upon yourself my errand? don't you know with what object I have come here, and if you do know, can you throw no light upon it?"

"You think I'm a conjuror, sir," replied Quilp, shrugging up his shoulders. "If I was, I should tell my own fortune—and make it."

"Ah! we have said all we need say, I see," returned the other, throwing himself impatiently upon a sofa. "Pray leave us, if you please."

"Willingly." returned Quilp. "Most willingly. Christopher's mother, my good soul, farewell. A pleasant journey—*back, sir*. Ahem!"

With these parting words, and with a grin upon his features altogether indescribable, but which seemed to be compounded of every monstrous grimace of which men or monkeys are capable, the dwarf slowly retreated and closed the door behind him.

"Oho!" he said when he had regained his own room, and sat himself down in a chair with his arms akimbo. "Oho! Are you there, my friend? In-deed!"

Chuckling as though in very great glee, and recompensing himself for the restraint he had lately put upon his countenance by twisting it into all imaginable varieties of ugliness, Mr Quilp, rocking himself to and fro in his chair and nursing his left leg at the same time, fell into certain meditations, of which it may be necessary to relate the substance.

First, he reviewed the circumstances which had led to his repairing to that spot, which were briefly these. Dropping in at Mr Sampson Brass's office on the previous evening, in the absence of that gentleman and his learned sister, he had lighted upon Mr Swiveller, who chanced at the moment to be sprinkling a glass of warm gin and water on the dust of the law, and to be moistening his clay, as the phrase goes, rather copiously. But as clay in the abstract, when too much moistened, becomes of a weak and uncertain consistency, breaking down in unexpected places, retaining impressions but faintly, and preserving no strength or steadiness of character, so Mr Swiveller's clay, having imbibed a considerable quantity of moisture, was in a very loose and slippery state, insomuch that the various ideas impressed upon it were fast losing their distinctive character, and running into each other. It is not uncommon for human clay in this condition to value itself above all things upon its great prudence and sagacity; and Mr Swiveller, especially prizing himself upon these qualities, took occasion to remark that he had made strange discoveries in connexion with the single gentleman who lodged above, which he had determined to keep within his own bosom, and which neither tortures nor cajolery should ever induce him to reveal. Of this determination Mr Quilp expressed his high approval, and setting himself in the same breath to goad Mr Swiveller on to further hints, soon made out that the single gentleman had been seen in communication with Kit, and that this was the secret which was never to be disclosed.

Possessed of this piece of information, Mr Quilp directly supposed, that the single gentleman above-stairs must be the same individual who had waited on him, and having assured himself by further inquiries that this surmise was correct, had no difficulty in arriving at the conclusion that the intent and object of his correspondence with Kit was the recovery of his old client and the child. Burning with curiosity to know what proceedings were afoot, he resolved to pounce upon Kit's mother as the person least able to resist his arts, and consequently the most likely to be entrapped into such revelations as he sought; so taking an abrupt leave of Mr Swiveller, he hurried to her house. The good woman being from home, he made inquiries of a neighbour, as Kit himself did soon afterwards, and being directed to the chapel betook himself there, in order to waylay her, at the conclusion of the service.

He had not sat in the chapel more than a quarter of an hour, and with his eyes piously fixed upon the ceiling was chuckling inwardly over the joke of his being there at all, when Kit himself appeared. Watchful as a lynx, one glance showed the dwarf that he had come on business. Absorbed in appearance, as we have seen, and feigning a profound abstraction, he noted every circumstance of his behaviour, and when he withdrew with his family, shot out after him. In fine, he traced them to the notary's house; learnt the destination of the carriage from one of the postilions; and knowing that a fast night-coach started for the same place, at the very hour which was on the point of striking, from a street hard by, darted round to the coach-office without more ado, and took his seat upon the roof. After passing and repassing the carriage on the road, and being passed and repassed by it sundry times in the course of the night, according as their stoppages were longer or shorter, or their rate of travelling varied, they reached the town almost together. Quilp kept the chaise in sight, mingled with the crowd, learnt the single gentleman's errand, and its failure, and having possessed himself of all that it was material to know, hurried off, reached the inn before him, had the interview just now detailed, and shut himself up in the little room in which he hastily reviewed all these occurrences.

"You are there, are you, my friend?" he repeated, greedily biting his nails. "I am suspected and thrown aside, and Kit's the confidential agent, is he? I shall have to dispose of him, I fear. If we had come up with them this morning," he continued, after a thoughtful pause, "I was ready to prove a pretty good claim. I could have made my profit. But for these canting hypocrites, the lad and his mother, I could get this fiery gentleman as comfortable into my net as our old friend—our mutual friend, ha! ha!—and chubby, rosy Nell. At the worst, it's a golden opportunity, not to be lost. Let us find them first, and I'll find means of draining you of some of your superfluous cash, sir, while there are prison bars, and bolts, and locks, to keep your friend or kinsman safely. I hate your virtuous people!" said the dwarf, throwing off a bumper of brandy, and smacking his lips, "ah! I hate 'em every one!"

This was not a mere empty vaunt, but a deliberate avowal of his real sentiments; for Mr Quilp, who loved nobody, had by little and little come to hate everybody nearly or remotely connected with his ruined client:—the old man himself, because he had been able to deceive him and elude his vigilance—the child, because she was the object of Mrs Quilp's commiseration and constant self-reproach—the single gentleman, because of his unconcealed aversion to himself—Kit and his mother, most mortally, for the reasons already shown. Above and beyond that general feeling of opposition to them, which would have been inseparable from his ravenous desire to enrich himself by these altered circumstances, Daniel Quilp hated them every one.

In this amiable mood, Mr Quilp enlivened himself and his hatreds with more brandy, and then, changing his quarters, withdrew to an obscure alehouse, under cover of which seclusion he instituted all possible inquiries that might lead to the discovery of the old man and his grandchild. But all was in vain. Not the slightest trace or clue could be obtained. They had left the town by night; no one had seen them go; no one had met them on the road: the driver of no coach, cart, or waggon, had seen any travellers answering their description; nobody had fallen in with them, or heard of them. Convinced at last that for the present all such attempts were hopeless, he appointed two or three scouts, with promises of large rewards in case of their forwarding him any intelligence, and returned to London by next day's coach.

It was some gratification to Mr Quilp to find, as he took his place upon the roof, that Kit's mother was alone inside; from which circumstance he derived in the course of the journey much cheerfulness of spirit, inasmuch as her solitary condition enabled him to terrify her with many extraordinary annoyances; such as hanging over the side of the coach at the risk of his life, and staring in with his great goggle eyes, which seemed in hers the more horrible from his face being upside-down; dodging her in this way from one window to another; getting nimbly down whenever they changed horses and thrusting his head in at the window with a dismal squint: which ingenious tortures had such an effect upon Mrs Nubbles, that she was quite unable for the time to resist the belief that Mr Quilp did in his own person represent and embody that Evil Power, who was so vigorously attacked at Little Bethel, and who, by reason of her backslidings in respect of Astley's and oysters, was now frolicsome and rampant.

Kit, having been apprised by letter of his mother's intended return, was waiting for her at the coach-office; and great was his surprise when he saw, leering over the coachman's shoulder like some familiar demon invisible to all eyes but his, the well-known face of Quilp.

"How are you, Christopher?" croaked the dwarf from the coach-top. "All right, Christopher. Mother's inside."

"Why, how did he come here, mother?" whispered Kit.

"I don't know how he came or why, my dear," rejoined Mrs Nubbles, dismounting with her son's assistance, "but he has been a terrifying of me out of my seven senses all this blessed day."

"He has?" cried Kit.

"You wouldn't believe it, that you wouldn't," replied his mother; "but don't say a word to him, for I really don't believe he's human. Hush! Don't turn round as if I was talking of him, but he's a squinting at me now in the full blaze of the coach-lamp, quite awful!"

In spite of his mother's injunction, Kit turned sharply round to look. Mr Quilp was serenely gazing at the stars, quite absorbed in celestial contemplation.

"Oh, he's the artfullest creetur!" cried Mrs Nubbles. "But come away. Don't speak to him for the world."

"Yes I will, mother. What nonsense. I say, sir——"

Mr Quilp affected to start, and looked smilingly round.

"You let my mother alone, will you?" said Kit. "How dare you tease a poor lone woman like her, making her miserable and melancholy as if she hadn't got enough to make her so, without you. An't you ashamed of yourself, you little monster?"

"Monster!" said Quilp inwardly, with a smile. "Ugliest dwarf that could be seen anywhere for a penny—monster—ah!"

"You show her any of your impudence again," resumed Kit, shouldering the bandbox, "and I tell you what, Mr Quilp, I won't bear with you any more. You have no right to do it; I'm sure we never interfered with you. This isn't the first time; and if ever you worry or frighten her again, you'll oblige me (though I should be very sorry to do it, on account of your size) to beat you."

Quilp said not a word in reply, but walking up so close to Kit as to bring his eyes within two or three inches of his face, looked fixedly at him, retreated a little distance without averting his gaze, approached again, again withdrew, and so on for half a dozen times, like a bead in a phantasmagoria. Kit stood his ground as if in expectation of an immediate assault, but finding that nothing came of these gestures, snapped his fingers and walked away; his mother dragging him off as fast as she could, and, even in the midst of his news of little Jacob and the baby, looking anxiously over her shoulder to see if Quilp were following.

Chapter XLIX

K IT'S mother might have spared herself the trouble of looking back so often, for nothing was further from Mr Quilp's thoughts than any intention of pursuing her and her son, or renewing the quarrel with which they had parted. He went his way, whistling from time to time some fragments of a tune; and with a face quite tranquil and composed, jogged pleasantly towards home; entertaining himself as he went with visions of the fears and terrors of Mrs Quilp, who, having received no intelligence of him for three whole days and two nights, and having had no previous notice of his absence, was doubtless by that time in a state of distraction, and constantly fainting away with anxiety and grief.

This facetious probability was so congenial to the dwarf's humour, and so exquisitely amusing to him, that he laughed as he went along until the tears ran down his cheeks; and more than once, when he found himself in a by-street, vented his delight in a shrill scream, which greatly terrifying any lonely passenger, who happened to be walking on before him expecting nothing so little, increased his mirth, and made him remarkably cheerful and light-hearted.

In this happy flow of spirits Mr Quilp reached Tower Hill, when, gazing up at the window of his own sitting-room, he thought he descried more light than is usual in a house of mourning. Drawing nearer, and listening attentively, he could hear several voices in earnest conversation, among which he could distinguish, not only those of his wife and mother-in-law, but the tongues of men.

"Ha!" cried the jealous dwarf. "What's this! Do they entertain such visitors while I'm away!"

A smothered cough from above, was the reply. He felt in his pockets for his latch-key, but had forgotten it. There was no resource but to knock at the door.

"A light in the passage," said Quilp, peeping through the keyhole. "A very soft knock; and, by your leave, my lady, I may yet steal upon you unawares. Soho!"

A very low and gentle rap received no answer from within. But after a second application to the knocker, no louder than the first, the door was softly opened by the boy from the wharf, whom Quilp instantly gagged with one hand, and dragged into the street with the other.

"You'll throttle me, master," whispered the boy. "Let go, will you?"

"Who's upstairs, you dog?" retorted Quilp in the same tone. "Tell me. And don't speak above your breath, or I'll choke you in good earnest."

The boy could only point to the window, and reply with a stifled giggle, expressive of such intense enjoyment, that Quilp clutched him by the throat again and might have carried his threat into execution, or at least have made very good progress towards that end, but for the boy's nimbly extricating himself from his grasp, and fortifying himself behind the nearest post, at which, after some fruitless attempts to catch him by the hair of his head, his master was obliged to come to a parley.

"Will you answer me?" said Quilp. "What's going on, above?"

"You won't let one speak," replied the boy. "They—ha, ha, ha!—they think you're—you're dead. Ha, ha, ha!"

"Dead!" cried Quilp, relaxing into a grim laugh himself. "No. Do they? Do they really, you dog?"

"They think you're—you're drowned," replied the boy, who in his malicious nature had a strong infusion of his master. "You was last seen on the brink of the wharf, and they think you tumbled over. Ha, ha!"

The prospect of playing the spy under such delicious circumstances, and of disappointing them all by walking in alive, gave more delight to Quilp than the greatest stroke of good fortune could possibly have inspired him with. He was no less tickled than his hopeful assistant, and they both stood for some seconds, grinning and gasping, and wagging their heads at each other, on either side of the post, like an unmatchable pair of Chinese idols.

"Not a word," said Quilp, making towards the door on tiptoe. "Not a sound, not so much as a creaking board, or a stumble against a cobweb. Drowned, eh, Mrs Quilp? Drowned!"

So saying, he blew out the candle, kicked off his shoes, and groped his way upstairs; leaving his delighted young friend in an ecstasy of summersets on the pavement.

The bedroom door on the staircase being unlocked, Mr Quilp slipped in, and planted himself behind the door of communication between that chamber and the sitting-room, which standing ajar to render both more airy, and having a very convenient chink (of which he had often availed himself for purposes of espial, and had indeed enlarged with his pocket-knife), enabled him not only to hear, but to see distinctly, what was passing.

Applying his eye to this convenient place, he descried Mr Brass seated at the table with pen, ink, and paper, and the case-bottle of rum—his own case-bottle, and his own particular Jamaica—convenient to his hand; with hot water, fragrant lemons, white lump sugar, and all things fitting; from which choice materials, Sampson, by no means insensible to their claims upon his attention, had compounded a mighty glass of punch reeking hot; which he was at that very moment stirring up with a teaspoon, and contemplating with looks in which a faint assumption of sentimental regret struggled but weakly with a bland and comfortable joy. At the same table, with both her elbows upon it, was Mrs Jiniwin: no longer sipping other people's punch feloniously with teaspoons, but taking deep draughts from a jorum of her own; while her daughter—not exactly with ashes on her head, or sackloth on her back, but preserving a very decent and becoming appearance of sorrow nevertheless—was reclining in an easy-chair, and soothing her grief with a smaller allowance of the same glib liquid. There were also present a couple of waterside men, bearing between them certain machines called drags; even these fellows were accommodated with a stiff glass a-piece; and as they drank with a great relish, and were naturally of a red-nosed, pimple-faced, convivial look, their presence rather increased than detracted from that decided appearance of comfort, which was the great characteristic of the party.

"If I could poison that dear old lady's rum and water," murmured Quilp, "I'd die happy."

"Ah!" said Mr Brass, breaking the silence, and raising his eyes to the ceiling with a sigh, "who knows but he may be looking down upon us now! Who knows but he may be surveying of us from—from somewheres or another, and contemplating us with a watchful eye! Oh, Lor!"

Here Mr Brass stopped to drink half his punch, and then resumed; looking at the other half, as he spoke, with a dejected smile.

"I can almost fancy," said the lawyer, shaking his head, "that I see his eye glistening down at the very bottom of my liquor. When shall we look upon his like again? Never, never! One minute we are here"—holding his tumbler before his eyes—"the next we are there"— gulping down its contents, and striking himself emphatically a little below the chest—"in the silent tomb. To think that I should be drinking his very rum! It seems like a dream."

With the view, no doubt, of testing the reality of his position, Mr Brass pushed his tumbler as he spoke towards Mrs Jiniwin for the purpose of being replenished; and turned towards the attendant mariners.

"The search has been quite unsuccessful then?"

"Quite, master. But I should say that if he turns up anywhere, he'll come ashore somewhere about Grinidge to-morrow, at ebb tide, eh, mate?"

The other gentleman assented, observing that he was expected at the Hospital, and that several pensioners would be ready to receive him whenever he arrived.

"Then we have nothing for it but resignation," said Mr Brass; "nothing but resignation, and expectation. It would be a comfort to have his body; it would be a dreary comfort."

"Oh, beyond a doubt," assented Mrs Jiniwin hastily; "if we once had that, we should be quite sure."

"With regard to the descriptive advertisement," said Sampson Brass, taking up his pen. "It is a melancholy pleasure to recall his traits. Respecting his legs now—"

"Crooked, certainly," said Mrs Jiniwin.

"Do you think they *were* crooked?" said Brass, in an insinuating tone. "I think I see them now coming up the street very wide apart, in nankeen pantaloons a little shrunk and without straps. Ah! what a vale of tears we live in. Do we say crooked?"

"I think they were a little so," observed Mrs Quilp with a sob.

"Legs crooked," said Brass, writing as he spoke. "Large head, short body, legs crooked——"

"Very crooked," suggested Mrs Jiniwin.

"We'll not say very crooked, ma'am," said Brass piously. "Let us not bear hard upon the weaknesses of the deceased. He is gone, ma'am, to where his legs will never come in question.—We will content ourselves with crooked, Mrs Jiniwin."

"I thought you wanted the truth," said the old lady. "That's all."

"Bless your eyes, how I love you," muttered Quilp. "There she goes again. Nothing but punch!"

"This is an occupation," said the lawyer, laying down his pen and emptying his glass, "which seems to bring him before my eyes like the Ghost of Hamlet's father, in the very clothes that he wore on work-a-days. His coat, his waistcoat, his shoes and stockings, his trousers, his hat, his wit and humour, his pathos and his umbrella, all come before me like visions of my youth. His linen!" said Mr Brass smiling fondly at the wall, "his linen which was always of a particular colour, for such was his whim and fancy—how plain I see his linen now!"

"You had better go on, sir," said Mrs Jiniwin impatiently.

"True, ma'am, true," cried Mr Brass. "Our faculties must not freeze with grief. I'll trouble you for a little more of that, ma'am. A question now arises, with relation to his nose."

"Flat," said Mrs Jiniwin.

"Aquiline!" cried Quilp, thrusting in his head, and striking the feature with his fist. "Aquiline, you hag. Do you see it? Do you call this flat? Do you? Eh?"

"Oh, capital, capital!" shouted Brass, from the mere force of habit. "Excellent! How very good he is! He's a most remarkable man—so extremely whimsical! Such an amazing power of taking people by surprise!"

Quilp paid no regard whatever to these compliments, nor to the dubious and frightened look into which the lawyer gradually subsided, nor to the shrieks of his wife and mother-in-law, nor to the latter's running from the room, nor to the former's fainting away. Keeping his eye fixed on Sampson Brass, he walked up to the table, and beginning with his glass, drank off the contents, and went regularly round until he had emptied the other two, when he seized the case-bottle, and hugging it under his arm, surveyed him with a most extraordinary leer.

"Not yet, Sampson," said Quilp. "Not just yet!"

"Oh, very good indeed!" cried Brass, recovering his spirits a little. "Ha, ha, ha! Oh, exceedingly good! There's not another man alive who could carry it off like that. A most difficult position to carry off. But he has such a flow of good-humour, such an amazing flow!"

"Good night," said the dwarf, nodding expressively.

"Good night, sir, good night" cried the lawyer, retreating backwards towards the door. "This is a joyful occasion indeed, extremely joyful. Ha, ha, ha! oh, very rich, very rich indeed, re-markably so!"

Waiting until Mr Brass's ejaculations died away in the distance (for he continued to pour them out, all the way downstairs), Quilp advanced towards the two men, who yet lingered in a kind of stupid amazement.

"Have you been dragging the river all day, gentlemen?" said the dwarf, holding the door open with great politeness.

"And yesterday too, master."

"Dear me, you've had a deal of trouble. Pray consider everything yours that you find upon the—upon the body. Good night!"

The men looked at each other, but had evidently no inclination to argue the point just then, and shuffled out of the room. This speedy clearance effected, Quilp locked the doors; and, still embracing the case-bottle with shrugged-up shoulders and folded arms, stood looking at his insensible wife like a dismounted nightmare.

Chapter L

MATRIMONIAL differences are usually discussed by the parties concerned in the form of dialogue, in which the lady bears at least her full half-share. Those of Mr and Mrs Quilp, however, were an exception to the general rule; the remarks which they occasioned being limited to a long soliloquy on the part of the gentleman, with perhaps a few deprecatory observations from the lady, not extending beyond a trembling mono-syllable uttered at long intervals, and in a very submissive and humble tone. On the present occasion, Mrs Quilp did not for a long time venture even upon this gentle defence, but when she had recovered from her fainting-fit sat in a tearful silence, meekly listening to the reproaches of her lord and master.

Of these Mr Quilp delivered himself with the utmost animation and rapidity, and with so many distortions of limb and feature, that even his wife, although tolerably well accustomed to his proficiency in these respects, was well-nigh beside herself with alarm. But the Jamaica rum, and the joy of having occasioned a heavy disappointment, by degrees cooled Mr Quilp's wrath; which, from being at savage heat, dropped slowly to the bantering or chuckling point, at which it steadily remained.

"So you thought I was dead and gone, did you?" said Quilp. "You thought you were a widow, eh? Ha, ha, ha, you jade!"

"Indeed, Quilp," returned his wife. "I'm very sorry——"

"Who doubts it!" cried the dwarf. "You very sorry! to be sure you are. Who doubts that you're *very* sorry!"

"I don't mean sorry that you have come home again alive and well," said his wife, "but sorry that I should have been led into such a belief. I am glad to see you, Quilp; indeed I am."

In truth Mrs Quilp did seem a great deal more glad to behold her lord than might have been expected, and did evince a degree of interest in his safety which, all things considered, was rather unaccountable. Upon Quilp, however, this circumstance made no impression, further than as it moved him to snap his fingers close to his wife's eyes, with divers grins of triumph and derision.

"How could you go away so long without saying a word to me or letting me hear of you or know anything about you?" asked the poor little woman, sobbing. "How could you be so cruel, Quilp?"

"How could I be so cruel! cruel!" cried the dwarf. "Because I was in the humour. I'm in the humour now. I shall be cruel when I like. I'm going away again."

"Not again!"

"Yes again. I'm going away now. I'm off directly. I mean to go and live wherever the fancy seizes me, at the wharf—at the counting-house—and be a jolly bachelor. You were a widow in anticipation. Damme," screamed the dwarf, "I'll be a bachelor in earnest."

"You can't be serious, Quilp," sobbed his wife.

"I tell you," said the dwarf, exulting in his project, "that I'll be a bachelor, a devil-may-care bachelor; and I'll have my bachelor's hall at the counting-house, and at such times come near it if you dare. And mind too that I don't pounce in upon you at unseasonable hours again, for I'll be a spy upon you, and come and go like a mole or a weazel. Tom Scott—where's Tom Scott?"

"Here I am, master," cried the voice of the boy, as Quilp threw up the window.

"Wait there, you dog," returned the dwarf, "to carry a bachelor's portmanteau. Pack it up, Mrs Quilp. Knock up the dear old lady to help; knock her up. Hallo there! Hallo!"

With these exclamations, Mr Quilp caught up the poker, and hurrying to the door of the good lady's sleeping-closet beat upon it therewith until she awoke in inexpressible terror, thinking that her amiable son-in-law surely intended to murder her in justification of the legs she had slandered. Impressed with this idea, she was no sooner fairly awake than she screamed violently, and would have quickly precipitated herself out of the window and through a neighbouring skylight, if her daughter had not hastened in to undeceive her, and implore her assistance. Somewhat reassured by her account of the service she was required to render, Mrs Jiniwin made her appearance in a flannel dressing-gown; and both mother and daughter, trembling with terror and cold—for the night was now far advanced—obeyed Mr Quilp's directions in submissive silence. Prolonging his preparations as much as possible, for their greater comfort, that eccentric gentleman superintended the packing of his wardrobe, and having added to it with his own hands, a plate, knife and fork, spoon, teacup and saucer, and other small household matters of that nature, strapped up the portmanteau, took it on his shoulders, and actually marched off without another word, and with the case-bottle (which he had never once put down) still tightly clasped under his arm. Consigning his heavier burden to the care of Tom Scott when he reached the street, taking a dram from the bottle for his own encouragement, and giving the boy a rap on the head with it as a small taste for himself, Quilp very deliberately led the way to the wharf, and reached it at between three and four o'clock in the morning.

"Snug!" said Quilp, when he had groped his way to the wooden counting-house, and opened the door with a key he carried about with him. "Beautifully snug! Call me at eight, you dog."

With no more formal leave-taking or explanation, he clutched the portmanteau, shut the door upon his attendant, and climbing on the desk, and rolling himself up as round as a hedgehog, in an old boat-cloak, fell fast asleep.

Being roused in the morning at the appointed time, and roused with difficulty, after his late fatigues, Quilp instructed Tom Scott to make a fire in the yard of sundry pieces of old timber, and to prepare some coffee for breakfast; for the better furnishing of which repast he entrusted him with certain small moneys, to be expended in the purchase of hot rolls, butter, sugar, Yarmouth bloaters, and other articles of housekeeping; so that in a few minutes a savoury meal was smoking on the board. With this substantial comfort, the dwarf regaled himself to his heart's content; and being highly satisfied with this free and gipsy mode of life (which he had often meditated, as offering, whenever he chose to avail himself of it, an agreeable freedom from the restraints of matrimony, and a choice means of keeping Mrs Quilp and her mother in a state of incessant agitation and suspense), bestirred himself to improve his retreat, and render it more commodious and comfortable.

With this view, he issued forth to a place hard by, where such stores were sold; purchased a second-hand hammock, and had it slung in seamanlike fashion from the ceiling of the counting-house. He also caused to be erected, in the same mouldy cabin, an old ship's stove with a rusty funnel to carry the smoke through the roof; and these arrangements completed, surveyed them with ineffable delight.

"I've got a country-house like Robinson Crusoe"—said the dwarf, ogling the accommodations; a solitary, sequestered, desolate-island sort of spot, where I can be quite alone when I have business on hand, and be secure from all spies and listeners. Nobody near me here, but rats, and they are fine stealthy secret fellows. I shall be as merry as a grig among these gentry. I'll look out for one like Christopher, and poison him—ha, ha, ha! Business though—business—we must be mindful of business in the midst of pleasure, and the time has flown this morning, I declare."

Enjoining Tom Scott to await his return, and not to stand upon his head, or throw a summerset, or so much as walk upon his hands meanwhile, on pain of lingering torments, the dwarf threw himself into a boat, and crossing to the other side of the river, and then speeding away on foot, reached Mr Swiveller's usual house of entertainment in Bevis Marks, just as that gentleman sat down alone to dinner in its dusky parlour.

"Dick"—said the dwarf, thrusting his head in at the door, "my pet, my pupil, the apple of my eye, hey, hey!"

"Oh, you're there, are you?" returned Mr Swiveller; *"how* are you?"

"How's Dick?" retorted Quilp. "How's the cream of clerkship, eh?"

"Why, rather sour, sir," replied Mr Swiveller. "Beginning to border upon cheesiness, in fact."

"What's the matter?" said the dwarf, advancing. "Has Sally proved unkind? 'Of all the girls that are so smart, there's none like——' Eh, Dick!"

"Certainly not," replied Mr Swiveller, eating his dinner with great gravity, "none like her. She's the sphynx of private life is Sally B."

"You're out of spirits," said Quilp, drawing up a chair. "What's the matter?"

"The law don't agree with me," returned Dick. "It isn't moist enough, and there's too much confinement. I have been thinking of running away."

"Bah!" said the dwarf. "Where would you run to, Dick?"

"I don't know," returned Mr Swiveller. "Towards Highgate, I suppose. Perhaps the bells might strike up 'Turn again Swiveller, Lord Mayor of London.' Whittington's name was Dick. I wish cats were scarcer."

Quilp looked at his companion with his eyes screwed up into a comical expression of curiosity, and patiently awaited his further explanation; upon which, however, Mr Swiveller appeared in no hurry to enter, as he ate a very long dinner in profound silence, and finally pushed away his plate, threw himself back into his chair, folded his arms, and stared ruefully at the fire, in which some ends of cigars were smoking on their own account, and sending up a fragrant odour.

"Perhaps you'd like a bit of cake"—said Dick, at last turning to the dwarf. "You're quite welcome to it. You ought to be, for it's of your making."

"What do you mean?" said Quilp.

Mr Swiveller replied by taking from his pocket a small and very greasy parcel, slowly unfolding it, and displaying a little slab of plum cake extremely indigestible in appearance, and bordered with a paste of white sugar an inch and a half deep.

"What should you say this was?" demanded Mr Swiveller.

"It looks like bride-cake," replied the dwarf, grinning.

"And whose should you say it was?" inquired Mr Swiveller, rubbing the pastry against his nose with a dreadful calmness. "Whose?"

"Not——"

"Yes," said Dick, "the same. You needn't mention her name. There's no such name now. Her name is Cheggs now, Sophy Cheggs. Yet loved I as man never loved that hadn't wooden legs, and my heart, my heart is breaking for the love of Sophy Cheggs."

With this extemporary adaptation of a popular ballad to the distressing circumstances of his own case, Mr Swiveller folded up the parcel again, beat it very flat between the palms of his hands, thrust it into his breast, buttoned his coat over it, and folded his arms upon the whole.

"Now I hope you're satisfied, sir," said Dick; "and I hope Fred's satisfied. You went partners in the mischief, and I hope you like it. This is the triumph I was to have, is it? It's like the old country-dance of that name, where there are two gentlemen to one lady, and one has her, and the other hasn't, but comes limping up behind to make out the figure. But it's Destiny, and mine's a crusher!"

Disguising his secret joy in Mr Swiveller's defeat, Daniel Quilp adopted the surest means of soothing him, by ringing the bell, and ordering in a supply of rosy wine (that is to say, of its usual representative), which he put about with great alacrity, calling upon Mr Swiveller to pledge him in various toasts derisive of Cheggs, and eulogistic of the happiness of single men. Such was their impression on Mr Swiveller, coupled with the reflection that no man could oppose his destiny, that in a very short space of time his spirits rose surprisingly, and he was enabled to give the dwarf an account of the receipt of the cake, which, it appeared, had been brought to Bevis Marks by the two surviving Miss Wackleses in person, and delivered at the office door with much giggling and joyfulness.

"Ha!" said Quilp. "It will be our turn to giggle soon. And that reminds me—you spoke of young Trent—where is he?"

Mr Swiveller explained that his respectable friend had recently accepted a responsible situation in a locomotive gaming-house, and was at that time absent on a professional tour among the adventurous spirits of Great Britain.

"That's unfortunate," said the dwarf, "for I came, in fact, to ask you about him. A thought has occurred to me, Dick; your friend over the way———"

"Which friend?"

"In the first floor."

"Yes?"

"Your friend in the first floor, Dick, may know him."

"No, he don't," said Mr Swiveller, shaking his head.

"Don't! No, because he has never seen him," rejoined Quilp; "but if we were to bring them together, who knows, Dick, but Fred, properly introduced, would serve his turn almost as well as little Nell or her grandfather—who knows but it might make the young fellow's fortune, and, through him, yours, eh?"

"Why, the fact is, you see," said Mr Swiveller, "that they *have been* brought together."

"Have been!" cried the dwarf, looking suspiciously at his companion. "Through whose means?"

"Through mine," said Dick, slightly confused. "Didn't I mention it to you the last time you called over yonder?"

"You know you didn't," returned the dwarf.

"I believe you're right," said Dick. "No. I didn't, I recollect. Oh, yes, I brought 'em together that very day. It was Fred's suggestion."

"And what came of it?"

"Why, instead of my friend's bursting into tears when he knew who Fred was, embracing him kindly, and telling him that he was his grandfather, or his grandmother in disguise (which we fully expected), he flew into a tremendous passion; called him all manner of names; said it was in a great measure his fault that little Nell and the old gentleman had ever been brought to poverty; didn't hint at our taking anything to drink;

and—and in short rather turned us out of the room than otherwise."

"That's strange," said the dwarf, musing.

"So we remarked to each other at the time," returned Dick coolly, "but quite true."

Quilp was plainly staggered by this intelligence, over which he brooded for some time in moody silence, often raising his eyes to Mr Swiveller's face, and sharply scanning its expression. As he could read in it, however, no additional information or anything to lead him to believe he had spoken falsely; and as Mr Swiveller, left to his own meditations, sighed deeply, and was evidently growing maudlin on the subject of Mrs Cheggs; the dwarf soon broke up the conference and took his departure, leaving the bereaved one to his melancholy ruminations.

"Have been brought together, eh?" said the dwarf as he walked the streets alone. "My friend has stolen a march upon me. It led him to nothing, and therefore is no great matter, save in the intention. I'm glad he has lost his mistress. Ha, ha! The blockhead mustn't leave the law at present. I'm sure of him where he is, whenever I want him for my own purposes, and, besides, he's a good unconscious spy on Brass, and tells, in his cups, all that he sees and hears. You're useful to me, Dick, and cost nothing but a little treating now and then. I am not sure that it may not be worth while, before long, to take credit with the stranger, Dick, by discovering your designs upon the child; but for the present, we'll remain the best friends in the world, with your good leave."

Pursuing these thoughts, and gasping as he went along, after his own peculiar fashion, Mr Quilp once more crossed the Thames and shut himself up in his Bachelor's Hall, which, by reason of its newly erected chimney depositing the smoke inside the room and carrying none of it off, was not quite so agreeable as more fastidious people might have desired. Such inconveniences, however, instead of disgusting the dwarf with his new abode, rather suited his humour; so, after dining luxuriously from the public-house, he lighted his pipe, and smoked against the chimney until nothing of him was visible through the mist but a pair of red and highly inflamed eyes, with sometimes a dim vision of his head and face, as, in a violent fit of coughing, he slightly stirred the smoke and scattered the heavy wreaths by which they were obscured. In the midst of this atmosphere, which must infallibly have smothered any other man, Mr Quilp passed the evening with great cheerfulness; solacing himself all the time with the pipe and the case-bottle; and occasionally entertaining himself with a melodious howl, intended for a song, but bearing not the faintest resemblance to any scrap of any piece of music, vocal or instrumental, ever invented by man. Thus he amused himself until nearly midnight, when he turned into his hammock with the utmost satisfaction.

The first sound that met his ears in the morning—as he half opened his eyes, and, finding himself so unusually near the ceiling, entertained a drowsy idea that he must have been transformed into a fly or blue-bottle in the course of the night—was that of a stifled sobbing and weeping in the room. Peeping cautiously over the side of his hammock, he descried Mrs Quilp, to whom, after contemplating her for some time in silence, he communicated a violent start by suddenly yelling out:

"Halloa!"

"Oh, Quilp!" cried his poor little wife, looking up. "How you frightened me!"

"I meant to, you jade," returned the dwarf. "What do you want here? I'm dead, an't I?"

"Oh, please come home, do come home," said Mrs Quilp, sobbing; "we'll never do so any more, Quilp, and after all it was only a mistake that grew out of our anxiety."

"Out of your anxiety," grinned the dwarf. "Yes, I know that—out of your anxiety for my death. I shall come home when I please, I tell you. I shall come home when I please, and go when I please. I'll be a Will o' the Wisp, now here, now there, dancing about you always, starting up when you least expect me, and keeping you in a constant state of restlessness and irritation. Will you begone?"

Mrs Quilp durst only make a gesture of entreaty.

"I tell you no," cried the dwarf. "No. If you dare to come here again unless you're sent for, I'll keep watch-dogs in the yard that'll growl and bite——I'll have man-traps, cunningly altered and improved for catching women——I'll have spring guns, that shall explode when you tread upon the wires, and blow you into little pieces. Will you begone?"

"Do forgive me. Do come back," said his wife earnestly.

"No-o-o-o-o!" roared Quilp. "Not till my own good time, and then I'll return again as often as I choose, and be accountable to nobody for my goings or comings. You see the door there. Will you go?"

Mr Quilp delivered this last command in such a very energetic voice, and moreover accompanied it with such a sudden gesture, indicative of an intention to spring out of his hammock, and, nightcapped as he was, bear his wife home again through the public streets, that she sped away like an arrow. Her worthy lord stretched his neck and eyes until she had crossed the yard, and then, not at all sorry to have had this opportunity of carrying his point, and asserting the sanctity of his castle, fell into an immoderate fit of laughter, and laid himself down to sleep again.

Chapter LI

T HE bland and open-hearted proprietor of Bachelor's Hall slept on amidst the congenial accompaniments of rain, mud, dirt, damp, fog, and rats, until late in the day; when, summoning his valet Tom Scott to assist him to rise, and to prepare breakfast, he quitted his couch, and made his toilet. This duty performed, and his repast ended, he again betook himself to Bevis Marks.

This visit was not intended for Mr Swiveller, but for his friend and employer Mr Sampson Brass. Both gentlemen, however, were from home, nor was the life and light of law, Miss Sally, at her post either. The fact of their joint desertion of the office was made known to all comers by a scrap of paper in the handwriting of Mr Swiveller, which was attached to the bell-handle, and which, giving the reader no clue to the time of day when it was first posted, furnished him with the rather vague and unsatisfactory information that that gentleman would "return in an hour."

"There's a servant, I suppose," said the dwarf, knocking at the house door. "She'll do."

After a sufficiently long interval, the door was opened, and a small voice immediately accosted him with, "Oh, please will you leave a card or message?"

"Eh?" said the dwarf, looking down (it was something quite new to him) upon the small servant.

To this, the child, conducting her conversation as upon the occasion of her first interview with Mr Swiveller, again replied, "Oh, please will you leave a card or message?"

"I'll write a note," said the dwarf, pushing past her into the office; "and mind your master has it directly he comes home." So Mr Quilp climbed up to the top of a tall stool to write the note, and the small servant, carefully tutored for such emergencies, looked on with her eyes wide open, ready, if he so much as abstracted a wafer, to rush into the street and give the alarm to the police.

As Mr Quilp folded his note (which was soon written: being a very short one) he encountered the gaze of the small servant. He looked at her long and earnestly.

"How are you?" said the dwarf, moistening a wafer with horrible grimaces.

The small servant, perhaps frightened by his looks, returned no audible reply; but it appeared from the motion of her lips that she was inwardly repeating the same form of expression concerning the note or message.

"Do they use you ill here? is your mistress a Tartar?" said Quilp with a chuckle.

In reply to the last interrogation, the small servant, with a look of infinite cunning mingled with fear, screwed up her mouth very tight and round, and nodded violently.

Whether there was anything in the peculiar slyness of her action which fascinated Mr. Quilp, or anything in the expression of her features at the moment which attracted his attention for some other reason; or whether it merely occurred to him as a pleasant whim to stare the small servant out of countenance; certain it is, that he planted his elbows square and firmly on the desk, and squeezing up his cheeks with his hands, looked at her fixedly.

"Where do you come from?" he said after a long pause, stroking his chin.

"I don't know."

"What's your name?"

"Nothing."

"Nonsense!" retorted Quilp. "What does your mistress call you when she wants you?"

"A little devil," said the child.

She added in the same breath, as if fearful of any further questioning, "But please will you leave a card or message?"

These unusual answers might naturally have provoked some more inquiries; Quilp, however, without uttering another word, withdrew his eyes from the small servant, stroked his chin more thoughtfully than before, and then, bending over the note as if to direct it with scrupulous and hair-breadth nicety, looked at her, covertly but very narrowly, from under his bushy eyebrows. The result of this secret survey was that he shaded his face with his hands, and laughed slyly and noiselessly, until every vein in it was swollen almost to bursting. Pulling his hat over his brow to conceal his mirth and its effects, he tossed the letter to the child, and hastily withdrew.

Once in the street, moved by some secret impulse, he laughed, and held his sides, and laughed again, and tried to peer through the dusty area railings as if to catch another glimpse of the child, until he was quite tired out. At last, he travelled back to the Wilderness, which was within rifle-shot of his bachelor retreat, and ordered tea in the wooden summer-house that afternoon for three persons; an invitation to Miss Sally Brass and her brother to partake of that entertainment at that place having been the object both of his journey and his note.

It was not precisely the kind of weather in which people usually take tea in summer-houses, far less in summer-houses in an advanced state of decay, and overlooking the slimy banks of a great river at low water. Nevertheless, it was in this choice retreat that Mr Quilp ordered a cold collation to be prepared, and it was beneath its cracked and leaky roof that he in due course of time received Mr Sampson and his sister Sally.

"You're fond of the beauties of nature," said Quilp with a grin. "Is this charming, Brass? Is it unusual, unsophisticated, primitive?"

"It's delightful indeed, sir," replied the lawyer.

"Cool?" said Quilp.

"N-not particularly so, I think, sir," rejoined Brass, with his teeth chattering in his head.

"Perhaps a little damp and ague-ish?" said Quilp.

"Just damp enough to be cheerful, sir," rejoined Brass. "Nothing more, sir, nothing more."

"And Sally?" said the delighted dwarf. "Does *she* like it?"

"She'll like it better," returned that strong-minded lady, "when she has tea; so let us have it, and don't bother."

"Sweet Sally?" cried Quilp, extending his arms as if about to embrace her. "Gentle, charming, overwhelming Sally."

"He's a very remarkable man indeed!" soliloquised Mr Brass. "He's quite a Troubadour, you know; quite a Troubadour!"

These complimentary expressions were uttered in a somewhat absent and distracted manner; for the unfortunate lawyer, besides having a bad cold in his head, had got wet in coming, and would have willingly borne some pecuniary sacrifice if he could have shifted his present raw quarters to a warm room, and have dried himself at a fire. Quilp, however—who, beyond the gratification of his demon whims, owed Sampson some acknowledgment of the part he had played in the mourning scene of which he had been a hidden witness, marked these symptoms of uneasiness with a delight past all expression, and derived from them a secret joy which the costliest banquet could never have afforded him.

It is worthy of remark, too, as illustrating a little feature in the character of Miss Sally Brass, that, although on her own account she would have borne the discomforts of the Wilderness with a very ill grace, and would probably, indeed, have walked off before the tea appeared, she no sooner beheld the latent uneasiness and misery of her brother than she developed a grim satisfaction, and began to enjoy herself after her own manner. Though the wet came stealing through the roof and trickling down upon their heads, Miss Brass uttered no complaint, but presided over the tea equipage with imperturbable composure. While Mr Quilp, in his uproarious hospitality, seated himself upon an empty beer-barrel, vaunted the place as the most beautiful and comfortable in the three kingdoms, and elevating his glass, drank to their next merry-meeting in that jovial spot; and Mr Brass, with the rain plashing down into his tea-cup, made a dismal attempt to pluck up his spirits and appear at his ease; and Tom Scott, who was in waiting at the door under an old umbrella, exulted in his agonies and bade fair to split his sides with laughing; while all this was passing, Miss Sally Brass, unmindful of the wet which dripped down upon her own feminine person and fair apparel, sat placidly behind the tea-board, erect and grizzly, contemplating the unhappiness of her brother with a mind at ease, and content, in her amiable disregard of self, to sit there all night, witnessing the torments which his avaricious and grovelling nature compelled him to endure and forbade him to resent. And this, it must be observed, or the illustration would be incomplete, although in a business point of view she had the strongest sympathy with Mr Sampson, and would have been beyond measure indignant if he had thwarted their client in any one respect.

In the height of his boisterous merriment, Mr Quilp, having on some pretence dismissed his attendant sprite for the moment, resumed his usual manner all at once, dismounted from his cask, and laid his hand upon the lawyer's sleeve.

"A word," said the dwarf, "before we go further. Sally, hark'ee for a minute."

Miss Sally drew closer, as if accustomed to business conferences with their host which were the better for not having air.

"Business," said the dwarf, glancing from brother to sister. "Very private business. Lay your heads together when you're by yourselves."

"Certainly, sir," returned Brass, taking out his pocket-book and pencil. "I'll take down the heads if you please, sir. Remarkable documents," added the lawyer, raising his eyes to the ceiling, "most remarkable documents. He states his points so clearly that it's a treat to have 'em! I don't know any Act of Parliament that's equal to him in clearness."

"I shall deprive you of a treat," said Quilp. "Put up your book. We don't want any documents. So. There's a lad named Kit———"

Miss Sally nodded, implying that she knew of him.

"Kit!" said Mr Sampson.—"Kit! Ha! I've heard the name before, but I don't exactly call to mind—I don't exactly———"

"You're as slow as a tortoise, and more thick-headed than a rhinoceros," returned his obliging client with an impatient gesture.

"He's extremely pleasant!" cried the obsequious Sampson. "His acquaintance with Natural History too is surprising. Quite a Buffoon, quite!"

There is no doubt that Mr Brass intended some compliment or other; and it has been argued with show of reason that he would have said Buffon, but made use of a super-fluous vowel. Be this as it may, Quilp gave him no time for correction, as he performed that office himself by more than tapping him on the head with the handle of his umbrella.

"Don't let's have any wrangling," said Miss Sally, staying his hand. "I've showed you that I know him, and that's enough."

"She's always foremost!" said the dwarf, patting her on the back and looking contemptuously at Sampson. "I don't like Kit, Sally."

"Nor I," rejoined Miss Brass.

"Nor I," said Sampson.

"Why, that's right!" cried Quilp. "Half our work is done already. This Kit is one of your honest people; one of your fair characters; a prowling prying hound; a hypocrite; a double-faced, white-livered, sneaking spy; a crouching cur to those that feed and coax him, and a barking yelping dog to all besides."

"Fearfully eloquent!" cried Brass with a sneeze. "Quite appalling!"

"Come to the point," said Miss Sally, "and don't talk so much."

"Right again!" exclaimed Quilp, with another contemptuous look at Sampson; "always foremost! I say, Sally, he is a yelping, insolent dog to all besides, and most of all, to me. In short, I owe him a grudge."

"That's enough, sir," said Sampson.

"No, it's not enough, sir," sneered Quilp; "will you hear me out? Besides that I owe him a grudge on that account, he thwarts me at this minute, and stands between me and an end which might otherwise prove a golden one to us all. Apart from that, I repeat that he crosses my humour, and I hate him. Now, you know the lad, and can guess the rest. Devise your own means of putting him out of my way, and execute them. Shall it be done?"

"It shall, sir," said Sampson.

"Then give me your hand," retorted Quilp. "Sally, girl, yours. I rely as much or more, on you than him. Tom Scott comes back. Lantern, pipes, more grog, and a jolly night of it!"

No other word was spoken, no other look exchanged, which had the slightest reference to this, the real occasion of their meeting. The trio were well accustomed to act together, and were linked to each other by ties of mutual interest and advantage, and nothing more was needed. Resuming his boisterous manner with the same ease with which he had thrown it off, Quilp was in an instant the same uproarious, reckless little savage he had been a few seconds before. It was ten o'clock at night before the amiable Sally supported her beloved and loving brother from the Wilderness, by which time he needed the utmost support her tender frame could render; his walk being for some unknown reason anything but steady, and his legs constantly doubling up in unexpected places.

Overpowered, notwithstanding his late prolonged slumbers, by the fatigues of the last few days, the dwarf lost no time in creeping to his dainty house, and was soon dreaming in his hammock. Leaving him to visions, in which perhaps the quiet figures we quitted in the old church porch were not without their share, be it our task to rejoin them as they sat and watched.

Chapter LII

AFTER a long time, the schoolmaster appeared at the wicket-gate of the churchyard, and hurried towards them, jingling in his hand, as he came along, a bundle of rusty keys. He was quite breathless with pleasure and haste when he reached the porch, and at first could only point towards the old building which the child had been contemplating so earnestly.

"You see those two old houses," he said at last.

"Yes, surely," replied Nell. "I have been looking at them nearly all the time you have been away."

"And you would have looked at them more curiously yet, if you could have guessed what I have to tell you," said the friend. "One of those houses is mine."

Without saying any more, or giving the child time to reply, the schoolmaster took her hand, and, his honest face quite radiant with exultation, led her to the place of which he spoke.

They stopped before its low arched door. After trying several of the keys in vain, the schoolmaster found one to fit the huge lock, which turned back, creaking, and admitted them into the house.

The room into which they entered was a vaulted chamber once nobly ornamented by cunning architects, and still retaining, in its beautiful groined roof and rich stone tracery, choice remnants of its ancient splendour. Foliage carved in the stone, and emulating the mastery of Nature's hand, yet remained to tell how many times the leaves outside had come and gone, while it lived on unchanged. The broken figures supporting the burden of the chimney-piece, though mutilated, were still distinguishable for what they had been—far different from the dust without—and showed sadly by the empty hearth, like creatures who had outlived their kind, and mourned their own too slow decay.

In some old time—for even change was old in that old place—a wooden partition had been constructed in one part of the chamber to form a sleeping-closet, into which the light was admitted at the same period by a rude window, or rather niche, cut in the solid wall. This screen, together with two seats in the broad chimney, had at some forgotten date been part of the church or convent; for the oak, hastily appropriated to its present purpose, had been little altered from its former shape, and presented to the eye a pile of fragments of rich carving from old monkish stalls.

An open door leading to a small room or cell, dim with the light that came through leaves of ivy, completed the interior of this portion of the ruin. It was not quite destitute of furniture. A few strange chairs, whose arms and legs looked as though they had dwindled away with age; a table, the very spectre of its race; a great old chest that had once held records in the church, with other quaintly fashioned domestic necessaries, and store of firewood for the winter, were scattered around, and gave evident tokens of its occupation as a dwelling-place at no very distant time.

The child looked around her, with that solemn feeling with which we contemplate the work of ages that have become but drops of water in the great ocean of eternity. The old man had followed them, but they were all three hushed for a space, and drew their breath softly, as if they feared to break the silence even by so slight a sound.

"It is a very beautiful place!" said the child, in a low voice.

"I almost feared you thought otherwise," returned the schoolmaster. "You shivered when we first came in, as if you felt it cold or gloomy."

"It was not that," said Nell, glancing round with a slight shudder. "Indeed, I cannot tell you what it was, but when I saw the outside, from the church porch, the same feeling came over me. It is its being so old and grey perhaps."

"A peaceful place to live in, don't you think so?" said her friend.

"Oh, yes," rejoined the child, clasping her hands earnestly. "A quiet, happy place—a place to live and learn to die in!" She would have said more, but that the energy of her thoughts caused her voice to falter, and come in trembling whispers from her lips.

"A place to live, and learn to live, and gather health of mind and body in," said the schoodmaster; "for this old house is yours."

"Ours!" cried the child.

"Ay," returned the schoolmaster gaily, "for many a merry year to come, I hope. I shall be a close neighbour—only next door—but this house is yours."

Having now disburdened himself of his great surprise, the schoolmaster sat down, and drawing Nell to his side, told her how he had learnt that that ancient tenement had been occupied for a very long time by an old person, nearly a hundred years of age, who kept the keys of the church, opened and closed it for the services, and showed it to strangers; how she had died not many weeks ago, and nobody had yet been found to fill the office; how, learning all this in an interview with the sexton, who was confined to his bed by rheumatism, he had been bold to make mention of his fellow-traveller, which had been so favourably received by that high authority, that he had taken courage, acting on his advice, to propound the matter to the clergyman. In a word, the result of his exertions was that Nell and her grandfather were to be carried before the last-named gentleman next day; and, his approval of their conduct and appearance reserved as a matter of form, that they were already appointed to the vacant post.

"There's a small allowance of money," said the schoolmaster. "It is not much, but still enough to live upon in this retired spot. By clubbing our funds together, we shall do bravely; no fear of that."

"Heaven bless and prosper you!" sobbed the child.

"Amen, my dear," returned her friend cheerfully; "and all of us, as it will, and has, in leading us through sorrow and trouble to this tranquil life. But we must look at *my* house now. Come!"

They repaired to the other tenement; tried the rusty keys as before; at length found the right one; and opened the worm-eaten door. It led into a chamber, vaulted and old, like that from which they had come, but not so spacious, and having only one other little room attached. It was not difficult to divine that the other house was of right the schoolmaster's, and that he had chosen for himself the least commodious, in his care and regard for them. Like the adjoining habitation, it held such old articles of furniture as were absolutely necessary, and had its stack of fire-wood.

To make these dwellings as habitable and full of comfort as they could, was now their pleasant care. In a short time, each had its cheerful fire glowing and crackling on the hearth, and reddening the pale old wall with a hale and healthy blush. Nell, busily plying her needle, repaired the tattered window-hangings, drew together the rents that time had worn in the threadbare scraps of carpet, and made them whole and decent. The schoolmaster swept and smoothed the ground before the door, trimmed the long grass, trained the ivy and creeping plants which hung their drooping heads in melancholy neglect; and gave to the outer walls a cheery air of home. The old man, sometimes by his side and sometimes with the child, lent his aid to both, went here and there on little patient services, and was happy. Neighbours too, as they came from work, proffered their help; or sent their children with such small presents or loans as the strangers needed most. It was a busy day; and night came on, and found them wondering that there was yet so much to do, and that it should be dark so soon.

They took their supper together, in the house which may be henceforth called the child's; and when they had finished their meal drew round the fire, and almost in whispers—their hearts were too quiet and glad for loud expression—discussed their future plans. Before they separated, the schoolmaster read some prayers aloud; and then, full of gratitude and happiness, they parted for the night.

At that silent hour, when her grandfather was sleeping peacefully in his bed, and every sound was hushed, the child lingered before the dying embers, and thought of her past fortunes as if they had been a dream and she only now awoke. The glare of the sinking flame, reflected in the oaken panels whose carved tops were dimly seen in the gloom of the dusky roof—the aged walls, where strange shadows came and went with every flickering of the fire—the solemn presence, within, of that decay which falls on senseless things the most enduring in their nature: and, without, and round about on every side, of Death—filled her with deep and thoughtful feelings, but with none of terror or alarm. A change had been gradually stealing over her, in the time of her loneliness and sorrow. With failing strength and heightening resolution, there had sprung up a purified and altered mind; there had grown in her bosom blessed thoughts and hopes, which are the portion of few but the weak and drooping. There were none to see the frail, perishable figure, as it glided from the fire and leaned pensively at the open casement; none but the stars, to look into the upturned face and read its history. The old church bell rang out the hour with a mournful sound, as if it had grown sad from so much communing with the dead and unheeded warning to the living; the fallen leaves rustled; the grass stirred upon the graves; all else was still and sleeping.

Some of those dreamless sleepers lay close within the shadow of the church—touching the wall, as if they clung to it for comfort and protection. Others had chosen to lie beneath the changing shade of trees; others by the path, that footsteps might come near them; others among the graves of little children. Some had desired to rest beneath the very ground they had trodden in their daily walks; some where the setting sun might shine upon their beds; some where its light would fall upon them when it rose. Perhaps not one of the imprisoned souls had been able quite to separate itself in living thought from its old companion. If any had, it had still felt for it a love like that which captives have been known to bear towards the cell in which they have been long confined, and even at parting hung upon its narrow bounds affectionately.

It was long before the child closed the window, and approached her bed. Again something of the same sensation as before—an involuntary chill—a momentary feeling akin to fear—but vanishing directly, and leaving no alarm behind. Again, too, dreams of the little scholar; of the roof opening, and a column of bright faces, rising far away into the sky, as she had seen in some old Scriptural picture once, and looking down on her, asleep. It was a sweet and happy dream. The quiet spot, outside, seemed to remain the same, saving that there was music in the air, and a sound of angels' wings. After a time the sisters came there hand in hand, and stood among the graves. And then the dream grew dim, and faded.

With the brightness and joy of morning, came the renewal of yesterday's labours, the revival of its pleasant thoughts, the restoration of its energies, cheerfulness, and hope. They worked gaily in ordering and arranging their houses until noon, and then went to visit the clergyman.

He was a simple-hearted old gentleman, of a shrinking, subdued spirit, accustomed to retirement, and very little acquainted with the world, which he had left many years before to come and settle in that place. His wife had died in the house in which he still lived, and he had long since lost sight of any earthly cares or hopes beyond it.

He received them very kindly, and at once showed an interest in Nell; asking her name, and age, her birthplace, the circumstances which had led her there, and so forth. The schoolmaster had already told her story. They had no other friends or home to leave, he said, and had come to share his fortunes. He loved the child as though she were his own.

"Well, well," said the clergyman. "Let it be as you desire. She is very young."

"Old in adversity and trial, sir," replied the schoolmaster.

"God help her! Let her rest, and forget them," said the old gentleman. "But an old church is a dull and gloomy place for one so young as you, my child."

"Oh, no, sir," returned Nell. "I have no such thoughts, indeed."

"I would rather see her dancing on the green at nights," said the old gentleman, laying his hand upon her head, and smiling sadly, "than have her sitting in the shadow of our mouldering arches. You must look to this, and see that her heart does not grow heavy among these solemn ruins. Your request is granted, friend."

After more kind words, they withdrew, and repaired to the child's house; where they were yet in conversation on their happy fortune, when another friend appeared.

This was a little old gentleman, who lived in the parsonage-house, and had resided there (so they learnt soon afterwards) ever since the death of the clergyman's wife, which had happened fifteen years before. He had been his college friend and always his close companion; in the first shock of his grief had come to console and comfort him; and from that time they had never parted company. The little old gentleman was the active spirit of the place; the adjuster of all differences, the promoter of all merry-makings, the dispenser of his friend's bounty, and of no small charity of his own besides; the universal mediator, comforter, and friend. None of the simple villagers had cared to ask his name, or, when they knew it, to store it in their memory. Perhaps from some vague rumour of his college honours which had been whispered abroad on his first arrival, perhaps because he was an unmarried, unencumbered gentleman, he had been called the Bachelor. The name pleased him, or suited him as well as any other, and the Bachelor he had ever since remained. And the bachelor it was, it may be added, who with his own hands had laid in the stock of fuel which the wanderers had found in their new habitation.

The bachelor, then—to call him by his usual appellation—lifted the latch, showed his little round mild face for a moment at the door, and stepped into the room like one who was no stranger to it.

"You are Mr Marton, the new schoolmaster?" he said, greeting Nell's kind friend.

"I am, sir."

"You come well recommended, and I am glad to see you. I should have been in the way yesterday, expecting you, but I rode across the country to carry a message from a sick mother to her daughter in service some miles off, and have but just now returned. This is our young church-keeper? You are not the less welcome, friend, for her sake, or for this old man's; nor the worse teacher for having learnt humanity."

"She has been ill, sir, very lately," said the schoolmaster, in answer to the look with which their visitor regarded Nell when he had kissed her cheek.

"Yes, yes. I know she has," he rejoined. "There have been suffering and heartache here."

"Indeed there have, sir."

The little old gentleman glanced at the grandfather, and back again at the child, whose hand he took tenderly in his, and held.

"You will be happier here," he said; "we will try, at least, to make you so. You have made great improvements here already. Are they the work of your hands?"

"Yes, sir."

"We may make some others—not better in themselves, but with better means perhaps," said the bachelor. "Let us see now, let us see."

Nell accompanied him into the other little rooms, and over both the houses, in which he found various small comforts wanting, which he engaged to supply from a certain collection of odds and ends he had at home, and which must have been a very miscellaneous and extensive one, as it comprehended the most opposite articles imaginable. They all came, however, and came without loss of time; for the little old gentleman, disappearing for some five or ten minutes, presently returned, laden with old shelves, rugs, blankets, and other household gear, and followed by a boy bearing a similar load. These being cast on the floor in a promiscuous heap, yielded a quantity of occupation in arranging, erecting, and putting away; the superintendence of which task evidently afforded the old gentleman extreme delight, and engaged him for some time with great briskness and activity. When nothing more was left to be done, he charged the boy to run off and bring his schoolmates to be marshalled before their new master, and solemnly reviewed.

"As good a set of fellows, Marton, as you'd wish to see," he said, turning to the schoolmaster when the boy was gone; "but I don't let 'em know I think so. That wouldn't do, at all."

The messenger soon returned at the head of a long row of urchins, great and small, who, being confronted by the bachelor at the house door, fell into various convulsions of politeness; clutching their hats and caps, squeezing them into the smallest possible dimensions, and making all manner of bows and scrapes, which the little old gentleman contemplated with excessive satisfaction, and expressed his approval of by a great many nods and smiles. Indeed, his approbation of the boys was by no means so scrupulously disguised as he had led the schoolmaster to suppose, inasmuch as it broke out in sundry loud whispers and confidential remarks which were perfectly audible to them every one.

"This first boy, schoolmaster," said the bachelor, "is John Owen; a lad of good parts, sir, and frank, honest temper; but too thoughtless, too playful, too light-headed by far. That boy, my good sir, would break his neck with pleasure, and deprive his parents of their chief comfort—and between ourselves, when you come to see him at hare and hounds, taking the fence and ditch by the finger-post, and sliding down the face of the little quarry, you'll never forget it. It's beautiful!"

John Owen having been thus rebuked, and being in perfect possession of the speech aside, the bachelor singled out another boy.

"Now, look at that lad, sir," said the bachelor. "You see that fellow? Richard Evans his name is, sir. An amazing boy to learn, blessed with a good memory, and a ready understanding, and moreover with a good voice and ear for psalm-singing, in which he is the best among us. Yet, sir, that boy will come to a bad end; he'll never die in his bed; he's always falling asleep in church in sermon-time—and to tell the truth, Mr Marton, I always did the same at his age, and feel quite certain that it was natural to my constitution and I couldn't help it."

This hopeful pupil edified by the above terrible reproval, the bachelor turned to another.

"But if we talk of examples to be shunned," said he, "if we come to boys that should be a warning and a beacon to all their fellows, here's the one, and I hope you won't spare him. This is the lad, sir; this one with the blue eyes and light hair. This is a swimmer, sir, this fellow—a diver, Lord save us! This is a boy, sir, who had a fancy for plunging into eighteen feet of water, with his clothes on, and bringing up a blind man's dog, who was being drowned by the weight of his chain and collar, while his master stood wringing his hands upon the bank, bewailing the loss of his guide and friend. I sent the boy two guineas anonymously, sir," added the bachelor, in his peculiar whisper, "directly I heard of it; but never mention it on any account, for he hasn't the least idea that it came from me."

Having disposed of this culprit, the bachelor turned to another, and from him to another, and so on through the whole array, laying for their wholesome restriction within due bounds, the same cutting emphasis on such of their propensities as were dearest to his heart and were unquestionably referable to his own precept and example. Thoroughly persuaded in the end, that he had made them miserable by his severity, he dismissed them with a small present, and an admonition to walk quietly home, without any leapings, scufflings, or turnings out of the way; which injunction (he informed the schoolmaster in the same audible confidence) he did not think he could have obeyed when he was a boy, had his life depended on it.

Hailing these little tokens of the bachelor's disposition as so many assurances of his own welcome course from that time, the schoolmaster parted from him with a light heart and joyous spirits, and deemed himself one of the happiest men on earth. The windows of the two old houses were ruddy again that night with the reflection of the cheerful fires that burnt within; and the bachelor and his friend, pausing to look upon them as they returned from their evening walk, spoke softly together of the beautiful child, and looked round upon the churchyard with a sigh.

Chapter LIII

NELL was stirring early in the morning; and having discharged her household tasks, and put everything in order for the good schoolmaster (though sorely against his will, for he would have spared her the pains), took down, from its nail by the fireside, a little bundle of keys with which the bachelor had formally invested her on the previous day, and went out alone to visit the old church.

The sky was serene and bright, the air clear, perfumed with the fresh scent of newly fallen leaves, and grateful to every sense. The neighbouring stream sparkled, and rolled onward with a tuneful sound; the dew glistened on the green mounds, like tears shed by Good Spirits over the dead.

Some young children sported among the tombs, and hid from each other, with laughing faces. They had an infant with them, and had laid it down asleep upon a child's grave, in a little bed of leaves. It was a new grave—the resting-place, perhaps, of some little creature, who, meek and patient in its illness, had often sat and watched them; and now seemed to their minds scarcely changed.

She drew near and asked one of them whose grave it was. The child answered that that was not its name; it was a garden—his brother's. It was greener, he said, than all the other gardens, and the birds loved it better because he had been used to feed them. When he had done speaking, he looked at her with a smile, and kneeling down and nestling for a moment with his cheek against the turf, bounded merrily away.

She passed the church, gazing upward at its old tower, went through the wicket-gate, and so into the village. The old sexton, leaning on a crutch, was taking the air at his cottage door, and gave her good morrow.

"You are better?" said the child, stopping to speak with him.

"Ay, surely," returned the old man. "I'm thankful to say much better."

"You will be quite well soon."

"With Heaven's leave, and a little patience. But come in, come in."

The old man limped on before, and warning her of the downward step, which he achieved himself with no small difficulty, led the way into his little cottage.

"It is but one room you see. There is another up above, but the stair has got harder to climb o' late years, and I never use it. I'm thinking of taking to it again next summer, though."

The child wondered how a grey-headed man like him—one of his trade too—could talk of time so easily. He saw her eyes wandering to the tools that hung upon the wall, and smiled.

"I warrant now," he said, "that you think all those are used in making graves."

"Indeed, I wondered that you wanted so many."

"And well you might. I am a gardener. I dig the ground, and plant things that are to live and grow. My works don't all moulder away and rot in the earth. You see that spade in the centre?"

"The very old one—so notched and worn? Yes."

"That's the sexton's spade, and it's a well-used one, as you see. We're healthy people here, but it has done a power of work. If it could speak now. that spade, it would tell you of many an unexpected job that it and I have done together; but I forget 'em, for my memory's a poor one. That's nothing new," he added hastily. "It always was."

"There are flowers and shrubs to speak to your other work," said the child.

"Oh, yes. And tall trees. But they are not so separated from the sexton's labours as you think."

"No!"

"Not in my mind, and recollection—such as it is," said the old man. "Indeed, they often help it. For say that I planted such a tree for such a man. There it stands to remind me that he died. When I look at its broad shadow, and remember what it was in his time, it helps me to the age of my other work, and I can tell you pretty nearly when I made his grave."

"But it may remind you of one who is still alive," said the child.

"Of twenty that are dead, in connexion with that one who lives, then," rejoined the old man; "wife, husband, parents, brothers, sisters, children, friends—a score at least. So it happens that the sexton's spade gets worn and battered. I shall need a new one—next summer."

The child looked quickly towards him, thinking that he jested with his age and infirmity: but the unconscious sexton was quite in earnest.

"Ah!" he said, after a brief silence. "People never learn. They never learn. It's only we who turn up the ground, where nothing grows and everything decays, who think of such things as these—who think of them properly, I mean. You have been into the church?"

"I am going there now," the child replied.

"There's an old well there," said the sexton, "right underneath the belfry; a deep, dark, echoing well. Forty year ago, you had only to let down the bucket till the first knot in the rope was free of the windlass, and you heard it splashing in the cold dull water. By little and little the water fell away, so that in ten year after that, a second knot was made, and you must unwind so much rope, or the bucket swung tight and empty at the end. In ten years' time, the water fell again, and a third knot was made. In ten years more the well dried up; and now, if you lower the bucket till your arms are tired and let out nearly all the cord, you'll hear it of a sudden clanking and rattling on the ground below, with a sound of being so deep and so far down, that your heart leaps into your mouth, and you start away as if you were falling in."

"A dreadful place to come on in the dark!" exclaimed the child, who had followed the old man's looks and words until she seemed to stand upon its brink.

"What is it but a grave!" said the sexton. "What else! And which of our old folks, knowing all this, thought, as the spring subsided, of their own failing strength, and lessening life? Not one!"

"Are you very old yourself?" asked the child, involuntarily.

"I shall be seventy-nine—next summer."

"You still work when you are well?"

"Work! To be sure. You shall see my gardens hereabout. Look at the window there. I made, and have kept, that plot of ground entirely with my own hands. By this time next year I shall hardly see the sky, the boughs will have grown so thick. I have my winter work at night besides."

He opened, as he spoke, a cupboard close to where he sat, and produced some miniature boxes, carved in a homely manner and made of old wood.

"Some gentlefolks who are fond of ancient days, and what belongs to them," he said, "like to buy these keepsakes from our church and ruins. Sometimes, I make them of scraps of oak, that turn up here and there; sometimes of bits of coffins which the vaults have long preserved. See here—this is a little chest of the last kind, clasped at the edges with fragments of brass plates that had writing on 'em once, though it would be hard to read it now. I haven't many by me at this time of year, but these shelves will be full—next summer."

The child admired and praised his work, and shortly afterwards departed; thinking as she went, how strange it was that this old man, drawing from his pursuits, and everything around him, one stern moral, never contemplated its application to himself; and, while he dwelt upon the uncertainty of human life, seemed both in word and deed to deem himself immortal. But her musings did not stop here, for she was wise enough to think that by a good and merciful adjustment this must be human nature, and that the old sexton, with his plans for next summer, was but a type of all mankind.

Full of these meditations, she reached the church. It was easy to find the key belonging to the outer door, for each was labelled on a scrap of yellow parchment. Its very turning in the lock awoke a hollow sound, and when she entered with a faltering step, the echoes that it raised in closing made her start.

Everything in our lives, whether of good or evil, affects us most by contrast. If the peace of the simple village had moved the child more strongly, because of the dark and troubled ways that lay beyond and through which she had journeyed with such failing feet, what was the deep impression of finding herself alone in that solemn building; where the very light, coming through sunken windows, seemed old and grey, and the air, redolent of earth and mould, seemed laden with decay, purified by time of all its grosser particles, and sighing through arch and aisle, and clustered pillars, like the breath of ages gone! Here was the broken pavement, worn so long ago by pious feet, that Time, stealing on the pilgrims' steps, had trodden out their track, and left but crumbling stones. Here were the rotten beam, the sinking arch, the sapped and mouldering wall, the lowly trench of earth, the stately tomb on which no epitaph remained—all—marble, stone, iron, wood, and dust, one common monument of ruin. The best work and the worst, the plainest and the richest, the stateliest and the least imposing—both of Heaven's work and Man's—all found one common level here, and told one common tale.

Some part of the edifice had been a baronial chapel, and here were effigies of warriors stretched upon their beds of stone with folded hands, crosslegged—those who had fought in the Holy Wars—girded with their swords, and cased in armour as they had lived. Some of these knights had their own weapons, helmets, coats of mail, hanging upon the walls hard by, and dangling from rusty hooks. Broken and dilapidated as they were, they yet retained their ancient form, and something of their ancient aspect. Thus violent deeds live after men upon the earth, and traces of war and bloodshed will survive in mournful shapes, long after those who worked the desolation are but atoms of earth themselves.

The child sat down in this old, silent place, among the stark figures on the tombs— they made it more quiet there, than elsewhere, to her fancy—and gazing round with a feeling of awe, tempered with a calm delight, felt that now she was happy, and at rest. She took a Bible from the shelf, and read; then, laying it down, thought of the summer days and the bright spring-time that would come—of the rays of sun that would fall in aslant upon the sleeping forms—of the leaves that would flutter at the window, and play in glistening shadows on the pavement—of the songs of birds, and growth of buds and blossoms out of doors—of the sweet air, that would steal in and gently wave the tattered banners overhead. What if the spot awakened thoughts of death! Die who would, it would still remain the same; these sights and sounds would still go on as happily as ever. It would be no pain to sleep amidst them.

She left the chapel—very slowly and often turning back to gaze again—and coming to a low door, which plainly led into the tower, opened it, and climbed the winding stair in darkness; save where she looked down through narrow loopholes on the place she had left, or caught a glimmering vision of the dusty bells. At length she gained the end of the ascent and stood upon the turret top.

Oh! the glory of the sudden burst of light; the freshness of the fields and woods, stretching away on every side and meeting the bright blue sky; the cattle grazing in the pasturage; the smoke, that, coming from among the trees, seemed to rise upward from the green earth; the children at their gambols down below—all, everything, so beautiful and happy! It was like passing from death to life; it was drawing nearer Heaven.

The children were gone by the time she emerged into the porch, and locked the door. As she passed the school-house she could hear the busy hum of voices. Her friend had begun his labours only that day. The noise grew louder, and, looking back, she saw the boys come trooping out and disperse themselves with merry shouts and play. "It's a good thing," thought the child, "I am very glad they pass the church." And then she stopped, to fancy how the noise would sound inside, and how gently it would seem to die away upon the ear.

Again that day, yes, twice again, she stole back to the old chapel, and in her former seat read from the same book, or indulged the same quiet train of thought. Even when it had grown dusk, and the shadows of coming night made it more solemn still, the child remained like one rooted to the spot, and had no fear, or thought of stirring.

They found her there at last, and took her home. She looked pale but very happy, until they separated for the night; and then, as the poor schoolmaster stooped down to kiss her cheek, he thought he felt a tear upon his face.

Chapter LIV

T HE bachelor, among his various occupations, found in the old church a constant source of interest and amusement. Taking that pride in it which men conceive for the wonders of their own little world, he had made its history his study; and many a summer day within its walls, and many a winter's night beside the parsonage fire, had found the bachelor still poring over and adding to his goodly store of tale and legend.

As he was not one of those rough spirits who would strip fair Truth of every little shadowy vestment in which time and teeming fancies love to array her—and some of which become her pleasantly enough, serving, like the waters of her well, to add new graces to the charms they half conceal and half suggest, and to awaken interest and pursuit rather than languor and indifference—as, unlike this stern and obdurate class, he loved to see the goddess crowned with those garlands of wild flowers which tradition wreathes for her gentle wearing, and which are often freshest in their homeliest shapes—he trod with a light step and bore with a light hand upon the dust of centuries, unwilling to demolish any of the airy shrines that had been raised above it, if one good feeling or affection of the human heart were hiding thereabouts. Thus, in the case of an ancient coffin of rough stone, supposed for many generations to contain the bones of a certain baron, who, after ravaging, with cut, and thrust, and plunder, in foreign lands, came back with a penitent and sorrowing heart to die at home, but which had been lately shown by learned antiquaries to be no such thing, as the baron in question (so they contended) had died hard in battle, gnashing his teeth and cursing with his latest breath—the bachelor stoutly maintained that the old tale was the true one; that the baron, repenting him of the evil, had done great charities and meekly given up the ghost; and that, if ever baron went to heaven, that baron was then at peace. In like manner, when the aforesaid antiquaries did argue and contend that a certain secret vault was not the tomb of a grey-haired lady who had been hanged and drawn and quartered by glorious Queen Bess for succouring a wretched priest who fainted of thirst and hunger at her door, the bachelor did solemnly maintain against all comers that the church was hallowed by the said poor lady's ashes; that her remains had been collected in the night from four of the city's gates, and thither in secret brought, and there deposited; and the bachelor did further (being highly excited at such times) deny the glory of Queen Bess, and assert the immeasurably greater glory of the meanest woman in her realm who had a merciful and tender heart. As to the assertion that the flat stone near the door was not the grave of the miser who had disowned his only child and left a sum of money to the church to buy a peal of bells, the bachelor did readily admit the same, and that the place had given birth to no such man. In a word, he would have had every stone, and plate of brass, the monument only of deeds whose memory should survive. All others he was willing to forget. They might be buried in consecrated ground, but he would have had them buried deep, and never brought to light again.

It was from the lips of such a tutor that the child learnt her easy task. Already impressed, beyond all telling, by the silent building and the peaceful beauty of the spot in which it stood—majestic age surrounded by perpetual youth—it seemed to her, when she heard these things, sacred to all goodness and virtue. It was another world, where sin and sorrow never came; a tranquil place of rest, where nothing evil entered.

When the bachelor had given her in connexion with almost every tomb and flat grave-stone some history of its own, he took her down into the old crypt, now a mere dull vault, and showed her how it had been lighted up in the time of the monks, and how, amid lamps depending from the roof, and swinging censers exhaling scented odours, and habits glittering with gold and silver, and pictures, and precious stuffs, and jewels all flashing and glistening through the low arches, the chant of aged voices had been many a time heard there at midnight in old days, while hooded figures knelt and prayed around, and told their rosaries of beads. Thence, he took her above ground again, and showed her, high up in the old walls, small galleries, where the nuns had been wont to glide along—dimly seen in their dark dresses so far off—or to pause like gloomy shadows, listening to the prayers. He showed her too, how the warriors, whose figures rested on the tombs, had worn those rotting scraps of armour up above—how this had been a helmet, and that a shield, and that a gauntlet—and how they had wielded the great two-handed swords, and beaten men down with yonder iron mace. All that he told the child she treasured in her mind; and sometimes, when she woke at night from dreams of those old times, and rising from her bed looked out at the dark church, she almost hoped to see the windows lighted up, and hear the organ's swell, and sound of voices, on the rushing wind.

The old sexton soon got better, and was about again. From him the child learnt many other things, though of a different kind. He was not able to work, but one day there was a grave to be made, and he came to overlook the man who dug it. He was in a talkative mood; and the child, at first standing by his side, and afterwards sitting on the grass at his feet, with her thoughtful face raised towards his, began to converse with him.

Now the man who did the sexton's duty was a little older than he, though much more active. But he was deaf; and when the sexton (who peradventure, on a pinch, might have walked a mile with great difficulty in half a dozen hours) exchanged a remark with him about his work, the child could not help noticing that he did so with an impatient kind of pity for his infirmity, as if he were himself the strongest and heartiest man alive.

"I'm sorry to see there is this to do," said the child, when she approached. "I heard of no one having died."

"She lived in another hamlet, my dear," returned the sexton. "Three mile away."

"Was she young?"

"Ye—yes," said the sexton; "not more than sixty-four, I think. David, was she more than sixty-four?"

David, who was digging hard, heard nothing of the question. The sexton, as he could not reach to touch him with his crutch, and was too infirm to rise without assistance, called his attention by throwing a little mould upon his red nightcap.

"What's the matter now?" said David, looking up.

"How old was Becky Morgan?" asked the sexton.

"Becky Morgan?" repeated David.

"Yes," replied the sexton; adding in a half-compassionate, half-irritable tone, which the old man couldn't hear, "you're getting very deaf, Davy, very deaf to be sure!"

The old man stopped in his work, and cleansing his spade with a piece of slate he had by him for the purpose—and scraping off, in the process, the essence of Heaven knows how many Becky Morgans—set himself to consider the subject.

"Let me think," quoth he. "I saw last night what they had put upon the coffin—was it seventy-nine?"

"No, no," said the sexton.

"Ah, yes, it was, though," returned the old man with a sigh. "For I remember thinking she was very near our age. Yes, it was seventy-nine."

"Are you sure you didn't mistake a figure, Davy?" asked the sexton, with signs of some emotion.

"What?" said the old man. "Say that again."

"He's very deaf. He's very deaf indeed," cried the sexton petulantly; "are you sure you're right about the figures?"

"Oh, quite," replied the old man. "Why not?"

"He's exceedingly deaf," muttered the sexton to himself. "I think he's getting foolish."

The child rather wondered what had led him to this belief, as to say the truth the old man seemed quite as sharp as he, and was infinitely more robust. As the sexton said nothing more just then, however, she forgot it for the time, and spoke again.

"You were telling me," she said, "about your gardening. Do you ever plant things here?"

"In the churchyard?" returned the sexton. "Not I."

"I have seen some flowers and little shrubs about," the child rejoined; "there are some over there, you see. I thought they were of your rearing, though indeed they grow but poorly."

"They grow as Heaven wills," said the old man; "and it kindly ordains that they shall never flourish here."

"I do not understand you."

"Why, this it is," said the sexton. "They mark the graves of those who had very tender, loving friends."

"I was sure they did!" the child exclaimed. "I am very glad to know they do!"

"Ay," returned the old man, "but stay. Look at them. See how they hang their heads, and droop, and wither. Do you guess the reason?"

"No," the child replied.

"Because the memory of those who lie below passes away so soon. At first they tend them, morning, noon, and night; they soon begin to come less frequently; from once a day, to once a week; from once a week to once a month; then, at long and uncertain intervals; then, not at all. Such tokens seldom flourish long. I have known the briefest summer flowers outlive them."

"I grieve to hear it," said the child.

"Ah! so say the gentlefolks who come down here to look about them," returned the old man, shaking his head, "but I say otherwise. 'It's a pretty custom you have in this part of the country,' they say to me sometimes, 'to plant the graves, but it's melancholy to see these things all withering or dead.' I crave their pardon and tell them that as I take it, 'tis a good sign for the happiness of the living. And so it is. It's nature."

"Perhaps the mourners learn to look to the blue sky by day, and to the stars by night, and to think that the dead are there, and not in graves," said the child in an earnest voice.

"Perhaps so," replied the old man doubtfully. "It may be."

"Whether it be as I believe it is, or no," thought the child within herself, "I'll make this place my garden. It will be no harm at least to work here day by day, and pleasant thoughts will come of it, I am sure."

Her glowing cheek and moistened eye passed unnoticed by the sexton, who turned towards old David, and called him by his name. It was plain that Becky Morgan's age still troubled him; though why, the child could scarcely understand.

The second or third repetition of his name attracted the old man's attention. Pausing from his work, he leant upon his spade, and put his hand to his dull ear.

"Did you call?" he said.

"I have been thinking, Davy," replied the sexton, "that she," he pointed to the grave, "must have been a deal older than you or me."

"Seventy-nine," answered the old man, with a sorrowful shake of the head; "I tell you that I saw it."

"Saw it?" replied the sexton; "ah, but, Davy, women don't always tell the truth about their age."

"That's true, indeed," said the other old man, with a sudden sparkle in his eye. "She might have been older."

"I'm sure she must have been. Why, only think how old she looked. You and I seemed but boys to her."

"She did look old," rejoined David. "You're right. She did look old."

"Call to mind how old she looked for many a long, long year, and say if she could be but seventy-nine at last—only our age," said the sexton.

"Five year older at the very least!" cried the other.

"Five!" retorted the sexton. "Ten. Good eighty-nine. I call to mind the time her daughter cried. She was eighty-nine if she was a day, and tries to pass upon us now, for ten year younger. Oh! human vanity!"

The other old man was not behindhand with some moral reflections on this fruitful theme, and both adduced a mass of evidence, of such weight as to render it doubtful— not whether the deceased was of the age suggested, but whether she had not almost reached the patriarchal term of a hundred. When they had settled this question to their mutual satisfaction, the sexton, with his friend's assistance, rose to go.

"It's chilly sitting here, and I must be careful—till the summer," he said, as he prepared to limp away.

"What?" asked old David.

"He's very deaf, poor fellow!" cried the sexton. "Good-bye."

"Ah!" said old David, looking after him. "He's failing very fast. He ages every day."

And so they parted: each persuaded that the other had less life in him than himself; and both greatly consoled and comforted by the little fiction they had agreed upon, respecting Becky Morgan, whose decease was no longer a precedent of uncomfortable application, and would be no business of theirs for half a score of years to come.

The child remained for some minutes, watching the deaf old man as he threw out the earth with his shovel, and, often stopping to cough and fetch his breath, still muttered to himself, with a kind of sober chuckle, that the sexton was wearing fast. At length she turned away, and walking thoughtfully through the churchyard, came unexpectedly upon the schoolmaster, who was sitting on a green grave in the sun, reading.

"Nell here?" he said cheerfully, as he closed his book. "It does me good to see you in the air and light. I feared you were again in the church, where you so often are."

"Feared!" replied the child, sitting down beside him. "Is it not a good place?"

"Yes, yes," said the schoolmaster. "But you must be gay sometimes—nay, don't shake your head and smile so very sadly."

"Not sadly, if you knew my heart. Do not look at me as if you thought me sorrowful. There is not a happier creature on the earth than I am now."

Full of grateful tenderness, the child took his hand, and folded it between her own. "It's God's will!" she said, when they had been silent for some time.

"What?"

"All this," she rejoined; "all this about us. But which of us is sad now? You see that *I* am smiling."

"And so am I," said the schoolmaster; "smiling to think how often we shall laugh in this same place. Were you not talking yonder?"

"Yes," the child rejoined.

"Of something that has made you sorrowful?"

There was a long pause.

"What was it?" said the schoolmaster tenderly. "Come. Tell me what it was."

"I rather grieve—I *do* rather grieve to think," said the child, bursting into tears, "that those who die about us are so soon forgotten."

"And do you think," said the schoolmaster, marking the glance she had thrown around, "that an unvisited grave, a withered tree, a faded flower or two, are tokens of forgetfulness or cold neglect? Do you think there are no deeds far away from here, in which these dead may be best remembered? Nell, Nell, there may be people busy in the world at this instant, in whose good actions and good thoughts these very graves— neglected as they look to us—are the chief instruments."

"Tell me no more," said the child quickly. "Tell me no more. I feel, I know it. How could *I* be unmindful of it, when I thought of you?"

"There is nothing," cried her friend, "no, nothing innocent or good, that dies, and is forgotten. Let us hold to that faith, or none. An infant, a prattling child, dying in its cradle, will live again in the better thoughts of those who loved it, and play its part, through them, in the redeeming actions of the world, though its body be burnt to ashes or drowned in the deepest sea. There is not an angel added to the Host of Heaven but does its blessed work on earth in those that loved it here. Forgotten! oh, if the good deeds of human creatures could be traced to their source, how beautifully would even death appear; for how much charity, mercy, and purified affection, would be seen to have their growth in dusty graves!"

"Yes," said the child, "it is the truth; I know it is. Who should feel its force so much as I, in whom your little scholar lives again! Dear, dear, good friend, if you knew the comfort you have given me!"

The poor schoolmaster made her no answer, but bent over her in silence; for his heart was full.

They were yet seated in the same place, when the grandfather approached. Before they had spoken many words together, the church clock struck the hour of school, and their friend withdrew.

"A good man," said the grandfather, looking after him; "a kind man. Surely *he* will never harm us, Nell. We are safe here, at last—eh? We will never go away from here?"

The child shook her head and smiled.

"She needs rest," said the old man, patting her cheek; "too pale—too pale. She is not like what she was."

"When?" asked the child.

"Ha!" said the old man, "to be sure—when? How many weeks ago? Could I count them on my fingers? Let them rest, though; they're better gone."

"Much better, dear," replied the child. "We will forget them; or, if we ever call them to mind, it shall be only as some uneasy dream that has passed away.

"Hush!" said the old man, motioning hastily to her with his hand and looking over his shoulder; "no more talk of the dream, and all the miseries it brought. There are no dreams here. 'Tis a quiet place, and they keep away. Let us never think about them, lest they should pursue us again. Sunken eyes and hollow cheeks—wet, cold, and famine— and horrors before them all, that were even worse—we must forget such things if we would be tranquil here."

"Thank Heaven!" inwardly exclaimed the child, "for this most happy change!"

"I will be patient," said the old man, "humble, very thankful and obedient, if you will let me stay. But do not hide from me; do not steal away alone; let me keep beside you. Indeed, I will be very true and faithful, Nell."

"I steal away alone! why that," replied the child, with assumed gaiety, "would be a pleasant jest indeed. See here, dear grandfather, we'll make this place our garden—why not? It is a very good one—and to-morrow we'll begin, and work together, side by side."

"It is a brave thought!" cried her grandfather. "Mind, darling—we begin to-morrow!"

Who so delighted as the old man, when they next day began their labour! Who so unconscious of all associations connected with the spot, as he! They plucked the long grass and nettles from the tombs, thinned the poor shrubs and roots, made the turf smooth, and cleared it of the leaves and weeds. They were yet in the ardour of their work, when the child, raising her head from the ground over which she bent, observed that the bachelor was sitting on the stile close by, watching them in silence.

"A kind office," said the little gentleman, nodding to Nell as she curtseyed to him. "Have you done all that this morning?"

"It is very little, sir," returned the child, with downcast eyes, "to what we mean to do."

"Good work, good work," said the bachelor. "But do you only labour at the graves of children, and young people?"

"We shall come to the others in good time, sir," replied Nell, turning her head aside, and speaking softly.

It was a slight incident, and might have been design or accident, or the child's unconscious sympathy with youth. But it seemed to strike upon her grandfather, though he had not noticed it before. He looked in a hurried manner at the graves, then anxiously at the child, then pressed her to his side, and bade her stop to rest. Something he had long forgotten appeared to struggle faintly in his mind. It did not pass away, as weightier things had done; but came uppermost again, and yet again, and many times that day, and often afterwards. Once, while they were yet at work, the child, seeing that he often turned and looked uneasily at her, as though he were trying to resolve some painful doubts or collect some scattered thoughts, urged him to tell the reason. But he said it was nothing—nothing—and, laying her head upon his arm, patted her fair cheek with his hand, and muttered that she grew stronger every day, and would be a woman soon.

Chapter LV

FROM that time, there sprang up in the old man's mind, a solicitude about the child which never slept or left him. There are chords in the human heart—strange, varying strings—which are only struck by accident; which will remain mute and sense-less to appeals the most passionate and earnest, and respond at last to the slightest casual touch. In the most insensible or childish minds, there is some train of reflection which art can seldom lead, or skill assist, but which will reveal itself, as great truths have done, by chance, and when the discoverer has the plainest and simplest end in view. From that time, the old man never for a moment forgot the weakness and devotion of the child: from the time of that slight incident, he, who had seen her toiling by his side through so much difficulty and suffering, and had scarcely thought of her otherwise than as the partner of miseries which he felt severely in his own person, and deplored for his own sake at least as much as hers, awoke to a sense of what he owed her, and what those miseries had made her. Never, no, never once, in one unguarded moment from that time to the end, did any care for himself, any thought of his own comfort, any selfish consideration or regard distract his thoughts from the gentle object of his love.

He would follow her up and down, waiting till she should tire and lean upon his arm—he would sit opposite to her in the chimney-corner, content to watch, and look, until she raised her head and smiled upon him as of old—he would discharge, by stealth, those household duties which tasked her powers too heavily—he would rise, in the cold dark nights, to listen to her breathing in her sleep, and sometimes crouch for hours by her bedside only to touch her hand. He Who knows all, can only know what hopes, and fears, and thoughts of deep affection, were in that one disordered brain, and what a change had fallen on the poor old man.

Sometimes—weeks had crept on, then—the child, exhausted, though with little fatigue, would pass whole evenings on a couch beside the fire. At such times, the schoolmaster would bring in books, and read to her aloud; and seldom an evening passed, but the bachelor came in, and took his turn of reading. The old man sat and listened—with little understanding for the words, but with his eyes fixed upon the child—and if she smiled or brightened with the story, he would say it was a good one, and conceive a fondness for the very book. When, in their evening talk, the bachelor told some tale that pleased her (as his tales were sure to do), the old man would painfully try to store it in his mind; nay, when the bachelor left them, he would sometimes slip out after him, and humbly beg that he would tell him such a part again, that he might learn to win a smile from Nell.

But these were rare occasions, happily; for the child yearned to be out of doors, and walking in her solemn garden. Parties, too, would come to see the church; and those who came, speaking to others of the child, sent more; so that even at that season of the year they had visitors almost daily. The old man would follow them at a little distance through the building, listening to the voice he loved so well; and when the strangers left, and parted from Nell, he would mingle with them to catch up fragments of their conversation; or he would stand for the same purpose, with his grey head uncovered, at the gate, as they passed through. They always praised the child, her sense and beauty, and he was proud to hear them! But what was that, so often added, which wrung his heart, and made him sob and weep alone, in some dull corner! Alas! even careless strangers—they who had no feeling for her, but the interest of the moment—they who would go away and forget next week that such a being lived—even they saw it—even they pitied her—even they bade him good day compassionately, and whispered as they passed.

The people of the village, too, of whom there was not one but grew to have a fondness for poor Nell; even among them, there was the same feeling; a tenderness towards her—a compassionate regard for her, increasing every day. The very school-boys, light-hearted and thoughtless as they were, even they cared for her. The roughest among them was sorry if he missed her in the usual place upon his way to school, and would turn out of the path to ask for her at the latticed window. If she were sitting in the church, they perhaps might peep in softly at the open door; but they never spoke to her, unless she rose and went to speak to them. Some feeling was abroad which raised the child above them all.

So, when Sunday came. They were all poor country people in the church, for the castle in which the old family had lived was an empty ruin, and there were none but humble folks for seven miles around. There, as elsewhere, they had an interest in Nell. They would gather round her in the porch, before and after service; young children would cluster at her skirts; and aged men and women forsake their gossips, to give her kindly greeting. None of them, young or old, thought of passing the child without a friendly word. Many who came from three or four miles distant, brought her little presents; the humblest and rudest had good wishes to bestow.

She had sought out the young children whom she first saw playing in the church-yard. One of these—he who had spoken of his brother—was her little favourite and friend, and often sat by her side in the church, or climbed with her to the tower-top. It was his delight to help her, or to fancy that he did so, and they soon became close companions.

It happened that, as she was reading in the old spot by herself one day, this child came running in with his eyes full of tears, and after holding her from him and looking at her eagerly for a moment, clasped his little arms passionately about her neck.

"What now?" said Nell, soothing him. "What is the matter?"

"She is not one yet!" cried the boy, embracing her still more closely. "No, no. Not yet."

She looked at him wonderingly, and putting his hair back from his face, and kissing him, asked what he meant.

"You must not be one, dear Nell," cried the boy. "We can't see them. They never come to play with us, or talk to us. Be what you are. You are better so."

"I do not understand you," said the child. "Tell me what you mean."

"Why, they say," replied the boy, looking up into her face, "that you will be an angel before the birds sing again. But you won't be, will you? Don't leave us, Nell, though the sky *is* bright. Do not leave us!"

The child drooped her head, and put her hands before her face.

"She cannot bear the thought!" cried the boy, exulting through his tears. "You will not go. You know how sorry we should be. Dear Nell, tell me that you'll stay amongst us. Oh! Pray, pray, tell me that you will."

The little creature folded his hands, and knelt down at her feet.

"Only look at me, Nell," said the boy, "and tell me that you'll stop, and then I shall know that they are wrong, and will cry no more. Won't you say yes, Nell?"

Still the drooping head and hidden face, and the child quite silent—save for her sobs.

"After a time," pursued the boy, trying to draw away her hand, "the kind angels will be glad to think that you are not among them, and that you stayed here to be with us. Willy went away, to join them; but if he had known how I should miss him in our little bed at night, he never would have left me, I am sure."

Yet the child could make him no answer, and sobbed as though her heart were bursting.

"Why would you go, dear Nell? I know you would not be happy when you heard that we were crying for your loss. They say that Willy is in Heaven now, and that it's always summer there, and yet I'm sure he grieves when I lie down upon his garden bed, and he cannot turn to kiss me. But if you do go, Nell," said the boy, caressing her, and pressing his face to hers, "be fond of him, for my sake. Tell him how I love him still, and how much I loved you; and when I think that you two are together, and are happy, I'll try to bear it, and never give you pain by doing wrong—indeed I never will!"

The child suffered him to move her hands, and put them round his neck. There was a tearful silence, but it was not long before she looked upon him with a smile, and promised him, in a very gentle, quiet voice, that she would stay, and be his friend, as long as Heaven would let her. He clapped his hands for joy, and thanked her many times; and being charged to tell no person what had passed between them, gave her an earnest promise that he never would.

Nor did he, so far as the child could learn; but was her quiet companion in all her walks and musings, and never again adverted to the theme, which he felt had given her pain, although he was unconscious of its cause. Something of distrust lingered about him still; for he would often come, even in the dark evenings, and call in a timid voice outside the door to know if she were safe within; and being answered yes, and bidden to enter, would take his station on a low stool at her feet, and sit there patiently until they came to seek, and take him home. Sure as the morning came, it found him lingering near the house to ask if she were well; and, morning, noon, or night, go where she would, he would forsake his playmates and his sports to bear her company.

"And a good little friend he is, too," said the old sexton to her once. "When his elder brother died—elder seems a strange word, for he was only seven year old—I remember this one took it sorely to heart."

The child thought of what the schoolmaster had told her, and felt how its truth was shadowed out even in this infant.

"It has given him something of a quiet way, I think," said the old man, "though for that he is merry enough at times. I'd wager now that you and he have been listening by the old well."

"Indeed we have not," the child replied. "I have been afraid to go near it; for I am not often down in that part of the church, and do not know the ground."

"Come down with me," said the old man. "I have known it from a boy. Come!"

They descended the narrow steps which led into the crypt, and paused among the gloomy arches, in a dim and murky spot.

"This is the place," said the old man. "Give me your hand while you throw back the cover, lest you should stumble and fall in. I am too old—I mean rheumatic—to stoop, myself."

"A black and dreadful place!" exclaimed the child.

"Look in," said the old man, pointing downward with his finger.

The child complied, and gazed down into the pit.

"It looks like a grave, itself," said the old man.

"It does," replied the child.

"I have often had the fancy," said the sexton, "that it might have been dug at first to make the old place more gloomy, and the old monks more religious. It's to be closed up, and built over."

The child still stood, looking thoughtfully into the vault.

"We shall see," said the sexton, "on what gay heads other earth will have closed, when the light is shut out from here. God knows! They'll close it up, next spring."

"The birds sing again in spring," thought the child, as she leant at her casement window, and gazed at the declining sun. "Spring! a beautiful and happy time!"

Chapter LVI

A DAY or two after the Quilp tea-party at the Wilderness, Mr Swiveller walked into Sampson Brass's office at the usual hour, and being alone in that Temple of Probity, placed his hat upon the desk, and taking from his pocket a small parcel of black crape, applied himself to folding and pinning the same upon it, after the manner of a hatband. Having completed the construction of this appendage, he surveyed his work with great complacency, and put his hat on again—very much over one eye, to increase the mournfulness of the effect. These arrangements perfected to his entire satisfaction, he thrust his hands into his pockets, and walked up and down the office with measured steps.

"It has always been the same with me," said Mr Swiveller, "always. 'Twas ever

thus—from childhood's hour I've seen my fondest hopes decay, I never loved a tree or
flower but 'twas the first to fade away. I never nursed a dear Gazelle, to glad me with
its soft black eye, but when it came to know me well, and love me, it was sure to marry
a market-gardener."

Overpowered by these reflections, Mr Swiveller stopped short at the clients' chair,
and flung himself into its open arms.

"And this," said Mr Swiveller, with a kind of bantering composure, "is life, I believe.
Oh, certainly. Why not! I'm quite satisfied. I shall wear," added Richard, taking off his
hat again and looking hard at it, as if he were only deterred by pecuniary considerations
from spurning it with his foot, "I shall wear this emblem of woman's perfidy, in remembrance of her with whom I shall never again thread the windings of the mazy; whom I
shall never more pledge in the rosy; who, during the short remainder of my existence,
will murder the balmy. Ha, ha, ha!"

It may be necessary to observe, lest there should appear any incongruity in the close
of this soliloquy, that Mr Swiveller did not wind up with a cheerful hilarious laugh, which
would have been undoubtedly at variance with his solemn reflections, but that, being in
a theatrical mood, he merely achieved that performance which is designated in melo-
dramas "laughing like a fiend"—for it seems that your fiends always laugh in syllables,
and always in three syllables, never more or less, which is a remarkable property in such
gentry, and one worthy of remembrance.

The baleful sounds had hardly died away, and Mr Swiveller was still sitting in a very
grim state in the clients' chair, when there came a ring—or, if we may adapt the sound
to his then humour, a knell—at the office bell. Opening the door with all speed, he
beheld the expressive countenance of Mr Chuckster, between whom and himself a
fraternal greeting ensued.

"You're devilish early at this pestiferous old slaughter-house," said that gentleman,
poising himself on one leg, and shaking the other in an easy manner.

"Rather," returned Dick.

"Rather!" retorted Mr Chuckster, with that air of graceful trifling which so well
became him. "I should think so. Why, my good feller, do you know what o'clock it
is—half-past nine A.M. in the morning?"

"Won't you come in?" said Dick. "All alone. Swiveller solus. ' 'Tis now the witch-
ing——' "

" 'Hour of night!' "

" 'When churchyards yawn.' "

" 'And graves give up their dead.' "

At the end of this quotation in dialogue, each gentleman struck an attitude, and
immediately subsiding into prose walked into the office. Such morsels of enthusiasm
were common among the Glorious Apollos, and were indeed the links that bound them
together, and raised them above the cold dull earth.

"Well, and how are you, my buck?" said Mr Chuckster, taking a stool. "I was forced
to come into the City upon some little private matters of my own, and couldn't pass the
corner of the street without looking in, but upon my soul I didn't expect to find you. It
is so everlastingly early."

Mr Swiveller expressed his acknowledgments; and it appearing on further conversation that he was in good health, and that Mr Chuckster was in the like enviable condition,
both gentlemen, in compliance with a solemn custom of the ancient Brotherhood to
which they belonged, joined in a fragment of the popular duet of *All's Well*, with a long
shake at the end.

"And what's the news?" said Richard.

"The town's as flat, my dear feller," replied Mr Chuckster, "as the surface of a Dutch oven. There's no news. By the bye, that lodger of yours is a most extraordinary person. He quite eludes the most vigorous comprehension, you know. Never was such a feller!"

"What has he been doing now?" said Dick.

"By Jove, sir," returned Mr Chuckster, taking out an oblong snuffbox, the lid whereof was ornamented with a fox's head curiously carved in brass, "that man is an unfathomable. Sir, that man has made friends with our articled clerk. There's no harm in him, but he is so amazingly slow and soft. Now, if he wanted a friend, why couldn't he have one that knew a thing or two, and could do him some good by his manners and conversation. I have my faults, sir," said Mr Chuckster——

"No, no," interposed Mr Swiveller.

"Oh, yes, I have, I have my faults, no man knows his faults better than I know mine. But," said Mr Chuckster, "I'm not meek. My worst enemies—every man has his enemies, sir, and I have mine—never accused me of being meek. And I tell you what, sir, if I hadn't more of these qualities that commonly endear man to man, than our articled clerk has, I'd steal a Cheshire cheese, tie it round my neck, and drown myself. I'd die degraded, as I had lived. I would upon my honour."

Mr Chuckster paused, rapped the fox's head exactly on the nose with the knuckle of the forefinger, took a pinch of snuff, and looked steadily at Mr Swiveller, as much as to say that if he thought he was going to sneeze, he would find himself mistaken.

"Not contented, sir," said Mr Chuckster, "with making friends with Abel, he has cultivated the acquaintance of his father and mother. Since he came home from that wild-goose chase, he has been there—actually been there. He patronises young Snobby besides; you'll find, sir, that he'll be constantly coming backwards and forwards to this place: yet I don't suppose that beyond the common forms of civility, he has ever exchanged half a dozen words with *me*. Now, upon my soul, you know," said Mr Chuckster, shaking his head gravely, as men are wont to do when they consider things are going a little too far, "this is altogether such a low-minded affair, that if I didn't feel for the governor, and know that he could never get on without me, I should be obliged to cut the connexion. I should have no alternative."

Mr Swiveller, who sat on another stool opposite to his friend, stirred the fire in an excess of sympathy, but said nothing.

"As to young Snob, sir," pursued Mr Chuckster with a prophetic look, "you'll find he'll turn out bad. In our profession we know something of human nature, and take my word for it, that the feller that came back to work out that shilling, will show himself one of these days in his true colours. He's a low thief, sir. He must be."

Mr Chuckster being roused, would probably have pursued this subject further, and in more emphatic language, but for a tap at the door, which seeming to announce the arrival of somebody on business, caused him to assume a greater appearance of meekness than was perhaps quite consistent with his late declaration. Mr Swiveller, hearing the same sound, caused his stool to revolve rapidly on one leg until it brought him to his desk, into which, having forgotten in the sudden flurry of his spirits to part with the poker, he thrust it as he cried "Come in!"

Who should present himself but that very Kit who had been the theme of Mr Chuckster's wrath! Never did man pluck up his courage so quickly, or look so fierce, as Mr Chuckster when he found it was he. Mr Swiveller stared at him for a moment, and then leaping from his stool, and drawing out the poker from its place of concealment, performed the broad-sword exercise with all the cuts and guards complete, in a species of frenzy.

"Is the gentleman at home?" said Kit, rather astonished by this uncommon reception.

Before Mr Swiveller could make any reply, Mr Chuckster took occasion to enter his indignant protest against this form of inquiry; which he held to be of a disrespectful and snobbish tendency, inasmuch as the inquirer, seeing two gentlemen then and there present, should have spoken of the other gentleman; or rather (for it was not impossible that the object of his search might be of inferior quality) should have mentioned his name, leaving it to his hearers to determine his degree as they thought proper. Mr Chuckster further remarked, that he had some reason to believe this form of address was personal to himself, and that he was not a man to be trifled with, as certain snobs (whom he did not more particularly mention or describe) might find, to their cost.

"I mean the gentleman upstairs," said Kit, turning to Richard Swiveller. "Is he at home?"

"Why?" rejoined Dick.

"Because if he is, I have a letter for him."

"From whom?" said Dick.

"From Mr Garland."

"Oh!" said Dick, with extreme politeness. "Then you may hand it over, sir. And if you're to wait for an answer, sir, you may wait in the passage, sir, which is an airy and well-ventilated apartment, sir."

"Thank you," returned Kit. "But I am to give it to himself, if you please."

The excessive audacity of this retort so overpowered Mr Chuckster and so moved his tender regard for his friend's honour, that he declared, if he were not restrained by official considerations, he must certainly have annihilated Kit upon the spot; a resentment of the affront which he did consider, under the extraordinary circumstances of aggravation attending it, could but have met with the proper sanction and approval of a jury of Englishmen, who, he had no doubt, would have returned a verdict of Justifiable Homicide, coupled with a high testimony to the morals and character of the Avenger. Mr Swiveller, without being quite so hot upon the matter, was rather shamed by his friend's excitement, and not a little puzzled how to act (Kit being quite cool and good-humoured), when the single gentleman was heard to call violently down the stairs.

"Didn't I see somebody for me come in?" cried the lodger.

"Yes, sir," replied Dick. "Certainly, sir."

"Then where is he?" roared the single gentleman.

"He's here, sir," rejoined Mr Swiveller. "Now young man, don't you hear you're to go upstairs? Are you deaf?"

Kit did not appear to think it worth his while to enter into any further altercation, but hurried off and left the Glorious Apollos gazing at each other in silence.

"Didn't I tell you so?" said Mr Chuckster. "What do you think of that?"

Mr Swiveller being in the main a good-natured fellow, and not perceiving in the conduct of Kit any villany of enormous magnitude, scarcely knew what answer to return. He was relieved from his perplexity, however, by the entrance of Mr Sampson and his sister, Sally, at sight of whom Mr Chuckster precipitately retired.

Mr Brass and his lovely companion appeared to have been holding a consultation over their temperate breakfast, upon some matter of great interest and importance. On the occasion of such conferences, they generally appeared in the office some half an hour after their usual time, and in a very smiling state, as though their late plots and designs had tranquillised their minds and shed a light upon their toilsome way. In the present instance, they seemed particularly gay; Miss Sally's aspect being of a most oily kind, and Mr Brass rubbing his hands in an exceedingly jocose and light-hearted manner.

"Well, Mr Richard," said Brass. "How are we this morning? Are we pretty fresh and cheerful, sir—eh, Mr Richard?"

"Pretty well, sir," replied Dick.

"That's well," said Brass. "Ha, ha! We should be gay as larks, Mr Richard—why not? It's a pleasant world we live in, sir, a very pleasant world. There are bad people in it, Mr Richard, but if there were no bad people, there would be no good lawyers. Ha, ha! Any letters by the post this morning, Mr Richard?"

Mr Swiveller answered in the negative.

"Ha!" said Brass, "no matter. If there's little business to-day, there'll be more to-morrow. A contented spirit, Mr Richard, is the sweetness of existence. Anybody been here, sir?"

"Only my friend"—replied Dick. " 'May we ne'er want a——' "

" 'Friend,' " Brass chimed in quickly, " 'or a bottle to give him.' Ha, ha! That's the way the song runs, isn't it? A very good song, Mr Richard, very good. I like the sentiment of it. Ha, ha! Your friend's the young man from Witherden's office, I think—yes—'May we ne'er want a——' Nobody else at all, been, Mr Richard?"

"Only somebody to the lodger," replied Mr Swiveller.

"Oh, indeed!" cried Brass. "Somebody to the lodger, eh? Ha, ha! 'May we ne'er want a friend, or a——' Somebody to the lodger, eh, Mr Richard?"

"Yes," said Dick, a little disconcerted by the excessive buoyancy of spirits which his employer displayed. "With him now."

"With him now!" cried Brass; "Ha, ha! There let 'em be, merry and free, toor rul lol le. Eh, Mr Richard? Ha, ha!"

"Oh, certainly," replied Dick.

"And who," said Brass, shuffling among his papers, "who is the lodger's visitor—not a lady visitor, I hope, eh, Mr Richard? The morals of the Marks you know, sir—'when lovely woman stoops to folly'—and all that—eh, Mr Richard?"

"Another young man, who belongs to Witherden's too, or half belongs there," returned Richard. "Kit, they call him."

"Kit, eh!" said Brass. "Strange name—name of a dancing-master's fiddle, eh, Mr Richard? Ha, ha! Kit's there, is he? Oh!"

Dick looked at Miss Sally, wondering that she didn't check this uncommon exuberance on the part of Mr Sampson; but as she made no attempt to do so, and rather appeared to exhibit a tacit acquiescence in it, he concluded that they had just been cheating somebody, and receiving the bill.

"Will you have the goodness, Mr Richard," said Brass, taking a letter from his desk, "just to step over to Peckham Rye with that? There's no answer, but it's rather particular and should go by hand. Charge the office with your coach-hire back, you know; don't spare the office; get as much out of it as you can—clerk's motto—eh, Mr Richard? Ha, ha!"

Mr Swiveller solemnly doffed the aquatic jacket, put on his coat, took down his hat from its peg, pocketed the letter, and departed. Directly he was gone, up rose Miss Sally Brass, and smiling sweetly at her brother (who nodded and smote his nose in return) withdrew also.

Sampson Brass was no sooner left alone, than he set the office-door wide open, and establishing himself at his desk directly opposite, so that he could not fail to see anybody who came downstairs and passed out at the street door, began to write with extreme cheerfulness and assiduity; humming as he did so, in a voice that was anything but musical, certain vocal snatches which appeared to have reference to the union between Church and State, inasmuch as they were compounded of the Evening Hymn and *God save the King*.

Thus, the attorney of Bevis Marks sat, and wrote, and hummed, for a long time, except when he stopped to listen with a very cunning face, and hearing nothing, went on humming louder, and writing slower than ever. At length, in one of these pauses, he heard his lodger's door opened and shut, and footsteps coming down the stairs. Then Mr Brass left off writing entirely, and with his pen in his hand hummed his very loudest; shaking his head meanwhile from side to side like a man whose whole soul was in the music, and smiling in a manner quite seraphic.

It was towards this moving spectacle that the staircase and the sweet sounds guided Kit, on whose arrival before his door, Mr Brass stopped his singing, but not his smiling, and nodded affably, at the same time beckoning to him with his pen.

"Kit," said Mr Brass, in the pleasantest way imaginable, "how do you do?"

Kit, being rather shy of his friend, made a suitable reply, and had his hand upon the lock of the street door when Mr Brass called him softly back.

"You are not to go, if you please, Kit," said the attorney in a mysterious and yet businesslike way. "You are to step in here, if you please. Dear me, dear me! When I look at you," said the lawyer, quitting his stool, and standing before the fire with his back towards it, "I am reminded of the sweetest little face that ever my eyes beheld. I remember your coming there twice or thrice when we were in possession. Ah, Kit, my dear fellow, gentlemen in my profession have such painful duties to perform sometimes, that you needn't envy us—you needn't indeed!"

"I don't, sir," said Kit, "though it isn't for the like of me to judge."

"Our only consolation, Kit," pursued the lawyer, looking at him in a sort of pensive abstraction, "is, that although we cannot turn away the wind, we can soften it; we can temper it, if I may say so, to the shorn lambs."

"Shorn indeed!" thought Kit. "Pretty close!" But he didn't say so.

"On that occasion, Kit," said Mr Brass, "on that occasion that I have just alluded to, I had a hard battle with Mr Quilp (for Mr Quilp is a very hard man) to obtain them the indulgence they had. It might have cost me a client. But suffering virtue inspired me, and I prevailed."

"He's not so bad after all," thought honest Kit, as the attorney pursed up his lips and looked like a man who was struggling with his better feelings.

"I respect *you*, Kit," said Brass with emotion. "I saw enough of your conduct at that time to respect you, though your station is humble, and your fortune lowly. It isn't the waistcoat that I look at. It is the heart. The checks in the waistcoat are but the wires of the cage. But the heart is the bird. Ah! How many sich birds are perpetually moulting, and putting their beaks through the wires to peck at all mankind!"

This poetic figure, which Kit took to be in special allusion to his own checked waistcoat, quite overcame him; Mr Brass's voice and manner added not a little to its effect, for he discoursed with all the mild austerity of a hermit, and wanted but a cord round the waist of his rusty surtout, and a skull on the chimney-piece, to be completely set up in that line of business.

"Well, well," said Sampson, smiling as good men smile when they compassionate their own weakness or that of their fellow-creatures "this is wide of the bull's-eye. You're to take that, if you please." As he spoke, he pointed to a couple of half-crowns upon the desk.

Kit looked at the coins, and then at Sampson, and hesitated.

"For yourself," said Brass.

"From——"

"No matter about the person they came from," replied the lawyer. "Say me, if you like. We have eccentric friends overhead, Kit, and we mustn't ask questions or talk too much—you understand? You're to take them, that's all; and between you and me, I don't think they'll be the last you'll have to take from the same place. I hope not. Good-bye, Kit. Good-bye!"

With many thanks, and many more self-reproaches for having on such slight grounds suspected one who in their very first conversation turned out such a different man from what he had supposed, Kit took the money and made the best of his way home. Mr Brass remained airing himself at the fire, and resumed his vocal exercise, and his seraphic smile, simultaneously.

"May I come in?" said Miss Sally, peeping.

"Oh, yes, you may come in," returned her brother.

"Ahem?" coughed Miss Brass interrogatively.

"Yes," returned Sampson, "I should say as good as done."

Chapter LVII

MR Chuckster's indignant apprehensions were not without foundation. Certainly the friendship between the single gentleman and Mr Garland was not suffered to cool, but had a rapid growth and flourished exceedingly. They were soon in habits of constant intercourse and communication; and the single gentleman labouring at this time under a slight attack of illness—the consequence most probably of his late excited feelings and subsequent disappointment—furnished a reason for their holding yet more frequent correspondence; so that some one of the inmates of Abel Cottage, Finchley, came backwards and forwards between that place and Bevis Marks, almost every day.

As the pony had now thrown off all disguise, and without any mincing of the matter or beating about the bush, sturdily refused to be driven by anybody but Kit, it generally happened that whether old Mr Garland came, or Mr Abel, Kit was of the party. Of all messages and inquiries, Kit was in right of his position the bearer; thus it came about that, while the single gentleman remained indisposed, Kit turned into Bevis Marks every morning with nearly as much regularity as the General Postman.

Mr Sampson Brass, who no doubt had his reasons for looking sharply about him, soon learnt to distinguish the pony's trot and the clatter of the little chaise at the corner of the street. Whenever this sound reached his ears, he would immediately lay down his pen and fall to rubbing his hands and exhibiting the greatest glee.

"Ha, ha!" he would cry. "Here's the pony again. Most remarkable pony, extremely docile, eh, Mr Richard, eh, sir?"

Dick would return some matter-of-course reply, and Mr Brass, standing on the bottom rail of his stool, so as to get a view of the street over the top of the window-blind, would take an observation of the visitors.

"The old gentleman again!" he would exclaim, "a very prepossessing old gentleman, Mr Richard—charming countenance, sir—extremely calm—benevolence in every feature, sir. He quite realises my idea of King Lear, as he appeared when in possession of his kingdom, Mr Richard—the same good-humour, the same white hair and partial baldness, the same liability to be imposed upon. Ah! A sweet subject for contemplation, sir, very sweet!"

Then, Mr Garland having alighted and gone upstairs, Sampson would nod and smile to Kit from the window, and presently walk out into the street to greet him, when some such conversation as the following would ensue.

"Admirably groomed, Kit"—Mr Brass is patting the pony—"does you great credit—amazingly sleek and bright to be sure. He literally looks as if he had been varnished all over."

Kit touches his hat, smiles, pats the pony himself, and expresses his conviction, "that Mr Brass will not find many like him."

"A beautiful animal indeed!" cries Brass. "Sagacious too!"

"Bless you!" replies Kit, "he knows what you say to him as well as a Christian does."

"Does he indeed!" cries Brass, who has heard the same thing in the same place from the same person in the same words a dozen times, but is paralysed with astonishment notwithstanding. "Dear me!"

"I little thought the first time I saw him, sir," says Kit, pleased with the attorney's strong interest in his favourite, "that I should come to be as intimate with him as I am now."

"Ah!" rejoins Mr Brass, brim-full of moral precepts and love of virtue. "A charming subject of reflection for you, very charming. A subject of proper pride and congratulation, Christopher. Honesty is the best policy.—I always find it so myself. I lost forty-seven pound ten by being honest this morning. But it's all gain, it's gain!"

Mr Brass slyly tickles his nose with his pen, and looks at Kit with the water standing in his eyes. Kit thinks that if ever there was a good man who belied his appearance, that man is Sampson Brass.

"A man," says Sampson, "who loses forty-seven pound ten in one morning by his honesty, is a man to be envied. If it had been eighty pound, the luxuriousness of feeling would have been increased. Every pound lost, would have been a hundredweight of happiness gained. The still, small voice, Christopher," cries Brass smiling, and tapping himself on the bosom, "is a-singing comic songs within me, and all is happiness and joy!"

Kit is so improved by the conversation, and finds it go so completely home to his feelings, that he is considering what he shall say, when Mr Garland appears. The old gentleman is helped into the chaise with great obsequiousness by Mr Sampson Brass; and the pony, after shaking his head several times, and standing for three or four minutes with all his four legs planted firmly on the ground as if he had made up his mind never to stir from that spot, but there to live and die, suddenly darts off without the smallest notice, at the rate of twelve English miles an hour. Then Mr Brass and his sister (who has joined him at the door) exchange an odd kind of smile—not at all a pleasant one in its expression—and return to the society of Mr Richard Swiveller, who during their absence has been regaling himself with various feats of pantomime, and is discovered at his desk, in a very flushed and heated condition, violently scratching out nothing with half a penknife.

Whenever Kit came along, and without the chaise, it always happened that Sampson Brass was reminded of some mission, calling Mr Swiveller, if not to Peckham Rye again, at all events to some pretty distant place from which he could not be expected to return for two or three hours, or in all probability a much longer period, as that gentleman was not, to say the truth, renowned for using great expedition on such occasions, but rather for protracting and spinning out the time to the very utmost limit of possibility. Mr Swiveller out of sight, Miss Sally immediately withdrew. Mr Brass would then set the office door wide open, hum his old tune with great gaiety of heart, and smile seraphically as before. Kit coming downstairs would be called in; entertained with some moral and agreeable conversation; perhaps entreated to mind the office for an instant while Mr Brass stepped over the way; and afterwards presented with one or two half-crowns as the case might be. This occurred so often, that Kit, nothing doubting but that they came from the single gentleman, who had already rewarded his mother with great liberality, could not enough admire his generosity; and brought so many cheap presents for her, and for little Jacob, and for the baby, and for Barbara to boot, that one or other of them was having some new trifle every day of their lives.

While these acts and deeds were in progress in and out of the office of Sampson Brass, Richard Swiveller, being often left alone therein, began to find the time hang heavy on his hands. For the better preservation of his cheerfulness therefore, and to prevent his faculties from rusting, he provided himself with a cribbage-board and pack of cards, and accustomed himself to play at cribbage with a dummy, for twenty, thirty, or sometimes even fifty thousand pounds aside, besides many hazardous bets to a considerable amount.

As these games were very silently conducted, notwithstanding the magnitude of the interests involved, Mr Swiveller began to think that on those evenings when Mr and Miss Brass were out (and they often went out now) he heard a kind of snorting or hard-breathing sound in the direction of the door, which it occurred to him, after some reflection, must proceed from the small servant, who always had a cold from damp living. Looking intently that way one night, he plainly distinguished an eye gleaming and glistening at the keyhole; and having now no doubt that his suspicions were correct, he stole softly to the door, and pounced upon her before she was aware of his approach.

"Oh! I didn't mean any harm indeed. Upon my word I didn't," cried the small servant, struggling like a much larger one. "It's so very dull, downstairs. Please don't you tell upon me; please don't."

"Tell upon you!" said Dick. "Do you mean to say you were looking through the keyhole for company?"

"Yes, upon my word I was," replied the small servant.

"How long have you been cooling your eye there?" said Dick.

"Oh, ever since you first began to play them cards, and long before."

Vague recollections of several fantastic exercises with which he had refreshed himself after the fatigues of business, and to all of which, no doubt, the small servant was a party, rarther disconcerted Mr Swiveller; but he was not very sensitive on such points, and recovered himself speedily.

"Well—come in"—he said, after a little consideration. "Here—sit down, and I'll teach you how to play."

"Oh! I durstn't do it," rejoined the small servant; "Miss Sally 'ud kill me, if she know'd I came up here."

"Have you got a fire downstairs?" said Dick.

"A very little one," replied the small servant.

"Miss Sally couldn't kill me if she know'd I went down there, so I'll come," said Richard, putting the cards into his pocket. "Why, how thin you are! What do you mean by it?"

"It an't my fault."

"Could you eat any bread and meat?" said Dick, taking down his hat. "Yes? Ah! I thought so. Did you ever taste beer?"

"I had a sip of it once," said the small servant.

"Here's a state of things!" cried Mr Swiveller, raising his eyes to the ceiling. "She *never* tasted it—it can't be tasted in a sip! Why, how old are you?"

"I don't know."

Mr Swiveller opened his eyes very wide, and appeared thoughtful for a moment; then, bidding the child mind the door until he came back, vanished straightway.

Presently he returned, followed by the boy from the public-house, who bore in one hand a plate of bread and beef, and in the other a great pot, filled with some very fragrant compound, which sent forth a grateful steam, and was indeed choice purl, made after a particular recipe which Mr Swiveller had imparted to the landlord at a period when he was deep in his books and desirous to conciliate his friendship. Relieving the boy of his burden at the door, and charging his little companion to fasten it to prevent surprise, Mr Swiveller followed her into the kitchen.

"There!" said Richard, putting the plate before her. "First of all, clear that off, and then you'll see what's next."

The small servant needed no second bidding, and the plate was soon empty.

"Next," said Dick, handing the purl, "take a pull at that; but moderate your transports, you know, for you're not used to it. Well, is it good?"

"Oh! isn't it?" said the small servant.

Mr Swiveller appeared gratified beyond all expression by this reply, and took a long draught himself, steadfastly regarding his companion while he did so. These preliminaries disposed of, he applied himself to teaching her the game, which she soon learnt tolerably well, being both sharp-witted and cunning.

"Now," said Mr Swiveller, putting two sixpences into a saucer, and trimming the wretched candle, when the cards had been cut and dealt, "those are the stakes. If you win, you get 'em all. If I win, I get 'em. To make it seem more real and pleasant, I shall call you the Marchioness, do you hear?"

The small servant nodded.

"Then, Marchioness," said Mr Swiveller, "fire away!"

The Marchioness, holding her cards very tight in both hands, considered which to play, and Mr Swiveller, assuming the gay and fashionable air which such society required, took another pull at the tankard, and waited for her lead.

Chapter LVIII

MR Swiveller and his partner played several rubbers with varying success, until the loss of three sixpences, the gradual sinking of the purl, and the striking of ten o'clock, combined to render that gentleman mindful of the flight of Time, and the expediency of withdrawing before Mr Sampson and Miss Sally Brass returned.

"With which object in view, Marchioness," said Mr Swiveller gravely, "I shall ask your ladyship's permission to put the board in my pocket, and to retire from the presence when I have finished this tankard; merely observing, Marchioness, that since life like a river is flowing, I care not how fast it rolls on, ma'am, on, while such purl on the bank still is growing, and such eyes light the waves as they run. Marchioness, your health. You will excuse my wearing my hat, but the palace is damp, and the marble floor is—if I may be allowed the expression—sloppy."

As a precaution against this latter inconvenience, Mr Swiveller had been sitting for some time with his feet on the hob, in which attitude he now gave utterance to these apologetic observations, and slowly sipped the last choice drops of nectar.

"The Baron Sampsono Brasso and his fair sister are (you tell me) at the Play?" said Mr Swiveller, leaning his left arm heavily upon the table, and raising his voice and his right leg after the manner of a theatrical bandit.

The Marchioness nodded.

"Ha!" said Mr Swiveller, with a portentous frown. " 'Tis well. Marchioness!—but no matter. Some wine there. Ho!" He illustrated these melodramatic morsels by handing the tankard to himself with great humility, receiving it haughtily, drinking from it thirstily, and smacking his lips fiercely.

The small servant, who was not so well acquainted with theatrical conventionalities as Mr Swiveller (having indeed never seen a play, or heard one spoken of, except by chance through chinks of doors and in other forbidden places), was rather alarmed by demonstrations so novel in their nature, and showed her concern so plainly in her looks, that Mr Swiveller felt it necessary to discharge his brigand manner for one more suitable to private life, as he asked:

"Do they often go where glory waits 'em, and leave you here?"

"Oh, yes; I believe you they do," returned the small servant. "Miss Sally's such a one-er for that, she is."

"Such a what?" said Dick.

"Such a one-er," returned the Marchioness.

After a moment's reflection, Mr Swiveller determined to forego his responsible duty of setting her right, and to suffer her to talk on; as it was evident that her tongue was loosened by the purl, and her opportunities for conversation were not so frequent as to render a momentary check of little consequence.

"They sometimes go to see Mr Quilp," said the small servant with a shrewd look; "they go to a many places, bless you."

"Is Mr Brass a wunner?" said Dick.

"Not half what Miss Sally is, he isn't," replied the small servant, shaking her head. "Bless you, he'd never do anything without her."

"Oh! He wouldn't, wouldn't he?" said Dick.

"Miss Sally keeps him in such order," said the small servant; "he always asks her advice, he does; and he catches it sometimes. Bless you, you wouldn't believe how much he catches it."

"I suppose," said Dick, "that they consult together a good deal, and talk about a great many people—about me, for instance, sometimes, eh, Marchioness?"

The Marchioness nodded amazingly.

"Complimentary?" said Mr Swiveller.

The Marchioness changed the motion of her head, which had not yet left off nodding, and suddenly began to shake it from side to side with a vehemence which threatened to dislocate her neck.

"Humph!" Dick muttered. "Would it be any breach of confidence, Marchioness, to relate what they say of the humble individual who has now the honour to——?"

"Miss Sally says you are a funny chap," replied his friend.

"Well, Marchioness," said Mr Swiveller, "that's not uncomplimentary. Merriment, Marchioness, is not a bad or degrading quality. Old King Cole was himself a merry old soul, if we may put any faith in the pages of history."

"But she says," pursued his companion, "that you an't to be trusted."

"Why, really, Marchioness," said Mr Swiveller thoughtfully; "several ladies and gentlemen—not exactly professional persons, but tradespeople, ma'am, tradespeople—have made the same remark. The obscure citizen who keeps the hotel over the way, inclined strongly to that opinion to-night when I ordered him to prepare the banquet. It's a popular prejudice, Marchioness; and yet I am sure I don't know why, for I have been trusted in my time to a considerable amount, and I can safely say that I never forsook my trust until it deserted me—never. Mr Brass is of the same opinion, I suppose?"

His friend nodded again, with a cunning look which seemed to hint that Mr Brass held stronger opinions on the subject than his sister; and seeming to recollect herself, added imploringly, "But don't you ever tell upon me, or I shall be beat to death."

"Marchioness," said Mr Swiveller, rising, "the word of a gentleman is as good as his bond—sometimes better; as in the present case, where his bond might prove but a doubtful sort of security. I am your friend, and I hope we shall play many more rubbers together in this same saloon. But, Marchioness," added Richard, stopping in his way to the door, and wheeling slowly round upon the small servant, who was following with the candle; "it occurs to me that you must be in the constant habit of airing your eye at keyholes, to know all this."

"I only wanted," replied the trembling Marchioness, "to know where the key of the safe was hid; that was all; and I wouldn't have taken much, if I had found it—only enough to squench my hunger."

"You didn't find it then?" said Dick. "But of course you didn't, or you'd be plumper. Good night, Marchioness. Fare thee well, and if for ever, then for ever fare thee well—and put up the chain, Marchioness, in case of accidents."

With this parting injunction, Mr Swiveller emerged from the house; and feeling that he had by this time taken quite as much to drink as promised to be good for his constitution (purl being a rather strong and heady compound), wisely resolved to betake himself to his lodgings, and to bed at once. Homeward he went therefore; and his apartments (for he still retained the plural fiction) being at no great distance from the office, he was soon seated in his own bed-chamber, where, having pulled off one boot and forgotten the other, he fell into deep cogitation.

"This Marchioness," said Mr Swiveller, folding his arms, "is a very extraordinary person—surrounded by mysteries, ignorant of the taste of beer, unacquainted with her own name (which is less remarkable), and taking a limited view of society through the keyholes of doors—can these things be her destiny, or has some unknown person started an opposition to the decrees of fate? It is a most inscrutable and unmitigated staggerer!"

When his meditations had attained this satisfactory point, he became aware of his remaining boot, of which, with unimpaired solemnity, he proceeded to divest himself; shaking his head with exceeding gravity all the time, and sighing deeply.

"These robbers," said Mr Swiveller, putting on his nightcap in exactly the same style as he wore his hat, "remind me of the matrimonial fireside. Cheggs's wife plays cribbage; all fours likewise. She rings the changes on 'em now. From sport to sport they hurry her, to banish her regrets, and when they win a smile from her, they think that she forgets— but she don't. By this time, I should say," added Richard, getting his left cheek into profile, and looking complacently at the reflection of a very little scrap of whisker in the looking-glass; "by this time, I should say, the iron has entered into her soul. It serves her right!"

Melting from this stern and obdurate, into the tender and pathetic mood, Mr Swiveller groaned a little, walked wildly up and down, and even made a show of tearing his hair, which however he thought better of, and wrenched the tassel from his nightcap instead. At last, undressing himself with a gloomy resolution, he got into bed.

Some men in his blighted position would have taken to drinking; but as Mr Swiveller had taken to that before, he only took, on receiving the news that Sophy Wackles was lost to him for ever, to playing the flute; thinking after mature consideration that it was a good, sound, dismal occupation, not only in unison with his own sad thoughts, but calculated to awaken a fellow-feeling in the bosoms of his neighbours. In pursuance of this resolution, he now drew a little table to his bedside, and arranging the light and a small oblong music-book to the best advantage, took his flute from its box, and began to play most mournfully.

The air was *Away with Melancholy*—a composition which, when it is played very slowly on the flute in bed, with the further disadvantage of being performed by a gentleman but imperfectly acquainted with the instrument, who repeats one note a great many times before he can find the next, has not a lively effect. Yet for half the night, or more, Mr Swiveller, lying sometimes on his back with his eyes upon the ceiling, and sometimes half out of bed to correct himself by the book, played this unhappy tune over and over again; never leaving off, save for a minute or two at a time to take breath and soliloquize about the Marchioness, and then beginning again with renewed vigour. It was not until he had quite exhausted his several subjects of meditation, and had breathed into the flute the whole sentiment of the purl down to its very dregs, and had nearly maddened the people of the house, and at both the next doors, and over the way—that he shut up the music-book, extinguished the candle, and finding himself greatly light-ened and relieved in his mind, turned round and fell asleep.

He awoke in the morning, much refreshed; and having taken half an hour's exercise at the flute, and graciously received a notice to quit from his landlady, who had been in waiting on the stairs for that purpose since the dawn of day, repaired to Bevis Marks; where the beautiful Sally was already at her post, bearing in her looks a radiance, mild as that which beameth from the virgin moon.

Mr Swiveller acknowledged her presence by a nod, and exchanged his coat for the aquatic jacket; which usually took some time fitting on, for in consequence of a tightness in the sleeves, it was only to be got into by a series of struggles. This difficulty overcome, he took his seat at the desk.

"I say"—quoth Miss Brass, abruptly breaking the silence, "you haven't seen a silver pencil-case this morning, have you?"

"I didn't meet many in the street," rejoined Mr Swiveller. "I saw one—a stout pencil-case of respectable appearance—but as he was in company with an elderly penknife and a young toothpick, with whom he was in earnest conversation, I felt a delicacy in speaking to him."

"No, but have you?" returned Miss Brass. "Seriously, you know."

"What a dull dog you must be to ask me such a question seriously," said Mr Swiveller. "Haven't I this moment come?"

"Well, all I know is," replied Miss Sally, "that it's not to be found, and that it disappeared one day this week, when I left it on the desk."

"Halloa!" thought Richard, "I hope the Marchioness hasn't been at work here."

"There was a knife, too," said Miss Sally, "of the same pattern. They were given to me by my father, years ago, and are both gone. You haven't missed anything yourself, have you?"

Mr Swiveller involuntarily clapped his hands to the jacket to be quite sure that it *was* a jacket and not a skirted coat; and having satisfied himself of the safety of this, his only moveable in Bevis Marks, made answer in the negative.

"It's a very unpleasant thing, Dick"—said Miss Brass, pulling out the tin box and refreshing herself with a pinch of snuff; "but between you and me—between friends you know, for if Sammy knew it, I should never hear the last of it—some of the office money, too, that has been left about, has gone in the same way. In particular, I have missed three half-crowns at three different times."

"You don't mean that?" cried Dick. "Be careful what you say, old boy, for this is a serious matter. Are you quite sure? Is there no mistake?"

"It is so, and there can't be any mistake at all," rejoined Miss Brass emphatically.

"Then by Jove," thought Richard, laying down his pen, "I'm afraid the Marchioness is done for!"

The more he discussed the subject in his thoughts, the more probable it appeared to Dick that the miserable little servant was the culprit. When he considered on what a spare allowance of food she lived, how neglected and untaught she was, and how her natural cunning had been sharpened by necessity and privation, he scarcely doubted it. And yet he pitied her so much, and felt so unwilling to have a matter of such gravity disturbing the oddity of their acquaintance, that he thought, and thought truly, that rather than receive fifty pounds, down, he would have the Marchioness proved innocent.

While he was plunged in very profound and serious meditation upon this theme, Miss Sally sat shaking her head with an air of great mystery and doubt; when the voice of her brother Sampson, carolling a cheerful strain, was heard in the passage, and that gentleman himself, beaming with virtuous smiles, appeared.

"Mr Richard, sir, good morning! Here we are again, sir, entering upon another day, with our bodies strengthened by slumber and breakfast, and our spirits fresh and flowing. Here we are, Mr Richard, rising with the sun to run our little course—our course of duty, sir—and, like him, get through our day's work with credit to ourselves and advantage to our fellow-creatures. A charming reflection, sir, very charming!"

While he addressed his clerk in these words, Mr Brass was somewhat ostentatiously engaged in minutely examining and holding up against the light a five-pound banknote, which he had brought in, in his hand.

Mr Richard not receiving his remarks with anything like enthusiasm, his employer turned his eyes to his face, and observed that it wore a troubled expression.

"You're out of spirits, sir," said Brass. "Mr Richard, sir, we should fall to work cheerfully, and not in a despondent state. It becomes us, Mr Richard, sir, to——"

Here the chaste Sarah heaved a loud sigh.

"Dear me!" said Mr Sampson, "you too! Is anything the matter? Mr Richard, sir——"

Dick, glancing at Miss Sally, saw that she was making signals to him, to acquaint her brother with the subject of their recent conversation. As his own position was not a very pleasant one until the matter was set at rest one way or other, he did so; and Miss Brass, plying her snuff-box at a most wasteful rate, corroborated his account.

The countenance of Sampson fell, and anxiety overspread his features. Instead of passionately bewailing the loss of his money, as Miss Sally had expected, he walked on tiptoe to the door, opened it, looked outside, shut it softly, returned on tiptoe, and said in a whisper,

"This is a most extraordinary and painful circumstance—Mr Richard, sir, a most painful circumstance. The fact is, that I myself have missed several small sums from the desk of late, and have refrained from mentioning it, hoping that accident would discover the offender; but it has not done so—it has not done so. Sally—Mr Richard, sir—this is a particularly distressing affair!"

As Sampson spoke, he laid the banknote upon the desk among some papers, in an absent manner, and thrust his hands into his pockets. Richard Swiveller pointed to it, and admonished him to take it up.

"No, Mr Richard, sir," rejoined Brass with emotion. "I will not take it up. I will let it lie there, sir. To take it up, Mr Richard, sir, would imply a doubt of you; and in you, sir, I have unlimited confidence. We will let it lie there, sir, if you please, and we will not take it up by any means." With that, Mr Brass patted him twice or thrice upon the shoulder, in a most friendly manner, and entreated him to believe that he had as much faith in his honesty as he had in his own.

Although at another time Mr Swiveller might have looked upon this as a doubtful compliment, he felt it, under the then-existing circumstances, a great relief to be assured that he was not wrongfully suspected. When he had made a suitable reply, Mr Brass wrung him by the hand, and fell into a brown study, as did Miss Sally likewise. Richard too remained in a thoughtful state; fearing every moment to hear the Marchioness impeached, and unable to resist the conviction that she must be guilty.

When they had severally remained in this condition for some minutes, Miss Sally all at once gave a loud rap upon the desk with her clenched fist, and cried, "I've hit it!"—as indeed she had, and chipped a piece out of it too; but that was not her meaning.

"Well," cried Brass anxiously. "Go on, will you?"

"Why," replied his sister with an air of triumph, "hasn't there been somebody always coming in and out of this office for the last three or four weeks; hasn't that somebody been left alone in it sometimes—thanks to you; and do you mean to tell me that that somebody isn't the thief!"

"What somebody?" blustered Brass.

"Why, what do you call him—Kit?"

"Mr Garland's young man?"

"To be sure."

"Never!" cried Brass. "Never. I'll not hear of it. Don't tell me"—said Sampson, shaking his head, and working with both his hands as if he were clearing away ten thousand cobwebs. "I'll never believe it of him. Never!"

"I say," repeated Miss Brass, taking another pinch of snuff, "that he's the thief."

"I say," returned Sampson violently, "that he is *not*. What do you mean? How dare you? Are characters to be whispered away like this? Do you know that he's the honestest and faithfullest fellow that ever lived, and that he has an irreproachable good name? Come in, come in!"

These last words were not addressed to Miss Sally, though they partook of the tone in which the indignant remonstrances that preceded them had been uttered. They were addressed to some person who had knocked at the office door; and they had hardly passed the lips of Mr Brass, when this very Kit himself looked in.

"Is the gentleman upstairs, sir, if you please?"

"Yes, Kit," said Brass, still fired with an honest indignation, and frowning with knotted brows upon his sister; "yes, Kit, he is. I am glad to see you, Kit, I am rejoiced to see you. Look in again, as you come downstairs, Kit. *That* lad a robber!" cried Brass when he had withdrawn, "with that frank and open countenance! I'd trust him with untold gold. Mr Richard, sir, have the goodness to step directly to Wrasp and Co.'s in Broad Street, and inquire if they have had instructions to appear in Carkem and Painter. *That* lad a robber," sneered Sampson, flushed and heated with his wrath. "Am I blind, deaf, silly; do I know nothing of human nature when I see it before me? Kit a robber! Bah!"

Flinging this final interjection at Miss Sally with immeasurable scorn and contempt, Sampson Brass thrust his head into his desk as if to shut the base world from his view, and breathed defiance from under its half-closed lid.

Chapter LIX

WHEN Kit, having discharged his errand, came downstairs from the single gentleman's apartment after the lapse of a quarter of an hour or so, Mr Sampson Brass was alone in the office. He was not singing as usual, nor was he seated at his desk. The open door showed him standing before the fire with his back towards it, and looking so very strange that Kit supposed he must have been suddenly taken ill.

"Is anything the matter, sir?" said Kit.

"Matter!" cried Brass. "No. Why anything the matter?"

"You are so very pale," said Kit, "that I should hardly have known you."

"Pooh, pooh! mere fancy," cried Brass, stooping to throw up the cinders. "Never better, Kit, never better in all my life. Merry too. Ha, ha! How's our friend abovestairs, eh?"

"A great deal better," said Kit.

"I'm glad to hear it," rejoined Brass; "thankful, I may say. An excellent gentleman— worthy, liberal, generous, gives very little trouble—an admirable lodger. Ha, ha! Mr Garland—he's well, I hope, Kit—and the pony—my friend, my particular friend, you know. Ha, ha!"

Kit gave a satisfactory account of all the little household at Abel Cottage. Mr Brass, who seemed remarkably inattentive and impatient, mounted on a stool, and beckoning him to come nearer, took him by the button-hole.

"I have been thinking, Kit," said the lawyer, "that I could throw some little emoluments into your mother's way—you have a mother, I think? If I recollect right, you told me——"

"Oh, yes, sir, yes certainly."

"A widow, I think? an industrious widow?"

"A harder-working woman or a better mother never lived, sir."

"Ah!" cried Brass. "That's affecting, truly affecting. A poor widow struggling to maintain her orphans in decency and comfort, is a delicious picture of human goodness.—Put down your hat, Kit."

"Thank you, sir, I must be going directly."

"Put it down while you stay, at any rate," said Brass, taking it from him and making some confusion among the papers, in finding a place for it on the desk. "I was thinking, Kit, that we have often houses to let for people we are concerned for, and matters of that sort. Now you know we're obliged to put people into those houses to take care of 'em—very often undeserving people that we can't depend upon. What's to prevent our having a person that we *can* depend upon, and enjoying the delight of doing a good action at the same time? I say, what's to prevent our employing this worthy woman, your mother? What with one job and another, there's lodging—and good lodging too—pretty well all the year round, rent free, and a weekly allowance besides, Kit, that would provide them with a great many comforts they don't at present enjoy. Now what do you think of that? Do you see any objection? My only desire is to serve you, Kit; therefore if you do, say so freely."

As Brass spoke, he moved the hat twice or thrice, and shuffled among the papers again, as if in search of something.

"How can I see any objection to such a kind offer, sir?" replied Kit with his whole heart. "I don't know how to thank you, sir, I don't indeed."

"Why, then," said Brass, suddenly turning upon him and thrusting his face close to Kit's with such a repulsive smile that the latter, even in the very height of his gratitude, drew back quite startled. "Why, then, *it's done.*"

Kit looked at him in some confusion.

"Done, I say"—added Sampson, rubbing his hands and veiling himself again in his usual oily manner. "Ha, ha! and so you shall find, Kit, so you shall find. But dear me," said Brass, "what a time Mr Richard is gone! A sad loiterer to be sure! Will you mind the office one minute, while I run upstairs? Only one minute. I'll not detain you an instant longer, on any account, Kit."

Talking as he went, Mr Brass bustled out of the office, and in a very short time returned. Mr Swiveller came back almost at the same instant; and as Kit was leaving the room hastily to make up for lost time, Miss Brass herself encountered him in the doorway.

"Oh!" sneered Sally, looking after him as she entered. "There goes your pet, Sammy, eh?"

"Ah! There he goes," replied Brass. "My pet, if you please. An honest fellow, Mr Richard, sir—a worthy fellow indeed!"

"Hem!" coughed Miss Brass.

"I tell you, you aggravating vagabond," said the angry Sampson, "that I'd stake my life upon his honesty. Am I never to hear the last of this? Am I always to be baited, and beset, by your mean suspicions? Have you no regard for true merit, you malignant fellow? If you come to that, I'd sooner suspect your honesty than his."

Miss Sally pulled out the tin snuff-box, and took a long, slow pinch: regarding her brother with a steady gaze all the time.

"She drives me wild, Mr Richard, sir," said Brass, "she exasperates me beyond all bearing. I am heated and excited, sir, I know I am. These are not business manners, sir, nor business looks, but she carries me out of myself."

"Why don't you leave him alone?" said Dick.

"Because she can't, sir," retorted Brass; "because to chafe and vex me is a part of her nature, sir, and she will and must do it, or I don't believe she'd have her health. But never mind," said Brass, "never mind. I've carried my point. I've shown my confidence in the lad. He has minded the office again. Ha, ha! Ugh, you viper!"

The beautiful virgin took another pinch, and put the snuff-box in her pocket; still looking at her brother with perfect composure.

"He has minded the office again," said Brass triumphantly; "he has had my confidence, and he shall continue to have it; he—why, where's the———"

"What have you lost?" inquired Mr Swiveller.

"Dear me!" said Brass, slapping all his pockets one after another, and looking into his desk, and under it, and upon it, and wildly tossing the papers about, "the note, Mr Richard, sir, the five-pound note—what can have become of it? I laid it down here—God bless me!"

"What!" cried Miss Sally, starting up, clapping her hands, and scattering the papers on the floor. "Gone! Now, who's right? Now, who's got it? Never mind five pounds— what's five pounds? He's honest you know, quite honest. It would be mean to suspect him. Don't run after him. No, no, not for the world!"

"Is it really gone, though?" said Dick, looking at Brass with a face as pale as his own.

"Upon my word, Mr Richard, sir," replied the lawyer, feeling in all his pockets with looks of the greatest agitation, "I fear this is a black business. It's certainly gone, sir. What's to be done?"

"Don't run after him," said Miss Sally, taking more snuff. "Don't run after him on any account. Give him time to get rid of it, you know. It would be cruel to find him out!"

Mr Swiveller and Sampson Brass looked from Miss Sally to each other in a state of utter bewilderment, and then, as by one impulse, caught up their hats and rushed out into the street—darting along in the middle of the road, and dashing aside all obstructions as though they were running for their lives.

It happened that Kit had been running too, though not so fast, and having the start of them by some few minutes, was a good distance ahead. As they were pretty certain of the road he must have taken, however, and kept on at a great pace, they came up with him, at the very moment when he had taken breath, and was breaking into a run again.

"Stop!" cried Sampson, laying his hand on one shoulder, while Mr Swiveller pounced upon the other. "Not so fast, sir. You're in a hurry?"

"Yes, I am," said Kit, looking from one to the other in great surprise.

"I—I—can hardly believe it," panted Sampson, "but something of value is missing from the office. I hope you don't know what."

"Know what! good Heaven, Mr Brass!" cried Kit, trembling from head to foot; "you don't suppose———"

"No, no," rejoined Brass quickly, "I don't suppose anything. Don't say *I* said you did. You'll come back quietly, I hope?"

"Of course I will," returned Kit. "Why not?"

"To be sure!" said Brass. "Why not? I hope there may turn out to be no why not. If you knew the trouble I've been in this morning through taking your part, Christopher, you'd be sorry for it."

"And I am sure you'll be sorry for having suspected me, sir," replied Kit. "Come. Let us make haste back."

"Certainly!" cried Brass, "the quicker, the better. Mr Richard—have the goodness, sir, to take that arm. I'll take this one. It's not easy walking three abreast, but under these circumstances it must be done, sir; there's no help for it."

Kit did turn from white to red, and from red to white again, when they secured him thus, and for a moment seemed disposed to resist. But, quickly recollecting himself, and remembering that if he made any struggle, he would perhaps be dragged by the collar through the public streets, he only repeated, with great earnestness and with the tears standing in his eyes, that they would be sorry for this—and suffered them to lead him off. While they were on the way back, Mr Swiveller, upon whom his present functions sat very irksomely, took an opportunity of whispering in his ear that if he would confess his guilt, even by so much as a nod, and promise not to do so any more, he would connive at his kicking Sampson Brass on the shins and escaping up a court; but Kit indignantly rejecting this proposal, Mr Richard had nothing for it, but to hold him tight until they reached Bevis Marks, and ushered him into the presence of the charming Sarah, who immediately took the precaution of locking the door.

"Now, you know," said Brass, "if this is a case of innocence, it is a case of that description, Christopher, where the fullest disclosure is the best satisfaction for everybody. Therefore if you'll consent to an examination," he demonstrated what kind of examination he meant by turning back the cuffs of his coat, "it will be a comfortable and pleasant thing for all parties."

"Search me," said Kit, proudly, holding up his arms. "But mind, sir—I know you'll be sorry for this, to the last day of your life."

"It is certainly a very painful occurrence," said Brass with a sigh, as he dived into one of Kit's pockets, and fished up a miscellaneous collection of small articles; "very painful. Nothing here, Mr Richard, sir, all perfectly satisfactory. Not here, sir. Nor in the waistcoat, Mr Richard, nor in the coat tails. So far, I am rejoiced, I am sure."

Richard Swiveller, holding Kit's hat in his hand, was watching the proceedings with great interest, and bore upon his face the slightest possible indication of a smile, as Brass, shutting one of his eyes, looked with the other up the inside of one of the poor fellow's sleeves as if it were a telescope, when Sampson turning hastily to him, bade him search the hat.

"Here's a handkerchief," said Dick.

"No harm in that, sir," rejoined Brass, applying his eye to the other sleeve, and speaking in the voice of one who was contemplating an immense extent of prospect. "No harm in a handkerchief, sir, whatever. The faculty don't consider it a healthy custom, I believe, Mr Richard, to carry one's handkerchief in one's hat—I have heard that it keeps the head too warm—but in every other point of view, its being there, is extremely satisfactory—ex-tremely so."

An exclamation, at once from Richard Swiveller, Miss Sally, and Kit himself, cut the lawyer short. He turned his head, and saw Dick standing with the banknote in his hand.

"In the hat?" cried Brass, in a sort of shriek.

"Under the handkerchief, and tucked beneath the lining," said Dick, aghast at the discovery.

Mr Brass looked at him, at his sister, at the walls, at the ceiling, at the floor—

everywhere but at Kit who stood quite stupefied and motionless.

"And this," cried Sampson, clasping his hands, "is the world that turns upon its own axis, and has Lunar influences, and revolutions round Heavenly Bodies, and various games of that sort! This is human natur, is it! Oh, natur, natur! This is the miscreant that I was going to benefit with all my little arts, and that even now I feel so much for, as to wish to let him go! But," added Mr Brass with greater fortitude, "I am myself a lawyer, and bound to set an example in carrying the laws of my happy country into effect. Sally, my dear, forgive me, and catch hold of him on the other side. Mr Richard, sir, have the goodness to run and fetch a constable. The weakness is past and over, sir, and moral strength returns. A constable, sir, if *you* please!"

Chapter LX

K IT stood as one entranced, with his eyes opened wide and fixed upon the ground, regardless alike of the tremulous hold which Mr Brass maintained on one side of his cravat, and of the firmer grasp of Miss Sally upon the other; although this latter detention was in itself no small inconvenience, as that fascinating woman, besides screwing her knuckles rather inconveniently into his throat from time to time, had fastened upon him in the first instance with so tight a grip that even in the disorder and distraction of his thoughts he could not divest himself of an uneasy sense of choking. Between the brother and sister he remained in this posture, quite unresisting and passive, until Mr Swiveller returned with a police constable at his heels.

This functionary, being of course well used to such scenes, looking upon all kinds of robbery from petty larceny up to house-breaking or ventures on the highway as matters in the regular course of business, and regarding the perpetrators in the light of so many customers coming to be served at the wholesale and retail shop of criminal law where he stood behind the counter, received Mr Brass's statement of facts with about as much interest and surprise, as an undertaker might evince if required to listen to a circumstantial account of the last illness of a person whom he was called in to wait upon professionally; and took Kit into custody with a decent indifference.

"We had better," said this subordinate minister of justice, "get to the office while there's a magistrate sitting. I shall want you to come along with us, Mr Brass, and the——" he looked at Miss Sally as if in some doubt whether she might not be a griffin or other fabulous monster.

"The lady, eh?" said Sampson.

"Ah!" replied the constable. "Yes—the lady. Likewise the young man that found the property."

"Mr Richard, sir," said Brass in a mournful voice. "A sad necessity. But the altar of our country, sir——"

"You'll have a hackney-coach, I suppose?" interrupted the constable, holding Kit (whom his other captors had released) carelessly by the arm, a little above the elbow. "Be so good as send for one, will you?"

"But hear me speak a word," cried Kit, raising his eyes and looking imploringly about him. "Hear me speak a word. I am no more guilty than any of you. Upon my soul I am not. I a thief! Oh, Mr Brass, you know me better. I am sure you know me better. This is not right of you, indeed."

"I give you my word, constable——" said Brass. But here the constable interposed with the constitutional principle "Words be blowed"; observing that words were but spoonmeat for babes and sucklings, and that oaths were the food for strong men.

"Quite true, constable," assented Brass in the same mournful tone. "Strictly correct. I give you my oath, constable, that down to a few minutes ago, when this fatal discovery was made, I had such confidence in that lad, that I'd have trusted him with—a hackney-coach, Mr Richard, sir; you're very slow, sir."

"Who is there that knows me," cried Kit, "that would not trust me—that does not? Ask anybody whether they have ever doubted me; whether I have ever wronged them of a farthing. Was I ever once dishonest when I was poor and hungry, and is it likely I would begin now! Oh, consider what you do. How can I meet the kindest friends that ever human creature had, with this dreadful charge upon me!"

Mr Brass rejoined that it would have been well for the prisoner if he had thought of that before, and was about to make some other gloomy observations, when the voice of the single gentleman was heard demanding from above-stairs what was the matter, and what was the cause of all that noise and hurry. Kit made an involuntary start towards the door in his anxiety to answer for himself, but being speedily detained by the constable, had the agony of seeing Sampson Brass run out alone to tell the story in his own way.

"And he can hardly believe it either," said Sampson, when he returned, "nor nobody will. I wish I could doubt the evidence of my senses, but their depositions are unimpeachable. It's of no use cross-examining my eyes," cried Sampson, winking and rubbing them, "they stick to their first account, and will. Now, Sarah, I hear the coach in the Marks; get on your bonnet, and we'll be off. A sad errand! a moral funeral, quite!"

"Mr Brass," said Kit, "do me one favour. Take me to Mr Witherden's first."

Sampson shook his head irresolutely.

"Do," said Kit. "My master's there. For Heaven's sake, take me there first."

"Well, I don't know," stammered Brass, who perhaps had his reasons for wishing to show as fair as possible in the eyes of the notary. "How do we stand in point of time, constable, eh?"

The constable, who had been chewing a straw all this while with great philosophy, replied that if they went away at once they would have time enough, but that if they stood shilly-shallying there any longer they must go straight to the Mansion House; and finally expressed his opinion that that was where it was, and that was all about it.

Mr Richard Swiveller having arrived inside the coach, and still remaining immovable in the most commodious corner with his face to the horses, Mr Brass instructed the officer to remove his prisoner, and declared himself quite ready. Therefore the constable, still holding Kit in the same manner, and pushing him on a little before him, so as to keep him at about three-quarters of an arm's length in advance (which is the professional mode), thrust him into the vehicle and followed himself. Miss Sally entered next; and there being now four inside, Sampson Brass got upon the box, and made the coachman drive on.

Still completely stunned by the sudden and terrible change which had taken place in his affairs, Kit sat gazing out of the coach window, almost hoping to see some monstrous phenomenon in the streets which might give him reason to believe he was in a dream. Alas! Everything was too real and familiar; the same succession of turnings, the same houses, the same streams of people running side by side in different directions upon the pavement, the same bustle of carts and carriages in the road, the same well-remembered objects in the shop windows; a regularity in the very noise and hurry which no dream ever mirrored. Dreamlike as the story was, it was true. He stood charged with robbery; the note had been found upon him, though he was innocent in thought and deed; and they were carrying him back, a prisoner.

Absorbed in these painful ruminations, thinking with a drooping heart of his mother and little Jacob, feeling as though even the consciousness of innocence would be insufficient to support him in the presence of his friends if they believed him guilty, and sinking in hope and courage more and more as they drew nearer to the notary's, poor Kit was looking earnestly out of the window, observant of nothing—when all at once, as though it had been conjured up by magic, he became aware of the face of Quilp.

And what a leer there was upon the face! It was from the open window of a tavern that it looked out; and the dwarf had so spread himself over it, with his elbows on the window-sill and his head resting on both his hands, that what between this attitude and his being swoln with suppressed laughter, he looked puffed and bloated into twice his usual breadth. Mr Brass on recognising him immediately stopped the coach. As it came to a halt directly opposite to where he stood, the dwarf pulled off his hat, and saluted the party with a hideous and grotesque politeness.

"Aha!" he cried. "Where now, Brass? where now? Sally with you too? Sweet Sally! And Dick? Pleasant Dick! And Kit? Honest Kit!"

"He's extremely cheerful!" said Brass to the coachman. "Very much so! Ah, sir—a sad business! Never believe in honesty any more, sir."

"Why not?" returned the dwarf. "Why not, you rogue of a lawyer, why not?"

"Banknote lost in our office, sir," said Brass, shaking his head. "Found in his hat, sir—he previously left alone there—no mistake at all, sir—chain of evidence complete—not a link wanting."

"What!" cried the dwarf, leaning half his body out of window. "Kit a thief! Kit a thief! Ha, ha, ha! Why, he's an uglier-looking thief than can be seen anywhere for a penny. Eh, Kit—eh? Ha, ha, ha! Have you taken Kit into custody before he had time and opportunity to beat me! Eh, Kit—eh?" And with that, he burst into a yell of laughter, manifestly to the great terror of the coachman, and pointed to a dyer's pole hard by, where a dangling suit of clothes bore some resemblance to a man upon a gibbet.

"Is it coming to that, Kit!" cried the dwarf, rubbing his hands violently. "Ha, ha, ha, ha! What a disappointment for little Jacob, and for his darling mother! Let him have the Bethel minister to comfort and console him, Brass. Eh, Kit—eh? Drive on, coachey, drive on. Bye-bye, Kit; all good go with you; keep up your spirits; my love to the Garlands—the dear old lady and gentleman. Say I inquired after 'em, will you? Blessings on 'em, on you, and on everybody, Kit. Blessings on all the world!"

With such good wishes and farewells, poured out in a rapid torrent until they were out of hearing, Quilp suffered them to depart; and when he could see the coach no longer, drew in his head, and rolled upon the ground in an ecstasy of enjoyment.

When they reached the notary's, which they were not long in doing, for they had encountered the dwarf in a bye-street at a very little distance from the house, Mr Brass dismounted; and opening the coach door with a melancholy visage, requested his sister to accompany him into the office, with the view of preparing the good people within for the mournful intelligence that awaited them. Miss Sally complying, he desired Mr

Swiveller to accompany them. So into the office they went; Mr Sampson and his sister arm in arm; and Mr Swiveller following, alone.

The notary was standing before the fire in the outer office, talking to Mr Abel and the elder Mr Garland, while Mr Chuckster sat writing at the desk, picking up such crumbs of their conversation as happened to fall in his way. This posture of affairs Mr Brass observed through the glass door as he was turning the handle, and seeing that the notary recognised him, he began to shake his head and sigh deeply while that partition yet divided them.

"Sir," said Sampson, taking off his hat, and kissing the two forefingers of his right-hand beaver glove, "my name is Brass—Brass of Bevis Marks, sir. I have had the honour and pleasure, sir, of being concerned against you in some little testamentary matters. How do you do, sir?"

"My clerk will attend to any business you may have come upon, Mr Brass," said the notary, turning away.

"Thank you, sir," said Brass, "thank you, I am sure. Allow me, sir, to introduce my sister—quite one of us, sir, although of the weaker sex—of great use in my business, sir, I assure you. Mr Richard, sir, have the goodness to come forward if you please—— No really," said Brass, stepping between the notary and his private office (towards which he had begun to retreat), and speaking in the tone of an injured man, "really, sir, I must, under favour, request a word or two with you, indeed."

"Mr Brass," said the other, in a decided tone, "I am engaged. You see that I am occupied with these gentlemen. If you will communicate your business to Mr. Chuckster yonder, you will receive every attention."

"Gentlemen," said Brass, laying his right hand on his waistcoat, and looking towards the father and son with a smooth smile—"Gentlemen, I appeal to you—really, gentlemen—consider, I beg of you. I am of the law. I am styled 'gentleman' by Act of Parliament. I maintain the title by the annual payment of twelve pounds sterling for a certificate. I am not one of your players of music, stage actors, writers of books, or painters of pictures, who assume a station that the laws of their country don't recognise. I am none of your strollers or vagabonds. If any man brings his action against me, he must describe me as a gentleman, or his action is null and void. I appeal to you—is this quite respectful? Really, gentlemen——"

"Well, will you have the goodness to state your business then, Mr Brass?" said the notary.

"Sir," rejoined Brass, "I will. Ah, Mr Witherden! you little know the—but I will not be tempted to travel from the point, sir. I believe the name of one of these gentlemen is Garland."

"Of both," said the notary.

"In-deed!" rejoined Brass, cringing excessively. "But I might have known that, from the uncommon likeness. Extremely happy, I am sure, to have the honour of an introduction to two such gentlemen, although the occasion is a most painful one. One of you gentlemen has a servant called Kit?"

"Both," replied the notary.

"Two Kits?" said Brass smiling. "Dear me!"

"One Kit, sir," returned Mr Witherden angrily, "who is employed by both gentlemen. What of him?"

"This of him, sir," rejoined Brass, dropping his voice impressively. "That young man, sir, that I have felt unbounded and unlimited confidence in, and always behaved to as if he was my equal—that young man has this morning committed a robbery in my office, and been taken almost in the fact."

"This must be some falsehood!" cried the notary.

"It is not possible," said Mr Abel.

"I'll not believe one word of it," exclaimed the old gentleman.

Mr Brass looked mildly round upon them, and rejoined:

"Mr Witherden, sir, *your* words are actionable, and if I was a man of low and mean standing, who couldn't afford to be slandered, I should proceed for damages. Hows'ever, sir, being what I am, I merely scorn such expressions. The honest warmth of the other gentleman I respect, and I'm truly sorry to be the messenger of such unpleasant news. I shouldn't have put myself in this painful position, I assure you, but that the lad himself desired to be brought here in the first instance, and I yielded to his prayers. Mr Chuckster, sir, will you have the goodness to tap at the window for the constable that's waiting in the coach?"

The three gentlemen looked at each other with blank faces when these words were uttered, and Mr Chuckster, doing as he was desired, and leaping off his stool with something of the excitement of an inspired prophet whose foretellings had in the fulness of time been realised, held the door open for the entrance of the wretched captive.

Such a scene as there was, when Kit came in, and bursting into the rude eloquence with which Truth at length inspired him, called Heaven to witness that he was innocent, and that how the property came to be found upon him he knew not! Such a confusion of tongues, before the circumstances were related, and the proofs disclosed! Such a dead silence when all was told, and his three friends exchanged looks of doubt and amazement!

"Is it not possible," said Mr Witherden, after a long pause, "that this note may have found its way into the hat by some accident—such as the removal of papers on the desk, for instance?"

But this was clearly shown to be quite impossible. Mr Swiveller, though an unwilling witness, could not help proving to demonstration, from the position in which it was found, that it must have been designedly secreted.

"It's very distressing," said Brass, "immensely distressing, I am sure. When he comes to be tried, I shall be very happy to recommend him to mercy on account of his previous good character. I did lose money before, certainly, but it doesn't quite follow that he took it. The presumption's against him—strongly against him—but we're Christians, I hope?"

"I suppose," said the constable, looking round, "that no gentleman here can give evidence as to whether he's been flush of money of late. Do you happen to know, sir?"

"He has had money from time to time, certainly," returned Mr Garland, to whom the man had put the question. "But that, as he always told me, was given him by Mr Brass himself."

"Yes to be sure," said Kit eagerly. "You can bear me out in that, sir?"

"Eh?" cried Brass, looking from face to face with an expression of stupid amazement.

"The money you know, the half-crowns, that you gave me—from the lodger," said Kit.

"Oh, dear me!" cried Brass, shaking his head and frowning heavily. "This is a bad case, I find; a very bad case indeed."

"What! Did you give him no money on account of anybody, sir?" asked Mr Garland, with great anxiety.

"*I* give him money, sir!" returned Sampson. "Oh, come you know, this is too barefaced. Constable, my good fellow, we had better be going."

"What!" shrieked Kit. "Does he deny that he did? ask him, somebody, pray. Ask him to tell you whether he did or not!"

"Did you, sir?" asked the notary.

"I tell you what, gentlemen," replied Brass, in a very grave manner, "he'll not serve his case this way, and really, if you feel any interest in him, you had better advise him to go upon some other tack. Did I, sir? Of course I never did."

"Gentlemen," cried Kit, on whom a light broke suddenly, "Master, Mr Abel, Mr Witherden, every one of you—he did it! What I have done to offend him I don't know, but this is a plot to ruin me. Mind, gentlemen, it's a plot, and whatever comes of it, I will say with my dying breath that he put that note in my hat himself! Look at him, gentlemen! see how he changes colour. Which of us looks the guilty person—he or I?"

"You hear him, gentlemen?" said Brass, smiling, "you hear him. Now, does this case strike you as assuming rather a black complexion, or does it not? Is it at all a treacherous case, do you think, or is it one of mere ordinary guilt? Perhaps, gentlemen, if he had not said this in your presence and I had reported it, you'd have held this to be impossible likewise, eh?"

With such pacific and bantering remarks did Mr Brass refut the foul aspersion on his character; but the virtuous Sarah, moved by stronger feelings, and having at heart, perhaps, a more jealous regard for the honour of her family, flew from her brother's side, without any previous intimation of her design, and darted at the prisoner with the utmost fury. It would undoubtedly have gone hard with Kit's face, but that the wary constable, foreseeing her design, drew him aside at the critical moment, and thus placed Mr Chuckster in circumstances of some jeopardy; for that gentleman happening to be next the object of Miss Brass's wrath; and rage being, like Love and Fortune, blind; was pounced upon by the fair enslaver, and had a false collar plucked up by the roots, and his hair very much dishevelled, before the exertions of the company could make her sensible of her mistake.

The constable, taking warning by this desperate attack, and thinking perhaps that it would be more satisfactory to the ends of justice if the prisoner was taken before a magistrate, whole, rather than in small pieces, led him back to the hackney-coach without more ado, and further insisted on Miss Brass becoming an outside passenger; to which proposal the charming creature, after a little angry discussion, yielded her consent; and so took her brother Sampson's place upon the box: Mr Brass with some reluctance agreeing to occupy her seat inside. These arrangements perfected, they drove to the justice-room with all speed, followed by the notary and his two friends in another coach. Mr Chuckster alone was left behind—greatly to his indignation; for he held the evidence he could have given, relative to Kit's returning to work out the shilling, to be so very material as bearing upon his hypocritical and designing character, that he considered its suppression little better than a compromise of felony.

At the justice-room, they found the single gentleman, who had gone straight there, and was expecting them with desperate impatience. But not fifty single gentlemen rolled into one could have helped poor Kit, who in half an hour afterwards was committed for trial, and was assured by a friendly officer on his way to prison that there was no occasion to be cast down, for the sessions would soon be on, and he would in all likelihood get his little affair disposed of, and be comfortably transported, in less than a fortnight.

Chapter LXI

L ET moralists and philosophers say what they may, it is very questionable whether a guilty man would have felt half as much misery that night, as Kit did, being innocent. The world, being in the constant commission of vast quantities of injustice, is a little too apt to comfort itself with the idea that if the victim of its falsehood and malice have a clear conscience, he cannot fail to be sustained under his trials, and somehow or other to come right at last; "in which case," say they who have hunted him down, "—though we certainly don't expect it—nobody will be better pleased than we." Whereas, the world would do well to reflect, that injustice is in itself, to every generous and properly constituted mind, an injury, of all others the most insufferable, the most torturing, and the most hard to bear; and that many clear consciences have gone to their account elsewhere, and many sound hearts have broken, because of this very reason; the knowledge of their own deserts only aggravating their sufferings, and rendering them the less endurable.

The world, however, was not in fault in Kit's case. But Kit was innocent; and knowing this, and feeling that his best friends deemed him guilty—that Mr and Mrs Garland would look upon him as a monster of ingratitude—that Barbara would associate him with all that was bad and criminal—that the pony would consider himself forsaken—and that even his own mother might perhaps yield to the strong appearances against him, and believe him to be the wretch he seemed—knowing and feeling all this, he experienced at first an agony of mind which no words can describe, and walked up and down the little cell in which he was locked up for the night, almost beside himself with grief.

Even when the violence of these emotions had in some degree subsided, and he was beginning to grow more calm, there came into his mind a new thought, the anguish of which was scarcely less. The child—the bright star of the simple fellow's life—she, who always came back upon him like a beautiful dream—who had made the poorest part of his existence, the happiest and best—who had ever been so gentle, and considerate, and good—if she were ever to hear of this, what would she think! As this idea occurred to him, the walls of the prison seemed to melt away, and the old place to reveal itself in their stead, as it was wont to be on winter nights—the fireside, the little supper-table, the old man's hat and coat, and stick—the half-opened door, leading to her little room—they were all there. And Nell herself was there, and he—both laughing heartily as they had often done—and when he had got as far as this, Kit could go no farther, but flung himself upon his poor bedstead and wept.

It was a long night, which seemed as though it would have no end; but he slept too, and dreamed—always of being at liberty, and roving about, now with one person and now with another, but ever with a vague dread of being recalled to prison; not that prison, but one which was in itself a dim idea, not of a place, but of a care and sorrow: of something oppressive and always present, and yet impossible to define. At last the morning dawned, and there was the jail itself—cold, black, and dreary, and very real indeed.

He was left to himself, however, and there was comfort in that. He had liberty to walk in a small paved yard at a certain hour, and learnt from the turnkey, who came to unlock his cell and show him where to wash, that there was a regular time for visiting, every day, and that if any of his friends came to see him, he would be fetched down to the grate. When he had given him this information, and a tin porringer containing his breakfast, the man locked him up again; and went clattering along the stone passage, opening and shutting a great many other doors, and raising numberless loud echoes which resounded through the building for a long time, as if they were in prison too, and unable to get out.

This turnkey had given him to understand that he was lodged, like some few others in the jail, apart from the mass of prisoners; because he was not supposed to be utterly depraved and irreclaimable, and had never occupied apartments in that mansion before. Kit was thankful for this indulgence, and sat reading the Church Catechism very attentively (though he had known it by heart from a little child), until he heard the key in the lock, and the man entered again.

"Now, then," he said, "come on!"

"Where to, sir?" asked Kit.

The man contented himself by briefly replying "Wisitors"; and taking him by the arm in exactly the same manner as the constable had done the day before, led him through several winding ways and strong gates into a passage, where he placed him at a grating, and turned upon his heel. Beyond this grating, at the distance of about four or five feet, was another exactly like it. In the space between, sat a turnkey reading a newspaper; and outside the further railing, Kit saw, with a palpitating heart, his mother with the baby in her arms; Barbara's mother with her never-failing umbrella; and poor little Jacob, staring in with all his might, as though he were looking for the bird, or the wild beast, and thought the men were mere accidents with whom the bars could have no possible concern.

But directly little Jacob saw his brother, and, thrusting his arms between the rails to hug him, found that he came no nearer, but still stood afar off with his head resting on the arm by which he held to one of the bars, he began to cry most piteously; whereupon, Kit's mother and Barbara's mother, who had restrained themselves as much as possible, burst out sobbing and weeping afresh. Poor Kit could not help joining them, and not one of them could speak a word.

During this melancholy pause, the turnkey read his newspaper with a waggish look (he had evidently got among the facetious paragraphs) until, happening to take his eyes off it for an instant, as if to get by dint of contemplation at the very marrow of some joke of a deeper sort than the rest, it appeared to occur to him for the first time that somebody was crying.

"Now, ladies, ladies," he said, looking round with surprise, "I'd advise you not to waste time like this. It's allowanced here, you know. You mustn't let that child make that noise either. It's against all rules."

"I'm his poor mother, sir," sobbed Mrs Nubbles, curtseying humbly, "and this is his brother, sir. Oh, dear me, dear me!"

"Well!" replied the turnkey, folding his paper on his knee, so as to get with greater convenience at the top of the next column. "It can't be helped, you know. He ain't the only one in the same fix. You mustn't make a noise about it!"

With that, he went on reading. The man was not unnaturally cruel or hard-hearted. He had come to look upon felony as a kind of disorder, like the scarlet fever or erysipelas: some people had it—some hadn't—just as it might be.

"Oh! my darling Kit"—said his mother, whom Barbara's mother had charitably relieved of the baby—"that I should see my poor boy here!"

"You don't believe that I did what they accuse me of, mother dear?" cried Kit, in a choking voice.

"*I* believe it!" exclaimed the poor woman, "*I* that never knew you to tell a lie, or do a bad action from your cradle—that have never had a moment's sorrow on your account, except it was for the poor meals that you have taken with such good-humour and content, that I forgot how little there was when I thought how kind and thoughtful you were, though you were but a child!—*I* believe it of the son that's been a comfort to me from the hour of his birth to this time, and that I never laid down one night in anger with! *I* believe it of you, Kit!——"

"Why, then, thank God!" said Kit, clutching the bars with an earnestness that shook them, "and I can bear it, mother. Come what may, I shall always have one drop of happiness in my heart when I think that you said that."

At this the poor woman fell a-crying again, and Barbara's mother too. And little Jacob, whose disjointed thoughts had by this time resolved themselves into a pretty distinct impression that Kit couldn't go out for a walk if he wanted, and that there were no birds, lions, tigers, or other natural curiosities behind those bars—nothing indeed, but a caged brother—added his tears to theirs with as little noise as possible.

Kit's mother, drying her eyes (and moistening them, poor soul, more than she dried them), now took from the ground a small basket, and submissively addressed herself to the turnkey, saying, would he please to listen to her for a minute? The turnkey, being in the very crisis and passion of a joke, motioned to her with his hand to keep silent one minute longer, for her life. Nor did he remove his hand into its former posture, but kept it in the same warning attitude until he had finished the paragraph, when he paused for a few seconds, with a smile upon his face, as who should say "This editor is a comical blade—a funny dog," and then asked her what she wanted.

"I have brought him a little something to eat," said the good woman. "If you please, sir, might he have it?"

"Yes—he may have it. There's no rule against that. Give it to me when you go, and I'll take care he has it."

"No, but if you please, sir—don't be angry with me, sir—I am his mother, and you had a mother once—if I might only see him eat a little bit, I should go away so much more satisfied that he was all comfortable."

And again the tears of Kit's mother burst forth, and of Barbara's mother, and of little Jacob. As to the baby, it was crowing and laughing with all its might—under the idea, apparently, that the whole scene had been invented and got up for its particular satisfaction.

The turnkey looked as if he thought the request a strange one and rather out of the common way, but nevertheless he laid down his paper, and coming round to where Kit's mother stood, took the basket from her, and after inspecting its contents, handed it to Kit, and went back to his place. It may be easily conceived that the prisoner had no great appetite, but he sat down upon the ground, and ate as hard as he could, while, at every morsel he put into his mouth, his mother sobbed and wept afresh, though with a softened grief that bespoke the satisfaction the sight afforded her.

While he was thus engaged, Kit made some anxious inquiries about his employers, whether they had expressed any opinion about him; but all he could learn was that Mr Abel had himself broken the intelligence to his mother with great kindness and delicacy late on the previous night, but had himself expressed no opinion of his innocence or guilt. Kit was on the point of mustering courage to ask Barbara's mother about Barbara, when the turnkey who had conducted him reappeared, a second turnkey appeared behind his visitors, and the third turnkey with the newspaper cried "Time's up!"—adding in the same breath "Now for the next party!" and then plunging deep into his newspaper again. Kit was taken off in an instant, with a blessing from his mother, and a scream from little Jacob, ringing in his ears. As he was crossing the next yard with the basket in his hand, under the guidance of his former conductor, another officer called to them to stop, and came up with a pint-pot of porter in his hand.

"This is Christopher Nubbles, isn't it, that come in last night for felony?" said the man.

His comrade replied that this was the chicken in question.

"Then here's your beer," said the other man to Christopher. "What are you looking at? There ain't a discharge in it."

"I beg your pardon," said Kit. "Who sent it me?"

"Why, your friend," replied the man. "You're to have it every day, he says. And so you will, if he pays for it."

"My friend!" repeated Kit.

"You're all abroad, seemingly," returned the other man. "There's his letter. Take hold!"

Kit took it, and when he was locked up again, read as follows:

> Drink of this cup. You'll find there's a spell in its every drop 'gainst the ills of mortality. Talk of the cordial that sparkled for Helen! *Her* cup was a fiction, but this is reality (Barclay and Co.'s). If they ever send it in a flat state, complain to the Governor.
>
> YOURS,
> R.S.

"R.S.!" said Kit, after some consideration. "It must be Mr Richard Swiveller. Well, it's very kind of him, and I thank him heartily."

Chapter LXII

A FAINT light, twinkling from the window of the counting-house on Quilp's wharf, and looking inflamed and red through the night-fog, as though it suffered from it like an eye, forewarned Mr Sampson Brass, as he approached the wooden cabin with a cautious step, that the excellent proprietor, his esteemed client, was inside, and probably waiting with his accustomed patience and sweetness of temper the fulfilment of the appointment which now brought Mr Brass within his fair domain.

"A treacherous place to pick one's steps in of a dark night," muttered Sampson, as he stumbled for the twentieth time over some stray lumber, and limped in pain. "I believe that boy strews the ground differently every day, on purpose to bruise and maim one; unless his master does it with his own hands, which is more than likely. I hate to come to this place without Sally. She's more protection than a dozen men."

As he paid this compliment to the merit of the absent charmer, Mr Brass came to a halt; looking doubtfully towards the light, and over his shoulder.

"What's he about, I wonder?" murmured the lawyer, standing on tiptoe and endeavouring to obtain a glimpse of what was passing inside, which at that distance was impossible—"drinking, I suppose—making himself more fiery and furious, and heating his malice and mischievousness till they boil. I'm always afraid to come here by myself, when his account's a pretty large one. I don't believe he'd mind throttling me, and dropping me softly into the river when the tide was at its strongest, any more than he'd mind killing a rat—indeed, I don't know whether he wouldn't consider it a pleasant joke. Hark! Now he's singing!"

Mr Quilp was certainly entertaining himself with vocal exercise, but it was rather a kind of chant than a song; being a monotonous repetition of one sentence in a very rapid manner, with a long stress upon the last word, which he swelled into a dismal roar. Nor did the burden of this performance bear any reference to love, or war, or wine, or loyalty, or any other, the standard topics of song, but to a subject not often set to music or generally known in ballads; the words being these: "The worthy magistrate, after remarking that the prisoner would find some difficulty in persuading a jury to believe his tale, committed him to take his trial at the approaching sessions; and directed the customary recognizances to be entered into for the pros-e-cu-tion."

Every time he came to this concluding word, and had exhausted all possible stress upon it, Quilp burst into a shriek of laughter, and began again.

"He's dreadfully imprudent," muttered Brass, after he had listened to two or three repetitions of the chant. "Horribly imprudent. I wish he was dumb. I wish he was deaf. I wish he was blind. Hang him," cried Brass, as the chant began again, "I wish he was dead!"

Giving utterance to these friendly aspirations in behalf of his client, Mr Sampson composed his face into its usual state of smoothness, and waiting until the shriek came again and was dying away, went up to the wooden house, and knocked at the door.

"Come in!" cried the dwarf.

"How do you do to-night, sir?" said Sampson, peeping in. "Ha, ha, ha! How do you do, sir? Oh, dear me, how very whimsical! Amazingly whimsical to be sure!"

"Come in, you fool!" returned the dwarf, "and don't stand there shaking your head and showing your teeth. Come in, you false witness, you perjurer, you suborner of evidence, come in!"

"He has the richest humour!" cried Brass, shutting the door behind him; "the most amazing vein of comicality! But isn't it *rather* injudicious, sir——?"

"What?" demanded Quilp. "What, Judas?"

"Judas!" cried Brass. "He has such extraordinary spirits! His humour is so extremely playful! Judas! Oh, yes—dear me, how very good! Ha, ha, ha!"

All this time, Sampson was rubbing his hands, and staring, with ludicrous surprise and dismay, at a great, goggle-eyed, blunt-nosed figurehead of some old ship, which was reared up against the wall in a corner near the stove, looking like a goblin or hideous idol whom the dwarf worshipped. A mass of timber on its head, carved into the dim and distant semblance of a cocked hat, together with a representation of a star on the left breast and epaulettes on the shoulders, denoted that it was intended for the effigy of some famous admiral; but, without those helps, any oberver might have supposed it the authentic portrait of a distinguished merman, or great sea-monster. Being originally much too large for the apartment which it was now employed to decorate, it had been sawn short off at the waist. Even in this state it reached from floor to ceiling; and thrusting itself forward with that excessively wide-awake aspect, and air of somewhat obtrusive politeness, by which figureheads are usually characterized, seemed to reduce everything else to mere pigmy proportions.

"Do you know it?" said the dwarf, watching Sampson's eyes. "Do you see the likeness?"

"Eh?" said Brass, holding his head on one side, and throwing it a little back, as connoisseurs do. "Now I look at it again, I fancy I see a——yes, there certainly is something in the smile that reminds me of——and yet upon my word I——"

Now, the fact was, that Sampson, having never seen anything in the smallest degree resembling this substantial phantom, was much perplexed; being uncertain whether Mr Quilp considered it like himself, and had therefore bought it for a family portrait; or whether he was pleased to consider it as the likeness of some enemy. He was not very long in doubt; for, while he was surveying it with that knowing look which people assume when they are contemplating for the first time portraits which they ought to recognise but don't, the dwarf threw down the newspaper from which he had been chanting the words already quoted, and seizing a rusty iron bar, which he used in lieu of poker, dealt the figure such a stroke on the nose that it rocked again.

"Is it like Kit——is it his picture, his image, his very self?" cried the dwarf, aiming a shower of blows at the insensible countenance, and covering it with deep dimples. "Is it the exact model and counterpart of the dog——is it——is it——is it?" And with every repetition of the question, he battered the great image until the perspiration streamed down his face with the violence of the exercise.

Although this might have been a very comical thing to look at from a secure gallery, as a bull-fight is found to be a comfortable spectacle by those who are not in the arena, and a house on fire is better than a play to people who don't live near it, there was something in the earnestness of Mr Quilp's manner which made his legal adviser feel that the counting-house was a little too small, and a great deal too lonely, for the due enjoyment of these humours. Therefore he stood as far off as he could while the dwarf was thus engaged; whimpering out but feeble applause; and when he left off and sat down again from pure exhaustion, approached with more obsequiousness than ever.

"Excellent indeed!" cried Brass. "He, he! Oh, very good, sir. You know," said Sampson, looking round as if in appeal to the bruised admiral, "he's quite a remarkable man——quite!"

"Sit down," said the dwarf. "I bought the dog yesterday. I've been screwing gimlets into him, and sticking forks in his eyes, and cutting my name on him. I mean to burn him at last."

"Ha, ha!" cried Brass. "Extremely entertaining, indeed!"

"Come here!" said Quilp, beckoning him to draw near. "What's injudicious, hey?"

"Nothing, sir——nothing. Scarcely worth mentioning, sir; but I thought that song—— admirably humorous in itself, you know——was perhaps rather——"

"Yes," said Quilp, "rather what?"

"Just bordering, or as one may say remotely verging upon the confines of injudiciousness perhaps, sir," returned Brass, looking timidly at the dwarf's cunning eyes, which were turned towards the fire and reflected its red light.

"Why?" inquired Quilp, without looking up.

"Why, you know, sir," returned Brass, venturing to be more familiar: "——the fact is,

sir, that any allusion to these little combinings together of friends for objects in themselves extremely laudable, but which the law terms conspiracies, are—you take me,
sir?—best kept snug and among friends, you know."

"Eh!" said Quilp, looking up with a perfectly vacant countenance. "What do you
mean?"

"Cautious, exceedingly cautious, very right and proper!" cried Brass, nodding his
head. "Mum, sir, even here—my meaning, sir, exactly."

"*Your* meaning exactly, you brazen scarecrow—what's your meaning?" retorted
Quilp. "Why do you talk to me of combining together? Do *I* combine? Do I know
anything about your combinings?"

"No, no, sir—certainly not; not by any means," returned Brass.

"If you so wink and nod at me," said the dwarf, looking about him as if for his poker,
"I'll spoil the expression of your monkey's face, I will."

"Don't put yourself out of the way I beg, sir," rejoined Brass, checking himself with
great alacrity. "You're quite right, sir, quite right. I shouldn't have mentioned the subject,
sir. It's much better not to. You're quite right, sir. Let us change it, if you please. You were
asking, sir, Sally told me, about our lodger. He has not returned, sir."

"No?" said Quilp, heating some rum in a little saucepan, and watching it to prevent
its boiling over. "Why not?"

"Why, sir," returned Brass, "he—dear me, Mr Quilp, sir———"

"What's the matter?" said the dwarf, stopping his hand in the act of carrying the
saucepan to his mouth.

"You have forgotten the water, sir," said Brass. "And—excuse me, sir—but it's
burning hot."

Deigning no other than a practical answer to this remonstrance, Mr Quilp raised the
hot saucepan to his lips, and deliberately drank off all the spirit it contained, which might
have been in quantity about half a pint, and had been but a moment before, when he
took it off the fire, bubbling and hissing fiercely. Having swallowed this gentle stimulant,
and shaken his fist at the admiral, he bade Mr Brass proceed.

"But first," said Quilp, with his accustomed grin, "have a drop yourself—a nice
drop—a good, warm, fiery drop."

"Why, sir," replied Brass, "if there was such a thing as a mouthful of water that could
be got without trouble———"

"There's no such thing to be had here," cried the dwarf. "Water for lawyers! Melted
lead and brimstone, you mean, nice hot blistering pitch and tar—that's the thing for
them—eh, Brass, eh?"

"Ha, ha, ha!" laughed Mr Brass. "Oh, very biting! and yet it's like being tickled—
there's a pleasure in it too, sir!"

"Drink that," said the dwarf, who had by this time heated some more. "Toss it off,
don't leave any heeltap, scorch your throat and be happy."

The wretched Sampson took a few short sips of the liquor, which immediately
distilled itself into burning tears, and in that form came rolling down his cheeks into the
pipkin again, turning the colour of his face and eyelids to a deep red, and giving rise to
a violent fit of coughing, in the midst of which he was still heard to declare, with the
constancy of a martyr, that it was "beautiful indeed!" While he was yet in unspeakable
agonies, the dwarf renewed their conversation.

"The lodger," said Quilp—"what about him?"

"He is still, sir," returned Brass, with intervals of coughing, "stopping with the
Garland family. He has only been home once, sir, since the day of the examination of

that culprit. He informed Mr Richard, sir, that he couldn't bear the house after what had taken place; that he was wretched in it; and that he looked upon himself as being in a certain kind of way the cause of the occurrence.—A very excellent lodger, sir. I hope we may not lose him."

"Yah!" cried the dwarf. "Never thinking of anybody but yourself—why don't you retrench then—scrape up, hoard, economize, eh?"

"Why, sir," replied Brass, "upon my word I think Sarah's as good an economizer as any going. I do indeed, Mr Quilp."

"Moisten your clay, wet the other eye, drink, man!" cried the dwarf. "You took a clerk to oblige me."

"Delighted, sir, I am sure, at any time," replied Sampson. "Yes, sir, I did."

"Then, now you may discharge him," said Quilp. "There's a means of retrenchment for you at once."

"Discharge Mr Richard, sir?" cried Brass.

"Have you more than one clerk, you parrot, that you ask the question? Yes."

"Upon my word, sir," said Brass, "I wasn't prepared for this——"

"How could you be?" sneered the dwarf, "when *I* wasn't. How often am I to tell you that I brought him to you that I might always have my eye on him and know where he was—and that I had a plot, a scheme, a little quiet piece of enjoyment afoot, of which the very cream and essence was, that this old man and grandchild (who have sunk underground I think) should be, while he and his precious friend believed them rich, in reality as poor as frozen rats?"

"I quite understood that, sir," rejoined Brass. "Thoroughly."

"Well, sir," retorted Quilp, "and do you understand now, that they're *not* poor— that they can't be, if they have such men as your lodger searching for them and scouring the country far and wide?"

"Of course I do, sir," said Sampson.

"Of course you do," retorted the dwarf, viciously snapping at his words. "Of course do you understand then, that it's no matter what comes of this fellow? Of course do you understand that for any other purpose he's no man for me, nor for you?"

"I have frequently said to Sarah, sir," returned Brass, "that he was of no use at all in the business. You can't put any confidence in him, sir. If you'll believe me I've found that fellow, in the commonest little matters of the office that have been trusted to him, blurting out the truth, though expressly cautioned. The aggravation of that chap, sir, has exceeded anything you can imagine, it has indeed. Nothing but the respect and obligation I owe to you, sir——"

As it was plain that Sampson was bent on a complimentary harangue, unless he received a timely interruption, Mr Quilp politely tapped him on the crown of his head with the little saucepan, and requested that he would be so obliging as to hold his peace.

"Practical, sir, practical," said Brass, rubbing the place and smiling; "but still extremely pleasant—immensely so!"

"Hearken to me, will you?" returned Quilp, "or I'll be a little more pleasant, presently. There's no chance of his comrade and friend returning. The scamp has been obliged to fly, as I learn, for some knavery, and has found his way abroad. Let him rot there."

"Certainly, sir. Quite proper.—Forcible!" cried Brass, glancing at the admiral again, as if he made a third in company. "Extremely forcible!"

"I hate him," said Quilp between his teeth, "and have always hated him, for family reasons. Besides, he was an intractable ruffian; otherwise *he* would have been of use.

This fellow is pigeon-hearted, and light-headed. I don't want him any longer. Let him hang or drown—starve—go to the devil."

"By all means, sir," returned Brass. "When would you wish him, sir, to—ha, ha!—to make that little excursion?"

"When this trial's over," said Quilp. "As soon as that's ended, send him about his business."

"It shall be done, sir," returned Brass; "by all means. It will be rather a blow to Sarah, sir, but she has all her feelings under control. Ah, Mr Quilp, I often think, sir, if it had only pleased Providence to bring you and Sarah together in earlier life, what blessed results would have flowed from such a union! You never saw our dear father, sir?—A charming gentleman. Sarah was his pride and joy, sir. He would have closed his eyes in bliss, would Foxey, Mr Quilp, if he could have found her such a partner. You esteem her, sir?"

"I love her," croaked the dwarf.

"You're very good, sir," returned Brass, "I am sure. Is there any other order, sir, that I can take a note of, besides this little matter of Mr Richard?"

"None," replied the dwarf, seizing the saucepan. "Let us drink the lovely Sarah."

"If we could do it in something, sir, that wasn't quite boiling," suggested Brass humbly, "perhaps it would be better. I think it will be more agreeable to her feelings, when she comes to hear from me of the honour you have done her, if she learns it was in liquor rather cooler than the last, sir."

But to these remonstrances Mr Quilp turned a deaf ear. Sampson Brass, who was by this time anything but sober, being compelled to take further draughts of the same strong bowl, found that, instead of at all contributing to his recovery, they had the novel effect of making the counting-house spin round and round with extreme velocity, and causing the floor and ceiling to heave in a very distressing manner. After a brief stupour, he awoke to a consciousness of being partly under the table and partly under the grate. This position not being the most comfortable one he could have chosen for himself, he managed to stagger to his feet, and, holding on by the admiral, looked round for his host.

Mr Brass's first impression was that his host was gone and had left him there alone—perhaps locked him in for the night. A strong smell of tobacco, however, suggested a new train of ideas, he looked upwards, and saw that the dwarf was smoking in his hammock.

"Good-bye, sir," cried Brass faintly. "Good-bye, sir."

"Won't you stop all night?" said the dwarf, peeping out. "Do stop all night."

"I couldn't indeed, sir," replied Brass, who was almost dead from nausea and the closeness of the room. "If you'd have the goodness to show me a light, so that I may see my way across the yard, sir——"

Quilp was out in an instant; not with his legs first, or his head first, or his arms first, but bodily—altogether.

"To be sure," he said, taking up a lantern, which was now the only light in the place. "Be careful how you go, my dear friend. Be sure to pick your way among the timber, for all the rusty nails are upwards. There's a dog in the lane. He bit a man last night, and a woman the night before, and last Tuesday he killed a child—but that was in play. Don't go too near him."

"Which side of the road is he, sir?" asked Brass, in great dismay.

"He lives on the right hand," said Quilp, "but sometimes he hides on the left, ready for a spring. He's uncertain in that respect. Mind you take care of yourself. I'll never forgive you if you don't. There's the light out—never mind—you know the way—straight on!"

Quilp had slily shaded the light by holding it against his breast, and now stood chuckling and shaking from head to foot in a rapture of delight, as he heard the lawyer stumbling up the yard, and now and then falling heavily down. At length, however, he got quit of the place, and was out of hearing.

The dwarf shut himself up again, and sprang once more into his hammock.

Chapter LXIII

THE professional gentleman who had given Kit that consolatory piece of information relative to the settlement of his trifle of business at the Old Bailey, and the probability of its being very soon disposed of, turned out to be quite correct in his prognostications. In eight days' time, the sessions commenced. In one day afterwards, the Grand Jury found a True Bill against Christopher Nubbles for felony; and in two days from that finding, the aforesaid Christopher Nubbles was called upon to plead Guilty or Not Guilty to an Indictment for that he the said Christopher did feloniously abstract and steal from the dwelling-house and office of one Sampson Brass, gentleman, one Bank Note for Five Pounds issued by the Governor and Company of the Bank of England; in contravention of the Statutes in that case made and provided, and against the peace of our Sovereign Lord the King, his crown, and dignity.

To this indictment, Christopher Nubbles, in a low and trembling voice, pleaded Not Guilty: and here let those who are in the habit of forming hasty judgments from appearances, and who would have had Christopher, if innocent, speak out very strong and loud, observe, that confinement and anxiety will subdue the stoutest hearts; and that to one who has been close shut up, though it be only for ten or eleven days, seeing but stone walls and a very few stony faces, the sudden entrance into a great hall filled with life is a rather disconcerting and startling circumstance. To this it must be added that life in a wig is to a large class of people much more terrifying and impressive than life with its own head of hair; and if, in addition to these considerations, there be further taken into account Kit's natural emotion on seeing the two Mr Garlands and the little notary looking on with pale and anxious faces, it will perhaps seem matter of no very great wonder that he should have been rather out of sorts, and unable to make himself exactly at home.

Although he had never seen either of the Mr Garlands, or Mr Witherden, since the time of his arrest, he had been given to understand that they had employed counsel for him. Therefore, when one of the gentlemen in wigs got up and said "I am for the prisoner, my Lord," Kit made him a bow; and when another gentleman in a wig got up and said "And I'm against him, my Lord," Kit trembled very much, and bowed to him too. And didn't he hope in his own heart that his gentleman was a match for the other gentleman, and would make him ashamed of himself in no time!

The gentleman who was against him had to speak first, and being in dreadfully good spirits (for he had, in the last trial, very nearly procured the acquittal of a young gentleman who had had the misfortune to murder his father) he spoke up you may be sure; telling the Jury that if they acquitted this prisoner they must expect to suffer no less pangs and agonies than he had told the other Jury they would certainly undergo if they convicted that prisoner. And when he had told them all about the case, and that he had never known a worse case, he stopped a little while, like a man who had something terrible to tell them, and then said that he understood an attempt would be made by his learned friend (and here he looked sideways at Kit's gentleman) to impeach the testimony of those immaculate witnesses whom he should call before them; but he did hope and trust that his learned friend would have a greater respect and veneration for the character of the prosecutor; than whom, as he well knew, there did not exist, and never had existed, a more honourable member of that most honourable profession to which he was attached. And then he said, did the Jury know Bevis Marks? And if they did know Bevis Marks (as he trusted, for their own characters, they did) did they know the historical and elevating associations connected with that most remarkable spot? Did they believe that a man like Brass could reside in a place like Bevis Marks, and not be a virtuous and most upright character? And when he had said a great deal to them on this point, he remembered that it was an insult to their understandings to make any remarks on what they must have felt so strongly without him, and therefore called Sampson Brass into the witness-box, straightway.

Then up comes Mr Brass, very brisk and fresh; and, having bowed to the judge, like a man who has had the pleasure of seeing him before and who hopes he has been pretty well since their last meeting, folds his arms, and looks at his gentleman as much as to say "Here I am—full of evidence—Tap me!" And the gentleman does tap him presently, and with great discretion too; drawing off the evidence by little and little, and making it run quite clear and bright in the eyes of all present. Then Kit's gentleman takes him in hand, but can make nothing of him; and after a great many very long questions and very short answers, Mr Sampson Brass goes down in glory.

To him succeeds Sarah, who in like manner is easy to be managed by Mr Brass's gentleman, but very obdurate to Kit's. In short, Kit's gentleman can get nothing out of her but a repetition of what she has said before (only a little stronger this time, as against his client), and therefore lets her go, in some confusion. Then Mr Brass's gentleman calls Richard Swiveller, and Richard Swiveller appears accordingly.

Now, Mr Brass's gentleman has it whispered in his ear that this witness is disposed to be friendly to the prisoner—which, to say the truth, he is rather glad to hear, as his strength is considered to lie in what is familiarly termed badgering. Wherefore, he begins by requesting the officer to be quite sure that this witness kisses the book, and then goes to work at him, tooth and nail.

"Mr Swiveller," says this gentleman to Dick, when he has told his tale with evident reluctance and a desire to make the best of it: "Pray, sir, where did you dine yesterday?"—"Where did I dine yesterday?"—"Ay, sir, where did you dine yesterday—was it near here, sir?"—"Oh, to be sure—yes—just over the way."—"To be sure. Yes. Just over the way," repeats Mr Brass's gentleman. with a glance at the Court—"Alone, sir?"—"I beg your pardon," says Mr Swiveller, who has not caught the question—"*Alone,* sir?" repeats Mr Brass's gentleman in a voice of thunder, "did you dine alone? Did you treat anybody, sir? Come!"—"Oh, yes, to be sure—yes, I did," says Mr Swiveller with a smile. "Have the goodness to banish a levity, sir, which is very ill-suited to the place in which you stand (though perhaps you have reason to be thankful that it's only that place)," says

Mr Brass's gentleman, with a nod of the head insinuating that the dock is Mr Swiveller's legitimate sphere of action; "and attend to me. You were waiting about here yesterday in expectation that this trial was coming on. You dined over the way. You treated somebody. Now, was that somebody brother to the prisoner at the bar?"—Mr Swiveller is proceeding to explain—"Yes or No, sir," cries Mr Brass's gentleman—"But will you allow me——" — "Yes or No, sir"—"Yes it was, but——" — "Yes it was," cries the gentleman, taking him up short—"And a very pretty witness *you* are!"

Down sits Mr Brass's gentleman. Kit's gentleman, not knowing how the matter really stands, is afraid to pursue the subject. Richard Swiveller retires abashed. Judge, jury and spectators have visions of his lounging about with an ill-looking, large-whiskered, dissolute young fellow of six feet high. The reality is, little Jacob, with the calves of his legs exposed to the open air, and himself tied up in a shawl. Nobody knows the truth, everybody believes a falsehood—and all because of the ingenuity of Mr Brass's gentleman!

Then come the witnesses to character, and here Mr Brass's gentleman shines again. It turns out that Mr Garland has had no character with Kit, no recommendation of him but from his own mother, and that he was suddenly dismissed by his former master for unknown reasons. "Really, Mr Garland," says Mr Brass's gentleman, "for a person who has arrived at your time of life, you are, to say the least of it, singularly indiscreet, I think." The Jury think so too, and find Kit guilty. He is taken off, humbly protesting his innocence. The spectators settle themselves in their places with renewed attention, for there are several female witnesses to be examined in the next case, and it has been rumoured that Mr Brass's gentleman will make great fun in cross-examining them for the prisoner.

Kit's mother, poor woman, is waiting at the grate below-stairs, accompanied by Barbara's mother (who, honest soul! never does anything but cry, and hold the baby), and a sad interview ensues. The newspaper-reading turnkey has told them all. He don't think it will be transportation for life, because there's time to prove the good character yet, and that is sure to serve him. He wonders what he did it for. "He never did it!" cries Kit's mother. "Well," says the turnkey, "I won't contradict you. It's all one now, whether he did or not."

Kit's mother can reach his hand through the bars, and clasps it—God, and those to whom he has given such tenderness, only know in how much agony. Kit bids her keep a good heart, and, under pretence of having the children lifted up to kiss him, prays Barbara's mother in a whisper to take her home.

"Some friend will rise up for us, mother," cries Kit, "I am sure. If not now, before long. My innocence will come out, mother, and I shall be brought back again; I feel confidence in that. You must teach little Jacob and the baby how all this was, for if they thought I had ever been dishonest, when they grow old enough to understand, it would break my heart to know it, if I was thousands of miles away.—Oh! is there no good gentleman here, who will take care of her!"

The hand slips out of his, for the poor creature sinks down upon the earth, insensible. Richard Swiveller comes hastily up, elbows the bystanders out of the way, takes her (after some trouble) in one arm after the manner of theatrical ravishers, and nodding to Kit, and commanding Barbara's mother to follow, for he has a coach waiting, bears her swiftly off.

Well; Richard took her home. And what astonishing absurdities in the way of quotation from song and poem he perpetrated on the road, no man knows. He took her home, and stayed till she was recovered; and, having no money to pay the coach, went back in state to Bevis Marks, bidding the driver (for it was Saturday night) wait at the door while he went in for "change."

"Mr Richard, sir," said Brass cheerfully, "good evening."

Monstrous as Kit's tale had appeared at first, Mr Richard did, that night, half suspect his affable employer of some deep villany. Perhaps it was but the misery he had just witnessed which gave his careless nature this impulse; but, be that as it may, it was very strong upon him, and he said in as few words as possible, what he wanted.

"Money!" cried Brass, taking out his purse. "Ha, ha! To be sure, Mr Richard, to be sure, sir. All men must live. You haven't change for a five-pound note, have you, sir?"

"No," returned Dick, shortly.

"Oh!" said Brass, "here's the very sum. That saves trouble. You're very welcome I'm sure.—Mr Richard, sir——"

Dick, who had by this time reached the door, turned round.

"You needn't," said Brass, "trouble yourself to come back any more, sir."

"Eh?"

"You see, Mr Richard," said Brass, thrusting his hands in his pockets and rocking himself to and fro upon his stool, "the fact is, that a man of your abilities is lost, sir, quite lost in our dry and mouldy line. It's terrible drudgery—shocking. I should say now that the stage, or the—or the army, Mr Richard—or something very superior in the licensed victualling way—was the kind of thing that would call out the genius of such a man as you. I hope you'll look in to see us now and then. Sally, sir, will be delighted I'm sure. She's extremely sorry to lose you, Mr Richard, but a sense of her duty to society reconciles her.—An amazing creature that, sir! You'll find the money quite correct, I think. There's a cracked window, sir, but I've not made any deduction on that account. Whenever we part with friends, Mr Richard, let us part liberally. A delightful sentiment, sir!"

To all these rambling observations, Mr Swiveller answered not one word, but, returning for the aquatic jacket, rolled it into a tight round ball, looking steadily at Brass meanwhile as if he had some intention of bowling him down with it. He only took it under his arm, however, and marched out of the office in profound silence. Directly he had closed the door, he opened it, stared in again for a few moments with the same portentous gravity; and nodding his head once, in a slow and ghost-like manner, vanished.

He paid the coachman and turned his back on Bevis Marks, big with great designs for the comforting of Kit's mother and the aid of Kit himself.

But the lives of gentlemen devoted to such pleasures as Richard Swiveller, are extremely precarious. The spiritual excitement of the last fortnight, working upon a system affected in no slight degree by the spirituous excitement of some years, proved a little too much for him. That very night, Mr Richard was seized with an alarming illness, and in twenty-four hours was stricken with a raging fever.

Chapter LXIV

TOSSING to and fro upon his hot, uneasy bed; tormented by a fierce thirst which nothing could appease; unable to find, in any change of posture, a moment's peace or ease; and rambling ever through deserts of thought where there was no resting-place, no sight or sound suggestive of refreshment or repose, nothing but a dull eternal weariness, with no change but the restless shiftings of his miserable body, and the weary wanderings of his mind, constant still to one ever-present anxiety—to a sense of something left undone, of some fearful obstacle to be surmounted, of some carking care that would not be driven away, and haunted the distempered brain, now in this form, now in that—always shadowy and dim, but recognisable for the same phantom in every shape it took, darkening every vision like an evil conscience, and making slumber horrible; in these slow tortures of his dread disease, the unfortunate Richard lay wasting and consuming inch by inch, until at last, when he seemed to fight and struggle to rise up, and to be held down by devils, he sank into a deep sleep, and dreamed no more.

He awoke; and, with a sensation of most blissful rest, better than sleep itself, began gradually to remember something of these sufferings, and to think what a long night it had been, and whether he had not been delirious twice or thrice. Happening in the midst of these cogitations to raise his hand, he was astonished to find how heavy it seemed, and yet how thin and light it really was. Still, he felt indifferent and happy; and having no curiosity to pursue the subject, remained in the same waking slumber until his attention was attracted by a cough. This made him doubt whether he had locked his door last night, and feel a little surprised at having a companion in the room. Still, he lacked energy to follow up this train of thought; and unconsciously fell, in a luxury of repose, to staring at some green stripes upon the bed-furniture, and associating them strangely with patches of fresh turf, while the yellow ground between made gravel-walks, and so helped out a long perspective of trim gardens.

He was rambling in imagination upon these terraces, and had quite lost himself among them indeed, when he heard the cough once more. The walks shrank into stripes again at the sound; and raising himself a little in the bed, and holding the curtain open with one hand, he looked out.

The same room certainly, and still by candlelight; but with what unbounded astonishment did he see all those bottles, and basins, and articles of linen airing by the fire, and such-like furniture of a sick-chamber—all very clean and neat, but all quite different from anything he had left there, when he went to bed! The atmosphere, too, filled with a cool smell of herbs and vinegar; the floor newly sprinkled; the—the what? The Marchioness? Yes; playing cribbage with herself at the table. There she sat, intent upon her game, coughing now and then in a subdued manner as if she feared to disturb him—shuffling the cards, cutting, dealing, playing, counting, pegging—going through all the mysteries of cribbage as though she had been in full practice from her cradle!

Mr Swiveller contemplated these things for a short time, and suffering the curtain to fall into its former position, laid his head upon the pillow again.

"I'm dreaming," thought Richard, "that's clear. When I went to bed, my hands were not made of egg-shells; and now I can almost see through 'em. If this is not a dream, I have woke up by mistake in an Arabian Night, instead of a London one. But I have no doubt I'm asleep. Not the least."

Here the small servant had another cough.

"Very remarkable!" thought Mr Swiveller. "I never dreamt such a real cough as that before. I don't know, indeed, that I ever dreamt either a cough or a sneeze. Perhaps it's part of the philosophy of dreams that one never does. There's another—and another—I say—I'm dreaming rather fast!"

For the purpose of testing his real condition, Mr Swiveller, after some reflection, pinched himself in the arm.

"Queerer still!" he thought. "I came to bed rather plump than otherwise, and now there's nothing to lay hold of. I'll take another survey."

The result of this further inspection was to convince Mr Swiveller that the objects by which he was surrounded were real, and that he saw them, beyond all question, with his waking eyes.

"It's an Arabian Night, that's what it is," said Richard. "I'm in Damascus or Grand Cairo. The Marchioness is a Genie, and having had a wager with another Genie about who is the handsomest young man alive, and the worthiest to be the husband of the Princess of China, has brought me away, room and all, to compare us together. Perhaps," said Mr Swiveller, turning languidly round upon his pillow, and looking on that side of his bed which was next the wall, "the Princess may be still—— No, she's gone."

Not feeling quite satisfied with this explanation, as, even taking it to be the correct one, it still involved a little mystery and doubt, Mr Swiveller raised the curtain again, determined to take the first favourable opportunity of addressing his companion. An occasion soon presented itself. The Marchioness dealt, turned up a knave, and omitted to take the usual advantage; upon which Mr Swiveller called out as loud as he could— "Two for his heels!"

The Marchioness jumped up quickly, and clapped her hands. "Arabian Night, certainly," thought Mr Swiveller; "they always clap their hands instead of ringing the bell. Now for the two thousand black slaves, with jars of jewels on their heads!"

It appeared, however, that she had only clapped her hands in joy; for directly afterwards she began to laugh, and then to cry; declaring, not in choice Arabic but in familiar English, that she was "so glad, she didn't know what to do."

"Marchioness," said Mr Swiveller thoughtfully, "be pleased to draw nearer. First of all, will you have the goodness to inform me where I shall find my voice; and secondly, what has become of my flesh?"

The Marchioness only shook her head mournfully, and cried again; whereupon Mr Swiveller (being very weak) felt his own eyes affected likewise.

"I begin to infer, from your manner and these appearances, Marchioness"—said Richard after a pause, and smiling with a trembling lip, "that I have been ill."

"You just have!" replied the small servant, wiping her eyes. "And haven't you been a-talking nonsense!"

"Oh!" said Dick. "Very ill, Marchioness, have I been?"

"Dead, all but," replied the small servant. "I never thought you'd get better. Thank Heaven you have!"

Mr Swiveller was silent for a long while. By and bye, he began to talk again— inquiring how long he had been there.

"Three weeks to-morrow," replied the small servant.

"Three what?" said Dick.

"Weeks," returned the Marchioness emphatically; "three long, slow weeks."

The bare thought of having been in such extremity caused Richard to fall into another silence, and to lie flat down again at his full length. The Marchioness, having arranged the bedclothes more comfortably, and felt that his hands and forehead were quite cool—a discovery that filled her with delight—cried a little more, and then applied herself to getting tea ready, and making some thin dry toast.

While she was thus engaged, Mr Swiveller looked on with a grateful heart, very much astonished to see how thoroughly at home she made herself, and attributing this attention, in its origin, to Sally Brass, whom, in his own mind, he could not thank enough. When the Marchioness had finished her toasting, she spread a clean cloth on a tray, and brought him some crisp slices and a great basin of weak tea, with which (she said) the doctor had left word he might refresh himself when he awoke. She propped him up with pillows, if not as skilfully as if she had been a professional nurse all her life, at least as tenderly; and looked on with unutterable satisfaction while the patient— stopping every now and then to shake her by the hand—took his poor meal with an appetite and relish which the greatest dainties of the earth, under any other circumstances, would have failed to provoke. Having cleared away, and disposed everything comfortably about him again, she sat down at the table to take her own tea.

"Marchioness," said Mr Swiveller, "how's Sally?"

The small servant screwed her face into an expression of the very uttermost entanglement of slyness, and shook her head.

"What, haven't you seen her lately?" said Dick.

"Seen her!" cried the small servant. "Bless you, I've run away!"

Mr Swiveller immediately laid himself down again quite flat, and so remained for about five minutes. By slow degrees he resumed his sitting posture after that lapse of time, and inquired:

"And where do you live, Marchioness?"

"Live!" cried the small servant. "Here!"

"Oh!" said Mr Swiveller.

And with that he fell down flat again, as suddenly as if he had been shot. Thus he remained, motionless and bereft of speech, until she had finished her meal, put everything in its place, and swept the hearth; when he motioned her to bring a chair to the bedside, and, being propped up again, opened a farther conversation.

"And so," said Dick, "you have run away?"

"Yes," said the Marchioness, "and they've been a-tizing of me."

"Been—I beg your pardon," said Dick—"what have they been doing?"

"Been a-tizing of me—tizing, you know—in the newspapers," rejoined the Marchioness.

"Ay, ay," said Dick, "advertising?"

The small servant nodded, and winked. Her eyes were so red with waking and crying, that the Tragic Muse might have winked with greater consistency. And so Dick felt.

"Tell me," said he, "how it was that you thought of coming here."

"Why, you see," returned the Marchioness, "when you was gone, I hadn't any friend at all, because the lodger he never come back, and I didn't know where either him or you was to be found, you know, but one morning, when I was——"

"Was near a keyhole?" suggested Mr Swiveller, observing that she faltered.

"Well, then," said the small servant, nodding; "when I was near the office keyhole— as you see me through, you know—I heard somebody saying that she lived here, and was the lady whose house you lodged at, and that you was took very bad, and wouldn't nobody come and take care of you. Mr Brass, he says, 'It's no business of mine'; and Miss Sally, she says, 'He's a funny chap, but it's no business of mine'; and the lady went away, and slammed the door to, when she went out, I can tell you. So I run away that night, and come here, and told 'em you was my brother, and they believed me, and I've been here ever since."

"This poor little Marchioness has been wearing herself to death!" cried Dick.

"No I haven't," she returned, "not a bit of it. Don't you mind about me. I like sitting up, and I've often had a sleep, bless you, in one of them chairs. But if you could have seen how you tried to jump out o' winder, and if you could have heard how you used to keep on singing and making speeches, you wouldn't have believed it—I'm so glad you're better, Mr Liverer."

"Liverer indeed!" said Dick thoughtfully. "It's well I *am* a liverer. I strongly suspect I should have died, Marchioness, but for you."

At this point, Mr Swiveller took the small servant's hand in his again, and being, as we have seen, but poorly, might in struggling to express his thanks have made his eyes as red as hers, but that she quickly changed the theme by making him lie down, and urging him to keep very quiet.

"The doctor," she told him, "said you was to be kept quite still, and there was to be no noise nor nothing. Now, take a rest, and then we'll talk again. I'll sit by you, you know. If you shut your eyes, perhaps you'll go to sleep. You'll be all the better for it, if you do."

The Marchioness, in saying these words, brought a little table to the bedside, took her seat at it, and began to work away at the concoction of some cooling drink, with the address of a score of chemists. Richard Swiveller, being indeed fatigued, fell into a slumber, and waking in about half an hour, inquired what time it was.

"Just gone half after six," replied his small friend, helping him to sit up again.

"Marchioness," said Richard, passing his hand over his forehead and turning suddenly round, as though the subject but that moment flashed upon him, "what has become of Kit?"

He had been sentenced to transportation for a great many years, she said.

"Has he gone?" asked Dick—"his mother—how is she—what has become of her?"

His nurse shook her head, and answered that she knew nothing about them.

"But, if I thought," said she very slowly, "that you'd keep quiet, and not put yourself into another fever, I could tell you—but I won't now."

"Yes, do," said Dick. "It will amuse me."

"Oh! would it though!" rejoined the small servant, with a horrified look. "I know better than that. Wait till you're better, and then I'll tell you."

Dick looked very earnestly at his little friend: and his eyes, being large and hollow from illness assisted the expression so much, that she was quite frightened, and besought him not to think any more about it. What had already fallen from her, however, had not only piqued his curiosity, but seriously alarmed him, wherefore he urged her to tell him the worst at once.

"Oh! there's no worst in it," said the small servant. "It hasn't anything to do with you."

"Has it anything to do with—is it anything you heard through chinks or keyholes—and that you were not intended to hear?" asked Dick, in a breathless state.

"Yes," replied the small servant.

"In—in Bevis Marks?" pursued Dick hastily. "Conversations between Brass and Sally?"

"Yes," cried the small servant again.

Richard Swiveller thrust his lank arm out of bed, and, gripping her by the wrist and drawing her close to him, bade her out with it, and freely too, or he would not answer for the consequences; being wholly unable to endure that state of excitement and expectation. She, seeing that he was greatly agitated, and that the effects of postponing her revelation might be much more injurious than any that were likely to ensue from its being made at once, promised compliance, on condition that the patient kept himself perfectly quiet, and abstained from starting up or tossing about.

"But if you begin to do that," said the small servant, "I'll leave off. And so I tell you."

"You can't leave off till you have gone on," said Dick. "And do go on, there's a darling. Speak, sister, speak. Pretty Polly say—— Oh, tell me when, and tell me where, pray Marchioness, I beseech you!"

Unable to resist these fervent adjurations, which Richard Swiveller poured out as passionately as if they had been of the most solemn and tremendous nature, his companion spoke thus:

"Well! Before I run away, I used to sleep in the kitchen—where we played cards, you know. Miss Sally used to keep the key of the kitchen door in her pocket, and she always come down at night to take away the candle and rake out the fire. When she had done that, she left me to go to bed in the dark, locked the door on the outside, put the key in her pocket again, and kept me locked up till she come down in the morning— very early I can tell you—and let me out. I was terrible afraid of being kept like this, because if there was a fire, I thought they might forget me and only take care of themselves you know. So whenever I see an old rusty key anywhere, I picked it up and tried if it would fit the door, and at last I found in the dust cellar a key that *did* fit it."

Here, Mr Swiveller made a violent demonstration with his legs. But the small servant immediately pausing in her talk, he subsided again, and, pleading a momentary forget-fulness of their compact, entreated her to proceed.

"They kept me very short," said the small servant. "Oh! you can't think how short they kept me! So I used to come out at night after they'd gone to bed, and feel about in the dark for bits of biscuit, or sangwitches that you'd left in the office, or even pieces of orange peel to put into cold water and make believe it was wine. Did you ever taste orange peel and water?"

Mr Swiveller replied that he had never tasted that ardent liquor; and once more urged his friend to resume the thread of her narrative.

"If you make believe very much, it's quite nice," said the small servant; "but if you don't, you know, it seems as if it would bear a little more seasoning, certainly. Well, sometimes I used to come out after they'd gone to bed, and sometimes before, you know; and one or two nights before there was all that precious noise in the office— when the young man was took, I mean—I come upstairs while Mr Brass and Miss Sally was a-sittin' at the office fire; and I'll tell you the truth, that I come to listen again about the key of the safe."

Mr Swiveller gathered up his knees so as to make a great cone of the bedclothes, and conveyed into his countenance an expression of the utmost concern. But the small servant pausing, and holding up her finger, the cone gently disappeared, though the look of concern did not.

"There was him and her," said the small servant, "a-sittin' by the fire, and talking softly together. Mr Brass says to Miss Sally, 'Upon my word,' he says, 'it's a dangerous thing, and it might get us into a world of trouble, and I don't half like it.' She says—you know her way—she says, 'You're the chickenest-hearted, feeblest, faintest man I ever see, and I think,' she says, 'that I ought to have been the brother, and you the sister. Isn't Quilp,' she says, 'our principal support?' 'He certainly is,' says Mr Brass. 'And an't we,' she says, 'constantly ruining somebody or other in the way of business?' 'We certainly are,' says Mr Brass. 'Then does it signify,' she says, 'about ruining this Kit when Quilp desires it?' 'It certainly does not signify,' says Brass. Then they whispered and laughed for a long time about there being no danger if it was well done, and then Mr Brass pulls out his pocket-book, and says, 'Well,' he says, 'here it is—Quilp's own five-pound note. We'll agree that way, then,' he says. 'Kit's coming to-morrow morning, I know. While he's upstairs, you'll get out of the way, and I'll clear off Mr Richard. Having Kit alone, I'll hold him in conversation, and put this property in his hat. I'll manage so, besides,' he says, 'that Mr Richard shall find it there, and be the evidence. And if that don't get Christopher out of Mr Quilp's way, and satisfy Mr Quilp's grudges,' he says, 'the Devil's in it.' Miss Sally laughed, and said that was the plan, and as they seemed to be moving away, and I was afraid to stop any longer, I went downstairs again.—There!"

The small servant had gradually worked herself into as much agitation as Mr Swiveller, and therefore made no effort to restrain him when he sat up in bed and hastily demanded whether this story had been told to anybody.

"How could it be?" replied his nurse. "I was almost afraid to think about it, and hoped the young man would be let off. When I heard 'em say they had found him guilty of what he didn't do, you was gone, and so was the lodger—though I think I should have been frightened to tell him, even if he'd been there. Ever since I come here, you've been out of your senses, and what would have been the good of telling you then?"

"Marchioness," said Mr Swiveller, plucking off his nightcap and flinging it to the other end of the room; "if you'll do me the favour to retire for a few minutes and see what sort of a night it is, I'll get up."

"You mustn't think of such a thing," cried his nurse.

"I must indeed," said the patient, looking round the room. "Whereabouts are my clothes?"

"Oh, I'm so glad—you haven't got any," replied the Marchioness.

"Ma'am!" said Mr Swiveller, in great astonishment.

"I've been obliged to sell them, every one, to get the things that was ordered for you. But don't take on about that," urged the Marchioness, as Dick fell back upon his pillow. "You're too weak to stand, indeed."

"I am afraid," said Richard dolefully, "that you're right. What ought I to do! what is to be done!"

It naturally occurred to him on very little reflection, that the first step to take would be to communicate with one of the Mr Garlands instantly. It was very possible that Mr Abel had not yet left the office. In as little time as it takes to tell it, the small servant had the address in pencil on a piece of paper; a verbal description of father and son, which would enable her to recognise either without difficulty; and a special caution to be shy of Mr Chuckster, in consequence of that gentleman's known antipathy to Kit. Armed with these slender powers, she hurried away, commissioned to bring either old Mr Garland or Mr Abel, bodily, to that apartment.

"I suppose," said Dick, as she closed the door slowly, and peeped into the room again to make sure that he was comfortable, "I suppose there's nothing left—not so much as a waistcoat even?"

"No, nothing."

"It's embarrassing," said Mr Swiveller, "in case of fire—even an umbrella would be something—but you did quite right, dear Marchioness. I should have died without you!"

Chapter LXV

IT was well for the small servant that she was of a sharp, quick nature, or the consequence of sending her out alone, from the very neighbourhood in which it was most dangerous for her to appear, would probably have been the restoration of Miss Sally Brass to the supreme authority over her person. Not unmindful of the risk she ran, however, the Marchioness no sooner left the house than she dived into the first dark by-way that presented itself, and, without any present reference to the point to which her journey tended, made it her first business to put two good miles of brick and mortar between herself and Bevis Marks.

When she had accomplished this object, she began to shape her course for the notary's office, to which—shrewdly inquiring of apple-women and oyster-sellers at street-corners, rather than in lighted shops or of well-dressed people, at the hazard of attracting notice—she easily procured a direction. As carrier-pigeons, on being first let loose in a strange place, beat the air at random for a short time, before darting off towards the spot for which they are designed, so did the Marchioness flutter round and round until she believed herself in safety, and then bear swiftly down upon the port for which she was bound.

She had no bonnet—nothing on her head but a great cap which in some old time had been worn by Sally Brass, whose taste in headdresses was, as we have seen, peculiar—and her speed was rather retarded than assisted by her shoes, which, being extremely large and slipshod, flew off every now and then, and were difficult to find again, among the crowd of passengers. Indeed, the poor little creature experienced so much trouble and delay from having to grope for these articles of dress in mud and kennel, and suffered in these researches so much jostling, pushing, squeezing, and bandying from hand to hand, that by the time she reached the street in which the notary lived, she was fairly worn out and exhausted, and could not refrain from tears.

But to have got there at last was a great comfort, especially as there were lights still burning in the office window, and therefore some hope that she was not too late. So, the Marchioness dried her eyes with the backs of her hands, and, stealing softly up the steps, peeped in through the glass door.

Mr Chuckster was standing behind the lid of his desk, making such preparations towards finishing off for the night as pulling down his wristbands and pulling up his shirt-collar, settling his neck more gracefully in his stock, and secretly arranging his whiskers by the aid of a little triangular bit of looking-glass. Before the ashes of the fire stood two gentlemen, one of whom she rightly judged to be the notary, and the other (who was buttoning his greatcoat, and was evidently about to depart immediately) Mr Abel Garland.

Having made these observations, the small spy took counsel with herself, and resolved to wait in the street until Mr Abel came out, as there would then be no fear of having to speak before Mr Chuckster, and less difficulty in delivering her message. With this purpose she slipped out again, and crossing the road, sat down upon a door-step just opposite.

She had hardly taken this position, when there came dancing up the street, with his legs all wrong, and his head everywhere by turns, a pony. This pony had a little phaeton behind him, and a man in it; but neither man nor phaeton seemed to embarrass him in the least, as he reared up on his hind-legs, or stopped, or went on, or stood still again, or backed, or went sideways, without the smallest reference to them—just as the fancy seized him, and as if he were the freest animal in creation. When they came to the notary's door, the man called out in a very respectful manner, "Woa, then"—intimating that if he might venture to express a wish, it would be that they stopped there. The pony made a moment's pause; but as if it occurred to him that to stop when he was required might be to establish an inconvenient and dangerous precedent, he immediately started off again, rattled at a fast trot to the street-corner, wheeled round, came back, and then stopped of his own accord.

"Oh! you're a precious creatur!" said the man—who didn't venture by the bye to come out in his true colors until he was safe on the pavement. "I wish I had the rewarding of you—I do."

"What has he been doing?" said Mr Abel, tying a shawl round his neck as he came down the steps.

"He's enough to fret a man's heart out," replied the hostler. "He is the most wicious rascal——Woa then, will you?"

"He'll never stand still, if you call him names," said Mr Abel, getting in, and taking the reins. "He's a very good fellow if you know how to manage him. This is the first time he has been out, this long while, for he has lost his old driver and wouldn't stir for anybody else, till this morning. The lamps are right, are they? That's well. Be here to take him to-morrow, if you please. Good night!"

And after one or two strange plunges, quite of his own invention, the pony yielded to Mr Abel's mildness, and trotted gently off.

All this time Mr Chuckster had been standing at the door, and the small servant had been afraid to approach. She had nothing for it now, therefore, but to run after the chaise, and to call to Mr Abel to stop. Being out of breath when she came up with it, she was unable to make him hear. The case was desperate; for the pony was quickening his pace. The Marchioness hung on behind for a few moments, and, feeling that she could go no farther, and must soon yield, clambered by a vigorous effort into the hinder seat, and in so doing lost one of the shoes for ever.

Mr Abel being in a thoughtful frame of mind, and having quite enough to do to keep the pony going, went jogging on without looking round; little dreaming of the strange figure that was close behind him, until the Marchioness, having in some degree recovered her breath, and the loss of her shoe, and the novelty of her position, uttered close to his ear, the words:

"I say, sir——"

He turned his head quickly enough then, and stopping the pony, cried, with some trepidation, "God bless me, what is this!"

"Don't be frightened, sir," replied the still panting messenger. "Oh, I've run such a way after you!"

"What do you want with me?" said Mr Abel. "How did you come here?"

"I got in behind," replied the Marchioness. "Oh, please drive on, sir—don't stop—and go towards the City, will you? And, oh, do please make haste, because it's of consequence. There's somebody wants to see you there. He sent me to say would you come directly, and that he knowed all about Kit, and could save him yet, and prove his innocence."

"What do you tell me, child?"

"The truth, upon my word and honour I do. But please to drive on—quick, please! I've been such a time gone, he'll think I'm lost."

Mr Abel involuntarily urged the pony forward. The pony, impelled by some secret sympathy or some new caprice, burst into a great pace, and neither slackened it, nor indulged in any eccentric performances, until they arrived at the door of Mr Swiveller's lodging, where, marvellous to relate, he consented to stop when Mr Abel checked him.

"See! It's that room up there," said the Marchioness, pointing to one where there was a faint light. "Come!"

Mr Abel, who was one of the simplest and most retiring creatures in existence, and naturally timid withal, hesitated; for he had heard of people being decoyed into strange places to be robbed and murdered, under circumstances very like the present, and, for anything he knew to the contrary, by guides very like the Marchioness. His regard for Kit, however, overcame every other consideration. So, entrusting Whisker to the charge of a man who was lingering hard by in expectation of the job, he suffered his companion to take his hand, and to lead him up the dark and narrow stairs.

He was not a little surprised to find himself conducted into a dimly lighted sick-chamber, where a man was sleeping tranquilly in bed.

"An't it nice to see him lying there so quiet?" said his guide, in an earnest whisper. "Oh! you'd say it was, if you had only seen him two or three days ago."

Mr Abel made no answer, and, to say the truth, kept a long way from the bed and very near the door. His guide, who appeared to understand his reluctance, trimmed the candle, and taking it in her hand, approached the bed. As she did so, the sleeper started up, and he recognised in the wasted face the features of Richard Swiveller.

"Why, how is this?" said Mr Abel kindly, as he hurried towards him. "You have been ill?"

"Very," replied Dick. "Nearly dead. You might have chanced to hear of your Richard on his bier, but for the friend I sent to fetch you. Another shake of the hand, Marchioness, if you please. Sit down, sir."

Mr Abel seemed rather astonished to hear of the quality of his guide, and took a chair by the bedside.

"I have sent for you, sir," said Dick—"but she told you on what account?"

"She did. I am quite bewildered by all this. I really don't know what to say or think," replied Mr Abel.

"You'll say that presently," retorted Dick. "Marchioness, take a seat on the bed, will you? Now, tell this gentleman all that you told me; and be particular. Don't you speak another word, sir."

The story was repeated; it was, in effect, exactly the same as before, without any deviation or omission. Richard Swiveller kept his eyes fixed on his visitor during its narration, and directly it was concluded, took the word again.

"You have heard it all, and you'll not forget it. I'm too giddy and too queer to suggest anything; but you and your friends will know what to do. After this long delay, every minute is an age. If ever you went home fast in your life, go home fast to-night. Don't stop to say one word to me, but go. She will be found here, whenever she's wanted; and as to me, you're pretty sure to find me at home, for a week or two. There are more reasons than one for that. Marchioness, a light! If you lose another minute in looking at me, sir, I'll never forgive you!"

Mr Abel needed no more remonstrance or persuasion. He was gone in an instant; and the Marchioness, returning from lighting him downstairs, reported that the pony, without any preliminary objection whatever, had dashed away at full gallop.

"That's right!" said Dick; "and hearty of him; and I honour him from this time. But get some supper and a mug of beer, for I am sure you must be tired. Do have a mug of beer. It will do me as much good to see you take it as if I might drink it myself."

Nothing but this assurance could have prevailed upon the small nurse to indulge in such a luxury. Having eaten and drunk to Mr Swiveller's extreme contentment, given him his drink, and put everything in neat order, she wrapped herself in an old coverlet and lay down upon the rug before the fire.

Mr Swiveller was by that time murmuring in his sleep, "Strew then, oh, strew, a bed of rushes. Here will we stay, till morning blushes. Good night, Marchioness!"

Chapter LXVI

ON awaking in the morning, Richard Swiveller became conscious by slow degrees of whispering voices in his room. Looking out between the curtains, he espied Mr Garland, Mr Abel, the notary, and the single gentleman, gathered round the Marchioness, and talking to her with great earnestness but in very subdued tones—fearing, no doubt, to disturb him. He lost no time in letting them know that this precaution was unnecessary, and all four gentlemen directly approached his bedside. Old Mr Garland was the first to stretch out his hand, and inquire how he felt.

Dick was about to answer that he felt much better, though still as weak as need be, when his little nurse, pushing the visitors aside and pressing up to his pillow as if in jealousy of their interference, set his breakfast before him, and insisted on his taking it before he underwent the fatigue of speaking or of being spoken to. Mr Swiveller, who was perfectly ravenous, and had had, all night, amazingly distinct and consistent dreams of mutton chops, double stout, and similar delicacies, felt even the weak tea and dry toast such irresistible temptations, that he consented to eat and drink upon one condition.

"And that is," said Dick, returning the pressure of Mr Garland's hand, "that you answer me this question truly, before I take a bit or drop. Is it too late?"

"For completing the work you began so well last night?" returned the old gentleman. "No. Set your mind at rest upon that point. It is not, I assure you."

Comforted by this intelligence, the patient applied himself to his food with a keen appetite, though evidently not with a greater zest in the eating than his nurse appeared to have in seeing him eat. The manner of his meal was this:—Mr Swiveller, holding the slice of toast or cup of tea in his left hand, and taking a bite or drink as the case might be, constantly kept, in his right, one palm of the Marchioness tight locked; and to shake, or even to kiss this imprisoned hand, he would stop every now and then, in the very act of swallowing, with perfect seriousness of intention, and the utmost gravity. As often as he put anything into his mouth, whether for eating or drinking, the face of the Marchioness lighted up beyond all description; but whenever he gave her one or other of these tokens of recognition, her countenance became overshadowed, and she began to sob. Now, whether she was in her laughing joy, or in her crying one, the Marchioness could not help turning to the visitors with an appealing look, which seemed to say, "You see this fellow—can I help this?"—and they being thus made, as it were, parties to the scene, as regularly answered by another look, "No. Certainly not." This dumb-show taking place during the whole time of the invalid's breakfast, and the invalid himself, pale and emaciated, performing no small part in the same, it may be fairly questioned whether at any meal, where no word, good or bad, was spoken from beginning to end, so much was expressed by gestures in themselves so slight and unimportant.

At length—and to say the truth before very long—Mr Swiveller had despatched as much toast and tea as in that stage of his recovery it was discreet to let him have. But the cares of the Marchioness did not stop here; for, disappearing for an instant and presently returning with a basin of fair water, she laved his face and hands, brushed his hair, and in short made him as spruce and smart as anybody under such circumstances could be made; and all this in as brisk and businesslike a manner, as if he were a very little boy, and she his grown-up nurse. To these various attentions, Mr Swiveller submitted in a kind of grateful astonishment beyond the reach of language. When they were at last brought to an end, and the Marchioness had withdrawn into a distant corner to take her own poor breakfast (cold enough by that time), he turned his face away for some few moments, and shook hands heartily with the air.

"Gentlemen," said Dick, rousing himself from this pause, and turning round again, "you'll excuse me. Men who have been brought so low as I have been, are easily fatigued. I am fresh again now, and fit for talking. We're short of chairs here, among other trifles, but if you'll do me the favour to sit upon the bed——"

"What can we do for you?" said Mr Garland kindly.

"If you could make the Marchioness yonder, a Marchioness in real, sober earnest," returned Dick, "I'd thank you to get it done off-hand. But as you can't, and as the question is not what you will do for me, but, what you will do for somebody else who has a better claim upon you, pray, sir, let me know what you intend doing."

"It's chiefly on that account that we have come just now," said the single gentleman, "for you will have another visitor presently. We feared you would be anxious unless you knew from ourselves what steps we intended to take, and therefore came to you before we stirred in the matter."

"Gentlemen," returned Dick, "I thank you. Anybody in the helpless state that you see me in, is naturally anxious. Don't let me interrupt you, sir."

"Then, you see, my good fellow," said the single gentleman, "that while we have no doubt whatever of the truth of this disclosure, which has so providentially come to light——"

"Meaning hers?" said Dick, pointing towards the Marchioness.

"—Meaning hers, of course. While we have no doubt of that, or that a proper use of it would procure the poor lad's immediate pardon and liberation, we have a great doubt whether it would, by itself, enable us to reach Quilp, the chief agent in this villainy. I should tell you that this doubt has been confirmed into something very nearly approaching certainty by the best opinions we have been enabled, in this short space of time, to take upon the subject. You'll agree with us, that to give him even the most distant chance of escape, if we could help it, would be monstrous. You say with us, no doubt, if somebody must escape, let it be any one but he."

"Yes," returned Dick, "certainly. That is if somebody *must*—but upon my word, I'm unwilling that anybody should. Since laws were made for every degree, to curb vice in others as well as in me—and so forth you know—doesn't it strike you in that light?"

The single gentleman smiled as if the light in which Mr. Swiveller had put the question were not the clearest in the world, and proceeded to explain that they contemplated proceeding by stratagem in the first instance; and that their design was to endeavour to extort a confession from the gentle Sarah.

"When she finds how much we know, and how we know it," he said, "and that she is clearly compromised already, we are not without strong hopes that we may be enabled through her means to punish the other two effectually. If we could do that, she might go scot-free for aught I cared."

Dick received this project in anything but a gracious manner, representing with as much warmth as he was then capable of showing, that they would find the old buck (meaning Sarah) more difficult to manage than Quilp himself—that for any tampering, terrifying, or cajolery, she was a very unpromising and unyielding subject—that she was of a kind of brass not easily melted or moulded into shape—in short, that they were no match for her, and would be signally defeated. But it was in vain to urge them to adopt some other course. The single gentleman has been described as explaining their joint intentions, but it should have been written that they all spoke together; that if any one of them by chance held his peace for a moment, he stood gasping and panting for an opportunity to strike in again: in a word, that they had reached that pitch of impatience and anxiety where men can neither be persuaded nor reasoned with; and that it would have been easier to turn the most impetuous wind that ever blew, than to prevail on them to reconsider their determination. So, after telling Mr Swiveller how they had not lost sight of Kit's mother and the children; how they had never once even lost sight of Kit himself, but had been unremitting in their endeavours to procure a mitigation of his sentence; how they had been perfectly distracted between the strong proofs of his guilt, and their own fading hopes of his innocence; and how he, Richard Swiveller, might keep his mind at rest, for everything should be happily adjusted between that time and night;—after telling him all this, and adding a great many kind and cordial expressions, personal to himself, which it is unnecessary to recite, Mr Garland, the notary, and the single gentleman, took their leaves at a very critical time, or Richard Swiveller must assuredly have been driven into another fever, whereof the results might have been fatal.

Mr Abel remained behind, very often looking at his watch and at the room door, until Mr Swiveller was roused from a short nap, by the setting-down on the landing-place outside, as from the shoulders of a porter, of some giant load, which seemed to shake the house, and made the little physic bottles on the mantel-shelf ring again. Directly this sound reached his ears, Mr Abel started up, and hobbled to the door, and opened it; and behold! there stood a strong man, with a mighty hamper, which, being hauled into the room and presently unpacked, disgorged such treasures of tea, and coffee, and wine, and rusks, and oranges, and grapes, and fowls ready trussed for boiling, and calves'-foot jelly, and arrow-root, and sago, and other delicate restoratives, that the small servant, who had never thought it possible that such things could be, except in shops, stood rooted to the spot in her one shoe, with her mouth and eyes watering in unison, and her power of speech quite gone. But not so Mr Abel; or the strong man who emptied the hamper, big as it was, in a twinkling; and not so the nice old lady, who appeared so suddenly that she might have come out of the hamper too (it was quite large enough), and who, bustling about on tiptoe and without noise—now here, now there, now everywhere at once—began to fill out the jelly in teacups, and to make chicken broth in small saucepans, and to peel oranges for the sick man and to cut them up in little pieces, and to ply the small servant with glasses of wine and choice bits of everything until more substantial meat could be prepared for her refreshment. The whole of which appearances were so unexpected and bewildering, that Mr Swiveller, when he had taken two oranges and a little jelly, and had seen the strong man walk off with the empty basket, plainly leaving all that abundance for his use and benefit, was fain to lie down and fall asleep again, from sheer inability to entertain such wonders in his mind.

Meanwhile the single gentleman, the notary, and Mr Garland, repaired to a certain coffee-house, and from that place indited and sent a letter to Miss Sally Brass, requesting her, in terms mysterious and brief, to favour an unknown friend, who wished to consult her, with her company there, as speedily as possible. The communication performed its errand so well, that within ten minutes of the messenger's return and report of its delivery, Miss Brass herself was announced.

"Pray, ma'am," said the single gentleman, whom she found alone in the room, "take a chair."

Miss Brass sat herself down in a very stiff and frigid state, and seemed—as indeed she was—not a little astonished to find that the lodger and her mysterious correspondent were one and the same person.

"You did not expect to see me?" said the single gentleman.

"I didn't think much about it," returned the beauty. "I supposed it was business of some kind or other. If it's about the apartments, of course you'll give my brother regular notice, you know—or money. That's very easily settled. You're a responsible party, and in such a case lawful money and lawful notice are pretty much the same."

"I am obliged to you for your good opinion," retorted the single gentleman, "and quite concur in those sentiments. But that is not the subject on which I wish to speak with you."

"Oh!" said Sally. "Then just state the particulars, will you? I suppose it's professional business?"

"Why, it *is* connected with the law, certainly."

"Very well," returned Miss Brass. "My brother and I are just the same. I can take any instructions, or give you any advice."

"As there are other parties interested besides myself," said the single gentleman, rising and opening the door of an inner room, "we had better confer together. Miss Brass is here, gentlemen!"

Mr Garland and the notary walked in, looking very grave; and drawing up two chairs, one on each side of the single gentleman, formed a kind of fence round the gentle Sarah, and penned her into a corner. Her brother Sampson under such circumstances would certainly have evinced some confusion or anxiety, but she—all composure— pulled out the tin box and calmly took a pinch of snuff.

"Miss Brass," said the notary, taking the word at this crisis, "we professional people understand each other, and, when we choose, can say what we have to say, in very few words. You advertised a runaway servant, the other day?"

"Well," returned Miss Sally, with a sudden flush overspreading her features, "what of that?"

"She is found, ma'am," said the notary, pulling out his pocket-handkerchief with a flourish. "She is found."

"Who found her?" demanded Sarah hastily.

"We did, ma'am—we three. Only last night, or you would have heard from us before."

"And now I *have* heard from you," said Miss Brass, folding her arms resolutely, as though she were about to deny something to the death, "what have you got to say? Something you have got into your heads about her, of course. Prove it, will you—that's all. Prove it. You have found her, you say. I can tell you (if you don't know it) that you have found the most artful, lying, pilfering, and devilish little minx that was ever born.— Have you got her here?" she added, looking sharply round.

"No, she is not here at present," returned the notary. "But she is quite safe."

"Ha!" cried Sally, twitching a pinch of snuff out of her box, as spitefully as if she were in the very act of wrenching off the small servant's nose; "she shall be safe enough from this time, I warrant you."

"I hope so," replied the notary.—"Did it occur to you for the first time when you found she had run away, that there were two keys to your kitchen door?"

Miss Sally took another pinch, and putting her head on one side, looked at her questioner with a curious kind of spasm about her mouth, but with a cunning aspect of immense expression.

"Two keys," repeated the notary; "one of which gave her the opportunities of roaming through the house at nights when you supposed her fast locked up, and of overhearing confidential consultations—among others, that particular conference to be described to-day before a justice, which you will have an opportunity of hearing her relate; that conference which you and Mr Brass held together on the night before that most unfortunate and innocent young man was accused of robbery, by a horrible device of which I will only say that it may be characterised by the epithets you have applied to this wretched little witness, and by a few stronger ones besides."

Sally took another pinch. Although her face was wonderfully composed, it was apparent that she was wholly taken by surprise, and that what she had expected to be taxed with, in connexion with her small servant, was something very different from this.

"Come, come, Miss Brass," said the notary, "you have great command of feature, but you feel, I see, that by a chance which never entered your imagination, this base design is revealed, and two of its plotters must be brought to justice. Now, you know the pains and penalties you are liable to, and so I need not dilate upon them, but I have a proposal to make to you. You have the honour of being sister to one of the greatest scoundrels unhung; and, if I may venture to say so to a lady, you are in every respect quite worthy of him. But, connected with you two is a third party, a villain of the name of Quilp, the prime mover of the whole diabolical device, who I believe to be worse than either. For his sake, Miss Brass, do us the favour to reveal the whole history of this affair. Let me remind you that your doing so at our instance will place you in a safe and comfortable position—your present one is not desirable—and cannot injure your brother, for against him and you we have quite sufficient evidence (as you hear) already. I will not say to you that we suggest this course in mercy (for, to tell you the truth, we do not entertain any regard for you), but it is a necessity to which we are reduced, and I recommend it to you as a matter of the very best policy. Time," said Mr Witherden, pulling out his watch, "in a business like this, is exceedingly precious. Favour us with your decision as speedily as possible, ma'am."

With a smile upon her face, and looking at each of the three by turns, Miss Brass took two or three more pinches of snuff, and having by this time very little left, travelled round and round the box with her forefinger and thumb, scraping up another. Having disposed of this likewise and put the box carefully in her pocket, she said:

"I am to accept or reject at once, am I?"

"Yes," said Mr Witherden.

The charming creature was opening her lips to speak in reply, when the door was hastily opened too, and the head of Sampson Brass was thrust into the room.

"Excuse me," said that gentleman hastily. "Wait a bit!"

So saying, and quite indifferent to the astonishment his presence occasioned, he crept in, shut the door, kissed his greasy glove as servilely as if it were the dust, and made a most abject bow.

"Sarah," said Brass, "hold your tongue if you please, and let me speak. Gentlemen, if I could express the pleasure it gives me to see three such men in a happy unity of feeling and concord of sentiment, I think you would hardly believe me. But though I am unfortunate—nay, gentlemen, criminal, if we are to use harsh expressions in a company like this—still I have my feelings like other men. I have heard of a poet, who remarked that feelings were the common lot of all. If he could have been a pig, gentlemen, and have uttered that sentiment, he would still have been immortal."

"If you're not an idiot," said Miss Brass harshly, "hold your peace."

"Sarah, my dear," returned her brother, "thank you. But I know what I am about, my love, and will take the liberty of expressing myself accordingly. Mr Witherden, sir, your handkerchief is hanging out of your pocket—would you allow me to——"

As Mr Brass advanced to remedy this accident, the notary shrank from him with an air of great disgust. Brass, who over and above his usual prepossessing qualities, had a scratched face, a green shade over one eye, and a hat grievously crushed, stopped short, and looked round with a pitiful smile.

"He shuns me," said Sampson, "even when I would, as I may say, heap coals of fire upon his head. Well! Ah! But I am a falling house, and the rats (if I may be allowed the expression in reference to a gentleman that I respect and love beyond everything) fly from me! Gentlemen—regarding your conversation just now, I happened to see my sister on her way here, and, wondering where she could be going to, and being—may I venture to say?—naturally of a suspicious turn, followed her. Since then, I have been listening."

"If you're not mad," interposed Miss Sally, "stop there, and say no more."

"Sarah, my dear," rejoined Brass with undiminished politeness, "I thank you kindly, but will still proceed. Mr Witherden, sir, as we have the honour to be members of the same profession—to say nothing of that other gentleman having been my lodger, and having partaken, as one might say, of the hospitality of my roof—I think you might have given me the refusal of this offer in the first instance. I do indeed. Now, my dear sir," cried Brass, seeing that the notary was about to interrupt him, "suffer me to speak, I beg."

Mr Witherden was silent, and Brass went on.

"If you will do me the favour," he said, holding up the green shade, and revealing an eye most horribly discoloured, "to look at this, you will naturally inquire in your own minds how did I get it. If you look from that, to my face, you will wonder what could have been the cause of all these scratches. And if from them to my hat, how it came into the state in which you see it. Gentlemen," said Brass, striking the hat fiercely with his clenched hand, "to all these questions I answer—Quilp!"

The three gentlemen looked at each other, but said nothing.

"I say," pursued Brass, glancing aside at his sister, as though he were talking for her information, and speaking with a snarling malignity, in violent contrast to his usual smoothness, "that I answer to all these questions—Quilp—Quilp, who deludes me into his infernal den, and takes a delight in looking on and chuckling while I scorch, and burn, and bruise, and maim myself—Quilp, who never once, no, never once, in all our communications together, has treated me otherwise than as a dog—Quilp, whom I have always hated with my whole heart, but never so much as lately. He gives me the cold shoulder on this very matter as if he had had nothing to do with it, instead of being the first to propose it. I can't trust him. In one of his howling, raving, blazing humours, I believe he'd let it out if it was murder, and never think of himself so long as he could terrify me. Now," said Brass, picking up his hat again, replacing the shade over his eye, and actually crouching down, in the excess of his servility, "What does all this lead me to?—what should you say it led me to, gentlemen?—could you guess at all near the mark?"

Nobody spoke. Brass stood smirking for a little while as if he had propounded some choice conundrum; and then said:

"To be short with you, then, it leads me to this. If the truth has come out, as it plainly has in a manner that there's no standing up against—and a very sublime and grand thing is Truth, gentlemen, in its way, though like other sublime and grand things, such as thunderstorms and that, we're not always over and above glad to see it—I had better turn upon this man than let this man turn upon me. It's clear to me that I am done for. Therefore, if anybody is to split, I had better be the person and have the advantage of it. Sarah, my dear, comparatively speaking, you're safe. I relate these circumstances for my own profit."

With that, Mr Brass, in a great hurry, revealed the whole story; bearing as heavily as possible on his amiable employer, and making himself out to be rather a saint-like and holy character, though subject—he acknowledged—to human weaknesses. He concluded thus:

"Now, gentlemen, I am not a man who does things by halves. Being in for a penny, I am ready, as the saying is, to be in for a pound. You must do with me what you please, and take me where you please. If you wish to have this in writing, we'll reduce it into manuscript immediately. You will be tender with me, I am sure. I am quite confident you will be tender with me. You are men of honour, and have feeling hearts. I yielded from necessity to Quilp, for though necessity has no law, she has her lawyers. I yield to you from necessity too; from policy besides; and because of feelings that have been a pretty long time working within me. Punish Quilp, gentlemen. Weigh heavily upon him. Grind him down. Tread him underfoot. He has done as much by me, for many and many a day."

Having now arrived at the conclusion of his discourse, Sampson checked the current of his wrath, kissed his glove again, and smiled as only parasites and cowards can.

"And this," said Miss Brass, raising her head, with which she had hitherto sat resting on her hands, and surveying him from head to foot with a bitter sneer, "this is my brother, is it! This is my brother, that I have worked and toiled for, and believed to have had something of the man in him!"

"Sarah, my dear," returned Sampson, rubbing his hands feebly; "you disturb our friends. Besides you—you're disappointed, Sarah, and, not knowing what you say, expose yourself."

"Yes, you pitiful dastard," retorted the lovely damsel, "I understand you. You feared that I should be beforehand with you. But do you think that *I* would have been enticed to say a word! I'd have scorned it, if they had tried and tempted me for twenty years."

"He, he!" simpered Brass, who in his deep debasement really seemed to have changed sexes with his sister, and to have made over to her any spark of manliness he might have possessed. "You think so, Sarah, you think so perhaps; but you would have acted quite different, my good fellow. You will not have forgotten that it was a maxim with Foxey—our revered father, gentlemen—'Always suspect everybody.' That's the maxim to go through life with! If you were not actually about to purchase your own safety when I showed myself, I suspect you'd have done it by this time. And therefore I've done it myself, and spared you the trouble as well as the shame. The shame, gentlemen," added Brass, allowing himself to be slightly overcome, "if there is any, is mine. It's better that a female should be spared it."

With deference to the better opinion of Mr Brass, and more particularly to the authority of his Great Ancestor, it may be doubted with humility whether the elevating principle laid down by the latter gentleman, and acted upon by his descendant, is always a prudent one, or attended in practice with the desired results. This is beyond question a bold and presumptuous doubt, inasmuch as many distinguished characters, called men of the world, long-headed customers, knowing dogs, shrewd fellows, capital hands at business, and the like, have made, and do daily make this axiom their polar star and compass. Still, the doubt may be gently insinuated. And in illustration it may be observed that if Mr Brass, not being over-suspicious, had, without prying and listening, left his sister to manage the conference on their joint behalf, or prying and listening, had not been in such a mighty hurry to anticipate her (which he would not have been, but for his distrust and jealousy), he would probably have found himself much better off in the end. Thus it will always happen that these men of the world, who go through it in armour, defend themselves from quite as much good as evil; to say nothing of the inconvenience and absurdity of mounting guard with a microscope at all times, and of wearing a coat of mail on the most innocent occasions.

The three gentlemen spoke together apart for a few moments. At the end of their consultation, which was very brief, the notary pointed to the writing-materials on the table, and informed Mr Brass that if he wished to make any statement in writing, he had the opportunity of doing so. At the same time he felt bound to tell him that they would require his attendance presently before a Justice of the Peace, and that in what he did or said, he was guided entirely by his own discretion.

"Gentlemen," said Brass, drawing off his gloves, and crawling in spirit upon the ground before them, "I will justify the tenderness with which I know I shall be treated; and as, without tenderness, I should, now that this discovery has been made, stand in the worst position of the three, you may depend upon it I will make a clean breast. Mr Witherden, sir, a kind of faintness is upon my spirits—if you would do me the favour to ring the bell and order up a glass of something warm and spicy, I shall, notwithstanding what has passed, have a melancholy pleasure in drinking your good health. I had hoped," said Brass, looking round with a mournful smile, "to have seen you three gentlemen one day or another with your legs under the mahogany in my humble parlour in the Marks. But hopes are fleeting. Dear me!"

Mr Brass found himself so exceedingly affected at this point that he could say or do nothing more until some refreshment arrived. Having partaken of it, pretty freely for one in his agitated state, he sat down to write.

The lovely Sarah, now with her arms folded, and now with her hands clasped behind her, paced the room with manly strides while her brother was thus employed, and sometimes stopped to pull out her snuff-box and bite the lid. She continued to pace up and down until she was quite tired, and then fell asleep on a chair near the door.

It has been since supposed with some reason that this slumber was a sham or feint, as she contrived to slip away unobserved in the dusk of the afternoon. Whether this was an intentional and waking departure, or a somnambulistic leave-taking and walking in her sleep, may remain a subject of contention; but on one point (and indeed the main one) all parties are agreed. In whatever state she walked away, she certainly did not walk back again.

Mention having been made of the dusk of the afternoon, it will be inferred that Mr Brass's task occupied some time in the completion. It was not finished until evening; but being done at last, that worthy person and the three friends adjourned in a hackney-coach to the private office of a Justice, who, giving Mr Brass a warm reception and detaining him in a secure place that he might insure to himself the pleasure of seeing him on the morrow, dismissed the others with the cheering assurance that a warrant could not fail to be granted next day for the apprehension of Mr Quilp, and that a proper application and statement of all the circumstances to the Secretary of State (who was fortunately in town), would no doubt procure Kit's free pardon and liberation without delay.

And now indeed it seemed that Quilp's malignant career was drawing to a close, and that retribution, which often travels slowly—especially when heaviest—had tracked his footsteps with a sure and certain scent and was gaining on him fast. Unmindful of her stealthy tread, her victim holds his course in fancied triumph. Still at his heels she comes, and once afoot, is never turned aside.

Their business ended, the three gentlemen hastened back to the lodgings of Mr Swiveller, whom they found progressing so favourably in his recovery as to have been able to sit up for half an hour, and to have conversed with cheerfulness. Mrs Garland had gone home some time since, but Mr Abel was still sitting with him. After telling him all they had done, the two Mr Garlands and the single gentleman, as if by some previous understanding, took their leaves for the night, leaving the invalid alone with the notary and the small servant.

"As you are so much better," said Mr Witherden, sitting down at the bedside, "I may venture to communicate to you a piece of news which has come to me professionally."

The idea of any professional intelligence from a gentleman connected with legal matters appeared to afford Richard anything but a pleasing anticipation. Perhaps he connected it in his own mind with one or two outstanding accounts, in reference to which he had already received divers threatening letters. His countenance fell as he replied,

"Certainly, sir. I hope it's not anything of a very disagreeable nature, though?"

"If I thought it so, I should choose some better time for communicating it," replied the notary. "Let me tell you, first, that my friends who have been here to-day, know nothing of it, and that their kindness to you has been quite spontaneous, and with no hope of return. It may do a thoughtless, careless man good to know that."

Dick thanked him, and said he hoped it would.

"I have been making some inquiries about you," said Mr Witherden, "little thinking that I should find you under such circumstances as those which have brought us together. You are the nephew of Rebecca Swiveller, spinster, deceased, of Cheselbourne in Dorsetshire."

"Deceased!" cried Dick.

"Deceased. If you had been another sort of nephew, you would have come into possession (so says the will, and I see no reason to doubt it) of five-and-twenty thousand pounds. As it is, you have fallen into an annuity of one hundred and fifty pounds a year; but I think I may congratulate you even upon that."

"Sir," said Dick, sobbing and laughing together, "you may. For, please God, we'll make a scholar of the poor Marchioness yet! And she shall walk in silk attire, and siller have to spare, or may I never rise from this bed again!"

Chapter LXVII

UNCONSCIOUS of the proceedings faithfully narrated in the last chapter, and little dreaming of the mine which had been sprung beneath him (for, to the end that he should have no warning of the business afoot, the profoundest secrecy was observed in the whole transaction), Mr Quilp remained shut up in his hermitage, undisturbed by any suspicion, and extremely well satisfied with the result of his machinations. Being engaged in the adjustment of some accounts—an occupation to which the silence and solitude of his retreat were very favourable—he had not strayed from his den for two whole days. The third day of his devotion to this pursuit found him still hard at work, and little disposed to stir abroad.

It was the day next after Mr Brass's confession, and consequently that which threatened the restriction of Mr Quilp's liberty, and the abrupt communication to him of some very unpleasant and unwelcome facts. Having no intuitive perception of the cloud which lowered upon his house, the dwarf was in his ordinary state of cheerfulness; and, when he found he was becoming too much engrossed by business with a due regard to his health and spirits, he varied its monotonous routine with a little screeching, or howling, or some other innocent relaxation of that nature.

He was attended, as usual, by Tom Scott, who sat crouching over the fire after the manner of a toad, and from time to time, when his master's back was turned, imitated his grimaces with a fearful exactness. The figurehead had not yet disappeared, but remained in its old place. The face, horribly seared by the frequent application of the red-hot poker, and further ornamented by the insertion in the tip of the nose of a tenpenny nail, yet smiled blandly in its less lacerated parts, and seemed, like a sturdy martyr, to provoke its tormentor to the commission of new outrages and insults.

The day, in the highest and brightest quarters of the town, was damp, dark, cold, and gloomy. In that low and marshy spot, the fog filled every nook and corner with a thick dense cloud. Every object was obscure at one or two yards' distance. The warning lights and fires upon the river were powerless beneath this pall, and, but for a raw and piercing chillness in the air, and now and then the cry of some bewildered boatman as he rested on his oars and tried to make out where he was, the river itself might have been miles away.

The mist, though sluggish and slow to move, was of a keenly searching kind. No muffling up in furs and broadcloth kept it out. It seemed to penetrate into the very bones of the shrinking wayfarers, and to rack them with cold and pains. Everything was wet, and clammy to the touch. The warm blaze alone defied it, and leaped and sparkled merrily. It was a day to be at home, crowding about the fire, telling stories of travellers who had lost their way in such weather on heaths and moors; and to love a warm hearth more than ever.

The dwarf's humour, as we know, was to have a fireside to himself; and when he was disposed to be convivial, to enjoy himself alone. By no means insensible to the comfort of being within doors, he ordered Tom Scott to pile the little stove with coals, and, dismissing his work for that day, determined to be jovial.

To this end, he lighted up fresh candles and heaped more fuel on the fire; and having dined off a beefsteak, which he cooked himself in somewhat of a savage and cannibal-like manner, brewed a great bowl of hot punch, lighted his pipe, and sat down to spend the evening.

At this moment, a low knocking at the cabin door arrested his attention. When it had been twice or thrice repeated, he softly opened the little window, and thrusting his head out, demanded who was there.

"Only me, Quilp," replied a woman's voice.

"Only you!" cried the dwarf, stretching his neck to obtain a better view of his visitor. "And what brings you here, you jade? How dare you approach the ogre's castle, eh?"

"I have come with some news," rejoined his spouse. "Don't be angry with me."

"Is it good news, pleasant news, news to make a man skip and snap his fingers?" said the dwarf. "Is the dear old lady dead?"

"I don't know what news it is, or whether it's good or bad," rejoined his wife.

"Then she's alive," said Quilp, "and there's nothing the matter with her. Go home again, you bird of evil note, go home!"

"I have brought a letter——" cried the meek little woman.

"Toss it in at the window here, and go your ways," said Quilp, interrupting her, "or I'll come out and scratch you."

"No, but please, Quilp—do hear me speak," urged his submissive wife, in tears. "Please do!"

"Speak then," growled the dwarf, with a malicious grin. "Be quick and short about it. Speak, will you?"

"It was left at our house this afternoon," said Mrs Quilp, trembling, "by a boy who said he didn't know from whom it came, but that it was given to him to leave, and that he was told to say it must be brought to you directly, for it was of the very greatest consequence.—But please," she added, as her husband stretched out his hand for it, "please let me in. You don't know how wet and cold I am, or how many times I have lost my way in coming here through this thick fog. Let me dry myself at the fire for five minutes. I'll go away directly you tell me to, Quilp. Upon my word I will."

Her amiable husband hesitated for a few moments; but bethinking himself that the letter might require some answer, of which she could be the bearer, closed the window, opened the door, and bade her enter. Mrs Quilp obeyed right willingly, and, kneeling down before the fire to warm her hands, delivered into his a little packet.

"I'm glad you're wet," said Quilp, snatching it, and squinting at her. "I'm glad you're cold. I'm glad you've lost your way. I'm glad your eyes are red with crying. It does my heart good to see your little nose so pinched and frosty."

"Oh, Quilp!" sobbed his wife. "How cruel it is of you!"

"Did she think I was dead!" said Quilp, wrinkling his face into a most extraordinary series of grimaces. "Did she think she was going to have all the money, and to marry somebody she liked! Ha, ha, ha! Did she?"

These taunts elicited no reply from the poor little woman, who remained on her knees, warming her hands, and sobbing, to Mr Quilp's great delight. But as he was contemplating her, and chuckling excessively, he happened to observe that Tom Scott was delighted too; wherefore, that he might have no presumptuous partner in his glee, the dwarf instantly collared him, dragged him to the door, and after a short scuffle, kicked him into the yard. In return for this mark of attention, Tom immediately walked upon his hands to the window, and—if the expression be allowable—looked in with his shoes: besides rattling his feet upon the glass like a Banshee upside-down. As a matter of course, Mr Quilp lost no time in resorting to the infallible poker, with which, after some dodging and lying in ambush, he paid his young friend one or two such unequivocal compliments that he vanished precipitately, and left him in quiet possession of the field.

"So! That little job being disposed of," said the dwarf, coolly, "I'll read my letter. Humph!" he muttered, looking at the direction. "I ought to know this writing. Beautiful Sally!"

Opening it, he read, in a fair, round, legal hand, as follows:

> Sammy has been practised upon, and has broken confidence. It has all come out. You had better not be in the way, for strangers are going to call upon you. They have been very quiet as yet, because they mean to surprise you. Don't lose time. I didn't. I am not to be found anywhere. If I was you, I wouldn't be, either.
>
> S. B., late of B. M.

To describe the changes that passed over Quilp's face as he read this letter half a dozen times, would require some new language; such, for power of expression, as was never written, read, or spoken. For a long time he did not utter one word; but after a considerable interval, during which Mrs Quilp was almost paralysed with the alarm his looks engendered, he contrived to gasp out:

"——If I had him here. If I only had him here——"

"Oh, Quilp!" said his wife, "what's the matter? Who are you angry with?"

"——I should drown him," said the dwarf, not heeding her. "Too easy a death, too short, too quick—but the river runs close at hand. Oh! If I had him here! Just to take him to the brink, coaxingly and pleasantly—holding him by the button-hole—joking with him—and, with a sudden push, to send him splashing down! Drowning men come to the surface three times, they say. Ah! To see him those three times, and mock him as his face came bobbing up—oh, what a rich treat that would be!"

"Quilp!" stammered his wife, venturing at the same time to touch him on the shoulder: "what has gone wrong?"

She was so terrified by the relish with which he pictured this pleasure to himself, that she could scarcely make herself intelligible.

"Such a bloodless cur!" said Quilp, rubbing his hands very slowly, and pressing them tight together. "I thought his cowardice and servility were the best guarantee for his keeping silence. Oh, Brass, Brass—my dear, good, affectionate, faithful, complimentary, charming friend—if I only had you here!"

His wife, who had retreated lest she should seem to listen to these mutterings, ventured to approach him again, and was about to speak, when he hurried to the door and called Tom Scott, who, remembering his late gentle admonition, deemed it prudent to appear immediately.

"There!" said the dwarf, pulling him in. "Take her home. Don't come here to-morrow, for this place will be shut up. Come back no more till you hear from me or see me. Do you mind?"

Tom nodded sulkily, and beckoned Mrs Quilp to lead the way.

"As for you," said the dwarf, addressing himself to her, "ask no questions about me, make no search for me, say nothing concerning me. I shall not be dead, Mistress, and that'll comfort you. He'll take care of you."

"But, Quilp? What is the matter? Where are you going? Do say something more."

"I'll say that," said the dwarf, seizing her by the arm, "and do that too, which undone and unsaid would be best for you unless you go directly."

"Has anything happened?" cried his wife. "Oh! Do tell me that."

"Yes," snarled the dwarf. "No. What matter which? I have told you what to do. Woe betide you if you fail to do it, or disobey me by a hair's breadth. Will you go!"

"I am going, I'll go directly; but," faltered his wife, "answer me one question first. Has this letter any connexion with dear little Nell? I must ask you that—I must indeed, Quilp. You cannot think what days and nights of sorrow I have had through having once deceived that child. I don't know what harm I may have brought about, but, great or little, I did it for you, Quilp. My conscience misgave me when I did it. Do answer me this question, if you please."

The exasperated dwarf returned no answer, but turned round and caught up his usual weapon with such vehemence, that Tom Scott dragged his charge away by main force, and as swiftly as he could. It was well he did so, for Quilp, who was nearly mad with rage, pursued them to the neighbouring lane, and might have prolonged the chase but for the dense mist which obscured them from his view, and appeared to thicken every moment.

"It will be a good night for travelling anonymously," he said, as he returned slowly, being pretty well breathed with his run. "Stay. We may look better here. This is too hospitable and free."

By a great exertion of strength, he closed the two old gates which were deeply sunken in the mud, and barred them with a heavy beam. That done, he shook his matted hair from about his eyes, and tried them.—Strong and fast.

"The fence between this wharf and the next is easily climbed," said the dwarf, when he had taken these precautions. "There's a back lane too from there. That shall be my way out. A man need know his road well, to find it in this lovely place to-night. I need fear no unwelcome visitors while this lasts, I think."

Almost reduced to the necessity of groping his way with his hands (it had grown so dark and the fog had so much increased), he returned to his lair; and, after musing for some time over the fire, busied himself in preparations for a speedy departure.

While he was collecting a few necessaries and cramming them into his pockets, he never once ceased communing with himself in a low voice, or unclenched his teeth, which he had ground together on finishing Miss Brass's note.

"Oh, Sampson!" he muttered, "good, worthy creature—if I could but hug you! If I could only fold you in my arms, and squeeze your ribs, as I *could* squeeze them if I once had you tight, what a meeting there would be between us! If we ever do cross each other again, Sampson, we'll have a greeting not easily to be forgotten, trust me. This time, Sampson, this moment when all had gone on so well, was so nicely chosen! It was so thoughtful of you, so penitent, so good. Oh, if we were face to face in this room again, my white-livered man of law, how well contented one of us would be!"

There he stopped; and raising the bowl of punch to his lips, drank a long deep draught, as if it were fair water and cooling to his parched mouth. Setting it down abruptly, and resuming his preparations, he went on with his soliloquy.

"There's Sally," he said with flashing eyes; "the woman has spirit, determination, purpose—was she asleep, or petrified? She could have stabbed him—poisoned him safely. She might have seen this coming on. Why does she give me notice when it's too late? When he sat there—yonder there, over there—with his white face, and red head, and sickly smile, why didn't I know what was passing in his heart? It should have stopped beating that night, if I had been in his secret; or there are no drugs to lull a man to sleep, and no fire to burn him!"

Another draught from the bowl; and, cowering over the fire with a ferocious aspect, he muttered to himself again.

"And this, like every other trouble and anxiety I have had of late times, springs from that old dotard and his darling child—two wretched feeble wanderers! I'll be their evil genius yet. And you, sweet Kit, honest Kit, virtuous, innocent Kit, look to yourself. Where I hate, I bite. I hate you, my darling fellow, with good cause, and proud as you are to-night, I'll have my turn.—What's that!"

A knocking at the gate he had closed. A loud and violent knocking. Then a pause; as if those who knocked had stopped to listen. Then the noise again, more clamorous and importunate than before.

"So soon!" said the dwarf. "And so eager! I am afraid I shall disappoint you. It's well I'm quite prepared. Sally, I thank you!"

As he spoke, he extinguished the candle. In his impetuous attempts to subdue the brightness of the fire, he overset the stove, which came tumbling forward, and fell with a crash upon the burning embers it had shot forth in its descent, leaving the room in pitchy darkness. The noise at the gate still continuing, he felt his way to the door, and stepped into the open air.

At that moment the knocking ceased. It was about eight o'clock; but the dead of the darkest night would have been as noon-day, in comparison with the thick cloud which then rested upon the earth, and shrouded everything from view. He darted forward for a few paces, as if into the mouth of some dim, yawning cavern; then, thinking he had gone wrong, changed the direction of his steps; then stood still, not knowing where to turn.

"If they would knock again," said Quilp, trying to peer into the gloom by which he was surrounded, "the sound might guide me. Come. Batter the gate once more!"

He stood listening intently, but the noise was not renewed. Nothing was to be heard in that deserted place, but at intervals the distant barking of dogs. The sound was far away—now in one quarter, now answered in another—nor was it any guide, for it often came from shipboard, as he knew.

"If I could find a wall or fence," said the dwarf, stretching out his arms, and walking slowly on, "I should know which way to turn. A good, black, devil's night this, to have my dear friend here! If I had but that wish, it might, for anything I cared, never be day again."

As the word passed his lips, he staggered and fell; and next moment was fighting with the cold, dark water.

For all its bubbling up and rushing in his ears, he could hear the knocking at the gate again—could hear a shout that followed it—could recognise the voice. For all his struggling and plashing, he could understand that they had lost their way, and had wandered back to the point from which they started; that they were all but looking on while he was drowned; that they were close at hand, but could not make an effort to save him; that he himself had shut and barred them out. He answered the shout—with a yell, which seemed to make the hundred fires that danced before his eyes tremble and flicker as if a gust of wind had stirred them. It was of no avail. The strong tide filled his throat, and bore him on, upon its rapid current.

Another mortal struggle, and he was up again, beating the water with his hands, and looking out with wild and glaring eyes that showed him some black object he was drifting close upon. The hull of a ship! If he could touch its smooth and slippery surface with his hand. One loud cry now—but the resistless water bore him down before he could give it utterance, and, driving him under it, carried away a corpse.

It toyed and sported with its ghastly freight, now bruising it against the slimy piles, now hiding it in mud or long rank grass, now dragging it heavily over rough stones and gravel, now feigning to yield it to its own element, and in the same action luring it away, until, tired of the ugly plaything, it flung it on a swamp—a dismal place where pirates had swung in chains, through many a wintry night—and left it there to bleach.

And there it lay, alone. The sky was red with flame, and the water that bore it there had been tinged with the sullen light as it flowed along. The place the deserted carcase had left so recently, a living man, was now a blazing ruin. There was something of the glare upon its face. The hair, stirred by the damp breeze, played in a kind of mockery of death—such a mockery as the dead man himself would have revelled in when alive—about its head, and its dress fluttered idly in the night wind.

Chapter LXVIII

L IGHTED rooms, bright fires, cheerful faces, the music of glad voices, words of love and welcome, warm hearts, and tears of happiness—what a change is this! But it is to such delights that Kit is hastening. They are awaiting him, he knows. He fears he will die of joy before he gets among them.

They have prepared him for this, all day. He is not to be carried off to-morrow with the rest, they tell him first. By degrees they let him know that doubts have arisen, that inquiries are to be made, and perhaps he may be pardoned after all. At last, the evening being come, they bring him to a room where some gentlemen are assembled. Foremost among them is his good old master, who comes and takes him by the hand. He hears that his innocence is established, and that he is pardoned. He cannot see the speaker, but he turns towards the voice, and in trying to answer, falls down insensible.

They recover him again, and tell him he must be composed, and bear this like a man. Somebody says he must think of his poor mother. It is because he does think of her so much, that the happy news had overpowered him. They crowd about him, and tell him that the truth has gone abroad, and that all the town and country ring with sympathy for his misfortunes. He has no ears for this. His thoughts as yet have no wider range than home. Does *she* know it? what did she say? who told her? He can speak of nothing else.

They make him drink a little wine, and talk kindly to him for a while, until he is more collected, and can listen, and thank them. He is free to go. Mr Garland thinks, if he feels better, it is time they went away. The gentlemen cluster round him, and shake hands with him. He feels very grateful to them for the interest they have in him, and for the kind promises they make; but the power of speech is gone again, and he has much ado to keep his feet, even though leaning on his master's arm.

As they pass through the dismal passages, some officers of the jail who are in waiting there, congratulate him in their rough way on his release. The newsmonger is of the number, but his manner is not quite hearty—there is something of surliness in his compliments. He looks upon Kit as an intruder, as one who has obtained admission to that place on false pretences, who has enjoyed a privilege without being duly qualified. He may be a very good sort of young man, he thinks but he has no business there, and the sooner he is gone, the better.

The last door shuts behind them. They have passed the outer wall, and stand in the open air—in the street he has so often pictured to himself when hemmed in by those gloomy stones, and which has been in all his dreams. It seems wider and more busy than it used to be. The night is bad, and yet how cheerful and gay in his eyes! One of the gentlemen, in taking leave of him, pressed some money into his hand. He has not counted it; but when they had gone a few paces beyond the box for poor prisoners, he hastily returns and drops it in.

Mr Garland has a coach waiting in a neighbouring street, and, taking Kit inside with him, bids the man drive home. At first they can only travel at a foot pace, and then with torches going on before, because of the heavy fog. But as they get farther from the river, and leave the closer portions of the town behind, they are able to dispense with this precaution and to proceed at a brisker rate. On the road, hard galloping would be too slow for Kit; but when they are drawing near their journey's end, he begs they may go more slowly, and when the house appears in sight, that they may stop—only for a minute or two, to give him time to breathe.

But there is no stopping then, for the old gentleman speaks stoutly to him, the horses mend their pace, and they are already at the garden gate. Next minute they are at the door. There is a noise of tongues, and tread of feet, inside. It opens. Kit rushes in, and finds his mother clinging round his neck.

And there, too, is the ever faithful Barbara's mother, still holding the baby as if she had never put it down since that sad day when they little hoped to have such joy as this—there she is, Heaven bless her, crying her eyes out, and sobbing as never woman sobbed before; and there is little Barbara—poor little Barbara, so much thinner and so much paler, and yet so very pretty—trembling like a leaf and supporting herself against the wall; and there is Mrs Garland, neater and nicer than ever, fainting away stone dead with nobody to help her; and there is Mr Abel, violently blowing his nose, and wanting to embrace everybody; and there is the single gentleman hovering round them all, and constant to nothing for an instant; and there is that good, dear, thoughtful little Jacob, sitting all alone by himself on the bottom stair, with his hands on his knees like an old man, roaring fearfully without giving any trouble to anybody; and each and all of them are for the time clean out of their wits, and so jointly and severally commit all manner of follies.

And even when the rest have in some measure come to themselves again, and can find words and smiles, Barbara—that soft-hearted, gentle, foolish little Barbara—is suddenly missed, and found to be in a swoon by herself in the back parlour, from which swoon she falls into hysterics, and from which hysterics into a swoon again, and is, indeed, so bad, that despite a mortal quantity of vinegar and cold water she is hardly a bit better at last than she was at first. Then Kit's mother comes in and says, will he come and speak to her; and Kit says "Yes," and goes; and he says in a kind voice "Barbara!" and Barbara's mother tells her that "it's only Kit"; and Barbara says (with her eyes closed all the time) "Oh! but is it him indeed?" and Barbara's mother says "To be sure it is, my dear; there's nothing the matter now." And in further assurance that he's safe and sound, Kit speaks to her again; and then Barbara goes off into another fit of laughter, and then into another fit of crying; and then Barbara's mother and Kit's mother nod to each other and pretend to scold her—but only to bring her to herself the faster, bless you—and being experienced matrons, and acute at perceiving the first dawning symptoms of recovery, they comfort Kit with the assurance that "she'll do now," and so dismiss him to the place from whence he came.

Well! In that place (which is the next room) there are decanters of wine, and all that sort of thing, set out as grand as if Kit and his friends were first-rate company; and there is little Jacob, walking, as the popular phrase is, into a home-made plum-cake at a most surprising pace, and keeping his eye on the figs and oranges which are to follow, and making the best use of his time, you may believe. Kit no sooner comes in, than that single gentleman (never was such a busy gentleman) charges all the glasses—bumpers—and drinks his health, and tells him he shall never want a friend while he lives; and so does Mr Garland, and so does Mrs Garland, and so does Mr Abel. But even this honour and distinction is not all, for the single gentleman forthwith pulls out of his pocket a massive silver watch—going hard, and right to half a second—and upon the back of this watch is engraved Kit's name, with flourishes all over; and in short it is Kit's watch, bought expressly for him, and presented to him on the spot. You may rest assured that Mr and Mrs Garland can't help hinting about their present in store, and that Mr Abel tells outright that he has his; and that Kit is the happiest of the happy.

There is one friend he has not seen yet, and as he cannot be conveniently introduced into the family circle, by reason of his being an iron-shod quadruped, Kit takes the first opportunity of slipping away and hurrying to the stable. The moment he lays his hand upon the latch, the pony neighs the loudest pony's greeting; before he has crossed the threshold, the pony is capering about his loose box (for he brooks not the indignity of a halter), mad to give him welcome; and when Kit goes up to caress and pat him, the pony rubs his nose against his coat, and fondles him more lovingly than ever pony fondled man. It is the crowning circumstance of his earnest, heartfelt reception; and Kit fairly puts his arm round Whisker's neck and hugs him.

But how comes Barbara to trip in there? and how smart she is again! she has been at her glass since she recovered. How comes Barbara in the stable, of all places in the world? Why, since Kit has been away, the pony would take his food from nobody but her, and Barbara, you see, not dreaming Christopher was there, and just looking in to see that everything was right, has come upon him unawares. Blushing little Barbara!

It may be that Kit has caressed the pony enough; it may be that there are even better things to caress than ponies. He leaves him for Barbara at any rate, and hopes she is better. Yes. Barbara is a great deal better. She is afraid—and here Barbara looks down and blushes more—that he must have thought her very foolish. "Not at all," says Kit. Barbara is glad of that, and coughs—Hem!—just the slightest cough possible—not more than that.

What a discreet pony, when he chooses! He is as quiet now, as if he were of marble. He has a very knowing look, but that he always has. "We have hardly had time to shake hands, Barbara," says Kit. Barbara gives him hers. Why, she is trembling now! Foolish, fluttering Barbara!

Arm's length! The length of an arm is not much. Barbara's was not a long arm by any means, and besides, she didn't hold it out straight, but bent a little. Kit was so near her when they shook hands, that he could see a small tiny tear, yet trembling on an eyelash. It was natural that he should look at it, unknown to Barbara. It was natural that Barbara should raise her eyes unconsciously, and find him out. Was it natural that at that instant, without any previous impulse or design, Kit should kiss Barbara? He did it, whether or no. Barbara said "for shame," but let him do it too—twice. He might have done it thrice, but the pony kicked up his heels and shook his head, as if he were suddenly taken with convulsions of delight, and Barbara being frightened, ran away—not straight to where her mother and Kit's mother were, though, lest they should see how red her cheeks were, and should ask her why. Sly little Barbara!

When the first transports of the whole party had subsided, and Kit and his mother, and Barbara and her mother, with little Jacob and the baby to boot, had had their suppers together—which there was no hurrying over, for they were going to stop there all night—Mr Garland called Kit to him, and taking him into a room where they could be alone, told him that he had something yet to say, which would surprise him greatly. Kit looked so anxious and turned so pale on hearing this, that the old gentleman hastened to add, he would be agreeably surprised; and asked him if he would be ready next morning for a journey.

"For a journey, sir!" cried Kit.

"In company with me and my friend in the next room. Can you guess its purpose?"

Kit turned paler yet, and shook his head.

"Oh, yes. I think you do already," said his master. "Try."

Kit murmured something rather rambling and unintelligible, but he plainly pronounced the words "Miss Nell," three or four times—shaking his head while he did so, as if he would add there was no hope of that.

But Mr Garland, instead of saying "Try again," as Kit had made sure he would, told him very seriously that he had guessed right.

"The place of their retreat is indeed discovered," he said, "at last. And that is our journey's end."

Kit faltered out such questions as, where was it, and how had it been found, and how long since, and was she well, and happy.

"Happy she is, beyond all doubt," said Mr Garland. "And well, I—I trust she will be soon. She has been weak and ailing, as I learn, but she was better when I heard this morning, and they were full of hope. Sit you down, and you shall hear the rest."

Scarcely venturing to draw his breath, Kit did as he was told. Mr Garland then related to him, how he had a brother (of whom he would remember to have heard him speak, and whose picture, taken when he was a young man, hung in the best room), and how this brother lived a long way off in a country-place, with an old clergyman who had been his early friend. How, although they loved each other as brothers should, they had not met for many years, but had communicated by letter from time to time, always looking forward to some period when they would take each other by the hand once more, and still letting the Present time steal on, as it was the habit of men to do, and suffering the Future to melt into the Past. How this brother, whose temper was very mild and quiet and retiring—such as Mr Abel's—was greatly beloved by the simple people among whom he dwelt, who quite revered the Bachelor (for so they called him), and had every one experienced his charity and benevolence. How even those slight circumstances had come to his knowledge, very slowly and in course of years, for the Bachelor was one of those whose goodness shuns the light, and who have more pleasure in discovering and extolling the good deeds of others, than in trumpeting their own, be they never so commendable. How, for that reason, he seldom told them of his village friends; but how, for all that, his mind had become so full of two among them—a child and an old man, to whom he had been very kind—that, in a letter received a few days before, he had dwelt upon them from first to last, and had told there such a tale of their wanderings, and mutual love, that few could read it without being moved to tears. How he, the recipient of that letter, was directly led to the belief that these must be the very wanderers for whom so much search had been made, and whom Heaven had directed to his brother's care. How he had written for such further information as would put the fact beyond all doubt; how it had that morning arrived; had confirmed his first impression into a certainty; and was the immediate cause of that journey being planned, which they were to take tomorrow.

"In the meantime," said the old gentleman rising, and laying his hand on Kit's shoulder, "you have great need of rest, for such a day as this would wear out the strongest man. Good night, and Heaven send our journey may have a prosperous ending!"

Chapter LXIX

K IT was no sluggard next morning, but, springing from his bed some time before day, began to prepare for his welcome expedition. The hurry of spirits consequent upon the events of yesterday, and the unexpected intelligence he had heard at night, had troubled his sleep through the long dark hours, and summoned such uneasy dreams about his pillow that it was rest to rise.

But had it been the beginning of some great labour with the same end in view—had it been the commencement of a long journey, to be performed on foot in that inclement season of the year; to be pursued under every privation and difficulty; and to be achieved only with great distress, fatigue, and suffering—had it been the dawn of some painful enterprise, certain to task his utmost powers of resolution and endurance, and to need his utmost fortitude, but only likely to end, if happily achieved, in good fortune and delight to Nell—Kit's cheerful zeal would have been as highly roused, Kit's ardour and impatience would have been at least the same.

Nor was he alone excited and eager. Before he had been up a quarter of an hour the whole house were astir and busy. Everybody hurried to do something towards facilitating the preparations. The single gentleman, it is true, could do nothing himself, but he overlooked everybody else and was more locomotive than anybody. The work of packing and making ready went briskly on, and by daybreak every preparation for the journey was completed. Then Kit began to wish they had not been quite so nimble; for the travelling carriage which had been hired for the occasion was not to arrive until nine o'clock, and there was nothing but breakfast to fill up the intervening blank of one hour and a half.

Yes there was, though. There was Barbara. Barbara was busy, to be sure, but so much the better—Kit could help her, and that would pass away the time better than any means that could be devised. Barbara had no objection to this arrangement, and Kit, tracking out the idea which had come upon him so suddenly overnight, began to think that surely Barbara was fond of him, and surely he was fond of Barbara.

Now, Barbara, if the truth must be told—as it must and ought to be—Barbara seemed, of all the little household, to take least pleasure in the bustle of the occasion; and when Kit, in the openness of his heart, told her how glad and overjoyed it made him, Barbara became more downcast still, and seemed to have even less pleasure in it than before!

"You have not been home so long, Christopher," said Barbara—and it is impossible to tell how carelessly she said it—"You have not been home so long, that you need be glad to go away again, I should think."

"But for such a purpose," returned Kit. "To bring back Miss Nell! To see her again! Only think of that! I am so pleased too to think that you will see her, Barbara, at last."

Barbara did not absolutely say that she felt no great gratification on this point, but she expressed the sentiment so plainly by one little toss of her head, that Kit was quite disconcerted, and wondered in his simplicity why she was so cool about it.

"You'll say she has the sweetest and beautifullest face you ever saw, I know," said Kit, rubbing his hands. "I'm sure you'll say that!"

Barbara tossed her head again.

"What's the matter, Barbara?" said Kit.

"Nothing," cried Barbara. And Barbara pouted—not sulkily, or in an ugly manner, but just enough to make her look more cherry-lipped than ever.

There is no school in which a pupil gets on so fast, as that in which Kit became a scholar when he gave Barbara the kiss. He saw what Barbara meant now—he had his lesson by heart all at once—she was the book—there it was before him as plain as print.

"Barbara," said Kit, "you're not cross with me?"

Oh, dear, no! Why should Barbara be cross? And what right had she to be cross? And what did it matter whether she was cross or no? Who minded *her!*

"Why, *I* do," said Kit. "Of course I do."

Barbara didn't see why it was of course, at all.

Kit was sure she must. Would she think again?

Certainly, Barbara would think again. No, she didn't see why it was of course. She didn't understand what Christopher meant. And besides she was sure they wanted her upstairs by this time, and she must go, indeed——

"No, but Barbara," said Kit, detaining her gently, "let us part friends. I was always thinking of you, in my troubles. I should have been a great deal more miserable than I was, if it hadn't been for you."

Goodness gracious, how pretty Barbara was when she coloured—and when she trembled, like a little shrinking bird!

"I am telling you the truth, Barbara, upon my word, but not half so strong as I could wish," said Kit earnestly. "When I want you to be pleased to see Miss Nell, it's only because I like you to be pleased with what pleases me—that's all. As to her, Barbara, I think I could almost die to do her service, but you would think so too if you knew her as I do. I am sure you would."

Barbara was touched, and sorry to have appeared indifferent.

"I have been used, you see," said Kit, "to talk and think of her, almost as if she was an angel. When I look forward to meeting her again, I think of her smiling as she used to do, and being glad to see me, and putting out her hand and saying, 'It's my own old Kit,' or some such words as those—like what she used to say. I think of seeing her happy, and with friends about her, and brought up as she deserves, and as she ought to be. When I think of myself, it's as her old servant, and one that loved her dearly, as his kind, good, gentle mistress; and who would have gone—yes, and still would go—through any harm to serve her. Once I couldn't help being afraid that if she came back with friends about her she might forget, or be ashamed of having known, a humble lad like me, and so speak coldly, which would have cut me, Barbara, deeper than I can tell. But when I came to think again, I felt sure that I was doing her wrong in this; and so I went on as I did at first, hoping to see her once more, just as she used to be. Hoping this, and remembering what she was, has made me feel as if I would always try to please her, and always be what I should like to seem to her if I was still her servant. If I'm the better for that—and I don't think I'm the worse—I am grateful to her for it, and love and honour her the more. That's the plain honest truth, dear Barbara, upon my word it is!"

Little Barbara was not of a wayward or capricious nature, and, being full of remorse, melted into tears. To what further conversation this might have led, we need not stop to inquire; for the wheels of the carriage were heard at that moment, and, being followed by a smart ring at the garden gate, caused the bustle in the house, which had lain dormant for a short time, to burst again into tenfold life and vigour.

Simultaneously with the travelling equipage, arrived Mr. Chuckster in a hackney-cab, with certain papers and supplies of money for the single gentleman, into whose hands he delivered them. This duty discharged, he subsided into the bosom of the family; and entertaining himself with a strolling or peripatetic breakfast, watched with a genteel indifference the process of loading the carriage.

"Snobby's in this I see, sir?" he said to Mr Abel Garland. "I thought he wasn't in the last trip because it was expected that his presence wouldn't be very acceptable to the ancient buffalo."

"To whom, sir?" demanded Mr Abel.

"To the old gentleman," returned Mr. Chuckster, slightly abashed.

"Our client prefers to take him now," said Mr Abel drily. "There is no longer any need for that precaution, as my father's relationship to a gentleman in whom the objects of his search have full confidence, will be a sufficient guarantee for the friendly nature of their errand."

"Ah!" thought Mr. Chuckster, looking out of window, "anybody but me! Snobby before me, of course. He didn't happen to take that particular five-pound note, but I have not the smallest doubt that he's always up to something of that sort. I always said it, long before this came out. Devilish pretty girl that! 'Pon my soul, an amazing little creature!"

Barbara was the subject of Mr. Chuckster's commendations; and as she was lingering near the carriage (all being now ready for its departure), that gentleman was suddenly seized with a strong interest in the proceedings, which impelled him to swagger down the garden, and take up his position at a convenient ogling distance. Having had great experience of the sex, and being perfectly acquainted with all those little artifices which find the readiest road to their hearts, Mr. Chuckster, on taking his ground, planted one hand on his hip, and with the other adjusted his flowing hair. This is a favourite attitude in the polite circles, and accompanied with a graceful whistling has been known to do immense execution.

Such, however, is the difference between town and country, that nobody took the smallest notice of this insinuating figure; the wretches being wholly engaged in bidding the travellers farewell, in kissing hands to each other, waving handkerchiefs, and the like tame and vulgar practices. For now the single gentleman and Mr Garland were in the carriage, and the postboy was in the saddle, and Kit, well wrapped and muffled up, was in the rumble behind; and Mrs Garland was there, and Mr Abel was there, and Kit's mother was there, and little Jacob was there, and Barbara's mother was visible in remote perspective, nursing the ever-wakeful baby; and all were nodding, beckoning, curtseying, or crying out "Good-bye!" with all the energy they could express. In another minute, the carriage was out of sight; and Mr. Chuckster remained alone upon the spot where it had lately been, with a vision of Kit standing up in the rumble waving his hand to Barbara, and of Barbara in the full light and lustre of his eyes—*his* eyes—Chuckster's—Chuckster the successful—on whom ladies of quality had looked with favour from phaetons in the parks on Sundays—waving hers to Kit!

How Mr. Chuckster, entranced by this monstrous fact, stood for some time rooted to the earth, protesting within himself that Kit was the Prince of felonious characters, and very Emperor or Great Mogul of Snobs, and how he clearly traced this revolting circumstance back to that old villainy of the shilling, are matters foreign to our purpose; which is to track the rolling wheels, and bear the travellers company on their cold, bleak journey.

It was a bitter day. A keen wind was blowing, and rushed against them fiercely: bleaching the hard ground, shaking the white frost from the trees and hedges, and whirling it away like dust. But little cared Kit for weather. There was a freedom and freshness in the wind, as it came howling by, which, let it cut never so sharp, was welcome. As it swept on with its cloud of frost, bearing down the dry twigs and boughs and withered leaves, and carrying them away pell-mell, it seemed as though some general sympathy had got abroad, and everything was in a hurry like themselves. The harder the gusts, the better progress they appeared to make. It was a good thing to go struggling and fighting forward, vanquishing them one by one; to watch them driving up, gathering strength and fury as they came along; to bend for a moment, as they whistled past; and then to look back and see them speed away, their hoarse noise dying in the distance, and the stout trees cowering down before them.

All day long it blew without cessation. The night was clear and starlight, but the wind had not fallen, and the cold was piercing. Sometimes—towards the end of a long stage—Kit could not help wishing it were a little warmer: but when they stopped to change horses, and he had had a good run; and what with that, and the bustle of paying the old postilion, and rousing the new one, and running to and from again until the horses were put to, he was so warm that the blood tingled and smarted in his fingers' ends; then he felt as if to have it one degree less cold would be to lose half the delight and glory of the journey: and up he jumped again right cheerily, singing to the merry music of the wheels as they rolled away, and, leaving the townspeople in their warm beds, pursued their course along the lonely road.

Meantime the two gentlemen inside, who were little disposed to sleep, beguiled the time with conversation. As both were anxious and expectant, it naturally turned upon the subject of their expedition, on the manner in which it had been brought about, and on the hopes and fears they entertained respecting it. Of the former they had many, of the latter few—none perhaps beyond that indefinable uneasiness which is inseparable from suddenly awakened hope, and protracted expectation.

In one of the pauses of their discourse, and when half the night had worn away, the single gentleman, who had gradually become more and more silent and thoughtful, turned to his companion and said abruptly:

"Are you a good listener?"

"Like most other men, I suppose," returned Mr Garland, smiling. "I can be, if I am interested; and if not interested I should still try to appear so. Why do you ask?"

"I have a short narrative on my lips," rejoined his friend, "and will try you with it. It is very brief."

Pausing for no reply, he laid his hand on the old gentleman's sleeve, and proceeded thus:

"There were once two brothers, who loved each other dearly. There was a disparity in their ages—some twelve years. I am not sure but they may insensibly have loved each other the better for that reason. Wide as the interval between them was, however, they became rivals too soon. The deepest and strongest affection of both their hearts settled upon one object.

"The youngest—there were reasons for *his* being sensitive and watchful—was the first to find this out. I will not tell you what misery he underwent, what agony of soul he knew, how great his mental struggle was. He had been a sickly child. His brother, patient and considerate in the midst of his own high health and strength, had many and many a day denied himself the sports he loved, to sit beside his couch, telling him old stories till his pale face lighted up with an unwonted glow; to carry him in his arms to some green spot, where he could tend the poor pensive boy as he looked upon the bright summer day, and saw all nature healthy but himself; to be in any way his fond and faithful nurse. I may not dwell on all he did, to make the poor, weak creature love him, or my tale would have no end. But when the time of trial came, the younger brother's heart was full of those old days. Heaven strengthened it to repay the sacrifices of inconsiderate youth by one of thoughtful manhood. He left his brother to be happy. The truth never passed his lips, and he quitted the country, hoping to die abroad.

"The elder brother married her. She was in Heaven before long, and left him with an infant daughter.

"If you have seen the picture-gallery of any one old family, you will remember how the same face and figure—often the fairest and slightest of them all—come upon you in different generations; and how you trace the same sweet girl through a long line of portraits—never growing old or changing—the Good Angel of the race—abiding by them in all reverses—redeeming all their sins——

"In this daughter the mother lived again. You may judge with what devotion he who lost that mother almost in the winning, clung to this girl, her breathing image. She grew to womanhood, and gave her heart to one who could not know its worth. Well! Her fond father could not see her pine and droop. He might be more deserving than he thought him. He surely might become so with a wife like her. He joined their hands, and they were married.

"Through all the misery that followed this union; through all the cold neglect and undeserved reproach; through all the poverty he brought upon her; through all the struggles of their daily life, too mean and pitiful to tell, but dreadful to endure; she toiled on, in the deep devotion of her spirit, and in her better nature, as only women can. Her means and substance wasted; her father nearly beggared by her husband's hand, and the hourly witness (for they lived now under one roof) of her ill-usage and unhappiness—she never, but for him, bewailed her fate. Patient, and upheld by strong affection to the last, she died a widow of some three weeks' date, leaving to her father's care two orphans; one a son of ten or twelve years old; the other a girl—such another infant child—the same in helplessness, in age, in form, in feature—as she had been herself when her young mother died.

"The elder brother, grandfather to these two children, was now a broken man; crushed and borne down, less by the weight of years than by the heavy hand of sorrow. With the wreck of his possessions, he began to trade—in pictures first, and then in curious ancient things. He had entertained a fondness for such matters from a boy, and the tastes he had cultivated were now to yield him an anxious and precarious subsistence.

"The boy grew like his father in mind and person; the girl so like her mother, that when the old man had her on his knee, and looked into her mild blue eyes, he felt as if awakening from a wretched dream, and his daughter were a little child again. The wayward boy soon spurned the shelter of his roof, and sought associates more congenial to his taste. The old man and the child dwelt alone together.

"It was then, when the love of two dead people who had been nearest and dearest to his heart, was all transferred to this slight creature; when her face, constantly before him, reminded him from hour to hour of the too early change he had seen in such another—of all the suffering he had watched and known, and all his child had undergone; when the young man's profligate and hardened course drained him of money as his father's had, and even sometimes occasioned them temporary privation and distress; it was then that there began to beset him, and to be ever in his mind, a gloomy dread of poverty and want. He had no thought for himself in this. His fear was for the child. It was a spectre in his house, and haunted him night and day.

"The younger brother had been a traveller in many countries, and had made his pilgrimage through life alone. His voluntary banishment had been misconstrued, and he had borne (not without pain) reproach and slight for doing that which had wrung his heart, and cast a mournful shadow on his path. Apart from this, communication between him and the elder was difficult, and uncertain, and often failed; still it was not so wholly broken off but that he learnt—with long blanks and gaps between each interval of information—all that I have told you now.

"Then, dreams of their young, happy life—happy to him though laden with pain and early care—visited his pillow yet oftener than before; and every night, a boy again, he was at his brother's side. With the utmost speed he could exert, he settled his affairs; converted into money all the goods he had; and, with honourable wealth enough for both, with open heart and hand, with limbs that trembled as they bore him on, with emotion such as men can hardly bear and live, arrived one evening at his brother's door!"

The narrator, whose voice had faltered lately, stopped. "The rest," said Mr Garland, pressing his hand, "I know."

"Yes," rejoined his friend, after a pause, "we may spare ourselves the sequel. You know the poor result of all my search. Even when, by dint of such inquiries as the utmost vigilance and sagacity could set on foot, we found they had been seen with two poor travelling showmen; and in time discovered the men themselves—and in time, the actual place of their retreat; even then, we were too late. Pray God we are not too late again!"

"We cannot be," said Mr Garland. "This time we must succeed."

"I have believed and hoped so," returned the other. "I try to believe and hope so still. But a heavy weight has fallen on my spirits, my good friend, and the sadness that gathers over me, will yield to neither hope nor reason."

"That does not surprise me," said Mr Garland; "it is a natural consequence of the events you have recalled; of this dreary time and place; and above all, of this wild and dismal night. A dismal night, indeed! Hark! how the wind is howling!"

Chapter LXX

DAY broke, and found them still upon their way. Since leaving home, they had halted here and there for necessary refreshment, and had frequently been delayed, especially in the night-time, by waiting for fresh horses. They had made no other stoppages, but the weather continued rough, and the roads were often steep and heavy. It would be night again before they reached their place of destination.

Kit, all bluff and hardened with the cold, went on manfully; and having enough to do to keep his blood circulating, to picture to himself the happy end of this adventurous journey, and to look about him and be amazed at everything, had little spare time for thinking of discomforts. Though his impatience, and that of his fellow-travellers, rapidly increased as the day waned, the hours did not stand still. The short daylight of winter soon faded away, and it was dark again when they had yet many miles to travel.

As it grew dusk, the wind fell; its distant moanings were more low and mournful; and as it came creeping up the road, and rattling covertly among the dry brambles on either hand, it seemed like some great phantom for whom the way was narrow, whose garments rustled as it stalked along. By degrees it lulled and died away; and then it came on to snow.

The flakes fell fast and thick, soon covering the ground some inches deep, and spreading abroad a solemn stillness. The rolling wheels were noiseless; and the sharp ring and clatter of the horses' hoofs became a dull, muffled tramp. The life of their progress seemed to be slowly hushed, and something deathlike to usurp its place.

Shading his eyes from the falling snow, which froze upon their lashes and obscured his sight, Kit often tried to catch the earliest glimpse of twinkling lights denoting their approach to some not distant town. He could descry objects enough at such times, but none correctly. Now a tall church-spire appeared in view, which presently became a tree, a barn, a shadow on the ground, thrown on it by their own bright lamps. Now there were horsemen, foot-passengers, carriages, going on before, or meeting them in narrow ways; which, when they were close upon them, turned to shadows too. A wall, a ruin, a sturdy gable-end, would rise up in the road; and when they were plunging headlong at it, would be the road itself. Strange turnings too, bridges, and sheets of water, appeared to start up here and there, making the way doubtful and uncertain; and yet they were on the same bare road, and these things, like the others, as they were passed, turned into dim illusions.

He descended slowly from his seat—for his limbs were numbed—when they arrived at a lone posting-house, and inquired how far they had to go to reach their journey's end. It was a late hour in such by-places, and the people were abed; but a voice answered from an upper window, "Ten miles." The ten minutes that ensued appeared an hour; but at the end of that time, a shivering figure led out the horses they required, and after another brief delay they were again in motion.

It was a cross-country road, full, after the first three or four miles, of holes and cart-ruts, which, being covered by the snow, were so many pitfalls to the trembling horses, and obliged them to keep a footpace. As it was next to impossible for men so much agitated as they were by this time, to sit still and move so slowly, all three got out and plodded on behind the carriage. The distance seemed interminable, and the walk was most laborious. As each was thinking within himself that the driver must have lost his way, a church bell, close at hand, struck the hour of midnight, and the carriage stopped. It had moved softly enough, but when it ceased to crunch the snow, the silence was as startling as if some great noise had been replaced by perfect stillness.

"This is the place, gentlemen," said the driver, dismounting from his horse, and knocking at the door of a little inn. "Halloa! Past twelve o'clock is the dead of night here."

The knocking was loud and long, but it failed to rouse the drowsy inmates. All continued dark and silent as before. They fell back a little, and looked up at the windows, which were mere black patches in the whitened house front. No light appeared. The house might have been deserted, or the sleepers dead, for any air of life it had about it.

They spoke together, with a strange inconsistency, in whispers; unwilling to disturb again the dreary echoes they had just now raised.

"Let us go on," said the younger brother, "and leave this good fellow to wake them, if he can. I cannot rest until I know that we are not too late. Let us go on, in the name of Heaven!"

They did so, leaving the postilion to order such accommodation as the house afforded, and to renew his knocking. Kit accompanied them with a little bundle, which he had hung in the carriage when they left home, and had not forgotten since—the bird in his old cage—just as she had left him. She would be glad to see her bird, he knew.

The road wound gently downward. As they proceeded, they lost sight of the church whose clock they had heard, and of the small village clustering round it. The knocking, which was now renewed, and which in that stillness they could plainly hear, troubled them. They wished the man would forbear, or that they had told him not to break the silence until they returned.

The old church-tower, clad in a ghostly garb of pure cold white, again rose up before them, and a few moments brought them close beside it. A venerable building— grey, even in the midst of the hoary landscape. An ancient sun-dial on the belfry wall was nearly hidden by the snow-drift, and scarcely to be known for what it was. Time itself seemed to have grown dull and old, as if no day were ever to displace the melancholy night.

A wicket-gate was close at hand, but there was more than one path across the churchyard to which it led, and, uncertain which to take, they came to a stand again.

The village street—if street that could be called which was an irregular cluster of poor cottages of many heights and ages, some with their fronts, some with their backs, and some with gable-ends towards the road, with here and there a signpost, or a shed encroaching on the path—was close at hand. There was a faint light in a chamber window not far off, and Kit ran towards that house to ask their way.

His first shout was answered by an old man within, who presently appeared at the casement, wrapping some garment round his throat as a protection from the cold, and demanded who was abroad at that unseasonable hour, wanting him.

" 'Tis hard weather this," he grumbled, "and not a night to call me up in. My trade is not of that kind that I need be roused from bed. The business on which folks want me, will keep cold, especially at this season. What do you want?"

"I would not have roused you, if I had known you were old and ill," said Kit.

"Old!" repeated the other peevishly. "How do you know I am old? Not so old as you think, friend, perhaps. As to being ill, you will find many young people in worse case than I am. More's the pity that it should be so—not that I should be strong and hearty for my years, I mean, but that they should be weak and tender. I ask your pardon, though," said the old man, "if I spoke rather rough at first. My eyes are not good at night—that's neither age nor illness; they never were—and I didn't see you were a stranger."

"I am sorry to call you from your bed," said Kit, "but those gentlemen you may see by the churchyard gate are strangers too, who have just arrived from a long journey, and seek the parsonage-house. You can direct us?"

"I should be able to," answered the old man, in a trembling voice, "for come next summer I have been sexton here good fifty years. The right-hand path, friend, is the road.—There is no ill news for our good gentleman, I hope?"

Kit thanked him, and made him a hasty answer in the negative; he was turning back, when his attention was caught by the voice of a child. Looking up, he saw a very little creature at a neighbouring window.

"What is that?" cried the child earnestly. "Has my dream come true? Pray speak to me, whoever that is, awake and up."

"Poor boy!" said the sexton, before Kit could answer, "how goes it, darling?"

"Has my dream come true?" exclaimed the child again, in a voice so fervent that it might have thrilled the heart of any listener. "But no, that can never be. How could it be—oh! how could it!"

"I guess his meaning," said the sexton. "To thy bed again, dear boy!"

"Ay!" cried the child, in a burst of despair, "I knew it could never be, I felt too sure of that, before I asked. But, all to-night and last night too, it was the same. I never fall asleep, but that cruel dream comes back."

"Try to sleep again," said the old man soothingly. "It will go, in time."

"No, no, I would rather that it staid—cruel as it is, I would rather that it staid," rejoined the child. "I am not afraid to have it in my sleep, but I am so sad—so very, very sad."

The old man blessed him, the child in tears replied good night, and Kit was again alone.

He hurried back, moved by what he had heard, though more by the child's manner than by anything he had said, as his meaning was hidden from him. They took the path indicated by the sexton, and soon arrived before the parsonage wall. Turning round to look about them when they had got thus far, they saw, among some ruined buildings at a distance, one single solitary light.

It shone from what appeared to be an old oriel window, and being surrounded by the deep shadows of overhanging walls, sparkled like a star. Bright and glimmering as the stars above their heads, lonely and motionless as they, it seemed to claim some kindred with the eternal lamps of Heaven, and to burn in fellowship with them.

"What light is that!" exclaimed the younger brother.

"It is surely," said Mr Garland, "in the ruin where they live. I see no other ruin hereabouts."

"They cannot," returned the brother hastily, "be waking at this late hour——"

Kit interposed directly, and begged that, while they rang and waited at the gate, they would let him make his way to where this light was shining and try to ascertain if any people were about. Obtaining the permission he desired, he darted off with breathless eagerness, and, still carrying the birdcage in his hand, made straight towards the spot.

It was not easy to hold that pace among the graves, and at another time he might have gone more slowly, or round by the path. Unmindful of all obstacles, however, he pressed forward without slackening his speed, and soon arrived within a few yards of the window.

He approached as softly as he could, and advancing so near the wall as to brush the whitened ivy with his dress, listened. There was no sound inside. The church itself was not more quiet. Touching the glass with his cheek, he listened again. No. And yet there was such a silence all around, that he felt sure he could have heard even the breathing of a sleeper, if there had been one there.

A strange circumstance, a light in such a place at that time of night, with no one near it.

A curtain was drawn across the lower portion of the window, and he could not see into the room. But there was no shadow thrown upon it from within. To have gained a footing on the wall and tried to look in from above, would have been attended with some danger—certainly with some noise, and the chance of terrifying the child, if that really were her habitation. Again and again he listened; again and again the same wearisome blank.

Leaving the spot with slow and cautious steps, and skirting the ruin for a few paces, he came at length to a door. He knocked. No answer. But there was a curious noise inside. It was difficult to determine what it was. It bore a resemblance to the low moaning of one in pain, but it was not that, being far too regular and constant. Now it seemed a kind of song, now a wail—seemed, that is, to his changing fancy, for the sound itself was never changed or checked. It was unlike anything he had ever heard, and in its tone there was something fearful, chilling, and unearthly.

The listener's blood ran colder now than ever it had done in frost and snow, but he knocked again. There was no answer, and the sound went on without any interruption. He laid his hand softly upon the latch, and put his knee against the door. It was not secured on the inside, but yielded to the pressure, and turned upon its hinges. He saw the glimmering of a fire upon the old walls, and entered.

Chapter LXXI

THE dull, red glow of a wood fire—for no lamp or candle burnt within the room— showed him a figure, seated on the hearth with its back towards him, bending over the fitful light. The attitude was that of one who sought the heat. It was, and yet was not. The stooping posture and the cowering form were there, but no hands were stretched out to meet the grateful warmth, no shrug or shiver compared its luxury with the piercing cold outside. With limbs huddled together, head bowed down, arms crossed upon the breast, and fingers tightly clenched, it rocked to and fro upon its seat without a moment's pause, accompanying the action with the mournful sound he had heard.

The heavy door closed behind him on his entrance, with a crash that made him start. The figure neither spoke nor turned to look, nor gave in any other way the faintest sign of having heard the noise. The form was that of an old man, his white head akin in colour to the mouldering embers upon which he gazed. He, and the failing light and dying fire, the time-worn room, the solitude, the wasted life, and gloom, were all in fellowship. Ashes, and dust, and ruin!

Kit tried to speak, and did pronounce some words, though what they were he scarcely knew. Still the same terrible low cry went on—still the same rocking in the chair—the same stricken figure was there, unchanged and heedless of his presence.

He had his hand upon the latch, when something in the form—distinctly seen as one log broke and fell, and, as it fell, blazed up—arrested it. He returned to where he had stood before—advanced a pace—another—another still. Another, and he saw the face. Yes! Changed as it was, he knew it well.

"Master!" he cried, stooping on one knee and catching at his hand. "Dear master. Speak to me!"

The old man turned slowly towards him; and muttered, in a hollow voice,

"This is another!—How many of these spirits there have been to-night!"

"No spirit, master. No one but your old servant. You know me now, I am sure? Miss Nell—where is she—where is she?"

"They all say that!" cried the old man. "They all ask the same question. A spirit!"

"Where is she?" demanded Kit. "Oh, tell me but that—but that, dear master!"

"She is asleep—yonder—in there."

"Thank God!"

"Ay! Thank God!" returned the old man. "I have prayed to Him, many, and many, and many a livelong night, when she has been asleep. He knows. Hark! Did she call?"

"I heard no voice."

"You did. You hear her now. Do you tell me that you don't hear *that?*"

He started up, and listened again.

"Nor that?" he cried, with a triumphant smile. "Can anybody know that voice so well as I! Hush! hush!"

Motioning to him to be silent, he stole away into another chamber. After a short absence (during which he could be heard to speak in a softened soothing tone) he returned, bearing in his hand a lamp.

"She is still asleep," he whispered. "You were right. She did not call—unless she did so in her slumber. She has called to me in her sleep before now, sir; as I sat by, watching, I have seen her lips move, and have known, though no sound came from them, that she spoke of me. I feared the light might dazzle her eyes and wake her, so I brought it here."

He spoke rather to himself than to the visitor, but when he had put the lamp upon the table, he took it up, as if impelled by some momentary recollection or curiosity, and held it near his face. Then, as if forgetting his motive in the very action, he turned away and put it down again.

"She is sleeping soundly," he said; "but no wonder. Angel hands have strewn the ground deep with snow, that the lightest footstep may be lighter yet; and the very birds are dead, that they may not wake her. She used to feed them, sir. Though never so cold and hungry, the timid things would fly from us. They never flew from her!"

Again he stopped to listen, and scarcely drawing breath, listened for a long, long time. That fancy past, he opened an old chest, took out some clothes as fondly as if they had been living things, and began to smooth and brush them with his hand.

"Why dost thou lie so idle there, dear Nell," he murmured, "when there are bright red berries out of doors waiting for thee to pluck them! Why dost thou lie so idle there, when thy little friends come creeping to the door, crying 'Where is Nell—sweet Nell?'—and sob, and weep, because they do not see thee. She was always gentle with children. The wildest would do her bidding—she had a tender way with them, indeed she had!"

Kit had no power to speak. His eyes were filled with tears.

"Her little homely dress—her favourite!" cried the old man, pressing it to his breast, and patting it with his shrivelled hand. "She will miss it when she wakes. They have hid it here in sport, but she shall have it—she shall have it. I would not vex my darling, for the wide world's riches. See here—these shoes—how worn they are—she kept them to remind her of our last long journey. You see where the little feet were bare upon the ground. They told me, afterwards, that the stones had cut and bruised them. *She* never told me that. No, no, God bless her! and, I have remembered since, she walked behind me, sir, that I might not see how lame she was—but yet she had my hand in hers, and seemed to lead me still."

He pressed them to his lips, and having carefully put them back again, went on communing with himself—looking wistfully from time to time towards the chamber he had lately visited.

"She was not wont to be a lie-abed; but she was well then. We must have patience. When she is well again, she will rise early, as she used to do, and ramble abroad in the healthy morning time. I often tried to track the way she had gone, but her small fairy footstep left no print upon the dewy ground, to guide me. Who is that? Shut the door. Quick!—Have we not enough to do to drive away that marble cold, and keep her warm!"

The door was indeed opened, for the entrance of Mr Garland and his friend, accompanied by two other persons. These were the schoolmaster, and the bachelor. The former held a light in his hand. He had, it seemed, but gone to his own cottage to replenish the exhausted lamp, at the moment when Kit came up and found the old man alone.

He softened again at sight of these two friends, and, laying aside the angry manner—if to anything so feeble and so sad the term can be applied—in which he had spoken when the door opened, resumed his former seat, and subsided, by little and little, into the old action, and the old, dull, wandering sound.

Of the strangers he took no heed whatever. He had seen them, but appeared quite incapable of interest or curiosity. The younger brother stood apart. The bachelor drew a chair towards the old man, and sat down close beside him. After a long silence, he ventured to speak.

"Another night, and not in bed!" he said softly; "I hoped you would be more mindful of your promise to me. Why do you not take some rest?"

"Sleep has left me," returned the old man. "It is all with her!"

"It would pain her very much to know that you were watching thus," said the bachelor. "You would not give her pain?"

"I am not so sure of that, if it would only rouse her. She has slept so very long. And yet I am rash to say so. It is a good and happy sleep—eh?"

"Indeed it is," returned the bachelor. "Indeed, indeed, it is!"

"That's well!—and the waking"—faltered the old man.

"Happy too. Happier than tongue can tell, or heart of man conceive."

They watched him as he rose and stole on tiptoe to the other chamber where the lamp had been replaced. They listened as he spoke again within its silent walls. They looked into the faces of each other, and no man's cheek was free from tears. He came back, whispering that she was still asleep, but that he thought she had moved. It was her hand, he said—a little—a very, very little—but he was pretty sure she had moved it—perhaps in seeking his. He had known her do that before now, though in the deepest sleep the while. And when he had said this, he dropped into his chair again, and, clasping his hands above his head, uttered a cry never to be forgotten.

The poor schoolmaster motioned to the bachelor that he would come upon the other side, and speak to him. They gently unlocked his fingers, which he had twisted in his grey hair, and pressed them in their own.

"He will hear me," said the schoolmaster, "I am sure. He will hear either me or you if we beseech him. She would, at all times."

"I will hear any voice she liked to hear," cried the old man. "I love all she loved!"

"I know you do," returned the schoolmaster. "I am certain of it. Think of her; think of all the sorrows and afflictions you have shared together; of all the trials, and all the peaceful pleasures, you have jointly known."

"I do. I do. I think of nothing else."

"I would have you think of nothing else to-night—of nothing but those things which will soften your heart, dear friend, and open it to old affections and old times. It is so that she would speak to you herself, and in her name it is that I speak now."

"You do well to speak softly," said the old man. "We will not wake her. I should be glad to see her eyes again, and to see her smile. There is a smile upon her young face now, but it is fixed and changeless. I would have it come and go. That shall be in Heaven's good time. We will not wake her."

"Let us not talk of her in her sleep, but as she used to be when you were journeying together, far away—as she was at home, in the old house from which you fled together—as she was in the old cheerful time," said the schoolmaster.

"She was always cheerful—very cheerful," cried the old man, looking steadfastly at him. "There was ever something mild and quiet about her, I remember, from the first; but she was of a happy nature."

"We have heard you say," pursued the schoolmaster, "that in this, and in all goodness, she was like her mother. You can think of, and remember her?"

He maintained his steadfast look, but gave no answer.

"Or even one before her," said the bachelor. "It is many years ago, and affliction makes the time longer, but you have not forgotten her whose death contributed to make this child so dear to you, even before you knew her worth or could read her heart? Say, that you could carry back your thoughts to very distant days—to the time of your early life—when, unlike this fair flower, you did not pass your youth alone. Say, that you could remember, long ago, another child who loved you dearly, you being but a child yourself. Say, that you had a brother, long forgotten, long unseen, long separated from you, who now, at last, in your utmost need came back to comfort and console you——"

"To be to you what you were once to him," cried the younger, falling on his knee before him; "to repay your old affection, brother dear, by constant care, solicitude, and love; to be, at your right hand, what he never ceased to be when oceans rolled between us; to call to witness his unchanging truth and mindfulness of bygone days, whole years of desolation. Give me but one word of recognition, brother—and never—no, never, in the brightest moment of our youngest days, when, poor silly boys, we thought to pass our lives together—have we been half as dear and precious to each other as we shall be from this time hence!"

The old man looked from face to face, and his lips moved; but no sound came from them in reply.

"If we were knit together then," pursued the younger brother, "what will be the bond between us now! Our love and fellowship began in childhood, when life was all before us, and will be resumed when we have proved it, and are but children at the last. As many restless spirits, who have hunted fortune, fame, or pleasure through the world, retire in their decline to where they first drew breath, vainly seeking to be children once again, before they die, so we, less fortunate than they in early life, but happier in its closing scenes, will set up our rest again among our boyish haunts; and going home with no hope realised, that had its growth in manhood—carrying back nothing that we brought away, but our old yearnings to each other—saving no fragment from the wreck of life, but that which first endeared it—may be indeed but children as at first. And even," he added in an altered voice, "even if what I dread to name has come to pass—even if that be so, or is to be (which Heaven forbid and spare us!)—still, dear brother, we are not apart, and have that comfort in our great affliction."

By little and little, the old man had drawn back towards the inner chamber, while these words were spoken. He pointed there, as he replied, with trembling lips,

"You plot among you to wean my heart from her. You never will do that—never while I have life. I have no relative or friend but her—I never had—I never will have. She is all in all to me. It is too late to part us now."

Waving them off with his hand, and calling softly to her as he went, he stole into the room. They who were left behind, drew close together, and after a few whispered words—not unbroken by emotion, or easily uttered—followed him. They moved so gently, that their footsteps made no noise; but there were sobs from among the group, and sounds of grief and mourning.

For she was dead. There, upon her little bed, she lay at rest. The solemn stillness was no marvel now.

She was dead. No sleep so beautiful and calm, so free from trace of pain, so fair to look upon. She seemed a creature fresh from the hand of God, and waiting for the breath of life; not one who had lived and suffered death.

Her couch was dressed with here and there some winter berries and green leaves, gathered in a spot she had been used to favour. "When I die, put near me something that has loved the light, and had the sky above it always." Those were her words.

She was dead. Dear, gentle, patient, noble Nell was dead. Her little bird—a poor slight thing the pressure of a finger would have crushed—was stirring nimbly in its cage; and the strong heart of its child-mistress was mute and motionless for ever.

Where were the traces of her early cares, her sufferings, and fatigues? All gone. Sorrow was dead indeed in her, but peace and perfect happiness were born; imaged in her tranquil beauty and profound repose.

And still her former self lay there, unaltered in this change. Yes. The old fireside had smiled upon that same sweet face; it had passed like a dream through haunts of misery and care; at the door of the poor schoolmaster on the summer evening, before the furnace fire upon the cold wet night, at the still bedside of the dying boy, there had been the same mild lovely look. So shall we know the angels in their majesty, after death.

The old man held one languid arm in his, and had the small hand tight folded to his breast, for warmth. It was the hand she had stretched out to him with her last smile—the hand that had led him on through all their wanderings. Ever and anon he pressed it to his lips; then hugged it to his breast again, murmuring that it was warmer now; and as he said it he looked, in agony, to those who stood around, as if imploring them to help her.

She was dead, and past all help, or need of it. The ancient rooms she had seemed to fill with life, even while her own was waning fast—the garden she had tended—the eyes she had gladdened—the noiseless haunts of many a thoughtful hour—the paths she had trodden as it were but yesterday—could know her no more.

"It is not," said the schoolmaster, as he bent down to kiss her on the cheek, and gave his tears free vent, "it is not on earth that Heaven's justice ends. Think what it is, compared with the World to which her young spirit has winged its early flight, and say, if one deliberate wish expressed in solemn terms above this bed could call her back to life, which of us would utter it!"

Chapter LXXII

WHEN morning came, and they could speak more calmly on the subject of their grief, they heard how her life had closed.

She had been dead two days. They were all about her at the time, knowing that the end was drawing on. She died soon after daybreak. They had read and talked to her in the earlier portion of the night, but as the hours crept on, she sank to sleep. They could tell, by what she faintly uttered in her dreams, that they were of her journeyings with the old man; they were of no painful scenes, but of those who had helped and used them kindly, for she often said "God bless you!" with great fervour. Waking, she never wandered in her mind but once, and that was of beautiful music which she said was in the air. God knows. It may have been.

Opening her eyes at last, from a very quiet sleep, she begged that they would kiss her once again. That done, she turned to the old man with a lovely smile upon her face—such, they said, as they had never seen, and never could forget—and clung with both her arms about his neck. They did not know that she was dead, at first.

She had spoken very often of the two sisters, who, she said, were like dear friends to her. She wished they could be told how much she thought about them, and how she had watched them as they had walked together, by the river-side at night. She would like to see poor Kit, she had often said of late. She wished there was somebody to take her love to Kit. And even then, she never thought or spoke about him, but with something of her old, clear, merry laugh.

For the rest, she had never murmured or complained; but, with a quiet mind, and manner quite unaltered—save that she every day became more earnest and more grateful to them—faded like the light upon a summer's evening.

The child who had been her little friend came there almost as soon as it was day, with an offering of dried flowers which he begged them to lay upon her breast. It was he who had come to the window overnight and spoken to the sexton, and they saw in the snow traces of small feet, where he had been lingering near the room in which she lay before he went to bed. He had a fancy, it seemed, that they had left her there alone; and could not bear the thought.

He told them of his dream again, and that it was of her being restored to them, just as she used to be. He begged hard to see her, saying that he would be very quiet, and that they need not fear his being alarmed, for he had sat alone by his young brother all day long, when *he* was dead, and had felt glad to be so near him. They let him have his wish; and indeed he kept his word, and was in his childish way a lesson to them all.

Up to that time, the old man had not spoken once—except to her—or stirred from the bedside. But when he saw her little favourite, he was moved as they had not seen him yet, and made as though he would have him come nearer. Then pointing to the bed, he burst into tears for the first time, and they who stood by, knowing that the sight of this child had done him good, left them alone together.

Soothing him with his artless talk of her, the child persuaded him to take some rest, to walk abroad, to do almost as he desired him. And when the day came on, which must remove her in her earthly shape from earthly eyes for ever, he led him away, that he might not know when she was taken from him.

They were to gather fresh leaves and berries for her bed. It was Sunday—a bright, clear, wintry afternoon—and as they traversed the village street, those who were walking in their path drew back to make way for them, and gave them a softened greeting. Some shook the old man kindly by the hand, some stood uncovered while he tottered by, and many cried, "God help him!" as he passed along.

"Neighbour!" said the old man, stopping at the cottage where his young guide's mother dwelt, "how is it that the folks are nearly all in black to-day? I have seen a mourning ribbon or a piece of crape on almost every one."

She could not tell, the woman said.

"Why, you yourself—you wear the colour too!" he cried. "Windows are closed that never used to be by day. What does this mean?"

Again the woman said she could not tell.

"We must go back," said the old man hurriedly. "We must see what this is."

"No, no," cried the child, detaining him. "Remember what you promised. Our way is to the old green lane, where she and I so often were, and where you found us more than once making those garlands for her garden. Do not turn back!"

"Where is she now?" said the old man. "Tell me that."

"Do you not know?" returned the child. "Did we not leave her, but just now?"

"True. True. It *was* her we left—was it!"

He pressed his hand upon his brow, looked vacantly round, and as if impelled by a sudden thought, crossed the road, and entered the sexton's house. He and his deaf assistant were sitting before the fire. Both rose up, on seeing who it was.

The child made a hasty sign to them with his hand. It was the action of an instant, but that, and the old man's look, were quite enough.

"Do you—do you bury any one to-day?" he said eagerly.

"No, no! Who should we bury, sir?" returned the sexton.

"Ay, who indeed! I say with you, who indeed?"

"It is a holiday with us, good sir," returned the sexton mildly. "We have no work to do to-day."

"Why, then, I'll go where you will," said the old man, turning to the child. "You're sure of what you tell me? You would not deceive me? I am changed even in the little time since you last saw me."

"Go thy ways with him, sir," cried the sexton, "and Heaven be with ye both!"

"I am quite ready," said the old man meekly. "Come, boy, come"—and so submitted to be led away.

And now the bell—the bell she had so often heard by night and day, and listened to with solemn pleasure almost as a living voice—rang its remorseless toll for her, so young, so beautiful, so good. Decrepit age, and vigorous life, and blooming youth, and helpless infancy, poured forth—on crutches, in the pride of strength and health, in the full blush of promise, in the mere dawn of life—to gather round her tomb. Old men were there, whose eyes were dim and senses failing—grandmothers, who might have died ten years ago, and still been old—the deaf, the blind, the lame, the palsied, the living dead in many shapes and forms, to see the closing of that early grave. What was the death it would shut in, to that which still could crawl and creep above it!

Along the crowded path they bore her now; pure as the newly fallen snow that covered it; whose day on earth had been as fleeting. Under that porch, where she had sat when Heaven in its mercy brought her to that peaceful spot, she passed again, and the old church received her in its quiet shade.

They carried her to one old nook, where she had many and many a time sat musing, and laid their burden softly on the pavement. The light streamed on it through the coloured window—a window, where the boughs of trees were ever rustling in the summer, and where the birds sang sweetly all day long. With every breath of air that stirred among those branches in the sunshine, some trembling, changing light would fall upon her grave.

Earth to earth, ashes to ashes, dust to dust. Many a young hand dropped in its little wreath, many a stifled sob was heard. Some—and they were not a few—knelt down. All were sincere and truthful in their sorrow.

The service done, the mourners stood apart, and the villagers closed round to look into the grave before the pavement-stone should be replaced. One called to mind how he had seen her sitting on that very spot, and how her book had fallen on her lap, and she was gazing with a pensive face upon the sky. Another told how he had wondered much that one so delicate as she, should be so bold; how she had never feared to enter the church alone at night, but had loved to linger there when all was quiet, and even to climb the tower stair, with no more light than that of the moon rays stealing through the loopholes in the thick old wall. A whisper went about among the oldest there, that she had seen and talked with angels; and when they called to mind how she had looked, and spoken, and her early death, some thought it might be so, indeed. Thus, coming to the grave in little knots, and glancing down, and giving place to others, and falling off in whispering groups of three or four, the church was cleared in time of all but the sexton and the mourning friends.

They saw the vault covered and the stone fixed down. Then, when the dusk of evening had come on, and not a sound disturbed the sacred stillness of the place—when the bright moon poured in her light on tomb and monument, on pillar, wall, and arch, and most of all (it seemed to them) upon her quiet grave—in that calm time, when all outward things and inward thoughts teem with assurances of immortality, and wordly hopes and fears are humbled in the dust before them—then, with tranquil and submissive hearts they turned away, and left the child with God.

Oh! it is hard to take to heart the lesson that such deaths will teach, but let no man reject it, for it is one that all must learn, and is a mighty, universal Truth. When Death strikes down the innocent and young, for every fragile form from which he lets the panting spirit free, a hundred virtues rise, in shapes of mercy, charity, and love, to walk the world, and bless it. Of every tear that sorrowing mortals shed on such green graves, some good is born, some gentler nature comes. In the Destroyer's steps there spring up bright creations that defy his power, and his dark path becomes a way of light to Heaven.

It was late when the old man came home. The boy had led him to his own dwelling, under some pretence, on their way back; and, rendered drowsy by his long ramble and late want of rest, he had sunk into a deep sleep by the fireside. He was perfectly exhausted, and they were careful not to rouse him. The slumber held him a long time, and when he at length awoke the moon was shining.

The younger brother, uneasy at his protracted absence, was watching at the door for his coming, when he appeared in the pathway with his little guide. He advanced to meet them, and tenderly obliging the old man to lean upon his arm, conducted him with slow and trembling steps towards the house.

He repaired to her chamber, straight. Not finding what he had left there, he returned with distracted looks to the room in which they were assembled. From that, he rushed into the schoolmaster's cottage, calling her name. They followed close upon him, and when he had vainly searched it, brought him home.

With such persuasive words as pity and affection could suggest, they prevailed upon him to sit among them and hear what they should tell him. Then, endeavouring by every little artifice to prepare his mind for what must come, and dwelling with many fervent words upon the happy lot to which she had been removed, they told him, at last, the truth. The moment it had passed their lips, he fell down among them like a murdered man.

For many hours, they had little hope of his surviving; but grief is strong, and he recovered.

If there be any who have never known the blank that follows death—the weary void—the sense of desolation that will come upon the strongest minds, when something familiar and beloved is missed at every turn—the connexion between inanimate and senseless things, and the object of recollection, when every household god becomes a monument and every room a grave—if there be any who have not known this, and proved it by their own experience, they can never faintly guess how, for many days, the old man pined and moped away the time, and wandered here and there as seeking something, and had no comfort.

Whatever power of thought or memory he retained, was all bound up in her. He never understood, or seemed to care to understand, about his brother. To every endearment and attention he continued listless. If they spoke to him on this, or any other theme—save one—he would hear them patiently for awhile, then turn away, and go on seeking as before.

On that one theme, which was in his and all their minds, it was impossible to touch. Dead! He could not hear or bear the word. The slightest hint of it would throw him into a paroxysm, like that he had had when it was first spoken. In what hope he lived, no man could tell; but that he had some hope of finding her again—some faint and shadowy hope, deferred from day to day, and making him from day to day more sick and sore at heart—was plain to all.

They bethought them of a removal from the scene of this last sorrow; of trying whether change of place would rouse or cheer him. His brother sought the advice of those who were accounted skilful in such matters, and they came and saw him. Some of the number staid upon the spot, conversed with him when he would converse, and watched him as he wandered up and down, alone and silent. Move him where they might, they said, he would ever seek to get back there. His mind would run upon that spot. If they confined him closely, and kept a strict guard upon him, they might hold him prisoner, but if he could by any means escape, he would surely wander back to that place, or die upon the road.

The boy, to whom he had submitted at first, had no longer any influence with him. At times he would suffer the child to walk by his side, or would even take such notice of his presence as giving him his hand, or would stop to kiss his cheek, or pat him on the head. At other times, he would entreat him—not unkindly—to be gone, and would not brook him near. But whether alone; or with this pliant friend; or with those who would have given him, at any cost or sacrifice, some consolation or some peace of mind, if happily the means could have been devised; he was at all times the same—with no love or care for anything in life—a broken-hearted man.

At length they found one day that he had risen early, and, with his knapsack on his back, his staff in hand, her own straw hat, and little basket full of such things as she had been used to carry, was gone. As they were making ready to pursue him far and wide, a frightened schoolboy came who had seen him, but a moment before, sitting in the church—upon her grave, he said.

They hastened there, and going softly to the door, espied him in the attitude of one who waited patiently. They did not disturb him then, but kept a watch upon him all that day. When it grew quite dark, he rose and returned home, and went to bed, murmuring to himself, "She will come to-morrow!"

Upon the morrow he was there again from sunrise until night; and still at night he laid him down to rest, and muttered, "She will come to-morrow!"

And thenceforth, every day, and all day long, he waited at her grave for her. How many pictures of new journeys over pleasant country, of resting-places under the free broad sky, of rambles in the fields and woods, and paths not often trodden—how many tones of that one well-remembered voice—how many glimpses of the form, the fluttering dress, the hair that waved so gaily in the wind—how many visions of what had been, and what he hoped was yet to be—rose up before him, in the old, dull, silent church! He never told them what he thought, or where he went. He would sit with them at night, pondering with a secret satisfaction, they could see, upon the flight that he and she would take before the night came again; and still they would hear him whisper in his prayers, "Oh! Let her come to-morrow!"

The last time was on a genial day in spring. He did not return at the usual hour, and they went to seek him. He was lying dead upon the stone.

They laid him by the side of her whom he had loved so well; and, in the church where they had often prayed, and mused, and lingered hand in hand, the child and the old man slept together.

Chapter the Last

THE magic reel, which, rolling on before, has led the chronicler thus far, now slackens in its pace, and stops. It lies before the goal; the pursuit is at an end.

It remains but to dismiss the leaders of the little crowd who have borne us company upon the road, and so to close the journey.

Foremost among them, smooth Sampson Brass and Sally, arm in arm, claim our polite attention.

Mr Sampson, then, being detained, as already has been shown, by the Justice upon whom he called, and being so strongly pressed to protract his stay that he could by no means refuse, remained under his protection for a considerable time, during which the great attention of his entertainer kept him so extremely close, that he was quite lost to society, and never even went abroad for exercise saving into a small paved yard. So well, indeed, was his modest and retiring temper understood by those with whom he had to deal, and so jealous were they of his absence, that they required a kind of friendly bond to be entered into by two substantial housekeepers, in the sum of fifteen hundred pounds a-piece, before they would suffer him to quit their hospitable roof—doubting, it appeared, that he would return, if once let loose, on any other terms. Mr Brass, struck with the humour of this jest, and carrying out its spirit to the utmost, sought from his wide connexion a pair of friends whose joint possessions fell some half-pence short of fifteen pence, and proffered them as bail—for that was the merry word agreed upon on both sides. These gentlemen being rejected after twenty-four hours' pleasantry, Mr Brass consented to remain, and did remain, until a club of choice spirits called a Grand Jury (who were in the joke) summoned him to a trial before twelve other wags for perjury and fraud, who in their turn found him guilty with a most facetious joy—nay, the very populace entered into the whim, and when Mr Brass was moving in a hackney-coach towards the building where these wags assembled, saluted him with rotten eggs and carcases of kittens, and feigned to wish to tear him into shreds, which greatly increased the comicality of the thing, and made him relish it the more, no doubt.

To work this sportive vein still further, Mr Brass, by his counsel, moved in arrest of judgment that he had been led to criminate himself, by assurances of safety and promises of pardon, and claimed the leniency which the law extends to such confiding natures as are thus deluded. After solemn argument, this point (with others of a technical nature, whose humorous extravagance it would be difficult to exaggerate) was referred to the judges for their decision, Sampson being meantime removed to his former quarters. Finally, some of the points were given in Sampson's favour, and some against him; and the upshot was that, instead of being desired to travel for a time in foreign parts, he was permitted to grace the mother country under certain insignificant restrictions.

These were that he should, for a term of years, reside in a spacious mansion where several other gentlemen were lodged and boarded at the public charge, who went clad in a sober uniform of grey turned up with yellow, had their hair cut extremely short, and chiefly lived on gruel and light soup. It was also required of him that he should partake of their exercise of constantly ascending an endless flight of stairs; and lest his legs, unused to such exertion, should be weakened by it, that he should wear upon one ankle an amulet or charm of iron. These conditions being arranged, he was removed one evening to his new abode, and enjoyed, in common with nine other gentlemen and two ladies, the privilege of being taken to his place of retirement in one of Royalty's own carriages.

Over and above these trifling penalties, his name was erased and blotted out from the roll of attorneys; which erasure has been always held in these latter times to be a great degradation and reproach, and to imply the commission of some amazing villany—as indeed would seem to be the case, when so many worthless names remain among its better records, unmolested.

Of Sally Brass, conflicting rumours went abroad. Some said with confidence that she had gone down to the docks in male attire, and had become a female sailor; others darkly whispered that she had enlisted as a private in the second regiment of Foot Guards, and had been seen in uniform and on duty, to wit, leaning on her musket and looking out of a sentry-box in St. James's Park one evening. There were many such whispers as these in circulation; but the truth appears to be that, after a lapse of some five years (during which there is no direct evidence of her having been seen at all), two wretched people were more than once observed to crawl at dusk from the inmost recesses of St. Giles's, and to take their way along the streets, with shuffling steps and cowering, shivering forms, looking into the roads and kennels as they went in search of refuse food or disregarded offal. These forms were never beheld but in those nights of cold and gloom, when the terrible spectres, who lie at all other times in the obscene hiding-places of London, in archways, dark vaults and cellars, venture to creep into the streets; the embodied spirits of Disease, and Vice, and Famine. It was whispered by those who should have known, that these were Sampson and his Sister Sally, and to this day, it is said, they sometimes pass, on bad nights, in the same loathsome guise, close at the elbow of the shrinking passenger.

The body of Quilp being found—though not until some days had elapsed—an inquest was held on it near the spot where it had been washed ashore. The general supposition was that he had committed suicide, and, this appearing to be favoured by all the circumstances of his death, the verdict was to that effect. He was left to be buried with a stake through his heart in the centre of four lonely roads.

It was rumoured afterwards that this horrible and barbarous ceremony had been dispensed with, and that the remains had been secretly given up to Tom Scott. But even here, opinion was divided; for some said Tom had dug them up at midnight, and carried them to a place indicated to him by the widow. It is probable that both these stories may have had their origin in the simple fact of Tom's shedding tears upon the inquest—which he certainly did, extraordinary as it may appear. He manifested besides, a strong desire to assault the jury; and being restrained and conducted out of court, darkened its only window by standing on his head upon the sill, until he was dexterously tilted upon his feet again by a cautious beadle.

Being cast upon the world by his master's death, he determined to go through it upon his head and hands, and accordingly began to tumble for his bread. Finding, however, his English birth an insurmountable obstacle to his advancement in this pursuit (notwithstanding that his art was in high repute and favour), he assumed the name of an Italian image lad, with whom he had become acquainted; and afterwards tumbled with extraordinary success, and to overflowing audiences.

Little Mrs Quilp never quite forgave herself the one deceit that lay so heavy on her conscience, and never spoke or thought of it but with bitter tears. Her husband had no relations, and she was rich. He had made no will, or she would probably have been poor. Having married the first time at her mother's instigation, she consulted in her second choice nobody but herself. It fell upon a smart young fellow enough; and as he made it a preliminary condition that Mrs Jiniwin should be thenceforth an out-pensioner, they lived together after marriage with no more than the average amount of quarrelling, and led a merry life upon the dead dwarf's money.

Mr and Mrs Garland, and Mr Abel, went on as usual (except that there was a change in their household, as will be seen presently), and in due time the latter went into partnership with his friend the notary, on which occasion there was a dinner, and a ball, and a great extent of dissipation. Unto this ball there happened to be invited the most bashful young lady that was ever seen, with whom Mr Abel happened to fall in love. *How* it happened, or how they found it out, or which of them first communicated the discovery to the other, nobody knows. But certain it is that in course of time they were married; and equally certain it is that they were the happiest of the happy; and no less certain it is that they deserved to be so. And it is pleasant to write down that they reared a family; because any propagation of goodness and benevolence is no small addition to the aristocracy of nature, and no small subject of rejoicing for mankind at large.

The pony preserved his character for independence and principle down to the last moment of his life; which was an unusually long one, and caused him to be looked upon, indeed, as the very Old Parr of ponies. He often went to and fro with the little phaeton between Mr Garland's and his son's, and, as the old people and the young were frequently together, had a stable of his own at the new establishment, into which he would walk of himself with surprising dignity. He condescended to play with the children, as they grew old enough to cultivate his friendship, and would run up and down the little paddock with them like a dog; but though he relaxed so far, and allowed them such small freedoms as caresses, or even to look at his shoes or hang on by his tail, he never permitted any one among them to mount his back or drive him; thus showing that even their familiarity must have its limits, and that there were points between them far too serious for trifling.

He was not unsusceptible of warm attachments in his later life, for when the good bachelor came to live with Mr Garland upon the clergyman's decease, he conceived a great friendship for him, and amiably submitted to be driven by his hands without the least resistance. He did no work for two or three years before he died, but lived in clover; and his last act (like a choleric old gentleman) was to kick his doctor.

Mr Swiveller, recovering very slowly from his illness, and entering into the receipt of his annuity, bought for the Marchioness a handsome stock of clothes, and put her to school forthwith, in redemption of the vow he had made upon his fevered bed. After casting about for some time for a name which should be worthy of her, he decided in favour of Sophronia Sphynx, as being euphonious and genteel, and furthermore indicative of mystery. Under this title the Marchioness repaired, in tears, to the school of his selection, from which, as she soon distanced all competitors, she was removed before the lapse of many quarters to one of a higher grade. It is but bare justice to Mr Swiveller to say, that, although the expenses of her education kept him in straitened circumstances for half a dozen years, he never slackened in his zeal, and always held himself sufficiently repaid by the accounts he heard (with great gravity) of her advancement, on his monthly visits to the governess, who looked upon him as a literary gentleman of eccentric habits, and of a most prodigious talent in quotation.

In a word, Mr Swiveller kept the Marchioness at this establishment until she was, at a moderate guess, full nineteen years of age—good-looking, clever, and good-humoured; when he began to consider seriously what was to be done next. On one of his periodical visits, while he was revolving this question in his mind, the Marchioness came down to him, alone, looking more smiling and more fresh than ever. Then it occurred to him, but not for the first time, that if she would marry him, how comfortable they might be! So Richard asked her; whatever she said, it wasn't No; and they were married in good earnest that day week, which gave Mr Swiveller frequent occasion to remark at divers subsequent periods that there had been a young lady saving up for him after all.

A little cottage at Hampstead being to let, which had in its garden a smoking-box, the envy of the civilised world, they agreed to become its tenants; and when the honeymoon was over, entered upon its occupation. To this retreat Mr Chuckster repaired regularly every Sunday to spend the day—usually beginning with breakfast; and here he was the great purveyor of general news and fashionable intelligence. For some years he continued a deadly foe to Kit, protesting that he had a better opinion of him when he was supposed to have stolen the five-pound note, that when he was shown to be perfectly free of the crime; inasmuch as his guilt would have had in it something daring and bold, whereas his innocence was but another proof of a sneaking and crafty disposition. By slow degrees, however, he was reconciled to him in the end; and even went so far as to honour him with his patronage, as one who had in some measure reformed, and was therefore to be forgiven. But he never forgot or pardoned that circumstance of the shilling; holding that if he had come back to get another he would have done well enough, but that his returning to work out the former gift was a stain upon his moral character which no penitence or contrition could ever wash away.

Mr Swiveller, having always been in some measure of a philosophic and reflective turn, grew immensely contemplative, at times, in the smoking-box, and was accustomed at such periods to debate in his own mind the mysterious question of Sophronia's parentage. Sophronia herself supposed she was an orphan; but Mr Swiveller, putting various slight circumstances together, often thought Miss Brass must know better than that; and, having heard from his wife of her strange interview with Quilp, entertained sundry misgivings whether that person, in his lifetime, might not also have been able to solve the riddle, had he chosen. These speculations, however, gave him no uneasiness; for Sophronia was ever a most cheerful, affectionate, and provident wife to him; and Dick (excepting for an occasional outbreak with Mr Chuckster, which she had the good sense rather to encourage than oppose) was to her an attached and domesticated husband. And they played many hundred thousand games of cribbage together. And let it be added, to Dick's honour, that, though we have called her Sophronia, he called her the Marchioness from first to last; and that upon every anniversary of the day on which he found her in his sickroom Mr Chuckster came to dinner, and there was great glorification.

The gamblers, Isaac List and Jowl, with their trusty confederate Mr James Groves of unimpeachable memory, pursued their course with varying success, until the failure of a spirited enterprise in the way of their profession, dispersed them in various directions, and caused their career to receive a sudden check from the long and strong arm of the law. This defeat had its origin in the untoward detection of a new associate—young Frederick Trent—who thus became the unconscious instrument of their punishment and his own.

For the young man himself, he rioted abroad for a brief term, living by his wits—which means by the abuse of every faculty that worthily employed raises man above the beasts, and so degraded, sinks him far below them. It was not long before his body was recognised by a stranger, who chanced to visit that hospital in Paris where the drowned are laid out to be owned; despite the bruises and disfigurements which were said to have been occasioned by some previous scuffle. But the stranger kept his own counsel until he returned home, and it was never claimed or cared for.

The younger brother, or the single gentleman, for that designation is more familiar, would have drawn the poor schoolmaster from his lone retreat, and made him his companion and friend. But the humble village teacher was timid of venturing into the noisy world, and had become fond of his dwelling in the old churchyard. Calmly happy in his school, and in the spot, and in the attachment of Her little mourner, he pursued his quiet course in peace; and was, through the righteous gratitude of his friend—let this brief mention suffice for that—a *poor* schoolmaster no more.

That friend—single gentleman, or younger brother, which you will—had at his heart a heavy sorrow; but it bred in him no misanthropy or monastic gloom. He went forth into the world, a lover of his kind. For a long, long time, it was his chief delight to travel in the steps of the old man and the child (so far as he could trace them from her last narrative), to halt where they had halted, sympathise where they had suffered, and rejoice where they had been made glad. Those who had been kind to them, did not escape his search. The sisters at the school—they who were her friends, because themselves so friendless—Mrs Jarley of the wax-work, Codlin, Short—he found them all; and trust me, that the man who fed the furnace fire was not forgotten.

Kit's story having got abroad, raised him up a host of friends, and many offers of provision for his future life. He had no idea at first of ever quitting Mr Garland's service; but, after serious remonstrance and advice from that gentleman, began to contemplate the possibility of such a change being brought about in time. A good post was procured for him, with a rapidity which took away his breath, by some of the gentlemen who had believed him guilty of the offence laid to his charge, and who had acted upon that belief. Through the same kind agency, his mother was secured from want, and made quite happy. Thus, as Kit often said, his great misfortune turned out to be the source of all his subsequent prosperity.

Did Kit live a single man all his days, or did he marry? Of course he married, and who should be his wife but Barbara? And the best of it was, he married so soon that little Jacob was an uncle, before the calves of his legs, already mentioned in this history, had ever been encased in broadcloth pantaloons—though that was not quite the best either, for of necessity the baby was an uncle too. The delight of Kit's mother and of Barbara's mother upon the great occasion is past all telling; finding they agreed so well on that, and on all other subjects, they took up their abode together, and were a most harmonious pair of friends from that time forth. And hadn't Astley's cause to bless itself for their all going together once a quarter—to the pit—and didn't Kit's mother always say, when they painted the outside, that Kit's last treat had helped to that, and wondered what the manager would feel if he but knew it as they passed his house!

When Kit had children six and seven years old, there was a Barbara among them, and a pretty Barbara she was. Nor was there wanting an exact facsimile and copy of little Jacob as he appeared in those remote times when they taught him what oysters meant. Of course there was an Abel, own godson to the Mr Garland of that name; and there was a Dick, whom Mr Swiveller did especially favour. The little group would often gather round him of a night and beg him to tell again that story of good Miss Nell who died. This Kit would do; and when they cried to hear it, wishing it longer too, he would teach them how she had gone to Heaven, as all good people did; and how, if they were good like her, they might hope to be there too one day, and to see and know her as he had done when he was quite a boy. Then he would relate to them how needy he used to be, and how she had taught him what he was otherwise too poor to learn, and how the old man had been used to say "she always laughs at Kit"; at which they would brush away their tears, and laugh themselves to think that she had done so, and be again quite merry.

He sometimes took them to the street where she had lived; but new improvements had altered it so much, it was not like the same. The old house had been long ago pulled down, and a fine broad road was in its place. At first he would draw with his stick a square upon the ground to show them where it used to stand. But he soon became uncertain of the spot, and could only say it was thereabouts, he thought, and that these alterations were confusing.

Such are the changes which a few years bring about, and so do things pass away, like a tale that is told!

ard
Times

For These Times

Inscribed

To

THOMAS CARLYLE

Contents

BOOK THE FIRST

Sowing

Chapter I

THE ONE THING NEEDFUL

NOW, what I want is, Facts. Teach these boys and girls nothing but Facts. Facts alone are wanted in life. Plant nothing else, and root out everything else. You can only form the minds of reasoning animals upon Facts: nothing else will ever be of any service to them. This is the principle on which I bring up my own children, and this is the principle on which I bring up these children. Stick to Facts, sir!"

The scene was a plain, bare, monotonous vault of a schoolroom, and the speaker's square forefinger emphasized his observations by underscoring every sentence with a line on the schoolmaster's sleeve. The emphasis was helped by the speaker's square wall of a forehead, which had his eyebrows for its base, while his eyes found commodious cellarage in two dark caves, overshadowed by the wall. The emphasis was helped by the speaker's mouth, which was wide, thin, and hard set. The emphasis was helped by the speaker's voice, which was inflexible, dry, and dictatorial. The emphasis was helped by the speaker's hair, which bristled on the skirts of his bald head, a plantation of firs to keep the wind from its shining surface, all covered with knobs, like the crust of a plum pie, as if the head had scarcely warehouse-room for the hard facts stored inside. The speaker's obstinate carriage, square coat, square legs, square shoulders—nay, his very neckcloth, trained to take him by the throat with an unaccommodating grasp, like a stubborn fact, as it was—all helped the emphasis.

"In this life, we want nothing but Facts, sir; nothing but Facts!"

The speaker, and the schoolmaster, and the third grown person present, all backed a little, and swept with their eyes the inclined plane of little vessels then and there arranged in order, ready to have imperial gallons of facts poured into them until they were full to the brim.

Chapter II

MURDERING THE INNOCENTS

THOMAS Gradgrind, sir. A man of realities. A man of fact and calculations. A man who proceeds upon the principle that two and two are four, and nothing over, and who is not to be talked into allowing for anything over. Thomas Gradgrind, sir—

peremptorily Thomas—Thomas Gradgrind. With a rule and a pair of scales, and the multiplication table always in his pocket, sir, ready to weigh and measure any parcel of human nature, and tell you exactly what it comes to. It is a mere question of figures, a case of simple arithmetic. You might hope to get some other nonsensical belief into the head of George Gradgrind, or Augustus Gradgrind, or John Gradgrind, or Joseph Gradgrind (all suppositious, non-existent persons), but into the head of Thomas Gradgrind—no, sir!

In such terms Mr Gradgrind always mentally introduced himself, whether to his private circle of acquaintance, or to the public in general. In such terms, no doubt, substituting the words "boys and girls," for "sir," Thomas Gradgrind now presented Thomas Gradgrind to the little pitchers before him, who were to be filled so full of facts.

Indeed, as he eagerly sparkled at them from the cellarage before mentioned, he seemed a kind of cannon loaded to the muzzle with facts, and prepared to blow them clean out of the regions of childhood at one discharge. He seemed a galvanizing apparatus, too, charged with a grim mechanical substitute for the tender young imaginations that were to be stormed away.

"Girl number twenty," said Mr Gradgrind, squarely pointing with his square forefinger, "I don't know that girl. Who is that girl?"

"Sissy Jupe, sir," explained number twenty, blushing, standing up, and curtseying.

"Sissy is not a name," said Mr Gradgrind. "Don't call yourself Sissy. Call yourself Cecilia."

"It's father as calls me Sissy, sir," returned the young girl in a trembling voice, and with another curtsey.

"Then he has no business to do it," said Mr Gradgrind. "Tell him he mustn't. Cecilia Jupe. Let me see. What is your father?"

"He belongs to the horse-riding, if you please, sir."

Mr Gradgrind frowned, and waved off the objectionable calling with his hand.

"We don't want to know anything about that, here. You mustn't tell us about that, here. Your father breaks horses, don't he?"

"If you please, sir, when they can get any to break, they do break horses in the ring, sir."

"You mustn't tell us about the ring, here. Very well, then. Describe your father as a horsebreaker. He doctors sick horses, I dare say?"

"Oh yes, sir."

"Very well, then. He is a veterinary surgeon, a farrier and horsebreaker. Give me your definition of a horse."

(Sissy Jupe thrown into the greatest alarm by this demand.)

"Girl number twenty unable to define a horse!" said Mr Gradgrind, for the general behoof of all the little pitchers. "Girl number twenty possessed of no facts, in reference to one of the commonest of animals! Some boy's definition of a horse. Bitzer, yours."

The square finger, moving here and there, lighted suddenly on Bitzer, perhaps because he chanced to sit in the same ray of sunlight which, darting in at one of the bare windows of the intensely whitewashed room, irradiated Sissy. For, the boys and girls sat on the face of the inclined plane in two compact bodies, divided up the centre by a narrow interval; and Sissy, being at the corner of a row on the sunny side, came in for the beginning of a sunbeam, of which Bitzer, being at the corner of a row on the other side, a few rows in advance, caught the end. But, whereas the girl was so dark-eyed and dark-haired, that she seemed to receive a deeper and more lustrous colour from the sun when it shone upon her, the boy was so light-eyed and light-haired that the self-same rays appeared to draw out of him what little colour he ever possessed. His cold eyes would hardly have been eyes, but for the short ends of lashes which, by bringing them into immediate contrast with something paler than themselves, expressed their form. His short-cropped hair might have been a mere continuation of the sandy freckles on his forehead and face. His skin was so unwholesomely deficient in the natural tinge, that he looked as though, if he were cut, he would bleed white.

"Bitzer," said Thomas Gradgrind. "Your definition of a horse."

"Quadruped. Graminivorous. Forty teeth, namely twenty-four grinders, four eye-teeth, and twelve incisive. Sheds coat in the spring; in marshy countries, sheds hoofs, too. Hoofs hard, but requiring to be shod with iron. Age known by marks in mouth." Thus (and much more) Bitzer.

"Now girl number twenty," said Mr Gradgrind. "You know what a horse is."

She curtseyed again, and would have blushed deeper, if she could have blushed deeper than she had blushed all this time. Bitzer, after rapidly blinking at Thomas Gradgrind with both eyes at once, and so catching the light upon his quivering ends of lashes that they looked like the antennae of busy insects, put his knuckles to his freckled forehead, and sat down again.

The third gentleman now stepped forth. A mighty man at cutting and drying, he was; a government officer; in his way (and in most other people's too), a professed pugilist; always in training, always with a system to force down the general throat like a bolus, always to be heard of at the bar of his little Public-office, ready to fight all England. To continue in fistic phraseology, he had a genius for coming up to the scratch, wherever and whatever it was, and proving himself an ugly customer. He would go in and damage any subject whatever with his right, follow up with his left, stop, exchange, counter, bore his opponent (he always fought All England) to the ropes, and fall upon him neatly. He was certain to knock the wind out of common-sense, and render that unlucky adversary deaf to the call of time. And he had it in charge from high authority to bring about the great public-office Millennium, when Commissioners should reign upon earth.

"Very well," said this gentleman, briskly smiling, and folding his arms. "That's a horse. Now, let me ask you girls and boys, Would you paper a room with representations of horses?"

After a pause, one half of the children cried in chorus, "Yes, sir!" Upon which the other half, seeing in the gentleman's face that Yes was wrong, cried out in chorus, "No, sir!"—as the custom is, in these examinations.

"Of course, No. Why wouldn't you?"

A pause. One corpulent slow boy, with a wheezy manner of breathing, ventured the answer, Because he wouldn't paper a room at all, but would paint it.

"You *must* paper it," said Thomas Gradgrind, "whether you like it or not. Don't tell *us* you wouldn't paper it. What do you mean, boy?"

"I'll explain to you, then," said the gentleman, after another and a dismal pause, "why you wouldn't paper a room with representations of horses. Do you ever see horses walking up and down the sides of rooms in reality—in fact? Do you?"

"Yes, sir!" from one half. "No, sir!" from the other.

"Of course no," said the gentleman, with an indignant look at the wrong half. "Why, then, you are not to see anywhere, what you don't see in fact; you are not to have anywhere, what you don't have in fact. What is called Taste, is only another name for Fact."

Thomas Gradgrind nodded his approbation.

"This is a new principle, a discovery, a great discovery," said the gentleman. "Now, I'll try you again. Suppose you were going to carpet a room. Would you use a carpet having a representation of flowers upon it?"

There being a general conviction by this time that "No, sir!" was always the right answer to this gentleman, the chorus of No was very strong. Only a few feeble stragglers said Yes; among them Sissy Jupe.

"Girl number twenty," said the gentleman, smiling in the calm strength of knowledge.

Sissy blushed, and stood up.

"So you would carpet your room—or your husband's room, if you were a grown woman, and had a husband—with representations of flowers, would you," said the gentleman. "Why would you?"

"If you please, sir, I am very fond of flowers," returned the girl.

"And is that why you would put tables and chairs upon them, and have people walking over them with heavy boots?"

"It wouldn't hurt them, sir. They wouldn't crush and wither if you please, sir. They would be the pictures of what was very pretty and pleasant, and I would fancy—"

"Ay, ay, ay! But you mustn't fancy," cried the gentleman, quite elated by coming so happily to his point. "That's it! You are never to fancy."

"You are not, Cecilia Jupe," Thomas Gradgrind solemnly repeated, "to do anything of that kind."

"Fact, fact, fact!" said the gentleman. And "Fact, fact, fact!" repeated Thomas Gradgrind.

"You are to be in all things regulated and governed," said the gentleman, "by fact. We hope to have, before long, a board of fact, composed of commissioners of fact, who will force the people to be a people of fact, and of nothing but fact. You must discard the word Fancy altogether. You have nothing to do with it. You are not to have, in any object of use or ornament, what would be a contradiction in fact. You don't walk upon flowers in fact; you cannot be allowed to walk upon flowers in carpets. You don't find that foreign birds and butterflies come and perch upon your crockery. You never meet with quadrupeds going up and down walls; you must not have quadrupeds represented upon walls. You must use," said the gentleman, "for all these purposes, combinations and modifications (in primary colours) of mathematical figures which are susceptible of proof and demonstration. This is the new discovery. This is fact. This is taste."

The girl curtseyed, and sat down. She was very young, and she looked as if she were frightened by the matter of fact prospect the world afforded.

"Now, if Mr M'Choakumchild," said the gentleman, "will proceed to give his first lesson here, Mr Gradgrind, I shall be happy, at your request, to observe his mode of procedure."

Mr Gradgrind was much obliged. "Mr M'Choakumchild, we only wait for you."

So, Mr M'Choakumchild began in his best manner. He and some one hundred and forty other schoolmasters, had been lately turned at the same time, in the same factory, on the same principles, like so many pianoforte legs. He had been put through an immense variety of paces, and had answered volumes of head-breaking questions. Orthography, etymology, syntax, and prosody, biography, astronomy, geography, and general cosmography, the sciences of compound proportion, algebra, land-surveying and levelling, vocal music, and drawing from models, were all at the ends of his ten chilled fingers. He had worked his stony way into Her Majesty's most Honourable Privy Council's Schedule B, and had taken the bloom off the higher branches of mathematics and physical science, French, German, Latin, and Greek. He knew all about all the Water Sheds of all the world (whatever they are), and all the histories of all the peoples, and all the names of all the rivers and mountains, and all the productions, manners, and customs of all the countries, and all their boundaries and bearings on the two and thirty points of the compass. Ah, rather overdone, M'Choakumchild. If he had only learnt a little less, how infinitely better he might have taught much more!

He went to work in this preparatory lesson, not unlike Morgiana in the Forty Thieves: looking into all the vessels ranged before him, one after another, to see what they contained. Say, good M'Choakumchild. When from thy boiling store, thou shalt fill each jar brim full by and by, dost thou think that thou wilt always kill outright the robber Fancy lurking within—or sometimes only maim him and distort him!

Chapter III

A LOOPHOLE

MR Gradgrind walked homeward from the school, in a state of considerable satisfaction. It was his school, and he intended it to be a model. He intended every child in it to be a model—just as the young Gradgrinds were all models.

There were five young Gradgrinds, and they were models every one. They had been lectured at, from their tenderest years; coursed, like little hares. Almost as soon as they could run alone, they had been made to run to the lecture-room. The first object with which they had an association, or of which they had a remembrance, was a large black board with a dry Ogre chalking ghastly white figures on it.

Not that they knew, by name or nature, anything about an Ogre. Fact forbid! I only use the word to express a monster in a lecturing castle, with Heaven knows how many heads manipulated into one, taking childhood captive, and dragging it into gloomy statistical dens by the hair.

No little Gradgrind had ever seen a face in the moon; it was up in the moon before it could speak distinctly. No little Gradgrind had ever learnt the silly jingle, Twinkle, twinkle, little star; how I wonder what you are! No little Gradgrind had ever known wonder on the subject, each little Gradgrind having at five years old dissected the Great Bear like a Professor Owen, and driven Charles's Wain like a locomotive engine-driver. No little Gradgrind had ever associated a cow in a field with that famous cow with the crumpled horn who tossed the dog who worried the cat who killed the rat who ate the malt, or with that yet more famous cow who swallowed Tom Thumb: it had never heard of those celebrities, and had only been introduced to a cow as a graminivorous ruminating quadruped with several stomachs.

To his matter of fact home, which was called Stone Lodge, Mr Gradgrind directed his steps. He had virtually retired from the wholesale hardware trade before he built Stone Lodge, and was now looking about for a suitable opportunity of making an arithmetical figure in Parliament. Stone Lodge was situated on a moor within a mile or two of a great town—called Coketown in the present faithful guide-book.

A very regular feature on the face of the country, Stone Lodge was. Not the least disguise toned down or shaded off that uncompromising fact in the landscape. A great square house, with a heavy portico darkening the principal windows, as its master's heavy brows overshadowed his eyes. A calculated, cast up, balanced, and proved house. Six windows on this side of the door, six on that side; a total of twelve in this wing, a total of twelve in the other wing: four and twenty carried over to the back wings. A lawn and garden and an infant avenue, all ruled straight like a botanical account-book. Gas and ventilation, drainage and water-service, all of the primest quality. Iron clamps and girders, fireproof from top to bottom; mechanical lifts for the housemaids, with all their brushes and brooms; everything that heart could desire.

Everything? Well, I suppose so. The little Gradgrinds had cabinets in various departments of science too. They had a little conchological cabinet, and a little metallurgical cabinet, and a little mineralogical cabinet; and the specimens were all arranged and labelled, and the bits of stone and ore looked as though they might have been broken from the parent substances by those tremendously hard instruments their own names; and, to paraphrase the idle legend of Peter Piper, who had never found his way into *their* nursery, If the greedy little Gradgrinds grasped at more than this, what was it for good gracious goodness sake, that the greedy little Gradgrinds grasped at!

Their father walked on in a hopeful and satisfied frame of mind. He was an affectionate father, after his manner; but he would probably have described himself (if he had been put, like Sissy Jupe, upon a definition) as "an eminently practical" father. He had a particular pride in the phrase eminently practical, which was considered to have a special application to him. Whatsoever the public meeting held in Coketown, and whatsoever the subject of such meeting, some Coketowner was sure to seize the occasion of alluding to his eminently practical friend Gradgrind. This always pleased the eminently practical friend. He knew it to be his due, but his due was acceptable.

He had reached the neutral ground upon the outskirts of the town, which was neither town nor country, and yet was either spoiled, when his ears were invaded by the sound of music. The clashing and banging band attached to the horse-riding establishment which had there set up its rest in a wooden pavilion, was in full bray. A flag, floating from the summit of the temple, proclaimed to mankind that it was "Sleary's Horse-riding" which claimed their suffrages. Sleary himself, a stout modern statue with a money-box at its elbow, in an ecclesiastical niche of early Gothic architecture, took the money. Miss Josephine Sleary, as some very long and very narrow strips of printed bill announced, was then inaugurating the entertainments with her graceful equestrian Tyrolean flower-act. Among the other pleasing but always strictly moral wonders which must be seen to be believed, Signor Jupe was that afternoon to "elucidate the diverting accomplishments of his highly trained performing dog Merrylegs." He was also to exhibit "his astounding feat of throwing seventy-five hundred-weight in rapid succession backhanded over his head thus forming a fountain of solid iron in mid-air, a feat never before attempted in this or any other country and which having elicited such rapturous plaudits from enthusiastic throngs it cannot be withdrawn." The same Signor Jupe was to "enliven the varied performances at frequent intervals with his chaste Shaksperean quips and retorts." Lastly, he has to wind them up by appearing in his favourite character of Mr William Button, of Tooley Street, in "the highly novel and laughable hippo-comedietta of The Tailor's Journey to Brentford."

Thomas Gradgrind took no heed of these trivialities of course, but passed on as a practical man ought to pass on, either brushing the noisy insects from his thoughts, or consigning them to the House of Correction. But, the turning of the road took him by the back of the booth, and at the back of the booth a number of children were congregated in a number of stealthy attitudes, striving to peep in at the hidden glories of the place.

This brought him to a stop. "Now, to think of these vagabonds," said he, "attracting the young rabble from a model school."

A space of stunted grass and dry rubbish being between him and the young rabble, he took his eyeglass out of his waistcoat to look for any child he knew by name, and might order off. Phenomenon almost incredible though distinctly seen, what did he then behold but his own metallurgical Louisa peeping with all her might through a hole in a deal board, and his own mathematical Thomas abasing himself on the ground to catch but a hoof of the graceful equestrian Tyrolean flower-act!

Dumb with amazement, Mr Gradgrind crossed to the spot where his family was thus disgraced, laid his hand upon each erring child, and said:

"Louisa!! Thomas!!"

Both rose, red and disconcerted. But, Louisa looked at her father with more boldness than Thomas did. Indeed, Thomas did not look at him, but gave himself up to be taken home like a machine.

"In the name of wonder, idleness, and folly!" said Mr Gradgrind, leading each away by a hand; "what do you do here?"

"Wanted to see what it was like," returned Louisa shortly.

"What it was like?"

"Yes, father."

There was an air of jaded sullenness in them both, and particularly in the girl: yet, struggling through the dissatisfaction of her face, there was a light with nothing to rest upon, a fire with nothing to burn, a starved imagination keeping life in itself somehow, which brightened its expression. Not with the brightness natural to cheerful youth, but with uncertain, eager, doubtful flashes, which had something painful in them, analogous to the changes on a blind face groping its way.

She was a child now, of fifteen or sixteen; but at no distant day would seem to become a woman all at once. Her father thought so as he looked at her. She was pretty. Would have been self-willed (he thought in his eminently practical way), but for her bringing-up.

"Thomas, though I have the fact before me, I find it difficult to believe that you, with your education and resources, should have brought your sister to a scene like this."

"I brought *him*, father," said Louisa, quickly. "I asked him to come."

"I am sorry to hear it. I am very sorry indeed to hear it. It makes Thomas no better, and it makes you worse, Louisa."

She looked at her father again, but no tear fell down her cheek.

"You! Thomas and you, to whom the circle of the sciences is open; Thomas and you, who may be said to be replete with facts; Thomas and you, who have been trained to mathematical exactness; Thomas and you, here!" cried Mr Gradgrind. "In this degraded position! I am amazed."

"I was tired. I have been tired a long time," said Louisa.

"Tired? Of what?" asked the astonished father.

"I don't know of what—of everything I think."

"Say not another word," returned Mr Gradgrind. "You are childish. I will hear no more." He did not speak again until they had walked some half-a-mile in silence, when he gravely broke out with: "What would your best friends say, Louisa? Do you attach no value to their good opinion? What would Mr Bounderby say?"

At the mention of this name, his daughter stole a look at him, remarkable for its intense and searching character. He saw nothing of it, for before he looked at her she had again cast down her eyes!

"What," he repeated presently, "would Mr Bounderby say!" All the way to Stone Lodge, as with grave indignation he led the two delinquents home, he repeated at intervals "What would Mr Bounderby say!"—as if Mr Bounderby had been Mrs Grundy.

Chapter IV

MR BOUNDERBY

NOT being Mrs Grundy, who *was* Mr Bounderby?

Why, Mr Bounderby was as near being Mr Gradgrind's bosom friend, as a man perfectly devoid of sentiment can approach that spiritual relationship towards another man perfectly devoid of sentiment. So near was Mr Bounderby—or, if the reader should prefer it, so far off.

He was a rich man: banker, merchant, manufacturer, and what not. A big, loud man, with a stare and a metallic laugh. A man made out of a coarse material, which seemed to have been stretched to make so much of him. A man with a great puffed head and forehead, swelled veins in his temples, and such a strained skin to his face that it seemed to hold his eyes open and lift his eyebrows up. A man with a pervading appearance on him of being inflated like a balloon, and ready to start. A man who could never sufficiently vaunt himself a self-made man. A man who was always proclaiming, through that brassy speaking-trumpet of a voice of his, his old ignorance and his old poverty. A man who was the Bully of humility.

A year or two younger than his eminently practical friend, Mr Bounderby looked older; his seven or eight and forty might have had the seven or eight added to it again, without surprising anybody. He had not much hair. One might have fancied he had talked it off; and that what was left, all standing up in disorder, was in that condition from being constantly blown about by his windy boastfulness.

In the formal drawing-room of Stone Lodge, standing on the hearth-rug, warming himself before the fire, Mr Bounderby delivered some observations to Mrs Gradgrind on the circumstance of its being his birthday. He stood before the fire, partly because it was a cool spring afternoon, though the sun shone; partly because the shade of Stone Lodge was always haunted by the ghost of damp mortar; partly because he thus took up a commanding position, from which to subdue Mrs Gradgrind.

"I hadn't a shoe to my foot. As to a stocking, I didn't know such a thing by name. I passed the day in a ditch, and the night in a pigsty. That's the way I spent my tenth birthday. Not that a ditch was new to me, for I was born in a ditch."

Mrs Gradgrind, a little, thin, white, pink-eyed bundle of shawls, of surpassing feebleness, mental and bodily; who was always taking physic without any effect, and who, whenever she showed a symptom of coming to life, was invariably stunned by some weighty piece of fact tumbling on her; Mrs Gradgrind hoped it was a dry ditch?

"No! As wet as a sop. A foot of water in it," said Mr Bounderby.

"Enough to give a baby cold," Mrs Gradgrind considered.

"Cold? I was born with inflammation of the lungs, and of everything else, I believe, that was capable of inflammation," returned Mr Bounderby. "For years, ma'am, I was one of the most miserable little wretches ever seen. I was so sickly, that I was always moaning and groaning. I was so ragged and dirty, that you wouldn't have touched me with a pair of tongs."

Mrs Gradgrind faintly looked at the tongs, as the most appropriate thing her imbecility could think of doing.

"How I fought through it, I don't know," said Bounderby. "I was determined, I suppose. I have been a determined character in later life, and I suppose I was then. Here I am, Mrs Gradgrind, anyhow, and nobody to thank for my being here but myself."

Mrs Gradgrind meekly and weakly hoped that his mother—

"*My* mother? Bolted, ma'am!" said Bounderby.

Mrs Gradgrind, stunned as usual, collapsed and gave it up.

"My mother left me to my grandmother," said Bounderby; "and, according to the best of my remembrance, my grandmother was the wickedest and the worst old woman that ever lived. If I got a little pair of shoes by any chance, she would take 'em off and sell 'em for drink. Why, I have known that grandmother of mine lie in her bed and drink her fourteen glasses of liquor before breakfast!"

Mrs Gradgrind, weakly smiling, and giving no other sign of vitality, looked (as she always did) like an indifferently executed transparency of a small female figure, without enough light behind it.

"She kept a chandler's shop," pursued Bounderby, "and kept me in an egg-box. That was the cot of my infancy; an old egg-box. As soon as I was big enough to run away, of course I ran away. Then I became a young vagabond; and instead of one old woman knocking me about and starving me, everybody of all ages knocked me about and starved me. They were right; they had no business to do anything else. I was a nuisance, an incumbrance, and a pest. I know that, very well."

His pride in having at any time of his life achieved such a great social distinction as to be a nuisance, an incumbrance, and a pest, was only to be satisfied by three sonorous repetitions of the boast.

"I was to pull through it I suppose, Mrs Gradgrind. Whether I was to do it or not, ma'am, I did it. I pulled through it, though nobody threw me out a rope. Vagabond, errand-boy, vagabond, labourer, porter, clerk, chief manager, small partner, Josiah Bounderby of Coketown. Those are the antecedents, and the culmination. Josiah Bounderby of Coketown learnt his letters from the outsides of the shops, Mrs Gradgrind, and was first able to tell the time upon a dial-plate, from studying the steeple clock of St Giles's Church, London, under the direction of a drunken cripple, who was a convicted thief and an incorrigible vagrant. Tell Josiah Bounderby of Coketown, of your district schools and your model schools, and your training schools, and your whole kettle-of-fish of schools; and Josiah Bounderby of Coketown, tells you plainly, all right, all correct—he hadn't such advantages—but let us have hard-headed, solid-fisted people—the education that made him won't do for everybody, he knows well—such and such his education was, however, and you may force him to swallow boiling fat, but you shall never force him to suppress the facts of his life."

Being heated when he arrived at this climax, Josiah Bounderby of Coketown stopped. He stopped just as his eminently practical friend, still accompanied by the two young culprits, entered the room. His eminently practical friend, on seeing him, stopped also, and gave Louisa a reproachful look that plainly said, "Behold your Bounderby!"

"Well!" blustered Mr Bounderby, "what's the matter? What is young Thomas in the dumps about?"

He spoke of young Thomas, but he looked at Louisa.

"We were peeping at the circus," muttered Louisa haughtily, without lifting up her eyes, "and father caught us."

"And Mrs Gradgrind," said her husband in a lofty manner, "I should as soon have expected to find my children reading poetry."

"Dear me," whimpered Mrs Gradgrind. "How can you, Louisa and Thomas! I wonder at you. I declare you're enough to make one regret ever having had a family at all. I have a great mind to say I wish I hadn't. *Then* what would you have done, I should like to know."

Mr Gradgrind did not seem favourably impressed by these cogent remarks. He frowned impatiently.

"As if, with my head in its present throbbing state, you couldn't go and look at the shells and minerals and things provided for you, instead of circuses!" said Mrs Gradgrind. "You know, as well as I do, no young people have circus masters, or keep circuses in cabinets, or attend lectures about circuses. What can you possibly want to know of circuses then? I am sure you have enough to do, if that's what you want. With my head in its present state, I couldn't remember the mere names of half the facts you have got to attend to."

"That's the reason!" pouted Louisa.

"Don't tell me that's the reason, because it can be nothing of the sort," said Mrs Gradgrind. "Go and be somethingological directly." Mrs Gradgrind was not a scientific character, and usually dismissed her children to their studies with this general injunction to choose their pursuit.

In truth, Mrs Gradgrind's stock of facts in general was woefully defective; but Mr Gradgrind in raising her to her high matrimonial position, had been influenced by two reasons. Firstly, she was most satisfactory as a question of figures; and, secondly, she had "no nonsense" about her. By nonsense he meant fancy; and truly it is probable she was as free from any alloy of that nature, as any human being not arrived at the perfection of an absolute idiot, ever was.

The simple circumstance of being left alone with her husband and Mr Bounderby, was sufficient to stun this admirable lady again, without collision between herself and any other fact. So, she once more died away, and nobody minded her.

"Bounderby," said Mr Gradgrind, drawing a chair to the fireside, "you are always so interested in my young people—particularly in Louisa—that I make no apology for saying to you, I am very much vexed by this discovery. I have systematically devoted myself (as you know) to the education of the reason of my family. The reason is (as you know) the only faculty to which education should be addressed. And yet, Bounderby, it would appear from this unexpected circumstance of today, though in itself a trifling one, as if something had crept into Thomas's and Louisa's minds which is—or rather, which is not—I don't know that I can express myself better than by saying—which has never been intended to be developed, and in which their reason has no part."

"There certainly is no reason in looking with interest at a parcel of vagabonds," returned Bounderby. "When I was a vagabond myself, nobody looked with any interest at *me;* I know that."

"Then comes the question," said the eminently practical father, with his eyes on the fire, "in what has this vulgar curiosity its rise?"

"I'll tell you in what. In idle imagination."

"I hope not," said eminently practical; "I confess, however, that the misgiving *has* crossed me on my way home."

"In idle imagination, Gradgrind," repeated Bounderby. "A very bad thing for any-body, but a cursed bad thing for a girl like Louisa. I should ask Mrs Gradgrind's pardon for strong expressions, but that she knows very well I am not a refined character. Whoever expects refinement in *me* will be disappointed. I hadn't a refined bringing up."

"Whether," said Mr Gradgrind, pondering with his hands in his pockets, and his cavernous eyes on the fire, "whether any instructor or servant can have suggested anything? Whether Louisa or Thomas can have been reading anything? Whether, in spite of all precautions, any idle story-book can have got into the house? Because, in minds that have been practically formed by rule and line, from the cradle upwards, this is so curious, so incomprehensible."

"Stop a bit!" cried Bounderby, who all this time had been standing, as before, on the hearth, bursting at the very furniture of the room with explosive humility. "You have one of those strollers' children in the school."

"Cecilia Jupe, by name," said Mr Gradgrind, with something of a stricken look at his friend.

"Now, stop a bit!" cried Bounderby again. "How did she come there?"

"Why, the fact is, I saw the girl myself, for the first time, only just now. She specially applied here at the house to be admitted, as not regularly belonging to our town, and—yes, you are right, Bounderby, you are right."

"Now, stop a bit!" cried Bounderby, once more, "Louisa saw her when she came?"

"Louisa certainly did see her, for she mentioned the application to me. But Louisa saw her, I have no doubt, in Mrs Gradgrind's presence."

"Pray, Mrs Gradgrind," said Bounderby, "what passed?"

"Oh, my poor health!" returned Mrs Gradgrind. "The girl wanted to come to the school, and Mr Gradgrind wanted girls to come to the school, and Louisa and Thomas both said that the girl wanted to come, and that Mr Gradgrind wanted girls to come, and how was it possible to contradict them when such was the fact!"

"Now I tell you what, Gradgrind!" said Mr Bounderby. "Turn this girl to the right about, and there's an end of it."

"I am much of your opinion."

"Do it at once," said Bounderby, "has always been my motto from a child. When I thought I would run away from my egg-box and my grandmother, I did it at once. Do you the same. Do this at once!"

"Are you walking?" asked his friend. "I have the father's address. Perhaps you would not mind walking to town with me?"

"Not the least in the world," said Mr Bounderby, "as long as you do it at once!"

So, Mr Bounderby threw his hat on—he always threw it on, as expressing a man who had been far too busily employed in making himself, to acquire any fashion of wearing his hat—and with his hands in his pockets, sauntered out into the hall. "I never wear gloves," it was his custom to say. "I didn't climb up the ladder in *them*. Shouldn't be so high up, if I had."

Being left to saunter in the hall a minute or two while Mr Gradgrind went upstairs for the address, he opened the door of the children's study and looked into that serene floor-clothed apartment, which, notwithstanding its book-cases and its cabinets and its variety of learned and philosophical appliances, had much of the genial aspect of a room devoted to hair-cutting. Louisa languidly leaned upon the window looking out, without looking at anything, while young Thomas stood sniffing revengefully at the fire. Adam Smith and Malthus, two younger Gradgrinds, were out at lecture in custody; and little Jane, after manufacturing a good deal of moist pipe-clay on her face with slate-pencil and tears, had fallen asleep over vulgar fractions.

"It's all right now, Louisa; it's all right, young Thomas," said Mr Bounderby; "you won't do so any more. I'll answer for it's being all over with father. Well, Louisa, that's worth a kiss, isn't it?"

"You can take one, Mr Bounderby," returned Louisa, when she had coldly paused, and slowly walked across the room, and ungraciously raised her cheek towards him, with her face turned away.

"Always my pet; an't you, Louisa?" said Mr Bounderby. "Good-bye, Louisa!"

He went his way, but she stood on the same spot, rubbing the cheek he had kissed, with her handkerchief, until it was burning red. She was still doing this, five minutes afterwards.

"What are you about, Loo?" her brother sulkily remonstrated. "You'll rub a hole in your face."

"You may cut the piece out with your penknife if you like, Tom. I wouldn't cry!"

Chapter V

THE KEY-NOTE

COKETOWN, to which Messrs. Bounderby and Gradgrind now walked, was a triumph of fact; it had no greater taint of fancy in it than Mrs Gradgrind herself. Let us strike the key-note, Coketown, before pursuing our tune.

It was a town of red brick, or of brick that would have been red if the smoke and ashes had allowed it; but, as matters stood it was a town of unnatural red and black like the painted face of a savage. It was a town of machinery and tall chimneys, out of which interminable serpents of smoke trailed themselves for ever and ever, and never got uncoiled. It had a black canal in it, and a river that ran purple with ill-smelling dye, and vast piles of building full of windows where there was a rattling and a trembling all day long, and where the piston of the steam-engine worked monotonously up and down, like the head of an elephant in a state of melancholy madness. It contained several large streets all very like one another, and many small streets still more like one another, inhabited by people equally like one another, who all went in and out at the same hours, with the same sound upon the same pavements, to do the same work, and to whom every day was the same as yesterday and tomorrow, and every year the counterpart of the last and the next.

These attributes of Coketown were in the main inseparable from the work by which it was sustained; against them were to be set off, comforts of life which found their way

all over the world, and elegancies of life which made, we will not ask how much of the
fine lady, who could scarcely bear to hear the place mentioned. The rest of its features
were voluntary, and they were these.

You saw nothing in Coketown but what was severely workful. If the members of
a religious persuasion built a chapel there—as the members of eighteen religious persuasions had done—they made it a pious warehouse of red brick, with sometimes (but this
only in highly ornamented examples) a bell in a bird-cage on the top of it. The solitary
exception was the New Church; a stuccoed edifice with a square steeple over the door,
terminating in four short pinnacles like florid wooden legs. All the public inscriptions in
the town were painted alike, in severe characters of black and white. The jail might have
been the infirmary, the infirmary might have been the jail, the town-hall might have been
either, or both, or anything else, for anything that appeared to the contrary in the graces
of their construction. Fact, fact, fact, everywhere in the material aspect of the town; fact,
fact, fact, everywhere in the immaterial. The M'Choakumchild school was all fact, and the
school of design was all fact, and the relations between master and man were all fact,
and everything was fact between the lying-in hospital and the cemetery, and what you
couldn't state in figures, or show to be purchaseable in the cheapest market and saleable
in the dearest, was not, and never should be, world without end, Amen.

A town so sacred to fact, and so triumphant in its assertion, of course got on well?
Why no, not quite well. No? Dear me!

No. Coketown did not come out of its own furnaces, in all respects like gold that
had stood the fire. First, the perplexing mystery of the place was, Who belonged to the
eighteen denominations? Because, whoever did, the labouring people did not. It was
very strange to walk through the streets on a Sunday morning, and note how few of *them*
the barbarous jangling of bells that was driving the sick and nervous mad, called away
from their own quarter, from their own close rooms, from the corners of their own
streets, where they lounged listlessly, gazing at all the church and chapel going, as at a
thing with which they had no manner of concern. Nor was it merely the stranger who
noticed this, because there was a native organization in Coketown itself, whose members
were to be heard of in the House of Commons every session, indignantly petitioning for
acts of parliament that should make these people religious by main force. Then, came
the Teetotal Society, who complained that these same people *would* get drunk, and
showed in tabular statements that they did get drunk, and proved at tea parties that no
inducement, human or Divine (except a medal), would induce them to forego their
custom of getting drunk. Then, came the chemist and druggist, with other tabular
statements, showing that when they didn't get drunk, they took opium. Then, came the
experienced chaplain of the jail, with more tabular statements, outdoing all the previous
tabular statements, and showing that the same people *would* resort to low haunts,
hidden from the public eye, where they heard low singing and saw low dancing, and
mayhap joined in it; and where A. B., aged twenty-four next birthday, and committed for
eighteen months' solitary, had himself said (not that he had ever shown himself particularly worthy of belief) his ruin began, as he was perfectly sure and confident that
otherwise he would have been a tip-top moral specimen. Then, came Mr Gradgrind and
Mr Bounderby, the two gentlemen at this present moment walking through Coketown,
and both eminently practical, who could, on occasion, furnish more tabular statements
derived from their own personal experience, and illustrated by cases they had known
and seen, from which it clearly appeared—in short it was the only clear thing in the
case—that these same people were a bad lot altogether, gentlemen; that do what you
would for them they were never thankful for it, gentlemen; that they were restless,

gentlemen; that they never knew what they wanted; that they lived upon the best, and bought fresh butter, and insisted on Mocha coffee, and rejected all but prime parts of meat, and yet were eternally dissatisfied and unmanageable. In short it was the moral of the old nursery fable:

> There was an old woman, and what do you think?
> She lived upon nothing but victuals and drink;
> Victuals and drink were the whole of her diet,
> And yet this old woman would NEVER be quiet.

Is it possible, I wonder, that there was any analogy between the case of the Coketown population and the case of the little Gradgrinds? Surely, none of us in our sober senses and acquainted with figures, are to be told at this time of day, that one of the foremost elements in the existence of the Coketown working people had been for scores of years, deliberately set at nought? That there was any Fancy in them demanding to be brought into healthy existence instead of struggling on in convulsions? That exactly in the ratio as they worked long and monotonously, the craving grew within them for some physical relief—some relaxation, encouraging good humour and good spirits, and giving them a vent—some recognized holiday, though it were but for an honest dance to a stirring band of music—some occasional light pie in which even M'Choakumchild had no finger—which craving must and would be satisfied aright, or must and would inevitably go wrong, until the laws of the Creation were repealed?

"This man lives at Pod's End, and I don't quite know Pod's End," said Mr Gradgrind. "Which is it, Bounderby?"

Mr Bounderby knew it was somewhere down town, but knew no more respecting it. So they stopped for a moment, looking about.

Almost as they did so, there came running round the corner of the street at a quick pace and with a frightened look, a girl whom Mr Gradgrind recognized. "Halloa!" said he. "Stop! Where are you going? Stop!" Girl number twenty stopped then, palpitating, and made him a curtsey.

"Why are you tearing about the streets," said Mr Gradgrind, "in this improper manner?"

"I was—I was run after, sir," the girl panted, "and I wanted to get away."

"Run after?" repeated Mr Gradgrind. "Who would run after *you?*"

The question was unexpectedly and suddenly answered for her, by the colourless boy, Bitzer, who came round the corner with such blind speed and so little anticipating a stoppage on the pavement, that he brought himself up against Mr Gradgrind's waistcoat, and rebounded into the road.

"What do you mean, boy?" said Mr Gradgrind. "What are you doing? How dare you dash against—everybody—in this manner?"

Bitzer picked up his cap, which the concussion had knocked off; and backing, and knuckling his forehead, pleaded that it was an accident.

"Was this boy running after you, Jupe?" asked Mr Gradgrind.

"Yes, sir," said the girl reluctantly.

"No, I wasn't, sir!" cried Bitzer. "Not till she run away from me. But the horse-riders never mind what they say, sir; they're famous for it. You know the horse-riders are famous for never minding what they say," addressing Sissy. "It's as well known in the town as—please, sir, as the multiplication table isn't known to the horse-riders." Bitzer tried Mr Bounderby with this.

"He frightened me so," said the girl, "with his cruel faces!"

"Oh!" cried Bitzer. "Oh! An't you one of the rest! An't you a horse-rider! I never looked at her, sir. I asked her if she would know how to define a horse tomorrow, and offered to tell her again, and she ran away, and I ran after her, sir, that she might know how to answer when she was asked. You wouldn't have thought of saying such mischief if you hadn't been a horse-rider!"

"Her calling seems to be pretty well known among 'em," observed Mr Bounderby. "You'd have had the whole school peeping in a row, in a week."

"Truly, I think so," returned his friend. "Bitzer, turn you about and take yourself home. Jupe, stay here a moment. Let me hear of your running in this manner any more, boy, and you will hear of me through the master of the school. You understand what I mean. Go along."

The boy stopped in his rapid blinking, knuckled his forehead again, glanced at Sissy, turned about, and retreated.

"Now, girl," said Mr Gradgrind, "take this gentleman and me to your father's; we are going there. What have you got in that bottle you are carrying?"

"Gin," said Mr Bounderby.

"Dear, no sir! It's the nine oils."

"The what?" cried Mr Bounderby.

"The nine oils, sir. To rub father with." Then, said Mr Bounderby, with a loud, short laugh, "what the devil do you rub your father with nine oils for?"

"It's what our people always use, sir, when they get any hurts in the ring," replied the girl, looking over her shoulder, to assure herself that her pursuer was gone. "They bruise themselves very bad sometimes."

"Serve 'em right," said Mr Bounderby, "for being idle." She glanced up at his face, with mingled astonishment and dread.

"By George!" said Mr Bounderby, "when I was four or five years younger than you, I had worse bruises upon me than ten oils, twenty oils, forty oils, would have rubbed off. I didn't get 'em by posture-making, but by being banged about. There was no rope-dancing for me; I danced on the bare ground and was larruped with the rope."

Mr Gradgrind, though hard enough, was by no means so rough a man as Mr Bounderby. His character was not unkind, all things considered; it might have been a very kind one indeed, if he had only made some round mistake in the arithmetic that balanced it, years ago. He said, in what he meant for a reassuring tone, as they turned down a narrow road, "And this is Pod's End; is it, Jupe?"

"This is it, sir, and—if you wouldn't mind, sir—this is the house."

She stopped, at twilight, at the door of a mean little public house, with dim red lights in it. As haggard and as shabby, as if, for want of custom, it had itself taken to drinking, and had gone the way all drunkards go, and was very near the end of it.

"It's only crossing the bar, sir, and up the stairs, if you wouldn't mind, and waiting there for a moment till I get a candle. If you should hear a dog, sir, it's only Merrylegs, and he only barks."

"Merrylegs and nine oils, eh!" said Mr Bounderby, entering last with his metallic laugh. "Pretty well this, for a self-made man!"

Chapter VI

SLEARY'S HORSEMANSHIP

THE name of the public house was the Pegasus's Arms. The Pegasus's legs might have been more to the purpose; but, underneath the winged horse upon the sign-board, the Pegasus's Arms was inscribed in Roman letters. Beneath that inscription again, in a flowing scroll, the painter had touched off the lines:

> Good malt makes good beer,
> Walk in, and they'll draw it here;
> Good wine makes good brandy,
> Give us a call, and you'll find it handy.

Framed and glazed upon the wall behind the dingy little bar, was another Pegasus—a theatrical one—with real gauze let in for his wings, golden stars stuck on all over him, and his ethereal harness made of red silk.

As it had grown too dusky without, to see the sign, and as it had not grown light enough within to see the picture, Mr Gradgrind and Mr Bounderby received no offence from these idealities. They followed the girl up some steep corner-stairs without meeting any one, and stopped in the dark while she went on for a candle. They expected every moment to hear Merrylegs give tongue, but the highly-trained performing dog had not barked when the girl and the candle appeared together.

"Father is not in our room, sir," she said, with a face of great surprise. "If you wouldn't mind walking in, I'll find him directly."

They walked in; and Sissy, having set two chairs for them, sped away with a quick light step. It was a mean, shabbily-furnished room, with a bed in it. The white night-cap, embellished with two peacock's feathers and a pigtail bolt upright, in which Signor Jupe had that very afternoon enlivened the varied performances with his chaste Shaksperean quips and retorts, hung upon a nail; but no other portion of his wardrobe, or other token of himself or his pursuits, was to be seen anywhere. As to Merrylegs, that respectable ancestor of the highly-trained animal who went aboard the ark, might have been accidentally shut out of it, for any sign of a dog that was manifest to eye or ear in the Pegasus's Arms.

They heard the doors of rooms above, opening and shutting as Sissy went from one to another in quest of her father; and presently they heard voices expressing surprise. She came bounding down again in a great hurry, opened a battered and mangey old hair trunk, found it empty, and looked round with her hands clasped and her face full of terror.

"Father must have gone down to the Booth, Sir. I don't know why he should go there, but he must be there; I'll bring him in a minute!" She was gone directly, without her bonnet; with her long, dark, childish hair streaming behind her.

"What does she mean!" said Mr Gradgrind. "Back in a minute? It's more than a mile off."

Before Mr Bounderby could reply, a young man appeared at the door, and introducing himself with the words, "By your leaves, gentlemen!" walked in with his hands in his pockets. His face, close-shaven, thin, and sallow, was shaded by a great quantity of dark hair brushed into a roll all round his head, and parted up the centre. His legs were very robust, but shorter than legs of good proportions should have been. His chest and back were as much too broad, as his legs were too short. He was dressed in a Newmarket coat and tight-fitting trousers; wore a shawl round his neck; smelt of lamp-oil, straw, orange-peel, horses' provender, and sawdust; and looked a most remarkable sort of Centaur, compounded of the stable and the play-house. Where the one began, and the other ended, nobody could have told with any precision. This gentleman was mentioned in the bills of the day as Mr E. W. B. Childers, so justly celebrated for his daring vaulting act as the Wild Huntsman of the North American Prairies; in which popular performance, a diminutive boy with an old face, who now accompanied him, assisted as his infant son: being carried upside down over his father's shoulder, by one foot, and held by the crown of his head, heels upwards, in the palm of his father's hand, according to the violent paternal manner in which wild huntsmen may be observed to fondle their offspring. Made up with curls, wreaths, wings, white bismuth, and carmine, this hopeful young person soared into so pleasing a Cupid as to constitute the chief delight of the maternal part of the spectators; but, in private, where his characteristics were a precocious cuta-way coat and an extremely gruff voice, he became of the Turf, turfy.

"By your leaves, gentlemen," said Mr E. W. B. Childers, glancing round the room. "It was you, I believe, that were wishing to see Jupe?"

"It was," said Mr Gradgrind. "His daughter has gone to fetch him, but I can't wait; therefore, if you please, I will leave a message for him with you."

"You see, my friend," Mr Bounderby put in, "we are the kind of people who know the value of time, and you are the kind of people who don't know the value of time."

"I have not," retorted Mr Childers, after surveying him from head to foot, "the honour of knowing *you;*—but if you mean that you can make more money of your time than I can of mine, I should judge from your appearance, that you are about right."

"And when you have made it, you can keep it too, I should think," said Cupid.

"Kidderminster, stow that!" said Mr Childers. (Master Kidderminster was Cupid's mortal name.)

"What does he come here cheeking us for, then?" cried Master Kidderminster, showing a very irascible temperament. "If you want to cheek us, pay your ochre at the doors and take it out."

"Kidderminster," said Mr Childers, raising his voice, "stow that!—Sir," to Mr Grad-grind, "I was addressing myself to you. You may or you may not be aware (for perhaps you have not been much in the audience), that Jupe has missed his tip very often lately."

"Has—what has he missed?" asked Mr Gradgrind, glancing at the potent Bounderby for assistance.

"Missed his tip."

"Offered at the Garters four times last night, and never done 'em once," said Master Kidderminster. "Missed his tip at the banners, too, and was loose in his ponging."

"Didn't do what he ought to do. Was short in his leaps and bad in his tumbling," Mr Childers interpreted.

"Oh!" said Mr Gradgrind, "that is tip, is it?"

"In a general way that's missing his tip," Mr E. W. B. Childers answered.

"Nine-oils, Merrylegs, missing tips, garters, banners, and Ponging, eh!" ejaculated Bounderby, with his laugh of laughs. "Queer sort of company, too, for a man who has raised himself."

"Lower yourself, then," retorted Cupid. "Oh Lord! if you've raised yourself so high as all that comes to, let yourself down a bit."

"This is a very obtrusive lad!" said Mr Gradgrind, turning, and knitting his brows on him.

"We'd have had a young gentleman to meet you, if we had known you were coming," retorted Master Kidderminster, nothing abashed. "It's a pity you don't have a bespeak, being so particular. You're on the Tight-Jeff, ain't you?"

"What does this unmannerly boy mean," asked Mr Gradgrind, eyeing him in a sort of desperation, "by Tight-Jeff?"

"There! Get out, get out!" said Mr Childers, thrusting his young friend from the room, rather in the prairie manner. "Tight-Jeff or Slack-Jeff, it don't much signify: it's only tight-rope and slack-rope. You were going to give me a message for Jupe?"

"Yes, I was."

"Then," continued Mr Childers, quickly, "my opinion is, he will never receive it. Do you know much of him?"

"I never saw the man in my life."

"I doubt if you ever *will* see him now. It's pretty plain to me, he's off."

"Do you mean that he has deserted his daughter?"

"Ay! I mean," said Mr Childers, with a nod, "that he has cut. He was goosed last night, he was goosed the night before last, he was goosed today. He has lately got in the way of being always goosed, and he can't stand it."

"Why has he been—so very much—Goosed?" asked Mr Gradgrind, forcing the word out of himself, with great solemnity and reluctance.

"His joints are turning stiff, and he is getting used up," said Childers. "He has his points as a Cackler still, but he can't get a living out of *them.*"

"A Cackler!" Bounderby repeated. "Here we go again!"

"A speaker, if the gentleman likes it better," said Mr E. W. B. Childers, superciliously throwing the interpretation over his shoulder, and accompanying it with a shake of his long hair—which all shook at once. "Now, it's a remarkable fact, sir, that it cut that man deeper, to know that his daughter knew of his being goosed, than to go through with it."

"Good!" interrupted Mr Bounderby. "This is good, Gradgrind! A man so fond of his daughter, that he runs away from her! This is devilish good! Ha! ha! Now, I'll tell you what, young man. I haven't always occupied my present station of life. I know what these things are. You may be astonished to hear it, but my mother ran away from *me.*"

E. W. B. Childers replied pointedly, that he was not at all astonished to hear it.

"Very well," said Bounderby. "I was born in a ditch, and my mother ran away from me. Do I excuse her for it? No. Have I ever excused her for it? Not I. What do I call her for it? I call her probably the very worst woman that ever lived in the world, except my drunken grandmother. There's no family pride about me, there's no imaginative senti-mental humbug about me. I call a spade a spade; and I call the mother of Josiah Bounderby of Coketown, without any fear or any favour, what I should call her if she had been the mother of Dick Jones of Wapping. So, with this man. He is a runaway rogue and a vagabond, that's what he is, in English."

"It's all the same to me what he is or what he is not, whether in English or whether in French," retorted Mr E. W. B. Childers, facing about. "I am telling your friend what's the fact; if you don't like to hear it, you can avail yourself of the open air. You give it mouth enough, you do; but give it mouth in your own building at least," remonstrated E. W. B. with stern irony. "Don't give it mouth in this building, till you're called upon. You have got some building of your own, I dare say, now?"

"Perhaps so," replied Mr Bounderby, rattling his money and laughing.

"Then give it mouth in your own building, will you, if you please?" said Childers.

"Because this isn't a strong building, and too much of you might bring it down!"

Eyeing Mr Bounderby from head to foot again, he turned from him, as from a man finally disposed of, to Mr Gradgrind.

"Jupe sent his daughter out on an errand not an hour ago, and then was seen to slip out himself, with his hat over his eyes and a bundle tied up in a handkerchief under his arm. She will never believe it of him, but he has cut away and left her."

"Pray," said Mr Gradgrind, "why will she never believe it of him?"

"Because those two were one. Because they were never asunder. Because, up to this time, he seemed to dote upon her," said Childers, taking a step or two to look into the empty trunk. Both Mr Childers and Master Kidderminster walked in a curious manner; with their legs wider apart than the general run of men, and with a very knowing assumption of being stiff in the knees. This walk was common to all the male members of Sleary's company, and was understood to express, that they were always on horseback.

"Poor Sissy! He had better have apprenticed her," said Childers, giving his hair another shake, as he looked up from the empty box. "Now, he leaves her without anything to take to."

"It is creditable to you who have never been apprenticed, to express that opinion," returned Mr Gradgrind, approvingly.

"I never apprenticed? I was apprenticed when I was seven year old."

"Oh! Indeed?" said Mr Gradgrind, rather resentfully, as having been defrauded of his good opinion. "I was not aware of its being the custom to apprentice young persons to—"

"Idleness," Mr Bounderby put in with a loud laugh. "No, by the Lord Harry! Nor I!"

"Her father always had it in his head," resumed Childers, feigning unconsciousness of Mr Bounderby's existence, "that she was to be taught the deuce-and-all of education. How it got into his head, I can't say; I can only say that it never got out. He has been picking up a bit of reading for her, here—and a bit of writing for her, there—and a bit of cyphering for her, somewhere else—these seven years."

Mr E. W. B. Childers took one of his hands out of his pockets, stroked his face and chin, and looked, with a good deal of doubt and a little hope, at Mr Gradgrind. From the first he had sought to conciliate that gentleman, for the sake of the deserted girl.

"When Sissy got into the school here," he pursued, "her father was as pleased as Punch. I couldn't altogether make out why, myself, as we were not stationary here, being but comers and goers anywhere. I suppose, however, he had this move in his mind—he was always half-cracked—and then considered her provided for. If you should happen to have looked in tonight, for the purpose of telling him that you were going to do her any little service," said Mr Childers, stroking his face again, and repeating his look, "it would be very fortunate and well timed; *very* fortunate and well-timed."

"On the contrary," returned Mr Gradgrind. "I came to tell him that her connexions made her not an object for the school, and that she must not attend any more. Still, if her father really has left her, without any connivance on her part—Bounderby, let me have a word with you."

Upon this, Mr Childers politely betook himself, with his equestrian walk, to the landing outside the door, and there stood stroking his face and softly whistling. While thus engaged, he overheard such phrases in Mr Bounderby's voice as "No. *I* say no. I advise you not. I say by no means." While, from Mr Gradgrind, he heard in his much lower tone the words, "But even as an example to Louisa, of what this pursuit which has been the subject of a vulgar curiosity, leads to and ends in. Think of it, Bounderby, in that point of view."

Meanwhile, the various members of Sleary's company gradually gathered together
from the upper regions, where they were quartered, and, from standing about, talking
in low voices to one another and to Mr Childers, gradually insinuated themselves and
him into the room. There were two or three handsome young women among them, with
their two or three husbands, and their two or three mothers, and their eight or nine little
children, who did the fairy business when required. The father of one of the families was
in the habit of balancing the father of another of the families on the top of a great pole;
the father of a third family often made a pyramid of both those fathers, with Master
Kidderminster for the apex, and himself for the base; all the fathers could dance upon
rolling casks, stand upon bottles, catch knives and balls, twirl hand-basins, ride upon
anything, jump over everything, and stick at nothing. All the mothers could (and did)
dance, upon the slack wire and the tight rope, and perform rapid acts on bare-backed
steeds; none of them were at all particular in respect of showing their legs; and one of
them, alone in a Greek chariot, drove six in hand into every town they came to. They
all assumed to be mighty rakish and knowing, they were not very tidy in their private
dresses, they were not at all orderly in their domestic arrangements, and the combined
literature of the whole company would have produced but a poor letter on any subject.
Yet there was a remarkable gentleness and childishness about these people, a special
inaptitude for any kind of sharp practice, and an untiring readiness to help and pity one
another, deserving, often of as much respect, and always of as much generous construction, as the everyday virtues of any class of people in the world.

Last of all appeared Mr Sleary: a stout man as already mentioned, with one fixed eye
and one loose eye, a voice (if it can be called so) like the efforts of a broken old pair of
bellows, a flabby surface, and a muddled head which was never sober and never drunk.

"Thquire!" said Mr Sleary, who was troubled with asthma, and whose breath came
far too thick and heavy for the letter s, "Your thervant! Thith ith a bad piethe of bithnith,
thith ith. You've heard of my Clown and hith dog being thuppothed to have morrithed?"

He addressed Mr Gradgrind, who answered "Yes."

"Well Thquire," he returned, taking off his hat, and rubbing the lining with his
pocket-handkerchief, which he kept inside it for the purpose. "Ith it your intenthion to
do anything for the poor girl, Thquire?"

"I shall have something to propose to her when she comes back," said Mr Gradgrind.

"Glad to hear it, Thquire. Not that I want to get rid of the child, any more than I want
to thtand in her way. I'm willing to take her prentith, though at her age ith late. My voithe
ith a little huthky, Thquire, and not eathy heard by them ath don't know me; but if you'd
been chilled and heated, heated and chilled, chilled and heated in the ring when you
wath young, ath often ath I have been, *your* voithe wouldn't have lathted out, Thquire,
no more then mine."

"I dare say not," said Mr Gradgrind.

"What thall it be, Thquire, while you wait? Thall it be Therry? Give it a name,
Thquire!" said Mr Sleary, with hospitable ease.

"Nothing for me, I thank you," said Mr Gradgrind.

"Don't thay nothing, Thquire. What doth your friend thay? If you haven't took your
feed yet, have a glath of bitterth."

Here his daughter Josephine—a pretty fair-haired girl of eighteen, who had been
tied on a horse at two years old, and had made a will at twelve, which she always carried
about with her, expressive of her dying desire to be drawn to the grave by the two
piebald ponies—cried "Father, hush! she has come back!" Then came Sissy Jupe, run-

ning into the room as she had run out of it. And when she saw them all assembled, and saw their looks, and saw no father there, she broke into a most deplorable cry, and took refuge on the bosom of the most accomplished tight-rope lady (herself in the family way), who knelt down on the floor to nurse her, and to weep over her.

"Ith an infernal thame, upon my thoul it ith," said Sleary.

"O my dear father, my good kind father, where are you gone? You are gone to try to do me some good, I know! You are gone away for my sake, I am sure. And how miserable and helpless you will be without me, poor, poor father, until you come back!" It was so pathetic to hear her saying many things of this kind, with her face turned upward, and her arms stretched out as if she were trying to stop his departing shadow and embrace it, that no one spoke a word until Mr Bounderby (growing impatient) took the case in hand.

"Now, good people all," said he, "this is wanton waste of time. Let the girl understand the fact. Let her take it from me, if you like, who have been run away from, myself. Here, what's your name! Your father has absconded—deserted you—and you mustn't expect to see him again as long as you live."

They cared so little for plain Fact, these people, and were in that advanced state of degeneracy on the subject, that instead of being impressed by the speaker's strong common sense, they took it in extraordinary dudgeon. The men muttered "Shame!" and the women "Brute!" and Sleary, in some haste, communicated the following hint, apart to Mr Bounderby.

"I tell you what, Thquire. To thpeak plain to you, my opinion ith that you had better cut it thort, and drop it. They're a very good natur'd people, my people, but they're accuthtomed to be quick in their movementh; and if you don't act upon my advithe, I'm damned if I don't believe they'll pith you out o' winder."

Mr Bounderby being restrained by this mild suggestion, Mr Gradgrind found an opening for his eminently practical exposition of the subject.

"It is of no moment, said he, "whether this person is to be expected back at any time, or the contrary. He is gone away, and there is no present expectation of his return. That, I believe, is agreed on all hands."

"Thath agreed, Thquire. Thtick to that!" From Sleary.

"Well then. I, who came here to inform the father of the poor girl, Jupe, that she could not be received at the school any more, in consequence of there being practical objections, into which I need not enter, to the reception there of the children of persons so employed, am prepared in these altered circumstances to make a proposal. I am willing to take charge of you, Jupe, and to educate you, and provide for you. The only condition (over and above your good behaviour) I make is, that you decide now, at once, whether to accompany me or remain here. Also, that if you accompany me now, it is understood that you communicate no more with any of your friends who are here present. These observations comprise the whole of the case."

"At the thame time," said Sleary, "I mutht put in my word, Thquire, tho that both thides of the banner may be equally theen. If you like, Thethilia, to be prentitht, you know the natur of the work and you know your companionth. Emma Gordon, in whothe lap you're a lyin' at prethent, would be a mother to you, and Joth'phine would be a thithter to you. I don't pretend to be of the angel breed mythelf, and I don't thay but what, when you mith'd your tip, you'd find me cut up rough, and thwear a oath or two at you. But what I thay, Thquire, ith, that good tempered or bad tempered, I never did a horthe a injury yet, no more than thwearing at him went, and that I don't expect I thall begin otherwithe at my time of life, with a rider. I never wath much of a Cackler, Thquire, and I have thed my thay."

The latter part of this speech was addressed to Mr Gradgrind, who received it with a grave inclination of his head, and then remarked:

"The only observation I will make to you, Jupe, in the way of influencing your decision, is, that it is highly desirable to have a sound practical education, and that even your father himself (from what I understand) appears, on your behalf, to have known and felt that much."

The last words had a visible effect upon her. She stopped in her wild crying, a little detached herself from Emma Gordon, and turned her face full upon her patron. The whole company perceived the force of the change, and drew a long breath together, that plainly said, "she will go!"

"Be sure you know your own mind, Jupe," Mr Gradgrind cautioned her; "I say no more. Be sure you know your own mind!"

"When father comes back," cried the girl, bursting into tears again after a minute's silence, "how will he ever find me if I go away!"

"You may be quite at ease," said Mr Gradgrind, calmly; he worked out the whole matter like a sum: "you may be quite at ease, Jupe, on that score. In such a case, your father, I apprehend, must find out Mr——."

"Thleary. Thath my name, Thquire. Not athamed of it. Known all over England, and alwayth payeth ith way."

"Must find out Mr Sleary, who would then let him know where you went. I should have no power of keeping you against his wish, and he would have no difficulty, at any time, in finding Mr Thomas Gradgrind of Coketown. I am well known."

"Well known," assented Mr Sleary, rolling his loose eye. "You're one of the thort, Thquire, that keepth a prethious thight of money out of the houthe. But never mind that at prethent."

There was another silence; and then she exclaimed, sobbing with her hands before her face, "Oh give me my clothes, give me my clothes, and let me go away before I break my heart!"

The women sadly bestirred themselves to get the clothes together—it was soon done, for they were not many—and to pack them in a basket which had often travelled with them. Sissy sat all the time, upon the ground, still sobbing and covering her eyes. Mr Gradgrind and his friend Bounderby stood near the door, ready to take her away. Mr Sleary stood in the middle of the room, with the male members of the company about him, exactly as he would have stood in the centre of the ring during his daughter Josephine's performance. He wanted nothing but his whip.

The basket packed in silence, they brought her bonnet to her, and smoothed her disordered hair, and put it on. Then they pressed about her, and bent over her in very natural attitudes, kissing and embracing her; and brought the children to take leave of her; and were a tender-hearted, simple, foolish set of women altogether.

"Now, Jupe," said Mr Gradgrind. "If you are quite determined, come!"

But she had to take her farewell of the male part of the company yet, and every one of them had to unfold his arms (for they all assumed the professional attitude when they found themselves near Sleary), and give her a parting kiss—Master Kidderminster excepted, in whose young nature there was an original flavour of the misanthrope, who was also known to have harboured matrimonial views, and who moodily withdrew. Mr Sleary was reserved until the last. Opening his arms wide he took her by both her hands, and would have sprung her up and down, after the riding-master manner of congratulating young ladies on their dismounting from a rapid act; but there was no rebound in Sissy, and she only stood before him crying.

"Goodbye, my dear!" said Sleary. "You'll make your fortun, I hope, and none of our poor folkth will ever trouble you, I'll pound it. I with your father hadn't taken hith dog with him; ith a ill-conwenienth to have the dog out of the billth. But on thecond thoughth, he wouldn't have performed without hith mathter, tho ith ath broad ath ith long!"

With that he regarded her attentively with his fixed eye, surveyed his company with his loose one, kissed her, shook his head, and handed her to Mr Gradgrind as to a horse.

"There the ith, Thquire," he said, sweeping her with a professional glance as if she were being adjusted in her seat, "and the'll do you juthtithe. Goodbye, Thethilia!"

"Goodbye, Cecilia!" "Goodbye, Sissy!" "God bless you, dear!" In a variety of voices from all the room.

But the riding-master eye had observed the bottle of the nine oils in her bosom, and he now interposed with "Leave the bottle, my dear; ith large to carry; it will be of no uthe to you now. Give it to me!"

"No, no!" she said, in another burst of tears. "Oh no! Pray let me keep it for father till he comes back! He will want it when he comes back. He had never thought of going away, when he sent me for it. I must keep it for him, if you please!"

"Tho be it, my dear. (You thee how it ith, Thquire!) Farewell, Thethilia! My latht wordth to you ith thith, Thtick to the termth of your engagement, be obedient to the Thquire, and forget uth. But if, when you're grown up and married and well off, you come upon any horthe-riding ever, don't be hard upon it, don't be croth with it, give it a Bethpeak if you can, and think you might do wurth. People must be amuthed, Thquire, thomehow," continued Sleary, rendered more pursy than ever, by so much talking; "they can't be alwayth a working, nor yet they can't be alwayth a learning. Make the betht of uth; not the wurtht. I've got my living out of horthe-riding all my life, I know; but I conthider that I lay down the philothophy of the thubject when I thay to you, Thquire, make the betht of uth: not the wurtht!"

The Sleary philosophy was propounded as they went downstairs; and the fixed eye of Philosophy—and its rolling eye, too—soon lost the three figures and the basket in the darkness of the street.

Chapter VII

MRS SPARSIT

M R Bounderby being a bachelor, an elderly lady presided over his establishment, in consideration of a certain annual stipend. Mrs Sparsit was this lady's name; and she was a prominent figure in attendance on Mr Bounderby's car, as it rolled along in triumph with the Bully of humility inside.

For, Mrs Sparsit had not only seen different days, but was highly connected. She had a great aunt living in these very times called Lady Scadgers. Mr Sparsit, deceased, of whom she was the relict, had been by the mother's side what Mrs Sparsit still called "a

Powler". Strangers of limited information and dull apprehension were sometimes observed not to know what a Powler was, and even to appear uncertain whether it might be a business, or a political party, or a profession of faith. The better class of minds, however, did not need to be informed that the Powlers were an ancient stock, who could trace themselves so exceedingly far back that it was not surprising if they sometimes lost themselves—which they had rather frequently done, as respected horse-flesh, blind-hookey, Hebrew monetary transactions, and the Insolvent Debtors Court.

The late Mr Sparsit, being by the mother's side a Powler, married this lady, being by the father's side a Scadgers. Lady Scadgers (an immensely fat old woman, with an inordinate appetite for butcher's meat, and a mysterious leg which had now refused to get out of bed for fourteen years) contrived the marriage, at a period when Sparsit was just of age, and chiefly noticeable for a slender body, weakly supported on two long slim props, and surmounted by no head worth mentioning. He inherited a fair fortune from his uncle, but owed it all before he came into it, and spent it twice over immediately afterwards. Thus, when he died, at twenty-four (the scene of his decease, Calais, and the cause brandy), he did not leave his widow, from whom he had been separated soon after the honeymoon, in affluent circumstances. That bereaved lady, fifteen years older than he, fell presently at deadly feud with her only relative, Lady Scadgers; and, partly to spite her ladyship, and partly to maintain herself, went out at a salary. And here she was now, in her elderly days, with the Coriolanian style of nose and the dense black eyebrows which had captivated Sparsit, making Mr Bounderby's tea as he took his breakfast.

If Bounderby had been a Conqueror, and Mrs Sparsit a captive Princess whom he took about as a feature in his state-processions, he could not have made a greater flourish with her than he habitually did. Just as it belonged to his boastfulness to depreciate his own extraction, so it belonged to it to exalt Mrs Sparsit's. In the measure that he would not allow his own youth to have been attended by a single favourable circumstance, he brightened Mrs Sparsit's juvenile career with every possible advantage, and showered wagon-loads of early roses all over that lady's path. "And yet, sir," he would say, "how does it turn out after all? Why here she is at a hundred a year (I give her a hundred, which she is pleased to term handsome), keeping the house of Josiah Bounderby of Coketown!"

Nay, he made this foil of his so very widely known, that third parties took it up, and handled it on some occasions with considerable briskness. It was one of the most exasperating attributes of Bounderby, that he not only sang his own praises but stimulated other men to sing them. There was a moral infection of clap-trap in him. Strangers, modest enough elsewhere, started up at dinners in Coketown, and boasted, in quite a rampant way, of Bounderby. They made him out to be the Royal arms, the Union-Jack, Magna Charta, John Bull, Habeas Corpus, the Bill of Rights, An Englishman's house is his castle, Church and State, and God save the Queen, all put together. And as often (and it was very often) as an orator of this kind brought into his peroration,

> Princes and Lords may flourish or may fade,
> A breath can make them, as a breath has made,

—it was, for certain, more or less understood among the company that he had heard of Mrs Sparsit.

"Mr Bounderby," said Mrs Sparsit, "you are unusually slow, sir, with your breakfast this morning."

"Why, ma'am," he returned, "I am thinking about Tom Gradgrind's whim"; Tom

Gradgrind, for a bluff independent manner of speaking—as if somebody were always endeavouring to bribe him with immense sums to say Thomas, and he wouldn't; "Tom Gradgrind's whim, ma'am, of bringing up the tumbling-girl."

"The girl is now waiting to know," said Mrs Sparsit, "whether she is to go straight to the school, or up to the Lodge."

"She must wait, ma'am," answered Bounderby, "till I know myself. We shall have Tom Gradgrind down here presently, I suppose. If he should wish her to remain here a day or two longer, of course she can, ma'am."

"Of course she can if you wish it, Mr Bounderby."

"I told him I would give her a shake-down here, last night, in order that he might sleep on it before he decided to let her have any association with Louisa."

"Indeed, Mr Bounderby? Very thoughtful of you!"

Mrs Sparsit's Coriolanian nose underwent a slight expansion of the nostrils, and her black eyebrows contracted as she took a sip of tea.

"It's tolerably clear to *me,*" said Bounderby, "that the little puss can get small good out of such companionship."

"Are you speaking of young Miss Gradgrind, Mr Bounderby?"

"Yes, ma'am, I am speaking of Louisa."

"Your observation being limited to 'little puss,' " said Mrs Sparsit, "and there being two little girls in question, I did not know which might be indicated by that expression."

"Louisa," repeated Mr Bounderby. "Louisa, Louisa."

"You are quite another father to Louisa, sir." Mrs Sparsit took a little more tea; and, as she bent her again contracted eyebrows over her steaming cup, rather looked as if her classical countenance were invoking the infernal gods.

"If you had said I was another father to Tom—young Tom, I mean, not my friend Tom Gradgrind—you might have been nearer the mark. I am going to take young Tom into my office. Going to have him under my wing, ma'am."

"Indeed? Rather young for that, is he not, sir?" Mrs Sparsit's "sir," in addressing Mr Bounderby, was a word of ceremony, rather exacting consideration for herself in the use, than honouring him.

"I'm not going to take him at once; he is to finish his educational cramming before then," said Bounderby. "By the Lord Harry, he'll have enough of it, first and last! He'd open his eyes, that boy would, if he knew how empty of learning *my* young maw was, at his time of life." Which, by the by, he probably did know, for he had heard of it often enough. "But it's extraordinary the difficulty I have on scores of such subjects, in speaking to any one on equal terms. Here, for example, I have been speaking to you this morning about tumblers. Why, what do *you* know about tumblers? At the time when, to have been a tumbler in the mud of the streets, would have been a godsend to me, a prize in the lottery to me, you were at the Italian Opera. You were coming out of the Italian Opera, ma'am, in white satin and jewels, a blaze of splendour, when I hadn't a penny to buy a link to light you."

"I certainly, sir," returned Mrs Sparsit, with a dignity serenely mournful, "was familiar with the Italian Opera at a very early age."

"Egad, ma'am, so was I," said Bounderby, "—with the wrong side of it. A hard bed the pavement of its Arcade used to make, I assure you. People like you, ma'am, accustomed from infancy to lie on Down feathers, have no idea *how* hard a paving-stone is, without trying it. No no, it's of no use my talking to *you* about tumblers. I should speak of foreign dancers, and the West End of London, and May Fair, and lords and ladies and honourables."

"I trust, sir," rejoined Mrs Sparsit, with decent resignation, "it is not necessary that you should do anything of that kind. I hope I have learnt how to accommodate myself to the changes of life. If I have acquired an interest in hearing of your instructive experiences, and can scarcely hear enough of them, I claim no merit for that, since I believe it is a general sentiment."

"Well, ma'am," said her patron, "perhaps some people may be pleased to say that they do like to hear, in his own unpolished way, what Josiah Bounderby of Coketown, has gone through. But you must confess that you were born in the lap of luxury, yourself. Come, ma'am, you know you were born in the lap of luxury."

"I do not, sir," returned Mrs Sparsit with a shake of her head, "deny it."

Mr Bounderby was obliged to get up from table, and stand with his back to the fire, looking at her; she was such an enhancement of his position.

"And you were in crack society. Devilish high society," he said, warming his legs.

"It is true, sir," returned Mrs Sparsit, with an affectation of humility the very opposite of his, and therefore in no danger of jostling it.

"You were in the tiptop fashion, and all the rest of it," said Mr Bounderby.

"Yes, sir," returned Mrs Sparsit, with a kind of social widowhood upon her. "It is unquestionably true."

Mr Bounderby, bending himself at the knees, literally embraced his legs in his great satisfaction and laughed aloud. Mr and Miss Gradgrind being then announced, he received the former with a shake of the hand, and the latter with a kiss.

"Can Jupe be sent here, Bounderby?" asked Mr Gradgrind.

Certainly. So Jupe was sent there. On coming in, she curtseyed to Mr Bounderby, and to his friend Tom Gradgrind, and also to Louisa; but in her confusion unluckily omitted Mrs Sparsit. Observing this, the blustrous Bounderby had the following remarks to make:

"Now, I tell you what, my girl. The name of that lady by the teapot, is Mrs Sparsit. That lady acts as mistress of this house, and she is a highly connected lady. Consequently, if ever you come again into any room in this house, you will make a short stay in it if you don't behave towards that lady in your most respectful manner. Now, I don't care a button what you do to *me,* because I don't affect to be anybody. So far from having high connexions I have no connexions at all, and I come of the scum of the earth. But towards that lady, I do care what you do; and you shall do what is deferential and respectful, or you shall not come here."

"I hope, Bounderby," said Mr Gradgrind, in a conciliatory voice, "that this was merely an oversight."

"My friend Tom Gradgrind suggests, Mrs Sparsit," said Bounderby, "that this was merely an oversight. Very likely. However, as you are aware, ma'am, I don't allow of even oversights towards you."

"You are very good indeed, sir," returned Mrs Sparsit, shaking her head with her State humility. "It is not worth speaking of."

Sissy, who all this time had been faintly excusing herself with tears in her eyes, was now waved over by the master of the house to Mr Gradgrind. She stood, looking intently at him, and Louisa stood coldly by, with her eyes upon the ground, while he proceeded thus:

"Jupe, I have made up my mind to take you into my house; and, when you are not in attendance at the school, to employ you about Mrs Gradgrind, who is rather an invalid. I have explained to Miss Louisa—this is Miss Louisa—the miserable but natural end of your late career; and you are to expressly understand that the whole of that subject is past, and is not to be referred to any more. From this time you begin your history. You are, at present, ignorant, I know."

"Yes, sir, very," she answered, curtseying.

"I shall have the satisfaction of causing you to be strictly educated; and you will be a living proof to all who come into communication with you, of the advantages of the training you will receive. You will be reclaimed and formed. You have been in the habit, now, of reading to your father, and those people I found you among, I dare say?" said Mr Gradgrind, beckoning her nearer to him before he said so, and dropping his voice.

"Only to father and Merrylegs, sir. At least I mean to father, when Merrylegs was always there."

"Never mind Merrylegs, Jupe," said Mr Gradgrind, with a passing frown. "I don't ask about him. I understand you to have been in the habit of reading to your father?"

"O yes, sir, thousands of times. They were the happiest—O, of all the happy times we had together, sir!"

It was only now, when her sorrow broke out, that Louisa looked at her.

"And what," asked Mr Gradgrind, in a still lower voice, "did you read to your father, Jupe?"

"About the Fairies, sir, and the Dwarf, and the Hunchback, and the Genies," she sobbed out; "and about—"

"Hush!" said Mr Gradgrind, "that is enough. Never breathe a word of such destructive nonsense any more. Bounderby, this is a case for rigid training, and I shall observe it with interest."

"Well," returned Mr Bounderby, "I have given you my opinion already, and I shouldn't do as you do. But, very well, very well. Since you are bent upon it, *very* well!"

So, Mr Gradgrind and his daughter took Cecilia Jupe off with them to Stone Lodge, and on the way Louisa never spoke one word, good or bad. And Mr Bounderby went about his daily pursuits. And Mrs Sparsit got behind her eyebrows and meditated in the gloom of that retreat, all the evening.

Chapter VIII

NEVER WONDER

LET us strike the key-note again, before pursuing the tune.

When she was half a dozen years younger, Louisa had been overheard to begin a conversation with her brother one day, by saying "Tom, I wonder"—upon which Mr Gradgrind, who was the person overhearing, stepped forth into the light, and said, "Louisa, never wonder!"

Herein lay the spring of the mechanical art and mystery of educating the reason without stooping to the cultivation of the sentiments and affections. Never wonder. By means of addition, subtraction, multiplication, and division, settle everything somehow, and never wonder. Bring to me, says M'Choakumchild, yonder baby just able to walk, and I will engage that it shall never wonder.

Now, besides very many babies just able to walk, there happened to be in Coketown a considerable population of babies who had been walking against time towards the infinite world, twenty, thirty, forty, fifty years and more. These portentous infants being alarming creatures to stalk about in any human society, the eighteen denominations incessantly scratched one another's faces and pulled one another's hair, by way of agreeing on the steps to be taken for their improvement—which they never did; a surprising circumstance, when the happy adaptation of the means to the end is considered. Still, although they differed in every other particular, conceivable and inconceivable (especially inconceivable), they were pretty well united on the point that these unlucky infants were never to wonder. Body number one, said they must take everything on trust. Body number two, said they must take everything on political economy. Body number three, wrote leaden little books for them, showing how the good grown-up baby invariably got to the Savings-bank, and the bad grown-up baby invariably got transported. Body number four, under dreary pretences of being droll (when it was very melancholy indeed), made the shallowest pretences of concealing pitfalls of knowledge, into which it was the duty of these babies to be smuggled and inveigled. But, all the bodies agreed that they were never to wonder.

There was a library in Coketown, to which general access was easy. Mr Gradgrind greatly tormented his mind about what the people read in this library: a point whereon little rivers of tabular statements periodically flowed into the howling ocean of tabular statements, which no diver ever got to any depth in and came up sane. It was a disheartening circumstance, but a melancholy fact, that even these readers persisted in wondering. They wondered about human nature, human passions, human hopes and fears, the struggles, triumphs and defeats, the cares and joys and sorrows, the lives and deaths, of common men and women! They sometimes, after fifteen hours' work, sat down to read mere fables about men and women, more or less like themselves, and about children, more or less like their own. They took De Foe to their bosoms, instead of Euclid, and seemed to be on the whole more comforted by Goldsmith than by Cocker. Mr Gradgrind was for ever working, in print and out of print, at this eccentric sum, and he never could make out how it yielded this unaccountable product.

"I am sick of my life, Loo. I hate it altogether, and I hate everybody except you," said the unnatural young Thomas Gradgrind in the hair-cutting chamber at twilight.

"You don't hate Sissy, Tom?"

"I hate to be obliged to call her Jupe. And she hates me," said Tom moodily.

"No she does not, Tom, I am sure."

"She must," said Tom. "She must just hate and detest the whole set-out of us. They'll bother her head off, I think, before they have done with her. Already she's getting as pale as wax, and as heavy as—I am."

Young Thomas expressed these sentiments, sitting astride of a chair before the fire, with his arms on the back, and his sulky face on his arms. His sister sat in the darker corner by the fireside, now looking at him, now looking at the bright sparks as they dropped upon the hearth.

"As to me," said Tom, tumbling his hair all manner of ways with his sulky hands, "I am a Donkey, that's what *I* am. I am as obstinate as one, I am more stupid than one, I get as much pleasure as one, and I should like to kick like one."

"Not me, I hope, Tom?"

"No, Loo; I wouldn't hurt *you*. I made an exception of you at first. I don't know what this—jolly old—Jaundiced Jail," Tom had paused to find a sufficiently complimentary and expressive name for the parental roof, and seemed to relieve his mind for a moment by the strong alliteration of this one, "would be without you."

"Indeed, Tom? Do you really and truly say so?"

"Why, of course I do. What's the use of talking about it!" returned Tom, chafing his face on his coat-sleeve, as if to mortify his flesh, and have it in unison with his spirit.

"Because Tom," said his sister, after silently watching the sparks awhile, "as I get older, and nearer growing up, I often sit wondering here, and think how unfortunate it is for me that I can't reconcile you to home better than I am able to do. I don't know what other girls know. I can't play to you, or sing to you. I can't talk to you so as to lighten your mind, for I never see any amusing sights or read any amusing books that it would be a pleasure or a relief to you to talk about, when you are tired."

"Well, no more do I. I am as bad as you in that respect; and I am a Mule too, which you're not. If father was determined to make me either a Prig or a Mule, and I am not a Prig, why, it stands to reason, I must be a Mule. And so I am," said Tom, desperately.

"It's a great pity," said Louisa, after another pause, and speaking thoughtfully out of her dark corner; "it's a great pity, Tom. It's very unfortunate for both of us."

"Oh! You," said Tom; "you are a girl, Loo, and a girl comes out of it better than a boy does. I don't miss anything in you. You are the only pleasure I have—you can brighten even this place—and you can always lead me as you like."

"You are a dear brother, Tom; and while you think I can do such things, I don't so much mind knowing better. Though I do know better, Tom, and am very sorry for it." She came and kissed him, and went back into her corner again.

"I wish I could collect all the Facts we hear so much about," said Tom, spitefully setting his teeth, "and all the Figures, and all the people who found them out; and I wish I could put a thousand barrels of gunpowder under them, and blow them all up together! However, when I go to live with old Bounderby, I'll have my revenge."

"Your revenge, Tom?"

"I mean, I'll enjoy myself a little, and go about and see something, and hear something. I'll recompense myself for the way in which I have been brought up."

"But don't disappoint yourself beforehand, Tom. Mr Bounderby thinks as father thinks, and is a great deal rougher, and not half so kind."

"Oh"; said Tom, laughing; "I don't mind that. I shall very well know how to manage and smoothe old Bounderby!"

Their shadows were defined upon the wall, but those of the high presses in the room were all blended together on the wall and on the ceiling, as if the brother and sister were overhung by a dark cavern. Or, a fanciful imagination—if such treason could have been there—might have made it out to be the shadow of their subject, and of its lowering association with their future.

"What is your great mode of smoothing and managing, Tom? Is it a secret?"

"Oh!" said Tom, "if it is a secret, it's not far off. It's you. You are his little pet, you are his favourite; he'll do anything for you. When he says to me what I don't like, I shall say to him, 'My sister Loo will be hurt and disappointed, Mr Bounderby. She always used to tell me she was sure you would be easier with me than this.' That'll bring him about, or nothing will."

After waiting for some answering remark, and getting none, Tom wearily relapsed into the present time, and twined himself yawning round and about the rails of his chair, and rumpled his head more and more, until he suddenly looked up, and asked:

"Have you gone to sleep, Loo?"

"No, Tom. I am looking at the fire."

"You seem to find more to look at in it than ever I could find," said Tom. "Another of the advantages, I suppose, of being a girl."

"Tom," inquired his sister, slowly, and in a curious tone, as if she were reading what she asked, in the fire, and it were not quite plainly written there, "do you look forward with any satisfaction to this change to Mr Bounderby's?"

"Why, there's one thing to be said of it," returned Tom, pushing his chair from him and standing up; "it will be getting away from home."

"There is one thing to be said of it," Louisa repeated in her former curious tone; "it will be getting away from home. Yes."

"Not but what I shall be very unwilling, both to leave you, Loo, and to leave you here. But I must go, you know, whether I like it or not; and I had better go where I can take with me some advantage of your influence, than where I should lose it altogether. Don't you see?"

"Yes, Tom."

The answer was so long in coming, though there was no indecision in it, that Tom went and leaned on the back of her chair, to contemplate the fire which so engrossed her, from her point of view, and see what he could make of it.

"Except that it is a fire," said Tom, "it looks to me as stupid and blank as everything else looks. What do you see in it? Not a circus?"

"I don't see anything in it, Tom, particularly. But since I have been looking at it, I have been wondering about you and me, grown up."

"Wondering again!" said Tom.

"I have such unmanageable thoughts," returned his sister, "that they *will* wonder."

"Then I beg of you, Louisa," said Mrs Gradgrind, who had opened the door without being heard, "to do nothing of that description, for goodness' sake you inconsiderate girl, or I shall never hear the last of it from your father. And Thomas, it is really shameful, with my poor head continually wearing me out, that a boy brought up as you have been, and whose education has cost what yours has, should be found encouraging his sister to wonder, when he knows his father has expressly said that she is not to do it."

Louisa denied Tom's participation in the offence; but her mother stopped her with the conclusive answer, "Louisa, don't tell me, in my state of health; for unless you had been encouraged, it is morally and physically impossible that you could have done it."

"I was encouraged by nothing, mother, but by looking at the red sparks dropping out of the fire, and whitening and dying. It made me think, after all, how short my life would be, and how little I could hope to do in it."

"Nonsense!" said Mrs Gradgrind, rendered almost energetic. "Nonsense! Don't stand there and tell me such stuff, Louisa, to my face, when you know very well that if it was ever to reach your father's ears I should never hear the last of it. After all the trouble that has been taken with you! After the lectures you have attended, and the experiments you have seen! After I have heard you myself, when the whole of my right side has been benumbed, going on with your master about combustion, and calcination, and calorification, and I may say every kind of ation that could drive a poor invalid distracted, to hear you talking in this absurd way about sparks and ashes! I wish," whimpered Mrs Gradgrind, taking a chair, and discharging her strongest point before succumbing under these mere shadows of facts, "yes, I really *do* wish that I had never had a family, and then you would have known what it was to do without me!"

Chapter IX

SISSY'S PROGRESS

SISSY Jupe had not an easy time of it, between Mr M'Choakumchild and Mrs Gradgrind, and was not without strong impulses, in the first months of her probation, to run away. It hailed facts all day long so very hard, and life in general was opened to her as such a closely-ruled cyphering-book, that assuredly she would have run away, but for only one restraint.

It is lamentable to think of; but this restraint was the result of no arithmetical process, was self-imposed in defiance of all calculation, and went dead against any table of probabilities that any Actuary would have drawn up from the premises. The girl believed that her father had not deserted her; she lived in the hope that he would come back, and in the faith that he would be made the happier by her remaining where she was.

The wretched ignorance with which Jupe clung to this consolation, rejecting the superior comfort of knowing, on a sound arithmetical basis, that her father was an unnatural vagabond, filled Mr Gradgrind with pity. Yet, what was to be done? M'Choakumchild reported that she had a very dense head for figures; that, once possessed with a general idea of the globe, she took the smallest conceivable interest in its exact measurements; that she was extremely slow in the acquisition of dates, unless some pitiful incident happened to be connected therewith; that she would burst into tears on being required (by the mental process) immediately to name the cost of two hundred and forty-seven muslin caps at fourteenpence halfpenny; that she was as low down, in the school, as low could be; that after eight weeks of induction into the elements of Political Economy, she had only yesterday been set right by a prattler three feet high, for returning to the question, "What is the first principle of this science?" the absurd answer, "To do unto others as I would that they should do unto me."

Mr Gradgrind observed, shaking his head, that all this was very bad; that it showed the necessity of infinite grinding at the mill of knowledge, as per system, schedule, blue book, report, and tabular statements A to Z; and that Jupe "must be kept to it". So Jupe was kept to it, and became low-spirited, but no wiser.

"It would be a fine thing to be you, Miss Louisa!" she said, one night, when Louisa had endeavoured to make her perplexities for next day something clearer to her.

"Do you think so?"

"I should know so much, Miss Louisa. All that is difficult to me now, would be so easy then."

"You might not be the better for it, Sissy."

Sissy submitted, after a little hesitation, "I should not be the worse, Miss Louisa." To which Miss Louisa answered, "I don't know that."

There had been so little communication between these two—both because life at Stone Lodge went monotonously round like a piece of machinery which discouraged human interference, and because of the prohibition relative to Sissy's past career—that they were still almost strangers. Sissy, with her dark eyes wonderingly directed to Louisa's face, was uncertain whether to say more or to remain silent.

"You are more useful to my mother, and more pleasant with her than I can ever be,"

Louisa resumed. "You are pleasanter to yourself, than *I* am to *my* self."

"But, if you please Miss Louisa," Sissy pleaded, "I am—O so stupid!"

Louisa, with a brighter laugh than usual, told her she would be wiser by and by.

"You don't know," said Sissy, half crying, "what a stupid girl I am. All through school hours I make mistakes. Mr and Mrs M'Choakumchild call me up, over and over again, regularly to make mistakes. I can't help them. They seem to come natural to me."

"Mr and Mrs M'Choakumchild never make any mistakes themselves, I suppose, Sissy?"

"O no!" she eagerly returned. "They know everything."

"Tell me some of your mistakes."

"I am almost ashamed," said Sissy, with reluctance. "But today, for instance, Mr M'Choakumchild was explaining to us about Natural Prosperity."

"National, I think it must have been," observed Louisa.

"Yes, it was.—But isn't it the same?" she timidly asked.

"You had better say, National, as he said so," returned Louisa, with her dry reserve.

"National Prosperity. And he said, Now, this schoolroom is a Nation. And in this nation, there are fifty millions of money. Isn't this a prosperous nation? Girl number twenty, isn't this a prosperous nation, and a'n't you in a thriving state?"

"What did you say?" asked Louisa.

"Miss Louisa, I said I didn't know. I thought I couldn't know whether it was a prosperous nation or not, and whether I was in a thriving state or not, unless I knew who had got the money, and whether any of it was mine. But that had nothing to do with it. It was not in the figures at all," said Sissy, wiping her eyes.

"That was a great mistake of yours," observed Louisa.

"Yes, Miss Louisa, I know it was, now. Then Mr M'Choakumchild said he would try me again. And he said, This schoolroom is an immense town, and in it there are a million of inhabitants, and only five-and-twenty are starved to death in the streets, in the course of a year. What is your remark on that proportion? And my remark was—for I couldn't think of a better one—that I thought it must be just as hard upon those who were starved, whether the others were a million, or a million million. And that was wrong, too."

"Of course it was."

"Then Mr M'Choakumchild said he would try me once more. And he said, Here are the stutterings—"

"Statistics," said Louisa.

"Yes, Miss Louisa—they always remind me of stutterings, and that's another of my mistakes—of accidents upon the sea. And I find (Mr M'Choakumchild said) that in a given time a hundred thousand persons went to sea on long voyages, and only five hundred of them were drowned or burnt to death. What is the percentage? And I said, Miss;" here Sissy fairly sobbed as confessing with extreme contrition to her greatest error; "I said it was nothing."

"Nothing, Sissy?"

"Nothing, Miss—to the relations and friends of the people who were killed. I shall never learn," said Sissy. "And the worst of all is, that although my poor father wished me so much to learn, and although I am so anxious to learn because he wished me to, I am afraid I don't like it."

Louisa stood looking at the pretty modest head, as it drooped abashed before her, until it was raised again to glance at her face. Then she asked:

"Did your father know so much himself, that he wished you to be well taught too, Sissy?"

Sissy hesitated before replying, and so plainly showed her sense that they were entering on forbidden ground, that Louisa added, "No one hears us; and if any one did, I am sure no harm could be found in such an innocent question."

"No, Miss Louisa," answered Sissy, upon this encouragement, shaking her head; "father knows very little indeed. It's as much as he can do to write; and it's more than people in general can do to read his writing. Though it's plain to *me.*"

"Your mother?"

"Father says she was quite a scholar. She died when I was born. She was;" Sissy made the terrible communication nervously; "she was a dancer."

"Did your father love her?" Louisa asked these questions with a strong, wild, wandering interest peculiar to her; an interest gone astray like a banished creature, and hiding in solitary places.

"O yes! As dearly as he loves me. Father loved me, first, for her sake. He carried me about with him when I was quite a baby. We have never been asunder from that time."

"Yet he leaves you now, Sissy?"

"Only for my good. Nobody understands him as I do; nobody knows him as I do. When he left me for my good—he never would have left me for his own—I know he was almost broken-hearted with the trial. He will not be happy for a single minute, till he comes back."

"Tell me more about him," said Louisa, "I will never ask you again. Where did you live?"

"We travelled about the country, and had no fixed place to live in. Father's a;" Sissy whispered the awful word; "a clown."

"To make the people laugh?" said Louisa, with a nod of intelligence.

"Yes. But they wouldn't laugh sometimes, and then father cried. Lately, they very often wouldn't laugh, and he used to come home despairing. Father's not like most. Those who didn't know him as well as I do, and didn't love him as dearly as I do, might believe he was not quite right. Sometimes they played tricks upon him; but they never knew how he felt them, and shrunk up, when he was alone with me. He was far, far timider than they thought!"

"And you were his comfort through everything?"

She nodded, with the tears rolling down her face. "I hope so, and father said I was. It was because he grew so scared and trembling, and because he felt himself to be a poor, weak, ignorant, helpless man (those used to be his words), that he wanted me so much to know a great deal and be different from him. I used to read to him to cheer his courage, and he was very fond of that. They were wrong books—I am never to speak of them here—but we didn't know there was any harm in them."

"And he liked them?" said Louisa, with her searching gaze on Sissy all this time.

"O very much! They kept him, many times, from what did him real harm. And often and often of a night, he used to forget all his troubles in wondering whether the Sultan would let the lady go on with the story, or would have her head cut off before it was finished."

"And your father was always kind? To the last?" asked Louisa; contravening the great principle, and wondering very much.

"Always, always!" returned Sissy, clasping her hands. "Kinder and kinder than I can tell. He was angry only one night, and that was not to me, but Merrylegs. Merrylegs;" she whispered the awful fact; "is his performing dog."

"Why was he angry with the dog?" Louisa demanded.

"Father, soon after they came home from performing, told Merrylegs to jump up on the backs of the two chairs and stand across them—which is one of his tricks. He looked at father, and didn't do it once. Everything of father's had gone wrong that night, and he hadn't pleased the public at all. He cried out that the very dog knew he was failing, and had no compassion on him. Then he beat the dog, and I was frightened, and said, 'Father, father! Pray don't hurt the creature who is so fond of you! O Heaven forgive you, father, stop!' And he stopped, and the dog was bloody, and father lay down crying on the floor with the dog in his arms, and the dog licked his face."

Louisa saw that she was sobbing; and going to her, kissed her; took her hand, and sat down beside her.

"Finish by telling me how your father left you, Sissy. Now that I have asked you so much, tell me the end. The blame, if there is any blame, is mine, not yours."

"Dear Miss Louisa," said Sissy, covering her eyes, and sobbing yet; "I came home from the school that afternoon, and found poor father just come home too, from the booth. And he sat rocking himself over the fire, as if he was in pain. And I said, 'Have you hurt yourself, father?' (as he did sometimes, like they all did), and he said, 'A little, my darling.' And when I came to stoop down and look up at his face, I saw that he was crying. The more I spoke to him, the more he hid his face; and at first he shook all over, and said nothing but 'My darling!' and 'My love!' "

Here Tom came lounging in, and stared at the two with a coolness not particularly savouring of interest in anything but himself, and not much of that at present.

"I am asking Sissy a few questions, Tom," observed his sister. "You have no occasion to go away; but don't interrupt us for a moment, Tom dear."

"Oh! very well!" returned Tom. "Only father has brought old Bounderby home, and I want you to come into the drawing-room. Because if you come, there's a good chance of old Bounderby's asking me to dinner; and if you don't, there's none."

"I'll come directly."

"I'll wait for you," said Tom, "to make sure."

Sissy resumed in a lower voice. "At last poor father said that he had given no satisfaction again, and never did give any satisfaction now, and that he was a shame and disgrace, and I should have done better without him all along. I said all the affectionate things to him that came into my heart, and presently he was quiet and I sat down by him, and told him all about the school and everything that had been said and done there. When I had no more left to tell, he put his arms round my neck, and kissed me a great many times. Then he asked me to fetch some of the stuff he used, for the little hurt he had had, and to get it at the best place, which was at the other end of town from there; and then, after kissing me again, he let me go. When I had gone down stairs, I turned back that I might be a little bit more company to him yet, and looked in at the door, and said, 'Father dear, shall I take Merrylegs?' Father shook his head and said, 'No, Sissy, no; take nothing that's known to be mine, my darling;' and I left him sitting by the fire. Then the thought must have come upon him, poor poor father! of going away to try something for my sake; for, when I came back, he was gone."

"I say! Look sharp for old Bounderby, Loo!" Tom remonstrated.

"There's no more to tell, Miss Louisa. I keep the nine oils ready for him, and I know he will come back. Every letter that I see in Mr Gradgrind's hand takes my breath away and blinds my eyes, for I think it comes from father, or from Mr Sleary about father. Mr

Sleary promised to write as soon as ever father should be heard of, and I trust to him to keep his word."

"Do look sharp for old Bounderby, Loo!" said Tom, with an impatient whistle. "He'll be off, if you don't look sharp!"

After this, whenever Sissy dropped a curtsey to Mr Gradgrind in the presence of his family, and said in a faltering way, "I beg your pardon, sir, for being troublesome—but—have you had any letter yet about me?" Louisa would suspend the occupation of the moment, whatever it was, and look for the reply as earnestly as Sissy did. And when Mr Gradgrind regularly answered, "No, Jupe, nothing of the sort," the trembling of Sissy's lip would be repeated in Louisa's face, and her eyes would follow Sissy with compassion to the door. Mr Gradgrind usually improved these occasions by remarking, when she was gone, that if Jupe had been properly trained from an early age she would have demonstrated to herself on sound principles the baselessness of these fantastic hopes. Yet it did seem (though not to him, for he saw nothing of it) as if fantastic hope could take as strong a hold as Fact.

This observation must be limited exclusively to his daughter. As to Tom, he was becoming that not unprecedented triumph of calculation which is usually at work on number one. As to Mrs Gradgrind, if she said anything on the subject, she would come a little way out of her wrappers, like a feminine dormouse, and say:

"Good gracious bless me how my poor head is vexed and worried by that girl Jupe's so perseveringly asking, over and over again, about her tiresome letters! Upon my word and honour I seem to be fated, and destined, and ordained, to live in the midst of things that I am never to hear the last of. It really is a most extraordinary circumstance that it appears as if I never was to hear the last of anything!"

At about this point, Mr Gradgrind's eye would fall upon her; and under the influence of that wintry piece of fact, she would become torpid again.

Chapter X

STEPHEN BLACKPOOL

I ENTERTAIN a weak idea that the English people are as hard-worked as any people upon whom the sun shines. I acknowledge to this ridiculous idiosyncrasy, as a reason why I would give them a little more play.

In the hardest working part of Coketown; in the innermost fortifications of that ugly citadel, where Nature was as strongly bricked out as killing airs and gases were bricked in; at the heart of the labyrinth of narrow courts upon courts, and close streets upon streets, which had come into existence piecemeal, every piece in a violent hurry for some one man's purpose, and the whole an unnatural family, shouldering, and trampling, and pressing one another to death; in the last close nook of this great exhausted receiver, where the chimneys, for want of air to make a draught, were built in an immense variety of stunted and crooked shapes as though every house put out a sign of the kind of people who might be expected to be born in it; among the multitude of Coketown, generically called "the Hands,"—a race who would have found more favour with some people, if Providence had seen fit to make them only hands, or, like the lower creatures of the seashore, only hands and stomachs—lived a certain Stephen Blackpool, forty years of age.

Stephen looked older, but he had had a hard life. It is said that every life has its roses and thorns; there seemed, however, to have been a misadventure or mistake in Stephen's case, whereby somebody else had become possessed of his roses, and he had become possessed of the same somebody else's thorns in addition to his own. He had known, to use his words, a peck of trouble. He was usually called Old Stephen, in a kind of rough homage to the fact.

A rather stooping man, with a knitted brow, a pondering expression of face, and a hard-looking head sufficiently capacious, on which his iron-grey hair lay long and thin, Old Stephen might have passed for a particularly intelligent man in his condition. Yet he was not. He took no place among those remarkable "Hands," who, piecing together their broken intervals of leisure through many years, had mastered difficult sciences, and acquired a knowledge of most unlikely things. He held no station among the Hands who could make speeches and carry on debates. Thousands of his compeers could talk much better than he, at any time. He was a good power-loom weaver, and a man of perfect integrity. What more he was, or what else he had in him, if anything, let him show for himself.

The lights in the great factories, which looked, when they were illuminated, like Fairy palaces—or the travellers by express-train said so—were all extinguished; and the bells had rung for knocking off for the night, and had ceased again; and the Hands, men and women, boy and girl, were clattering home. Old Stephen was standing in the street, with the odd sensation upon him which the stoppage of the machinery always produced—the sensation of its having worked and stopped in his own head.

"Yet I don't see Rachael, still!" said he.

It was a wet night, and many groups of young women passed him, with their shawls drawn over their bare heads and held close under their chins to keep the rain out. He knew Rachael well, for a glance at any one of these groups was sufficient to show him that she was not there. At last, there were no more to come; and then he turned away, saying in a tone of disappointment, "Why, then, I ha' missed her!"

But, he had not gone the length of three streets, when he saw another of the shawled figures in advance of him, at which he looked so keenly that perhaps its mere shadow indistinctly reflected on the wet pavement—if he could have seen it without the figure itself moving along from lamp to lamp, brightening and fading as it went—would have been enough to tell him who was there. Making his pace at once much quicker and much softer, he darted on until he was very near this figure, then fell into his former walk, and called "Rachael!"

She turned, being then in the brightness of a lamp; and raising her hood a little, showed a quiet oval face, dark and rather delicate, irradiated by a pair of very gentle eyes, and further set off by the perfect order of her shining black hair. It was not a face in its first bloom; she was a woman five and thirty years of age.

"Ah, lad! 'Tis thou?" When she had said this, with a smile which would have been quite expressed, though nothing of her had been seen but her pleasant eyes, she replaced her hood again, and they went on together.

"I thought thou wast ahind me, Rachael?"

"No."

"Early t'night, lass?"

" 'Times I'm a little early, Stephen; 'times a little late. I'm never to be counted on, going home."

"Nor going t'other way, neither, t'seems to me, Rachael?"

"No, Stephen."

He looked at her with some disappointment in his face, but with a respectful and patient conviction that she must be right in whatever she did. The expression was not lost upon her; she laid her hand lightly on his arm a moment, as if to thank him for it.

"We are such true friends, lad, and such old friends, and getting to be such old folk, now."

"No, Rachael, thou'rt as young as ever thou wast."

"One of us would be puzzled how to get old, Stephen, without t'other getting so too, both being alive," she answered, laughing; "but, anyways, we're such old friends, that t'hide a word of honest truth fro' one another would be a sin and a pity. 'Tis better not to walk too much together. 'Times, yes! 'Twould be hard, indeed, if 'twas not to be at all," she said, with a cheerfulness she sought to communicate to him.

" 'Tis hard, anyways, Rachael."

"Try to think not; and 'twill seem better."

"I've tried a long time, and 'ta'nt got better. But thou'rt right; 'tmight mak fok talk, even of thee. Thou hast been that to me, Rachael, through so many year: thou hast done me so much good, and heartened of me in that cheering way, that thy word is a law to me. Ah lass, and a bright good law! Better than some real ones."

"Never fret about them, Stephen," she answered quickly, and not without an anxious glance at his face. "Let the laws be."

"Yes," he said, with a slow nod or two. "Let 'em be. Let everything be. Let all sorts alone. 'Tis a muddle, and that's aw."

"Always a muddle?" said Rachael, with another gentle touch upon his arm, as if to recall him out of the thoughtfulness, in which he was biting the long ends of his loose neckerchief as he walked along. The touch had its instantaneous effect. He let them fall, turned a smiling face upon her, and said, as he broke into a good-humoured laugh, "Ay, Rachael, lass, awlus a muddle. That's where I stick. I come to the muddle many times and agen, and I never get beyond it."

They had walked some distance, and were near their own homes. The woman's was the first reached. It was in one of the many small streets for which the favourite undertaker (who turned a handsome sum out of the one poor ghastly pomp of the neighbourhood) kept a black ladder, in order that those who had done their daily groping up and down the narrow stairs might slide out of this working world by the windows. She stopped at the corner, and putting her hand in his, wished him good night.

"Good night, dear lass; good night!"

She went, with her neat figure and her sober womanly step, down the dark street, and he stood looking after her until she turned into one of the small houses. There was not a flutter of her coarse shawl, perhaps, but had its interest in this man's eyes; not a tone of her voice but had its echo in his innermost heart.

When she was lost to his view, he pursued his homeward way, glancing up sometimes at the sky, where the clouds were sailing fast and wildly. But, they were broken now, and the rain had ceased, and the moon shone—looking down the high chimneys of Coketown on the deep furnaces below, and casting Titanic shadows of the steam engines at rest, upon the walls where they were lodged. The man seemed to have brightened with the night, as he went on.

His home, in such another street as the first, saving that it was narrower, was over a little shop. How it came to pass that any people found it worth their while to sell or buy the wretched little toys, mixed up in its window with cheap newspapers and pork (there was a leg to be raffled for tomorrow night), matters not here. He took his end of candle from a shelf, lighted it at another end of candle on the counter, without disturbing the mistress of the shop who was asleep in her little room, and went up stairs into his lodging.

It was a room, not unacquainted with the black ladder under various tenants; but as neat, at present, as such a room could be. A few books and writings were on an old bureau in a corner, the furniture was decent and sufficient, and, though the atmosphere was tainted, the room was clean.

Going to the hearth to set the candle down upon a round three-legged table standing there, he stumbled against something. As he recoiled, looking down at it, it raised itself up into the form of a woman in a sitting attitude.

"Heaven's mercy, woman!" he cried, falling farther off from the figure. "Hast thou come back again!"

Such a woman! A disabled, drunken creature, barely able to preserve her sitting posture by steadying herself with one begrimed hand on the floor, while the other was so purposeless in trying to push away her tangled hair from her face, that it only blinded her the more with the dirt upon it. A creature so foul to look at, in her tatters, stains, and splashes, but so much fouler than that in her moral infamy, that it was a shameful thing even to see her.

After an impatient oath or two, and some stupid clawing of herself with the hand not necessary to her support, she got her hair away from her eyes sufficiently to obtain a sight of him. Then she sat swaying her body to and fro, and making gestures with her unnerved arm, which seemed intended as the accompaniment to a fit of laughter, though her face was stolid and drowsy.

"Eigh lad? What, yo'r there?" Some hoarse sounds meant for this, came mockingly out of her at last; and her head dropped forward on her breast.

"Back agen?" she screeched, after some minutes, as if he had that moment said it. "Yes! And back agen. Back agen ever and ever so often. Back? Yes, back. Why not?"

Roused by the unmeaning violence with which she cried it out, she scrambled up, and stood supporting herself with her shoulders against the wall; dangling in one hand by the string, a dunghill-fragment of a bonnet, and trying to look scornfully at him.

"I'll sell thee off again, and I'll sell thee off again, and I'll sell thee off a score of times!" she cried, with something between a furious menace and an effort at a defiant dance. "Come awa' from th' bed!" He was sitting on the side of it, with his face hidden in his hands. "Come awa' from 't. 'Tis mine, and I've a right to't!"

As she staggered to it, he avoided her with a shudder, and passed—his face still hidden—to the opposite end of the room. She threw herself upon the bed heavily, and soon was snoring hard. He sunk into a chair, and moved but once all that night. It was to throw a covering over her; as if his hands were not enough to hide her, even in the darkness.

Chapter XI

NO WAY OUT

THE Fairy palaces burst into illumination, before pale morning showed the monstrous serpents of smoke trailing themselves over Coketown. A clattering of clogs upon the pavement; a rapid ringing of bells; and all the melancholy-mad elephants, polished and oiled up for the day's monotony, were at their heavy exercise again.

Stephen bent over his loom, quiet, watchful, and steady. A special contrast, as every man was in the forest of looms where Stephen worked, to the crashing, smashing, tearing piece of mechanism at which he laboured. Never fear, good people of an anxious turn of mind, that Art will consign Nature to oblivion. Set anywhere, side by side, the work of GOD and the work of man; and the former, even though it be a troop of Hands of very small account, will gain in dignity from the comparison.

So many hundred Hands in this Mill; so many hundred horse Steam Power. It is known, to the force of a single pound weight, what the engine will do; but, not all the calculators of the National Debt can tell me the capacity for good or evil, for love or hatred, for patriotism or discontent, for the decomposition of virtue into vice, or the reverse, at any single moment in the soul of one of these its quiet servants, with the composed faces and the regulated actions. There is no mystery in it; there is an unfathomable mystery in the meanest of them, for ever.—Supposing we were to reserve our arithmetic for material objects, and to govern these awful unknown quantities by other means!

The day grew strong, and showed itself outside, even against the flaming lights within. The lights were turned out, and the work went on. The rain fell, and the Smoke-serpents, submissive to the curse of all that tribe, trailed themselves upon the earth. In the waste-yard outside, the steam from the escape-pipe, the litter of barrels and old iron, the shining heaps of coals, the ashes everywhere, were shrouded in a veil of mist and rain.

The work went on, until the noon-bell rang. More clattering upon the pavements. The looms, and wheels, and Hands, all out of gear for an hour.

Stephen came out of the hot mill into the damp wind and cold wet streets, haggard and worn. He turned from his own class and his own quarter, taking nothing but a little bread as he walked along, towards the hill on which his principal employer lived, in a red house with black outside shutters, green inside blinds, a black street door, up two white steps, BOUNDERBY (in letters very like himself) upon a brazen plate, and a round brazen door-handle underneath it like a brazen full-stop.

Mr Bounderby was at his lunch. So Stephen had expected. Would his servant say that one of the Hands begged leave to speak to him? Message in return, requiring name of such Hand. Stephen Blackpool. There was nothing troublesome against Stephen Blackpool; yes, he might come in.

Stephen Blackpool in the parlour. Mr Bounderby (whom he just knew by sight), at lunch on chop and sherry. Mrs Sparsit netting at the fire-side, in a side-saddle attitude, with one foot in a cotton stirrup. It was a part, at once of Mrs Sparsit's dignity and service, not to lunch. She supervised the meal officially, but implied that in her own stately person she considered lunch a weakness.

"Now, Stephen," said Mr Bounderby, "what's the matter with *you?*"

Stephen made a bow. Not a servile one—these Hands will never do that! Lord bless you, sir, you'll never catch them at that, if they have been with you twenty years!—and, as a complimentary toilet for Mrs Sparsit, tucked his neckerchief ends into his waistcoat.

"Now, you know," said Mr Bounderby, taking some sherry, "we have never had any difficulty with you, and you have never been one of the unreasonable ones. You don't expect to be set up in a coach and six, and to be fed on turtle soup and venison, with a gold spoon, as a good many of 'em do!" Mr Bounderby always represented this to be the sole, immediate, and direct object of any Hand who was not entirely satisfied; "and therefore I know already that you have not come here to make a complaint. Now, you know, I am certain of that, beforehand."

"No, sir, sure I ha' not coom for nowt o' th' kind."

Mr Bounderby seemed agreeably surprised, notwithstanding his previous strong conviction. "Very well," he returned. "You're a steady Hand, and I was not mistaken. Now, let me hear what it's all about. As it's not that, let me hear what it is. What have you got to say? Out with it, lad!"

Stephen happened to glance towards Mrs Sparsit. "I can go, Mr Bounderby, if you wish it," said that self-sacrificing lady, making a feint of taking her foot out of the stirrup.

Mr Bounderby stayed her, by holding a mouthful of chop in suspension before swallowing it, and putting out his left hand. Then, withdrawing his hand and swallowing his mouthful of chop, he said to Stephen:

"Now, you know, this good lady is a born lady, a high lady. You are not to suppose because she keeps my house for me, that she hasn't been very high up the tree—ah, up at the top of the tree! Now, if you have got anything to say that can't be said before a born lady, this lady will leave the room. If what you have got to say *can* be said before a born lady, this lady will stay where she is."

"Sir, I hope I never had nowt to say, not fitten for a born lady to year, sin' I were born mysen," was the reply, accompanied with a slight flush.

"Very well," said Mr Bounderby, pushing away his plate, and leaning back. "Fire away!"

"I ha' coom," Stephen began, raising his eyes from the floor, after a moment's consideration, "to ask yo yor advice. I need't overmuch. I were married on Eas'r Monday nineteen year sin, long and dree. She were a young lass—pretty enow—wi' good accounts of herseln. Well! She went bad—soon. Not along of me. Gonnows I were not a unkind husband to her."

"I have heard all this before," said Mr Bounderby. "She took to drinking, left off working, sold the furniture, pawned the clothes, and played old Gooseberry."

"I were patient wi' her."

("The more fool you, I think," said Mr Bounderby, in confidence to his wine-glass.)

"I were very patient wi' her. I tried to wean her fra't, ower and ower agen. I tried this, I tried that, I tried t'other. I ha' gone home, many's the time, and found all vanished as I had in the world, and her without a sense left to bless herseln lying on bare ground. I ha' dun't not once, not twice—twenty time!"

Every line in his face deepened as he said it, and put in its affecting evidence of the suffering he had undergone.

"From bad to worse, from worse to worsen. She left me. She disgraced herseln everyways, bitter and bad. She coom back, she coom back, she coom back. What could I do t' hinder her? I ha' walked the streets nights long, ere ever I'd go home. I ha' gone t' th' brigg, minded to fling myseln ower, and ha' no more on't. I ha' bore that much, that I were owd when I were young."

Mrs Sparsit, easily ambling along with her netting-needles, raised the Coriolanian eyebrows and shook her head, as much as to say, "The great know trouble as well as the small. Please to turn your humble eye in My direction."

"I ha' paid her to keep awa' fra' me. These five year I ha' paid her. I ha' gotten decent fewtrils about me agen. I ha' lived hard and sad, but not ashamed and fearfo' a' the minnits o' my life. Last night, I went home. There she lay upon my har-stone! There she is!"

In the strength of his misfortune, and the energy of his distress, he fired for the moment like a proud man. In another moment, he stood as he had stood all the time—his usual stoop upon him; his pondering face addressed to Mr Bounderby, with a curious expression on it, half shrewd, half perplexed, as if his mind were set upon unravelling something very difficult; his hat held tight in his left hand, which rested on his hip; his right arm, with a rugged propriety and force of action, very earnestly emphasizing what he said: not least so when it always paused, a little bent, but not withdrawn, as he paused.

"I was acquainted with all this, you know," said Mr Bounderby, "except the last clause, long ago. It's a bad job; that's what it is. You had better have been satisfied as you were, and not have got married. However, it's too late to say that."

"Was it an unequal marriage, sir, in point of years?" asked Mrs Sparsit.

"You hear what this lady asks. Was it an unequal marriage in point of years, this unlucky job of yours?" said Mr Bounderby.

"Not e'en so. I were one-and-twenty myseln; she were twenty nighbut."

"Indeed, sir?" said Mrs Sparsit to her Chief, with great placidity. "I inferred, from its being so miserable a marriage, that it was probably an unequal one in point of years."

Mr Bounderby looked very hard at the good lady in a sidelong way that had an odd sheepishness about it. He fortified himself with a little more sherry.

"Well? Why don't you go on?" he then asked, turning rather irritably on Stephen Blackpool.

"I ha' coom to ask yo, sir, how I am to be ridded o' this woman." Stephen infused a yet deeper gravity into the mixed expression of his attentive face. Mrs Sparsit uttered a gentle ejaculation, as having received a moral shock.

"What do you mean?" said Bounderby, getting up to lean his back against the chimney-piece. "What are you talking about? You took her for better for worse."

"I mun' be ridden o' her. I cannot bear't nommore. I ha' lived under't so long, for that I ha' had'n the pity and comforting words o' th' best lass living or dead. Haply, but for her, I should ha' gone hottering mad."

"He wishes to be free, to marry the female of whom he speaks, I fear, sir," observed Mrs Sparsit in an undertone, and much dejected by the immorality of the people.

"I do. The lady says what's right. I do. I were a coming to't. I ha' read i' th' papers that great fok (fair faw 'em a'! I wishes 'em no hurt!) are not bonded together for better for worse so fast, but that they can be set free fro' *their* misfortnet marriages, an marry ower agen. When they dunnot agree, for that their tempers is ill-sorted, they has rooms o' one kind an another in their houses, above a bit, and they can live asunders. We fok ha' only one room, an we can't. When that won't do, they ha' gowd an other cash, an they can say 'This for yo, an that for me,' an they can go their separate ways. We can't.

Spite o' all that, they can be set free for smaller wrongs than mine. So, I mun be ridden o' this woman, an I want t'know how?"

"No how," returned Mr Bounderby.

"If I do her any hurt, sir, there's a law to punish me?"

"Of course there is."

"If I flee from her, there's a law to punish me?"

"Of course there is."

"If I marry t'oother dear lass, there's a law to punish me?"

"Of course there is."

"If I was to live wi' her an not marry her—saying such a thing could be, which it never could or would, an her so good—there's a law to punish me, in every innocent child belonging to me?"

"Of course there is."

"Now, a' God's name," said Stephen Blackpool, "show me the law to help me!"

"Hem! There's a sanctity in this relation of life," said Mr Bounderby, "and—and—it must be kept up."

"No no, dunnot say that, sir. 'Tan't kep' up that way. Not that way. 'Tis kep' down that way. I'm a weaver, I were in a fact'ry when a chilt, but I ha' gotten een to see wi' and eern to year wi'. I read in th' papers every 'Sizes, every Sessions—and you read too—I know it!—with dismay—how th' supposed unpossibility o' ever getting un-chained from one another, at any price, on any terms, brings blood upon this land, and brings many common married fok to battle, murder, and sudden death. Let us ha' this, right understood. Mine's a grievous case, an I want—if yo will be so good—t'know the law that helps me."

"Now, I tell you what!" said Mr Bounderby, putting his hands in his pockets. "There *is* such a law."

Stephen, subsiding into his quiet manner, and never wandering in his attention, gave a nod.

"But it's not for you at all. It costs money. It costs a mint of money."

How much might that be? Stephen calmly asked.

"Why, you'd have to go to Doctors' Commons with a suit, and you'd have to go to a court of Common Law with a suit, and you'd have to go to the House of Lords with a suit, and you'd have to get an Act of Parliament to enable you to marry again, and it would cost you (if it was a case of very plain-sailing), I suppose from a thousand to fifteen hundred pound," said Mr Bounderby. "Perhaps twice the money."

"There's no other law?"

"Certainly not."

"Why then, sir," said Stephen, turning white, and motioning with that right hand of his, as if he gave everything to the four winds, " 'tis a muddle. 'Tis just a muddle a'toogether, an the sooner I am dead, the better."

(Mrs Sparsit again dejected by the impiety of the people.)

"Pooh, pooh! Don't you talk nonsense, my good fellow," said Mr Bounderby, "about things you don't understand; and don't you call the Institutions of your country a muddle, or you'll get yourself into a real muddle one of these fine mornings. The institutions of your country are not your piece-work, and the only thing you have got to do, is, to mind your piece-work. You didn't take your wife for fast and for loose; but for better for worse. If she has turned out worse—why, all we have got to say is, she might have turned out better."

" 'Tis a muddle," said Stephen, shaking his head as he moved to the door. " 'Tis a' a muddle!"

"Now, I'll tell you what!" Mr Bounderby resumed, as a valedictory address. "With what I shall call your unhallowed opinions, you have been quite shocking this lady: who, as I have already told you, is a born lady, and who, as I have not already told you, has had her own marriage misfortunes to the tune of tens of thousands of pounds—tens of Thou-sands of Pounds!" (he repeated it with great relish). "Now, you have always been a steady Hand hitherto; but my opinion is, and so I tell you plainly, that you are turning into the wrong road. You have been listening to some mischievous stranger or other— they're always about—and the best thing you can do is, to come out of that. Now you know;" here his countenance expressed marvellous acuteness; "I can see as far into a grindstone as another man; farther than a good many, perhaps, because I had my nose well kept to it when I was young. I see traces of the turtle soup, and venison, and gold spoon in this. Yes, I do!" cried Mr Bounderby, shaking his head with obstinate cunning. "By the Lord Harry, I do!"

With a very different shake of the head and a deep sigh, Stephen said, "Thank you, sir, I wish you good day." So he left Mr Bounderby swelling at his own portrait on the wall, as if he were going to explode himself into it; and Mrs Sparsit still ambling on with her foot in her stirrup, looking quite cast down by the popular vices.

Chapter XII

THE OLD WOMAN

OLD Stephen descended the two white steps, shutting the black door with the brazen door-plate, by the aid of the brazen full-stop, to which he gave a parting polish with the sleeve of his coat, observing that his hot hand clouded it. He crossed the street with his eyes bent upon the ground, and thus was walking sorrowfully away, when he felt a touch upon his arm.

It was not the touch he needed most at such a moment—the touch that could calm the wild waters of his soul, as the uplifted hand of the sublimest love and patience could abate the raging of the sea—yet it was a woman's hand too. It was an old woman, tall and shapely still, though withered by Time, on whom his eyes fell when he stopped and turned. She was very cleanly and plainly dressed, had country mud upon her shoes, and was newly come from a journey. The flutter of her manner, in the unwonted noise of the streets; the spare shawl, carried unfolded on her arm; the heavy umbrella, and little basket; the loose long-fingered gloves, to which her hands were unused; all bespoke an old woman from the country, in her plain holiday clothes, come into Coketown on an expedition of rare occurrence. Remarking this at a glance, with the quick observation of his class, Stephen Blackpool bent his attentive face—his face, which, like the faces of many of his order, by dint of long working with eyes and hands in the midst of a prodigious noise, had acquired the concentrated look with which we are familiar in the countenances of the deaf—the better to hear what she asked him.

"Pray, sir," said the old woman, "didn't I see you come out of that gentleman's house?" pointing back to Mr Bounderby's. "I believe it was you, unless I have had the bad luck to mistake the person in following?"

"Yes, missus," returned Stephen, "it were me."

"Have you—you'll excuse an old woman's curiosity—have you seen the gentleman?"

"Yes, missus."

"And how did he look, sir? Was he portly, bold, outspoken, and hearty?" As she straightened her own figure, and held up her head in adapting her action to her words, the idea crossed Stephen that he had seen this old woman before, and had not quite liked her.

"O yes," he returned, observing her more attentively, "he were all that."

"And healthy," said the old woman, "as the fresh wind?"

"Yes," returned Stephen. "He were ett'n and drinking—as large and as loud as a Hummobee."

"Thank you!" said the old woman with infinite content. "Thank you!"

He certainly never had seen this old woman before. Yet there was a vague remembrance in his mind, as if he had more than once dreamed of some old woman like her.

She walked along at his side, and, gently accommodating himself to her humour, he said Coketown was a busy place, was it not? To which she answered "Eigh sure! Dreadful busy!" Then he said, she came from the country, he saw? To which she answered in the affirmative.

"By Parliamentary, this morning. I came forty mile by Parliamentary this morning, and I'm going back the same forty mile this afternoon. I walked nine mile to the station this morning, and if I find nobody on the road to give me a lift, I shall walk the nine mile back tonight. That's pretty well, sir, at my age!" said the chatty old woman, her eye brightening with exultation.

"'Deed 'tis. Don't do't too often, missus."

"No, no. Once a year," she answered, shaking her head. "I spend my savings so, once every year. I come regular, to tramp about the streets, and see the gentlemen."

"Only to see 'em?" returned Stephen.

"That's enough for me," she replied, with great earnestness and interest of manner. "I ask no more! I have been standing about, on this side of the way, to see that gentleman," turning her head back towards Mr Bounderby's again, "come out. But, he's late this year, and I have not seen him. You came out, instead. Now, if I am obliged to go back without a glimpse of him—I only want a glimpse—well! I have seen you, and you have seen him, and I must make that do." Saying this, she looked at Stephen as if to fix his features in her mind, and her eye was not so bright as it had been.

With a large allowance for difference of tastes, and with all submission to the patricians of Coketown, this seemed so extraordinary a source of interest to take so much trouble about, that it perplexed him. But they were passing the church now, and as his eye caught the clock, he quickened his pace.

He was going to his work? the old woman said, quickening hers, too, quite easily. Yes, time was nearly out. On his telling her where he worked, the old woman became a more singular old woman than before.

"An't you happy?" she asked him.

"Why—there's awmost nobbody but has their troubles, missus." He answered evasively, because the old woman appeared to take it for granted that he would be very happy indeed, and he had not the heart to disappoint her. He knew that there was trouble enough in the world; and if the old woman had lived so long, and could count upon his having so little, why so much the better for her, and none the worse for him.

"Ay, ay! You have your troubles at home, you mean?" she said.

"Times. Just now and then," he answered slightly.

"But, working under such a gentleman, they don't follow you to the Factory?"

No, no; they didn't follow him there, said Stephen. All correct there. Everything accordant there. (He did not go so far as to say, for her pleasure, that there was a sort of Divine Right there; but, I have heard claims almost as magnificent of late years.)

They were now in the black by-road near the place, and the Hands were crowding in. The bell was ringing, and the Serpent was a Serpent of many coils, and the Elephant was getting ready. The strange old woman was delighted with the very bell. It was the beautifullest bell she had ever heard, she said, and sounded grand!

She asked him, when he stopped good-naturedly to shake hands with her before going in, how long he had worked there?

"A dozen year," he told her.

"I must kiss the hand," said she, "that has worked in this fine factory for a dozen year!" And she lifted it, though he would have prevented her, and put it to her lips. What harmony, besides her age and her simplicity, surrounded her, he did not know, but even in this fantastic action there was a something neither out of time nor place: a something which it seemed as if nobody else could have made as serious, or done with such a natural and touching air.

He had been at his loom full half an hour, thinking about this old woman, when, having occasion to move round the loom for its adjustment, he glanced through a window which was in his corner, and saw her still looking up at the pile of building, lost in admiration. Heedless of the smoke and mud and wet, and of her two long journeys, she was gazing at it, as if the heavy thrum that issued from its many stories were proud music to her.

She was gone by and by, and the day went after her, and the lights sprung up again, and the Express whirled in full sight of the Fairy Palace over the arches near: little felt amid the jarring of the machinery, and scarcely heard above its crash and rattle. Long before then, his thoughts had gone back to the dreary room above the little shop, and to the shameful figure heavy on the bed, but heavier on his heart.

Machinery slackened; throbbing feebly like a fainting pulse; stopped. The bell again; the glare of light and heat dispelled; the factories, looming heavy in the black wet night—their tall chimneys rising up into the air like competing Towers of Babel.

He had spoken to Rachael only last night, it was true, and had walked with her a little way; but he had his new misfortune on him in which no one else could give him a moment's relief, and, for the sake of it, and because he knew himself to want that softening of his anger which no voice but hers could effect, he felt he might so far disregard what she had said as to wait for her again. He waited, but she had eluded him. She was gone. On no other night in the year could he so ill have spared her patient face.

O! Better to have no home in which to lay his head, than to have a home and dread to go to it, through such a cause. He ate and drank, for he was exhausted—but, he little knew or cared what; and he wandered about in the chill rain, thinking and thinking, and brooding and brooding.

No word of a new marriage had ever passed between them; but Rachael had taken great pity on him years ago, and to her alone he had opened his closed heart all this time, on the subject of his miseries; and he knew very well that if he were free to ask her, she would take him. He thought of the home he might at that moment have been seeking with pleasure and pride; of the different man he might have been that night; of the lightness then in his now heavy-laden breast; of the then restored honour, self-respect, and tranquillity, now all torn to pieces. He thought of the waste of the best part of his life, of the change it made in his character for the worse every day, of the dreadful nature of his existence, bound hand and foot to a dead woman, and tormented by a demon in her shape. He thought of Rachael, how young when they were first brought together in these circumstances, how mature now, how soon to grow old. He thought of the number of girls and women she had seen marry, how many homes with children in them she had seen grow up around her, how she had contentedly pursued her own lone quiet path—for him—and how he had sometimes seen a shade of melancholy on her blessed face, that smote him with remorse and despair. He set the picture of her up, beside the infamous image of last night; and thought, Could it be, that the whole earthly course of one so gentle, good, and self-denying, was subjugate to such a wretch as that!

Filled with these thoughts—so filled that he had an unwholesome sense of growing larger, of being placed in some new and diseased relation towards the objects among which he passed, of seeing the iris round every misty light turn red—he went home for shelter.

Chapter XIII

RACHAEL

A CANDLE faintly burned in the window, to which the black ladder had often been raised for the sliding away of all that was most precious in this world to a striving wife and a brood of hungry babies; and Stephen added to his other thoughts the stern reflection, that of all the casualties of this existence upon earth, not one was dealt out with so unequal a hand as Death. The inequality of Birth was nothing to it. For, say that the child of a King and the child of a Weaver were born tonight in the same moment, what was that disparity, to the death of any human creature who was serviceable to, or beloved by, another, while this abandoned woman lived on!

From the outside of his home he gloomily passed to the inside, with suspended breath and with a slow footstep. He went up to his door, opened it, and so into the room.

Quiet and peace were there. Rachael was there, sitting by the bed.

She turned her head, and the light of her face shone in upon the midnight of his mind. She sat by the bed, watching and tending his wife. That is to say, he saw that some one lay there, and he knew too well it must be she; but Rachael's hands had put a curtain up, so that she was screened from his eyes. Her disgraceful garments were removed, and some of Rachael's were in the room. Everything was in its place and order as he had always kept it, the little fire was newly trimmed, and the hearth was freshly swept. It appeared to him that he saw all this in Rachael's face, and looked at nothing besides. While looking at it, it was shut out from his view by the softened tears that filled his eyes; but, not before he had seen how earnestly she looked at him, and how her own eyes were filled too.

She turned again towards the bed, and satisfying herself that all was quiet there, spoke in a low, calm, cheerful voice.

"I am glad you have come at last, Stephen. You are very late."

"I ha' been walking up an down."

"I thought so. But 'tis too bad a night for that. The rain falls very heavy, and the wind has risen."

The wind? True. It was blowing hard. Hark to the thundering in the chimney, and the surging noise! To have been out in such a wind, and not to have known it was blowing!

"I have been here once before, today, Stephen. Landlady came round for me at dinner-time. There was some one here that needed looking to, she said. And 'deed she was right. All wandering and lost, Stephen. Wounded too, and bruised."

He slowly moved to a chair and sat down, drooping his head before her.

"I came to do what little I could, Stephen; first, for that she worked with me when we were girls both, and for that you courted her and married her when I was her friend—"

He laid his furrowed forehead on his hand, with a low groan.

"And next, for that I know your heart, and am right sure and certain that 'tis far too merciful to let her die, or even so much as suffer, for want of aid. Thou knowest who said, 'Let him who is without sin among you, cast the first stone at her!' There have been plenty to do that. Thou art not the man to cast the last stone, Stephen, when she is brought so low."

"O Rachael, Rachael!"

"Thou hast been a cruel sufferer, Heaven reward thee!" she said, in compassionate accents. "I am thy poor friend, with all my heart and mind."

The wounds of which she had spoken, seemed to be about the neck of the self-made outcast. She dressed them now, still without showing her. She steeped a piece of linen in a basin, into which she poured some liquid from a bottle, and laid it with a gentle hand upon the sore. The three-legged table had been drawn close to the bedside, and on it there were two bottles. This was one.

It was not so far off, but that Stephen, following her hands with his eyes, could read what was printed on it, in large letters. He turned of a deadly hue, and a sudden horror seemed to fall upon him.

"I will stay here, Stephen," said Rachael, quietly resuming her seat, 'till the bells go Three. 'Tis to be done again at three, and then she may be left till morning."

"But thy rest agen tomorrow's work, my dear."

"I slept sound last night. I can wake many nights, when I am put to it. 'Tis thou who art in need of rest—so white and tired. Try to sleep in the chair there, while I watch. Thou hadst no sleep last night, I can well believe. Tomorrow's work is far harder for thee than for me."

He heard the thundering and surging out of doors, and it seemed to him as if his late angry mood were going about trying to get at him. She had cast it out; she would keep it out; he trusted to her to defend him from himself.

"She don't know me, Stephen; she just drowsily mutters and stares. I have spoken to her times and again, but she don't notice! 'Tis as well so. When she comes to her right mind once more, I shall have done what I can, and she never the wiser."

"How long, Rachael, is't looked for, that she'll be so?"

"Doctor said she would haply come to her mind tomorrow."

His eyes again fell on the bottle, and a tremble passed over him, causing him to shiver in every limb. She thought he was chilled with the wet. "No," he said, "it was not that. He had had a fright."

"A fright?"

"Ay, ay! coming in. When I were walking. When I were thinking. When I——" It seized him again; and he stood up, holding by the mantel-shelf, as he pressed his dank cold hair down with a hand that shook as if it were palsied.

"Stephen!"

She was coming to him, but he stretched out his arm to stop her.

"No! Don't please; don't! Let me see thee setten by the bed. Let me see thee, a' so good, and so forgiving. Let me see thee as I see thee when I coom in. I can never see thee better than so. Never, never, never!"

He had a violent fit of trembling, and then sunk into his chair. After a time he controlled himself, and, resting with an elbow on one knee, and his head upon that hand, could look towards Rachael. Seen across the dim candle with his moistened eyes, she looked as if she had a glory shining round her head. He could have believed she had. He did believe it, as the noise without shook the window, rattled at the door below, and went about the house clamouring and lamenting.

"When she gets better, Stephen, 'tis to be hoped she'll leave thee to thyself again, and do thee no more hurt. Anyways we will hope so now. And now I shall keep silence, for I want thee to sleep."

He closed his eyes, more to please her than to rest his weary head; but, by slow degrees as he listened to the great noise of the wind, he ceased to hear it, or it changed into the working of his loom, or even into the voices of the day (his own included) saying what had been really said. Even this imperfect consciousness faded away at last, and he dreamed a long, troubled dream.

He thought that he, and some one on whom his heart had long been set—but she was not Rachael, and that surprised him, even in the midst of his imaginary happiness—stood in the church being married. While the ceremony was performing, and while he recognized among the witnesses some whom he knew to be living, and many whom he knew to be dead, darkness came on, succeeded by the shining of a tremendous light. It broke from one line in the table of commandments at the altar, and illuminated the building with the words. They were sounded through the church too, as if there were voices in the fiery letters. Upon this, the whole appearance before him and around him changed, and nothing was left as it had been, but himself and the clergyman. They stood in the daylight before a crowd so vast, that if all the people in the world could have been brought together into one space, they could not have looked, he thought, more numerous; and they all abhorred him, and there was not one pitying or friendly eye among the millions that were fastened on his face. He stood on a raised stage, under his own loom; and, looking up at the shape the loom took, and hearing the burial service distinctly read, he knew that he was there to suffer death. In an instant what he stood on fell below him, and he was gone.

Out of what mystery he came back to his usual life, and to places that he knew, he was unable to consider; but, he was back in those places by some means, and with this condemnation upon him, that he was never, in this world or the next, through all the unimaginable ages of eternity, to look on Rachael's face or hear her voice. Wandering to and fro, unceasingly, without hope, and in search of he knew not what (he only knew that he was doomed to seek it), he was the subject of a nameless, horrible dread, a mortal fear of one particular shape which everything took. Whatsoever he looked at, grew into that form sooner or later. The object of his miserable existence was to prevent its recognition by any one among the various people he encountered. Hopeless labour! If he led them out of rooms where it was, if he shut up drawers and closets where it stood, if he drew the curious from places where he knew it to be secreted, and got them out into the streets, the very chimneys of the mills assumed that shape, and round them was the printed word.

The wind was blowing again, the rain was beating on the housetops, and the larger spaces through which he had strayed contracted to the four walls of his room. Saving that the fire had died out, it was as his eyes had closed upon it. Rachael seemed to have fallen into a doze, in the chair by the bed. She sat wrapped in her shawl, perfectly still. The table stood in the same place, close by the bedside, and on it, in its real proportions and appearance, was the shape so often repeated.

He thought he saw the curtain move. He looked again, and he was sure it moved. He saw a hand come forth, and grope about a little. Then the curtain moved more perceptibly, and the woman in the bed put it back, and sat up.

With her woful eyes, so haggard and wild, so heavy and large, she looked all round the room, and passed the corner where he slept in his chair. Her eyes returned to that corner, and she put her hand over them as a shade, while she looked into it. Again they went all round the room, scarcely heeding Rachael if at all, and returned to that corner. He thought, as she once more shaded them—not so much looking at him, as looking for him with a brutish instinct that he was there—that no single trace was left in those debauched features, or in the mind that went along with them, of the woman he had married eighteen years before. But that he had seen her come to this by inches, he never could have believed her to be the same.

All this time, as if a spell were on him, he was motionless and powerless, except to watch her.

Stupidly dozing, or communing with her incapable self about nothing, she sat for a little while with her hands at her ears, and her head resting on them. Presently, she resumed her staring round the room. And now, for the first time, her eyes stopped at the table with the bottles on it.

Straightway she turned her eyes back to his corner, with the defiance of last night, and, moving very cautiously and softly, stretched out her greedy hand. She drew a mug into the bed, and sat for a while considering which of the two bottles she should choose. Finally, she laid her insensate grasp upon the bottle that had swift and certain death in it, and, before his eyes, pulled out the cork with her teeth.

Dream or reality, he had no voice, nor had he power to stir. If this be real, and her allotted time be not yet come, wake, Rachael, wake!

She thought of that, too. She looked at Rachael, and very slowly, very cautiously, poured out the contents. The draught was at her lips. A moment and she would be past all help, let the whole world wake and come about her with its utmost power. But, in that moment Rachael started up with a suppressed cry. The creature struggled, struck her, seized her by the hair; but Rachael had the cup.

Stephen broke out of his chair. "Rachael, am I wakin' or dreamin' this dreadfo' night!"

" 'Tis all well, Stephen. I have been asleep myself. 'Tis near three. Hush! I hear the bells."

The wind brought the sounds of the church clock to the window. They listened, and it struck three. Stephen looked at her, saw how pale she was, noted the disorder of her hair, and the red marks of fingers on her forehead, and felt assured that his senses of sight and hearing had been awake. She held the cup in her hand even now.

"I thought it must be near three," she said, calmly pouring from the cup into the basin, and steeping the linen as before. "I am thankful I stayed! 'Tis done now, when I have put this on. Three! And now she's quiet again. The few drops in the basin I'll pour away, for 'tis bad stuff to leave about, though ever so little of it." As she spoke, she drained the basin into the ashes of the fire, and broke the bottle on the hearth.

She had nothing to do, then, but to cover herself with her shawl before going out into the wind and rain.

"Thou'lt let me walk wi' thee at this hour, Rachael?"

"No, Stephen. 'Tis but a minute and I'm home."

"Thou'rt not fearfo';" he said it in a low voice, as they went out at the door; "to leave me alone wi' her!"

As she looked at him, saying "Stephen?" he went down on his knee before her, on the poor mean stairs, and put an end of her shawl to his lips.

"Thou art an Angel. Bless thee, bless thee!"

"I am, as I have told thee, Stephen, thy poor friend. Angels are not like me. Between them, and a working woman fu' of faults, there is a deep gulf set. My little sister is among them, but she is changed."

She raised her eyes for a moment as she said the words; and then they fell again, in all their gentleness and mildness, on his face.

"Thou changest me from bad to good. Thou mak'st me humbly wishfo' to be more like thee, and fearfo' to lose thee when this life is ower, an' a' the muddle cleared awa'. Thou'rt an Angel; it may be, thou hast saved my soul alive!"

She looked at him, on his knee at her feet, with her shawl still in his hand, and the reproof on her lips died away when she saw the working of his face.

"I coom home desp'rate. I coom home wi'out a hope, and mad wi' thinking that when I said a word o' complaint, I was reckoned a onreasonable Hand. I told thee I had had a fright. It were the Poison-bottle on table. I never hurt a livin' creetur; but happenin' so suddenly upon't, I thowt, 'How can *I* say what I might ha' done to myseln, or her, or both!' "

She put her two hands on his mouth, with a face of terror, to stop him from saying more. He caught them in his unoccupied hand, and holding them, and still clasping the border of her shawl, said, hurriedly:

"But I see thee, Rachel, setten by the bed. I ha' seen thee, aw this night. In my troublous sleep I ha' known thee still to be there. Evermore I will see thee there. I nevermore will see her or think o' her, but thou shalt be beside her. I nevermore will see or think o' anything that angers me, but thou, so much better than me, shalt be by th' side on't. And so I will try t' look t' th' time, and so I will try t' trust t' th' time, when thou and me at last shall walk together far awa', beyond the deep gulf, in th' country where thy little sister is."

He kissed the border of her shawl again, and let her go. She bade him good night in a broken voice, and went out into the street.

The wind blew from the quarter where the day would soon appear, and still blew strongly. It had cleared the sky before it, and the rain had spent itself or travelled elsewhere, and the stars were bright. He stood bare-headed in the road, watching her quick disappearance. As the shining stars were to the heavy candle in the window, so was Rachael, in the rugged fancy of this man, to the common experiences of his life.

Chapter XIV

THE GREAT MANUFACTURER

T IME went on in Coketown like its own machinery: so much material wrought up, so much fuel consumed, so many powers worn out, so much money made. But, less inexorable than iron, steel, and brass, it brought its varying seasons even into that wilderness of smoke and brick, and made the only stand that ever *was* made in the place against its direful uniformity.

"Louisa is becoming," said Mr Gradgrind, "almost a young woman."

Time, with his innumerable horse-power, worked away, not minding what anybody said, and presently turned out young Thomas a foot taller than when his father had last taken particular notice of him.

"Thomas is becoming," said Mr Gradgrind, "almost a young man."

Time passed Thomas on in the mill, while his father was thinking about it, and there he stood in a long-tailed coat and a stiff shirt-collar.

"Really," said Mr Gradgrind, "the period has arrived when Thomas ought to go to Bounderby."

Time, sticking to him, passed him on into Bounderby's Bank, made him an inmate of Bounderby's house, necessitated the purchase of his first razor, and exercised him diligently in his calculations relative to number one.

The same great manufacturer, always with an immense variety of work on hand, in every stage of development, passed Sissy onward in his mill, and worked her up into a very pretty article indeed.

"I fear, Jupe," said Mr Gradgrind, "that your continuance at the school any longer, would be useless."

"I am afraid it would, sir," Sissy answered with a curtsey.

"I cannot disguise from you, Jupe," said Mr Gradgrind, knitting his brow, "that the result of your probation there has disappointed me; has greatly disappointed me. You have not acquired, under Mr and Mrs M'Choakumchild, anything like that amount of exact knowledge which I looked for. You are extremely deficient in your facts. Your acquaintance with figures is very limited. You are altogether backward, and below the mark."

"I am sorry, sir," she returned; "but I know it is quite true. Yet I have tried hard, sir."

"Yes," said Mr Gradgrind, "yes, I believe you have tried hard; I have observed you, and I can find no fault in that respect."

"Thank you, sir. I have thought sometimes;" Sissy very timid here; "that perhaps I tried to learn too much, and that if I had asked to be allowed to try a little less, I might have—"

"No, Jupe, no," said Mr Gradgrind, shaking his head in his profoundest and most eminently practical way. "No. The course you pursued, you pursued according to the system—the system—and there is no more to be said about it. I can only suppose that the circumstances of your early life were too unfavourable to the development of your reasoning powers, and that we began too late. Still, as I have said already, I am disappointed."

"I wish I could have made a better acknowledgement, sir, of your kindness to a poor forlorn girl who had no claim upon you, and of your protection of her."

"Don't shed tears," said Mr Gradgrind. "Don't shed tears. I don't complain of you. You are an affectionate, earnest, good young woman, and—and we must make that do."

"Thank you, sir, very much," said Sissy, with a grateful curtsey.

"You are useful to Mrs Gradgrind, and (in a generally pervading way) you are serviceable in the family also; so I understand from Miss Louisa, and, indeed, so I have observed myself. I therefore hope," said Mr Gradgrind, "that you can make yourself happy in those relations."

"I should have nothing to wish, sir, if—"

"I understand you," said Mr Gradgrind; "you still refer to your father. I have heard from Miss Louisa that you still preserve that bottle. Well! If your training in the science of arriving at exact results had been more successful, you would have been wiser on these points. I will say no more."

He really liked Sissy too well to have a contempt for her; otherwise he held her calculating powers in such very slight estimation that he must have fallen upon that conclusion. Somehow or other, he had become possessed by an idea that there was something in this girl which could hardly be set forth in a tabular form. Her capacity of definition might be easily stated at a very low figure, her mathematical knowledge at nothing; yet he was not sure that if he had been required, for example, to tick her off into columns in parliamentary return, he would have quite known how to divide her.

In some stages of his manufacture of the human fabric, the processes of Time are very rapid. Young Thomas and Sissy being both at such a stage of their working up, these changes were effected in a year or two; while Mr Gradgrind himself seemed stationary in his course, and underwent no alteration.

Except one, which was apart from his necessary progress through the mill. Time hustled him into a little noisy and rather dirty machinery, in a by-corner, and made him Member of Parliament for Coketown: one of the respected members for ounce weights and measures, one of the representatives of the multiplication table, one of the deaf honourable gentlemen, dumb honourable gentlemen, blind honourable gentlemen, lame honourable gentlemen, dead honourable gentlemen, to every other consideration. Else wherefore live we in a Christian land, eighteen hundred and odd years after our Master?

All this while, Louisa had been passing on, so quiet and reserved, and so much given to watching the bright ashes at twilight as they fell into the grate and became extinct, that from the period when her father had said she was almost a young woman—which seemed but yesterday—she had scarcely attracted his notice again, when he found her quite a young woman.

"Quite a young woman," said Mr Gradgrind, musing. "Dear me!"

Soon after this discovery, he became more thoughtful than usual for several days, and seemed much engrossed by one subject. On a certain night, when he was going out, and Louisa came to bid him good-bye before his departure—as he was not to be home until late and she would not see him again until the morning—he held her in his arms, looking at her in his kindest manner, and said:

"My dear Louisa, you are a woman!"

She answered with the old, quick, searching look of the night when she was found at the Circus; then cast down her eyes. "Yes, father."

"My dear," said Mr Gradgrind, "I must speak with you alone and seriously. Come to me in my room after breakfast tomorrow, will you?"

"Yes, father."

"Your hands are rather cold, Louisa. Are you not well?"

"Quite well, father."

"And cheerful?"

She looked at him again, and smiled in her peculiar manner. "I am as cheerful, father, as I usually am, or usually have been."

"That's well," said Mr Gradgrind. So, he kissed her and went away; and Louisa returned to the serene apartment of the haircutting character, and leaning her elbow on her hand, looked again at the short-lived sparks that so soon subsided into ashes.

"Are you there, Loo?" said her brother, looking in at the door. He was quite a young gentleman of pleasure now, and not quite a prepossessing one.

"Dear Tom," she answered, rising and embracing him, "how long it is since you have been to see me!"

"Why, I have been otherwise engaged, Loo, in the evenings; and in the daytime old Bounderby has been keeping me at it rather. But I touch him up with you, when he comes it too strong, and so we preserve an understanding. I say! Has father said anything particular to you, today or yesterday, Loo?"

"No, Tom. But he told me tonight that he wished to do so in the morning."

"Ah! That's what I mean," said Tom. "Do you know where he is tonight?"—with a very deep expression.

"No."

"Then I'll tell you. He's with old Bounderby. They are having a regular confab together, up at the Bank. Why at the Bank, do you think? Well, I'll tell you again. To keep Mrs Sparsit's ears as far off as possible, I expect."

With her hand upon her brother's shoulder, Louisa still stood looking at the fire. Her brother glanced at her face with greater interest than usual, and, encircling her waist with his arm, drew her coaxingly to him.

"You are very fond of me, an't you, Loo?"

"Indeed I am, Tom, though you do let such long intervals go by without coming to see me."

"Well, sister of mine," said Tom, "when you say that, you are near my thoughts. We might be so much oftener together—mightn't we? Always together, almost—mightn't we? It would do me a great deal of good if you were to make up your mind to I know what, Loo. It would be a splendid thing for me. It would be uncommonly jolly!"

Her thoughtfulness baffled his cunning scrutiny. He could make nothing of her face. He pressed her in his arm, and kissed her cheek. She returned the kiss, but still looked at the fire.

"I say, Loo! I thought I'd come, and just hint to you what was going on: though I supposed you'd most likely guess, even if you didn't know. I can't stay, because I'm engaged to some fellows tonight. You won't forget how fond you are of me?"

"No, dear Tom, I won't forget."

"That's a capital girl," said Tom. "Good-bye, Loo."

She gave him an affectionate good night, and went out with him to the door, whence the fires of Coketown could be seen, making the distance lurid. She stood there, looking steadfastly towards them, and listening to his departing steps. They retreated quickly, as glad to get away from Stone Lodge; and she stood there yet, when he was gone and all was quiet. It seemed as if, first in her own fire within the house, and then in the fiery haze without, she tried to discover what kind of woof Old Time, that greatest and longest-established Spinner of all, would weave from the threads he had already spun into a woman. But, his factory is a secret place, his work is noiseless, and his Hands are mutes.

Chapter XV

FATHER AND DAUGHTER

ALTHOUGH Mr Gradgrind did not take after Blue Beard, his room was quite a blue chamber in its abundance of blue books. Whatever they could prove (which is usually anything you like), they proved there, in an army constantly strengthening by the arrival of new recruits. In that charmed apartment, the most complicated social questions were cast up, got into exact totals, and finally settled—if those concerned could only have been brought to know it. As if an astronomical observatory should be made without any windows, and the astronomer within should arrange the starry universe solely by pen, ink and paper, so Mr Gradgrind, in *his* Observatory (and there are many like it), had no need to cast an eye upon the teeming myriads of human beings around him, but could settle all their destinies on a slate, and wipe out all their tears with one dirty little bit of sponge.

To this Observatory, then: a stern room, with a deadly-statistical clock in it, which measured every second with a beat like a rap upon a coffin-lid: Louisa repaired on the appointed morning. A window looked towards Coketown; and when she sat down near her father's table, she saw the high chimneys and the long tracts of smoke looming in the heavy distance gloomily.

"My dear Louisa," said her father, "I prepared you last night to give me your serious attention in the conversation we are now going to have together. You have been so well trained, and you do, I am happy to say, so much justice to the education you have received, that I have perfect confidence in your good sense. You are not impulsive, you are not romantic, you are accustomed to view everything from the strong dispassionate ground of reasons and calculation. From that ground alone, I know you will view and consider what I am going to communicate."

He waited, as if he would have been glad that she said something. But she said never a word.

"Louisa my dear, you are the subject of a proposal of marriage that has been made to me."

Again he waited, and again she answered not one word. This so far surprised him, as to induce him gently to repeat, "a proposal of marriage, my dear." To which she returned, without any visible emotion whatever:

"I hear you, father. I am attending, I assure you."

"Well!" said Mr Gradgrind, breaking into a smile, after being for the moment at a loss, "you are even more dispassionate than I expected, Louisa. Or, perhaps, you are not unprepared for the announcement I have it in charge to make?"

"I cannot say that, father, until I hear it. Prepared or unprepared, I wish to hear it all from you. I wish to hear you state it to me, father."

Strange to relate, Mr Gradgrind was not so collected at this moment as his daughter was. He took a paper-knife in his hand, turned it over, laid it down, took it up again, and even then had to look along the blade of it, considering how to go on.

"What you say, my dear Louisa, is perfectly reasonable. I have undertaken then to let you know that—in short, that Mr Bounderby has informed me that he has long watched your progress with particular interest and pleasure, and has long hoped that the time might ultimately arrive when he should offer you his hand in marriage. That time, to which he has so long, and certainly with great constancy, looked forward, is now come. Mr Bounderby has made his proposal of marriage to me, and has entreated me to make it known to you, and to express his hope that you will take it into your favourable consideration."

Silence between them. The deadly-statistical clock very hollow. The distant smoke very black and heavy.

"Father," said Louisa, "do you think I love Mr Bounderby?"

Mr Gradgrind was extremely discomfited by this unexpected question. "Well, my child," he returned, "I—really—cannot take upon myself to say."

"Father," pursued Louisa in exactly the same voice as before, "do you ask me to love Mr Bounderby?"

"My dear Louisa, no. No. I ask nothing."

"Father," she still pursued, "does Mr Bounderby ask me to love him?"

"Really, my dear," said Mr Gradgrind, "it is difficult to answer your question—"

"Difficult to answer it, Yes or No, father?"

"Certainly, my dear. Because"; here was something to demonstrate, and it set him up again; "because the reply depends so materially, Louisa, on the sense in which we use the expression. Now, Mr Bounderby does not do you the injustice, and does not do himself the injustice, of pretending to anything fanciful, fantastic or (I am using synony-mous terms) sentimental. Mr Bounderby would have seen you grow up under his eyes, to very little purpose, if he could so far forget what is due to your good sense, not to say to his, as to address you from any such ground. Therefore, perhaps the expression itself—I merely suggest this to you, my dear—may be a little misplaced."

"What would you advise me to use in its stead, father?"

"Why, my dear Louisa," said Mr Gradgrind, completely recovered by this time, "I would advise you (since you ask me) to consider this question, as you have been accustomed to consider every other question, simply as one of tangible Fact. The igno-rant and the giddy may embarrass such subjects with irrelevant fancies, and other absurdities that have no existence, properly viewed—really no existence—but it is no compliment to you to say, that you know better. Now, what are the Facts of this case? You are, we will say in round numbers, twenty years of age; Mr Bounderby is, we will say in round numbers, fifty. There is some disparity in your respective years, but in your means and positions there is none; on the contrary, there is a great suitability. Then the question arises, Is this one disparity sufficient to operate as a bar to such a marriage? In considering this question, it is not unimportant to take into account the statistics of marriage, so far as they have yet been obtained, in England and Wales. I find on reference to the figures, that a large proportion of these marriages are contracted between parties of very unequal ages, and that the elder of these contracting parties is, in rather more than three-fourths of these instances, the bridegroom. It is remarkable as showing the wide prevalence of this law, that among the natives of the British possessions in India, also in a considerable part of China, and among the Calmucks of Tartary, the best means of computation yet furnished us by travellers, yield similar results. The disparity I have mentioned, therefore, almost ceases to be disparity, and (virtually) all but disappears."

"What do you recommend, father," asked Louisa, her reserved composure not in the least affected by these gratifying results, "that I should substitute for the term I used just now? For the misplaced expression?"

"Louisa," returned her father, "it appears to me that nothing can be plainer. Confining yourself rigidly to Fact, the question of Fact you state to yourself is: Does Mr Bounderby ask me to marry him? Yes, he does. The sole remaining question then is: Shall I marry him? I think nothing can be plainer than that."

"Shall I marry him?" repeated Louisa, with great deliberation.

"Precisely. And it is satisfactory to me, as your father, my dear Louisa, to know that you do not come to the consideration of that question with the previous habits of mind, and habits of life, that belong to many young women."

"No, father," she returned, "I do not."

"I now leave you to judge for yourself," said Mr Gradgrind. "I have stated the case, as such cases are usually stated among practical minds; I have stated it, as the case of your mother and myself was stated in its time. The rest, my dear Louisa, is for you to decide."

From the beginning, she had sat looking at him fixedly. As he now leaned back in his chair, and bent his deep-set eyes upon her in his turn, perhaps he might have seen one wavering moment in her, when she was impelled to throw herself upon his breast, and give him the pent-up confidences of her heart. But, to see it, he must have over-leaped at a bound the artificial barriers he had for many years been erecting, between himself and all those subtle essences of humanity which will elude the utmost cunning of algebra until the last trumpet ever to be sounded shall blow even algebra to wreck. The barriers were too many and too high for such a leap. With his unbending, utilitarian, matter-of-fact face, he hardened her again, and the moment shot away into the plumbless depths of the past, to mingle with all the lost opportunities that are drowned there.

Removing her eyes from him, she sat so long looking silently towards the town, that he said, at length: "Are you consulting the chimneys of the Coketown works, Louisa?"

"There seems to be nothing there, but languid and monotonous smoke. Yet when the night comes, Fire bursts out, father!" she answered, turning quickly.

"Of course I know that, Louisa. I do not see the application of the remark." To do him justice he did not, at all.

She passed it away with a slight motion of her hand, and concentrating her attention upon him again, said, "Father, I have often thought that life is very short."—This was so distinctly one of his subjects that he interposed:

"It is short, no doubt, my dear. Still, the average duration of human life is proved to have increased of late years. The calculations of various life assurance and annuity offices, among other figures which cannot go wrong, have established the fact."

"I speak of my own life, father."

"O indeed? Still," said Mr Gradgrind, "I need not point out to you, Louisa, that it is governed by the laws which govern lives in the aggregate."

"While it lasts, I would wish to do the little I can, and the little I am fit for. What does it matter!"

Mr Gradgrind seemed rather at a loss to understand the last four words; replying, "How, matter? What, matter, my dear?"

"Mr Bounderby," she went on in a steady, straight way, without regarding this, "asks me to marry him. The question I have to ask myself is, shall I marry him? That is so, father, is it not? You have told me so, father. Have you not?"

"Certainly, my dear."

"Let it be so. Since Mr Bounderby likes to take me thus, I am satisfied to accept his proposal. Tell him, father, as soon as you please, that this was my answer. Repeat it, word for word, if you can, because I should wish him to know what I said."

"It is quite right, my dear," retorted her father, approvingly, "to be exact. I will observe your very proper request. Have you any wish, in reference to the period of your marriage, my child?"

"None, father. What does it matter!"

Mr Gradgrind had drawn his chair a little nearer to her, and taken her hand. But, her repetition of these words seemed to strike with some little discord on his ear. He paused to look at her, and, still holding her hand, said:

"Louisa, I have not considered it essential to ask you one question, because the possibility implied in it appeared to me to be too remote. But, perhaps I ought to do so. You have never entertained in secret any other proposal?"

"Father," she returned, almost scornfully, "what other proposal can have been made to *me?* Whom have I seen? Where have I been? What are my heart's experiences?"

"My dear Louisa," returned Mr Gradgrind, reassured and satisfied, "you correct me justly. I merely wished to discharge my duty."

"What do *I* know, father," said Louisa in her quiet manner, "of tastes and fancies; of aspirations and affections; of all that part of my nature in which such light things might have been nourished? What escape have I had from problems that could be demonstrated, and realities that could be grasped?" As she said it, she unconsciously closed her hand, as if upon a solid object, and slowly opened it as though she were releasing dust or ash.

"My dear," assented her eminently practical parent, "quite true, quite true."

"Why, father," she pursued, "what a strange question to ask *me!* The baby-preference that even I have heard of as common among children, has never had its innocent resting-place in my breast. You have been so careful of me, that I never had a child's heart. You have trained me so well, that I never dreamed a child's dream. You have dealt so wisely with me, father, from my cradle to this hour, that I never had a child's belief or a child's fear."

Mr Gradgrind was quite moved by his success, and by this testimony to it. "My dear Louisa," said he, "you abundantly repay my care. Kiss me, my dear girl."

So his daughter kissed him. Detaining her in his embrace, he said, "I may assure you now, my favourite child, that I am made happy by the sound decision at which you have arrived. Mr Bounderby is a very remarkable man; and what little disparity can be said to exist between you—if any—is more than counterbalanced by the tone your mind has acquired. It has always been my object so to educate you, as that you might, while still in your early youth, be (if I may so express myself) almost any age. Kiss me once more, Louisa. Now, let us go and find your mother."

Accordingly, they went down to the drawing-room, where the esteemed lady with no nonsense about her, was recumbent as usual, while Sissy worked beside her. She gave some feeble signs of returning animation when they entered, and presently the faint transparency was presented in a sitting attitude.

"Mrs Gradgrind," said her husband, who had waited for the achievement of this feat with some impatience, "allow me to present to you Mrs Bounderby."

"Oh!" said Mrs Gradgrind, "so you have settled it! Well, I'm sure I hope your health may be good, Louisa; for if your head begins to split as soon as you are married, which was the case with mine, I cannot consider that you are to be envied, though I have no doubt you think you are, as all girls do. However, I give you joy, my dear—and I hope you may now turn all your ological studies to good account, I am sure I do! I must give you a kiss of congratulation, Louisa; but don't touch my right shoulder, for there's something running down it all day long. And now you see," whimpered Mrs Gradgrind, adjusting her shawls after the affectionate ceremony, "I shall be worrying myself, morning, noon, and night, to know what I am to call him!"

"Mrs Gradgrind," said her husband, solemnly, "what do you mean?"

"Whatever I am to call him, Mr Gradgrind, when he is married to Louisa! I must call him something. It's impossible," said Mrs Gradgrind, with a mingled sense of politeness and injury, "to be constantly addressing him, and never giving him a name. I cannot call him Josiah, for the name is insupportable to me. You yourself wouldn't hear of Joe, you very well know. Am I to call my own son-in-law, Mister? Not, I believe, unless the time has arrived when, as an invalid, I am to be trampled upon by my relations. Then, what am I to call him!"

Nobody present having any suggestion to offer in the remarkable emergency, Mrs Gradgrind departed this life for the time being, after delivering the following codicil to her remarks already executed:

"As to the wedding, all I ask, Louisa, is,—and I ask it with a fluttering in my chest, which actually extends to the soles of my feet,—that it may take place soon. Otherwise, I know it is one of those subjects I shall never hear the last of."

When Mr Gradgrind had presented Mrs Bounderby, Sissy had suddenly turned her head, and looked, in wonder, in pity, in sorrow, in doubt, in a multitude of emotions, towards Louisa. Louisa had known it, and seen it, without looking at her. From that moment she was impassive, proud, and cold—held Sissy at a distance—changed to her altogether.

Chapter XVI

HUSBAND AND WIFE

MR Bounderby's first disquietude, on hearing of his happiness, was occasioned by the necessity of imparting it to Mrs Sparsit. He could not make up his mind how to do that, or what the consequences of the step might be. Whether she would instantly depart, bag and baggage, to Lady Scadgers, or would positively refuse to budge from the premises; whether she would be plaintive or abusive, tearful or tearing; whether she would break her heart, or break the looking-glass; Mr Bounderby could not at all foresee. However, as it must be done, he had no choice but to do it; so, after attempting several letters, and failing in them all, he resolved to do it by word of mouth.

On his way home, on the evening he set aside for this momentous purpose, he took the precaution of stepping into a chemist's shop and buying a bottle of the very strongest smelling-salts. "By George!" said Mr Bounderby, "if she takes it in the fainting way, I'll have the skin off her nose, at all events!" But, in spite of being thus forearmed, he entered his own house with anything but a courageous air; and appeared before the object of his misgivings, like a dog who was conscious of coming direct from the pantry.

"Good evening, Mr Bounderby!"

"Good evening, ma'am, good evening." He drew up his chair, and Mrs Sparsit drew back hers, as who should say, "Your fireside, sir. I freely admit it. It is for you to occupy it all, if you think proper."

"Don't go to the North Pole, ma'am!" said Mr Bounderby.

"Thank you, sir," said Mrs Sparsit, and returned, though short of her former position.

Mr Bounderby sat looking at her, as, with the points of a stiff, sharp pair of scissors, she picked out holes for some inscrutable ornamental purpose, in a piece of cambric. An operation which, taken in connexion with the bushy eyebrows and the Roman nose, suggested with some liveliness the idea of a hawk engaged upon the eyes of a tough little bird. She was so steadfastly occupied, that many minutes elapsed before she looked up from her work; when she did so, Mr Bounderby bespoke her attention with a hitch of his head.

"Mrs Sparsit ma'am," said Mr Bounderby, putting his hands in his pockets, and assuring himself with his right hand that the cork of the little bottle was ready for use, "I have no occasion to say to you, that you are not only a lady born and bred, but a devilish sensible woman."

"Sir," returned the lady, "this is indeed not the first time that you have honoured me with similar expressions of your good opinion."

"Mrs Sparsit ma'am," said Mr Bounderby, "I am going to astonish you."

"Yes, sir?" returned Mrs Sparsit, interrogatively, and in the most tranquil manner possible. She generally wore mittens, and she now laid down her work, and smoothed those mittens.

"I am going, ma'am," said Bounderby, "to marry Tom Gradgrind's daughter."

"Yes, sir?" returned Mrs Sparsit. "I hope you may be happy, Mr Bounderby. Oh, indeed I hope you may be happy, sir!" And she said it with such great condescension, as well as with such great compassion for him, that Bounderby,—far more disconcerted than if she had thrown her work-box at the mirror, or swooned on the hearth-rug,—corked up the smelling-salts tight in his pocket, and thought, "Now con-found this woman, who could have ever guessed that she would take it in this way!"

"I wish with all my heart, sir," said Mrs Sparsit, in a highly superior manner; somehow she seemed, in a moment, to have established a right to pity him ever afterwards; "that you may be in all respects very happy."

"Well, ma'am," returned Bounderby, with some resentment in his tone: which was clearly lowered, though in spite of himself, "I am obliged to you. I hope I shall be."

"*Do* you, sir!" said Mrs Sparsit, with great affability. "But naturally you do; of course you do."

A very awkward pause on Mr Bounderby's part, succeeded. Mrs Sparsit sedately resumed her work, and occasionally gave a small cough, which sounded like the cough of conscious strength and forbearance.

"Well, ma'am," resumed Bounderby, "under these circumstances, I imagine it would not be agreeable to a character like yours to remain here, though you would be very welcome here?"

"Oh dear no, sir, I could on no account think of that!" Mrs Sparsit shook her head, still in her highly superior manner, and a little changed the small cough—coughing now, as if the spirit of prophecy rose within her, but had better be coughed down.

"However, ma'am," said Bounderby, "there are apartments at the Bank, where a born and bred lady, as keeper of the place, would be rather a catch than otherwise; and if the same terms—"

"I beg your pardon, sir. You were so good as to promise that you would always substitute the phrase, annual compliment."

"Well, ma'am, annual compliment. If the same annual compliment would be accept-able there, why I see nothing to part us unless you do."

"Sir," returned Mrs Sparsit. "The proposal is like yourself, and if the position I should assume at the Bank is one that I could occupy without descending lower in the social scale—"

"Why, of course it is," said Bounderby. "If it was not, ma'am, you don't suppose that I should offer it to a lady who has moved in the society you have moved in. Not that *I* care for such society, you know! But *you* do."

"Mr Bounderby, you are very considerate."

"You'll have your own private apartments, and you'll have your coals and your candles and all the rest of it, and you'll have your maid to attend upon you, and you'll have your light porter to protect you, and you'll be what I take the liberty of considering precious comfortable," said Bounderby.

"Sir," rejoined Mrs Sparsit, "say no more. In yielding up my trust here, I shall not be freed from the necessity of eating the bread of dependence:" she might have said the sweetbread, for that delicate article in a savoury brown sauce was her favourite supper: "and I would rather receive it from your hand, than from any other. Therefore, sir, I accept your offer gratefully, and with many sincere acknowledgements for past favours. And I hope sir," said Mrs Sparsit, concluding in an impressively compassionate manner, "I fondly hope that Miss Gradgrind may be all you desire, and deserve!"

Nothing moved Mrs Sparsit from that position any more. It was in vain for Bound-erby to bluster, or to assert himself in any of his explosive ways; Mrs Sparsit was resolved to have compassion on him, as a Victim. She was polite, obliging, cheerful, hopeful; but, the more polite, the more obliging, the more cheerful, the more hopeful, the more exemplary altogether, she; the forlorner Sacrifice and Victim, he. She had that tenderness for his melancholy fate, that his great red countenance used to break out into cold perspirations when she looked at him.

Meanwhile the marriage was appointed to be solemnized in eight weeks' time, and Mr Bounderby went every evening to Stone Lodge as an accepted wooer. Love was made on these occasions in the form of bracelets; and, on all occasions during the period of betrothal, took a manufacturing aspect. Dresses were made, jewellery was made, cakes and gloves were made, settlements were made, and an extensive assortment of Facts did appropriate honour to the contract. The business was all Fact, from first to last. The Hours did not go through any of those rosy performances, which foolish poets have ascribed to them at such times; neither did the clocks go any faster, or any slower, than at other seasons. The deadly-statistical recorder in the Gradgrind observatory knocked every second on the head as it was born, and buried it with his accustomed regularity.

So the day came, as all other days come to people who will only stick to reason; and when it came, there were married in the church of the florid wooden legs—that popular order of architecture—Josiah Bounderby Esquire of Coketown, to Louisa eldest daughter of Thomas Gradgrind Esquire of Stone Lodge, M.P. for that borough. And when they were united in holy matrimony, they went home to breakfast at Stone Lodge aforesaid.

There was an improving party assembled on the auspicious occasion, who knew what everything they had to eat and drink was made of, and how it was imported or exported, and in what quantities, and in what bottoms, whether native or foreign, and all about it. The bridesmaids, down to little Jane Gradgrind, were, in an intellectual point of view, fit helpmates for the calculating boy; and there was no nonsense about any of the company.

After breakfast, the bridegroom addressed them in the following terms.

"Ladies and gentlemen, I am Josiah Bounderby of Coketown. Since you have done my wife and myself the honour of drinking our healths and happiness, I suppose I must acknowledge the same; though, as you all know me, and know what I am, and what my extraction was, you won't expect a speech from a man who, when he sees a Post, says 'that's a Post,' and when he sees a Pump, says 'that's a Pump,' and is not to be got to call a Post a Pump. or a Pump a Post, or either of them a Toothpick. If you want a speech this morning, my friend and father-in-law, Tom Gradgrind, is a Member of Parliament, and you know where to get it. I am not your man. However, if I feel a little independent when I look around this table today, and reflect how little I thought of marrying Tom Gradgrind's daughter when I was a ragged street-boy, who never washed his face unless it was at a pump, and that not oftener than once a fortnight, I hope I may be excused. So, I hope you like my feeling independent; if you don't, I can't help it. I *do* feel independent. Now. I have mentioned, and you have mentioned, that I am this day married to Tom Gradgrind's daughter. I am very glad to be so. It has long been my wish to be so. I have watched her bringing-up, and I believe she is worthy of me. At the same time—not to deceive you—I believe I am worthy of her. So, I thank you, on both our parts, for the goodwill you have shown towards us; and the best wish I can give the unmarried part of the present company, is this: I hope every bachelor may find as good a wife as I have found. And I hope every spinster may find as good a husband as my wife has found."

Shortly after which oration, as they were going on a nuptial trip to Lyons, in order that Mr Bounderby might take the opportunity of seeing how the Hands got on in those parts, and whether they, too, required to be fed with gold spoons; the happy pair departed for the railroad. The bride, in passing down stairs, dressed for her journey, found Tom waiting for her—flushed, either with his feelings or the vinous part of the breakfast.

"What a game girl you are, to be such a first-rate sister, Loo!" whispered Tom.

She clung to him, as she should have clung to some far better nature that day, and was a little shaken in her reserved composure for the first time.

"Old Bounderby's quite ready," said Tom. "Time's up. Good-bye! I shall be on the look-out for you, when you come back. I say, my dear Loo! An't it uncommonly jolly now!"

BOOK THE SECOND

Reaping

Chapter I

EFFECTS IN THE BANK

A SUNNY midsummer day. There was such a thing sometimes, even in Coketown. Seen from a distance in such weather, Coketown lay shrouded in a haze of its own, which appeared impervious to the sun's rays. You only knew the town was there, because you knew there could have been no such sulky blotch upon the prospect without a town. A blur of soot and smoke, now confusedly tending this way, now that way, now aspiring to the vault of Heaven, now murkily creeping along the earth, as the wind rose and fell, or changed its quarter: a dense formless jumble, with sheets of cross light in it, that showed nothing but masses of darkness:—Coketown in the distance was suggestive of itself, though not a brick of it could be seen.

The wonder was, it was there at all. It had been ruined so often, that it was amazing how it had borne so many shocks. Surely there never was such fragile china-ware as that of which the millers of Coketown were made. Handle them never so lightly, and they fell to pieces with such ease that you might suspect them of having been flawed before. They were ruined, when they were required to send labouring children to school; they were ruined, when inspectors were appointed to look into their works; they were ruined when such inspectors considered it doubtful whether they were quite justified in chopping people up with their machinery; they were utterly undone, when it was hinted that perhaps they need not always make quite so much smoke. Besides Mr Bounderby's gold spoon which was generally received in Coketown, another prevalent fiction was very popular there. It took the form of a threat. Whenever a Coketowner felt he was ill-used—that is to say, whenever he was not left entirely alone, and it was proposed to hold him accountable for the consequences of any of his acts—he was sure to come out with the awful menace, that he would "sooner pitch his property into the Atlantic." This had terrified the Home Secretary within an inch of his life, on several occasions.

However, the Coketowners were so patriotic after all, that they never had pitched their property into the Atlantic yet, but on the contrary, had been kind enough to take mighty good care of it. So there it was, in the haze yonder; and it increased and multiplied.

The streets were hot and dusty on the summer day, and the sun was so bright that it even shone through the heavy vapour drooping over Coketown, and could not be looked at steadily. Stokers emerged from low underground doorways into factory yards, and sat on steps, and posts, and palings, wiping their swarthy visages, and contemplating coals. The whole town seemed to be frying in oil. There was a stifling smell of hot oil everywhere. The steam-engines shone with it, the dresses of the Hands were soiled with it, the mills throughout their many stories oozed and trickled it. The atmosphere of those Fairy palaces was like the breath of the simoom; and their inhabitants, wasting with heat, toiled languidly in the desert. But no temperature made the melancholy mad elephants more mad or more sane. Their wearisome heads went up and down at the same rate, in hot weather and cold, wet weather and dry, fair weather and foul. The measured motion of their shadows on the walls, was the substitute Coketown had to show for the shadows of rustling woods; while, for the summer hum of insects, it could offer, all the year round, from the dawn of Monday to the night of Saturday, the whirr of shafts and wheels.

Drowsily they whirred all through this sunny day, making the passenger more sleepy and more hot as he passed the humming walls of the mills. Sun-blinds, and sprinklings of water, a little cooled the main streets and the shops; but the mills, and the courts and alleys, baked at a fierce heat. Down upon the river that was black and thick with dye, some Coketown boys who were at large—a rare sight there—rowed a crazy boat, which made a spumous track upon the water as it jogged along, while every dip of an oar stirred up vile smells. But the sun itself, however beneficent generally, was less kind to Coketown than hard frost, and rarely looked intently into any of its closer regions without engendering more death than life. So does the eye of Heaven itself become an evil eye, when incapable or sordid hands are interposed between it and the things it looks upon to bless.

Mrs Sparsit sat in her afternoon apartment at the Bank, on the shadier side of the frying street. Office-hours were over: and at that period of the day, in warm weather, she usually embellished with her genteel presence, a managerial board-room over the public office. Her own private sitting-room was a storey higher, at the window of which post of observation she was ready, every morning, to greet Mr Bounderby as he came across the road, with the sympathizing recognition appropriate to a Victim. He had been married now, a year; and Mrs Sparsit had never released him from her determined pity a moment.

The Bank offered no violence to the wholesome monotony of the town. It was another red brick house, with black outside shutters, green inside blinds, a black street-door up two white steps, a brazen door-plate, and a brazen door-handle full stop. It was a size larger than Mr Bounderby's house, as other houses were from a size to half-a-dozen sizes smaller; in all other particulars, it was strictly according to pattern.

Mrs Sparsit was conscious that by coming in the evening-tide among the desks and writing implements, she shed a feminine, not to say also aristocratic, grace upon the office. Seated, with her needlework or netting apparatus, at the window, she had a self-laudatory sense of correcting, by her ladylike deportment, the rude business aspect of the place. With this impression of her interesting character upon her, Mrs Sparsit considered herself, in some sort, the Bank Fairy. The townspeople who, in their passing and repassing, saw her there, regarded her as the Bank Dragon, keeping watch over the treasures of the mine.

What those treasures were, Mrs Sparsit knew as little as they did. Gold and silver coin, precious paper, secrets that if divulged would bring vague destruction upon vague persons (generally, however, people whom she disliked), were the chief items in her ideal catalogue thereof. For the rest, she knew that after office-hours, she reigned supreme over all the office furniture, and over a locked-up iron room with three locks, against the door of which strong chamber the light porter laid his head every night, on a truckle bed, that disappeared at cockcrow. Further, she was lady paramount over certain vaults in the basement, sharply spiked off from communication with the preda-tory world; and over the relics of the current day's work, consisting of blots of ink, worn-out pens, fragments of wafers, and scraps of paper torn so small, that nothing interesting could ever be deciphered on them when Mrs Sparsit tried. Lastly she was guardian over a little armoury of cutlasses and carbines, arrayed in vengeful order above one of the official chimney-pieces; and over that respectable tradition never to be separated from a place of business claiming to be wealthy—a row of fire-buckets—vessels calculated to be of no physical utility on any occasion, but observed to exercise a fine moral influence, almost equal to bullion, on most beholders.

A deaf serving-woman and the light porter completed Mrs Sparsit's empire. The deaf serving-woman was rumoured to be wealthy; and a saying had for years gone about among the lower orders of Coketown, that she would be murdered some night when the Bank was shut, for the sake of her money. It was generally considered, indeed, that she had been due some time, and ought to have fallen long ago; but she had kept her life, and her situation, with an ill-conditioned tenacity that occasioned much offence and disappointment.

Mrs Sparsit's tea was just set for her on a pert little table, with its tripod of legs in an attitude, which she insinuated after office-hours, into the company of the stern, leathern-topped, long board-table that bestrode the middle of the room. The light porter placed the tea-tray on it, knuckling his forehead as a form of homage.

"Thank you, Bitzer," said Mrs Sparsit.

"Thank *you*, ma'am," returned the light porter. He was a very light porter indeed; as light as in the days when he blinkingly defined a horse, for girl number twenty.

"All is shut up, Bitzer?" said Mrs Sparsit.

"All is shut up, ma'am."

"And what," said Mrs Sparsit, pouring out her tea, "is the news of the day? Anything?"

"Well, ma'am, I can't say that I have heard anything particular. Our people are a bad lot, ma'am; but that is no news, unfortunately."

"What are the restless wretches doing now?" asked Mrs Sparsit.

"Merely going on in the old way, ma'am. Uniting, and leaguing, and engaging to stand by one another."

"It is much to be regretted," said Mrs Sparsit, making her nose more Roman and her eyebrows more Coriolanian in the strength of her severity, "that the united masters allow of any such class-combinations."

"Yes, ma'am," said Bitzer.

"Being united themselves, they ought one and all to set their faces against employing any man who is united with any other man," said Mrs Sparsit.

"They have done that, ma'am," returned Bitzer; "but it rather fell through, ma'am."

"I do not pretend to understand these things," said Mrs Sparsit, with dignity, "my lot having been originally cast in a widely different sphere; and Mr Sparsit, as a Powler, being also quite out of the pale of any such dissensions. I only know that these people must be conquered, and that it's high time it was done, once for all."

"Yes, ma'am," returned Bitzer, with a demonstration of great respect for Mrs Sparsit's oracular authority. "You couldn't put it clearer, I am sure, ma'am."

As this was his usual hour for having a little confidential chat with Mrs Sparsit, and as he had already caught her eye and seen that she was going to ask him something, he made a pretence of arranging the rulers, inkstands, and so forth, while that lady went on with her tea, glancing through the open window down into the street.

"Has it been a busy day, Bitzer?" asked Mrs Sparsit.

"Not a very busy day, my lady. About an average day." He now and then slided into my lady, instead of ma'am, as an involuntary acknowledgement of Mrs Sparsit's personal dignity and claims to reverence.

"The clerks," said Mrs Sparsit, carefully brushing an imperceptible crumb of bread and butter from her left-hand mitten, "are trustworthy, punctual, and industrious, of course?"

"Yes, ma'am, pretty fair, ma'am. With the usual exception."

He held the respectable office of general spy and informer in the establishment, for which volunteer service he received a present at Christmas, over and above his weekly wage. He had grown into an extremely clear-headed, cautious, prudent young man, who was safe to rise in the world. His mind was so exactly regulated, that he had no affections or passions. All his proceedings were the result of the nicest and coldest calculation; and it was not without cause that Mrs Sparsit habitually observed of him, that he was a young man of the steadiest principle she had ever known. Having satisfied himself, on his father's death, that his mother had a right of settlement in Coketown, this excellent young economist had asserted that right for her with such a steadfast adherence to the principle of the case, that she had been shut up in the workhouse ever since. It must be admitted that he allowed her half a pound of tea a year, which was weak in him: first, because all gifts have an inevitable tendency to pauperize the recipient, and secondly, because his only reasonable transaction in that commodity would have been to buy it for as little as he could possibly give, and sell it for as much as he could possibly get; it having been clearly ascertained by philosophers that in this is comprised the whole duty of man—not a part of man's duty, but the whole.

"Pretty fair, ma'am. With the usual exception, ma'am," repeated Bitzer.

"Ah—h!" said Mrs Sparsit, shaking her head over her tea-cup, and taking a long gulp.

"Mr Thomas, ma'am, I doubt Mr Thomas very much, ma'am, I don't like his ways at all."

"Bitzer," said Mrs Sparsit, in a very impressive manner, "do you recollect my having said anything to you respecting names?"

"I beg your pardon, ma'am. It's quite true that you did object to names being used, and they're always best avoided."

"Please to remember that I have a charge here," said Mrs Sparsit, with her air of state. "I hold a trust here, Bitzer, under Mr Bounderby. However improbable both Mr Bounderby and myself might have deemed it years ago, that he would ever become my patron, making me an annual compliment, I cannot but regard him in that light. From Mr Bounderby I have received every acknowledgement of my social station, and every recognition of my family descent, that I could possibly expect. More, far more. Therefore, to my patron I will be scrupulously true. And I do not consider, I will not consider, I cannot consider," said Mrs Sparsit, with a most extensive stock on hand of honour and morality, "that I *should* be scrupulously true, if I allowed names to be mentioned under this roof, that are unfortunately—most unfortunately—no doubt of that—connected with his."

Bitzer knuckled his forehead again, and again begged pardon.

"No, Bitzer," continued Mrs Sparsit, "say an individual, and I will hear you; say Mr Thomas, and you must excuse me."

"With the usual exception, ma'am," said Bitzer, trying back, "of an individual."

"Ah—h!" Mrs Sparsit repeated the ejaculation, the shake of the head over her tea-cup, and the long gulp, as taking up the conversation again at the point where it had been interrupted.

"An individual, ma'am," said Bitzer, "has never been what he ought to have been, since he first came into the place. He is a dissipated, extravagant idler. He is not worth his salt, ma'am. He wouldn't get it either, if he hadn't a friend and relation at court, ma'am!"

"Ah——h!" said Mrs Sparsit, with another melancholy shake of her head.

"I only hope, ma'am," pursued Bitzer, "that his friend and relation may not supply him with the means of carrying on. Otherwise, ma'am, we know out of whose pocket *that* money comes."

"Ah——h!" sighed Mrs Sparsit again, with another melancholy shake of her head.

"He is to be pitied, ma'am. The last party I have alluded to, is to be pitied, ma'am," said Bitzer.

"Yes, Bitzer," said Mrs Sparsit. "I have always pitied the delusion, always."

"As to an individual, ma'am," said Bitzer, dropping his voice and drawing nearer, "he is as improvident as any of the people in this town. And you know what *their* improvidence is, ma'am. No one could wish to know it better than a lady of your eminence does."

"They would do well," returned Mrs Sparsit, "to take example by you, Bitzer."

"Thank you, ma'am. But, since you do refer to me, now look at me, ma'am. I have put by a little, ma'am, already. That gratuity which I receive at Christmas, ma'am: I never touch it. I don't even go the length of my wages, though they're not high, ma'am. Why can't they do as I have done, ma'am? What one person can do, another can do."

This, again, was among the fictions of Coketown. Any capitalist there, who had made sixty thousand pounds out of sixpence, always professed to wonder why the sixty thousand nearest Hands didn't each make sixty thousand pounds out of sixpence, and more or less reproached them every one for not accomplishing the little feat. What I did you can do. Why don't you go and do it?

"As to their wanting recreations, ma'am," said Bitzer, "it's stuff and nonsense. *I* don't want recreations. I never did, and I never shall; I don't like 'em. As to their combining together; there are many of them, I have no doubt, that by watching and informing upon one another could earn a trifle now and then, whether in money or good will, and improve their livelihood. Then, why don't they improve it, ma'am? It's the first consideration of a rational creature, and it's what they pretend to want."

"Pretend indeed!" said Mrs Sparsit.

"I am sure we are constantly hearing ma'am, till it becomes quite nauseous, concerning their wives and families," said Bitzer. "Why, look at me, ma'am! I don't want a wife and family. Why should they?"

"Because they are improvident," said Mrs Sparsit.

"Yes, ma'am," returned Bitzer, "that's where it is. If they were more provident, and less perverse, ma'am, what would they do? They would say, 'While my hat covers my family', or, 'while my bonnet covers my family'—as the case might be, ma'am—'I have only one to feed, and that's the person I most like to feed.' "

"To be sure," assented Mrs Sparsit, eating muffin.

"Thank you, ma'am," said Bitzer, knuckling his forehead again in return for the favour of Mrs Sparsit's improving conversation. "Would you wish a little more hot water, ma'am, or is there anything else that I could fetch you?"

"Nothing just now, Bitzer."

"Thank you, ma'am. I shouldn't wish to disturb you at your meals, ma'am, particularly tea, knowing your partiality for it," said Bitzer, craning a little to look over into the street from where he stood; "but there's a gentleman been looking up here for a minute or so, ma'am, and he has come across as if he was going to knock. That *is* his knock, ma'am, no doubt."

He stepped to the window; and looking out, and drawing in his head again, confirmed himself with, "Yes, ma'am. Would you wish the gentleman to be shown in, ma'am?"

"I don't know who it can be," said Mrs Sparsit, wiping her mouth and arranging her mittens.

"A stranger, ma'am, evidently."

"What a stranger can want at the Bank at this time of the evening, unless he comes upon some business for which he is too late, I don't know," said Mrs Sparsit; "but I hold a charge in this establishment from Mr Bounderby, and I will never shrink from it. If to see him is any part of the duty I have accepted, I will see him. Use your own discretion, Bitzer."

Here, the visitor, all unconscious of Mrs Sparsit's magnanimous words, repeated his knock so loudly that the light porter hastened down to open the door; while Mrs Sparsit took the precaution of concealing her little table, with all its appliances upon it, in a cupboard, and then decamped up stairs that she might appear, if needful, with the greater dignity.

"If you please, ma'am, the gentleman would wish to see you," said Bitzer, with his light eye at Mrs Sparsit's keyhole. So, Mrs Sparsit, who had improved the interval by touching up her cap, took her classical features down stairs again, and entered the board-room in the manner of a Roman matron going outside the city walls to treat with an invading general.

The visitor having strolled to the window, and being then engaged in looking carelessly out, was as unmoved by this impressive entry as man could possibly be. He stood whistling to himself with all imaginable coolness, with his hat still on, and a certain air of exhaustion upon him, in part arising from excessive summer, and in part from excessive gentility. For, it was to be seen with half an eye that he was a thorough gentleman, made to the model of the time; weary of everything and putting no more faith in anything than Lucifer.

"I believe, sir," quoth Mrs Sparsit, "you wished to see me."

"I beg your pardon," he said, turning and removing his hat; "pray excuse me."

"Humph!" thought Mrs Sparsit, as she made a stately bend. "Five and thirty, good-looking, good figure, good teeth, good voice, good breeding, well-dressed, dark hair, bold eyes." All which Mrs Sparsit observed in her womanly way—like the Sultan who put his head in the pail of water—merely in dipping down and coming up again.

"Please to be seated, sir," said Mrs Sparsit.

"Thank you. Allow me." He placed a chair for her, but remained himself carelessly lounging against the table. "I left my servant at the railway looking after the luggage—very heavy train and vast quantity of it in the van—and strolled on, looking about me. Exceedingly odd place. Will you allow me to ask you if it's *always* as black as this?"

"In general much blacker," returned Mrs Sparsit, in her uncompromising way.

"Is it possible! Excuse me: you are not a native, I think?"

"No, sir," returned Mrs Sparsit. "It was once my good or ill fortune, as it may be—before I became a widow—to move in a very different sphere. My husband was a Powler."

"Beg your pardon, really!" said the stranger. "Was—?"

Mrs Sparsit repeated, "A Powler." "Powler Family," said the stranger, after reflecting a few moments. Mrs Sparsit signified assent. The stranger seemed a little more fatigued than before.

"You must be very much bored here?" was the inference he drew from the communication.

"I am the servant of circumstances, sir," said Mrs Sparsit, "and I have long adapted myself to the governing power of my life."

"Very philosophical," returned the stranger, "and very exemplary and laudable, and—" It seemed to be scarcely worth his while to finish the sentence, so he played with his watch-chain wearily.

"May I be permitted to ask, sir," said Mrs Sparsit, "to what I am indebted for the favour of—"

"Assuredly," said the stranger. "Much obliged to you for reminding me. I am the bearer of a letter of introduction to Mr Bounderby the banker. Walking through this extraordinarily black town, while they were getting dinner ready at the hotel, I asked a fellow whom I met; one of the working people; who appeared to have been taking a shower-bath of something fluffy, which I assume to be the raw material;—"

Mrs Sparsit inclined her head.

"—Raw material—where Mr Bounderby the banker, might reside. Upon which, misled no doubt by the word Banker, he directed me to the Bank. Fact being, I presume, that Mr Bounderby the Banker, does *not* reside in the edifice in which I have the honour of offering this explanation?"

"No, sir," returned Mrs Sparsit, "he does not."

"Thank you. I had no intention of delivering my letter at the present moment, nor have I. But, strolling on to the Bank to kill time, and having the good fortune to observe at the window," towards which he languidly waved his hand, then slightly bowed, "a lady of a very superior and agreeable appearance, I considered that I could not do better than take the liberty of asking that lady where Mr Bounderby the Banker, *does* live. Which I accordingly venture, with all suitable apologies, to do."

The inattention and indolence of his manner were sufficiently relieved, to Mrs Sparsit's thinking, by a certain gallantry at ease, which offered her homage too. Here he was, for instance, at this moment, all but sitting on the table, and yet lazily bending over her, as if he acknowledged an attraction in her that made her charming—in her way.

"Banks, I know, are always suspicious, and officially must be," said the stranger, whose lightness and smoothness of speech were pleasant likewise; suggesting matter far more sensible and humorous than it ever contained—which was perhaps a shrewd device of the founder of this numerous sect, whosoever may have been that great man; "therefore I may observe that my letter—here it is—is from the member for this place— Gradgrind—whom I have had the pleasure of knowing in London."

Mrs Sparsit recognized the hand, intimated that such confirmation was quite unnecessary, and gave Mr Bounderby's address, with all needful clues and directions in aid.

"Thousand thanks," said the stranger. "Of course you know the Banker well?"

"Yes, sir," rejoined Mrs Sparsit. "In my dependent relation towards him, I have known him ten years."

"Quite an eternity! I think he married Gradgrind's daughter?"

"Yes," said Mrs Sparsit, suddenly compressing her mouth. "He had that—honour."

"The lady is quite a philosopher, I am told?"

"Indeed, sir," said Mrs Sparsit. "*Is* she?"

"Excuse my impertinent curiosity," pursued the stranger, fluttering over Mrs Sparsit's eyebrows, with a propitiatory air, "but you know the family, and know the world. I am about to know the family, and may have much to do with them. Is the lady so very alarming? Her father gives her such a portentously hard-headed reputation, that I have a burning desire to know. Is she absolutely unapproachable? Repellently and stunningly clever? I see, by your meaning smile, you think not. You have poured balm into my anxious soul. As to age, now. Forty! Five and thirty?"

Mrs Sparsit laughed outright. "A chit," said she. "Not twenty when she was married."

"I give you my honour, Mrs Powler," returned the stranger, detaching himself from the table, "that I never was so astonished in my life!"

It really did seem to impress him, to the utmost extent of his capacity of being impressed. He looked at his informant for full a quarter of a minute, and appeared to have the surprise in his mind all the time. "I assure you, Mrs Powler," he then said, much exhausted, "that the father's manner prepared me for a grim and stony maturity. I am obliged to you, of all things, for correcting so absurd a mistake. Pray excuse my intrusion. Many thanks. Good day!"

He bowed himself out; and Mrs Sparsit, hiding in the window-curtain, saw him languishing down the street on the shady side of the way, observed of all the town.

"What do you think of the gentleman, Bitzer?" she asked the light porter, when he came to take away.

"Spends a deal of money on his dress, ma'am."

"It must be admitted," said Mrs Sparsit, "that it's very tasteful."

"Yes, ma'am," returned Bitzer, "if that's worth the money."

"Besides which, ma'am," resumed Bitzer, while he was polishing the table, "he looks to me as if he gamed."

"It's immoral to game," said Mrs Sparsit.

"It's ridiculous, ma'am," said Bitzer, "because the chances are against the players."

Whether it was that the heat prevented Mrs Sparsit from working, or whether it was that her hand was out, she did no work that night. She sat at the window, when the sun began to sink behind the smoke; she sat there, when the smoke was burning red, when the colour faded from it, when darkness seemed to rise slowly out of the ground, and creep upward, upward, up to the house-tops, up the church steeple, up to the summits of the factory chimneys, up to the sky. Without a candle in the room, Mrs Sparsit sat at the window, with her hands before her, not thinking much of the sounds of evening: the whooping of boys, the barking of dogs, the rumbling of wheels, the steps and voices of passengers, the shrill street cries, the clogs upon the pavement when it was their hour for going by, the shutting-up of shop-shutters. Not until the light porter announced that her nocturnal sweetbread was ready, did Mrs Sparsit arouse herself from her reverie, and convey her dense black eyebrows—by that time creased with meditation, as if they needed ironing out—up stairs.

"O, you Fool!" said Mrs Sparsit, when she was alone at her supper. Whom she meant, she did not say; but she could scarcely have meant the sweetbread.

Chapter II

MR JAMES HARTHOUSE

THE Gradgrind party wanted assistance in cutting the throats of the Graces. They went about recruiting; and where could they enlist recruits more hopefully, than among the fine gentlemen who, having found out everything to be worth nothing, were equally ready for anything?

Moreover, the healthy spirits who had mounted to this sublime height were attractive to many of the Gradgrind school. They liked fine gentlemen; they pretended that they did not, but they did. They became exhausted in imitation of them; and they yaw-yawed in their speech like them; and they served out, with an enervated air, the little mouldy rations of political economy, on which they regaled their disciples. There never before was seen on earth such a wonderful hybrid race as was thus produced.

Among the fine gentlemen not regularly belonging to the Gradgrind school, there was one of a good family and a better appearance, with a happy turn of humour which had told immensely with the House of Commons on the occasion of his entertaining it with his (and the Board of Directors') view of a railway accident, in which the most careful officers ever known, employed by the most liberal managers ever heard of, assisted by the finest mechanical contrivances ever devised, the whole in action on the best line ever constructed, had killed five people and wounded thirty-two, by a casualty without which the excellence of the whole system would have been positively incomplete. Among the slain was a cow, and among the scattered articles unowned, a widow's cap. And the honourable member had so tickled the House (which has a delicate sense of humour) by putting the cap on the cow, that it became impatient of any serious reference to the Coroner's Inquest, and brought the railway off with Cheers and Laughter.

Now, this gentleman had a younger brother of still better appearance than himself, who had tried life as a Cornet of Dragoons, and found it a bore; and had afterwards tried it in the train of an English minister abroad, and found it a bore; and had then strolled to Jerusalem, and got bored there; and had then gone yachting about the world, and got bored everywhere. To whom this honourable and jocular member fraternally said one day, "Jem, there's a good opening among the hard Fact fellows, and they want men. I wonder you don't go in for statistics." Jem, rather taken by the novelty of the idea, and very hard up for a change, was as ready to "go in" for statistics as for anything else. So, he went in. He coached himself up with a blue book or two; and his brother put it about among the hard Fact fellows, and said, "If you want to bring in, for any place, a handsome dog who can make you a devilish good speech, look after my brother Jem, for he's your man." After a few dashes in the public meeting way, Mr Gradgrind and a council of political sages approved of Jem, and it was resolved to send him down to Coketown, to become known there and in the neighbourhood. Hence the letter Jem had last night shown to Mrs Sparsit, which Mr Bounderby now held in his hand; super-scribed, "Josiah Bounderby, Esquire, Banker, Coketown. Specially to introduce James Harthouse, Esquire. Thomas Gradgrind."

Within an hour of the receipt of this dispatch and Mr James Harthouse's card, Mr Bounderby put on his hat and went down to the Hotel. There he found Mr James

Harthouse looking out of window, in a state of mind so disconsolate, that he was already half disposed to "go in" for something else.

"My name, sir," said his visitor, "is Josiah Bounderby of Coketown."

Mr James Harthouse was very happy indeed (though he scarcely looked so), to have a pleasure he had long expected.

"Coketown, sir," said Bounderby, obstinately taking a chair, "is not the kind of place you have been accustomed to. Therefore, if you'll allow me—or whether you will or not, for I am a plain man—I'll tell you something about it before we go any further."

Mr Harthouse would be charmed.

"Don't be too sure of that," said Bounderby. "I don't promise it. First of all, you see our smoke. That's meat and drink to us. It's the healthiest thing in the world in all respects, and particularly for the lungs. If you are one of those who want us to consume it, I differ from you. We are not going to wear the bottoms of our boilers out any faster than we wear 'em out now, for all the humbugging sentiment in Great Britain and Ireland."

By way of "going in" to the fullest extent, Mr Harthouse rejoined, "Mr Bounderby, I assure you I am entirely and completely of your way of thinking. On conviction."

"I am glad to hear it," said Bounderby. "Now, you have heard a lot of talk about the work in our mills, no doubt. You have? Very good. I'll state the fact of it to you. It's the pleasantest work there is, and it's the lightest work there is, and it's the best paid work there is. More than that, we couldn't improve the mills themselves, unless we laid down Turkey carpets on the floors. Which we're not a-going to do."

"Mr Bounderby, perfectly right."

"Lastly," said Bounderby, "as to our Hands. There's not a Hand in this town, sir, man, woman, or child, but has one ultimate object in life. That object is, to be fed on turtle soup and venison with a gold spoon. Now, they're not a-going—none of 'em— ever to be fed on turtle soup and venison with a gold spoon. And now you know the place."

Mr Harthouse professed himself in the highest degree instructed and refreshed, by this condensed epitome of the whole Coketown question.

"Why, you see," replied Mr Bounderby, "it suits my disposition to have a full understanding with a man, particularly with a public man, when I make his acquaintance. I have only one thing more to say to you, Mr Harthouse, before assuring you of the pleasure with which I shall respond to the utmost of my poor ability, to my friend Tom Gradgrind's letter of introduction. You are a man of family. Don't you deceive yourself by supposing for a moment that I am a man of family. I am a bit of dirty riff-raff, and a genuine scrap of tag, rag, and bobtail."

If anything could have exalted Jem's interest in Mr Bounderby, it would have been this very circumstance. Or, so he told him.

"So now," said Bounderby, "we may shake hands on equal terms. I say, equal terms, because although I know what I am, and the exact depth of the gutter I have lifted myself out of, better than any man does, I am as proud as you are. I am just as proud as you are. Having now asserted my independence in a proper manner, I may come to how do you find yourself, and I hope you're pretty well."

The better, Mr Harthouse gave him to understand as they shook hands, for the salubrious air of Coketown. Mr Bounderby received the answer with favour.

"Perhaps you know," said he, "or perhaps you don't know, I married Tom Gradgrind's daughter. If you have nothing better to do than to walk up town with me, I shall be glad to introduce you to Tom Gradgrind's daughter."

"Mr Bounderby," said Jem, "you anticipate my dearest wishes."

They went out without further discourse; and Mr Bounderby piloted the new acquaintance who so strongly contrasted with him, to the private red brick dwelling, with the black outside shutters, the green inside blinds, and the black street door up the two white steps. In the drawing-room of which mansion, there presently entered to them the most remarkable girl Mr James Harthouse had ever seen. She was so constrained, and yet so careless; so reserved, and yet so watchful; so cold and proud, and yet so sensitively ashamed of her husband's braggart humility—from which she shrunk as if every example of it were a cut or a blow; that it was quite a new sensation to observe her. In face she was no less remarkable than in manner. Her features were handsome; but their natural play was so locked up, that it seemed impossible to guess at their genuine expression. Utterly indifferent, perfectly self-reliant, never at a loss, and yet never at her ease, with her figure in company with them there, and her mind apparently quite alone—it was of no use "going in" yet awhile to comprehend this girl, for she baffled all penetration.

From the mistress of the house, the visitor glanced to the house itself. There was no mute sign of a woman in the room. No graceful little adornment, no fanciful little device, however trivial, anywhere expressed her influence. Cheerless and comfortless, boastfully and doggedly rich, there the room stared at its present occupants, unsoftened and unrelieved by the least trace of any womanly occupation. As Mr Bounderby stood in the midst of his household gods, so those unrelenting divinities occupied their places around Mr Bounderby, and they were worthy of one another, and well matched.

"This, sir," said Bounderby, "is my wife, Mrs Bounderby: Tom Gradgrind's eldest daughter. Loo, Mr James Harthouse. Mr Harthouse has joined your father's muster-roll. If he is not Tom Gradgrind's colleague before long, I believe we shall at least hear of him in connexion with one of our neighbouring towns. You observe, Mr Harthouse, that my wife is my junior. I don't know what she saw in me to marry me, but she saw something in me, I suppose, or she wouldn't have married me. She has lots of expensive knowledge, sir, political and otherwise. If you want to cram for anything, I should be troubled to recommend you to a better adviser than Loo Bounderby."

To a more agreeable adviser, or one from whom he would be more likely to learn, Mr Harthouse could never be recommended.

"Come!" said his host. "If you're in the complimentary line, you'll get on here, for you'll meet with no competition. I have never been in the way of learning compliments myself, and I don't profess to understand the art of paying 'em. In fact, despise 'em. But, your bringing-up was different from mine; mine was a real thing, by George! You're a gentleman, and I don't pretend to be one. I am Josiah Bounderby of Coketown, and that's enough for me. However, though *I* am not influenced by manners and station, Loo Bounderby may be. She hadn't my advantages—disadvantages you would call 'em, but I call 'em advantages—so you'll not waste your power, I dare say."

"Mr Bounderby," said Jem, turning with a smile to Louisa, "is a noble animal in a comparatively natural state, quite free from the harness in which a conventional hack like myself works."

"You respect Mr Bounderby very much," she quietly returned. "It is natural that you should."

He was disgracefully thrown out, for a gentleman who had seen so much of the world, and thought, "Now, how am I to take this?"

"You are going to devote yourself, as I gather from what Mr Bounderby has said, to the service of your country. You have made up your mind," said Louisa, still standing before him where she had first stopped—in all the singular contrariety of her self-possession, and her being obviously very ill at ease—"to show the nation the way out of all its difficulties."

"Mrs Bounderby," he returned, laughing, "upon my honour, no. I will make no such pretence to you. I have seen a little, here and there, up and down; I have found it all to be very worthless, as everybody has, and as some confess they have, and some do not; and I am going in for your respected father's opinions—really because I have no choice of opinions, and may as well back them as anything else."

"Have you none of your own?" asked Louisa.

"I have not so much as the slightest predilection left. I assure you I attach not the least importance to any opinions. The result of the varieties of boredom I have undergone, is a conviction (unless conviction is too industrious a word for the lazy sentiment I entertain on the subject), that any set of ideas will do just as much good as any other set, and just as much harm as any other set. There's an English family with a charming Italian motto. What will be, will be. It's the only truth going!"

This vicious assumption of honesty in dishonesty—a vice so dangerous, so deadly, and so common—seemed, he observed, a little to impress her in his favour. He followed up the advantage, by saying in his pleasantest manner: a manner to which she might attach as much or as little meaning as she pleased: "The side that can prove anything in a line of units, tens, hundreds, and thousands, Mrs Bounderby, seems to me to afford the most fun and to give a man the best chance. I am quite as much attached to it as if I believed it. I am quite ready to go in for it, to the same extent as if I believed it. And what more could I possibly do, if I did believe it!"

"You're a singular politician," said Louisa.

"Pardon me; I have not even that merit. We are the largest party in the state, I assure you, Mrs Bounderby, if we all fell out of our adopted ranks and were reviewed together."

Mr Bounderby, who had been in danger of bursting in silence, interposed here with a project for postponing the family dinner till half-past six, and taking Mr James Harthouse in the meantime on a round of visits to the voting and interesting notabilities of Coketown and its vicinity. The round of visits was made; and Mr James Harthouse, with a discreet use of his blue coaching, came off triumphantly, though with a considerable accession of boredom.

In the evening, he found the dinner-table laid for four, but they sat down only three. It was an appropriate occasion for Mr Bounderby to discuss the flavour of the hap'orth of stewed eels he had purchased in the streets at eight years old; and also of the inferior water, specially used for laying the dust, with which he had washed down that repast. He likewise entertained his guest, over the soup and fish, with the calculation that he (Bounderby) had eaten in his youth at least three horses under the guise of polonies and saveloys. These recitals, Jem, in a languid manner, received with "charming!" every now and then; and they probably would have decided him to "go in" for Jerusalem again tomorrow morning, had he been less curious respecting Louisa.

"Is there nothing," he thought, glancing at her as she sat at the head of the table, where her youthful figure, small and slight, but very graceful, looked as pretty as it looked misplaced; "is there nothing that will move that face?"

Yes! By Jupiter, there was something, and here it was, in an unexpected shape! Tom appeared. She changed as the door opened, and broke into a beaming smile.

A beautiful smile. Mr James Harthouse might not have thought so much of it, but that he had wondered so long at her impassive face. She put out her hand—a pretty little soft hand; and her fingers closed upon her brother's, as if she would have carried them to her lips.

"Ay, ay?" thought the visitor. "This whelp is the only creature she cares for. So, so!"

The whelp was presented, and took his chair. The appellation was not flattering, but not unmerited.

"When I was your age, young Tom," said Bounderby, "I was punctual, or I got no dinner!"

"When you were my age," returned Tom, "you hadn't a wrong balance to get right, and hadn't to dress afterwards."

"Never mind that now," said Bounderby.

"Well, then," grumbled Tom. "Don't begin with me."

"Mrs Bounderby," said Harthouse, perfectly hearing this under-strain as it went on; "your brother's face is quite familiar to me. Can I have seen him abroad? Or at some public school perhaps?"

"No," she returned, quite interested, "he has never been abroad yet, and was educated here, at home. Tom, love, I am telling Mr Harthouse that he never saw you abroad."

"No such luck, sir," said Tom.

There was little enough in him to brighten her face, for he was a sullen young fellow, and ungracious in his manner even to her. So much the greater must have been the solitude of her heart, and her need of someone on whom to bestow it. "So much the more is this whelp the only creature she has ever cared for," thought Mr James Harthouse, turning it over and over. "So much the more. So much the more."

Both in his sister's presence, and after she had left the room, the whelp took no pains to hide his contempt for Mr Bounderby, whenever he could indulge it without the observation of that independent man, by making wry faces, or shutting one eye. Without responding to these telegraphic communications, Mr Harthouse encouraged him much in the course of the evening, and showed an unusual liking for him. At last, when he rose to return to his hotel, and was a little doubtful whether he knew the way by night, the whelp immediately proffered his services as guide, and turned out with him to escort him thither.

Chapter III

THE WHELP

I T was very remarkable that a young gentleman who had been brought up under one continuous system of unnatural restraint, should be a hypocrite; but it was certainly the case with Tom. It was very strange that a young gentleman who had never been left to his own guidance for five consecutive minutes, should be incapable at last of governing himself; but so it was with Tom. It was altogether unaccountable that a young gentleman whose imagination had been strangled in his cradle, should be still inconvenienced by its ghost in the form of grovelling sensualities; but such a monster, beyond all doubt, was Tom.

"Do you smoke?" asked Mr James Harthouse, when they came to the hotel.

"I believe you!" said Tom.

He could do no less than ask Tom up; and Tom could do no less than go up. What with a cooling drink adapted to the weather, but not so weak as cool; and what with a rarer tobacco than was to be bought in those parts; Tom was soon in a highly free and easy state at his end of the sofa, and more than ever disposed to admire his new friend at the other end.

Tom blew his smoke aside, after he had been smoking a little while, and took an observation of his friend. "He don't seem to care about his dress," thought Tom, "and yet how capitally he does it. What an easy swell he is!"

Mr James Harthouse, happening to catch Tom's eye, remarked that he drank nothing, and filled his glass with his own negligent hand.

"Thank'ee," said Tom. "Thank'ee. Well, Mr Harthouse, I hope you have had about a dose of old Bounderby tonight." Tom said this with one eye shut up again, and looking over his glass knowingly, at his entertainer.

"A very good fellow indeed!" returned Mr James Harthouse.

"You think so, don't you?" said Tom. And shut up his eye again.

Mr James Harthouse smiled; and rising from his end of the sofa, and lounging with his back against the chimney-piece, so that he stood before the empty fire-grate as he smoked, in front of Tom and looking down at him, observed:

"What a comical brother-in-law you are!"

"What a comical brother-in-law old Bounderby is, I think you mean," said Tom.

"You are a piece of caustic, Tom," retorted Mr James Harthouse.

There was something so very agreeable in being so intimate with such a waistcoat; in being called Tom, in such an intimate way, by such a voice; in being on such off-hand terms so soon, with such a pair of whiskers; that Tom was uncommonly pleased with himself.

"Oh! I don't care for old Bounderby," said he, "if you mean that. I have always called old Bounderby by the same name when I have talked about him, and I have always thought of him in the same way. I am not going to begin to be polite now, about old Bounderby. It would be rather late in the day."

"Don't mind me," returned James; "but take care when his wife is by, you know."

"His wife?" said Tom. "My sister Loo? O yes!" And he laughed, and took a little more of the cooling drink.

James Harthouse continued to lounge in the same place and attitude, smoking his cigar in his own easy way, and looking pleasantly at the whelp, as if he knew himself to be a kind of agreeable demon who had only to hover over him, and he must give up his whole soul if required. It certainly did seem that the whelp yielded to this influence. He looked at his companion sneakingly, he looked at him admiringly, he looked at him boldly, and put up one leg on the sofa.

"My sister Loo?" said Tom. "*She* never cared for old Bounderby."

"That's the past tense, Tom," returned Mr James Harthouse, striking the ash from his cigar with his little finger. "We are in the present tense, now."

"Verb neuter, not to care. Indicative mood, present tense. First person singular, I do not care; second person singular, thou dost not care; third person singular, she does not care," returned Tom.

"Good! Very quaint!" said his friend. "Though you don't mean it."

"But I *do* mean it," cried Tom. "Upon my honour! Why, you won't tell me, Mr Harthouse, that you really suppose my sister Loo does care for old Bounderby."

"My dear fellow," returned the other, "what am I bound to suppose, when I find two married people living in harmony and happiness?"

Tom had by this time got both his legs on the sofa. If his second leg had not been already there when he was called a dear fellow, he would have put it up at that great stage of the conversation. Feeling it necessary to do something then, he stretched himself out at greater length, and, reclining with the back of his head on the end of the sofa, and smoking with an infinite assumption of negligence, turned his common face, and not too sober eyes, towards the face looking down upon him so carelessly yet so potently.

"You know our governor, Mr Harthouse," said Tom, "and therefore you needn't be surprised that Loo married old Bounderby. She never had a lover, and the governor proposed old Bounderby, and she took him."

"Very dutiful in your interesting sister," said Mr James Harthouse.

"Yes, but she wouldn't have been as dutiful, and it would not have come off as easily," returned the whelp, "if it hadn't been for me."

The tempter merely lifted his eyebrows; but the whelp was obliged to go on.

"*I* persuaded her," he said, with an edifying air of superiority. "I was stuck into old Bounderby's bank (where I never wanted to be), and I knew I should get into scrapes there, if she put old Bounderby's pipe out; so I told her my wishes, and she came into them. She would do anything for me. It was very game of her, wasn't it?"

"It was charming, Tom!"

"Not that it was altogether so important to her as it was to me," continued Tom coolly, "because my liberty and comfort, and perhaps my getting on, depended on it; and she had no other lover, and staying at home was like staying in jail—especially when I was gone. It wasn't as if she gave up another lover for old Bounderby; but still it was a good thing in her."

"Perfectly delightful. And she gets on so placidly."

"Oh," returned Tom, with contemptuous patronage, "she's a regular girl. A girl can get on anywhere. She has settled down to the life, and *she* don't mind. It does just as well as another. Besides, though Loo is a girl, she's not a common sort of girl. She can shut herself up within herself, and think—as I have often known her sit and watch the fire—for an hour at a stretch."

"Ay, ay? Has resources of her own," said Harthouse, smoking quietly.

"Not so much of that as you may suppose," returned Tom; "for our governor had her crammed with all sorts of dry bones and sawdust. It's his system."

"Formed his daughter on his own model?" suggested Harthouse.

"His daughter? Ah! and everybody else. Why, he formed Me that way," said Tom.

"Impossible!"

"He did though," said Tom, shaking his head. "I mean to say, Mr Harthouse, that when I first left home and went to old Bounderby's, I was as flat as a warming-pan, and knew no more about life, than any oyster does."

"Come, Tom! I can hardly believe that. A joke's a joke."

"Upon my soul!" said the whelp. "I am serious; I am indeed!" He smoked with great gravity and dignity for a little while, and then added, in a highly complacent tone, "Oh! I have picked up a little since. I don't deny that. But I have done it myself; no thanks to the governor."

"And your intelligent sister?"

"My intelligent sister is about where she was. She used to complain to me that she had nothing to fall back upon, that girls usually fall back upon; and I don't see how she is to have got over that since. But *she* don't mind," he sagaciously added, puffing at his cigar again. "Girls can always get on, somehow."

"Calling at the Bank yesterday evening, for Mr Bounderby's address, I found an ancient lady there, who seems to entertain great admiration for your sister," observed Mr James Harthouse, throwing away the last small remnant of the cigar he had now smoked out.

"Mother Sparsit?" said Tom. "What! you have seen her already, have you?"

His friend nodded. Tom took his cigar out of his mouth, to shut up his eye (which had grown rather unmanageable) with the greater expression, and to tap his nose several times with his finger.

"Mother Sparsit's feeling for Loo is more than admiration, I should think," said Tom. "Say affection and devotion. Mother Sparsit never set her cap at Bounderby when he was a bachelor. Oh no!"

These were the last words spoken by the whelp, before a giddy drowsiness came upon him, followed by complete oblivion. He was roused from the latter state by an uneasy dream of being stirred up with a boot, and also of a voice saying: "Come, it's late. Be off!"

"Well!" he said, scrambling from the sofa. "I must take my leave of you though. I say. Yours is very good tobacco. But it's too mild."

"Yes, it's too mild," returned his entertainer.

"It's—it's ridiculously mild," said Tom. "Where's the door? Good night!"

He had another odd dream of being taken by a waiter through a mist, which, after giving him some trouble and difficulty, resolved itself into the main street, in which he stood alone. He then walked home pretty easily, though not yet free from an impression of the presence and influence of his new friend—as if he were lounging somewhere in the air, in the same negligent attitude, regarding him with the same look.

The whelp went home, and went to bed. If he had had any sense of what he had done that night, and had been less of a whelp and more of a brother, he might have turned short on the road, might have gone down to the ill-smelling river that was dyed black, might have gone to bed in it for good and all, and have curtained his head for ever with its filthy waters.

Chapter IV

MEN AND BROTHERS

OH my friends, the down-trodden operatives of Coketown! Oh my friends and fellow countrymen, the slaves of an iron-handed and a grinding despotism! Oh my friends and fellow-sufferers, and fellow-workmen, and fellow-men! I tell you that the hour is come, when we must rally round one another as One united power, and crumble into dust the oppressors that too long have battened upon the plunder of our families, upon the sweat of our brows, upon the labour of our hands, upon the strength of our sinews, upon the God-created glorious rights of Humanity, and upon the holy and eternal privileges of Brotherhood!"

"Good!" "Hear, hear, hear!" "Hurrah!" and other cries arose in many voices from various parts of the densely crowded and suffocatingly close Hall, in which the orator, perched on a stage, delivered himself of this and what other froth and fume he had in him. He had declaimed himself into a violent heat, and was as hoarse as he was hot. By dint of roaring at the top of his voice under a flaring gas-light, clenching his fists, knitting his brows, setting his teeth, and pounding with his arms, he had taken so much out of himself by this time, that he was brought to a stop and called for a glass of water.

As he stood there, trying to quench his fiery face with his drink of water, the comparison between the orator and the crowd of attentive faces turned towards him, was extremely to his disadvantage. Judging him by Nature's evidence, he was above the mass in very little but the stage on which he stood. In many great respects, he was essentially below them. He was not so honest, he was not so manly, he was not so good-humoured; he substituted cunning for their simplicity, and passion for their safe solid sense. An ill-made high-shouldered man, with lowering brows, and his features crushed into an habitually sour expression, he contrasted most unfavourably, even in his mongrel dress, with the great body of his hearers in their plain working clothes. Strange as it always is to consider any assembly in the act of submissively resigning itself to the dreariness of some complacent person, lord or commoner, whom three-fourths of it could, by no human means, raise out of the slough of inanity to their own intellectual level, it was particularly strange, and it was even particularly affecting, to see this crowd of earnest faces, whose honesty in the main no competent observer free from bias could doubt, so agitated by such a leader.

Good! Hear, hear! Hurrah! The eagerness, both of attention and intention, exhibited in all the countenances, made them a most impressive sight. There was no carelessness, no languor, no idle curiosity; none of the many shades of indifference to be seen in all other assemblies, visible for one moment there. That every man felt his condition to be, somehow or other, worse than it might be; that every man considered it incumbent on him to join the rest, towards the making of it better; that every man felt his only hope to be in his allying himself to the comrades by whom he was surrounded; and that in this belief, right or wrong (unhappily wrong then), the whole of that crowd were gravely, deeply, faithfully in earnest; must have been as plain to any one who chose to see what was there, as the bare beams of the roof, and the whitened brick walls. Nor could any such spectator fail to know in his own breast, that these men, through their very delusions, showed great qualities, susceptible of being turned to the happiest and best account; and that to pretend (on the strength of sweeping axioms, howsoever cut and dried) that they went astray wholly without cause, and of their own irrational wills, was to pretend that there could be smoke without fire, death without birth, harvest without seed, anything or everything produced from nothing.

The orator having refreshed himself, wiped his corrugated forehead from left to right several times with his handkerchief folded into a pad, and concentrated all his revived forces in a sneer of great disdain and bitterness.

"But, oh my friends and brothers! Oh men and Englishmen, the down-trodden operatives of Coketown! What shall we say of that man—that working-man, that I should find it necessary so to libel the glorious name—who, being practically and well acquainted with the grievances and wrongs of you, the injured pith and marrow of this land, and having heard you, with a noble and majestic unanimity that will make Tyrants tremble, resolve for to subscribe to the funds of the United Aggregate Tribunal, and to abide by the injunctions issued by that body for your benefit, whatever they may be—what, I ask you, will you say of that working-man, since such I must acknowledge him to be, who, at such a time, deserts his post, and sells his flag; who, at such a time, turns a traitor and a craven and a recreant; who, at such a time, is not ashamed to make to you the dastardly and humiliating avowal that he will hold himself aloof and will *not* be one of those associated in the gallant stand for Freedom and for Right?"

The assembly was divided at this point. There were some groans and hisses, but the general sense of honour was much too strong for the condemnation of a man unheard. "Be sure you're right, Slackbridge!" "Put him up!" "Let's hear him!" Such things were said on many sides. Finally, one strong voice called out, "Is the man heer? If the man's heer, Slackbridge, let's hear the man himseln, 'stead o' yo." Which was received with a round of applause.

Slackbridge, the orator, looked about him with a withering smile; and, holding out his right hand at arm's length (as the manner of all Slackbridges is), to still the thundering sea, waited until there was a profound silence.

"Oh my friends and fellow-men!" said Slackbridge then, shaking his head with violent scorn, "I do not wonder that you, the prostrate sons of labour, are incredulous of the existence of such a man. But he who sold his birthright for a mess of pottage existed, and Judas Iscariot existed, and Castlereagh existed, and this man exists!"

Here, a brief press and confusion near the stage, ended in the man himself standing at the orator's side before the concourse. He was pale and a little moved in the face—his lips especially showed it; but he stood quiet, with his left hand at his chin, waiting to be heard. There was a chairman to regulate the proceedings, and this functionary now took the case into his own hands.

"My friends," said he, "by virtue o' my office as your president, I ashes o' our friend Slackbridge, who may be a little over hetter in this business, to take his seat, whiles this man Stephen Blackpool is heern. You all know this man Stephen Blackpool. You know him awlung o' his misfort'ns, and his good name."

With that, the chairman shook him frankly by the hand, and sat down again. Slackbridge likewise sat down, wiping his hot forehead—always from left to right, and never the reverse way.

"My friends," Stephen began, in the midst of a dead calm; "I ha' hed what's been spok'n o' me, and 'tis lickly that I shan't mend it. But I'd liefer you'd hearn the truth concernin myseln, fro my lips than for onny other man's, though I never cud'n speak afore so monny, wi'out bein moydert and muddled."

Slackbridge shook his head as if he would shake it off, in his bitterness.

"I'm th' one single Hand in Bounderby's mill, o' a' the men theer, as don't coom in wi' th' proposed reg'lations. I canna 'coom in wi' 'em. My friends, I doubt their doin' yo onny good. Licker they'll do yo hurt."

Slackbridge laughed, folded his arms, and frowned sarcastically.

"But 't ant sommuch for that as I stands out. If that were aw, I'd coom in wi' th' rest. But I ha' my reasons—mine, yo see—for being hindered; not on'y now, but awlus—awlus—life long!"

Slackbridge jumped up and stood beside him, gnashing and tearing. "Oh my friends, what but this did I tell you? Oh my fellow-countrymen, what warning but this did I give you? And how shows this recreant conduct in a man on whom unequal laws are known to have fallen heavy? Oh you Englishmen, I ask you how does this subornation show in one of yourselves, who is thus consenting to his own undoing and to yours, and to your children's and your children's children?"

There was some applause, and some crying of Shame upon the man; but the greater part of the audience were quiet. They looked at Stephen's worn face, rendered more pathetic by the homely emotions it evinced; and, in the kindness of their nature, they were more sorry than indignant.

" 'Tis this Delegate's trade for t' speak," said Stephen, "an he's paid for't, and he knows his work. Let him keep to't. Let him give no heed to what I ha' had'n to bear. That's not for him. That's not for nobbody but me."

There was a propriety, not to say a dignity in these words, that made the hearers yet more quiet and attentive. The same strong voice called out, "Slackbridge, let the man be heern, and howd thee tongue!" Then the place was wonderfully still.

"My brothers," said Stephen, whose low voice was distinctly heard, "and my fellow-workmen—for that yo are to me, though not, as I knows on, to this delegate heer—I ha' but a word to sen, and I could sen nommore if I was to speak till Strike o' day. I know weel, aw what's afore me. I know weel that yo are aw resolved to ha' nommore ado wi' a man who is not wi' yo in this matther. I know weel that if I was a lyin' parisht i' th' road, yo'd feel it right to pass me by, as a forrenner and stranger. What I ha' getn, I mun mak th' best on."

"Stephen Blackpool," said the chairman, rising, "think on't agen. Think on't once agen, lad, afore thour't shunned by aw owd friends."

There was an universal murmur to the same effect, though no man articulated a word. Every eye was fixed on Stephen's face. To repent of his determination, would be to take a load from all their minds. He looked around him, and knew that it was so. Not a grain of anger with them was in his heart; he knew them, far below their surface weaknesses and misconceptions, as no one but their fellow-labourer could.

"I ha' thowt on't, above a bit, sir. I simply canna coom in. I mun go th' way as lays afore me. I mun tak my leave o' aw heer."

He made a sort of reverence to them by holding up his arms, and stood for the moment in that attitude: not speaking until they slowly dropped at his sides.

"Monny's the pleasant word as soom heer has spok'n wi' me; monny's the face I see heer, as I first seen when I were yoong and lighter heart'n than now. I ha' never had no fratch afore, sin ever I were born, wi' any o' my like; Gonnows I ha' none now that's o' my makin'. Yo'll ca' me traitor and that—yo I mean t'say," addressing Slackbridge, "but 'tis easier to ca' than mak' out. So let be."

He had moved away a pace or two to come down from the platform, when he remembered something he had not said, and returned again.

"Haply," he said, turning his furrowed face slowly about that he might as it were individually address the whole audience, those both near and distant; "haply, when this question has been tak'n up and discoosed, there'll be a threat to turn out if I'm let to work among yo. I hope I shall die ere ever such a time cooms, and I shall work solitary among yo unless it cooms—truly, I mun do't, my friends; not to brave yo, but to live. I ha' nobbut work to live by; and wheerever can I go, I who ha' worked sin I were no heighth at aw, in Coketown heer? I mak' no complaints o' bein turned to the wa', o' being outcasten and overlooken fro this time forrard, but I hope I shall be let to work. If there is any right for me at aw, my friends, I think 'tis that."

Not a word was spoken. Not a sound was audible in the building, but the slight rustle of men moving a little apart, all along the centre of the room, to open a means of passing out, to the man with whom they had all bound themselves to renounce companionship. Looking at no one, and going his way with a lowly steadiness upon him that asserted nothing and sought nothing, Old Stephen, with all his troubles on his head, left the scene.

Then Slackbridge, who had kept his oratorical arm extended during the going out, as if he were repressing with infinite solicitude and by a wonderful moral power the vehement passions of the multitude, applied himself to raising their spirits. Had not the Roman Brutus, oh my British countrymen, condemned his son to death; and had not the Spartan mothers, oh my soon to be victorious friends, driven their flying children on the points of their enemies' swords? Then was it not the sacred duty of the men of Coketown, with forefathers before them, an admiring world in company with them, and a posterity to come after them, to hurl out traitors from the tents they had pitched in a sacred and a Godlike cause? The winds of Heaven answered Yes; and bore Yes, east, west, north, and south. And consequently three cheers for the United Aggregate Tribunal!

Slackbridge acted as fugleman, and gave the time. The multitude of doubtful faces (a little conscience-stricken) brightened at the sound, and took it up. Private feeling must yield to the common cause. Hurrah! The roof yet vibrated with the cheering, when the assembly dispersed.

Thus easily did Stephen Blackpool fall into the loneliest of lives, the life of solitude among a familiar crowd. The stranger in the land who looks into ten thousand faces for some answering look and never finds it, is in cheering society as compared with him who passes ten averted faces daily, that were once the countenances of friends. Such experience was to be Stephen's now, in every waking moment of his life; at his work, on his way to it and from it, at his door, at his window, everywhere. By general consent, they even avoided that side of the street on which he habitually walked; and left it, of all the working men, to him only.

He had been for many years, a quiet silent man, associating but little with other men, and used to companionship with his own thoughts. He had never known before, the strength of the want in his heart for the frequent recognition of a nod, a look, a word; or the immense amount of relief that had been poured into it by drops, through such small means. It was even harder than he could have believed possible, to separate in his own conscience his abandonment by all his fellows, from a baseless sense of shame and disgrace.

The first four days of his endurance were days so long and heavy, that he began to be appalled by the prospect before him. Not only did he see no Rachael all the time, but he avoided every chance of seeing her; for, although he knew that the prohibition did not yet formally extend to the women working in the factories, he found that some of them with whom he was acquainted were changed to him, and he feared to try others, and dreaded that Rachael might be even singled out from the rest if she were seen in his company. So, he had been quite alone during the four days, and had spoken to no one, when, as he was leaving his work at night, a young man of a very light complexion accosted him in the street.

"Your name's Blackpool, an't it?" said the young man.

Stephen coloured to find himself with his hat in his hand, in his gratitude for being spoken to, or in the suddenness of it, or both. He made a feint of adjusting the lining, and said, "Yes."

"You are the Hand they have sent to Coventry, I mean?" said Bitzer, the very light young man in question.

Stephen answered "Yes," again.

"I supposed so, from their all appearing to keep away from you. Mr Bounderby wants to speak to you. You know his house, don't you?"

Stephen said "Yes," again.

"Then go straight up there, will you?" said Bitzer. "You're expected, and have only to tell the servant it's you. I belong to the Bank; so, if you go straight up without me (I was sent to fetch you), you'll save me a walk."

Stephen, whose way had been in the contrary direction, turned about, and betook himself as in duty bound, to the red brick castle of the giant Bounderby.

Chapter V

MEN AND MASTERS

W ELL Stephen," said Bounderby, in his windy manner, "what's this I hear? What have these pests of the earth been doing to *you?* Come in, and speak up."

It was into the drawing-room that he was thus bidden. A tea-table was set out; and Mr Bounderby's young wife, and her brother, and a great gentleman from London, were present. To whom Stephen made his obeisance, closing the door and standing near it, with his hat in his hand.

"This is the man I was telling you about, Harthouse," said Mr Bounderby. The gentleman he addressed, who was talking to Mrs Bounderby on the sofa, got up, saying in an indolent way, "Oh really?" and dawdled to the hearthrug where Mr Bounderby stood.

"Now," said Bounderby, "speak up!"

After the four days he had passed, this address fell rudely and discordantly on Stephen's ear. Besides being a rough handling of his wounded mind, it seemed to assume that he really was the self-interested deserter he had been called.

"What were it, sir," said Stephen, "as yo were pleased to want wi' me?"

"Why, I have told you," returned Bounderby. "Speak up like a man, since you are a man, and tell us about yourself and this Combination."

"Wi' yor pardon, sir," said Stephen Blackpool, "I ha' nowt to sen about it."

Mr Bounderby, who was always more or less like a Wind, finding something in his way here, began to blow at it directly.

"Now, look here, Harthouse," said he, "here's a specimen of 'em. When this man was here once before, I warned this man against the mischievous strangers who are always about—and who ought to be hanged wherever they are found—and I told this man that he was going in the wrong direction. Now, would you believe it, although they have put this mark upon him, he is such a slave to them still, that he's afraid to open his lips about them?"

"I sed as I had nowt to sen, sir; not as I was fearfo' o' openin' my lips."

"You said. Ah! *I* know what you said; more than that, I know what you mean, you see. Not always the same thing, by the Lord Harry! Quite different things. You had better tell us at once, that that fellow Slackbridge is not in the town, stirring up the people to mutiny; and that he is not a regular qualified leader of the people: that is, a most confounded scoundrel. You had better tell us so at once; you can't deceive me. You want to tell us so. Why don't you?"

"I'm as sooary as yo, sir, when the people's leaders is bad," said Stephen, shaking his head. "They taks such as offers. Haply 'tis na' the sma'est o' their misfortuns when they can get no better."

The wind began to be boisterous.

"Now, you'll think this pretty well, Harthouse," said Mr Bounderby. "You'll think this tolerably strong. You'll say, upon my soul this is a tidy specimen of what my friends have to deal with; but this is nothing, sir! You shall hear me ask this man a question. Pray, Mr Blackpool"—wind springing up very fast—"may I take the liberty of asking you how it happens that you refused to be in this Combination?"

"How 't happens?"

"Ah!" said Mr Bounderby, with his thumbs in the arms of his coat, and jerking his head and shutting his eyes in confidence with the opposite wall: "how it happens."

"I'd leefer not coom to't, sir; but sin you put th' question—an not want'n t'be ill-manner'n—I'll answer. I ha passed a promess."

"Not to me, you know," said Bounderby. (Gusty weather with deceitful calms. One now prevailing.)

"O no, sir. Not to yo."

"As for me, any consideration for me has had just nothing at all to do with it," said Bounderby, still in confidence with the wall. "If only Josiah Bounderby of Coketown had been in question, you would have joined and made no bones about it?"

"Why yes, sir. 'Tis true."

"Though he knows," said Mr Bounderby, now blowing a gale, "that these are a set of rascals and rebels whom transportation is too good for! Now, Mr Harthouse, you have been knocking about in the world some time. Did you ever meet with anything like that man out of this blessed country?" And Mr Bounderby pointed him out for inspection, with an angry finger.

"Nay, ma'am," said Stephen Blackpool, staunchly protesting against the words that had been used, and instinctively addressing himself to Louisa, after glancing at her face. "Not rebels, nor yet rascals. Nowt o' th' kind, ma'am, nowt o th' kind. They've not doon me a kindness, ma'am, as I know and feel. But there's not a dozen men amoong 'em, ma'am—a dozen? Not six—but what believes as he has doon his duty by the rest and by himseln. God forbid as I, that ha' known an hadn' experience o' these men aw my life—I, that ha' ett'n an droonken wi' em, an seet'n wi' em, and toil'n wi' em, and lov'n 'em, should fail fur to stan by 'em wi' the truth, let 'em ha doon to me what they may!"

He spoke with the rugged earnestness of his place and character—deepened perhaps by a proud consciousness that he was faithful to his class under all their mistrust; but he fully remembered where he was, and did not even raise his voice.

"No, ma'am, no. They're true to one another, faithfo' to one another, 'fectionate to one another, e'en to death. Be poor amoong 'em, be sick amoong 'em, grieve amoong 'em for onny o' th' monny causes that carries grief to the poor man's door, an they'll be tender wi' yo, gentle wi' yo, comfortable wi' yo, Chrisen wi' yo. Be sure o' that, ma'am. They'd be riven to bits, ere ever they'd be different."

"In short," said Mr Bounderby, "it's because they are so full of virtues that they have turned you adrift. Go through with it while you are about it. Out with it."

"How 'tis, ma'am," resumed Stephen, appearing still to find his natural refuge in

Louisa's face, "that what is best in us fok, seems to turn us most to trouble an misfort'n an mistake, I dunno. But 'tis so. I know 'tis, as I know the heavens is over me ahint the smoke. We're patient too, an wants in general to do right. An' I canna think the fawt is aw wi' us."

"Now, my friend," said Mr Bounderby, whom he could not have exasperated more, quite unconscious of it though he was, than by seeming to appeal to anyone else, "if you will favour me with your attention for half a minute, I should like to have a word or two with you. You said just now, that you had nothing to tell us about this business. You are quite sure of that, before we go any further?"

"Sir, I am sure on't."

"Here's a gentleman from London present," Mr Bounderby made a back-handed point at Mr James Harthouse with his thumb, "a Parliament gentleman. I should like him to hear a short bit of dialogue between you and me, instead of taking the substance of it—for I know precious well, beforehand, what it will be; nobody knows better than I do, take notice!—instead of receiving it on trust, from my mouth."

Stephen bent his head to the gentleman from London, and showed a rather more troubled mind than usual. He turned his eyes involuntarily to his former refuge, but at a look from that quarter (expressive though instantaneous) he settled them on Mr Bounderby's face.

"Now, what do you complain of?" asked Mr Bounderby.

"I ha' not coom here, sir," Stephen reminded him, "to complain. I coom for that I were sent for."

"What," repeated Mr Bounderby, folding his arms, "do you people, in a general way, complain of?"

Stephen looked at him with some little irresolution for a moment, and then seemed to make up his mind.

"Sir, I were never good at showin o't, though I ha' had'n my share in feeling o't. 'Deed we are in a muddle, sir. Look round town—so rich as 'tis—and see the numbers o' people as has been broughten into bein heer, fur to weave, an to card, an to piece out a livin', aw the same one way, somehows, twixt their cradles and their graves. Look how we live, an wheer we live, an in what numbers, an by what chances, an wi' what sameness; and look how the mills is awlus a goin, and how they never works us no nigher to ony dis'ant object—ceptin awlus, Death. Look how you considers of us, an writes of us, an talks of us, and goes up wi' yor deputations to Secretaries o' State 'bout us, and how yo are awlus right, and how we are awlus wrong, and never had'n no reason in us sin ever we were born. Look how this ha' growen and growen, sir, bigger an bigger, broader an broader, harder an harder, fro year to year, fro generation unto generation. Who can look on't, sir, and fairly tell a man 'tis not a muddle?"

"Of course," said Mr Bounderby. "Now perhaps you'll let the gentleman know, how you would set this muddle (as you're so fond of calling it) to rights."

"I donno, sir. I canna be expecten to't. 'Tis not me as should be looken to for that, sir. 'Tis them as is put ower me, and ower aw the rest of us. What do they tak upon themseln, sir, if not to do't?"

"I'll tell you something towards it, at any rate," returned Mr Bounderby. "We will make an example of half a dozen Slackbridges. We'll indict the blackguards for felony, and get 'em shipped off to penal settlements."

Stephen gravely shook his head.

"Don't tell me we won't, man," said Mr Bounderby, by this time blowing a hurri-cane, "because we will, I tell you!"

"Sir," returned Stephen, with the quiet confidence of absolute certainty, "if yo was t' tak a hundred Slackbridges—aw as there is, and aw the number ten times towd—an was t' sew 'em up in separate sacks, an sink 'em in the deepest ocean as were made ere ever dry land coom to be, yo'd leave the muddle just wheer 'tis. Mischeevous strangers!" said Stephen, with an anxious smile; "when ha' we not heern, I am sure, sin ever we can call to mind, o' th' mischeevous strangers! 'Tis not by *them* the trouble's made, sir. 'Tis not wi' *them* 't commences. I ha' no favour for 'em—I ha' no reason to favour 'em—but 'tis hopeless an useless to dream o' takin' them fro their trade, 'stead o' takin their trade fro them! Aw that's now about me in this room were heer afore I coom, an will be heer when I am gone. Put that clock aboard a ship an pack it off to Norfolk Island, an the time will go on just the same. So 'tis wi' Slackbridge every bit."

Reverting for a moment to his former refuge, he observed a cautionary movement of her eyes towards the door. Stepping back, he put his hand upon the lock. But, he had not spoken out of his own will and desire; and he felt it in his heart a noble return for his late injurious treatment, to be faithful to the last to those who had repudiated him. He stayed to finish what was in his mind.

"Sir, I canna, wi' my little learning an my common way, tell the genelman what will better aw this—though some working men o' this town could, above my powers—but I can tell him what I know will never do't. The strong hand will never do't. Victory and triumph will never do't. Agreeing fur to mak one side unnat'rally awlus and for ever right, and toother side unnat'rally awlus and for ever wrong, will never, never do't. Nor yet lettin alone will never do't. Let thousands upon thousands alone, aw leadin the like lives and aw faw'en into the like muddle, and they will be as one, and yo will be as anoother, wi' a black unpassable world betwixt yo, just as long or short a time as sitch-like misery can last. Not drawin' nigh to fok, wi' kindness and patience an cheery ways, that so draws nigh to one another in their monny troubles, and so cherishes one another in their distresses wi' what they need themseln—like, I humbly believe, as no people the genelman ha' seen in aw his travels can beat—will never do't till th' Sun turns t' ice. Most o' aw, ratin 'em as so much Power, and reg'latin 'em as if they was figures in a soom, or machines: wi'out loves and likeins, wi'out memories and inclinations, wi'out souls to weary and souls to hope—when aw goes quiet, draggin on wi' 'em as if they'd nowt o' th' kind, an when aw goes onquiet, reproachin 'e, for their want o' sitch humanly feelins in their dealins wi' yo—this will never do't, sir, till God's work is onmade."

Stephen stood with the open door in his hand, waiting to know if anything more were expected of him.

"Just stop a moment," said Mr Bounderby, excessively red in the face. "I told you, the last time you were here with a grievance, that you had better turn about and come out of that. And I also told you, if you remember, that I was up to the gold spoon look-out."

"I were not up to't myseln, sir; I do assure yo."

"Now, it's clear to me," said Mr Bounderby, "that you are one of those chaps who have always got a grievance. And you go about, sowing it and raising crops. That's the business of *your* life, my friend."

Stephen shook his head, mutely protesting that indeed he had other business to do for his life.

"You are such a waspish, raspish, ill-conditioned chap, you see," said Mr Bounderby, "that even your own Union, the men who know you best, will have nothing to do with you. I never thought those fellows could be right in anything; but I tell you what! I so far go along with them for a novelty, that *I'll* have nothing to do with you either."

Stephen raised his eyes quickly to his face.

"You can finish off what you're at," said Mr Bounderby, with a meaning nod, "and then go elsewhere."

"Sir, yo know weel," said Stephen expressively, "that if I canna get work wi' yo, I canna get it elsewheer."

The reply was, "What I know, I know; and what you know, you know. I have no more to say about it."

Stephen glanced at Louisa again, but her eyes were raised to his no more; therefore, with a sigh, and saying, barely above his breath, "Heaven help us aw in this world!" he departed.

Chapter VI

FADING AWAY

IT was falling dark when Stephen came out of Mr Bounderby's house. The shadows of night had gathered so fast, that he did not look about him when he closed the door, but plodded straight along the street. Nothing was further from his thoughts than the curious old woman he had encountered on his previous visit to the same house, when he heard a step behind him that he knew, and, turning, saw her in Rachael's company.

He saw Rachael first, as he had heard her only.

"Ah Rachael, my dear! Missus, thou wi' her!"

"Well, and now you are surprised to be sure, and with reason I must say," the old woman returned. "Here I am again, you see."

"But how wi' Rachael?" said Stephen, falling into their step, walking between them, and looking from the one to the other.

"Why, I come to be with this good lass pretty much as I came to be with you," said the old woman cheerfully, taking the reply upon herself. "My visiting time is later this year than usual, for I have been rather troubled with shortness of breath, and so put it off till the weather was fine and warm. For the same reason I don't make all my journey in one day, but divide it into two days, and get a bed tonight at the Travellers' Coffee House down by the railroad (a nice clean house), and go back Parliamentary, at six in the morning. Well, but what has this to do with this good lass, says you? I'm going to tell you. I have heard of Mr Bounderby being married. I read it in the paper, where it looked grand—oh, it looked fine!" the old woman dwelt on it with strange enthusiasm; "and I want to see his wife. I have never seen her yet. Now, if you'll believe me, she hasn't come out of that house since noon today. So, not to give her up too easily, I was waiting about, a little last bit more, when I passed close to this good lass two or three times; and her face being so friendly I spoke to her, and she spoke to me. There!" said the old woman to Stephen, "you can make all the rest out for yourself now, a deal shorter than I can, I dare say!"

Once again, Stephen had to conquer an instinctive propensity to dislike this old woman, though her manner was as honest and simple as a manner possibly could be. With a gentleness that was as natural to him as he knew it to be to Rachael, he pursued the subject that interested her in her old age.

"Well, missus," said he, "I ha' seen the lady, and she were yoong and hansom. Wi' fine dark thinkin' eyes, and a still way, Rachael, as I ha' never seen the like on."

"Young and handsome. Yes!" cried the old woman, quite delighted. "As bonny as a rose! And what a happy wife!"

"Aye, missus, I suppose she be," said Stephen. But with a doubtful glance at Rachael.

"Suppose she be? She must be. She's your master's wife," returned the old woman.

Stephen nodded assent. "Though as to master," said he, glancing again at Rachael, "not master onny more. That's aw enden twixt him and me."

"Have you left his work, Stephen?" asked Rachael, anxiously and quickly.

"Why Rachael," he replied, "whether I ha' lef'n his work, or whether his work ha' left'n me, cooms t' th' same. His work and me are parted. 'Tis as weel so—better, I were thinkin when yo coom up wi' me. It would ha' brought'n trouble upon trouble if I had stayed theer. Haply 'tis a kindness to monny that I go; haply 'tis a kindness to myseln; anyways it mun be done. I mun turn my face fro Coketown fur th' time, and seek a fort'n, dear, by beginnin fresh."

"Where will you go, Stephen?"

"I donno t'night," said he, lifting off his hat, and smoothing his thin hair with the flat of his hand. "But I'm not goin' t'night, Rachael; nor yet t'morrow. Tan't easy over-much, t'know wheer t' turn, but a good heart will coom to me."

Herein, too, the sense of even thinking unselfishly aided him. Before he had so much as closed Mr Bounderby's door, he had reflected that at least his being obliged to go away was good for her, as it would save her from the chance of being brought into question for not withdrawing from him. Though it would cost him a hard pang to leave her, and though he could think of no similar place in which his condemnation would not pursue him, perhaps it was almost a relief to be forced away from the endurance of the last four days even to unknown difficulties and distresses.

So he said, with truth, "I'm more leetsome, Rachael, under't, than I couldn ha' believed." It was not her part to make his burden heavier. She answered with her comforting smile, and the three walked on together.

Age, especially when it strives to be self-reliant and cheerful, finds much considera-tion among the poor. The old woman was so decent and contented, and made so light of her infirmities, though they had increased upon her since her former interview with Stephen, that they both took an interest in her. She was too sprightly to allow of their walking at a slow pace on her account, but she was very grateful to be talked to, and very willing to talk to any extent: so, when they came to their part of the town, she was more brisk and vivacious than ever.

"Coom to my poor place, missus," said Stephen, "and tak a coop o' tea. Rachael will coom then; and arterwards I'll see thee safe t' thy Travellers' lodgin. 'T may be long, Rachael, ere ever I ha' th' chance o' thy coompany agen."

They complied, and the three went on to the house where he lodged. When they turned into a narrow street, Stephen glanced at his window with a dread that always haunted his desolate home; but it was open, as he had left it, and no one was there. The evil spirit of his life had flitted away again, months ago, and he had heard no more of her since. The only evidences of her last return now, were the scantier moveables in his room, and the greyer hair upon his head.

He lighted a candle, set out his little tea-board, got hot water from below, and brought in small portions of tea and sugar, a loaf, and some butter, from the nearest shop. The bread was new and crusty, the butter fresh, and the sugar lump, of course—in fulfilment of the standard testimony of the Coketown magnates, that these people lived like princes, sir. Rachael made the tea (so large a party necessitated the borrowing of a cup), and the visitor enjoyed it mightily. It was the first glimpse of sociality the host had had for many days. He too, with the world a wide heath before him, enjoyed the meal—again in corroboration of the magnates, as exemplifying the utter want of calculation on the part of these people, sir.

"I ha never thowt yet, missus," said Stephen, "o' askin thy name."

The old lady announced herself as "Mrs Pegler."

"A widder, I think?" said Stephen.

"Oh, many long years!" Mrs Pegler's husband (one of the best on record) was already dead, by Mrs Pegler's calculation, when Stephen was born.

" 'Twere a bad job too, to lose so good a one," said Stephen. "Onny children?"

Mrs Pegler's cup, rattling against her saucer as she held it, denoted some nervousness on her part. "No," she said. "Not now, not now."

"Dead, Stephen," Rachael softly hinted.

"I'm sooary I ha spok'n on't," said Stephen, "I ought t' hadn in my mind as I might touch a sore place. I—I blame myseln."

While he excused himself, the old lady's cup rattled more and more. "I had a son," she said, curiously distressed, and not by any of the usual appearances of sorrow; "and he did well, wonderfully well. But he is not to be spoken of if you please. He is—" Putting down her cup, she moved her hands as if she would have added, by her action, "dead!" Then she said, aloud, "I have lost him."

Stephen had not yet got the better of his having given the old lady pain, when his landlady came stumbling up the narrow stairs, and calling him to the door, whispered in his ear. Mrs Pegler was by no means deaf, for she caught a word as it was uttered.

"Bounderby!" she cried, in a suppressed voice, starting up from the table. "Oh hide me! Don't let me be seen for the world. Don't let him come up till I've got away. Pray, pray!" She trembled, and was excessively agitated; getting behind Rachael, when Rachael tried to reassure her; and not seeming to know what she was about.

"But hearken, missus, hearken;" said Stephen, astonished, " 'Tisn't Mr Bounderby; 'tis his wife. Yor not fearfo' o' her. Yo was hey-go-mad about her, but an hour sin."

"But are you sure it's the lady, and not the gentleman?" she asked still trembling. "Certain sure!"

"Well then, pray, don't speak to me, nor yet take any notice of me," said the old woman. "Let me be quite to myself in this corner."

Stephen nodded; looking to Rachael for an explanation, which she was quite unable to give him; took the candle, went downstairs, and in a few moments returned, lighting Louisa into the room. She was followed by the whelp.

Rachael had risen, and stood apart with her shawl and bonnet in her hand, when Stephen, himself profoundly astonished by this visit, put the candle on the table. Then he too stood, with his doubled hand upon the table near it, waiting to be addressed.

For the first time in her life, Louisa had come into one of the dwellings of the Coketown Hands; for the first time in her life, she was face to face with anything like individuality in connexion with them. She knew of their existence by hundreds and by thousands. She knew what results in work a given number of them would produce, in a given space of time. She knew them in crowds passing to and from their nests, like ants or beetles. But she knew from her reading infinitely more of the ways of toiling insects than of these toiling men and women.

Something to be worked so much and paid so much, and there ended; something to be infallibly settled by laws of supply and demand; something that blundered against those laws, and floundered into difficulty; something that was a little pinched when wheat was dear, and over-ate itself when wheat was cheap; something that increased at such a rate of percentage, and yielded such another percentage of crime, and such another percentage of pauperism; something wholesale, of which vast fortunes were made; something that occasionally rose like a sea, and did some harm and waste (chiefly to itself), and fell again; this she knew the Coketown Hands to be. But, she had scarcely thought more of separating them into units, than of separating the sea itself into its component drops.

She stood for some moments looking round the room. From the few chairs, the few books, the common prints, and the bed, she glanced to the two women, and to Stephen.

"I have come to speak to you, in consequence of what passed just now. I should like to be serviceable to you, if you will let me. Is this your wife?"

Rachael raised her eyes, and they sufficiently answered no, and dropped again.

"I remember," said Louisa, reddening at her mistake; "I recollect, now, to have heard your domestic misfortunes spoken of, though I was not attending to the particulars at the time. It was not my meaning to ask a question that would give pain to any one here. If I should ask any other question that may happen to have that result, give me credit, if you please, for being in ignorance how to speak to you as I ought."

As Stephen had but a little while ago instinctively addressed himself to her, so she now instinctively addressed herself to Rachael. Her manner was short and abrupt, yet faltering and timid.

"He has told you what has passed between himself and my husband? You would be his first resource, I think."

"I have heard the end of it, young lady," said Rachael.

"Did I understand, that, being rejected by one employer, he would probably be rejected by all? I thought he said as much?"

"The chances are very small, young lady—next to nothing—for a man who gets a bad name among them."

"What shall I understand that you mean by a bad name?"

"The name of being troublesome."

"Then, by the prejudices of his own class, and by the prejudices of the other, he is sacrificed alike? Are the two so deeply separated in this town, that there is no place whatever, for an honest workman between them?"

Rachael shook her head in silence.

"He fell into suspicion," said Louisa, "with his fellow-weavers, because he had made a promise not to be one of them. I think it must have been to you that he made that promise. Might I ask you why he made it?"

Rachael burst into tears. "I didn't seek it of him, poor lad. I prayed him to avoid trouble for his own good, little thinking he'd come to it through me. But I know he'd die a hundred deaths, ere ever he'd break his word. I know that of him well."

Stephen had remained quietly attentive, in his usual thoughtful attitude, with his hand at his chin. He now spoke in a voice rather less steady than usual.

"No one, excepting myseln, can ever know what honour, an what love, an respect, I bear to Rachael, or wi' what cause. When I passed that promess, I towd her true, she were th' Angel o' my life. 'Twere a solemn promess. 'Tis gone fro me, for ever."

Louisa turned her head to him, and bent it with a deference that was new in her. She looked from him to Rachael, and her features softened. "What will you do?" she asked him. And her voice had softened too.

"Weel, ma'am," said Stephen, making the best of it, with a smile; "when I ha' finished off, I mun quit this part, an try another. Fortnet or misfortnet, a man can but try; there's nowt to be done wi'out tryin'—cept laying down an dying."

"How will you travel?"

"Afoot, my kind ledy, afoot."

Louisa coloured, and a purse appeared in her hand. The rustling of a bank-note was audible, as she unfolded one and laid it on the table.

"Rachael, will you tell him—for you know how, without offence—that this is freely his, to help him on his way? Will you entreat him to take it?"

"I canna do that, young lady," she answered, turning her head aside; "Bless you for thinking o' the poor lad wi' such tenderness. But 'tis for him to know his heart, and what is right according to it."

Louisa looked, in part incredulous, in part frightened, in part overcome with quick sympathy, when this man of so much self-command, who had been so plain and steady through the late interview, lost his composure in a moment, and now stood with his hand before his face. She stretched out hers, as if she would have touched him; then checked herself, and remained still.

"Not e'en Rachael," said Stephen, when he stood again with his face uncovered, "could mak sitch a kind offerin, by onny words, kinder. T' show that I'm not a man wi'out reason and gratitude, I'll tak two pound. I'll borrow't for t' pay't back. 'Twill be the sweetest work as ever I ha' done, that puts it in my power t'acknowledge once more my lastin thankfulness for this present action."

She was fain to take up the note again, and to substitute the much smaller sum he had named. He was neither courtly, nor handsome, nor picturesque, in any respect; and yet his manner of accepting it, and of expressing his thanks without more words, had a grace in it that Lord Chesterfield could not have taught his son in a century.

Tom had sat upon the bed, swinging one leg and sucking his walking-stick with sufficient unconcern, until the visit had attained this stage. Seeing his sister ready to depart, he got up, rather hurriedly, and put in a word.

"Just wait a moment, Loo! Before we go, I should like to speak to him a moment. Something comes into my head. If you'll step out on the stairs, Blackpool, I'll mention it. Never mind a light, man!" Tom was remarkably impatient of his moving towards the cupboard, to get one. "It don't want a light."

Stephen followed him out, and Tom closed the room door, and held the lock in his hand.

"I say!" he whispered. "I think I can do you a good turn. Don't ask me what it is, because it may not come to anything. But there's no harm in my trying."

His breath fell like a flame of fire on Stephen's ear, it was so hot.

"That was our light porter at the Bank," said Tom, "who brought you the message tonight. I call him our light porter, because I belong to the Bank too."

Stephen thought "What a hurry he is in!" He spoke so confusedly.

"Well!" said Tom. "Now look here! When are you off?"

"T'day's Monday," replied Stephen, considering. "Why, sir, Friday or Saturday, nigh 'bout."

"Friday or Saturday," said Tom. "Now look here! I am not sure that I can do you the good turn I want to do you—that's my sister, you know, in your room—but I may be able to, and if I should not be able to, there's no harm done. So I tell you what. You'll know our light porter again?"

"Yes sure," said Stephen.

"Very well," returned Tom. "When you leave work of a night, between this and your going away, just hang about the Bank an hour or so, will you? Don't take on, as if you meant anything, if he should see you hanging about there; because I shan't put him up to speak to you, unless I find I can do you the service I want to do you. In that case he'll have a note or a message for you, but not else. Now look here! You are sure you understand."

He had wormed a finger, in the darkness, through a buttonhole of Stephen's coat, and was screwing that corner of the garment tight up, round and round, in an extraordinary manner.

"I understand, sir," said Stephen.

"Now look here!" repeated Tom. "Be sure you don't make any mistake then, and don't forget. I shall tell my sister as we go home, what I have in view, and she'll approve, I know. Now look here! You're all right, are you? You understand all about it? Very well then. Come along, Loo!"

He pushed the door open as he called to her, but did not return into the room, or wait to be lighted down the narrow stairs. He was at the bottom when she began to descend, and was in the street before she could take his arm.

Mrs Pegler remained in her corner until the brother and sister were gone, and until Stephen came back with the candle in his hand. She was in a state of inexpressible admiration of Mrs Bounderby, and, like an unaccountable old woman, wept, "because she was such a pretty dear." Yet Mrs Pegler was so flurried lest the object of her admiration should return by chance, or anybody else should come, that her cheerfulness was ended for that night. It was late too, to people who rose early and worked hard; therefore the party broke up; and Stephen and Rachael escorted their mysterious acquaintance to the door of the Travellers' Coffee House, where they parted from her.

They walked back together to the corner of the street where Rachael lived, and as they drew nearer and nearer to it, silence crept upon them. When they came to the dark corner where their unfrequent meetings always ended, they stopped, still silent, as if both were afraid to speak.

"I shall strive t' see thee agen, Rachael, afore I go, but if not——"

"Thou wilt not, Stephen, I know. 'Tis better that we make up our minds to be open wi' one another."

"Thou'rt awlus right. 'Tis bolder and better. I ha' been thinkin then, Rachael, that as 'tis but a day or two that remains, 'twere better for thee, my dear, not t' be seen wi' me. 'T might bring thee into trouble, fur no good."

"'Tis not for that, Stephen, that I mind. But thou know'st our old agreement. 'Tis for that."

"Well, well," said he. "'Tis better, onnyways."

"Thou'lt write to me, and tell me all that happens, Stephen?"

"Yes. What can I say now, but Heaven be wi' thee, Heaven bless thee, Heaven thank thee and reward thee?"

"May it bless thee, Stephen, too, in all thy wanderings, and send thee peace and rest at last!"

"I towd thee, my dear," said Stephen Blackpool—"that night—that I would never see or think o' onnything that angered me, but thou, so much better than me, should'st

be beside it. Thou'rt beside it now. Thou mak'st me see it wi' a better eye. Bless thee.
Good night. Good-bye!"

It was but a hurried parting in the common street, yet it was a sacred remembrance
to these two common people. Utilitarian economists, skeletons of schoolmasters, Commissioners of Fact, genteel and used-up infidels, gabblers of many little dog's-eared
creeds, the poor you will have always with you. Cultivate in them, while there is yet time,
the utmost graces of the fancies and affections to adorn their lives so much in need of
ornament; or, in the day of your triumph, when romance is utterly driven out of their
souls, and they and a bare existence stand face to face, Reality will take a wolfish turn,
and make an end of you!

Stephen worked the next day, and the next, uncheered by a word from any one, and
shunned in all his comings and goings as before. At the end of the second day, he saw
land; at the end of the third, his loom stood empty.

He had overstayed his hour in the street outside the Bank, on each of the two first
evenings; and nothing had happened there, good or bad. That he might not be remiss
in his part of the engagement, he resolved to wait full two hours, on this third and last
night.

There was the lady who had once kept Mr Bounderby's house, sitting at the first
floor window as he had seen her before; and there was the light porter, sometimes
talking with her there, and sometimes looking over the blind below which had BANK
upon it, and sometimes coming to the door and standing on the steps for a breath of air.
When he first came out, Stephen thought he might be looking for him, and passed near;
but the light porter only cast his winking eyes upon him slightly, and said nothing.

Two hours were a long stretch of lounging about, after a long day's labour. Stephen
sat upon the step of a door, leaned against a wall under an archway, strolled up and
down, listened for the church clock, stopped and watched children playing in the street.
Some purpose or other is so natural to every one, that a mere loiterer always looks and
feels remarkable. When the first hour was out, Stephen even began to have an uncomfortable sensation upon him of being for the time a disreputable character.

Then came the lamplighter, and two lengthening lines of light all down the long
perspective of the street, until they were blended and lost in the distance. Mrs Sparsit
closed the first floor window, drew down the blind, and went up stairs. Presently, a light
went up stairs after her, passing first the fanlight of the door, and afterwards the two
stair-case windows, on its way up. By and by, one corner of the second floor blind was
disturbed, as if Mrs Sparsit's eye were there; also the other corner, as if the light porter's
eye were on that side. Still, no communication was made to Stephen. Much relieved
when the two hours were at last accomplished, he went away at a quick pace, as a
recompense for so much loitering.

He had only to take leave of his landlady, and lie down on his temporary bed upon
the floor; for his bundle was made up for tomorrow, and all was arranged for his
departure. He meant to be clear of the town very early; before the Hands were in the
streets.

It was barely daybreak, when, with a parting look round his room, mournfully
wondering whether he should ever see it again, he went out. The town was as entirely
deserted as if the inhabitants had abandoned it, rather than hold communication with
him. Everything looked wan at that hour. Even the coming sun made but a pale waste
in the sky, like a sad sea.

By the place where Rachael lived, though it was not in his way; by the red brick streets; by the great silent factories, not trembling yet; by the railway, where the danger-lights were waning in the strengthening day; by the railway's crazy neighbourhood, half pulled down and half built up; by scattered red brick villas, where the besmoked evergreens were sprinkled with a dirty powder, like untidy snuff-takers; by coal-dust paths and many varieties of ugliness; Stephen got to the top of the hill, and looked back.

Day was shining radiantly upon the town then, and the bells were going for the morning work. Domestic fires were not yet lighted, and the high chimneys had the sky to themselves. Puffing out their poisonous volumes, they would not be long in hiding it; but, for half an hour, some of the many windows were golden, which showed the Coketown people a sun eternally in eclipse, through a medium of smoked glass.

So strange to turn from the chimneys to the birds. So strange to have the road-dust on his feet instead of the coal-grit. So strange to have lived to his time of life, and yet to be beginning like a boy this summer morning! With these musings in his mind, and his bundle under his arm, Stephen took his attentive face along the high road. And the trees arched over him, whispering that he left a true and loving heart behind.

Chapter VII

GUNPOWDER

M R James Harthouse, "going in" for his adopted party, soon began to score. With the aid of a little more coaching for the political sages, a little more genteel listlessness for the general society, and a tolerable management of the assumed honesty in dishonesty, most effective and most patronized of the polite deadly sins, he speedily came to be considered of much promise. The not being troubled with earnestness was a grand point in his favour, enabling him to take to the hard Fact fellows with as good a grace as if he had been born one of the tribe, and to throw all other tribes overboard, as conscious hypocrites.

"Whom none of us believe, my dear Mrs Bounderby, and who do not believe themselves. The only difference between us and the professors of virtue or benevolence, or philanthropy—never mind the name—is, that we know it is all meaningless, and say so; while they know it equally and will never say so."

Why should she be shocked or warned by this reiteration? It was not so unlike her father's principles, and her early training, that it need startle her. Where was the great difference between the two schools, when each chained her down to material realities, and inspired her with no faith in anything else? What was there in her soul for James Harthouse to destroy, which Thomas Gradgrind had nurtured there in its state of inno-cence!

It was even the worse for her at this pass, that in her mind—implanted there before her eminently practical father began to form it—a struggling disposition to believe in a wider and nobler humanity than she had ever heard of, constantly strove with doubts and resentments. With doubts, because the aspiration had been so laid waste in her youth. With resentments, because of the wrong that had been done her, if it were indeed a whisper of the truth. Upon a nature long accustomed to self-suppression, thus torn and divided, the Harthouse philosophy came as a relief and justification. Everything being hollow and worthless, she had missed nothing and sacrificed nothing. What did it matter, she had said to her father, when he proposed her husband. What did it matter, she said still. With a scornful self-reliance, she asked herself, What did anything matter—and went on.

Towards what? Step by step, onward and downward, towards some end, yet so gradually, that she believed herself to remain motionless. As to Mr Harthouse, whither *he* tended, he neither considered nor cared. He had no particular design or plan before him: no energetic wickedness ruffled his lassitude. He was as much amused and interested, at present, as it became so fine a gentleman to be; perhaps even more than it would have been consistent with his reputation to confess. Soon after his arrival he languidly wrote to his brother, the honourable and jocular member, that the Bounderbys were "great fun"; and further, that the female Bounderby, instead of being the Gorgon he had expected, was young, and remarkably pretty. After that, he wrote no more about them, and devoted his leisure chiefly to their house. He was very often in their house, in his flittings and visitings about the Coketown district; and was much encouraged by Mr Bounderby. It was quite in Mr Bounderby's gusty way to boast to all his world that *he* didn't care about your highly connected people, but that if his wife Tom Gradgrind's daughter did, she was welcome to their company.

Mr James Harthouse began to think it would be a new sensation, if the face which changed so beautifully for the whelp, would change for him.

He was quick enough to observe; he had a good memory, and did not forget a word of the brother's revelations. He interwove them with everything he saw of the sister, and he began to understand her. To be sure, the better and profounder part of her character was not within his scope of perception; for in natures, as in seas, depth answers unto depth; but he soon began to read the rest with a student's eye.

Mr Bounderby had taken possession of a house and grounds, about fifteen miles from the town, and accessible within a mile or two, by a railway striding on many arches over a wild country, undermined by deserted coal-shafts, and spotted at night by fires and black shapes of stationary engines at pits' mouths. This country, gradually softening towards the neighbourhood of Mr Bounderby's retreat, there mellowed into a rustic landscape, golden with heath, and snowy with hawthorn in the spring of the year, and tremulous with leaves and their shadows all the summer time. The bank had foreclosed a mortgage effected on the property thus pleasantly situated, by one of the Coketown magnates, who, in his determination to make a shorter cut than usual to an enormous fortune, overspeculated himself by about two hundred thousand pounds. These accidents did sometimes happen in the best-regulated families of Coketown, but the bankrupts had no connexion whatever with the improvident classes.

It afforded Mr Bounderby supreme satisfaction to instal himself in this snug little estate, and with demonstrative humility to grow cabbages in the flower-garden. He delighted to live, barrack-fashion, among the elegant furniture, and he bullied the very pictures with his origin. "Why, sir," he would say to a visitor, "I am told that Nickits," the late owner, "gave seven hundred pound for that Sea-beach. Now, to be plain with you, if I ever, in the whole course of my life, take seven looks at it, at a hundred pound a look, it will be as much as I shall do. No, by George! I don't forget that I am Josiah Bounderby of Coketown. For years upon years, the only pictures in my possession, or that I could have got into my possession by any means, unless I stole 'em, were the engravings of a man shaving himself in a boot, on the blacking bottles that I was overjoyed to use in cleaning boots with, and that I sold when they were empty for a farthing a-piece, and glad to get it!"

Then he would address Mr Harthouse in the same style.

"Harthouse, you have a couple of horses down here. Bring half a dozen more if you like, and we'll find room for 'em. There's stabling in this place for a dozen horses; and unless Nickits is belied, he kept the full number. A round dozen of 'em, sir. When that man was a boy, he went to Westminster School. Went to Westminster School as a King's Scholar, when I was principally living on garbage, and sleeping in market baskets. Why, if I wanted to keep a dozen horses—which I don't, for one's enough for me—I couldn't bear to see 'em in their stalls here, and think what my own lodging used to be. I couldn't look at 'em, sir, and not order 'em out. Yet so things come round. You see this place; you know what sort of a place it is; you are aware that there's not a completer place of its size in this kingdom or elsewhere—I don't care where—and here, got into the middle of it, like a maggot into a nut, is Josiah Bounderby. While Nickits (as a man came into my office, and told me yesterday), Nickits, who used to act in Latin, in the Westminster School plays, with the chief-justices and nobility of this country applauding him till they were black in the face, is drivelling at this minute—drivelling, sir!—in a fifth floor, up a narrow dark back street in Antwerp."

It was among the leafy shadows of this retirement, in the long sultry summer days, that Mr Harthouse began to prove the face which had set him wondering when he first saw it, and to try if it would change for him.

"Mrs Bounderby, I esteem it a most fortunate accident that I find you alone here. I have for some time had a particular wish to speak to you."

It was not by any wonderful accident that he found her, the time of day being that at which she was always alone, and the place being her favourite resort. It was an opening in a dark wood, where some felled trees lay, and where she would sit watching the fallen leaves of last year, as she had watched the falling ashes at home.

He sat down beside her, with a glance at her face.

"Your brother. My young friend Tom—"

Her colour brightened, and she turned to him with a look of interest. "I never in my life," he thought, "saw anything so remarkable and so captivating as the lighting of those features!" His face betrayed his thoughts—perhaps without betraying him, for it might have been according to its instructions so to do.

"Pardon me. The expression of your sisterly interest is so beautiful—Tom should be so proud of it—I know this is inexcusable, but I am so compelled to admire."

"Being so impulsive," she said composedly.

"Mrs Bounderby, no: you know I make no pretence with you. You know I am a sordid piece of human nature, ready to sell myself at any time for any reasonable sum, and altogether incapable of any Arcadian proceeding whatever."

"I am waiting," she returned, "for your further reference to my brother."

"You are rigid with me, and I deserve it. I am as worthless a dog as you will find, except that I am not false—not false. But you surprised and started me from my subject, which was your brother. I have an interest in him."

"Have you an interest in anything, Mr Harthouse?" she asked, half incredulously and half gratefully.

"If you had asked me when I first came here, I should have said no. I must say now—even at the hazard of appearing to make a pretence, and of justly awakening your incredulity—yes."

She made a slight movement, as if she were trying to speak, but could not find voice; at length she said, "Mr Harthouse, I give you credit for being interested in my brother."

"Thank you. I claim to deserve it. You know how little I do claim, but I will go that length. You have done so much for him, you are so fond of him; your whole life, Mrs Bounderby, expresses such charming self-forgetfulness on his account—pardon me again—I am running wide of the subject. I am interested in him for his own sake."

She had made the slightest action possible, as if she would have risen in a hurry and gone away. He had turned the course of what he said at that instant, and she remained.

"Mrs Bounderby," he resumed, in a lighter manner, and yet with a show of effort in assuming it, which was even more expressive than the manner he dismissed; "it is no irrevocable offence in a young fellow of your brother's years, if he is heedless, inconsiderate, and expensive—a little dissipated, in the common phrase. Is he?"

"Yes."

"Allow me to be frank. Do you think he games at all?"

"I think he makes bets." Mr Harthouse waiting, as if that were not her whole answer, she added, "I know he does."

"Of course he loses?"

"Yes."

"Everybody does lose who bets. May I hint at the probability of your sometimes supplying him with money for these purposes?"

She sat looking down; but, at this question, raised her eyes searchingly and a little resentfully.

"Acquit me of impertinent curiosity, my dear Mrs Bounderby. I think Tom may be gradually falling into trouble, and I wish to stretch out a helping hand to him from the depths of my wicked experience.—Shall I say again, for his sake? Is that necessary?"

She seemed to try to answer, but nothing came of it.

"Candidly to confess everything that has occurred to me," said James Harthouse, again gliding with the same appearance of effort into his more airy manner; "I will confide to you my doubt whether he has had many advantages. Whether—forgive my plainness—whether any great amount of confidence is likely to have been established between himself and his most worthy father."

"I do not," said Louisa, flushing with her own great remembrance in that wise, "think it likely."

"Or, between himself, and—I may trust to your perfect understanding of my meaning, I am sure—and his highly esteemed brother-in-law."

She flushed deeper and deeper, and was burning red when she replied in a fainter voice, "I do not think that likely, either."

"Mrs Bounderby," said Harthouse, after a short silence, "may there be a better confidence between yourself and me? Tom has borrowed a considerable sum of you?"

"You will understand, Mr Harthouse," she returned, after some indecision: she had been more or less uncertain, and troubled throughout the conversation, and yet had in the main preserved her self-contained manner; "you will understand that if I tell you what you press to know, it is not by way of complaint or regret. I would never complain of anything, and what I have done I do not in the least regret."

"So spirited, too!" thought James Harthouse.

"When I married, I found that my brother was even at that time heavily in debt. Heavily for him, I mean. Heavily enough to oblige me to sell some trinkets. They were no sacrifice. I sold them very willingly. I attached no value to them. They were quite worthless to me."

Either she saw in his face that he knew, or she only feared in her conscience that he knew, that she spoke of some of her husband's gifts. She stopped, and reddened again. If he had not known it before, he would have known it then, though he had been a much duller man than he was.

"Since then, I have given my brother, at various times, what money I could spare: in short, what money I have had. Confiding in you at all, on the faith of the interest you profess for him, I will not do so by halves. Since you have been in the habit of visiting here, he has wanted in one sum as much as a hundred pounds. I have not been able to give it to him. I have felt uneasy for the consequences of his being so involved, but I have kept these secrets until now, when I trust them to your honour. I have held no confidence with any one, because—you anticipated my reason just now." She abruptly broke off.

He was a ready man, and he saw, and seized, an opportunity here of presenting her own image to her, slightly disguised as her brother.

"Mrs Bounderby, though a graceless person, of the world worldly, I feel the utmost interest, I assure you, in what you tell me. I cannot possibly be hard upon your brother. I understand and share the wise consideration with which you regard his errors. With all possible respect both for Mr Gradgrind and for Mr Bounderby, I think I perceive that he has not been fortunate in his training. Bred at a disadvantage towards the society in which he has to play, he rushes into these extremes for himself, from opposite extremes that have long been forced—with the very best intentions we have no doubt—upon him. Mr Bounderby's fine bluff English independence, though a most charming characteristic, does not—as we have agreed—invite confidence. If I might venture to remark that it is the least in the world deficient in that delicacy to which a youth mistaken, a character misconceived, and abilities misdirected, would turn for relief and guidance, I should express what it presents to my own view."

As she sat looking straight before her, across the changing lights upon the grass into the darkness of the wood beyond, he saw in her face her application of his very distinctly uttered words.

"All allowance," he continued, "must be made. I have one great fault to find with Tom, however, which I cannot forgive, and for which I take him heavily to account."

Louisa turned her eyes to his face, and asked him what fault was that?

"Perhaps," he returned, "I have said enough. Perhaps it would have been better, on the whole, if no allusion to it had escaped me."

"You alarm me, Mr Harthouse. Pray let me know it."

"To relieve you from needless apprehension—and as this confidence regarding your brother, which I prize I am sure above all possible things, has been established between us—I obey. I cannot forgive him for not being more sensible, in every word, look, and act of his life, of the affection of his best friend; of the devotion of his best friend; of her unselfishness; of her sacrifice. The return he makes her, within my observation, is a very poor one. What she has done for him demands his constant love and gratitude, not his ill-humour and caprice. Careless fellow as I am, I am not so indifferent, Mrs Bounderby, as to be regardless of this vice in your brother, or inclined to consider it a venial offence."

The wood floated before her, for her eyes were suffused with tears. They rose from a deep well, long concealed, and her heart was filled with acute pain that found no relief in them.

"In a word, it is to correct your brother in this, Mrs Bounderby, that I must aspire. My better knowledge of his circumstances, and my direction and advice in extricating him—rather valuable, I hope, as coming from a scapegrace on a much larger scale—will give me some influence over him, and all I gain I shall certainly use towards this end. I have said enough, and more than enough. I seem to be protesting that I am a sort of good fellow, when, upon my honour, I have not the least intention to make any protestation to that effect, and openly announce that I am nothing of the sort. Yonder, among the trees," he added, having lifted up his eyes and looked about; for he had watched her closely until now; "is your brother himself; no doubt, just come down. As he seems to be loitering in this direction, it may be as well, perhaps, to walk towards him, and throw ourselves in his way. He has been very silent and doleful of late. Perhaps, his brotherly conscience is touched—if there are such things as consciences. Though, upon my honour, I hear of them much too often to believe in them."

He assisted her to rise, and she took his arm, and they advanced to meet the whelp. He was idly beating the branches as he lounged along: or he stooped viciously to rip the moss from the trees with his stick. He was startled when they came upon him while he was engaged in this latter pastime, and his colour changed.

"Holloa!" he stammered; "I didn't know you were here."

"Whose name, Tom," said Mr Harthouse, putting his hand upon his shoulder and turning him, so that they all three walked towards the house together, "have you been carving on the trees?"

"Whose name?" returned Tom. "Oh! You mean what girl's name?"

"You have a suspicious appearance of inscribing some fair creature's on the bark, Tom."

"Not much of that, Mr Harthouse, unless some fair creature with a slashing fortune at her own disposal would take a fancy to me. Or she might be as ugly as she was rich, without any fear of losing me. I'd carve her name as often as she liked."

"I'm afraid you are mercenary, Tom."

"Mercenary," repeated Tom. "Who is not mercenary? Ask my sister."

"Have you so proved it to be a failing of mine, Tom?" said Louisa, showing no other sense of his discontent and ill-nature.

"You know whether the cap fits you, Loo," returned her brother sulkily. "If it does, you can wear it."

"Tom is misanthropical today, as all bored people are now and then," said Mr Harthouse. "Don't believe him, Mrs Bounderby. He knows much better. I shall disclose some of his opinions of you, privately expressed to me, unless he relents a little."

"At all events, Mr Harthouse," said Tom, softening in his admiration of his patron, but shaking his head sullenly too, "you can't tell her that I ever praised her for being mercenary. I may have praised her for being the contrary, and I should do it again if I had as good reason. However, never mind this now; it's not very interesting to you, and I am sick of the subject."

They walked on to the house, where Louisa quitted her visitor's arm and went in. He stood looking after her, as she ascended the steps, and passed into the shadow of the door; then put his hand upon her brother's shoulder again, and invited him with a confidential nod to a walk in the garden.

"Tom, my fine fellow, I want to have a word with you."

They had stopped among a disorder of roses—it was part of Mr Bounderby's humility to keep Nickits's roses on a reduced scale—and Tom sat down on a terrace-parapet, plucking buds and picking them to pieces; while his powerful Familiar stood over him, with a foot upon the parapet, and his figure easily resting on the arm supported by that knee. They were just visible from her window. Perhaps she saw them.

"Tom, what's the matter?"

"Oh! Mr Harthouse," said Tom, with a groan, "I am hard up, and bothered out of my life."

"My good fellow, so am I."

"You!" returned Tom. "You are the picture of independence. Mr Harthouse, I am in a horrible mess. You have no idea what a state I have got myself into—what a state my sister might have got me out of, if she would only have done it."

He took to biting the rose-buds now, and tearing them away from his teeth with a hand that trembled like an infirm old man's. After one exceedingly observant look at him, his companion relapsed into his lightest air.

"Tom, you are inconsiderate: you expect too much of your sister. You have had money of her, you dog, you know you have."

"Well, Mr Harthouse, I know I have. How else was I to get it? Here's old Bounderby always boasting that at my age he lived upon two-pence a month, or something of that sort. Here's my father drawing what he calls a line, and tying me down to it from a baby, neck and heels. Here's my mother who never has anything of her own, except her complaints. What *is* a fellow to do for money, and where *am* I to look for it, if not to my sister?"

He was almost crying, and scattered the buds about by dozens. Mr Harthouse took him persuasively by the coat.

"But, my dear Tom, if your sister has not got it—"

"Not got it, Mr Harthouse? I don't say she has got it. I may have wanted more than she was likely to have got. But then she ought to get it. She could get it. It's of no use pretending to make a secret of matters now, after what I have told you already; you know she didn't marry old Bounderby for her own sake, or for his sake, but for my sake. Then why doesn't she get what I want, out of him, for my sake? She is not obliged to say what she is going to do with it; she is sharp enough; she could manage to coax it out of him, if she chose. Then why doesn't she choose, when I tell her of what consequence it is? But no. There she sits in his company like a stone, instead of making herself agreeable and getting it easily. I don't know what you may call this, but *I* call it unnatural conduct."

There was a piece of ornamental water immediately below the parapet, on the other side, into which Mr James Harthouse had a very strong inclination to pitch Mr Thomas Gradgrind Junior, as the injured men of Coketown threatened to pitch their property into the Atlantic. But he preserved his easy attitude; and nothing more solid went over the stone balustrades than the accumulated rosebuds now floating about, a little surface-island.

"My dear Tom," said Harthouse, "let me try to be your banker."

"For God's sake," replied Tom, suddenly, "don't talk about bankers!" And very white he looked, in contrast with the roses. Very white.

Mr Harthouse, as a thoroughly well bred man, accustomed to the best society, was not to be surprised—he could as soon have been affected—but he raised his eyelids a little more, as if they were lifted by a feeble touch of wonder. Albeit it was as much against the precepts of his school to wonder, as it was against the doctrines of the Gradgrind College.

"What is the present need, Tom? Three figures? Out with them. Say what they are."

"Mr Harthouse," returned Tom, now actually crying; and his tears were better than his injuries, however pitiful a figure he made; "it's too late; the money is of no use to me at present. I should have had it before, to be of use to me. But I am very much obliged to you; you're a true friend."

A true friend! "Whelp, whelp!" thought Mr Harthouse, lazily; "what an Ass you are!"

"And I take your offer as a great kindness," said Tom grasping his hand. "As a great kindness, Mr Harthouse."

"Well," returned the other, "it may be of more use by and by. And, my good fellow, if you will open your bedevilments to me when they come thick upon you, I may show you better ways out of them than you can find for yourself."

"Thank you," said Tom, shaking his head dismally, and chewing rosebuds. "I wish I had known you sooner, Mr Harthouse."

"Now, you see, Tom," said Mr Harthouse in conclusion, himself tossing over a rose or two, as a contribution to the island, which was always drifting to the wall as if it wanted to become a part of the mainland; "every man is selfish in everything he does, and I am exactly like the rest of my fellow creatures. I am desperately intent;" the languor of his desperation being quite tropical; "on your softening towards your sister—which you ought to do; and on your being a more loving and agreeable sort of brother—which you ought to be."

"I will be, Mr Harthouse."

"No time like the present, Tom. Begin at once."

"Certainly I will. And my sister Loo shall say so."

"Having made which bargain, Tom," said Harthouse, clapping him on the shoulder again, with an air which left him at liberty to infer—as he did, poor fool—that this condition was imposed upon him in mere careless good nature, to lessen his sense of obligation, "we will tear ourselves asunder until dinner-time."

When Tom appeared before dinner, though his mind seemed heavy enough, his body was on the alert; and he appeared before Mr Bounderby came in. "I didn't mean to be cross, Loo," he said, giving her his hand, and kissing her. "I know you are fond of me, and you know I am fond of you."

After this, there was a smile upon Louisa's face that day, for some one else. Alas, for some one else!

"So much the less is the whelp the only creature that she cares for," thought James Harthouse, reversing the reflection of his first day's knowledge of her pretty face. "So much the less, so much the less."

Chapter VIII

EXPLOSION

THE next morning was too bright a morning for sleep, and James Harthouse rose early, and sat in the pleasant bay window of his dressing-room, smoking the rare tobacco that had had so wholesome an influence on his young friend. Reposing in the sunlight, with the fragrance of his eastern pipe about him, and the dreamy smoke vanishing into the air, so rich and soft with summer odours, he reckoned up his advantages as an idle winner might count his gains. He was not at all bored for the time, and could give his mind to it.

He had established a confidence with her, from which her husband was excluded. He had established a confidence with her, that absolutely turned upon her indifference towards her husband, and the absence, now and at all times, of any congeniality between them. He had artfully, but plainly assured her, that he knew her heart in its last most delicate recesses; he had come so near to her through its tenderest sentiment; he had associated himself with that feeling; and the barrier behind which she lived, had melted away. All very odd, and very satisfactory!

And yet he had not, even now, any earnest wickedness of purpose in him. Publicly and privately, it were much better for the age in which he lived, that he and the legion of whom he was one were designedly bad, than indifferent and purposeless. It is the drifting icebergs setting with any current anywhere, that wreck the ships.

When the Devil goeth about like a roaring lion, he goeth about in a shape by which few but savages and hunters are attracted. But, when he is trimmed, smoothed, and varnished, according to the mode: when he is aweary of vice, and aweary of virtue, used up as to brimstone, and used up as to bliss; then, whether he take to the serving out of red tape, or to the kindling of red fire, he is the very Devil.

So, James Harthouse reclined in the window, indolently smoking, and reckoning up the steps he had taken on the road by which he happened to be travelling. The end to which it led was before him, pretty plainly; but he troubled himself with no calculations about it. What will be, will be.

As he had rather a long ride to take that day—for there was a public occasion "to do" at some distance, which afforded a tolerable opportunity of going in for the Grad-grind men—he dressed early, and went down to breakfast. He was anxious to see if she had relapsed since the previous evening. No. He resumed where he had left off. There was a look of interest for him again.

He got through the day as much (or as little) to his own satisfaction, as was to be expected under the fatiguing circumstances; and came riding back at six o'clock. There was a sweep of some half mile between the lodge and the house, and he was riding along at a foot pace over the smooth gravel, once Nickits's, when Mr Bounderby burst out of the shrubbery, with such violence as to make his horse shy across the road.

"Harthouse!" cried Mr Bounderby. "Have you heard?"

"Heard what?" said Harthouse, soothing his horse, and inwardly favouring Mr Bounderby with no good wishes.

"Then you *haven't* heard!"

"I have heard you, and so has this brute. I have heard nothing else."

Mr Bounderby, red and hot, planted himself in the centre of the path before the horse's head, to explode his bombshell with more effect.

"The Bank's robbed!"

"You don't mean it!"

"Robbed last night, sir. Robbed in an extraordinary manner. Robbed with a false key."

"Of much?"

Mr Bounderby, in his desire to make the most of it, really seemed mortified by being obliged to reply, "Why, no; not of very much. But it might have been."

"Of how much?"

"Oh! as a sum—if you stick to a sum—of not more than a hundred and fifty pound," said Bounderby, with impatience. "But it's not the sum; it's the fact. It's the fact of the Bank being robbed, that's the important circumstance. I am surprised you don't see it."

"My dear Bounderby," said James, dismounting, and giving his bridle to his servant, "I *do* see it; and am as overcome as you can possibly desire me to be, by the spectacle afforded to my mental view. Nevertheless, I may be allowed, I hope, to congratulate you—which I do with all my soul, I assure you—on your not having sustained a greater loss."

"Thank'ee," replied Bounderby, in a short, ungracious manner. "But I tell you what. It might have been twenty thousand pound."

"I suppose it might."

"Suppose it might! By the Lord, you *may* suppose so. By George!" said Mr Bounderby, with sundry menacing nods and shakes of his head. "it might have been twice twenty. There's no knowing what it would have been, or wouldn't have been, as it was, but for the fellows' being disturbed."

Louisa had come up now, and Mrs Sparsit, and Bitzer.

"Here's Tom Gradgrind's daughter knows pretty well what it might have been, if you don't," blustered Bounderby. "Dropped, sir, as if she was shot when I told her! Never knew her do such a thing before. Does her credit, under the circumstances, in my opinion!"

She still looked faint and pale. James Harthouse begged her to take his arm; and as they moved on very slowly, asked her how the robbery had been committed.

"Why, I am going to tell you," said Bounderby, irritably giving his arm to Mrs Sparsit. "If you hadn't been so mighty particular about the sum, I should have begun to tell you before. You know this lady (for she *is* a lady), Mrs Sparsit?"

"I have already had the honour"—

"Very well. And this young man, Bitzer, you saw him too on the same occasion?" Mr Harthouse inclined his head in assent, and Bitzer knuckled his forehead.

"Very well. They live at the Bank. You know they live at the Bank, perhaps? Very well. Yesterday afternoon, at the close of business hours, everything was put away as usual. In the iron room that this young fellow sleeps outside of, there was never mind how much. In the little safe in young Tom's closet, the safe used for petty purposes, there was a hundred and fifty odd pound."

"A hundred and fifty-four, seven, one," said Bitzer.

"Come!" retorted Bounderby, stopping to wheel round upon him, "let's have none of *your* interruptions. It's enough to be robbed while you're snoring because you're too comfortable, without being put right with *your* four seven ones. I didn't snore, myself, when I was your age, let me tell you. I hadn't victuals enough to snore. And I didn't four seven one. Not if I knew it."

Bitzer knuckled his forehead again, in a sneaking manner, and seemed at once particularly impressed and depressed by the instance last given of Mr Bounderby's moral abstinence.

"A hundred and fifty odd pound," resumed Mr Bounderby. "That sum of money, young Tom locked in his safe; not a very strong safe, but that's no matter now. Everything was left. all right. Some time in the night, while this young fellow snored—Mrs Sparsit, ma'am, you say you have heard him snore?"

"Sir," returned Mrs Sparsit, "I cannot say that I have heard him precisely snore, and therefore must not make that statement. But on winter evenings, when he has fallen asleep at his table, I have heard him, what I should prefer to describe as partially choke. I have heard him on such occasions produce sounds of a nature similar to what may be sometimes heard in Dutch clocks. Not," said Mrs Sparsit, with a lofty sense of giving strict evidence, "that I would convey any imputation on his moral character. Far from it, I have always considered Bitzer a young man of the most upright principle; and to that I beg to bear my testimony."

"Well!" said the exasperated Bounderby, "while he was snoring, *or* choking, *or* Dutch-clocking, *or* something or other—being asleep—some fellows, somehow, whether previously concealed in the house or not remains to be seen, got to young Tom's safe, forced it, and abstracted the contents. Being then disturbed, they made off; letting themselves out at the main door, and double-locking it again (it was double-locked, and the key under Mrs Sparsit's pillow) with a false key, which was picked up in the street near the Bank, about twelve o'clock today. No alarm takes place, till this chap, Bitzer, turns out this morning and begins to open and prepare the offices for business. Then, looking at Tom's safe, he sees the door ajar, and finds the lock forced, and the money gone."

"Where is Tom, by the by?" asked Harthouse, glancing round.

"He has been helping the police," said Bounderby, "and stays behind at the Bank. I wish these fellows had tried to rob me when I was at his time of life. They would have been out of pocket, if they had invested eighteenpence in the job; I can tell 'em that."

"Is anybody suspected?"

"Suspected? I should think there was somebody suspected. Egod!" said Bounderby, relinquishing Mrs Sparsit's arm to wipe his heated head. "Josiah Bounderby of Coketown, is not to be plundered and nobody suspected. No, thank you!"

Might Mr Harthouse inquire Who was suspected?

"Well," said Bounderby, stopping and facing about to confront them all, "I'll tell you. It's not to be mentioned everywhere; it's not to be mentioned anywhere: in order that the scoundrels concerned (there's a gang of 'em) may be thrown off their guard. So take this in confidence. Now wait a bit." Mr Bounderby wiped his head again. "What should you say to;" here he violently exploded: "to a Hand being in it?"

"I hope," said Harthouse, lazily, "not our friend Blackpot?"

"Say Pool instead of Pot, sir," returned Bounderby, "and that's the man."

Louisa faintly uttered some word of incredulity and surprise.

"O yes! I know!" said Bounderby, immediately catching at the sound. "I know! I am used to that. I know all about it. They are the finest people in the world, these fellows are. They have got the gift of the gab, they have. They only want to have their rights explained to them, they do. But I tell you what. Show me a dissatisfied Hand, and I'll show you a man that's fit for anything bad, I don't care what it is."

Another of the popular fictions of Coketown, which some pains had been taken to disseminate—and which some people really believed.

"But I am acquainted with these chaps," said Bounderby. "I can read 'em off, like books. Mrs Sparsit, ma'am, I appeal to you. What warning did I give that fellow, the first time he set foot in the house, when the express object of his visit was to know how he could knock Religion over, and floor the Established Church? Mrs Sparsit, in point of high connexions, you are on a level with the aristocracy,—did I say, or did I not say, to that fellow, 'you can't hide the truth from me: you are not the kind of fellow I like; you'll come to no good.'?"

"Assuredly, sir," returned Mrs Sparsit, "you did, in a highly impressive manner, give him such an admonition."

"When he shocked you, ma'am," said Bounderby; "when he shocked your feelings?"

"Yes, sir," returned Mrs Sparsit, with a meek shake of her head, "he certainly did so.

Though I do not mean to say but that my feelings may be weaker on such points—more foolish, if the term is preferred—than they might have been, if I had always occupied my present position."

Mr Bounderby stared with a bursting pride at Mr Harthouse, as much as to say, "I am the proprietor of this female, and she's worth your attention, I think." Then, resumed his discourse.

"You can recall for yourself, Harthouse, what I said to him when you saw him. I didn't mince the matter with him. I am never mealy with 'em. I KNOW 'em. Very well, sir. Three days after that, he bolted. Went off, nobody knows where: as my mother did in my infancy—only with this difference, that he is a worse subject than my mother, if possible. What did he do before he went? What do you say;" Mr Bounderby, with his hat in his hand, gave a beat upon the crown at every little division of his sentence, as if it were a tambourine; "to his being seen—night after night—watching the Bank?—to his lurking about there—after dark?—To its striking Mrs Sparsit—that he could be lurking for no good—To her calling Bitzer's attention to him, and their both taking notice of him—And to its appearing on inquiry today—that he was also noticed by the neighbours?" Having come to the climax, Mr Bounderby, like an oriental dancer, put his tambourine on his head.

"Suspicious," said James Harthouse, "certainly."

"I think so, sir," said Bounderby, with a defiant nod. "I think so. But there are more of 'em in it. There's an old woman. One never hears of these things till the mischief's done; all sorts of defects are found out in the stable door after the horse is stolen; there's an old woman turns up now. An old woman who seems to have been flying into town on a broomstick, every now and then. *She* watches the place a whole day before this fellow begins, and, on the night when you saw him, she steals away with him and holds a council with him—I suppose, to make her report on going off duty, and be damned to her."

There was such a person in the room that night, and she shrunk from observation, thought Louisa.

"This is not all of 'em, even as we already know 'em," said Bounderby, with many nods of hidden meaning. "But I have said enough for the present. You'll have the goodness to keep it quiet, and mention it to no one. It may take time, but we shall have 'em. It's policy to give 'em line enough, and there's no objection to that."

"Of course, they will be punished with the utmost rigour of the law, as notice-boards observe," replied James Harthouse, "and serve them right. Fellows who go in for Banks must take the consequences. If there were no consequences, we should all go in for Banks." He had gently taken Louisa's parasol from her hand, and had put it up for her; and she walked under its shade, though the sun did not shine there.

"For the present, Loo Bounderby," said her husband, "here's Mrs Sparsit to look after. Mrs Sparsit's nerves have been acted upon by this business, and she'll stay here a day or two. So, make her comfortable."

"Thank you very much, sir," that discreet lady observed, "but pray do not let My comfort be a consideration. Anything will do for Me."

It soon appeared that if Mrs Sparsit had a failing in her association with that domestic establishment, it was that she was so excessively regardless of herself and regardful of others, as to be a nuisance. On being shown her chamber, she was so dreadfully sensible of its comforts as to suggest the inference that she would have preferred to pass the night on the mangle in the laundry. True, the Powlers and the Scadgerses were accustomed to splendour, "but it is my duty to remember," Mrs Sparsit was fond of observing with a lofty grace: particularly when any of the domestics were present, "that what I was, I am no longer. Indeed," said she, "if I could altogether cancel the remembrance that Mr Sparsit was a Powler, or that I myself am related to the Scadgers family; or if I could even revoke the fact, and make myself a person of common descent and ordinary connexions; I would gladly do so. I should think it, under existing circumstances, right to do so." The same Hermitical state of mind led to her renunciation of made dishes and wines at dinner, until fairly commanded by Mr Bounderby to take them; when she said, "Indeed you are very good, sir;" and departed from a resolution of which she had made rather formal and public announcement, to "wait for the simple mutton." She was likewise deeply apologetic for wanting the salt; and, feeling amiably bound to bear out Mr Bounderby to the fullest extent in the testimony he had borne to her nerves, occasionally sat back in her chair and silently wept; at which periods a tear of large dimensions, like a crystal ear-ring, might be observed (or rather, must be, for it insisted on public notice) sliding down her Roman nose.

But Mrs Sparsit's greatest point, first and last, was her determination to pity Mr Bounderby. There were occasions when in looking at him she was involuntarily moved to shake her head, as who would say, "Alas poor Yorick!" After allowing herself to be betrayed into these evidences of emotion, she would force a lambent brightness, and would be fitfully cheerful, and would say, "You have still good spirits, sir, I am thankful to find;" and would appear to hail it as a blessed dispensation that Mr Bounderby bore up as he did. One idiosyncrasy for which she often apologized, she found it excessively difficult to conquer. She had a curious propensity to call Mrs Bounderby "Miss Grad-grind," and yielded to it some three or four score times in the course of the evening. Her repetition of this mistake covered Mrs Sparsit with modest confusion; but indeed, she said, it seemed so natural to say Miss Gradgrind: whereas, to persuade herself that the young lady whom she had had the happiness of knowing from a child could be really and truly Mrs Bounderby, she found almost impossible. It was a further singularity of this remarkable case, that the more she thought about it, the more impossible it appeared; "the differences," she observed, "being such."

In the drawing-room after dinner, Mr Bounderby tried the case of the robbery, examined the witnesses, made notes of the evidence, found the suspected persons guilty, and sentenced them to the extreme punishment of the law. That done, Bitzer was dismissed to town with instructions to recommend Tom to come home by the mail-train.

When candles were brought, Mrs Sparsit murmured, "Don't be low, sir. Pray let me see you cheerful, sir, as I used to do." Mr Bounderby, upon whom these consolations had begun to produce the effect of making him, in a bull-headed blundering way, sentimen-tal, sighed like some large sea-animal. "I cannot bear to see you so, sir," said Mrs Sparsit. "Try a hand at backgammon, sir, as you used to do when I had the honour of living under your roof." "I haven't played backgammon, ma'am," said Mr Bounderby, "since that time." "No, sir," said Mrs Sparsit, soothingly, "I am aware that you have not. I remember that Miss Gradgrind takes no interest in the game. But I shall be happy, sir, if you will condescend."

They played near a window, opening on the garden. It was a fine night: not moonlight, but sultry and fragrant. Louisa and Mr Harthouse strolled out into the garden, where their voices could be heard in the stillness, though not what they said. Mrs Sparsit, from her place at the backgammon board, was constantly straining her eyes to pierce the shadows without. "What's the matter, ma'am?" said Mr Bounderby; "you don't see a Fire, do you?" "Oh dear no, sir," returned Mrs Sparsit, "I was thinking of the dew." "What have you got to do with the dew, ma'am?" said Mr Bounderby. "It's not myself, sir," returned

Mrs Sparsit, "I am fearful of Miss Gradgrind's taking cold." "She never takes cold," said Mr Bounderby. "Really, sir?" said Mrs Sparsit. And was affected with a cough in her throat.

When the time drew near for retiring, Mr Bounderby took a glass of water. "Oh, sir?" said Mrs Sparsit. "Not your sherry warm, with lemon-peel and nutmeg?" "Why I have got out of the habit of taking it now, ma'am," said Mr Bounderby. "The more's the pity, sir," returned Mrs Sparsit; "you are losing all your good old habits. Cheer up, sir! If Miss Gradgrind will permit me, I will offer to make it for you, as I have often done."

Miss Gradgrind readily permitting Mrs Sparsit to do anything she pleased, that considerate lady made the beverage, and handed it to Mr Bounderby. "It will do you good, sir. It will warm your heart. It is the sort of thing you want, and ought to take, sir." And when Mr Bounderby said, "Your health, ma'am!" she answered with great feeling. "Thank you, sir. The same to you, and happiness also." Finally, she wished him good night, with great pathos; and Mr Bounderby went to bed, with a maudlin persuasion that he had been crossed in something tender, though he could not, for his life, have mentioned what it was.

Long after Louisa had undressed and lain down, she watched and waited for her brother's coming home. That could hardly be, she knew, until an hour past midnight; but in the country silence, which did anything but calm the trouble of her thoughts, time lagged wearily. At last, when the darkness and stillness had seemed for hours to thicken one another, she heard the bell at the gate. She felt as though she would have been glad that it rang on until daylight; but it ceased, and the circles of its last sound spread out fainter and wider in the air, and all was dead again.

She waited yet some quarter of an hour, as she judged. Then she arose, put on a loose robe, and went out of her room in the dark, and up the staircase to her brother's room. His door being shut, she softly opened it and spoke to him, approaching his bed with a noiseless step.

She kneeled down beside it, passed her arm over his neck, and drew his face to hers. She knew that he only feigned to be asleep, but she said nothing to him.

He started by and by as if he were just then awakened, and asked who that was, and what was the matter?

"Tom, have you anything to tell me? If ever you loved me in your life, and have anything concealed from every one besides, tell it to me."

"I don't know what you mean, Loo. You have been dreaming."

"My dear brother:" she laid her head down on his pillow, and her hair flowed over him as if she would hide him from every one but herself: "is there nothing that you have to tell me? Is there nothing you can tell me, if you will? You can tell me nothing that will change me. O Tom, tell me the truth!"

"I don't know what you mean, Loo!"

"As you lie here alone, my dear, in the melancholy night, so you must lie somewhere one night, when even I, if I am living then, shall have left you. As I am here beside you, barefoot, unclothed, undistinguishable in darkness, so must I lie through all the night of my decay, until I am dust. In the name of that time, Tom, tell me the truth now!"

"What is it you want to know?"

"You may be certain:" in the energy of her love she took him to her bosom as if he were a child: "that I will not reproach you. You may be certain that I will be compassionate and true to you. You may be certain that I will save you at whatever cost. O Tom, have you nothing to tell me? Whisper very softly. Say only 'yes,' and I shall understand you!"

She turned her ear to his lips, but he remained doggedly silent.

"Not a word, Tom?"

"How can I say Yes, or how can I say No, when I don't know what you mean? Loo, you are a brave, kind girl, worthy I begin to think of a better brother than I am. But I have nothing more to say. Go to bed, go to bed."

"You are tired," she whispered presently, more in her usual way.

"Yes, I am quite tired out."

"You have been so hurried and disturbed today. Have any fresh discoveries been made?"

"Only those you have heard of, from—him."

"Tom, have you said to any one that we made a visit to those people, and that we saw those three together?"

"No. Didn't you yourself particularly ask me to keep it quiet, when you asked me to go there with you?"

"Yes. But I did not know then what was going to happen."

"Nor I neither. How could I?"

He was very quick upon her with this retort.

"Ought I to say, after what has happened," said his sister, standing by the bed—she had gradually withdrawn herself and risen, "that I made that visit? Should I say so? Must I say so?"

"Good Heavens, Loo," returned her brother, "you are not in the habit of asking my advice. Say what you like. If you keep it to yourself, I shall keep it to *my*self. If you disclose it, there's an end of it."

It was too dark for either to see the other's face; but each seemed very attentive, and to consider before speaking.

"Tom, do you believe the man I gave the money to, is really implicated in this crime?"

"I don't know. I don't see why he shouldn't be."

"He seemed to me an honest man."

"Another person may seem to you dishonest, and yet not be so."

There was a pause, for he had hesitated and stopped.

"In short," resumed Tom, as if he had made up his mind, "if you come to that, perhaps I was so far from being altogether in his favour, that I took him outside the door to tell him quietly, that I thought he might consider himself very well off to get such a windfall as he had got from my sister, and that I hoped he would make good use of it. You remember whether I took him out or not. I say nothing against the man; he may be a very good fellow, for anything I know; I hope he is."

"Was he offended by what you said?"

"No, he took it pretty well; he was civil enough. Where are you, Loo?" He sat up in bed and kissed her. "Good night, my dear, good night!"

"You have nothing more to tell me?"

"No. What should I have? You wouldn't have me tell you a lie?"

"I wouldn't have you do that tonight, Tom, of all the nights in your life; many and much happier as I hope they will be."

"Thank you, my dear Loo. I am so tired, that I am sure I wonder I don't say anything, to get to sleep. Go to bed, go to bed."

Kissing her again, he turned round, drew the coverlet over his head, and lay as still as if that time had come by which she had adjured him. She stood for some time at the bedside before she slowly moved away. She stopped at the door, looked back when she had opened it, and asked him if he had called her? But he lay still, and she softly closed the door and returned to her room.

Then the wretched boy looked cautiously up and found her gone, crept out of bed, fastened his door, and threw himself upon his pillow again: tearing his hair, morosely crying, grudgingly loving her, hatefully but impenitently spurning himself, and no less hatefully and unprofitably spurning all the good in the world.

Chapter IX

HEARING THE LAST OF IT

M RS Sparsit, lying by to recover the tone of her nerves in Mr Bounderby's retreat, kept such a sharp look-out, night and day, under her Coriolanian eyebrows, that her eyes, like a couple of lighthouses on an iron-bound coast, might have warned all prudent mariners from that bold rock her Roman nose and the dark and craggy region in its neighbourhood, but for the placidity of her manner. Although it was hard to believe that her retiring for the night could be anything but a form, so severely wide awake were those classical eyes of hers, and so impossible did it seem that her rigid nose could yield to any relaxing influence, yet her manner of sitting, smoothing her uncomfortable, not to say, gritty, mittens (they were constructed of a cool fabric like a meat-safe), or of ambling to unknown places of destination with her foot in her cotton stirrup, was so perfectly serene, that most observers would have been constrained to suppose her a dove, embodied, by some freak of nature, in the earthly tabernacle of a bird of the hook-beaked order.

She was a most wonderful woman for prowling about the house. How she got from storey to storey, was a mystery beyond solution. A lady so decorous in herself, and so highly connected, was not to be suspected of dropping over the banisters or sliding down them, yet her extraordinary facility of locomotion suggested the wild idea. Another noticeable circumstance in Mrs Sparsit was, that she was never hurried. She would shoot with consummate velocity from the roof to the hall, yet would be in full possession of her breath and dignity on the moment of her arrival there. Neither was she ever seen by human vision to go at a great pace.

She took very kindly to Mr Harthouse, and had some pleasant conversation with him soon after her arrival. She made him her stately curtsey in the garden, one morning before breakfast.

"It appears but yesterday, sir," said Mrs Sparsit, "that I had the honour of receiving you at the Bank, when you were so good as to wish to be made acquainted with Mr Bounderby's address."

"An occasion, I am sure, not to be forgotten by myself in the course of Ages," said Mr Harthouse, inclining his head to Mrs Sparsit with the most indolent of all possible airs.

"We live in a singular world, sir," said Mrs Sparsit.

"I have had the honour, by a coincidence of which I am proud, to have made a remark, similar in effect, though not so epigrammatically expressed."

"A singular world, I would say, sir," pursued Mrs Sparsit; after acknowledging the compliment with a drooping of her dark eyebrows, not altogether so mild in its expression as her voice was in its dulcet tones; "as regards the intimacies we form at one time, with individuals we were quite ignorant of, at another. I recall, sir, that on that occasion you went so far as to say you were actually apprehensive of Miss Gradgrind."

"Your memory does me more honour than my insignificance deserves. I availed myself of your obliging hints to correct my timidity, and it is unnecessary to add that they were perfectly accurate. Mrs Sparsit's talent for—in fact for anything requiring accuracy—with a combination of strength of mind—and Family—is too habitually developed to admit of any question." He was almost falling asleep over this compliment; it took him so long to get through, and his mind wandered so much in the course of its execution.

"You found Miss Gradgrind—I really cannot call her Mrs Bounderby; it's very absurd of me—as youthful as I described her?" asked Mrs Sparsit, sweetly.

"You drew her portrait perfectly," said Mr Harthouse. "Presented her dead image."

"Very engaging, sir," said Mrs Sparsit, causing her mittens slowly to revolve over one another.

"Highly so."

"It used to be considered," said Mrs Sparsit, "that Miss Gradgrind was wanting in animation, but I confess she appears to me considerably and strikingly improved in that respect. Ay, and indeed here *is* Mr Bounderby!" cried Mrs Sparsit, nodding her head a great many times, as if she had been talking and thinking of no one else. "How do you find yourself this morning, sir? Pray let us see you cheerful, sir."

Now, these persistent assuagements of his misery, and lightenings of his load, had by this time begun to have the effect of making Mr Bounderby softer than usual towards Mrs Sparsit, and harder than usual to most other people from his wife downward. So, when Mrs Sparsit said with forced lightness of heart, "You want your breakfast, sir, but I daresay Miss Gradgrind will soon be here to preside at the table," Mr Bounderby replied, "If I waited to be taken care of by my wife, ma'am, I believe you know pretty well I should wait till Doomsday, so I'll trouble *you* to take charge of the teapot." Mrs Sparsit complied, and assumed her old position at table.

This again made the excellent woman vastly sentimental. She was so humble withal, that when Louisa appeared, she rose, protesting she never could think of sitting in that place under existing circumstances, often as she had had the honour of making Mr Bounderby's breakfast, before Mrs Gradgrind—she begged pardon, she meant to say, Miss Bounderby—she hoped to be excused, but she really could not get it right yet, though she trusted to become familiar with it by and by—had assumed her present position. It was only (she observed) because Miss Gradgrind happened to be a little late, and Mr Bounderby's time was so very precious, and she knew it of old to be so essential that he should breakfast to the moment, that she had taken the liberty of complying with his request: long as his will had been a law to her.

"There! Stop where you are, ma'am," said Mr Bounderby, "stop where you are! Mrs Bounderby will be very glad to be relieved of the trouble, I believe."

"Don't say that, sir," returned Mrs Sparsit, almost with severity, "because that is very unkind to Mrs Bounderby. And to be unkind is not to be you, sir."

"You may set your mind at rest, ma'am.—You can take it very quietly, can't you, Loo?" said Mr Bounderby, in a blustering way to his wife.

"Of course. It is of no moment. Why should it be of any importance to me?"

"Why should it be of any importance to any one, Mrs Sparsit, ma'am?" said Mr Bounderby, swelling with a sense of slight. "You attach too much importance to these things, ma'am. By George, you'll be corrupted in some of your notions here. You are old-fashioned, ma'am. You are behind Tom Gradgrind's children's time."

"What is the matter with you?" asked Louisa, coldly surprised. "What has given you offence?"

"Offence!" repeated Bounderby. "Do you suppose if there was any offence given me, I shouldn't name it, and request to have it corrected? I am a straightforward man, I believe. I don't go beating about for side-winds."

"I suppose no one ever had occasion to think you too diffident, or too delicate," Louisa answered him composedly: "I have never made that objection to you, either as a child or as a woman. I don't understand what you would have."

"Have?" returned Mr Bounderby. "Nothing. Otherwise, don't you, Loo Bounderby, know thoroughly well that I, Josiah Bounderby of Coketown, would have it?"

She looked at him, as he struck the table and made the teacups ring, with a proud colour in her face that was a new change, Mr Harthouse thought. "You are incomprehensible this morning," said Louisa. "Pray take no further trouble to explain yourself. I am not curious to know your meaning. What does it matter!"

Nothing more was said on this theme, and Mr Harthouse was soon idly gay on indifferent subjects. But from this day, the Sparsit action upon Mr Bounderby threw Louisa and James Harthouse more together, and strengthened the dangerous alienation from her husband and confidence against him with another, into which she had fallen by degrees so fine that she could not retrace them if she tried. But, whether she ever tried or no, lay hidden in her own closed heart.

Mrs Sparsit was so much affected on this particular occasion, that, assisting Mr Bounderby to his hat after breakfast, and being then alone with him in the hall, she imprinted a chaste kiss upon his hand, murmured "My benefactor!" and retired, over-whelmed with grief. Yet it is an indubitable fact, within the cognizance of this history, that five minutes after he had left the house in the self-same hat, the same descendant of the Scadgerses and connexion by matrimony of the Powlers, shook her right-hand mitten at his portrait, made a contemptuous grimace at that work of art, and said "Serve you right, you Noodle, and I am glad of it!"

Mr Bounderby had not been long gone, when Bitzer appeared. Bitzer had come down by train, shrieking and rattling over the long line of arches that bestrode the wild country of past and present coal-pits, with an express from Stone Lodge. It was a hasty note to inform Louisa, that Mrs Gradgrind lay very ill. She had never been well, within her daughter's knowledge; but, she had declined within the last few days, had continued sinking all through the night, and was now as nearly dead, as her limited capacity of being in any state that implied the ghost of an intention to get out of it, allowed.

Accompanied by the lightest of porters, fit colourless servitor at Death's door when Mrs Gradgrind knocked, Louisa rumbled to Coketown, over the coal-pits past and present, and was whirled into its smoky jaws. She dismissed the messenger to his own devices, and rode away to her old home.

She had seldom been there, since her marriage. Her father was usually sifting and sifting at his parliamentary cinder-heap in London (without being observed to turn up many precious articles among the rubbish), and was still hard at it in the national dust-yard. Her mother had taken it rather as a disturbance than otherwise, to be visited, as she reclined upon her sofa; young people, Louisa felt herself all unfit for; Sissy she had never softened to again, since the night when the stroller's child had raised her eyes to look at Mr Bounderby's intended wife. She had no inducements to go back, and had rarely gone.

Neither, as she approached her old home now, did any of the best influences of old home descend upon her. The dreams of childhood—its airy fables; its graceful, beautiful, humane, impossible adornments of the world beyond: so good to be believed in once, so good to be remembered when outgrown, for then the least among them rises to the stature of a great Charity in the heart, suffering little children to come into the midst of it, and to keep with their pure hands a garden in the stony ways of this world, wherein it were better for all the children of Adam that they should oftener sun themselves, simple and trustful, and not worldly-wise—what had she to do with these? Remembrances of how she had journeyed to the little that she knew, by the enchanted roads of what she and millions of innocent creatures had hoped and imagined; of how, first coming upon Reason through the tender light of Fancy, she had seen it a beneficent god, deferring to gods as great as itself: not a grim Idol, cruel and cold, with its victims bound hand to foot, and its big dumb shape set up with a sightless stare, never to be moved by anything but so many calculated tons of leverage—what had she to do with these? Her remembrances of home and childhood, were remembrances of the drying up of every spring and fountain in her young heart as it gushed out. The golden waters were not there. They were flowing for the fertilization of the land where grapes are gathered from thorns, and figs from thistles.

She went, with a heavy, hardened kind of sorrow upon her, into the house and into her mother's room. Since the time of her leaving home, Sissy had lived with the rest of the family on equal terms. Sissy was at her mother's side; and Jane, her sister, now ten or twelve years old, was in the room.

There was great trouble before it could be made known to Mrs Gradgrind that her eldest child was there. She reclined, propped up, from mere habit, on a couch: as nearly in her old usual attitude, as anything so helpless could be kept in. She had positively refused to take to her bed; on the ground that if she did, she would never hear the last of it.

Her feeble voice sounded so far away in her bundle of shawls, and the sound of another voice addressing her seemed to take such a long time in getting down to her ears, that she might have been lying at the bottom of a well. The poor lady was nearer Truth than she ever had been: which had much to do with it.

On being told that Mrs Bounderby was there, she replied, at cross-purposes, that she had never called him by that name since he married Louisa; that pending her choice of an unobjectionable name, she had called him J; and that she could not at present depart from that regulation, not being yet provided with a permanent substitute. Louisa had sat by her for some minutes, and had spoken to her often, before she arrived at a clear understanding who it was. She then seemed to come to it all at once.

"Well, my dear," said Mrs Gradgrind, "and I hope you are going on satisfactorily to yourself. It was all your father's doing. He set his heart upon it. And he ought to know."

"I want to hear of you, mother; not of myself."

"You want to hear of me, my dear? That's something new, I am sure, when anybody wants to hear of me. Not at all well, Louisa. Very faint and giddy."

"Are you in pain, dear mother?"

"I think there's a pain somewhere in the room," said Mrs Gradgrind, "but I couldn't positively say that I have got it."

After this strange speech, she lay silent for some time. Louisa holding her hand, could feel no pulse; but kissing it, could see a slight thin thread of life in fluttering motion.

"You very seldom see your sister," said Mrs Gradgrind. "She grows like you. I wish you would look at her. Sissy, bring her here."

She was brought, and stood with her hand in her sister's. Louisa had observed her with her arm round Sissy's neck, and she felt the difference of this approach.

"Do you see the likeness, Louisa?"

"Yes, mother. I should think her like me. But"—

"Eh? Yes, I always say so," Mrs Gradgrind cried, with unexpected quickness. "And that reminds me. I—I want to speak to you, my dear. Sissy, my good girl, leave us alone a minute."

Louisa had relinquished the hand: had thought that her sister's was a better and brighter face than hers had ever been: had seen in it, not without a rising feeling of resentment, even in that place and at that time, something of the gentleness of the other face in the room: the sweet face with the trusting eyes, made paler than watching and sympathy made it, by the rich dark hair.

Left alone with her mother, Louisa saw her lying with an awful lull upon her face, like one who was floating away upon some great water, all resistance over, content to be carried down the stream. She put the shadow of a hand to her lips again, and recalled her.

"You were going to speak to me, mother."

"Eh? Yes, to be sure, my dear. You know your father is almost always away now, and therefore I must write to him about it."

"About what, mother? Don't be troubled. About what?"

"You must remember, my dear, that whenever I have said anything, on any subject, I have never heard the last of it; and consequently, that I have long left off saying anything."

"I can hear you, mother." But, it was only by dint of bending down to her ear, and at the same time attentively watching the lips as they moved, that she could link such faint and broken sounds into any chain of connexion.

"You learnt a great deal, Louisa, and so did your brother. Ologies of all kinds, from morning to night. If there is any Ology left, of any description, that has not been worn to rags in this house, all I can say is, I hope I shall never hear its name."

"I can hear you, mother, when you have strength to go on." This, to keep her from floating away.

"But there is something—not an Ology at all—that your father has missed, or forgotten, Louisa. I don't know what it is. I have often sat with Sissy near me, and thought about it. I shall never get its name now. But your father may. It makes me restless. I want to write to him, to find out for God's sake, what it is. Give me a pen, give me a pen."

Even the power of restlessness was gone, except from the poor head, which could just turn from side to side.

She fancied, however, that her request had been complied with, and that the pen she could not have held was in her hand. It matters little what figures of wonderful no-meaning she began to trace upon her wrappers. The hand soon stopped in the midst of them; the light that had always been feeble and dim behind the weak transparency, went out; and even Mrs Gradgrind, emerged from the shadow in which man walketh and disquieteth himself in vain, took upon her the dread solemnity of the sages and patriarchs.

Chapter X

MRS SPARSIT'S STAIRCASE

MRS Sparsit's nerves being slow to recover their tone, the worthy woman made a stay of some weeks in duration at Mr Bounderby's retreat, where, notwithstanding her anchorite turn of mind based upon her becoming consciousness of her altered station, she resigned herself with noble fortitude, to lodging, as one may say, in clover, and feeding on the fat of the land. During the whole term of this recess from the guardianship of the Bank, Mrs Sparsit was a pattern of consistency; continuing to take such pity on Mr Bounderby to his face, as is rarely taken on man, and to call his portrait a Noodle to *its* face, with the greatest acrimony and contempt.

Mr Bounderby, having got it into his explosive composition that Mrs Sparsit was a highly superior woman to perceive that he had that general cross upon him in his deserts (for he had not yet settled what it was), and further that Louisa would have objected to her as a frequent visitor if it had comported with his greatness that she should object to anything he chose to do, resolved not to lose sight of Mrs Sparsit easily. So, when her nerves were strung up to the pitch of again consuming sweet-breads in solitude, he said to her at the dinner-table, on the day before her departure, "I tell you what, ma'am; you shall come down here of a Saturday while the fine weather lasts, and stay till Monday." To which Mrs Sparsit returned, in effect, though not of the Mahommedan persuasion: "To hear is to obey."

Now, Mrs Sparsit was not a poetical woman; but she took an idea, in the nature of an allegorical fancy, into her head. Much watching of Louisa, and much consequent observation of her impenetrable demeanour, which keenly whetted and sharpened Mrs Sparsit's edge, must have given her as it were a lift, in the way of inspiration. She erected in her mind a mighty Staircase, with a dark pit of shame and ruin at the bottom; and down those stairs, from day to day and hour to hour, she saw Louisa coming.

It became the business of Mrs Sparsit's life, to look up at her staircase, and to watch Louisa coming down. Sometimes slowly, sometimes quickly, sometimes several steps at one bout, sometimes stopping, never turning back. If she had once turned back, it might have been the death of Mrs Sparsit in spleen and grief.

She had been descending steadily, to the day, and on the day, when Mr Bounderby issued the weekly invitation recorded above. Mrs Sparsit was in good spirits, and inclined to be conversational.

"And pray, sir," said she, "if I may venture to ask a question appertaining to any subject on which you show reserve—which is indeed hardy in me, for I well know you have a reason for everything you do—have you received intelligence respecting the robbery?"

"Why, ma'am, no; not yet. Under the circumstances, I didn't expect it yet. Rome wasn't built in a day, ma'am."

"Very true, sir," said Mrs Sparsit, shaking her head.

"Nor yet in a week, ma'am."

"No, indeed, sir," returned Mrs Sparsit, with a gentle melancholy upon her.

"In a similar manner, ma'am," said Bounderby, "I can wait, you know. If Romulus and Remus could wait, Josiah Bounderby can wait. They were better off in their youth than I was, however. They had a she-wolf for a nurse; *I* had only a she-wolf for a grandmother. She didn't give any milk, ma'am; she gave bruises. She was a regular Alderney at that."

"Ah!" Mrs Sparsit sighed and shuddered.

"No, ma'am," continued Bounderby, "I have not heard anything more about it. It's in hand, though; and young Tom, who rather sticks to business at present—something new for him; he hadn't the schooling *I* had—is helping. My injunction is, Keep it quiet, and let it seem to blow over. Do what you like under the rose, but don't give a sign of what you're about; or half a hundred of 'em will combine together and get this fellow who has bolted, out of reach for good. Keep it quiet, and the thieves will grow in confidence by little and little, and we shall have 'em."

"Very sagacious indeed, sir," said Mrs Sparsit. "Very interesting. The old woman you mentioned, sir—"

"The old woman I mentioned, ma'am," said Bounderby, cutting the matter short, as it was nothing to boast about, "is not laid hold of; but, she may take her oath she will be, if that is any satisfaction to her villainous old mind. In the mean time, ma'am, I am of opinion, if you ask me my opinion, that the less she is talked about, the better."

That same evening, Mrs Sparsit, in her chamber window, resting from her packing operations, looked towards her great staircase and saw Louisa still descending.

She sat by Mr Harthouse, in an alcove in the garden, talking very low, he stood leaning over her, as they whispered together, and his face almost touched her hair. "If not quite!" said Mrs Sparsit, straining her hawk's eyes to the utmost. Mrs Sparsit was too distant to hear a word of their discourse, or even to know that they were speaking softly, otherwise than from the expression of their figures; but what they said was this:

"You recollect the man, Mr Harthouse?"

"Oh, perfectly!"

"His face, and his manner, and what he said?"

"Perfectly. And an infinitely dreary person he appeared to me to be. Lengthy and prosy in the extreme. It was knowing to hold forth, in the humble-virtue school of eloquence; but, I assure you I thought at the time, "My good fellow, you are over-doing this!' "

"It has been very difficult to me to think ill of that man."

"My dear Louisa—as Tom says." Which he never did say. "You know no good of the fellow?"

"No, certainly."

"Nor of any other such person?"

"How can I," she returned, with more of her first manner on her than he had lately seen, "when I know nothing of them, men or women?"

"My dear Louisa, then consent to receive the submissive representation of your devoted friend, who knows something of several varieties of his excellent fellow-creatures—for excellent they are, I am quite ready to believe, in spite of such little foibles as always helping themselves to what they can get hold of. This fellow talks. Well; every fellow talks. He professes morality. Well; all sorts of humbugs profess morality. From the House of Commons to the House of Correction, there is a general profession of morality, except among our people; it really is that exception which makes our people quite reviving. You saw and heard the case. Here was one of the fluffy classes pulled up extremely short by my esteemed friend Mr Bounderby—who, as we know, is not possessed of that delicacy which would soften so tight a hand. The member of the fluffy classes was injured, exasperated, left the house grumbling, met somebody who proposed to him to go in for some share in this Bank business, went in, put something in his pocket which had nothing in it before, and relieved his mind extremely. Really he would have been an uncommon, instead of a common, fellow, if he had not availed himself of such an opportunity. Or he may have originated it altogether, if he had the cleverness."

"I almost feel as though it must be bad in me," returned Louisa, after sitting thoughtful awhile, "to be so ready to agree with you, and to be so lightened in my heart by what you say."

"I only say what is reasonable; nothing worse. I have talked it over with my friend Tom more than once—of course I remain on terms of perfect confidence with Tom —and he is quite of my opinion, and I am quite of his. Will you walk?"

They strolled away, among the lanes beginning to be indistinct in the twilight—she leaning on his arm—and she little thought how she was going down, down, down, Mrs Sparsit's staircase.

Night and day, Mrs Sparsit kept it standing. When Louisa had arrived at the bottom and disappeared in the gulf, it might fall in upon her if it would; but, until then, there it was to be, a Building, before Mrs Sparsit's eyes. And there Louisa always was, upon it. And always gliding down, down, down!

Mrs Sparsit saw James Harthouse come and go; she heard of him here and there; she saw the changes of the face he had studied; she, too, remarked to a nicety how and when it clouded, how and when it cleared; she kept her black eyes wide open, with no touch of pity, with no touch of compunction, all absorbed in interest. In the interest of seeing her, ever drawing, with no hand to stay her, nearer and nearer to the bottom of this new Giants' Staircase.

With all her deference for Mr Bounderby as contra-distinguished from his portrait, Mrs Sparsit had not the smallest intention of interrupting the descent. Eager to see it accomplished, and yet patient, she waited for the last fall, as for the ripeness and fulness of the harvest of her hopes. Hushed in expectancy, she kept her wary gaze upon the stairs; and seldom so much as darkly shook her right mitten (with her fist in it), at the figure coming down.

Chapter XI

LOWER AND LOWER

THE figure descended the great stairs, steadily, steadily; always verging, like a weight in deep water, to the black gulf at the bottom.

Mr Gradgrind, apprised of his wife's decease, made an expedition from London, and buried her in a business-like manner. He then returned with promptitude to the national cinder-heap, and resumed his sifting for the odds and ends he wanted, and his throwing of the dust about into the eyes of other people who wanted other odds and ends—in fact, resumed his parliamentary duties.

In the meantime, Mrs Sparsit kept unwinking watch and ward. Separated from her staircase, all the week, by the length of iron road dividing Coketown from the country-house, she yet maintained her cat-like observation of Louisa, through her husband, through her brother, through James Harthouse, through the outsides of letters and packets, through everything animate and inanimate that at any time went near the stairs. "Your foot on the last step, my lady," said Mrs Sparsit, apostrophizing the descending figure, with the aid of her threatening mitten, "and all your art shall never blind me."

Art or nature though, the original stock of Louisa's character or the graft of circum-stances upon it,—her curious reserve did baffle, while it stimulated, one as sagacious as Mrs Sparsit. There were times when Mr James Harthouse was not sure of her. There were times when he could not read the face he had studied so long; and when this lonely girl was a greater mystery to him, than any woman of the world with a ring of satellites to help her.

So the time went on; until it happened that Mr Bounderby was called away from home by business which required his presence elsewhere, for three or four days. It was on a Friday that he intimated this to Mrs Sparsit at the Bank, adding: "But you'll go down tomorrow. ma'am, all the same. You'll go down just as if I was there. It will make no difference to you."

"Pray, sir," returned Mrs Sparsit, reproachfully, "let me beg you not to say that. Your absence will make a vast difference to me, sir, as I think you very well know."

"Well, ma'am, then you must get on in my absence as well as you can," said Bounderby, not displeased.

"Mr Bounderby," retorted Mrs Sparsit, "your will is to me a law, sir; otherwise, it might be my inclination to dispute your kind commands, not feeling sure that it will be quite so agreeable to Miss Gradgrind to receive me, as it ever is to your own munificent hospitality. But you shall say no more, sir. I will go, upon your invitation."

"Why, when I invite you to my house, ma'am," said Bounderby, opening his eyes, "I should hope you want no other invitation."

"No indeed, sir," returned Mrs Sparsit, "I should hope not. Say no more, sir. I would, sir, I could see you gay again."

"What do you mean, ma'am?" blustered Bounderby.

"Sir," rejoined Mrs Sparsit, "there was wont to be an elasticity in you which I sadly miss. Be buoyant, sir!"

Mr Bounderby, under the influence of this difficult adjuration, backed up by her compassionate eye, could only scratch his head in a feeble and ridiculous manner, and afterwards assert himself at a distance, by being heard to bully the small fry of business all the morning.

"Bitzer," said Mrs Sparsit that afternoon, when her patron was gone on his journey, and the Bank was closing, "present my compliments to young Mr Thomas, and ask him if he would step up and partake of a lamb chop and walnut ketchup, with a glass of India ale?" Young Mr Thomas being usually ready for anything in that way, returned a gracious answer, and followed on its heels. "Mr Thomas," said Mrs Sparsit, "these plain viands being on table, I thought you might be tempted." "Thank'ee, Mrs Sparsit," said the whelp. And gloomily fell to.

"How is Mr Harthouse, Mr Tom?" asked Mrs Sparsit.

"Oh, he's all right," said Tom.

"Where may he be at present?" Mrs Sparsit asked in a light conversational manner, after mentally devoting the whelp to the Furies for being so uncommunicative.

"He is shooting in Yorkshire," said Tom. "Sent Loo a basket half as big as a church, yesterday."

"The kind of gentleman, now," said Mrs Sparsit, sweetly, "whom one might wager to be a good shot!"

"Crack," said Tom.

He had long been a down-looking young fellow, but this characteristic had so increased of late, that he never raised his eyes to any face for three seconds together. Mrs Sparsit consequently had ample means of watching his looks, if she were so inclined.

"Mr Harthouse is a great favourite of mine," said Mrs Sparsit, "as indeed he is of most people. May we expect to see him again shortly, Mr Tom?"

"Why, I expect to see him tomorrow," returned the whelp.

"Good news!" cried Mrs Sparsit, blandly.

"I have got an appointment with him to meet him in the evening at the station here," said Tom, "and I am going to dine with him afterwards, I believe. He is not coming down to the country house for a week or so, being due somewhere else. At least, he says so; but I shouldn't wonder if he was to stop here over Sunday, and stray that way."

"Which reminds me!" said Mrs Sparsit. "Would you remember a message to your sister, Mr Tom, if I was to charge you with one?"

"Well? I'll try," returned the reluctant whelp, "if it isn't a long un."

"It is merely my respectful compliments," said Mrs Sparsit, "and I fear I may not trouble her with my society this week; being still a little nervous, and better perhaps by my poor self."

"Oh! If that's all," observed Tom, "it wouldn't much matter, even if I was to forget it, for Loo's not likely to think of you unless she sees you."

Having paid for his entertainment with this agreeable compliment, he relapsed into a hangdog silence until there was no more India ale left, when he said, "Well, Mrs Sparsit, I must be off!" and went off.

Next day, Saturday, Mrs Sparsit sat at her window all day long: looking at the customers coming in and out, watching the postmen, keeping an eye on the general traffic of the street, revolving many things in her mind, but, above all, keeping her attention on her staircase. The evening come, she put on her bonnet and shawl, and went quietly out: having her reasons for hovering in a furtive way about the station by which a passenger would arrive from Yorkshire, and for preferring to peep into it round pillars and corners, and out of ladies' waiting-room windows, to appearing in its precincts openly.

Tom was in attendance, and loitered about until the expected train came in. It brought no Mr Harthouse. Tom waited until the crowd had dispersed, and the bustle was over; and then referred to a posted list of trains, and took counsel with porters. That done, he strolled away idly, stopping in the street and looking up it and down it, and lifting his hat off and putting it on again, and yawning and stretching himself, and exhibiting all the symptoms of mortal weariness to be expected in one who had still to wait until the next train should come in, an hour and forty minutes hence.

"This is a device to keep him out of the way," said Mrs Sparsit, starting from the dull office window whence she had watched him last. "Harthouse is with his sister now!"

It was the conception of an inspired moment, and she shot off with her utmost swiftness to work it out. The station for the country house was at the opposite end of the town, the time was short, the road not easy; but she was so quick in pouncing on a disengaged coach, so quick in darting out of it, producing her money, seizing her ticket, and diving into the train, that she was borne along the arches spanning the land of coal-pits past and present, as if she had been caught up in a cloud and whirled away.

All the journey, immovable in the air though never left behind; plain to the dark eyes of her mind, as the electric wires which ruled a colossal strip of music-paper out of the evening sky, were plain to the dark eyes of her body; Mrs Sparsit saw her staircase, with the figure coming down. Very near the bottom now. Upon the brink of the abyss.

An overcast September evening, just at nightfall, saw beneath its drooping eyelid Mrs Sparsit glide out of her carriage, pass down the wooden steps of the little station into a stony road, cross it into a green lane, and become hidden in a summer-growth of leaves and branches. One or two late birds sleepily chirping in their nests, and a bat heavily crossing and recrossing her, and the reek of her own tread in the thick dust that felt like velvet, were all Mrs Sparsit heard or saw until she very softly closed a gate.

She went up to the house, keeping within the shrubbery, and went round it, peeping between the leaves at the lower windows. Most of them were open, as they usually were in such warm weather, but there were no lights yet, and all was silent. She tried the garden with no better effect. She thought of the wood, and stole towards it, heedless of long grass and briers: of worms, snails, and slugs, and all the creeping things that be. With her dark eyes and her hook nose warily in advance of her, Mrs Sparsit softly crushed her way through the thick undergrowth, so intent upon her object that she probably would have done no less, if the wood had been a wood of adders.

Hark!

The smaller birds might have tumbled out of their nests, fascinated by the glittering of Mrs Sparsit's eyes in the gloom, as she stopped and listened.

Low voices close at hand. His voice and hers. The appointment *was* a device to keep the brother away! There they were yonder, by the felled tree.

Bending low among the dewy grass, Mrs Sparsit advanced closer to them. She drew herself up, and stood behind a tree, like Robinson Crusoe in his ambuscade against the savages; so near to them that at a spring, and that no great one, she could have touched them both. He was there secretly, and had not shown himself at the house. He had come on horseback, and must have passed through the neighbouring fields; for his horse was tied to the meadow side of the fence, within a few paces.

"My dearest love," said he, "what could I do? Knowing you were alone, was it possible that I could stay away?"

"You may hang your head, to make yourself the more attractive; I don't know what they see in you when you hold it up," thought Mrs Sparsit; "but you little think, my dearest love, whose eyes are on you!"

That she hung her head, was certain. She urged him to go away, she commanded him to go away; but she neither turned her face to him, nor raised it. Yet it was remarkable that she sat as still, as ever the amiable woman in ambuscade had seen her sit, at any period in her life. Her hands rested in one another, like the hands of a statue; and even her manner of speaking was not hurried.

"My dear child," said Harthouse; Mrs Sparsit saw with delight that his arm embraced her; "will you not bear with my society for a little while?"

"Not here."

"Where, Louisa?"

"Not here."

"But we have so little time to make so much of, and I have come so far, and am altogether so devoted, and distracted. There never was a slave at once so devoted and ill-used by his mistress. To look for your sunny welcome that has warmed me into life, and to be received in your frozen manner, is heart-rending."

"Am I to say again, that I must be left to myself here?"

"But we must meet, my dear Louisa. Where shall we meet?"

They both started. The listener started guiltily, too; for she thought there was another listener among the trees. It was only rain, beginning to fall fast, in heavy drops.

"Shall I ride up to the house a few minutes hence, innocently supposing that its master is at home and will be charmed to receive me?"

"No!"

"Your cruel commands are implicitly to be obeyed; though I am the most unfortunate fellow in the world, I believe, to have been insensible to all other women, and to have fallen prostrate at last under the foot of the most beautiful, and the most engaging, and the most imperious. My dearest Louisa, I cannot go myself, or let you go, in this hard abuse of your power."

Mrs Sparsit saw him detain her with his encircling arm, and heard him then and there, within her (Mrs Sparsit's) greedy hearing, tell her how he loved her, and how she was the stake for which he ardently desired to play away all that he had in life. The objects he had lately pursued, turned worthless beside her; such success as was almost in his grasp, he flung away from him like the dirt it was, compared with her. Its pursuit, nevertheless, if it kept him near her, or its renunciation if it took him from her, or flight if she shared it, or secrecy if she commanded it, or any fate, or every fate, all was alike to him, so that she was true to him,—the man who had seen how cast away she was, whom she had inspired at their first meeting with an admiration, an interest, of which he had thought himself incapable, whom she had received into her confidence, who was devoted to her and adored her. All this, and more, in his hurry, and in hers, in the whirl of her own gratified malice, in the dread of being discovered, in the rapidly increasing noise of heavy rain among the leaves, and a thunder-storm rolling up—Mrs Sparsit received into her mind, set off with such an unavoidable halo of confusion and indistinctness, that when at length he climbed the fence and led his horse away, she was not sure where they were to meet, or when, except that they had said it was to be that night.

But one of them yet remained in the darkness before her; and while she tracked that one she must be right. "Oh, my dearest love," thought Mrs Sparsit, "you little think how well attended you are."

Mrs Sparsit saw her out of the wood, and saw her enter the house. What to do next? It rained now, in a sheet of water. Mrs Sparsit's white stockings were of many colours, green predominating; prickly things were in her shoes; caterpillars slung themselves, in hammocks of their own making, from various parts of her dress; rills ran from her bonnet, and her Roman nose. In such condition, Mrs Sparsit stood hidden in the density of the shrubbery, considering what next?

Lo, Louisa coming out of the house! Hastily cloaked and muffled, and stealing away. She elopes! She falls from the lowermost stair, and is swallowed up in the gulf!

Indifferent to the rain, and moving with a quick determined step, she struck into a side-path parallel with the ride. Mrs Sparsit followed in the shadow of the trees, at but a short distance; for it was not easy to keep a figure in view going quickly through the umbrageous darkness.

When she stopped to close the side-gate without noise, Mrs Sparsit stopped. When she went on, Mrs Sparsit went on. She went by the way Mrs Sparsit had come, emerged from the green lane, crossed the stony road, and ascended the wooden steps to the railroad. A train for Coketown would come through presently, Mrs Sparsit knew; so she understood Coketown to be her first place of destination.

In Mrs Sparsit's limp and streaming state, no extensive precautions were necessary to change her usual appearance; but, she stopped under the lee of the station wall, tumbled her shawl into a new shape, and put it on over her bonnet. So disguised, she had no fear of being recognized when she followed up the railroad steps, and paid her money in the small office. Louisa sat waiting in a corner. Mrs Sparsit sat waiting in another corner. Both listened to the thunder, which was loud, and to the rain, as it washed off the roof, and pattered on the parapets of the arches. Two or three lamps were rained out and blown out; so, both saw the lightning to advantage as it quivered and zig-zagged on the iron tracks.

The seizure of the station with a fit of trembling, gradually deepening to a complaint of the heart, announced the train. Fire and steam, and smoke, and red light; a hiss, a crash, a bell, and a shriek; Louisa put into one carriage, Mrs Sparsit put into another: the little station a desert speck in the thunder-storm.

Though her teeth chattered in her head from wet and cold, Mrs Sparsit exulted hugely. The figure had plunged down the precipice, and she felt herself, as it were, attending on the body. Could she, who had been so active in the getting up of the funeral triumph, do less than exult? "She will be at Coketown long before him," thought Mrs Sparsit, "though his horse is never so good. Where will she wait for him? And where will they go together? Patience. We shall see."

The tremendous rain occasioned infinite confusion, when the train stopped at its destination. Gutters and pipes had burst, drains had overflowed, and streets were under water. In the first instant of alighting, Mrs Sparsit turned her distracted eyes towards the waiting coaches, which were in great request. "She will get into one," she considered, "and will be away before I can follow in another. At all risks of being run over, I must see the number, and hear the order given to the coachman."

But Mrs Sparsit was wrong in her calculation. Louisa got into no coach, and was already gone. The black eyes kept upon the railroad-carriage in which she had travelled, settled upon it a moment too late. The door not being opened after several minutes, Mrs Sparsit passed it and repassed it, saw nothing, looked in, and found it empty. Wet through and through: with her feet squelching and squashing in her shoes whenever she moved; with a rash of rain upon her classical visage; with a bonnet like an over-ripe fig; with all her clothes spoiled; with damp impressions of every button, string, and hook-and-eye she wore, printed off upon her highly-connected back; with a stagnant verdure on her general exterior, such as accumulates on an old park fence in a mouldy lane; Mrs Sparsit had no resource but to burst into tears of bitterness and say, "I have lost her!"

Chapter XII

DOWN

T HE national dustmen, after entertaining one another with a great many noisy little fights among themselves, had dispersed for the present, and Mr Gradgrind was at home for the vacation.

He sat writing in the room with the deadly-statistical clock, proving something no doubt—probably, in the main, that the Good Samaritan was a Bad Economist. The noise of the rain did not disturb him much; but it attracted his attention sufficiently to make him raise his head sometimes, as if he were rather remonstrating with the elements. When it thundered very loudly, he glanced towards Coketown, having it in his mind that some of the tall chimneys might be struck by lightning.

The thunder was rolling into distance, and the rain was pouring down like a deluge, when the door of his room opened. He looked round the lamp upon his table, and saw, with amazement, his eldest daughter.

"Louisa!"

"Father, I want to speak to you."

"What is the matter? How strange you look! And good Heaven," said Mr Gradgrind, wondering more and more, "have you come here exposed to this storm?"

She put her hands to her dress, as if she hardly knew. "Yes." Then she uncovered her head, and letting her cloak and hood fall where they might, stood looking at him: so colourless, so dishevelled, so defiant and despairing, that he was afraid of her.

"What is it? I conjure you, Louisa, tell me what is the matter."

She dropped into a chair before him, and put her cold hand on his arm.

"Father, you have trained me from my cradle."

"Yes, Louisa."

"I curse the hour in which I was born to such a destiny."

He looked at her in doubt and dread, vacantly repeating, "Curse the hour? Curse the hour?"

"How could you give me life, and take from me all the inappreciable things that raise it from the state of conscious death? Where are the graces of my soul? Where are the sentiments of my heart? What have you done, O father, what have you done, with the garden that should have bloomed once, in this great wilderness here!"

She struck herself with both her hands upon her bosom.

"If it had ever been here, its ashes alone would save me from the void in which my whole life sinks. I did not mean to say this; but, father, you remember the last time we conversed in this room?"

He had been so wholly unprepared for what he heard now, that it was with difficulty he answered, "Yes, Louisa."

"What has risen to my lips now, would have risen to my lips then, if you had given me a moment's help. I don't reproach you, father. What you have never nurtured in me, you have never nurtured in yourself; but O! if you had only done so long ago, or if you had only neglected me, what a much better and much happier creature I should have been this day!"

On hearing this, after all his care, he bowed his head upon his hand and groaned aloud.

"Father, if you had known, when we were last together here, what even I feared while I strove against it—as it has been my task from infancy to strive against every natural prompting that has arisen in my heart; if you had known that there lingered in my breast, sensibilities, affections, weaknesses capable of being cherished into strength, defying all the calculations ever made by man, and no more known to his arithmetic than his Creator is,—would you have given me to the husband whom I am now sure that I hate?"

He said, "No. No, my poor child."

"Would you have doomed me, at any time, to the frost and blight that have hardened and spoiled me? Would you have robbed me—for no one's enrichment—only for the greater desolation of this world—of the immaterial part of my life, the spring and summer of my belief, my refuge from what is sordid and bad in the real things around me, my school in which I should have learned to be more humble and more trusting with them, and to hope in my little sphere to make them better?"

"O no, no. No, Louisa."

"Yet, father, if I had been stone blind; if I had groped my way by my sense of touch, and had been free, while I knew the shapes and surfaces of things, to exercise my fancy somewhat, in regard to them; I should have been a million times wiser, happier, more loving, more contented, more innocent and human in all good respects, than I am with the eyes I have. Now, hear what I have come to say."

He moved, to support her with his arm. She rising as he did so, they stood close together: she, with a hand upon his shoulder, looking fixedly in his face.

"With a hunger and thirst upon me, father, which have never been for a moment appeased; with an ardent impulse towards some region where rules, and figures, and definitions were not quite absolute; I have grown up, battling every inch of my way."

"I never knew you were unhappy, my child."

"Father, I always knew it. In this strife I have almost repulsed and crushed my better angel into a demon. What I have learned has left me doubting, misbelieving, despising, regretting, what I have not learned; and my dismal resource has been to think that life would soon go by, and that nothing in it could be worth the pain and trouble of a contest."

"And you so young, Louisa!" he said with pity.

"And I so young. In this condition, father—for I show you now, without fear or favour, the ordinary deadened state of my mind as I know it—you proposed my husband to me. I took him. I never made a pretence to him or you that I loved him. I knew, and, father, you knew, and he knew, that I never did. I was not wholly indifferent, for I had a hope of being pleasant and useful to Tom. I made that wild escape into something visionary, and have slowly found out how wild it was. But Tom had been the subject of all the little tenderness of my life; perhaps he became so because I knew so well how to pity him. It matters little now, except as it may dispose you to think more leniently of his errors."

As her father held her in his arms, she put her other hand upon his other shoulder, and still looking fixedly in his face, went on.

"When I was irrevocably married, there rose up into rebellion against the tie, the old strife, made fiercer by all those causes of disparity which arise out of our two individual natures, and which no general laws shall ever rule or state for me, father, until they shall be able to direct the anatomist where to strike his knife into the secrets of my soul."

"Louisa!" he said, and said imploringly; for he well remembered what had passed between them in their former interview.

"I do not reproach you, father, I make no complaint. I am here with another object."

"What can I do, child? Ask me what you will."

"I am coming to it. Father, chance then threw into my way a new acquaintance; a man such as I had had no experience of; used to the world; light, polished, easy; making no pretences; avowing the low estimate of everything, that I was half afraid to form in secret; conveying to me almost immediately, though I don't know how or by what degrees, that he understood me, and read my thoughts. I could not find that he was worse than I. There seemed to be a near affinity between us. I only wondered it should be worth his while, who cared for nothing else, to care so much for me."

"For you, Louisa!"

Her father might instinctively have loosened his hold, but that he felt her strength departing from her, and saw a wild dilating fire in the eyes steadfastly regarding him.

"I say nothing of his plea for claiming my confidence. It matters very little how he gained it. Father, he did gain it. What you know of the story of my marriage, he soon knew, just as well."

Her father's face was ashy white, and he held her in both his arms.

"I have done no worse, I have not disgraced you. But if you ask me whether I have loved him, or do love him, I tell you plainly, father, that it may be so. I don't know!"

She took her hands suddenly from his shoulders and pressed them both upon her side; while in her face, not like itself—and in her figure, drawn up, resolute to finish by a last effort what she had to say—the feelings long suppressed broke loose.

"This night, my husband being away, he has been with me, declaring himself my lover. This minute he expects me, for I could release myself of his presence by no other means. I do not know that I am sorry, I do not know that I am ashamed, I do not know that I am degraded in my own esteem. All that I know is, your philosophy and your teaching will not save me. Now, father, you have brought me to this. Save me by some other means!"

He tightened his hold in time to prevent her sinking on the floor, but she cried out in a terrible voice, "I shall die if you hold me! Let me fall upon the ground!" And he laid her down there, and saw the pride of his heart and the triumph of his system, lying, an insensible heap, at his feet.

BOOK THE THIRD

Garnering

Chapter I

ANOTHER THING NEEDFUL

LOUISA awoke from a torpor, and her eyes languidly opened on her old bed at home, and her old room. It seemed, at first, as if all that had happened since the days when these objects were familiar to her were the shadows of a dream; but gradually, as the objects became more real to her sight, the events became more real to her mind.

She could scarcely move her head for pain and heaviness, her eyes were strained and sore, and she was very weak. A curious passive inattention had such possession of her, that the presence of her little sister in the room did not attract her notice for some time. Even when their eyes had met, and her sister had approached the bed, Louisa lay for minutes looking at her in silence, and suffering her timidly to hold her passive hand, before she asked:

"When was I brought to this room?"

"Last night, Louisa."

"Who brought me here?"

"Sissy, I believe."

"Why do you believe so?"

"Because I found her here this morning. She didn't come to my bedside to wake me, as she always does; and I went to look for her. She was not in her own room either; and I went looking for her all over the house, until I found her here, taking care of you and cooling your head. Will you see father? Sissy said I was to tell him when you woke."

"What a beaming face you have, Jane!" said Louisa, as her young sister—timidly still—bent down to kiss her.

"Have I? I am very glad you think so. I am sure it must be Sissy's doing."

The arm Louisa had begun to twine about her neck, unbent itself. "You can tell father, if you will." Then, staying her a moment, she said, "It was you who made my room so cheerful, and gave it this look of welcome?"

"Oh no, Louisa, it was done before I came. It was—"

Louisa turned upon her pillow, and heard no more. When her sister had withdrawn, she turned her head back again, and lay with her face towards the door, until it opened and her father entered.

He had a jaded anxious look upon him, and his hand, usually steady, trembled in hers. He sat down at the side of the bed, tenderly asking how she was, and dwelling on the necessity of her keeping very quiet after her agitation and exposure to the weather last night. He spoke in a subdued and troubled voice, very different from his usual dictatorial manner; and was often at a loss for words.

"My dear Louisa. My poor daughter." He was so much at a loss at that place, that he stopped altogether. He tried again.

"My unfortunate child." The place was so difficult to get over, that he tried again.

"It would be hopeless for me, Louisa, to endeavour to tell you how overwhelmed

I have been, and still am, by what broke upon me last night. The ground on which I stand has ceased to be solid under my feet. The only support on which I leaned, and the strength of which it seemed and still does seem, impossible to question, has given way in an instant. I am stunned by these discoveries. I have no selfish meaning in what I say; but I find the shock of what broke upon me last night, to be very heavy indeed."

She could give him no comfort herein. She had suffered the wreck of her whole life upon the rock.

"I will not say, Louisa, that if you had by any happy chance undeceived me some time ago, it would have been better for us both; better for your peace, and better for mine. For I am sensible that it may not have been a part of my system to invite any confidence of that kind. I have proved my—my system to myself, and I have rigidly administered it; and I must bear the responsibility of its failures. I only entreat you to believe, my favourite child, I have meant to do right."

He said it earnestly, and to do him justice he had. In gauging fathomless deeps with his little mean excise-rod, and in staggering over the universe with his rusty stiff-legged compasses, he had meant to do great things. Within the limits of his short tether he had tumbled about, annihilating the flowers of existence with greater singleness of purpose than many of the blatant personages whose company he kept.

"I am well assured of what you say, father. I know I have been your favourite child. I know you have intended to make me happy. I have never blamed you, and I never shall."

He took her outstretched hand, and retained it in his.

"My dear, I have remained all night at my table, pondering again and again on what has so painfully passed between us. When I consider your character; when I consider that what has been known to me for hours, has been concealed by you for years; when I consider under what immediate pressure it has been forced from you at last; I come to the conclusion that I cannot but mistrust myself."

He might have added more than all, when he saw the face now looking at him. He did add it in effect, perhaps, as he softly moved her scattered hair from her forehead with his hand. Such little actions, slight in another man, were very noticeable in him; and his daughter received them as if they had been words of contrition.

"But," said Mr Gradgrind, slowly, and with hesitation, as well as with a wretched sense of helplessness, "if I see reason to mistrust myself for the past, Louisa, I should also mistrust myself for the present and the future. To speak unreservedly to you, I do. I am far from feeling convinced now, however differently I might have felt only this time yesterday, that I am fit for the trust you repose in me; that I know how to respond to the appeal you have come home to make to me; that I have the right instinct—supposing it for the moment to be some quality of that nature—how to help you, and to set you right, my child."

She had turned upon her pillow, and lay with her face upon her arm, so that he could not see it. All her wildness and passion had subsided; but, though softened, she was not in tears. Her father was changed in nothing so much as in the respect that he would have been glad to see her in tears.

"Some persons hold," he pursued, still hesitating, "that there is a wisdom of the Head, and that there is a wisdom of the Heart. I have not supposed so; but, as I have said, I mistrust myself now. I have supposed the Head to be all-sufficient. It may not be all-sufficient; how can I venture this morning to say it is! If that other kind of wisdom should be what I have neglected, and should be the instinct that is wanted, Louisa—"

He suggested it very doubtfully, as if he were half unwilling to admit it even now. She made him no answer; lying before him on her bed, still half-dressed, much as he had seen her lying on the floor of his room last night.

"Louisa," and his hand rested on her hair again, "I have been absent from here, my dear, a good deal of late; and though your sister's training has been pursued according to—the system," he appeared to come to that word with great reluctance always, "it has necessarily been modified by daily associations begun, in her case, at an early age. I ask you—ignorantly and humbly, my daughter—for the better, do you think?"

"Father," she replied, without stirring, "if any harmony has been awakened in her young breast that was mute in mine until it turned to discord, let her thank Heaven for it, and go upon her happier way, taking it as her greatest blessing that she has avoided my way."

"O my child, my child!" he said, in a forlorn manner, "I am an unhappy man to see you thus! What avails it to me that you do not reproach me, if I so bitterly reproach myself!" He bent his head, and spoke low to her. "Louisa, I have a misgiving that some change may have been slowly working about me in this house, by mere love and gratitude; that what the Head had left undone and could not do, the Heart may have been doing silently. Can it be so?"

She made him no reply.

"I am not too proud to believe it, Louisa. How could I be arrogant, and you before me! Can it be so? Is it so, my dear?"

He looked upon her, once more, lying cast away there; and without another word went out of the room. He had not been long gone, when she heard a light tread near the door, and knew that some one stood beside her.

She did not raise her head. A dull anger that she should be seen in her distress, and that the involuntary look she had so resented should come to this fulfilment, smouldered within her like an unwholesome fire. All closely imprisoned forces rend and destroy. The air that would be healthful to the earth, the water that would enrich it, the heat that would ripen it, tear it when caged up. So in her bosom even now; the strongest qualities she possessed, long turned upon themselves, became a heap of obduracy, that rose against a friend.

It was well that soft touch came upon her neck, and that she understood herself to be supposed to have fallen asleep. The sympathetic hand did not claim her resentment. Let it lie there, let it lie.

It lay there, warming into life a crowd of gentler thoughts; and she rested. As she softened with the quiet, and the consciousness of being so watched, some tears made their way into her eyes. The face touched hers, and she knew that there were tears upon it too, and she the cause of them.

As Louisa feigned to rouse herself, and sat up, Sissy retired, so that she stood placidly near the bed-side.

"I hope I have not disturbed you. I have come to ask if you would let me stay with you."

"Why should you stay with me? My sister will miss you. You are everything to her."

"Am I?" returned Sissy, shaking her head. "I would be something to you, if I might."

"What?" said Louisa, almost sternly.

"Whatever you want most, if I could be that. At all events, I would like to try to be as near it as I can. And however far off that may be, I will never tire of trying. Will you let me?"

"My father sent you to ask me."

"No indeed," replied Sissy. "He told me that I might come in now, but he sent me away from the room this morning—or at least—" She hesitated and stopped.

"At least, what?" said Louisa, with her searching eyes upon her.

"I thought it best myself that I should be sent away, for I felt very uncertain whether you would like to find me here."

"Have I always hated you so much?"

"I hope not, for I have always loved you, and have always wished that you should know it. But you changed to me a little, shortly before you left home. Not that I wondered at it. You knew so much, and I knew so little, and it was so natural in many ways, going as you were among other friends, that I had nothing to complain of, and was not at all hurt."

Her colour rose as she said it modestly and hurriedly. Louisa understood the loving pretence, and her heart smote her.

"May I try?" said Sissy, emboldened to raise her hand to the neck that was insensibly drooping towards her.

Louisa, taking down the hand that would have embraced her in another moment, held it in one of hers, and answered:

"First, Sissy, do you know what I am? I am so proud and so hardened, so confused and so troubled, so resentful and unjust to every one and to myself, that everything is stormy, dark, and wicked to me. Does not that repel you?"

"No!"

"I am so unhappy, and all that should have made me otherwise is so laid waste, that if I had been bereft of sense to this hour, and instead of being as learned as you think me, had to begin to acquire the simplest truths, I could not want a guide to peace, contentment, honour, all the good of which I am quite devoid, more abjectly than I do. Does not that repel you?"

"No!"

In the innocence of her brave affection, and the brimming up of her old devoted spirit, the once deserted girl shone like a beautiful light upon the darkness of the other.

Louisa raised the hand that it might clasp her neck, and join its fellow there. She fell upon her knees, and clinging to this stroller's child looked up at her almost with veneration.

"Forgive me, pity me, help me! Have compassion on my great need, and let me lay this head of mine upon a loving heart!"

"O lay it here!" cried Sissy. "Lay it here, my dear."

Chapter II

VERY RIDICULOUS

MR James Harthouse passed a whole night and a day in a state of so much hurry, that the World, with its best glass in its eye, would scarcely have recognized him during that insane interval, as the brother Jem of the honourable and jocular member. He was positively agitated. He several times spoke with an emphasis, similar to the vulgar manner. He went in and went out in an unaccountable way, like a man without an object. He rode like a highwayman. In a word, he was so horribly bored by existing circumstances, that he forgot to go in for boredom in the manner prescribed by the authorities.

After putting his horse at Coketown through the storm, as if it were a leap, he waited up all night: from time to time ringing his bell with the greatest fury, charging the porter who kept watch with delinquency in withholding letters or messages that could not fail to have been entrusted to him, and demanding restitution on the spot. The dawn coming, the morning coming, and the day coming, and neither message nor letter coming with either, he went down to the country-house. There, the report was, Mr Bounderby away, and Mrs Bounderby in town. Left for town suddenly last evening. Not even known to be gone until receipt of message, importing that her return was not to be expected for the present.

In these circumstances he had nothing for it but to follow her to town. He went to the house in town. Mrs Bounderby not there. He looked in at the Bank. Mr Bounderby away, and Mrs Sparsit away. Mrs Sparsit away? Who could have been reduced to sudden extremity for the company of that griffin!

"Well! I don't know," said Tom, who had his own reasons for being uneasy about it. "She was off somewhere at daybreak this morning. She's always full of mystery; I hate her. So I do that white chap; he's always got his blinking eyes upon a fellow."

"Where were you last night, Tom?"

"Where was I last night!" said Tom. "Come! I like that. I was waiting for you, Mr Harthouse, till it came down as *I* never saw it come down before. Where was I too! Where were you, you mean."

"I was prevented from coming—detained."

"Detained!" murmured Tom. "Two of us were detained. I was detained looking for you, till I lost every train but the mail. It would have been a pleasant job to go down by that on such a night, and have to walk home through a pond. I was obliged to sleep in town after all."

"Where?"

"Where? Why, in my own bed at Bounderby's."

"Did you see your sister?"

"How the deuce," returned Tom, staring, "could I see my sister when she was fifteen miles off?"

Cursing these quick retorts of the young gentleman to whom he was so true a friend, Mr Harthouse disembarrassed himself of that interview with the smallest conceivable amount of ceremony, and debated for the hundredth time what all this could mean? He made only one thing clear. It was, that whether she was in town or out of town, whether he had been premature with her who was so hard to comprehend, or she had lost courage, or they were discovered, or some mischance or mistake, at present incomprehensible had occurred, he must remain to confront his fortune, whatever it was. The hotel where he was known to live when condemned to that region of blackness, was the stake to which he was tied. As to all the rest—What will be, will be.

"So, whether I am waiting for a hostile message, or an assignation, or a penitent remonstrance, or an impromptu wrestle with my friend Bounderby in the Lancashire manner—which would seem as likely as anything else in the present state of affairs—I'll dine," said Mr James Harthouse. "Bounderby has the advantage in point of weight; and if anything of a British nature is to come off between us, it may be as well to be in training."

Therefore he rang the bell, and tossing himself negligently on a sofa, ordered "Some dinner at six—with a beefsteak in it," and got through the intervening time as well as he could. That was not particularly well; for he remained in the greatest perplexity, and, as the hours went on, and no kind of explanation offered itself, his perplexity augmented at compound interest.

However, he took affairs as coolly as it was in human nature to do, and entertained himself with the facetious idea of the training more than once. "It wouldn't be bad," he yawned at one time, "to give the waiter five shillings, and throw him." At another time it occurred to him, "Or a fellow of about thirteen or fourteen stone might be hired by the hour." But these jests did not tell materially on the afternoon, or his suspense; and, sooth to say, they both lagged fearfully.

It was impossible, even before dinner, to avoid often walking about in the pattern of the carpet, looking out of the window, listening at the door for footsteps, and occasionally becoming rather hot when any steps approached that room. But, after dinner, when the day turned to twilight, and the twilight turned to night, and still no communication was made to him, it began to be as he expressed it, "like the Holy Office and slow torture." However, still true to his conviction that indifference was the genuine high-breeding (the only conviction he had), he seized this crisis as the opportunity for ordering candles and a newspaper.

He had been trying in vain, for half an hour, to read this newspaper, when the waiter appeared and said, at once mysteriously and apologetically:

"Beg your pardon, sir. You're wanted, sir, if you please."

A general recollection that this was the kind of thing the Police said to the swell mob, caused Mr Harthouse to ask the waiter in return, with bristling indignation, what the Devil he meant by "wanted"?

"Beg your pardon, sir. Young lady outside, sir, wishes to see you."

"Outside? Where?"

"Outside this door, sir."

Giving the waiter to the personage before-mentioned, as a blockhead duly qualified for that consignment, Mr Harthouse hurried into the gallery. A young woman whom he had never seen stood there. Plainly dressed, very quiet, very pretty. As he conducted her into the room and placed a chair for her, he observed, by the light of the candles, that she was even prettier than he had at first believed. Her face was innocent and youthful, and its expression remarkably pleasant. She was not afraid of him, or in any way disconcerted; she seemed to have her mind entirely preoccupied with the occasion of her visit, and to have substituted that consideration for herself.

"I speak to Mr Harthouse?" she said, when they were alone.

"To Mr Harthouse." He added in his mind, "And you speak to him with the most confiding eyes I ever saw, and the most earnest voice (though so quiet) I ever heard."

"If I do not understand—and I do not, sir"—said Sissy, "what your honour as a gentleman binds you to, in other matters:" the blood really rose in his face as she began in these words: "I am sure I may rely upon it to keep my visit secret, and to keep secret what I am going to say. I will rely upon it, if you will tell me I may so far trust—"

"You may, I assure you."

"I am young, as you see; I am alone, as you see. In coming to you, sir, I have no advice or encouragement beyond my own hope."

He thought, "But that is very strong," as he followed the momentary upward glance of her eyes. He thought besides, "This is a very odd beginning. I don't see where we are going."

"I think," said Sissy, "you have already guessed whom I left just now?"

"I have been in the greatest concern and uneasiness during the last four-and-twenty hours (which have appeared as many years)," he returned, "on a lady's account. The hopes I have been encouraged to form that you come from that lady, do not deceive me, I trust."

"I left her within an hour."

"At—?"

"At her father's."

Mr Harthouse's face lengthened in spite of his coolness, and his perplexity increased. "Then I certainly," he thought, "do *not* see where we are going."

"She hurried there last night. She arrived there in great agitation, and was insensible all through the night. I live at her father's, and was with her. You may be sure, sir, you will never see her again as long as you live."

Mr Harthouse drew a long breath; and, if ever man found himself in the position of not knowing what to say, made the discovery beyond all question that he was so circumstanced. The child-like ingenuousness with which his visitor spoke, her modest fearlessness, her truthfulness which put all artifice aside, her entire forgetfulness of herself in her earnest quiet holding to the object with which she had come; all this, together with her reliance on his easily-given promise—which in itself shamed him—presented something in which he was so inexperienced, and against which he knew any of his usual weapons would fall so powerless; that not a word could he rally to his relief.

At last he said:

"So startling an announcement, so confidently made, and by such lips, is really disconcerting in the last degree. May I be permitted to inquire, if you are charged to convey that information to me in those hopeless words, by the lady of whom we speak."

"I have no charge from her."

"The drowning man catches at the straw. With no disrespect for your judgement, and with no doubt of your sincerity, excuse my saying that I cling to the belief that there is yet hope that I am not condemned to perpetual exile from that lady's presence."

"There is not the least hope. The first object of my coming here, sir, is to assure you that you must believe that there is no more hope of your ever speaking with her again, than there would be if she had died when she came home last night."

"Must believe? But if I can't—or if I should, by infirmity of nature, be obstinate—and won't—"

"It is still true. There is no hope."

James Harthouse looked at her with an incredulous smile upon his lips; but her mind looked over and beyond him, and the smile was quite thrown away.

He bit his lip, and took a little time for consideration.

"Well! If it should unhappily appear," he said, "after due pains and duty on my part, that I am brought to a position so desolate as this banishment, I shall not become the lady's persecutor. But you said you had no commission from her?"

"I have only the commission of my love for her, and her love for me. I have no other trust, than that I have been with her since she came home, and that she has given me her confidence. I have no further trust, than that I know something of her character and her marriage. O Mr Harthouse, I think you had that trust too!"

He was touched in the cavity where his heart should have been—in that nest of addled eggs, where the birds of heaven would have lived if they had not been whistled away—by the fervour of this reproach.

"I am not a moral sort of fellow," he said, "and I never make any pretensions to the character of a moral sort of fellow. I am as immoral as need be. At the same time, in bringing any distress upon the lady who is the subject of the present conversation, or in unfortunately compromising her in any way, or in committing myself by any expression of sentiments towards her, not perfectly reconcilable with—in fact with—the domestic hearth; or in taking any advantage of her father's being a machine, or of her brother's being a whelp, or of her husband's being a bear; I beg to be allowed to assure you that I have had no particularly evil intentions, but have glided on from one step to another with a smoothness so perfectly diabolical, that I had not the slightest idea the catalogue was half so long until I began to turn it over. Whereas I find," said Mr James Harthouse, in conclusion, "that it is really in several volumes."

Though he said all this in his frivolous way, the way seemed, for that once, a conscious polishing of but an ugly surface. He was silent for a moment; and then proceeded with a more self-possessed air, though with traces of vexation and disappointment that would not be polished out.

"After what has been just now represented to me, in a manner I find it impossible to doubt—I know of hardly any other source from which I could have accepted it so readily—I feel bound to say to you, in whom the confidence you have mentioned has been reposed, that I cannot refuse to contemplate the possibility (however unexpected) of my seeing the lady no more. I am solely to blame for the thing having come to this—and—and, I cannot say," he added, rather hard up for a general peroration, "that I have any sanguine expectation of ever becoming a moral sort of fellow, or that I have any belief in any moral sort of fellow whatever."

Sissy's face sufficiently showed that her appeal to him was not finished.

"You spoke," he resumed, as she raised her eyes to him again, "of your first object. I may assume that there is a second to be mentioned?"

"Yes."

"Will you oblige me by confiding it?"

"Mr Harthouse," returned Sissy, with a blending of gentleness and steadiness that quite defeated him, and with a simple confidence in his being bound to do what she required, that held him at a singular disadvantage, "the only reparation that remains with you, is to leave here immediately and finally. I am quite sure that you can mitigate in no other way the wrong and harm you have done. I am quite sure that it is the only compensation you have left it in your power to make. I do not say that it is much, or that it is enough; but it is something, and it is necessary. Therefore, though without any other authority than I have given you, and even without the knowledge of any other person than yourself and myself, I ask you to depart from this place tonight, under an obligation never to return to it."

If she had asserted any influence over him beyond her plain faith in the truth and right of what she said; if she had concealed the least doubt or irresolution, or had harboured for the best purpose any reserve or pretence; if she had shown, or felt, the lightest trace of any sensitiveness to his ridicule or his astonishment, or any remonstrance he might offer; he would have carried it against her at this point. But he could as easily have changed a clear sky by looking at it in surprise, as affect her.

"But do you know," he asked, quite at a loss, "the extent of what you ask? You probably are not aware that I am here on a public kind of business, preposterous enough in itself, but which I have gone in for, and sworn by, and am supposed to be devoted to in quite a desperate manner? You probably are not aware of that, but I assure you it's the fact."

It had no effect on Sissy, fact or no fact.

"Besides which," said Mr Harthouse, taking a turn or two across the room, dubiously, "it's so alarmingly absurd. It would make a man so ridiculous, after going in for these fellows, to back out in such an incomprehensible way."

"I am quite sure," repeated Sissy, "that it is the only reparation in your power, sir. I am quite sure, or I would not have come here."

He glanced at her face, and walked about again. "Upon my soul, I don't know what to say. So immensely absurd!"

It fell to his lot, now, to stipulate for secrecy.

"If I were to do such a very ridiculous thing," he said, stopping again presently, and leaning against the chimney-piece, "it could only be in the most inviolable confidence."

"I will trust to you, sir," returned Sissy, "and you will trust to me."

His leaning against the chimney-piece reminded him of the night with the whelp. It was the self-same chimney-piece, and somehow he felt as if *he* were the whelp tonight. He could make no way at all.

"I suppose a man never was placed in a more ridiculous position," he said, after looking down, and looking up, and laughing, and frowning, and walking off, and walking back again. "But I see no way out of it. What will be, will be. *This* will be, I suppose. I must take off myself, I imagine—in short, I engage to do it."

Sissy rose. She was not surprised by the result, but she was happy in it, and her face beamed brightly.

"You will permit me to say," continued Mr James Harthouse, "that I doubt if any other ambassador, or ambassadress, could have addressed me with the same success. I must not only regard myself as being in a very ridiculous position, but as being vanquished at all points. Will you allow me the privilege of remembering my enemy's name?"

"*My* name?" said the ambassadress.

"The only name I could possibly care to know, tonight."

"Sissy Jupe."

"Pardon my curiosity at parting. Related to the family?"

"I am only a poor girl," returned Sissy. "I was separated from my father—he was only a stroller—and taken pity on by Mr Gradgrind. I have lived in the house ever since."

She was gone.

"It wanted this to complete the defeat," said Mr James Harthouse, sinking, with a resigned air, on the sofa, after standing transfixed a little while. "The defeat may now be considered perfectly accomplished. Only a poor girl—only a stroller—only James Harthouse made nothing of—only James Harthouse a Great Pyramid of failure."

The Great Pyramid put it into his head to go up the Nile. He took a pen upon the instant, and wrote the following note (in appropriate hieroglyphics) to his brother:

DEAR JACK
    All up at Coketown. Bored out of the place, and going in for camels. Affectionately,

                                                         JEM.

He rang the bell.

"Send my fellow here."

"Gone to bed, sir."

"Tell him to get up, and pack up."

He wrote two more notes. One, to Mr Bounderby, announcing his retirement from that part of the country, and showing where he would be found for the next fortnight.

The other, similar in effect, to Mr Gradgrind. Almost as soon as the ink was dry upon their superscriptions, he had left the tall chimneys of Coketown behind, and was in a railway carriage, tearing and glaring over the dark landscape.

The moral sort of fellows might suppose that Mr James Harthouse derived some comfortable reflections afterwards, from this prompt retreat, as one of his few actions that made any amends for anything, and as a token to himself that he had escaped the climax of a very bad business. But it was not so, at all. A secret sense of having failed and been ridiculous—a dread of what other fellows who went in for similar sorts of things, would say at his expense if they knew it—so oppressed him, that what was about the very best passage in his life was the one of all others he would not have owned to on any account, and the only one that made him ashamed of himself.

Chapter III

VERY DECIDED

THE indefatigable Mrs Sparsit, with a violent cold upon her, her voice reduced to a whisper, and her stately frame so racked by continual sneezes that it seemed in danger of dismemberment, gave chase to her patron until she found him in the metropolis; and there, majestically sweeping in upon him at his hotel in St James's Street, exploded the combustibles with which she was charged, and blew up. Having executed her mission with infinite relish, this high-minded woman then fainted away on Mr Bounderby's coat-collar.

Mr Bounderby's first procedure was to shake Mrs Sparsit off, and leave her to progress as she might through various stages of suffering on the floor. He next had recourse to the administration of potent restoratives, such as screwing the patient's thumbs, smiting her hands, abundantly watering her face, and inserting salt in her mouth. When these attentions had recovered her (which they speedily did), he hustled her into a fast train without offering any other refreshment, and carried her back to Coketown more dead than alive.

Regarded as a classical ruin, Mrs Sparsit was an interesting spectacle on her arrival at her journey's end; but considered in any other light, the amount of damage she had by that time sustained was excessive, and impaired her claims to admiration. Utterly heedless of the wear and tear of her clothes and constitution, and adamant to her pathetic sneezes, Mr Bounderby immediately crammed her into a coach, and bore her off to Stone Lodge.

"Now, Tom Gradgrind," said Bounderby, bursting into his father-in-law's room late at night; "here's a lady here—Mrs Sparsit—you know Mrs Sparsit—who has something to say to you that will strike you dumb."

"You have missed my letter!" exclaimed Mr Gradgrind, surprised by the apparition.

"Missed your letter, sir!" bawled Bounderby. "The present time is no time for letters. No man shall talk to Josiah Bounderby of Coketown about letters, with his mind in the state it's in now."

"Bounderby," said Mr Gradgrind, in a tone of temperate remonstrance, "I speak of a very special letter I have written to you, in reference to Louisa."

"Tom Gradgrind," replied Bounderby, knocking the flat of his hand several times with great vehemence on the table, "I speak of a very special messenger that has come to me, in reference to Louisa. Mrs Sparsit ma'am, stand forward!"

That unfortunate lady hereupon essaying to offer testimony, without any voice and with painful gestures expressive of an inflamed throat, became so aggravating and underwent so many facial contortions, that Mr Bounderby, unable to bear it, seized her by the arm and shook her.

"If you can't get it out ma'am," said Bounderby, "leave *me* to get it out. This is not a time for a lady, however highly connected, to be totally inaudible, and seemingly swallowing marbles. Tom Gradgrind, Mrs Sparsit latterly found herself, by accident, in a situation to overhear a conversation out of doors between your daughter and your precious gentleman-friend, Mr James Harthouse."

"Indeed?" said Mr Gradgrind.

"Ah! Indeed!" cried Bounderby. "And in that conversation——"

"It is not necessary to repeat its tenor, Bounderby. I know what passed."

"You do? Perhaps," said Bounderby, starting with all his might at his so quiet and assuasive father-in-law, "you know where your daughter is at the present time?"

"Undoubtedly. She is here."

"Here?"

"My dear Bounderby, let me beg you to restrain these loud outbreaks, on all accounts. Louisa is here. The moment she could detach herself from that interview with the person of whom you speak, and whom I deeply regret to have been the means of introducing to you, Louisa hurried here, for protection. I myself had not been at home many hours, when I received her—here, in this room. She hurried by the train to town, she ran from town to this house through a raging storm, and presented herself before me in a state of distraction. Of course, she has remained here ever since. Let me entreat you, for your own sake and for hers, to be more quiet."

Mr Bounderby silently gazed about him for some moments, in every direction except Mrs Sparsit's direction; and then, abruptly turning upon the niece of Lady Scadgers, said to that wretched woman:

"Now, ma'am! We shall be happy to hear any little apology you may think proper to offer, for going about the country at express pace, with no other luggage than a Cock-and-a-Bull, ma'am!"

"Sir," whispered Mrs Sparsit, "my nerves are at present too much shaken, and my health is at present too much impaired, in your service, to admit of my doing more than taking refuge in tears."

(Which she did.)

"Well, ma'am," said Bounderby, "without making any observation to you that may not be made with propriety to a woman of good family, what I have got to add to that, is, that there's something else in which it appears to me you may take refuge, namely a coach. And the coach in which we came here, being at the door, you'll allow me to hand you down to it, and pack you home to the Bank: where the best course for you to pursue, will be to put your feet into the hottest water you can bear, and take a glass of scalding rum and butter after you get into bed." With these words, Mr Bounderby extended his right hand to the weeping lady and escorted her to the conveyance in question, shedding many plaintive sneezes by the way. He soon returned alone.

"Now, as you showed me in your face, Tom Gradgrind, that you wanted to speak to me," he resumed, "here I am. But, I am not in a very agreeable state, I tell you plainly; not relishing this business even as it is, and not considering that I am at any time as dutifully and submissively treated by your daughter, as Josiah Bounderby of Coketown ought to be treated by his wife. You have your opinion, I dare say; and I have mine, I know. If you mean to say anything to me tonight, that goes against this candid remark, you had better let it alone."

Mr Gradgrind, it will be observed, being much softened, Mr Bounderby took particular pains to harden himself at all points. It was his amiable nature.

"My dear Bounderby," Mr Gradgrind began in reply.

"Now, you'll excuse me," said Bounderby, "but I don't want to be too dear. That, to start with. When I begin to be dear to a man, I generally find that his intention is to come over me. I am not speaking to you politely; but, as you are aware, I am *not* polite. If you like politeness, you know where to get it. You have your gentleman-friends you know, and they'll serve you with as much of the article as you want. I don't keep it myself."

"Bounderby," urged Mr Gradgrind, "we are all liable to mistakes——"

"I thought you couldn't make 'em," interrupted Bounderby.

"Perhaps I thought so. But, I say we are all liable to mistakes; and I should feel sensible of your delicacy, and grateful for it, if you would spare me these references to Harthouse. I shall not associate him in our conversation with your intimacy and encouragement; pray do not persist in connecting him with mine."

"I never mentioned his name!" said Bounderby.

"Well, well!" returned Mr Gradgrind, with a patient, even a submissive, air. And he sat for a little while pondering. "Bounderby, I see reason to doubt whether we have ever quite understood Louisa."

"Who do you mean by We?"

"Let me say I, then," he returned, in answer to the coarsely blurted question; "I doubt whether I have understood Louisa. I doubt whether I have been quite right in the manner of her education."

"There you hit it," returned Bounderby. "There I agree with you. You have found it out at last, have you? Education! I'll tell you what education is——To be tumbled out of doors, neck and crop, and put upon the shortest allowance of everything except blows. That's what *I* call education."

"I think your good sense will perceive," Mr Gradgrind remonstrated in all humility, "that whatever the merits of such a system may be, it would be difficult of general application to girls."

"I don't see it at all, sir," returned the obstinate Bounderby.

"Well," sighed Mr Gradgrind, "we will not enter into the question. I assure you I have no desire to be controversial. I seek to repair what is amiss, if I possibly can; and I hope you will assist me in a good spirit, Bounderby, for I have been very much distressed."

"I don't understand you, yet," said Bounderby, with determined obstinacy, "and therefore I won't make any promises."

"In the course of a few hours, my dear Bounderby," Mr Gradgrind proceeded, in the same depressed and propitiatory manner, "I appear to myself to have become better informed as to Louisa's character, than in previous years. The enlightenment has been forced upon me, and the discovery is not mine. I think there are——Bounderby, you will be surprised to hear me say this——I think there are qualities in Louisa, which——which have been harshly neglected, and——and a little perverted. And——and I would suggest to you, that—that if you would kindly meet me in a timely endeavour to leave her to her better nature for a while—and to encourage it to develop itself by tenderness and consideration—it—it would be the better for the happiness of all of us. Louisa," said Mr Gradgrind, shading his face with his hand, "has always been my favourite child."

The blustrous Bounderby crimsoned and swelled to such an extent on hearing these words, that he seemed to be, and probably was, on the brink of a fit. With his very ears a bright purple shot with crimson, he pent up his indignation, however, and said:

"You'd like to keep her here for a time?"

"I—I had intended to recommend, my dear Bounderby, that you should allow Louisa to remain here on a visit, and be attended by Sissy (I mean of course Cecilia Jupe), who understands her, and in whom she trusts."

"I gather from all this, Tom Gradgrind," said Bounderby, standing up with his hands in his pockets, "that you are of opinion that there's what people call some incompatibility between Loo Bounderby and myself."

"I fear there is at present a general incompatibility between Louisa, and—and—almost all the relations in which I have placed her," was her father's sorrowful reply.

"Now, look you here, Tom Gradgrind," said Bounderby the flushed, confronting him with his legs wide apart, his hands deeper in his pockets, and his hair like a hayfield wherein his windy anger was boisterous. "You have said your say; I am going to say mine. I am a Coketown man. I am Josiah Bounderby of Coketown. I know the bricks of this town, and I know the works of this town, and I know the chimneys of this town, and I know the smoke of this town, and I know the Hands of this town. I know 'em all pretty well. They're real. When a man tells me anything about imaginative qualities, I always tell that man, whoever he is, that I know what he means. He means turtle-soup and venison, with a gold spoon, and that he wants to be set up with a coach and six. That's what your daughter wants. Since you are of opinion that she ought to have what she wants, I recommend you to provide it for her. Because, Tom Gradgrind, she will never have it from me."

"Bounderby," said Mr Gradgrind, "I hoped, after my entreaty, you would have taken a different tone."

"Just wait a bit," retorted Bounderby, "you have said your say, I believe. I heard you out; hear me out, if you please. Don't make yourself a spectacle of unfairness as well as inconsistency, because, although I am sorry to see Tom Gradgrind reduced to his present position, I should be doubly sorry to see him brought so low as that. Now, there's an incompatibility of some sort or another, I am given to understand by you, between your daughter and me. I'll give *you* to understand, in reply to that, that there unquestionably is an incompatibility of the first magnitude—to be summed up in this—that your daughter don't properly know her husband's merits, and is not impressed with such a sense as would become her, by George! of the honour of his alliance. That's plain speaking, I hope."

"Bounderby," urged Mr Gradgrind, "this is unreasonable."

"Is it?" said Bounderby. "I am glad to hear you say so. Because when Tom Gradgrind with his new lights, tells me that what I say is unreasonable, I am convinced at once it must be devilish sensible. With your permission I am going on. You know my origin; and you know that for a good many years of my life I didn't want a shoeing-horn, in consequence of not having a shoe. Yet you may believe it or not, as you think proper, that there are ladies—born ladies—belonging to families—Families!—who next to worship the ground I walk on."

He discharged this, like a Rocket, at his father-in-law's head.

"Whereas your daughter," proceeded Bounderby, "is far from being a born lady. That you know, yourself. Not that I care a pinch of candle-snuff about such things, for you are very well aware I don't; but that such is the fact, and you, Tom Gradgrind, can't change it. Why do I say this?"

"Not, I fear," observed Mr Gradgrind, in a low voice, "to spare me."

"Hear me out," said Bounderby, "and refrain from cutting in till your turn comes round. I say this, because highly connected females have been astonished to see the way in which your daughter has conducted herself, and to witness her insensibility. They have wondered how I have suffered it. And I wonder myself now, and I won't suffer it."

"Bounderby," returned Mr Gradgrind, rising, "the less we say tonight the better, I think."

"On the contrary, Tom Gradgrind, the more we say tonight, the better, I think. That is," the consideration checked him, "till I have said all I mean to say, and then I don't care how soon we stop. I come to a question that may shorten the business. What do you mean by the proposal you made just now?"

"What do I mean, Bounderby?"

"By your visiting proposition," said Bounderby, with an inflexible jerk of the hay-field.

"I mean that I hope you may be induced to arrange, in a friendly manner, for allowing Louisa a period of repose and reflection here, which may tend to a gradual alteration for the better in many respects."

"To a softening down of your ideas of the incompatibility?" said Bounderby.

"If you put it in those terms."

"What made you think of this?" said Bounderby.

"I have already said, I fear Louisa has not been understood. Is it asking too much, Bounderby, that you, so far her elder, should aid in trying to set her right? You have accepted a great charge of her; for better for worse, for——"

Mr Bounderby may have been annoyed by the repetition of his own words to Stephen Blackpool, but he cut the quotation short with an angry start.

"Come!" said he, "I don't want to be told about that. I know what I took her for, as well as you do. Never you mind what I took her for; that's my look-out."

"I was merely going on to remark, Bounderby, that we may all be more or less in the wrong, not even excepting you; and that some yielding on your part, remembering the trust you have accepted, may not only be an act of true kindness, but perhaps a debt incurred towards Louisa."

"I think differently," blustered Bounderby. "I am going to finish this business according to my own opinions. Now, I don't want to make a quarrel of it with you, Tom Gradgrind. To tell you the truth, I don't think it would be worthy of my reputation to quarrel on such a subject. As to your gentleman-friend, he may take himself off, wherever he likes best. If he falls in my way, I shall tell him my mind; if he don't fall in my way, I shan't, for it won't be worth my while to do it. As to your daughter, whom I made Loo Bounderby, and might have done better by leaving Loo Gradgrind, if she don't come home tomorrow by twelve o'clock at noon, I shall understand that she prefers to stay away, and I shall send her wearing apparel and so forth over here, and you'll take charge of her for the future. What I shall say to people in general, of the incompatibility that led to my so laying down the law, will be this. I am Josiah Bounderby, and I had my bringing-up; she's the daughter of Tom Gradgrind, and she had her bringing-up; and the two horses wouldn't pull together. I am pretty well known to be rather an uncommon man, I believe; and most people will understand fast enough that it must be a woman rather out of the common, also, who, in the long run, would come up to my mark."

"Let me seriously entreat you to re-consider this, Bounderby," urged Mr Gradgrind, "before you commit yourself to such a decision."

"I always come to a decision," said Bounderby, tossing his hat on: "and whatever I do, I do at once. I should be surprised at Tom Gradgrind's addressing such a remark to Josiah Bounderby of Coketown, knowing what he knows of him, if I could be surprised by anything Tom Gradgrind did, after his making himself a party to sentimental humbug. I have given you my decision, and I have got no more to say. Good-night!"

So Mr Bounderby went home to his town house to bed. At five minutes past twelve o'clock next day, he directed Mrs Bounderby's property to be carefully packed up and sent to Tom Gradgrind's; advertised his country retreat for sale by private contract; and resumed a bachelor life.

Chapter IV

LOST

THE robbery at the Bank had not languished before, and did not cease to occupy a front place in the attention of the principal of that establishment now. In boastful proof of his promptitude and activity, as a remarkable man, and a self-made man, and a commercial wonder more admirable than Venus, who had risen out of the mud instead of the sea, he liked to show how little his domestic affairs abated his business ardour. Consequently, in the first few weeks of his resumed bachelorhood, he even advanced upon his usual display of bustle, and every day made such a rout in renewing his investigations into the robbery, that the officers who had it in hand almost wished it had never been committed.

They were at fault too, and off the scent. Although they had been so quiet since the first outbreak of the matter, that most people really did suppose it to have been abandoned as hopeless, nothing new occurred. No implicated man or woman took untimely courage, or made a self-betraying step. More remarkable yet, Stephen Blackpool could not be heard of, and the mysterious old woman remained a mystery.

Things having come to this pass, and showing no latent signs of stirring beyond it, the upshot of Mr Bounderby's investigations was, that he resolved to hazard a bold burst. He drew up a placard, offering Twenty Pounds reward for the apprehension of Stephen Blackpool, suspected of complicity in the robbery of the Coketown Bank on such a night; he described the said Stephen Blackpool by dress, complexion, estimated height, and manner, as minutely as he could; he recited how he had left the town, and in what direction he had been last seen going; he had the whole printed in great black letters on a staring broadsheet; and he caused the walls to be posted with it in the dead of night, so that it should strike upon the sight of the whole population at one blow.

The factory-bells had need to ring their loudest that morning to disperse the groups of workers who stood in the tardy daybreak, collected round the placards, devouring them with eager eyes. Not the least eager of the eyes assembled, were the eyes of those who could not read. These people, as they listened to the friendly voice that read aloud—there was always some such ready to help them—stared at the characters which meant so much with a vague awe and respect that would have been half ludicrous if any aspect of public ignorance could ever be otherwise than threatening and full of evil. Many ears and eyes were busy with a vision of the matter of these placards, among turning spindles, rattling looms, and whirring wheels, for hours afterwards; and when the Hands cleared out again into the streets, there were still as many readers as before.

Slackbridge, the delegate, had to address his audience too that night; and Slackbridge had obtained a clean bill from the printer, and had brought it in his pocket. Oh my friends and fellow countrymen, the down-trodden operatives of Coketown, oh my fellow brothers and fellow workmen and fellow citizens and fellow men, what a to-do was there, when Slackbridge unfolded what he called "that damning document," and held it up to the gaze, and for the execration, of the working-man community! "Oh my fellow men, behold of what a traitor in the camp of those great spirits who are enrolled upon the holy scroll of Justice and of Union, is appropriately capable! Oh my prostrate friends, with the galling yoke of tyrants on your necks and the iron foot of despotism treading down your fallen forms into the dust of the earth, upon which right glad would your oppressors be to see you creeping on your bellies all the days of your lives, like the serpent in the garden—oh my brothers, and shall I as a man not add, my sisters too, what do you say, *now,* of Stephen Blackpool, with a slight stoop in his shoulders and about five foot seven in height, as set forth in this degrading and disgusting document, this blighting bill, this pernicious placard, this abominable advertisement; and with what majesty of denouncement will you crush the viper, who would bring this stain and shame upon the Godlike race that happily has cast him out for ever! Yes, my compatriots, happily cast him out and sent him forth! For you remember how he stood here before you on this platform; you remember how, face to face and foot to foot, I pursued him through all his intricate windings; you remember how he sneaked, and slunk, and sidled, and splitted of straws, until, with not an inch of ground to which to cling, I hurled him out from amongst us: an object for the undying finger of scorn to point at, and for the avenging fire of every free and thinking mind, to scorch and sear! And now my friends— my labouring friends, for I rejoice and triumph in that stigma—my friends whose hard but honest beds are made in toil, and whose scanty but independent pots are boiled in hardship; and, now I say, my friends, what appellation has that dastard craven taken to himself, when, with the mask torn from his features, he stands before us in all his native deformity, a What? A thief! A plunderer! A proscribed fugitive, with a price upon his head; a fester and a wound upon the noble character of the Coketown operative! Therefore, my band of brothers in a sacred bond, to which your children and your children's children yet unborn have set their infant hands and seals, I propose to you on the part of the United Aggregate Tribunal, ever watchful for your welfare, ever zealous for your benefit, that this meeting does Resolve: That Stephen Blackpool, weaver, referred to in this placard, having been already solemnly disowned by the community of Coketown Hands, the same are free from the shame of his misdeeds, and cannot as a class be reproached with his dishonest actions!"

Thus Slackbridge; gnashing and perspiring after a prodigious sort. A few stern voices called out "No!" and a score or two hailed, with assenting cries of "Hear hear!" the caution from one man, "Slackbridge, y'or over hetter int; y'or a goen too fast!" But these were pigmies against an army; the general assemblage subscribed to the gospel according to Slackbridge, and gave three cheers for him, as he sat demonstratively panting at them.

These men and women were yet in the streets, passing quietly to their homes, when Sissy, who had been called away from Louisa some minutes before, returned.

"Who is it?" asked Louisa.

"It is Mr Bounderby," said Sissy, timid of the name, "and your brother Mr Tom, and a young woman who says her name is Rachael, and that you know her."

"What do they want, Sissy dear?"

"They want to see you. Rachael has been crying, and seems angry."

"Father," said Louisa, for he was present, "I cannot refuse to see them, for a reason that will explain itself. Shall they come in here?"

As he answered in the affirmative, Sissy went away to bring them. She reappeared with them directly. Tom was last; and remained standing in the obscurest part of the room, near the door.

"Mrs Bounderby," said her husband, entering with a cool nod, "I don't disturb you, I hope. This is an unseasonable hour, but here is a young woman who has been making statements which render my visit necessary. Tom Gradgrind, as your son, young Tom, refuses for some obstinate reason or other to say anything at all about those statements, good or bad, I am obliged to confront her with your daughter."

"You have seen me once before, young lady," said Rachael, standing in front of Louisa.

Tom coughed.

"You have seen me, young lady," repeated Rachael, as she did not answer, "once before."

Tom coughed again.

"I have."

Rachael cast her eyes proudly towards Mr Bounderby, and said, "Will you make it known, young lady, where, and who was there?"

"I went to the house where Stephen Blackpool lodged, on the night of his discharge from his work, and I saw you there. He was there too: and an old woman who did not speak, and whom I could scarcely see, stood in a dark corner. My brother was with me."

"Why couldn't you say so, young Tom?" demanded Bounderby.

"I promised my sister I wouldn't." Which Louisa hastily confirmed. "And besides," said the whelp bitterly, "she tells her own story so precious well—and so full—that what business had I to take it out of her mouth!"

"Say, young lady, if you please," pursued Rachael, "why in an evil hour, you ever came to Stephen's that night."

"I felt compassion for him," said Louisa, her colour deepening, "and I wished to know what he was going to do, and wished to offer him assistance."

"Thank you, ma'am," said Bounderby. "Much flattered and obliged."

"Did you offer him," asked Rachael, "a bank note?"

"Yes; but he refused it, and would only take two pounds in gold."

Rachael cast her eyes towards Mr Bounderby again.

"Oh certainly!" said Bounderby. "If you put the question whether your ridiculous and improbable account was true or not, I am bound to say it's confirmed."

"Young lady," said Rachael, "Stephen Blackpool is now named as a thief in public print all over this town, and where else! There have been a meeting tonight where he have been spoken of in the same shameful way. Stephen! The honestest lad, the truest lad, the best!" Her indignation failed her, and she broke off, sobbing.

"I am very, very sorry," said Louisa.

"O young lady, young lady," returned Rachael, "I hope you may be, but I don't know! I can't say what you may ha' done! The like of you don't know us, don't care for us, don't belong to us. I am not sure why you may ha' come that night. I can't tell but what you may ha' come wi' some aim of your own, not mindin to what trouble you brought such as the poor lad. I said then, Bless you for coming; and I said it of my heart, you seemed to take so pitifully to him; but I don't know now, I don't know!"

Louisa could not reproach her for her unjust suspicions; she was so faithful to her idea of the man, and so afflicted.

"And when I think," said Rachael through her sobs, "that the poor lad was so grateful, thinkin' you so good to him—when I mind that he put his hand over his hard-worken face to hide the tears that you brought up there—O, I hope you may be sorry, and ha' no bad cause to be it; but I don't know, I don't know!"

"You're a pretty article," growled the whelp, moving uneasily in his dark corner, "to come here with these precious imputations! You ought to be bundled out for not knowing how to behave yourself, and you would be by rights."

She said nothing in reply; and her low weeping was the only sound that was heard, until Mr Bounderby spoke.

"Come!" said he, "you know what you have engaged to do. You had better give your mind to that; not this."

"'Deed, I am loath," returned Rachael, drying her eyes, "that any here should see me like this; but I won't be seen so again. Young lady, when I had read what's put in print of Stephen—and what has just as much truth in it as if it had been put in print of you—I went straight to the Bank to say I knew where Stephen was, and to give a sure and certain promise that he should be here in two days. I couldn't meet wi' Mr Bounderby then, and your brother sent me away, and I tried to find you, but you was not to be found, and I went back to work. Soon as I come out of the Mill tonight, I hastened to hear what was said of Stephen—for I know wi' pride he will come back to shame it!—and then I went again to seek Mr Bounderby, and I found him, and I told him every word I knew; and he believed no word I said, and brought me here."

"So far, that's true enough," assented Mr Bounderby, with his hands in his pockets and his hat on. "But I have known you people before today, you'll observe, and I know you never die for want of talking. Now, I recommend you not so much to mind talking just now, as doing. You have undertaken to do something; all I remark upon that at present is, do it!"

"I have written to Stephen by the post that went out this afternoon, as I have written to him once before sin' he went away," said Rachael; "and he will be here, at furthest, in two days."

"Then, I'll tell you something. You are not aware, perhaps," retorted Mr Bounderby, "that you yourself have been looked after now and then, not being considered quite free from suspicion in this business, on account of most people being judged according to the company they keep. The post-office hasn't been forgotten either. What I'll tell you, is, that no letter to Stephen Blackpool has ever got into it. Therefore, what has become of yours, I leave you to guess. Perhaps you're mistaken, and never wrote any."

"He hadn't been gone from here, young lady," said Rachael, turning appealingly to Louisa, "as much as a week, when he sent me the only letter I have had from him, saying that he was forced to seek work in another name."

"Oh, by George!" cried Bounderby, shaking his head, with a whistle, "he changes his name, does he! That's rather unlucky, too, for such an immaculate chap. It's considered a little suspicious in Courts of Justice, I believe, when an Innocent happens to have many names."

"What," said Rachael, with the tears in her eyes again, "what, young lady, in the name of Mercy, was left the poor lad to do! The masters against him on one hand, the men against him on the other, he only wantin to work hard in peace, and do what he felt right. Can a man have no soul of his own, no mind of his own? Must he go wrong all through wi' this side, or must he go wrong all through wi' that, or else be hunted like a hare?"

"Indeed, indeed, I pity him from my heart," returned Louisa; "and I hope that he will clear himself."

"You need have no fear of that, young lady. He is sure!"

"All the surer, I suppose," said Mr Bounderby, "for your refusing to tell where he is? Eh?"

"He shall not, through any act of mine, come back wi' the unmerited reproach of being brought back. He shall come back of his own accord to clear himself, and put all those that have injured his good character, and he not here for its defence, to shame. I have told him what has been done against him," said Rachael, throwing off all distrust as a rock throws off the sea, "and he will be here, at furthest, in two days."

"Notwithstanding which," added Mr Bounderby, "if he can be laid hold of any sooner, he shall have an earlier opportunity of clearing himself. As to you, I have nothing against you; what you came and told me turns out to be true, and I have given you the means of proving it to be true, and there's an end of it. I wish you good night all! I must be off to look a little further into this."

Tom came out of his corner when Mr Bounderby moved, moved with him, kept close to him, and went away with him. The only parting salutation of which he delivered himself was a sulky "Good night, father!" With a brief speech, and a scowl at his sister, he left the house.

Since his sheet-anchor had come home, Mr Gradgrind had been sparing of speech. He still sat silent, when Louisa mildly said:

"Rachael, you will not distrust me one day, when you know me better."

"It goes against me," Rachael answered, in a gentler manner, "to mistrust any one; but when I am so mistrusted—when we all are—I cannot keep such things quite out of my mind. I ask your pardon for having done you an injury. I don't think what I said now. Yet I might come to think it again, wi' the poor lad so wronged."

"Did you tell him in your letter," inquired Sissy, "that suspicion seemed to have fallen upon him, because he had been seen about the bank at night? He would then know what he would have to explain on coming back, and would be ready."

"Yes, dear," she returned; "but I can't guess what can have ever taken him there. He never used to go there. It was never in his way. His way was the same as mine, and not near it."

Sissy had already been at her side asking her where she lived, and whether she might come tomorrow-night, to inquire if there were news of him.

"I doubt," said Rachael, "if he can be here till next day."

"Then I will come next night too," said Sissy.

When Rachael, assenting to this, was gone, Mr Gradgrind lifted up his head, and said to his daughter:

"Louisa, my dear, I have never, that I know of, seen this man. Do you believe him to be implicated?"

"I think I have believed it, father, though with great difficulty. I do not believe it now."

"That is to say, you once persuaded yourself to believe it, from knowing him to be suspected. His appearance and manner; are they so honest?"

"Very honest."

"And her confidence not to be shaken! I ask myself," said Mr Gradgrind, musing, "does the real culprit know of these accusations? Where is he? Who is he?"

His hair had latterly begun to change its colour. As he leaned upon his hand again, looking grey and old, Louisa, with a face of fear and pity, hurriedly went over to him, and sat close at his side. Her eyes by accident met Sissy's at the moment. Sissy flushed and started, and Louisa put her finger on her lip.

Next night, when Sissy returned home and told Louisa that Stephen was not come, she told it in a whisper. Next night again, when she came home with the same account, and added that he had not been heard of, she spoke in the same low frightened tone. From the moment of that interchange of looks, they never uttered his name, or any reference to him, aloud; nor ever pursued the subject of the robbery, when Mr Gradgrind spoke of it.

The two appointed days ran out, three days and nights ran out, and Stephen Blackpool was not come, and remained unheard of. On the fourth day, Rachael, with unabated confidence, but considering her dispatch to have miscarried, went up to the Bank, and showed her letter from him with his address, at a working colony, one of many, not upon the main road, sixty miles away. Messengers were sent to that place, and the whole town looked for Stephen to be brought in next day.

During this whole time the whelp moved about with Mr Bounderby like his shadow, assisting in all the proceedings. He was greatly excited, horribly fevered, bit his nails down to the quick, spoke in a hard rattling voice, and with lips that were black and burnt up. At the hour when the suspected man was looked for, the whelp was at the station; offering to wager that he had made off before the arrival of those who were sent in quest of him, and that he would not appear.

The whelp was right. The messengers returned alone. Rachael's letter had gone, Rachael's letter had been delivered, Stephen Blackpool had decamped in that same hour; and no soul knew more of him. The only doubt in Coketown was, whether Rachael had written in good faith, believing that he really would come back, or warning him to fly. On this point opinion was divided.

Six days, seven days, far on into another week. The wretched whelp plucked up a ghastly courage, and began to grow defiant. "*Was* the suspected fellow the thief? A pretty question! If not, where was the man, and why did he not come back?"

Where was the man, and why did he not come back? In the dead of night the echoes of his own words, which had rolled Heaven knows how far away in the daytime, came back instead, and abided by him until morning.

Chapter V

FOUND

D AY and night again, day and night again. No Stephen Blackpool. Where was the man, and why did he not come back?

Every night, Sissy went to Rachael's lodging, and sat with her in her small neat room. All day, Rachael toiled as such people must toil, whatever their anxieties. The smoke-serpents were indifferent who was lost or found, who turned out bad or good; the melancholy mad elephants, like the Hard Fact men, abated nothing of their set routine, whatever happened. Day and night again, day and night again. The monotony was unbroken. Even Stephen Blackpool's disappearance was falling into the general way, and becoming as monotonous a wonder as any piece of machinery in Coketown.

"I misdoubt," said Rachael, "if there is as many as twenty left in all this place, who have any trust in the poor dear lad now."

She said it to Sissy, as they sat in her lodging, lighted only by the lamp at the street corner. Sissy had come there when it was already dark, to await her return from work; and they had since sat at the window where Rachael had found her, wanting no brighter light to shine on their sorrowful talk.

"If it hadn't been mercifully brought about, that I was to have you to speak to," pursued Rachael, "times are, when I think my mind would not have kept right. But I get hope and strength through you; and you believe that though appearances may rise against him, he will be proved clear?"

"I do believe so," returned Sissy, "with my whole heart. I feel so certain, Rachael, that the confidence you hold in yours against all discouragement, is not like to be wrong, that I have no more doubt of him than if I had known him through as many years of trial as you have."

"And I, my dear," said Rachael, with a tremble in her voice, "have known him through them all, to be, according to his quiet ways, so faithful to everything honest and good, that if he was never to be heard of more, and I was to live to be a hundred years old, I could say with my last breath, God knows my heart. I have never once left trusting Stephen Blackpool!"

"We all believe, up at the Lodge, Rachael, that he will be freed from suspicion, sooner or later."

"The better I know it to be so believed there, my dear," said Rachael, "and the kinder I feel that you come away from there, purposely to comfort me, and keep my company, and be seen wi' me when I am not yet free from all suspicion myself, the more grieved I am that I should ever have spoken those mistrusting words to the young lady. And yet—"

"You don't mistrust her now, Rachael?"

"Now that you have brought us more together, no. But I can't at all times keep out of my mind—"

Her voice so sunk into a low and slow communing with herself, that Sissy, sitting by her side, was obliged to listen with attention.

"I can't at all times keep out of my mind, mistrustings of some one. I can't think who 'tis, I can't think how or why it may be done, but I mistrust that some one has put Stephen out of the way. I mistrust that by his coming back of his own accord, and showing himself innocent before them all, some one would be confounded, who—to prevent that—has stopped him, and put him out of the way."

"That is a dreadful thought," said Sissy, turning pale.

"It *is* a dreadful thought to think he may be murdered."

Sissy shuddered, and turned paler yet.

"When it makes its way into my mind, dear," said Rachael, "and it will come sometimes, though I do all I can to keep it out, wi' counting on to high numbers as I work, and saying over and over again pieces that I knew when I were a child—I fall into such a wild, hot hurry, that, however tired I am, I want to walk fast, miles and miles. I must get the better of this before bed-time. I'll walk home wi' you."

"He might fall ill upon the journey back," said Sissy, faintly offering a worn-out scrap of hope; "and in such a case, there are many places on the road where he might stop."

"But he is in none of them. He has been sought for in all, and he's not there."

"True," was Sissy's reluctant admission.

"He'd walk the journey in two days. If he was footsore and couldn't walk, I sent him, in the letter he got, the money to ride, lest he should have none of his own to spare."

"Let us hope that tomorrow will bring something better, Rachael. Come into the air!"

Her gentle hand adjusted Rachael's shawl upon her shining black hair in the usual manner of her wearing it, and they went out. The night being fine, little knots of Hands were here and there lingering at street-corners; but it was supper-time with the greater part of them, and there were but few people in the streets.

"You're not so hurried now, Rachael, and your hand is cooler."

"I get better dear, if I can only walk, and breathe a little fresh. 'Times when I can't, I turn weak and confused."

"But you must not begin to fail, Rachael, for you may be wanted at any time to stand by Stephen. Tomorrow is Saturday. If no news comes tomorrow, let us walk in the country on Sunday morning, and strengthen you for another week. Will you go?"

"Yes, dear."

They were by this time in the street where Mr Bounderby's house stood. The way to Sissy's destination led them past the door, and they were going straight towards it. Some train had newly arrived in Coketown, which had put a number of vehicles in motion, and scattered a considerable bustle about the town. Several coaches were rattling before them and behind them as they approached Mr Bounderby's, and one of the latter drew up with such briskness as they were in the act of passing the house, that they looked round involuntarily. The bright gaslight over Mr Bounderby's steps showed them Mrs Sparsit in the coach, in an ecstacy of excitement, struggling to open the door; Mrs Sparsit seeing them at the same moment, called to them to stop.

"It's a coincidence," exclaimed Mrs Sparsit, as she was released by the coachman. "It's a Providence! Come out, ma'am!" then said Mrs Sparsit, to some one inside, "come out, or we'll have you dragged out!"

Hereupon, no other than the mysterious old woman descended. Whom Mrs Sparsit incontinently collared.

"Leave her alone, everybody!" cried Mrs Sparsit, with great energy. "Let nobody touch her. She belongs to me. Come in, ma'am!" then said Mrs Sparsit, reversing her former word of command. "Come in, ma'am, or we'll have you dragged in!"

The spectacle of a matron of classical deportment, seizing an ancient woman by the throat, and haling her into a dwelling-house, would have been, under any circumstances, sufficient temptation to all true English stragglers so blest as to witness it, to force a way into that dwelling-house and see the matter out. But when the phenomenon was enhanced by the notoriety and mystery by this time associated all over the town, with the Bank robbery, it would have lured the stragglers in, with an irresistible attraction, though the roof had been expected to fall upon their heads. Accordingly, the chance witnesses on the ground, consisting of the busiest of the neighbours to the number of some five-and-twenty, closed in after Sissy and Rachael, as they closed in after Mrs Sparsit and her prize; and the whole body made a disorderly irruption into Mr Bounderby's dining-room, where the people behind lost not a moment's time in mounting on the chairs, to get the better of the people in front.

"Fetch Mr Bounderby down!" cried Mrs Sparsit. "Rachael, young woman; you know who this is?"

"It's Mrs Pegler," said Rachael.

"I should think it is!" cried Mrs Sparsit, exulting. "Fetch Mr Bounderby. Stand away, everybody!" Here old Mrs Pegler, muffling herself up, and shrinking from observation, whispered a word of entreaty. "Don't tell me," said Mrs Sparsit, aloud, "I have told you twenty times, coming along, that I will *not* leave you till I have handed you over to him myself."

Mr Bounderby now appeared, accompanied by Mr Gradgrind, and the whelp, with whom he had been holding conference upstairs. Mr Bounderby looked more astonished than hospitable, at sight of this uninvited party in his dining-room.

"Why, what's the matter now!" said he. "Mrs Sparsit, ma'am?"

"Sir," explained that worthy woman, "I trust it is my good fortune to produce a person you have much desired to find. Stimulated by my wish to relieve your mind, sir, and connecting together such imperfect clues to the part of the country in which that person might be supposed to reside, as have been afforded by the young woman Rachael, fortunately now present to identify, I have had the happiness to succeed, and to bring that person with me—I need not say most unwillingly on her part. It has not been, sir, without some trouble that I have effected this; but trouble in your service is to me a pleasure, and hunger, thirst, and cold a real gratification."

Here Mrs Sparsit ceased; for Mr Bounderby's visage exhibited an extraordinary combination of all possible colours and expressions of discomfiture, as old Mrs Pegler was disclosed to his view.

"Why, what do you mean by this?" was his highly unexpected demand, in great warmth. "I ask you, what do you mean by this, Mrs Sparsit, ma'am?"

"Sir!" exclaimed Mrs Sparsit, faintly.

"Why don't you mind your own business, ma'am?" roared Bounderby. "How dare you go and poke your officious nose into my family affairs?"

This allusion to her favourite feature overpowered Mrs Sparsit. She sat down stiffly in a chair, as if she were frozen; and, with a fixed stare at Mr Bounderby, slowly grated her mittens against one another, as if they were frozen too.

"My dear Josiah!" cried Mrs Pegler, trembling. "My darling boy! I am not to blame. It's not my fault, Josiah. I told this lady over and over again, that I knew she was doing what would not be agreeable to you, but she would do it."

"What did you let her bring you for? Couldn't you knock her cap off, or her tooth out, or scratch her, or do something or other to her?" asked Bounderby.

"My own boy! She threatened me that if I resisted her, I should be brought by constables, and it was better to come quietly than make that stir in such a—" Mrs Pegler glanced timidly but proudly round the walls—"such a fine house as this. Indeed, indeed, it is not my fault! My dear, noble, stately boy! I have always lived quiet and secret, Josiah, my dear. I have never broken the condition once. I have never said I was your mother. I have admired you at a distance; and if I have come to town sometimes, with long times between, to take a proud peep at you, I have done it unbeknown, my love, and gone away again."

Mr Bounderby, with his hands in his pockets, walked in impatient mortification up and down at the side of the long dining-table, while the spectators greedily took in every syllable of Mrs Pegler's appeal, and at each succeeding syllable became more and more round-eyed. Mr Bounderby still walking up and down when Mrs Pegler had done, Mr Gradgrind addressed that maligned old lady:

"I am surprised, madam," he observed with severity, "that in your old age you have the face to claim Mr Bounderby for your son, after your unnatural and inhuman treatment of him."

"*Me* unnatural!" cried poor old Mrs Pegler. "*Me* inhuman! To my dear boy?"

"Dear!" repeated Mr Gradgrind. "Yes; dear in his self-made prosperity, madam, I dare say. Not very dear, however, when you deserted him in his infancy, and left him to the brutality of a drunken grandmother."

"*I* deserted my Josiah!" cried Mrs Pegler, clasping her hands. "Now, Lord forgive you, sir, for your wicked imaginations, and for your scandal against the memory of my poor mother, who died in my arms before Josiah was born. May you repent of it, sir, and live to know better!"

She was so very earnest and injured, that Mr Gradgrind, shocked by the possibility which dawned upon him, said in a gentler tone:

"Do you deny, then, madam, that you left your son to—to be brought up in the gutter?"

"Josiah in the gutter!" exclaimed Mrs Pegler. "No such a thing, sir. Never! For shame on you! My dear boy knows, and will give *you* to know, that though he come of humble parents, he come of parents that loved him as dear as the best could, and never thought it hardship on themselves to pinch a bit that he might write and cypher beautiful, and I've his books at home to show it! Aye, have I!" said Mrs Pegler, with indignant pride. "And my dear boy knows, and will give *you* to know, sir, that after his beloved father died when he was eight years old, his mother, too, could pinch a bit, as it was her duty and her pleasure and her pride to do it, to help him out in life, and put him 'prentice. And a steady lad he was, and a kind master he had to lend him a hand, and well he worked his own way forward to be rich and thriving. And *I'll* give you to know, sir—for this my dear boy won't—that though his mother kept but a little village shop, he never forgot her, but pensioned me on thirty pound a-year—more than I want, for I put by out of it—only making the condition that I was to keep down in my own part, and make no boasts about him, and not trouble him. And I never have, except with looking at him once a year, when he has never knowed it. And it's right," said poor old Mrs Pegler, in affectionate championship, "that I *should* keep down in my own part, and I have no doubts that if I was here I should do a many unbefitting things, and I am well contented, and I can keep my pride in my Josiah to myself, and I can love for love's own sake! And I am ashamed of you, sir," said Mrs Pegler, lastly, "for your slanders and suspicions. And I never stood here before, nor never wanted to stand here when my dear son said no. And I shouldn't be here now, if it hadn't been for being brought here. And for shame upon you, O for shame, to accuse me of being a bad mother to my son, with my son standing here to tell you so different!"

The bystanders, on and off the dining-room chairs, raised a murmur of sympathy with Mrs Pegler, and Mr Gradgrind felt himself innocently placed in a very distressing predicament, when Mr Bounderby, who had never ceased walking up and down, and had every moment swelled larger and larger, and grown redder and redder, stopped short.

"I don't exactly know," said Mr Bounderby, "how I come to be favoured with the attendance of the present company, but I don't inquire. When they're quite satisfied, perhaps they'll be so good as to disperse; whether they're satisfied or not, perhaps they'll be so good as to disperse. I'm not bound to deliver a lecture on my family affairs, I have not undertaken to do it, and I'm not a-going to do it. Therefore those who expect any explanation whatever upon that branch of the subject, will be disappointed—particularly Tom Gradgrind, and he can't know it too soon. In reference to the Bank robbery, there has been a mistake made, concerning my mother. If there hadn't been over-officiousness it wouldn't have been made, and I hate over-officiousness at all times, whether or no. Good evening!"

Although Mr Bounderby carried it off in these terms, holding the door open for the company to depart, there was a blustering sheepishness upon him, at once extremely crest-fallen and superlatively absurd. Detected as the Bully of humility, who had built his windy reputation upon lies, and in his boastfulness had put the honest truth as far away from him as if he had advanced the mean claim (there is no meaner) to tack himself on to a pedigree, he cut a most ridiculous figure. With the people filing off at the door he held, who he knew would carry what had passed to the whole town, to be given to the four winds, he could not have looked a Bully more shorn and forlorn, if he had had his ears cropped. Even that unlucky female, Mrs Sparsit, fallen from her pinnacle of exultation into the Slough of Despond, was not in so bad a plight as that remarkable man and self-made Humbug, Josiah Bounderby of Coketown.

Rachael and Sissy, leaving Mrs Pegler to occupy a bed at her son's for that night, walked together to the gate of Stone Lodge and there parted. Mr Gradgrind joined them before they had gone very far, and spoke with much interest of Stephen Blackpool; for whom he thought this signal failure of the suspicions against Mrs Pegler was likely to work well.

As to the whelp; throughout this scene as on all other late occasions, he had stuck close to Bounderby. He seemed to feel that as long as Bounderby could make no discovery without his knowledge, he was so far safe. He never visited his sister, and had only seen her once since she went home: that is to say, on the night when he still stuck close to Bounderby, as already related.

There was one dim unformed fear lingering about his sister's mind, to which she never gave utterance, which surrounded the graceless and ungrateful boy with a dreadful mystery. The same dark possibility had presented itself in the same shapeless guise, this very day, to Sissy, when Rachael spoke of someone who would be confounded by Stephen's return, having put him out of the way. Louisa had never spoken of harbouring any suspicion of her brother, in connexion with the robbery; she and Sissy had held no confidence on the subject, save in that one interchange of looks when the unconscious father rested his grey head on his hand; but it was understood between them, and they both knew it. This other fear was so awful, that it hovered about each of them like a ghostly shadow; neither daring to think of its being near herself, far less of its being near the other.

And still the forced spirit which the whelp had plucked up, throve with him. If Stephen Blackpool was not the thief, let him show himself. Why didn't he?

Another night. Another day and night. No Stephen Blackpool. Where was the man, and why did he not come back?

Chapter VI

THE STARLIGHT

THE Sunday was a bright Sunday in autumn, clear and cool, when early in the morning Sissy and Rachael met, to walk in the country.

As Coketown cast ashes not only on its own head but on the neighbourhood's too—after the manner of those pious persons who do penance for their own sins by putting other people into sackcloth—it was customary for those who now and then thirsted for a draught of pure air, which is not absolutely the most wicked among the vanities of life, to get a few miles away by the railroad, and then begin their walk, or their lounge in the fields. Sissy and Rachael helped themselves out of the smoke by the usual means, and were put down at a station about midway between the town and Mr Bounderby's retreat.

Though the green landscape was blotted here and there with heaps of coal, it was green elsewhere, and there were trees to see, and there were larks singing (though it was Sunday), and there were pleasant scents in the air, and all was overarched by a bright blue sky. In the distance one way, Coketown showed as a black mist; in another distance, hills began to rise; in a third, there was a faint change in the light of the horizon, where it shone upon the far-off sea. Under their feet, the grass was fresh; beautiful shadows of branches flickered upon it, and speckled it; hedgerows were luxuriant; everything was at peace. Engines at pits' mouths, and lean old horses that had worn the circle of their daily labour into the ground, were alike quiet; wheels had ceased for a short space to turn; and the great wheel of earth seemed to revolve without the shocks and noises of another time.

They walked on across the fields and down the shady lanes, sometimes getting over a fragment of a fence so rotten that it dropped at a touch of the foot, sometimes passing near a wreck of bricks and beams overgrown with grass, marking the site of deserted works. They followed paths and tracks, however slight. Mounds where the grass was rank and high, and where brambles, dock-weed, and such-like vegetation, were confusedly heaped together, they always avoided; for dismal stories were told in that country of the old pits hidden beneath such indications.

The sun was high when they sat down to rest. They had seen no one, near or distant, for a long time; and the solitude remained unbroken. "It is so still here, Rachael, and the way is so untrodden, that I think we must be the first who have been here all the summer."

As Sissy said it, her eyes were attracted by another of those rotten fragments of fence upon the ground. She got up to look at it. "And yet I don't know. This has not been broken very long. The wood is quite fresh where it gave way. Here are footsteps too.—O Rachael!"

She ran back, and caught her round the neck. Rachael had already started up.

"What is the matter?"

"I don't know. There is a hat lying in the grass."

They went forward together. Rachael took it up, shaking from head to foot. She broke into a passion of tears and lamentations: Stephen Blackpool was written in his own hand on the inside.

"O the poor lad, the poor lad! He has been made away with. He is lying murdered here!"

"Is there—has the hat any blood upon it?" Sissy faltered.

They were afraid to look; but they did examine it, and found no mark of violence, inside or out. It had been lying there some days, for rain and dew had stained it, and the mark of its shape was on the grass where it had fallen. They looked fearfully about them, without moving, but could see nothing more. "Rachael," Sissy whispered, "I will go on a little by myself."

She had unclasped her hand, and was in the act of stepping forward, when Rachael caught her in both arms with a scream that resounded over the wide landscape. Before them, at their very feet, was the brink of a black ragged chasm, hidden by the thick grass. They sprang back, and fell upon their knees, each hiding her face upon the other's neck.

"O, my good Lord! He's down there! Down there!" At first this, and her terrific screams, were all that could be got from Rachael, by any tears, by any prayers, by any representations, by any means. It was impossible to hush her; and it was deadly necessary to hold her, or she would have flung herself down the shaft.

"Rachael, dear Rachael, good Rachael, for the love of Heaven not these dreadful cries! Think of Stephen, think of Stephen, think of Stephen!"

By an earnest repetition of this entreaty, poured out in all the agony of such a moment, Sissy at last brought her to be silent, and to look at her with a tearless face of stone.

"Rachael, Stephen may be living. You wouldn't leave him lying maimed at the bottom of this dreadful place, a moment, if you could bring help to him!"

"No, no, no!"

"Don't stir from here, for his sake! Let me go and listen."

She shuddered to approach the pit; but she crept towards it on her hands and knees, and called to him as loud as she could call. She listened, but no sound replied. She called again and listened; still no answering sound. She did this, twenty, thirty, times. She took a little clod of earth from the broken ground where he had stumbled, and threw it in. She could not hear it fall.

The wide prospect, so beautiful in its stillness but a few minutes ago, almost carried despair to her brave heart, as she rose and looked all round her, seeing no help. "Rachael, we must lose not a moment. We must go in different directions, seeking aid. You shall go by the way we have come, and I will go forward by the path. Tell any one you see, and every one what has happened. Think of Stephen, think of Stephen!"

She knew by Rachael's face that she might trust her now. And after standing for a moment to see her running, wringing her hands as she ran, she turned and went upon her own search; she stopped at the hedge to tie her shawl there as a guide to the place, then threw her bonnet aside, and ran as she had never run before.

Run, Sissy, run, in Heaven's name! Don't stop for breath. Run, run! Quickening herself by carrying such entreaties in her thoughts, she ran from field to field, and lane to lane, and place to place, as she had never run before; until she came to a shed by an engine-house, where two men lay in the shade, asleep on straw.

First to wake them, and next to tell them, all so wild and breathless as she was, what had brought her there, were difficulties; but they no sooner understood her than their spirits were on fire like hers. One of the men was in a drunken slumber, but on his comrade's shouting to him that a man had fallen down the Old Hell Shaft, he started out to a pool of dirty water, put his head in it, and came back sober.

With these two men she ran to another half-a-mile further, and with that one to another, while they ran elsewhere. Then a horse was found; and she got another man to ride for life or death to the railroad, and send a message to Louisa, which she wrote and gave him. By this time a whole village was up; and windlasses, ropes, poles, candles, lanterns, all things necessary, were fast collecting and being brought into one place, to be carried to the Old Hell Shaft.

It seemed now hours and hours since she had left the lost man lying in the grave where he had been buried alive. She could not bear to remain away from it any longer—it was like deserting him—and she hurried swiftly back, accompanied by half-a-dozen labourers, including the drunken man whom the news had sobered, and who was the best man of all. When they came to the Old Hell Shaft, they found it as lonely as she had left it. The men called and listened as she had done, and examined the edge of the chasm, and settled how it had happened, and then sat down to wait until the implements they wanted should come up.

Every sound of insects in the air, every stirring of the leaves, every whisper among these men, made Sissy tremble, for she thought it was a cry at the bottom of the pit. But the wind blew idly over it, and no sound arose to the surface, and they sat upon the grass, waiting and waiting. After they had waited some time, straggling people who had heard of the accident began to come up; then the real help of implements began to arrive. In the midst of this, Rachael returned; and with her party there was a surgeon, who brought some wine and medicines. But, the expectation among the people that the man would be found alive, was very slight indeed.

There being now people enough present, to impede the work, the sobered man put himself at the head of the rest, or was put there by the general consent, and made a large ring round the Old Hell Shaft, and appointed men to keep it. Besides such volunteers as were accepted to work, only Sissy and Rachael were at first permitted within this ring; but, later in the day, when the message brought an express from Coketown, Mr Gradgrind and Louisa, and Mr Bounderby, and the whelp, were also there.

The sun was four hours lower than when Sissy and Rachael had first sat down upon the grass, before a means of enabling two men to descend securely was rigged with poles and ropes. Difficulties had arisen in the construction of this machine, simple as it was; requisites had been found wanting, and messages had had to go and return. It was five o'clock in the afternoon of the bright autumnal Sunday, before a candle was sent down to try the air, while three or four rough faces stood crowded close together, attentively watching it: the men at the windlass lowering as they were told. The candle was brought up again, feebly burning, and then some water was cast in. Then the bucket was hooked on; and the sobered man and another got in with lights, giving the word "Lower away!"

As the rope went out, tight and strained, and the windlass creaked, there was not a breath among the one or two hundred men and women looking on, that came as it was wont to come. The signal was given and the windlass stopped, with abundant rope to spare. Apparently so long an interval ensued with the men at the windlass standing idle, that some women shrieked that another accident had happened! But the surgeon who held the watch, declared five minutes not to have elapsed yet, and sternly admonished them to keep silence. He had not well done speaking, when the windlass was reversed and worked again. Practised eyes knew that it did not go as heavily as it would if both workmen had been coming up, and that only one was returning.

The rope came in tight and strained; and ring after ring was coiled upon the barrel of the windlass, and all eyes were fastened on the pit. The sobered man was brought up, and leaped out briskly on the grass. There was an universal cry of "Alive or dead?" and then a deep, profound hush.

When he said "Alive!" a great shout arose, and many eyes had tears in them.

"But he's hurt very bad," he added, as soon as he could make himself heard again. "Where's doctor? He's hurt so very bad, sir, that we donno how to get him up."

They all consulted together, and looked anxiously at the surgeon, as he asked some questions, and shook his head on receiving the replies. The sun was setting now; and the red light in the evening sky touched every face there, and caused it to be distinctly seen in all its wrapt suspense.

The consultation ended in the men returning to the windlass, and the pitman going down again, carrying the wine and some other small matters with him. Then the other man came up. In the meantime, under the surgeon's directions, some men brought a hurdle, on which others made a thick bed of spare clothes covered with loose straw, while he himself contrived some bandages and slings from shawls and handkerchiefs. As these were made, they were hung upon an arm of the pitman who had last come up, with instructions how to use them; and as he stood, shown by the light he carried, leaning his powerful loose hand upon one of the poles, and sometimes glancing down the pit, and sometimes glancing round upon the people, he was not the least conspicuous figure in the scene. It was dark now, and torches were kindled.

It appeared from the little this man said to those about him, which was quickly repeated all over the circle, that the lost man had fallen upon a mass of crumbled rubbish with which the pit was half choked up, and that his fall had been further broken by some jagged earth at the side. He lay upon his back with one arm doubled under him, and according to his own belief had hardly stirred since he fell, except that he had moved his free hand to a side pocket, in which he remembered to have some bread and meat (of which he had swallowed crumbs), and had likewise scooped up a little water in it now and then. He had come straight away from his work, on being written to, and had walked the whole journey; and was on his way to Mr Bounderby's country-house after dark, when he fell. He was crossing that dangerous country at such a dangerous time, because he was innocent of what was laid to his charge, and couldn't rest from coming the nearest way to deliver himself up. The Old Hell Shaft, the pitman said, with a curse upon it, was worthy of its bad name to the last; for, though Stephen could speak now, he believed it would soon be found to have mangled the life out of him.

When all was ready, this man, still taking his last hurried charges from his comrades and the surgeon after the windlass had begun to lower him, disappeared into the pit. The rope went out as before, the signal was made as before, and the windlass stopped. No man removed his hand from it now. Every one waited with his grasp set, and his body bent down to the work, ready to reverse and wind in. At length the signal was given, and all the ring leaned forward.

For, now, the rope came in, tightened and strained to its utmost as it appeared, and the men turned heavily, and the windlass complained. It was scarcely endurable to look at the rope, and think of its giving way. But, ring after ring was coiled upon the barrel of the windlass safely, and the connecting chains appeared, and finally the bucket with the two men holding on at the sides—a sight to make the head swim, and oppress the heart—and tenderly supporting between them, slung and tied within, the figure of a poor, crushed, human creature.

A low murmur of pity went round the throng, and the women wept aloud, as this form, almost without form, was moved very slowly from its iron deliverance, and laid upon the bed of straw. At first, none but the surgeon went close to it. He did what he could in its adjustment on the couch, but the best that he could do was to cover it. That gently done, he called to him Rachael and Sissy. And at that time the pale, worn, patient face was seen looking up at the sky, with the broken right hand lying bare on the outside of the covering garments, as if waiting to be taken by another hand.

They gave him drink, moistened his face with water, and administered some drops of cordial and wine. Though he lay quite motionless looking up at the sky, he smiled and said, "Rachael".

She stooped down on the grass at his side, and bent over him until her eyes were between his and the sky, for he could not so much as turn them to look at her.

"Rachael, my dear."

She took his hand. He smiled again and said, "Don't let 't go."

"Thou'rt in great pain, my own dear Stephen?"

"I ha' been, but not now. I ha' been—dreadful, and dree, and long, my dear—but 'tis ower now. Ah, Rachael, aw a muddle! Fro' first to last, a muddle!"

The spectre of his old look seemed to pass as he said the word.

"I ha' fell into th' pit, my dear, as have cost wi'in the knowledge o' old fok now livin, hundreds and hundreds o' men's lives—fathers, sons, brothers, dear to thousands an thousands, an keepin 'em fro' want and hunger. I ha' fell into a pit that ha' been wi' the' Fire-damp crueller than battle. I ha' read on't in the public petition, as onny one may read, fro' the men that works in pits, in which they ha' pray'n and pray'n the lawmakers for Christ's sake not to let their work be murder to 'em, but to spare 'em for th' wives and children that they loves as well as gentlefok loves theirs. When it were in work, it killed wi'out need; when 'tis let alone, it kills wi'out need. See how we die an no need, one way an another—in a muddle—every day!"

He faintly said it, without any anger against any one. Merely as the truth.

"Thy little sister, Rachael, thou hast not forgot her. Thou'rt not like to forget her now, and me so nigh her. Thou know'st—poor, patient, suff'rin, dear—how thou didst work for her, seet'n all day long in her little chair at thy winder, and how she died, young and misshapen, awlung o' sickly air as had'n no need to be, an awlung o' working people's miserable homes. A muddle! Aw a muddle!"

Louisa approached him; but he could not see her, lying with his face turned up to the night sky.

"If aw th' things that tooches us, my dear, was not so muddled, I should'n ha' had'n need to coom heer. If we was not in a muddle among ourseln, I should'n ha' been, by my own fellow weavers and workin' brothers, so mistook. If Mr Bounderby had ever know'd me right—if he'd ever know'd me at aw—he would'n ha' took'n offence wi' me. He would'n ha' suspect'n me. But look up yonder, Rachael! Look aboove!"

Following his eyes, she saw that he was gazing at a star.

"It ha' shined upon me," he said reverently, "in my pain and trouble down below. It ha' shined into my mind. I ha' lookn at 't an thowt o' thee, Rachael, till the muddle in my mind have cleared awa, above a bit, I hope. If soom ha' been wantin' in unnerstan'in me better, I, too, ha' been wantin' in unnerstan'in them better. When I got thy letter, I easily believen that what the yoong ledy sen an done to me, an what her brother sen an done to me, was one, an that there were a wicked plot betwixt'em. When I fell, I were in anger wi' her, an hurryin on t' be as onjust t' her as oothers was t' me. But in our judgements, like as in our doins, we mun bear and forbear. In my pain an trouble, lookin up yonder,—wi' it shinin' on me—I ha' seen more clear, and ha' made it my dyin prayer that aw th' world may on'y coom toogether more, an get a better unnerstan'in o'one another, than when I were in't my own weak seln."

Louisa hearing what he said, bent over him on the opposite side to Rachael, so that he could see her.

"You ha' heard?" he said after a few moments' silence. "I ha' not forgot yo, ledy."

"Yes, Stephen, I have heard you. And your prayer is mine."

"You ha' a father. Will yo tak' a message to him?"

"He is here," said Louisa, with dread. "Shall I bring him to you?"

"If yo please."

Louisa returned with her father. Standing hand-in-hand, they both looked down upon the solemn countenance.

"Sir, yo will clear me an mak my name good wi' aw men. This I leave to yo."

Mr Gradgrind was troubled and asked how?

"Sir," was the reply; "yor son will tell yo how. Ask him. I mak no charges: I leave none ahint me: not a single word. I ha' seen and spok'n wi' yor son, one night. I ask no more o' yo than that yo clear me—an I trust to yo to do't."

The bearers being now ready to carry him away, and the surgeon being anxious for his removal, those who had torches or lanterns, prepared to go in front of the litter. Before it was raised, and while they were arranging how to go, he said to Rachael, looking upward at the star:

"Often as I coom to myseln, and found it shinin on me down there in my trouble, I thowt it were the star as guided to Our Saviour's home. I awmust think it be the very star!"

They lifted him up, and he was overjoyed to find that they were about to take him in the direction whither the star seemed to him to lead.

"Rachael, beloved lass! Don't let go my hand. We may walk toogether t'night, my dear!"

"I will hold thy hand, and keep beside thee, Stephen, all the way."

"Bless thee! Will somebody be pleased to coover my face!"

They carried him very gently along the fields, and down the lanes, and over the wide landscape; Rachael always holding the hand in hers. Very few whispers broke the mournful silence. It was soon a funeral procession. The star had shown him where to find the God of the poor; and through humility, and sorrow, and forgiveness, he had gone to his Redeemer's rest.

Chapter VII

WHELP-HUNTING

BEFORE the ring formed round the Old Hell Shaft was broken, one figure had disappeared from within it. Mr Bounderby and his shadow had not stood near Louisa, who held her father's arm, but in a retired place by themselves. When Mr Gradgrind was summoned to the couch, Sissy, attentive to all that happened, slipped behind that wicked shadow—a sight in the horror of his face, if there had been eyes there for any sight but one—and whispered in his ear. Without turning his head, he conferred with her a few moments, and vanished. Thus the whelp had gone out of the circle before the people moved.

When the father reached home, he sent a message to Mr Bounderby's, desiring his son to come to him directly. The reply was, that Mr Bounderby having missed him in the crowd, and seeing nothing of him since, had supposed him to be at Stone Lodge.

"I believe, father," said Louisa, "he will not come back to town tonight." Mr Gradgrind turned away, and said no more.

In the morning, he went down to the Bank himself as soon as it was opened, and seeing his son's place empty (he had not the courage to look in at first), went back along the street to meet Mr Bounderby on his way there. To whom he said that, for reasons he would soon explain, but entreated not then to be asked for, he had found it necessary to employ his son at a distance for a little while. Also, that he was charged with the duty of vindicating Stephen Blackpool's memory, and declaring the thief. Mr Bounderby, quite confounded, stood stock-still in the street after his father-in-law had left him, swelling like an immense soap-bubble, without its beauty.

Mr Gradgrind went home, locked himself in his room, and kept it all that day. When Sissy and Louisa tapped at his door, he said, without opening it, "Not now, my dears; in the evening." On their return in the evening, he said, "I am not able yet—tomorrow." He ate nothing all day, and had no candle after dark; and they heard him walking to and fro late at night.

But, in the morning he appeared at breakfast at the usual hour, and took his usual place at the table. Aged and bent he looked, and quite bowed down; and yet he looked a wiser man, and a better man, than in the days when in this life he wanted nothing but Facts. Before he left the room, he appointed a time for them to come to him; and so, with his grey head drooping, went away.

"Dear father," said Louisa, when they kept their appointment, "you have three young children left. They will be different, *I* will be different yet, with Heaven's help."

She gave her hand to Sissy, as if she meant with her help too.

"Your wretched brother," said Mr Gradgrind. "Do you think he had planned this robbery, when he went with you to the lodging?"

"I fear so, father. I know he had wanted money very much, and had spent a great deal."

"The poor man being about to leave the town, it came into his evil brain to cast suspicion on him?"

"I think it must have flashed upon him while he sat there, father. For, I asked him to go there with me. The visit did not originate with him."

"He had some conversation with the poor man. Did he take him aside?"

"He took him out of the room. I asked him afterwards, why he had done so, and he made a plausible excuse; but since last night, father, and when I remember the circumstances by its light, I am afraid I can imagine too truly what passed between them."

"Let me know," said her father, "if your thoughts present your guilty brother in the same dark view as mine."

"I fear, father," hesitated Louisa, "that he must have made some representation to Stephen Blackpool—perhaps in my name, perhaps in his own—which induced him to do in good faith and honesty, what he had never done before, and to wait about the Bank those two or three nights before he left the town."

"Too plain!" returned the father. "Too plain!"

He shaded his face, and remained silent for some moments. Recovering himself, he said:

"And now, how is he to be found? How is he to be saved from justice? In the few hours that I can possibly allow to elapse before I publish the truth, how is he to be found by us, and only by us? Ten thousand pounds could not effect it."

"Sissy has effected it, father."

He raised his eyes to where she stood, like a good fairy in his house, and said in a tone of softened gratitude and grateful kindness, "It is always you, my child!"

"We had our fears," Sissy explained, glancing at Louisa, "before yesterday; and when I saw you brought to the side of the litter last night, and heard what passed (being close to Rachael all the time), I went to him when no one saw, and said to him, 'Don't look at me. See where your father is. Escape at once for his sake and your own!' He was in a tremble before I whispered to him, and he started and trembled more then, and said, 'Where can I go? I have very little money, and I don't know who will hide me!' I thought of father's old circus. I have not forgotten where Mr Sleary goes at this time of year, and I read of him in a paper only the other day. I told him to hurry there, and tell his name, and ask Mr Sleary to hide him till I came. 'I'll get to him before the morning,' he said. And I saw him shrink away among the people."

"Thank Heaven!" exclaimed his father. "He may be got abroad yet."

It was the more hopeful as the town to which Sissy had directed him was within three hours' journey of Liverpool, whence he could be swiftly dispatched to any part of the world. But, caution being necessary in communicating with him—for there was a greater danger every moment of his being suspected now, and nobody could be sure at heart but that Mr Bounderby himself, in a bullying vein of public zeal, might play a Roman part—it was consented that Sissy and Louisa should repair to the place in question, by a circuitous course, alone; and that the unhappy father, setting forth in an opposite direction, should get round to the same bourne by another and wider route. It was further agreed that he should not present himself to Mr Sleary, lest his intentions should be mistrusted, or the intelligence of his arrival should cause his son to take flight anew; but, that the communication should be left to Sissy and Louisa to open; and that they should inform the cause of so much misery and disgrace, of his father's being at hand and of the purpose for which they had come. When these arrangements had been well considered and were fully understood by all three, it was time to begin to carry them into execution. Early in the afternoon, Mr Gradgrind walked direct from his own house into the country, to be taken up on the line by which he was to travel; and at night the remaining two set forth upon their different course, encouraged by not seeing any face they knew.

The two travelled all night, except when they were left, for odd numbers of minutes, at branch-places up illimitable flights of steps, or down wells—which was the only variety of those branches—and, early in the morning, were turned out on a swamp, a mile or two from the town they sought. From this dismal spot they were rescued by a savage old postilion, who happened to be up early, kicking a horse in a fly; and so were smuggled into the town by all the back lanes where the pigs lived: which, although not a magnificent or even savoury approach, was, as is usual in such cases, the legitimate highway.

The first thing they saw on entering the town was the skeleton of Sleary's Circus. The company had departed for another town more than twenty miles off, and had opened there last night. The connexion between the two places was by a hilly turnpike-road, and the travelling on that road was very slow. Though they took but a hasty breakfast, and no rest (which it would have been in vain to seek under such anxious circumstances), it was noon before they began to find the bills of Sleary's Horseriding on barns and walls, and one o'clock when they stopped in the market-place.

A Grand Morning Performance by the Riders, commencing at that very hour, was in course of announcement by the bellman as they set their feet upon the stones of the street. Sissy recommended that, to avoid making inquiries and attracting attention in the town, they should present themselves to pay at the door. If Mr Sleary were taking the money, he would be sure to know her, and would proceed with discretion. If he were not, he would be sure to see them inside; and, knowing what he had done with the fugitive, would proceed with discretion still.

Therefore they repaired, with fluttering hearts, to the well-remembered booth. The flag with the inscription SLEARY'S HORSERIDING, was there; and the Gothic niche was there; but Mr Sleary was not there. Master Kidderminster, grown too maturely turfy to be received by the wildest credulity as Cupid any more, had yielded to the invincible force of circumstances (and his beard), and, in the capacity of a man who made himself generally useful, presided on this occasion over the exchequer—having also a drum in reserve, on which to expend his leisure moments and superfluous forces. In the extreme sharpness of his look out for base coin, Mr Kidderminster, as at present situated, never saw anything but money; so Sissy passed him unrecognized, and they went in.

The Emperor of Japan, on a steady old white horse stencilled with black spots, was twirling five wash-hand basins at once, as it is the favourite recreation of that monarch to do. Sissy, though well acquainted with his Royal line, had no personal knowledge of the present Emperor, and his reign was peaceful. Miss Josephine Sleary, in her celebrated graceful Equestrian Tyrolean Flower-Act, was then announced by a new clown (who humorously said Cauliflower Act), and Mr Sleary appeared, leading her in.

Mr Sleary had only made one cut at the Clown with his long whip-lash, and the Clown had only said, "If you do it again, I'll throw the horse at you!" when Sissy was recognized both by father and daughter. But they got through the Act with great self-possession; and Mr Sleary, saving for the first instant, conveyed no more expression into his locomotive eye than into his fixed one. The performance seemed a little long to Sissy and Louisa, particularly when it stopped to afford the Clown an opportunity of telling Mr Sleary (who said "Indeed, sir!" to all his observations in the calmest way, and with his eye on the house), about two legs sitting on three legs looking at one leg, when in came four legs, and laid hold of one leg, and up got two legs, caught hold of three legs, and threw 'em at four legs, who ran away with one leg. For, although an ingenious Allegory relating to a butcher, a three-legged stool, a dog, and a leg of mutton, this narrative consumed time; and they were in great suspense. At last, however, little fair-haired Josephine made her curtsey amid great applause; and the Clown, left alone in the ring, had just warmed himself, and said, "Now *I'll* have a turn!" when Sissy was touched on the shoulder, and beckoned out.

She took Louisa with her; and they were received by Mr Sleary in a very little private apartment, with canvas sides, a grass floor, and a wooden ceiling all aslant, on which the box company stamped their approbation as if they were coming through. "Thethilia," said Mr Sleary, who had brandy and water at hand, "it doth me good to thee you. You wath alwayth a favourite with uth, and you've done uth credit thinth the old timeth I'm thure. You mutht thee our people, my dear, afore we thpeak of bithnith, or they'll break their hearth—ethpethially the women. Here'th Jothphine hath been and got married to E. W. B. Childerth, and thee hath got a boy, and though he'th only three yearth old, he thtickth on to any pony you can bring againtht him. He'th named The Little Wonder Of Thcolathtic Equitation; and if you don't hear of that boy at Athley'th, you'll hear of him at Parith. And you recollect Kidderminthter, that wath thought to be rather thweet upon yourthelf? Well. He'th married too. Married a widder. Old enough to be hith mother.

Thee wath Tightrope, thee wath, and now thee'th nothing—on accounth of fat. They've got two children, tho we're throng in the Fairy bithnith and the Nurthery dodge. If you wath to thee our Children in the Wood, with their father and mother both a dyin' on a horthe—their uncle a rethieving of 'em ath hith wardth, upon a horthe—themthelvth both a goin' a blackberryin' on a horthe—and the Robinth a coming in to cover 'em with leavth, upon a horthe—you'd thay it wath the completetht thing ath ever you thet your eyeth on! And you remember Emma Gordon, my dear, ath wath a'motht a mother to you? Of courthe you do; I needn't athk. Well! Emma, thee lotht her huthband. He wath throw'd a heavy back-fall off a Elephant in a thort of a Pagoda thing ath the Thultan of the Indieth, and he never got the better of it; and thee married a thecond time—married a Cheethemonger ath fell in love with her from the front—and he'th a Overtheer and makin' a fortun."

These various changes, Mr Sleary, very short of breath now, related with great heartiness, and with a wonderful kind of innocence, considering what a bleary and brandy-and-watery old veteran he was. Afterwards he brought in Josephine, and E. W. B. Childers (rather deeply-lined in the jaws by daylight), and The Little Wonder of Scholastic Equitation, and, in a word, all the company. Amazing creatures they were in Louisa's eyes, so white and pink of complexion, so scant of dress, and so demonstrative of leg; but it was very agreeable to see them crowding about Sissy, and very natural in Sissy to be unable to refrain from tears.

"There! Now Thethilia hath kithd all the children, and hugged all the women, and thaken handth all round with all the men, clear, every one of you, and ring in the band for the thecond part!"

As soon as they were gone, he continued in a low tone. "Now, Thethilia, I don't athk to know any thecreth, but I thuppothe I may conthider thith to be Mith Thquire."

"This is his sister. Yes."

"And t'other one'th daughter. That'h what I mean. Hope I thee you well, mith. And I hope the Thquire'th well?"

"My father will be here soon," said Louisa, anxious to bring him to the point. "Is my brother safe?"

"Thafe and thound!" he replied. "I want you jutht to take a peep at the Ring, mith, through here. Thethilia, you know the dodgeth; find a thpy-hole for yourthelf."

They each looked through a chink in the boards.

"That'h Jack the Giant Killer—piethe of comic infant bithnith," said Sleary. "There'th a property-houthe, you thee, for Jack to hide in; there'th my Clown with a thauthepan-lid and a thpit, for Jack'th thervant; there'th little Jack himthelf in a thplendid thoot of armour; there'th two comic black thervanth twithe ath big ath the houthe, to thtand by it and to bring it in and clear it; and the Giant (a very ecthpenthive bathket one), he an't on yet. Now, do you thee 'em all?"

"Yes," they both said.

"Look at 'em again," said Sleary, "look at 'em well. You thee 'em all? Very good. Now, mith;" he put a form for them to sit on; "I have my opinionth, and the Thquire your father hath hith. I don't want to know what your brother'th been up to; ith better for me not to know. All I thay ith, the Thquire hath thtood by Thethilia, and I'll thtand by the Thquire. Your brother ith one o' them black thervanth."

Louisa uttered an exclamation, partly of distress, partly of satisfaction.

"Ith a fact," said Sleary, "and even knowin' it, you couldn't put your finger on him. Let the Thquire come. I thall keep your brother here after the performanth. I thant undreth him, nor yet wath hith paint off. Let the Thquire come here after the performanth, and you thall find your brother, and have the whole plathe to talk to him in. Never mind the lookth of him, ath long ath he'th well hid."

Louisa, with many thanks and with a lightened load, detained Mr Sleary no longer then. She left her love for her brother, with her eyes full of tears; and she and Sissy went away until later in the afternoon.

Mr Gradgrind arrived within an hour afterwards. He too had encountered no one whom he knew; and was now sanguine, with Sleary's assistance, of getting his disgraced son to Liverpool in the night. As neither of the three could be his companion without almost identifying him under any disguise, he prepared a letter to a correspondent whom he could trust, beseeching him to ship the bearer off, at any cost, to North or South America, or any distant part of the world to which he could be the most speedily and privately dispatched. This done, they walked about, waiting for the Circus to be quite vacated; not only by the audience, but by the company and by the horses. After watching it a long time, they saw Mr Sleary bring out a chair and sit down by the side-door, smoking; as if that were his signal that they might approach.

"Your thervant, Thquire," was his cautious salutation as they passed in. "If you want me you'll find me here. You muthn't mind your thon having a comic livery on."

They all three went in; and Mr Gradgrind sat down, forlorn, on the Clown's performing chair in the middle of the ring. On one of the back benches, remote in the subdued light and the strangeness of the place, sat the villainous whelp, sulky to the last, whom he had the misery to call his son.

In a preposterous coat, like a beadle's, with cuffs and flaps exaggerated to an unspeakable extent; in an immense waistcoat, knee-breeches, buckled shoes, and a mad cocked hat; with nothing fitting him, and everything of coarse material, moth-eaten, and full of holes; with seams in his black face, where fear and heat had started through the greasy composition daubed all over it; anything so grimly, detestably, ridiculously shameful as the whelp in his comic livery, Mr Gradgrind never could by any other means have believed in, weighable and measurable fact though it was. And one of his model children had come to this!

At first the whelp would not draw any nearer, but persisted in remaining up there by himself. Yielding at length, if any concession so sullenly made can be called yielding, to the entreaties of Sissy—for Louisa he disowned altogether—he came down, bench by bench, until he stood in the sawdust, on the verge of the circle, as far as possible, within its limits, from where his father sat.

"How was this done?" asked the father.

"How was what done?" moodily answered the son.

"This robbery," said the father, raising his voice upon the word.

"I forced the safe myself over night, and shut it up ajar before I went away. I had had the key that was found, made long before. I dropped it that morning, that it might be supposed to have been used. I didn't take the money all at once. I pretended to put my balance away every night, but I didn't. Now you know all about it."

"If a thunderbolt had fallen on me," said the father, "it would have shocked me less than this!"

"I don't see why," grumbled the son. "So many people are employed in situations of trust; so many people, out of so many, will be dishonest. I have heard you talk, a hundred times, of its being a law. How can I help laws? You have comforted others with such things, father. Comfort yourself!"

The father buried his face in his hands, and the son stood in his disgraceful grotesqueness, biting straw: his hands, with the black partly worn away inside, looking like the hands of a monkey. The evening was fast closing in; and, from time to time, he turned the whites of his eyes restlessly and impatiently towards his father. They were the only parts of his face that showed any life or expression, the pigment upon it was so thick.

"You must be got to Liverpool, and sent abroad."

"I suppose I must. I can't be more miserable anywhere," whimpered the whelp, "than I have been here, ever since I can remember. That's one thing."

Mr Gradgrind went to the door, and returned with Sleary, to whom he submitted the question, How to get this deplorable object away?

"Why, I've been thinking of it, Thquire. There'th not muth time to lothe, tho you muth thay yeth or no. Ith over twenty mileth to the rail. Thereth a coath in half an hour, that goeth *to* the rail, 'purpothe to cath the mail train. That train will take him right to Liverpool."

"But look at him," groaned Mr Gradgrind. "Will any coach——"

"I don't mean that he thould go in the comic livery," said Sleary. "Thay the word, and I'll make a Jothkin of him, out of the wardrobe, in five minutes."

"I don't understand," said Mr Gradgrind.

"A Jothkin——a Carter. Make up your mind quick, Thquire. There'll be beer to feth. I've never met with nothing but beer ath'll ever clean a comic blackamoor."

Mr Gradgrind rapidly assented; Mr Sleary rapidly turned out from a box, a smock frock, a felt hat, and other essentials; the whelp rapidly changed clothes behind a screen of baize; Mr Sleary rapidly brought beer, and washed him white again.

"Now," said Sleary, "come along to the coath, and jump up behind; I'll go with you there, and they'll thuppothe you one of my people. Thay farewell to your family, and tharp'th the word!" With which he delicately retired.

"Here is your letter," said Mr Gradgrind. "All necessary means will be provided for you. Atone, by repentance and better conduct, for the shocking action you have committed, and the dreadful consequences to which it has led. Give me your hand, my poor boy, and may God forgive you as I do!"

The culprit was moved to a few abject tears by these words and their pathetic tone. But, when Louisa opened her arms, he repulsed her afresh.

"Not you. I don't want to have anything to say to you!"

"O Tom, Tom, do we end so, after all my love!"

"After all your love!" he returned, obdurately. "Pretty love! Leaving old Bounderby to himself, and packing my best friend Mr Harthouse off, and going home, just when I was in the greatest danger. Pretty love that! Coming out with every word about our having gone to that place, when you saw the net was gathering round me. Pretty love that! You have regularly given me up. You never cared for me."

"Tharp'th the word!" said Sleary at the door.

They all confusedly went out: Louisa crying to him that she forgave him, and loved him still, and that he would one day be sorry to have left her so, and glad to think of these her last words, far away: when some one ran against them. Mr Gradgrind and Sissy, who were both before him while his sister yet clung to his shoulder, stopped and recoiled.

For, there was Bitzer, out of breath, his thin lips parted, his thin nostrils distended, his white eyelashes quivering, his colourless face more colourless than ever, as if he ran himself into a white heat, when other people ran themselves into a glow. There he stood, panting and heaving, as if he had never stopped since the night, now long ago, when he had run them down before.

"I'm sorry to interfere with your plans," said Bitzer, shaking his head, "but I can't allow myself to be done by horseriders. I must have young Mr Tom; he mustn't be got away by horseriders; here he is in a smock frock, and I must have him!"

By the collar, too, it seemed. For, so he took possession of him.

Chapter VIII

PHILOSOPHICAL

T HEY went back into the booth, Sleary shutting the door to keep intruders out. Bitzer, still holding the paralysed culprit by the collar, stood in the Ring, blinking at his old patron through the darkness of the twilight.

"Bitzer," said Mr Gradgrind, broken down, and miserably submissive to him, "have you a heart?"

"The circulation, sir," returned Bitzer, smiling at the oddity of the question, "couldn't be carried on without one. No man, sir, acquainted with the facts established by Harvey relating to the circulation of the blood, can doubt that I have a heart."

"Is it accessible," cried Mr Gradgrind, "to any compassionate influence?"

"It is accessible to Reason, sir," returned the excellent young man. "And to nothing else."

They stood looking at each other; Mr Gradgrind's face as white as the pursuer's.

"What motive—even what motive in reason—can you have for preventing the escape of this wretched youth," said Mr Gradgrind, "and crushing his miserable father? See his sister here. Pity us!"

"Sir," returned Bitzer, in a very business-like and logical manner, "since you ask me what motive I have in reason, for taking young Mr Tom back to Coketown, it is only reasonable to let you know. I have suspected young Mr Tom of this bank-robbery from the first. I had had my eye upon him before that time, for I knew his ways. I have kept my observations to myself, but I have made them; and I have got ample proofs against him now, besides his running away, and besides his own confession, which I was just in time to overhear. I had the pleasure of watching your house yesterday morning, and following you here. I am going to take young Mr Tom back to Coketown, in order to deliver him over to Mr Bounderby. Sir, I have no doubt whatever that Mr Bounderby will then promote me to young Mr Tom's situation. And I wish to have his situation, sir, for it will be a rise to me, and will do me good."

"If this is solely a question of self-interest with you——" Mr Gradgrind began.

"I beg your pardon for interrupting you, sir," returned Bitzer; "but I am sure you know that the whole social system is a question of self-interest. What you must always appeal to, is a person's self-interest. It's your only hold. We are so constituted. I was brought up in that catechism when I was very young, sir, as you are aware."

"What sum of money," said Mr Gradgrind, "will you set against your expected promotion?"

"Thank you, sir," returned Bitzer, "for hinting at the proposal; but I will not set any sum against it. Knowing that your clear head would propose that alternative, I have gone over the calculations in my mind; and I find that to compound a felony, even on very high terms indeed, would not be as safe and good for me as my improved prospects in the Bank."

"Bitzer," said Mr Gradgrind, stretching out his hands as though he would have said, See how miserable I am! "Bitzer, I have but one chance left to soften you. You were many years at my school. If, in remembrance of the pains bestowed upon you there—you can persuade yourself in any degree to disregard your present interest and release my son, I entreat and pray you to give him the benefit of that remembrance."

"I really wonder, sir," rejoined the old pupil in an argumentative manner, "to find you taking a position so untenable. My schooling was paid for; it was a bargain; and when I came away, the bargain ended."

It was a fundamental principle of the Gradgrind philosophy, that everything was to be paid for. Nobody was ever on any account to give anybody anything, or render anybody help without purchase. Gratitude was to be abolished, and the virtues springing from it were not to be. Every inch of the existence of mankind, from birth to death, was to be a bargain across a counter. And if we didn't get to Heaven that way, it was not a politico-economical place, and we had no business there.

"I don't deny," added Bitzer, "that my schooling was cheap. But that comes right, sir. I was made in the cheapest market, and have to dispose of myself in the dearest."

He was a little troubled here, by Louisa and Sissy crying.

"Pray don't do that," said he, "it's of no use doing that: it only worries. You seem to think that I have some animosity against young Mr Tom; whereas I have none at all. I am only going, on the reasonable grounds I have mentioned, to take him back to Coketown. If he was to resist, I should set up the cry of Stop Thief! But, he won't resist, you may depend upon it."

Mr Sleary, who, with his mouth open and his rolling eye as immoveably jammed in his head as his fixed one, had listened to these doctrines with profound attention, here stepped forward.

"Thquire, you know perfectly well, and your daughter knowth perfectly well (better than you, becauthe I thed it to her), that I didn't know what your thon had done, and that I didn't want to know—I thed it wath better not, though I only thought, then, it wath thkylarking. However, thith young man having made it known to be a robbery of a bank, why, that'th a theriouth thing; muth too theriouth a thing for me to compound, ath thith young man hath very properly called it. Conthequently, Thquire, you muth'nt quarrel with me if I take thith young man'th thide, and thay he'th right and there'th no help for it. But I tell you what I'll do, Thquire; I'll drive your thon and thith young man over to the rail, and prevent expothure here. I can't conthent to do more, but I'll do that."

Fresh lamentations from Louisa, and deeper affliction on Mr Gradgrind's part, followed this desertion of them by their last friend. But, Sissy glanced at him with great attention; nor did she in her own breast misunderstand him. As they were all going out again, he favoured her with one slight roll of his moveable eye, desiring her to linger behind. As he locked the door, he said excitedly:

"The Thquire thtood by you, Thethilia, and I'll thtand by the Thquire. More than that: thith ith a prethiouth rathcal, and belongth to that bluthering Cove that my people nearly pitht out o' winder. It'll be a dark night; I've got a horthe that'll do anything but thpeak; I've got a pony that'll go fifteen mile an hour with Childerth driving of him; I've got a dog that'll keep a man to one plathe four-and-twenty hourth. Get a word with the young Thquire. Tell him, when he theeth our horthe begin to danthe, not to be afraid of being thpilt, but to look out for a pony-gig coming up. Tell him, when he theeth that gig clothe by, to jump down, and it'll take him off at a rattling pathe. If my dog leth thith young man thtir a peg on foot, I give him leave to go. And if my horthe ever thtirth from that thpot where he beginth a danthing, till the morning—I don't know him!—Tharp'th the word!"

The word was so sharp, that in ten minutes Mr Childers, sauntering about the market-place in a pair of slippers, had his cue, and Mr Sleary's equipage was ready. It was a fine sight, to behold the learned dog barking round it, and Mr Sleary instructing him, with his one practicable eye, that Bitzer was the object of his particular attentions. Soon after dark they all three got in and started; the learned dog (a formidable creature) already pinning Bitzer with his eye, and sticking close to the wheel on his side, that he might be ready for him in the event of his showing the slightest disposition to alight.

The other three sat up at the inn all night in great suspense. At eight o'clock in the morning Mr Sleary and the dog re-appeared: both in high spirits.

"All right, Thquire!" said Mr Sleary, "your thon may be aboard-a-thip by thith time. Childerth took him off, an hour and a half after we left here latht night. The horthe danthed the Polka till he wath dead beat (he would have walthed, if he hadn't been in harneth), and then I gave him the word and he went to thleep comfortable. When that prethiouth young Rathcal thed he'd go for'ard afoot, the dog hung on to hith neck-hankercher with all four legth in the air and pulled him down and rolled him over. Tho he come back into the drag, and there he that, 'till I turned the horthe'th head, at halfpatht thixth thith morning."

Mr Gradgrind overwhelmed him with thanks, of course; and hinted as delicately as he could, at a handsome remuneration in money.

"I don't want money mythelf, Thquire; but Childerth ith a family man, and if you wath to like to offer him a five-pound note, it mightn't be unactheptable. Likewithe if you wath to thtand a collar for the dog, or a thet of bellth for the horthe, I thould be very glad to take 'em. Brandy and water I alwayth take." He had already called for a glass, and now called for another. "If you wouldn't think it going too far, Thquire, to make a little thpread for the company at about three and thixth ahead, not reckoning Luth, it would make 'em happy."

All these little tokens of his gratitude, Mr Gradgrind very willingly undertook to render. Though he thought them far too slight, he said, for such a service.

"Very well, Thquire; then, if you'll only give a Horthe-Riding, a bethpeak, whenever you can, you'll more than balanthe the account. Now, Thquire, if your daughter will ethcuthe me, I thould like one parting word with you."

Louisa and Sissy withdrew into an adjoining room; Mr Sleary, stirring and drinking his brandy and water as he stood, went on:

"Thquire, you don't need to be told that dogth ith wonderful animalth."

"Their instinct," said Mr Gradgrind, "is surprising."

"Whatever you call it—and I'm bletht if I know what to call it"—said Sleary, "it ith athtonithing. The way in with a dog'll find you—the dithtanthe he'll come!"

"His scent," said Mr Gradgrind, "being so fine."

"I'm bletht if I know what to call it," repeated Sleary, shaking his head, "but I have had dogth find me, Thquire, in a way that made me think whether that dog hadn't gone to another dog, and thed, 'You don't happen to know a perthon of the name of Thleary, do you? Perthon of the name of Thleary, in the Horthe-Riding way—thtout man—game eye?' And whether that dog mightn't have thed, 'Well, I can't thay I know him mythelf, but I know a dog that I think would be likely to be acquainted with him." And whether that dog mightn't have thought it over, and thed, 'Thleary, Thleary! O yeth, to be thure! A friend of mine menthioned him to me at one time. I can get you hith addreth directly.' In conthequenth of my being afore the public, and going about tho muth, you thee, there mutht be a number of dogth acquainted with me, Thquire, that *I* don't know!"

Mr Gradgrind seemed to be quite confounded by this speculation.

"Any way," said Sleary, after putting his lips to his brandy and water, "ith fourteen month ago, Thquire, thinthe we wath at Chethter. We wath getting up our Children in the Wood one morning, when there cometh into our Ring, by the thtage door, a dog. He had travelled a long way, he wath in very bad condithon, he wath lame, and pretty well blind. He went round to our children, one after another, as if he wath a theeking for a child he know'd; and then he come to me, and throwd hithelf up behind, and thtood on hith two fore-legth, weak ath he wath, and then he wagged hith tail and died. Thquire, that dog wath Merrylegth."

"Sissy's father's dog!"

"Thethilia'th father'th old dog. Now, Thquire, I can take my oath, from my knowledge of that dog, that that man wath dead—and buried—afore that dog come back to me. Joth'phine and Childerth and me talked it over a long time, whether I thould write or not. But we agreed, 'No. There'th nothing comfortable to tell; why unthettle her mind, and make her unhappy?' Tho, whether her father bathely detherted her; or whether he broke hith own heart alone, rather than pull her down along with him; never will be known, now, Thquire, till—no, not till we know how the dogth findth uth out!"

"She keeps the bottle that he sent her for, to this hour; and she will believe in his affection to the last moment of her life," said Mr Gradgrind.

"It theemth to prethent two thingth to a perthon, don't it, Thquire?" said Mr Sleary, musing as he looked down into the depths of his brandy and water: "one, that there ith a love in the world, not all Thelf-interetht after all, but thomething very different; t'other, that it hath a way of ith own of calculating or not calculating, whith thomehow or another ith at leatht ath hard to give a name to, ath the wayth of the dogth ith!"

Mr Gradgrind looked out of window, and made no reply. Mr Sleary emptied his glass and recalled the ladies.

"Thethilia my dear, kith me and good-bye! Mith Thquire, to thee you treating of her like a thithter, and a thithter that you trutht and honour with all your heart and more, ith a very pretty thight to me. I hope your brother may live to be better detherving of you, and a greater comfort to you. Thquire, thake handth, firtht and latht! Don't be croth with uth poor vagabondth. People mutht be amuthed. They can't be alwayth a learning, nor yet they can't be alwayth a working, they an't made for it. You *muth* have uth, Thquire. Do the withe thing and the kind thing too, and make the betht of uth; not the wurtht!"

"And I never thought before," said Mr Sleary, putting his head in at the door again to say it, "that I wath tho muth of a Cackler!"

Chapter IX

FINAL

I T is a dangerous thing to see anything in the sphere of a vain blusterer, before the vain blusterer sees it himself. Mr Bounderby felt that Mrs Sparsit had audaciously anticipated him, and presumed to be wiser than he. Inappeasably indignant with her for her triumphant discovery of Mrs Pegler, he turned this presumption, on the part of a woman in her dependent position, over and over in his mind, until it accumulated with turning like a great snowball. At last he made the discovery that to discharge this highly-connected female—to have it in his power to say, "She was a woman of family, and wanted to stick to me, but I wouldn't have it, and got rid of her"—would be to get the utmost possible amount of crowning glory out of the connexion, and at the same time to punish Mrs Sparsit according to her deserts.

Filled fuller than ever, with this great idea, Mr Bounderby came in to lunch, and sat himself down in the dining-room of former days, where his portrait was. Mrs Sparsit sat by the fire, with her foot in her cotton stirrup, little thinking whither she was posting.

Since the Pegler affair, this gentlewoman had covered her pity for Mr Bounderby with a veil of quiet melancholy and contrition. In virtue thereof, it had become her habit to assume a woful look; which woful look she now bestowed upon her patron.

"What's the matter now, ma'am?" said Mr Bounderby, in a very short, rough way.

"Pray, sir," returned Mrs Sparsit, "do not bite my nose off."

"Bite your nose off, ma'am?" repeated Mr Bounderby. "*Your* nose!" meaning, as Mrs Sparsit conceived, that it was too developed a nose for the purpose. After which offensive implication, he cut himself a crust of bread, and threw the knife down with a noise.

Mrs Sparsit took her foot out of her stirrup, and said, "Mr Bounderby, sir!"

"Well, ma'am?" retorted Mr Bounderby. "What are you staring at?"

"May I ask, sir," said Mrs Sparsit, "have you been ruffled this morning?"

"Yes, ma'am."

"May I inquire, sir," pursued the injured woman, "whether I am the unfortunate cause of your having lost your temper?"

"Now, I'll tell you what, ma'am," said Bounderby, "I am not come here to be bullied. A female may be highly connected, but she can't be permitted to bother and badger a man in my position, and I am not going to put up with it." (Mr Bounderby felt it necessary to get on; foreseeing that if he allowed of details, he would be beaten.)

Mrs Sparsit first elevated, then knitted, her Coriolanian eyebrows; gathered up her work into its proper basket; and rose.

"Sir," said she, majestically. "It is apparent to me that I am in your way at present. I will retire to my own apartment."

"Allow me to open the door, ma'am."

"Thank you, sir; I can do it for myself."

"You had better allow me, ma'am," said Bounderby, passing her, and getting his hand upon the lock; "because I can take the opportunity of saying a word to you, before you go. Mrs Sparsit, ma'am, I rather think you are cramped here, do you know? It appears to me, that, under my humble roof, there's hardly opening enough for a lady of your genius in other people's affairs."

Mrs Sparsit gave him a look of the darkest scorn, and said with great politeness, "Really, sir?"

"I have been thinking it over, you see, since the late affairs have happened, ma'am," said Bounderby; "and it appears to my poor judgement——"

"Oh! Pray, sir," Mrs Sparsit interposed, with sprightly cheerfulness, "don't disparage your judgement. Everybody knows how unerring Mr Bounderby's judgement is. Everybody has had proofs of it. It must be the theme of general conversation. Disparage anything in yourself but your judgement, sir," said Mrs Sparsit, laughing.

Mr Bounderby, very red and uncomfortable, resumed:

"It appears to me, ma'am, I say, that a different sort of establishment altogether, would bring out a lady of *your* powers. Such an establishment as your relation, Lady Scadgers's, now. Don't you think you might find some affairs there, ma'am, to interfere with?"

"It never occurred to me before, sir," returned Mrs Sparsit; "but now you mention it, I should think it highly probable."

"Then suppose you try, ma'am," said Bounderby, laying an envelope with a cheque in it, in her little basket. "You can take your own time for going, ma'am; but perhaps in the meanwhile, it will be more agreeable to a lady of your powers of mind, to eat her meals by herself, and not to be intruded upon. I really ought to apologize to you——being only Josiah Bounderby of Coketown——for having stood in your light so long."

"Pray don't name it, sir," returned Mrs Sparsit. "If that portrait could speak, sir,——but it has the advantage over the original of not possessing the power of committing itself and disgusting others,——it would testify, that a long period has elapsed since I first habitually addressed it as the picture of a Noodle. Nothing that a Noodle does, can awaken surprise or indignation; the proceedings of a Noodle can only inspire contempt."

Thus saying, Mrs Sparsit, with her Roman features like a medal struck to commemorate her scorn of Mr Bounderby, surveyed him fixedly from head to foot, swept disdainfully past him, and ascended the staircase. Mr Bounderby closed the door, and stood before the fire; projecting himself after his old explosive manner into his portrait——and into futurity.

Into how much of futurity? He saw Mrs Sparsit fighting out a daily fight, at the points of all the weapons in the female armoury, with the grudging, smarting, peevish, tormenting Lady Scadgers, still laid up in bed with her mysterious leg, and gobbling her insufficient income down by about the middle of every quarter, in a mean little airless lodging, a mere closet for one, a mere crib for two; but did he see more? Did he catch any glimpse of himself making a show of Bitzer to strangers, as the rising young man, so devoted to his master's great merits, who had won young Tom's place, and had almost captured young Tom himself, in the times when by various rascals he was spirited away? Did he see any faint reflection of his own image making a vain-glorious will, whereby five-and-twenty Humbugs, past five and fifty years of age, each taking upon himself the name, Josiah Bounderby of Coketown, should for ever dine in Bounderby Hall, for ever lodge in Bounderby buildings, for ever attend a Bounderby chapel, for ever go to sleep under a Bounderby chaplain, for ever be supported out of a Bounderby estate, and for ever nauseate all healthy stomachs with a vast amount of Bounderby balderdash and bluster? Had he any prescience of the day, five years to come, when Josiah Bounderby of Coketown was to die of a fit in the Coketown street, and this same precious will was to begin its long career of quibble, plunder, false pretences, vile example, little service and much law? Probably not. Yet the portrait was to see it all out.

Here was Mr Gradgrind on the same day, and in the same hour, sitting thoughtful in his own room. How much of futurity did *he* see? Did he see himself, a white-haired decrepit man, bending his hitherto inflexible theories to appointed circumstances; making his facts and figures subservient to Faith, Hope, and Charity; and no longer trying to grind that Heavenly trio in his dusty little mills? Did he catch sight of himself, therefore much despised by his late political associates? Did he see them, in the era of its being quite settled that the national dustmen have only to do with one another, and owe no duty to an abstraction called a People, "taunting the honourable gentleman" with this and with that and with what not, five nights a-week, until the small hours of the morning? Probably he had that much fore-knowledge, knowing his men.

Here was Louisa on the night of the same day, watching the fire as in days of yore, though with a gentler and a humbler face. How much of the future might arise before *her* vision? Broadsides in the streets, signed with her father's name, exonerating the late Stephen Blackpool, weaver, from misplaced suspicion, and publishing the guilt of his own son, with such extenuation as his years and temptation (he could not bring himself to add, his education) might beseech; were of the Present. So, Stephen Blackpool's tombstone, with her father's record of his death, was almost of the Present, for she knew it was to be. These things she could plainly see. But, how much of the Future?

A working woman, christened Rachael, after a long illness once again appearing at the ringing of the Factory bell, and passing to and fro at the set hours, among the Coketown Hands; a woman of a pensive beauty, always dressed in black, but sweet-tempered and serene, and even cheerful; who, of all the people in the place, alone appeared to have compassion on a degraded, drunken wretch of her own sex, who was sometimes seen in the town secretly begging of her, and crying to her; a woman working, ever working, but content to do it, and preferring to do it as her natural lot, until she should be too old to labour any more? Did Louisa see this? Such a thing was to be.

A lonely brother, many thousands of miles away, writing, on paper blotted with tears, that her words had too soon come true, and that all the treasures in the world would be cheaply bartered for a sight of her dear face? At length this brother coming nearer home, with hope of seeing her, and being delayed by illness; and then a letter in a strange hand, saying "he died in hospital, of fever, such a day, and died in penitence and love of you: his last word being your name?" Did Louisa see these things? Such things were to be.

Herself again a wife—a mother—lovingly watchful of her children, ever careful that they should have a childhood of the mind no less than a childhood of the body, as knowing it to be even a more beautiful thing, and a possession, any hoarded scrap of which, is a blessing and happiness to the wisest? Did Louisa see this? Such a thing was never to be.

But, happy Sissy's happy children loving her; all children loving her; she, grown learned in childish lore; thinking no innocent and pretty fancy ever to be despised; trying hard to know her humbler fellow-creatures, and to beautify their lives of machinery and reality with those imaginative graces and delights, without which the heart of infancy will wither up, the sturdiest physical manhood will be morally stark death, and the plainest national prosperity figures can show, will be the Writing on the Wall,—she holding this course as part of no fantastic vow, or bond, or brotherhood, or sisterhood, or pledge, or covenant, or fancy dress, or fancy fair; but simply as a duty to be done,—did Louisa see these things of herself? These things were to be.

Dear reader! It rests with you and me, whether, in our two fields of action, similar things shall be or not. Let them be! We shall sit with lighter bosoms on the hearth, to see the ashes of our fires turn gray and cold.